THE BURNING GOD

Praise for *The Burning God*

"Bringing her complex Poppy War trilogy to a poignant conclusion, Kuang shines a searing light on the devastating price and valiant sacrifices that warfare requires of all involved." —*Booklist*

"An incredible end to this epic trilogy. Mixing historical parallels of Chinese history, the themes of war, politics, and colonialism are balanced with terrific, flawed characters and amazing worldbuilding." —*Library Journal*

"A dark and devastating conclusion that transcends its roots in historical fact to examine brutal truths." —*Kirkus Reviews*

"Kuang's Poppy War series, the saga of a young shaman fighting to bring the old gods back to her homeland, comes to a striking close in this gritty finale." —*Publishers Weekly*

"In *The Burning God*, the third and final entry in the Poppy War trilogy, R. F. Kuang finds new ways to bring life, horror, and excitement to this saga about a nation torn apart by war." —*BookPage*

"Readers will get . . . a gut-wrenching ride. The book . . . goes beyond exploring the moral ambiguity war creates to ask whether it even matters who is ultimately right or victorious, if all that's left at the end is death and devastation." —*Tor.com*

"You know you have read a *really* good book when all you can do when you sit down to write a review of it is stare at a blank document for hours, trying to remember how to make words and turn them into coherent sentences. *The Burning God* was one of those *really* good books. . . . Kuang has always excelled at writing vividly rendered, immensely gripping battle scenes . . . She has genuinely outdone herself." —The Nerd Daily

Praise for *The Dragon Republic*

"Her story's refreshing, shocking, and there's some sort of invisible phoenix fire god controlling everything. Behold the horizons of fantasy expand." —*Wired*

"R. F. Kuang's sophomore novel continues an enthralling saga from one of fantasy's exciting new voices." —*Paste*

"This stunning sequel to *The Poppy War* is an epic journey of vengeance, friendship, and power. . . . Kuang has created a young woman torn by her connections to friends and family, searching for love and belonging and given power beyond her imagining. Her story is unforgettable." —*Library Journal*

"Kuang brings brilliance to this invigorating and complex military fantasy sequel to *The Poppy War*." —*Publishers Weekly*

"Kuang's descriptive storytelling reveals the grueling psychological and material cost of war on combatants and those they are supposed to protect. Fans of epic military fantasy will be eager for the next volume." —*Booklist*

"Kuang does a wonderful job of showing the effects of that pain in the initial period of this book, as well as the impact of addiction and PTSD. Rin seems destined to find war wherever she goes, and Kuang is fantastic at putting us in Rin's head to witness her internal conflict." —*BookPage*

"It's not a sequel readers will want to miss." —Culturess

"*The Dragon Republic* is straight up incredible. . . . It's big, bold, beautiful, and badass." —Fantasy Hive

"*The Dragon Republic* is a brilliantly unputdownable sequel that deflects the infamous middle book syndrome with brutal precision. With *The Dragon Republic*, Kuang has proven that her debut wasn't a one-hit wonder, further establishing herself as the new rising queen of fantasy." —Novel Notions

"A sequel born of flames and emerging not unscathed, but anew. Enter *The Dragon Republic*." —Utopia State of Mind

Praise for *The Poppy War*

"A thrilling, action-packed fantasy of gods and mythology. . . . The ambitious heroine's rise from poverty to ruthless military commander makes for a gripping read, and I eagerly await the next installment." —Julie C. Dao, author of *Forest of a Thousand Lanterns*

"A blistering, powerful epic of war and revenge that will captivate you to the bitter end." —Kameron Hurley, author of *The Stars Are Legion*

"I have no doubt this will end up being the best fantasy debut of the year. . . . I have absolutely no doubt that [Kuang's] name will be up there with the likes of Robin Hobb and N. K. Jemisin." —BookNest

"The best fantasy debut of 2018. . . . This year's Potter." —*Wired*

"The 'year's best debut' buzz around this one was warranted; it really is that good." —B&N Sci-fi and Fantasy Blog

"Debut novelist Kuang creates an ambitious fantasy reimagining of Asian history populated by martial artists, philosopher-generals, and gods. . . . This is a strong and dramatic launch to Kuang's career." —*Publishers Weekly*

"The book starts as an epic bildungsroman, and just when you think it can't get any darker, it does. . . . Kuang pulls from East Asian history, including the brutality of the Second Sino-Japanese War, to weave a wholly unique experience." —*Washington Post*

"[*The Poppy War* is] strikingly grim military fantasy that summons readers into an East Asian–inspired world of battles, opium, gods, and monsters. Fans of Ken Liu's *The Grace of Kings* will snap this one up." —*Library Journal*

"This isn't just another magical, fantasy world with artificially fabricated stakes. Rin's journey and the war against the Federation feel incredibly urgent and powerful. . . . R. F. Kuang is one of the most exciting new authors I've had the privilege of reading." —The Roarbots

"I can safely say that this will be the finest debut of 2018 and I'd be surprised if it isn't one of the top three books of the year full stop. Spectacular, master class, brilliant, awesome. . . . Simply put, R. F. Kuang's *The Poppy War* is a towering achievement of modern fantasy." —Fantasy Book Review

"The narrative is an impactful, impressive symphony of words that grant life to this incredible morality tale. Setting the stage for an epic fantasy is an understandably enormous undertaking, but Kuang does an exceptional job of world and character building." —RT Book Reviews

"Kuang ambitiously begins a trilogy that doesn't shy away from the darkest sides of her characters, wrapped in a confectionery of high-fantasy pulp. . . . The future of Rin in this world may appear quite dark, but that of the series seems bright indeed." —*Daily News* (New York)

"A young woman's determination and drive to succeed and excel at any cost runs into the horrors of war, conflict and ancient, suppressed forces in R. F. Kuang's excellent debut novel, *The Poppy War*." —*The Skiffy and Fanty Show*

"*The Poppy War* feels entirely immersive and rich in a way that kind of sucks you in. . . . It's a treasure trove." —Utopia State of Mind

ALSO BY R. F. KUANG

The Poppy War

The Dragon Republic

THE BURNING GOD

THE POPPY WAR, BOOK THREE

R. F. KUANG

HARPER Voyager
An Imprint of HarperCollinsPublishers

This is a work of fiction. Names, characters, places, and incidents are products of the author's imagination or are used fictitiously and are not to be construed as real. Any resemblance to actual events, locales, organizations, or persons, living or dead, is entirely coincidental.

THE BURNING GOD. Copyright © 2020 by R. F. Kuang. All rights reserved. "The Drowning Faith" © 2020 by R. F. Kuang. Printed in the United States of America. No part of this book may be used or reproduced in any manner whatsoever without written permission except in the case of brief quotations embodied in critical articles and reviews. For information, address HarperCollins Publishers, 195 Broadway, New York, NY 10007.

HarperCollins books may be purchased for educational, business, or sales promotional use. For information, please email the Special Markets Department at SPsales@harpercollins.com.

Harper Voyager and design are trademarks of HarperCollins Publishers LLC.

A hardcover edition of this book was published in 2020 by Harper Voyager, an imprint of HarperCollins Publishers.

FIRST HARPER VOYAGER PAPERBACK EDITION PUBLISHED 2021.

Designed by Paula Russell Szafranski
Frontispiece © Jannarong / Shutterstock.com
Map by Eric Gunther and copyright © 2017 Springer Cartographics

Library of Congress Cataloging-in-Publication Data has been applied for.

ISBN 978-0-06-266264-4

25 26 27 28 29 LBC 22 21 20 19 18

To my dear readers,

who stayed with this series until the end,

and came prepared with a bucket for their tears

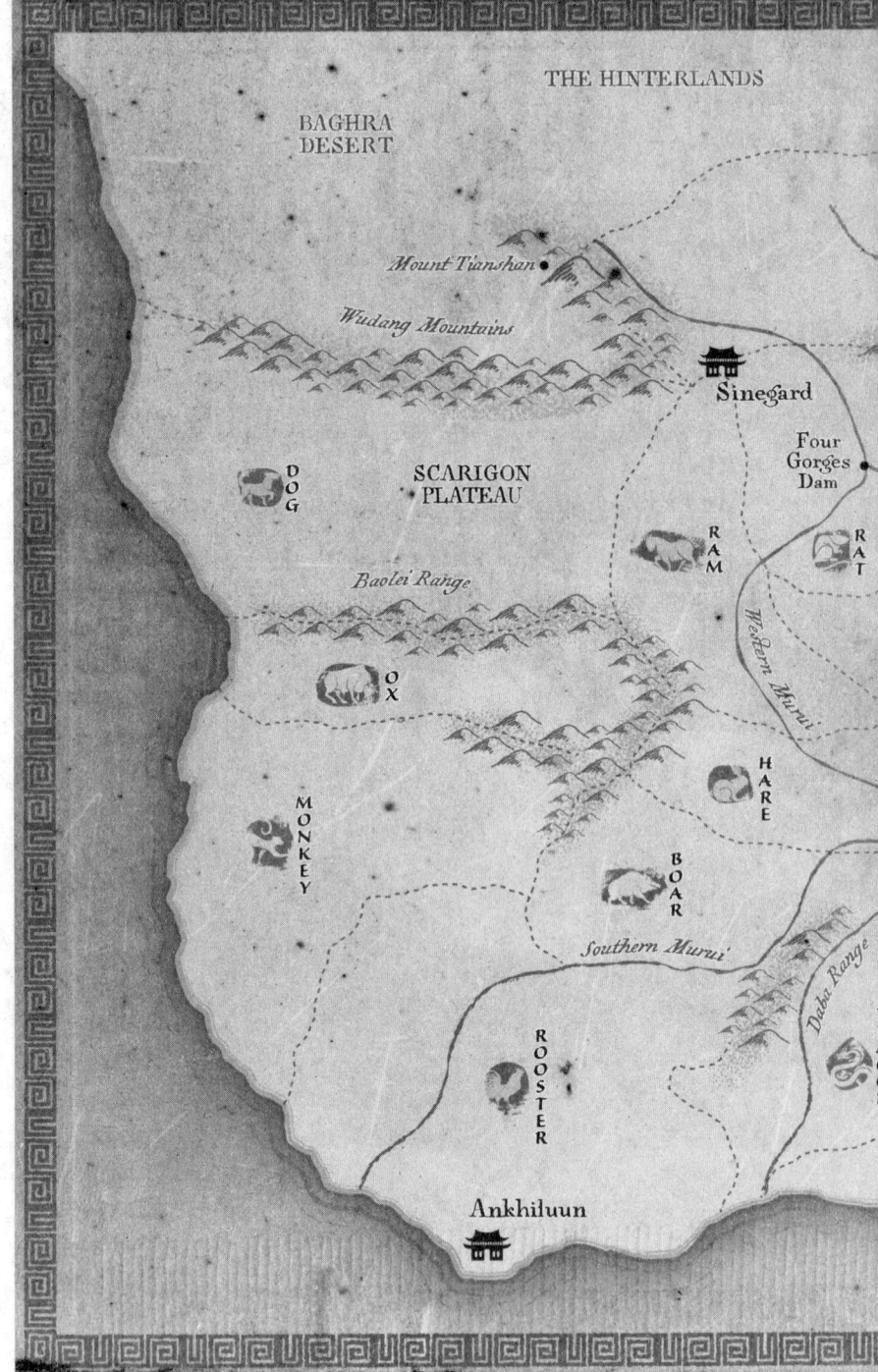

THE BURNING GOD

PROLOGUE

"We shouldn't be doing this," Daji said.

The campfire burned an unnatural shade of purple, sparking and hissing reproachfully as if it could sense her guilt. Tendrils of flame reached out like grasping hands that transformed into flickering faces that, months later, still made Daji's stomach twist with shame. She looked away.

But the dead were seared into the backs of her eyelids, their mouths still open in shock at her betrayal. Their whispers echoed in her mind, the same way they echoed every night in her dreams.

Murderer, they said. *Ingrate. Whore.*

Fear squeezed her chest. "Riga, I don't think—"

"Too late for second guesses now, sweetheart." Across the fire, Riga was binding a struggling deer with his usual brutal, callous efficiency. He'd already arranged three serrated knives, all looted from the corpses of Ketreyid archers, in a perfect triangle around the fire. Daji hadn't touched hers. She'd been too scared—the glinting metal looked poisonous, resentful. "We're far past the point of no return, don't you think?"

The deer arched its neck, straining to break free. Riga grasped its antlers with one hand and slammed its head to the ground.

The flames jumped higher; the whispers intensified. Daji flinched. "This feels wrong."

Riga snorted. "When did you become such a coward?"

"I'm just worried. Tseveri said—"

"Who cares what she said?" Riga sounded brittle, defensive. Daji knew he, too, was ashamed. She could tell some small part of him wished they'd never started down this path. But he could never admit that. If he did, he'd break.

Riga, pinning the deer's neck down with one knee, jerked twine around its front legs. The deer's mouth opened as if to scream, but the only sound it could make was a hoarse, eerie rasp. "Tseveri's always been full of shit. Prophecy, my ass—don't believe that babble. She was just saying whatever the Sorqan Sira wanted us to hear."

"She said this would kill us," Daji said.

"That's not precisely what she said."

"It's close enough."

"Oh, Daji." Riga tightened the last knot with a cruel yank, examined his handiwork for a moment, then moved to sit down beside her. His hand massaged her back in slow circles. He meant to be comforting. It felt like a trap. "Do you think I'd ever let anything happen to you?"

Daji struggled to keep her breathing even.

Do what he says, she reminded herself. That was the deal she'd made with Ziya. *Keep your head down and obey, or Riga will find some way to get rid of you.* She should be glad for this ritual. It was protection—the ultimate guarantee that Riga could not kill her without killing himself, a shield for her and Ziya both.

But still she was so afraid. What if this was worse than death?

She found her voice. "There has to be some other way—"

"There isn't," Riga snapped. "We won't last much longer like this. This war's gotten too big. Our enemies have grown too many." He gestured with his knife toward the forest. "And if Ziya keeps acting like that, he won't last another day."

He won't last because you've pushed him, Daji wanted to snap back. But she held her tongue for fear of stoking his temper. His cruelty.

You don't have another choice. She'd realized long ago that she needed to make herself absolutely necessary to Riga if she wanted to stay safe. Indispensable, anchored and chained to his very life.

"Come on, Ziya." Riga cupped his hands around his mouth and called out. "Let's get this over with."

The trees were silent.

Riga raised his voice. "*Ziya.* I know you're out there."

Maybe he ran, Daji thought. *Clever bastard*.

She wondered what Riga might do if Ziya really did try to escape. He'd chase him, of course, and likely catch him—Riga had always been the strongest and fastest of them all. The punishment would be terrible. But Daji might fend Riga off for a few minutes, buy Ziya some time, and even if that cost her her life at least one of them would be spared.

But seconds later Ziya came wandering through the forest, stumbling as if drunk. His eyes had that bemused, wild look that Daji had recently grown accustomed to seeing on his face. She knew it meant danger. Her hand crept toward her knife.

Riga stood and approached Ziya like a keeper might a tiger, hands spread cautiously out before him. "How are you?"

"How am I?" Ziya tilted his head. "Whatever do you mean?"

Daji saw Riga's throat pulse.

"Can you come sit down?" Riga asked.

Ziya shook his head, snickering.

"This isn't funny," Riga snarled. "Come here, Ziya."

"Ziya?" Ziya's eyes tipped to the sky. "Who's that?"

Riga reached for his sword. Daji raised her knife. They'd prepared for this, all three of them, with Ziya's consent. They had to strike just before he opened the gate—

Ziya's face split into a horrible grin. "Kidding."

Riga relaxed. "Fuck you."

Daji exhaled and tried to slow her frantically beating heart.

Ziya sat down cross-legged in front of the fire. His eyes flickered toward the bound deer with a cursory interest. "It's acting very tame, isn't it?"

He picked his own knife up from the ground and dangled it before the deer. Fire glinted off the serrated edge. The deer lay still, indifferent. It might have been dead save for its resigned, labored breathing.

"Daji shoved a wad of opium down its mouth," Riga said.

"Ah." Ziya winked at her. "Clever girl."

Daji wished the drug had taken effect earlier. She wished Riga had given it time. But that would require empathy—a trait he most certainly did not possess.

"Look alive, Daji." Riga brandished his knife at her. "Let's not drag this out."

Daji sat frozen in place. For a brief moment she considered running. Her knees trembled.

No. There's no way out. If she didn't do this for herself, she at least had to do it for Ziya.

He liked to fucking joke. He'd never been able to take anything seriously; only he would be amused by the prospect of losing his own mind. But her fear—hers and Riga's—was real. Ziya had been careening on the line between sanity and madness for months, and they didn't know when he'd tip into the void for good. Only this could bring him back.

But oh, how it had cost them.

"Knives up," Riga said.

They obeyed. The deer was tame beneath the blades, eyes open and glassy.

Riga began to speak. Every word of the incantation they'd lied, tortured, and murdered to obtain made the fire rise higher and higher, until flames ten feet high jumped toward the night sky. When Tseveri had spoken these words, they had sounded like music. On Riga's tongue, they sounded like a curse. Daji squeezed her eyes shut, trying to block out the screams in her mind.

Riga finished chanting. Nothing happened.

They sat there for a long time, their confusion mounting, until Ziya's laughter broke the silence.

"What the fuck is wrong with you?" Riga demanded.

"You're saying it wrong," Ziya said.

"The fuck does that mean?"

"It's your accent. This won't work with you butchering the words like that."

"You do it, then." Riga spat something else under his breath. Mugenese words, a slur he'd picked up as a child. *Horse lover.*

"I don't know the words," Ziya said.

"Yes, you do." A malicious edge crept into Riga's voice. "She taught them to you first."

Ziya stiffened.

Don't do it, Daji thought. *Let's kill him and run.*

Ziya began the incantation. His voice turned gradually from a hoarse whisper to a shout, forceful and fluid. This time the words sounded closer to how they'd sounded on Tseveri's tongue. This time they held power.

"Now," Riga whispered, and they raised their knives to slaughter the last necessary innocent.

When it was over, the void flung them back into their material bodies with a shock like icy water. Daji lurched forward, gasping. The earth felt so solid under her legs, the air so sweet. The world became the familiar made strange—solid and beautiful and mystifying. Daji was burning inside, shaking from the sheer power arcing through her body.

She felt more alive than she'd ever been. Now she was three souls instead of one; now she was complete; now she was *more*.

They hadn't fully returned yet from the world of spirit. Their connection hadn't severed. She was still reading into Ziya's and Riga's souls, and their thoughts crashed into her mind so loudly she struggled to separate them from her own.

From Ziya, she felt cold and naked fear combined with a terrible relief. He didn't want this. He'd never wanted any of this. He was so scared of what he might become but also grateful for his deliverance from the alternative. He was grateful to be bound.

From Riga, she felt both giddy delight and a dizzying rush of ambition. He wanted more. He wasn't even paying attention to the panic radiating from Ziya. His thoughts were on greater things. He saw them on a battlefield, at a negotiating table, on three thrones.

To Riga, this had been the last obstacle. Now they were tipping forward into the future he'd always imagined for them.

Daji wanted it, too. She just wasn't sure she'd survive it.

Slowly she opened her eyes. The blood coating her hands looked black in the moonlight. The fire had nearly gone out, yet the smoke threatened to suffocate. Daji almost fell forward into the embers, almost smothered her face in the ash and let it end there.

Strong fingers gripped her shoulder and dragged her back.

"Easy." Riga grinned.

Daji couldn't share in his euphoria.

Years later, when she tortured herself with memories of the three of them at the beginning, before everything had gone so dreadfully wrong, she could never remember how it felt when they were first anchored. Couldn't remember the thrill of power, or the terrifying yet delightful sense of being known. All she remembered was a curdling dread—the certainty that one day, the secrets they'd stolen would be paid for in blood.

And Tseveri. Always in her mind she saw the dead girl's wretched face, and heard so clearly the last warning she'd uttered before Ziya ripped her heart out of her chest.

Here's a prophecy for you, she'd said.
One will die.
One will rule.
And one will sleep for eternity.

PART I

CHAPTER 1

Rin's wrist throbbed.

The air always felt different on the morning of an ambush, as if an electric charge, the crackling residue of a thunderstorm, thrummed through her and every soldier around her. Rin had never felt energy like this when she'd fought for the Republic. In the beginning, Yin Vaisra's troops had been consummate professionals—sullen, grim, there to finish the job and get out. By the end, they'd been fearful. Desperate.

But the soldiers of the Southern Coalition were *angry*, and that force alone had driven them through grueling weeks of basic training, had quickly shaped them into capable killers even though not so long ago many of them had never even touched a sword.

It helped that their fight was personal. Khudla wasn't their town, but this was their province, and everyone in Monkey Province had suffered the same way under Mugenese occupation. Displacement, looting, rape, murder, mass executions. A thousand Golyn Niis–level massacres had played out over the land, and no one had cared, because no one in the Republic or the Empire had ever cared much about the south.

But some in the south had survived to avenge their dead, and those were the men and women who comprised Rin's troops.

As the minutes trickled past, the gathered ranks bristled in anticipation like hunting dogs straining against the leash. And Rin's wrist stung like a conducting rod, a million little jolts of pain shooting through her elbow every second.

"Stop rubbing," Kitay admonished. "You're irritating it."

"It hurts," she said.

"Because you're rubbing it. Leave it alone and it'll heal faster."

Rin ran her fingers over the cracked, bumpy skin that covered the bone of her wrist where it should have extended into a right hand. She clenched her jaw, trying to resist the urge to dig her nails into flesh long rubbed raw.

She'd had the hand amputated the night they made port in Ankhiluun. By then, after two weeks at sea, the appendage had all but rotted into a gangrenous mess. For all of the Black Lily physician's efforts to sterilize the wound, there had remained so many points of exposure in her skin that it was a miracle the infection hadn't spread farther up her arm. The procedure was short. Moag's personal physician had cut away Rin's hand, trimmed down the rotting flesh, and sewed her skin into a neat flap over the exposed bone.

The wound itself healed cleanly enough. But when Rin stopped taking laudanum, the wrist became a torch of unbearable agony. Phantom pains flashed through fingers she no longer had several times an hour. Sometimes they were so bad she slammed her hand at the wall to dull the pricks with a greater pain, only to remember that the hand wasn't there. The pain was imaginary. And she couldn't dull pain that existed purely in her mind.

"You're going to make it bleed," Kitay said.

Rin had, without thinking, begun to scratch again. She cupped her fingers over the stump and squeezed hard, trying to drive out the itching with sheer, numbing pressure. "It's driving me mad. It's not just the itching, it's the fingers. It's like I can still feel them, and they're being pricked with a thousand needles, only I can't do anything about it."

"I think I get it," Kitay said. "I feel it, too, sometimes. Little tremors out of nowhere. Which is strange, if you think about it—I'm the one with fingers, but the pain is coming from you."

Before her surgery, they'd worried that cutting away her rotted right hand might also sever Kitay's. They didn't know the limits of their anchor bond. They knew that death for one meant death for both. They felt each other's pain, and injuries to one manifested in pale, faintly visible scars for the other. But they didn't know what that meant for amputations.

By the time they docked in Ankhiluun, however, Rin's infections were so inflamed that the pain for both of them was unbearable, and Kitay had declared through gritted teeth that if Rin wouldn't cut away the hand, he'd gnaw it off himself.

To their great relief, his own arm remained intact. A ridged white line appeared around his wrist like a bracelet where the incision was made, but his fingers were still functional, if somewhat stiff. Occasionally Rin saw him struggling to hold an ink brush, and he now took much longer to dress in the mornings. But he still had his hand, and though Rin was relieved, she couldn't help but feel a constant, lingering jealousy.

"Can you see it?" She waved her wrist at him. "A little ghost hand?"

"You should put a hook on that," he said.

"I'm not putting a fucking hook on it."

"A blade, then. Then maybe you'd start practicing."

She shot him an irritated look. "I'll get around to it."

"You're never going to get around to it," he said. "Keep acting like this and the first time you pick up a sword will be the last."

"I won't need to—"

"You know you might. Think, Rin, what happens when—"

"Not now," she snapped. "I don't want to talk about this now."

She hated practicing with a sword. She hated fumbling at

things with her left hand that her right hand had once done unconsciously. It made her feel helpless and stupid and inadequate, and she had spent such a long time trying to convince herself that she wasn't powerless anymore. The first time she'd grasped a sword, a week after her surgery, her left arm had shaken with such debilitating weakness that she'd immediately flung the blade to the ground in disgust. She couldn't bear feeling like that again.

"I see the problem," Kitay said. "You're nervous."

"I don't get nervous."

"Bullshit. You're terrified. That's why you're fidgeting. You're scared."

For good fucking reason, Rin thought.

Her throbbing wrist wasn't the problem, just the symptom. She was searching for something, anything to go wrong. Their position could have been compromised. The Mugenese could know they were coming.

Or they might simply lose.

She hadn't dealt with defenses this good before. The Mugenese at Khudla knew Rin's troops were coming; their guard had been up for days. And they were primed to fear nighttime attacks now, even though most ambushing forces wouldn't dare launch such a tricky operation without adequate light. This would be no easy, devastating raid.

But Rin couldn't fail today.

Khudla was a test. She'd been begging the Monkey Warlord for a command position ever since they'd escaped Arlong, only to be told over and over that she couldn't lead entire columns into battle until she had the experience. Today, at last, he'd put her in charge.

Liberating Khudla was her mission, and hers alone. Until now she'd been fighting like a unit of one, a juggernaut of fire that the Southern Coalition threw into battles like a wide-range missile. Now she was leading a brigade of hundreds.

These soldiers fought under her command. That terrified her. What if they died under her command?

"We have this down like clockwork. The guard changes every

thirty minutes," Kitay said. They'd been over this a dozen times before, but he was repeating it to calm her down. "You'll know when the voices change. Get as close as you can before sunset, and then hit during the transition. Do you know the signals?"

She took a deep breath. "Yes."

"Then you've got nothing to worry about."

If only saying it made it so.

The minutes crawled past. Rin watched the sun dipping toward the mountains, dropping reluctantly, as if dragged downward by some creature in the valley below.

After Rin had raised the Phoenix on the Isle of Speer and ended the Third Poppy War, there was no formal surrender by the Federation of Mugen. Emperor Ryohai and his progeny were turned instantly into charcoal statues under mountains of ash. No one in the Mugenese imperial family survived to negotiate for peace.

So there had been no armistice, no treaty. No Mugenese generals provided a map of their troop placements and turned their weapons over to the Nikara leadership. Instead, all remaining Federation soldiers on the mainland became rogue threats—highly skilled roving soldiers without mission or nation. Yin Vaisra, the former Dragon Warlord and newly elected President of the Nikara Republic, could have dealt conclusively with them months ago, but he'd let them roam free to undercut his own allies in a long-term ploy to strengthen his grasp on the crumbling Nikara Empire. Now those scattered platoons had organized into several large independent bands terrorizing the south. For all intents and purposes, the Nikara and the Mugenese remained at war. Even without support from the longbow island, the Mugenese had essentially colonized the south in a matter of months. And Rin had let them, obsessed as she'd been with Vaisra's insurrection while the real war was being fought at home.

She'd failed the south once. She wouldn't do it again.

"Kazuo says the ships are still coming," spoke a voice in Mugini. It was a boy's voice, thin and reedy.

"Kazuo is a fucking idiot," said his companion.

Rin and Kitay crouched hidden behind the tall grass. They'd crept close enough to the Mugenese camp that they could hear patrolmen gossiping idly, their hushed voices traveling far over still night air. Still, Rin's Mugini was rusty from more than a year of disuse, and she had to strain her ears to understand what they were saying.

"This language is like insect chitter," Nezha had once complained, back when they'd been stupid young children crammed into a classroom at Sinegard, when they had yet to realize that the war they were training to fight wasn't hypothetical.

Nezha had hated Mugini lessons, Rin remembered. He hadn't been able to comprehend the language when spoken at its standard rapid clip, so he'd spent class each day mocking it, making his fellow students laugh with gibberish that sounded so much like real sentences.

"*Click click click*," he'd said, and made scuttling noises between his teeth. "Like little bugs."

Like crickets, Rin thought. They'd started calling the Mugenese that in the countryside. Rin didn't know if it was a new slur or an old insult recycled from a time before her birth. She wouldn't have been surprised by the latter. History moved in circles—she'd learned that very well by now.

"Kazuo said that ships have started coming into the ports in Tiger Province," said the first voice she'd heard, the boy's voice. "They're docking in the shadows, ferrying us back handful by handful—"

The second patrolman snorted. "That's bullshit. We'd know by now if they had."

There was a brief silence. Someone stirred in the grass. The patrolmen were lying down, Rin realized. Perhaps they were stargazing. That was stupid of them, wildly irresponsible. But they sounded so very young; they sounded not like soldiers but like children. Did they simply not know any better?

"The moon is different here," the first patrolman said wistfully.

Rin recognized that phrase. She'd learned it at Sinegard—it was an old Mugini expression, some aphorism derived from a myth about a ferryman who loved a woman who lived on a distant star, who built her a bridge between two worlds so that they could finally embrace.

The moon is different here. He meant he wanted to go home.

The Mugenese were always talking about going home. She heard about it every time she eavesdropped on them. They spoke about home like it still existed, like the longbow island was some beautiful paradise where they could easily return if only the ships would come to harbor. They spoke about their mothers, fathers, sisters, and brothers who awaited them on their shores, spared somehow from the scorching pyroclastic flows.

"You'd better get used to this moon," said the second patrolman.

The more they spoke, the younger they sounded. Rin pictured their faces in her head; their voices brought to mind gangly limbs and fuzzy upper lips. They couldn't be older than her—they had to be just over twenty, possibly younger.

She remembered fighting a boy her age during the siege at Khurdalain, what seemed like an eternity ago. Remembered his wide moonlike face and soft hands. Remembered how his eyes bulged when she ran her blade through his stomach.

He must have been so scared. He might have been as scared as she was.

She felt Kitay stiffen beside her.

"They don't want to be here, either." He'd told her this weeks ago. He'd been interrogating some of their Mugenese prisoners, and he'd come away far more sympathetic to them than she was comfortable with. "They're just kids. A quarter of them are younger than we are, and they didn't sign up for this war. Most of them were pulled from their homes and thrown into vicious training camps so that their families wouldn't go to prison or starve. They don't want to kill, they just want to go home."

But their home didn't exist anymore. Those boys had nowhere to escape to. If the gates of reconciliation had ever been open, if there'd ever been the option of repatriating enemy combatants and building slowly toward peace, Rin had slammed them shut long ago.

A wide chasm of guilt, her ever-faithful friend, yawned in the back of her mind.

She pushed it away.

She'd done such a good job of burying her memories; that was the only way she could keep herself sane.

Children can be murderers, she reminded herself. *Little boys can be monsters.*

The lines of war had become far too blurred. Every Mugenese soldier who'd ever put on a uniform was complicit, and Rin didn't have the patience to separate the guilty from the innocent. Speerly justice was absolute. Her retribution was conclusive. She didn't have time to dawdle on what could have been; she had a homeland to liberate.

Her wrist had started to throb again. She exhaled slowly, closed her eyes, and repeated their plan of attack over and over in her mind in an attempt to shake off her nerves.

She traced her fingers across the scars on her stomach. Let them linger on the spot where Altan's handprint was burned into her like a brand. She envisioned those boy patrolmen and transformed them into targets.

I've killed millions of you before, she thought. *This is routine now. This is nothing.*

The sun was a little crimson dot now, the top of it barely visible over the mountaintops. The patrolmen had rotated from their post. The fields, for now, were empty.

"It's time," Kitay murmured.

Rin stood up. They faced each other, hands clasped between them.

"At dawn," she said.

"At dawn," he agreed. He put his hands on her shoulders and kissed her forehead.

This was their standard way of parting, the way they said everything they never spoke out loud. *Fight well. Keep us safe. I love you.*

Every goodbye had to be so much harder for Kitay, who wagered his life on hers every time she set foot on the battlefield.

Rin wished she didn't have that vulnerability. If she could cut out the part of the soul that endangered Kitay—that was endangered by Kitay—then she would.

But the fact that his life was at stake lent an edge to her fighting. It made her sharper, warier, less likely to take risks and more likely to strike hard and fast when she could. She no longer fought from pure rage. She fought to protect him—and that, she had discovered, changed everything.

Kitay gave her one last nod, then disappeared behind the ranks.

"Does he always stay behind?" Officer Shen asked.

Rin liked Officer Shen. A Monkey Province native and veteran of the last two Poppy Wars, Shen Sainang was brusque, efficient, and pragmatic. She despised factional politics, which perhaps explained why she was one of the few officers who had volunteered to follow Rin into her first battle as commander. Rin was grateful for that.

But Shen was too observant. Always asking too many questions.

"Kitay doesn't fight," Rin said.

"Why not?" Shen asked. "He's Sinegard-trained, isn't he?"

Because Kitay was Rin's single link to the heavens. Because Kitay needed to be in a safe and quiet place so that his mind could function as a channel between her and the Phoenix. Because every time Kitay was exposed and vulnerable it doubled Rin's chances of dying.

That was Rin's greatest secret. If the Monkey Warlord knew Kitay was her anchor, he'd know the only way to kill her. And Rin didn't trust him or the Southern Coalition enough to give them that chance.

"He's a Sinegard-trained strategist," Rin said. "Not a foot soldier."

Shen looked unconvinced. "He carries a sword like one."

"Yes, and his mind's more valuable than the sword," Rin said curtly, shutting down the discussion. She nodded toward Khudla. "It's time."

Adrenaline rushed her veins then. Her heartbeat began pounding in her ears, an internal countdown to the slaughter. Across the village perimeter, eight pairs of eyes were trained on Rin—eight squadron leaders, waiting at their vantage points, watching for the flame.

At last, Rin saw a line of Mugenese troops moving down the field. There it was—the patrol switch.

She raised her left hand and gave the signal—a thin stream of fire, burning the air ten feet over her head before it winked away.

The fields moved. Soldiers poured in from the northern and eastern fronts. They flooded out of hiding points in riverbanks, ravines, and forests like ants storming out of an anthill. Rin watched with satisfaction. So what if her columns were thinner than the defense? The Mugenese wouldn't know the first place to look.

She heard a series of signal whistles, clear indications that every squadron had moved successfully into position. Officer Shen's troops took the east. Officer Lin's troops took the north.

Rin stormed the southern quarter alone.

The Mugenese weren't ready. Most had been asleep or preparing to go to sleep. They staggered out of their tents and barracks, rubbing at their eyes. Rin almost laughed at the way their faces morphed into uniform expressions of horror when they saw what had turned the night air so very warm.

She lifted her arms. Wings shot out of her shoulders, glowing ten feet high.

Kitay had once accused her of being too flamboyant, of sacrificing efficiency for attention.

What did it matter? There was no point to subtlety when everyone knew what she was. And Rin wanted this image burned into their eyelids, the last thing they saw before they died—a Speerly and her god.

Men scattered before her like startled hens. One or two had the sense to hurl swords in her direction. Their movements were panicked, their aim poor. Rin advanced, hand splayed outward, fire ensconcing everything she saw.

Then the screaming started, and the ecstasy set in.

Rin had spent so long hating how she felt when she burned, hating her fire and her god. Not anymore. She could admit to herself now that she liked it. She liked letting her basest instincts take over. She reveled in it.

She didn't have to think hard to summon the rage. She only had to remember the corpses at Golyn Niis. The corpses in the research laboratory. Altan burning on the pier, a miserable end to the miserable life they'd given him.

Hate was a funny thing. It gnawed at her insides like poison. It made every muscle in her body tense, made her veins boil so hot she thought her head might split in half, and yet it fueled everything she did. Hate was its own kind of fire and if you had nothing else, it kept you warm.

Once, Rin had wielded fire like a blunt instrument, letting the Phoenix's will control her as if she were the weapon and not the other way around. Once, she'd only known how to act as a gateway for a torrent of divine fire. But such unrestrained explosions were only useful when one intended genocide. Campaigns for liberation demanded precision.

She had spent weeks with Kitay practicing the intricacies of calling the flame. She'd learned to shape it like a sword. To lash it out in tendrils like a whip. She'd learned to mold it into moving, dancing entities—lions, tigers, phoenixes.

She'd learned so many ways to kill with fire. She liked going for the eyes the best. Burning limbs to ash took too long. The human body could sustain a burn for a surprisingly long time, and she wanted her fights over quickly. Really, the entire face presented an excellent target—hair would keep burning, and light head wounds fazed combatants more than other minor wounds could. But if she aimed for the eyes, she could scorch retinas, seal eyelids shut, or blister the surrounding skin, all of which would blind her opponents in seconds.

She saw a flash of movement to her right. Someone was trying to charge her.

The Phoenix cackled. *The audacity.*

Half a second before he reached her, she opened her palm toward his face.

His eyes popped one by one. Viscous fluid dribbled down his cheeks. He opened his mouth to scream, and Rin sent flames pouring down his throat.

This was only grotesque if she saw her opponents as human. But she didn't see humans, because Sinegard and Altan had taught her to compartmentalize and detach. *Learn to look and see not a man but a body. The soul is not there. The body is simply a composite of different targets, and all of them burn so bright.*

"Do you know where the Mugenese come from?" Altan had asked her once. "Do you know what kind of race they are?"

They had been sailing down the Murui toward Khurdalain then. The Third Poppy War had just begun. She'd been fresh out of Sinegard, stupid and naive, a student who was struggling with the fact that she was now a soldier. Altan had just become her commander and she had hung on his every word, so in awe of him she could barely string together a sentence.

She'd realized he was waiting for her to answer, so she'd said the first thing that came to mind. "They're. Um. Related to us?"

"Do you know how?"

She could have repeated any textbook answer to him. Migration induced by droughts or flooding. Exiled aristocracy. Clan warfare dating back to the days of the Red Emperor. No one was really certain. She'd been taught many theories that were all equally plausible. But she'd suspected that Altan wasn't really interested in her answer, so she had shaken her head instead.

She'd guessed right. He'd wanted to tell a story.

"A long time ago the Red Emperor had a pet," he'd said. "It was a beastly thing, some very intelligent ape he'd found in the mountains. One ugly, vicious fucker. Do you know this tale?"

"I don't," she'd whispered. "Tell me."

"The Red Emperor kept it in a cage in his palace," he continued. "Occasionally he brought it out for guests to see. They liked to watch it kill things. They'd release pigs or roosters into its cage to watch it dismember them. I imagine they had great fun. Until one day the beast sprang free of its cage, killed a minister with its bare hands, kidnapped the Red Emperor's daughter, and escaped back to the mountains."

"I didn't know the Red Emperor had a daughter," Rin had said, stupidly. For some reason, she'd found this the most striking detail. History only remembered the princes—the Red Emperor's sons.

"No one does. He would have erased her from the record, after what happened. She became pregnant by the beast but couldn't find any means of expelling the fetus from her womb, not while she was its prisoner, so she gave birth to a little brood of half-men and raised them in the mountains. Years later the Red Emperor sent his generals to chase them out of the Empire, and they fled to the longbow island."

Rin had never heard that iteration of the story, but it made sense. The Nikara did like to compare the Mugenese to monkeys. Half-men, they called them; short and little—even though when she had finally seen a Federation soldier with her own eyes she wouldn't have been able to tell him apart from a Nikara villager.

Altan had paused then, watching her, waiting for her response.

But she'd only had one question, which she hadn't wanted to ask, because she'd known Altan wouldn't have an answer.

If they were beasts, how did they kill us?

Who decided who counted as human? The Nikara thought the Speerlies were beasts, too, and they'd made them warrior slaves for centuries. The enemy was not human—fine. But if they were animals, then they must be inferior. If the Mugenese were inferior, though, then how could they have been the victors? Did that mean that, in this world, one had to be a beast to survive?

Maybe no one was truly a beast. Maybe that was just how murder became possible. You took away someone's humanity, and then you killed them. At Sinegard, Strategy Master Irjah had taught them once that during the heat of battle, they should regard their opponents as objects, abstract and disparate parts and not the sum, because that would make it easier to plunge a blade into a pumping heart. But maybe if you looked at someone as not an object but an animal, you could not only commit the murder without flinching, you could let yourself take some pleasure in it. Then it felt good, the same way kicking down anthills felt good.

"Monkeys raping humans. Half-breed brats. Beastly freaks. Stupid savages." Altan had said the last words with bitter relish, and Rin had thought that perhaps it was because those were the same words so many others used to describe him. "That's where the Mugenese come from."

Rin carved her way through the camp in minutes. The Mugenese presented almost no resistance. The soldiers she'd faced at Sinegard and Khurdalain had been well trained and lethally armed, with lines of glinting swords and an endless supply of chemical weapons they hurled into civilian centers at will. But these soldiers ran instead of fighting, and they died with an ease that astounded her.

This was all too simple, so simple that it made Rin slow down. She wanted to savor this power differential. *Once I was your screaming victim, begging for your mercy. And now you cower before me.*

She shouldn't have slowed.

Because once she slowed, she noticed how unprepared they were. How utterly unlike soldiers they seemed. How young they looked.

The boy before her had a sword, but he wasn't using it. He

didn't even try to fight, only stumbled back with his arms raised, begging for her mercy.

"Please don't," he kept saying.

He might have been the patrolman from before; he spoke in that same reedy, wobbly voice. "*Please.*"

She stayed her hand only because she realized he was speaking Nikara.

She considered him for a moment. *Was* he Nikara? Was he a prisoner of war? He wasn't wearing a Mugenese uniform, he might have been an innocent . . .

"Please," he said again. "Don't—"

His accent sealed his fate. His tones were too clipped. He wasn't Nikara after all, just a clever Mugenese soldier who thought he might fool her into taking mercy.

"Burn," she said.

The boy fell backward. She saw his mouth open, saw his face curdle into a piteous scream just as it blackened and solidified, but she couldn't bring herself to care.

In the end, it was always so easy to kill her heart. It didn't matter that they looked like boys. That they were nothing, nothing like the monsters she had once known. In this war of racial totality, none of that mattered. If they were Mugenese, that meant they were crickets and that meant when she crushed them under her heel, the universe hardly registered their loss.

Once, Altan had made her watch him burn a squirrel alive.

He'd caught it for their breakfast with a simple netted trap. It was still alive when he retrieved it from the trees, wriggling in his grasp. But instead of snapping its neck, he'd decided to teach her a lesson.

"Do you know how exactly fire kills a person?" he'd asked.

She'd shaken her head. She'd watched, entranced, as he conjured fire into his palms.

Altan had such remarkable control over the shape of fire. He was a puppeteer, casually twisting flames into the loveliest shapes:

now a flying bird, now a twisting dragon, now a human figure, flailing inside the cage he made with his fingers until he clamped his palms shut.

She'd been captivated, watching his fingers dance through the air. His question had caught her off guard, and when she spoke, her words were clumsy and stupid. "Through heat? I mean, um . . ."

His lip had curled. "Fire is such an inefficient way to kill. Did you know the moment of death is actually quite painless? The fire eats up all the breathable air around the victim, and they choke to death."

She blinked at him. "You don't want that?"

"Why would you want that? If you want a quick death, you use a sword. Or an arrow." He'd twirled a stream of flame around his fingers. "You don't throw Speerlies into battle unless you want to terrorize. We want our victims to suffer first. We want them to burn, and slowly."

He'd picked up the bound squirrel and wrapped his fingers around its middle. The squirrel couldn't scream, but Rin had imagined the sound, quivering little gasps that corresponded to its twitching limbs.

"Watch the skin," he'd said.

Once the fur burned off, she'd been able to glimpse the pink underneath, bubbling, crackling, hardening to black. "First it boils. Then it starts to slough off. Watch the color. Once you've turned it black, and once that black spreads, there's nothing that can bring them back."

He had held the squirrel out toward her. "Hungry?"

She had glanced down at its little black eyes, bulging and glassy, and her stomach roiled. And she hadn't known what was worse, the way the animal's legs twitched in its death throes, or the fact that the roasted flesh smelled so terribly good.

By the time she'd finished in the southern quarter, the rest of her soldiers had corralled the last Mugenese holdouts into a corner in Khudla's eastern district. They parted to let her through to the front.

"Took you a while," Officer Shen said.

"Got held up," Rin said. "Having too much fun."

"The southern quarter—"

"Finished." Rin rubbed her fingers together, and crackled blood burned black fell to the ground. "Why aren't we attacking?"

"They've taken hostages inside the temple," Shen said.

That was smart. Rin regarded the structure. It was one of the nicer village temples she'd seen in a while, made from stone and not wood. It wouldn't burn easily, and the Mugenese artillery inside had good vantage points from the upper floors.

"They're going to shoot us out," Shen said.

As if to prove her point, a fire rocket shrieked overhead and exploded against the tree ten paces from where they crouched.

"So storm them," Rin said.

"We're afraid they might have gas."

"They would have used it by now."

"They could be waiting for you," Shen pointed out.

That was fair logic. "Then we'll burn it."

"We can't get past the stone—"

"*You* can't get past stone." Rin wiggled her fingers in the air. A fiery dragon danced around her palm. She squinted at the temple, considering. It fell easily within her range; she could extend her flames to a radius of fifty yards. She only needed to sneak a flame through a window. Once past stone, her fire would find plenty of things to burn.

"How many hostages?" Rin asked.

"Does it matter?" Shen asked.

"It does to me."

Shen paused for a long moment, and then nodded. "Maybe five, six. No more than eight."

"Are they important?" Women and children could die without many ramifications. Local leadership likely couldn't.

"Not as far as I can tell. Souji's people are on the other side of town. And he doesn't have family."

Rin mulled over her options one last time.

She could still have her troops storm the temple, but she'd suffer casualties, especially if the Mugenese really did have gas canisters. The Southern Army couldn't afford casualties; their numbers were low enough already.

And her margin of victory mattered. This was her great test. If she came home from this not just victorious but with minimal losses, the Monkey Warlord would give her an army. The decision, then, was clear; she wasn't slinking back with only half her troops.

"Who else knows about the hostages?" she asked Shen.

"Just the men here."

"What about the villagers?"

"We've evacuated everyone we could find," Shen said, which was code for *No one will speak of what you did*.

Rin nodded. "Get your men out of here. At least a hundred paces. I don't want them to inhale any smoke."

Shen looked pale. "General—"

Rin raised her voice. "I wasn't asking."

Shen nodded and broke into a run. The field cleared in seconds. Rin stood alone in the yard, rubbing her fingers against her palm.

Can you feel this, Kitay? Can you tell what I'm doing?

No time for hesitation. She had to do this before the Mugenese ventured out to investigate the silence.

She turned her palm out. Fire roared. She directed the core of the flame toward the locks on the temple doors. She saw the metal warping, twisting into an unbreakable shape.

Then the Mugenese must have caught on, because someone inside started to scream.

Rin increased the heat to a roar loud enough to drown it out, yet somehow it pierced the wall of sound. It was a high squeal of pain. Maybe a woman's, maybe a child's. It almost sounded like a baby. But that didn't mean anything—she knew how shrilly a grown man could scream.

She increased the force of her flame, made it roar so loudly that she couldn't hear herself think. But still the scream penetrated the wall of fire.

She squeezed her eyes shut. She imagined herself falling backward into the Phoenix's warmth, into that distant space where nothing mattered but rage. The thin wail wavered.

Burn, she thought, *shut up and burn.*

CHAPTER 2

"Well done," Kitay said.

She threw her arms around him, pulled him tight against her, and lingered in his embrace for a long while. By now she should have become used to their brief separations, but leaving him behind felt harder and harder every time.

She tried to convince herself that it wasn't solely because Kitay was the one source of her power. That it wasn't just because of her selfish concern that if anything happened to him, she was useless.

No, she also felt responsible for him. *Guilty*, rather. Kitay's mind was stretched like a rope between her and the Phoenix, and between the rage and hatred and shame, he felt *everything*. He kept her safe from madness, and she subjected him to madness in return. Nothing she ever did could repay that debt.

"You're shaking," she said.

"I'm all right," he said. "It's nothing."

"You're lying." Even in the dim light of dawn, Rin could see his legs were trembling. He was far from all right—he could barely stand. They had this same argument after every battle. Every time she came back and saw what she'd done to him, saw his pale, drawn face and knew that to him, it felt like torture. Every time he denied it.

She'd limit her use of flame if only he asked. He never asked.

"I'll be fine," he amended gently. He nodded over her shoulder. "And you're drawing a bit of attention."

Rin turned and saw Khudla's survivors.

This had happened often enough that she knew what to expect.

First they wandered forward in little, tentative clumps. Curious whispering, terrified pointing. Then, when they realized that this new army was not Mugenese but Nikara, not Militia but something new entirely, and that Rin's soldiers were not here to replace their oppressors, they grew braver.

Is she the Speerly? they asked. *Are you the Speerly?*

Are you one of us?

And then the whispers grew louder as the crowd swelled, bodies coalescing around her. They spoke her name, her race, her god. Her legend had already spread to this place; she could hear it rippling through the field.

They reached out to touch her.

Rin's chest constricted. Her breathing quickened; her throat felt blocked.

Kitay's hand tightened around her arm. He didn't have to ask what was wrong; he knew.

"Are you—" he began.

"It's fine," she murmured. "It's fine."

These hands were not the enemy's. She was not in danger. She knew that, but her body didn't. She took a deep breath and composed her face. She had to play the part—had to look like not the scared girl she'd once been or the tired soldier that she was, but the leader they needed.

"You're free," she told them. Her voice quivered with exhaustion; she cleared her throat. "Go."

A hush ran through the crowd when they saw that she spoke

their language—not the abrasive Nikara of the north, but the slow, rolling dialect of the south.

They still regarded her with a kind of awed terror. But she knew this was the kind of fear that turned into love.

Rin raised her voice and spoke, this time without a tremor. "Go tell your families that they've been saved. Tell them the Mugenese can't harm you any longer. And when they ask who broke your shackles, tell them the Southern Coalition is marching across the Empire with the Phoenix at its fore. Tell them we're taking back our home."

As the sun climbed through the sky, Rin commenced Khudla's liberation.

This was supposed to be the fun part. It was supposed to feel good, telling grateful villagers that their erstwhile occupiers were smoldering piles of ash.

But Rin dreaded liberation. Combing through a half-destroyed village to find survivors only meant yet another survey of the extent of Federation cruelty. She'd rather face the battlefield again than confront that suffering. It didn't matter that she'd already seen the worst at Golyn Niis, that she'd witnessed the worst things one could do to a human body dozens of times over. It never got easier.

She'd learned by now that the Mugenese implemented the same three measures every time they occupied a city, three directives so clean and textbook that she could have written a full treatise on how to subdue a population herself.

First, the Mugenese rounded up every Nikara man who resisted their occupation, marched them to the killing fields, and either shot or beheaded them. Beheading was more common; arrows were valuable resources and couldn't always be retrieved intact. They didn't kill all the local men, just those who had threatened to make trouble. They needed laborers.

Second, the Mugenese either repurposed or stripped away the village infrastructure. Anything sturdy they turned into soldiers' barracks, and anything flimsy they tore apart for firewood. When the loose wood was gone, they scoured the homes for furniture, blankets, valuables, and ceramics with which to furnish their barracks. They were very efficient at turning villages into empty shells. Rin often found liberated villagers crowded in pigsties, cramped together knee to knee just to keep warm.

Third, the Mugenese co-opted the local leadership. After all, what did you do when you didn't speak the local language? When you didn't grasp the nuances of regional politics? You didn't supplant the existing leadership structure—that would result in chaos. You grafted yourself onto it. You got the local bullies to do your dirty work for you.

Rin hated the Nikara collaborators. Their crimes, to her, seemed almost worse than those of the Federation. The Mugenese were at least targeting the enemy race—a natural instinct in wartime. But collaborators helped the Mugenese murder, mutilate, and violate their own kind. That was inconceivable. Unforgivable.

Rin and Kitay were always split on how to handle the captured collaborators. Kitay begged for lenience. They were desperate, he argued. They were trying to save their own skins. They might have saved some villagers' skins. *Sometimes compliance saves you pain. Compliance might have saved us at Golyn Niis.*

Bullshit, Rin retorted. Compliance was cowardice. She had no respect for anyone who would rather die than fight. She wanted the collaborators to burn.

But the matter was out of their hands. The villagers invariably settled things themselves. Sometime in the next week, if not in the next day, they would drag the collaborators into the middle of the square, extract their confessions, and then flay, whip, beat, or stone them. Rin never had to intervene. The south delivered its own justice. The catharsis of violence hadn't happened yet in Khudla—it was too early in the morning for a public execution, and the villagers were too starved and exhausted to form a mob—but Rin knew that soon enough, she would hear screaming.

Meanwhile, she had survivors to find. She was looking for

prisoners. The Federation always took captives—political dissidents, soldiers too willful to control but too useful to let die, or hostages they hoped might dissuade their incoming attackers. Sometimes the bodies were freshly dead—either from one last act of vengeance by desperate Mugenese soldiers under siege, or suffocated by smoke from Rin's flames.

More often, however, she found them alive. You couldn't kill hostages if you ever meant to use them.

Kitay led soldiers to search in the eastern edge of the village through the Mugenese-occupied buildings that had escaped the brunt of the destruction. He had a particular talent for finding survivors. He'd once hidden for weeks behind a bricked-up wall at Golyn Niis, cringing and hugging his knees while Federation soldiers dragged Nikara soldiers from their hiding spots and shot them on the streets. He knew how to look for the signs—tarps or stacked debris that seemed out of place, faint footprints in the dust, echoes of shallow breathing in frightened silence.

Rin alone took on the burned wreckage.

She dreaded this task: pulling charred boards aside to find bodies broken and bleeding but still breathing. Too many times they were beyond saving. Half the time she'd caused the destruction herself. Once flames started burning, they were difficult to put out.

Still, she had to try.

"Is anyone here?" she called repeatedly. "Make a noise. Any noise. I'm listening."

She went through every cellar, every abandoned lot and well; shouted out for survivors many times and made sure she listened hard to the echoing silence. It would be a horrible fate to be chained up, slowly starving or suffocating to death because your village had been liberated but the survivors forgot about you. Her eyes watered as she stumbled through a smoky grain cellar. She doubted she'd find anything—already she'd stumbled over two corpses—but she waited a moment before she left. Just in case.

Her patience rewarded her.

"In the back," called a voice.

Rin pulled a flame into her hand, illuminating the far wall of the cellar. She couldn't see anything but empty grain sacks. She stepped closer.

"Who are you?" she demanded.

"Souji." She heard the clink of chains. "Likely the man you're looking for."

She decided she wasn't dealing with an ambush. She knew that flat-tongued, rustic accent. The best Mugenese spies couldn't imitate it; they'd all trained only to speak the curt Sinegardian dialect.

She crossed to the other end of the cellar, stopped, and amplified her torchlight.

Her first goal at Khudla had been liberation. Her second goal was to locate Yang Souji, the famed rebel leader and local hero who had until recently been fending off the Mugenese in southern Monkey Province. The closer she'd marched to Khudla, the more myths and rumors she'd heard about him. Yang Souji had eyes that could see for ten thousand miles. He could speak to animals; he knew when the Mugenese were coming because the birds always warned him. His skin was invulnerable to all kinds of metal—swords, arrowheads, axes, spears.

The man chained to the floor was none of those things. He looked surprisingly young—he couldn't be more than a few years older than she was. A scraggly beard had sprouted over his neck and chin, some indication of how long he'd been chained up, but he sat up straight with his shoulders rolled back, and his eyes shone bright in the firelight.

Despite herself, Rin found him surprisingly handsome.

"So you're the Speerly," he said. "I thought you'd be taller."

"And I thought you'd be older," she said.

"Then we're both a disappointment." He jangled his chains at her. "Took you long enough. Did you really need all night?"

She knelt down and began working at the locks. "Not even a thank-you?"

"You're going to do that one-handed?" he asked skeptically.

She fumbled with the pin. "Look, if you're going to—"

"Give me that." He plucked the pin from her fingers. "Just hold the lock up where I can see it and give me some light—there you go."

As she watched him work at the lock with remarkable dexterity, she couldn't help but feel a flicker of jealousy. It still stung, how the simplest things—picking locks, getting dressed, filling her canteen—had become so damnably difficult overnight.

She'd lost her hand to such a stupid turn of events. If they'd only had a key back then. If they'd just been able to steal a motherfucking *key*.

Her stump itched. She clenched her teeth and willed herself not to scratch it.

Souji undid the lock in less than a minute. He shook his hands free and sighed, cradling his wrists. He bent over toward the chains around his ankles. "That's better. Can you give me some more light?"

She moved the flame closer to the lock, careful not to singe his skin.

She noticed the middle finger on his right hand was missing its top joint. It didn't look like an accident—the middle finger on his left hand was missing a joint as well.

"What's wrong with your hands?" she asked.

"My mother's first two children died in infancy," he explained. "She thought that the gods were stealing them because they were so lovely. So when I entered the world she gnawed the first joint off both my middle fingers." He wiggled his left hand at her. "Made me a bit less attractive."

Rin snorted. "The gods don't want fingers."

"So what do they want?"

"Pain," she said. "Pain, and your sanity."

Souji popped the lock, shook the chains away, and clambered to his feet. "I suppose you would know."

After all likely survivors had been rescued from the wreckage, Rin's troops fell on the battlefield like vultures.

The first time the newly minted soldiers of the Southern Coalition had scavenged for supplies in the wake of a battle, they'd been reluctant to touch the corpses. They'd been superstitious, scared of angering vengeful ghosts of the unburied dead who couldn't return home. Now they raided bodies with hardened disregard, stripping them of anything of value. They looked for weapons, leather, clean linens—Mugenese uniforms were blue, but could be easily dyed—and, prized above all, shoes.

The Southern Coalition's troops suffered terribly from shoddy footwear. They fought in straw sandals, and cotton if they could obtain it, but those cotton shoes were more like slippers, sewn weeks before the battle by wives, mothers, and sisters. Most were fighting in footwear of plaited straw that broke midmarch, fell apart in sticky mud, and offered no protection against the cold.

The Mugenese, however, had sailed over the Nariin Sea wearing leather boots—fine, solid, warm, and waterproof. Rin's soldiers had become very adept at untying the laces, yanking boots off stiffening feet, and tossing them into wheelbarrows to be redistributed later according to size.

While Rin's soldiers combed through the fields, Souji led her toward the former village headman's office, which the Mugenese had repurposed into a headquarters. He provided running commentary on the ruins as they walked, like a disgruntled host apologetic that his home had been found in such a mess.

"It looked loads better than this months ago. Khudla's a nice village—had some lovely historic architecture, until they tore down everything for firewood. And *we* made those barricades," he said somewhat sulkily, pointing to the sandbags around the headquarters. "They just stole them."

For a simple village's defenses, Souji's barricades had been surprisingly well constructed. He'd organized pillboxes the way she would have done it—wooden stakes driven into the ground to provide a lattice framework for layers of sandbags. She'd been taught that method at Sinegard. These defenses, Rin realized, had been built according to Militia guidelines.

"Then how did they get through in the end?" she asked.

Souji blinked at her as if she were an idiot. "They had *gas*."

So Officer Shen was right. Rin stifled a shudder, imagining the impact of the noxious yellow fumes on unsuspecting civilians. "How much?"

"Just one canister," Souji said. "I think they'd been hoarding it, because they didn't use it when they first came. Waited until the third day of fighting, when they had us all barricaded into one place, and then they popped it over the wall. We fell apart pretty quickly after that."

They reached the headquarters. Souji tried the door. It swung open without trouble; no one was left to lock it from the inside.

Food littered the table of the central conference room. Souji picked a wheat bun off its place, tore off a bite, then spat it back out. "Disgusting."

"What, too stale for you?"

"No. It's got too much salt. Gross." Souji tossed the wheat bun back onto the table. "Salt doesn't belong in buns."

Rin's mouth watered. "They have salt?"

She hadn't tasted salt in weeks. Most salt in the Empire was imported from the basins of Dog Province, but those trade networks had completely broken down during Vaisra's civil war. Out in the arid eastern Monkey Province, Rin's army had been subsisting on the blandest rice gruel and boiled vegetables. There were rumored to be a few jars of fermented soy paste hidden in the kitchens at Ruijin, but if they existed, Rin had never seen nor tasted them.

"*We* had salt," Souji corrected. He bent over to examine the contents of a barrel. "Looks like they've eaten through most of it. There's only a handful left."

"Take that back to the public kitchen. We'll treat everyone." Rin leaned over the commander's desk. Documents were strewn all over its surface. Rin found troop numbers, food ration records, and letters written in a scrawled, messy script that she could barely read. Here and there she could make out a few words. *Wife. Home. Emperor.*

She collected them into a neat pile. She and Kitay would pore over them later, see if they bore any meaningful news about the Mugenese. But they were likely months old, like the other correspondence they'd found. Every dead Mugenese general kept letters from the mainland on their desk, as if rereading those Mugini characters could maintain their connection to a motherland they must have known was gone.

"They were reading Sunzi?" Rin picked up the slim text—a Nikara edition, not a translation. "And the *Bodhidharma*? Where'd they get these?"

"Those were mine. Stole them out of the Sinegard library way back in the day." Souji plucked the booklet from her hand. "I take them with me everywhere I go. Those bastards wouldn't have been able to make head or tail of them."

Rin glanced at him, surprised. "You're a Sinegard graduate?"

"Not a graduate. I was there for two years. Then the famine struck, so I went home. Jima didn't let me back in when I returned. But I still needed a paycheck, so I enlisted in the Militia."

So he'd passed the Keju. That was rare for someone from his background—Rin should know. She regarded Souji with a newfound respect. "Why wouldn't they?"

"Because they thought that if I left once, then I'd do it again. That I'd always prioritize my family over my military career. Guess they were right. I would have left the ranks the moment we got wind of the Mugenese invasion."

"And what about now?"

"Whole family's dead." His voice was flat. "Died this past year."

"I'm sorry. Was it the Federation?"

"No. The flood." Souji jerked out a shrug. "We're usually pretty good at seeing floods coming. Not hard to read the weather if you know what you're doing. But not this time. This was man-made."

"The Empress broke the dams," Rin said automatically. Chaghan and Qara felt like such a distant memory that she could speak this lie without struggle. Best that Souji didn't know that the Cike, her old regiment, had deliberately caused the flood that killed his family.

"Broke the dams to stem an enemy that she'd invited in herself." Souji's voice turned bitter. "I know. I'd learned to swim at Sinegard. They hadn't. There's nothing where my village used to be."

Rin felt a stab of guilt. She did her best to ignore it. She shouldn't have to shoulder the blame for that particular atrocity. That flood had been the fault of the twins, an act of environmental warfare to slow the Federation's progress inland.

Who could say if it had worked, or if it had even mattered? What was done was done. The only way to live with your transgressions, Rin had learned, was to lock them away in your mind and leave them in the abyss.

"Why can't you just blow them up?" Souji asked abruptly.

She blinked at him. "What?"

"When you ended the war. When the longbow island went up in smoke. What's stopping you from doing that again in the south?"

"Prudence," she said. "If I burn them, I burn everyone. Fire on that scale doesn't discriminate. A massive genocide on our own territory would—"

"We don't need a massive genocide. Just a little one would do."

"You don't know what you're asking for." She turned away; she didn't want to meet his eyes. "Even the little fires hurt people they shouldn't."

She'd grown tired of this question. That was what everyone wanted to know—why she couldn't simply snap her fingers and incinerate the Mugenese camp like she'd done to their entire island. If she'd finished off a nation once, why couldn't she do it again? Why couldn't she end this whole war in seconds? Wasn't that *so obviously* the next move?

She wished she could do it. There were times when she wanted so badly to send walls of flame roaring across the entire south, clearing out the Mugenese the way one might raze a field of blighted crops, with no regard for the collateral damage.

But every time that desire surged within her, she ran up against the same pulsing black venom that clouded her mind—Su Daji's parting gift, the Seal that cut her off from direct access to the Pantheon.

Maybe it was a blessing that her mind remained blocked by the Seal, that she was forced to use Kitay as a conduit for her power. Kitay kept her sane. Stable. He let her call the fire, but only in targeted, limited bursts.

Without Kitay, Rin was terrified of what she might do.

"If I were you," Souji said, "I would have gotten rid of them all. One single blaze, and the south would be clean. Fuck prudence."

She shot him a wry look. "Then you'd be dead, too."

"Just as well," he said, and sounded like he meant it.

Rin felt as if eternity had passed by the time the sun set. Twenty-four hours ago, she had led troops into battle for the first time. That afternoon, she'd liberated a village. Now her wrist throbbed, her knees shook, and a headache pounded behind her eyes.

She could not silence the memory of that scream in the temple. She needed to silence it.

Back in her tent, she dug a packet of opium out from the bottom of her traveling satchel and pressed a nugget into a pipe.

"Do you have to?" Kitay asked. It wasn't really a question. They'd had this argument a thousand times, and every time arrived at the same lack of resolution. He just felt obligated to express his displeasure. By now they were simply going through the motions.

"It's not your business," she said.

"You need to sleep. You've been up nearly forty-eight hours."

"I'll sleep after this. I can't relax without it."

"It smells awful."

"So go sleep somewhere else."

Silently Kitay stood up and walked out of the tent.

Rin didn't watch him go. She lifted the pipe to her mouth, lit the bowl with her fingers, and breathed in deep. Then she curled over on her side and drew her knees into her chest.

In seconds she saw the Seal—a live, pulsing thing, reeking so strongly of the Vipress's venom that Su Daji might have been standing in the tent right next to her. She used to curse the Seal, used to barrel pointlessly against the immutable barrier of venom that wouldn't leave her mind.

But she'd since found a better use for it.

Rin drifted toward the glistening characters. The Seal tilted toward her, opened, and swallowed her. There was a brief moment of blinding, terrifying darkness, and then she was in a dark room with no doors or windows.

Daji's poison was composed of desire—the things she would kill for, the things she missed so badly she wanted to die.

Altan materialized on cue.

Rin used to be so afraid of him. She'd felt a little thrill of fear every time she'd looked at him, and she'd *liked* it. When he was alive, she'd never known if he was going to caress or throttle her. The first time she'd seen him inside the Seal, he'd nearly convinced her to follow him into oblivion. But now she kept him leashed in her mind, firmly under control, and he spoke only when she wanted him to.

Still the fear remained. She couldn't help it, nor did she want to. She needed someone who could still scare her.

"There you are." He reached a hand out to stroke her cheek. "Did you miss me?"

"Get back," she said. "Sit down."

He held his hands up and obeyed, crossing his legs on the dark floor. "Whatever you say, darling."

She sat down across from him. "I killed dozens of people last night. Probably some of them innocent."

Altan tilted his head to the side. "And how did that make you feel?" His tone was perfectly neutral, without judgment.

Even so, she felt a swell in her chest, a familiar toxic squeeze, like her lungs were eroding under the sheer weight of her guilt. She exhaled, fighting to remain calm. Altan stayed under her control only so long as she was calm. "You would have done it."

"And why would I have done it, kiddo?"

"Because you were ruthless," she said. "You did strategy by the numbers. You would have known you had to do it. You couldn't risk your troops. Soldiers are worth more than civilians, it's just math."

"So there it is." He gave her a patronizing smile. "You did what you needed to. You're a hero. Did you enjoy it?"

She didn't lie. Why would she? Altan was her secret, her conjuration, and no one would ever know what she said here. Not even Kitay.

"Yes."

"Show it to me," Altan said. Hunger was etched across his face. "Show me everything."

She let him see. Relived it all, second by second, in vivid, lurid detail. She showed him the bodies doubling over. The babble of terrified voices pleading for mercy—*No, no, please, no.* The temple transforming into a pillar of flame.

"Good," said Altan. "That's very good. Show me more."

She brought out the memories of ashes, of pristine white bone poking out from charred black piles. She could never burn the bones away entirely, no matter how hard she tried. Some fragment always remained.

She stayed for another minute to let herself feel it—feel all of it, the guilt, the remorse, the horror. She could only feel them in *this* space, where they wouldn't be debilitating, where they wouldn't make her want to crawl across the floor and scratch long streaks of blood into her forearms and thighs.

Then she left the memories alone. Interred here, they wouldn't haunt her again.

She always felt so clean afterward. Like the world was covered in stains and with every enemy she reduced to ash, it became just a little bit more pure.

This was both her absolution and her penance. Once she self-flagellated in her mind, once she replayed the atrocities over and over so much the images lost meaning, then she'd given the dead their due respect. She owed them nothing more.

She opened her eyes. The memory of Altan threatened to resurge in her thoughts, but she forced it back down. He appeared only when she allowed it, only when she wanted to see him.

Once, her memories of Altan had nearly driven her mad. Now his company was one of the only things keeping her sane.

She was finding it easier and easier to cut him off. She'd learned now to divide her mind into clean, convenient compartments. Thoughts could be blocked. Memories suppressed. Life was so much easier when she blockaded off the part of her that agonized over what she'd done. And as long as she kept those parts of her mind separate—the part that felt pain and the part that fought wars—then she would be all right.

"You think they're going to join up?" Kitay asked.

"I'm not sure," Rin said. "They've been a bit surly about everything so far. Ingrates."

They watched, arms crossed, as the men who called themselves the Iron Wolves carried salvageable wreckage out of the village center.

The Iron Wolves were Souji's troops. More of them had survived Khudla's occupation than Rin had feared—their numbers ranked at least five hundred. That was a relief. The Southern Army desperately needed new troops, but suitable recruits were difficult to find in Mugenese-occupied villages. Most young men with any inclination to fight were already buried in the killing fields. The lucky survivors were either too young or too old—or too frightened—to make good soldiers.

But Souji's Iron Wolves were strong, healthy men with plenty of combat experience. Until now, they had been roving protectors of the Monkey Province's backwaters. Many had fled into the forests when Khudla fell. Now they'd returned in hordes. They would make excellent soldiers—but the question was whether they could be convinced to join the Coalition.

Rin wasn't sure. So far the Iron Wolves had been less than grateful to their liberators. In fact the rescue operations had taken a heated turn; Souji's men were terribly territorial and reluctant to take commands that didn't come from Souji himself. They were irked, it seemed, that someone else had swooped in to claim the title of savior. Already Kitay had mediated three quarrels over resource allocation between Iron Wolves and soldiers of the Southern Coalition.

"What's going on there?" Rin asked suddenly.

She pointed. Two of Souji's yellow-banded troops were marching toward their camp, both lugging sacks of rice behind them.

"Ah, fuck." Kitay looked exasperated. "Not this again."

"Hey!" Rin stood up and cupped her hand around her mouth. "You! Stop there."

They kept walking as if they hadn't heard her. She had to run at them, shouting, before they finally stopped.

"Where are you taking that?" she demanded.

They exchanged looks of obvious irritation. The taller one spoke. "Souji told us to bring some rice out to the tents."

"We've set up a communal kitchen." Rin pointed. "You can eat there. That's where all the salvaged food goes. All the scavenging teams were ordered to—"

The shorter one cut her off. "Well, see, we don't take orders from you."

She blinked at him. "I *liberated* this place."

"And that's very kind of you, miss. But we've got this village under control now."

Rin was amazed when, without so much as a final look of disdain, they slung the rice sacks up onto their shoulders and stalked insolently off.

I'll teach you to listen. Her palm sang with heat. She raised her fist, pointed it toward their retreating backs—

"Don't." Kitay caught her by the wrist. "Now isn't the time to start a fight."

"They should be terrified of me," she snarled. "The sheer *nerve*—"

"You can't be mad about stupidity. Just let them go. If we want them on our side, you can't go around burning their balls off."

"What the hell is Souji telling his men?" she hissed. "He knows I'm in command!"

"I doubt he's passed that on."

"They're in for a rude awakening, then."

"And while that's true, you don't have to convince the *soldiers*," Kitay said. "You've got to convince Souji. He's the problem."

"Should have just left him in the cellar," Rin grumbled. "Or we could kill him now."

"Too hard to pull off," Kitay said, unfazed. Rin suggested casual murder on such a regular basis that he'd learned to brush it off. "The timing would be too suspicious. We'd certainly lose his men. You could try to make it look like an accident, but even then it'd be difficult to spin. Souji's not the type to go around tripping off cliffs."

"Then we have to undercut him," Rin said. "Knock him off his pedestal."

But how? She pondered this for a moment. Discrediting him would be too hard. Those men loved Souji. She couldn't sever those bonds overnight.

"That's not necessary," Kitay said. "Don't cut the head off the snake if you can tame it. You've just got to convince him where his interests lie."

"But how?"

He shot her a droll look. "Oh, I think you're good enough at that."

She rubbed her wrist stump into the palm of her good fist. "I'll go have a nice long chat with him then, shall I?"

He sighed. "Be nice."

∞

"To what do I owe the pleasure?" Souji asked. He was crouched over a campfire, digging into a bowl of steaming white rice that smelled much better than the vats of barley porridge in the communal kitchen.

"Get up," Rin said. "We're going for a walk."

"Why?"

"For privacy."

Souji's eyes narrowed. He must have known what was coming, because he gave a nearly imperceptible shake of his head to the closest Iron Wolves. *Leave us*, it said. *I'm fine.*

The men turned and left. Souji stood up. "All right, Princess. I'll walk with you."

Rin wrinkled her nose. "Princess?"

"Sinegard educated? Former Militia elite? That's royalty in my book."

He didn't make it sound like a compliment. Rin chose not to retort; she held her tongue until they'd walked deep into the forest, out of earshot from camp. She might as well let Souji keep his dignity with his men. He'd be less grumpy about taking orders if she did.

She tried a diplomatic opening. "I'm sure you've realized by now we have men and resources that you don't."

"Stop." He held up a hand. "I know what you want. We're not joining any coalitions. Your war isn't my problem."

She scoffed. "You were happy enough about taking our aid yesterday."

"The *Mugenese* are my problem. But don't pretend that this is all about the Federation. Your Southern Coalition is baiting the Republic and you're an idiot if you think I'm getting involved with that."

"Soon enough you won't have a choice. Yin Vaisra—"

Souji rolled his eyes. "Vaisra doesn't care about us."

"He will," she insisted. "You think Vaisra's going to stop after he's conquered the north? I've met the Hesperians, I know their intentions. They won't stop until they've put a church in each of our villages—"

Souji picked at his teeth with the nail of his little finger. "Churches never killed anyone."

"They prop up regime ideologies that do."

"Come on, you're grasping at straws—"

"Am I? You've dealt with them before, have you? No, you'll regret saying that when you're all under Hesperian rule. I've spoken to them. I know how they look at us. None of this—our villages, our people, our freedom—will survive under their intended world order."

"Don't talk to me about survival," Souji snapped. "I've been keeping our people alive for months while you've been playing the hunting dog over at Vaisra's court. What did that get you?"

"I was a fool," Rin said bluntly. "I know that. I was stupid then and I should have seen the signs. But I'm back in the south now, and we can build this army, if you bring your Iron Wolves—"

He cut her off with a laugh. "That's a no, Princess."

"I don't think you understand," she said. "That was an order. Not a request."

He reached out and flicked her on the nose. "And you don't understand: we are not, and never will be, under your command."

Rin blinked, stunned that he would even *dare*.

So this was how things were going to go.

"Oh, Souji." She pulled a flame into her palm. "You don't understand how this works."

She darted toward him just as he reached for his sword. She'd anticipated that. As he swung, she dodged his blade and jammed a foot hard into his left kneecap. He buckled. She swept the other leg out from under him and jumped down onto his chest as he fell, fingers grasping for his neck. She squeezed.

"You don't know who you're dealing with." She leaned down close until her lips brushed his skin, until her breath scorched the side of his face. "I'm not Sinegardian elite. I'm that savage, mud-skinned Speerly bitch that wiped a country off the map. And sometimes when I get a little too angry, I *snap*."

She let just the faintest trickle of fire seep from under her fingers. Souji's eyes bulged. She dug her fingertips farther into his skin.

"You're coming back with me to Ruijin. The Iron Wolves now fight under my command. You'll keep your position as their leader, but you'll make the hierarchy clear to your men. And if you try to mutiny, I'll pick this up where I left off. Understand?"

Souji's throat bobbed. He pawed feebly at her arm.

She tightened her grip. "You're my bitch now, Souji. You do anything I ask without complaint. You'll lick the dirt off my boots if I want. Is that clear?"

He nodded, patting frantically at her wrist.

She didn't budge. Blisters formed and popped under his chin. "I didn't hear an answer."

"Yes," he croaked.

"Yes, what?" She relaxed her grip just enough to let him speak.

"Yes, I'm your bitch. I'll do what you want. Anything. Just—please—"

She released him and let him stand. Little tendrils of smoke wafted out from his neck. Visible beneath his collar was a first-degree burn, a pale red imprint of her skinny fingers.

It would heal quickly, but that scar would never disappear. Souji might cover it with his collar and hide it from his men, but it would be clear as day to him every time he so much as glanced at his reflection.

"Why don't you go put a poultice on that?" she asked. "Wouldn't want it infected."

He backed away from her. "You're insane."

"Everyone vying for this country is insane," she said. "But none of them have skin as dark as ours. I'm the least terrible option you've got."

Souji stared at her for a long time. Rin couldn't read his expression, couldn't tell if his eyes glinted with rage or humiliation. She curled her fist and tensed, ready for another round.

To her surprise, he began to laugh. "All right. You win, you fucking bitch."

"Don't call me a bitch."

"You win, General." He held his hands up in a gesture of mock surrender. "I'll march back with you. Where are we going? Dalian? Heirjiang?"

"I told you," she said. "Ruijin."

He raised a brow. "Why Ruijin?"

"It's built into the mountains. Keeps us safe from almost everything. Why not?"

"I just assumed you'd be somewhere farther south. Near Rooster Province, if your goal is liberation."

"What are you talking about? The occupied areas are clustered at the Monkey border."

"No, they aren't. Most of them are bunched down south in Rooster Province."

"Where, the capital?" Rin frowned. None of this tracked with her intelligence.

"No, somewhere farther down south," Souji said. "A few weeks' march from the ocean. A cluster of tiny villages, you won't know it."

"Tikany," she said automatically.

A little township no one had ever heard of. A dusty, arid place with no riches and no special culture; nothing except a docile population still addicted to opium from the second invasion. A place where Rin had once hoped she would never in her life return.

"Yeah." Souji arched an eyebrow. "That's one of them. Why, do you know the place?"

He said something else after that, but she didn't hear it.

Tikany. The Mugenese were still in Tikany.

We're fools, she thought. *We've been fighting on the wrong front this entire time.*

"Tell your men to pack up," she said. "We head out for Ruijin in two hours."

CHAPTER 3

That evening they began their march back to the base camp of the Southern Coalition. Ruijin lay within the backwoods of the Monkey Province, a poor and calcified land racked by years of banditry, warlord campaigns, famines, and epidemics. It had been the capital of the Monkey Province in antiquity, a lush city famed for its stone shrines built elegantly into the topiary of surrounding bamboo groves. Now it comprised ruins of its former splendor, half eroded by rain and half devoured by the forest.

That made it an excellent place to hide. For centuries, the people of Monkey Province prided themselves on their ability to blend into the mountains during troubled times. They built houses on stilts or up in the trees to keep safe from tigers. They paved winding paths through the dark forest invisible to the untrained eye. In all the stories of old, the Monkeys were stereotyped as backward mountain people—cowards who hid away in trees and caves while the wars of the world passed them by. But those were the same traits that kept them alive.

"Where are we going?" Souji grumbled a week into a continuously uphill hike, during which they'd encountered nothing but endless bumpy paths through hilly forest. "There's nothing up here."

"That's what you think." Rin bent low to check the scores against the base of a poplar tree—a clue that they were still on the right path—and motioned for the column to follow.

The way up the pass was easier than she had remembered it. The sheen had melted off the edges of the ice. She could see plenty of green beneath sheets of snow that hadn't been visible when she'd set out two weeks ago. Against all odds, the Southern Coalition had made it to spring.

Winter in the Monkey Province had been a frigid, arid ordeal for the Southern Coalition. It didn't snow, it hailed. The cold, dry air robbed their breaths from under their noses. The ground turned into a hard, brittle thing. Nothing grew. They'd come so close to starving, and likely would have if an ambushed Mugenese enclave ten miles away hadn't turned out to possess a shocking amount of food stores.

The soldiers hadn't distributed their spoils. Rin couldn't forget the faces of the villagers who'd come out from hiding, thin and exhausted, their relief quickly turning to horror when they realized their liberators were here simply to cart their grain away.

She pushed the memory from her mind. That was a necessary sacrifice. The future of the entire country hinged on the Southern Coalition. What difference did a few lives make?

"Well, this clarifies some things," Souji muttered as he pushed through the undergrowth.

"What are you talking about?"

"You don't hide in the mountains if you're a liberating force."

"No?"

"If you're trying to take back territory, you inhabit the villages you've freed. You expand your base. You set up defenses to make sure the Mugenese don't come back again. But you're just predatory extractors. You'll liberate places, but only for the tribute."

"I didn't hear you complaining when I freed you from that cellar."

"Whatever you say, Princess." Souji's voice took on a judging, mocking tone. "You aren't the salvation of the south. You're just hiding out here until the whole thing blows over."

Several scathing responses leaped to mind. Rin bit them back.

The trouble was that he was right. The Southern Coalition had been too passive, too slow to initiate the wider campaign the rest of the country clearly needed, and she hated it.

The coalition leadership's priority at Ruijin was still sheer survival, which meant ensconcing themselves in the mountains and biding their time while Vaisra's Republic battled for control of the north. But they were barely even surviving. This wouldn't last forever. Ruijin kept them safe for now, for the same reasons it was slowly becoming their tomb.

Not if Rin got her way. Not if they sent every soldier in their army south.

"That's about to change." She jammed her hiking pole into the rocky path and hauled herself up a steep incline. "You'll see."

"You're lost," Souji accused.

"I'm not lost."

She was helplessly lost. She knew they were close, but she had no idea where to go from here. Three months and dozens of expeditions later, Rin still couldn't find the precise entrance to Ruijin. It was a hideout designed to stay invisible. She had to send an intricate flare spiraling high into the air and wait until two sentries emerged from the undergrowth to guide them onto a path that, previously invisible, now seemed obvious. Rin followed along, ignoring Souji's smirk.

Half an hour's hike later, the camp emerged from the trees like an optical illusion; everything was camouflaged so artfully that Rin sometimes thought if she blinked, it might all disappear.

Just past the wall of bamboo stakes surrounding the camp, an excited crowd had gathered around something on the ground.

"What's this about?" Rin asked the closest sentry.

"They finally killed that tiger," he told her.

"Really?"

"Found the corpse this morning. We're going to skin it, but nobody can agree on who gets the pelt."

The tiger had been plaguing the camp since before Rin's troops had left for Khudla. Its growling haunted the soldiers on patrol duty. Dried fish kept disappearing nightly from the food stores. After the tiger dragged an infant out of its tent and left its mauled, half-eaten body by the creek, the Monkey Warlord had ordered a hunting expedition. But the hunters came back empty-handed and exhausted, limbs scratched up by thorns.

"How'd they manage it?" Kitay asked.

"We poisoned a horse," said the sentry. "It was already dying from a peptic ulcer, else we wouldn't have spared the animal. Injected opium and strychnine into the carcass and left it out for the tiger to find. We found the bastard this morning. Stiff as a board."

"You see," Rin told Kitay. "It's a good plan."

"This has nothing to do with your plan."

"Opium kills tigers. Literal and metaphorical."

"It's lost this country two wars," he said. "I don't mean to call you stupid, because I love you, but that plan is so stupid."

"We have the arable land! Moag's happy to buy it up; if we just planted it in a few regions we'd get all the silver we need—"

"And an army full of addicts. Let's not kid ourselves, Rin. Is that what you want?"

Rin opened her mouth to respond, but something over Kitay's shoulder caught her eye.

A tall man stood a little way off from the crowd, arms crossed as he watched her. Waiting. He was Du Zhuden—the right-hand man of the bandit leader Ma Lien. He raised an eyebrow when he saw her glancing his way, and she nodded in response. He jerked his head toward the forest, turned, and disappeared into the trees.

Rin touched Kitay on the arm. "I'll be back."

He'd seen Zhuden, too. He sighed. "You're still going through with this?"

"I don't see any other option."

He was quiet for a moment. "Me neither," he said at last. "But be careful. The monkey's men are watching."

Rin met Zhuden at their usual spot—a crooked rowan tree a mile outside the camp, at the juncture of a small creek burbling just loudly enough to conceal their voices from eavesdroppers.

"You found Yang Souji?" Zhuden's eyes darted warily around as he spoke. The Monkey Warlord had spies everywhere in Ruijin; Rin would not have been surprised if someone had followed her out of camp.

She nodded. "Took a little convincing, but he's here."

"What's he like?"

"Arrogant. Annoying." She grimaced, thinking of Souji's smug, leering grin.

"So he's just like you?"

"Very funny," she drawled. "He's competent, though. Knows the terrain well. Has strong local contacts—he might be better keyed into the intelligence network here than we are. And he comes with five hundred experienced soldiers. They'd die for him."

"Well done," Zhuden said. "We'll just have to make sure they start dying for you."

Rin shot him a grin.

Zhuden wasn't native to Monkey Province. He was a war orphan from Rat Province who had wound up in Ma Lien's band from the usual combination of homelessness, desperation, and a callous willingness to do whatever it took to get ahead. Most importantly, unlike the rest of the southern leadership, he wasn't a mere survivalist.

He, too, thought they were dying slowly in Ruijin. He wanted to expand farther south. And, like Rin, he'd decided on drastic measures to shake things up.

"How's Ma Lien doing?" Rin asked.

"Getting worse," Zhuden said. "Honestly, he might just croak on his own, given time, but we still don't want to risk the off chance that he gets better. You'll want to act soon." He passed her a single vial filled with a viscous piss-yellow fluid. "Careful you don't break that."

She pinched it by the neck and gingerly dropped it into her front pocket. "Did you extract this yourself?"

"Yep. Can't say I enjoyed it."

She patted her pocket. "Thank you."

"Are you going now?" he asked.

"Tonight," she said. "I'm due to meet with Gurubai right now. I'll try one last time to convince him."

They both knew that meeting would come to nothing. She'd been having the same argument with the Monkey Warlord for weeks. She wanted to march out of Ruijin. He wanted to remain in the mountains, and his allies in the leadership of the Southern Coalition agreed. They outnumbered her three votes to one.

Rin was about to flip those numbers.

But not just yet. No need to act in haste; she'd show her hand too early. One thing at a time. She'd give the Monkey Warlord one last chance first, make him think she'd come back cooperative and complacent. She had learned, since her days at Sinegard, to rein in her impulses. The best plans were a secret until their execution. The hidden knife cut the deepest.

"Welcome back," said the Monkey Warlord.

Liu Gurubai had set up his headquarters in one of the few old architectural beauties in Ruijin that still stood, a square stone temple with three walls eaten over by moss. He'd chosen it for security, not comfort. The insides were sparsely furnished, with only a stove dug into the corner wall, two rugs, and a simple council table in the center of the cold, drafty room.

Rin and Kitay sat down across him, resembling two students arriving at their tutor's home for a lesson.

"I brought presents," said Rin.

"Oh, I saw," Gurubai said. "Couldn't help but leave a little mark, could you?"

"I thought they should know who's commanding them."

"Well, I assumed Souji would." Gurubai raised an eyebrow. "Unless you were planning on decapitating him?"

Rin gave him a thin smile and wished fervently she could force a flaming fist down his throat.

When she'd hurtled out of Arlong on a Black Lily ship with her hand a bloody mess, she'd thought that the Monkey Warlord might be different from the series of horrible men she'd hitherto thrown in her lot with. That he'd keep his promises. That he'd treat her not as a weapon but as an ally. That he'd put her in charge.

She'd been so wrong.

She'd underestimated Gurubai. He was brilliant; he'd been the sole survivor of Vaisra's violent purge at Arlong for a reason. He understood power politics in a way she never would, because he'd spent his entire life practicing it. Gurubai understood what made men pledge their support, what won him trust and love. He was used now, after two decades, to calling all the shots. And he did not relinquish power.

"I thought we had agreed," she said lightly, "if the Khudla experiment worked out—"

"Oh, it worked out. You can keep that contingent. Officers Shen and Lin were quite happy with your performance."

"I don't want a single contingent, I want the army."

"Let's not pretend you could handle that."

"I just liberated an entire village with minimal casualties—"

"Your supreme talent for burning things down does not qualify you to be a commander." Gurubai drew out the last syllable of each word as if she wouldn't have understood him otherwise. "You're still learning to manage communication and logistics. Don't rush it, child. Give yourself the space to learn. This isn't Sinegard, where we throw children into war with no preparation. We'll find you something better to do in time."

The condescension in his voice made her fist curl. Her eyes focused on the veins in his neck. They protruded so visibly; it would be so easy to slice them open.

If only. Speerly or no, if she hurt Liu Gurubai, she wouldn't make it out of Ruijin alive.

Kitay kicked her lightly under the table. *Don't.*

She grimaced at him. *I know.*

If Rin was a Speerly outsider and Kitay a Sinegardian elite, then the Monkey Warlord was the true product of the south, a rough-hewn man with shoulders broadened from years of labor, whose gleaming, intelligent eyes were set deep in a face lined like the forest.

Rin had left the south at the first chance she got. The Monkey Warlord had fought and suffered in the south his entire life. He'd watched his grandmother begging for rice in the streets during the Lunar New Year. He'd walked miles to tend water buffalo for a single copper a day. He'd fought in the ragged provincial brigades that rallied to the Trifecta's cause during the Second Poppy War. He hadn't become a warlord through inheritance or sheer ambition; he'd simply moved slowly up through the line of succession as the soldiers around him died. He'd been drafted into an army at thirteen years old for the promise of a single silver coin a month, and he'd stayed in the army for the rest of his life.

His younger brothers had both died fighting the Federation. His clan, once a sprawling village family, had withered away from opium addiction. He'd survived the worst of the past century, and so survival became his greatest skill. He'd become a soldier out of necessity, and that made him a leader whose legitimacy was nigh unquestionable.

Most importantly, he *belonged*. These mountains were part of his blood. Anyone could see it in the tired way he carried his shoulders, the hard glint in his eyes.

Rin may have been a figurehead of power, but Liu Gurubai symbolized the very identity of the south. If she hurt him, Monkey Province would tear her to pieces.

So for now, she compromised.

"I hear there have been developments in the north." She

changed the subject, forcing her tone to stay neutral. "Anything you want to show me?"

"Several updates." If Gurubai was surprised by her sudden acquiescence, he didn't show it. He slid a sheaf of letters across the table. "Your friend wrote back. These arrived yesterday."

Rin snatched up the first page and started poring hungrily down the lines, passing the pages to Kitay once she was done. News from the north always trickled in by little bursts—weeks passed with nothing, and then they received sudden gluts of information. The Southern Coalition had only a handful of spies in the Republic, and most of them were Moag's girls; the few pale-skinned Black Lilies who had been shipped to Arlong with carefully disguised accents to work in teahouses and gambling dens.

Venka had gone north, too. With her pale, pretty face and flawless Sinegardian diction, she blended in perfectly among the aristocrats of the formal capital. At first Rin had been worried she'd be recognized—she was the missing daughter of the former finance minister; she couldn't be more high-profile—but based on Venka's reports, she'd completely transformed with only a wig and several gobs of cosmetics.

No one pays much attention to my face, Venka had written shortly after she arrived. *The dolls of Sinegard, it turns out, are shockingly interchangeable.*

Her report now contained nothing surprising. *Vaisra's still battling it out in the north. Warlords and their successors dropping dead like flies. They can't hold out for long, they're overstretched. Vaisra's turned the siege cities into death zones. It'll all be over soon.*

That wasn't news, only a slow intensification of what they'd known for weeks. Vaisra's Hesperians were ravaging the countryside in their dirigibles, leaving craters and bombed-out hellscapes in their wake.

"Any mention of a southern turn?" Rin asked Gurubai.

"None yet. What you're holding is everything we have."

"Then we're being ignored," she said.

"We're getting *lucky*," Kitay amended. "It's only a matter of time."

The Dragon Warlord Yin Vaisra's great democracy, the one he'd sacked cities and turned the Murui crimson for, had never come into existence. He'd never meant it to. Days after he defeated the Imperial Navy at Arlong, he'd assassinated the Boar Warlord and Rooster Warlord, and then declared himself the sole President of the Nikara Republic.

But he didn't yet have a country to rule. Many former Militia officers, not least of whom included the Empress's former favorite soldier, General Jun Loran, had escaped the purge at Arlong and fled north to Tiger Province. Now the combined forces of the Militia's remnants were almost proving to be a challenge for the Hesperians.

Almost. With each new report that reached Ruijin, the Republic appeared to have extended its reach farther and farther north. That meant Rin was sitting on borrowed time. The Southern Coalition was only one rebellion among many. For the time being Vaisra had his hands tied up with Jun's insurgency, not to mention a country chock-full of bandit gangs that had sprung up in local power vacuums immediately after the war's end. But he wouldn't stay busy for long. Jun couldn't hope to beat Vaisra's forces, not with Hesperian dirigibles at Vaisra's back. Not when thousands of Hesperian soldiers with arquebuses were pumping bullets into Jun's armies.

Rin was grateful that Jun had bought them such a long reprieve. But sooner or later, Vaisra would turn his attention to the south. He'd have to, so long as Rin was alive. A reckoning was inevitable. And when it came, she wanted to be on the offensive.

"You know my feelings on this," she told Gurubai.

"Yes, Runin, I do." He regarded her like an exhausted parent might a troublesome child. "And again, I'm telling you—"

"We're *dying* up here. If we don't take the offensive now, then Nezha will. We need to catch him by surprise, and right now is—"

"I'm not the only one you have to convince. *None* of the Southern Coalition want to overextend themselves. These mountains are their home. And when the wolves come, you protect what's behind your walls."

"It's only home for some of you."

He shrugged. "You're free to leave whenever you like."

He could make that bluff. He knew she had nowhere else to turn.

Her nostrils flared. "We need to at least discuss this, Gurubai—"

"Then we'll discuss it at council." His tone made it very clear that their audience was finished. "You can make your case again to the others, if you're so inclined. Although to be quite honest, it's become a bit repetitive."

"I'm going to keep saying it until someone listens," Rin snapped.

"Whatever you like," Gurubai said. "You do so love to be difficult."

Kitay kicked her beneath the table again just as they stood up to leave.

"I know," Rin muttered. "I *know*."

Some little part of her heart sank as she walked out the door. She wished Gurubai had said yes. She was trying to cooperate. She hated to be the lone contrarian; she *did* want to work with the coalition. This all would have been so much easier if he'd said yes.

But if he wasn't going to budge, then she'd have to force his hand.

Dinner was a rapid affair. Rin and Kitay emptied their bowls in seconds. Not because they were hungry—it was just easier to ignore the mold sprouting on the greens and the tiny maggots squirming around the rice if they wolfed it down without thinking. The fare in the mess halls became worse and worse every time she returned to Ruijin, and the cooks had gone from keeping insects out of the vats to encouraging them on the grounds that the carcasses contained badly needed nutrients. Ant porridge was now a dish Rin ate regularly, though she always had to suppress her gag reflex before she could take the first bite.

The only staple that hadn't started to rot was shanyu root—the starchy white yam that stuck like glue in her throat every time she swallowed. Shanyu tubers, having proved remarkably resistant to frost, grew everywhere on the mountainside. For a time Rin had been quite fond of them; they were filling, easy to steam, and had the slightly sweet taste of fresh-baked bread.

That was months ago. She'd since grown so sick of the taste of raw shanyu, dried shanyu, steamed shanyu, and mashed shanyu that the smell was enough to induce nausea. Still, it was the only fresh food with nutrients she could get her hands on. She forced it down as well.

When she was finished, she stood up and prepared to go pay a visit to the bandit chief Ma Lien.

Kitay moved to follow, but she shook her head. "I can do this alone. You don't need to see this."

He didn't argue the point. She knew he didn't want to come. "Fine. You've got the medicine?"

"In my front pocket."

"And you're *sure* that—"

"Please don't." She cut him off. "We've had this debate a thousand times. Can you think of a better option?"

He sighed. "Just do it quickly. Don't linger."

"Why on earth would I linger?"

"*Rin.*"

"All right." She clapped him on the shoulder and strode toward the forest.

Ma Lien's quarters were built into the cave wall near Ruijin's northern perimeter. It should have been near impossible for Rin to get this close to his private residence without at least three blades at her neck, but in recent days Ma Lien's guards had reevaluated their loyalties. When they saw Rin approach, they nodded silently and let her pass through. None of them would meet her eyes.

Ma Lien's wife and daughter sat outside the cave entrance. They stood up when they saw her, their eyes wide with fear and desperation.

They already know, Rin thought. They'd heard the whispers. Or someone in the ranks—perhaps even Zhuden—had already told them what was about to happen in an effort to save their lives.

"You shouldn't be here," she said.

Ma Lien's wife seized Rin's wrist just as she entered the cave. "Please," she begged. "Don't."

"Necessity calls." Rin shrugged her hand away. "Don't try to stop me."

"You can spare him, he'll do what you say, you don't have to—"

"He won't," Rin said. "And I do. I hope you've said goodbye."

They knew what would happen next. Ma Lien's men knew. And Rin suspected that, on some level, the Monkey Warlord had to know, too. He might even sanction it. She would, if she were in his position. What did you do when one of your generals kept agitating to fight a war you knew you couldn't win?

You cut your losses.

The cave smelled like sick, a stomach-turning mix of fumes from bitter herbal medicines and the odor of stale vomit. Ma Lien had been suffering from the bloody lung fever since before she'd left for Khudla. The timing was perfect. She'd struck a deal with Zhuden the morning she marched out—if Ma Lien was still ill by the time she returned, and the odds of his recovery seemed slim, then they would seize their chance.

Still, she hadn't expected Ma Lien to disintegrate so quickly. He lay shriveled and desiccated against his sheets. He seemed to have shrunk to half his body weight. Crusted blood lined the edges of his lips. Every time he breathed, an awful rattle echoed through the cave.

Ma Lien was already half-gone. From the looks of it, what Rin was about to do couldn't even properly be called murder. She was only hastening the inevitable.

"Hello, General." She perched herself by the edge of his bed.

His eyes cracked open at the sound of her voice.

She'd been told the illness had taken his vocal cords. *He bleeds when he tries to speak*, Zhuden had said. *And if he gets agitated, he starts choking on it.* She felt a little thrill at the thought. He couldn't mock her, couldn't curse at her, couldn't scream for help. She could taunt him as much as she liked. And all he could do was lie there and listen.

She should have just done the job and left. The smarter, pragmatic part of her was screaming at her to go—it was a risk to stay for so long, to speak where Gurubai's spies might hear her.

But this encounter had been a long time coming. She wanted him to know every reason why he had to die. She wanted to relish this moment. She'd earned this.

She recalled vividly the way he'd shouted her down when she first suggested deploying troops to Rooster Province. He'd called her a savage, sentimental, dirt-skinned, warmongering bitch. He'd railed at Gurubai for letting a little girl into the war council in the first place. He'd suggested she'd be better off dead with the rest of her kind.

He probably didn't remember saying that. Ma Lien was one of those loud, garrulous types. Always tossing insults out like the wind. Always assuming that his bodily strength and the loyalty of his men would insulate him from resentment.

"Do you remember what you said when I first asked for command?" Rin asked.

Spit bubbled by the side of Ma Lien's mouth. She picked a bloodstained bed rag up from the floor and gently rubbed it away.

"You said I was a dumb bitch with no command experience and a genetic lack of rationality." She chuckled. "Your words. You said I was an empty-headed little fool with more power than I knew what to do with. You said I should know my place. You said Speerlies weren't meant to make decisions but to obey."

Ma Lien mouthed something incoherent. She smoothed tendrils of his hair back from his mouth. He was sweating so hard he looked like he'd been drenched in oil. Poor man.

"I didn't come south to be someone's pet again," she said. "You should have understood that about me."

She'd laid her loyalty at the feet of two masters before. Each had betrayed her in turn. She'd trusted first Daji and then Vaisra, and they'd both sold her away without blinking. From now on Rin took charge of her own fate.

She reached into her pocket and pulled out the vial.

Fat yellow scorpions infested the forests around Ruijin. The soldiers had learned to ward them away from the camp by burning lavender and setting traps, but they couldn't wander ten feet into the trees without stumbling upon a nest. And a single nest was all it took to extract a vial's worth of venom.

"I'm not sorry for this," she said. "You shouldn't have gotten in my way."

She tipped the vial toward Ma Lien's mouth. He thrashed, trying to cough the poison out, but she seized his jaw and forced it shut, pinching his nose between her fingers until the liquid seeped down into his throat. After a minute he stopped resisting. She let go.

"You're not going to die immediately," she said. "Scorpion venom paralyzes. Locks up all your muscles."

She dabbed saliva and venom off his chin with the bed rag. "In a while, it'll feel a little hard to breathe. You'll try to call for help, but you'll find your jaw won't move. I'm sure your wife will come in to check on you, but she knows there's nothing she can do. She knows what I'm doing right now. She's probably imagining it all in her head. But maybe she'll love you enough to see you through to the end. Or, if she really loves you, she'll slit your throat."

She stood up. An odd thrill rushed through her head. Her knees shook. She felt giddy, shot through with a bizarre and unexpected energy.

This wasn't her first kill. But this was her first deliberate, premeditated murder. This was the first person she'd killed not out of desperation but with cool, malicious intent.

It felt—

It felt *good*.

She didn't need her pipe to show this to Altan; she heard his laughter as loudly as if he were standing right next to her. She felt divine. She felt like she could leap across mountains if she wanted to. Her hand couldn't stop shaking. The vial dropped from her fingers and shattered against the floor.

Heart pounding, blood pumping with a euphoria that confused her, she left the cave.

"I want to lead two contingents into Rooster Province," Rin said. "Souji says they've clustered there because the flat terrain is easier to navigate. We've been shoring up for a fight on the wrong front. They're not going to push up into the mountains here because they don't need to. They're just going to expand farther south."

The leadership of the Southern Coalition sat assembled around a table in the Monkey Warlord's headquarters. Gurubai, the natural leader, sat at the front. Liu Dai, a former county official and Gurubai's longtime ally, sat on his right. Zhuden was seated to Liu Dai's right as Ma Lien's substitute, but an empty chair remained at the table out of respect. Souji sat in the back left corner, arms crossed, smirking, as if he'd already called this charade for what it was.

"If we strike quickly," Rin continued, "that is, if we take the main nodes before they've gotten the chance to regroup, we could end this whole thing in one drive."

"Just this morning you wanted to turn north to face Vaisra," Gurubai said. "Now you want to drive south. You can't fight a war on two fronts, Rin. Which is it?"

"We've got to go south *just so* we can get the strength to muster a defense against the Hesperians," Rin said. "If we win the south, we get warm bodies. Food stores. Access to river routes, armories, and who knows what else we've been relinquishing to the Mugenese. Our armies will swell by thousands, and we'll have the supply lines to support them. But if we don't clear out the Mugenese first, then we'll be trapped inside the mountains—"

"We're *safe* inside the mountains," Liu Dai interrupted. "No one has invaded Ruijin in centuries, the terrain is too hostile—"

"There's no food here," Rin said. "The wells are drying up. This won't last forever."

"We understand that," Gurubai said. "But you're asking too much of this army. Half these boys only picked up a sword for the first time two months ago. You need to give them time."

"Vaisra won't give them time," Rin snapped. "The moment he's done with Jun, he will bury us."

She'd already lost them. She could tell from their bored, skeptical expressions. She knew this was pointless; this was just another iteration of the same argument they'd rehashed a dozen times now. They were at a stalemate—she had the fire, but they had everything else. And they were seasoned, war-hardened men who, despite everything they publicly proclaimed, couldn't be less happy about sharing power with a girl half their age.

Rin knew that. She was just constitutionally unable to keep silent.

"Rooster Province is finished," Gurubai said. "The Mugenese have overrun the place like ants. Our strategy now should be survival. We can *keep* the Monkey Province. They cannot survive in the mountains. Don't throw this away, Rin."

He spoke like he'd come to this conclusion long ago. A sudden suspicion struck Rin.

"You knew," she said. "You knew they'd taken Rooster Province."

Gurubai exchanged a glance with Liu Dai. "Runin . . ."

"You've known that all along." Her voice rose in pitch. Her cheeks were burning. This wasn't just his standard patronization, this was appalling condescension. *The fucking nerve.* "You knew this entire time and you didn't tell me."

"It wouldn't have made a difference—"

"Did they all know?" She gestured around the room. Little sparks of flame burst forth from her fingers; she couldn't help it. The coalition members cringed back, but that gave her no pleasure. She was far too embarrassed.

What else hadn't they told her?

Gurubai cleared his throat. "Given your impulses, we didn't think it prudent—"

"Fuck you!" she exclaimed. "I'm a member of this council, I've been winning your battles for you, *I deserve to*—"

"The fact remains that you are impulsive and reckless, as evidenced by your repeated demands for command—"

"I deserve full command! That's what I was promised!"

Gurubai sighed. "We are not discussing this again."

"Look." She slammed her hand on the table. "If none of you are willing to make the first move, then just send me. Give me two thousand troops. Just twice the number I took to Khudla. That'll be enough."

"You and I both know why that's not possible."

"But that's our only chance at staying alive—"

"Is it?" Gurubai asked. "Do you really believe that we can't survive in the mountains? Or do you just want your chance to go after Yin Nezha?"

She could have slapped him. But she wasn't stupid enough to take the bait.

"The Yins will not let us live free in this country," she said. She knew how Vaisra operated. He identified his threats—past, current, and potential—and patiently isolated, captured, and destroyed them. He didn't forgive past wrongs. He never failed to wrap up loose ends. And Rin, once his most precious weapon, was now his biggest loose end. "The Republic doesn't want to split territory, they want to wipe us off the map. So pardon me for thinking it might be a good idea to strike first."

"Vaisra is not coming for us." The Monkey Warlord stood up. "He's coming for *you*."

The implication of that sat heavy in the air between them.

The door opened. All hands in the room twitched toward swords. A camp aide stepped in, breathless. "Sir—"

"Not now," snapped the Monkey Warlord.

"No, sir—" The aide swallowed. "Sir, Ma Lien's passed away."

Rin exhaled slowly. There it was.

Gurubai stared at the aide, speechless.

Rin spoke up before anyone else could. "So there's a vacancy."

Liu Dai looked appalled. "Have some respect."

She ignored that. "There's a vacancy, and I'm the most qualified person to fill it."

"You're hardly in the chain of command," Gurubai said.

She rolled her eyes. "The chain of command matters for real armies, not bandit camps squatting in the mountains hoping dirigibles won't see us when they fly overhead."

"Those men won't obey you," Gurubai said. "They hardly know you—"

For the first time Zhuden spoke. "We're with the girl."

Gurubai trailed off, staring at Zhuden in disbelief.

Rin suppressed a snicker.

"She's right," Zhuden said. "We're dying up here. We need to march while we've got fight left in us. And if you won't lead us, we're going with her."

"You don't control the entire army," Gurubai said. "You'll be fifteen hundred men at the most."

"Two thousand," Souji said.

Rin shot him a startled look.

Souji shrugged. "The Iron Wolves are going south, too. Been itching for that fight for a while."

"You said you didn't care about the Southern Coalition," Rin said.

"I said I didn't care about the rest of the Empire," Souji said. "This is different. Those are my people. And from what I've seen, you're the only one with balls enough to go after them instead of sitting here, waiting to die."

Rin could have shrieked with laughter. She looked around the table, chin out, daring anyone to object. Liu Dai shifted in his seat. Souji winked at her. Gurubai, utterly defeated, said nothing.

She could tell he knew what she had done. It was no secret. She'd admit it out loud if he asked. But he couldn't prove it, and nobody would want to believe him. The hearts of at least a third of his men had turned against him.

This wasn't news. This only made official whispers that had been circulating for a long, long time.

Zhuden nodded to her. "Your move, General Fang."

She liked the sound of those words so much she couldn't help but grin.

"Well, that's settled." She glanced around the table. "I'm taking the Third Division and the Iron Wolves to Rooster Province. We march at dawn."

CHAPTER 4

"I want fresh troops when we get to the Beehive," Rin said. "If we take the pace down to four-fifths our usual marching speed, we can still get there in twelve days. We'll take detours here and here to avoid known Mugenese outposts. It adds distance, but I'd prefer to keep the element of surprise as long as we can. It'll cut down their preparation time."

She spoke with more confidence than she felt. She thought her voice sounded inordinately high and squeaky, though she could barely hear it, her blood was pumping so hard in her ears. Now that she'd finally gotten what she wanted, her giddiness had died away, replaced by a frightful mix of exhaustion and nerves.

Night had fallen on their first day of marching out of Ruijin. They'd stopped to make camp in the forest. A circle of soldiers—Kitay, Zhuden, Souji, and a smattering of officers—sat clustered in Rin's tent, watching with rapt attention as she drew thick, inky lines across the maps before them.

Her hand kept shaking, scattering droplets across the parchment. It was so hard to write with her left hand. She felt as if she were taking an exam she hadn't studied for. She should have been relishing this moment, but she couldn't shake the feeling that she was a fraud.

You are a fraud. She had never led a proper campaign by herself before. Her brief stints as the commander of the Cike had always ended in disaster. She didn't know how to manage logistics on this scale. And worst of all, she was currently describing an attack strategy that she wasn't at all sure would work.

Altan's laughter echoed in her mind.

Little fool, he said. *Finally got yourself an army, and now you don't know what to do with it.*

She blinked and forced his specter to disappear.

"If all goes according to plan," she continued, "Leiyang will be ours by the next moon."

Leiyang was the biggest township in northern Rooster Province. She'd passed through there only once in her life, nearly five years ago when she'd made the long caravan trip north to start school at Sinegard. It was a central trading hub connected to dozens of smaller villages by two creeks and several wide roads so old they'd been paved in the days of the Red Emperor. Compared to any northern capital it was a shoddy, run-down market in the outskirts of nowhere, but back then Rin had found it the busiest market town she'd ever seen.

Kitay had dubbed the network around Leiyang the Beehive. Mugenese troops exercised some control over all villages in northern Rooster Province, but based on their troops' patrol and travel patterns, Leiyang was the central node.

Something important lay in that township. Kitay thought it was likely a high-ranking general who, after his homeland's demise, continued to wield regional authority. Or, as Rin feared, it was a weapons base that they didn't know about. Leiyang could be sitting on cans of yellow gas. They had no way of knowing.

That was the root of their problem. Rin's intelligence on Leiyang was terrible. She'd updated her maps with Souji's detailed descriptions of the surrounding terrain, but everything else he knew had been outdated for months. A handful of Iron Wolves were escaped survivors from Leiyang, but their reports of Mugenese troop presence varied wildly. They'd been the opposite of helpful.

Survivors almost always gave them bad information—either their terror made them exaggerate the threat, or they downplayed it in hopes they could entice a rescue force to help their village.

Rin had sent scouts ahead, but those scouts would have to be exceedingly cautious. Anything that tipped the Mugenese off to an impending ambush would spell disaster. That meant she could speculate as much as they liked, but she wouldn't know the full power of the fighting force at Leiyang until just before the battle began.

"How are you going to draw them out from behind the gates?" Zhuden asked. "We don't want to hit too close to civilians."

Well, that's obvious. Rin couldn't tell if he was being condescending or simply careful. It had suddenly become very hard not to read everything like a challenge to her authority.

"We'll give as much advance warning as we can without betraying our location. Souji has some local connections. But really we'll just have to adapt to contingencies," she added, knowing full well that was a bunch of babble that meant nothing.

She didn't have a better answer. Zhuden's question got to the critical strategic puzzle that, despite hours spent racking her brains with Kitay, she still hadn't cracked.

The problem was that the Mugenese troops near Leiyang were not clustered in one area, where a well-coordinated ambush could have herded them into a singular burning ground, but spread out over an entire village network.

Rin needed to figure out a way to draw the Mugenese out onto an open battlefield. In Khudla it had been easy to minimize civilian casualties—the majority of Mugenese troops had lived in camps separate from the village itself. But all the Iron Wolves she'd questioned had reported that the Mugenese at Leiyang had integrated fully into the township. They'd formed some strange occupational system of predatory symbiosis. That made distinguishing targets from innocents much, much harder.

"We can't make those calls now without more intelligence," Rin said. "Our priority for now is to get as close as we can to

Leiyang without any patrols seeing us coming. We don't want a citywide hostage situation." She glanced up. "Everyone clear?"

They nodded.

"Good," she said. "Zhuden, post some men to first watch."

"Yes, General." Zhuden stood up.

The other officers filed out behind him. But Souji remained cross-legged on the floor, leaning back against his outstretched arms. A single stalk of grain hung annoyingly out the side of his mouth like a judgmental, wagging finger.

Rin shot him a wary look. "Is something the matter?"

"Your plans are all wrong," he said.

"Excuse me?"

"Sorry, should have spoken up earlier. Just didn't want you to lose face."

She scowled. "If you're here just to whine—"

"No, listen." Souji straightened up, leaned forward, and tapped his finger at the little star that indicated Leiyang on the map. "For starters, you can't take your army through these back roads. They'll have sentries posted across every path, not just the main roads, and you *know* you don't have the numbers to survive a prepared defense."

"There's no other route except those back roads," Kitay said.

"Well, you're just not being very creative, then."

Irritation flickered across Kitay's face. "You can't drag supply carts through thick forest, there's no way—"

"Do you two just refuse to listen to anyone who's got advice to offer?" Souji spat the grain stalk out of his mouth. It landed on the map, smudging Rin's carefully drawn routes. "I'm just trying to help, you know."

"And we're Sinegard-trained strategists who know what we're doing," Rin snapped. "So if you haven't got anything more helpful to say than 'your plans are all wrong,' then—"

"You know that the Monkey Warlord wants you to fail, right?" Souji interrupted.

"Excuse me?"

"The Southern Coalition don't like you at all. Gurubai, Liu Dai, the whole cohort. They talk about you every time you're not in the room. Fuck, I'd just *gotten* there, and they were already trying to turn me against you. It's a boys' club, Princess, and you're the odd one out."

Rin kept her voice carefully neutral. "And what did they say about me?"

"That you're a little fool who thinks three years at Sinegard and a few months in the Militia can replace decades in the field," Souji said calmly. "That you wouldn't be worth keeping around if it weren't for your nice little party trick. And that you'll probably die at Leiyang because you're too stupid to know what you're up against, but then they'll at least be rid of one nuisance."

Rin couldn't stop the heat rising in her cheeks. "That's nothing new."

"Look, Speerly." Souji leaned forward. "I'm on your side. But Gurubai's right about some things. You *don't* know how to command, and you *are* inexperienced, especially in this kind of warfare. But I know how to fight these battles. And if my men are being dragged into them, then you're going to fucking listen."

"You're not giving me orders," Rin said.

"If you go in there according to those plans, then you'll die."

"Look, asshole—"

"Hold on." Kitay held up a hand. "Rin, just—listen to him for a second."

"But he's—"

"He's been here longer than we have. If he's got information, we need to hear it." Kitay nodded to Souji. "Go on."

"Thank you." Souji cleared his throat like a master about to deliver a lecture. "You're both going about all this wrong. You can't keep fighting like this is a war between two proper armies—open field combat, and all that. This isn't the same. This is about liberation, and liberation means small-scale tactics and deception."

"And those worked so well for you in Khudla," Rin muttered.

"Got overwhelmed at Khudla," Souji admitted. "Like I said.

We couldn't win on the battlefield. We didn't have the numbers, and we should have resorted to smaller tactics. You'd better learn from my mistakes."

"So what are you proposing?" Rin's voice had lost its edge. She was listening now.

"Go through the forest," Souji said. "I'll get your precious supply carts through. There are hidden pathways all over that area and I have men who can find them. Then establish contact with Leiyang's resistance leadership before you move in. Right now you don't have the numbers."

"Numbers?" Rin repeated. "I can—"

"You can burn a whole squadron down yourself, Speerly, I'm well aware. But you're only useful in your radius, and your radius by definition can't be too close to civilians. You need people to run interference. Keep the Mugenese off the very people you're trying to save. Right now you don't have the numbers for that, which is why I suspect you keep wincing every time you glance at your maps."

Souji, Rin realized reluctantly, was extraordinarily astute.

"And you've got a magic fix for that?" she asked.

"It's not magic. I've been to those villages. They've got underground resistance bands. Strong men, willing to fight. They just need someone to push them over the edge."

"You're talking a handful of peasants with pitchforks," Kitay said.

"I'm talking an extra hundred men wherever we go."

"Bullshit," Rin said.

"I'm from this region," Souji said. "I have contacts. I can win Leiyang for you, if you'll both just trust me. Can you manage that?"

He extended his hand toward her.

Rin and Kitay exchanged a doubtful glance.

"This isn't a trap," Souji said, exasperated. "Come on, you two. I'm just as eager to go home as you are."

Rin paused, then reached out to grasp his hand.

The tent flap swung open the moment their palms touched. A sentry stepped inside. "Mugenese patrol," he said breathlessly. "Two miles out."

"Everyone hide," Souji said. "There's tree cover for half a mile on both sides, have the men pack up and go."

"No—what?" Rin scrambled to her feet, fumbling to gather up the maps. "I'm the one giving orders here—"

He shot her an exasperated look. "So order them to hide."

"Fuck that," she said. "We fight."

The Mugenese had a single patrol group. They had an army. How was this a debate?

But before she could shout the order, Souji stuck his head out the tent flap, jammed two fingers in his mouth, and whistled thrice in succession so loudly Rin felt like knives had been driven through her ears.

The response astonished her. At once, the Iron Wolves got up and began packing their gear. In under two minutes they had rolled up their tents, bagged up their equipment, and disappeared completely from the campsite into the forest. They left no trace behind—their campfires were leveled, their litter cleaned. They'd even filled in the holes their tent pegs made in the dirt. No casual observer would ever guess this had once been a campsite.

Rin didn't know if she was furious or impressed.

"Still going to fight?" Souji inquired.

"You little shit."

"Better come with."

"Please, I've got a god—"

"And all it takes is one arrow to shut you up, Princess. No one's covering for you now. I'd follow along."

Cheeks flaming, Rin ordered Zhuden's men to clear their campsites and retreat into the trees.

They ran, pushing through branches that left thousands of tiny cuts in their exposed skin, before they stopped and hoisted themselves up into the trees. Rin had never felt so humiliated as she crouched, perched beside Souji, peeking through the leaves to track the incoming patrol.

Was Souji's plan to just wait the Mugenese out? He couldn't possibly intend to attack—it'd be suicide. This didn't check any of the prerequisites for an ambush they'd been hardwired for in Strategy class—they didn't have fixed artillery stations, they didn't have clear lines of communication or signal visibility between the ranks. By retreating into the forest they'd only scattered and disorganized their numbers, while Rin was now trapped in a fighting zone where her flames would easily grow out of control.

Several minutes later Rin saw the Mugenese patrol moving down the main road.

"We could have taken them in the clearing," she hissed at Souji. "Why—"

He clamped a hand over her mouth. "*Look.*"

The patrol came thundering into clear view. Rin counted about twenty of them. They rode on sleek warhorses, no doubt fed with grain stolen from starving villagers, moving slowly as they examined the abandoned campsite.

"Come on," Souji muttered. "Move along."

No way, Rin thought. Her men were efficient, but not that efficient. Ten minutes wasn't enough to evacuate a campsite without leaving a single trace behind.

Sure enough, it took only a minute before the Mugenese captain shouted something and pointed at the ground. Rin didn't know what he'd seen—a footprint, a peg hole, a discarded belt—but it didn't matter. They'd been made.

"Now watch." Souji stuck his fingers into his mouth again and whistled, this time twice in succession.

The Iron Wolves loosed a round of arrows into the clearing.

They aimed true. Half the Mugenese patrollers dropped from the horses. The other half bolted and made to run, but another round of arrows hissed through the air, burrowing into throats, temples, mouths, and eyes. The last three patrollers raced farther down the road, only to be felled by a final group of archers stationed nearly a mile from where Rin hid.

"And that's the last of them." Souji dropped from the tree and extended a hand to help her down. "Was that so bad?"

"That was unnecessary." Rin batted Souji's hand away and climbed down herself. Her left arm buckled from the strain; she let go, dropped the last few inches, and nearly fell flat on her bum. Hastily she recovered. "We could have taken them head-on, we didn't have to hide—"

"How many troops do you think they had?" Souji inquired.

"Twenty. Thirty, maybe, I didn't—"

"And how many do you think we shot?"

"Well, all of them, but—"

"And how many casualties do we have?"

"None," she muttered.

"And do the Mugenese back in the Beehive know we're coming?"

"No."

"So there you go," he said smugly. "Tell me that was unnecessary."

She wanted to slap that look off his face. "*Hiding* was unnecessary. We could have just taken them—"

"And what, given them an extra day to muster defenses? The very first thing that Mugenese patrol teams do when they sense a fight coming is send back a designated survivor to report it."

She frowned. "I didn't know that."

"Course you didn't. You would have burned most of them where they stood, fine. But you can't outrun a horse. None of us have steeds faster than what they're riding. You slip up a *single time*, and you've given up all advantage of surprise."

"But that's absurd," she said. "We're not going to keep ourselves concealed all the way until we reach Leiyang."

"Fair enough. But we should *try* to keep our numbers concealed at least until we attack our next targets. Tiny strategic adjustments like this matter. Don't think about absolutes, think about the details. Every day, every *hour* that you can maintain an information asymmetry, you do it. It means the difference between two casualties and twenty."

"Got it," she said, chastened.

She wasn't too stubborn to admit when she'd been wrong. It stung to realize that she *had* been thinking about strategies in terms of absolutes. She'd gotten so used to it—the details had never seemed to matter much when her strategies boiled down to extermination by fire.

Cheeks burning, she brushed the leaves off her pants, and then uttered the words she knew Souji was waiting to hear. "You win, okay? You're right."

He grinned, vindicated. "I've been doing this for years, Princess. You may as well pay attention."

They made camp two miles south of where they'd seen the patrol, under tree cover so thick the leaves would dissipate the smoke from their campfires before it could furl higher into the air. Even so, Rin set strict limits—no more than one fire to every seven men, and all evidence would have to be tamped down and thoroughly concealed with leaves and dirt before they picked up again to march in the morning.

Dinner was measly, baked cornmeal wotou and unseasoned rice gruel. The Monkey Warlord hadn't let Rin take anything but the stalest provision sacks out of Ruijin, arguing that if she failed on this expedition then she at least shouldn't starve Ruijin at the same time. Rin hadn't pressed the point; she didn't want to push her luck.

But the Iron Wolves were eating suspiciously well. Rin didn't know where they'd found the ingredients, but the steam wafting from their bubbling cauldrons smelled *good*. Had they stolen extra rations from Ruijin? She wouldn't put it past Souji; he was enough of an asshole.

"If it's bothering you then just go ask them," Kitay said.

"That's stupid," Rin muttered. "I'm not going to make a fuss—"

But Souji was already walking toward them, carrying stacked bamboo steamers in both hands. His eyes alighted on their rations. His lip curled. "Looks appetizing."

Rin curled her fingers possessively around her wotou. "It's enough."

Souji sat down across from them and set the steamers on the ground. "You haven't learned to forage for yourselves?"

"Of course we can, there's just nothing edible on this stretch—"

"Really?" Souji lifted the steamer lids. "Look. Bamboo shoots. Freshly killed partridges. Cook all this up with a little salt and vinegar, and you have a three-course meal."

"But there's none of that around here," Kitay said.

"Right, we picked it up on the march. There was a bamboo grove right at the base of Ruijin, didn't you see it? Lots of baby saplings. Whenever you see something edible, you put it in your sack. First rule of march, no?"

The smell of partridge meat was making Rin salivate. She eyed the steamers with envy. "And how'd you catch the birds?"

"Simple. You can rig up a trap with next to nothing as long as you've got some cornmeal for bait. We can set some overnight and wake up to crackling partridge wings. I can teach you how."

Rin pointed to something yellow and mushy buried under the bamboo shoots. "What's that?"

"Bajiao bananas."

"Do they taste good?"

"You've never eaten these before?" Souji gave her an incredulous look. "They grow everywhere in these parts."

"We thought they might be poisonous," Kitay admitted. "They gave some men at Ruijin a bad stomachache, so we've stayed clear of them since."

"Ah, no, that's just when they're not ripe. If you can't tell from the color—darkish brown, you see?—you can peel it open and tell from the smell. If it's sour, put it back. None of your men knew about that?"

"None at our camp."

"Incredible," Souji said. "I suppose after a few centuries you start to forget the little things."

Rin pointed to a bowl of what looked like black, crispy, oversize beans. "What's that?"

"Bees," Souji said casually. "They're very tasty when you fry them up. You've just got to make sure you take all the stingers out."

She stared. "I can't tell if you're kidding or not."

"I'm not kidding." He picked one up and showed her the husk. "See? The legs are the best part. They soak up all the oil." He popped it into his mouth and chewed loudly. "Incredible. You want?"

"I'm good," she muttered.

"You're from the south. Thought you could eat anything."

"We never ate bugs in Tikany."

He laughed. "Tikany's hardly the poorest village in the south. Makes sense that you've never known famine."

She had to admit that was true. She'd gone hungry on plenty of nights, both in Tikany and at the Academy in Sinegard, but that was because of food withheld and not the sheer lack of it. Even after the Third Poppy War kicked off in earnest, when villagers across the Empire grew so desperate they resorted to eating wood bark, Rin had been able to rely on at least two square meals from army rations every day.

Of course. When things got bad, soldiers were fed first, and everyone else was left to die. Rin had been living so long on the extractive capabilities of the empire she fought for, she'd never learned to forage for herself.

"That wasn't an insult. Just being frank." Souji held the bowl of bees out toward her. "Want to try?"

They smelled terribly good. Rin's stomach let loose an embarrassingly loud growl.

"Eat up." Souji chuckled. "We've got rations to spare."

They continued their march at dawn, trailing by the edge of the road, always ready to bolt back into the trees at the first signal from the scouts ahead. They quickened their pace slightly from the day before. Rin had wanted to make straight for the Beehive, but Souji had drawn a zigzag pattern on her map instead, creating a circuitous route that took them all around local power bases but avoided the center until the very end.

"But then they'll know we're coming," Rin said. "Isn't the whole point to keep the element of surprise until Leiyang?"

Souji shook his head. "No, they'll know we're out here in five days at most. We can't keep our approach a secret for that much longer, so we may as well get some good hits in when we can."

"Then what is the point of all these measures?"

"Think, Princess. They know we're coming. That's *all* they know. They don't know how many we are. We could be a band of ten. We could be an army of a million. They've got absolutely no clue what to be on the guard for, and the threat of the unknown hamstrings defense preparations. Preserve that."

Of course Rin had learned at Sinegard to strategize accounting for the enemy's state of mind. But she'd always thought of it as a matter of dominant strategies. What, given the circumstances, was their best option? And how should she prepare for their best option? The issues Souji obsessed over—fear, apprehension, anxiety, irrationality—were details she'd never much considered. But now, in this war of uncertainty and unbalanced forces, they seemed paramount.

So whenever the Southern Coalition encountered Mugenese soldiers, they either hid in the trees and watched them march past if they appeared not to have noticed anything, or pulled the same kind of lure tactic the Iron Wolves had used the first day. And whenever they came past occupied hamlets, they employed much the same sort of strategy—cautious baiting accompanied by strikes of limited force, just enough to achieve limited tactical objectives without ever escalating into a real battle.

Over eight days and numerous engagements, Rin witnessed the full range of Souji's favorite tactics. They revolved almost entirely around deception, and they were brilliant. The Iron Wolves were fond of waylaying small groups of Mugenese soldiers, always at night and never twice in the same spot. When the Mugenese returned with larger bands, the guerrillas were long gone. They feigned beggars, farmers, and village drunkards to draw Mugenese attacks. They deliberately created false campsites to agitate Mugenese patrols. Souji's favorite ploy was to send a group of Iron Wolves, all young women, out to fields near Mugenese encampments wearing the most brightly colored, provocative clothing that village women had access to. They were, without fail, assaulted. But girls with fire rockets and knives were harder to take down than the Mugenese soldiers' usual prey.

"You're fond of pretending to be weaklings," Rin observed. "Does that always work?"

"Almost every time. The Mugenese are terribly attracted to easy targets."

"And they never catch on?"

"Not as far as I've noticed. See, they're bullies. Weakness is what they want to see. They're so convinced that we're just base, cowardly animals, they won't stop to question it. They don't *want* to believe we can fight back, so they won't."

"But we're not really fighting back," Rin said. "We're only annoying them."

Souji knew that she wasn't thrilled with this tentative campaign—this sort of half fighting, of provoking from the shadows instead of facing the enemy head-on. It defied every strategic principle she'd ever been taught. She'd been taught to win, and to win conclusively to preempt a later counterattack. Souji, on the other hand, flirted with victory but never took the spoils. He left chess pieces open all over the board, like a dog might bury bones to savor later.

But Souji insisted she was still thinking about war the wrong way.

"You don't have a conventional army," he said. "You can't move into Leiyang and mow them down like you did when you fought for the Republic."

"Yes, I could," she said.

"You're good nine times out of ten, Princess. Then a stray arrow or javelin finds its way into your temple, and your luck's run out. Don't take chances. Err on the side of caution."

"But I hate this constant *running*—"

"It's not running. That's what you don't get. This is disruption. Think about how your calculations change if you're on the receiving end. You change your patrol pattern to keep up with the random attacks, but you can't anticipate when they'll happen. Your nerves get frayed. You can't rest or sleep because you're not sure what's coming next."

"So your plan is to annoy them to death," Kitay said.

"Bad morale is a big weapon," Souji said. "Don't underestimate it."

"I'm not," Rin said. "But it feels like we're just constantly retreating."

"The entire point is that *only you* have the ability to retreat. They don't; they're stuck in the places they've occupied because they can't give them up. Try to wrap your head around this, you two. Your default model of warfare won't work for you anymore. At Sinegard you're taught to lead large forces into major battles. But you don't have that anymore. What you *can* do is strike against isolated forces, multiple times, and delay their reinforcements. You have to deploy small operational units who have the latitude to make their own calls. And you want to delay head-on battles on the open field for as long as you possibly can."

"This is all bonkers." Kitay had the wide-eyed, slightly panicked look on his face he got when his mind was chewing frantically through new concepts. Rin could almost hear the whirring in his brain. "This cuts against everything the Classics ever said about warfare."

"Not really," Souji said. "What did Sunzi say was the fundamental theorem of war?"

"Subjugate the enemy without fighting," Kitay said automatically. "But that doesn't apply to—"

Souji cut him off. "And what does that mean?"

"It means you pacify an enemy with sheer, overwhelming superiority," Rin said impatiently. "If not in numbers, then in technology or position. You make him realize his inferiority so he surrenders without fighting. Saves your troops a battle, and keeps the battlefields clean. The only problem is that they *aren't* inferior on any plane. So that's not going to work."

"But that's not what Sunzi means." Souji looked frustratingly smug, like a teacher waiting for a very slow student to arrive at the right answer.

Kitay had lost his patience. "What, was half the text written in invisible ink?"

Souji raised his hands. "Look, I went to Sinegard, too. I know the way your minds work. But they trained you for conventional warfare, and this is not that."

"Then kindly explain what this is," Kitay said.

"You can't concentrate superior force all at once, so you need to do it in little parts. Mobile operations. Night movements. Deception, surprise, all that fun stuff—the stuff we've been doing—that's how you focus your optimal alignment, or whatever bogus word Sunzi calls it." Souji made a pincer motion with his hands. "You're like ants swarming an injured rat. You whittle it down with little bites. You never engage in a full-fledged battlefield encounter, you just fucking exhaust them.

"Sinegard's problem was that it was teaching you to fight an ancient enemy. They saw everything through the Red Emperor's eyes. But that method of warfare doesn't work anymore. It didn't even work against the Mugenese when you *had* the armies. And what's more, Sinegard assumed that the enemy would be a conquering force from the outside." Souji grinned. "They weren't in the business of teaching rebels."

∞

Despite her initial skepticism, Rin had to admit that Souji's tactics worked. And they *kept* working. The closer they got to Leiyang, the more supplies and intelligence they acquired, all without evidence that the Mugenese at Leiyang knew what was coming. Souji planned his attacks so that even Mugenese survivors wouldn't be able to report more than ten or twenty sighted troops at once; the full size of their army remained well concealed. And if Rin ever called the fire, she made sure she left no witnesses.

But their luck had to be running out. Souji's small-scale tactics worked for tiny targets—hamlets where the Mugenese guard numbered no more than fifty men. But Leiyang was one of the largest townships in the province. More and more reports corroborated the fact that their numbers were in the thousands.

You couldn't fool an army of thousands with skirts and firecrackers. Sooner or later, they'd have to stand face-to-face with their enemy and fight.

CHAPTER 5

On the twelfth day of their march, after an eternity of navigating winding, treacherous forest footpaths, they reached a vast plain filled with red stalks of sorghum. Against the otherwise overgrown wilderness, the sparse and dying trees that littered the roadside, those neatly cultivated fields stood out like a red flag of warning.

Armies only maintained fields once they'd settled down for permanent occupation. They'd reached the edge of the Beehive.

Rin's men wanted to move on Leiyang that night. They'd marched at a leisurely pace for the last two days; the forest routes didn't permit them to go any faster. They had energy, pent up and raging. They wanted blood.

Souji was the only holdout. "You've got to contact the local leadership first."

Rin humored him. "Fine. Where are they?"

"Well." Souji scratched his ear. "On the inside."

"Are you mad?"

"The civilians suffer the most from your little liberations," Souji said. "Or did you not count the casualties at Khudla?"

"Listen, we *freed* Khudla—"

"And burned a temple full of civilians to death," Souji said.

"Don't think I didn't know about that. We need to give them advance warning."

"That's too risky," Kitay said. "We don't know how many collaborators they have. If the wrong person sees you, they'll crack down on the civilians regardless."

"No one's going to report us," Souji said. "I know these people. Their loyalty runs thicker than blood."

Rin gave him a skeptical look. "You'd be willing to stake the lives of everyone in this army on that?"

"I'm staking the lives of everyone in that township on it," Souji said. "I've gotten you this far, Speerly. Trust me just a little longer."

So Rin found herself walking with Souji into the center of the Beehive, dressed in peasant rags, without her sword and without reinforcements. Souji had identified a lapse in the northern patrol, a thirty-second pocket of time between revolving guards that allowed them to sneak past the fields and over the city gates unnoticed.

What Rin saw inside Leiyang astonished her.

She'd never before encountered a Mugenese-occupied township where corpses weren't stacked in rotting, haphazard piles around every corner. Where the residents weren't utterly, uniformly, brutally crushed into submission.

But here in Leiyang, the Mugenese had embarked on something more like occupational state-building. And this, somehow, was scarier.

The civilians here were thin, haggard, clearly downtrodden, but alive—and not just alive, but *free*. They weren't locked up in holding pens, nor were they crouching inside their homes in fear. Civilians—visibly Nikara civilians—strode around the township so casually that if Rin didn't know better she wouldn't have guessed there was a Mugenese presence at all. As they snuck deeper into the township, Rin saw a band of men—laborers with farming implements that could easily be used as weapons—walking toward the fields without so much as a single armed guard. Closer to the town center, there were long queues looping around an unbelievable sight—a rationing station, where Mugenese troops doled out daily portions of barley grain to civilians waiting patiently with copper bowls.

She could barely form the question. "How—?"

"Collaboration," Souji said. "It's how most of us have been getting along. The Mugenese figured out pretty quickly that their original depopulation policy was only going to work if they were getting supplies from the island. Island's gone, and there's no point to clearing out space anymore. What's more, they need someone to do their cooking and cleaning."

So the soldiers without a home had formed a sick symbiosis with their intended victims. The Mugenese had merged with the Nikara into a society that, if not necessarily nonviolent, at least looked stable and sustainable.

Rin found evidence of wary coexistence everywhere she looked. She saw Mugenese soldiers eating at Nikara food stands. She saw Mugenese patrolmen escorting a group of Nikara farmers back through the city gates. No blades were drawn; no hands were bound. This looked routine. She even saw a Mugenese soldier fondly stroke the head of a Nikara child as they passed each other on the street.

Her stomach churned.

She didn't know what to do with this. She was so used to absolute destruction, a complete binary of the extremities of war, that she couldn't work her mind around this bizarre middle ground. How did it feel to live with a sword hanging over your head? How did it feel to look these men in the eyes, day by day, knowing full well what they were capable of?

Rin followed closely behind Souji as they moved through the streets, her eyes darting nervously about with every turn. No one had reported, or even seemed to care about, their presence. Occasionally someone narrowed their eyes at Souji in questioning recognition, but no one so much as breathed a word.

Souji didn't stop walking until they'd reached the far edge of the township, where he pointed to a small, thatched-roof hut half-hidden behind a cluster of trees. "The chief of Leiyang is a man named Lien Wen. His daughter-in-law came from the same village as my mother. He's expecting us."

Rin frowned. "How?"

"I told you." Souji shrugged. "I know these people."

A skinny, plain-faced girl about seven years old sat outside the door, hand-grinding sorghum grain in a small stone bowl. She scrambled to her feet when they approached and, without a word, gestured for them to follow her inside the hut.

Souji nudged Rin forward. "Go on."

For the home of a township chief, Lien Wen's was not particularly luxurious. The interior would barely have fit ten men standing shoulder to shoulder. A square tea table occupied the center, surrounded by three-legged stools. Rin squatted down on the nearest stool. The uneven, scratched-up legs wobbled every time she shifted position. That was oddly calming—this kind of poverty felt familiar.

"Weapons over there. Father's orders." The girl pointed at a cracked vase in the corner.

Rin's fingers twitched toward the knives hidden inside her shirt. "But—"

"Of course." Souji shot Rin a stern look. "Whatever Chief Lien asks."

Rin reluctantly dropped the blades into the vase.

The girl disappeared for several seconds, returned with a plate of coarse-grain steamed buns, and set it down on the tea table.

"Dinner," she said, then retreated to the corner.

The starchy grain smelled terribly good. Rin hadn't seen proper steamed buns in ages; in Ruijin, they'd long ago run out of yeast. She reached out for a bun, but Souji slapped her hand away.

"Don't," he muttered. "That's more than she eats in a week."

"Then why—"

"Leave it. They'll save it for later if you don't touch it, but if you touch it and put it down then they'll insist you take it with you when you leave."

Stomach growling, Rin returned her hand to her lap.

"I didn't think you'd come back."

A tall, broad-shouldered man filled the doorframe. Rin found his age impossible to place—his lined eyes and white whiskers could have made him as old as her grandfather, but he carried himself with his back straight and chin up, a warrior with decades of fight left in his body.

"Chief Lien." Souji stood up, cupped his hands, and bowed deeply at the waist. Rin hastily followed suit.

"Sit," Chief Lien grumbled. "This hut isn't big enough for all this commotion."

Rin and Souji returned to their stools. Chief Lien merely shoved his out of the way and sat down cross-legged on the dirt floor, which made Rin feel suddenly very childish, squatting as she was.

Chief Lien folded his arms across his chest. "So you're the ones who've been causing trouble up north."

"Guilty." Souji beamed. "Next up is—"

"Stop it," Chief Lien said. "I don't care what's next. Take your army, leave here, and don't come back."

Souji trailed off, looking hurt. Rin would have found that funny if she weren't also confused.

"They think our men are doing it," Chief Lien said. "They made the elders line up in the square the morning after the first patrolmen went missing and said they'd shoot them one by one until the culprits confessed. No one stepped forward, so they beat my mother within an inch of her life. That was over a week ago. She's not recovered. She'll be lucky if she makes it through tonight."

"We have a physician," Souji said. "We'll bring him to you, or we can just carry her out to our camps. We've got men in those fields, we can move on the crickets tonight—"

"No," Chief Lien said firmly. "You will turn around and disappear. We know how this story ends, and we can't suffer the consequences. Compliance is the only thing keeping us alive—"

"*Compliance?*" Souji had warned Rin to keep quiet and let him do the talking, but she couldn't help but interject. "That's your word for slavery? You like walking the streets with your head down, cringing when they approach you, licking their boots to win their goodwill?"

"Our township still has all our men," said Chief Lien.

"Then you have soldiers," Rin said. "And you should be fighting."

Chief Lien merely regarded her through his lined, tired eyes.

In the passing silence, Rin noticed for the first time a series of ropy scars etched across his arms. Others snaked up the side of his neck. Those weren't the kind of scars you got from a whip. Those were from knives.

His gaze made her feel so tiny.

Finally he asked, "Did you know that they take young girls with the darkest skin they can find and burn them alive?"

She flinched. "What?"

But then the explanation rose to her mind, slow and dreadful, just as Chief Lien spelled it out aloud. "The Mugenese tell stories about you. They know what happened to the longbow island. They know it was a dark-skinned girl with red eyes. And they know you're near."

Of course they know. They'd massacred the Speerlies twenty years ago; surely the myth of the dark-skinned, red-eyed race who called fire still circulated in their younger generations. And certainly they'd heard whispers in the south. The Mugenese troops who could understand Nikara would have picked up on whispered stories of the goddess incarnate, the reason why they could never go home. They would have tortured to discover the details. They would have learned very quickly who they needed to target.

But they couldn't find her, so they'd targeted anyone who might possibly look like her instead.

Guilt twisted in her stomach like a knife.

She heard the sudden noise of steel scraping against steel. She jumped and turned. The little girl, still sitting in the corner of the hut, had started fiddling with their weapons.

Chief Lien turned to look over his shoulder. "Don't touch that."

"She's all right," Souji said easily. "She ought to learn how to handle steel. You like that knife?"

"Yes," said the girl, testing the blade's balance on one finger.

"Keep it. You'll need it."

The girl peered up at them. "Are you soldiers?"

"Yes," Souji said.

"Then why don't you have uniforms?"

"Because we don't have any money." Souji gave her a toothy smile. "Would you like to sew us some uniforms?"

The girl ignored this question. "The Mugenese have uniforms."

"That's true."

"So do they have more money than you?"

"Not if we and your baba have anything to do with it." Souji turned back to Chief Lien. "Please, Chief. Just hear us out."

Chief Lien shook his head. "I won't risk the reprisals."

"There won't be reprisals—"

"How can you guarantee that?"

"Because everything they say about me is true," Rin interrupted. Little arcs of flame danced around her arms and shoulders, just enough to cast long shadows across her face. To make her look utterly inhuman.

She saw a faint look of surprise flicker across Chief Lien's face. She knew, despite the rumors, that until now he hadn't really believed what she was. She could understand that. It was hard to believe in the gods, to *truly* believe, until they stared you in the face.

She'd made believers of the Mugenese. She'd make him believe, too.

"They're killing those girls because they're afraid," she said. "They should be. I sank the longbow island. I can destroy everything around me in a fifty-yard radius. When we attack it won't be like the previous attempts. There will be no chance of defeat and no reprisals, because I cannot lose. I have a god. I only need you to bring the civilians out of range. We'll do the rest."

Chief Lien's jaw had lost its stubborn set. She'd won him over, she knew. She saw it in his eyes—for the first time, he was considering something other than compliance. He was thinking about how freedom might taste.

"You can ambush them at the northern border," he said at last. "Not many civilians live up there, and we can evacuate the ones who do. The reeds would be tall enough to conceal you—you could fit about five hundred men in those fields alone. They won't know you're here until you choose to reveal yourselves."

"Understood," Souji said. "Thank you."

"You'll only have a bit of time to get in position. They send troops with dogs and staves every few hours to track anyone who might be hiding in the fields."

"Combing their hair for lice," said the girl. "That's what they call it."

"We'll have to be clever lice, then," Souji said. Relief shone clear on his face. This wasn't a negotiation anymore; now it was just about logistics. "And do you know how many men they have?"

"About three thousand," Chief Lien said.

"That's very precise," Rin said. "How do you know?"

"They commission their grains from us. We know how much they eat."

"And you can calculate that by the *grain*?"

"It's simple multiplication," Chief Lien said. "We're not stupid."

Rin sat back, impressed. "All right. Three thousand, then."

"We can draw them two hundred yards out of the township if we split half our forces around and drive them into the fields," Souji said. "That's out of Rin's range—"

"No," said Chief Lien. "Four hundred."

"That might not be possible," Rin said.

"Make it possible," Chief Lien said. "You keep your fight away from this township."

"I understand," Rin said. Her voice turned hard. "You want your liberation without suffering the consequences."

Chief Lien stood up. The message was clear; this audience was over. "If you lose, they will come for us. And you know what they can do."

"Doesn't matter," Rin said. "We won't lose."

Chief Lien said nothing. His eyes followed them silently, judging, as they left the hut. In the corner, his daughter hummed and continued to scrape steel against steel.

"That went well," Rin muttered.

"Sure did." Souji was beaming.

"What are you so happy about? He's made this ten times harder than it had to be, and he hasn't given us anything in return—"

"That's not true. He gave us permission."

"Permission? Who the fuck needs *permission*—"

"You always need permission." Souji stopped walking. The grin slid off his face. "Every time you bring a fight to a village, you put every innocent civilian's life in danger. It's your obligation to warn them."

"Look, if every army behaved like that, then—"

"Listen. You're not fighting a campaign for this land, you're fighting for the people. And if you learn to trust them, they'll be your best weapons. They'll be your eyes and ears on the ground. They'll be natural extensions of your army. But you never, *ever* endanger them against their will. Do you understand?"

He glared at her until she nodded.

"Good," he said, and strode briskly toward the gate. Chastened, she followed.

Someone stood awaiting them in the shadows.

Rin pulled a flame into her hand, but Souji grabbed her elbow. "Don't. It's a friendly."

The man at the gate was, indeed, Nikara. He had to be—his clothes, ratty and faded, hung from his gaunt frame. None of the Mugenese soldiers were starving.

He was quite young—hardly more than a boy. He seemed terribly excited to see them. He took one look at Rin, and his entire face lit up. "Are you the Speerly?"

Something about him struck her as familiar—his thick eyebrows, his broad shoulders. He carried himself like a born leader, confident and resolute.

"You're Chief Lien's son," Rin said. "Aren't you?"

"Guilty," he said. "Lien Qinen. It's good to meet you."

"Come here, you bastard." Souji grasped Qinen's arm and pulled him into a tight embrace. "Does your father know you're here?"

"Father thinks I'm still hiding out in the woods." Qinen turned to Rin. "So *are* you the Speerly? You're smaller than I expected."

She bristled at that. "Oh, am I?"

He held out his hands. "No, no, I wasn't—I—wow." He blinked several times. "Sorry. I've just heard so much about you, I was expecting—I didn't know what to expect. It's good to meet you."

He wasn't being rude, Rin realized. He was *nervous*. Her expression softened. "Yes, I'm the Speerly. And you're here because—"

"I'm your ally." Qinen reached out quickly to shake her hand. His palms were slick with sweat. He gawked at her, mouth hanging slightly agape, as if he'd just watched her descend from the heavens on a staircase of clouds. Then he blinked and cleared his throat. "We're going to help you fight. I've got men prepared to come out for you, just say the word and we'll—"

"You'll do nothing," Souji said. "You know what your father demanded."

Qinen's face twisted in contempt. "My father's a coward."

"He's just trying to keep you alive," Souji said.

"Alive?" Qinen scowled. "He's sentenced us to a living hell. He thinks compliance means lenience, but he doesn't listen to reports from villages all around us. He doesn't know what they do to the women. Or he doesn't care." His fists tightened. "Thirty miles from here, a village tried to hide girls in nearby mines, and when the Mugenese found out, they sealed off the exits and let them suffocate over three days. When they finally let the villagers retrieve the corpses, they found the girls dead with their fingers cracked and bleeding from trying to claw their way out. But Father doesn't understand. He's been—I mean, since my brother died, he's . . ." His throat bobbed. "He's wrong. We aren't safe here; we'll never be. Let us fight beside you. If we die, then at least let us die like men."

This isn't about permission, Rin realized. Souji was wrong. Qinen was going to fight whether they agreed to let him or not. This was about validation. After everything Qinen had seen, he needed absolution for the guilt of remaining alive, and he could get that only by putting his life on the line. She knew that feeling.

"You and your friends aren't soldiers," Souji said quietly.

"We can be," Qinen said. "Did you think we'd just lie down and wait to be rescued? I'm glad to see you, brother, but we would have started this fight without you. You'll need us. We've been laying down our own preparations, we've already set your stage—"

"What?" Souji shot him a sharp glance. "What have you been doing?"

"Everything my father's been too scared to try." Qinen lifted his chin with pride. "We've taken down their patrol routes to the minute. They're all written down in a code they can't read. We've sent round signals so the villagers know exactly when to run or hide. We've made sure every household has a weapon. Knives made from stakes, or farming implements we've snuck out of the sheds one at a time. We're ready for this fight."

"If they found out they'd kill you," Souji said.

"We're braver than that," Qinen scoffed. "You saw my baby sister?"

"The girl in the hut?" Rin asked.

He nodded. "She's with us, too. The Mugenese have her working in the mess hall—that's where they force the children to work—so she slips a handful of water hemlock into a few bowls every time. It doesn't do much. Just induces some vomiting and diarrhea—but it weakens them, and no one ever suspects it's her."

Watching Qinen's face—his earnest, furious, desperate face—

Rin couldn't help but feel a mix of admiration and pity. His courage amazed her. These civilians were poking the dragon's nest, risking their lives every day, preparing for a rebellion that they must have known they wouldn't win.

What did they really think they could accomplish? They were farmers and children. Their little acts of resistance might infuriate the Mugenese, but wouldn't drive them away.

Maybe, Rin thought, under these circumstances, that kind of resistance—no matter how futile—was the only way to live.

"We can help you," Qinen insisted. "Just tell us where to be and when."

The ruthless side of her wanted to say yes. She could use Qinen. It was so easy to go through cannon fodder. Even the most inexperienced commander could buy seconds, even minutes, by throwing bodies at the enemy.

But she couldn't forget the look in Chief Lien's eyes.

She'd learned, now, what it meant to bring the war to the south.

She read the expression on Souji's face. *Don't you dare.*

And she knew that if she said the wrong thing now, then she'd lose the support of both Chief Lien and the Iron Wolves.

"Souji's right." She reached out to touch Qinen lightly on the arm. "This isn't your fight."

"The hell it isn't," Qinen snapped. "This is my home."

"I know." She tried to sound like she meant what she was saying. "And the best thing you can do is keep your countrymen safe when we attack."

Qinen looked crestfallen. "But that's nothing."

"You're wrong," said Souji. "That's everything."

Night had fallen by the time Rin and Souji rejoined the camp. They'd planned their attack for the following sunset. They had considered striking right then, under cover of darkness, and before any news had leaked of their arrival. But they'd decided to hold off until the next evening; Chief Lien needed time to orchestrate the villagers' evacuation, and the Southern Army needed time to scope out the terrain, to position their troops optimally within the fields. The general staff spent the next few hours huddled around maps, marking out lines of entry.

It was far past midnight when at last they disbanded to rest. When Rin returned to her tent, she found a slim scroll placed neatly at the top of her travel pack.

She reached out, paused, and then withdrew her hand. This wasn't right. Nobody at camp was receiving personal parcels. The Southern Coalition owned only one carrier pigeon, and it was trained to take a one-way message to Ankhiluun. Every instinct screamed that this was a trap. The scroll's exterior could be laced with venom—countless Nikara generals of old had tried that trick before.

She leaned over the scroll with a small flame bobbing in her palm, carefully illuminating its every angle. She couldn't see anything dangerous—no thin needles, no dark sheen on the parchment edge. Still, she used her teeth to pull her sleeve over her fingers before she picked the scroll up and unrolled it. Then she nearly dropped it.

The wax seal bore the dragon insignia of the House of Yin.

She exhaled slowly, trying to slow her racing heart. This had to be a joke—someone had pulled a deeply unfunny prank, and she would make sure they suffered for it.

The note inside was scrawled in a wobbly, childish font; the characters were so smudged and messy she had to squint to read it.

> Hello, Rin,
> They told me to write this in my own hand, but I don't see how it could have made a difference seeing as I could barely write when you left, so you wouldn't have recognized it anyway.

"This isn't funny," she muttered to herself.

But she knew this wasn't a joke. Nobody at camp could have done this. Nobody *knew*.

This is Kesegi, if you hadn't pieced that together. I've been in the New City prisons for a while and it was my fault, I got stupid and bragged to some people that you were my sister and I knew you, and then the talk trickled up to the guards so now here I am.

I'm sorry I did this to you. I really am.

Your friend says to tell you that this doesn't have to be difficult. He said to tell you I walk free if you'll come to the New City yourself, but if you bring an army then they'll behead me above the city gates. He says that this doesn't have to end in bloodshed, and that he only wants to speak. He says he doesn't want a war. He's prepared to grant clemency to every one of your allies. He only wants you.

Although to be honest—

The rest of the message had been scratched out with thick inky lines.

Rin snatched the scroll up and ran outside her tent.

She accosted the first sentry she saw. "Who delivered this?"

He gave her a blank stare. "Delivered what?"

She waved the scroll at him. "This was inside my travel pack. Did anyone deliver this to you?"

"N-No—"

"Did you see anyone going through my things?"

"No, but my watch has only just started, you'd have to ask Ginsen, he was here for three hours before that, and he should be—General, are you all right?"

Rin couldn't stop trembling.

Nezha knew where she was. Nezha knew where she *slept*.

"General?" the sentry asked again. "Is everything all right?"

She crumpled the scroll in her fist. "Get me Kitay."

"Shit." Kitay lowered the letter.

"I know," Rin said.

"Is this real?"

"What does that mean?"

"I mean, is there any chance this is a forgery? That this isn't really Kesegi?"

"I don't know," she admitted. "I've no idea."

She couldn't tell if that was really Kesegi's handwriting. Frankly, she wasn't even sure Kesegi knew how to read; her foster brother had rarely attended school. She couldn't tell if the letter sounded like him, either. Certainly she could imagine the words in his voice, could picture him sitting at a writing desk, wrists shackled, his thin face trembling as Nezha dictated the words to him one by one. But how could she know for sure? She'd barely spoken to Kesegi in years.

"And what if it's not?" Kitay asked.

"I don't think we should respond," Rin said in the calmest tone she could muster. "Either way."

She'd worked through the possibilities in the minutes it had taken Kitay to arrive. She'd weighed the cost of her foster brother's life, and she'd decided she could afford to lose him.

Kesegi wasn't a general, wasn't even a soldier. Nezha couldn't torture him for information. Kesegi knew nothing of importance about either the Southern Coalition or Rin. Everything he knew of Rin was the biography of a little girl that she'd killed long ago at Sinegard, a naive Tikany shopgirl who existed only in suppressed memories.

"Rin." Kitay put a hand on her arm. "Do you want to go after him?"

She hated how he was looking at her, eyes wide with pity, as if she were on the verge of tears. It made her feel so fragile.

But that's just what Nezha wants. She refused to let this shake her. Nezha had manipulated her with sentiment before. The Cike had died for her sentiment.

"The problem is not Kesegi," she said. "It's Nezha's troop placements. It's his fucking *reach*—I mean, he put a letter in my fucking *tent*, Kitay. We're just supposed to ignore that?"

"Rin, if you need to—"

"We need to discuss whether Nezha's forces are in the south." She had to keep talking; they had to move the conversation on to something else, because she was afraid of how her chest would feel if they didn't. "Which I don't think is possible—Venka says he's leading his father's troops in Tiger Province. But if they're in the south, they've hidden so well that not a *single* one of our scouts has seen any troops, dirigibles, or supply wagons."

"I don't think he's in the south," Kitay said. "I think he's just fucking with you. He's gathering information; he just wants to see how you'll respond."

"He won't get a response. We're not going to take the bait."

"We can discuss that."

"This isn't a discussion," she snapped. "This letter is a forgery. And Nezha's terms are absurd."

Her fingers clenched around the scroll. The remainder of the message had been written in Nezha's smooth, elegant calligraphy.

Hello, Rin,
It's about time we talked.
    You and I both know this war benefits no one. Our country has cracked apart. Our homeland has been ravaged, by war, by environmental catastrophe, by mindless evil. Nikan now faces her greatest test. And the Hesperians are watching us, waiting to see if we might stand strong or become another slave society for them to exploit.
    I understand why you hate them. I am not blind to their intentions, and I will not let them turn our Republic into their mining ground. I will not see this land ruled by foreign hands. I know you don't want that, either.
    Please, Rin. Come to reason. I need you at my side.

The terms he listed were simple and unacceptable. A truce, full-scale demobilization and disarmament, and Kesegi returned safely in exchange for Rin. The Southern Coalition would be allowed to walk free, or join the Republican Army if they wished.

Nezha hadn't specified what would happen to Rin. She suspected it involved hourly doses of laudanum and an operating table.

"I'm not crazy, right?" she asked. "This is clearly a trap?"

"I'm not sure," Kitay said. "I think there's a world where Nezha does want you alive. He's not stupid, he knows you'd be useful to him. He might try to talk you around—"

"The Hesperians are never going to let me walk free."

"If you take Nezha at face value, then it looks like he's trying to defy the Hesperians."

She snorted. "You really think he'd do that?"

"I don't know. The Yins . . . the House of Yin is far more comfortable working with foreigners than any Nikara leaders ever have been. It's the reason why they're rolling in silver. They might be fine with remaining stewards for the blue-eyed devils. But Nezha . . ."

"Nezha's a shaman."

"Yes."

"And you think the Hesperians know."

"I think *Nezha* knows that he cannot exist in a Hesperian-dominated world," Kitay said. "It's a world that labels him an abomination. Their vision of order demands his death and yours."

Was that what Nezha was trying to imply? That he'd changed his mind about shamans? That if she joined him at his side, he might break the alliance his father had forged?

"But I've had this argument with Nezha," she said. "And he thinks they're right. That we *are* abominations, and that we're better off dead. Only he can't die."

"So then we're back to square one. We have no idea what this letter implies. And we have no reason to trust Nezha."

Rin sighed. "So what's our move, then?"

"I think we start with deciding what to do about your brother."

"My foster brother," she corrected. "And I've told you, we're doing nothing."

"Why don't you even want to talk about this?"

"Because he's just my brother." She gave him a helpless look.

"And I am the last great hope of the south. How do you think history will judge me if I throw away its fate for one person?"

Kitay opened his mouth, paused, and closed it. Rin knew his mind was racing; he was trying to come up with a way to save Kesegi, a way to foil Nezha, or a justification why one life might be worth more than thousands.

They didn't exist. She knew that. She loved him for trying.

"Please," she said. "Please just let this go."

She was grateful he did not argue.

"Then we have a battle to win." He handed the scroll back to her. "And I think we can both agree that showing this to anyone else gets us nothing."

Rin understood his implication. The Southern Coalition could never know about this. Not Souji, not Zhuden, and certainly not Gurubai. The offer was admittedly attractive—even she found it tempting, might even have sacrificed herself for it if she weren't so sure that what lay at the other end were lies.

If this got out, the factional infighting would explode. The Monkey Warlord had taught her that much about southern politics. This had to remain her secret.

"Of course," she said.

She drew a ball of flame into her palm under the scroll. For a moment Nezha's words burned bright, searing red. The parchment edges blackened, crinkled, then curled in on themselves like the legs of a dying spider.

Rin spent the next few hours attempting to catch short bursts of fitful sleep. She didn't know why she tried; she could never sleep before battle. At last she gave up and passed the last hours until dawn pacing around the camp, watching for the sun to rise. She couldn't bear sitting still with her thoughts. She couldn't keep torturing herself with the possibilities—whether Kesegi was alive, whether Nezha was telling the truth, whether she should have responded to the letter rather than ignore it.

She needed a distraction. She needed this battle.

She felt good about their positions. They'd arranged their troops in a four-point formation. One squadron, the one she led, would spearhead the attack and tie the Mugenese soldiers down at the front near the sorghum fields, while two smaller squadrons would circle around the Mugenese flanks, hemming them inside a triangle to form a wedge between the village and the battlefield. Souji's Iron Wolves, the fourth squadron, would drive holes through the enemy lines in the back, preventing a rout toward the civilians' evacuation zone.

Preparations proceeded smoothly as the day wore on. Thanks to the Liens, they were operating with far more information than she'd ever been used to on the battlefield. She knew exactly where the Mugenese slept. When they ate. Where and when they patrolled. It was almost like a textbook case of an ambush, a test question on an exam she would have taken at Sinegard.

As the sun began its downward slope, Rin went over final instructions before she dispatched her squadron commanders to their spots. Their plans had come together with clockwork efficiency. They avoided the patrols they knew were coming. Their map directions lined up perfectly with the actual terrain. All squadron commanders fully understood their signals and timetables.

The only hiccup was their uniforms.

Chief Lien had requested they wear uniforms to distinguish themselves from civilians. Rin had protested that they didn't have any.

"Tough," Chief Lien said. "Find some, or your ambush is off."

They'd compromised at headbands—thin strips of cloth tied around their foreheads. But an hour before they were due to move out, the squadron leaders started reporting they didn't have enough excess cloth. Their soldiers were already marching in threadbare uniforms; they didn't have any spares to cut up. Zhuden asked Rin if they should start ripping strips from their trouser legs.

"Forget that," Rin grumbled. "Let's just send them out."

"You can't," Souji said. "You made a promise."

"It's idiotic! Who's going to care about uniforms at nighttime?"

"The Mugenese might care," Kitay said. "Killing their labor source doesn't work in a symbiotic relationship. It's a small measure, but it's the least you can do. It's the difference between ten lives and a thousand."

In the end they had their troops smear their faces with bright red mud from a nearby pond. It left crimson patches on their clothes wherever they touched, and it caked onto their skin in dry, rusty streaks that didn't rub off without water.

"We look stupid." Rin surveyed the ranks. "We look like children playing past our dinnertime."

"No, we look like a clay army." Souji dragged two fingers across his cheek, leaving a thick, clearly visible streak. "The Red Emperor's very finest, baked fresh from southern dirt."

Thirty minutes until sunset, Rin crouched low amid the sorghum stalks. The smell of oil hung heavy in the air—the two thousand men behind her held dripping torches, ready to light at her signal.

The Southern Coalition's soldiers had been trained to fight in the darkness as they had at Khudla. It hurt their visibility, yes, but the psychological advantage was significant. Troops under ambush in pitch-black night reacted with panic, confusion, and cowardice.

But tonight, Rin wanted the battlefield well lit. The Mugenese might fall back on the civilians in the chaotic dark. She needed to draw them out into the grain fields, which meant she needed to show them precisely where their enemy lay.

Are you ready, little warrior?

The Phoenix crooned in the back of her mind, eager, waiting. Rin let the old rage leak in, familiar and warming as a hearth fire, let it seep into her limbs while visions of destruction played in her head.

Oh, how she'd craved this fight.

I'm ready.

"Rin!"

She whipped around. Souji pushed his way through the sorghum stalks, red-faced and panting for breath.

Her stomach dropped. He wasn't supposed to be here. He was supposed to be on the eastern flank with his Iron Wolves, poised and ready to attack.

"What are you doing?" she hissed.

"Hold up." He doubled over, wheezing. "Don't give the signal. Something's wrong."

"What are you talking about? We're ready, it's time—"

"No. Look." He rummaged in his pockets, pulled out a spyglass, and tossed it toward her. "Look *carefully*."

She raised it to her eye at the township walls. She struggled to make anything out in the dark. "I don't see anything."

"Move to the west. Just over the fields."

Rin moved the lens. What she saw didn't make any sense.

Mugenese soldiers clustered around the township walls. More poured out with every passing second. They knew about the ambush. Something—or someone—had tipped them off.

But they weren't charging forward. Their blades weren't pointed outward. They weren't even arranging themselves into defensive formations of the kind Rin would have expected from an army under attack.

No—their weapons were pointed at the city gates. They weren't preventing the attackers from coming in, they were keeping the residents from coming out.

Then Rin understood their strategy.

They weren't going to fight a fair fight. They weren't planning to engage the Southern Coalition at all.

They'd simply taken all Leiyang hostage.

Rin grabbed the arm of the nearest field officer and hissed, "*Find Kitay.*"

He sprinted back toward the camp.

"Fuck." Rin slammed a fist against her knee. "Fuck—*how*?"

"I don't know." For the first time, the confident swagger was wiped from Souji's face. He looked terrified. "I've no idea, I don't know what we're going to do—"

What had given them away? They'd prepared this ambush with twice their usual caution. The patrols couldn't possibly have seen them; they'd worked around the guard schedule with clockwork precision. Had someone seen her and Souji leaving the township? That was possible, but then how would the Mugenese have known when the ambush was scheduled? And how did they know it would come from the north?

It didn't matter how. Even if there were spies within her ranks, she couldn't solve that now; she had a more pressing problem to deal with.

The Mugenese were holding Leiyang's civilians at knifepoint.

A small contingent of Mugenese soldiers started moving toward the ambush line. One of them waved a red flag. They wanted to negotiate.

Rin worked frantically through all the possible ways this could end, and couldn't come up with one where both the civilians and the Southern Army were safe. The Mugenese would have to secure a guarantee that Rin's troops would never come back.

They were going to demand a blood sacrifice. Most likely they'd massacre Rin's troops, one for every civilian kept alive.

Rin didn't know if she could pay that price.

"What's going on?"

Kitay, at last. Rin turned toward him, trying not to slip into a panicked babble as she started to explain what was happening, but the moment she twisted around she saw Souji's expression morph into horror as he lifted a finger, pointing, toward the village.

A second later, she heard an arrow shriek through the air.

The Mugenese flag-bearer dropped to the ground.

Instinctively she whipped her head around, searching the ranks for a raised bow, a twanging bowstring—who'd done it, which absolute *idiot* had—

"My gods," Souji murmured. His eyes were still fixed on the village.

Rin turned back around and thought she was hallucinating. What else explained that great column moving out of the township gates, a crowd nearly the size of an army?

She raised the spyglass back to her eye.

Qinen. It had to be. He'd mobilized his resistance band—no, from the looks of it, he'd mobilized the entire township. The column wasn't just the fighting men of Leiyang; they were the women, elders, and even some of the children. They held torches, plows, field hoes, kitchen knives, and clubs clearly made from legs torn from chairs.

They charged.

They knew their lives were the price of this battle. Rin's attack couldn't proceed so long as they were held hostage. They'd known the Mugenese would force her to choose.

They'd made this decision for her.

The Mugenese archers turned toward the township to commence the massacre. Their commander signaled an order.

Civilian bodies fell from the front of the column in a clean sweep. But the villagers kept marching over their dead, pressing inexorably forward like ants bursting forth. Another round of arrows. Another line of bodies. The villagers kept marching.

The Mugenese soldiers couldn't shoot quickly enough to keep them at bay. This was a clash of steel and bodies now, an utterly mismatched comedy of a melee. Federation soldiers cut the villagers down as quickly as they came. They knocked the weapons out of their hands, pierced them easily in their necks and chests because their victims had never been trained to parry.

The villagers kept marching.

The bodies piled up on the field. Rin watched, horrified, as a blade went clean through an old woman's shoulder. But the woman lifted her trembling hands and clenched the wrist of her attacker, held him still long enough for an arrow to find his forehead.

The villagers kept marching.

Souji's hand landed on her shoulder. His voice came out a strangled rasp. "What are you waiting for?"

She reached into the back of her mind, through the channel of Kitay's soul, to the god who lay patiently waiting.

Avenge this, she ordered.

Whatever you ask, said the Phoenix.

And Rin strode forward through the sorghum fields to rip the world open with fire. She killed indiscriminately. She turned them all to ash, civilians and enemies alike. Leiyang's civilians welcomed her flames with smiles.

This was their choice. Their sacrifice.

Her troops surged forth around her, blades glinting in the fiery night. They'd broken formation, but formation didn't matter anymore, only bodies, blood, and steel.

This is how we win the south, she thought as her surroundings dissolved into a blurry wave of heat. That made it easier to keep going. She couldn't see faces, couldn't see the pain. All she saw were shapes. *Not with our blades, but our bodies.*

They would take back the south with sheer numbers. The Mugenese and the Republic were strong, but the south was many. And if southerners were dirt like all the legends said, then they would crush their enemies with the overwhelming force of the earth until they could only dream of breathing. They would bury them with their bodies. They would drown them in their blood.

CHAPTER 6

After that, it was just cleanup.

Rin walked dazedly through the sorghum fields, razed now to a level sheet of dark gray ash. Smoke curled out of her clothes in lazy, indolent spirals. She hadn't touched opium since they'd set out on this march. But she was high now on a familiar euphoria, an exhilarating buzz that started in her fingertips and thrummed through her chest to her heart.

In Tikany, summer season was always overrun with ants. The vicious red creatures were driven into a frenzy by the dry heat, attacking whatever small children and animals crossed their paths. One bite alone raised a welt; a dozen could be fatal. The villagers retaliated with acid, using long poles to tip jars onto the anthills from a distance. Rin remembered how as a child she would crouch by the ground with empty jars in hand, squinting as destroyed civilizations frothed and burned under the sunlight.

She'd always lingered too long. She liked to listen to the acid hissing as it burrowed into the ants' deepest tunnels. Liked to see the ants pouring frantically out the top, fleeing straight into the pools of acid she'd laid carefully in a ring around the nest. Liked to watch their little legs wiggle as they frothed and dissolved.

She felt a similar kind of pleasure now, the sadistic glee of watching lives evaporate and knowing she'd done it. Of knowing she had that *power*.

What is wrong with me?

She felt the same bizarre, confused elation that'd come over her when she'd poisoned Ma Lien. This time she didn't push it away. She drank it in. Her power was derived from rage, and what she felt now was the other side of the coin—vengeance fulfilled.

Leiyang hadn't been completely lost. When Rin's soldiers searched the ruins for any civilians with breath left in their lungs, they found that the rate of survival was surprisingly high. The Mugenese attackers had been careless, acting from a frenzied panic rather than a calculated cruelty. They'd slammed steel haphazardly into any exposed flesh they saw instead of aiming for vital organs as they should have.

Leiyang the township was dead. Chief Lien's people couldn't live here any longer. Their numbers were too few; their homes and belongings were destroyed. They'd have to march south with Rin's army to seek new homes, would have to see their numbers cannibalized into whatever villages would take them.

But Leiyang's survivors were free. That, at least, was worth it.

Qinen, by some miracle, had made it out alive. Rin went to see him the moment she heard he was conscious.

The Southern Coalition's handful of physicians had set up a triage center in a butchery, one of the few structures in Leiyang's city center that hadn't burned to the ground. They'd sanitized the structurally intact interior to the best of their ability, but couldn't scourge the taint of burned pig intestines. By the end of the day the air was thick with the hot, tangy smell of blood, human and animal alike.

Rin found Qinen lying on a sheet outdoors, where the physicians had sent every patient not under immediate surgery. He looked awful. The burns that covered the right side of his body had twisted the skin on his face so badly that he could only speak in a hoarse, garbled whisper. His eyes were open but swollen, his right eye covered by a filmy white layer. Rin wasn't sure that he could see her until his face broke into an awful, painful smile.

"I'm sorry—" she started, but he reached out and seized her wrist with a force that surprised her.

"I told you," he rasped. "I told you we'd fight."

Qinen's band of resistance fighters hadn't been acting alone. Similar organizations had existed all throughout the Beehive. This Rin discovered when, one by one, the villages clustered around Leiyang began to liberate themselves with startling speed.

Without the central leadership at Leiyang, the remaining ranks of Mugenese soldiers were isolated, cut off from all communications, resources, or reinforcements. Villagers armed with knives and plows now stood a fighting chance. Reports began flooding in about the villagers all throughout Rooster Province rising up, taking up arms, and purging their villages of their former rulers.

After Rin sent squadrons of Zhuden's troops throughout the Beehive to speed up the process, the battle for the surrounding area took no more than two weeks. Some Mugenese troops put up a fight and went down in explosions of fire, yellow gas, steel, and blood. Others took their chances and surrendered, begging for exile or leniency, and were invariably executed by village committees.

When Rin toured the Beehive, she found herself witness to a wave of violence sweeping across the province.

In some hamlets, the civilians had already decapitated their Mugenese guards and strung their heads upside down along the town gates like a welcoming display of holiday lanterns. In other villages, Rin arrived while the executions were ongoing. These were drawn out over a period of days, a twisted parade whose centerpiece entertainment was an orgy of violence.

The sheer creativity astounded her. The liberated southerners marched the Mugenese naked in chains along the streets while onlookers reached out with knives to slice their flesh. They forced the Mugenese to kneel for hours on broken bricks with millstones hung around their necks. They buried the Mugenese alive, dismembered them, shot them, throttled them, and threw their bodies into dirty, rotting piles.

The victims were not limited to Mugenese troops. The victorious liberators' harshest punishments fell on the collaborators—the magistrates, merchants, and delegates who had succumbed to Federation rule. In one village three miles south of Leiyang, Rin stumbled upon a public ceremony where three men were tied to posts, naked and gagged with rags to muffle their screams. In the corner, two women held long knives over a barrel fire. The blades glowed a vicious orange.

Rin could guess this would end in castration.

She turned to Souji. "Do you know what those men did?"

"Sure," he said. "Traded girls."

"They—*what*?"

He spelled it out for her. "They struck a deal to stop the Mugenese from grabbing women off the street. Every day they'd take a few women—usually the poor ones, or the orphans, who had no one to fight for them—and deliver them to the Mugenese general headquarters. Then they'd go back at sunrise, retrieve the girls, clean them up best they could, and send them home. It kept the younger girls and the pregnant women safe, though I don't think the women they picked were too happy." He watched, unflinching, as a girl who couldn't have been more than fourteen ascended the stage and poured a vat of boiling oil over the men's heads. "They said it was for the good of the village. Guess not everyone agreed."

Loud sizzles mixed with the screams. Rin's stomach grumbled, tricked into thinking she'd smelled freshly cooked meat. She hugged her arms over her chest and looked away, suppressing the urge to vomit.

Souji chuckled. "What's wrong, Princess?"

"I just . . ." Rin wasn't sure how to articulate her unease, much less distinguish it from obvious hypocrisy. "Isn't this a bit much?"

"'A bit much'?" He scoffed. "Really? This from you?"

"It's different when . . ." She trailed off. How exactly was it different? What right did she have to judge? Why did she feel shame and disgust now, when the pain she regularly inflicted on the battlefield was a thousand times worse? "It's different when it's civilians doing it. It . . . it feels *wrong*."

"How did it feel when you called the Phoenix at Speer?"

She flinched. "What does that matter?"

"It was good, wasn't it?" His lip curled. "Oh, it was horrific, I'm sure, must have left a mental scar the size of a crater. But it was also the best thing you'd ever felt, wasn't it? It felt like you'd put the universe back in place. Like you were balancing the scales. Didn't it?"

He pointed to the men on the stage. They weren't screaming anymore. Only one was still twitching. "You don't know what these men have done. They might look like innocent Nikara faces, but you weren't here during occupation, and you don't know the pain they caused. The south doesn't burn its own unless there's a reason. You have no idea what these villagers are healing from. So don't take this from them."

His voice grew louder. "You don't fix hurts by pretending they never happened. You treat them like infected wounds. You dig deep with a burning knife and gouge out the rotten flesh and then, maybe, you have a chance to heal."

So when the south reclaimed itself in a sea of blood, Rin didn't stop it. She could only watch as the tide of peasant violence rose to a fever pitch that she wasn't sure she could control, even if she'd wanted to. Nobody would admit out loud how satisfying this was—the villagers had to pretend that this was a ritual of necessity and not of indulgence—but Rin saw the hungry gleams in their eyes as they drank in the screams.

This was catharsis. They needed to spill blood like they needed to breathe. Of course she understood that impulse; at night, alone with her pipe, she showed those bloody scenes over and over again to Altan so that her mind could find some semblance of peace while he could drink them hungrily in. The south needed retribution to keep going. How could she deprive them?

Only Kitay kept agitating to put an end to the riots. He could allow for the death penalty but he wanted order; he wanted public trials that weren't a sham and sentences more moderate than execution.

"Some of those people are innocent," he said. "Some of them were just trying to stay alive."

"Bullshit," Souji said. "They made their choice."

"Do you understand the choices they got?" Kitay pointed across the courtyard to where a man had been hanging upside down by his ankles for the past three days. "He served as one of their translators for seven months. Why? Because the Mugenese captured his wife and daughter and told him he could serve, or he could watch them be buried alive. Then they started torturing his daughter in front of him to drive home the point. What do you think he picked?"

Souji was utterly unmoved. "He helped them kill other Nikara."

"*Everyone* helped them kill other Nikara," Kitay insisted. "Ideological purity is well and fine, but some people were just trying to survive."

"You know, the Mugenese gave my sister a choice," Souji said. "Said she could be one of their double agents and rat on her fellow villagers, or they'd rape and kill her. You know what she picked?"

Kitay's cheeks flushed red. "I'm not saying—"

"Did you know the Mugenese liked to play games to fill their kill quota?" Souji inquired.

"I know," Kitay said. "At Golyn Niis—"

"I know what they did at Golyn Niis." Souji's voice was like steel. "Want to know what they did here? They'd drive mobs of villagers up to the roofs of the tallest buildings they could find. Then they'd tear down the stairs, set the bottom floors on fire, and stand back in a circle to watch while they screamed. *That's* what those collaborators had a hand in. Tell me we're supposed to forgive that."

"Kitay," Rin said quietly. "Drop it."

He didn't. "But they're not just targeting the Mugenese and their collaborators."

"Kitay, please—"

"They're targeting everyone who's ever been *remotely* suspected of collaboration," Kitay hissed. "This isn't justice, it's a killing frenzy, and whispers and pointed fingers are ending lives. You can't tell who's truly guilty and who's fallen on the bad side of their neighbors. It's not justice, it's chaos."

"So what?" Souji shrugged. "Hunt a rat, you're going to smash some dishes. This is a revolution. It's not a fucking tea party."

They marched in silent exhaustion on the road back to Leiyang. The thrill of victory had long since died off. Two weeks of screams and torture, no matter who the victims were, had left them all somewhat haggard and pale.

They were half a day's march out when a hooded rider appeared on the road. Rin's officers rushed forward, spears leveled, shouting for the rider to stop. The rider halted, raising their hands to indicate the lack of weapon.

"Get down!" Zhuden insisted. "Who are you?"

"Oh, for heaven's sake." Venka threw the hood off her face and dismounted from her horse. She strode forth, batting spear points away with one hand as if swatting at a cloud of gnats. "What the fuck, Rin? Call off these fools."

"Venka!" Rin darted forward and embraced Venka, but quickly let go; the stench was too much to bear. Venka smelled like a tannery on fire. "Great Tortoise, when's the last time you had a bath?"

"Cut me a fucking break," Venka said. "I've been fleeing for my life."

"You had time to put on fresh face paint," Kitay pointed out.

"Everyone was doing it in Sinegard. I had some left in my bag. Easier to access than soap, all right?"

Rin could only laugh. What else did they expect? Sring Venka was a prim, spoiled Sinegardian princess turned lethal soldier turned brittle survivor; of course she'd walk into a war zone with red paint on her lips simply because she felt like it.

"Anyway, it took you long enough to get back," Venka griped. "I've been pacing this patch of road since yesterday. They told me you were based in Leiyang."

"We were," Rin said. "Are. Left to do some cleaning up."

"What happened?" Kitay asked. "Thought you were just fine in the Republic."

Venka gave a dramatic sigh. "Broke my cover. It was the stupidest thing. There I was, an utterly invisible servant girl in a magistrate's household, and then the lady of the house started thinking I was trying to seduce her husband and dragged me out into the street."

"Were you—?" Kitay began.

Venka shot him a scathing look. "Of course not. It's not my fault that the stupid man couldn't keep his eyes off my ass."

Kitay looked flustered. "I was just going to ask if you were recognized."

"Oh. No, but it was a near thing. His wife had me fired, then she went around telling all the other households not to hire me. That brought a bit too much attention. So I looted the armory in the middle of the night, sweet-talked the stable boy into lending me a horse, and made my way down south." She recounted all this with such brazen flippancy she might have been chatting about Sinegard's latest fashions. "At Ruijin they said you'd gone south, so I followed the trail of bodies. Didn't take me long to track you down."

"We've, ah, split with Ruijin," Rin said.

"So I figured." Venka nodded to the waiting troops. "How'd you wrestle an army from Gurubai?"

"Created a vacancy." Rin glanced over her shoulder at her troops. Souji and the other officers were paused in the middle of the road, watching them curiously.

"She's an ally," Rin told them. "Carry on."

The column resumed its march toward Leiyang. Rin kept her

voice low as she spoke to Venka, glancing around to make sure Souji did not overhear.

"Listen, has Nezha started sending anyone south?"

Venka arched an eyebrow. "Not the last I heard. Why?"

"Are you sure?"

"Supposedly he's still cooped up in the palace. Rumor has it he's not doing so well, actually; he's been out of commission for a few weeks."

"What?" Rin asked sharply. Her heart was suddenly beating very quickly. "What does that mean?"

Kitay shot her a curious look. She ignored it. "Was he injured?" she asked.

"I don't think so," Venka said. "He hasn't been out on the field in weeks. Vaisra recalled him from Tiger Province last month. He's spent a lot of time with the Hesperians, negotiating with their delegates, and I think the prevailing rumor was that he's fallen ill. He looks weak, he's got shadows under his eyes, or so they say. It's hard to tell what's gossip and what's fact, since no one I knew had actually gotten a good look at him, but it seems serious."

Rin felt a stupid, instinctive stab of worry, the residue of concern. She quashed it. "You think he's going to die?"

"Not sure," Venka said. "They say he's got all the best Hesperian doctors working on him, though that might be doing more harm than good. I doubt he'll be leading troops out anytime soon."

Did that mean she was safe? Had Nezha just been fucking around with her? His illness did not negate the fact that he had spies in her camp, that he knew where she laid her head every night. But if Venka was right, and if Nezha and his father were indeed still preoccupied with the north, they might not have to worry about an impending ambush for the time being.

This reprieve might not last for long. But she'd take every extra day she had.

"What's the matter?" Venka asked. "You spooked about something?"

Rin exchanged a glance with Kitay. They'd come to an unspoken agreement—they wouldn't tell Venka about the letter. The fewer people who knew, the better.

"Nothing," Rin said. "Just—just wanted to make sure we're not getting blindsided."

"Trust me." Venka snorted. "I don't think he's even in a fit state to walk."

They rode for a few moments in silence. Rin could see the silhouette of Leiyang emerging from the horizon; from here on it was only flat roads.

"So what in the sixty-four gods has been happening here?" Venka asked after a while. "I passed a few villages on my way up here. They've all gone completely mad."

"Throes of victory," Rin said. "Growing pains."

"They're skinning people alive," Venka said.

"Because they traded little girls for food rations."

"Oh. Fair enough." Venka flicked an invisible speck of dust from her wrist. "I hope they castrated them, too."

Later that afternoon, as Rin headed to the fields to supervise basic training, she was accosted by a wizened old woman dragging two skinny girls along by their wrists.

"We heard you were taking girls," she said. "Will they do?"

Rin was so startled by her pushy irreverence that rather than directing the woman to the enlistment stand, she paused and looked. She was puzzled by what she saw. The girls were thin and scrawny, certainly no older than fifteen, and they cowered behind the old woman as if terrified of being seen. They couldn't possibly be volunteers—every other woman who had enlisted in the Southern Army had done so proudly and of her own volition.

"You're taking girls," the old woman prompted.

Rin hesitated. "Yes, but—"

"They're sisters. You can have them for two silvers."

Rin blinked. "Pardon?"

"One silver?" the woman suggested impatiently.

"I'm not paying you anything." Rin's brow furrowed. "That's not what—"

"They're good girls," said the woman. "Quick. Obedient. And neither are virgins—"

"*Virgins?*" Rin repeated. "What do you think we're doing here?"

The woman looked at her as if she were mad. "They said you were taking girls. For the army."

Then the pieces fell together. Rin's gut twisted. "We aren't hiring *prostitutes*."

The woman was undaunted. "One silver."

"Get out of here," Rin snapped. "Or I'll have you thrown in jail."

The woman spat a gob of saliva at Rin's feet and stormed off, tugging the girls behind her.

"Hold it," Rin said. "Leave them."

The woman paused, looking for a moment like she might protest. So Rin let a stream of fire, ever so delicate, slip through her fingers and dance around her wrist. "I wasn't asking."

Hastily, the woman left without another word.

Rin turned to the girls. They had barely moved this whole time. Neither would meet her eyes. They stood still, arms hanging loose by their sides, heads lowered deferentially like house servants waiting for commands.

Rin had the oddest temptation to pinch their arms, check their muscles, turn up their chins, and open their mouths to see if their teeth were good. *What is wrong with me?*

She asked, for want of anything better to say, "Do you want to be soldiers?"

The older girl shot Rin a fleeting glance, then gave a dull shrug. The other didn't react at all; her eyes remained fixed on an empty patch of air before her.

Rin tried something else. "What are your names?"

"Pipaji," said the older girl.

The younger girl's eyes dropped to the ground.

"What's wrong with her?" Rin asked.

"She doesn't speak," snapped Pipaji. Rin saw a sudden flash of anger in her eyes—a sharp defensiveness, and she understood then that Pipaji had spent her entire life shielding her sister from other people.

"I understand," Rin said. "You speak for her. What's her name?"

The hostility eased somewhat from Pipaji's face. "Jiuto."

"Jiuto and Pipaji," Rin said. "Do you have a family name?"

Silence.

"Where are you from?"

Pipaji gave her a sullen look. "Not here."

"I see. They took your home, too, huh?"

Pipaji gave a listless shrug, as if she found this question incredibly stupid.

"Listen," Rin said. Her patience was running out. She wanted to be on the field with her troops, not coaxing words from sullen little girls. "I haven't got time for this. You're free of that woman, so you can do whatever you like. You can join this army if you want—"

"Do we get food?" Pipaji interrupted.

"Yes. Twice a day."

Pipaji considered this for a moment, then nodded. "Okay."

Her tone made it clear she had no further questions. Rin watched them both for a moment, then shrugged and pointed. "Good. Barracks are over there."

CHAPTER 7

Two weeks later they reached Tikany.

Rin had been prepared to fight for her hometown. But when her troops approached Tikany's earthen walls, the fields were quiet. The trenches lay empty; the gates hung wide open, with no sentries in sight. This wasn't the deceptive stillness of a waiting ambush but the listless silence of a place abandoned. Whatever Mugenese troops had once terrorized Tikany had already fled. Rin passed completely unobstructed through the northern gates into a place she hadn't seen since she'd left it nearly five years ago.

She didn't recognize it.

Not because she'd forgotten. As much as she'd once wanted to, she'd never erase the texture of this place from her mind—not the clouds of red dust that blew through the streets on windy days, covering everything with a fine sheen of crimson; not the abandoned shrines and temples around every corner, remnants of more superstitious days; not the rickety wooden buildings emerging from dirt like angry, resilient scars. She knew Tikany's streets like she knew the back of her hand; knew its alleys, hidden tunnels, and opium drop-off sites; knew the best hiding corners wherein to take refuge when Auntie Fang's temper bubbled over into violence.

But Tikany had changed. The whole place felt empty, hollowed, like someone had gouged its intestines out with a knife and devoured them, leaving behind a fragile, traumatized shell. Tikany had never been one of the Empire's great cities, but it had held life. It had been, like so many of the southern cities, a locus of small autonomy, carved defiantly into the hard soil.

The Federation had turned it into a city of the dead.

Most of the ramshackle buildings were gone, long since burned down or dismantled. The Mugenese had turned what was left into a spare military camp. The library, the outdoor opera stage, and schoolhouse—the only places in Tikany that had ever brought Rin any happiness—were skeletal structures that showed signs of deliberate deconstruction. Rin guessed the Mugenese had stripped down their walls for firewood.

In the pleasure district, the whorehouses alone remained standing.

"Take twelve troops—women, if possible—and scour every one of those buildings for survivors," Rin told the closest officer. "Hurry."

She knew by now what they would likely find. She knew she should have gone herself. She wasn't brave enough for it.

She kept walking. Closer to the township center, near the magistrate's hall and public ceremonies office, she found evidence of the public executions. Stage floorboards painted brown with months-old stains. Whips tossed onto careless piles under the spot where once, a lifetime ago, she'd read her Keju test score and realized she was going to Sinegard.

What she didn't see were corpses. In Golyn Niis, they'd been stacked up on every street corner. Tikany's streets were empty.

But that made sense. When your goal was occupation, you always cleaned up your corpses. Otherwise they stank.

"Great Tortoise." Souji whistled under his breath as he strode beside her, hands in his pockets, peering about the devastation like a child perusing a holiday market. "They really did a number on this place."

"Shut up," Rin said.

"What's the matter? Did they tear down your favorite teahouse?"

"I said *shut up*."

She hated the thought of crying in front of him, yet she could barely breathe for the weight crushing her chest. Her head felt terribly light; her temples throbbed. She dug her nails into her palm to ward off the tears.

She'd seen large-scale devastation like this only once before, and it had almost broken her. But this was worse than Golyn Niis, because at least in Golyn Niis, most everyone was *dead*. She would almost have rather seen corpses than the survivors she saw now, crawling out from whatever safe houses remained standing, blinking at her with the dazed confusion of animals who had spent too long living in the dark.

"Are they gone?" they asked her. "Are we freed?"

"You're freed," she said. "They're gone. Forever."

They registered these words with fearful, doubtful looks, as if they expected the Mugenese to return any moment and smite them for their temerity. Then they grew braver. More and more of them emerged from huts, shacks, and hiding holes, more than Rin had dared hope remained alive. Whispers arced through the ghost town, and gradually the survivors began to fill the square, crowding around the soldiers, homing in on Rin.

"Are you . . . ?" they asked.

"I am," she said. She let them touch her so that they knew she was real. She let them see her flames, spiraling high in delicate patterns, silently conveying the words she couldn't bring herself to say out loud.

It's me. I'm back. I'm sorry.

"They need to wash," Kitay said. "Almost everyone here's got a lice problem; we need to contain it before it spreads to our troops. And they need a good meal, we should get the rations in order—"

"Can you handle it?" she asked. Her voice rang oddly in her

ears when she spoke, as if coming from the other side of a thick wooden door. "I want—I need to keep walking."

He touched her arm. "Rin—"

"I'm all right," she said.

"You don't have to do this alone."

"But I do. You can't understand." She stepped away from him. Kitay knew every part of her soul, but he couldn't share this with her. This was about roots, about dirt. He wasn't from here; he couldn't know how it felt. "You—you take care of the survivors. Let me go. Please."

He squeezed her hand and nodded. "Just be careful."

Rin broke away from the crowd, disappeared down a side alley while no one was watching, and then walked alone across town to her old neighborhood.

She didn't bother going to the Fang residence. There was nothing for her there. She knew Uncle Fang was dead. She knew Auntie Fang and Kesegi had most likely died in Arlong. And aside from Kesegi, her memories of that house contained nothing but misery.

She went straight to Tutor Feyrik's house.

His quarters were empty. She couldn't find a single trace of him in any of the bare rooms; he might never have lived there at all. The books were gone, every last one. Even the bookshelves were missing. All that remained was a little stool, which she suspected the Mugenese had left alone because it was carved from stone and not wood.

She remembered that stool. She'd perched there so many nights as a child, listening to Tutor Feyrik talk about places she never thought she would see. She'd sat there the night before the exam, sobbing into her hands while he gently patted her shoulders and murmured that she'd be all right. *A girl like you? You'll always be all right.*

He might still be alive. He might have fled early, at the first warnings of danger; he might be in one of the refugee camps up north. If she tried hard enough, she could maintain the delusion that he was somewhere out there, safe and happy, simply out of her orbit. She tried to find comfort in that thought, but the uncertainty of not knowing, perhaps never knowing, only hurt more.

She tasted salt on her lips, and realized her face was wet with tears.

Abruptly, violently, she wiped them away.

Why do you need to find him? She heard the question in Altan's voice. *Why does it fucking matter?*

She'd hardly thought about Tutor Feyrik in years. She'd cut him out of her mind the same way she'd alienated herself from her sixteen years in Tikany, a snakeskin shed so she could reinvent herself from war orphan to student and soldier. She clung to his memory now out of some pathetic, cowardly nostalgia. He was only a relic—a reminder from an easier time when she was a little girl trying to memorize the Classics, and he was a kind teacher who'd shown her her only way out.

She was searching for a life she'd never have again. And Rin knew far too well by now that nostalgia could kill her.

"Find anything?" Kitay asked when she returned.

"No," she said. "There's nothing here."

Rin chose to make her headquarters in the Mugenese general's complex, partly because she felt like it was her right as liberator and partly because it was the safest place in the encampment. Before they moved in, she and Souji scoured each room, checking for any lurking assassins.

They encountered nothing but messy rooms still littered with dirty dishes, uniforms, and spare weapons. It was like the Mugenese had vanished into thin air, leaving all their belongings behind. Even the main office looked as if the general had simply stepped into the next room for a cup of tea.

Rin rooted through the general's desk, pulling out stacks of memos, maps, and letters. In one drawer she found sheaves of paper, all charcoal sketches of the same woman. This general had apparently considered himself an artist. The sketches weren't half bad—the general had rather painstakingly tried to capture his lover's eyes, to the neglect of other anatomical accuracies. The same Mugenese characters accompanied each sketch—*hudie*, meaning "butterfly" in Nikara; she'd forgotten its Mugenese pronunciation. It was likely not a proper name but an endearment.

He was lonely, she thought. How had he felt when he learned the fate of the longbow island? When he learned that no ships were ever sailing back across the Nariin Sea?

She found a note written on a folded sheet of paper wedged in between the last two sketches. The Mugenese script was not so different from Nikara—it borrowed heavily from Nikara characters, though their pronunciations were entirely different—but it took her several minutes of parsing through messy, scrawled ink to decipher what it said.

> If it means I have a traitorous heart then yes, I wish our Emperor had not summoned you for duty, for he has ripped you from my arms.
> The entirety of the eastern continent—no, the riches of this universe—means nothing to me in your absence.
> I pray every day for the seas to bring your return.
> Your butterfly.

It was an extract torn out of a longer letter. Rin couldn't find the rest.

She felt oddly guilty as she leafed through the general's things. Absurdly enough, she felt like an intruder. She'd spent so much time figuring out how to kill the Mugenese that the very idea that they could be people, with private lives and loves and hopes and dreams, made her feel vaguely nauseated.

"Look at those walls," Souji said.

Rin followed his gaze. The general had kept a detailed wall calendar, filled in neat, tiny handwriting. It was far more legible than the letter. She flipped to the very first page. "They arrived here just three months ago."

"That's just when they started keeping the calendar," Souji said. "Trust me, they've been in the south far longer than that."

His unspoken accusation lingered in the air between them. Three months ago she could have come south. She could have stopped this.

Rin had long since accepted that charge. She knew this was her fault. She could have taken the Empress's hand that day in Lusan, could have killed Vaisra's rebellion in the cradle and led her troops straight down south. But instead she'd played at revolution, and all that won her was a scar snaking across her back and an aching stump where her hand should have been.

She hated how nakedly transparent Vaisra's strategy had been from the start, and hated herself more for failing to see it. In retrospect it was so clear why the south had to burn, why Vaisra had withheld his aid even when the southern warlords came begging at his feet.

He could have easily stopped those massacres. He'd known the Hesperian fleet was coming to his aid; he could have dispatched half his army to answer the pleas of a dying nation. He'd deliberately crippled the south instead. He didn't have to grapple with the southern Warlords for political authority if he just let the Mugenese do his dirty work for him. And then, when the smoke cleared, when the Empire lay in fractured shambles, he would have marched in with the Republican Army and burned out the Mugenese with dirigibles and arquebuses. By then southern autonomy would have seemed laughable—whatever survivors remained would have fallen on their knees and worshipped him as their savior.

What if he had told you? Altan—Rin's hallucination of Altan—had asked her once. *What if he'd made you fully complicit? Would you have switched your allegiance?*

Rin didn't know. She had despised the southerners back then. She'd hated her own people, had hated them the moment she saw them in the camps. She'd hated their darkness, their flat-tongued rural accents and fearful, dull-eyed stares. It was so easy to mistake sheer terror for stupidity, and she'd been desperate to think of them as stupid because she knew *she* wasn't stupid, and she needed any reason to set herself apart.

Back then her self-loathing had run so deep that if Vaisra had simply told her every part of his plan, she might have taken his evil for brilliance and laughed. If he hadn't traded her away, she might never have left his side.

Anger coiled in her gut. She tore the calendar down from the wall and crushed it in her fingers.

"I was a fool for Vaisra," she said. "I shouldn't have counted on his virtue. But he didn't count on my survival."

Once they'd deemed the general's complex safe as a home base, Rin walked across town to the whorehouses. She didn't want to; she was hungry and exhausted, her eyes and throat felt sore from suppressed tears, and all she wanted to do was curl up in a corner with her pipe.

But she was General Fang the Speerly, and she owed this to the survivors.

Venka was already there. She'd begun the difficult work of marshaling the women from the whorehouses. Puddles and overturned buckets covered the cold stone floors where the women had showered, next to thick, dark piles of lice-ridden locks shorn from newly bald heads.

Venka stood now at the center of the square courtyard, hands clasped behind her back like a drill sergeant. The women clustered around her in a sullen circle, blankets clutched around their skinny shoulders, their eyes dull and unfocused.

"You have to eat," Venka said. "I'm not leaving you alone until I see you swallow."

"I can't." The girl in front of Venka could have been anywhere from thirteen to thirty—her skin was stretched so tight over her fragile, birdlike bones that Rin couldn't tell.

Venka grabbed the girl's shoulder with one hand; with the other, she held a steamed bun up so close to the girl's face that Rin thought she might start mashing it into her lips. "*Eat.*"

The girl pressed her mouth shut and squirmed in Venka's grasp, whimpering.

"What's wrong with you?" Venka shouted. "*Eat!* Take care of yourself!"

The girl wriggled free and backed away, eyes scrunched up in tears, shoulders hunched as if she expected a beating.

"Venka!" Rin hurried forward and pulled Venka back by the wrist. "What are you doing?"

"What the fuck do you think?" Venka's cheeks were chalk-pale with fury. "Everyone else has eaten, but this little bitch thinks she's too good for her food—"

One of the other women put an arm around the girl. "She's still in shock. Let her be."

"Shut up." Venka shot the girl a scathing glare. "Do you want to die?"

After a long pause, the girl gave a timid shake of her head.

"So *eat.*" Venka flung the bun at her. It bounced off her chest and landed on the dirt. "Right now you're the luckiest fucking girl in the world. You're alive. You have food. You're saved from the brink of starvation. All you have to do is put that bun in your fucking mouth."

The girl began to cry.

"Stop that," Venka ordered. "Don't be pathetic."

"You don't understand," choked the girl. "I don't—you can't—"

"I do understand," Venka said flatly. "Same thing happened to me at Golyn Niis."

The girl lifted her eyes. "Then you're a whore, too. And we should both be dead."

Venka drew her arm back and slapped the girl hard across the face.

"Venka, *stop*." Rin seized Venka's arm and pulled her out of the courtyard. Venka didn't resist; rather, she stumbled along willingly as if in a daze.

She wasn't angry, Rin realized. If anything, Venka seemed about to collapse.

This wasn't about the food.

Rin knew, deep down, that Venka hadn't turned her back on her home province and joined the Southern Coalition—a rebellion formed of people with skin several shades darker than hers—out of any real loyalty to their cause. She'd done it because of what had happened at Golyn Niis. Because the Dragon Warlord Yin Vaisra had knowingly let those atrocities at Golyn Niis happen, had let them happen across the entire south, and hadn't lifted a finger to stop them.

Venka had taken it upon herself to fight those battles. But as she and Rin had both discovered, the battles were easy. Destroying was easy. The hard part was the aftermath.

"Are you all right?" Rin asked quietly.

Venka's voice trembled. "I'm just trying to make this easier."

"I know," Rin said. "But not everyone is as strong as you."

"They'd better learn to be, or they'll be dead in a few weeks."

"They'll survive. The Mugenese are gone."

"Oh, you think it just ends like that?" Venka gave a brittle laugh. "You think it's all over? Once they're gone?"

"I didn't mean—"

"They're never gone. Do you understand? They still come for you in your sleep. Only this time they're dream-wraiths, not real, and there's no escape from them because they're living in your own mind."

"Venka, I'm sorry, I didn't—"

Venka continued like she hadn't heard. "Do you know that after Golyn Niis, the other two survivors from that pleasure house drank lye? Do you want to guess how many of these girls are going to hang themselves? They have no space to be weak, Rin. They don't have time to be *in shock*. That can't be an option. That's how they die."

"I understand that," Rin said. "But you can't take your shit out on them. You're here to protect. You're a soldier. Act like it."

Venka's eyes widened. For a moment Rin thought Venka might slap her, too. But the moment passed, and Venka's shoulders slumped, like all the fight had drained out of her at once.

"Fine. Put them under someone else's charge, then. I'm finished here." She pointed to the whorehouses. "And burn that place to the ground."

"We can't," Rin said. "They're some of the only walled structures still standing. Until we can rebuild some shelters—"

"Burn it," Venka snarled. "Or I'll get some oil and do it myself. Now, I'm not very good at arson. So you can set a controlled fire, or deal with an inferno. You pick."

A scout's arrival saved Rin the burden of a response.

"We found it," he reported. "Looks like there was only one."

Rin's stomach twisted. Not this. Not now. She wasn't ready; after the whorehouses, she just wanted to shrink into a ball somewhere and hide. "Where was it?"

"About half a mile south of the city border. It's muddy out there; you'll want to lace on some thicker boots. Lieutenant Chen told me to tell you he's already on the way. Shall I take you?"

Rin hesitated. "Venka . . ."

"Count me out. I don't want to see that." Venka turned on her heel and called over her shoulder as she stalked off, "I want the whorehouses in ashes by dawn, or I'll assume it's my job."

Rin wanted to chase after her. She wanted to pull Venka back by the wrist, hug her tight, and hold her close until they were able to sob, until their sobs subsided. But Venka would interpret that as pity, and Venka detested pity more than anything. She read pity as an insult—as confirmation that, after all this time, everyone still thought her fragile and broken, on the verge of falling apart. Rin couldn't do that to her.

She'd burn the whorehouses, she decided. The survivors could survive a few nights in the open air. She had fire enough to keep them warm.

"General?" the scout asked quietly.

Rin blinked. She'd been staring after Venka's retreating figure. "Give me a moment. I'll meet you at the east gate."

She returned to the general's complex to change her boots and ask around the barracks until someone lent her a spare shovel. Then she followed the scout to the killing fields.

The walk was shorter than she expected.

She knew the site from a quarter-mile off. She knew it from the smell, the rancid odor of decay under a thin sheen of dust; from the fat insects scurrying into the ground and the carrion birds that perched casually on white bone fragments sticking out of the ground. She knew it from the discolored and displaced soil, and the traces of hair and clothes strewn across the dirt where the Mugenese had hardly bothered to bury them.

She stopped ten feet before she reached the graves. She needed to breathe before she could bring herself to go any farther.

"Let someone else do this." Kitay put a hand on her shoulder. "You're allowed to go back."

"I'm not," she said. "And I can't. This has to be me."

It had to be her because this was her fault. She was obligated to look. She needed to afford the dead at least that modicum of respect.

She wanted to bury it all, to pile mounds of soil over this shallow grave, tamp it tightly against the ground with shovels, and then roll wagons over it to flatten this site so that it might fade back into the landscape until one day they could pretend it had never existed.

But they had to identify the bodies. So many southerners were currently trapped in that horrifying limbo of uncertainty with no way to know if their loved ones were dead, and that uncertainty could hurt more than grief. Once they found the bodies, at least they could mourn.

And then, because burial rituals were so important in the south, the bodies needed to be cleaned. In peacetime, funerals in Tikany were daylong affairs. Hordes of mourners—sometimes including hired professionals to inflate the ranks, if the deceased's family could afford it—moaned and wailed as they followed the coffin out of town to carefully prepared ancestral plots. The souls of the dead needed to be properly coaxed into their graves so they would rest instead of haunting the living; this demanded regular offerings of burned paper goods and incense to soothe them into the world beyond.

Rin had an idea of what the afterlife looked like now. She knew it was not some cute parallel ghost city where burned paper offerings might be translated into real treasures. But still, to leave a loved one's body to rot in the open was shameful.

She'd thrown away most of her Rooster heritage. She'd lost her dialect and her mannerisms; since her first year at school, she'd dressed and spoken like a Sinegardian elite. She didn't believe in southern superstition, and she wasn't going to start pretending now.

But death was sacred. Death demanded respect.

Kitay had taken on the gray-green pallor of someone about to vomit.

She reached for his shovel. "You don't need to stay if you can't. These aren't your people."

"We're bound." He pulled his shovel back from her grasp and gave her a wan, exhausted smile. "Your pain will always be mine."

Together they began to dig.

It wasn't difficult. The Mugenese had covered their handiwork with only a thin layer of soil, barely enough to conceal the tangled mass of limbs underneath. Whenever Rin had uncovered enough dirt to reveal the top layer of a corpse, she stopped and moved on, not wanting to break apart the already soft, decomposing bodies.

"In the north, we burn our dead," Kitay said after an hour. He reached up to wipe the sweat off his forehead, leaving behind a streak of mud. "It's cleaner."

"So we're vulgar," Rin said. "So what?"

She didn't have the energy to defend what they were doing. Earthen burial was the oldest of southern rituals. The Roosters were people of the earth, and their bodies and souls belonged in the ground—ancestral land that was marked, possessed, inhabited by generations stretching back as long as the history of the province. So what if that made them the Empire's mud-skinned refuse? The earth was permanent, unforgiving. The earth would rise up and swallow its invaders whole.

"They won't be able to recognize half these bodies," Kitay said. "They're too far decomposed, look—"

"They still have their clothes. Jewelry. Hair. Teeth. They'll find them."

They kept digging. No matter how many faces they uncovered, the shallow graves seemed to stretch on without end.

"Are you looking for someone?" Kitay asked after a while.

"No," Rin said.

She meant it. She had briefly considered searching for Tutor Feyrik. She'd tried to think of the distinct markers that might identify him. His height and build were too average. She could have searched for his beard, perhaps—but there were hundreds of old men in Tikany with beards just like his. His clothes had always been nondescript; perhaps he might have his lucky gambling dice in his front pocket, but Rin couldn't bear the thought of walking down the lines, ramming her hand down every bearded corpse's pocket to verify someone had already died.

She was never going to see Tutor Feyrik again. She already knew that.

Hours later, Rin at last called for a stop. They'd been digging for three hours. The sun drooped low in the sky; soon, it would be too dark to tell whether their shovel blades were hitting soil or flesh.

"Back to the village," she rasped. She desperately needed a drink of water. "We'll return tomorrow when the sun's come up—"

"Hold on," called a soldier farther down the path. "Something's moving over here."

At first Rin thought the slight movement she saw was a trick of light glinting against buried metal, or perhaps a lone vulture pecking at carrion. Then she drew closer and saw it was a hand—a scrawny hand forced through a gap in the pile of bodies, waving ever so faintly.

Her troops hastened to drag the corpses out of the way. Six bodies removed finally revealed the owner of the hand—a thin, coughing boy covered entirely in dried blood.

He was still conscious when they pulled him out of the grave. He blinked up at them, dazed. Then his eyes closed, and his head slumped to the side.

Rin sent a runner into the township for a physician. Meanwhile, they laid the boy out on the grass and wiped away the blood and dirt caked to his skin as best they could using water from their canteens. Rin watched the boy's chest throughout—it was bloody and discolored, caked over with dried blood and bruises, but still it rose and fell in a steady, determined rhythm.

When a physician arrived and cleaned the boy's torso with alcohol, they learned that the source of the blood wasn't deep—the wound was just a cut about two inches deep into his left shoulder. Enough to agonize but not to kill. The dirt had acted as a poultice, stemming a tide of blood that would have killed him otherwise.

"Hold him tight," said the physician. He uncorked a bottle of rice wine and tipped it over the wound.

The boy jerked awake, hissing in pain. His eyes fluttered open and locked on Rin's.

"You're okay," she said as she pinned his arms against the ground. "You're alive. Be brave."

His eyes bulged. A vein pulsed in his clenched jaw as he writhed under their hands, but never once did he scream.

He couldn't have survived out here for more than a few days.

The infection, and lack of water, would have killed him if it had been any longer than that. That meant the killing fields were fresh. The Mugenese had slaughtered them just days before the Southern Army arrived.

Rin tried to figure out what that meant.

Why would you mass-slaughter a town just before another army arrived?

To make Rin's victory shallow? To spit venom at an army they knew they couldn't beat? To leave one last, cruel message?

No. Gods, no, please, that could not be the truth.

But she couldn't think of any other rationale. Blood rushed to her temples as she watched the boy's eyes roll into the back of his head. She was afraid to stand; she thought she, too, might faint.

You did this, taunted the burial fields. *You made us kill them. We would have left this town alone unless you came, but you did, and so all this is your fault.*

Rin sent her soldiers back to the township ahead of her. She hung back, waiting for the sun to set. She wanted a few minutes of silence. She wanted to stand alone with the graves.

"There's nothing left alive here," Kitay said. "Let's go."

"You go," she said. "I'll be right behind you."

He paused in his steps. "Will this make you feel better?"

He didn't elaborate, but she knew what he meant. "Don't suggest that."

"But I'm right," he pressed. "It makes it easier."

She couldn't deny that. He knew what she couldn't admit out loud; he could read her mind like an open book.

"Please," she said. "Just let me have this. Please just go."

He knew better than to argue. He nodded, squeezed her hand, and left with the others.

Kitay was right. He knew what kind of absolution she sought from the killing fields. He knew that she needed to stay because if she seared the sight of what the Mugenese had done into her eyes, if she breathed the scent of half-rotted corpses, if she reminded herself why she had a reason to hate and keep hating, then it became easier to come to terms with what she had done to the longbow island.

It didn't matter how shrill the screams of dying Mugenese boys sounded in her dreams. They were still monsters, heartless things who deserved everything she had ever done and would ever do to them.

That had to be her truth, or she would shatter.

She didn't know how long she stood there. But when she finally moved to return to camp, the sun had disappeared entirely, and the uncovered graves had seared such a deep impression in her mind that every detail would remain forever. The arrangement of bones. How they curved and arched around one another. How they shone under the last rays of the dying sun.

You won't forget, assured Altan. *I won't let you.*

She pressed her eyes shut, took a deep breath, then turned back toward the village.

She made it two steps before she froze. Something gave her pause. She squinted at the trees. Yes—there it was, the flash of motion that had caught her eye the first time. Someone was running into the forest.

Rin dug her heels into the ground and gave chase.

"Hold it!"

She crashed through the trees, arms backlit with flame, casting hot light on the darkness all around her.

Then she stumbled to a halt. Her target had stopped—it wasn't a soldier or spy but a little girl, crouched at the bottom of a shallow ravine, arms wrapped around her legs and head ducked down while her lips moved like she was counting numbers.

Someone had taught her to do this. Someone had drilled her in it. Rin had been taught the very same lesson as a little girl—if they are chasing you, if you cannot outrun them, find somewhere to hide and count until they've gone away.

"Hey." She approached slowly, arms out, the fingers of her left hand splayed out in what she hoped was a nonthreatening gesture. "It's okay."

The girl shook her head and continued counting, eyes squeezed shut like if she couldn't see Rin, then she might disappear.

"I'm not Mugenese." Rin dragged her vowels out, trying to replicate an accent she'd long ago lost. "I'm a Rooster. One of you."

The girl's eyes opened. Slowly she lifted her head.

Rin stepped closer. "Are you alone?"

The girl shook her head.

"How many are you?"

"Three," whispered the girl.

Rin saw another pair of eyes in the darkness, wide and terrified. They ducked behind a tree as soon as they caught her looking back at them.

She quickly pulled a larger ring of fire into the air around her, just enough to illuminate the clearing. It revealed two emaciated little girls staring up at her with naked fascination. Their eyes looked huge on their hollow faces.

"What are you doing?" Footsteps crashed through the thicket. Rin spun around. A third figure—the girls' mother, or an older sister, she couldn't tell—dashed into the clearing and reached for the girls' wrists, dragging them away from Rin.

"Are you mad?" The woman shook the taller girl by the shoulders. "What were you thinking?"

"She was dressed in fire," said the girl.

"What?"

The girl hadn't stopped staring at Rin. "I wanted to look."

"You're in no danger," Rin said quickly. "I'm Nikara, I'm from Tikany. I'm a Rooster. I'm here to protect you."

But she already knew she didn't have to explain. The woman's eyes had widened in recognition, and she seemed to have realized, for the first time, that the flames lighting the clearing came not from a torch but from Rin's skin.

The woman spoke in a whisper. "You're the Speerly."

"Yes."

Her mouth worked for a few seconds before words came out. "Then are you—have they—"

"Yes," Rin said. "They're gone."

"Truly?"

"Yes. They're all dead. You're safe."

She saw no joy on the woman's face, only a stark, stunned disbelief. Upon a closer look the woman wasn't as old as Rin had thought. She was emaciated and terribly filthy, but beneath a thick layer of grime was the face of someone not so much older than herself.

"What are you doing in the forest?" Rin asked her.

"We ran," said the woman. "As soon as we heard the Mugenese were coming. I'd heard what they do to Nikara women. I wasn't going to—I mean, they weren't—"

"They're your sisters?"

"No," said the woman. "Just two girls who lived in my alley. I tried to get more to come with me. They wouldn't leave."

"You were wise to go," Rin said. "How have you survived all this time?"

The woman hesitated. Rin could read the lie assembling behind her eyes. The woman had an answer, she just wasn't sure if she should speak it.

The smallest girl piped up. "The lady in the hut."

The woman's face tightened, which meant the girl had told the truth.

"What lady?" Rin asked.

"She protects us," said the girl. "She knows things. She tells us when to hide and which roots we can eat and where to lay traps for birds. She said that as long as we obeyed her, then we would be safe."

"Then she should have taken you far away from this place," said Rin.

"She can't. She won't leave here."

Rin felt a sudden, scorching suspicion of who this lady was.

"And why can't she leave?" she asked.

"Shush," the woman told the girl, but the girl kept speaking.

"Because she says she lost her daughter in the Dragon King's palace, and she's waiting for her to come back."

Rin's mouth filled with the taste of blood. Her knees buckled.

What is she doing here?

The woman put a tentative hand on Rin's elbow. "Are—are you all right?"

"She's here," Rin murmured. The words felt thick and coppery on her tongue. "Take me to her."

She had to go. She had no choice. She was a fly caught in a web; she was a hypnotized mouse crawling straight into a viper's jaws. She could not walk away now, not until she knew what Su Daji wanted.

CHAPTER 8

Rin followed the girls along a winding path deep into the heart of the forest. Moonlight did not penetrate the upper canopy; the trees seemed packed with threats that hissed, buzzed, and lurked hidden within the shadows. Rin kept a small flame burning in her hand to serve as a lamp, but the trees loomed so thick she was afraid to grow her fire any larger lest they catch ablaze.

She willed her racing heart to slow. She wasn't some scared little girl. She wasn't afraid of the dark.

But she couldn't quell her dread of what lay within.

"This way," said the woman.

Rin ducked beneath a cluster of leaves and pushed through the underbrush, wincing as thorny branches scraped at her knees.

What am I doing?

If Kitay were here, he'd call her an idiot. He'd suggest she set the whole forest on fire and be done with it, Trifecta be damned. Instead, Rin was walking straight into Daji's lair like dazed, entranced prey. Was stumbling right up to the woman who, for the better part of the last year, had spared no effort trying to torture, capture, or manipulate her.

But Daji didn't want to kill her. She hadn't ever before, and she didn't now. Rin was sure of that. If Daji had wanted Rin dead, she would have killed her at the base of the Red Cliffs. She would have pressed a shard of shrapnel deep into Rin's arteries and watched, smiling, as Rin bled out on the sand at her feet.

Rin had survived the Red Cliffs only because of Daji's design. The Vipress still needed something from her, and Rin had to at least find out what it was.

"We're here," said the woman.

Cautiously, Rin expanded her flame to illuminate their surroundings. They had stopped before a tiny hut constructed with tree branches, vines, and deer hides. The interior couldn't possibly fit more than two people.

The woman called toward the hut, "My lady, we've returned."

"I hear four pairs of footsteps." A feeble, trembling voice drifted from within. "What have you brought me?"

"A visitor," Rin said.

A short pause. "Come alone."

Rin dropped to her knees and crawled into the hut.

The former Empress of Nikan sat shrouded in darkness. Gone were her robes and jewelry. She was rank and filthy, wrapped in tattered clothes caked so thoroughly with dirt that Rin couldn't tell their original color. Her hair had lost its luster; the tantalizing gleam had disappeared from her eyes. She looked like she had aged twenty years in the span of months. This wasn't just the toll of war, wasn't the stress of scraping for survival while a nation fell apart. Something supernatural had gnawed at Daji's visage, had torn viciously at her beauty in a way time and hardship could not.

For a moment Rin stared in shock, wondering if she'd been wrong after all; if this was not the Vipress before her but just some old hag in the woods.

But then Daji locked her good eye onto Rin, and her cracked lips curved into an all-too-familiar smile. "Took you long enough."

Blood rushed to Rin's head, pounded in her ears. She glanced back to the entrance of the hut, outside of which the girls stood waiting.

"Leave us," she ordered.

The girls didn't budge. They looked to Daji, awaiting her command.

"Go," Daji told them. "Go back to the village. *Run.*"

They scattered.

The moment they were gone, Rin yanked a knife from her belt and jammed the edge at the soft flesh beneath Daji's chin. "Break the Seal."

Daji only laughed, white throat pulsing against the blade's tip. "You're not going to kill me."

"I swear to the gods—"

"You would have done it already." Daji batted at the knife the way a kitten might swat a fly. "Enough with the histrionics. You need me alive."

Rin held the knife firm. "*Break the Seal.*"

Her vision pulsed red. She had to focus to keep her hand from slipping, from accidentally slicing skin. She had spent so many hours fantasizing about what she'd do if she ever found Daji at her mercy. If she could force Daji to remove the block on her mind, she'd never have to rely on Kitay again. She'd never again wake up in the middle of the night, mouth dry from nightmares, head swimming with visions of his death. She'd never have to see the evidence of how much she hurt him—the ghost-white pallor of his face, the crescent marks dug into his palm—every single time she called the fire.

"It's killing you, isn't it?" Daji tilted her head back, studying her with a lazy, amused smile. "Does he suffer?"

"*Break the Seal.* I won't ask again."

"What, the Sorqan Sira couldn't do it?"

"You know she couldn't," Rin snarled. "You're the one who put it on, it's *your* mark, and you're the only one who can take it off."

Daji shrugged. "Pity."

Rin pressed the blade harder into Daji's skin. How hard would she have to push to draw blood? Perhaps she shouldn't aim at the neck—it would be too easy to hit an artery, and then Daji would bleed out before she did anything useful. She moved the sharp, gleaming tip down to Daji's collarbone. "Perhaps some decorations will persuade. Which side do you favor?"

Daji feigned a yawn. "Torture won't help you."

"Don't think I won't do it."

"I know you won't. You're not Altan."

"Don't fucking test me." Rin sent a rivulet of fire arcing down the edge of the blade, just hot enough to singe. "I'm not living my whole life like a beast on a leash."

Daji watched her for a long moment. The glowing metal sizzled against her collarbone, burning dark marks into her flesh, yet Daji didn't even flinch. At last she lifted her hands in supplication. "I don't know how."

"You're lying."

"Dear child, I swear to you I can't."

"But you—" Rin couldn't stop her voice from catching. "Why not?"

"Oh, Runin." Daji gave her a pitying look. "Don't you think I've tried? You think I haven't been trying since you were born?"

She wasn't mocking Rin then. There wasn't a trace of condescension in her voice. This was an honest admission—that sorrow in her voice belied genuine vulnerability.

Rin wished so badly that Daji were mocking her.

"I'd do anything to break that Seal," Daji whispered. "I've been trying to break it for decades."

She didn't mean the Seal she'd put on Rin. She was speaking about her own.

Rin lowered the knife. Her flames receded. "Then why did you do it?"

"You were trying to kill me, darling."

"Not to me. To *them*."

"I didn't want to. But I thought that they were going to kill each other. And I didn't want to die." Daji met her eyes. "Surely you understand."

Rin understood.

She didn't know the full story—no one but Jiang and Daji knew the full story, and they'd both concealed it from her for reasons she might never know—but she knew enough. Once upon a time Daji had cursed the other two members of the Trifecta, the Dragon Emperor and the Gatekeeper, with a Seal that inhibited them all. And she hadn't been able to take it off. One fight, one mysterious fight two decades ago over reasons no one in the Empire understood, and the Trifecta had been reduced to nothing, because Daji *couldn't take it off*.

One will die, the Ketreyid girl Tseveri had said, just before the Trifecta tore her heart out of her chest. *One will rule, and one will sleep for eternity*.

In the end, Tseveri had gotten her revenge.

Rin sank back against her heels. All the fight had suddenly drained from her body. She should have been angry. She *wanted* to be angry, wanted to simply take Daji's head off in an unthinking rage. But all she could feel, looking at this old and desperate creature, was bitter, exhausted pity.

"I should kill you." The knife dropped from her hand. "Why can't I kill you?"

"Because you still need me," Daji said softly.

"Why did you come here?"

"To wait for you. Of course." Daji reached out and touched two fingers to Rin's cheek. Rin didn't flinch. The gesture wasn't cruel, wasn't condescending. It felt, bizarrely, like some attempt at comfort. "I meant what I said in Lusan. I wish you'd let me help you. There are so few of us left."

"But how did you—"

"How did I know you'd come to Tikany?" Daji sighed, chuckling. "Because you Speerlies are all the same. You're bound to your roots, they're what define you. You thought you could utterly reinvent yourself at Sinegard and kill the girl you used to be. But you can't help drifting back to the place you came from. Speerlies are like that. You belong to the tribe."

"My tribe is dead," Rin said. "This isn't my tribe."

"Oh, you know that's not true." Daji's mouth twisted into a pitying smile. "You are the south now. Rooster Province is part of your founding myth. You need it to be. You have nothing else left."

"This is insane," Kitay said.

"Well, we can't put her anywhere else," Rin said.

"So you're keeping her here?" Kitay flung his hands up, gesturing wildly around the general's office. "We *sleep* here!"

"So she'll sleep in another room—"

"You know that's not what I fucking meant. Are you going to tell Souji? Zhuden?"

"Obviously not, and neither should you—"

"Is this the anchor?" Daji asked from the doorway. Her eyes darted over Kitay, drinking in the sight of him as if he were some particularly juicy morsel of prey. "Are you sleeping with him?"

Kitay visibly flinched. Rin stared at Daji, momentarily too stunned to respond. "I—what?"

"You should try it sometime. The bond makes it something quite special." Daji stepped forward, lip curling as she continued to examine Kitay. "Ah, I remember you. From the Academy. Irjah's student. You're a smart boy."

Kitay's hand moved to his belt for his knife. "Take one step closer and I'll kill you."

"She's not our enemy," Rin said hastily. "She wants to help us—"

He barked out a laugh. "Have you gone mad?"

"She won't hurt us. If she wanted to hurt me she would have done it at the Red Cliffs. The balance of power has shifted now, she's got no reason to—"

"That bitch," Kitay said slowly, "is the reason why my father is dead."

Rin faltered.

"I am so sorry," Daji said. Oddly enough, she looked it—her

eyes were solemn, and the mocking curl had disappeared from her lips. "Minister Chen was a faithful servant. I wish the war had not taken him."

Kitay looked astonished that she had even dared to address him. "You are a monster."

"I spent three years living with the Ketreyids and I know infinitely more about the Pantheon than either of you do," Daji said. "I'm the only one who's ever fought a war against the Hesperians, or against Yin Vaisra, for that matter. You need me if you want any chance of surviving what's coming, so you'd best stop making threats, little boy. Is this the best intelligence you have?"

Daji turned abruptly toward Kitay's desk and started riffling through his carefully marked maps. Kitay moved to stop her, but Rin blocked his way.

"Just hear her out," she muttered.

"*Hear her out?* We're better off taking off her head!"

"Just *listen*," Rin insisted. "And if she's full of shit, we'll tell the villagers who she is and let them carry out their justice. You can take the first blow."

"I'd rather take it now."

Daji glanced up from the desk. "You're going to lose."

"Did anyone ask you?" Kitay snapped.

Daji tapped her fingernails against the maps. "It is so obvious how this will go. You might beat the Mugenese. You're not finished with this campaign yet, you know—you need to chase them south to prevent a regrouping. But you have momentum now. Train that little peasant army well, and you'll likely win. But the moment the Republic turns south, Vaisra will grind you into dust."

Daji's tone changed drastically as she spoke. The feeble, grandmotherly tremor disappeared, and her pitch deepened. Her words rang out clear, crisp, and assured. She sounded how she used to. She sounded like a ruler.

"We've been doing well enough on our own," Kitay said.

Daji snorted. "You barely survived on a single front. You didn't liberate Tikany, you occupied a graveyard. And you've no defenses against the Republic whatsoever. Did you think they'd forgotten you? Once you've cleaned the Federation out for them, they will strike, hard and fast, and you won't know what hit you."

"Our army is thousands strong and growing," Kitay said.

"Aren't you supposed to be the smart one? Against dirigibles and arquebuses, you'll need five times your current numbers." Daji arched an eyebrow. "Or you need shamans."

Kitay rolled his eyes. "We have a shaman."

"Little Runin is a single soldier with a limited battlefield range and a rather obvious vulnerability." Daji flicked her hand dismissively at Kitay. "And you can't hide out every battle, darling. Unless Rin unleashes a catastrophe on the scale of what she did to the Federation, then you are no match for Yin Vaisra and his army."

"I've buried a god," Rin said. "I can handle dirigibles."

Daji laughed. "I assure you, you cannot. You've never seen a full fleet of dirigibles in action. I have. Their combat craft are light and agile as birds. They may as well be calling gods of their own. You might call the fire, but they will bury you in missiles." She smacked her palm against the maps. "You are dreadfully outnumbered and overpowered and you need to take steps to correct that *now*."

Rin could see Kitay's expression morphing from indignant to curious. He understood Daji's logic—angry as he was, he was too smart to refuse the truth when he saw it. And he'd realized just as she had that Daji, unfortunately, had a point.

The question was what to do about it.

Rin knew her answer. She saw Daji watching her expectantly, waiting for her to voice her conclusion.

"We need more shamans," she said.

"Correct, dear. You need an army of them."

This statement was so absurd that for a moment Rin and Kitay could only gape at her. But at the same time Kitay was coming up with objections—and Rin knew he would only have objections, she could already tell from his expression—Rin was trying to imagine a world where this might succeed.

"That's what Altan wanted," Rin murmured. "Altan always wanted to release the Chuluu Korikh, he wanted an army of madmen—"

"Altan was an idiot," Daji said dismissively. "You can't bring back someone who's gone to the stone mountain. Their minds are shattered."

"Then how—"

"Come on, Runin. This is easy. You simply train new ones."

"But we don't have the time," Rin said lamely, because this, of all the possible objections, seemed the easiest to explain.

Daji shrugged. "Then how much time do you need?"

"This conversation isn't happening," Kitay said haplessly to the wall. "This isn't really happening."

"It took me years to recognize that the Pantheon existed," Rin said. "And we barely have weeks, we can't—"

"It would have taken you weeks if Jiang hadn't been so determined to drive the Phoenix from your mind," Daji said. "And half of your problem was eroding your preconceived notions of the world. Your mind didn't allow the possibility of shamanism. Those assumptions are broken now. The Nikara realize that this is a world where gods walk in men. They've seen you burn. They're already true believers." Daji reached out with a thin, pale finger and tapped Rin on the forehead. "And all you need to do is give them access."

"You want us to raise an army of people just like me." Rin knew she sounded idiotic, repeating a point that had been made clear over and over again, but she had to say it out loud for it to ring true.

She understood Kitay's incredulity. This solution was horrific. This was so inhumane, so atrociously irresponsible that in all the months she'd been on the run from the Hesperians, she had never once seriously considered it. It had crossed her mind, certainly, but she'd always dismissed it within seconds, because—

Because what?

Because it was dangerous? Every option on the table was dangerous. They'd opened the floodgates now; the entire country was at open war between three factions, one of which ruled the skies and possessed the power to reduce the terrain to ash in seconds, and if Rin didn't correct their power asymmetry somehow, *soon*, then she might as well deliver herself to Nezha in a coffin.

Because this was monstrous? But they were at the stage of war where every choice would be monstrous, and the only question now was which choice kept them alive.

"This is so simple, children," Daji said. "Bring religion back to this country. Show the Hesperians the truth about the gods."

She wasn't talking to Kitay anymore. Kitay might as well have not been in the room; neither of them had acknowledged a single one of his objections. Daji spoke directly to Rin, one shaman to another.

"Do you know what your problem is?" Daji asked. "You've been fighting this entire war on the defensive. You're still thinking like someone on the run. But it's time you started thinking like a ruler."

"You're not seriously considering this," Kitay said.

Daji was gone, banished to a corner room of the complex with a coterie of guards. This precaution was largely a bluff—Rin had no doubt Daji could take down an entire squadron if she wanted to—but the guards were equipped with signal horns. If anything happened, at least they could raise an alarm.

Rin remained in the office with Kitay. Her head felt dizzy, swimming with possibilities she'd never even considered. Several minutes passed in silence. Kitay had sunk into some kind of furious, speechless daze; Rin watched him warily, afraid he might explode.

"You're not even thinking about it?" she asked.

"You're joking," he said.

"Daji might be right. It would balance things out—"

"Are you shitting me? Seriously, Rin? She's manipulating you, that's what she *does*, and you're just eating shit straight out of her hand."

Rin supposed that was possible. Daji could be trying to orchestrate her ruin, and this would be the most sadistic way to do it. But she'd seen the look on Daji's face when she spoke about the Hesperians. She'd seen a glimpse of a girl not so much older than she was, a girl with more power than she knew what to do with, a girl who had just won her country back and was terrified it might be ripped away again.

"The stakes have changed," Rin said. "She's not the Empress anymore. She needs us just as much as we need her."

Kitay folded his arms over his chest. "I think you're entranced."

"What is that supposed to mean?"

"I mean that the Vipress has some weird effect on you—no, Rin, don't deny it, you know it's true. You don't behave rationally around her, you never do. You always overreact, do the opposite of what's prudent—"

"What? No, I don't—"

"What about at Lusan? The Red Cliffs? Twice now you've had the opportunity to kill her and you haven't. Why, Rin?"

"I would have! But she overpowered me—"

"Did she? Or did you let her?" Kitay's voice had gone furiously, dangerously quiet. Rin hated this; she would have preferred that he scream. "The Vipress makes you do shit that makes *no sense*, and I don't know if it's because she's still hypnotizing you, or if it's something else, but you've got to get your mind straight. You're thinking exactly what Daji wants you to think. She's seduced you, and I *know* you're not too stupid to realize that."

Rin blinked. Was he right? Had Daji left some taint of poison on her mind? Was she hypnotizing Rin through the Seal?

She stood silent for a moment, trying to think through this calmly. Objectively. Yes—if she was being honest with herself, Daji *did* have a strange, outsize effect on her psyche. When she was around the Vipress she found it hard to breathe. Her limbs shook, her flames seared, and she trembled from the desire to choke her, to *kill* her, or—

Or to be her.

That was it. Rin wanted what Daji had. She wanted her easy confidence, her calm authority. She wanted her power.

"You can't deny Daji's right about one thing," she said. "The southern front is a distraction. Our biggest problem now is how we're going to deal with Nezha."

Kitay sighed. "By creating an army of people like you?"

"Is that so wrong?" Rin was finding it harder and harder to come up with a good objection. Daji had presented the idea like a glittering gem and now she couldn't stop turning it over and over in her mind, ruminating on the possibilities.

Imagine an army of shamans, whispered a quiet voice in her mind. Altan's voice. *Imagine the sheer firepower. Imagine having the Cike back. Imagine getting a second chance.*

"We should at least talk this through," she said.

"No," Kitay said firmly. "We are ruling it out, now and forever."

"But why—"

"Because you can't *do* this to people," he snapped. "Ignore the realistic chances of global apocalypse for a moment—which I'm shocked you haven't considered, by the way. You know what it does to a person's mind. This isn't something you can inflict on anyone."

"I think I turned out all right."

"*All right* is not a term anyone would use to describe you."

"I'm functional," she said. "Which is all you need."

"Barely," he said, in the cruelest tone he could muster. "And you had training. But Jiang's gone, and the Sorqan Sira's dead. If you do this to anyone else, it's a death sentence."

"The Cike went through it," Rin pointed out.

"And you're willing to inflict the Cike's fate on anyone?"

Rin winced. There were, and only ever had been, two possible fates for the Cike—death or the Chuluu Korikh. Rin had heard this warning repeated countless times from the moment she joined the Bizarre Children, and she'd watched it play out, inevitably and brutally, over and over again. She'd seen Altan engulfed in flame. She'd seen Baji torn apart by bullets. She'd seen Suni and Feylen imprisoned in their own minds by demons that they couldn't exorcise. She'd almost succumbed to that fate herself.

Could she force it on someone else?

Yes. If that was their only hope against a fleet of dirigibles, then absolutely yes. For the future of the Nikara south, for the sake of their survival—yes.

"It's been done before," she said.

"But not by us. Never by us. We can't do this to other people." Kitay's voice trembled. "I won't be complicit in that."

She had to laugh. "This is the moral line you won't cross? Come on, Kitay."

"Do you not understand how that feels? Look at what happened to Nezha. You forced him to call his god and—"

"I never forced him to do shit," she snapped.

"Don't lie to yourself. You pushed him past his limits when you knew it was torture to him and look what that got you, a scar in your back the size of Mount Tianshan."

She recoiled. "Fuck you."

That was a low blow. Kitay knew that; he knew exactly where she hurt the most, and still he'd stabbed and twisted the blade.

He didn't apologize. Instead, he raised his voice. "If you'd put aside your wild dreams of conquest for a fucking second, if you'd stop getting drunk off the Vipress's very *presence*, you'd realize this is one of the worst things you could do to someone."

"Oh, like you'd fucking know."

"You think I don't know?" His eyes widened, incredulous. "Rin, I was at *Golyn Niis*, and the Phoenix ripping through my mind is still the cruelest torture I've ever felt."

That shut her up.

She wanted to kick herself for forgetting that she could call the fire only because he let her, because every day he let a vicious god claw through his mind into the material world. He'd borne it all in silence because he didn't want her to worry. He'd borne it so well that she'd stopped thinking about it entirely.

"I'm sorry," she said. She reached for his shoulder. "I'm sorry, I didn't think—"

"No, Rin." Kitay brushed her hand away. He wouldn't be appeased; he was finished talking. They weren't moving past this, at least not now. "You never do."

Rin walked through Tikany alone. Kitay had stormed off somewhere inside the general's complex, and she didn't bother trying to find him.

They had fought like this before. Not so frequently after the Battle of the Red Cliffs, but every few weeks the same argument bubbled up between them, a chasm they couldn't bridge. It always boiled down to the same fundamental impasse, with a hundred different manifestations. Kitay found her callous. Astonishingly careless with human life, he'd once put it. And she found him weak, too hesitant to take decisive action. She'd always been convinced that he didn't quite grasp the stakes at hand, that he clung still to some bizarre, pacifist hope of diplomacy. Yet somehow their fights always left her feeling guilty and strangely embarrassed, like a child who had acted out in the classroom.

Fuck this, she thought. Forget Kitay. Forget his morals. She needed to remind herself of the stakes.

Her troops had constructed a public kitchen in the town square. Soldiers doled out bowls of rice gruel and steamed shanyu to long lines of waiting civilians. Camp aides walked along the lines reminding the civilians not to eat too quickly; if their stomachs began to hurt, they should stop immediately. After prolonged periods of starvation, ruptured stomachs from overeating could prove fatal.

Rin cut the line and grabbed two bowls piled high with shanyu root, balancing one nimbly in the crook of her right elbow.

The tent complex in Tikany's northern quarter couldn't be

properly called an infirmary. It was more like an emergency triage center, constructed from the wreckage of what used to be the town hall. Cloth-covered bamboo mats had been laid out in neat lines outside the surgery room, through which harried-looking assistants ferried antiseptics and painkillers to peasants whose wounds had been festering for months.

Rin approached the nearest physician and asked for the boy from the killing fields.

"Over there in the corner," he told her. "See if you can get him to eat. He hasn't touched a thing."

The boy's torso was wrapped in bandages, and he looked just as pale and wan as when they'd found him in the graves. But he was sitting up, alert and conscious.

Rin sat down on the dirt beside him. "Hello."

He blinked owlishly at her.

"I'm Runin," she prompted. "Rin. I pulled you from the grave."

His voice was a breathy rasp. "I know who you are."

"And what's your name?" she asked softly.

"Zhen," he started, and then coughed. He pressed a hand against his chest and winced. "Zhen Dulin."

"Looks like you got lucky, Dulin."

He snorted at that.

She placed one bowl on the ground and held out the other. "Are you hungry?"

He shook his head.

"If you starve yourself to death, then you're just letting them win."

He shrugged.

She tried something else. "It's got salt."

"Bullshit," Dulin said.

She couldn't help but grin. Nobody south of Monkey Province had tasted salt in months. It was easy to take such a common condiment for granted during peacetime, but after months of bland vegetables, salt became as valuable as gold.

"I'm not lying." She waved the bowl under his nose. "Try it."

Dulin hesitated, then nodded. She passed the bowl carefully into his trembling fingers.

He brought a spoonful of steamed shanyu to his mouth and nibbled at the edge. Then his eyes widened and he stopped bothering with the spoon, gulping the rest down like Rin might snatch it away from him at any moment.

"Take it slow," she cautioned. "There's plenty more. Stop if your stomach starts to cramp."

He didn't speak again until he'd nearly finished the bowl. He paused and sucked in a deep breath, eyelids fluttering. "I'd forgotten how salt tasted."

"Me too."

"You know how desperate we got?" He lowered the bowl. "We scraped the white deposits off tombstones and boiled it down because it resembled the taste. Tombs." His hands trembled. "My father's *tomb*."

"Don't think about that," Rin said quietly. "Just enjoy this."

She let him eat in silence for a while. At last he placed his empty bowl on the ground and sighed, both hands clutching his stomach. Then he twisted around to face her. "Why are you here?"

"I want you to tell me what happened," she said.

He seemed to shrink. "You mean at the—"

"Yes. Please. If you remember. As much as you can."

"Why?"

"Because I have to hear it."

He was silent for a long time, his gaze fixed on something far away.

"I thought I had died," he said at last. "When they struck me it hurt so much that everything turned black, and I thought that's what death was. I remember feeling glad that at least it was over. I didn't have to be scared anymore. But then I—"

He broke off. His entire body was shaking.

"You can stop," Rin said, suddenly ashamed. "I'm sorry, I shouldn't have made you."

But Dulin shook his head and kept going. "But then I woke

up in the field, and I saw the sun shining over me, and I realized I'd survived. But they were piling the bodies on top of me then, and I didn't want them to realize I was alive. So I lay still. They kept stacking the bodies, one after the other, until I could barely breathe. And then they packed on the dirt."

A pang of pain shot through Rin's palm, and she realized her fingernails had dug grooves into her skin. She forced them to relax before they drew blood.

"They never saw you?" she asked.

"They weren't looking. They're not thorough. They don't care. They just wanted it over with."

The unspoken implication, of course, was that Dulin might not have been the only one. Rather, it was more likely there *had* been other victims, injured but not dead, who toppled into an early grave and were slowly suffocated by dirt and the weight of bodies.

Rin exhaled slowly.

Somewhere in the back of her mind, Altan was appeased. This was her answer. This justified everything she'd done. This was the face of her enemy.

Kitay could spout on and on about ethics. She didn't care. She needed revenge. She wanted her army.

Dulin's shoulders started to heave. He was sobbing.

Rin reached out and patted him awkwardly on the shoulder. "Hey. You're all right—it's all right."

"It's not. I shouldn't be the only one, I should be dead—"

"Don't say that."

His face contorted. "But it shouldn't have been me."

"I used to hate myself for living, too," she said. "I didn't think it was fair that I'd survived. That others had died in my place."

"It's *not* fair," Dulin whispered. "I should be in the ground with them."

"And there will be days you'll wish you were." Rin didn't understand why she needed so urgently to comfort this boy, this stranger, only that she wished someone had told her the same thing months before. "It doesn't go away. It never will. But when it hurts, lean into it. It's so much harder to stay alive. That doesn't mean you don't deserve to live. It means you're brave."

Life returned to Tikany that night.

Rin had retreated early to the general's complex, intent on falling asleep the moment her face hit her mattress. But then a knock came at the door, and she opened it to find not the sentry or messenger she'd expected but a circle of women, eyes tilted sheepishly down, nudging one another as if daring someone else to be the first to speak.

"What is it?" Rin asked warily.

"Come with us," said the woman at the front.

Rin blinked at them, puzzled. "Where?"

The woman's face broke into a smile. "To dance."

Then Rin remembered that despite everything, this day had been a liberation, and liberations deserved to be celebrated.

So she followed them into the town center, where a crowd of hundreds had formed, holding bamboo torches and floating lanterns up against the moonless night. Drums beat incessantly, accompanying lilting flute melodies that seemed to come from everywhere, while firecrackers went off every few seconds like musical punctuation.

Dancers whirled in the center of the square. There were dozens of them, mostly young girls, all moving without choreography or order. None of this had been rehearsed. It couldn't possibly have been. Each dancer moved from memory, pulling together fragments of performances from earlier times, moving for the sheer joy of being alive and free.

It should have been an utter mess. It was the most beautiful thing Rin had ever seen.

The women entreated Rin to join. But she refused, preferring to sit down on an overturned barrel and watch. She'd never joined the dances when she'd lived here. Those dances were for rich girls, joyful girls, girls whose marriages were events to be celebrated and not feared. They weren't for war orphans. Rin had only ever watched. She wanted desperately to join them now, but she was afraid she wouldn't know how to move.

The drums sped up. The dancers became a hypnotic vision, ankles and arms moving faster and faster until they seemed a blur in the firelight, moving to a tempo that felt in tune with Rin's own pulse. She blinked, and for a moment she saw a different dance, heard a different song. She saw brown bodies dancing by the campfire, singing words that she'd heard a long time ago in a language that she couldn't speak but could almost remember.

She'd been seeing this vision since the first time she'd met the Phoenix. She knew this vision ended in death.

But this time the dancing bodies did not turn into skeletons, but instead remained furiously, resolutely, alive. *Here we are*, they said. *Watch us thrive. We've escaped the past, and we own the future.*

"Hey."

Rin blinked, and the vision disappeared. Souji stood before her, holding two mugs of millet wine. He held one out to her. "Mind if I sit?"

She shifted to make room for him. They clinked their mugs and drank. Rin sloshed the millet wine around her tongue, savoring the heady, sour tang.

"I'm surprised you haven't disappeared into an alley with one of them." Rin nodded to the dancers. Women seemed attracted to Souji like moths to a flame; Rin had seen him disappear into his tent with at least eight different companions since they'd left Ruijin.

"Still trying to pick," Souji said. "Where's your better half?"

"I'm not sure." She'd been scanning the crowd for Kitay since she arrived, but hadn't found him. "He might be asleep."

She didn't tell Souji that they'd fought. She and Kitay were a pair against the world; no one else should know about their rifts.

"He's missing out." Souji leaned back, watching the dancers with an amused, half-lidded expression. Rin could tell he was already quite drunk; his movements were slow and careless, and a cloud of sour fumes wafted toward her every time he spoke. "This is it, Princess. This is as good as it gets. Enjoy this while it lasts."

She gazed at the bonfire and tried to take Souji's advice, to lose herself in the music, the laughing, and the drums. But an uneasy darkness lingered in the pit of her stomach, a hard knot of fear that wouldn't dissipate no matter how hard she smiled.

She couldn't derive any joy from this.

Was this what liberation felt like? This couldn't be it. Freedom was supposed to feel like safety. She was supposed to feel like no one could ever harm her again.

No, it was more than that.

She wanted to go *back*. She couldn't remember a moment in the last two years that she had ever felt safe closing her eyes. If she chased that memory down, it would have last been when she was at the Academy, when the world seemed contained in books and exams, when war was a game mirroring something that might never come to pass.

And she knew she could never get that back again.

But she could get something close. Safety. Security. And that demanded total victory.

It didn't matter whether she wanted war. The Republic would bring war to her, would hunt her down until she was dead or it was. And the only way to be safe was to strike first.

Your life is not your own, Vaisra had once told her, and he had elaborated many times in the weeks that followed. *You do not have a right to happiness when you hold this much power in your hands.*

When you hear screaming, run toward it. His precise words. He'd only been trying to manipulate her; she knew that now. Still, the words rang true.

But where was the screaming now?

"What's wrong?" Souji asked.

She blinked and straightened up. "Hmm?"

"You look like someone's shat all over your ancestors' graves."

"I don't know, I just . . ." She struggled to name her discomfort. "This isn't right."

Souji snorted. "What, the dancing, or the music? Didn't know you were so picky."

"They're happy. Everyone's too happy." Her words spilled out faster and faster, spurred on by the millet wine burning in her gut. "They're dancing because they don't know what's coming, they can't see the entire world's about to end because this isn't the end of one war, it's the start, and—"

Souji's hand closed over hers. Rin glanced down, startled. His palm was rough and callused but warm; it felt surprisingly good. She didn't pull away.

"Learn to relax, Princess." His thumb stroked the top of her hand. "This life you've chosen, you won't get many moments like this again. But it's the nights like this that keep you alive. All you think about is who you're fighting against. But that?" He swung his mug toward the dancers. "That's what you're fighting for."

Several hours later Souji was so drunk that Rin didn't trust him to find the general's complex on his own. They walked up the dark, rocky path together, his arm draped heavily over her shoulders. Halfway up the hill his foot snagged on a rock and he pitched forward, looping his arm around her waist for balance.

The ploy was quite transparent. Rin rolled her eyes and extricated herself from his grasp. He fumbled for her breasts. She smacked his hand away. "Don't try that shit with me. I'll burn your balls off, I've done that before."

"Come on, Princess," he said. He wrapped his arm back around her shoulders, pulling her in close. His skin felt terribly hot.

Despite herself, Rin found herself curving into that heat.

"No one's here." His lips brushed her ear. "Why don't we have some fun?"

The embarrassing thing was that she *did* feel some interest, a faint, unfamiliar stirring in the pit of her stomach. She quashed it. *Don't be a fucking idiot.*

Souji didn't want her. Souji was the last man in the world to find her beautiful. He had his pick of willing conquests among the camp, all likely prettier and easier to deal with in the morning than Rin would be.

This wasn't about lust, this was about power. This was about possession. He wanted to dominate her just so that later he could crow that he had.

And Rin, admittedly, was tempted. Souji was undeniably handsome, and certainly experienced. He'd know what to do with their bodies even if she hadn't the faintest clue. He could show her how to do all the things she'd only heard of, had only imagined.

But she'd be stupid to go to bed with him. Once the word spread, no one would look at her the same way again. She'd been around soldiers long enough to know how this worked. The man got bragging rights. The woman, already likely the only female soldier in her squadron, became the camp whore.

"Let's get you back to your bed," she said.

"It'd be good for you." Souji didn't remove his arm from her shoulder. "You're too tense. All that pent-up anger. It'd do you good to let loose once in a while, Princess. Have some fun."

He caressed her collarbone. She shuddered. "Souji, *stop*."

"What's the matter? Are you a virgin?"

He asked this so bluntly that for a moment all Rin could do was stare.

His eyebrows shot up. "No. Really, Princess?"

She shoved his arm away. "It's none of your business."

But he'd found her weak spot. He knew it—he grinned, teeth glinting in the moonlight. "Is it true you have no womb?"

"*What?*"

"Heard a rumor around camp. Said you burned your womb out back at Sinegard. Doesn't surprise me. Smart, really. Pity about the Speerlies, though. Now you're the last. Do you ever regret it?"

She hissed through clenched teeth. "I've never regretted it."

"Pity." He put a hand on her stomach. "We could have made some nice brown babies. My brains, your abilities. Kings of the south."

That was enough. She jerked away from him, fist raised and knees crouched. "Touch me again and I'll kill you."

He just scoffed. His eyes roved up and down her body, as if evaluating how much force it would take to pin her to the ground.

Rin's breath caught in her throat.

What was wrong with her? She'd started and ended wars. She'd buried a god. She'd incinerated a country. There wasn't an entity on the planet that could face her in a fair fight and win. She was certain of her own strength; she'd sacrificed everything to make sure she never felt powerless again.

So why was she so afraid?

At last, he raised his hands in a gesture of surrender. "Just offering. No need to be like that."

"Get away from me." Her voice rang through the dark, louder than she'd intended. Someone might overhear. Perhaps that was what she should want—for someone, anyone, to come running. "*Now*, Souji."

"Are you always like this? Great Tortoise, that explains why—"

She cut him off. "Do you hear that?"

She thought she heard a faint whining drone—a sound like a faraway swarm of bees, growing louder and louder with every passing second.

Souji fell silent, brows furrowed. "What are you—"

"Shut up," Rin hissed. "Just listen."

Yes—the droning was distinct now. The noise wasn't just in her head. She wasn't panicking over nothing. This was real.

Souji's eyes widened. He'd heard it, too.

"Get down," he gasped, and lunged at her just before the first bombs exploded.

CHAPTER 9

They hit the ground together, Souji's elbows digging painfully into Rin's ribs. There was the briefest moment of silence, then an eerie ringing in her ears. She peered up from beneath Souji's splayed body, groaning, just as Tikany lit up in a flash of orange light.

Then the bombing resumed, a roll of thunder that just kept going.

Souji rolled off of Rin. She scrambled unsteadily to her feet. *Kitay.* Her vision was half-gone, along with her balance; as she stumbled toward the general's complex she kept lurching to the side like a drunkard. *I have to find Kitay.*

A high, tortured keen sounded behind her. She turned around. By firelight she could just make out a young officer's face, one of Zhuden's men whose name she'd never learned. He lay on the ground several yards away. She stared at him for a moment, utterly confused. She and Souji had been alone in the street until now; all the other officers had remained at the bonfire, a good five minutes' walk from here.

Was it the blast? Could the force of the explosion have hurled him this far?

But the officer looked fine—his head, shoulders, and torso were all intact, unbloodied. Unburned, even. Why was he—

The black smudges cleared slowly from Rin's vision, and she saw what had at first been hidden by smoke and darkness. The officer's legs had been blown away from the upper thigh.

He was looking at her. Gods, he was still conscious. He lifted a trembling hand toward her. His mouth moved. No sound came out, at least none that she could hear, but she understood.

Please.

She reached for the knife at her belt, but her fingers fumbled clumsily against the sheath.

"I'll do it." Souji's voice rang as loud as a gong against her ears. He seemed to have sobered completely, his alcohol-drenched sluggishness evaporated by the same adrenaline pounding through her veins. He seemed far more in command of himself than she felt. With a brisk efficiency, he pulled the knife out of her hand and bent down to slit the officer's throat.

She stared, swaying on her feet.

We weren't ready.

She'd thought she had more time. When she'd destroyed Kesegi's message she'd known Nezha had her in his sights, but she'd thought she might have the chance to train her newly won Southern Army while the Republic finished their campaign in the north. She'd thought, after the Beehive fell, that they could take a moment to breathe.

She hadn't known Nezha was on their fucking doorstep.

Air cannons boomed continuously in harmony with the drone of dirigible engines. *A celestial orchestra*, Rin thought, dazed. The gods were playing a dirge to their demise.

She heard screaming from the town center. She knew that there was no mounted ground defense, no chance of fending the airships off. Her troops were flush with victory and drunk from revels. They'd only posted a skeleton guard at the township gates because they'd thought, for once, they were safe.

And the fucking *bonfires*—gods, the bonfires must have been like beacons, screaming out their location from the ground.

The shouts grew louder. Panicked, scattered crowds were flooding through the streets, away from the bonfires. A little girl ran screaming in Rin's direction, and Rin didn't have time to yell, *No, stop, get down*, before a blast rocked the air and flames shrouded the tiny body.

The same explosion knocked Rin off her feet. She rolled onto her back and moaned, her good hand pressed against her left ear. The bombing was so frequent that she could no longer hear any pause between drops, only an incessant rumble while fiery orange flares went off everywhere she looked.

She pushed her hand against the ground and forced herself to stand.

"We need to get out of here." Souji yanked her up by the wrist and dragged her toward the forest. Explosions went off so close that she felt the heat sear her face, but the dirigibles weren't firing over the forests.

They were only aiming at the campfires—at open, vulnerable civilians.

"Hold on," she said. "Kitay—"

Souji wouldn't let go of her arm. "We'll move farther into the trees. They haven't got visibility near the forest. We'll take the mountain routes, get as far as we can before—"

She struggled against his grip. "We have to get Kitay!"

"He'll make his own way out," Souji said. "But you'll be dead in seconds if you—"

"I'll manage." She didn't know how she'd fend off the dirigibles—they didn't seem to have weak points she could easily burn—but she might aim fire at the steering mechanisms, the ammunition basket, *something*. But she couldn't leave without Kitay.

Was he still in the general's complex, or had he gone to the center square? The complex up the hill was still untouched, hidden under the cover of darkness, but the square was now an inferno.

He couldn't be critically injured—if he were, she would feel it, and right now she didn't feel anything, which meant—

"Hold on." Souji's fingers tightened around her wrist. "It's stopped."

The sky had turned silent. The buzzing had died away.

They're landing, Rin realized. This was a ground assault. The dirigibles didn't want to eradicate all Tikany by air. They wanted prisoners.

But didn't they understand the dangers of a ground assault? They might have their arquebuses, but she had a *god*, and she would smite them down the moment they approached. They only bore a fighting chance against her if they hovered out of her range. They had to understand that sending down troops was suicide.

Unless—

Unless.

An icy chill crept through her veins.

She saw it now. The Hesperians didn't want her bombed. She was their favorite test subject; they didn't want her blown to pieces. They wanted her captured alive, delivered whole and writhing to the Gray Company's laboratories, so they'd brought the only person in the world who could face her in hand-to-hand combat and win.

Nezha, whose wounds stitched themselves back together as quickly as they opened.

Nezha, whose powers flowed from the sea.

"Run," she told Souji, just as another round of missiles tore them apart.

For a moment the world was silent.

All was darkness, and then colors began to return—only red at first, red everywhere she looked, and then muddled clumps of red and green. Rin didn't know how she managed to stand, only that one moment she was lying on the ground and the next she was staggering through the forest, lurching from tree to tree because her balance was broken and she couldn't stand up straight. She tasted blood on her lip, but she couldn't tell where she'd been hurt;

the pain was like a shroud, pulsing uniformly across her body with every step she took.

"Souji?"

No response. She wasn't sure if she'd gotten the sounds out—she couldn't hear her own voice, except for an odd muffle deep inside her skull.

"Souji?"

Still nothing.

She stumbled forward, rubbing at her eyes, trying to gain some better grasp on the world and her senses other than it hurt, it *hurt* . . .

A familiar smell suffused the air. Something nauseatingly, sickly sweet, something that made her stomach roil and her veins ache with longing.

The Republicans had set off opium bombs.

They knew her weakness. They intended to incapacitate her.

Rin took a deep breath and pulled a ball of flame into her hand. She had a higher opium tolerance than most, a gift of months and months of opium addiction and failed rehabilitation. All those nights spent high out of her mind, conversing with hallucinations of Altan, might buy her a few extra minutes before she was cut off from the Phoenix.

That meant she had to find Nezha *now*.

"Come on," she murmured. She sent the flame into the air above and around her. Nezha wouldn't be able to resist the flare; it'd function like a beacon. He was searching for her. He'd come.

"Where are you?" she shouted.

Lightning split the air in response. Then a sheet of rain abruptly hammered down so hard that Rin nearly fell.

This wasn't natural rain. The sky had been clear just a moment ago, there hadn't even been a whisper of clouds, and even if a storm had been brewing it couldn't have moved in so quickly, so coincidentally . . .

But since when could Nezha summon the *rain*?

In some awful way it made sense. Dragons controlled the rain, so said the myths. Even in Tikany, a place where religion had long been diminished to children's bedtime stories, the magistrates lit incense offerings to the dragon lords of the river during drought years to induce heavy showers.

But that meant Nezha's domain wasn't just the river but all the water around him. And if he could summon it, control it . . .

If this rain was his doing, he'd become so much more powerful than she'd feared.

"General?"

Rin turned. A band of troops had clustered around her. New recruits, she didn't recognize them—they'd survived, bless them; they were rallying toward her, even when they'd just seen their comrades ripped apart.

Their loyalty amazed her. But their deaths would accomplish nothing.

"Get away," she ordered.

They didn't move. The one in the front spoke. "We'll fight with you, General."

"Don't even try," she said. "He will kill you all."

She'd seen Nezha at the height of his abilities once before. He'd raised an entire lake to protect his fleet. If he'd perfected his skills since, then not a single one of them would survive for more than a few seconds.

This wasn't a war of men anymore. This was a war of gods. This had to end between her and Nezha, shaman to shaman.

All she could do before then was minimize the fallout.

"Go help the villagers," she told them. "Get them away from here, as many as you can. Seek cover under darkness and don't stop running until you're out of range of the rain. *Hurry.*"

They obeyed, leaving her alone in the storm. The rainfall was deafening. She couldn't see a single Republican soldier, Nikara or Hesperian, around her, which meant Nezha, too, had sent away his reinforcements.

He would have done it out of nobility. Typical. He was always the righteous ruler, the noble aristocrat. She could just imagine

Nezha giving the order in his arrogant, assured voice. *Leave her to me.*

Fire flickered around her body, winking in and out as sheets of rain kept crushing it away. The water was now coming down so hard it felt like repeated smacks from the flat side of a sword. She struggled to stand up straight. Her fingers trembled on the hilt of her blade.

Then at last she saw him, striding through rain that parted cleanly around him whenever he moved.

Pain arced through the knotted scar in her lower back. Memories stabbed her mind like daggers. A touch, a whisper, a kiss. She clenched her jaw tight to keep from trembling.

He looked older, though only several months had passed since she last saw him. Taller. He moved differently; his stride was more assertive, imbued with a new sense of authority. With Jinzha dead, Nezha was the crown prince of Arlong, the Young Marshal of his father's army, and the heir apparent to the Nikara Republic. Nezha was about to own the entire country, and only Rin stood in his way.

They regarded each other for a moment in a silence that seemed to stretch on for an eternity, the weight of their shared past hanging heavy between them. Rin felt a sudden pang of nostalgia, that complicated mix of longing and regret, and couldn't make it go away. She'd spent so long fighting by his side, she had to make herself remember how to hate him.

He stood close enough that she could see his grotesque smile, the tortured ripple that pulled at the scar lines drawn into the left half of his face. His cheeks and jaw, once angular perfection, were shattered porcelain. Cracked tiles. A map of the country falling apart.

Venka had claimed he was ill. He looked the furthest thing from ill—Rin couldn't detect a shred of weakness in the way he carried himself. He was primed for battle, lethal.

"Hello, Rin," he called. His voice seemed deeper, crueler. He sounded a near match to his father. "What happened to your hand?"

She opened her palm. Flame roared at his face. Dismissively he waved a hand, and a gust of rain extinguished the fire long before it reached him.

Fuck. Rin could feel her fingers going numb. She was running out of time.

"This doesn't have to be hard," he said. "Come quietly and no one else has to die."

She braced her heels against the dirt. "You're going home in a coffin."

He shrugged. The rain began to pound even harder, pummeling so vigorously that her knees buckled.

She gritted her teeth, fighting to stay upright.

She would not kneel to him.

She had to get past that rain; it was functioning too well as a shield. But the solution was so simple. She'd learned it long ago at Sinegard. Years later, the basic pattern of their fights remained the same. Nezha was stronger than she was. His limbs were longer. Then and now, she only stood a chance when she got in close, where his reach didn't matter.

She lunged. Nezha crouched, whipping his sword out. But she'd aimed lower than he'd anticipated. She wasn't going for his head—she wanted his center of gravity. He came down easier than she'd expected. She scrambled for control as they fell. She was so much lighter than he was, she'd only pin him down if she caught him at just the right angle—but he slashed upward, and she lost her balance as she ducked.

He landed heavily atop her. She thrashed. He jabbed his sword down, twice missing her face for mud.

She opened her mouth and spat fire.

It engulfed his face for one glorious moment. She saw skin crinkling and peeling back. She caught a glimpse of bone. Then a wall of water crashed over both of them, extinguishing her flame, leaving them both sputtering for breath.

She recovered first. She got her knee up in his solar plexus. He flailed backward. She wriggled out from under him and settled into a crouch.

The rain's stopped, she realized. The pressure was gone; the forest fell silent.

At the same time she felt a woozy tilt in her limbs, a heady rush in her temples.

So this was it. The opium had seeped too deep into her bloodstream. She didn't have the fire, and her only advantage was that he'd lost the water. This was now a matter of blades and fists and teeth.

She unsheathed her knife. They dueled for only a moment. It was no contest. He disarmed her first, and easily, sent her blade spinning far away into the dark.

No matter. She knew she couldn't match him with blades. The moment the hilt left her palm, she aimed a savage kick at Nezha's wrist.

It worked. He dropped his sword. Now they had only their fists. That was a relief. This was so much easier, more direct, more brutal. She clawed at his eyes. He slapped her hand away. She bit at his elbow. He shoved it at her mouth. Her head jerked back.

Blood stung her eyes and clouded her vision. She punched without looking. Nezha was doing the same. His blows came at her too fast for her to dodge or block but she gave as good as she got, landed just as many as he did, until she forgot she didn't have a right hand to punch with. She lashed out with her stump. He blocked it with his elbow. Awful, blinding pain ripped through the right half of her torso. For a moment she forgot how to breathe.

Nezha broke free of her grasp, jumped to his feet, and kicked down at her ribs. She curled into a ball, too winded to scream. He stomped on her stump. Her vision flashed white.

He kicked her in the side, again and again until she was lying on her back, too stunned to do anything but gasp like a fish out of water. He stumbled back, chest heaving. Then he dropped to his knees, straddled her chest, and pinned her arms down with his hands.

"I told you," he panted, "to come quietly."

She spat blood in his face.

He slammed his knuckles into her right eye. Her head thudded against the wet dirt. He wiped the back of his hand against his shirt, then drew it back to deliver a second punch to her left eye. She took the beating like a limp doll, without sound, without response. He punched her five, six, seven times. She lost count. She was dazed with pain and opium; the blows felt like raindrops.

But the fact that he was beating her meant something—the fact that she wasn't dead *meant something*. She should be dead right now. He should have just stabbed her in the heart or slashed her throat; it would have been easier. And Nezha wasn't sadistic, wasn't prone to torture over efficiency.

He's not aiming to kill, she realized. Nezha wanted her alive. He wanted to incapacitate. And right now, he just wanted to hurt.

That was the difference between them. *His loss.*

"You should have killed me at Arlong," she hissed.

The punches stopped.

Nezha reached down for her neck and began to squeeze.

She scrabbled frantically at his hands. Altan had taught her to escape chokeholds—hands were strong, single fingers weren't so much, so all you had to do was separate them. *One at a time.* She dug her fingers under his middle finger and detached it from the others, then pulled backward hard, harder—

He wasn't letting go.

Alternate means, then. She jammed her thumb toward his eyes. He twisted his face away. Her nails dug into his cheek instead, and she compensated by digging in so hard she drew blood. Three neat crimson streaks sliced down his right jaw.

His grip loosened, just the slightest bit, for a brief moment. That was all she needed.

She reached behind her, scrabbling to find his blade. She'd seen him drop it, it had to be within reach . . . but the first thing her fingers closed around was not the hilt but a stone, heavy and jagged, just about the size of her palm.

That would do.

She swung the stone up against Nezha's temple. It connected

with bone with a satisfying crunch. His grip loosened. She summoned every remaining ounce of her strength into her left arm and struck his head again. Blood gathered inside a gash by his right eye, as if hesitating, then started pouring out in thick rivulets.

He slumped to the side.

She wriggled out from beneath him. He toppled to the ground.

Was that it? Had she knocked him unconscious? Could this have been so easy? She leaned cautiously over him, hefting the rock in her hand for a third and final blow.

Then she paused, startled.

The blood flow had stopped. Nezha's skin was stitching itself together, pale skin growing back over red pulp as if time had simply reversed.

She watched in disbelief. Nezha could recover from blows with terrifying speed, she knew that, but the process had taken hours before. Now his body was erasing wounds in mere seconds.

She'd burned him earlier. Badly. There was no evidence of that, either.

What if she ripped his heart from his chest? Would a new one sprout? If she buried his sword between his ribs, would his heart grow around it?

Only one way to find out. She picked the sword up off the ground and knelt above him, straddling his torso with her knees.

Nezha made a soft moaning noise. His eyelids fluttered.

Rin raised her left hand high, blade pointed straight down. Her arm trembled; her fingers felt awkward around the hilt. But she couldn't miss, not from this angle. She had an immobile victim and a clear, open target; she couldn't possibly fuck this up.

One hard blow to the chest. That was all it would take. One blow, perhaps a twist for good measure, and all this would be over.

But she couldn't bring her arm down. Something stayed her hand. Her arm was like some foreign object, moving of its own will. She clenched her teeth and tried again. The blade remained suspended in the air.

She screamed in frustration, lunging forward over Nezha's

limp form, yet she still couldn't bring the blade anywhere near his flesh.

Nezha's eyes shot open just as a droning noise buzzed over their heads.

Rin glanced up. A dirigible approached, swooping low toward the clearing at a frightening speed. She dropped the sword and scrambled off Nezha's chest.

The dirigible landed only ten yards away. The basket had barely hit the ground before soldiers jumped out, shouting words that Rin couldn't understand.

She dove for the trees. For the next several moments she crawled desperately through the bushes, ignoring the thorns and branches scratching at her eyes, lacerating her skin. *Elbow, knee, elbow, knee.* She didn't dare look back. She just had to get away, quickly as she could. If they caught her now she was nothing; she had no sword, no fire, no army. If they caught her now, she was dead. Pain screamed for her to stop and fear propelled her forward.

She kept waiting for the shouts to catch up to her. For the cold steel at the back of her neck.

They never came.

At last, when her lungs burned red-hot and her heart felt like it would explode out of her chest, she stopped and peered behind her.

The dirigible rose slowly into the air. She watched, heart pounding, as it ascended above the trees. It teetered for a moment, as if unsure of where it was going, and then it veered sharply to the left and retreated.

They hadn't found her. They hadn't even tried.

Rin attempted to stand and failed. Her muscles wouldn't obey. She couldn't even sit up. The pummeling she'd just taken hit her all at once, a million different pains and bruises that kept her on the ground like firm hands pushing her down.

She lay curled on her side, helpless and immobile, shrieking in frustration. She'd squandered her chance. She wouldn't get it back. Nezha was gone, and she was alone in the mud, the dark, and the smoke.

CHAPTER 10

She awoke choking on mud. She'd rolled into it while unconscious, and it had caked over the lower half of her face. She couldn't breathe and couldn't see; she clawed agitatedly at her eyes, nose, and mouth, terrified a rocket had blown them off. The mud came away in sharp, sticky tiles that left her skin raw and stinging, and her panic subsided.

She lay still for a moment, breathing deep, and then rose slowly to her feet.

She could stand without swaying. The opium high was fading. She knew this stage of the comedown—was familiar with the numb dryness of her tongue and the faint, disorienting buzzing in her temples. She needed hours still before her mind fully cleared, but at least she could walk.

Everything hurt. She didn't want to stop and take stock of her wounds. She didn't want to know the full list of what was wrong with her, not now. She could move all four limbs. She could see, breathe, hear, and walk. That was good enough. The rest had to wait.

She staggered back toward the village, wincing with every step.

The sun was just starting to rise. The attack had occurred

just after midnight. That meant she'd been lying out there for five hours at least. That boded ill—if her army was still intact then their very *first* task would have been to search for her—their general, their Speerly.

But no one had come.

She knew they'd lost. That was a foregone conclusion; they'd never had a ground-based air defense to begin with. But how bad was the damage?

Silence met her in the town square. Small fires still crackled around every corner, smoldering inside bomb craters. A handful of soldiers moved through the streets, combing through the ruins and pulling bodies from the wreckage. So few of those bodies were moving. So few of those bodies were whole. Rin saw scattered parts wherever she looked: an arm here, a headless torso there, a pair of little feet on the dirt path right in front of her.

She couldn't even muster the strength to vomit. Still dazed, she focused on just breathing, on staying calm and figuring out what to do next.

Should they hide? Should she round up the survivors and send them fleeing to the nearest caves? Or were they temporarily safe, now that the dirigibles had gone? Kitay would know what to do—

Kitay.

Where was Kitay?

When she reached for the Phoenix, all she met was a wall of silence. She tried to suppress a rising wave of panic. If the back door wasn't working, then it only meant that Kitay was asleep or unconscious. It didn't mean he was gone. He *couldn't* be gone.

"Where is Kitay?"

She asked every person she saw. She shook exhausted soldiers and half-conscious survivors alike and screamed the question into their faces. But no one had any answers; they returned her pleas with stricken, glassy-eyed silence.

For hours she shouted his name around Tikany, limping through the lanes of wounded bodies, scanning the wreckage for any sign of his wiry, overgrown hair and his slender freckled limbs. When she found Venka, miraculously unhurt, they searched together, checking every street, alley, and dead end, even in the districts that had been far removed from the center of the bombing. They checked twice. Thrice.

He had to be here. He had to be fine. She had searched for him like this once before, in Golyn Niis, where his odds of survival had been far worse. Yet still he had answered then, and she hoped that he might again, that she would hear his thin voice carrying once more through the still air.

She knew he was alive. She knew he wasn't too badly wounded, not more than she was, because she would have felt it. *He has to be here.* She didn't dare consider the alternatives because the alternatives were too awful, because without Kitay she was just—

She was just—

Her whole body trembled.

Oh, gods.

"He's gone." Finally Venka said out loud what they both knew, wrapping her arms tight around Rin's waist as if she were afraid Rin might hurt herself if she moved. "They took him. He's not lost, he's gone."

Rin shook her head. "We have to keep looking—"

"We've walked twice through every square foot in a mile's radius," Venka said. "He's not here. We've got other things to worry about, Rin."

"But Kitay—we can't—"

"He might still be all right." Venka's voice was inordinately gentle; she was making a valiant effort to comfort. "There's no body."

Of course there was no body. If Kitay were dead then Rin wouldn't be standing—which left only one conclusion.

Nezha had taken him prisoner.

And what a valuable prisoner he was, a hostage worth his weight in gold. He was so smart, he was too fucking smart, and that made him vulnerable to anyone who had the faintest idea of who he was and what his mind could do. The Pirate Queen Moag had once locked Kitay in a safe house and assigned him to balance Ankhiluun's books. Yin Vaisra had made him a senior strategist.

What would Nezha use him for? How cruel would he be?

This was her fault. She should have killed him, she *couldn't* kill him, and now he had Kitay.

"Calm down." Venka gripped her by the shoulders. "You have to calm down, you're shaking. Let's get you to a physician—"

Rin jerked out of her grasp, more violently than she'd intended. "Don't touch me."

Venka recoiled, startled. Rin staggered away. She would have run off, but her left ankle screamed in protest every time she moved. She hobbled resolutely forward, trying to breathe, trying not to cry. It didn't matter where she was going, she just had to get away from these bodies—the smoke, the embers, the dying, and the dead.

Venka didn't follow.

Then Rin was halfway to the killing fields, alone on the dusty plain. No soldiers in sight, no spies or witnesses.

She tilted her head to the sky, shut her eyes, and reached for the fire.

Come on. Come on . . .

Of course the fire didn't come. She knew it wouldn't; she was trying only because she needed to confirm it, like the way one prodded the sore gap left by a wrenched tooth to examine the extent of the loss. When she groped for the void, tried to tilt backward into the Pantheon like she had done so many times before with ease, she came away with nothing.

Nothing but the Seal—always lurking, taunting, Altan's laughter echoing louder and louder to match her despair.

Kitay? She tried sending her thoughts out to him. That wasn't how the anchor bond worked; they couldn't communicate telepathically, they could only feel each other's pain. But regardless of distance, their souls were still linked—didn't that count for something?

Please. She threw her thoughts against the barrier in her mind, praying they might somehow reach him. *Please, I need you. Where are you?*

She was met with deafening silence.

She clutched her head, shaking, breathing in short and frantic bursts. Then came the sheer and utter terror as she realized what this meant.

She didn't have the fire.

She didn't have the fire.

Kitay was gone, truly gone, and without him she was vulnerable. Powerless. A girl who didn't have a fighting arm or the shamanic ability that justified her inability to wield a blade. Not a Speerly, not a soldier, not a goddess.

What army would follow her now?

Desperate, she gripped her knife and carved a shaky question mark into her upper thigh, deep enough to leave scars that might reappear as thin white lines on Kitay's skin. They'd communicated this way once before; it had to work again. She carved another mark. Then another. She sliced her thigh bloody. But Kitay never answered.

Tikany was shrouded in terrified silence when she returned from the fields. No one seemed to know what to do. Here and there Rin saw desultory efforts at rescue and reconstruction. A triage center was set up on the bonfire grounds, where the bombs had hit hardest, but Rin saw only two physicians and one assistant, hardly enough to deal with the lines of the wounded stretching around the square. Here and there she saw soldiers clearing away rubble or making futile attempts to create temporary shelters from the hollowed pits where once had stood buildings. But most of the survivors, civilians and soldiers both, just stood around looking dazed, as if they still couldn't quite believe what had just happened.

No one was giving orders.

Rin supposed *she* should have been the one giving the orders. But she, too, walked about in a helpless fugue. She didn't know what to say. Every order, every action she could possibly take seemed utterly pointless. How could they come back from this?

She couldn't turn back time. She couldn't bring back the dead.

Don't be pathetic, Altan would have said. She could hear his voice loud and clear, as if he were standing right beside her. *Stop being such a little brat. So you lost. You're still alive. Pick up the pieces and figure out how to start over.*

She took a deep breath, squared her shoulders, and tried to at least act like she knew what she was doing.

Back to the basics. She had to know what assets she still had, and what she had lost. She needed to determine what her fighting capabilities were. She had to gather her officers.

She seized the arm of the first Iron Wolf she saw. "Where's Souji?"

She wouldn't have been surprised if he said he didn't know. Most of the Iron Wolves were milling about, looking just as confused and disoriented as the rest. But she wasn't prepared for the look of terror that came over his face.

He looked as if she'd just threatened to kill him.

He paused before he answered. "Ah, not here, ma'am—"

"I can see that," she snapped. "Find him for me. Tell him I want to see him. Right now."

The Iron Wolf seemed to be trying to decide something. He had a strange look in his eye that Rin couldn't quite read. Defiance? Mere disorientation? She opened her mouth to ask again, but he gave her a curt nod and headed off toward the wreckage.

She returned to the general's complex, one of the few buildings left intact thanks to its solid stone foundations. She sat behind the desk, pulled out a sheaf of planning documents from a drawer, and spread them on her desk. Then she started to think.

The opium was nearly gone from her bloodstream. Her mental clarity had returned. Her mind went back to the cool, logical plane where strategy existed outside the friction of war. It felt familiar, calming. She could do this. She'd been trained for this.

For a moment she forgot the trauma of what she'd just seen,

forgot the million hurts lacerating her body, and busied herself with next steps. She'd start with the tasks that she didn't need Souji for. First things first: She gathered a handful of reliable runners and ordered them to make assessments as quickly as possible. She took stock of how many men she had left based on triage reports and corpse counts. She wrote down a list of basic necessities the army would need to recover, find, or build within the next twenty-four hours—means of transportation, food stores, and shelter. She reread spy reports on the Republic's last known troop positions. That intelligence was clearly outdated, but it helped to know where the gaps in their knowledge were.

Then she tried to work out a way to destroy those damned dirigibles.

She could deal with arquebuses—they were more or less just faster, more lethal crossbows. But the fucking *airships* changed the landscape of battle, added an extra dimension on which she couldn't compete. She needed a way to bring them down.

She started by sketching out her best recollection of their build. She wished they'd managed to ground even one of those dirigibles for study, but memory would have to do for now. The images in her mind's eye were fuzzy; she had to focus through visions of smoke and thunder to recall where the cannons were positioned, how the passenger cradles were affixed to the balloons.

She knew one thing—the airships were frustratingly well-designed. They were heavily armored from below, with no visible chinks at which to aim, and they floated too high in the air for arrows or cannons to reach. The balloons that kept the dirigibles afloat made more promising targets. If she could puncture them she could send the whole ship crashing down. But they seemed to have been plated with some kind of light metal just strong enough to deflect arrowheads, and she'd never gotten a cannonball high enough to see what happened when they collided.

Rockets, then? Could they get the trajectory right? How much explosive force would those rockets need? And how would she organize those ground artillery forces?

She crumpled her diagram in frustration. These sorts of problems were Kitay's domain. He was her engineer, her problem solver. She devised grand schemes, but Kitay figured out the details. He would have cracked this already, would have already begun crafting together some idiotic invention that still somehow *worked*.

A pain that had nothing to do with her injuries stabbed at her chest and spread like blades splintering into daggers, gouging at her heart like grappling hooks. She gasped, then clenched her mouth with her hand.

Tears dripped down her fingers. She couldn't do this alone. Gods, she missed him so much.

Stop that, Altan admonished. *Stop being such a fucking baby.*

Kitay was gone. Bitching and moaning wouldn't change that. All she could do now was focus on getting him back.

She set her drawings aside. She wouldn't be able to solve this now. She had to think about basic survival, had to get what was left of the army through the night. For that she needed Souji, but he still hadn't appeared.

She frowned. *Why* hadn't he appeared? It had been over an hour. She hadn't seen him since the attack, but surely he wasn't dead or captured—she would have known by now. She stood up and strode to the door. She jumped, startled, when she saw the same Iron Wolf from earlier standing on the other side, hand raised as if he'd been about to knock. Souji was nowhere in sight.

"Where is he?" she demanded.

The Iron Wolf cleared his throat. "Souji requests that you meet him in his tent."

That immediately struck Rin as suspicious. Souji had made his quarters in the general's complex like the rest of the army leadership. What the hell was he doing in his tent? "Is he joking? I've been waiting for over an hour now, and he thinks he can just summon me?"

The Iron Wolf's expression remained studiedly blank. "That's all he said. I can take you if you like."

For a moment Rin considered refusing the summons. Who did Souji think he was? She outranked him. He wore the collar of authority around his neck. How dare he make her wait, how *dare*—

She bit her tongue before she said something rash.

Don't be an idiot. She couldn't afford a display of power now. Kitay was gone and the fire was gone. She had no leverage. This wasn't the time to bluff. For once, she'd have to be diplomatic.

"Fine," she said tightly, and followed the Iron Wolf out the door.

Souji wasn't waiting in his tent.

Rin stopped short at the entrance. "*You.*"

The Monkey Warlord rose from his seat. "Hello, Runin."

"What are you—" She inhaled sharply, then composed herself. "Get out."

"Why don't you sit down?" He gestured to the table. "We've much to discuss."

"Get out," she said again. Anger superseded her confusion. She didn't know why Gurubai was here, but she didn't care—she wanted him gone. He didn't deserve to be here. This wasn't his victory, his troops hadn't bled at Leiyang, and the very sight of him standing here in Rooster Province, where her people had died while he cowered in Ruijin, was almost too much to bear. If she still had the fire, she would have incinerated him where he stood.

"You should be glad we arrived when we did," he said. "My troops have been leading the rescue efforts, have you not noticed? Without us, hundreds more of you would be dead."

She barked out a laugh. "So that was your plan? Hide out in your mountains until I'd won your battles, follow us, and then claim our victory?"

Gurubai sighed. "I would hardly call this a victory."

The tent flaps parted before she could retort. Souji strode in, followed by three Iron Wolves and several of Zhuden's junior officers.

Rin looked at them in surprise. She'd been waiting for those officers just as long as she'd been waiting for Souji. Was this why no one had responded? Had they spent all this time together? Doing *what*?

"Oh, good," Souji said. "We're all here."

"Where the hell have you all been?" Rin demanded. "I've been sending for you since noon."

He sighed and shook his head. "Oh, Rin."

"What?" she demanded. "What's going on?"

None of Zhuden's officers would meet her eye.

Souji shot her an apologetic smile. His fingers played at the hilt of his sword. "You still haven't figured this out?"

Too late Rin realized she was alone.

Alone, and without her fire.

Her hand flew to her knife. Souji charged her. She unsheathed her blade, parried clumsily, and didn't last three seconds. He twisted her knife from her grip with a move used by novice swordsmen, then kicked it far out of her reach.

"Where's your fire?" he taunted.

She threw herself at his waist. Again, he overpowered her with ease. At the peak of her training she could have put up a good fight, could have scratched out his eyeballs or gotten a good, vicious grip on his crotch. But he was bigger and heavier, and he had both his hands. In two moves, he had her pinned to the ground.

"So it's true," he observed. "You've lost it."

She thrashed, shrieking.

"Shhh." Souji's fingers closed around her throat and squeezed. "Not so loud. Hurts my ears."

"What are you doing?" she gasped. "What the *fuck* are you—"

Gurubai raised his voice. "'He said to tell you I walk free if you'll come to the New City yourself.'"

He was reading from a scroll. Rin stared at him, bemused. Her mind was so fogged with panic it took her a moment to recognize those words. Where had she read those—

Oh.

Oh, no.

"'He says that this doesn't have to end in bloodshed,'" Gurubai continued, "'and that he only wants to speak. He says he doesn't want a war. He's prepared to grant clemency to every one of your allies. He only wants you.'" Gurubai set the scroll down. "Rather cold, I think, to sacrifice your only family."

"You snake," she hissed.

He had to have learned this from his spies—his fucking ubiquitous spies, eavesdropping on her wherever she went, even after they were leagues away from Ruijin. Who was it? The sentries? The guard outside her tent? Had he opened and copied the scroll before she'd ever seen it?

She thought she'd outplayed him, had finally gotten the upper hand. But he'd been playing the long game this entire time.

"When were you going to tell us there was a peace offer on the table?" Gurubai inquired. "Before or after you sacrificed us to an unnecessary war?"

"Nezha's a lying bastard," she choked. "He doesn't want to negotiate—"

"On the contrary," Gurubai said. "He seemed quite keen on our proposal. You see, *we* don't want to die. And we've no qualms about sacrificing you, particularly since you seemed so ready to do the same to us."

"Are you deluded? You need me—"

"We needed you in the south," Gurubai said. "We have the south. Now you're just a liability, and the only obstacle to a cease-fire with the Republic."

"If you think you're getting a truce, you're so stupid you deserve to die," she spat. "The Yins don't keep their word. I swear to the gods, if you deliver me then you're dead."

"And we're dead if we don't," Gurubai said. "We'll take our chances. Souji?"

Souji's grip tightened around her neck. "Sorry, Princess."

Rin writhed, just hard enough to force Souji to lean forward and use his weight to press her back against the dirt. That brought his wrist close enough to her mouth. She bared her teeth and bit down. She broke skin; she tasted copper and salt on her tongue. Souji shrieked. The pressure on her neck disappeared. Something slammed into the side of her head.

She fell back, temples ringing, blood dribbling onto her chin.

She saw two Soujis looming over her, and both looked so outraged that she couldn't help but laugh.

"You taste good," she said.

He responded with a slap to her face. Then another. The blows stung like lightning; head swimming, ears ringing, she could do nothing but lie still and absorb them like a corpse.

"Not so chatty now, are you?"

She gurgled something incomprehensible. He pulled his fist back, and that was the last thing she saw.

She was lying on the same floor when she awoke. Everything hurt. When she twitched, she felt the stretch of bruises along her back, bruises from blows she didn't remember taking. Souji had kept kicking long after she'd passed out.

Breathing was agony. She had to learn to take small, suffocatingly insufficient breaths, expanding her lungs just enough not to crack her likely broken ribs.

After a few seconds, her fear gave way to confusion.

She ought to be dead.

Why wasn't she dead yet?

"There you go." Souji's voice. She saw his boots standing several feet away. "I'm assuming we don't have to verify her identity."

Who was he talking to? Rin tried to crane her neck to see, but her puffy eyes limited her view, and she couldn't tilt her head up any farther than thirty degrees. She lay curled on her side; her field of vision was restricted to the dirt floor and the wall of the tent.

Footsteps sounded close to her head. Someone put the heel of their boot on her neck.

"The Young Marshal wants her alive," spoke an unfamiliar voice.

Rin stiffened. *The Young Marshal.* This man was Nezha's envoy.

"His orders were to take her alive if we can manage, and dead if she puts up a fight," said the envoy. "I say we preempt a resistance. I've seen what she can do when she's awake."

"We can keep her dosed," spoke another voice across the room. "We brought enough opium for the journey. That keeps her harmless."

"You're going to stake your lives on that?" Souji asked. "Go on, press a little harder. None of us will tattle."

Rin winced, bracing herself for the impact. But it never came—suddenly the boot lifted from her neck, and footsteps sounded away from her head. She heard the tent flaps rustle.

"You can't kill her."

Her eyes widened. *Daji?*

"Who's this hag?" Souji asked. "Someone toss her out."

There was a flurry of movement, a clash of steel, then a loud clatter as weapons dropped to the floor.

"Don't touch me," Daji said, very slowly, very calmly. "Now step away."

The tent fell silent.

"She's a chosen manifestation of the gods." Daji's voice grew louder as she crossed the tent toward Rin. "Her body is a bridge between this world and the Pantheon. If you hurt her, then her god will come flooding through in full force to our realm. Have you ever encountered the Phoenix? You will be ash before you can blink."

That's not true, Rin thought, befuddled. *That's not how it works.* If they hurt her now, without Kitay, the Phoenix could do nothing to help her.

But none of them knew that. No one objected. The men were utterly silent, hanging on Daji's every word.

Rin could imagine what was happening. She'd suffered the Vipress's hypnosis before. Daji's eyes induced paralysis—those bright, yellow serpent's eyes that enticed and beckoned; those pupils that engorged to become gates into dark and lovely visions of butterfly wings and wretched nostalgia. The Vipress made her prey desire. Yearn. Hurt.

When Souji at last spoke, his voice sounded different—dazed, hesitant. "Then what do we do?"

"There is a mountain in Snake Province," Daji said. "Not far from here. It will be quite a march, but—"

"We have a dirigible," said one of Nezha's envoys. He spoke eagerly, like he was trying to impress. If Rin weren't so terrified, she would have laughed. "We have the fuel. We could fly there in less than a day."

"Very good, officer," Daji cooed.

No one objected. Daji had these men well and truly trapped. *Good*, Rin thought. *Now gut them.*

But Daji didn't move.

"I've heard of this mountain," Souji said after a pause. "It's impossible to find."

"Only for those who don't know where they're going," Daji said. "But I have been there many times."

"And who are you?" Souji asked. The question didn't sound like a challenge. He sounded confused, rather, like a man who had just awoken from a deep slumber to find himself in unfamiliar forest. Souji was groping through the mist, trying desperately to catch hold of clarity.

Daji gave a low chuckle. "Only an old woman who has seen a fair bit of the world."

"But you don't . . ." Souji trailed off. His question dissipated into nothing. Rin wished she could see his face.

"The Young Marshal will want to see her first," said the first of Nezha's envoys, the one who had put his boot on Rin's neck. "He'll want to know that she—"

"Your Young Marshal will be content with your report," Daji said smoothly. "You are his loyal lieutenants. He'll trust your word. Wait any longer and you risk that she wakes."

"But we were tasked to—"

"Yin Nezha is weak and ailing," Daji said. "He cannot face the Speerly right now. What do you think he will do if she strikes? She will burn him in his bed, and you will be known as the men who brought this monster to his lair. Would you murder your own general?"

"But he said she'd lost the fire," said the soldier.

"And you trust this man?" Daji pressed. "You'll wager the Young Marshal's life on the words of a guerrilla commander?"

"No," the soldier murmured. "But we—"

"Don't think," Daji whispered. Her voice was like gossamer silk. "Why think? Don't trouble yourself with such thoughts. It's much easier to obey, remember? You only have to do as I say, and you'll be at peace."

Another meek silence descended over the room.

"Good," Daji cooed. "Good boys."

Rin couldn't see Daji's eyes, not from this angle, but even she felt drowsy, lured into the soft, comforting undulations of Daji's voice.

Daji bent over Rin and smoothed the hair away from her face. Her fingers lingered over Rin's exposed neck. "Now, you'll want to sedate her for the trip."

The trip.

This wasn't all just a ploy, then. They really were taking her to the Chuluu Korikh. The stone prison, the hell inside the mountain, the place where shamans who had gone mad were taken to be locked in stone, trapped forever, unable to call their gods and unable to die.

Gods, no. Not there.

Rin had been to the Chuluu Korikh once. The very thought of returning made her feel as if she were drowning.

She tried to lift her head. Tried to say something, to do anything. But Daji's whispers washed over her thoughts like a cool, cleansing stream.

"Don't think." Rin barely heard distinct words anymore, just music, just tinkling notes that soothed her mind like a lullaby.

"Give up, darling. Trust me, this is easier. This is so much easier."

PART II

CHAPTER 11

"Before humans lived on this earth, the god of water and the god of fire quarreled and split the sky apart," Riga said. "All that shiny blue ceramic cracked and fell to Earth, and the Earth in its greenery was exposed to the darkness like yolk inside a shattered egg. That's a nice image, isn't it?"

Daji moved cautiously toward him, fingers outstretched as if she were approaching a wild animal. She didn't know what to expect from him. Nothing Riga did was predictable anymore; these days she couldn't tell from second to second whether he was about to kiss her or hit her.

She would have been less surprised if he were shouting, slamming things and people against the walls because things had gone wrong, had been going wrong for weeks.

But Riga was reading. Everything they had built over the past few years, every rock of their castle, was falling apart around them, and he was standing by the window with a book of children's myths, flipping idly through its pages, fucking *reading out loud* like he thought she needed a bedtime story.

She kept her voice low so as not to startle him. "Riga, what's happening out there?"

He ignored her question. "You know, I think I've figured out where you get all that self-righteousness." He flipped the book around to show her the painted illustrations. "Nüwa mends the sky. You've heard this myth, haven't you? The men wreck the world, and the woman has to piece it back together. The goddess Nüwa patched up that rift they'd made in the sky, rock by rock, and the world was right again."

Daji stared at him, casting wildly about for something to say.

She never understood what he was talking about anymore. She didn't know when the changes had begun—perhaps after Lusan, or perhaps since the Hinterlands. It had started so gradually, like little dribbles of water that eventually burst forth through a dam, and now Riga had transformed into an utterly different person, a person who lashed out and hurt those around him and delighted in torturing her with riddles he knew she couldn't answer.

He used to only inflict his strength on others. Now the person whose fear he seemed to enjoy the most was hers.

Come back to me, she wanted to cry every time they spoke. Something had broken between them, some invisible wound. It had started with Tseveri's death and grown like gangrenous rot, and now it loomed behind every word they spoke, every order they gave.

One will die, one will rule, and one will sleep for eternity.

"You're rambling," she said.

He just laughed. "Isn't it obvious?" He nodded toward the window. "Our stories move in circles. The Classics predicted how this whole thing is going to go. Ziya and I are going to break the world. And you're going to mend it."

Daji could glimpse the burning shore from where she stood. She didn't need General Tsolin's powerful astrological scopes to see what was happening across the strait. A simple spyglass was enough.

Spots of orange lit up the night. If she didn't know better, she would have thought they were firecrackers.

She wondered, because she couldn't help it, if any of the children Shiro hadn't taken had at least made it off the island, if their parents had packed them away in boats and told them to row on, never looking back. But she knew better than to hope. The Mugenese were too thorough.

She knew that by morning, no one on that island would be left alive.

Riga's doomed us.

This was the end. She knew this like a fundamental truth, as certain as the Earth's rotation around the sun. They would suffer dearly for their sacrifice of Speerly blood. This kind of evil would not go unpunished—the gods would not allow it.

Everything they'd fought for, everything they'd built—gone up in smoke. All for some stupid, stupid gamble.

"Do you like what you see?" Riga approached her from behind and put his hands on her hips.

Did he find this erotic? He *would*.

She lowered the spyglass, trying to mask the frantic pounding of her heart. She turned around and attempted a smile. Riga liked her so much better when she smiled.

"Does Ziya know yet?" she asked.

"He'll be here soon enough," Riga said. "Didn't think he'd want to miss this."

"That's cruel."

He shrugged. "It'll be good for him. He's going too soft, we've got to whet that edge."

"And what happens when that edge turns against you?"

"He'd never." Riga squeezed her waist, chuckling. "He loves us."

The door burst open. Ziya stormed in, right on cue.

"What's happening?" he demanded. "They said Speer's under attack."

"Oh, Speer's been attacked." Riga gestured at the window. "This is just the aftermath."

"That's impossible." Ziya grabbed the spyglass out of Daji's hands. He tried to train it on the shore, but his hands trembled too badly to hold it still. "Where were Vaisra's ships?"

Riga, looking smug, didn't answer.

Daji put a hand on Ziya's arm. "You should—"

"*Where were Vaisra's ships?*" Ziya shouted. He was shaking, barely in control. Daji could see the faint silhouettes of inky creatures under his skin, straining to pour out from within him.

"Come on, Ziya." Riga sighed. "You know what we had to do."

Ziya's mouth worked soundlessly. Daji watched as his eyes darted between Riga's face and the window.

Poor Ziya. He'd always been so fond of Hanelai. There were moments when she'd feared he might try to marry that spirited little Speerly general of his. Riga wouldn't have allowed it, of course—he'd always been a stickler about Nikara purity, and he loathed Hanelai besides—but Ziya might have forced it anyway.

Misguided love. Jealous friends. She longed for the time when those were their biggest problems.

"I have to get to Speer," Ziya said. "I have to—I have to find her."

"Oh, come now. You know what you'll find." Riga gestured grandly at the burning shore. "You can see the island clearly enough from here. They're all dead, every single one of them. The crickets are nothing if not thorough. It's already over. Whatever fighting is happening now is just cleanup. Hanelai's dead, Ziya. I did tell you it was foolish to let her go."

Ziya looked as if Riga had taken a dagger and twisted it into his heart.

Riga clapped him on the back. "It's for the best."

"You didn't have the right," Ziya whispered.

Riga laughed a deep, cruel laugh. "Now is when you grow a spine?"

"Their blood is on you. You killed them."

"'*You killed them*,'" Riga imitated. "Don't speak to me about killing innocents. Who leveled the Scarigon Plateau? Who tore Tseveri's heart out of her chest?"

"Tseveri wasn't my fault—"

"Oh, it's never your fault," Riga sneered. "You just lose control and people *accidentally* end up dead, and then you wake up and start whining about the people who are bold enough to do what's necessary while fully conscious. Get a grip, brother. You murdered Tseveri. You let Hanelai go to her death. Why? Because you know what's necessary and what's at stake, and you know that in the grand scheme of things, those two little whores of yours were obstacles not worth mentioning. Think of what happened as a kindness. You know it probably was. You know the Speerlies would have botched self-rule the moment they got it, would have probably started butchering each other the moment we let them take charge. You know people like Hanelai were never particularly good at being free."

"I hate you," Ziya said. "I wish we were all dead."

Riga lifted a hand and casually backhanded him across the face. The crack echoed through the room.

"I freed you from your shackles." Riga advanced on the cringing Ziya, slowly unsheathing his sword. "I dragged both of you out of the occupied zone. I found the Hinterlanders, I took us to Mount Tianshan, and I brought you to the Pantheon. And you dare to defy me?"

The air thrummed, thick with something powerful, suffocating, and terrible.

Just bow, Daji wanted to cry at Ziya. *Bow and it'll be over.*

But she was mute, rooted in place by fear.

Ziya hadn't moved, either. The sight was bizarre, a grown man cowering like a child, but Daji knew what made him do it.

Fear was inscribed in Ziya's bones, just like it was in hers. Blow by blow, cut by cut—over the last decade, since they were children, Riga had made sure of it.

She realized that both of them were glaring at her. Demanding a response. But what was the question? What could she possibly do to fix this?

"Nothing?" Ziya demanded.

"She won't say anything," Riga scoffed. "Little Daji knows what's best for us."

"You're a coward," Ziya snarled at her. "You've always been."

"Oh, don't bully her—"

"Fuck you." Ziya slammed his staff against the floor. The sound made Daji jump.

Riga laughed. "You want to do this now?"

"Don't," Daji murmured, but the word came out in a terrified squeak. Neither of them heard.

Ziya flew at Riga. Riga opened his palm and immediately Ziya dropped to the ground, howling in pain.

Riga sighed theatrically. "You would lift your hand against me, brother?"

"You're not my brother," Ziya gasped.

A void opened in the air behind them. Shadowy beasts poured through, one after the other. Ziya pointed. They surged, but Riga sliced them down like paper animals, fast as they came.

"Please," Riga said. The smile never dropped from his face. "You can do better than that."

Ziya raised his staff high. Riga lifted his sword.

Somehow Daji found the strength to move. She flung herself into the space between them just before they rushed each other with enough force to split cracks in the stone floor, a force that shattered the world like it was an eggshell. Decades later she would wonder if she had known what she was doing back then, when she threw her hands against their chests and spoke the incantation she did. Had she known and accepted the consequences? Or had she done it by accident? Was everything that happened after a cruelty of chance?

All she knew in that moment was that all sound and motion stopped. Time hung still for an eternity. A strange venom, something she'd never summoned before, seeped through the air, rooted itself into all three of their minds, and unfurled to take a shape none of them had ever seen or experienced. Then Riga collapsed to the floor and Ziya reeled backward, and they both might have shouted, but the only thing Daji could hear past the blood thundering in her ears was the ghostly echo of Tseveri's cold, mirthless laughter.

CHAPTER 12

Private Memorandum on the Nikara Republic, formerly known as the Nikara Empire or the Empire of Nikan, to the Office of Foreign Affairs of the Republic of Hesperia.

Open trade in the Nikara territories continues to reveal assets justifying the Consortium's investment, and efforts to acquire these assets proceed smoothly as anticipated. The Consortium has secured the rights to several critical mining deposits with surprisingly little struggle (in truth, I imagine the Nikara are ignorant to the riches beneath their feet). Beyond tea and minerals, our agents have discovered a number of local goods that will find an eager market at home. Nikara porcelain has a shine and translucency that, quite honestly, bests our domestic wares. Nikara carved jade figurines will no doubt attract customers looking for novel interior decoration (see Box 3, attached). The local textile craftsmanship is impressive given their lack of automated looms—their artisans have developed particularly clever mechanisms to harness the power of water to spin cloth far faster than a single weaver could. (I expect our ladies will be parading the streets in silk robes and parasols before too long!)

∞

The Gray Company representatives of the Order of the Holy Maker have encountered more significant difficulties. Indigenous opposition to conversion proves thorny (see the attached letter from Sister Petra Ignatius of the Second Spire). This is not so much because of an existing religion that defies replacement—indeed, most of the natives seem to be quite indifferent to the question of religion—but because of the social discipline that religion entails. They find regular weekly worship a waste of time and resent being corralled to chapel. They are used to their squalid, superstitious ways and seem unable to accept the blinding proof of the Maker's eminence, even when laid out slowly before them in their own language. But our efforts will continue, surely if slowly; our duty to the Architect to bring order upon every corner of the world necessitates no less.

We find minimal risk that Nikara natives could mount a concentrated armed uprising. Our studies of the Empire have long indicated that their strategic culture is made pacifist and stagnant by an Empire with no inclination to territorial expansion. The Republic has never mounted a seafaring expedition to conquer another nation. Save for their conquest of the Isle of Speer, the Republic has only ever absorbed foreign aggression. Now that Yin Vaisra has finished quelling the remnants of Su Daji's regime in the north, we expect that over a five-year timeline our fears of domestic warfare can be put to rest.

The greatest threats now are the indigenous guerrilla movements in the south, whose bases are concentrated in Rooster and Monkey Provinces. Their perceived trump card is the Speerly Fang Runin, whose pyrotechnic displays have convinced them of a pagan shamanistic belief that rivals the Order of the Holy Maker. (Our liaisons in the Gray Company believe these shamanic abilities to be heretofore unseen manifestations of Chaos—see Addendum

1: Nikara Shamanism.) This threat should not terribly worry the Consortium. The numbers of shamans are few—aside from the Speerly and Yin Vaisra's heir, the Gray Company have identified no others on the continent. The southern rebels are still centuries behind even the old Federation of Mugen on every front, and they attempt to fight dirigibles with sticks and stones.

Their so-called gods will not save them. Sister Petra assures me that in addition to improved opium missiles, which we have confirmed negates shamanic ability, research efforts to devise countermeasures proceed smoothly, and that in several weeks we will have weapons even the Speerly cannot best. (See Addendum 2: Research Notes on Yin Nezha.) The south will fall when the Speerly falls. Absent some divine intervention, we shall promptly produce upon this barbarous nation every effect we could desire.

In the Name of the Divine Architect,
    Major General Josephus Belial Tarcquet

CHAPTER 13

When Rin awoke, her head was fuzzy, her mouth felt like it had been stuffed with silkworm cocoons, and a throbbing ache snaked from the scars in her back through every muscle in her lower body. She heard a roar so loud it seemed to envelop her, drowning out her thoughts, making her bones thrum with its reverberations.

Her gut dropped; the floor seemed to lurch. Was she *in a dirigible*?

Something cool and wet rubbed against her forehead. She forced her throbbing eyelids open. Daji's face came gradually into focus. She was wiping Rin's face with a washcloth.

"Finally," Daji said. "I was starting to worry."

Rin sat up and glanced around. Up close, the dirigible carriage was much larger than she'd always imagined. They sat alone in a room the size of a ship's cabin, which had to be one of many, for none of the Republican soldiers were in sight. "Get away from me."

"Oh, shush." Daji rolled her eyes as she continued scrubbing grime from Rin's cheeks. The washcloth had turned rust brown from dried blood. "I've just saved your life."

"I'm not going . . ." Rin struggled to make sense of her

thoughts, trying to remember why she was afraid. "The mountain. *The mountain.* I'm not going—"

"Eat." Daji pressed a hard, stale bun into her hand. "You need your strength. You won't survive immurement otherwise."

Rin stared helplessly at her. She didn't lift the bun; her fingers hardly had the strength to close around it. "Why are you doing this?"

"I am saving us both," Daji said. "Maybe your incipient southern empire, too, if you'll stop with the hysterics and *listen*."

"The army—"

"Your army has abandoned you. Your loyal officers are in no position to help. You've been ousted by the Southern Coalition, and you can't call the fire." Daji smoothed Rin's hair back behind her ears. "I am guaranteeing us safe passage to the Chuluu Korikh."

"But *why*—"

"Because my strength now is not enough. We need an ally. A mutual friend, who to the best of my knowledge is currently whiling away eternity in a mountain."

Rin blinked. She understood Daji's words, but she didn't understand what she *meant*; it took a moment of thoughts churning sluggishly through her mind before the pieces fell together.

Then she balked.

She hadn't thought about Jiang for nearly a year. She hadn't let herself; the memories hurt too much. He'd been not just her teacher but her master. She'd trusted him; he'd promised to keep her safe. And then, the moment her world descended into war, he'd simply abandoned her. He'd left her to seal himself in a fucking rock.

"He won't come out," Rin said hoarsely. "He's too scared."

Daji's lip curled. "Is that what you think?"

"He wants to hide. He won't leave. He's—there's something wrong—"

"His Seal is eroding," Daji said fiercely. Her good eye glimmered. "I know. I've felt it, too. He's getting stronger—he's coming back to himself. I didn't know what I was doing when I Sealed the three of us, but I'd always suspected—hoped—I hadn't done it right. And I didn't. The Seal was a broken, imperfect thing, and now it's fading. Now I—*we*—get a second chance."

"Doesn't matter." Rin shook her head weakly. "He won't leave."

"Oh, he'll have to." Daji resumed dabbing at Rin's temples. "I need him."

"But *I* needed him," Rin said. She felt a sharp pang in her chest, a wrenching mix of frustration and despair that until now she'd been so good at suppressing. She wanted to kick something; she wanted to cry. How, after so much time, could old hurts sting so sharp?

"Perhaps you did." Daji gave Rin a pitying look. "But Ziya's not your anchor. He's mine."

The rest of the journey could have taken minutes or hours. Rin didn't know; she passed it in a painful daze, slipping in and out of consciousness as her body ached from its myriad contusions. Daji lapsed into silence, cautious of eavesdroppers. At last the engine roar slowed to a whine, then stopped. Rin jolted fully awake as the carriage thudded against the ground at an angle and screeched as it dragged several feet to a halt. Then Republican soldiers came into her compartment, loaded her bound form onto a wooden stretcher, and carried her out into the icy mountain air.

She didn't resist. Daji wanted her to play helpless.

She knew they had reached Snake Province. She recognized the shape of these mountains; she'd traveled this way before. But some part of her mind could not accept that they were really, truly, in the Kukhonin Mountains.

Less than a day had passed since Souji betrayed her in Tikany. They'd crossed half the country in the time since. But that couldn't be right—this journey should have taken weeks. Rin had seen dirigibles fly, she knew how fast they moved, but this was absurd. This took her ingrained conceptions of time, space, and distance, and ripped them to shreds.

Was this how the Hesperians regularly traveled? She tried to imagine spatiality from their perspective. What would society be like if one could traverse the continent in mere days? If she could wake up one morning in Sinegard, and go to bed in Arlong that evening?

No wonder they acted as if they owned the world. To them it must seem so small.

"Which way?" asked a soldier.

"Up," Daji said. "The entrance lies near the summit. There won't be space up there to land a craft. We'll have to climb."

Rin was strapped down so tightly to the stretcher she could barely lift her head. She couldn't see how much farther they had to march, but she suspected it would take hours. The only walking path to the entrance of the Chuluu Korikh grew treacherously narrow with altitude. There wouldn't have been space to land anything as large as a dirigible more than a third of the way up.

At least she didn't have to climb. As the soldiers hoisted her up the mountain, the rocking stretcher lulled her into a kind of half sleep. Her head felt light and fuzzy. She wasn't sure if they had sedated her, or if her body was breaking down from wounds sustained earlier. She passed the march in a barely conscious fugue, just dazed enough that the bruises from Souji's boot produced no more than a dull, nearly pleasant ache.

She didn't realize they'd reached the Chuluu Korikh until she heard the scrape of the stone door sliding open.

"We need a light," Daji said.

Rin heard a crackle as someone lit a torch.

Now, she thought. This was when Daji would turn on the soldiers, surely. She'd gotten what she wanted; she'd secured safe passage to the Chuluu Korikh, and now she only had to hypnotize them, lure them to the precipice, and push.

"Go on," Daji said. "There's nothing to fear here. Just statues."

The soldiers bore Rin into the looming dark. An immense pressure slammed over her, like an invisible hand clamped over her nose and mouth.

Rin gasped, arching her back against the stretcher. She gulped down huge mouthfuls of air, but it was thin and insufficient, and did nothing to stop the black spots creeping in at the edges of her vision. She could breathe so hard she ruptured her lungs and it still wouldn't be enough. The inside of the Chuluu Korikh was so *grounded*, so firmly material, a solid place with no possible crossover into the plane of spirit.

It felt worse than drowning.

Rin had barely tolerated the pressure the first time she'd come here with Altan. It was far worse now that she had lived and breathed for years with divinity just a glancing thought away. The Phoenix had become a part of her, a constant and reassuring presence in her mind. Even in Kitay's absence, she'd still felt the barest thread of a connection to her god, but now even that was gone. Now she felt as if the weight of the mountain might shatter her from inside.

The soldier at the front rapped his knuckles against her forehead. "Ah, shut up."

Rin hadn't even realized she was screaming.

Someone stuffed a rag in her mouth. That made the suffocation worse. Rational thought fled. She forgot that this was all a feint, all part of Daji's plan. How could Daji—*Su Daji*, who had lived with the voice of her god longer than Rin had been alive—withstand this? How could she walk calmly forward without screaming while Rin writhed, arrested in the last moment of drowning before death?

"All these were shamans?" The soldier bearing her legs whistled, a low sound that echoed through the mountain. "Great Tortoise. How long have they been here?"

"As long as this Empire has been alive," Daji said. "And they'll be here long after we're dead."

"They can't die?"

"No. Their bodies are no longer mortal. They have become open conduits to the gods, and so they are trapped here so they don't destroy the world."

"Fucking hell." The soldier clicked his tongue. "That's rough."

The soldiers halted and lowered Rin's stretcher to the floor. The one at her head leaned above her; his teeth gleamed yellow in the torchlight. "This is your stop, Speerly."

She stared past him at rows and rows of empty plinths, stretching farther into the mountain than Rin could see. Her mind was half-gone with fear. She flailed, helpless, as the soldiers unstrapped her from the stretcher and hauled her up toward the nearest pedestal.

Her eyes flashed to Daji, begging silently to no avail. *Why isn't she doing anything?* Hadn't this charade gone on long enough? Daji didn't need Rin immured. She only needed safe passage to the Chuluu Korikh. She had no use for the Republican soldiers anymore; she should have already disposed of them.

But Daji was just *standing* there, eyes lidded, face calm, watching as the soldiers positioned Rin on the center of the plinth.

A horrible thought crossed Rin's mind.

Daji hadn't just been bluffing.

Daji needed safe passage to the Chuluu Korikh. She needed Master Jiang. But nothing about her plan required Rin.

Oh, gods.

She had to get out of here. She wouldn't escape this—there was no way she could make it to the door and down the mountain ahead of them in her state, not with her legs bound so tightly. But she could get to the edge of the corridor. She could jump.

Anything was better than an eternity in the rock.

She stopped struggling and slouched against the soldiers' arms, pretending she'd fainted. It worked. Their grip loosened, just barely enough for her to wrench her torso free. She ducked beneath their hands and lunged toward the ledge. Her legs were tied so tightly she could only manage a lurching shuffle, but she was so close—it was only mere feet, she could evade them just two paces—

But then she reached the edge and saw the yawning abyss, and her limbs turned to lead.

Jump.

She couldn't.

It didn't matter that she knew eternity in the Chuluu Korikh was worse than death. She still couldn't do it. She didn't want to die.

"Come on." Strong arms wrapped around her midriff and dragged her back from the edge. "You're not getting off that easy."

The soldiers pulled her legs up so that between them they carried her like a sack of rice. Together, they flipped her up into a standing position and arranged her on the pedestal.

"Stop," Rin shrieked, but her words came muffled and meaningless behind her gag. "Stop, please don't—Daji! *Daji! Tell them!*"

Daji didn't meet her eyes.

"Make sure her feet are in the center," she said calmly, as if instructing servants on where to move a table. "Prop her up so that she's standing straight. The stone will do the rest."

Rin tried everything to escape—kicking, thrashing, writhing, and going limp. They didn't let go. They were too strong and she was too weak—famished, injured, dehydrated.

She had no more outs. She was trapped, and she couldn't even die.

"Now what?" one of them asked.

"Now the mountain does its work." Daji began to chant in Ketreyid, and the rocks came alive.

Rin watched the base of the pedestal in horror. At first its movement seemed a trick of the torchlight, but then she felt the icy touch of stone around her ankles as the plinth crept up and consumed her, solidifying into an immobile coat over the surface of her skin. She had no time to struggle; in seconds, it was up to her knees. The soldier holding her upright let go of her arms and sprang away when the rock reached her waist. Her upper body was now free but it made no difference; much as she flailed she couldn't break the stone's hold against her legs. Moments later it reached her chest, arrested her elbows where she'd bent them, and crept up her neck. She tilted her head up, desperate to get her nose away from the rock. It didn't matter. The stone crawled over her face. Closed over her eyes.

Then she saw nothing. Heard nothing. She did not feel the stone against her; it had become a part of her, a natural outer coating that rendered her completely still.

She couldn't move.

She couldn't *move*.

She strained against the rock but nothing budged even a fragment, and all that did was flood her nerves with such anxiety that she strained harder and harder while panic exploded inside her, intensifying second by second with no possible release.

She couldn't breathe. And at first she was at least grateful for that—without air, surely she'd soon lose consciousness, and then this torture would end. She could feel her lungs bursting, burning. Soon she'd black out. Soon it'd be over.

But nothing happened.

She was drowning, forever drowning, but *she couldn't die.*

She needed to scream and couldn't. She wanted so badly to writhe and flail that her heart almost burst out of her chest and even *that* would have been better because then she would at least be dead, but instead she hung still in a never-ending moment stretching on into a definite eternity.

The knowledge that this could and would continue, for days upon seasons upon years, was torture beyond belief.

I should have jumped, she thought. *I wish I were dead.*

The thought repeated in her mind over and over, the only salve against her new and terrifying reality.

I wish I were dead.

I wish I were dead.

I wish—

The mere thought of oblivion became a fantasy. She imagined she really had jumped, imagined the short, euphoric fall and the satisfying crunch of her bones against the bottom of the pit, followed by a blissful nothing. She repeated the sequence so many times in her mind that for brief seconds at a time she fooled herself into thinking she'd really done it.

She could not sustain her panic forever. Eventually it ebbed away, replaced by a dull, empty helplessness. Her body at last resigned itself to the truth—she would not escape. She would not die. She would remain standing here, half-dead and half-alive, conscious and thinking for eternity.

She had nothing now except for her own mind.

Once upon a time Jiang had taught her to meditate, to empty her mind for hours at a time while her body settled into the peaceful daze of an empty vessel. That was, no doubt, how he had survived in here all this time, why he had ever entered this place willingly. Rin wished she had that skill. But she had never once achieved that inner stillness. Her mind rebelled against boredom. Her thoughts had to wander.

She had nothing else to do but probe through memories for entertainment. She pored over them, picked them apart and stretched them out and relished them, prolonging every last detail. She remembered Tikany. Remembered those delicious warm afternoons she spent in Tutor Feyrik's room discussing every detail of the books he'd just lent her, stretching her arms to receive more. Remembered playing games with baby Kesegi in the yard, pretending to be every known beast in the Emperor's Menagerie, roaring and hissing just to get him to laugh. Remembered quiet, stolen minutes in the dark, brief interludes when she was all alone, free of the shop and of Auntie Fang, able to breathe without fear.

When Tikany failed to satisfy she turned her mind to Sinegard—that harsh, intimidating place that, paradoxically, now contained her happiest memories. She remembered studying in the cool basement chambers of the Academy library with Kitay, watching him pushing spindly fingers through his worried hairline as he riffled through scroll after scroll. Remembered sparring in the early mornings with Jiang in the Lore garden, parrying his blows with a blindfold tied around her head.

She got very good at exploring the crevices of her mind, excavating memories that she didn't know she still had. Memories she hadn't let herself acknowledge until now for fear they would break her.

She remembered the first time she'd ever laid eyes on Nezha, and then all the times thereafter.

It hurt to see him. It hurt *so much*.

They'd been so innocent once. It was agony to recall the face he wore just a year ago: pretty and cocky and unbearable at once, alternately grinning with delight or wearing the absurd snarl of an agitated puppy. But she was trapped here for an eternity. Those memories were the only things she had now, and the pain was the only way she'd feel anything ever again.

She retraced their entire history from the moment she met him first at Sinegard to the moment she felt his blade sliding into the muscles of her back. She remembered how childishly handsome he used to be, how she'd been both drawn to and repulsed by that haughty, sculpted face. She remembered how Sinegard had transformed him from a spoiled, petty princeling to a hardened soldier in training. She remembered the first time they'd sparred against each other and the first time they'd fought side by side in battle—how their animosity and partnership had both felt like such a natural fit, like slipping on a lost glove, like finding her other half.

She remembered how much taller than her he'd grown, how when they embraced, her head fit neatly under his chin. She remembered how dark his eyes had looked under the moonlight that night by the docks. Right when she thought he'd kiss her. Right before he'd pressed a blade into her back.

It hurt so much to riffle through those memories. It was humiliating to remember how readily she'd believed his lies. She felt like such a fool, for trusting him, for loving him, for thinking any of those thousands of tiny moments they'd shared during her brief time in Vaisra's army meant that he really, truly cared for her, when in truth Nezha had been manipulating her just like his father had.

She relived those interactions so many times that they began to lose all meaning. Their sting faded to a dull burn, and then nothing at all. She'd numbed herself to their significance. She'd grown bored of her own pain.

So she turned to the last thing that could still hurt her. She went looking for the Seal and found that it was still there, ready and waiting in the back of her mind, daring her to enter.

She wondered briefly why the Seal had not disappeared. It was the product of the goddess Nüwa's magic, and there was no connection to the gods in the Chuluu Korikh. But perhaps when Daji had brought the magic into the world, the connection severed, the same way venom lingered after the snake had died.

Rin was grateful for it. Here was at least a single distraction from her own mind. Something she could play with, flirt with. For prisoners in solitary confinement, a knife was better entertainment than nothing.

What happened if she touched it now? She might never come back. Here, with nothing from reality to distract her, she might end up trapped in a poison-soaked lie forever.

But she had nothing else. No reality to come back to, save her own stale memories.

She leaned forward and fell through the gate.

"Hello," said Altan. "How did we end up here?"

He was standing far too close. Only inches separated them.

"Stay back," she said. "Don't touch me."

"And I thought you wanted to see me." Ignoring her command he reached out, took her chin in his fingers, and tilted her head up. "What's happened to you, darling?"

"I've been betrayed."

"'*I've been betrayed*,'" he mimicked. "Fuck that nonsense. You threw everything away. You had an army. You had Leiyang. You had the south in the palm of your hand and you fucked it all up, you mangy, dirt-skinned piece of shit—"

Why was she so afraid? She knew she had control. Altan was her imagination; Altan was *dead*. "Get back."

He only moved closer.

She felt a flash of panic. Where were his chains? Why wouldn't he obey?

He cast her a mocking smile. "You can't tell me what to do."

"You're not real. You only exist in my mind—"

"My darling, I *am* your mind. I'm you. I'm all you've got left. It's just you and me now, and I'm not going anywhere. You don't want peace. You want accountability. You want to know exactly what you've done and you don't want to forget it. So let's begin." His fingers tightened around her chin. "Admit what you did."

"I lost the south."

He smacked a palm against her temple. She knew the blow wasn't real, that everything she felt was a hallucination, but still it stung. She'd *let* it sting. This was her imagination, and she'd decided she deserved this punishment.

"You didn't just *lose* the south. You gave it away. You had Nezha at your mercy. You had your blade pressed to his skin. All you had to do was bring your arm down and you would have won. You could have killed him. Why didn't you?"

"I don't know."

"*I* know." Another ringing blow, this time to her left temple. Rin's head jerked to the side. Altan seized her throat and dug his fingernails into the skin around her larynx. The pain was excruciating. "Because you're pathetic. You need to be someone's dog. You need someone's boots to lick."

Rin's blood ran cold—not with self-induced misery, but with true, uncontrolled fear. She didn't know where this was going; she couldn't predict what her mind would do next. She wanted to stop. She should have left the Seal alone.

"You're weak," Altan spat. "You're a stupid, sentimental, sniveling brat who betrayed everyone around her because she couldn't get over her schoolyard *crush*. Did you think he loved you? Do you think he ever loved you?"

He drew his fist back again. A tremor rippled through the Seal. Altan's image wavered like a reflection on a lake dispelled by a stone. There came a second tremor. Altan disappeared. Then Rin understood this wasn't a hallucination—something was slamming into the stone inches from her face.

The third time, she felt it, a shake that started in her nose and vibrated through her entire body. Her teeth rattled.

Her teeth rattled.

Movement. Which meant—

A fourth tremor. The stone shattered. Rin spilled off the plinth and tumbled hard onto the stone floor. Pain shot up her knees; it felt wonderful. She spat the rag out of her mouth. The air inside the mountain, stale and dank as it was, tasted delicious. The suffocation she'd felt earlier was gone; compared to immurement, the open air tasted like the difference between mild humidity and being underwater. For a long time she knelt with her head hanging between her shoulders and just *breathed*, marveling at how it felt when air rushed in and out of her lungs.

She flexed her fingers. Touched her face, felt her fingers on her cheeks. The bliss of those sensations, of the sheer freedom of movement, made her want to cry.

"Great Tortoise," said a voice she hadn't heard in a lifetime. "Someone clearly never learned to meditate."

Rin's eyes took a moment to adjust to the torchlight. Two silhouettes stood over her. To the left, Daji. And on the right was Jiang, covered from head to toe with gray dust, smiling widely in greeting as if they'd seen each other only yesterday.

"You've got dirt in your hair." He reached down to unbind her legs. "My gods, it's everywhere. We're going to have to dunk you into a creek."

Rin recoiled from his touch. "Get away from me."

"You all right, kid?" His tone was so light. So casual.

She stared at him, amazed. He'd been gone for a year. It had felt like decades. How could he act as if everything were normal?

"Hello?" Jiang waved a hand in front of her face. "Are you just going to sit there?"

She found her voice. "You abandoned me."

His smile dropped. "Ah, child."

"You *left* me." His wounded expression only made her angrier.

It felt like a mockery. Jiang didn't get to skirt this conversation like he skirted everything, dodging responsibility by feigning madness so well that they all believed it. He'd never been as crazy as everyone thought. She wouldn't start falling for it now. "I needed you—Altan needed you—and all you did was, was—"

Jiang spoke so quietly she almost couldn't hear him. "I couldn't save Altan."

Her voice broke. "But you could have saved me."

He looked stricken. For once he had no quippy retort, no excuse or deflection.

She thought he might apologize.

But then he cocked his head to the side, mouth quirking back into a grin. "Why, and spoil all your fun?"

Once upon a time Jiang's humor had been irritating at worst, a welcome salve in an otherwise dreadful environment at best. Once upon a time he'd been the only person who regularly made her laugh.

Now she saw red.

She didn't think. She lashed out at him, fingers curling into a fist midway to his face. His hand flashed out of his sleeve. He caught her wrist, forced her arm away with more strength than she'd expected.

She always forgot how strong Jiang was. All that power, concealed inside a reedy, whimsical frame.

He held her fist suspended between them. "Will it make you feel better to hit me?"

"Yes."

"Will it really?"

She glared at him for a moment, breathing heavily. Then she let her hand go limp.

"You ran away," she said. It wasn't a fair accusation. She knew that. But there was a part of her that had never stopped being his student. The part that was terrified and needed, still needed, his protection.

"You left." She couldn't keep her voice from breaking. "You left me alone."

"Oh, Rin." His voice turned gentle. "Do you think this place was anything like a refuge?"

Rin didn't want to forgive. She wanted to stay angry. She'd been nursing this resentment for too long. She couldn't just let this go; she felt like she'd been cheated of something she was owed.

But the horror of immurement was too immediate. She had just escaped her stone prison. And nothing, *nothing*, could make her enter it again. She'd fling herself off the ledge first.

"Then why did you do it?" she asked.

"To protect you," he said. "To protect everyone around me. I'm sorry I couldn't think of a better way how."

She had no response to that. His words terrified her. If Jiang had seen this hell as the best of alternatives, then what had he been afraid of?

"I'm sorry, child." Jiang stretched out his hands in a conciliatory gesture. "I am so sorry."

She turned away and shook her head, hugging her arms to her chest. She couldn't forgive so easily. She needed time to let her anger burn down its wick. She couldn't meet his eyes; she was glad the firelight was too dim for him to see her tears.

"So what's changed?" she asked, wiping at her cheeks. "Your Seal has eroded. You're not afraid of what will come through?"

"Oh, I am terrified," Jiang said. "I have no idea what my freedom might cause. But suspending myself in time is no answer. This story must end, one way or another."

"This story will end." Daji had been watching their exchange in silence, her mouth twisted in an unreadable expression. Now, her cool voice sliced the air like a knife. "The way it was always meant to."

Jiang put his hand on Rin's shoulder. "Come, child. Let's see how the world has broken while I was gone."

Again, he offered her his hand. This time, she took it. Together they approached the open door, a circle of blinding light.

The sheer whiteness of the sun on snow was agony. But Rin relished the pain shooting through her eyes just as much as she delighted in the cold bite of wind on her face, stone and half-melted snow under her toes. She opened her mouth and took a deep breath of icy mountain air. In that moment, it was the loveliest thing she'd ever tasted.

"Be ready to march," said Daji. "I can't fly that airship. We'll have to go by foot until we can find some horses."

Rin glanced back at her and then blinked, startled.

The old hag from Tikany was gone. Entire decades had melted from Daji's face. The lines around her eyes had disappeared, the skin around her gouged eye was smooth and unscarred, and the eyeball somehow, miraculously, healed.

Jiang, too, was more vividly alive than she'd ever seen him. He didn't just look younger. That wasn't new—Jiang had always had an ageless quality about him, like he'd been ripped from a place out of time. But now he seemed *solid*. Powerful. He had a different look in his eyes—less whimsical, less placidly amused, and more focused than she'd ever seen him.

This man had fought in the Poppy Wars. This man had nearly ruled the empire.

"Something wrong?" he asked.

Rin shook her head, blinking. "Nothing. I just—um, where are Nezha's troops?"

Daji shrugged. "Dealt with them as soon as they got you in the mountain."

Rin was indignant. "And you couldn't have freed me a bit earlier?"

Daji cast her an icy smile. "I thought you should know how it felt."

They made shelter that night under a small alcove near the base of the mountain. Humming, Jiang set about constructing a fire. Daji disappeared into the trees and, twenty minutes later, returned with a string of dead rats, which she then proceeded to skin with a dagger.

Rin slumped back against a tree trunk, trying to keep her eyes open. The absurdity of this scene would have amazed her if she had the energy. She was sitting at a campfire with two of the most powerful figures in Nikara history, figures that to most people existed only in shadow puppet plays, watching as they prepared dinner. Anyone else would have been slack-jawed in awe.

But Rin was too exhausted to even think. The climb downhill hadn't been arduous, but the Chuluu Korikh had drained her; she felt like she'd barely survived tumbling down a waterfall. She had nearly drifted into sleep when Jiang poked her in the stomach with a stick.

She jumped. "What?"

He poked her again. "You're being very quiet."

She rubbed her side. "I just want to sit for a second. In peace. Can I do that?"

"Well, now you're just being rude."

She lifted a languid hand and whacked him on the shin.

He ignored that and sat down beside her. "We need to talk next moves."

She sighed. "Then talk."

"Now, Daji's only caught me up on a little bit." He rubbed his hands together and held them out over the flames. "It's been a very distressing day for me."

"Same," Rin muttered.

"But the way I understand it, you've gone and split the country in half."

"That wasn't my fault."

"Oh, I know. Yin Vaisra's always been a bloodthirsty little gremlin." Jiang winked at her. "So what shall we do now? Raze Arlong to the ground?"

She gaped at him for a moment, waiting for him to chuckle, before she realized he was being utterly serious. His gaze was earnest.

She had no idea what this new Jiang was capable of, but she had to take his words at face value.

"We can't do that," she said. "We have to infiltrate them first. They've—they've got someone."

"Who?"

Daji interjected from across the fire. "Her anchor."

"She has an anchor?" Jiang arched an eyebrow. "Since when? You might have told me."

"I only retrieved you from rock this afternoon," Daji said.

"But that seems *relevant*—"

"Kitay," Rin snapped. "Chen Kitay. He was in my class at Sinegard. Nezha took him from Tikany, and we need to get him back."

"I remember him." Jiang rubbed his chin. "Skinny kid? Big ears, hair like an overgrown forest? Too smart for his own good?"

"That's the one."

"Does the Republic know he's your anchor?" Daji asked.

"No." Aside from Chaghan, everyone who knew she had an anchor had died at Lake Boyang. "No one possibly could."

"And they don't have a reason to hurt him?" Daji pressed.

"Nezha wouldn't do that," Rin said. "They're friends."

"Friends don't send dirigible bombers after friends," said Jiang.

"The point is that Kitay is alive," Rin said, exasperated. "And the first thing we need to do is get him back."

Jiang and Daji exchanged a long, deliberating look.

"Please," Rin said. "I'll follow any plan you two want, but I need Kitay. Otherwise I'm useless."

"We'll get him back," Jiang assured her. "Is there any chance we can get you an army?"

Daji snorted.

Rin sighed again. "My troops betrayed me to the Republic, and their leader probably wants me dead."

"That's not great," Jiang said.

"No," Rin agreed.

"Then who owns the resistance army?"

"The Southern Coalition."

"Then that's who we'll deal with. Walk me through their politics."

If he wasn't going to let her sleep, Rin decided, then she might as well entertain him. "The Monkey Warlord Liu Gurubai controls the core of the army. Yang Souji commands the Iron Wolves. Ma Lien led the second-largest contingent, the bandit troops, before he died. Zhuden was his second-in-command. They were loyal to me for a bit, until . . . well. They thought they'd trade me for immunity."

"And who is the leadership now?"

"Gurubai, definitely. And Souji."

"I see." Jiang pondered this for a moment, then said in a cheerful tone, "You'll have to kill them all, of course."

"Sorry, what?"

He lounged back against the trunk, stretched out his legs, and propped one ankle over the other. "Strike as soon as you can after you rendezvous with the coalition. Get them in their sleep. Sometimes it's easier to take them out in battle, but that tends to leave a nasty public impression. Bad form, and all that."

Rin stared at him in disbelief. She didn't know what shocked her more—his suggestion, or the cavalier tone in which he said it. The Jiang she knew liked to blow bubbles in the creek with a reed for fun. This Jiang discussed murder as if relaying a recipe for porridge.

"What did you think would happen when you returned?" Daji asked.

"I don't know, I thought maybe—maybe they'd realize they need me." Rin hadn't thought that far. She had some half-formed notion that she might be able to talk her way into their good graces, now that they'd learned she was right about the Republic.

But now that she considered it, they were just as likely to shoot her on sight.

"You are so bad at this," Jiang said. "It's cute."

"You can't fight a war on multiple fronts." Daji slid a thin whittled branch through the skinned rats, then propped them over the crackling fire. "The moment you hear whispers of dissent in your own ranks, you flush it out. With all the force necessary."

"Is that what you did?" Rin asked.

"Oh, yes," Jiang said happily. "All the time. I handled the public murders, of course. Riga only had to utter the name, and I'd have the beasts rip them up from head to toe. The point was the spectacle, to dissuade anyone else from defection." He nodded at Daji. "And this one took care of everything we wanted to keep quiet. Good times."

"But they hated you," Rin said.

She knew little of the Trifecta's reign except from what Vaisra had told her, but she knew they'd been resented by almost everyone. The Trifecta had sustained political support through sheer violence. No one had loved them, but everyone had feared them. After Riga disappeared, the only reason why the Twelve Warlords never unseated Daji from the throne was because they hated one another just as much.

"Elites with entrenched interests will always hate you," Daji said. "That's inevitable. But the elites don't matter, the masses do. What you have to do is shroud yourself in myth. Your enemies' deaths become part of your legend. Eventually you become so far removed from reality that right and wrong don't apply to you. Your identity becomes part and parcel of the idea of the nation itself. They'll love you no matter what you do."

"I feel like you're underestimating the public," Rin asked.

"How do you mean?"

"I mean—nobody becomes a legend overnight. People aren't blind. I wouldn't worship an icon like that."

"Didn't you worship Altan?" Daji asked.

Jiang whistled through his teeth. "Low blow."

"Fuck you," Rin said.

Daji just smiled. "People are attracted to power, darling. They can't help themselves. Power seduces. Exert it, make a show of it, and they'll follow you."

"I can't just bully people into getting what I want," Rin said.

"Really?" Daji cocked her head. "How did you get command of Ma Lien's troops, then?"

"I let him die," Rin said.

"Rephrase," Daji said.

"All right. I killed him." That felt surprisingly good to say out loud. She said it again. "I killed him. And I don't feel bad about it. He was a shitty leader, he was squandering his troops, he humiliated me, and I needed him out of the way—"

"And that's not how you feel about the others?" Daji pressed.

Rin paused. How hard would it be to murder the entire southern leadership—Souji, Gurubai, and Liu Dai? She considered the details. What about their guards? Would she have to strike them all at once, in case they warned one another?

It scared her that this was no longer a question of whether to do it, but *how*.

"You can't lead by committee," Daji said. "The entire bloody history of this country is proof of that. You've seen the Warlord councils. You know they can't get anything done on their own. Do you know how the succession wars kicked off? One of the Red Emperor's favorite generals demanded that his rival give him a troupe of Hinterlander musicians captured in a raid on the borderlands. His rival sent him the musicians, but smashed all their instruments. The first general slaughtered the musicians in retaliation, and that kicked off nearly a century of warfare. That's how petty multifactional government becomes. Save yourself the headaches, child. Kill your rivals on sight."

"But that's not . . ." Rin paused, trying to tease out the exact nature of her objection. Why was it so hard to make the argument? "They don't deserve that. It'd be one thing if they were Republican officers, but they're fighting for the south. It's wrong to just—"

"Dear girl." Daji sighed heavily. "Stop pretending to care about ethics, it's embarrassing. At some point, you'll have to convince yourself that you're above right and wrong. Morality doesn't apply to you."

She turned the skewered rats over the fire, exposing their uncooked underbellies to the flames. "Get that in your head. You'll have to get more decisive if you're ever going to lead. You're not a little girl anymore, and you're not just a soldier, either. You're in the running for the throne, and you've got a god on your side. You want full command of that army? This *country*? You take it."

"And how," Rin said tiredly, "do you propose to do that?"

Daji and Jiang exchanged a look.

Rin couldn't read it, and she didn't like it. It was a look loaded with decades of shared history, with secrets and allusions that she couldn't begin to understand. Suddenly she felt like a little child sitting between them—a peasant girl among legends, a mortal among gods, woefully inexperienced and utterly out of place.

"Easily," Daji said at last. "We'll retrieve your anchor. And then we'll go wake ours."

CHAPTER 14

The next morning they set off for the heart of enemy territory. They'd decided the Republican wartime headquarters was the most likely candidate for Kitay's location. Nezha and Vaisra had to be on the front lines, and if they were making use of Kitay as anyone in their position should, then he'd be right there with them.

The battlefront had moved far west in a very short period of time. They traversed through Snake Province and crossed over the northern tip of Dragon Province, and found the juncture of the Western Murui and Southern Murui in Hare Province, where they stole a raft and made a quick trip into Boar Province. Every passing mile where Rin did not find evidence of the Southern Coalition's resistance felt like another punch to the gut.

It meant Nezha had already pushed them this far across the country. It might mean they'd already been obliterated.

They tried their best to avoid civilians on their journey. That wasn't hard. This stretch of central Nikan was a war-stricken cesspool, much of which had lain straight in the paths of the destroyed Four Gorges Dam. The refugees who remained were scarce, and the few straggling souls they glimpsed tended to keep to themselves.

Rin stared at the banks as their raft floated through Boar Province, trying to imagine how this region would have looked barely a year ago. Whole villages, townships, and cities had thrived here once. Then the dam broke with no warning, and hundreds of thousands of villagers had either drowned or fled down south toward Arlong. When the survivors returned, they found their villages submerged still under floodwaters, ancestral lands that had housed generations lost to the river.

The region still hadn't recovered. The fields where once sorghum and barley crops grew lay under a sheet of water three inches thick, now rank from decomposing corpses. Occasionally, Rin glimpsed signs of life on the banks—either small camps of tents or tiny hamlets of no more than six or seven thatched huts. Never anything larger. These were subsistence hideaways, not long-term settlements.

It would take a long time for this region to sprout cities again. The destruction of the dam hadn't been the only source of devastation. The Murui was already a fickle river, prone to breaking its banks on unpredictably rainy years, and by destroying all vegetation cover, this great flood had destroyed the region's natural defenses. And before that, on their warpath inland, Mugenese soldiers had slashed and burned so many fields that they had ensured local starvation for years. Back in Ruijin, Rin had heard stories of children playing in the fields who had dug up explosives buried long ago, of children accidentally wiping out half their villages because they'd opened gas canisters in curiosity.

How many of those canisters still lurked hidden in the fields? Who was going to volunteer to find out?

Every day since the end of the Third Poppy War, Rin had learned that her victory on Speer mattered less and less. War hadn't ended when Emperor Ryohai perished on the longbow island. War hadn't ended when Vaisra's army defeated the Imperial Navy at the Red Cliffs.

She'd been so stupid to once think that if she ended the Federation then she'd ended the hurting. War didn't end, not so cleanly—it just kept building up in little hurts that piled on one another until they exploded afresh into raw new wounds.

Only when they reached the heart of Boar Province did they find evidence of recent fighting.

No—not fighting. *Destruction* was the better word. Rin saw the wreckage of thatched houses that still lay clumped near their foundations, instead of scattered in the patterns of older ruins. She saw scorch marks that hadn't yet been wiped away by wind and rain. Here and there, in ditches and along the stands, she saw bodies that hadn't fully decomposed—rotting flesh lumped over bones that hadn't yet been picked clean.

This proved the civil war wasn't over. Rin had been right—Vaisra hadn't rewarded the south for betraying her. He must have turned his dirigibles on the Southern Coalition the moment Rin and Daji left for the Chuluu Korikh. He'd chased them into Boar Province, and Boar Province must have put up a resistance. They had no reason to trust the Republic; their warlord had been unceremoniously decapitated at Arlong days after Daji's defeat. They must have rallied to the Southern Coalition's side.

From the looks of it, Vaisra had thrashed them for their impudence.

Rin whistled. "What happened here?"

They'd turned a corner of the river onto a bizarre shoreline; the area where trees should have stood was burned and flattened, like some flaming giant had come trampling through on a mindless rampage.

"Same thing that happened last time," Daji said. "They bring their bombers, and if they can't find their enemy they attack indiscriminately. They flatten the terrain to make it harder for the rebels to hide."

"But those aren't bombing marks," Rin said, still confused. "They're not all in crater patterns."

"No, that's the jelly," Jiang said.

"Jelly?"

"It's what they used last time. Something the Gray Company invented in their towers. It catches fire when it hits any living things—plants, animals, people. We never figured out how to put it out—water and smothering don't work. You have to wait for it to burn all the way through. And that takes a very long time."

The implications terrified Rin. This meant the Hesperians didn't just rule the skies; they also had flames that rivaled her own.

The destruction here was so much worse than the wreckage at Tikany. Boar Province must have fought so hard; that was the only thing that warranted retaliation on this scale. But they must have known they couldn't win. How did it feel when the heavens rained down a fire that wouldn't die? What was it like to fight the sky itself? She tried to imagine the moment when this forest turned into a chessboard of green, black, green, and black, when civilians running terrified through trees turned twitching and smoking into charcoal.

"The air campaigns are very clever, actually." Daji trailed her fingers idly through the water. "You drop bombs over dense areas with no built-in defenses, so they think they're entirely vulnerable. Then you fly your dirigibles over the widest possible area, so they know no one is safe no matter where they hide."

She wasn't speaking from conjecture, Rin realized. This was all from experience. Daji had fought this same war, decades before.

"You fly the airships at random schedules," Daji continued. "Sometimes at day and night, until the locals are terrified even of going outside, even though they're safer where their house won't collapse on them. Then you've robbed them of everything. Sleep, food, comfort, security. No one dares move in the open, so you've cut off communications and industry, too."

"Stop." Rin didn't want to hear any more. "I understand."

Daji ignored her. "You drive them into total collapse. Fear turns into despair, despair to panic, and then panic into utter submission. It's incredible, the power of psychological warfare. And all it takes is a couple of bombs."

"Then what did you do?" Rin asked.

Daji blinked slowly at her as if the answer were obvious. "We went to the Pantheon, darling."

"Things got a lot easier after that," Jiang said. "I used to snatch them out of the sky like mosquitoes. Riga and I made it a game. Record time was four crafts in five seconds."

He said this so casually that Rin couldn't help but stare. Immediately, like a gnat had buzzed into his ear, he shook his head quickly and looked away.

Whoever had emerged from the Chuluu Korikh was not the man she'd known at Sinegard. The Master Jiang at Sinegard had no recollection of the Second Poppy War. But this Jiang made constant offhand references about it and then backpedaled quickly, as if he were dipping his toes in an ocean of memory just to see if he'd like it, then cringing away because the water was too cold.

The memory lapses weren't the things about Jiang that bothered her. Ever since they'd left the Chuluu Korikh, she had been watching him, following his movements and vocal patterns to track the differences. He was refreshingly familiar and jarringly different all at once, often within the span of the same sentence. She couldn't predict the switches in the timbre of his voice, the sudden sharpness of his gaze. Sometimes he was affable, eccentric. And other times he carried himself like a man who had fought and won wars.

Rin knew his Seal was eroding. But what did it mean? Did it happen gradually, one regained memory at a time, until he collected everything that he'd lost? Or would it be erratic and unpredictable, like the way Jiang approached everything else?

What confused her even more were the times when Jiang slipped almost fully back into his former skin, when he acted so much like the teacher she'd once known that every day, for brief pockets of time, she almost forgot that anything had changed.

He would tease her about her hair, which was shorn so messily near her temples that she looked like she'd been raised in the wild. He would tease her about her stump ("Kitay's right, you should fix a blade on that"), about the Southern Coalition ("Losing a belt is one feat, losing an entire army is something else entirely"), about Altan ("You couldn't even mention him without blushing, you hopeless child"), about Nezha ("Well, there's no accounting for taste"). Those jokes would have prompted a slap if they'd come from anyone else, but when uttered in Jiang's detached, deadpan delivery, they somehow made her laugh.

During long, boring afternoons floating down empty stretches of river, he would tilt his head back at the clear sky and belt out bawdy, ribald songs whose lyrics made Daji snort and Rin blush. Occasionally, he'd even spar with her, teetering back and forth on the uneven raft, teaching her mental tricks to fix her balance, and jabbing her in the side with his staff until she corrected her form.

At those times Rin felt like a student again, eager and happy, learning from a master she adored. But inevitably, his smile always slipped, his shoulders tensed, and the laughter went out of his eyes, as if the ghost of who he had been had abruptly fled.

Only once, nearly three weeks into their journey, when Daji had fallen asleep during Jiang's watch rotation, did Rin work up the nerve to ask him about it.

"Get on with it," Jiang said promptly as soon as she opened her mouth.

"Um—sorry, what?"

"You've been eyeing me like a lovestruck village girl since we left the mountain," he said. "Go on. Proposition me."

She wanted to both laugh and hit him. A pang of nostalgia hit her stomach like a club, and her questions scattered on her tongue. She couldn't remember what she had wanted to ask him. She didn't even know where to start.

His expression softened. "Are you trying to see if I remember you? Because I do, you know. You're difficult to forget."

"I know you do, but . . ." She felt tongue-tied and bewildered, the way she'd often felt during the years she'd spent as Jiang's apprentice, groping at the truth about the gods before she even understood what she was looking for. She felt the absence of knowledge like a gap inside her. But she didn't know how to phrase her questions, couldn't trace the contours of what she lacked. "I suppose I wanted to know . . . well, the Seal, Daji said that—"

"You want to know what the Seal is doing to me." Jiang's voice took on a hard edge. "You're wondering if I am the same man who trained you. I am not."

Rin shuddered as memories rose unbidden to her mind: flashes of the vision the Sorqan Sira had once showed her, a nightmare of savaged corpses and manic laughter. "Then are you . . ."

"The Gatekeeper?" Jiang tilted his head. "Riga's right hand? The man who overthrew the Mugenese? No. I don't think I am him, either."

"I don't understand."

"How can I describe it?" He paused, tapping at his chin. "It's like seeing a warped reflection in a mirror. Sometimes we are the same and sometimes we are not; sometimes he moves with me, and sometimes he acts of his own volition. Sometimes I catch glimpses of his past, but it's like I'm watching from far away like a helpless observer, and that—"

He broke off, wincing, and pressed his fingers against his temples. Rin watched the headache pass; she'd witnessed these spasms before. They never lasted more than several seconds.

"And other times?" she prompted, after the lines around his eyes relaxed.

"Other times the memories are from my perspective, but it's like I'm experiencing them for the first time. For him, it's a memory. He already knows what happened. But for me, it's like watching a story unfold, but I don't know its ending. The only thing I do know, with absolute certainty, is that I did it. I see the bodies, and I know I'm responsible."

Rin tried to wrap her head around this, and failed. She couldn't see how one could live with two different sets of memories, belonging to two different personalities, and still remain sane.

"Does it hurt?" she asked.

"Knowing what I've done? Yes, it hurts. Unlike anything you could ever imagine."

Rin didn't have to imagine. She knew very well how it felt for a chasm of guilt to eat at her soul, to try to sleep when an abyss of vengeful souls whispered that she'd put them there, and for that she deserved to die.

But she had owned her memories. She knew what she'd done, and she'd come to terms with it. How did Jiang relate to his crimes? How could he take responsibility for them if he still couldn't identify with the person who had done them? And if he couldn't face his own past, couldn't even recognize it as *his*, was he doomed to remain a divided man, trapped in the schism of his psyche?

She phrased her next question carefully. She could tell she'd pushed him to the edge—he looked pale and skittish, ready to bolt if she said the wrong thing. She was reminded of her time at the Academy, when she'd had to mince and contort her words so that Jiang wouldn't mock them, skirt them, or simply pretend she hadn't spoken.

She understood now what he had been afraid of.

"Do you think . . ." She swallowed, shook her head, and started over. "Do you think you'll transform back to the person you were supposed to be? Before the Seal?"

"Is that who you want me to become?" he inquired.

"I think that's the man we need," she said. She blurted out her next words before her boldness receded. "But the Sorqan Sira said that man was a monster."

He didn't answer for a while. He sat back, watching the shore, trailing his fingers through the murky water. She couldn't tell what was going on behind those pale, pale eyes.

"The Sorqan Sira was right," he said at last.

Rin had thought—hoped, really—that when she came near enough to Kitay, she'd start sensing his presence, a warm familiarity that might gradually strengthen as she drew closer. She didn't think it would be so sudden. One morning she woke up shaking and gasping, nerves tingling like she'd been set on fire.

"What's wrong?" Daji asked sharply.

"Nothing, I'm . . ." Rin took several deep breaths, trying to pin down what had changed. She felt as if she'd been slowly drowning without realizing it until one day, abruptly, she broke for air. "I think we're close."

"It's your anchor." It wasn't a question; Jiang sounded certain. "How do you feel?"

"It's like—like I'm whole again." She struggled to articulate the feeling. It wasn't as if she could read Kitay's thoughts or sense his emotions. She still hadn't received any messages from him, not even scars in her skin. But she knew, as surely as she knew that the sun would set, that he was close. "It's as if—you know how when you're ill for a long time, you forget how it feels to be healthy? You get used to your head ringing, your ears being blocked, or your nose being stuffed—and you don't even notice you're not right anymore. Until you are."

She wasn't sure she'd made sense; the words sounded stupid tumbling out of her mouth. But Jiang and Daji only nodded.

Of course they understood. They were the only ones who could understand.

"Soon you'll start feeling his pain," Daji said. "If he's suffered any. That'll give us some clue about how he's been treated. And that feeling will get stronger and stronger the closer we get. Convenient, no? Our very own homing pigeon."

Their suspicions had been correct—Kitay was being held right on the Republican battlefront. The next morning, after long weeks on a road that seemed composed of never-ending bomb craters and ghost villages, the New City rose out of the horizon like a garish dash of color against a scorched background.

It made sense that the Republic would stake their base here, in one of the bloodiest cities in Nikara history. The New City, once named Arabak, had served as a military bastion since the campaigns of the Red Emperor. Originally it was a string of defensive forts over which warlords had fought for so long that the border between Boar and Hare Province was drawn in blood. The war machine required labor and talent, so over the years, civilians—physicians, farmers, craftsmen, and artisans—had moved with their families into the fortress complexes, which grew to accommodate the masses of people whose sole business was fighting.

Now, the New City was the frontier hub of the Republican Army and the air base of the Hesperian dirigible fleet. The Republican's senior military command was stationed behind those walls, and so was Kitay.

Rin, Jiang, and Daji had to get creative as they got closer to the city. They started traveling only at night, and even then in short, careful bursts, hiding in the forest undergrowth to avoid the dirigibles that circled the city in regular patrols, shining unnaturally strong lights at the ground below. They altered their appearances—Daji clipped her hair short above her ears, Rin started hiding her eyes behind messy shanks of hair, and Jiang dyed his white locks a rich brown with a mix of walnut hulls and ochre, ingredients that he found so easily that Rin had to assume he'd done it before. They agreed on a cover story in case they were stopped by sentries—they were a family of refugees, Rin their daughter, traveling from Snake Province to reunite with Daji's brother, a low-level bureaucrat in Dragon Province.

Rin found this last ploy ridiculous.

"No one's going to think I'm your daughter," she said.

"Why not?" Jiang asked.

"We look nothing alike! For one, your skin's infinitely paler than mine—"

"Ah, darling." He patted her on the head. "That's your fault. What did I tell you about staying out in the sun?"

Half a mile out from the gates they found crowds. Actual refugees, it turned out, had flocked to the New City in hordes. Those fortresses were the only thing within miles that guaranteed safety from the bombing campaigns.

"How are we going to get in?" Rin asked.

"The way you approach any other city," Daji said, as if this were obvious. "Right through the gates."

Rin cast a doubtful look at the lines snaking from the gates around the fortress walls. "They're not letting anyone in."

"I'm very persuasive," Daji said.

"You're not afraid they'll recognize you?"

Daji gave her a droll look. "Not if I instruct them to forget."

Surely it couldn't be so easy. Rin followed along, bewildered, as Daji led them straight to the gates, ignoring the cries of complaint from everyone else in the queue, and demanded so boldly to be let through that Rin was sure they were going to be shot.

But the soldiers only blinked, nodded, and parted.

"This never happened," Daji said as she passed. They nodded, eyes glazed. "You never saw me, and you have no idea what I look like."

She gestured for Jiang and Rin to follow. Astonished, Rin obeyed.

"Bothered?" Jiang asked.

"She just told them what to do," she muttered. "She just *told* them, without even—I mean, she wasn't even trying."

"Oh, yes." Jiang gave Daji a fond look. "We told you she's persuasive."

Persuasive didn't describe half of it. Rin knew about Daji's hypnosis. She'd been victim to it herself many times. But in the past, Daji's illusions had taken several long moments of careful coaxing. Never had Rin seen her utter such casual, dismissive commands with the full expectation that they would be obeyed.

Was it because Jiang was now freed from the Chuluu Korikh? Did Daji's powers amplify when her anchors grew stronger? And if so, then what would happen when they woke Riga?

Behind its walls, the New City felt like a punch to the face.

Rin had panicked the first time she'd ever left Tikany, when she'd woken up on the second morning of her journey to Sinegard and her caravan had traveled far enough that her surroundings felt truly foreign. It took her days to get used to the morphing landscape, the receding mountains, the terrifying reality that when she went to sleep at night on her cramped mat in the caravan wagon, Tikany's packed-earth walls no longer protected her.

She had traveled the Nikara Empire since then. She had been swept up in the overwhelming clamor of Sinegard, had walked the planks of the Floating City at Ankhiluun, had entered the Autumn Palace in lush, regal Lusan. She'd thought she understood the range of cities in the empire, spanning from the dusty poverty of Tikany to the winding disorder of Khurdalain's oceanside shacks to the sapphire-blue canals of Arlong.

But the New City was foreign on a different scale. The Hesperians had been here for only months—they could not possibly have dismantled and built over Nikara stone fortresses that had stood there for centuries. Yet its architectural skeleton seemed drastically altered—the old fortresses were augmented by a number of new installations that imposed a blockish sense of order, transforming the cityscape into a place of straight lines instead of the curved, winding alleys that Rin was used to.

Gone, too, were all Nikara-style decorations. She saw no lanterns, no wall banners, no sloping pagoda roofs or latticed windows, which would have appeared even in this sparsely utilitarian military city. Instead, everywhere she looked, she saw glass—clear glass on most windows, and colored patterns in the larger buildings, stained illustrations depicting scenes she did not recognize.

The effect was startling. Arabak, a city with more than a thousand years of history, seemed to have simply been erased.

This wasn't the first time Rin had seen Hesperian architecture. Khurdalain and Sinegard, too, had both been rebuilt by foreign occupation. But those were cities built first on Nikara roots, and later reclaimed by the Nikara. There, western architecture had been curious remnants of the past. The New City, on the other hand, felt as if a piece of Hesperia had simply been carved out and dropped whole into Nikan.

Rin found herself staring at things she had never dreamed could exist. On every street corner she saw blinking lights of every conceivable color powered not by flame, but by some energy source she couldn't see. She saw what looked like a monstrous black carriage mounted on steel tracks, chugging ponderously over the well-paved streets as thin trails of steam emitted from its head. Nothing pushed or pulled it—no laborers, no horses. She saw miniature dirigibles humming around the city, machines so perfectly small that she at first mistook them for loud birds. But their whine was unmistakable: a thinner, higher version of the airship engine whine she now associated with death.

No one controlled them. No one pulled their strings or even shouted out commands. The miniature airships seemed to have minds of their own; autonomously they dipped and swerved through the spaces between buildings, dodging deftly into windows to deliver letters and parcels.

Rin knew she couldn't keep gawking like this. The longer she stood here, eyes darting around at a million new and startling sights, the more she stood out. But she couldn't move. She felt dizzy, disoriented, like she had been plucked off the Earth and tossed adrift into an entirely different universe. She'd spent much of her life feeling like she didn't belong, but this was the first time she'd felt truly *foreign*.

Six months. Six months, and the Hesperians had transformed a riverside municipality into something like this.

How long would it take them to reconfigure the entire nation?

A whirring, apparently self-driving brass wagon across the street caught her eye, and she was so astonished that she didn't notice she was standing on two thin steel tracks. She didn't see the black horseless carriage sliding noiselessly in her direction until it was mere feet away, barreling straight toward her.

"*Move!*"

Jiang tackled her to the ground. The carriage zoomed past them both, chugging indifferently along its preordained route.

Heart pounding, Rin crawled to her feet.

"What is wrong with you?" Daji yanked her up by the wrist

and dragged her off the main road. They were attracting bystanders; Rin saw a Hesperian sentry eyeing them cautiously, arms cradling his arquebus. "Do you want to get caught?"

"I'm sorry." Rin followed her past a thicket of civilians into a narrow alley. She still felt terribly dizzy. She leaned against the cool, dark wall and took a breath. "It's just—this place, I didn't—"

To her surprise, Daji looked sympathetic. "I know. I feel it, too."

"I don't understand." Rin couldn't put her discomfort into words. She could barely breathe. "I don't know why—"

"I do," Daji said. "It's realizing that the future doesn't include you."

"Let's not dawdle." Jiang's tone was brusque, almost cold. Rin didn't recognize it at all. "We're wasting time. Where is Kitay?"

She shot him a puzzled glance. "How would I know?"

He looked impatient. "Surely you've sent a message."

"But there's no—" She faltered. "Oh. I see."

She glanced around the alley. It was thin and narrow, less a passageway and more a tight strip of space between two square buildings. "Can you cover me?"

Daji nodded. "Be quick."

They moved to guard either side of the alley. Rin sat down against a wall and pulled her knife out of her belt. She sent a probing question to the back of her mind, tentative, hopeful. *Are you there?*

To her surprise, a small flame flickered to life in her hand. She could have screamed in relief. She made a cage with her fingers over the blade, waiting until the tip glowed orange. She just needed to scar, not mutilate; a quick burn would be easier than drawing blood.

But Daji shook her head. "You have to press it in deep. You've got to bleed. Or he won't even feel it."

"Fine." Rin held the tip over the fleshy back of her lower left leg, but found that she couldn't stop her fingers from shaking.

"Would you like me to do it?" Daji asked.

"No—no, I'll do it." Rin clenched her teeth tight to make sure she wouldn't bite her tongue. She took a breath. Then she pushed the tip into her skin.

Her calf screamed. Every impulse told her to draw her hand away, but she kept the metal embedded inside her flesh.

She couldn't keep her fingers from shaking. The knife clattered to the ground.

She picked it up, embarrassed, unable to meet Daji's eyes.

Why was the pain so terrible now? She'd inflicted worse harms on herself before. She still had faint white burn scars on her arms from the candle wax she'd once dripped on herself to stay awake. Ridged, puckered marks covering her thighs where she'd once stabbed herself to escape her own hallucinations.

But those wounds were the product of fevered, desperate outbursts. She was sober right now, clear-minded and calm, and her full presence of mind made it so much harder to deliberately inflict pain.

She squeezed her eyes shut.

Get a grip, Altan said.

She thought of when a javelin had slammed her out of the sky over the Red Cliffs. Of when Daji had pinned her under a mast. Of when Kitay had smashed her hand apart, then pulled the mangled remnants through iron cuffs. Her body had been through so much worse than a shallow cut from a clean blade. This was a small pain. This was nothing.

She dug the metal under her skin. This time her hand held steady as she carved out a single character in clear, even strokes.

Where?

Minutes passed. Kitay didn't respond.

Rin glanced at her arm every several seconds, watching for pale scars that didn't emerge.

She tried not to panic. There were a million reasons why he

hadn't yet answered. He might be asleep. He might be drugged. He might have seen the message, but either lacked any means of responding, or couldn't because he was under surveillance. He needed time.

Meanwhile, they had nothing to do but wait.

Daji wanted to remain in hiding inside the alley, but Jiang suggested that they walk the length of the New City. This was purportedly to gather intelligence. He wanted to map out exit routes and mark down the guard post locations, so that if and when Kitay responded, they could smoothly get him out.

But Rin suspected that Jiang, like her, wanted to explore the New City simply out of sheer, sick fascination. To see how much had changed, to fully understand what the Hesperians were capable of.

"It's been decades," he told Daji when she objected. "We need to know what we're up against."

And so, scarves wrapped tight over their noses, they ventured back out onto the street.

The first thing Rin noticed was that the New City was *clean*.

She quickly discovered why. Ordinances printed on giant sheets of parchment were pasted all along the walls in Hesperian and Nikara characters. No urinating in the street. No dumping garbage from windows. No unlicensed sale of alcohol. No unleashed animals on the street. No fireworks, gambling, brawling, fighting, or shouting.

Rin had seen such ordinances before—Nikara magistrates often posted public notices like these in futile attempts to clean up their unruly cities. But here the ordinances were *followed*. The New City was far from pristine; it had all the crowded din of every large city. But that was a function of its swollen population, not their habits. The streets were dusty, but free from litter. The air smelled not of filth, excrement, or rotted trash, but of the normal stench of many tired humans crowded into one place.

"Look at that." Jiang paused by a metal plaque nailed to a streetlamp, engraved in alternating Nikara and Hesperian script.

The Four Cardinal Principles of Order
Propriety
Righteousness
Frugality
Modesty

Below that was a list of rules for the "Maintenance of Societal Order." *Do not spit. Queue politely in line to await your turn. Practice hygiene.* Under that last rule was another, indented list that clarified:

Practices that are unhygienic include:
Failure to wash hands before one cooks or eats.
Preparing raw meat with the same blade as vegetables.
Reusing cooking oil.

It went on for eight more lines.

"That's obnoxious." Rin had the sudden urge to rip it down, but the gleaming plaque looked so grand and official she was afraid one of the miniature dirigibles would start attacking her if she did.

"What's wrong with washing your hands?" Jiang asked. "Sounds fair to me."

"There's nothing *wrong*, it's just . . ." Rin trailed off, unsure how to phrase her discomfort. She felt like a little child being admonished to finish her rice. She didn't hate the idea of hygiene itself, but rather the presumption that the Nikara were so backward, so barbaric, that the Hesperians had to remind them in huge, clear text how not to behave like animals. "I mean, we know all this already."

"Do we?" Jiang chuckled. "Have you ever been to Sinegard?"

"There's nothing wrong with Sinegard." Rin didn't know why she was defending the old Nikara capital. She *knew* Sinegard was disgusting. The first time she'd traveled north, she'd been warned to eat nothing from dirt-cheap street vendors, since they produced their soy sauce from human hair and sewage. Yet now, for some reason, she felt territorial. Sinegard was the capital; Sinegard was a shining delight, and she would have far preferred its bustling din to this freak show of a city. "Let's just keep walking."

Her discomfort didn't ebb as they traveled farther into the New City. It worsened. Every time she turned a corner she saw something—new decorations, new technologies, new attire—that reinforced how *bizarre* this place was.

Even the background noise threw her off. She'd gotten used to the soundscape of her country; it was all she'd ever known. She knew its roadside shouts, its creaking wheels, its jabbering hagglers and crowded footsteps. She knew its language, had come to expect certain vowel-consonant combinations and vocal intonations. But the noises of the New City sounded on an entirely different register. From teahouses and street buskers she heard new strains of music, awful and discordant. She heard too many voices speaking Hesperian, or some accented attempt at Hesperian.

Nikara cities were loud, but their loudness was of a different type—local, discrete, irregular. The New City seemed run on an ever-present mechanical heartbeat, its thousand machines whirring, humming, and whining without end. Once Rin noticed it, she couldn't get it out of her head. She couldn't imagine living against this backdrop; it would drive her mad. How did anyone *sleep* in this city?

"Are you all right?" Jiang asked.

"What? Of course—"

"You're sweating."

Rin glanced down, and realized that the front of her tunic was soaked through.

What was wrong with her? She had never felt a panic like this before—this low, crescendoing distress of gradual suffocation. She felt like she'd been dropped blindfolded into a fairy realm. She did not want to be here. She wanted to run, back out past the walls and into the forests; anything to get away from this hopeless, confused alienation.

"This is how we felt last time." Daji's tone was uncharacteristically gentle. "They came in, rebuilt our cities, and transformed them according to their principles of order, and we almost couldn't bear it."

"But they have their own cities," Rin said. "What do they want here?"

"They want to erase us. It's their divine mandate. They want to make us better, to *improve* us, by turning us into a mirror of themselves. The Hesperians understand culture as a straight line." Daji dragged her finger through the air. "One starting point, and one destination. They are at the end of the line. They loved the Mugenese because they came close. But any culture or state that diverges is necessarily inferior. *We* are inferior, until we speak, dress, act, and worship just like them."

That terrified Rin.

Until now she had perceived the Hesperian threat in terms of hard power—through memories of airship fleets, smoking arquebuses, and exploding missiles. She'd seen them as an enemy on the battlefield.

She'd never considered that this alternate form of soft erasure might be far worse.

But what if the Nikara *wanted* this future? The New City was full of Nikara residents—they had to outnumber the Hesperians five to one—and they seemed completely fine with their new arrangement. Happy, even.

How had things changed so quickly? Once upon a time any Nikara on the continent would have run from the mere sight of the blue-eyed devils. They'd been primed for xenophobia by centuries of rumors and stereotypes, stories that Rin had half believed until she'd met the Hesperians in the flesh. *They eat their food raw. They steal orphan babies to cook them into stews. Their penises* are three times larger than normal, and their women's openings are cavernous to accommodate.*

But the Nikara in the New City seemed to adore their new neighbors. They nodded, smiled, and saluted Hesperian soldiers as they passed. They sold Hesperian food from carts parked on street corners—rocklike brown pastries, hard yellow rounds that gave off pungent odors, and varieties of fish so stinkingly moist Rin was surprised they hadn't rotted. They—the upper class, at least—had begun to imitate Hesperian dress. Merchants, bureaucrats, and officers walked down the streets garbed in tight trousers, thick white socks pulled up to their knees, and strange coats that buttoned over their waists but draped in the back past their buttocks like duck tails.

They'd even started learning Hesperian. It sounded like bad Hesperian—a clipped, pidgin dialect that morphed the two languages and made them, oddly, mutually understandable. Foreign phrases peppered exchanges between merchants and customers, soldiers and civilians—*Good day. How much? Which ones? Thank you.*

But despite all their pretensions and efforts, they were not the Hesperians' equals. They couldn't be, by virtue of their race. This Rin noticed soon enough—it was clear from the ways the Nikara bowed and scraped, nodding obsequiously while the Hesperians ordered them about. This wasn't a surprise. This was the Hesperians' idea of a natural social order.

Sister Petra's words rose to her mind. *The Nikara are a particularly herdlike nation. You listen well, but independent thought is difficult for you. Your brains, which we know to be an indicator of your rational capacity, are by nature smaller.*

"Look," Jiang murmured. "They've started bringing their women."

Rin followed his gaze and saw a tall, wheat-haired woman stepping out of the horseless carriage, her waist enveloped in massive bunches of ruffled fabric. She stretched out a gloved hand. A

Nikara foot servant ran up to help her off, then stooped to pick up her bags.

Rin couldn't stop staring at the woman's skirts, which arced out from her waist in the unnatural shape of an overturned teacup. "Are they—"

"Wooden frame," Jiang said, anticipating her confusion. "Don't fret, it's still legs underneath. They think it's fashionable."

"*Why?*"

Jiang shrugged. "Beyond me."

Before now, Rin had never seen regular Hesperian civilians—Hesperians who were not soldiers, nor part of the Gray Company. Hesperians who purportedly had no official business in Nikan other than to keep their husbands company. Now they strolled the New City's streets as if they belonged.

She shuddered to think of what that meant. If the Hesperians were shipping in their wives, it meant they intended to stay.

A sudden sharp prickle stung her left shin. She dropped to her knee and tugged her pant leg up, hoping fervently that the pain would continue.

For a few seconds she felt nothing. Then came another stab of pain so sharp she felt as if a needle had pierced all the way through her flesh and emerged out the other side. She uttered a quiet moan of relief.

"What's wrong?" Daji asked sharply.

"It's Kitay," Rin whispered. "He's writing back, look—"

"Not here," Daji hissed. She yanked Rin up by the arm and pulled her down the street. Pain continued to lance up Rin's left leg, the agony intensifying by the second.

Kitay likely didn't have access to a sharp, clean blade. He was probably carving his flesh with a nail, a piece of scrap wood, or the jagged edge of a shattered vase. Perhaps he was using his own fingernails to carve out the long, jagged strokes that dragged in sharp twists down the length of her shin, creating scars she couldn't wait to see.

It didn't matter how badly it hurt. This felt *good*. Every stab was proof that Kitay was here, he'd heard her, and he was writing back.

At last they reached an empty street corner. Daji let go of Rin's arm. "What does it say?"

Rin rolled her pant leg up to the knee. Kitay had written four characters, engraved in pale white lines along her inner calf.

"Three, six," Rin said. "Northeast."

"Coordinates," Jiang guessed. "Has to be. The intersection of the third and sixth streets. That makes sense, this city's arranged like a grid."

"Then which one's the vertical coordinate?" Daji asked.

Rin thought for a moment. "How do you read wikki positions?"

"The board game?" Jiang thought for a moment. "Vertical first, then horizontal, origin point in the southwest. Does he—"

"Yes," Rin said. "He loves it." Kitay was wild about the strategy game. He'd always tried to get other students to play with him at Sinegard, but no one ever would. Losing to Kitay was too annoying; he kept lecturing you on all your strategic missteps as he cleaned your pieces off the board. "Third street north. Sixth street east."

None of them could place themselves in relation to the grid, so they had to first find the southwest corner of the city, then count the blocks as they moved northeast. It took them the better part of the hour. All the while Jiang complained under his breath, "Stupid directions, that boy; there are four sides of an intersection, he could be in any one of them, should have included a *description*."

But they didn't need one. When Rin turned the corner toward the sixth street, Kitay's location became obvious.

A massive building dominated the block in front of them. Unlike the other buildings, which were Hesperian scaffolds built over Nikara foundations, this had clearly been constructed from scratch. The red bricks gleamed. Stained-glass windows stretched along every wall, depicting various insignia—scrolls, scales, and ladders.

At the center was a symbol Rin knew too well: an intricate circle inscribed with the pattern of a timepiece, complicated gears interlocking in a symmetrical pattern. The symbol of the Gray Company. The Architect's perfect design.

Jiang whistled. "Well, that's not a prison."

"It's worse," Rin said. "That's a church."

CHAPTER 15

"This is easy enough," Jiang said. They stood huddled against the wall of a tea shop across the street, eyeing the church's thick double doors. "We'll just kill and impersonate one of those missionary fellows. Drag them into a corner, strip off their cassock—"

"You can't do that," Rin said. "You're Nikara. All the Gray Company are Hesperians."

"Hmm." Jiang rubbed his chin. "A devastatingly good point."

"Servant's entrance, then?" Daji suggested. "They've always got some Nikara on hand to sweep their floors, and I can talk them down until you've found Kitay."

"Too risky," Jiang said. "We don't know how many there are, and we need to buy more than five minutes to search."

"So I'll ask them what I need, then stick them with needles."

Jiang reached out to tuck a lock of hair behind her ear. "Darling, people pay you less attention when you don't leave a trail of bodies in your wake."

Daji rolled her eyes.

Rin glanced back toward the church. Then the solution struck her—it was so blindingly obvious, she almost laughed.

"We don't have to do any of that." She pointed to the line of

Nikara civilians stretching out the front of the building. As if on cue, the heavy double doors swung open, and a brother of the Gray Company stepped outside, hands stretched wide in welcome to the congregation. "We can just walk right in."

They shuffled into the church with their heads bowed, following obediently behind the rest of the crowd in a single-file line. Rin tensed as they passed the gray-cassocked priest standing at the doors, but all he did was place a hand on her shoulder and murmur low words of greeting as he welcomed her inside, just as he had every person in line before her. He never even glanced at her face.

The church interior was a single wide room with high beams, crammed with low benches arranged in neat double columns. Sunlight streaming through the stained glass windows cast colorful, oddly beautiful splotches onto the smooth wooden floor. At the front stood a podium on a raised platform where half a dozen gray-robed Hesperians stood waiting, watching imperiously as the Nikara took their seats.

Rin glanced about the room, trying to find doors that might lead to hidden chambers or passageways.

"There." Jiang nodded across to the other end of the hall, where Rin glimpsed a door tucked behind a curtain. A single priest stood in front of it; a circle of keys hung visibly from his belt.

"Wait here." Daji broke from the line and strode confidently across the room. The priest's eyes widened in confusion as she approached, but lost focus as Daji began to speak. Seconds later, the priest passed the keys into Daji's hands, opened the door, and then walked off in the other direction.

Daji turned over her shoulder and waved impatiently for Rin to join her.

"Go." She pushed the keys into Rin's palm. "These open the cell doors. You should be clear for an hour and a half, and then you can join the crowd as they leave."

"But aren't you—"

"We'll cover your exits from up here." Daji pushed Rin toward the door. "Be quick."

The Nikara had nearly finished filing into their seats; only a handful of people were still standing. Daji hurried back to Jiang's side, and together they sat down in the very back row.

Rin almost laughed at the absurdity. She'd come to the New City with two of the most powerful shamans in Nikara history, beings from myths and legends, and here they were paying obeisance to a false god.

A great screech echoed through the hall as the double doors swung closed, trapping them inside. Heart pounding, Rin slipped through the door and hastened down the stairs.

Behind the door lay a winding staircase that emptied out into a dark hallway. Rin pulled a small flame in her hand and held it before her like a torch. They were right—this whole basement had been converted into a prison, cells lining either side of the passageway. Rin shielded her face as she walked, glancing to either side to check for Kitay. She needn't have bothered. The prisoners were hardly alert. Most were slumped in the corners of their cells, either sleeping or staring into space. A few were moaning quietly, but none gave any indication they'd even noticed her.

How quaint, Rin thought. It made sense that the Hesperians would keep their sinners and believers under the same roof. The Gray Company liked their symmetry. The Divine Architect rallying against Chaos. Light against dark. Worshippers on the top, and sinners on the bottom, the unseen side of the ruthless, unsparing quest from barbarism toward a well-ordered civilization.

Kitay's cell was at the end of the next corridor. She knew right as she turned the corner. All she saw by her faint flame was the curve of his shoulder and the silhouette of his head, turned away from the bars. But she knew. Her whole body thrummed with longing anticipation, like a magnet straining for its opposite. She *knew*.

She broke into a run.

He was asleep when she reached his cell, curled up on a cot with his knees drawn up to his chest. He looked so small. His left pant leg was soaked through with blood.

Rin fumbled clumsily with the keys, trying several before she found the one that fit the lock. She yanked hard at the door. It scraped open with a loud metallic screech that echoed down the corridor.

Kitay gave a start and jerked to a sitting position, fists up as if ready to fight.

"It's me," she whispered.

He blinked blearily, as if unsure whether or not he was dreaming. "Oh, hello."

She rushed toward him.

They collided over his cot. He rose halfway to meet her, but she knocked him right back down, arms wrapped tightly around his skinny frame. She had to hold him, feel the weight of him, know that he was real and solid and there. The void in her chest, that aching sense of absence she'd felt since Tikany, finally melted away.

She felt like herself again. She felt whole.

"Took you long enough," he murmured into her shoulder.

"Could you tell I was coming?"

"Sensed you yesterday." He drew back, grinning. "I woke up, and it felt like I'd been doused with cold water. Never been happier."

He looked better than she'd feared. He was thin, of course, but he'd been painfully thin since Ruijin, and his cheekbones protruded no more than they already had. His arms and legs were unbound save for an iron cuff around his left ankle, attached to a chain with enough slack to give him free movement around the cell. He didn't look like he'd been tortured. There were no cuts, welts, or bruises on his pale skin. The only wounds he'd suffered recently were the gashes he'd opened in his shin.

His index finger was crusted over in dried blood. He'd done it with his nail.

She reached for his leg. "Are you—"

"It's fine. It's stopped bleeding, I'll clean it up later." Kitay stood up. "Who are you here with?"

"Two-thirds of the Trifecta."

He didn't miss a beat. "Which two?"

"The Vipress and the Gatekeeper."

"Of course. And when are we meeting the Dragon Emperor?"

"We'll discuss that later." She jangled the keys at him. "Let's get you out first. Padlocks?"

He shook his ankle at her, looking impressed. "How did you—"

"Daji is persuasive." She held a flame up to the lock and began flipping through the keys to find one that looked like it matched. "No more bone smashing for us."

He snorted. "Thank the gods."

She'd just found a silver key that looked about the right size when she heard the unmistakable screech of a door sliding open, followed by a faint patter of footsteps echoing through the corridor. She froze. Daji had promised her more than an hour; she'd been planning to hide out downstairs until whatever ritual was going on in the main chamber had ended. Had something gone wrong upstairs?

"Hide," Kitay hissed.

"Where?"

He pointed to his cot. Rin didn't see how that could possibly work—it was a flimsy, narrow structure, barely two feet wide, with crossed wooden legs that wouldn't conceal a rabbit.

"Get under this." Kitay tugged at his blanket. The cotton sheet was thin but solidly opaque; hanging off the edge of the bed, it was just long enough to stretch to the floor.

Rin crawled underneath the cot and shrank in on herself, fighting to make her breathing inaudible. She heard the lock click back into place as Kitay pushed the cell door shut.

She poked her head out from the blankets, confused. "Wait, why don't we just—"

"Shh," he whispered. "I said *hide*."

Footsteps grew louder and louder in the corridor, then stopped just outside the cell.

"Hello, Kitay."

Rin dug her nails into her palm, madly clenching her teeth in an attempt to keep quiet. She knew only one person who could speak with that precise mixture of confidence, condescension, and feigned camaraderie.

"Good evening." Kitay's tone was all light, cheery indifference. "Good timing. I've just taken my nap."

The door screeched open. Rin hardly dared to breathe.

If he made any moves toward the cot, she'd kill him. She held two advantages—the element of surprise and the fire. She wouldn't hesitate this time. First a torrent of flame to his face to startle and blind him, then four white-hot fingers in a claw around his neck. She'd rip out his artery before he even realized what was happening.

"How have you been?" Nezha was standing right above her. "Accommodations still adequate?"

"I'd like some new books," Kitay said. "And my reading lamps are running low."

"I'll see to that."

"Thank you," Kitay said stiffly. "And how is the lab rat life?"

"Don't be a prick, Kitay."

"My apologies," Kitay drawled. "You were just so quick to send Rin to the same fate, I'm always stunned by the irony."

"Listen, asshole—"

"Why do you let them do it?" Kitay asked. "I'm just curious. Certainly you don't *enjoy* getting hurt."

"It doesn't hurt," Nezha said quietly. "It's the only time it doesn't hurt."

There was a pause, which stretched into a longer, more awkward silence.

"I take it the council's still giving you grief?" Kitay finally asked.

She heard a shuffling noise. Nezha was sitting down. "They're madmen. All of them."

Kitay chuckled. "At least we agree about something."

Rin was astonished by how quickly they settled into amiable chitchat. No—*amiable* wasn't quite the right word; they sounded far from friendly. But they also didn't sound like a prisoner and his interrogator. They sounded like second-year students at Sinegard complaining about Jima's sentence-diagramming homework. They were old acquaintances taking their seats at a wikki board, resuming a game right where they'd left off.

But was this really so surprising? Nostalgia gnawed Rin's chest at the mere sound of Nezha's voice. She wanted this familiarity with him back, too. Never mind that thirty seconds ago she'd been ready to kill him. His voice, his very *presence*, made her heart ache—she wished desperately they could be caught in a stalemate, that for just one minute the wars surrounding them could be suspended, so that they might speak like friends again. Just once.

"Our northern allies won't commit further troops to Arabak until they get relief," Nezha said. "They think I'm rolling in silver, that I'm just withholding it—but damn it, Kitay, they don't understand. The coffers are empty."

"And where's the money gone?" Kitay asked.

He said it lightly, but he'd clearly meant to strike a nerve. Nezha's tone turned sharp. "Don't you dare accuse—"

"You're getting far too much aid from the Hesperians for your army to be so poorly outfitted. Someone's bleeding you dry. Come on, Nezha, we've been over this already. Get your house in order."

"You're making baseless accusations—"

"I'm just telling you what's right in front of you," Kitay said. "You know I'm right. You wouldn't keep coming here if you didn't think I could be useful."

"Say something useful, then." Nezha sounded so nasally petty then, so much like how he'd sounded their first year at Sinegard, that Rin almost laughed.

"I've been telling you things so obvious a child could see them," Kitay said. "Your generals are siphoning away funds meant for relief—probably squirreling them away to their summer palaces, so that's the first place you'll want to check. That's the problem with all that Hesperian silver. Your entire base has gotten corrupted. You might start with cutting down on the bribes."

"But you have to bribe them to keep them on your side," Nezha said, frustrated. "Otherwise they won't present a united front, and if we don't have a united front then the Hesperians just run roughshod over us like our government doesn't even exist."

"Poor Nezha," Kitay said. "They've tied your hands behind your back, haven't they?"

"This is all so fucking stupid. I need unified army command. I need freedom to put absolute priority on the southern front, and I want to divert forces from the north to deal with Rin without making all these compromises. I just don't know *why*—"

"I know why. You're not the grand marshal, you're the *Young* Marshal. That's your nickname, right? The generals and the Hesperians both think you're just a spoiled, stupid princeling who doesn't know what he's doing. They think you're just like Jinzha. And they wouldn't put you in charge of their dirigibles if you sank to your knees and begged."

Rin didn't know what surprised her most—Kitay's frankness, that Nezha hadn't yet punished him for it, or that anything Kitay was saying might be *true*.

None of this made sense. She had assumed Nezha was wallowing in power. That he had the entire dirigible fleet at his disposal. He'd seemed so dominant when he'd descended on Tikany, she'd thought he had the entire Republic at his back.

But this was her first indication that Nezha was not holding together as well as she'd thought. Here, alone in the basement with his old classmate and prisoner, perhaps the only person he could be honest with, Nezha just sounded scared.

"I'm guessing things haven't gotten better with Tarcquet, either," Kitay said.

"He's a patronizing fuck," Nezha snarled. "You know what he's blamed the last campaign on? Our lack of fighting spirit. He said that the Nikara inherently *don't have fighting spirit*."

"A rather bold claim given our history, I think."

Nezha didn't laugh. "There's nothing wrong with our troops. They're incredibly well trained, they're excellent on the field, but the problem is the restructuring and integrated forces—"

"The what now?"

"Another one of Tarcquet's ideas." Nezha spat the name like it was poison. "They want coordinated air and ground assault teams."

"Interesting," Kitay said. "I'd have thought they were too up their own asses for that."

"It's not real integration. It means they want us to lug their coal wagons for them wherever they decide to go. Means we're just their fucking mules—"

"There are worse roles to play on the battlefront."

"Not if we're ever going to earn their respect."

"I think we both know your chances of winning Hesperian respect sailed a long time ago," Kitay said lightly. "So who are you dropping bombs on next? Has Boar Province capitulated?"

A tinge of exasperation crept into Nezha's voice. "If you'd agree to help with planning, I could tell you."

Kitay sighed. "Alas, I'm not that desperate to leave this cell."

"No, you seem to like captivity."

"I like knowing that the words out of my mouth won't cause the deaths of people I've become quite fond of. It's this thing called ethics. You might try it sometime."

"No one has to die," Nezha said. "No one ever had to die. But Rin's suckered those fools into waging everything on an all-or-nothing outcome."

Rin flinched at the sound of her name from his mouth this time. He said it with such violence.

"Rin's not behind this," Kitay said cautiously. "Rin's dead."

"Bullshit. The whole country would be talking if she were gone."

"Oh, you think that your lovely airships managed to miss her?"

"She can't be dead," Nezha insisted. "She's just in hiding, she has to be. They never found a body, and the south wouldn't be fighting this hard if they knew she was gone. She's the only thing they're rallying around. Without her they have no hope. They would have surrendered."

Rin heard a rustle of clothing. Kitay might have been shrugging.

"I suppose you know better than me."

Another silence filled the cell. Rin lay utterly still, her heartbeat ringing so loudly she was amazed she had not been discovered.

"I didn't want this war," Nezha said at last. His voice sounded oddly brittle—defensive, even. Rin didn't know what to make of it. "I never did. Why couldn't she understand that?"

"Well, you did put a blade in her back."

"I didn't want things to be like this."

"Oh, gods, let's not go down this road again."

"We'd let her have the south if she'd just come to the table. Gods know we're grateful she got rid of the Mugenese for us. And she's a good soldier. The very best. We'd happily have her back on our side; we'd make her a general in a heartbeat—"

"You seem to have mistaken me for a dullard," Kitay said.

"It's a tragedy we're on different sides, Kitay. You know that. We would have been so good united, all three of us."

"We *were* united. And we *were* good. Your father had other plans."

"We can come back from this," Nezha insisted. "Yes, we've messed up—I've messed up, I'll admit that—but think about what the Republic could accomplish, if we really fought to make it work. You're too smart to ignore its potential—"

"You're still on about that shit? Please don't patronize me, Nezha."

"Help me," Nezha begged. "Together we could end this whole thing in weeks, regardless of whether Rin is dead or alive. You're the smartest person I've ever met. If you had access to our resources—"

"See, it's hard to take you seriously when you do things like drop bombs on innocent children."

"That ambush was a mistake—"

"Sleeping in past roll call is a mistake," Kitay snapped. "Neglecting to deliver my meals on time was a *mistake*. What you did was cold-hearted murder. And Rin and I know that if we join you, it'll happen again, because we and the south are utterly disposable to you. You and your father think we are tools to be traded or thrown away at your convenience, which is precisely what you did."

"I didn't have a choice—"

"You had a thousand choices. You drew the lines at Arlong. You started this war, and it's not my fault if you haven't got the balls to finish it. So tell Vaisra he might as well lop my head off, because then he could at least use it for decoration."

Nezha said nothing. Rin heard a rustle of cloth as he stood. He was leaving; his footsteps sounded hard and angry against the stone. She wished she could see his face. She hoped he might give some rejoinder, any kind of reaction, just so she would know if Kitay had rattled him or not. But she heard only the screech as he pushed the door shut behind him, and then the click of the lock.

"Sorry I didn't have time to warn you." Kitay pulled the blanket off the cot and helped Rin to her feet. "Just thought you should hear."

She passed him the keys. "How long has he been at it?"

"Every day since I got here. He was actually on pretty good behavior today; you didn't get to see him at his worst. He's tried a million different things to break me." Kitay bent over to unlock his shackles. "But he should have remembered he never figured out how. Not at Sinegard, and certainly not now."

Rin felt an aching burst of pride. She forgot sometimes how resilient Kitay could be. One would never have suspected it by looking at him—the archetypal reedy and anxious scholar—but he bore hardship with iron fortitude. Sinegard hadn't worn him down. Even Golyn Niis hadn't destroyed him. Nezha could never have broken him.

No, whispered the little voice in her head that sounded too much like Altan. *The only person capable of breaking him is you.*

"Behind you," Kitay said suddenly.

Rin twisted around, expecting a soldier. But it was just one of the Gray Company—a young man in a cassock, carrying a meal tray in his hands.

His mouth fell open when he saw her. His eyes flitted, confused, between her and Kitay, as if he was trying to determine the appropriate number of people for one cell. "You—"

Kitay twisted the key and jerked the cell door open.

Too late, the missionary turned to run. Rin dug her heels into the ground and chased him down. His legs were much longer than hers, and he might have gotten away, but he tripped over his cassock just as he reached the corner. He stumbled—only for a split second, but that was enough. Rin grabbed his arm, yanked him further off balance, and kicked at the backs of his knees. He fell. She called the fire into her palm. It came back so quickly, so naturally, a well-worn glove slipping over waiting fingers.

She jammed her clawed hand onto his throat. Soft flesh gave way to her burning nails like tofu parting under steel. Easy. It was done in seconds. He went without so much as a whimper; she'd chosen his throat because she didn't want him to scream.

She straightened up, exhaled, and wiped her hand on the wall. The magnitude of what she'd just done hadn't hit her; it had happened so quickly, it didn't even seem real. She hadn't decided to kill the missionary; she hadn't even thought about it. She'd simply needed to protect Kitay. The rest was an instinct.

She felt a sudden, bizarre urge to laugh.

She cocked her head, observing the crimson streaks shining wet and bright on marble. For some reason, it gave her a dizzying rush of delight, the same confusing ecstasy she'd felt when she poisoned Ma Lien.

It wasn't about the violence.

It was about the *power*.

It wasn't as good as killing Nezha, but it felt close. For a wild, untethered moment, she considered dragging her bloody finger along the wall and drawing him a flower.

No. No. Too indulgent. She didn't have time. The wave of vertigo passed. She came back to her senses; she was in control.

Focus.

"Come here," she called down the corridor. "Help me drag him into your cell. We'll put him on the cot, cover him with a blanket—it'll buy some time."

Kitay wandered out two steps from his cell, keeled over, and vomited.

Their escape from the church proceeded with astonishing ease. Rin and Kitay waited by the door to the dungeons, listening against the wood to an ongoing Hesperian sermon, until they heard the Nikara civilians standing up from their pews. Then they opened it a crack and slid out to join the press of moving bodies, invisible in the crowd. Jiang and Daji rejoined them as they spilled out of the doors, but none of them spoke until they'd walked for several minutes down to the other end of the street.

"You've gotten taller," Jiang told Kitay once they'd turned the corner. "Good to see you again."

Kitay stared at him for a moment, as if unsure how to respond. "So you're the Gatekeeper."

"That's me."

"And you've been hiding in Sinegard all this time."

"Lost my mind for a bit," Jiang said. "Just starting to get it back now."

"Makes sense," Kitay said weakly.

All considered, Rin thought, he was taking this rather well.

"Questions later." Daji tossed Kitay a brown tunic, which was far less conspicuous than the tattered rags he'd been wearing since Tikany. "Put this on and let's go."

They left the New City in a horse-drawn laundry wagon. Its original driver had carried a gate permit to take infirmary linens to the river for washing; Daji had charmed him into relinquishing the wagon and permit both. While Daji drove the wagon confidently through the streets, Rin, Kitay, and Jiang hid under piles of linen stacked so tall they could hardly breathe. Rin squirmed, hot and itchy, trying not to think about the brown stains surrounding her. She felt the wagon stop only once. Rin heard Daji answering a guardsman's questions in very convincing pidgin Hesperian, and then they passed through the gates.

Daji kept driving. She didn't let them emerge from the linen piles until over an hour later, when the New City was nothing but a tiny outline behind them, until the sound of dirigibles had faded away and the only noise around them was the constant hum of cicadas.

Rin was relieved when the New City faded out of her sight. If she could help it, she never wanted to set foot in that place again.

That night, over a meal of dried shanyu root and a stolen loaf of thick, chewy Hesperian bread, Daji and Jiang interrogated Kitay for every shred of information he'd gleaned about the Republic. He had no solid details on troop placements or campaign plans—Nezha had fed him only enough information to seek his advice without creating a liability—but the little he did know was tremendously useful.

"They're in endgame now, but it's taking longer than it needs to," Kitay said. "Vaisra turned on the Southern Coalition the moment they failed to produce your body, as you would have expected. But the Monkey Warlord—well, really it's probably Souji's work—rallied a surprisingly strong defense. They learned pretty quickly to create decent bomb shelters. Once he realized the airships weren't getting the job done, Vaisra sent in ground forces. The south have beaten a retreat back to the corner of Boar Province for now. They've holed up under the mountains and forced a standstill for weeks, hence why everyone's centered in Arabak."

"The New City," Rin amended.

He shook his head. "It's still Arabak. No one here calls it the New City but the Hesperians, or Nikara in Hesperian company."

"So the holdup is just a consequence of the terrain?" Daji

asked. "What about the Young Marshal? Word on the street is he's falling apart."

Rin shot her a surprised look. "Where'd you hear that?"

"A pair of old women were gossiping in the pew behind us," Daji said. "They said if Yin Jinzha were in charge then all the southern rebels would have been exterminated months ago."

"Jinzha?" Jiang frowned, digging his little finger into his ear. "The older Yin brat?"

"Yes," Daji said.

"I think I taught him at Sinegard. Utter asshole. Whatever happened to him?"

"He got plucky," Daji said. "I turned him to mincemeat and sent him back to Vaisra in a dumpling basket."

Jiang arched an eyebrow. "Darling, fucking *what*?"

"Nezha's exhausted." Kitay quickly returned to the subject. "It's not entirely his fault. His Hesperian advisers keep making insane demands that he can't accommodate, and the Republican cabinet are pulling him in twenty different directions so that he doesn't even know which way to shatter."

"I don't get it," Rin said. "You'd still think he'd be faring better with his advantages."

"It's not so simple. This remains a war on multiple fronts. The Republic's pretty much conquered the north—Jun's dead, by the way; they flayed him alive on a dais a few weeks ago—but there are still a few provinces holding out."

"Really?" Rin perked up. That was the first piece of good news she'd heard in a long time. "Any provinces that are armed?"

"Ox Province is putting up the best resistance for now, but they'll all be dead in a few weeks," Kitay said. "They've got no organization. They're split into three factions that aren't communicating—which was their advantage for a while, actually, because Nezha never knew what the individual battalions were going to do next. But that's not a sustainable defense strategy. Nezha just needs to take care of them one by one.

"And then there's Dog Province, which has always been so peripheral to the Empire that no one's thought to care much about them. But that's made them value their autonomy. And they're even less likely to bow to Vaisra now that the Hesperians want to go in and turn the whole region into coal mines."

"How many men do they have?" Daji asked.

"They haven't needed men yet. The Republic hasn't even sent a delegate to negotiate. For now, they're not on Nezha's map." Kitay sighed. "But once they are, they're finished. They're too sparsely populated; they won't have nearly enough troops to survive the first wave of attacks."

"Then we should join them!" Rin exclaimed. "That's perfect—we break our troops out past the blockade, send a sentry ahead and then rendezvous with the Dog Warlord—"

"It's a bad guest that shows up unannounced," Daji said.

"Not if a third guest is holding a knife to the host's throat," Rin said.

"This analogy has lost me," Jiang said.

"It's not the worst idea," Kitay said. "Nezha was convinced that Souji and Gurubai intended to send to Dog Province for help. So it's the predictable option, but it's also our only option left. We need allies where we can get them. Divided, we're carrion."

Rin frowned at him. Something sounded off about Kitay's tone, though she couldn't quite put her finger on it. He didn't sound as sharp and engaged as he usually did at strategy councils. Instead, the words came out in a flat monotone, as if he were half-heartedly reciting a memorized test answer.

What had happened to him in Arabak? He hadn't been physically tortured, but he'd been alone with Nezha for weeks. Had he turned against her? Was he only pretending to be their ally now? The possibility made her shudder.

But Kitay couldn't conceal a lie like that. Their souls were bound. She'd feel it. At least, she *hoped* she'd feel it.

Why, then, was he speaking like a man who had already lost?

"Dog Province, then. Interesting." Jiang turned to Daji. "What do you say? The route to their capital takes us close to the Tianshan range, and it'd be nice to have ground cover for at least part of it."

"Fine." Daji shrugged. "But I don't see why we need the Southern Coalition for that."

"It's thousands of warm bodies."

"Thousands we have to drag along through the mountains. What's more, they sold her out." Daji jerked her chin toward Rin. "They deserve to be left behind."

"That's the leadership's fault. The masses are malleable, you know that."

"It'll be messy."

"I've just escaped from the stone mountain. Let me stretch a little, dear. Get some exercise. It's good for the mind."

"Fair enough." Daji sighed. "Dog Province it is."

"I'm sorry." Kitay looked between them. "Did I miss something?"

Rin shared his confusion. The exchange between Daji and Jiang had passed so quickly that she'd barely followed what was happening. The two often spoke in a shorthand peppered with allusions to their shared past, a code that had made Rin feel constantly like an outsider on their journey to Arabak. It was a regular reminder that no matter how much power she wielded, the Trifecta had decades of history behind them that she knew only as stories. They'd seen so much more. Done so much more.

"It's decided," Daji said. "We'll go get your army and take them north. Agreed?"

Kitay looked baffled. "But—what about the blockade?"

Jiang stretched his arms over his head, yawning. "Oh, we'll break them out."

Kitay blinked at him. "But how are you going to do that?"

Daji chuckled. Jiang gave him a bemused look, as if surprised that Kitay had even asked.

"I'm the Gatekeeper," he said simply, as if that fact were answer enough.

The night was comfortably warm, so they doused the campfire after they'd eaten and slept on the wagon in shifts. Kitay volunteered to take first watch. Rin hadn't rested since sunrise—she was bone-tired, temples still throbbing from the sensory shock of the New City—but she put off sleep for several minutes so she could sit beside him. She wanted these few minutes with him alone.

"I'm glad you're here," she said. Shallow words and a shallow sentiment that didn't come close to expressing how she felt.

But Kitay just nodded. He understood.

She felt a spark of warmth from every point of contact between them—her hand lying against his, his arm curved around her waist, her head nestled between his chin and shoulder. She craved the feeling of his skin against hers. Every touch was a reassurance that he was real, he was alive, and he was *here*.

She shifted against him. "What's on your mind?"

"Nothing." He still spoke in that flat, wan tone. "I'm just tired."

"Don't lie to me." She wanted everything laid out in the open. She couldn't stand another moment of Kitay's strange resignation; she couldn't bear thinking there was a part of him that she didn't understand. "What's bothering you?"

He was silent for a long moment before he spoke. "It's just . . . I don't know, Rin. Arabak was—"

"It's awful."

"It's not necessarily awful, it's just strange. And I was there for so long, and now I'm out, I still can't stop thinking about the Hesperians."

"What about them?"

"I don't know, I just . . ." His fingers fidgeted in his lap; he was clearly struggling with how much he wanted to tell her. Nothing could have prepared her for what he said next. "Do you think they might just be *better* than us?"

"Kitay." She twisted around to stare at him. "What the *fuck* does that mean?"

"When Nezha first brought me into Arabak, he spent the first two days giving me a tour of the city," he said. "Showing me everything that they'd built in just a few weeks. Do you remember how insufferable he was when we first got to Arlong? Couldn't stop jabbering about this naval innovation and that. But this time, everything I saw really was a marvel. Everywhere I looked I saw things that I never dreamed could exist."

She folded her arms against her chest. "So what?"

"So how did they build them? How did they create objects that defy every known law of the natural world? Their knowledge of so many fields—mathematics, physics, mechanics, engineering—eclipses ours to a terrifying degree. Everything we're discovering at Yuelu Mountain, they must have known already for centuries." His fingers twisted in his lap. "Why? What do they have that we don't have?"

"I don't know," she said. "But it doesn't mean they're just naturally *better*, whatever the fuck that means—"

"But could it? Every member of the Gray Company I've met believes that they are just innately, biologically superior to us. And they don't say this to be cruel or condescending. They see it as fact. A scientific fact, as simple as the fact that the ocean is salty and that the sun rises every morning." His fingers wouldn't stop twisting. Rin had the sudden impulse to slap them. "They see human evolution as a ladder, and they're at its top, or at least as far as it can reach for now. And we—the Nikara—are clinging on to the lower rungs. Closer to animals than human."

"That's bullshit."

"Is it? They built dirigibles. Not only can they fly, they've been flying for *decades*, and here we are with only a rudimentary knowledge of seafaring because we bombed our own navies to bits in civil wars over nothing. Why?"

Dread twisted Rin's stomach. She didn't want to hear these words from Kitay's mouth. This felt worse than betrayal. This felt like discovering her best friend was an utter stranger.

She would be lying if she said she'd never asked these questions herself. Of course she had. She'd asked them during all those weeks she'd spent undergoing examinations in Sister Petra's cabin, putting her naked, helpless body at the Hesperian's disposal, letting her take measurements and write them down while explaining in a cold, matter-of-fact tone that Rin's brain was smaller, her stature was shorter, and her eyes saw less because of her race.

Of course she'd wondered, often, whether the Hesperians were right. But she hated how Kitay spoke as if he'd already decided they were.

"They could be horribly wrong about us," he said. "But they're right about almost everything else; they couldn't have built all that if they weren't. Look at a city they threw up in weeks. Compare that to the finest cities in the Empire. Can't you at least see where I'm coming from?"

Rin thought of the New City's spotless streets, its neat gridlike layout, and its quick, efficient modes of transportation. The Nikara had never built something like that. Even in Sinegard, the Red Emperor's capital and the crown jewel of the Empire, sewage had rushed freely down the streets like rainwater.

"Maybe it's their Maker." She tried to inject some levity into her voice. He was tired, she was tired; perhaps by morning, after they'd slept, this entire conversation would seem like a joke. "Maybe those prayers are working."

He didn't smile. "It's not their religion. Perhaps that's related—the Divine Architect is certainly more friendly to scientific research than any of our gods are. But I don't think they need deities at all. They have machines, and that's perhaps more powerful than anything they could summon. They rewrite the script of the world, just like you do. And they don't need to sacrifice their sanity to do it."

Rin had no rebuttal to that.

Jiang would have an answer. Jiang, who was so sure that the Pantheon lay at the center of the universe, had warned her once against treating the material world like a thing to be mechanized, dominated, and militarized. He'd believed firmly that the Hesperian and Mugenese societies had long ago forgotten their essential oneness with universal being, and were spiritually lost as a result.

But Rin had never been interested in cosmology or theology. She'd only been interested in the gods for what power they could give her, and she couldn't formulate what little she remembered of Jiang's ramblings into any sort of valid objection.

"So what?" she asked finally. "So what does that mean for us?"

She already knew Kitay's conclusion. She just wanted to hear him say it out loud, to see if he would dare. Because the logical conclusion was terrifying. If they were so deeply separated by race, if the Hesperians were innately more intelligent, more capable, and more powerful—then what was the point of resistance? Why shouldn't the world be theirs?

He hesitated. "Rin, I just think—"

"You think we should just surrender," she accused. "That we'd be better off under their rule."

"I don't," he said. "But I do think it might be inevitable."

"It's not inevitable. Nothing ever is." Rin pointed toward the wagon, where Jiang and Daji lay asleep. "They were children in the occupied north. They didn't have arquebuses or airships, and they expelled the Hesperians and united the Empire—"

"And they lost it just two decades later. Our odds aren't looking much better the second time around."

"We'll be stronger this time."

"You know that's not true, Rin. As a country, as a people, we're weaker than we've ever been. If we beat them, it will be due to a massive stroke of good fortune, and it will come at a great cost to human life. So don't blame me for wondering whether it's worth the struggle."

"Do you know what Sinegard was like for me?" she asked suddenly.

He frowned. "Why does that—"

"No, listen. Do you know what it was like to be the country idiot who everyone thought was barely literate because my tongue was flat, my skin was dark, and I didn't know that you're supposed to bow to the master at the end of every class?"

"I'm not saying—"

"I thought there was something inherently wrong with me," she said. "That I was just born uglier, weaker, and less intelligent than everyone around me. I thought that, because that's what everyone told me. And you're arguing that means I had no right to defy them."

"That's not what I meant."

"But it's analogous. If the Hesperians are so *innately better*, then the next rung on the ladder is pale-skinned northerners like you, and the Speerlies are sitting on the bottom." She was burning a handprint into the grass they were sitting on; smoke wafted around them. "And then, by your logic, it's fine that the Empire turned us into slaves. It's fine that they wiped us off the map, and that the official histories mention us only in footnotes. It's only natural."

"You know I'd never argue that," Kitay said.

"That's the implication of your logic," she said. "And I won't accept that. I can't."

"But that doesn't matter." He drew his knees up to his chest. He looked so small then, a much diminished version of the Kitay she'd always known. "Don't you get it? There is still no foreseeable path that leads to our victory. What do you think is going to happen after we get to Dog Province? You can hide from the airships for a little bit, but how the fuck are you going to defeat it?"

"Simple," she said. "We've got a plan."

He gave a shaky, helpless laugh. "Let's hear it, then."

"We've got a problem of power asymmetry now," she said.

"Which means we only win if this war occurs in three phases. The first is a strategic retreat. That's what is happening now, intentionally or not. Second is the long stalemate. Then, at last, the counteroffensive."

He sighed. "And how are you going to launch this counteroffensive? You have maybe a tenth of their ranged capabilities."

"That's fine. We have gods."

"You can't win this war with just a handful of shamans."

"I beat the Federation on my own, didn't I?"

"Well, barring *genocide*—"

"We can beat them with shamanism constrained to armed combatants on the battlefield," she insisted. "The same way we've been hunting down the Mugenese now."

"Maybe. But it's just you and Jiang and the Vipress, that's not nearly—"

"Enough?" She lifted her chin. "What if there were more?"

"Don't you dare open the Chuluu Korikh," Kitay said.

"No." She shuddered at the thought of that place. "We won't go back to that mountain. But Jiang and Daji want to march north. Up to Mount Tianshan."

"So I heard." He eyed her skeptically. "What's in Mount Tianshan?"

"Come on, Kitay. You can figure this out."

His gaze wandered over toward the Trifecta. She saw his eyes widen as the pieces clicked in his mind.

"You're crazy," he said.

"Probably."

His mouth worked for several seconds before he got the words out. "But—the stories—I mean, the Dragon Emperor's dead."

"The Dragon Emperor's sleeping," Rin said. "And he's been asleep for a very long time. But the Seal is eroding. Jiang's remembering who he was, what he once could do, which means Riga is about to wake up. And once he does, once we've reunited the Trifecta, then we'll show Hesperia what true divinity looks like."

CHAPTER 16

The battlefront under the Baolei Mountains was a conundrum.

The valleys were silent. Dirigibles weren't buzzing, swords weren't clashing, and the air wasn't thick with the acrid burn of fire powder. Rin neither saw nor heard any signs of active combat, at least not for the seven days it took for their party to reach the front lines.

Only when they drew closer did she realize why. The Southern Coalition was trapped. The Republic had pinned them against the mountainside behind a series of makeshift forts, each planted half a mile within the other, surrounded by lines of cannons and mounted arquebuses prepared to mow down any who tried to break out of the impasse. The forts were temporary constructions but they looked brick solid, supported by piles of sandbags, their stone walls impenetrable save for tiny slits just large enough for the firing end of an arquebus. Archery was certainly futile against those forts, and Rin suspected that rudimentary cannons of the type the Southern Coalition possessed would barely make a dent, either.

But the Republic also couldn't penetrate the mountainside. The ravines and caves along the southern Baolei range functioned as natural bomb shelters, which meant sustained dirigible attacks would only be a waste of ammunition. The underground terrain couldn't be mapped from the air, which gave the southerners a significant defensive advantage. This, Rin assumed, was the only reason the Republic hadn't yet mounted a ground assault.

The Southern Coalition didn't have the manpower to break out. The Republic didn't want to bleed the forces necessary to break in. For now, both sides remained holed up in their respective stations. But this standoff would end, as all sieges did, the moment the southerners finally ran out of food and water.

"Your old classmate is unfortunately very good at siege warfare," Daji said. They had spent the morning circling the blockade perimeter in the laundry wagon, searching for a way to sneak past Republican lines unnoticed. "He's got them fenced in at every critical juncture. No easy way to slip past those pillboxes unless we make a scene."

"I think a scene is exactly what we want," Rin said.

"No, that's what you want when you break *out*," Kitay pointed out. "But we've got to get inside and rally the forces first. We don't know what condition they're in. Making a scene puts a hard time limit on how long it takes the southerners to mobilize."

So the question remained: How did one sneak past the greatest assembly of military power ever seen on the continent?

"We could swim in," Kitay suggested after a pause. "I think I saw a stream a mile back."

"They'd shoot us in the water," Rin said.

"They're guarding the river flows leading out," Kitay pointed out. "They don't care so much about people sneaking in. We get some bamboo reeds, swim down in the bottom layers where it's muddy—best to do it when it's raining, too; that'll maximize our water cover."

He glanced around the wagon. Daji shrugged, silent.

"So we'll swim," Rin said, since it didn't appear anyone had a better plan. "What next?"

"You need to go through the old mining tunnels." Rin was

startled when Jiang spoke up. He'd been silent all morning, gazing placidly around the battlefront like he was touring a botanical garden. Now suddenly his gaze was focused, his voice firm and assured. "You won't be underground for long. Just until you emerge on the other side into the forests. It's not a perfect exit route—those tunnels aren't well lit, and quite a few people are probably going to fall down the pits and break their necks. But there's no other route that keeps you safe from the dirigibles."

Once again, his switch in demeanor was so abrupt that Rin couldn't help but stare. Jiang was acting like a seasoned general, casually spinning together pieces of a strategy like someone who'd planned ambushes like this a hundred times before. This wasn't him. This was a stranger.

"The real challenge is getting the southerners to follow you out," he continued. "You'll have to be discreet about it. If Souji tried selling you to Vaisra once, he might do so again. Is there anyone in the coalition you still trust?"

"Venka," Rin said immediately. "Qinen, too, probably, if he's still alive. We could try to swing Zhuden's officers, but they'll take convincing."

"Can Venka mobilize at least half the army?" Daji asked.

Rin considered that for a moment. She didn't know how much sway Venka held. Venka wasn't terribly popular among the southerners; she was by nature curt and abrasive, a pale-skinned northerner with a harsh Sinegardian accent who clearly didn't belong. But she could be charming when she wanted to be. She might have managed to talk her way out of any suspected ties to Rin. Or Souji might have had her killed long ago.

Rin decided to be optimistic. "Probably. We can get her to scare up a crowd, and once the battle's started, the rest should follow."

"I suppose we can't do better than that." Jiang pointed to Rin and Kitay. "You two go in first and find your people. Round up as many of them as you can within the next twenty-four hours, and tell them to press hard to the west-facing mines when we break through the front lines. If you have to break cover before then, just send up a flare and we'll break the front early."

"There are at least two thousand Republican troops on the front," Kitay said.

Jiang surveyed the forts for a moment, and then shook his head. "Oh, no. Double that, at least."

Kitay furrowed his brows. "Then how are you going to . . . ?"

"I said we'll break the front," Jiang said very calmly.

Kitay blinked at him, clearly at a loss for words.

"Just trust him," Rin muttered.

She thought back to memories of howling screeches, shapes of darkness furling out of nowhere. She thought of Tseveri's stricken face as Jiang's clawed fingers went into her rib cage.

She didn't trust this newly confident, capable Jiang. She had no idea who he was, or what he could do. But she feared him, which meant the Republic should, too.

"Fine." Kitay still looked baffled, but he didn't push the point. "What's your signal, then?"

Jiang just chuckled. "Oh, I think you'll know."

"You're shitting me," Venka said.

She looked terrible. She'd lost a startling amount of weight. She was wrung out, rangier, sharp cheekbones jutting beneath hollow, purple-ringed eyes.

She hadn't been easy to find. Rin and Kitay had climbed out of the river into what looked like a long-deserted army camp. The sentry posts nearest them were unmanned; the few sandbags visible were scattered uselessly across the dirt. Rin would have assumed the Southern Coalition had already fled, except that the charred logs near the mountainside were evidence of freshly doused campfires, and the latrine dugouts stank of fresh shit.

The entire army, it appeared, had gone underground.

Rin and Kitay had ventured into the tunnels, ambushed the first soldier they encountered, and demanded he lead them to

Venka. He sat tamely now in the corner of the dimly lit room, gagged with rope, eyes darting back and forth in equal parts terror and confusion.

"Hello to you, too." Kitay headed for a pile of maps lying on the floor and began to rummage through them. "Are these up to date? Mind if I take a look?"

"Do whatever you want," Venka said faintly. She didn't even glance at him. Her eyes, still wide in disbelief, were fixed on Rin. "I thought they carted you to that mountain. Souji kept crowing on and on about that, said you were stuck in stone for good."

"Some old friends broke me out," Rin said. "Looks like you've been doing far worse."

"Gods, Rin, it's been a nightmare." Venka pressed her palms against her temples. "I honestly don't know what Souji's plan is at this point. I was starting to think we'd be buried here."

"So Souji's in charge?" Rin asked.

"He and Gurubai together." Venka looked abashed. "You, ah, might hear about some things I said. I mean, after Tikany, they were out for me, too, and I—"

"I'm sure you said whatever you needed to to get them off your back," Rin said. "I don't care about that. Just fill us in on what's happened."

Venka nodded. "The Republic launched a second assault a few days after the first air raid. Souji led us in a retreat north—the idea was to get back to Ruijin—but the Republic kept pushing us eastward, so we got trapped up against these mountains instead. We're calling this the Anvil, because they keep slamming up against us and we've got nowhere to run. I'm sure they'll be making their final push any day now; they know we're nearly out of supplies."

"I'm shocked you made it to the mountains at all." Kitay looked up from the maps. "How on earth did you hold them off this long?"

"It's their artillery's fault," Venka said. "They keep shooting themselves in the feet. Literally. Nezha's got his army outfitted with new Hesperian technology, but they don't know how to use it, and I guess they moved out before they were properly trained, so half the time they try to hit us they blow themselves up in the process."

No wonder Nezha had sounded so rattled when complaining about force integration. Rin couldn't help but grin.

"Something funny?" Venka asked.

"Nothing," Rin said. "It's just—remember that night on the tower, how Nezha kept bragging about how Hesperian technology was going to win the Empire for us?"

"Yes, they've had growing pains," Venka said drily. "Unfortunately, a misfired cannonball hurts just as bad."

Kitay held up a map and tapped at an arrow snaking south. "Is this how you were going to get them out? A hard press by the southern border?"

"That's what Souji's planning," Venka said. "It seemed like our best bet. Nezha doesn't have his own men on that border; it's under the domain of the new Ox Warlord. Bai Lin. There are massive tungsten deposits on the Monkey Province side of the border, and Gurubai's offered to mine it for him if he'll carve us an escape corridor."

"That won't work," Kitay said.

Venka gave him an exasperated look. "We've been planning this for weeks."

"Sure, but I know Bai Lin. He used to come over to our estate in Sinegard to play wikki with my parents all the time. The man hasn't got a backbone—Father used to call him the Empire's greatest brownnoser. There's no way he'll risk pissing Vaisra off. He'll let Nezha decimate you and send laborers in to mine the tungsten himself."

"Fine." Venka jutted her chin out. "You come up with something better, then."

Kitay tapped a northern point on the blockade. "We have to go through the old mining tunnels. They'll bring us out onto the other side of the Baolei range."

"We've tried those tunnels," Venka said. "They're blocked up."

"Then we'll blow a hole through the entrance," Kitay said.

Venka looked doubtful. "You'd need a lot of firepower."

"Oh dear," Rin drawled. "I wonder how we'll manage that."

Venka snorted. "None of the cave tunnels here lead to the mines. We'd still have to get through the dead zone, which is at least a mile long. Nezha's got half his infantry stationed right outside. We're working with two-thirds the numbers we had at Tikany, and we don't have an air defense. This can't work."

"It'll work," Kitay said. "We've got allies."

"Who?" Venka perked up. "How many?"

"Two," Rin said.

"You assholes—"

"Rin brought the Trifecta," Kitay clarified.

Venka squinted at them. "What, like the shadow puppets?"

"The original Trifecta," Rin said. "Two of them, at least. The Empress. Master Jiang. They're the Vipress and the Gatekeeper."

"Are you telling me," Venka said slowly, "that Lore Master Jiang, the man who kept a *drug garden* at Sinegard, is going to single-handedly spring us out of this blockade?"

Kitay scratched his chin. "Pretty much, yeah."

"He's only the most powerful shaman in Nikan," Rin said. "I mean, so we think. Word's still out on the Dragon Emperor."

Venka looked like she didn't know whether to laugh or cry. A vein twitched beneath her left eye. "The last time I saw Jiang he was trying to snip my hair off with garden shears."

"He's about the same now," Rin said. "But he can summon beasts that can wipe out entire platoons in seconds, if history is anything to go by, so we've got a bit more to work with."

"I don't—I just—you know what? Fine. Sure. This might as well be happening." Venka dragged her palms down her face and groaned. "Fucking hell, Rin. I wish you'd gotten here just a few days earlier. You picked a dreadful time to show up."

"Why's that?" Rin asked.

"Vaisra's making his tour to inspect the troops tomorrow."

"Tour?" Kitay repeated. "Vaisra doesn't command?"

"No, Nezha's in command. Vaisra stays behind at Arlong, rules over his new kingdom, and plays nice with the Hesperians."

Of course, Rin thought. Why would she have expected otherwise? Vaisra had fought the civil war from his throne room in Arlong, sending Rin out like an obedient hunting dog while he sat back and reaped the rewards. Vaisra never dirtied his own hands. He just turned people into weapons and then disposed of them.

"He comes out to Arabak every three weeks," Venka said. "Then he flies out here to conduct a troop appraisal right before he leaves. A rallying ceremony of sorts—it's insufferable. We've figured out the schedule because they always start firing into the air when he's here."

"Why is that a problem?" Kitay asked. "That's good for us."

Venka wrinkled her nose. "How so? It means the entire front line will be fully armed and at attention, and that we'll have to deal with Vaisra's private guard on top of that."

"It also puts them on the defensive," Kitay said. "Because now they've got a target to protect."

"But you're not . . ." Venka glanced between them. "Oh. Oh, you're not fucking serious. *That's* your plan?"

Rin hadn't thought of targeting Vaisra until Kitay said it out loud. But it made perfect sense. If the Republic's most important figure was going to put himself on the front lines, then of course she should aim his way. At the very least, it would split the Republican Army's attention—if they were busy rallying around Vaisra, that drew troops away from the Southern Coalition's escape route.

"He's had it coming," she said. "Why not now?"

"I—sure." Venka was past the point of disbelief; now she simply looked resigned. "And you're *sure* Master Jiang can clear the dead zone?"

"We'll worry about breaking the front," she said. "You handle evacuation. How many people here will listen to you?"

"Probably a lot, if I tell them you're back," Venka said. "Souji and Gurubai haven't got much goodwill among the ranks right now."

"Good," Rin said. "Tell every officer you can find to drive north in a wedge formation when things start exploding at the border. When does Vaisra arrive?"

"Typically in the mornings. That's when they've had their parades the last two times he's visited."

"Crack of dawn?" Kitay asked.

"A little later. Twenty minutes, maybe?"

"Then we'll break to the mines twenty minutes after dawn." Rin turned to the gagged soldier in the corner. "Are you going to help us?"

He nodded frantically. She strode toward him and pulled the rope out of his mouth. He coughed to clear his throat.

"I have no idea what is going on," he said, eyes watering. "And I'm fairly sure that we're all about to die."

"That's fine," Rin said. "Just so long as you'll do as I say."

For the rest of the night Rin followed Venka through the caves and tunnels, whispering the same message to everyone who cared to listen. *The Speerly is back. She's brought allies. Pack your things and ready your arms. Spread the word. At dawn, we break.*

But when at last the hour came, the tunnels were depressingly quiet. Rin had seen this coming. The Southern Coalition was a threadbare army living on stretched rations. Exhaustion plagued the ranks; even those who fully believed in her didn't have the energy to lead the charge. They were suffering a collective action problem—everyone was hoping someone else would make the first move.

Rin was happy to do just that.

"Give them a kick in the ass if they won't mobilize," Jiang had told her. "Bring hell to their doorstep."

So twenty minutes after the sun rose, once faint notes of parade music began carrying over the still morning air from the Republican line, Rin walked out in front of the cave mouths, stretched her hand toward the sky, and called down a column of bright orange fire.

The flames formed a thick pillar stretching to the heavens. A beacon, an invitation. She stood with her eyes closed and arms outstretched, relishing the caress of hot air against her skin, basking in its deafening roar. A minute later, she saw through the heat shimmer a cluster of black dots—dirigibles rising to meet her.

Then the southerners burst out of their caves and tunnels like ants foaming from the dirt. They ran past her, half-packed satchels hanging from their shoulders, bare feet padding against the dirt.

Rin stood still at the center of the frenzied panic.

Time seemed to dilate for a moment. She knew she should join the fleeing crowd. She knew she had to rally them, to use her flame to corral their confused panic into a concentrated assault. In a moment, she would.

But right now, she wanted to enjoy this.

At last this war was back under her control. She'd chosen this battle. She'd determined its time and place. She spoke the word, and the world exploded into action.

This was chaos, but chaos was where she thrived. A world at peace, at stalemate, at cease-fire, had no use for her. She understood now what she needed to do to cling to power: submerge the world in chaos, and forge her authority from the broken pieces.

The Republican Army awaited them at the northern front.

The infantry stood behind several rows of cannons, mounted arquebuses, and archers—three types of artillery, a mix of Nikara and Hesperian technologies designed to rip flesh apart at a distance. Six dirigibles hovered in the sky above them like guardian deities.

Rin's heart sank as she scanned the horizon. Jiang was nowhere to be seen. He'd promised them safe passage. This was a death trap.

Where is he?

Her mouth filled with the taste of ash. This was her fault. Despite his clear mental volatility, she'd trusted him. She'd placed her life and the fate of the south in his hands with all the naivete of a pupil at Sinegard. And once again, he'd failed her.

"It's a suicide drive, then." Venka, to her great credit, did not sound the least bit afraid. She reached for her sword, as if that could do anything against the impending air assault. "I suppose this had to end sometime. It's been fun, kids."

"Hold on." Kitay pointed to the front line just as Jiang strode, seemingly out of nowhere, into the empty space between the two armies.

He wielded no weapon and carried no shield. He loped casually with slouched shoulders across the field, hands in his pockets, as if he had just stepped out his front door for a mild afternoon stroll. He didn't stop until he reached the very center of the line of dirigibles. Then he turned around to face them, head tilted sideways like a fascinated child.

Rin dug her nails into her palm.

She couldn't breathe.

This was it. She'd wagered the lives of everyone in the Southern Coalition on what happened next. The fate of the south hung on one man, one clearly unstable man, and Rin could not truthfully say whether she believed in Jiang or not.

The dirigibles dipped down slightly toward him, like predators stalking their prey. Miraculously, they had not yet begun to fire.

Did they intend to be merciful? Did they want to spare the Southern Coalition so that they could take them alive, to be tortured and interrogated later? Or were they so confused and amazed by this solitary, suicidal fool that they wanted to draw in closer for a better look?

Did they have any idea what he was?

Someone on the Republican front must have shouted an order, because the entire artillery swiveled their barrels around to aim at Jiang.

Something invisible pulsed through the air.

Jiang hadn't moved, but something about the world had shifted, had knocked its sounds and colors slightly off-kilter. The hairs stood up on Rin's arm. She felt intensely, deliciously light-headed. A strange, exhilarating energy thrummed just beneath her skin, an incredible sense of *potential*. She felt like a cotton ball suffused in oil, just waiting for the smallest spark to ignite.

Jiang raised one hand into the air. His fingers splayed out. The air around him shimmered and distorted. Then the sky exploded into shadow like an ink bottle shattered on parchment.

Rin saw the effects before the cause. Bodies fell. The entire archery line collapsed. The dirigible closest to Jiang careened to the side and struck its neighbor, sending both crashing to the ground in a ball of fire.

Only after the wave of smoke cleared did Rin see the source of the destruction—black, mist-like wraiths snaked through the air, shooting through bodies, weapons, and shields with uniform ease. At times they hung still and, ever so briefly, she could just barely make out their shapes—a lion, a dragon, a kirin—before they disappeared back into formless shadow. They followed no known laws of the physical world. Metal passed through them as if they were immaterial, but their fangs ripped through flesh just as easily as the sharpest of swords.

Jiang had called down every beast of the Emperor's Menagerie, and they were tearing through the material world like steel through paper.

The other four dirigibles never managed to fire. A fleet of black birdlike shadows ripped through the balloons that kept them afloat, puncturing the centers and flying out the other side in neat, straight lines. The balloons popped into nothing. The dirigible baskets plummeted with startling velocity, where Jiang's beasts continued wreaking havoc on the ground forces. The Republican soldiers struggled valiantly against the wraiths, swinging their blades desperately against the onslaught, but they might as well have been fighting the wind.

"Holy shit." Venka stood gaping, arms hanging by her side.

She should have been leading the charge toward the mines, but neither she nor any of the Southern Coalition had moved an inch. All that any of them seemed able to do was watch.

"Told you," Rin murmured. "He's a shaman."

"I didn't think shamans were *that* powerful."

Rin shot her an indignant look. "You've seen me call flame!"

Venka pointed to Jiang. He was still alone in the dead zone. He was so open, so vulnerable. But no bullets seemed able to pierce his skin, and every arrow aimed his way dropped harmlessly onto the ground long before it reached him. Everywhere he pointed, explosions followed.

"You," Venka said reverently, "cannot do *that*."

She was right. Rin felt a pang of jealousy as she watched Jiang conducting his wraiths like a musician, each sweep of his arm prompting another charge of shadowy havoc.

She'd thought she understood the limits of shamanic destruction. She'd leveled a field of bodies before. She'd leveled a *country*.

But what she'd done to the longbow island had been a singular episode of divine intervention. It could never—*should* never be repeated. In conventional combat, on a battlefield where discriminating between ally and enemy actually mattered, she couldn't compete with Jiang. She could burn a handful of soldiers at once, dozens if she had a clear, clustered target. But Jiang was blowing through entire squadrons with mere waves of his hand.

No wonder he'd acted so cavalier before. This wasn't a fight for him, this was child's play.

Rin wanted power like that.

She could see now how the Trifecta had become legend. This was how they had massacred the Ketreyids. This was how they had reunited a country, declared themselves its rulers, and yanked it back from both Hesperia and the Federation.

So how had they ever lost it?

At last the Southern Coalition came to their senses. Under Venka and Kitay's direction they began a frenzied drive toward the scattered blockade. Jiang's shadow wraiths parted to let them through unscathed. His control was astonishing—there must have been more than a hundred beasts on the field, each weaving autonomously through the mass of bodies, all distinguishing perfectly between southerners and Republicans.

Rin and Jiang alone remained behind the front lines.

This wasn't over. A second fleet of dirigibles was approaching fast from the east. Deafening booms split the sky. The air was suddenly thick with missiles. Rin threw herself to the ground, wincing as explosions thundered above her.

The Republican troops had realized their only viable strategy. They'd noticed Jiang's limits—his beasts might be able to knock missiles out of the air, but their numbers were constrained to a pack the size of a small field. He couldn't tear through the ground troops and defend against the dirigibles at the same time. He couldn't summon an unending horde.

Rin lifted her head just as three airships peeled away from the fleet and veered toward the mines. She understood their plan in an instant—they couldn't count on taking Jiang out, so they were going to take out the Southern Coalition instead.

They were going to fire on Kitay.

Oh, *fuck* no.

Your turn, Rin told the Phoenix. *Show them everything we've got.*

The god responded with glee.

Her world burst into orange. Rin had never called flames so great into battle before. She had always kept the fire reined in within a twenty-yard radius; any farther than that and she risked collateral damage to allies and civilians. But now she had clear targets across an empty field. Now she could send great roaring columns fifty yards high into the sky, could shroud the dirigible baskets in flame, could scorch the troops inside, could char the balloons until they imploded.

One by one the dirigibles dropped.

This felt deliriously good. It wasn't just the freedom of range, the permission to destroy without constraint. Everything felt so *easy*. She wasn't calling the flame, she *was* the flame; those great columns were natural extensions of her body, as simple to command as her fingers and toes. She felt the Phoenix's presence so closely she might have been in the world of spirit. She might have been on Speer.

This was Jiang's doing. He'd opened the gate to the void to let the beasts in, and now the gap between worlds had thinned just a little more. Such small shreds of reality separated them from a churning cosmos of infinite possibility, and that made the material world so very malleable. It made her feel divine.

She noticed one more dirigible flying in the opposite direction of the fleet. Its guns weren't firing. Its flight pattern seemed erratic—she couldn't tell if the dirigible had been damaged, or if something was wrong with the crew. It climbed several feet in altitude above the rest of the fleet, teetered for a moment, and then turned back in the direction of the New City.

Rin knew then exactly who was on that dirigible. Someone who badly needed protection. Someone who had to be extracted from the fracas, immediately.

"Master!" She shouted, pointing. Her flames couldn't reach that high, but perhaps his beasts could. "Bring down that ship!"

Jiang didn't answer. She wasn't even sure that he'd heard her. His pale eyes had gone entirely blank; he seemed trapped in the throes of his own symphony of ruin.

But then a small cluster of shadows peeled away from the rest, hurtled upward through the air, and fell on the balloon like a ravenous pack of wolves. Moments later the carriage started tumbling to the ground.

The crash shook the earth. Rin sprinted toward the wreckage.

Most of the crew had died on impact. She made short work of the survivors. Two Hesperian soldiers made staggering advances when they saw her coming. One had an arquebus, so she took him out first, shrouding his head and shoulders in a ball of flame before he had time to pull the trigger. The other soldier had a knife. But he'd been injured in the crash, and his movements were comically slow. Rin let him approach, twisted the hilt from his hand, and jammed the blade into his neck so hard the point came up through his eye.

Then she started digging through the debris.

Yin Vaisra was still alive. She found him pinned beneath part of the basket hull and the corpses of two of his guards, gasping hoarsely as he struggled to free himself. His eyes widened when he saw her. The twist of fear was visible for only an instant before his face resumed its habitual mask of calm, but Rin saw. She felt a vicious pulse of glee.

He reached for a knife lying by his waist. She wedged her toe beneath its hilt and flicked it out of his reach. She sat back and waited, expecting him to produce another weapon, but he seemed otherwise unarmed. All he could do was squirm.

Easy. This was so *easy*. She could kill him where he lay, could gut him with his own knife with no more ceremony than a butcher slaughtering a pig. But that would be so terribly unsatisfying. She wanted to milk this moment for all it was worth.

She braced herself under the carriage hull and pushed her legs against the ground. The hull was heavier than it looked. Those things seemed so elegant and lightweight in the air; now it took all her strength to shift it off Vaisra's legs.

At last, he struggled out from beneath the corpses. She dropped the hull.

"Get up," she ordered.

To her surprise, he obeyed.

Slowly he rose to his feet. It hurt him terribly to stand—she could tell from the stoop of his shoulders and the way he winced as his left leg shook beneath him. But he didn't make a sound of protest.

No, the first President of the Nikara Republic had too much dignity for that.

They stood face-to-face for a moment in silence. Rin looked

him up and down, etching every detail of him into her memory. She wanted to remember everything about this moment.

He really was the spitting image of Nezha—an older, crueler version, an unsettling premonition of everything Nezha was supposed to be. Small wonder she'd so eagerly cast him her loyalty. She'd been attracted to him; she could admit this to herself, now that it didn't matter. It couldn't humiliate her anymore. She could concede that not so long ago, she'd wanted to be commanded and owned by someone who looked like *Nezha*.

Gods, she'd been so stupid.

Every day since her escape from Arlong, she'd wondered what she would say to Vaisra if she ever saw him again. What she might do if he were ever at her mercy. She'd fantasized about this moment so many times, but now, as he stood weakened and vulnerable before her, she couldn't think of anything to say.

There was nothing more to be said. She sought no answers or explanations from him. She knew very well why he'd betrayed her. She knew he considered her less human than animal. She didn't need his acknowledgment or respect. She needed nothing from him at all.

She just needed him gone. Out of the equation; off the chessboard.

"You do realize they're going to destroy you," he said.

She lifted her chin. "Are those your last words?"

"Everything you do convinces them you should not exist." Blood trickled from his lips. He knew he was a dead man; all he could do now was try to rattle her. "Every time you call the fire, you remind the Gray Order why you cannot remain free. The only reason you stand here now is because you've been useful in the south. But they'll come for you soon, my dear. These are your final days. Enjoy them."

Rin didn't flinch.

If he thought he could unsettle her with words, he was wrong. Once, perhaps, he could manipulate her with coaxing, praise, and insults like she was clay in his hands. Once, she'd clung to everything he said because she was weak and drifting, flailing about for anything solid to hold on to. But nothing he said could shake her now.

She couldn't feel the revulsion she'd anticipated at the sight of him. She'd spent so long thinking of Vaisra as a monster. This man had traded everything for power—his southern allies, all three of his sons, and Rin herself. But she found she couldn't fault him for that. Like her, like the Trifecta, Vaisra had only been pursuing his vision for Nikan with a ruthless and single-minded determination. The only difference between them was that he'd lost.

"Do you know your biggest mistake?" she asked softly. "You should have gambled on me."

Before Vaisra could respond, she seized his chin and brought his mouth to hers. He tried to twist away. She gripped the back of his head and kept it pressed against her face. He struggled, but he was so weak. He bit desperately at her lips. The taste of blood filled her mouth, but she just pressed her lips harder against his.

Then she funneled flame into his mouth.

It wasn't enough simply to kill him. She had to humiliate and mutilate him. She had to force an inferno down his throat and char him from the inside, to feel his burned flesh sloughing away under her fingers. She wanted overkill. She had to reduce him to a pile of something unfixable, unrecognizable.

This couldn't undo the past. It couldn't bring Suni, Baji, or Ramsa back, couldn't erase all the tortures she'd suffered at his commands. Couldn't erase the scar on her back or restore her missing hand. But it felt good. The point of revenge wasn't to heal. The point was that the exhilaration, however temporary, drowned out the hurt.

He went limp against her. She let his body drop; he fell forward, chest curled over his knees, as if he were bowing to her.

She breathed deep, inhaling the smoky tang of his burning innards. She knew this ecstasy wouldn't last. It would fade away in minutes, and then she'd want more. She almost wished that he would come back to life so she could kill him again, and then again, that she might keep experiencing the thrill of glimpsing the wretched fear in his eyes before her flames extinguished their light.

She felt the same way now that she did every time she destroyed a Mugenese contingent. She knew revenge was a drug. She knew it couldn't sustain her forever. But right now, while she was riding the high, before her adrenaline crashed and the weight and horror of what she'd just done flooded back through the crevices of her mind, while she stood breathing hard over the blackened ashes of the man who had destroyed almost everything she loved, it felt better than anything in the world.

She didn't see the last dirigible swooping low through the smoke at Jiang until it was too late.

"*Watch out!*" she screamed, but the boom of cannons drowned out her voice.

Jiang dropped like a puppet with cut strings. His beasts vanished. The dirigible veered tentatively backward, as if trying to assess the damage before it took a second shot. She flung her head back and screamed fire. A single jet of flame ripped through the airship balloon. The carriage spiraled into the ground and exploded.

Rin sprinted through the raining wreckage to Jiang.

He lay still where he had fallen. She pressed her fingers into his neck. She felt a pulse, strong and insistent. Good. She patted her hand over his body, trying to check the extent of his wounds. But there was no blood—his clothes were dry.

They weren't safe yet. Arquebuses went off all around them; Jiang had not finished off the Republican artillery.

"Get him up." Daji materialized, seemingly from nowhere. Her eyes were wild and frantic; her hair and clothes singed black. She jammed her hands under Jiang's arms and hoisted him to a sitting position. "Hurry."

"What's wrong with him?" Rin asked. "He's not even—"

Daji shook her head just as the crack of arquebus fire echoed around them. They both ducked.

"Quickly!" Daji hissed.

Rin pulled one of Jiang's arms around her shoulder. Daji took the other. Together they staggered to their feet and ran for cover, Jiang lolling between them like a drunkard.

Somehow they made it unscathed to the Southern Coalition's rear guard. Venka and a line of defenders stood at the base of the mountains, firing back at the Republicans as the civilians clustered around the blocked tunnel entrances.

"Oh, thank fuck, there you are." Venka dropped her crossbow to help them hoist Jiang toward a wagon. "Is he hurt?"

"I can't tell." Rin helped Daji push Jiang's legs up over the cart. He didn't *look* wounded. In fact, he was still conscious. He pulled his knees up into a crouched sitting position, rocking back and forth, emitting bursts of low, nervous giggles.

Rin couldn't look at him. This was wrong, this was so wrong. Her gut wrenched with a mix of horror and shame; she wanted to vomit.

"Riga," Jiang whispered suddenly. He'd stopped giggling. He sat utterly still, eyes fixed at something Rin couldn't see.

Daji recoiled like she'd been slapped.

"Riga?" Rin repeated. "What—"

"He's here," Jiang said. His shoulders began to tremble.

"He's not here." The blood had drained from Daji's face. She looked terrified. "Ziya, listen to me—"

"He's going to kill me," Jiang whispered.

His eyes rolled up to the back of his head. He shuddered so hard his teeth clacked. Then he slumped to the side and lay still.

CHAPTER 17

The mining tunnels felt more like a tomb than an escape. After Rin blew open the entrances with flame and several well-placed barrels of fire powder, the Southern Coalition filed in a packed column of bodies through a passage wide enough to fit only three men walking side by side. It seemed to stretch on for miles. All around them was cold stone, stale air, and a looming black that seemed to constrict like a vise as they pressed farther into the belly of the deep.

They stumbled through the dark, groping at the tunnel walls and tapping the floor before them to check for sudden drop-offs. Rin hated this—she wanted to light every inch of her body aflame and become a human lantern—but she knew that in such packed quarters, fire would suffocate. Altan had showed her once, with a pigeon in a glass vase, how quickly flames could eat up all the breathable air. She remembered clearly the eager fascination in his eyes as he watched the pigeon's little neck pulse frantically, then go still.

So she walked at the head of the column, illuminating the way with a tiny flame flickering inside a cupped hand, while the back of the line followed in complete darkness.

An hour into their journey, the soldiers behind her began

begging that they stop. Everyone wanted to rest. They were exhausted; many of them were marching with undressed open wounds dripping blood into the dirt. The dirigibles couldn't reach them underground, they argued. Surely they would be safe for twenty minutes.

Rin refused. She and Jiang might have decimated the Republican front lines, but Nezha was certainly still alive, and she didn't trust him to give up. He would have called for reinforcements long ago. Ground troops might be preparing to enter the tunnels as they marched. Nezha could use explosives and poisonous gas to smoke them out like rats right now, and then the Southern Coalition would disappear with muffled screams beneath the earth, and the only evidence they had ever existed would be ossified bones revealed eons later as the mountains eroded.

She ordered that they continue until they emerged out the other side. To her pleasant surprise, the troops obeyed her without question. She had expected to hear at least a little pushback—she had only just rejoined their ranks, with no explanation or apology, before she thrust them into a war zone wreaked by gods.

But she had broken them out of the Anvil. She'd done what the Southern Coalition had failed to do for months. Right now, her word was divine command.

At last, after what felt like an eternity, they emerged into a marvelous accident of nature—a cavern whose ceiling split into a jagged crack in the darkness, revealing the sky above. Rin stopped walking and tilted her head up at the stars. After a day spent underground trying to convince her racing heart at every second that she wasn't being buried alive, she felt like she'd come up from drowning.

Had the night sky always shone so bright?

"We should rest here." Kitay pointed to a ridge in the opposite wall. Rin squinted and saw a staircase carved into the stone—a narrow, precipitous set of steps, likely built by miners who hadn't revisited these tunnels in years. "If anything starts coming through those tunnels, we've got a way out."

"All right." Rin suddenly felt a wave of exhaustion that until now had been kept at bay by adrenaline and fear. She was still afraid. But she couldn't push herself or the army any farther, or they'd collapse. "Just until dawn. We start moving the moment the sun comes up."

A collective moan of relief echoed through the tunnels when she gave the order. The southerners set down their packs, spread out through the cavern and its adjacent tunnels, and unfurled sleeping mats on the dirt. Rin wanted nothing more than to curl up in a corner and close her eyes.

But she was in charge now, and she had work to do.

She walked through the huddled masses of soldiers and civilians, taking stock of what kind of numbers she had left. She lit their torches and warmed them with her flame. She answered honestly every question they asked about where she'd been—she told them about the Chuluu Korikh, the Trifecta's return, and her break-in to Arabak.

She found, to her surprise, a great deal of new faces not from Monkey or Rooster Provinces, but from the north—mostly young and middle-aged men with the hardy physique of laborers.

"I don't understand," she told Venka. "Where'd they come from?"

"They're miners," Venka said. "The Hesperians set up tungsten mines all over the Daba range after they took over Arlong. They've got these drilling machines that blast through mountainside like you've never seen. But they still needed warm bodies to do the dangerous work—crawling into tunnels, loading the carts, testing the rock face. The northerners came down to work."

"I guess they didn't like it much," Rin said.

"What do you expect? No one flees a good job to join rebel bandits. From what I've heard, those mines were hell. The machines were death traps. Some of those men weren't allowed to see sunlight for days. They joined up the minute they saw us coming."

It took Rin nearly two hours to move through the tunnels. Everyone wanted to speak to her, to hear her voice, to touch her.

They didn't believe that she was back or that she was alive. They had to see her fire with their own eyes.

"I'm real," she assured them, over and over again. "I'm back. And I've got a plan."

Quickly their doubt and confusion turned to wonder, then gratitude, and then clear and adamant loyalty. The more Rin spoke to the troops, the more she understood how the past day had played out in their minds. They had been on the brink of extermination, trapped for weeks in tunnels without enough food or water, awaiting imminent death from bullets, incineration, or starvation. Then Rin had shown up, returned from the stone mountain with barely a scratch and two of the Trifecta in tow, and reversed their fortunes in a single chaotic morning.

To them, what had just happened was divine intervention.

They might have been skeptical of her before. They couldn't be skeptical now. She'd proven without a shadow of a doubt that Souji was wrong—that the Republic would never show them mercy, and that she was the south's best hope for survival. And Rin realized, as she walked through the crowds of awed, grateful faces, that this army was finally hers for good.

Jiang wasn't getting better.

He had recovered consciousness shortly after they reached the cavern, but he hadn't spoken an intelligible word since. He gave no indication that he saw Rin as she approached his sleeping mat, where he sat like a child with his knees drawn up into his chest. He seemed lost somewhere inside himself, somewhere troubled and terrifying, and although Rin could tell from the way his mouth twitched and his eyes darted back and forth that he was fighting to claw his way back, she had no idea how to reach him.

"Hello, Master," she said.

He acted as if he hadn't heard her. His fingers fidgeted mindlessly at the hem of his shirt. He'd turned ghastly pale, sapphire veins visible under his skin like watery calligraphy.

She knelt down beside him. "I suppose we should thank you."

She put her hand on his, hoping that physical contact might calm him. He yanked it away. Only then did he look directly at her. Rin saw fear in his eyes—not the momentary flinch of surprise, but a deep, bone-wrenching terror from which he couldn't break free.

"He's been like that for hours," Daji said. She was curled up against the wall several feet away, gnawing at a strip of dried pork. "You won't get any other response. Leave him alone, he'll be fine."

Rin couldn't believe how indifferent she sounded. "He doesn't look fine."

"He'll get over it. He's been like that before."

"I'm sure you'd know. You did that to him."

Rin knew she was being cruel. But she meant to hurt. She wanted her words to twist like daggers, because the pained expression they elicited on Daji's face was the only outlet for the confused dread she felt when she looked at Jiang.

"I am the only reason why he's alive at all," Daji said in a hard voice. "I did what I had to do to give him the only chance at peace he'd ever get."

Rin glanced back at Jiang, who was now hunched over, whispering nonsense into his curled fingers. "And that's peace?"

"Back then his mind was killing him," Daji said. "I silenced it."

"We've got a problem," Kitay announced, appearing around the cavern wall. "You need to do something about Souji and Gurubai."

Rin groaned. "Shit."

She hadn't seen a glimpse of Souji or Gurubai since the breakout began. They hadn't even crossed her mind. She'd been so caught up in the exhilaration of the escape, in the sole objective of rescuing the south, she'd completely forgotten that not all of them might welcome her back.

"They're making noises," Kitay continued. "Telling their troops they need to split off when we've found the exit. We fix this tonight, or we're facing a desertion or coup in the morning."

"The boy is right," Daji said. "You need to act now."

"But there's nothing to—oh." Rin's exhausted mind finally grasped what Daji was implying. "I see."

She stood.

"What?" Kitay's eyes darted back and forth between her and Daji. "We haven't—what are you—"

"Execution." Rin said. "Plain and simple. Do you know where they are?"

"Wait." Kitay blinked at her, stunned by this sudden escalation. "That doesn't mean—I mean, you just saved their lives—"

"Those two sold her to the Republic without a second thought," Daji drawled. "If you think they won't betray you again, then you're too stupid to live."

Kitay glared at Rin. "Was this her idea?"

"It's the only option you've got," Daji said.

"Is that how you ruled?" Kitay inquired. "Killing everyone who disagreed with you?"

"Of course," Daji said, unfazed. "You cannot lead effectively when you have dissidents with this much influence. Riga had many enemies. Ziya and I took care of them for him. That was how we kept the Nikara front united."

"That didn't last very long."

"*They* didn't last very long. I lasted twenty years." Daji arched an eyebrow. "And it wasn't by being lenient."

"We've done this before," Rin told Kitay. "Ma Lien—"

"Ma Lien was on his deathbed," Kitay snapped. "And that was different. We were operating from a point of weakness then, we didn't have any other choices—"

"We've got no other choices now," Rin said. "The ranks might obey me for the time being, but that loyalty isn't sustainable. Not where we're going. And Gurubai and Souji are too clever. They're intensely charismatic in a way that I'll never be, and given time and space they *will* find a way to oust me."

"That's not predetermined," Kitay said. "Mistakes aside, they're good leaders. You could work with them."

It was a weak argument, and Rin could tell that he knew it. They all knew that this night had to end in blood. Rin could not continue sharing power with a coalition that had defied, obstructed, and betrayed her at every turn. If she was going to lead the south, she had to do it by her own vision. Alone and unopposed.

Kitay stopped trying to argue. They both knew there was nothing he could say. They had only one option; he was too smart not to see it. He might hate her for this, but he would forgive her, as he always did. He'd always had to forgive her for necessity.

Daji calmly pulled her knife from its sheath and handed it hilt-first to Rin.

"I don't need that," Rin said.

"Blades are quieter," Daji said. "Fire agonizes. And you don't want their screams to disturb the sleeping."

Rin dealt with the Monkey Warlord first.

Gurubai had known she was coming. He was standing in the tunnels with his officers, the only people in the cavern who didn't appear to be asleep. They were quietly discussing something. They fell silent when they saw her approach, but they didn't move for their weapons.

"Leave us," Gurubai said.

His officers departed without another word. They kept their heads down as they filed past; none gave Rin so much as a parting glance.

"They're good soldiers," Gurubai told Rin. "You've no cause to hurt them."

"I know," she said. "I won't."

She meant it. Without Gurubai to lead them, none of his officers had any reason to betray her. She knew those men. They weren't ambitious power grabbers; they were capable, rational-minded soldiers. They cared about the south, and they knew now she was their best chance at survival.

Gurubai regarded her for a moment. "Will you burn me?"

"No." She drew the knife Daji had given her. "You deserve better."

Gurubai raised his arms in the air. He didn't reach for a weapon. He'd resigned himself to his fate, Rin realized. There was no fight left in him.

He had lost so thoroughly. He'd been cornered in the mountains and starved out by a boy general, and then his only salvation had been the Speerly he thought he'd sold to his enemy. If his gamble had worked, if Vaisra and the Republic had kept their word, then Gurubai would have become a national hero. The savior of the south.

But it hadn't, so he would die a disgraced traitor. So cruel were the whims of history.

"You are the worst thing to happen to this country," Gurubai said. His voice carried no anger or invective, just resignation. He wasn't trying to hurt her. He was delivering his final testimony. "These people deserve better than you."

"I'm exactly what they deserve," she said. "They don't want peace, they want revenge. I'm it."

"Revenge doesn't make a stable nation."

"Neither does cowardice," she said. "That's where you failed. You were only ever fighting to survive, Gurubai. I was fighting to win. And history doesn't favor stability, it favors initiative."

She pointed the blade at his heart and jerked her hand forward in one quick, smooth motion. His eyes bulged. She yanked the blade out and stepped back just before he crumpled, clutching at his chest.

She'd aimed badly. She'd known that as soon as she felt the blade make contact. Her left hand was clumsy and weak; she'd pierced not his heart but an inch below it. She had put him in excruciating pain, but his heart wouldn't stop beating until he bled out.

Gurubai writhed at her feet, but he didn't make a single sound. No screams, no whimpers. She respected that.

"You would have been a wonderful peacetime leader," she

said. He had been honest with her; she might as well afford him the same in return. "But we don't need peace right now. We need blood."

Footsteps sounded behind her. She swiveled around, then relaxed—it was just Kitay. He stepped forward and stood over Gurubai's silent, twitching form, mouth curling in distaste.

"I see you started without me," he said.

"I didn't think you wanted to come." Her voice felt detached from her body. Her hand shook as she watched Gurubai's blood pooling over the stone floor. Her entire *body* shook; she could hear her teeth clattering in her skull. She registered this physiological reaction with a bemused, distant curiosity.

What was wrong with her?

She'd felt this same nervous ecstasy when she killed Ma Lien. When she killed the priest in Arabak. All three times she'd killed not with fire, but with her own hand. She was capable of such cruelties, even without the Phoenix's power, and that both delighted and scared her.

Gurubai grabbed at Kitay's ankle, choking. Blood bubbled out of his mouth.

"Don't be cruel, Rin." Kitay took the knife from her hand, knelt over Gurubai, and traced the sharp tip along the artery in his neck. Blood sprayed the cavern wall. Gurubai gave a final, violent thrash, and then he stopped moving.

Rin caught Souji as he was trying to flee.

Someone in Gurubai's camp had warned him to run. They'd been too late. By the time Souji and his Iron Wolves made it to the cavern's western exit, Rin was already waiting in the tunnel.

She waved. "Going somewhere?"

Souji stumbled to a halt. His usual confident smirk was gone, replaced with the desperate, dangerous look of a cornered wolf.

"Get out of my way," he snarled.

Rin drew her index finger through the air. Casual streams of flame arced out the tip and danced along the tunnel walls.

"As you can see," she said, "I have my fire back."

Souji pulled out his sword. To Rin's surprise, the Iron Wolves didn't follow suit. They weren't crowded close behind Souji like loyal followers would be. No—if they were loyal, they would have already joined him in the charge.

Instead they hung back, waiting.

Rin read the looks in their eyes—identical expressions of calculating uncertainty—and took a wild gamble.

"Disarm him," she ordered.

They obeyed immediately.

Souji lunged at Rin. The Iron Wolves yanked him back. Two forced him to his knees. One wrenched the blade out of his hands and tossed it across the tunnel. The third jerked his head back so that he was forced to gaze up at Rin.

"What the fuck are you doing?" Souji screamed. "Let me go!"

None of the Iron Wolves spoke a word.

"Oh, Souji." Rin strode toward him and bent down to ruffle his hair. He snapped like a dog, but he couldn't reach her fingers. "What did you think was going to happen?"

Her heart pounded with giddy disbelief. This had gone wonderfully, ridiculously smoothly; she couldn't have imagined a better outcome.

She patted his head. "You can beg now, if you like."

He spat a gob of saliva onto her front. She slammed the toe of her boot into his stomach. He sagged to the side.

"Drop him," Rin ordered.

The Iron Wolves let Souji crumple to the ground. She kept kicking.

She didn't brutalize him like he had her. She kept her kicks confined to his gut, his thighs, and his groin. She didn't aim to crack his ribs or his kneecaps—no, she needed him able to stand in front of a crowd.

But it felt good to hear the little girlish gasps escape from his throat. It kept that nervous ecstasy pounding through her veins.

She couldn't believe she'd once, however briefly, considered sleeping with him. She thought about the weight of his arm around her waist, the heat of his breath against her ear. She kicked harder.

"You cunt," Souji gasped.

"I love the way you talk to me," she cooed.

He tried to hiss out another insult, but she slammed her foot into his mouth. Felt her toes split his lip against his teeth. She had never before mutilated an opponent with pure brute force. She'd done it plenty with fire, of course. But this was a different kind of satisfaction, like the pleasure she derived from hearing fabric rip.

Human bodies were so breakable, she marveled. So soft. Just meat on bones.

She restrained herself from kicking his skull in. She needed Souji's face intact. Broken, maybe, but recognizable.

She and Kitay had decided not to kill him now. His death had to be a public display, a spectacle to legitimize her authority and to transform her takeover from an open secret to a universally acknowledged fact.

Daji, who had done this sort of thing quite often, had emphasized the importance of performative execution.

Don't just let them fear, she'd said. *Let them know.*

"Tie him up," Rin told the Iron Wolves. She knew, with certainty, she could trust them. No one wanted to burn. "Guard him in shifts during the night. We'll finish this in the morning."

At dawn Rin stood at the center of the cavern, right beneath the single shaft of sunlight that pierced through the cracked stone ceiling. She was aware of how absurdly symbolic this looked— the way her skin shone like polished bronze, the way she was the brightest figure in the darkness. It didn't matter that the watching crowd knew this was orchestrated. This imagery would be seared into their minds forever.

Souji knelt beside her, hands bound behind his back. Dried blood crackled over every inch of his exposed skin.

"You may have asked where I've been these past months. Why I disappeared after the attack on Tikany." She pointed to Souji's bowed head. He didn't stir; he was only half-conscious. "This man ambushed me and sent me to the Chuluu Korikh to rot. He betrayed me to the Young Marshal. And he betrayed all of you."

The cavern was so silent that the only sound Rin heard in response was the echo of her own words.

The crowd was with her. She could see it in the grim set of their faces and the coldly furious glint in their eyes. Every person in this cavern wanted to see Souji die.

"This man trapped you in the Anvil. He tried to kill the only person who could save you. Why?" Rin aimed a hard kick at Souji's back. He lurched forward and gave a muffled moan. He couldn't speak up in his own defense; his mouth was stuffed with cloth. "Because he was jealous. Yang Souji couldn't stand to see a Speerly leading his men. He needed to take charge himself. He wanted to own the Southern Coalition."

She didn't know where her words were coming from, but they poured out with ridiculous ease. She felt like a stage actor, chanting lines from some classical play, each dramatic phrase delivered in a deep, powerful voice that sounded nothing like her own.

When had she learned to act like this? Deep down, a fragment of her was scared that any minute the facade would drop, that her voice would falter, and that they'd all see her for the terrified girl she was.

Play the part, she thought. That, too, was Daji's advice. *You only have to wear this skin long enough for it to become a piece of you.*

"The Southern Coalition is now finished," she declared.

Her words met with dead silence. No one reacted. They waited.

She raised her voice. "Yang Souji and the Monkey Warlord are proof of the failures of coalition politics. They nearly destroyed you with their infighting. They had no strategy. They betrayed me and led you astray. But I have returned. I am your liberation. And now I alone will make the decisions for this army. Does anyone object?"

Of course no one objected. She had them in the palm of her

hand. She was their Speerly, their savior, the only one who time after time had rescued them from certain death.

"Good." She pointed down to Souji. She knew no one would try to protect him. Not a single person had spoken up in his defense. They weren't watching to see whether she would kill him. They were watching to see how she would do it.

"This is what happens to those who defy me." She looked to one of the Iron Wolves. "Remove the gag."

The Iron Wolf stepped up and pulled the bunched-up rag from Souji's mouth. Souji lurched forward, gasping.

Rin pressed the point of her knife under his chin and forced his gaze up to the crowd. "Confess your sins."

Souji snarled and mumbled something incoherent.

Rin pushed the blade just a bit harder against Souji's flesh, watching with pleasure as his throat bobbed tensely against steel.

"All you have to do is confess," she said softly. "Then this all ends."

Kitay hadn't wanted her to force a confession. Kitay thought that Souji would rebel and lash out, that his dying words could only damage her. But Rin couldn't let Souji die with his dignity, because then her detractors might take solace in his memory.

She had to annihilate him. Rin knew that his betrayal hadn't been his decision alone—every person in this cavern was in some way complicit in his treachery. But she couldn't execute them all. Souji had to be the scapegoat. His body had to take on the burden of everyone's guilt. This leadership transition demanded public catharsis, and Souji was its sacrificial lamb.

She gave the knife another jab. Blood beaded on the tip. "*Confess.*"

"I didn't do anything," Souji said hoarsely.

"You sold me to Nezha," she said. "And you trapped them in this mountain to die."

That wasn't strictly true. Souji had only ever meant to protect the south. For all she knew, Souji had made the best strategic decisions possible given the Republic's overwhelming superiority.

Souji certainly thought he was the only reason why the Southern Coalition had survived as long as they had. Perhaps he was even right.

But logic didn't matter in this ritual. Fury and resentment did.

"Say it," she demanded. "You sold me. You betrayed them."

He turned to face her. "You belong in that mountain, you cunt."

She just laughed. She wouldn't lash out with flame, no matter how tempting that was. She had to maintain a facade of indifferent calm to exacerbate the difference between them—he the angry, snapping, cornered wolf and she the icy voice of unflappable authority.

"You sold me," she repeated steadily. "You betrayed them."

"You would have driven them to their deaths," Souji said. "I did what I had to do to save them from you."

"Then we'll let the people decide." Rin turned to the crowd. "Does anyone think this man saved you?"

Again, no one spoke up.

"Nezha told me he only wanted the Speerly." Souji raised his voice to address the crowd. His voice cracked with fear. "He promised that's all it would take, he *said*—"

Rin spoke over him. "Does anyone believe this man was stupid enough to make such a simple mistake?"

The implication was clear. She'd just accused Souji of collaboration. This was of course a lie, but she didn't need to show proof. She didn't even need to make a real argument. All she had to do was insinuate. These people would accept whatever narrative she gave them because they wanted to feed their anger. The judgment had concluded before the trial started.

"Show him." Rin pointed to Souji like a hunter indicating a target to a pack of dogs. "Show him what the south does to its traitors."

She stepped back. There followed a brief, anticipatory silence. Then the crowd surged forth, and Souji disappeared beneath a mass of bodies.

They didn't just beat him. They tore his flesh apart. He must have screamed, but Rin couldn't hear him. She couldn't see him, either; she caught only the faintest glimpses of blood shining through the crowd. It was incredible, really, how easily a mass of weakened, half-starved men and women could together wrench entire limbs from a torso. She saw pieces of Souji's uniform fly through the air. Beneath the feet of the crowd rolled what looked like an eyeball.

She didn't join in. She didn't have to.

"This is chaos." Kitay's face had turned a sickly gray. "This is dangerous."

"Not to us," Rin said.

This was violence, but it wasn't chaos. This anger was utterly controlled, fine-tuned, directed, a massive swell of power that only she could control.

And it wasn't just fueled by resentment toward Souji. In a sense, this massacre wasn't about Souji at all. This was about demonstrating a change in loyalty, a gruesome apology by anyone who had ever spoken against her before. This was a blood sacrifice to a new figurehead.

And if anyone still doubted her leadership, then the screaming would at least strike fear deep into their hearts. Anyone on the fringes now understood the cost of opposition. Through love or hate, adoration or fear, she would have them one way or another.

Daji, standing at the far end of the crowd, caught Rin's eye and smiled.

Rin's heart was pounding so hard she could barely hear.

She understood what Daji had meant now. She could achieve so much with a simple show of strength. All she had to do was become the symbolic embodiment of power and liberation, and she could kill a man by pointing. She could make these people do anything.

You've got a god on your side. You want this nation? You take it.

Gradually the frenzy ceased. The crowd dispersed from the

center of the cavern like a pack of wolves retreating when the meat was gone and the bones picked clean.

Souji was long dead. Not just dead—mutilated, his corpse so thoroughly desecrated that not a single part remained that looked recognizably human. The crowd had destroyed his body and in doing so demonstrated their rejection of everything he'd stood for—a wily mix of guerrilla resistance and clever politicking that, in different circumstances, might have succeeded. In different circumstances, Yang Souji might have liberated the south.

But so fell the whims of fate. Souji was dead, his officers were converted, and the takeover was complete.

CHAPTER 18

The soil inside the cavern was too stiff to dig a grave, so Rin and Kitay piled Gurubai's and Souji's remains together onto a messy pyramid in the center of the caverns, soaked them with oil, and stood back to watch them burn.

It took nearly half an hour for the corpses to disintegrate. Rin wanted to speed the process with her own flames, but Kitay wouldn't let her; he demanded they sit vigil before the pyre while the southerners marched on without them. Rin found this a colossal waste of time, but Kitay couldn't be dissuaded. He thought they owed this to their victims, that otherwise Rin would come off like a callous murderer instead of a proper leader.

Twenty minutes in, he clearly regretted it. His cheeks had gone ashen; he looked like he wanted to vomit.

"You know what I'll never get over?" he asked.

"What?" she asked.

"It smells so much like pork. It makes me hungry. I mean—I couldn't eat now if I tried to, but I can't stop my mouth from watering. Is that disgusting?"

"It's not disgusting," Rin said, privately relieved. "I thought it was just me."

But she *could* eat right now, even sitting before the corpses.

She hadn't eaten since the previous afternoon, and she was starving. She had a ration of dried shanyu roots in her pocket, but it felt wrong to chew on it while the air still crackled with the scent of roasted meat. Only when the corpses had shriveled into pitch-black lumps and the air smelled of charcoal instead of flesh did she feel comfortable enough to pull the rations out. She chewed slowly on the coin-shaped root slivers, working her tongue around the starchy chunks until her saliva softened them enough to swallow, while the last remains of Souji and Gurubai puttered into bones and ash.

Then she rose and joined her army in their march.

After they emerged out the other side of the mining tunnels, they continued along the forest with the mountain to their rear. She told the southerners they were moving north to rendezvous with the Dog Warlord and his rebels to form the last organized holdout against the Republic left in the Empire. They would fare better with their numbers combined. She wasn't lying. She did intend to seek the Dog Warlord's aid. If the rumors were true that he had swords and bodies, she'd be a fool to ignore them.

But she didn't tell anyone but Kitay about their plan to climb Mount Tianshan. She'd learned now that she always had to assume someone in her ranks was spying for the Republic. The Monkey Warlord's coup had proved that point. The last thing she wanted was for the Hesperians to raid Mount Tianshan before she reached it.

She also withheld the truth for a more fundamental reason. She needed her soldiers to believe that they mattered. That their blood and sweat were the only things that could turn the wheels of history. She intended to win this war with shamans, yes, but she couldn't keep her hold on the country without the people's hearts. For that she needed them to believe that they wrote the script of the universe. Not the gods.

The skies above were clear and silent. Nezha and his airships had held off for now, and perhaps indefinitely. Rin didn't know how long their grace period would last, but she wasn't going to sit and wait it out.

Her nerves were on edge as they moved along the foothills. Her troops were too exposed and vulnerable, and they moved at a frustratingly slow pace. It wasn't due to poor discipline. Her soldiers, already weakened by months under siege, were weighed down with wagons carrying weapons arsenals, medical equipment, and their scant remaining food supplies. And the relentless rain, which had started that afternoon as a drizzle and quickly turned into thick, heavy sheets, turned their roads into nothing but mud for miles.

"We won't make ten miles today at this rate," Kitay said. "We've got to offload."

So Rin gave the order to dump as many supplies as they could bear to lose. Food and medicine were invaluable, but almost everything else had to go. Everyone chose two changes of clothes and discarded the rest, largely light summer tunics that would offer no shelter from the mountain snow. They also got rid of many of their weapons and ammunition—they simply didn't have the men to keep lugging along the mounted crossbows, chests of fire powder, and spare armor that they'd dragged all this way from Ruijin.

Rin hated this. They all hated it. The sight of so much sheer waste was unbearable; it hurt to watch the weapons piled up in stacks ready to be burned just so that the Republic couldn't find and repurpose them.

"When the final battles commence, it won't come down to swords and halberds," Daji told Rin. "The fate of this nation depends on how quickly we get to Mount Tianshan. The rest is inconsequential."

Their marching rate sped up considerably after they had shed their supplies. But shortly thereafter, the rain shifted from a heavy shower into a violent and torrential downpour that showed no signs of ceasing throughout the afternoon. The mud became a nightmare. On parts of the road, they waded through black sludge up to their ankles. Their flimsy cotton and straw shoes couldn't keep it out; none of them were dressed for such a wet climate.

Rin's mind spiraled into panic as she considered the consequences. Mud like this wasn't just a nuisance, it was a serious threat to her army's health. Few of them had boots; likely they were all going to get infections. Then their toes would rot and fall off, and they'd have to sit down by the roadside to die because they couldn't keep walking. And if they escaped foot infections, they might still contract gangrene from wounds they'd sustained when the blockade broke, because there weren't near enough medical supplies to go around. Or they might simply starve, because she had no idea how they were going to forage at such high altitudes, or—

Her breath quickened. Her vision dimmed. She felt so dizzy she had to stop walking for a moment and breathe, her one good hand pressed against her pulsing chest.

The magnitude of this journey was starting to sink in. Now that the adrenaline of the morning had worn off, now that she wasn't reeling from a heady mixture of insane confidence and drunk exhilaration, she was beginning to understand the stakes of the path she'd charted for the southerners.

And it was very likely that they were all going to die.

Huge losses were inevitable. Their survival was uncertain. If they ventured on, they might write themselves out of history just as completely as if they had never existed.

But if they stayed where they were, they died. If they parleyed for surrender, they died. If they took their chances now against Nezha, three shamans and a weakened army against the combined military might of the Republic and the west, they died. But if they made it to Mount Tianshan, if they could wake the Dragon Emperor, then the playing field would become very, very different.

This could be the end of their story or the beginning of a glorious chapter. And Rin had no choice now but to drag them across the mountain range by her teeth.

∞

It was the weather, not the dirigibles, that quickly proved to be their greatest obstacle. They'd ascended the Baolei range in the middle of the late summer thaw, and that meant raging river torrents, roads slippery with mud, and rain showers that went on for days at a time. At several crossings the mud reached up to their waists, and they could proceed only after cutting down log strips of bamboo and building a makeshift bridge so that the supply wagons, at least, would not sink beneath the surface.

At night they sought shelter in caves if they could find them, for those offered a shield against the rain and ever-present threat of air raids. But, as Rin quickly discovered, they provided no protection against insects and vermin—bulging nests of spiders, little snakes huddled together in horrific, writhing balls, and sharp-toothed rats nearly the size of house cats. The route they'd chosen was so rarely traveled by humans that the pests seemed to have doubled their numbers to compensate. One evening Rin had just put a bedroll down when a scorpion the length of her hand skittered up to her, tail poised, stinger wafting back and forth in the air.

She froze, too scared to scream.

An arrow thudded into the dirt just inches before the scorpion. It skittered backward and vanished into a crack in the cave wall.

Venka lowered her bow. "You all right?"

"Yeah." Rin exhaled. Her head felt dizzyingly light. "Great fucking Tortoise."

"Burn some lavender and tung oil." Venka pulled a pouch out of her pocket and handed it to Rin. "Then rub the residue on your skin. They hate the smell."

Rin burned the mixture in her palm and rubbed it around her neck. "When did you figure that out?"

"The tunnels by the Anvil were crawling with those things," Venka said. "Didn't learn about it until after a couple soldiers woke up swollen and choking, and then we started sleeping in shifts and clearing out the walls with incense every evening. Sorry about that one. Someone should have warned you."

"Thanks regardless." Rin offered her hand to Venka. Venka scraped the residual ointment from Rin's skin and dabbed it around her collarbones. Then she set her mat next to Rin's, sat down, and pressed her palms against her temples.

"It's been a fucking week," she groaned.

Rin joined her on the bedroll. "Yeah."

For a moment they sat beside each other in silence, breathing slowly, watching the cracks in the wall for the scorpion's return. The cave was cramped and bone-achingly cold, so they pressed tight against each other, misty breaths intermingling in the icy air.

It felt good to have Venka back by her side. Funny how people changed, Rin thought. She would never have dreamed that Venka—Sring Venka, the pretty, pampered Sinegardian turned lean, ferocious warrior—would become such a source of comfort.

Once not so long ago they'd hated each other with the particular intensity only schoolgirls could summon. Rin used to grit her teeth every time she heard Venka's high, petulant voice, used to fantasize about gouging Venka's eyes out with her fingernails. They would have brawled like wildcats in the school courtyard if they hadn't been so afraid of expulsion.

None of that mattered anymore. They weren't stupid little girls anymore. They weren't students anymore. War had transformed them both into wholly unimaginable creatures, and their relationship had transformed with them. They had never commented on how it had happened. They didn't need to. Theirs was a bond forged from necessity, hurt, and a shared, intimate understanding of hell.

"Tell me the truth," Venka murmured. "Where the fuck are we going?"

"Dog Province," Rin yawned. She was already half-asleep; after a full day of climbing, her limbs felt heavier than lead. "Thought I made that clear."

"But that's just a fiction, isn't it?" Venka pressed. "The Dog Warlord's army isn't really there, is it?"

Rin paused, considering.

Telling Venka the truth was risky, yes. It was risky now to share secrets with anyone who didn't strictly need to know. But Venka was, startlingly, one of the most loyal people she knew. Venka had readily turned her back on her family to follow a group of southerners in revolt against her home province. She'd never once looked back. Venka could be rude and brittle, but she didn't have a capricious bone in her body. She was blunt and honest, often to the point of cruelty, and she demanded honesty in return.

"I'm not a fucking spy," Venka said, when Rin's silence dragged on for too long.

"I know," Rin said quickly. "It's just—you're right." Her eyes darted around the cave, making sure no one was listening. "I have no clue what's in Dog Province."

Venka raised her eyebrows. "Sorry?"

"That's the truth. I don't know if they have an army. They could be legion. Enough to push the Republic back. Or they could all have defected, or have died. My intelligence is based on Kitay's, and his is based on offhand comments Nezha made weeks ago."

"Then what's up north?" Venka demanded. "Where are you going? I don't care what you tell everyone else, Rin, but you have to tell *me*." She examined Rin's face for a moment. "You're going to wake the third, aren't you?"

Rin blinked, surprised. "How did you guess?"

"Isn't it obvious?" Venka asked. "You've dragged back Master Jiang and the Empress. The Gatekeeper and the Vipress. There's only one missing, and no one ever confirmed that he's dead. So where is he? Somewhere in the Baolei range, I'm assuming?"

"The Wudang Mountains," Rin answered automatically, disconcerted by Venka's matter-of-fact tone. "We have to get through Dog Province first. But how are—I mean, that's fine with you? You don't think that's insane?"

"I've seen stranger things in the past week," Venka said. "You wield fire like it's a sword. Jiang—I mean, Master *fucking* Jiang, the grand idiot of Sinegard, just ripped an entire fleet from the sky. I don't know what's insane anymore. I just hope you know what you're doing."

"I don't," Rin said. "I've no idea."

She was being honest. She didn't have the faintest clue what the Dragon Emperor could do. Daji and Jiang had been frustratingly cagey on the topic. Daji, when asked, gave only the vaguest descriptions—*he's powerful, he's legendary, he's like nothing you've ever seen*. Meanwhile, half the time Jiang acted as if he'd never heard the name Riga. The only thing Rin had to go on was that both of them seemed so very sure that the Dragon Emperor, once awakened, could flatten the Republic.

"All I know is that he scares Jiang," she told Venka. "And whatever scares *him* ought to terrify the world."

Their misery intensified in the following days, because at last they'd reached an altitude high enough that everything was paved with ice.

Rin was initially undaunted. She'd had some half-baked idea that she might be able to ease their journey with the sheer force of flame. It worked at first. She became a human torch. She melted the slippery roads until they were walkable sludge, boiled water to drink, lit campfires by pointing, and kept the train warm by walking among the ranks.

But after two days of this continuous flame, a numbing exhaustion set in, and she found it harder and harder to reach for a force that drained her and tortured Kitay.

"I'm sorry," she said every time she found him shaking atop a wagon, ghostly pale, fingers pressed into his temples so hard they left little grooves.

"I'm fine," he said every time.

But she knew he was lying. She couldn't keep pushing him like this; it would destroy them both. She started calling the fire only several hours a day, and then only to clear the roads ahead. The troops now had only their dwindling supply of torches to rely on for heat. Frostbite and hypothermia eroded their ranks. Soldiers stopped waking up after they'd gone to sleep.

Jiang, meanwhile, was deteriorating at a terrifying rate.

This march was killing him. There was no other way to describe it. He'd grown gaunt and pale, and he wasn't eating. He couldn't walk on his own anymore; they had to drag him along on a wagon. He hadn't regained his lucidity, either. Sometimes he was mercifully placid, affable, and easy to order about like a child. More often he turned in on himself, gripped by some terrible visions that the rest of them couldn't see, lashing out whenever anyone tried to help him. Then he became dangerous. Then the shadows started to creep.

Under Daji's advice they often kept him in a sedated state, plying him with laudanum tea until he sank back against the corners of the wagon in a stupor. It made Rin sick to see his eyes dulled and uncomprehending, drool leaking out the side of his mouth, but she couldn't think of any better options. They needed to keep him stable until they got to Mount Tianshan.

She didn't know what Jiang was capable of when unhinged.

But they couldn't sedate him constantly without doing permanent damage to his mind. He still needed regular stretches of sobriety, and these were so painful and humiliating that Rin couldn't bring herself to watch.

One night Jiang woke the camp with such tortured screaming that Rin dashed immediately out of the tent where she slept and rushed to his side.

"Master?" She clenched his hand. "What's wrong?"

His eyes flew open. He regarded her with his wide, pale eyes, and for a moment, he seemed almost calm.

"Hanelai?"

Rin reeled.

She'd heard that name before. Just once, just briefly, but she'd never forget it. She remembered kneeling on the freezing forest floor, her ankle throbbing, while Chaghan's aunt, the Sorqan Sira, gripped her face in her hands and spoke a name that made the surrounding Ketreyids bristle. *She looks like Hanelai.*

"Master..." She swallowed. "Who—"

"I know where we're going." Jiang's arm trembled violently. She tightened her grasp, but that only seemed to increase his agitation. "And I don't—we can't—*don't make me wake him.*"

"Do you mean Riga?" she asked cautiously. She wasn't prepared for the way he flinched at the name.

He gave her a look of sheer, abject terror. "He is evil incarnate."

"What are you talking about?" she demanded. "He's your anchor, why won't—"

"*Listen to me.*" Jiang reached out with his other hand and gripped her arm above the elbow. "I know what she wants to do. She's lying to you. You cannot go."

His nails dug painfully into her flesh. Rin squirmed, but Jiang's grip was like iron.

"You're hurting me," she said.

He didn't let go. He stared at her, eyes wild and intense like she had never seen them. Something was lost behind them. Something was broken, suppressed, desperately trying to claw its way out.

"You don't understand what you're about to do," Jiang said urgently. "Don't climb that mountain. Kill me first. Kill *her.*"

His grip tightened. Rin's eyes watered from the pain, but she didn't wrench her arm away; she was too afraid of startling him. "Master, please..."

"End this before it begins," he hissed.

Rin didn't know what to do or say. Where on earth was Daji? Only she knew how to keep Jiang calm; only she could whisper the right combination of words to stop his raving.

"What's on Mount Tianshan?" she asked. "Why are you afraid of Riga? Who is Hanelai?"

Jiang relaxed his fingers. His eyes widened just the slightest bit, and Rin thought she saw some fragment of rationality and recognition dawning on his face. He opened his mouth. But just when she thought he was on the verge of an answer, he threw his head back and laughed.

I should leave, Rin thought, suddenly terrified. She should never have approached him. She should have just left him to his screaming until it died away on its own. She should leave now, walk away, and when morning came, Jiang would be calm again and everything would be normal and they'd never speak of this again.

She knew he was trying to tell her something. There was a hidden truth here, something awful and terrible, but she didn't want to know. She just wanted to run away and cry.

"Altan," Jiang said suddenly.

Rin froze, crouched halfway between sitting down and standing up.

"I'm sorry." Jiang stared her in the eyes; he was addressing *her*. "I'm so sorry. I could have protected you. But they—"

"Stop." Rin shook her head. "Please, Master, stop—"

"You don't understand." Jiang reached out for her wrist. "They hurt me and they said they'd hurt you worse so I had to let you go, don't you understand—"

"*Shut up!*" Rin screamed.

Jiang recoiled as if she had hit him. His entire body started to shake so hard she was afraid he might actually shatter like a porcelain vase, but then, abruptly, he went still. He wasn't breathing; his chest did not rise or fall. For a long time he sat with his head bent and his eyes closed. When at last he opened them, they were a bright, terrible white.

"You should not be here."

Rin didn't know who was speaking through his mouth, but that wasn't Jiang.

Then he smiled, and it was the most horrible sight she'd ever seen.

"Don't you know better?" he asked. "He wants you all dead."

He rose and advanced toward her. She scrambled to her feet and took a single, trembling step backward. *Run*, whispered a small voice in her mind. *Run, you idiot.* But she couldn't move, couldn't take her eyes off his face. She was rooted in place, simultaneously terrified and fascinated.

"Riga's going to kill you when he finds you." He laughed again, a high and unnerving sound. "Because of Hanelai. Because of what Hanelai did. He'll kill you all."

He gripped her by the shoulders and shook her hard. Rin felt an icy chill as she realized for the first time that she wasn't safe here, *physically* was not safe, because she had no idea what Jiang could or would do to her.

Jiang leaned closer. He didn't have a weapon. But Rin knew he'd never needed one.

"You're all scum," he sneered. "And I should have just done what he fucking wanted."

Rin reached for the fire.

"Ziya, *stop*!"

Daji ran into the tent. Rin flinched back, heart pounding with relief. Jiang turned toward Daji, that horrible sneer still etched across his face. For a moment Rin thought that he would strike her, but Daji grabbed his arm before he could move and jammed a needle into his vein. He stood stock-still, swaying on his feet. His expression turned placid, and then he dropped to his knees.

"*You*," he slurred. "You cunt. This is all your fault."

"Go to sleep," Daji said. "Just go to sleep."

Jiang said something else, but it was slurred and nonsensical. One arm scrabbled for the floor—Rin thought he was reaching for the needle, and tensed for a fight—but then he tilted forward and collapsed to the ground.

"Get away from here." Daji hustled Rin out of the tent into the cold night air. Rin stumbled along, too dazed to protest. Once they'd walked onto an icy ledge out of earshot of the main camp, Daji spun Rin around and shook her by the shoulders as if she were a disobedient child. "What were you thinking? Have you gone mad?"

"What was that?" Rin shrieked. She wiped frantically at her cheeks. Hot tears kept spilling down her face, but she couldn't make them stop. "*What is he?*"

Daji shook her head and pressed her hand against her chest. It took Rin a moment to realize she wasn't just posturing. Something was wrong.

"A flame," Daji whispered urgently. Her lips had turned a dark, shocking violet. "Please."

Rin lit a fire in her palm and held it out between them. "Here."

Daji hunched over the warmth. She stayed like that for a long time, eyes closed, fingers twitching over the fire. Slowly the color came back to her face.

"You know what that was," she said at last. "He's getting his mind back."

"But—" Rin swallowed, trying to wrap her mind around her racing questions, to configure them into an order that made sense. "But that's not him. He's not like that, surely he was never like *that*—"

"You didn't know the real Jiang. You knew a shade of a man. You knew a fake, an imitation. That's not Jiang, that never was."

"And *this* is?" Rin shrieked. "He was going to kill me!"

"He's adjusting." Daji didn't answer her question. "He's just . . . confused, is all—"

"*Confused?* Haven't you heard him? He's afraid. He's *terrified* of what's happening to him, and he doesn't want to become that person because he knows something—something you won't tell me. We can't do this to him." Rin's voice trembled. "We have to turn back."

"No." Daji violently shook her head. Her eyes glinted in the moonlight; with her disheveled hair and her hungry, desperate expression, she looked nearly as mad as Jiang. "There is no turning back. I've waited too long for this."

"I don't give a fuck what you want."

"You don't understand. I've had to watch him all these years, had to keep him confined to Sinegard knowing full well that I'd reduced him to a dithering idiot." Daji's voice trembled. "I took his mind from him. Now he has a chance to get it back. And I can't take that from him. Not even if he's happier like this."

"But you can't," Rin said. "He's so scared."

"It doesn't matter what this Jiang thinks. This Jiang isn't real. The *real* Jiang needs to come back." Daji looked like she was on the verge of tears. "I need him back."

Then Rin saw the tears glistening on Daji's cheeks. Daji, the Vipress, the former Empress of Nikan, was crying. The Vipress was fucking *crying*.

Rin was too upset for sympathy. No. No, Daji didn't get to do this, didn't get to stand here and whimper like she was innocent in the horrifying mental collapse they were witnessing, when Daji was the entire reason why Jiang was broken.

"Then you shouldn't have Sealed him," Rin said.

"You think I couldn't feel what I'd done?" Daji's eyes were red around the rims. "We are linked. You know what that's like. I felt his confusion. I felt how lost he was, I felt him probing at the corners of his mind for something he didn't know he'd lost, acutely so because I *knew* what he didn't have access to."

"Then why did you have to do it?" Rin asked miserably.

What was so terrible, so earth-wrenchingly terrible, that Daji would risk her own life and fracture Jiang's soul to stop it?

They quarreled, Daji had once told her.

Over what?

Daji just shook her head. Her pale neck bobbed. "Never ask me this."

"I have a right to know."

"You have a right to nothing," Daji said coldly. "They fought. I stopped them. That's all there is—"

"Bullshit." Rin's voice rose as the flame grew, stretching dangerously, threateningly close to Daji's skin. "There's more, there's something you're not telling me, *I deserve to know*—"

"Runin."

Daji's eyes glinted a snakelike yellow. Rin's limbs locked suddenly into place. She couldn't wrench her gaze from Daji's face. She understood immediately that this was a challenge—a battle of divine wills.

Do you dare?

Once Rin might have fought. She could have forced Daji into submission; she'd done it before. But she was so exhausted, stretched thin from day after day of pulling the Phoenix through Kitay's aching mind. She couldn't summon rage after what she'd just seen. She felt like a thin shard of frost, one touch from shattering apart.

Rin pulled her flame back into her hand.

Daji's pupils turned back to their normal, lovely black. Rin sagged, released from their grip.

"If I were you, I would stop worrying." Daji had stopped crying; the red around her eyes had faded away. Gone, too, was the fragile hitch in her voice, replaced by a cool, detached confidence. "Jiang's episodes will get worse. But he will not die. He cannot die—you can trust me on that. But the more you try to prod into his mind, try to retrieve whatever you think you've lost, the more you'll torture yourself. Let go of the man you remember. You're never going to get him back."

They returned together to Jiang's tent. Rin sat down next to where Jiang lay and watched him, her heart twisting with pity. He looked so miserable, even in dreamless, morphine-induced sleep. His features were pressed into a worried frown, his fingers clenching his blankets as if he were hanging on to the edge of a cliff.

This wasn't the last time she'd see him suffer like this, she realized. He was going to get worse and worse the closer they got to the mountain. He'd deteriorate until he finally snapped, and a victor emerged between the personalities battling in his mind.

Could she do this to him?

It would be easier if the Jiang who had been Sealed were truly derivative, if he were truly a pale shade of the other, genuine personality. But the Jiang she'd known at Sinegard was a full person in his own right, a person with wants and memories and desires.

That Jiang was so scared of who he used to be—who he was about to become. He'd found a refuge in his partitioned mind. How could she take that from him?

She tried to imagine how Jiang's Seal must have felt all those years he'd lived at Sinegard. What if she were blocked not only from the Pantheon but from her own memories? What if she were held captive behind a wall in her mind, screeching in silent anguish as a bumbling idiot took control of her limbs and tongue?

If she were him, of course she'd want to be free.

But what if someone could erase all memories of what she'd done?

No more guilt. No more nightmares. She wouldn't have flaring pockets in her memory like gaping wounds that hurt to touch. She wouldn't hear screams when she tried to sleep. She wouldn't see bodies burning every time she closed her eyes.

Maybe that was the coward's asylum. But she'd want it, too.

The next morning, Jiang had regained some degree of lucidity. Sleep, however forced, had helped—the shadows disappeared from under his eyes, and his face lost its rictus of dread, settling back into a placid calm.

"Hello, Master," she said when he awoke. "How are you feeling?"

He yawned. "I'm afraid I don't know what you mean."

She decided to push her luck. "You had a bad night."

"Did I?"

His amused indifference annoyed her. "You called me Altan."

"Oh, really?" He scratched the back of his head. "I'm sorry, that was terribly rude. I know you used to follow him around with those shining puppy eyes."

She brushed that off. *Shut up*, spoke a little voice in her mind. *Stop talking, walk away.* But she wasn't done. She wanted to push him, to see how much he remembered. "And you asked me to kill you."

She couldn't tell if his laugh sounded nervous, or if that was the way Jiang had always laughed—high, unsettling, and foolish.

"My goodness, Runin." He reached out to pat her on the shoulder. "Surely I taught you better than to fret over the little things."

Jiang's advice had been flippant. But as their altitude increased and the air grew thinner, Rin lost the mental energy to think about anything except the daily exigencies of the march. Her flames barely made the mountain pathways tolerable; the ice refroze almost as quickly as she melted it. At night, when the temperatures dropped dangerously low, the soldiers started sleeping only in one-hour shifts to prevent anyone from succumbing to the numb, beckoning dark.

At least the environment, not the Republic, formed the bulk of their problems. The first few days on the march Rin had kept her eyes trained on the pale gray sky, expecting dark shapes to materialize from the clouds any moment. But the fleet never came. Kitay floated a number of theories for why they weren't being pursued—the Hesperians were low on fuel, the misty mountain terrain made blind flying dangerous, or the fleet had been so badly damaged at the Anvil that the Hesperians wouldn't sanction sending out the remaining ships in pursuit of an enemy that could summon shadows from nothing.

"They've just seen what we can do," he told the officers, his tone so obviously full of artificial confidence. "They know it's suicide to come after us. They might be tracing where we are. But they won't risk an attack."

Rin hoped to the gods he was right.

Another week passed and the skies remained empty, but that didn't come close to putting her at ease. So what if Nezha chose to let them live for another day? He might change his mind tomorrow. He might cave under internal pressure for a quick victory. They couldn't be hard to pick out against the terrain—he might decide that following them through the mountains wasn't worth it, that the drain on fuel and resources was too great a cost to justify ferreting out whatever hotbed of shamanism he might find.

She was well aware that with every step she took, she moved under the threat of immediate extermination. The Republic was capable of inflicting mass death in seconds. They could end this at any time. But all she could do was forge ahead and hope that it would be far too late by the time Nezha realized he should have killed her long ago.

CHAPTER 19

Rin's journey by airship to the Chuluu Korikh had made the world seem so small. But their trek through the Baolei range felt infinite, and the mountains, which before now she had only ever known as little marks on a map, seemed to encompass a territory greater than the Empire itself. Exhausting weeks stretched into grueling, monotonous months and somehow, when the march had gone on for so long it seemed there had never been a time when they weren't climbing, the daily horrors they faced became routine.

They learned to scale tricky, narrow passages with rope and knives in lieu of ice picks. They learned to pour warm water over their genitals when they relieved themselves because otherwise the freezing temperatures would give them frostbite. They learned to drink boiled chili water constantly because that was the only thing that would keep them warm, which meant they spent half their nights crouching to relieve their diarrhea.

They learned how frightening snow blindness could be when their eyes grew red and itchy and their vision blinked out for hours at a time. They learned to focus on the dull gray of the paths beneath their feet instead of the snow that surrounded them. At noon, when the sun glinted so glaringly off the white peaks that it gave them headaches, they stopped and sat in their shaded tents until the brightness had dimmed.

They adapted in these ways and more. They had decided that if the best of Hesperian technology couldn't kill them, then the mountains certainly wouldn't, so they learned dozens of ways to stay alive in a terrain intent on burying them.

Jiang didn't recover, but his condition didn't become noticeably worse. Most days he sat obediently on the wagon, whittling sculptures of deformed animals out of half-frozen bark with a dull, worn knife because Rin and Daji didn't trust him with sharper objects.

His ramblings continued. They had spiraled past his usual nonsensical babbles. Every time Rin visited him, he launched into invectives involving people and events she had never heard of. Over and over, he addressed her as either Altan or Hanelai. Rarely did he call her by her name. Even more rarely did he look at her at all; more often he spoke to the snow, muttering with a hushed urgency, as if she were a chronicler present to record a history quickly slipping away from his grasp.

Daji remained tight-lipped when Rin pressed her about anything regarding the circumstances that led to Jiang's Seal. But, as if in exchange, she acquiesced to answering questions about Jiang's other utterances. Each night when they made camp, she sat with Rin and Kitay, recounting histories that Rin could never have found in the libraries of Sinegard. These discussions took the form of direct interrogations. Rin fired questions at Daji, one after the other, and Daji responded to everything that she could, often in great detail, as if by jabbering on about minor anecdotes, she could distract Rin from the important questions.

Rin knew what Daji was doing. She knew she was being deceived about *something*. But she took what she could get. Access to Daji was like an open scroll containing all the hidden secrets of Nikara history. She would be foolish not to play along.

"Why does Riga look so much like the House of Yin?" she asked.

"Because he's one of them," Daji said. "That should have been obvious. His father was Yin Zexu, the younger brother to the Dragon Warlord."

"Vaisra's brother?"

"No, Vaisra's uncle. The Dragon Warlord back then was Yin Vara. Vaisra's father."

So Nezha was Riga's nephew. Rin wondered if their power was passed through blood, like the Speerly affinity for the Phoenix. But the Yins had such different relationships to the Dragon. Riga was a true shaman, one who had been to the Pantheon and become imbued with a power freely given and freely received. Nezha was a slave to some perverted, corrupted thing, a creature that should never have existed in the material world.

"Zexu should have been the Warlord all along," Daji said. "He was a born leader. Decisive, ruthless, and capable. Vara was the eldest, but he was a child. Meek, terrified of confrontation. Always bowing to the men he feared, bending because he was so afraid to break. A few years into the occupation, the Hesperians decided they wanted to transport shipments of Mugenese opium into the harbor at the Red Cliffs. Vara agreed, and sent his younger brother out to guide the Hesperian cargo ships through the channel. Instead Zexu rigged the harbor with explosives and sank the Mugenese fleet."

"I like Zexu," Rin said.

"He was dead by the time I first heard his name," Daji said. "But Riga told me so much about him. He always admired his father. He was terribly hotheaded and impulsive. Never could stand an insult. You'd have gotten along splendidly, but only if you didn't kill each other first."

"I'm guessing the Hesperians had him shot," Rin said.

"They very much would have liked to," Daji said. "But open war hadn't broken out yet, and they didn't want to provoke it by killing a member of an elite family. Vara had Zexu exiled to the occupied zone in northern Horse Province instead. Sent his whole family away and cut him out of the lineage records. That's why you'll never find a portrait of him in the palace at Arlong. Riga was an orphan by the time we met. The Mugenese had worked his father to death in a labor camp, and the gods know what happened to his poor mother. When I first saw him, Riga was a pathetic thing, just skin and bones, scraping to tomorrow by stealing food out of trash heaps."

"So you met as children," Kitay said.

"We all grew up in the occupied north. Jiang and I might have been natives. Or children of refugees." Daji shrugged. "Now it's impossible to remember. We all lost our parents early on, before they could tell us what provinces we were from. Perhaps that's why we were so bent on unification. We were from nowhere, so we wanted to rule everywhere."

It felt bizarre to picture the Trifecta as young children. In Rin's mind, they had sprung fully formed into the world, powerful and godly. She'd rarely considered that there was a time when they were mere mortals just like she had once been. Young. Terrified. Weak.

They'd grown up during the bleakest period of Nikara history. Rin had known a country at relative peace before the third war, but the Trifecta had been born into misery. They'd grown up knowing nothing but oppression, humiliation, and suffering.

Small wonder they'd committed the atrocities they did. Small wonder they'd found them completely justified.

"How did you get out?" Rin asked.

"The Mugenese cared about grown soldiers, not children. No one noticed us. The hardest part, in fact, was getting me past the mistresses at the whorehouse." Some unrecognizable emotion flickered across Daji's face, a twist of her lip and a quirk of her eyebrow that quickly disappeared. "We didn't know where we were going, only that we wanted to get out. Once we crossed the border, we wandered for days on the steppe and nearly starved to death before the Ketreyids found us. They took us in. They trained us."

"And then you killed them," Rin said.

"Yes." Daji sighed. "That was unfortunate."

"They still hate you for it," Rin said, just to see how Daji might react. "They want you dead. You know that, right? They're just figuring out a way to get it done."

"Let them hate." Daji shrugged. "Back then our entire strategy was founded on crushing dissent. Wherever we could find it. In times like that, you couldn't let sleeping threats lie. I'm sorry Tseveri died. I know Jiang loved her. But I don't regret a thing."

Daji, it turned out, had done a terrible number of things worth regretting. Rin pried for details about all of them. She made her talk about the lies she had told. The rivals she had killed. The innocents she had sacrificed in the bloody calculus of strategy. Over talks that spanned days, and then weeks, Daji colored in a picture of a Trifecta who were so much more ruthless and capable than Rin had ever imagined.

But it wasn't enough. Daji always spoke only of the amusing stories, the minor details. She never spoke of the day she had Sealed her anchors. And unless prompted, she never spoke of Riga himself. She would answer any of Rin's questions about his past, but she only ever gave the barest, vaguest details about his abilities or his character.

"What was he like?" Rin asked.

"Glorious. Beautiful."

Rin made a noise of exasperation. "You're talking about a painting, not a man."

"There is no other way to describe him. He was magnificent. Everything you could want from a leader and more."

Rin found that deeply unsatisfying, but knew that line of questioning would only yield the same answers. "Then why did you put him to sleep?"

"You know why."

Rin tried to catch her off guard. "Then why are you afraid of him?"

Daji's voice retained its careful, icy calm. "I'm not afraid of him."

"That's bullshit. Both of you are."

"I am *not*—"

"Jiang is, at least. He screams Riga's name in his sleep. He flinches every time I mention him. And he seems convinced we're dragging him up the mountain to his death. Why?"

"We loved Riga," Daji said, unfazed. "And if we ever feared him, it was because he was great, and great rulers always inspire fear in the hearts of the weak."

Frustrated, Rin changed tack once again. "Who is Hanelai?"

For once, Daji looked startled. "Where did you hear that name?"

"Answer the question."

Daji arched an eyebrow, betraying nothing. "You first."

"The Sorqan Sira said once that I resembled Hanelai. Did you know her?"

Something shifted in Daji's expression. Rin couldn't quite read it—amusement? Relief? She seemed less on edge than she'd been just a moment ago, but Rin didn't know what had changed. "Hanelai doesn't matter to you. Hanelai's dead."

"Who was she?" Rin pressed. "A Speerly? Did you know her?"

"Yes," Daji said. "I knew her. And yes, she was a Speerly. A general, in fact. She fought alongside us in the Second Poppy War. She was an admirable woman. Very brave, and very stupid."

"Stupid? Why—"

"Because she defied Riga." Daji stood up, clearly finished. "Nobody defied Riga if they were smart."

The conversation stopped there. Rin tried many times again to broach the subject, but Daji refused to reveal anything more. She never spoke a word about what, precisely, Riga could do. Never a word about what Riga had done to Jiang, or the night that Jiang lost his mind, or how someone so supposedly great and powerful could possibly have missed the attack on Speer. Those gaps alone were enough for Rin to piece together the vaguest of theories, though she hated where it went.

She didn't want it to be true. The implications hurt too much.

She knew Daji was lying to her about something, but part of her didn't want to know. She wanted to just keep marching in a state of suspended disbelief, to keep assuming this war would be ended once they woke the Dragon Emperor. But the past kept prodding her mind like a tongue at an open sore, and the agony of not knowing, of being kept in the dark, grew too great to bear.

Finally, Rin decided to get her answers from Jiang instead.

That would be tricky. She'd have to get him alone. Daji was constantly at Jiang's side, day and night. They slept, marched, and ate together. In camp, they often sat with their heads pressed together, murmuring things that Rin could only guess at. Every time Rin attempted to speak to Jiang, Daji was present, hovering just within earshot.

She had to incapacitate Daji, if only for several hours.

"Can you get me a strong dose of laudanum?" she asked Kitay. "Discreetly?"

He gave her a concerned look. "Why?"

"Not for me," she said hastily. "For the Vipress."

Understanding dawned on his face. "You're playing a dangerous game there."

"I don't care," she said. "I have to know."

Daji proved shockingly easy to drug. She may have been vigilant as a hawk, but the demands of the march exhausted her just as much as they did everyone else. She still had to sleep. Rin only had to creep into Daji's tent and clamp a laudanum-soaked towel over her mouth for half a minute until her face went utterly slack. She snapped her fingers next to Daji's ears several times to check that she was fully unconscious. Daji didn't budge.

Then she shook Jiang awake.

He was trapped in another one of his nightmares. Sweat beaded on his temples as he twitched in his sleep, muttering invocations in a gibberish that sounded like a mixture of Mugini and Ketreyid.

Rin pinched his arm, then clamped a palm over his mouth. His eyes shot open.

"Don't scream," she said. "I just want to talk. Nod if you understand."

Miraculously, the fear withdrew from his face. To her great relief, he nodded.

He rose to a sitting position. His pale eyes moved about the tent and landed on Daji's limp form. His lips curled in amusement, as if he'd guessed exactly what Rin had done. "She's not dead, is she?"

"Only asleep." Rin stood up and gestured to the door. "Come on. Outside."

Obediently, he followed. Once they were out near the ledge, where the howling winds would drown out anything they said from eavesdroppers, she turned to Jiang and demanded, "Who is Hanelai?"

His face went slack.

"Who is Hanelai?" Rin repeated fiercely.

She knew from experience she might only get a minute or two of lucidity from him, so she needed to make the best use of that short window. She had spent that entire day with Kitay figuring out what to ask first. It was like trying to survey new territory in pitch darkness; there was simply too much they didn't know.

In the end, they had decided on Hanelai. Hanelai, aside from Altan, was the name Jiang called Rin most often whenever he forgot who she was. He uttered that name constantly, either in sleep or during his daily fitful hallucinations. She was a person he clearly associated with pain, fear, and dread. Hanelai linked the Trifecta with the Speerlies. Whatever Jiang was hiding from them, Hanelai was the key.

Her suspicions were right. Jiang shuddered at the word.

"Don't do this," he said.

"Do what?"

"Please don't make me remember." His eyes were like a child's, huge with fear.

He's not an innocent, Rin reminded herself. He was as much a monster as she and Daji were. He'd slaughtered the Sorqan Sira's daughter and half the Ketreyid clan with a smile on his face, even if he pretended not to remember.

"You don't get to forget," Rin said. "Whatever you did, you don't deserve to forget. Tell me about Hanelai."

"You don't understand." He shook his head frantically. "The more you press, the closer *he* comes, the other one—"

"He's going to come back regardless," she snapped. "You're just a front. You're an illusion you've constructed because you're too scared to face up to what you did. But you can't keep hiding, Master. If there's any shred of courage left in you, then you'll tell me. You owe that to me. You owe that to *her*."

She spat those last few words so forcefully that Jiang flinched.

She had been grasping at straws, throwing phrases out to see what stuck. She didn't know what Hanelai meant to Jiang. She hadn't known how he would react. But to her surprise, it seemed to work. Jiang didn't run away. He didn't shut down, the way he had so often before, when his eyes went glassy and his mind retreated back inside itself. He stared at her for a long time, looking not afraid, not confused, but *thoughtful*.

For the first time in a long time, he seemed like the man Rin had known at Sinegard.

"Hanelai." He drew the name out slowly, every syllable a sigh. "She was my mistake."

"What happened?" Rin asked. "Did you kill her?"

"I . . ." Jiang swallowed. The next words spilled out of him fast and quiet, as if he were spitting out a poison he'd been holding under his tongue. "I didn't want—that's not what I chose. Riga decided without me, and Daji didn't tell me until it was too late, but I tried to warn her—"

"Hold on," Rin said, overwhelmed. "Warn her about *what*?"

"I should have stopped Hanelai." He kept talking as if he hadn't heard. This wasn't a conversation anymore; he wasn't speaking to her, he was speaking to himself, unleashing a torrent of words like he was afraid if he didn't speak now then he'd never have the chance again. "She shouldn't have told him. She wanted help, but she was never going to get it, and I knew that. She should have left, if it hadn't been for the children—"

"Children?" Rin repeated. *What children?* What was Jiang talking about? This story had just become so much more complex and terrifying. Her mind spun, trying to fit together a narrative that made sense of it all, but everything it suggested horrified her. "Children like Altan? Like me?"

"Altan?" Jiang blinked. "No, no—poor boy, he never made it out—"

"Made it out of *where*?" Rin grasped Jiang by the collar, trying to catch the truth before it fled. "Jiang, who am I?"

But the moment had passed. Jiang stared down at her, his pale eyes vacant. The man who had the answers was gone.

"*Fuck!*" Rin screamed. Sparks flew out of her fist, singeing the front of Jiang's tunic.

He flinched back. "I'm sorry," he said in a small voice. "I can't—don't hurt me."

"Oh, for fuck's sake." She couldn't bear seeing him cower like this, a fully grown man acting like a child. She wanted to vomit from the shame.

She grabbed his arm and dragged him back toward his tent. He obeyed her instructions without a word, crawling meekly onto his blanket without even a glance at Daji's sprawled form.

Before Rin left she made him swallow a cup of laudanum tea. His sleep would be peaceful, dreamless. And tomorrow, if Jiang tried to tell anyone what had happened, she could easily pretend whatever he said was just his usual babbling nonsense.

"That's all he said?" Kitay asked for what felt like the hundredth time. "'If it hadn't been for the children'?"

"It's all I could get." Rin dragged one heavy foot before the other and pushed herself up the incline. They'd only been marching for an hour since sunrise, but she was already so exhausted she didn't know how she'd make it through the day. She hadn't been able to sleep, not with Jiang's words echoing over and over in her mind. They made no more sense now than they had when he'd first uttered them; her thousand unanswered questions had only sprouted a thousand more. "He didn't say whose, he didn't say where—"

"I mean, it's got to be the Speerly children," Kitay said. "Right? With Hanelai involved, there's no one else."

He'd said that already. They'd been running up against the same wall all morning, but that was the only conclusion they could deduce with any degree of certainty. Jiang had done something to Hanelai and the Speerly children, and he was still rotting with guilt over it.

But *what*?

"This is pointless," Kitay declared after a silence. "There are too many unknowns. We can't piece together a story through conjecture. We've no clue what happened twenty years ago."

"Unless we do that again," Rin said.

He shot her a sideways look. "*Are* you going to do that again?"

"Rin." Before Rin could respond, Venka pushed her way up to the front of the column, her face flushed red. This was rare. Typically Venka marched near the back of the line, overseeing the rear to keep an eye out for stragglers and deserters. "There's a problem."

Rin motioned for the troops to halt. "What's happened?"

"It's two girls." Venka had a strange expression on her face. "The soldiers are—ah, I mean, they're—"

"Have they touched them?" Rin asked sharply. She'd made her policy on sexual assault very clear. The first time two soldiers were caught cornering a young woman alone at midnight, she and Venka had castrated the soldiers and left them to bleed out in the dirt with their cocks shoved in their mouths. It hadn't happened again.

"It's not that," Venka said quickly. "But they've ganged up on them. They want punishment."

Rin furrowed her brow. "For what?"

Venka looked deeply uncomfortable. "For violating the bodies."

Hastily, Rin followed Venka down the column.

The first thing she saw when they broke through the gathered crowd was a corpse. She recognized the face of one of the Monkey Warlord's former officers. His body was splayed in the snow, arms and legs stretched wide as if he'd been prepared for a dissection. His midsection looked as if a bear had taken two large bites from his flesh—one around his chest, and one near his stomach.

Then Rin saw the girls, both kneeling with their hands tied behind their backs. Their hands were bloody. So were their mouths and chins.

Rin's stomach churned as she realized what had happened.

"They should burn," snarled a soldier—another one of Gurubai's men. He stood over the taller girl, one hand on his sword as if ready to behead her right then and there.

"Did they kill him?" Rin asked quickly.

"He was dead." The taller girl jerked her head up, eyes flashing with defiance. "He was already dead, he was sick, we didn't—"

"Shut up, you little whore." The soldier jammed his boot into the small of her back. The girl's mouth snapped shut and her eyes widened with pain, but she didn't whimper.

"Unbind them," Rin said.

The soldiers didn't move.

"What is this, a trial?" Rin raised her voice, trying to imbue it with that same ring that had come so easily in the cavern. "Justice is mine to deal, not yours. Unbind them and leave them be."

Sullenly they obeyed, then dispersed back to the marching column. Rin knelt down in front of the girls. She hadn't recognized them at first, but now she saw they were the girls she'd recruited at the Beehive—the pale, pretty waif and her shy, freckled sister. Their faces were gaunt and shrunken, but she recognized that hard, flinty look in their eyes.

"Pipaji?" At last their names came to mind. "Jiuto?"

They gave no indication that they had heard. Pipaji rubbed at Jiuto's arms, soothing her sister's whimpers with hushed whispers.

"You ate him," Rin said, because she wasn't sure what else to say. This was too bizarre, too unexpected. She didn't know what she was supposed to do next.

"I told you he was already dead." If Pipaji was scared, she did a remarkable job of hiding it. "He wasn't breathing when we found him."

Beside her, Jiuto sucked at her fingertips.

Rin stared at them, astonished. "You can't do that. That's not—I mean, that's a violation. That's disgusting."

"It's food." Pipaji gave her a very bored look—the sort of gaunt, indifferent stare that only starvation produced. *Go ahead*, said her eyes. *Kill me. I won't even feel it.*

Rin noticed then that the corpse was not so brutally savaged as it had first appeared. The bloodstained snow only made it seem that way. The girls had only made two neat incisions. One over the heart, and one over the liver. They'd gone straight for organs that would provide the most sustenance, which meant they'd harvested meat from bodies before. They were well practiced at this by now—this was just the first time they'd been caught.

But what was Rin supposed to do about it? Force them to starve? She couldn't tell them to subsist on rations. There wasn't enough of anything to go around. Rin had sufficient rations because of course she did; she was the general, the Speerly, the one person in this column who could not be allowed to go hungry. Meanwhile Pipaji and Jiuto were no one of importance, not even trained soldiers. They were expendable.

Could she punish these girls for wanting to survive?

"Take everything you want and put it in a bag," she said finally. She could barely believe the words coming out of her mouth, but in that instant, they seemed like the only appropriate things to say. "Wrap it in leaves so that the blood doesn't leak. Eat only when no one is looking. If they catch you again, they'll tear you apart, and I won't be able to help you. Do you understand?"

Pipaji's tongue darted out to lick the blood off the corner of her bottom lip.

"Do you understand?" Rin repeated.

"Whatever you say," Pipaji muttered. She gave Jiuto a nod. Without another word, they knelt back over the body and resumed deftly pulling the organs out of the carcass.

Pipaji and Jiuto were not the only ones who resorted to eating human flesh. They were just the first. The longer the march stretched on, the more it became apparent that their food supplies were not going to last. The army was subsisting on one ration of dried salted mayau and one cup of rice gruel a day. They foraged the best they could—some of the soldiers had even started swallowing tree bark to stifle their pangs of hunger—but at this altitude, vegetation was scarce and there was no wildlife in sight.

So Rin wasn't surprised when rumors circulated of corpses—usually victims of frostbite or starvation—divvied up and eaten raw, roasted, or parceled out for the road.

"Say nothing," Kitay advised her. "If you sanction it, you'll horrify them. If you denounce it, they'll resent you. But if you keep quiet, you get plausible deniability."

Rin couldn't see what other choice she had. She'd known this march would be hard, but their prospects looked bleaker with each passing day. Morale, which had been so blazingly strong at the start of their journey, began to wilt. Whispers of dissent and complaints about Rin riddled the column. *She doesn't know where she's going. Sinegard-trained, and she can't find her way through a damned mountain. She's led us up here to die.* Order collapsed along the column. Troops routinely ignored, or didn't hear, her commands. It took nearly an hour to rouse the camp into marching in the mornings. At first, the deserters numbered in handfuls, and then dozens.

Venka suggested sending search parties to chase them down,

but Rin couldn't see the point. What good would that do? The deserters had sentenced themselves to death—alone, they would freeze or starve in days. Their numbers made no difference to her ultimate victory or defeat.

All that mattered was Mount Tianshan. Their future was laid out in stark black and white now—either they woke Riga, or they died.

The days began blurring together. There was no difference between one instance of monotonous suffering and the next. Rin, fatigued beyond belief, started feeling a profound sense of detachment. She felt like an observer, not a participant, like she was watching a shadow puppet show about a beautiful and suicidal struggle, something that had already happened in the past and been enshrined in myth.

They weren't humans, they were stories; they were paintings winding their way across wall scrolls. The terrain transformed around them as they marched, became brighter, sharper, and lovelier, as if warping to match the mythic status of their journey. The snow gleamed a purer white. The mist grew thicker, and the mountains it shrouded seemed less solid, more blurred at the edges. The sky turned a paler shade of blue, not the cheery hue of a bright summer's day but the faded shade of water paint swept absently onto canvas with a thick rabbit-hair brush.

They saw crimson birds whose tails swept thrice the length of their bodies. They saw human faces etched into tree bark, not carved but organically grown—calm, beatific expressions that watched them go with no urgency or resentment. They saw pale white deer who stood utterly still when they approached, calm enough for Rin to run her hand over their soft ears. They tried hunting them for food, to no avail—the deer fled at the sight of steel. And Rin felt secretly relieved, because it didn't feel right to devour anything that beautiful.

Rin didn't know if they were hallucinations brought on by feverish fatigue. But if they were, then they were group hallucinations—shared visions of a lovely, mythical, incipient nation in becoming.

For it was wonderful to remember that this land could still be so breathtakingly beautiful, that there was more sewn into the heart of the Twelve Provinces than blood and steel and dirt. That centuries of warfare later, this country was still a canvas for the gods, that their celestial essence still seeped through the cracks between worlds.

Perhaps this was why the Hesperians so badly wanted to make Nikan their own. Rin could only picture their country by extrapolating from their abandoned colonial quarters, but she envisioned it as a dull place, gray and drab as the cloaks they wore, and maybe that was why they had to erect their garish cities of flashing lights and screaming noises: to deny the fact that their world was fundamentally without divinity.

Maybe that was what had driven the Federation, too. Why else would you murder children and hold a country hostage except for the promise of learning to speak to gods? The great empires of the waking world were driven so mad by what they had forgotten that they decided to slaughter the only people who could still dream.

That was what kept Rin going when her feet had gone so numb from the cold she could barely feel them as she dragged them through the snow, when her temples throbbed so badly from the glaring white that bright red flashes darted through her vision—the idea that survival was promised, victory was foreordained, because the truth of the universe was on their side. Because only the chaotic, incomprehensible Pantheon could explain the vast and eerie beauty of this land, which was something the Hesperians, with their obsessive, desperate clinging to order, could never understand.

So Rin marched because she knew that, at the end of their journey, divine salvation was waiting. She marched because every step brought her closer to the gods.

She marched until one morning Kitay abruptly stopped a few steps ahead of her. She tensed, heart already racing with dread, but when he turned around, she saw he was smiling.

He pointed, and she followed his gaze down the path to a single blue orchid pushing tentatively through the snow.

She exhaled and choked down the urge to cry.

Orchids couldn't grow at the altitudes at which they'd been marching. They could only grow in the lower elevations, in the valleys and foothills.

They'd crossed into Dog Province. They'd begun their descent. From here on out, they were marching down.

CHAPTER 20

Of all twelve provinces, Dog Province was the true wasteland of the Empire.

Rat Province was dirt poor, Monkey Province was an agriculturally barren backwater, and Boar Province was a lawless plain crawling with bandits. But Dog Province was remote, mountainous, and so sparsely populated that the yaks outnumbered the people—the only reason, perhaps, that it had not yet been invaded by the Republic.

When Rin and her troops descended the mountains over the border into the Scarigon Plateau, they saw no sign of human civilization.

She supposed it had been a foolish hope, that the Dog Warlord and his army might be waiting for them with open arms at the foothills of the Baolei Mountains. That rendezvous had always been an empty dream, a lie she'd told the southerners from the outset of the march to give them a reason to keep going. It had just been so long since they'd escaped from the Anvil that she'd started to believe it herself.

They might still find allies. Dog Province was a vast, open land, and they had only reached the southeastern edge of its border. Perhaps they might still find the nomadic herds of sheep and yaks that the Dog Province was known for. But Rin knew it would drive her mad to keep her eyes fixed on distant plains, hoping for silhouettes to appear on the horizon.

They could not assume aid would come. Their only option was to keep pushing forward to Mount Tianshan, alone.

The march across the plateau proceeded far more easily than their journey through the mountains. They were still exhausted; their numbers were still dwindling from starvation and disease. But now that the ground did not slip treacherously under their feet and the air couldn't bite hard enough to kill, they covered thrice the distance each day as they had on the Baolei range. Morale improved. The whispers of dissent grew quieter. And as the distant Tianshan range grew closer day by day, no longer a hazy line on the horizon but a distinct, ridged silhouette against the north sky, Rin began daring to hope that they might actually make it. That all their plans, all their talk of the Trifecta that up until now had seemed like a distant fantasy, might actually come to pass.

She just still hadn't figured out what she might do if they did.

"Rin." Kitay nudged her shoulder. "Look."

She'd been stumbling along in a daze, half-asleep from fatigue. "What?"

He tilted her chin up to stop her staring at the ground. He pointed. "Over there."

She didn't believe it when she saw it, but then a cheer went up through the column that confirmed everyone saw what she did—the outline of a village, clearly visible against the steppe. Thick clouds of smoke billowing up from rooftops of rounded huts that promised shelter, warmth, and a cooked dinner.

The column quickened its pace.

"Wait," Rin said. "We don't know if they're friendly."

Kitay shot her a wry look. Around them, the southerners marched with their hands on their weapons. "I don't think it matters much whether we're invited."

∞

"You're smaller than I thought you'd be," said the Dog Warlord, Quan Cholang.

Rin shrugged. "The last time a person said that to me, I had him torn apart by a mob."

She didn't elaborate. She was too busy chewing her way through the spread on the mat before her—tough, dry mutton; grainy steamed buns; sheep-stock gruel; and a cold, sour glass of yak's milk to wash it down. It was, by any standard, awful—Dog Province was often lampooned for its tough, tasteless food. But after months in the mountains, her tongue craved any flavors other than the dull sting of chili-boiled water.

She knew she was being rude. But as long as no one was actively trying to kill her, she was going to eat.

She sucked the last juicy mouthful of sheep marrow from bone, took a deep and satisfied breath, then wiped her hand on her pants.

"I don't recognize you at all," she said bluntly. "Leadership transition?"

She'd met the former Dog Warlord once before, just briefly, at the Empress's postwar summit in Lusan. He hadn't made much of an impression; she could only barely remember his features well enough to know that the man she dined with now was thinner, taller, and far younger. But she could also detect some family resemblances in his features—Cholang had the same long, narrow eyes and high forehead as the man Rin assumed had been his father.

Cholang sighed. "I told my father not to answer Vaisra's summons. He should have known better to assume the Dragon Warlord merely wanted to talk."

"Stupid of him," Kitay agreed. "Did Vaisra send back his head?"

"Vaisra would never be so compassionate." Cholang's voice hardened. "He sent me a series of scrolls threatening to skin my father alive and deliver to me his tanned hide if Dog Province didn't capitulate."

Kitay's tone was utterly neutral, without judgment. "So you let your father die."

"I know the kind of man my father was," Cholang said. "He would have fallen on his own blade rather than bow. Vaisra did send a parcel. I never opened it; I buried it."

His voice shook, just barely, as he finished speaking. *He's young*, Rin realized. Cholang carried himself like a general, and his men clearly treated him as such, but his voice betrayed a fragility that his sun-weathered skin and bushy beard couldn't hide.

He was just like them. Young, scared, without a clue about what he was doing, yet trying his best to pretend otherwise.

Kitay gestured around the camp. "I take it this is not the permanent capital?"

Cholang shook his head. "Gorulan is a lovely place. Temples carved into the mountainside, great statues the height of buildings everywhere you look. We abandoned it the moment they sent what I presume was my father's head back in a basket. Wasn't keen to get stabbed in my bed."

"Looks like you've been given a stay of execution for now," Rin said.

Cholang shot her a wry look. "Only because we've never figured largely on the Nikara chessboard before. No one quite knows what to do with us."

That was true. Dog Province had always been an outlier in Imperial politics. They were too distant from centers of power to feel the yoke of any regime, but none of the heartland emperors had ever tried very hard to exert more control, because the sparse, arid plateau held so very little worth controlling. The Dogs herded livestock for subsistence and they didn't trade. Their land wasn't worth cultivating; nothing but grass could take root in the thin, rocky soil.

"But you must know the Republic won't ignore you forever," Rin said.

"We're well aware." Cholang sighed. "It's about principle, I expect. Regime change requires total domination. Otherwise, if you've got cracks in your foundation even before you've begun to rule, that sets a poor precedent."

"It's not just that," Kitay said. "It's your minerals. Nezha told me the Hesperians were discussing it. They think there's coal, tungsten, and silver under this plateau. They're very excited about it—they've prepared all kinds of machines to drill beneath the earth's surface once they know it's safe to move in."

Cholang seemed unsurprised. "And I expect their definition of *safe* involves our complete removal."

"More or less," Kitay said.

"Then we're on the same page," Rin said eagerly. Perhaps too eagerly—she could hear the naked hunger in her own voice—but the Southern Army had marched for so long on only the smallest shreds of hope that she was desperate to solidify this alliance. "You need us. We need you. We'll take whatever hospitality you can offer—my soldiers are starved, but they're disciplined—and then we can take stock of how many forces we've got—"

Cholang held up a hand to cut her off. "You won't find your alliance here, Speerly."

She faltered. "But the Republic is your enemy."

"The Republic has enforced sanctions on the plateau since your march began." Cholang's voice bore no trace of hostility, only wary resignation. "We're barely holding out ourselves. And we have no defenses to mount. Our population has always been a fraction of those of other provinces, and we have no weapons other than bows and farming implements. Certainly no fire powder. I can offer you a good meal and a night's rest. But if you're looking for an army here, you won't find it."

Rin knew that. She'd noticed the obvious poverty in Cholang's camp. She could guess the extent of Dog Province's forces based on his paltry personal guard. She knew this was not a base from which she could mount a resistance—it was too bare, too open, too vulnerable to air raids. She knew there was no army here, and certainly not one that could defeat a horde of dirigibles.

But she hadn't come here for the army.

"This isn't about troop numbers," she said. "We just need a guide up the mountains."

Cholang's eyes narrowed. "Where are you trying to go?"

She nodded to the ridges in the distance.

His eyes widened. "Mount Tianshan?"

"There's something up there that will help us win," Rin said. "But you've got to escort us there."

He looked skeptical. "Are you planning on telling me what it is?"

Rin exchanged a glance with Kitay, who shook his head.

"It's best you don't know," she said truthfully. "Even my own officers don't know."

Cholang was quiet, examining her.

Rin understood his hesitation. He was a newly minted Warlord, saddled with his murdered father's legacy, trying to find some way to keep his people alive when all the options looked bleak. And here she was, the Republic's most wanted fugitive, asking him to defy caution to help her climb a distant mountain for a purpose he couldn't discern.

This proposal was ludicrous. But he had to know, after the death of his father, that this was the only choice he had. Defiance was ludicrous. *Hope* was ludicrous. And the longer Cholang sat in silence, brows furrowed, the surer Rin was that he'd realized this as well.

"They tell stories about that mountain," he said at last.

"What stories?" she asked.

"The mists up there are dense as walls," he said. "The paths don't act like paths should; they twist and loop back on themselves and send you walking in circles. If you lose your way, you'll never find it again. And no one who's ventured to the peak has come back alive."

"Three people have," Rin said. "And it's about to be four."

Cholang offered them hospitality in his settlement for the night. "It's not much of a shelter," he apologized. "This is a temporary outpost; it won't be very comfortable. And we haven't got the space to house everyone. But we can feed you, give you blankets, and send our physicians to tend to your wounded. My quarters are yours, if you want them."

At first Rin declined out of etiquette, insisting that her tent was enough. But then Cholang showed her and Kitay to his rounded hut, an impressively sturdy structure that could provide far better shelter against the howling night winds than the flimsy, tattered walls of her tent, and she immediately acquiesced.

"Take it," Cholang said. "I'll sleep under the stars tonight."

It had been so long since anyone had offered Rin such a simple kindness with no expectation of anything in return that it took her a moment to remember how to respond. "Thank you. Truly."

"Rest well, Speerly." He turned to leave. "We'll march for Tianshan at dawn."

A padded sleeping mat, at least two inches thick, occupied the center of the hut. Rin's back and shoulders ached just looking at it. After weeks sleeping curled on the cold, hard dirt, it seemed an unimaginable luxury.

"Nice digs," Kitay said, echoing her thoughts. "Do you want me to take the first watch?"

"No, you go ahead and sleep," she said. "I want to think."

She knew he was exhausted; she'd caught his eyes slipping closed more than once during their audience with Cholang. She sat cross-legged next to the mat, waited for Kitay to crawl under the covers, and then took his hand.

His fingers curled around hers. "Rin."

"Yeah?"

His voice sounded very small in the dark. "I hope we know what we're doing."

She took a deep breath, exhaled slowly, and squeezed his fingers. "Me too."

It was a meaningless, inadequate exchange, and didn't come close to expressing the worries that weighed on both their minds, nor the enormity of what was coming next. But she knew what he meant. She knew his confusion, his fear, and his deep, bone-rattling terror that none of their choices were good—that they were navigating a jungle of snakes carrying the weight of the south's future on their shoulders, and a single misstep would destroy it all.

They were going to wake Riga.

This, after many whispered debates, they'd decided. The calculation hadn't changed.

They weren't fools. They understood the risks, understood Jiang's cryptic warnings. They knew the Trifecta would not be so benevolent as Daji claimed—that whatever Riga was, when at last he awoke, might be more dangerous than Nezha or the Republic.

But the Trifecta were Nikara. Yin Riga, unlike his nephew, would never bow to the Hesperians. They might have committed atrocities, and they might do so again, but their regime at least was anathema to Hesperian encroachment.

To mount an armed resistance without them was suicide; to surrender to the Republic would lead them to a fate worse than death. The Trifecta had been monsters—and Rin knew with certainty that they would become so again—but she needed monsters on her side. What other choice did they have?

Necessity didn't make this any easier. Rin still felt, with every step they took toward Mount Tianshan, like a small animal walking into a trap. But they'd made their choice, and there was nothing they could do now but see it through and hope they came out alive.

She sat still in the darkness, holding Kitay's hand tight until finally his breaths settled into a slow, easy rhythm.

"Don't panic."

Rin jumped to her feet. Fire shrouded her body. She crouched, ready to spring. She'd have to fight with flame—her sword was lying on the other side of the sleeping mat, too far to reach.

Should have known better. Her thoughts raced. *Shouldn't have trusted Cholang so easily, should have known he'd sell us out—*

"Don't panic," the intruder said again, hands stretched out before him.

This time, his voice gave her pause. Rin recognized that voice. And she recognized the intruder's face, too, once he stepped forward and his features became visible in the dim firelight.

"Holy fuck." Despite herself, she burst out laughing. "It's *you*."

"Hello," said Chaghan. "Could I steal you for a chat?"

"How did you know I would be here?" Rin asked.

They walked through Cholang's camp unbothered. The sentries dipped their heads as they approached the perimeter and let them leave without question.

So Cholang must have known Chaghan was here. What's more, he must have permitted him entry into her hut without warning her.

Asshole, Rin thought.

"I've been tracking you since you left Arabak," Chaghan said. "I'm sorry for the surprise, by the way. I didn't want to announce my presence."

"How'd you convince Cholang to let you sneak through his camp?"

"The Hundred Clans have close ties to the frontier provinces," Chaghan said. "In the Red Emperor's time, Sinegard posted their poor bottom-ranked graduates out there to kill us."

"I take it that's not how things turned out."

"When you're alone on the front, waging unprovoked warfare is the last thing you want to do," Chaghan said. "We established strong trade relations a long time ago. We liked the Dog Province soldiers. We drew unofficial lines in the sand and agreed not to cross them, so long as they refrained from encroaching on our territory. It's worked so far."

Rin kept glancing sideways at him as they walked, amazed by how different he seemed. He was so much more *solid*. Before he'd been like a wraith, an ethereal spirit moving through the world like light passes through the air, present but never quite belonging. But now when he walked, he seemed as if he actually left footsteps.

"You're staring at me," he said.

"I'm curious," she said. "You look different."

"I feel different," he said. "When I leave the material plane now, there's no one on the other side pulling me back. I've had to learn to be my own anchor. It feels . . ."

She didn't ask what it was like to miss Qara, every second of every day. She didn't have to guess at the gaping pain, the clawing absence of that loss. She knew.

A thought struck her. "Then are you—"

"No. I'm dying," he said bluntly. He didn't seem bothered by this; he said it as casually as if informing her that he'd be going to market next week. "It gets harder every time—reaching the gods, I mean. I'm never going to be able to go as far out, or to stay as long, as I used to. Not if I want to wake up again. But I can't stand spending all my time in this realm, this horribly . . . *solid* place." He gestured about the steppe with disdain. "So I can't stop. And one day I'll go out too far. And I'm not going to come back."

"Chaghan." She stopped walking. She didn't know what to say. "I . . ."

"I'm not particularly worried," he said, and sounded like he meant it. "And I'd very much like to talk about something else."

She changed the subject. "So how did you get on back home?" The last time she'd seen Chaghan, he'd been racing north on a warhorse following his cousin Bekter's murderous coup. Back then, she'd feared he was riding to his death. But from the looks of it, he'd emerged from that power struggle unscathed, in charge, and with ample troops and resources.

"Well enough," said Chaghan. "Obviously, Bekter's not a problem anymore."

Rin was impressed, if not terribly surprised. "How did you manage that?"

"Murder and conspiracy. The usual means, of course."

"Of course. You lead the Ketreyids now, then?"

"Please, Rin." He shot her a thin-lipped smile. "I lead the Hundred Clans. For the first time in a century we are united, and I speak here on their behalf."

He nodded toward something in front of them. Rin glanced up. She had assumed they were only walking out of earshot of anyone in Cholang's settlement, but when she followed Chaghan's line of sight she saw campfires and lean silhouettes against the moonlight. They drew closer, and she made out dozens of cloth tents, resting horses, and sentries with bows at the ready. An army camp.

"You've brought a full contingent," she said.

"Of course," Chaghan said. "I wouldn't march against the Trifecta with anything less."

Rin stopped walking. The camaraderie between them vanished. She curled her palm into a fist, readying herself for a fight. "Chaghan—"

"I am here as a friend." He held his hands up to display that he had no weapon, though Rin knew that with Chaghan, it didn't matter. "But I know what you intend to do, and we desperately need to speak. Will you sit?"

"I want all your archers to leave their bows and quivers in a pile beside me," she said. "And I want you to swear on your mother's grave that I'll be back safe with the southerners before dawn."

"Rin, come on. It's me."

She held firm. "I'm not joking."

She'd last parted with Chaghan on friendly terms. She knew their interests, at least in regard to the Republic, were aligned. But she still didn't trust Chaghan, nor any of the Ketreyids, not to put an arrow in her forehead if they decided she was a threat. She'd dealt with Ketreyid justice before; she knew she'd only escaped because the Sorqan Sira had deemed her useful.

"As you wish." Chaghan signaled to his men, who reluctantly obeyed. "I swear on the grave of Kalagan of the Naimads that we won't harm you. Better?"

"Much." Rin sat and crossed her legs. "Go on."

"Thank you." Chaghan knelt down opposite her. He unrolled his satchel, pulled out a vial of cobalt-blue powder, and popped the cork off before offering it to her. "Lick your fingertip and dab it onto your tongue. Once should do. And get comfortable. It takes effect quickly, you remember—"

"Hold on." She didn't touch the vial. "Tell me what's going on before I hurl my spirit into the abyss with you. Which god are we visiting now?"

"Not the gods," he said. "The dead."

Her heart skipped a beat. "Altan? Did you find him?"

"No." A shadow of discomfort flitted across Chaghan's face. "He's not—I've never—no. But she is a Speerly. Most spirits dissolve into nothing when they pass. That's why it's hard to commune with the dead; they've already disappeared from the realm of conscious things. But your kind linger. They're bound by resentment and a god that feeds on it, which means often they can't let go. They're hungry ghosts."

Rin licked the tip of her index finger and poked it into the vial, swiveling it around until soft, downy powder coated her skin up to the first joint. "Are we speaking to Tearza?"

"No." Chaghan took the vial back and did the same. "Someone more recent. I don't believe you've met."

She glanced up. "Who?"

"Hanelai," Chaghan said bluntly.

Without hesitation Rin put her powder-covered finger in her mouth and sucked.

Immediately the Ketreyid campsite blurred and dissolved like paints swirled in water. Rin closed her eyes. She felt her spirit flying up, fleeing her heavy body, that clumsy sack of bones and organs and flesh, soaring toward the heavens like a bird freed from its cage.

"We'll wait here," Chaghan said. They floated together in a dark expanse—a plane not quite pitch-black, but rather shrouded in hazy twilight. "When I found out you were marching to Tianshan, I went searching. I needed to understand the risks. I know there's no one alive who could push you off the path you've chosen." He nodded toward a red ball of light in the void, a distant star that grew larger as it approached. "But she might."

The star became a pillar of flame and then a woman, drawn close before them, glowing red-hot like she was burning up from the inside.

Rin stared, speechless.

She knew this face. Knew that pointed chin, that straight jaw, and those hard, sullen eyes. She'd seen that face staring back at her from mirrors.

"Hello, Hanelai," Chaghan said. "This is the friend I've told you so much about."

Hanelai turned toward Rin, eyes roving imperiously over her like a queen surveying her subject. A curious feeling seized Rin's heart, some strange and unnameable longing. She'd felt it only once before, two years ago, when she'd held her fingers up against Altan's and marveled at how their dusky skin matched. She never thought she'd feel it again.

She suspected her relation to Hanelai. She'd suspected it for a long time. Now, staring at that face, she knew it was undeniable. She knew the word for it, a word she'd never used with anyone before. She dared not say it out loud.

Yet Hanelai showed no hint of recognition.

"You are the one traveling with Jiang Ziya?" she asked.

"Yes," Rin said. "And you're—"

Hanelai snarled. Her eyes glowed red. Her flames jumped and unfurled like an explosion suspended in time, deathly orange petals blooming outward at Rin.

"Don't be afraid," Chaghan said quickly. "The dead can't harm you. Those flames aren't real, they're only projections."

He was right. Hanelai frothed and snarled, screaming incoherently as fire shot out of every part of her body. But she never drew closer to Rin. Her flames bore no heat; though they curled and jumped, the twilight plane remained as neutrally cool as it had always been.

Still, she was terrifying. It took all Rin's willpower not to shrink away. "What's wrong with her?"

"She's dead," Chaghan said. "She's been dead for a long time.

And when souls don't fade back into the abyss, they need tethers, their lingering hatreds that keep them from passing. She's not a person anymore. She's rage."

"But I've seen Tearza before. Tearza wasn't—"

"Tearza had control," Chaghan said. "Her rage was tempered, because she chose the circumstances of her own death. Hanelai didn't."

Rin regarded Hanelai. Now her pulsing flames and twisted scowl didn't seem so frightening. They seemed wretched.

How long had Hanelai been drifting in her fury?

"You've nothing to be afraid of," Chaghan said. "She wants to talk to you, she just doesn't know how. If you speak to her, she'll answer. Go ahead."

Rin knew what she had to ask.

This was her chance, at last, to excavate the truth—the secret that had festered so long between her, Jiang, and Daji. She didn't want to know; she was afraid to know. It was like digging a knife into a poisoned wound to draw out the venom; the pain was daunting. But even if this secret destroyed her, she had to hear it. She had to climb that mountain with clear eyes.

She looked straight into Hanelai's furious, anguished face.

"What did he do to you?" she asked.

Hanelai howled.

Voices flew at Rin like an assault of arrows—not all of them Hanelai's, not all of them adult. Fragments of hundreds of grievances assaulted her like a mosaic of pain, cobbling together the details of a painting which, until now, she'd only glimpsed from a distance.

—*Riga*—

—*when they took our children*—

—*no other choice*—

—*would you have chosen?*—

—*it didn't matter, none of it mattered*—

—*they wanted the gods, they only ever wanted the gods, and we felt sorry for them because we could not imagine*—

—for our children—
—Riga—
—would have left us alone—
—just leave us alone, we never wanted—
—then Riga—
—Riga—
—Riga!—

"I understand," Rin said. She didn't, not fully, but she'd heard enough to piece together the outline and that was enough; she couldn't bear to hear more; she couldn't think of *Jiang* like that. "I understand, stop—"

But the voices did not stop, they only built, screams stacking upon screams at an unbearable volume.

—and Jiang didn't—
—Jiang never—
—he promised—
—when Riga—
—Ziya—
—he said he loved us—
He said he loved me.

"Stop it," Rin said. "I can't—"

"Can't?" Chaghan's voice cut through her mind like a shard of ice. "Or you don't want to know?"

The voices consolidated back into one.

"Traitor," Hanelai screeched, flying at Rin. "Stupid, imperialist, pathetic traitor—"

Her voice distorted into deep double timbre, which then split into a chorus. When Hanelai spoke, her mouth moved not only for herself but for a crowd of deceased. Rin could almost see them, a horde of Speerlies behind Hanelai, all spitting rage in her face.

"You hear our testimony and you refuse us, you defile the graves of your ancestors, you who escaped, you who carry our blood, how dare you call yourself a Speerly, *how dare you—*"

"Enough," Rin said. "Make her stop—"

"Listen to her," Chaghan said.

Fury surged in Rin. "I said *enough*."

Every time she'd used this drug before, Chaghan had guided her back from the world of spirit, dragging her bewildered, terrified soul into the land of the living. But Rin was done with wandering around like a lost child. Done with letting Chaghan manipulate her with wraiths and shadows.

The moment her soul hit her body, jolting her back into awareness like a swimmer breaking the surface, Rin clambered to her knees and seized him by the shoulders.

"What the hell was that?"

"You had to know," Chaghan said. "You weren't going to believe it from anyone else's mouth."

"So what, you were going to scare me off with a fucking ghost?"

"*Rin*. You're talking about reviving the man who murdered your race."

"The Mugenese murdered the Speerlies—"

"And Riga let them. Did you hear Hanelai? That's the full story. That's what the Vipress was never going to tell you. The Federation kidnapped Speerly children and demanded the secrets to shamanism as a ransom. Riga knew Hanelai was going to reveal everything to the Mugenese, he knew she cared more about those twenty children than the fate of the mainland, and he slaughtered her people for it. He thought the Speerlies were animals. Disposable. And you think he'll treat you any differently? Your ancestors would be disgusted. Altan wouldn't—"

"Don't," she said harshly. "Don't speak to me of Altan. You know very well what Altan would have done."

He opened his mouth to retort, saw the look on her face, and then closed it. He swallowed. "Rin, I'm just—"

"Riga is our best and only chance at winning this war," she said firmly.

"Perhaps. But what comes after that? Who rules the Empire then, you or them?"

"I don't know. Who cares?"

"You can't be this daft," he said, exasperated. "Surely you've considered this power struggle. It's not just about the enemy. It's about what the world looks like after. And if you intend to stay in charge, then you'd better start weighing your chances against the Trifecta combined. You think you can take them?"

"I don't know," she said again. "But I know one thing for certain. Without them, I have absolutely no chance against the Republic and the Hesperians. And they're the only opponents who matter right now."

"That's not true. Hesperian occupation will be difficult. But it is survivable—"

"Survivable to you," she scoffed, "only because you hide in a desert wasteland so dry and dead that no one would bother encroaching on your territory. Don't debate the stakes with me, Chaghan. You'll be just fine up north in your shithole no matter what happens."

"Watch how you speak to me," Chaghan said sharply.

Rin glared at him, incredulous. She remembered now why she had always resented him so, why she had always felt such an urge to smack the grim, all-knowing expression off his face. It was the sheer condescension. The way he always spoke as if he knew better, as if he were lecturing foolish children.

"I'm not the girl you met at Khurdalain anymore," she said. "I'm not the failed commander of the Cike. I know what I'm doing now. You're trying to protect your people. I understand that. But I'm trying to protect mine. I know what the Trifecta did to you, and I know you want your vengeance, but right now I need them. And you can't give me orders."

"Your obstinacy is going to destroy you."

She arched an eyebrow. "Is that a threat?"

"Don't start with that," he said, exasperated. "Rin, I came here as a friend."

She summoned a tiny spark of flame into her palm. "So did I."

"I'm not going to fight you. But you should know what you're getting into—"

"I know very well," she said loudly. "I know exactly what kind of man Jiang is, I know exactly what Daji is planning, and I *don't care*. Without Riga we have nothing. No army. No weapons. The dirigibles will bomb us out in seconds and that'll be it; this whole struggle will be over and we'll be nothing more than a blip in history. But the Trifecta give us a fighting chance. I'll deal with the fallout later. But I'm not crawling into oblivion with a whimper, and you should have known that before you came here. If you were this afraid of the Trifecta, then you should have tried to kill me. You shouldn't even have given me the choice."

She stood up. The Ketreyid archers swiveled to face her, alarmed, but she ignored them. She knew they wouldn't dare hurt her. "But you can't, can you? Because your hands are tied, too. Because you know that when the Hesperians are done with us, they'll come for you. You know about their Maker and how they look at the world. And you know their vision for the future of this continent does not include you. Your territories will shrink smaller and smaller, until the day the Hesperians decide they want you off the map, too. And you need me for that fight. The Sorqan Sira knew that. You're doomed without me."

She picked her knife off the floor. This audience was over. "I'm setting out for Mount Tianshan tomorrow. There's nothing you can do to stop me."

Chaghan regarded her with narrow, calculating eyes. "My men will be outside that mountain, ready to shoot at whatever emerges."

"Then aim well," she said. "So long as you're not aiming at me."

CHAPTER 21

Seven days later Rin stood with Jiang and Daji at the base of Mount Tianshan, preparing to make the final climb. Jiang carried a fawn slung over his shoulders, its skinny legs bound with rope. Rin tried not to look at its large, blinking eyes. There was power in a fleeing life, she knew. The incantation to break the eroding Seal required death.

The mountain loomed tall above them, deceptively pretty in its lush greenery and patches of clean snow, shrouded by its famous mists so thick she could barely see half a mile up the path. At twenty-five thousand feet, it was the tallest peak in the Empire, but the Heavenly Temple was only two-thirds of the way up the mountain. Still, it would take them the full day to climb, and they likely would not reach the temple until sunset.

"Well." Rin turned around to face Kitay. "See you tonight."

He wasn't coming with her. Despite his protests, they'd both agreed he would only be a liability on the mountain—he'd be safer in the valley, surrounded by Cholang's troops.

"Tonight," he agreed, leaning down to give her a tight, brief hug. His lips brushed against her ear. "Don't fuck this up."

"Can't promise anything." Rin gave him a wry chuckle. She had to laugh, to mask her apprehension with callous humor, otherwise she'd splinter from the fear. "It's only a day, dearest, don't miss me too much."

He didn't laugh.

"Come back down," he said, his expression suddenly grim. His fingers clenched tight around hers. "Listen, Rin. I don't care what else happens up there. But you come back to me."

The road up Mount Tianshan was a sacred path.

In all the myths, Tianshan was the site from which the gods descended. Where Lei Gong stood when he carved lightning into the sky with his staff. Where the Queen Mother of the West tended the peach tree of immortality that had sentenced the Moon Lady Chang'e to an eternity of torment. Where Sanshengmu, sister of the vengeful Erlang Shen, had fallen when the heavens banished her for loving a mortal.

It was clear why the gods would choose this place, where the rarefied air was cool and sweet, where the flowers that laced the road bloomed in colors so bright they did not seem real. The path, so rarely trodden it had nearly faded away, was silent as they walked. No one spoke. Save for their footsteps, Rin heard nothing—not the chirping of birds nor the hum of insects. Mount Tianshan, for all its natural loveliness, seemed devoid of any other life.

The dirigibles came at midday.

Rin thought she'd imagined the buzzing at first; it was so faint. She thought the droning was a fear-induced flashback, brought on by the nerves and pounding exhaustion.

But then Daji froze in her steps, and Rin realized she'd heard it, too.

Jiang glanced up at the sky and groaned. "Fucking hell."

Slowly the aircraft emerged from the thick white misty wall, one after another, black shapes half-hidden in clouds like lurking monsters.

Rin, Jiang, and Daji stood still below, exposed against the white snow, three targets laid bare before a firing squad.

How long had Nezha known where she was? Since she'd reached Dog Province? Since she'd begun the march? He must have tailed the southerners with reconnaissance crafts, lurking unseen beyond the horizon, tracing their movements across the Baolei range, waiting to see where they led him like a hunter following a baby deer to its herd. He must have realized they were marching west to seek salvation. And following his devastating loss at the Anvil, in desperate need of a victory to hand the Hesperians, he must have decided to wait to eliminate the resistance at its source.

"What are you waiting for?" Daji hissed. "Hit them."

Jiang shook his head. "They're not in range."

He was right. The airships crept hesitantly through the mist, patient predators watching to see where their prey scurried next. But they remained hovering at such a distance that they were only hazy shapes in the sky, where they knew Jiang's shades could not reach. They didn't approach. And they didn't fire.

Nezha knows, Rin thought. She was certain; that was the only explanation. Somehow, Nezha understood what she was attempting, or at least an approximation of it. He wasn't ready to murder the Trifecta just yet. He needed to find out, for the sake of his Hesperian overseers, what precisely lay in that chamber.

"Then hurry up," Daji said curtly, turning her gaze back to the path. "*Climb.*"

There was no other option but to follow.

Rin scrambled up the slippery rock, all reservations driven from her mind by sheer icy fear. Her questions about the Trifecta didn't matter now. Whatever Jiang had done, whatever he was hiding from her, whoever the children were—it didn't matter. Nezha lurked above her, ready to turn her bones to dust with a single order. She had one path to survival and that was Riga.

She could be about to wake a monster. She didn't care.

Farther up, the path was ensconced inside fog so thick that Rin could barely see or breathe. This was the famous mist of Mount Tianshan, the so-called impenetrable shroud of the Empress of the

Four Skies, cast down to keep mortals from discovering the doors to the heavens. The humidity was so dense she felt almost as if she were moving through water. She couldn't see even a foot in front of her; she had to scrabble along on all fours, listening desperately for the sound of Daji's footsteps.

She could still hear the dirigible fleet, but she couldn't see them at all now. The droning had become fainter, too, as if the fleet had first approached the mountain and then retreated backward.

Could they not see where they were going? That must be it—if the mist was hazardous to climbers, it must be doubly so for the aircraft. They must have fallen back to clearer skies, waiting until they figured out the precise location of their targets.

How long did that give them? Hours? Minutes?

She was finding it harder and harder to breathe. She had grown used to thin air on the march, but rarely had they ascended to such altitudes. Fatigue crept up her legs and arms and intensified to a screaming burn. Every step felt like torture. She slowed to a third of her initial speed, dragging her feet forward with every last ounce of energy she could squeeze from her muscles.

She couldn't stop. They'd initially agreed to camp halfway up the mountain if they tired too quickly, but with dirigibles following overhead, that was no longer an option.

One at a time, she told herself. One step. Then another. And then another, until at last, the steep path gave way to flat stone. She dropped to all fours, chest heaving, desperate for just a few seconds' reprieve.

"There," Daji whispered behind her.

Rin lifted her head, squinting through the fog, until the Heavenly Temple emerged through the mist—an imposing nine-story pagoda with red walls and slanted cobalt roofs, gleaming pristinely as if it had been built only yesterday.

The temple had no doors. A square hole was carved into the wall where one should have been, revealing nothing but darkness within. There was no barrier against the wind and the cold. Whatever lay inside needed no defenses—the interior pulsed with some dark, crackling power of its own. Rin could feel it in the air, growing thicker as she approached—a vague tension that made her skin prickle with unease.

Here, the boundary between the world of gods and the world of men blurred. This place was blessed. This place was cursed. She didn't know which.

The temple's dark entrance beckoned, inviting. Rin was seized by a sudden, heart-clenching impulse to flee.

"Well," Daji said behind her. "Go on."

Rin swallowed and stepped over the raised panel at the threshold, casting flames into the darkness to light her way. The room on the ground level wasn't warm. It wasn't cool, either. It was nothing at all, the absence of temperature, a place perfectly conditioned to leave her untouched. The air didn't stir. There was no dust. This was a space carved out of the boundaries of the natural world, a chamber outside of time.

Slowly her eyes adjusted to the dim interior.

The Heavenly Temple had no windows. The walls on all nine floors were solid stone. Even the ceiling, unlike ceilings in every pagoda Rin had ever seen, was closed off to the sky, blocking out all light except for the red glow in her palm.

Cautiously, she cast her flames higher and wider, trying to bring light to every corner of the room without setting anything ablaze. She made out the shapes of the sixty-four gods above her, statues perched on plinths exactly like those she'd always seen in the Pantheon. The flames distorted their shadows, made them loom large and menacing on the high stone walls.

Yes—the gods were undeniably present here. She didn't just feel them, she could *hear* them. Odd whispers arced around her, speaking fleeting words that disappeared just as she tried to catch them. She lingered under the plinth of the Phoenix. Its eyes gazed down at her—fond, mocking, daring. *Long time no see, little one.*

In the middle of the room stood an altar.

"Great Tortoise," Jiang said. "You really did a number on him."

The Dragon Emperor lay still on a bed of pure jade, hands

folded serenely over his chest. He didn't look like someone who had been comatose without food or water for two decades. He didn't look like a living person at all. He seemed a part of the temple, as still and permanent as stone. His chest did not rise or fall; Rin couldn't tell if he still breathed.

The Yin family resemblance was uncanny. His face was sculpted porcelain: strong brows, straight nose, a lovely arrangement of sharp angles. His long, raven-black hair draped elegantly over his shoulders. Rin felt dizzy as her eyes traced his noble sleeping features. She felt as if she were staring down at Nezha's corpse.

"Let's not draw this out," Daji said. "Ziya?"

Jiang moved fast. Before Rin could blink, he'd dropped the fawn onto the stone tiles and wedged a blade into its neck.

The fawn's mouth worked furiously, but no scream came out, only agonized gurgles and an astonishing tide of blood.

"Quickly now, before he's gone." Daji pulled Rin out of the way as Jiang dragged the fawn's writhing form against the base of the altar.

The fawn's choking went on for a torturously long time. Finally, its struggling dwindled to minute shudders as its blood seeped across the floor, running in straight, clean rivulets where the stone tiles met. All the while Daji knelt over it, one hand pressed against its flank, murmuring something under her breath.

A crackling noise filled the cave, a long, unceasing roll of thunder that grew louder and louder until it seemed the pagoda was about to explode. Rin felt power in the air. Too much power—it cloyed in her throat, choking her. She crouched back against the wall, suddenly terrified.

Daji spoke faster and faster, unintelligible words tumbling eagerly from her lips.

Jiang was utterly still. His face twisted in some strange and unfamiliar grimace; Rin couldn't tell if he was horrified or ecstatic.

Then shone a burst of white light, followed by a noise like a thunderclap. Rin didn't realize she'd been thrown off her feet until she felt her back slam against the far wall.

Stars exploded behind her eyelids. The pain was excruciating. She wanted to curl up into a ball and rock back and forth until it stopped, but fear dominated; fear made her crawl to her knees, coughing, squinting as she waited for her vision to return.

Jiang stood with his back against the opposite wall, unmoving, his expression blank. Daji was collapsed against the base of the altar. A thin trail of blood ran out from between her lips. Rin stumbled forth to help her up, but Daji shook her head and pointed to the altar, where, for the first time in over twenty years, Yin Riga rose.

The Dragon Emperor's eyes were pure, gleaming cobalt. They roved slowly about the room as he sat up, drinking in the sights of the pagoda.

Rin couldn't move. She couldn't even speak—all words seemed insufficient. Some force seemed to be clenching her jaw shut, some gravity that made the air in the temple thicker than rock.

"Can you hear me?" Daji, rising to her knees, pulled Riga's hands into her own. "Riga?"

He stared at her for a long time. Then he croaked, in a voice like scraping gravel, "Daji."

Jiang made a choking noise.

Riga's gaze flickered briefly toward him, then returned to Daji. "How long have I been gone?"

"Twenty years." Daji cleared her throat. "Do—do you know where you are?"

Riga sat silent for a moment, eyebrows furrowed.

"I've been drifting," he said. At least he sounded nothing like Nezha—his voice was hoarse from disuse, a rusted blade dragging against stone. "I don't know where. It was dark, and the gods were silent. And I couldn't get back. I couldn't find the way. And I kept wondering, who could possibly have . . ." His eyes refocused suddenly on Daji, as if he had just realized he was speaking out loud. "I remember now. We quarreled."

Daji's pale throat bobbed. "Yes."

"And you stopped it." His gaze lingered on Daji's face for a long while. Something passed between them that Rin did not understand—something full of remorse, longing, and resentment. Something dangerous.

Abruptly, Riga turned away.

"Ziya," he commanded. His voice grew smoother, louder, resounding off the pagoda walls.

Jiang's head jerked up. "Yes."

"You've come around, then?" Riga rose to his feet, shrugging off Daji's proffered arm. He was much taller than Nezha—if they'd been standing side by side, he would have made Nezha look like a child. "Have you gotten over that stupid girl? That's why we fought, wasn't it?"

Jiang's face was unreadable as stone. "It's good to see you again."

Riga turned toward Rin. "And what's this?"

Rin still couldn't speak. She tried to take a step backward, but to her horror she found herself frozen in place. Riga's gaze was like steel spikes nailing her feet to the ground, paralyzing her with seemingly no effort at all.

"How interesting." Riga tilted his head, eyes roving up and down her form as if surveying a pack animal at market. "I thought they killed them all."

Rin tried to draw her knife. Her arm wouldn't listen.

"Kneel," Riga said softly.

She obeyed instantly. His voice was like a physical force on its own, capable of bending her knees and forcing her gaze to the ground. It vibrated in her bones. It shook the very foundations of the pagoda.

Riga strode slowly toward her. "She's shorter than the others. Why is that?"

No one answered. He made a humming noise. "I suppose Hanelai was short. Does she follow orders?"

At last, Rin managed to spit out a word. "*Orders?*"

"Rin, be quiet," Daji said sharply.

Riga just laughed. "I'm impressed, Ziya. You really found another one to keep around, did you? You always did like your pets."

"I'm not his *pet*," Rin snarled.

"Oh, it talks."

Riga leaned down and gave her a wide, terrible smile. Then he reached out, seized her collar, and pulled her up into the air in one smooth, easy motion. Rin gasped as his thumbs dug painfully into her windpipe. She kicked out with her feet, but she was swinging entire inches off the ground, and all she could do was brush Riga's knees with her toes. All her flailing had no more effect than a child throwing a tantrum. Riga pulled her toward him until their eyes were level, their faces so close that she could feel the heat of his breath on her cheeks when he spoke.

"I've been asleep for a very long time, little Speerly," he whispered. "I'm not in the mood for contradiction."

"Oh, let her go," Daji said. "You're going to kill her like that."

Riga shot her a glare. "Did I give you permission to speak?"

"She's useful," Daji insisted. "She's strong, she helped us get here—"

"Really? That's pathetic. You used to get these things done on your own." Riga's lip curled in amusement. "What is it? Did Ziya fuck this one, too? I must say, his standards have dropped."

"It's nothing like that," Daji said quickly. "She's just a child, Riga, don't hurt her—"

"What's this, darling?" Riga gave a low chuckle. "Finally developing a conscience?"

Daji's voice became shrill. "Riga, listen to me, *let her go*."

Riga opened his fingers.

Rin dropped to the ground, clutching noiselessly at her throat. Riga's legs loomed above her. She cringed, bracing herself for a vicious kick, but he merely stepped over her as if she were a footstool.

He was headed for Daji.

"Riga—" Daji started, just before Riga drew his hand back

and slapped her across the face. Daji's head whipped to the side. She cried out and clutched her cheek.

"Shut up," Riga said, and slapped her again. Then again, and again, until a vivid crimson handprint bloomed on Daji's paper-white cheek. "*Shut up*, you fucking whore."

Rin watched them from where she lay, astonished.

For the longest time she had considered Daji—Su Daji, the Vipress, former Empress of Nikan—the most powerful being on earth. From the moment she'd met her, she'd feared her. She'd wanted terribly to *be* her.

But here Daji stood, shoulders hunched like she was trying to shrivel into nothing while Riga battered her like she was a dog. And she was just *taking* it.

"Did you think I'd forgotten?" Riga asked hoarsely. "You treacherous little bitch, did you think I don't know who put me here?"

He raised his hand high. Daji shrank against the wall and loosed a whimpering sob.

"Oh, don't be like that." He put his fingers under Daji's chin and forced her head up. He sighed. "You used to be so pretty when you cried. When did you stop being so pretty?"

Rin wanted to vomit.

Surely Daji wouldn't take this. Surely she would strike back. Surely Jiang would defend her.

But they only looked away—Daji at her hands, Jiang at the ground. They were both trembling. Then Rin realized that this was nothing new for them; this was a trained response to a terror they'd lived with for years. A terror so incapacitating that now, twenty years later, after half a lifetime of freedom from the man they'd hated, they still cowered meekly before him like whipped dogs.

Rin was astounded.

What had Riga done to them?

And if she brought him back down the mountain, what would he do to *her*?

Kill him, said the Phoenix. *Kill him now.*

Riga's back was turned to her. She could end this in seconds; all it took was a quick hop, lunge, and stab. She clasped the hilt of her knife, rose to her feet as silently as she could, and dug her heels into the ground. She could call on the Phoenix, but sometimes steel was faster than fire—

No. No. If she hurt the Trifecta, then she was alone. She'd come this far. He was her last, best hope; she couldn't throw this away.

She knew she'd woken a monster. But she'd known this from the start; she'd known she needed monsters on her side.

"I'm not your enemy," she said. "And I'm not your servant, either. I'm the last Speerly. And I came to seek your help."

Riga didn't turn around, but his hand dropped from Daji's chin. He stood very still, head cocked. Daji stumbled back, rubbing her jaw, staring at Rin with wide-eyed astonishment.

"I know what you did." Rin's words came out shaky and girlish; she couldn't help it. "I know everything. And I don't care. The past doesn't matter. Nikan is in danger *now*, and I need you."

Riga turned. His eyes were wide, his mouth half-open in an incredulous smile.

"You know?" He strode toward her, his steps low and menacing like a tiger approaching its prey. "What do you think you know?"

"Speer." Rin took a step back without thinking. Everything about him radiated danger; that grin on his face made her want to spin around and run. "I saw—I know—I know you gave it up. I know you let them."

"Is that what you think?" He bent toward her. "Then why don't you want to kill me, child?"

"Because I don't care," she breathed. "Because there's another enemy at our shores that's ten times worse than you, and I need you to destroy them. You made a necessary choice at Speer. I get it. I've traded lives, too."

Riga regarded her for a long moment in silence. Rin did her

best to meet his gaze, heart pounding so furiously she was afraid it might burst.

She couldn't read his expression. She had no idea what he was thinking. Something was off, something was wrong—she could tell from Daji's terrified expression—but she couldn't flee, she had to see this through.

Then Riga threw his head back and laughed. His cackle was a horrible thing, so like Nezha's, and so gleefully cruel. "You don't know shit."

"I don't *care*," Rin repeated desperately. "The Hesperians are *here*, Riga, they're right outside, you need to work with me—"

He lifted a hand. "Oh, shut up."

An invisible force slammed her forward into the ground. Her kneecaps screamed in agony. She hunched over on all fours, trying and failing to get up.

Riga knelt down before her and clasped her face in his hands. "Look at me."

Rin squeezed her eyes shut.

It didn't matter. Riga's fingertips dug so hard into her temples she thought he was about to shatter her skull in his hands. A cruel, cold presence forced its way into her mind, digging through her memories with callous disregard, wrenching out everything that made Rin go dry-mouthed in fright. Auntie Fang, twisting skin to form welts under her clothes where no one could see. Shiro, carelessly jamming needles into her veins with brutish force. Petra, tracing cold metal against her naked body, thin lips curling with amusement every time Rin flinched.

It went on for what seemed like an eternity. Rin wasn't aware she was screaming until her throat convulsed from the strain.

"Ah," Riga said. "Here we are."

The memories paused. She found herself bent over the floor, panting, drool dripping from her mouth.

"Look at me," Riga said again, and this time she wearily obeyed.

There was no fight left in her. She just wanted this over. If she just did what he said, would it be over?

"Is this what you wanted to see?" Riga inquired.

His face morphed into Altan's. He grinned.

And then, at last, Rin understood what Daji had meant when she said that Riga's power lay in fear.

He didn't just terrorize with brute force. He terrorized with pure, overwhelming *power*. He'd probed her memory for the one person she'd once thought so intimidatingly strong that she couldn't help but obey—no, *longed* to obey, because fear and love were really just opposite sides of the same coin.

She saw now what bound Jiang and Daji to Riga. It was the same reason she'd once been drawn to Altan. With Altan, it had always been so easy. She never had to think. He raged and she followed, blind and unquestioning, because marveling at his purpose was simpler than coming up with one of her own. He'd terrified her. She would have died for him.

"Altan Trengsin," Riga mused. "I remember the name. Hanelai's nephew, wasn't he, Ziya? Pride of the island?"

New images invaded her mind.

She saw waves crashing against a jagged shore. She saw a boy wading through the shallows. He was very young, no more than four or five. He stood alone on the beach, trident in his hand, his dark eyes narrowed in concentration as he watched the waves. His inky-black hair fell in soft curls around sun-bronzed cheeks, and his face was tight with a mature, intense focus that belonged to someone much older. Slowly, without glancing away from the water, he lifted the trident over his shoulder in a practiced stance Rin had seen many times before.

She realized with a jolt that she was looking at Altan.

"Come," said a voice—Riga's voice from her mouth, for this was Riga's memory, and she was experiencing something Riga had already done from within his body.

Twenty years ago, Yin Riga approached Altan Trengsin and said, "Come now. Your aunt is waiting."

Riga extended his hand. And Altan, without question or hesitation, took it.

She heard Riga's laughter ringing in her mind. *Now do you see?*

Rin stumbled back, horrified, but she was still caught in the vision, forced to watch as long as Riga wanted her to, and she couldn't bring herself back to her senses. She couldn't bring herself back to her body, couldn't return to Mount Tianshan—could only keep watching as Riga led Altan to a boat waiting down the shore, a boat flying Federation colors.

Other children were waiting on the decks. Dozens of them. And standing among them, one man—a thin, spindly man whose hands moved across the children's shoulders, whose narrow eyes danced with curious glee as he observed them the same way he had once observed Rin, whose narrow, sharp-chinned face had hovered above her in the worst moments of her life and haunted her nightmares even now.

Shiro.

Twenty years ago, Dr. Eyimchi Shiro took Altan's hand and guided him on board.

Then it all fit together; the final, horrible piece of the puzzle fell into place. The Federation had not kidnapped Speer's children. It was the Trifecta. It had been Riga all along; Riga who delivered the children to the Federation; Riga who forced Hanelai's hand when she dissented, and then watched her island go up in smoke when she made the wrong choice.

"You're right." Riga removed his hands from Rin's temples, leaving her gasping on her knees. "I make hard choices. I do whatever I must. But I do not work with Speerlies. I tried with Hanelai. That bitch tried to defect. Your kind don't serve, they only cause trouble. And you'll be no different."

Rin's head throbbed. She heaved for breath, glaring at the floor until her vision stopped spinning, trying to buy a few seconds.

She'd been so terribly wrong. There was no appeasing Riga. She couldn't beg an alliance from someone who didn't think her human.

This wasn't about humiliation.

This was about survival.

Then the calculus became starkly clear.

She'd hoped so desperately for a different outcome. She'd climbed that mountain willing to do almost anything for the Trifecta. She'd known they had done awful things. She would have overlooked those things, if only she could borrow their power. If it meant victory against the Republic, she would have forgiven the Trifecta for almost anything.

But not this.

She lifted her head. "Thank you."

Riga's mouth twisted into a sneer. "What for, little girl?"

"For making this easy." She closed her eyes, focusing through her pain onto a singular point of rage. Then she turned her palm out.

The burst of flame lasted for only two seconds, just long enough to singe Riga's clothes before it died away.

The Phoenix hadn't disappeared. Rin could still feel her link to the god, clearer than ever in the Heavenly Temple. But the Phoenix was suppressed, screeching, struggling against an enemy that Rin could not perceive.

Somewhere on the spiritual plane, the gods were at war.

Hand-to-hand combat, then.

Rin drew her sword. Riga pulled his blade from atop the altar just before she charged at him, parrying with a force that sent shock waves ripping through her arm.

He was unexpectedly slow. Bizarrely clumsy. He made the right moves, but always a split second behind, as if he were still remembering how to channel thoughts into actions. After twenty years asleep, Riga had yet to acclimate to his physical body, and only that disadvantage was keeping Rin alive.

It wasn't enough. Her swordplay was awful. She never practiced with her left hand. She had no balance. Slow as he was, she only barely managed to keep pace, and in seconds he put her on the defensive. She couldn't even think about striking back; she was so focused on avoiding his blade.

Riga raised his sword overhead. She jerked her blade up just in time to meet a blow meant to cleave her in two. Her shoulder buckled from the impact. She tensed, anticipating a side strike, but Riga did not lift his blade from hers. He pressed down, harder and harder, until the crossed steel was inches from Rin's face.

"Kneel," he said.

Rin's knees shook.

"I will be merciful," he said. "I will permit you to serve. You need only kneel."

Her arm gave out. He sliced down. She dove to the left, barely avoiding his blade, as her own sword dropped from her numb fingers to the floor. Riga scraped his foot over the hilt and kicked it to the other side of the room.

"Ziya." He glanced over his shoulder. "Get rid of that."

Jiang was still standing where he'd frozen when Riga stepped off the altar. At the sound of his name, he lifted his head, brows furrowed in confusion.

"Master," Rin breathed. "Please . . ."

Jiang moved slowly toward the sword, bent over to pick it up, then hesitated. His eyes landed on Rin and he frowned, squinting as if he was trying to remember where he had seen her before.

"Come now, Ziya." Riga sounded bored. "Don't dawdle."

Jiang blinked, then lifted the sword off the ground.

Rin hastened to her feet, hand scrabbling for her knife only to remember that she was reaching with phantom fingers, that her right hand *wasn't there.*

She lunged at Riga's legs. If she could just knock him off balance, get him on the ground—

He saw her coming. He stepped aside and swept his knee up high into her sternum. Something cracked in her rib cage. She dropped to the floor, unable to even gasp.

"Had enough?" He bent down, seized her collar, and dragged her up to face him. Then he slammed a fist into her stomach.

The blow sent her careening back until she hit the wall. Her head cracked against stone. Stars exploded behind her eyes. She slid bonelessly to the ground, choking. She couldn't breathe. Couldn't move. Couldn't perceive anything but pulsing, white-hot flashes of pain.

She had no weapon, no shield, and no fire.

For the first time, it sank in that she might not leave this temple alive.

"I hate to do this." Riga tapped his blade to the side of her neck, as if practicing his swing before he took it. "Killing off the last of you. It's so final. But you Speerlies never gave me a choice. You always had to be so very *troublesome*."

He drew his sword back. Rin squeezed her eyes shut and waited for the blade to land.

It never did.

She heard a splintering crack. She opened her eyes. Jiang stood between her and Riga. His staff was in splinters, and crimson stained both his torso and Riga's blade. Jiang twisted around. Their eyes met.

"Run," he whispered.

Riga swung his sword again. Something black whistled through the air, and Riga's blade skidded across the ground.

"I forgot," Riga sneered. "You always had a soft spot for Speerlies."

He aimed a savage kick at the wound in Jiang's side. Jiang doubled over. In the corner, Daji gasped and clutched her stomach, her faced pinched with pain.

Rin hesitated, torn between Jiang and the door.

"He can't kill me," Jiang hissed. "*Run.*"

She staggered to her feet. The door was ten feet away. That was nothing. Her legs hurt so much, everything hurt so much, but she bit down the pain and forced herself to keep moving. Five feet—

A bang exploded behind her. She tripped and fell.

"*Run*," Jiang repeated, though his voice sounded strained. Rin smelled blood. She wanted to look back but knew she couldn't, knew she had to keep moving. Three feet. She was so close.

"Call them," Jiang shouted. "End this."

Rin knew precisely what he meant.

Outside, she stumbled into the fog.

She refused to feel guilt for this. This was her only option; this was what Jiang wanted. He'd made his choice, and now she made hers. She turned an open palm to the sky.

I unleash you.

This time the Phoenix came. The Dragon was distracted, struggling against the Gatekeeper, and so her god was free. The fire surged through her arm and up into the mist, a shining beacon against a backdrop of gray.

The Phoenix shrieked, delighted. In that moment Rin felt its divine presence closer, more intimately than she ever had, a synchronicity that surpassed what she had once felt on Speer. Here where the boundary between man and god was blurred, their wills overlapped until they were not separate beings, one channeled through the other, but a single entity, ripping through the fabric of the world to rewrite history.

Fire pierced the dense mist, spiraling into a pillar so tall and bright that Rin thought it must be visible to the entire world. The clouds that shrouded Mount Tianshan shriveled away, exposing the pagoda against the bare face of stone.

Nezha must have seen. Rin was counting on it. He'd been following her all this way, and now she'd delivered to him everything he and the Hesperians wanted—all the world's most powerful shamans clustered in one place, open targets trapped atop the mountain.

Here's your chance, Nezha. Now take it.

One by one, the airships appeared from behind the clouds, blurry black shapes that homed in on her unmistakable beacon. They had been hovering, waiting, searching for a target. Now they had it.

They flew into a semicircular formation, surrounding the pagoda from every angle. Rin couldn't see Nezha from this distance, but she imagined he was riding in the center of the fleet, eyes trained on her. She raised her hand and waved.

"Hello there," she murmured. "You're welcome."

Then she extinguished her flames and ran, just as every dirigible in the sky turned its cannons toward the mountain and fired.

Booms split the sky. They didn't fade. They rolled on like endless thunder, growing louder and louder until Rin couldn't hear her own thoughts. She couldn't tell if she'd been knocked off the ground; she moved her legs but couldn't feel anything below her knees except deep reverberations in her bones. She moved like she was floating, buoyed by a numbing shock that muted all pain.

Something pulsed in the air. Not a noise, but a *sensation*—she could feel it, thick like congealed porridge, a crackling stillness that by now was all too familiar.

She hazarded a glance behind her. Beasts poured out of the pagoda—not the malformed, shadowy entities that Rin had seen Jiang summon before, but solid creatures, infinite in number, color, size, and shape, as if Jiang had really opened the gates to the Emperor's Menagerie and let every single one of those clawed, fanged, winged, and screeching creatures into the mortal world.

They shifted endlessly between forms. Rin watched as a phoenix became a kirin became a lion became some winged *thing* that shot toward the dirigible fleet like an arrow, accompanied by the screeching cacophony of its brothers and sisters.

The Hesperians fired back. The rumbling grew so loud that the mountain itself seemed to shake.

Good, Rin thought. *Hit them with everything you have.*

Let this be the ultimate test. Let this prove that even the most legendary shamans in Nikara history could not stand up to the machines of the Divine Architect.

Can you see this, Sister Petra? Is this vindicating?

She wanted to stand still and watch, to marvel at destruction that for once was not her own doing. She wanted to see, the same way little children ripped down birds' nests with glee, just how great a scar the two self-proclaimed great powers on this earth could rip into the fabric of the world.

A missile exploded overhead. Rin flung herself forward just as a boulder crashed into the dirt behind her. Shards of debris, still red-hot from impact, splattered the backs of her legs.

Get a fucking grip, said Altan's voice as she clambered upright, heart slamming against her ribs. *And get the fuck off this mountain.*

She needed a quicker way down. The missiles hadn't hit her yet, but they inevitably would; when dirigibles fired en masse they were not discriminate.

She paused, considering the fleet.

The airships weren't going to land. That would be stupid. But they had to get in close. They couldn't aim properly at the pagoda from too far away; they had to dip down to get a good shot at the Trifecta.

Which gave Rin a single, obvious way out.

She exhaled sharply. *Ah, fuck.*

She saw only one dirigible in jumping range, and she wasn't sure she'd be able to make that leap. In top fighting condition, she'd have taken it with confidence. But she was exhausted. Every part of her body was battered and hurting. Her legs felt weighed down with anchors, and her lungs burned for breath.

The closest dirigible was veering upward. If it scaled too high she'd never catch it—she couldn't jump at that trajectory.

No more time to think. It was now or never. She crouched low, pushed her feet against the dirt, and summoned every last ounce of her strength as she took a running leap off the cliff.

Her fingers just snagged an iron rod at the bottom of the carriage. The dirigible tilted dangerously to one side, jerked down by her sudden weight. Rin curled her fingers tighter as her other wrist flailed uselessly in the air. The dirigible readjusted its balance. Its pilot must have known she was there—he swerved back and forth, trying to shake her off. The thin metal rod dug into her flesh, nearly slicing through her joints. She screamed in pain.

Something—one of Jiang's beasts, a misfired missile, or flying debris; Rin couldn't see—struck the opposite side of the carriage.

The dirigible lurched, flipping her upward. She strained to maintain her grip. They weren't anywhere near solid ground yet—if she let go now she'd fall to her death.

She made the mistake of looking down. The chasm loomed. Her heart skipped a beat, and she squeezed her eyes shut.

The dirigible kept rising. She felt it turn away from the mountain, retreating to safer skies. The lurching had stopped.

The pilot had figured out who she was. He wanted to take her alive.

No. Oh, no no no . . .

Something shrieked above her head. Rin glanced up. Something had punctured the side of the dirigible—the balloon deflated as air escaped the hole with a deafening whistle.

The dirigible's movements grew erratic, dipping toward the mountain one moment and twisting away the next. Rin fought to keep a hold but her fingers were slick with sweat; her thumb slipped off the iron bar, numb, and then it was just four fingers between her and the chasm.

The pilot had lost all control. The dirigible was starting to nosedive.

But—thank the gods—it was careening *toward* the mountain.

Rin eyed the craggy surface, fighting to stay calm. She had to jump as soon as she was close enough, just before the airship crushed her in its wreckage.

The rock face loomed closer and closer.

She took a deep breath.

Three, two, one. She exhaled and let go.

Am I dead?

The world was black. Her body was on fire, and she could not see.

But death would not hurt so much. Death was easy; she'd come close so many times now that she knew dying was like falling backward into a black pit of comforting nothingness. Death made the pain go away. But hers only intensified.

Ah, Rin. Altan's voice rang in her temples—amused, teasing. *Ever the surprise.*

For once she did not recoil from his presence. She was grateful for the company. She needed him to filter through the horror.

Something wrong?

"I'm the only one now," she said. "They . . . they're not . . . I'm the only one."

It's nice to be the only one.

"But I wanted allies."

He just laughed. *Shouldn't you know better by now?*

And he was right—she should have known better than to put her fate in the hands of people more powerful than she. She should have learned, many times over, that everyone she pledged her faith to would inevitably use and abuse her.

But she'd *wanted* to follow the Trifecta. She wanted someone else to fight her battles for her, because she was so, so exhausted. She wanted Jiang back, and she wanted to believe Daji was the woman she hoped she'd be. She'd wanted to believe she could foist this war onto someone else. And she'd always clung far too hard to her illusions.

Forget those assholes, Altan said. *We can do this on our own.*

She snorted, tasting blood. "Yeah."

After a long time, the explosions stopped. By then, Rin's vision was fully restored. At first she'd seen only blotches of color—great patches of red against the white sky, flaring with every boom. Then her vision clarified, differentiated between billows of smoke and the fires that created them.

She lay flat on her back, head tilted to the sky, and laughed.

She'd done it.

She'd fucking done it.

In one blow, she'd rid herself of the Trifecta and the Hesperian fleet. Two of the greatest forces the Empire had ever seen—gone, wiped off the face of the earth with no monument but ash. The entire balance of the world had just changed. She saw the forces reversing in her mind.

For so long she'd been fighting a mad, hopeless, desperate war. And now it looked so very, very winnable.

Ever so faintly in the back of her mind, though muted and strained by the spiritual back door that ran through Kitay's mind, she heard the Phoenix laughing, too—the low, harsh cackle of a deity who had finally gotten everything it had wanted.

"Fuck you all," she whispered at the coiling smoke that dissipated up into the reforming mist. She made a rude gesture with her hand. "That's for Speer."

She would have seen something if anyone in the Heavenly Temple were still alive. She would have seen movement. As she stared, the mountain mist played tricks on her eyes, kept making her believe she'd caught the faintest glimpse of a silhouette stumbling out of the pagoda. But whenever she looked closer, all she saw was smoke.

It took a few moments for her rational mind to start working again.

Basics first. First she had to get off this mountain. Then she had to get medical care. Her open wounds weren't deep, and most of them had stopped bleeding, but a million other things—exposure, cracked ribs, bruised organs—might kill her if she didn't move fast.

But moving was agony. Her knees buckled with every step. Her ribs shrieked in protest every time she breathed. She clenched her teeth and willed herself to trudge forward. She couldn't manage more than a pathetic lurch with every step. The pain in her legs intensified—something, somewhere, was broken. It didn't matter. Kitay was waiting for her below. She just had to get back to Kitay.

Silent wreckage littered the base of Mount Tianshan. Not just the debris of ruined dirigibles—Nezha's bombers had also decimated Cholang's troops. She saw fragments of ground cannons mixed in with airship shells. Craters formed horribly clean hemispheres in the dirt.

She stood a moment in the silence, breathing in the ash. Nothing moved. She was the only survivor in sight.

Then she heard it—a distorted hum, the sloping whine of a dying engine. She spun around. Looked up.

In the moonlight she saw only its black silhouette—small but growing, flying straight toward her. It wouldn't make it. Whatever kept it alight was ruined—she saw smoke trailing out the back in thick, billowing clouds.

But it was still firing.

Fuck.

Rin dropped to the ground.

The bullets scattered pointlessly across scorched ground. The pilot wasn't aiming, he just needed to destroy something, anything, before his life spiraled out of his hands. The dirigible loosed one last round of cannons, then careened into the side of the mountain and exploded in a ball of fire.

She stood up, unscathed.

"You missed me!" she screamed at the mountainside, at the spot where plumes furled up from the last dirigible's wreckage. "*You fucking missed!*"

Of course no one answered. Her voice, thin and reedy, faded without echo into the frigid air.

But she screamed it again, and then again, and then again. It felt so good to say that she'd survived, that she'd fucking finally come out on top, that she didn't even care that she was screaming to corpses.

PART III

CHAPTER 22

ARLONG, NINE YEARS PRIOR

"Nezha." Yin Vaisra beckoned with one finger. "Come here."

Delighted, Nezha ran to his side. He'd been in the middle of a grueling Classics lesson, but his tutor had bowed and left the room as soon as his father appeared in the doorway.

"How go your studies?" Vaisra asked. "Are you working hard?"

Nezha swallowed his instinct to babble, instead mulling carefully over his response. Vaisra had never asked him questions like this before; he'd never displayed much interest in any of his children except Jinzha. Nezha didn't want his father to think him a braggart or a fool.

"Tutor Chau says I'm progressing well," he said cautiously. "I've mastered the fundamentals of Old Nikara grammar, and I can now recite one hundred and twenty-two poems from the Jin dynasty. Next week we'll—"

"Good." Vaisra sounded neither particularly interested nor pleased. He turned. "Walk with me."

Somewhat crestfallen, Nezha followed his father out of the eastern wing into the main reception hall. He wasn't quite sure where they were going. The palace of Arlong was a grand, chilly place consisting mostly of empty air and long, high-ceilinged hallways draped with tapestries depicting the history of the Dragon Province dating back to the fall of the Red Emperor's dynasty.

Vaisra paused before a detailed portrait of Yin Vara, the former Dragon Warlord before the Second Poppy War. Nezha had always hated this tapestry. He'd never known his grandfather, but Vara's stern, gaunt visage made him feel small and insignificant every time he passed beneath.

"Have you ever wanted to rule, Nezha?" Vaisra asked.

Nezha frowned, confused. "Why would I?"

Ruling had never been in his stars. Jinzha, the firstborn son, stood to inherit the title of Dragon Warlord and all the responsibilities that came with it. Nezha was only the second son. He was destined to become a soldier, his brother's most loyal general.

"You've never considered it?"

Nezha felt vaguely as if he were failing a test, but he didn't know what else to say. "It's not my place."

"No, I suppose not." Vaisra was silent for a moment. Then he asked, "Would you like to hear a story?"

A *story*? Nezha hesitated, unsure of how to respond. Vaisra never told him stories. But although Nezha had no idea how to converse with his father, he couldn't bear to let this opportunity pass.

"Yes," he said carefully. "I would."

Vaisra glanced down at him. "Do you know why we don't let you go to those grottoes?"

Nezha perked up. "Because of the monsters?"

Would this be a monster story? He hoped it would be. He felt a flicker of excitement. His childhood nurses knew that his favorite tales were about the myriad beasts rumored to lurk in the grottoes—the dragons, the cannibal crabs, the fish-women who made you love them and then drowned you once you got too close.

"Monsters?" Vaisra chuckled. Nezha had never heard his father chuckle before. "Do you like the grotto stories?"

Nezha nodded. "Very much."

Vaisra put a hand on his shoulder.

Nezha suppressed a flinch. He wasn't afraid of his father's touch—Vaisra had never been violent toward him. But Vaisra had never caressed him like this, either. Hugs, kisses, reassuring touches—those belonged to Nezha's mother, Lady Saikhara, who nearly suffocated her children with affection.

Nezha had always thought of his father as a statue—remote, foreboding, and untouchable. Vaisra seemed to him less like a man than a god, the perfect ideal of everything he'd been raised to become. Every word Yin Vaisra articulated was direct and concise, every action efficient and deliberate. Never did he show his children affection beyond the odd somber nod of approval. Never did he tell fairy tales.

So what was going on?

For the first time Nezha noticed that his father's eyes looked somewhat glassy, that his speech seemed much slower than usual. And his breath . . . a pungent, sour smell wafted into Nezha's face every time Vaisra spoke. Nezha had smelled that odor twice before—once in the servants' quarters, when he'd been wandering around past bedtime where he shouldn't have been, and once in Jinzha's room.

He squirmed under Vaisra's hand, suddenly uncomfortable. He didn't want a story anymore. He wanted to get back to his lesson.

"I'll tell you a grotto story," Vaisra said. "You know Arlong rose as a southern power in the decades of warfare after the Red Emperor's death. But in the last years of the Red Emperor's reign, after he abandoned Dragon Province to build a new capital at Sinegard, Arlong was regarded as a cursed place. These islands lay inside a valley of death, of crashing waves and flooding riverbanks. No ships that sailed past the Red Cliffs survived. Everything smashed to death against those rocks."

Nezha kept utterly still as he listened. He had never heard this story before. He wasn't sure that he liked it.

"Finally," Vaisra continued, "a man named Yu, learned in shamanic arts, called down the Dragon Lord of the Western River and begged his help to control the rivers. Overnight, Arlong transformed. The waters turned calm. The flooding ceased. Arlong's people built canals and rice paddies between the islands. In a few short years, Dragon Province became the jewel of the Nikara Empire, a land of beauty and plenty." Vaisra paused. "Only Yu continued to suffer."

Vaisra seemed caught in a reverie, speaking not to Nezha but at the tapestries, as if he were reciting dynastic lineage into the silent hall.

"Um." Nezha swallowed. "Why—"

"Nature can't be altered," Vaisra said. "Only held at bay. Always, the waters of Arlong threatened to break their leash and drown the new city in their fury. Yu was forced to spend his life in a state of shamanic hallucination, always calling upon the Dragon, always hearing its whispers in his ears. After several dozen years of this, Yu wanted desperately to end his life. And when the god's takeover was complete, when he could no longer die, he wanted to ensconce himself in the Chuluu Korikh. But he knew that if he sought peace, someone had to take up his mantle. Yu could not be that cruel, nor that selfish. So what happened?"

Nezha didn't know. But he could put this together like the pieces of a logic puzzle, like the kind that his tutors were always training him to solve for the Keju exam.

Father said this was a grotto story. And grotto stories were about monsters.

"Yu transformed," Nezha said. "He became the monster."

"Not a monster, Nezha." Vaisra stroked a lock of hair behind Nezha's ear. "A savior. He made the ultimate sacrifice for Arlong. But Arlong forgot him almost immediately. They saw his horrifying new form, his winding coils and sharp scales, and they received him with not gratitude but fear. Even his own wife did not recognize him. She took one look at him and screamed. Her brothers threw rocks at him and drove him out of the village, back into the grotto where he had spent decades praying to protect them. He . . ."

Vaisra's voice trailed away.

Nezha glanced up. "Father?"

Vaisra was gazing silently at the tapestries. Confused, Nezha followed his eyes. None of these tapestries contained the story he'd just heard. They were all dynastic portraits, an endless row of finely embroidered likenesses of Nezha's long-dead predecessors.

What was Father trying to tell him?

What sacrifices had the House of Yin made for Arlong?

"Your tutors told me you wanted to visit the grottoes," Vaisra said suddenly.

Nezha stiffened. Was that what this was about? Was he in trouble? Yes, he'd asked, many more times than he should have. He'd begged and whined, pledging to keep to the shallows or even the opposite riverbank if only they'd let him get near enough to catch a glimpse inside the cave mouths.

"I apologize, Father," he said. "I won't ask again—I was just curious—"

"About what?"

"I thought—I mean, I'd heard about treasures, and I thought . . ." Nezha trailed off. His cheeks flamed. His words sounded stupid and childish as he uttered them. Silently he swore never to disobey his father's word again.

But Vaisra didn't chide him. He just gazed at Nezha for a very long time, his expression inscrutable. At last, he patted Nezha again on the shoulder.

"Don't go to those grottoes, Nezha." He sounded very tired then. "Don't take on the burden of an entire nation. It's too heavy. And you aren't strong enough."

CHAPTER 23

"If I counted right, the explosions on Mount Tianshan destroyed almost two-thirds of the Hesperian fleet in Nikan," Kitay said. "That's . . . that's a lot."

"Just two-thirds?" Cholang asked. "Not all?"

"Nezha didn't send the entire fleet west," Kitay said. "The last I heard, the Consortium had lent him forty-eight aircraft. We brought down six at the Anvil. I saw about thirty at the mountain. And we know that two escaped back west."

"With any luck, Nezha wasn't on them," Venka muttered.

Rin rubbed at her aching eyes, too exhausted to laugh. The four of them—herself, Cholang, Kitay, and Venka—stood around the table in Cholang's hut. They were all wan and twitchy with fatigue, yet their conference felt suffused with an urgent, burning energy. A quiet, astonished confidence; a taste of hope that none of them had felt for months.

This was the difference between fleeing for their lives and planning an assault. They all understood the magnitude of what might be in reach. It was madness. It was thrilling.

"How quickly do you think the Hesperians will send replacements?" Rin asked.

"I'm not sure," Kitay said. "They're probably vacillating. When

I was in Arabak, I kept hearing rumors that the Consortium was reconsidering their investments. The longer Nezha took to solidify the south, the touchier they got about military aid. The Consortium's a tricky entity—they need a unanimous vote from all member countries to commit troops in any foreign location. And their constituents are getting less comfortable losing lives—and the costs of airships, which are considerable—to a power they can't understand."

"So they're cowards," Cholang said. "Paper tigers. They came in ready to win our wars for us, but the moment they get scared, they're all going to back off?"

"It won't end this easily," Rin said. "They've had designs on this continent for too long. We won't scare them away with mere threats. We have to make it real." She swallowed and lifted her chin. "If we want to finish this for good, we'll have to occupy Arlong."

No one laughed.

It was amazing how that simple sentence, which a week ago would have just sounded like a cruel joke, now seemed completely feasible. Defeating the Republic wasn't a daydream anymore. It was a question of time frame.

Rin had survived the long march with only the barest fragments of an army. The numbers Kitay had collected were depressing. Half the soldiers who had left the Anvil were now dead or missing. The casualty rate for civilians reached two-thirds.

But Rin still commanded the survivors. And right now, she held the biggest military advantage she'd possessed since this war began.

The Hesperians were rattled. Nezha had just suffered a defeat of epic proportions. Instead of bombing her to pieces under open skies, he'd followed Rin to Mount Tianshan and lost most of his fleet. This disaster fell on his shoulders, and the Consortium surely knew it. For once, the southerners had a fighting chance at defeating the Republic. But to capitalize on their momentum, they had to move out as quickly as they could.

"We should attack on two fronts." Rin made a pincer movement with her hand. "A double-pronged strategy from the north and south, like the one the Mugenese tried during the Third Poppy War."

"Didn't work so well for them," Venka said.

"Save for me, it would have," Rin said. "They had the right idea—they forced the Empire to split reinforcements along two vulnerable fronts. What's more, Nezha knows he's running low on manpower. He'll throw everything he has at us if we're concentrated in a single front. I don't want to take that gamble. I'd rather bleed him dry."

"Then we hit him from the northwest and the northeast." Seamlessly, Kitay picked up Rin's thoughts and spun them out loud into an articulable plan. "We send a first column through Ram, Rat, and Tiger Provinces. Then the main force will strike in the heartland, right when he's spread his forces thin trying to maintain territory that he's just gotten his hands on. If we act fast, we could have this wrapped up within six months."

"Hold on," said Cholang. "You'll accomplish all this with what army?"

"Well," Kitay said, "yours."

"I lost eighty soldiers at Mount Tianshan," Cholang said. "I'm not about to send more to their deaths."

"You'll die if you stay here," Rin said. "Did you think Nezha would leave you alone now that you've cast your lot? You're already dead men walking. It's a question of when and how."

"You might buy a few extra months while he's occupied with us," Kitay added. "But if the Republic can finish us off, then you certainly have no chance. Ask yourself if it's worth several more months living in tents on the plains."

Cholang said nothing.

"You won't think of a rejoinder," Venka informed him. "He's thought about five arguments ahead."

Cholang scowled. "Go on, then."

"The northeastern front will obviously be a feint—it doesn't determine the endgame—but we still gain a hard material advantage from striking there early," Kitay said. "It's got bases of wartime industry—armories, shipyards, all that good stuff. So even if Nezha doesn't take us seriously up north, it's a win either way." He nodded to Venka. "You go with Cholang. Take a couple hundred men from the Southern Army; you pick."

"Not that I'm refusing this assignment," Venka said, "but suppose you've miscalculated, and we head straight into a bloodbath?"

"That won't happen," Kitay assured her. "Nezha doesn't have a loyal local base in the north. They've only recently bowed to the Republic, and the civilians couldn't care less who wins this fight. They've lost their Empress, they've lost Jun Loran, and they're rankling under Arlong's rule just as much as we are. They don't have an ideological stake in this."

"They're the north, though," Venka said. "Part of their ideology is hating you lot. They won't bow to peasants."

"Then it's a good thing we're sending Sring Venka," Kitay said. "You porcelain-faced Sinegardian princess, you."

Venka snickered. "Fine."

"But what are you doing on the southeastern front?" Cholang asked. "We'd be leaving you with shards of an army."

"That's fine," Rin said. "We've got shamans."

"What shamans?" Cholang asked. "You're the only one left."

"I don't have to be."

It was as if she'd placed a lit fuse on the center of the table. The room fell silent. Kitay stiffened. Venka and Cholang stared at her, openmouthed.

Rin refused to let that faze her. She wouldn't get defensive; that would only justify their incredulity. She had been wondering how to introduce this proposal since she descended from the mountain. And then it became obvious—to make madness seem normal, she merely had to discuss it as if it were common sense. She just had to distort their idea of *normal*.

"Su Daji had the right idea," she continued calmly. "The only way we have a chance against the Hesperians is to match their Maker with our own gods. The Trifecta could have managed it. They might even have seized the Empire by now, if I'd let Riga have his way. But they were despots. Over time, they would have done more harm than good."

Now for the crucial leap of logic. "But if we haven't got them, we need our own shamans. We've got hundreds of soldiers who would be willing to do it. We just need to train them. We've set a campaign schedule of six months. I can get recruits in fighting form in two weeks."

She looked around the table, waiting for someone to object.

Everything hinged on what happened next. Rin was testing the boundaries of her authority in the aftermath of a tectonic shift in power. This felt so different from the first time she'd vaulted herself into leadership, mere months ago when she'd addressed Ma Lien's men with a dry mouth and quivering knees. Back then she'd been scared, grasping for straws, and disguising her utter lack of a strategy with feigned bravado.

Now she knew exactly what she needed to do. She just needed to force everyone onto the same page. She had a vision for the future—something horrifying, something grand. Could she speak it into reality?

"But back when . . ." Venka opened her mouth, closed it, then opened it again. "Rin, I'm just—you told me once that—"

"I understand the risks," Rin said. "Back then I didn't think they were worth it. But you saw what happened on that mountain. It's clear now that they are. The Hesperians still have at least fourteen airships, and that gives them an advantage we can't counter. Not without more of—well, *me*."

There was another silence.

Then Cholang shook his head and sighed. "Look. If any of my men want to volunteer, I won't stop them."

"Thank you," Rin said.

Good enough—that was as much of an endorsement as she was

going to get. So long as Cholang didn't try to stop her, she didn't care how uncomfortable he looked.

She glanced to her right. "Kitay?"

She needed to hear him speak before she could continue. She wasn't waiting for his permission—she'd never needed his permission for anything—but she wanted to hear his confirmation. She wanted someone else, someone whose mind worked far faster than hers ever would, to assess the forces at play and the lives at stake and say, *Yes, these calculations are valid. This sacrifice is necessary. You aren't mad. The world is.*

For a long time Kitay stood still, staring at the table, fingers tapping erratically against the wooden surface. Then he looked up at her. No, he looked right through her. His mind was already somewhere else. He was already thinking past this conversation. "No more than several—"

"We won't need more than a handful," she assured him. "Three at most—just enough that we can spread an attack around multiple planes."

"One for every cardinal direction," he murmured. "Because the impact is exponential if . . ."

"Right," she said. "I get a lot done. I'm not enough. But even one other shaman throws off defense formations like we couldn't dream."

"Fucking hell," Venka said. "How long have you been thinking about this?"

Rin didn't miss a beat. "Since Tikany."

She still hadn't fully won them over. She saw doubt lingering in their eyes—they might not have raised objections, but they still didn't like it.

She felt a pulse of frustration. How could she make them *see*? They had long surpassed wars of steel and bodies clashing on mortal fields. War happened on the divine plane now—her gods versus the Hesperians' Maker. What she'd seen on Mount Tianshan was a vision of the future, of how this would inevitably end.

They couldn't flinch away from that future. They had to fight the kind of war that moved mountains.

"The west does not conceive of this war as a material struggle," she said. "This is about contesting interpretations of divinity. They imagine that because they obey the Divine Architect, they can crush us like ants. We've just proven them wrong. We'll do it again."

She leaned forward, pressing her palm against the table. "We have one chance right now—probably the only chance we'll ever get—to seize this country back. The Republic is reeling, but they're going to recover. We've got to hit them hard before then. And when we do, it can't be a half-hearted assault. We need *overkill*. We need to scare Nezha's allies so badly that they'll scuttle back to their hemisphere and never dare to come back here again."

No one objected. She knew they wouldn't. The objections didn't exist.

"What's your plan for when they lose control?" Kitay asked quietly.

He'd said *when*. Not *if*. This wasn't a hypothetical. They'd moved into the realm of logistics now, which meant she'd already won.

"They won't," she said. The next words she spoke felt like reopened scars, familiar and painful, words that bore the weight of all the guilt that she'd tried so long to suppress. Words belonging to a legacy that now, she knew, she had no choice but to face. "Because we'll be Cike. And the first rule of the Cike is that we cull."

The world looked different when Rin walked out of Cholang's hut.

She saw the same haphazard army camp that she'd encountered walking in. She passed the same flimsy fires flickering under harsh steppe winds; the same clusters of underweight soldiers and civilians with too little to eat, drink, or wear; the same thin, worn, and hungry eyes.

But Rin didn't see weakness here.

She saw an army rebuilding. A nation in the making. Gods, it excited her. Did they understand what they were about to become?

"Look," Kitay said. "They're telling myths about you already."

Rin followed his gaze. A handful of younger soldiers had erected a stage in the center of the camp by pushing two tables together. A white sheet stretched taut between two poles, behind which a small lamp burned, throwing distorted silhouettes onto the blank canvas.

She paused to watch.

The sight of the canvas brought back memories so sweet they hurt: four days of summer among the hot, sticky crowds of Sinegard; the cool relief of the marble flooring in Kitay's family's estate; five-course banquet meals of rich foods she'd never tasted before and hadn't touched since. This puppet show wasn't a fraction as professional as the performance she'd seen during the Summer Festival in Sinegard, which had involved puppets that moved so smoothly, their rods and strings so invisible that Rin almost believed there were little creatures dancing on the other side. These puppeteers were quite visible behind the stage, wearing shabby, hastily stitched props on their hands that vaguely resembled people.

Rin didn't realize that the formless blue figure in front was Nezha until the play began.

"I am the Young Marshal!" The puppeteer adopted the nasal, reedy voice of a petulant child. "My father said we were supposed to win this war!"

"You've led our fleet to disaster!" The other actor spoke in guttural, broken Nikara, signifying a Hesperian soldier. "You idiot boy! Why would you fire on the Trifecta?"

"I didn't know they could fire *back*!"

The following scenes were equally bad, line after line of crude, stupid humor. But in the aftermath of Tianshan, crude humor was what the southerners wanted. They reveled in Nezha's humiliation. It made their impending fight seem winnable.

"Come on." Kitay resumed walking. "It's just more of the same."

"What else are they saying?" Rin asked.

"Who cares?"

"I don't care what they say about Nezha. What are they saying about me?"

"Ah."

He knew what she was really asking. *What do they know?*

"No one knows you turned on the Trifecta," he said after a pause. "They know you went to Mount Tianshan to seek help, and that the shamans inside sacrificed themselves to save us from the dirigible fleet. That's all they know."

"So they think the Trifecta died heroes."

"Wouldn't you assume the same?" Kitay raised an eyebrow at her. "Are you going to correct them?"

She considered that for a moment, and found herself in the curious position of determining a nation's historical narrative.

Did she let the Trifecta's legacy survive?

She could ruin them. She *ought* to ruin them, for what they had done to her.

But the hero narrative was halfway true. One of the Trifecta had died for honor. One, at least, deserved to be remembered as a good man. And that made a lovely myth—the shamans of a previous era of Nikara greatness had given up their lives to ensure a dawn of a new one.

Rin had ended the Trifecta. She could afford them dignity in death, if that was what she chose. She loved that she had the power to choose.

"No," she decided. "Let them linger on in legend."

She could be generous to the Trifecta's ghosts. They could become legends—legends were all they would ever be. For all of Riga, Jiang, and Daji's dreams of glory, their story had ended in the Heavenly Temple. She could allow them to occupy this little prelude in history. She had the far more delightful task of shaping the future. And when she was finished, no one would even remember the Trifecta's names.

Rin had another audience that night before she slept.

She set out alone to meet Chaghan in his camp. The Ketreyids were packing up. Their campfires were stamped out and the evidence buried; their yurts and blankets were rolled up and lashed onto their horses.

"You're not sticking around?" she asked.

"I did what I came here to do." Chaghan didn't ask her what had happened on the mountain. He clearly already knew; he'd greeted her with an impressed grin and a shake of his head. "Well done, Speerly. That was clever."

"Thank you," she said, pleased in spite of herself. Chaghan had never paid her a compliment before. For nearly the entirety of their relationship, since the day they'd first met at Khurdalain, he had treated her like some wayward child incapable of rational decisions.

Now, for the first time, he acted as if he truly respected her.

"Do you think they're dead?" she asked him. "I mean, there's no chance they—"

"Absolutely," he said. "They were powerful, but their anchor bond kept them in command of their own bodies, which means they were always mortal. They've passed on. I've felt it. And good riddance."

She nodded, relieved. "It's what you're owed. For Tseveri."

His lip curled. "Let's not pretend you did that for a blood debt."

"It was a blood debt," she said. "Just not yours. And now you must know what I have to do next."

He exhaled slowly. "I can guess."

"You're not going to try to stop me?"

"You confuse me with my aunt, Rin."

"The Sorqan Sira would have killed me on the spot."

"Oh, she would have assassinated you long ago." Chaghan ran his hand gently across the length of his horse's neck. Rin realized that she knew the creature—it was the same black warhorse that Chaghan had ridden out of the forests by Lake Boyang the last time she'd seen him. He adjusted his saddle as he spoke, tightening every knot with practiced care. "The Sorqan Sira was petrified of the resurgence of Nikara shamanism. She thought it would spell the end of the world."

"And you don't?"

"The world is already ending. You see, the Hundred Clans know that time moves in a circle. There are never any new stories, just old ones told again and again as this universe moves through its cycles of civilization and crumbles into despair. We are on the brink of an age of chaos again, and there's nothing we can do to stop it. I just prefer to back certain horses in the race."

"But you're going to watch the rest from a safe distance," Rin said.

She was being facetious. She knew better than to ask Chaghan to stay and help. She wasn't that selfish—the Nikara had exploited Chaghan's people enough.

If she had to be honest, she would have liked Chaghan to come south with her. She'd never been able to stand him before, but the sight of him brought back memories of the Cike. Of Suni, Baji, Ramsa, and Qara. Of Altan. Of all the Bizarre Children, they were the only ones left, both tasked independently with bringing order to their fracturing nations. Chaghan, somehow, had already succeeded. Rin desperately wished he might lend her his power.

But she'd taken so much from him already. She couldn't demand more.

"With you, I've learned it's best to keep a safe distance from the fallout." Chaghan yanked tight the last knot and patted the horse behind its ears. "Good luck, Speerly. You're mad as they come, but you're not quite as mad as Trengsin."

"I'll take that as a compliment."

"It's the only reason I think you might win."

"Thank you," Rin said, surprised. "For everything."

He acknowledged that with a thin-lipped smile. "There's one last thing before you go. I didn't just want to say goodbye. We need to talk about Nezha."

She tensed. "Yes?"

The horse, as if sensing her unease, whinnied in agitation and stamped its front hooves against the dirt. Chaghan hastily handed its reins off to the nearest rider.

"Sit down," he told her.

She obeyed. Her heart was pounding very hard. "What do you know?"

He sat cross-legged across from her. "I started looking into the Yins after I heard what happened at the Red Cliffs. It was difficult to parse truth from legend—the House of Yin is shrouded in rumors, and they're good at protecting their secrets. But I think I've gotten a better idea of what happened to Nezha. Why he is the way he is." He tilted his head at her. "What do you know about where Nezha derived his abilities?"

"He told me a story once," she said. "It's . . . it's odd. It's not how I thought shamanism worked."

"How so?" Chaghan pressed.

Why did it suddenly feel like her head was swimming? Rin pressed her nails into her palm, trying to slow down her breathing. It shouldn't be this hard to talk about Nezha. She'd been discussing how to kill him with Kitay for months now.

But Chaghan's question brought back memories of Arlong, of rare moments of vulnerability and harsh words she regretted. They made her feel. And she didn't want to feel.

She forced her voice to keep level. "When we need our gods, we call them. But Nezha never sought the dragon. He told me he encountered one when he was young, but when he spoke about it, he made it sound . . . real."

"All gods are real."

"Real on *this* plane," she clarified. "In the material world. He said that when he was a child, he wandered into an underwater grotto and met a dragon, which killed his brother and claimed him—whatever that means. He made it sound like his god walks this earth."

"I see." Chaghan rubbed his chin. "Yes. That's what I thought."

"But—that's—can they *do* that?"

"It's not inconceivable. There are pockets of this world where the boundary between our world and the world of spirit is thinner." Chaghan pressed his palms together to demonstrate. "Mount

Tianshan is one. The Speerly Temple is another. The Nine Curves Grotto is a third. That cave is the source of all Nezha's power.

"The Yins have been linked to the Dragon for a long time. The waters of Arlong are old, and those cliffs are powerful with their history of the dead. Magic flows smoothly through those waters. Have you ever wondered how Arlong is so rich, so lush, even when its surrounding provinces are barren? A divine power has protected the region for centuries."

"But how—"

"You've been to the Dead Island. You see how nothing grows there. Have you ever wondered why?"

"I thought—I mean, wasn't that just Mugenese chemical warfare? Didn't they just poison it?"

Chaghan shook his head. "That's not all. The Phoenix's aura pulses through the island, just like water pulses through Arlong."

"So then the Dragon . . ."

"The Dragon. If you can call it that." Chaghan made a disgusted face. "More like a poor enchanted creature that might have once been a lobster, starfish, or dolphin. It must have swum in the web of the true Dragon's magic and unwittingly become a physical manifestation of the ocean, whose desire is to—"

"To destroy?"

"No. The Phoenix's impulse is to destroy. The ocean wishes to drown, to possess. The treasures of all great civilizations have inevitably fallen into its dark depths, and the Dragon yearns to possess them all. It likes to collect beautiful things."

The way he said it made Rin cringe. "And it's collecting Nezha."

"That's a nice euphemism for it. But the word is too tame. The Dragon doesn't just want to *collect* Nezha like he's some priceless vase or painting. It wants to own him, body and soul."

Bile rose up in Rin's throat as she recalled the way Nezha had shuddered when he spoke of the Dragon.

What did I do to him?

For the first time, she felt a twinge of guilt for pushing Nezha to the edge, for calling him a coward for refusing to invoke the power that might have saved them.

Back then she'd thought Nezha was just acting spoiled and selfish. She'd never understood how he could loathe his gifts so much when they were so clearly useful. She'd hated him for calling them both abominations.

She'd never taken a moment to consider that unlike her, he hadn't chosen his pain as tribute. He couldn't derive satisfaction from it like she could, because for him, it wasn't the necessary price of a way out. For him, it was only torture.

"He's drawn to that creature," Chaghan said. "And he's drawn to that place. He's physically anchored. It is the source of all his power."

Rin took a deep breath. *Focus on what matters.* "That doesn't tell me how to kill him."

"But it tells you where to strike," Chaghan said. "If you want to end Nezha, you'll have to go to the source."

She understood. "I have to take Arlong."

"You must *destroy* Arlong," he agreed. "Otherwise the water will keep healing him. It'll keep protecting him. And you should know by now that when you leave your enemies alive, wars don't end."

CHAPTER 24

The next morning, Rin stepped out of Cholang's hut to discover a crowd of people so vast she couldn't see where it ended.

Kitay had sent out a call summoning volunteers the night before, specifying soldiers older than fifteen but younger than twenty-five. Rin wanted recruits around her age. She needed their rage to be all-consuming and untempered; she needed soldiers who would throw their souls into the void without the cautious timidity she'd grown to associate with men twice and thrice her age.

But it was clear no one had heeded the age limit. The people in the crowd ranged from civilians over sixty to children as young as seven.

Rin stood before the crowd and let herself imagine, just for a moment, what might happen if she made shamans of them all. It wasn't a true option, just an awful, indulgent fantasy. She pictured deserts shifting like whirlpools. Oceans towering like mountains. She saw the whole world turned upside down, frothing with primordial chaos, and it tickled her something awful to know that if she wanted to make that happen, she could.

You would have been so proud, Altan. This is what you always wanted.

"The parameters were fifteen to twenty-five," she told the crowd. "When I come back I don't want to see anyone who doesn't qualify."

She turned and walked back into the hut.

"What now?" Kitay asked, amused. "A written exam?"

"Make them wait," she said. "We'll see who really wants it."

She let them sit for hours. As the day stretched on, more and more trickled away, disabused by the blinding sun and relentless wind. Most of them—the ones that Rin suspected had volunteered out of a temporary, unsustainable bravado—left within the first hour. She was glad to see them go. She was also relieved when the youngest volunteers finally stood and left, either on their own or dragged along by their mothers.

But that still left a crowd of nearly fifty. Still far too many.

Late in the afternoon, after the sun had cut its scorching arc through the sky, Rin came back out to address them.

"Dig a blade under the nail of your fourth finger from the tip to the bed," she commanded. It was a good test of pain tolerance. She'd learned from Altan that that sort of wound healed easily and wasn't prone to infection, but it *hurt*. "If you want this, show me your blood."

Murmurs of hesitation rippled through the crowd. For a moment no one moved, as if they were all trying to decide whether or not she was joking.

"I'm not joking," Rin said. "I have knives if you need them."

Eight volunteers dug their knives into their nail beds as she'd asked. Dark red droplets splattered the dirt. Two screamed; the other six suppressed their cries with clenched jaws.

Rin dismissed everyone else and brought the silent six into the hut.

She recognized only two of them. There was Dulin—the boy she'd found buried alive in Tikany. She was glad to see he had survived the march. Then, to her surprise, there was Pipaji.

"Where's your sister?" Rin asked.

"She's fine," Pipaji said, and didn't elaborate.

Rin regarded her for a moment, then shrugged and surveyed the others. "Did any of you make the march with your families?"

Two of them, both boy soldiers with the faintest hint of whiskers, nodded.

"Do you love them?"

They nodded again.

"If you do this you'll never see them again," Rin said. It wasn't quite the truth, but she had to test their resolve. "It's too dangerous. Your power will be volatile, and I don't have the experience to help you rein it in around civilians, which means you'll only be permitted to spend time around other people in this squadron. Think carefully."

After a long, uneasy silence, both boys stood up and left. Four remained.

"Understand the sacrifice you're making," Rin told them. She felt by now she was belaboring the point. But she owed it to them to reiterate this warning as many times as she could. She didn't need all four shamans. She needed troops who wouldn't lose their nerve halfway through training or scare the others off. "I'm asking you to gamble with your sanity. If you go into the void you'll find monsters on the other side. And you might not be strong enough to claw your way back. My masters died before they could teach me everything they knew. I'll only be a halfway decent guide."

No one said a word. Were they too terrified to speak, or did they just not care?

"You could lose control of your body and mind," she said. "And if that happens, I'll have to kill you."

Again, no reaction.

Dulin raised his hand.

She nodded to him. "Yes?"

"Will we be able to do what you do?" he asked.

"Not so well," she said. "And not so easily. I'm used to it. It will be painful for you."

"How painful?"

"It will be the worst thing you've ever known." She had to be honest; she could not ensnare them in something they didn't understand. "If you fail, then you will lose your mind forever. If you succeed, you'll still never have your mind to yourself again. You'll live on the precipice of insanity. You'll be constantly afraid. Drinking laudanum might become the only way you can get a good night's sleep. You might kill innocent people around you because you don't know what you're doing. You might kill yourself."

Her words were met with blank stares. Rin waited, fully prepared for all of them to stand up and leave.

"General?" Again Dulin raised his hand. "With all due respect, could we stop fucking around and get started?"

So Rin set about the task of creating shamans.

They spent the first evening sitting in a circle on the floor of the hut, resembling village schoolchildren about to learn to write their first characters. First Rin asked for their names. Lianhua was a willowy, wide-eyed girl from Dog Province who bore a series of terrible scars on both arms, her collarbones, and down her back as far as Rin could see. She did not explain them, and nobody was bold enough to ask.

Rin wasn't sure about her. She seemed so terribly frail—she even spoke in a tremulous, barely audible whisper. But Rin knew very well by now that delicate veneers could conceal steel. Either Lianhua would prove her worth, or she'd break down in two days and stop wasting her time.

Merchi, a tall and rangy man a few years older than Rin, was the only experienced soldier among their ranks. He'd been serving in the Fourth Division of the Imperial Militia when the Mugenese invaded; he'd been part of the liberation force on the eastern coast after the longbow island fell, and he'd witnessed the aftermath of Golyn Niis. He'd first seen combat at the Battle of Sinegard.

"I was in the city when you burned half of it down," he told

Rin. "They were whispering about a Speerly then. Never thought I'd be here now."

The one thing that bound them all was unspeakable horror. They had all seen the worst the world had to offer, and they had all come out of the experience alive.

That was important. If you didn't have an anchor, you needed something to help you return from the world of spirit—something thoroughly mortal and human. Altan had his hatred. Rin had her vengeance. And these four recruits had the ferocious, undaunted will to survive under impossible odds.

"What happens now?" Pipaji asked once introductions were finished.

"Now I'm going to give you religion," Rin said.

She and Kitay had struggled all day to come up with a way to introduce the Pantheon to novices. At Sinegard, it had taken Rin nearly an entire year to prepare her mind to process the gods. Under Jiang's instruction she'd solved riddles, meditated for hours, and read dozens of texts on theology and philosophy, all so that she could accept that her presumptions about the natural world were founded on illusions.

Her recruits didn't have that luxury. They'd have to claw their way into heaven.

The necessary, fundamental change lay in their paradigms of the natural world. The Hesperians and the majority of the Nikara both saw the universe as cleanly divided between body and mind. They saw the material world as something separate, immutable, and permanent. But calling the gods required the basic understanding that the world was fluid—that existence itself was fluid—and that the waking world was nothing more than a script that could be written if they could find the right brush, a pattern they could weave in completely different colors if they just knew how to work the loom.

The hardest part of Rin's training had been belief. But it was so easy to believe when the evidence of supernatural power was right in front of you.

"We trust that the sun will rise every morning even if we don't know what moves it," Kitay had said. "So just show them the sun."

Rin opened her palm toward the recruits. A little string of fire danced between her fingers, weaving in and out like a carp among reeds.

"What am I doing right now?" she asked.

She didn't expect any of them to know the answer, but she needed to be clear on their preconceptions.

"Magic," Dulin said.

"Not helpful. 'Magic' is a word for effects with causes we can't explain. How am I causing this?"

They exchanged hesitant glances.

"You called the gods for help?" Pipaji ventured.

Rin closed her fist. "And what are the gods?"

More hesitation. Rin sensed a budding annoyance among the recruits. She decided to skip over the next line of questioning. All she'd ever wanted from Jiang were direct answers, but he'd withheld them from her for months. She didn't need to repeat that frustration. "The first thing you must accept is that the gods exist. They are real and tangible, as present and visible as any of us are. Perhaps even more so. Can you believe that?"

"Of course," Dulin said.

The others nodded in agreement.

"Good. The gods reside in a plane beyond this one. You can think of it as the heavens. Our task as shamans is to call them down to affect the matter around us. We act as the conduit—the gateway to divine power."

"What kind of place is the heavens?" Pipaji asked.

Rin paused, wondering how best to explain. How had Jiang once described it? "The only place that's real. The place where nothing is decided. The place you visit when you dream."

This met with puzzled stares. Rin realized she wasn't getting anywhere. She decided to start over, trying to think of the right words to explain concepts that by now were as familiar to her as breathing.

"You've got to stop thinking of our world as the one true domain," she said. "This world isn't permanent. It does not objectively exist, whatever that means. The great sage Zhuangzi once said that he didn't know whether he dreamed of transforming into a butterfly at night, or whether he was always living in a butterfly's dream. This world is a butterfly's dream. This world is the gods' dream. And when we dream of the gods, that just means we've woken up. Does that make sense?"

The recruits looked bewildered.

"Not in the least," Merchi said.

Fair enough. Rin could hear how much her own words sounded like gibberish, even though she also fully believed them to be true.

Small wonder she'd once thought Jiang mad. How on earth did you explain the cosmos while appearing sane?

She tried a different approach. "Don't overthink it. Just conceive of it like this. Our world is a puppet show, and the things we think of as objectively material are only shadows. Everything is constantly changing, constantly in flux. And the gods lurk behind the scenes, wielding the puppets."

"But you want us to seize the puppets," Pipaji said.

"Right!" Rin said. "Good. That's all shamanism is. It's recasting reality."

"Then why would they let us?" Pipaji asked. "If I were a god I wouldn't want to just lend someone my power."

"The gods don't care about things like that. They don't think like people; they're not selfish actors. They're . . . they're *instincts*. They have a single, focusing drive. In the Pantheon, they're kept in balance by all the rest. But when you open the gate, you let them inflict their will on the world."

"What is the will of your god?" Pipaji asked.

"To burn," Rin said easily. "To devour and cleanse. But every god is different. The Monkey God wants chaos. The Dragon wants to possess."

"And how many gods are there?" Pipaji pressed.

"Sixty-four," Rin said. "Sixty-four gods of the Pantheon, all opposing forces that make up this world."

"Opposing forces," Pipaji repeated slowly. "So they are all different instincts. And they all want different things."

"Yes! Excellent."

"So then how do we choose?" Pipaji asked. "Or do they choose us? Did the god of fire choose you because you're a Speerly, or—"

"Hold on," Merchi interrupted. "Can we bring this down from the level of abstraction? The gods, the Pantheon—great, fine, whatever. How do we call them?"

"One thing at a time," Rin told him. "We've just got to get through basic theory—"

"The drugs are the key, right?" Merchi asked. "That's what I've heard."

"We'll get there. The drugs give you access, yes, but first you have to understand what you're accessing—"

"So the drugs give you abilities?" Merchi interrupted again. "Which drugs? Laughing mushrooms? Poppy seeds?"

"That's not—we're not—no. Have you even been listening?" Rin had the sudden urge to smack him on the temple, like Jiang used to whenever he thought she was getting too impatient. She was starting to understand, now, what an insufferable student she must have been. "The drugs don't bestow abilities. They don't do anything except allow you to see the world as it really is. The gods bear the power. They *are* the power. All we can do is let them through."

"Why don't you ever need to take drugs?" Pipaji asked.

That caught Rin off guard. "How do you know that?"

"I was watching you during the march," Pipaji said. "You had a fire in your hand from day to night, but you always seemed so lucid. You can't have been swallowing poppy seeds the entire time. You would have walked straight off the side of the mountain."

The other recruits giggled nervously. But Pipaji stared expectantly at Rin with an intensity that made her uncomfortable.

"I'm past that point," Rin said.

Pipaji looked unconvinced. "Sounds like you're at the point where we need to be."

"Absolutely not. You don't want that. You never want that."

"But *why*—"

"Because then the god is always in your head," Rin snapped. "They're always screaming at you, trying to get you to bend to their will. Trying to *erase* you. Then there's no escape. Your body isn't mortal anymore, so you can't die, but you can't take back control, so the only way to keep the world safe from you is to lock you up in a stone mountain with the other hundreds of shamans who have made that mistake." Rin gazed around the room, staring levelly into each of their eyes in turn. "And I'll put a fist through your hearts before it comes to that. It's kinder that way."

They stopped giggling.

Late that evening, after several more hours of describing precisely how it felt to enter the Pantheon, Rin gave her recruits their first doses of poppy seeds.

Nothing much happened. All of them became stupidly, giddily high. They rolled around on the floor, tracing patterns through the air with their fingers and droning on and on about inane profundities that made Rin want to put her eyes out with her thumb. Lianhua was overcome with a fit of high-pitched giggles every time someone spoke a word in her direction. Merchi kept stroking the ground and murmuring about how soft it was. Pipaji and Dulin sat absolutely still, eyes pressed shut with something Rin hoped might be concentration, until Dulin began to snore.

Then they all came down and vomited.

"It didn't work," Pipaji groaned, rubbing at her bloodshot eyes.

"It's because you weren't trying to see," Rin said. She hadn't expected any of them to succeed on the first try, but she had been hoping for *something*. The faintest hint of a divine encounter. Not just four hours of idiocy.

"There's nothing *to* see," Merchi complained. "Whenever I

tried to tilt back, or whatever you said it felt like, all I saw was darkness."

"That's because you wouldn't concentrate."

"I was trying."

"Well, you weren't trying hard enough," Rin said testily. Supervising a group of tripping idiots was hardly fun when she was the only sober person in the room. "You might have at least *thought* about the Pantheon, instead of trying to do unspeakable things to a mound of dirt."

"I thought plenty about it," Merchi snapped. "You might have given us clearer instructions than *get high and summon a god*."

Rin knew he was right. The fault lay with her teaching. She just didn't know how to explain things more clearly than she had. She wished she still had Chaghan with her, who knew the cosmos and its mysteries so well that he could easily break it into concepts they could understand. She wished she had Daji or even the Sorqan Sira, who could implant a vision in their minds that would shatter their conceptions of real or not real. She needed some way to break the logic in their brains like Jiang had done to her, but she had no idea how to replicate his yearlong syllabus, much less condense it down to two weeks.

She stretched her arms over her head. She'd been sitting in a hunched position for hours, and her shoulders felt terribly sore.

"Head back to your tents and go to sleep," she told them. "We'll try again in the morning."

"Maybe this was a stupid idea," she admitted to Kitay after the third night of getting her recruits high with no results. "Their minds are like rocks. I can't get anything in, and they think everything I say is stupid."

He rubbed her shoulder in sympathy. "Look at it from their perspective. You thought everything was stupid when you first pledged Lore. You thought Jiang was clearly off his rocker."

"But that was because I didn't know what the fuck we were doing!"

"You must have had some idea."

He had a point. Back in her second year, she hadn't known Jiang's true identity, but she had known he could do things that he shouldn't be able to. She'd seen him call shadows without moving. She'd felt the wind blow and the water stir at his command. She'd known he had power, and she'd been so hungry to acquire that power, she hadn't cared what sort of mental hurdles he made her jump. And it had still taken her nearly a year.

But most of that year had been taken up by Jiang's endless series of precautions to prevent her from becoming precisely what she ultimately became. Rin didn't need to bother with safety or long-term stability. She just needed troops from whom she could squeeze, at maximum, several months' utility.

"Take your mind off it for a bit," Kitay suggested. "No point bashing your head against the wall. Come see what I've been working on."

She followed him out of the tent. Kitay had set up an outdoor work station a ten-minute walk from the camp, which consisted of tools strewn across the ground, diagrams held down with rocks to keep them from flying away in the relentless plateau winds, and one massive structure covered with a heavy canvas tarp. He reached up and pulled the tarp away with both hands, revealing a dirigible flipped on its side and split in two, its inner workings on display like a gutted animal's intestines.

"You're not the only one leveling out the power asymmetry," he said.

Rin moved in closer to inspect the airship engine's interior, running her fingers over the hull's outer lining. It wasn't made of any material she could recognize—not wood, not bamboo, and certainly not heavy metal. The power mechanisms appeared even more foreign, a complicated, interlocking set of gears and screws that brought to mind Sister Petra's round, fist-size clock, that perfectly intricate machine that the Hesperians believed to be irrefutable proof that the world was designed by some grand architect.

"It's the only craft that remained relatively intact," Kitay said.

"The rest were burned, shattered wreckage. But this one must have only lost power when it was fairly close to the ground. Its gears are all still working."

"Hold on," Rin said sharply. She'd thought Kitay had only been studying how they worked, not how to operate them. "You're telling me we can *fly* this?"

"Maybe. I'm still a few days from attempting a test flight. But yes, once we get the basket fitted together, I theoretically should be able to get it up . . ."

"Tiger's tits." Rin's pulse quickened just thinking about what this could mean. All kinds of tactical maneuvers opened up if they had a working dirigible. They still couldn't go toe-to-toe with the Hesperian fleet in the open air—they'd simply be outnumbered—but they could use air travel for so many other purposes. "This solves so much. Bulk transportation. Quick supply movements. River crossings—"

"Not so fast." Kitay tapped a winding copper cylinder at the center of the intestinal mess. "I've finally figured out its fuel source. It burns coal, but very inefficiently. These things are built with material that is as lightweight as possible, but they're still awfully heavy. They can't remain afloat for more than a day, and they can't carry enough coal to lengthen their journey otherwise they'll sink."

"I see," she said, disappointed.

So that partly solved the central mystery of why Nezha had used the fleet with such restraint during the march over the Baolei Mountains. Dirigibles were a decent quick show of force. But they did not give the Hesperians full reign over the sky. They still depended on ground support for fuel.

"It's still better than nothing," Kitay said. "I'll try to have it flying within the next week."

"You're incredible," Rin murmured. Kitay had always been so wonderfully clever—really, she should have stopped feeling surprised by his inventions after he'd found a way to make her *fly*—but learning to work a dirigible was an achievement on an entirely different scale. This was alien technology, technology supposedly centuries ahead of Nikara achievements, and somehow he'd pieced together its workings in mere days. "Did you figure this out just by looking at it?"

"I took apart the pieces that seemed removable, and spent a long time staring at the pieces that didn't." He pushed his fingers through his bangs, surveying the engine. "The basic principles were easy enough. There's still a lot I don't know."

"But then—then how." She blinked at the complex metal gears. They looked dauntingly sophisticated. She wouldn't have known where to start. "I mean, how did you figure out the science?"

"I didn't." He shrugged. "I can't. I don't know what half these things are or what they do. They're a mystery to me and will remain so until I'm versed in the fundamentals of this technology, which I won't be until I've studied in their Gray Towers."

"But if you didn't even have the fundamentals, then how—"

"I didn't need them, see? It doesn't matter. We're not building any dirigibles of our own, we just have to learn how to fly this one. I've only got to poke around until I re-create the original working circumstances."

She froze. "What did you say?"

"I said, I've only got to poke around until—" He broke off and gave her an odd look. "You all right?"

"Yes," she said, dazed. Kitay's words echoed in her mind like ringing gongs. *The original working circumstances.*

Great Tortoise, was it that easy?

"Fuck," she said. "Kitay, I've got it."

At last, Rin dragged her recruits to the Pantheon by force.

It was such a simple solution. Why hadn't she seen it before? She should have started here, by re-creating the original working circumstances of her own encounter with divinity.

She had first called the Phoenix a full year before Jiang took her to the Pantheon. She hadn't known what she was doing. All she remembered was that she'd beaten Nezha in a combat ring, had pummeled him within an inch of his life because he had slapped her and she couldn't *bear* the indignation, and then she'd rushed out of the building into the cool air outside because she couldn't contain the wave of power surging inside her.

She hadn't summoned fire that day. But she *had* touched the Pantheon. And that was the catalyst for everything that had happened thereafter—once she'd met the gods, it ripped a hole in her world that nothing but repeated encounters with divinity could fill.

What had driven her to the gods before she ever knew their names?

Anger. Burning, resentful anger.

And fear.

"What's the worst thing that's ever happened to you?" Rin asked her recruits.

As usual, they responded with puzzled hesitation.

"You don't . . ." Pipaji hesitated. "You don't actually want us to *say*, do—"

"I do," Rin said. "Tell me. Describe the very worst thing you've ever been through. Something you never want to happen again."

Pipaji flinched. "I'm not fucking—"

"I know it's hard to relive," Rin said. "But pain is the quickest way to the Pantheon. Find your scars. Drag a knife through them. Push yourself. What memory just surfaced in your mind?"

Two high spots of color rose up in Pipaji's face. She began blinking very rapidly.

"Fine. Take a moment to think about it." Rin turned to Dulin. "How long did you spend in that burial pit?"

He balked. "I . . ."

"Two days? Three? You looked close to decomposing when we found you."

Dulin's voice was strangled. "I don't want to think about that."

"You *have* to," Rin insisted. "This is the only way this works. Let's try a different question. What do you see when you see the face of the Mugenese?"

"Easy," Merchi said. "I see a fucking bug."

"Good," Rin said, though she knew that was bravado, not the corrosive resentment she needed from them. "And what would you do to them if you could? How would you crush them?"

When this elicited awkward stares, she hardened her voice. "Don't act so shocked. You're here to learn to kill, that's why you signed up. Not for self-defense, and not out of nobility. Every one of you wants blood. *What would you do to them?*"

"I want them helpless like I was," Pipaji burst out. "I want to stand over their faces and spit venom into their eyes. I want them to wither at my touch."

"Why?"

"Because they touched me," Pipaji said. "And it made me want to die."

"Good." Rin held the bowl of poppy seeds out toward her. "Now let's try this again."

Pipaji succeeded first.

The last few times Pipaji had gotten high she'd rocked back and forth on the ground, giggling to herself at jokes that only she could hear. But this time she sat perfectly still for several minutes before suddenly falling backward like a puppet with cut strings. Her eyes remained open but were terrifyingly white; her pupils had rolled entirely into the back of her head.

"Help!" Lianhua gripped Pipaji's shoulders. "Help, I think she's—"

But Pipaji's hand shot up into the air, fingers splayed outward in a firm and unquestionable gesture. *Stop.*

"Let her lie," Rin said sharply. "Don't touch her."

Pipaji's fingers curled like claws against the ground, digging long grooves into the dirt. Low, guttural moans emitted from her throat.

"She's in pain," Merchi insisted. He scooped her up from the floor and pulled her into his lap, patting her cheeks frantically. "Hey. *Hey.* Can you hear me?"

Pipaji's lips moved very quickly, uttering a stream of syllables that formed no language Rin could recognize. The tips of her fingers had turned a rotted purple beneath the dirt. When her eyes fluttered open, all Rin saw beneath her lashes were dark pools, black all the way through.

Finally. Rin felt a pulse of fierce, vicious pride, accompanied by the faintest pang of fear. What kind of deity had Pipaji called back from across the void? Was it stronger than she was?

Merchi's voice faltered. "Pipaji?"

Pipaji lifted a trembling hand to his face. "I . . ."

Her face spasmed and stretched into a wide smile with tortured eyes, like something inside her, something that didn't understand human expressions, was wearing her skin like a mask.

"Get back," Rin whispered.

The other recruits had already retreated to the opposite end of the hut. Merchi looked down, and his face went slack with confusion. Black streaks covered his arms everywhere his skin had touched Pipaji's.

Pipaji blinked and sat up, peering around as if she'd just awoken from a deeply absorbing dream. Her eyes were still the same unsettling obsidian. "Where are we?"

"Merchi, *get back*," Rin shouted.

Merchi pushed Pipaji away. She collapsed into a pile on the floor, limbs shaking. He shrank away, wiping furiously at his forearms as if he could rub his skin clean. But the black didn't stop spreading. It looked as if every vein in Merchi's body had risen to the surface of his skin, thickening like creeks transforming into rivers.

I have to help him, Rin thought. *I did this, this is my fault*—

But she couldn't bring herself to move. She didn't know what she would do if she could.

Merchi's eyes bulged wide. He opened his mouth to retch, then toppled sideways, writhing.

Pipaji shuffled backward, fingers clenched over her mouth. Sharp, hiccuping breaths escaped from behind her fingers.

"Oh, gods," she whispered, over and over. "Oh, *gods*. What did I do?"

Dulin and Lianhua were backed up against the opposite wall. Lianhua kept eyeing the door, as if considering bolting away. Pipaji's whimpers rose to a screaming wail. She crawled over to Merchi and shook his shoulders, trying to revive him, but all she did was dig craters into desiccated flesh wherever her fingers met his skin.

Finally Rin came to her senses.

"Get in the corner," she ordered Pipaji. "Sit on your hands. Touch no one."

To her great relief, Pipaji obeyed. Rin turned her attention to Merchi. His thrashing had subsided to a faint twitching, and black and purple blotches now covered every visible inch of skin, under which his veins bulged like they had crystallized into stone.

She had no idea what Cholang's physicians could possibly do for him, but she owed it to him to try.

"Someone help me lift him," she ordered. But neither Dulin nor Lianhua moved; they were frozen with shock.

She'd have to drag Merchi out herself, then. He was too tall for her to hoist up onto her shoulder; her only choice was to drag him by a leg. She bent and grasped his shin, careful not to brush against his exposed skin. Her shoulder throbbed from his weight as she pulled, but her adrenaline kicked in, counteracting the pain, and somehow she found the energy to drag him out of the hut and toward the infirmary.

"Hang in there," she told him. "Just breathe. We'll fix this."

She might as well have been talking to a rock. When she glanced back moments later to check how he was doing, his eyes had gone glassy, and his flesh had deteriorated so much he looked like a three-day-old corpse. He didn't respond when she shook him. His pulse was gone. She didn't know when he'd stopped breathing.

She kept limping forward. But she knew, long before she reached the infirmary, that she didn't need a physician now but a gravedigger.

∞

Pipaji was gone when Rin returned to the hut.

"Where is she?" she demanded.

Dulin and Lianhua were sitting shell-shocked against the wall where she'd left them. They'd clearly been crying; Dulin's eyes were bloodshot and unfocused, while Lianhua sat trembling with her fists balled up against her eyes.

"She ran," Dulin said. "Said she couldn't be here anymore."

"And you *let* her?" Rin wanted to slap him, just to wipe that dull, dazed expression off his face. "Do you know where she went?"

"I think up toward the hill, maybe, she said—"

Rin set out at a run.

Pipaji was thankfully easy to track; her slender footprints were stamped fresh in the snow. Rin caught up to her at a ledge twenty feet up the hill. She was doubled over, coughing, exhausted by the sprint.

"Where do you think you're going?" Rin called.

Pipaji didn't respond. She straightened up and faced the ledge, stretching out one slim ankle as if testing out the empty space before she hurtled forward.

"Pipaji, get away from there." Rin measured the distance between them, calculating. If she took a running leap she might seize Pipaji by the legs before she jumped, but only if Pipaji hesitated. The girl looked ready to spring—any sudden movements could startle her off the edge.

"You're confused." Rin kept her tone low and gentle, hand stretched out as if approaching a wild animal. "You're overwhelmed, I understand, but this is normal . . ."

"It's horrible." Pipaji didn't turn around. "This is—I didn't—I can't . . ."

She was dawdling. She wasn't sure yet whether she wanted to die. *Good.*

Her fingers, Rin noticed, were no longer purple. She'd wrested some control back over herself. That made her safe to touch.

Rin lunged forward and tackled her by the waist. They landed sprawled together in the snow. Rin clambered up, jerked the unresisting Pipaji back from the ledge by her shirt, then pinned her down with a knee against her stomach so that she couldn't flee.

"Are you going to jump?" Rin asked.

Pipaji's narrow chest heaved. "No."

"Then get up." Rin stood and extended Pipaji her hand.

But Pipaji remained on the ground, shoulders shaking violently, her face contorted again into sobs.

"Stop crying. Look at me." Rin leaned down and grabbed Pipaji by the chin. She didn't know what compelled her to do it. She'd never acted like this before. But Vaisra had done this to her once, and it had worked to command her attention, if only by shocking the fear into the back of her mind. "Do you want to quit?"

Pipaji stared mutely at her, tears streaking her face. She seemed stunned into silence.

"Because you can quit," Rin said. "I'll let you go right now, if that's what you want. No one's forcing you to be a shaman. You don't ever have to go to the Pantheon again. You can quit this army, too, if you'd prefer. You can go back to your sister and find somewhere to live in Dog Province. Is that what you want?"

"But I don't . . ." Pipaji's sobs subsided. She looked bewildered. "I don't know. I don't know what I . . ."

"I know," Rin said. "I know you don't want to quit. Because that felt good, didn't it? When you brought down the god? That rush of power was the best thing you've ever felt and you know it. How good is it to realize what you can *do*? Unfortunate that your first victim was an ally, but imagine laying your hands on enemy troops. Imagine felling armies with just a single *touch*."

"She told me . . ." Pipaji took a deep, rattling breath. "The goddess, I mean . . . she told me I'll never be afraid again."

"That's power," Rin said. "And you're not giving that up. I know you. You're *me*."

Pipaji stared, not quite at Rin, but at the blank space behind her. She seemed lost in her own mind.

Rin sat down beside Pipaji so that they were side by side, looking out over the ledge together. "What did you see when you swallowed the seeds?"

Pipaji bit her lip and glanced away.

"Tell me."

"I can't, it's . . ."

"Look at me." Rin lifted her shirt. Her upper torso was wrapped tight in bandages, ribs still cracked from where Riga had kicked her. But Altan's black handprint, etched just as clearly as the day he'd left it, was visible just below her sternum. Rin let Pipaji stare long enough to understand its shape, and then twisted to the side to show her the raised, bumpy ridges where Nezha had once slid a blade in her lower back.

Pipaji's face went white at the sight. "How . . . ?"

"I received both these scars from men I thought I loved," Rin said. "One is dead now. One will be. I understand how humiliation feels. Keep your secrets if you want. But there's nothing you can say that will make me think any less of you."

Pipaji stared for a long time at Altan's handprint. When she spoke at last, it was in such a low whisper that Rin had to lean in close to hear her over the wind.

"We were in the whorehouse when they came. They started marching up the stairs, and I told Jiuto to hide. She—" Pipaji's voice caught. She took a shaky breath, then continued. "She didn't have time to get out the door, so she hid under the blankets. I piled them on her. Piles and piles of winter coats. And I told her not to move, not to make a single sound, no matter what happened, no matter what she heard. Then they came in, and they found me, and they—they—" Pipaji swallowed. "And Jiuto didn't move."

"You protected her," Rin said gently.

"No." Pipaji gave her head a violent shake. "I didn't. Because—because after they'd gone, I opened the cabinet. And I took the blankets off. And Jiuto wasn't moving." Her face crumpled. "She hadn't moved. She was suffocating, she couldn't fucking *breathe* under there, and still she hadn't moved because that's what I told her. I thought I'd killed her. And I didn't, because she started breathing again, but I'm the reason why . . ."

She gave a little wail and pressed her face into her hands. She didn't continue. She didn't need to; Rin could piece the rest of this story together herself.

That explained why Jiuto followed her sister everywhere. Why Pipaji had never left her alone until now. Why Jiuto didn't—*couldn't*—speak. Why she responded to everyone who spoke to her with a dead, haunted stare.

Rin wanted to put an arm around Pipaji's shaking shoulders, hold her tight, and tell her she had nothing to be ashamed of and nothing to repent for. That she'd survived, and survival was enough. She wanted to tell her to go to her sister and run far away from this place and to never think about the Pantheon again. She wanted to tell Pipaji it was over.

Instead, she said in the hardest voice she could imagine, "Stop crying."

Pipaji lifted her head, startled.

"You're living in a country at war," Rin said. "Did you think you're special? You think you're the only one who's suffered? Look around. At least you're *alive*. There are thousands of others who weren't nearly as lucky. And there are thousands more who will meet the same fate if you can't accept the power you could have."

She heard a steely, ruthless timbre in her own voice that she had never used before. It was a stranger's voice. But she knew exactly where it came from, for everything she said was an echo of things Vaisra had once told her, the only true gift he'd ever given her.

When you hear screaming, run toward it.

"Everything you just told me? That's your key to the gods. Hold that in your mind and never forget the way you're feeling right now. That's what gives you power. And that's what is going to keep you human."

Rin seized Pipaji's fingers. They were slender fingers, dirty and scarred. Nothing like how a pretty young girl's fingers were supposed to look. They were fingers that had broken bodies. Fingers just like hers.

"You have the power to poison anyone you touch," she said. "You can make sure no one ever suffers like you and your sister again. *Use it*."

The other breakthroughs came much faster after Pipaji's success. Two days later, Lianhua gave a little whimper and slumped over on her side. At first Rin was afraid she'd overdosed and fainted, but then she noticed that the scars across Lianhua's arms and collarbones were disappearing—smooth new skin knitted over areas that had previously been cruelly crosshatched by a blade.

"What did you see?" Rin asked when Lianhua awoke.

"A beautiful woman," Lianhua murmured. "She held a lotus flower in one hand, and a set of reed pipes in the other. She smiled at me and said she could fix me."

"Do you think she could help you fix others?" Rin asked.

"I think so," Lianhua said. "She put something in my hands. It was white and hot, and I saw it shining through my fingers, like—like I was holding the sun itself."

Great Tortoise. Rin's heart leaped at the implications. *We can use this.*

When Lianhua managed to call her goddess while retaining consciousness, Rin had her test her abilities on a succession of injured animals—squirrels with shattered legs, birds with broken wings, and rabbits burned half to death. Lianhua had the good sense not to ask where the animals were coming from. When she restored all the creatures to full health without any apparent side effects, Rin let Lianhua experiment on her own body.

"It's these two ribs that are giving me trouble," she said, lifting her shirt up. "Do you need the bandages off, too?"

"I don't think so." Lianhua trailed her fingers over the linen strips so lightly they tickled. Then Rin felt a searing heat at an intensity straddling the line between relief and torment. Seconds later, the pain in her ribs was gone. For the first time since ascending Mount Tianshan, she could breathe without wincing.

"Great Tortoise." Rin marveled as she twisted her upper body back and forth. "*Thank you.*"

"Do you . . ." Lianhua's fingers hovered in the air over Rin's right arm, as if awaiting permission. She was staring at the stump. "Um, do you want me to try?"

The question caught Rin by surprise. She hadn't even considered trying to restore her lost hand. She blinked, not answering, caught between saying the obvious *yes, please, try it now,* and the fear of letting herself hope.

"I don't know if I can," Lianhua said quickly. "And I mean—if you don't want to—"

"No—no, sorry," Rin said hastily. "Of course I want to. Yes. Go ahead."

Lianhua peeled the sleeve back from over her stump and rested her cool fingers where Rin's wrist ended in a smooth mound. Several minutes passed. Lianhua sat still, her eyes squeezed tight in concentration, but Rin felt nothing—no heat, no prickle—except a phantom tingle where her hand ought to be. Minutes trickled by, but the tingle, if it was ever real, never intensified into anything else.

"Stop it," she said at last. She couldn't do this anymore. "That's enough."

Lianhua seemed to shrink in apology. "I guess, um, there are limits. But maybe I can try again, if . . ."

"Don't worry." Rin yanked the sleeve back over her wrist, hoping that Lianhua didn't notice the catch in her voice. Why did her chest feel so tight? She'd known it wouldn't work; it'd been stupid to imagine. "It's fine. There are some things you can't fix."

In terms of sheer spectacle, Dulin trumped all of them. One week later, after so many failed attempts that Rin considered putting him out of his misery, he took an extra dose of poppy seeds with a look of stubborn determination on his face and promptly summoned the Great Tortoise.

In every myth Rin had ever been told, the Tortoise was a patient, protective, and benevolent creature. It was the dark guardian of the earth, representing longevity and cool, fertile soil. Villagers in Tikany wore jade pendants etched like tortoiseshells to bring good luck and stability. In Sinegard, great stone tortoises were often planted in front of tombs to safeguard the spirits of the dead.

Dulin evoked none of that. He opened a sinkhole in the ground.

It happened without warning. One moment the dirt was steady beneath their feet, and the next a circle with a diameter of about five feet appeared inside the hut, dropping down to pitch-black, uncertain depths. By some miracle none of them fell inside; shrieking, Pipaji and Lianhua scrambled away from the edge.

The sinkhole ended right at Dulin's feet. It had stopped growing, but the soil and rocks at the edges were still crumbling into the hole, echoing into nowhere.

Rin spoke slowly, trying not to startle Dulin in case he accidentally buried them all. "Very good. Now do you think you might be able to close that thing back up?"

He looked dazed, gaping at the sinkhole as if trying to convince himself that not only did it exist, he was in fact the one who had created it. "I don't know."

He was trembling. Lightly, she placed a hand on his shoulder. "What are you feeling?"

"It's—it's *hungry*." Dulin sounded confused. "I think—it wants more."

"More what?"

"More . . . exposure. It wants to see the sunlight." His voice caught. Rin could guess which memory he'd invoked when he reached the Pantheon. She knew he was remembering how it felt to be buried alive. "It wants to be free."

"Fair enough," Rin said. "But perhaps try that when you're a good distance away from the rest of us."

Dulin swallowed hard, then nodded. The pit stopped rumbling.

"General Fang?" Pipaji called from across the sinkhole. "I think we need a bigger hut."

The next day Rin and her recruits set out before sunrise to trek out into the desert plateau, where nothing they summoned could hurt anyone at Cholang's settlement.

"How far out are you going?" Kitay asked.

"Five miles," she said.

"Not far enough. Go at least ten."

"I'll be out of your range!"

"Eight, then," he said. "But get them as far away from here as you can. There's no point wiping us out before Nezha does it for us."

So Rin slung a satchel stuffed with four days' worth of provisions and enough drugs to kill an elephant over her back, then led her recruits out toward the vast expanse of the Scarigon Plateau. They marched for the better part of the morning, and didn't stop until the sun climbed high into the cloudless, intensely blue sky, baking the air into a scorching heat that even the winds couldn't dissipate.

"Here is good," Rin decided. Flat, arid steppe extended in every direction as far as her eye could see. They were nowhere near any trees, boulders, or hills that could serve as shelter, but that would be all right; they'd packed canvas for two tents, and the skies didn't promise any precipitation for several days at least.

She pulled her satchel off and let it drop on the ground. "Everyone have a drink of water, then we'll get to work."

Pipaji was already suckling greedily from her canteen. She hiccuped and wiped her mouth with the back of her hand. "What exactly are we doing?"

Rin grinned. "Stand back."

They took a few steps backward, watching her warily.

"Farther."

She waited until they were at least twenty paces away. Then she stretched a hand into the sky and called down the fire.

It rippled through her like a bolt of lightning. It was delicious. She pulled forth more, reveling in the wanton release of power, the reckless indulgence that brought echoes of the sheer ecstasy she'd experienced on Mount Tianshan.

She saw their faces, wide-eyed with admiration and delight, and she laughed.

She lingered in the column of heat for just a few more delectable seconds, and then pulled the flames back into her body.

"Your turn," she said.

For the next few hours Rin supervised as Pipaji and Lianhua pitted their skills against each other. Pipaji would kneel down and press her hands against the dirt. Seconds later all kinds of creatures—worms, snakes, long-legged steppe rats, burrowing birds—would bubble up to the surface, writhing and screeching, clawing desperately at the black veins that shot through their bulging forms.

"Stop," Rin would say, and Lianhua would hastily begin the process of reversal, healing the creatures one by one until the rot had faded away.

The limits to Lianhua's skills quickly became obvious. She could make superficial wounds disappear in under a minute, and she could heal broken bones and internal hemorrhaging if given a little more time, but she seemed only able to reverse injuries that were not life-threatening. Most of Pipaji's targets were close to death within seconds, and even Lianhua's best efforts could not bring them back.

Pipaji's limits were less clear. At first Rin had thought she required skin-to-skin contact with her victims, but then it became clear her poison could seep through dirt, reaching organisms up to several feet away.

"Try the pond water," Rin suggested. A horrible, exciting thought had just occurred to her, but she didn't want to voice it aloud until she had confirmation. "See if that speeds up dissemination."

"We need that water to drink," Dulin protested. "The next pond's a mile away."

"So fill up your canteens now, and then we'll move our camp to the other pond once Pipaji's finished," Rin said.

They obeyed. Once all the canteens were full, Pipaji crouched over the pond, frowning in concentration as she dipped her fingertips into the water. Nothing happened. Rin was hoping to see black streaks shooting through the pond, but the water remained a murky greenish-brown. Then fish began floating belly-up to the surface, bloated and discolored.

"Gross," Dulin said. "I guess we're catching dinner somewhere else."

Rin didn't comment. She was clenching her fist so hard her knuckles had turned white.

This was it. This was how she beat Nezha.

Nezha couldn't be killed because the Dragon was always protecting him, stitching his wounds back together seconds after they opened. But Chaghan had told her that the source of his power was the river running through the grottoes of Arlong.

What if she attacked the river itself?

"Can I stop?" Pipaji asked. Fish, toads, tadpoles, and insects were still bubbling up dead in the water around her. "This feels, um, excessive."

"Fine," Rin murmured. "Stop."

Pipaji stood up, looking disgusted, and quickly wiped her fingers on her trousers.

Rin couldn't stop staring at the pond. The water was pitch-black now, an inkwell of corpses.

Nezha had never met Pipaji before. He would have no idea who she was or what she could do. All he would see was a thin, pretty girl with long-lashed doe's eyes, looking utterly out of place on the battlefield, right before she turned his veins to sludge.

∞

Next Rin focused her attentions on Dulin. He had a penchant for sinkholes—by the first day, he could easily summon one on command of any shape or size within a diameter of ten feet. But the sinkholes had to open up right next to where he stood; his feet had to be at the edge of the crevice.

This posed a problem. Certainly the sinkholes had great potential for tactical disruption, but only if Dulin was standing directly in the line of fire.

"Can you do anything more with the earth?" Rin asked him. "If you can move it down, can you move it up? Sideways? Vibrate in place?"

She wasn't sure what she had in mind. She had some vague picture of great pillars of dirt thrashing through the air like vipers. Or perhaps earthquakes—those could disorient and scatter defensive lines without excessive civilian casualties.

"I'll try." He lowered his chin, brows furrowed in concentration.

Rin felt tremors under her feet, so faint at first that she was unsure whether she was imagining them. They grew stronger. The thought that perhaps she should get back briefly crossed her mind before she went flying.

Her back slammed against the ground. Her head followed with a snap. She stared at the sky, mouth open like a fish, trying to breathe. She couldn't feel her fingertips. Or her toes.

She heard screaming. Dulin's and Lianhua's faces appeared above her. Pipaji was shouting something, but her voice was muffled and muted. Rin felt Lianhua's hands moving under her shirt, pushing up to rest on her ribs, and then a wonderful, scorching heat spread through her torso and head until Dulin's shouting sharpened into intelligible words.

"Are you all right?"

"Fine," she gasped. "I'm fine."

When Lianhua took her hands away, Rin curled onto her side

and laughed. She couldn't help herself; it spilled out of her like a waterfall, urgent and exhilarating.

Lianhua looked deeply concerned. "General, are you . . . ?"

"We're going to win," Rin said hoarsely. She couldn't understand why she was the only one laughing. Why weren't they laughing? Why weren't they beside themselves with delight? "Oh, my gods. Holy fucking shit. This is it. We're going to *win*."

They spent the last two days fine-tuning their response times, limitations, and necessary dosages. They determined how long it took after ingesting seeds for their highs to kick in—twenty minutes for Pipaji and Lianhua, ten for Dulin. They learned how long they were useful on their high—no more than an hour for any of them—and how long it took for them to come down from their useless, drooling state.

Their skills remained an imperfect art—they couldn't possibly achieve in two weeks the military efficiency of the original Cike. But they'd become sufficiently accustomed to reaching for their gods that they could replicate their results on the battlefield. That was as good as they were going to get.

Rin told them to return to the base camp without her. She wanted to journey out a bit farther before she turned back. They didn't ask where she was going, and she didn't tell them.

Alone, she walked until she found a secluded area at the base of a hill, in full view of the distant Mount Tianshan.

She picked up the largest rocks she could find and arranged them in a circular pile facing the setting sun. It was a shabby memorial, but it would stay in place. Barely anyone visited this mountain. In time, the wind, snow, and storms would eradicate every trace of these rocks, but for now, this was good enough.

Jiang didn't deserve much. But he deserved *something*.

She'd seen the look on his face before she escaped the temple. He knew full well what he'd done. In that moment he was complete and aware, reconciled with his past, and fully in control. And he'd chosen to save her.

"Thank you," she said. Her voice sounded reedy and insufficient against the chilly, dense air. Her chest felt very tight.

She'd loved him like a father once.

He'd taught her everything he'd known. He'd led her to the Pantheon. Then he'd abandoned her, returned to her, betrayed her, and saved her.

He'd let so many others die—he'd let *her people* die—but he had saved her.

What the fuck was she supposed to do with a legacy like that?

Hot tears welled up in her eyes. Irritated, she wiped them away. She wasn't here to cry. Jiang didn't deserve her tears. This wasn't about grief, this was about paying respects.

"Goodbye," she muttered.

She didn't know what else to say.

No, that wasn't true. Something else weighed on her mind, something she couldn't leave unsaid. She'd never dared to say it to his face when he was alive, though she'd thought it many times. She couldn't keep silent now. She kicked at the rocks and swallowed again, but the lump in her throat wouldn't go away. She cleared her throat, tears streaming down her cheeks.

"You were always such a fucking coward."

"We're marching out," she told Kitay when she returned. She bustled around the hut, flinging things into her travel bag—two shirts, a pair of trousers, knives, pouches of poppy seeds. She'd been walking for six hours straight, but somehow felt bursting with energy. "I'll tell Cholang to have his men ready to march in the morning. Is the dirigible ready to go?"

"Sure, but—hold on, slow down, Rin." Kitay looked concerned. "So soon? Really?"

"It has to be now," Rin said. She couldn't stay in Cholang's settlement, the capital of bum-fuck nowhere in the Scarigon Plateau, any longer. Her mind spun with possibilities for the campaign ahead. Never before had the cards lain so clearly in her favor. The Republic had one shaman in Nezha against Rin's four, and their best defense mechanism was opium bombs, which incapacitated troops on both sides without discrimination.

Of course Rin's recruits could have used another week of training. Of course it would have been ideal if they'd had time to fine-tune their abilities, to learn consistently to force the gods back out of their minds when the voices became too loud. But Rin also knew that every day they waited to move out east was another day Nezha had to prepare.

Nezha was licking his wounds now. She had to acquire as much territory as possible before he was ready to strike back. Armies were marching one way or another, and she wanted to be the first.

"For once, time's on our side," she said. "We won't get this chance again."

"You're sure they're ready?"

She shrugged. "About as ready as I was."

He sighed. "I'm sure you know that thought gives me no comfort at all."

CHAPTER 25

Rin's first major metropolitan target in Republican territory was Jinzhou—the Golden City, the opulent pearl of the Nikara mideast. After three weeks' march it rose out of the treetops, all high walls and thin, reaching pagodas. Its blue, dragon-emblazoned flags streamed from atop sentry towers like a glaring invitation to attack.

Jinzhou's other, less savory moniker was the Whore. It sat square on the intersection of three provinces and, thanks to its proximity to thriving mulberry farms that provided wagonfuls of silkworm cocoons and some of the largest coal deposits in the Empire, could afford to pay taxes to all three. In return, Jinzhou had received thrice the military aid throughout the Poppy Wars. Not once in recent history had it been sacked; it had only ever been passed from ruler to ruler, trading compliance and riches for protection.

Rin intended to end that streak.

The military strategist Sunzi once wrote that it was best to take enemy cities intact. Prolonged, destructive campaigns benefited no one. Jinzhou, which offered a potential taxation base and was positioned well against multiple transport routes, would have served better as a sustained resource base than as a ruined city left in the Southern Army's wake.

Once again, Rin rejected Sunzi's advice.

In the south she'd been fighting to claim territory back from the Federation. That was a war of liberation. But now her army was homeless, fighting in territory where they'd never lived, and they could never return to their home provinces in peace while the Republic was still angling for control. The problem with trying to hold on to territory was that she would bleed troops expending them to maintain conquered areas. That was the same reason why Nezha was bound to lose—he'd been forced to split his troops across both the northern and southern fronts.

The upshot of all this was that Jinzhou was expendable.

Rin didn't care about preserving it. She didn't want Jinzhou's economy, she wanted to cut Nezha off from its riches.

What I can't have, he can't have.

Jinzhou was a flagrant display of power. Jinzhou was a message.

As her troops approached the city's thick stone gates, Rin didn't feel the same nervous flutter she always had before a fight. She wasn't anxious about the outcome, because this was not a contest of strategy, numbers, or timing. This wasn't a battle of chance.

This time the victor was guaranteed. She had seen what her shamans could do and knew, no matter how good the city's defenses, they had nothing that could defy an army that could move the earth itself.

Jinzhou's fate was already a foregone conclusion. Rin was just curious to see how badly they could break it.

But first, they had to settle the question of battlefield etiquette. Prudence prevailed, because Kitay prevailed. Rin couldn't feed and clothe her army if she didn't amass resources as they went, and those were harder to obtain from burned, sacked cities.

"I know you want a fight out of this," Kitay said. "But if you start tearing walls down without giving them the chance to surrender, then you're just being stupid."

"Negotiations give them time to prepare defenses," she objected.

He rolled his eyes at that. "What defenses could they possibly mount against you?"

The first messenger they sent returned almost immediately. "No surrender," he reported. "They, ah, laughed in my face."

"That's it, then." Rin stood up. "We'll head out in five. Someone get Dulin and Pipaji—"

"Hold on," Kitay said. "We haven't given them fair warning."

"Fair warning? We just offered them surrender!"

"They think you're a scruffy peasant army with rusty swords and no artillery to speak of." Kitay gave her a stern look. "They don't know what they're sentencing themselves to. And you're not being fair."

"Sunzi said—"

"I think we both agree Sunzi's playbook stopped being relevant a long time ago. And when Sunzi wrote about preserving information asymmetries so that your enemy would underestimate you, he was talking about troop numbers and supplies. Not earth-shattering, godlike powers." Kitay smoothed a piece of parchment over the table. He didn't even wait for her response before he began penning another missive. "We give them another chance."

She made a noise of protest. "What, you're just going to reveal our new weapons before they've even seen their first battle?"

"I'm a bit concerned that you're referring to people as weapons. And no, Rin, I'm only telling them that they ought to consider the many innocent lives at risk. I won't include details." Kitay scribbled for a bit longer, glanced up, and reached toward his forehead to tug at a hank of hair. "This confirms one thing, though. Nezha's not in the city."

Rin frowned. "How do you figure?"

They'd decided there was perhaps a fifty-fifty chance that Nezha would remain at the front to defend Jinzhou in person. On one hand, Jinzhou was such a massive treasure trove it was hard to imagine the Republic would relinquish it so easily—the coal stockpiles alone could have kept the airships flying indefinitely. On the other hand, every report they received indicated that Nezha had fled east as far as he could. And Jinzhou, though rich, did not have the strongest defense structures—it was a city founded on trade, and trading cities were designed to invite the outside world in, not to keep it out. This would have been a stupid place for Nezha to make his last stand.

"We know he's not here because the magistrate would have invoked his name if he was," Kitay said. "Or he would have shown up to negotiate himself. The whole country knows what he can do now. They know he'd be a better deterrent than anything else they could muster."

"He could be trying to ambush us," Rin said.

"Maybe. But Nezha sticks even harder to Sunzi's principles than you do. Don't push where there's already resistance; don't bleed troops where you're already at a disadvantage." Kitay shook his head. "I suppose we can't be certain. But if I were Nezha, I wouldn't try to kill you here. Not enough water access. No, I think he's going to give you this one."

"How romantic," she sneered. "Then let's make him regret it."

They camped outside Jinzhou's walls for a while, passing the spyglass back and forth as they waited for their delegation to return. Minutes passed, then hours. After a while Rin got bored and went back inside her tent, where her recruits sat in a circle on the floor, waiting for the summons.

"They're not going to surrender," she told them. "Everyone ready?"

Lianhua chewed her bottom lip. Dulin was shaking; he kept rubbing his elbows as if he were freezing. They looked so much like nervous Sinegard students about to take an exam that Rin couldn't help but feel a small flicker of amusement. Only Pipaji looked completely and utterly calm, sitting back against the wall with her arms crossed as if she were a patron at a teahouse waiting to be served.

"Remember, it's different when there are bodies," Rin said. They'd discussed many times by now how everything changed in the heat of battle, how the safe predictability of practice in no way resembled actual warfare, but she wanted to drill it into their skulls again. She wanted it to be the last thing on their minds before they saw combat. "The blood will startle you. And it gets much harder when you hear the screams. The gods get excited. They're like wild dogs sniffing for fear—once they get a whiff of chaos, they'll try much harder to take over."

"We've all seen bodies," Pipaji said.

"It's different when you're the one who broke them," Rin said. Dulin blanched.

"I'm not trying to scare you," Rin said quickly. "I just want you on guard. But you can do this. You've practiced this, you know what to expect, and you'll stay in control. What do you do if you feel the god taking over?"

They chanted in unison like schoolchildren. "Chew the nuggets."

Each of them carried enough opium for a fatal overdose in their pockets. They knew precisely how much to swallow to knock themselves unconscious.

"And what do you do if your comrades are out of control?"

Pipaji flexed her fingers. "Deal with them before they deal with us."

"Good girl," Rin said.

The door swung open. All of them jumped.

It was a scout. "Jinzhou's sent word, General. No surrender."

"More's their loss." Rin motioned for them to stand. "Let's go show them what you can do."

At Sinegard, Strategy Master Irjah had once taught Rin's second-year class how to play an ancient game called shaqqi. He'd made them play plenty of common strategy games before—wikki for foresight and decisiveness, mahjong for diplomacy and exploiting information asymmetry. But shaqqi wasn't a game Rin had ever encountered before. Its list of basic rules went on for three booklets, and that didn't include the many supplemental scrolls that dictated standard opening maneuvers.

Kitay was the only one in the class who had even played shaqqi, so Master Irjah chose him to help demonstrate. They spent the first twenty minutes drawing random tiles determining their share of pieces representing troops, equipment, weaponry, and terrain allocations. When all the pieces were finally on the map, Master Irjah and Kitay had sat opposite each other with their eyes trained on the board. Neither of them spoke. The rest of the class watched, increasingly bored and irritated as the face-off stretched on for nearly an hour.

At long last, Kitay had sighed, tipped his emperor piece over with one finger, and shook his head.

"What's going on?" Nezha had demanded. "You didn't even play."

But they had played. Rin had only realized that near the last five minutes of the game. The entire match had taken place through silent mental calculations, both sides considering the balance of power created by their randomly assigned lots. Kitay had eventually come to the conclusion that he couldn't possibly win.

"Warfare rarely works this way," Irjah had lectured as he scooped up the pieces. "In real battle, the fog of war—*friction*, that is—overrides everything else. Even the best-laid plans fall victim to accident and chance. Only idiots think warfare is a simple matter of clever stratagems."

"Then what's the point of this game?" Venka had complained.

"That asymmetries do matter," Irjah said. "Underdogs can often find a way out, but not always. Particularly not if the side with the upper hand has anticipated, as well as is possible given the information at hand, everything that *could* go wrong. Because then it becomes an issue of winning in the most elegant, confident way possible. You learn to close off every possible exit. You foresee all the ways they could try to upset your advantage, and you must do it all ahead of time. On the flip side, sometimes you have no possible path to victory. Sometimes engaging in battle means suicide. It's important to know when. That's the purpose of this game. The gameplay doesn't matter half so much as the thinking exercise."

"But what if the players don't agree who has the advantage?" Nezha had asked. "If no one surrenders?"

"Then you play it out until someone does," Irjah said. "But then it's doubly embarrassing for the loser, who should have conceded from the outset. The point is to train your mind to see all the strategic possibilities at once so that you learn when you can't win."

Shaqqi, it turned out, had been the only strategy game that Rin never managed to grasp. They played many times in class throughout the year, but never could she bring herself to surrender. She'd played the role of the underdog since she could remember. It seemed so ludicrous to ever give up, to simply acknowledge defeat as if the future might not offer some chance, however slim, to reverse her fortunes. She'd been relying on those slim chances for her entire life.

But now, standing with her army outside Jinzhou's city gates, she was on the other side of the table. Now she possessed the overwhelming advantage, and her puzzle was how one should leverage three people who could rewrite reality in a conventional battle without killing everyone around them.

Victory was already assured. Right now she only had to worry about the loose ends.

This was the sort of puzzle that Altan had been constantly trying to solve when he'd commanded the Cike. How did you win a game of chess when your pieces were the most freakishly powerful things on the board, and the opponent was only equipped with pawns? When the objective is no longer victory, but victory with the lowest casualty rates possible?

Rin and Kitay had agreed early on that the battle hinged on Dulin. Lianhua's involvement was out of the question—they would keep her busy in the infirmary for days on end after the battle concluded, but she had no place on the battlefield. Pipaji was more lethal in close quarters, but Dulin had the wider range of impact. He could set off earthquakes and sinkholes in a ten-yard radius around him, whereas Pipaji had to enter deep into the fray to inflict her poison. That posed too great a risk—Rin needed Pipaji out of harm's way until she reached Arlong.

But Rin was quite sure she could shatter Jinzhou's resistance with Dulin alone.

"You get two major hits," Rin told him. "Both right at the start of the fighting. Our opening salvos. They'll think the first was a freak act of nature, or some very powerful conventional weapon. After the second, they'll know we have a shaman. Beyond that point, our forces will have mixed too much for you to get in a discriminate hit."

"I don't have to be in the melee, though," Dulin said. "I mean, couldn't I just target the city?"

"And then what?" Kitay asked sharply. "You'll massacre all the innocent civilians inside?"

Dulin's cheeks colored. The thought had clearly never even crossed his mind. "I hadn't—"

"I know you haven't thought it through," Kitay said. "But you've got to put your head back on straight. Just because you can alter the world on a ridiculous scale doesn't mean the normal calculations no longer apply. If anything, you must now be doubly careful. Do you understand?"

"Yes, sir." Dulin looked duly chastened. "Where do you want your sinkholes, then?"

"Jinzhou's got six walls," Kitay said. "Take your pick."

One hour later, a squadron of fewer than fifty soldiers charged out from the forest toward Jinzhou's western gate. Rin and Kitay waited in the trees with the rest of their army, watching through spyglasses as their troops rushed the high stone walls.

This first assault was a decoy. Jinzhou's leadership had to understand what Rin could do. After the Battle of the Red Cliffs, her abilities were no longer a frightful rumor but a well-known fact. So if Jinzhou's magistrate had rebuffed her offer of lenience for surrender, then he had to be very confident in his defenses against her fire. Rin wasn't stupid enough to enter the fray until she knew what Jinzhou had up its sleeve.

It had been so easy to design a dummy probe. Shamanic fire was the simplest weapon to simulate. It only took seconds for fifty soldiers wielding torches, gunpowder, and oil-soaked flags to create a scorching wave of flame that, when caught by the wind, towered close to the heights that Rin could summon herself.

Jinzhou's defenders responded seconds later. First came the standard volley of arrows. Then followed a thicker round of missiles—bombs that did not burst into balls of flame, but rather leaked a slow, greenish smoke as they hit the ground.

"Opium bombs," Kitay observed. "Is that all they had?"

He looked disappointed. Rin, too, couldn't help a fleeting sense of dismay. Jinzhou had refused negotiations with such confidence that Rin had seriously wondered, even hoped, that they could display some secret, innovative defense to back it up.

But instead, they'd merely signed their own death warrants.

The decoy squadron was breaking up. They were allowed to fall back—they'd only been charged with drawing out the artillery, not breaking Jinzhou's defenses. The wave of fire disintegrated into dozens of individual torches, snuffed out as fleeing soldiers dropped them on the dirt.

The retreat looked messy, but those troops would be fine. They'd gone in prepared with cloth masks soaked in water. It wouldn't keep the opium out for long, but it bought them sufficient time to scatter and retreat.

Rin turned to Dulin. He held his spyglass very still to his face. His right hand was curled in a fist, beating out an erratic pattern against his knee.

Battle nerves, Rin thought. *Adorable*. And she wished, just briefly, she were not so accustomed to war so that she could still feel that lurching, electrifying thrill of sheer nervous distress.

"Your turn," she told him. "Let's go."

They broke out of the trees to meet with a hail of arrows. Jinzhou's defenders hadn't been foolish enough to imagine the probe constituted Rin's entire attack. They'd fortified all six of their walls with artillerymen, and more rushed toward the eastern wall when Rin's troops began pouring out the forest.

The southerners locked shields over their heads as they surged toward the gates in a clustered formation. Rin's arm shook as arrow after arrow slammed into the inch of wood separating iron from skin. Then it went numb. She gritted her teeth and pushed forward, eyes locked on the great stone walls ahead. In training, she'd determined that Dulin could open a sinkhole from a distance of ten yards. Ninety yards to go.

A boom echoed ahead to her left. Blood and bone splattered the air; bodies hit the ground. Rin kept moving, stepping over the gore. Seventy yards.

"Holy shit," Dulin whispered. "Holy shit, I can't . . ."

"Shut up and move," Rin said.

Fifty yards. Something shrieked overhead. They both ducked but kept running. The missile exploded behind them, accompanied by screams. Ten yards.

Rin halted. "Close enough for you?"

Troops locked their shields in a protective shell over Dulin as he stood still, eyes tightly shut. Rin watched his twitching face, waiting.

The seconds that followed felt like an eternity.

He's too scared. She was suddenly anxious. *He can't focus, it's too much . . .* The missiles and arrows landing around them suddenly seemed so close. They'd been wildly fortunate, really, to have lasted so long without being hit. But now they were open, unmoving targets, and one of those volleys had to land eventually . . .

Then the ground shook, rippling in a way that soil was not supposed to move. The stone walls vibrated, which looked so absurd that Rin thought surely she must be the one shaking and not that massive structure, but then dust and pebbles poured down the walls in trickles that turned to torrents.

The wall came down.

It didn't collapse. Didn't implode. There was no messy, cascading collision of faults in stone shattering in a chain reaction, then crumbling under its own weight, the way a broken wall was *supposed* to fall. Instead, the ground beneath opened into a gaping maw. And the wall simply *disappeared*, taking the artillery line with it, exposing the city inside like a layer of flesh peeled away from pulsing organs.

The air was still. The firing had stopped.

Dulin sank dazed to his knees.

"Well done," Rin told him.

He looked like he was about to vomit.

He'll be fine, she thought. *Break a few more cities, and it'll feel routine.* She didn't have time to play wet nurse now; she had a city to conquer. She raised her left arm in the air in a signal to charge, and the Southern Army burst over the rubble through the missing wall.

Squadrons split off to the north and south to drive through Jinzhou's defenses, while Rin alone took the center quadrant. She heard panicked shouting as she approached. As flames licked up her shoulders, she heard her targets screaming for reinforcements—high-pitched voices called over and over again for opium bombs—but it was too late. Far too late. They'd directed their opium missiles to the western wall, and by the time they brought them anywhere near her this battle would be finished.

All Jinzhou's soldiers had now were their conventional weapons, and those were so miserably insufficient. Their sword hilts burned white-hot in their hands. Everything they hurled at her—arrows, spears, javelins—turned to ash in midair. No one could come within a ten-foot distance of her, for she was ensconced inside a searing, impenetrable column of flame.

They tumbled before her like sticks.

She tilted her head back, opened her mouth, and let fire rip forth through her throat.

Gods, this release felt good. She hadn't realized how much she missed this. She'd reached such a delirious thrill on Mount Tianshan and then on the training grounds on the plateau, when she'd let the flames roar unrestrained through her body. Every waking moment since then had felt muted and muzzled. But now she got what she wanted—mindless, careless, untrammeled destruction.

But something felt off. A niggling sensation chewed at her gut, a guilty compunction that only grew as the screams intensified and the bodies around her crumpled, blackened, and folded in on themselves.

She felt no rage. This had nothing to do with vengeance. These troops hadn't done anything to her. She had no reason to hate them. This didn't feel righteous, this just felt *cruel*.

Her flames sagged, then shrank back inside her.

What was wrong with her? It was usually so easy to sink into that rhapsodic space where rage met purpose. She'd never had to struggle to find anger before; she carried it around with her like a warm coal, forever burning.

She'd turned her fire on her fellow Nikara before. She'd done it easily at the Red Cliffs; she'd set entire ships aflame without thinking twice. But this was the first time she'd ever burned an enemy that hadn't attacked her first.

This wasn't self-defense or vengeance. This was plain, simple aggression.

But they chose this, she reminded herself. *We gave them two chances to surrender, and they refused. They knew what I am. They dug their graves.*

She reached deep into a dark pit inside her, and her column of fire burst forth anew, blazing this time with a wicked kind of energy.

She wielded now a different fire; a fiercer, hungrier fire; one that wanted to burn not as a reaction to fear and pain, but with a rage that sprang from *power*. The fury of being disrespected, of being defied.

This fire felt hotter. Darker.

Rin realized with a shudder that she rather liked this feeling.

She was as close to invincible as humans could get, and Jinzhou was about to fall into her lap.

Never grow cocky, Irjah had been so fond of repeating. *True warfare never goes according to plan.*

Oh, but it did, when the powers at play were this unbalanced, for even the inevitability of chance could not undo the infinite disparity between gods and men. She watched the battle unfold, mapping perfectly onto the chessboard in her mind's eye. Pieces toppled with the push of a finger, all because she'd willed them to. Cities shattered.

It took her a long moment to notice that the clang of steel had long since died down, that no one was shooting at her, that no one was charging forward. Only when she called the flames away did she see the white flags, now blackened at the edges, waving from every door of every building. The city had surrendered to the Southern Army long ago. The only one still fighting was her.

The battle had ended barely an hour after it had begun. Rin accepted Jinzhou's surrender, and her soldiers switched from the frenzied rush of battle to the somber business of occupation. Yet even as order was restored to the city, the ground continued to shake, rocked by a series of faraway booms that reverberated so strongly that Rin's teeth shook in her skull.

Dulin had lost control.

But she had expected this. This was the worst, and likeliest, outcome. She'd prepared for it. If Dulin couldn't summon the awareness to calm his mind with opium, she'd force it into him.

She turned on her heel and dashed back through the charred city toward the open wall. Her flames flickered and disappeared—

she was too panicked to focus on rage now—but no one bothered attacking her. Civilians and soldiers on both sides were all fleeing the shuddering city, dodging and weaving as great chunks of stone tore from the sides of buildings and smashed into the dirt.

The booms grew louder. Great crevices started ripping through the earth like gaping wounds left by some invisible beast. Rin saw two men in front of her disappear, screaming, as the ground opened up beneath them. For the first time on this campaign, a dagger of fear broke through her calm. The Great Tortoise had gotten a taste of freedom. It wanted more. If this continued, Dulin would put the entire city into the earth.

But miraculously, the ground seemed calmer the closer Rin got to the eastern wall. She realized the tremors were spreading out in a circular pattern, and the damage rippled out inversely, gaining destruction rather than fading at larger diameters. But the epicenter—the ground under Dulin's feet—was calm.

Of course. The Great Tortoise wanted liberation. It wanted to see the sky. It might bury everything in its vicinity, but it would not bury its mortal host.

Dulin was bent over where she'd left him, hands clutching at his head as he screamed. Rin spied Pipaji crouched several yards away, half kneeling like she couldn't decide whether or not to spring at him. Her eyes widened when she saw Rin. "Should I—"

"Not yet." Rin pushed her out of the way. "Get back."

Dulin's thrashing meant that he was still fighting. The Great Tortoise hadn't yet won; she could still bring him back. She fleetingly considered trying to shout him down, the way Altan had done for Suni so many times.

But Jinzhou was crumbling. She didn't have the time.

She ran forward, lowered her head, and tackled him at the waist.

He hit the ground with no resistance. Rin had forgotten how weak he really was, a spindly adolescent who'd been chronically malnourished over many months. He flailed beneath her, but to no avail; she held him still using only her knees.

The rumbling grew louder. She heard another ear-splitting

crash from within the city boundaries. Another building had just gone down. She fumbled hastily in her back pocket for the opium pouch, ripped it open with her teeth, and shook its contents out onto the dirt.

Dulin arched his back, twisting beneath her. Dreadful gargling sounds escaped his throat. His eyes flitted back and forth, alternating brown and shiny black every time he blinked.

"Hold still," she hissed.

His eyes fixed on hers. She felt a flutter of fear as something ancient and alien bore into her soul. Dulin's features contorted in an expression of absolute terror, and he began rasping out guttural words in no language she could recognize.

Rin snatched the nuggets off the dirt and shoved them all in his mouth.

His eyes bulged. She lurched forward and clamped her hand tight over his mouth, clenching his jaw shut as best she could. Dulin struggled but Rin squeezed harder, pressing her stump against his neck for leverage, until at last she saw his throat bob. Several minutes later, once the opium had seeped into his bloodstream, the earth at last fell silent.

Rin let go of Dulin's jaw and reached under his neck to feel for his pulse. Faint, but insistent. His chest was still rising and falling. Good—she hadn't choked him to death.

"Get Lianhua," she called to a cowering Pipaji. Foam bubbled out the sides of Dulin's clammy lips, and Rin wondered vaguely how quickly opium poisoning could kill a person. "Be quick."

As Jinzhou was falling, its city magistrate had realized that defeat likely meant death, so he'd fled out the back gates concealed under pig carcasses in a livestock cart. He left his pregnant wife and three children behind, barricaded in the inner chamber of their mansion, where several hours later they were found suffocated under collapsed rubble.

Rin learned all this as her troops took swift, efficient command of the city.

"Everyone we've interrogated confirms he's heading east," said Commander Miragha. She was a brutally efficient young woman, one of Cholang's subordinates from Dog Province, and she'd rapidly become one of Rin's most capable officers. "He's got allies in the next province over. What do you want to do?"

"Pursue him," Rin ordered. "Pursue anyone who's fled the city, and don't let up until you've dragged them back into the jails. I don't want anyone outside Jinzhou to know what happened here today."

Of all Souji's lessons, the one that had struck the hardest was that in campaigns of resistance, information asymmetry mattered more than anything. The playing field had leveled somewhat now, but Rin still didn't want Nezha to know her army had new shamans until Dulin and Pipaji became impossible to conceal. She knew she couldn't keep this secret for long, but there was no point giving Nezha extra time to prepare.

"Kill or capture?" Miragha pressed.

Rin paused, considering.

That question had bearing on the larger issue of how to handle Jinzhou's occupation. Most civil wars, like Vaisra's campaign, were fought by redefining territorial borders. Enemy land was hard to maintain, so grafting onto local power structures had historically been the easiest way to seamlessly take control of a city without breakdown of civil functions. If Rin had wanted Jinzhou to resume normal functions, then she'd try to keep as many fleeing officials alive as she could. But she was focused on obtaining resources, not territory—she didn't have the troops to station in every city that stood between her and Arlong.

Of course, that wasn't a strategy for sustained long-term rule. But Rin wasn't concerned with long-term rule right now. She wanted Nezha dead, the Republic collapsed, the south freed, and the Hesperians banished. She didn't care much what happened to the Nikara heartland in the interim.

This region would likely fall into a temporary chaos while local powers either reestablished themselves or became victim to opportunistic coups. Small-scale wars were bound to break out. Bandits would run rampant.

She had to bracket all that as a problem for later. It couldn't be hard to reassert control after she'd defeated the Republic. She'd be the only alternative left. Who could possibly challenge her?

"Capture them if you can," she told Miragha. "But no need to go out of your way."

For the rest of the afternoon, Rin's troops plundered Jinzhou for its riches.

They did it as politely as possible, with minimal brutality. Rin gave strict orders for her soldiers to leave the terrified civilians and their households alone. Even accounting for the buildings shattered by Dulin's earthquake, Jinzhou wallowed in so much wealth that the destruction had barely made a dent; the warehouses, granaries, and shops that remained standing still burst with enough goods to sustain the army for weeks. Rin's troops loaded their wagons with sacks of rice, grain, salt, and dried meat; restocked their stores of bandages and tinctures; and replaced their rusty, broken-down carts with new vehicles with wheels and axles that glinted silver in the sunlight.

By far their best discovery was bolts and bolts of cotton linen and silk stacked up in massive piles inside a textile warehouse. Now they could make bandages. Now they could repair their shoes, which were in such tatters after the march over Baolei that many of Rin's soldiers had fought the battle of Jinzhou barefoot. And now, for the first time in its short history, the Southern Army would have a uniform.

Up until now they'd been fighting in the same rags they'd worn out of the Southern Province. In battle they distinguished themselves with streaks of mud like Souji had suggested back when they'd broken the Beehive, or by putting on anything that wasn't blue and hoping they weren't killed by friendly fire. But now Rin had cloth, dyes, and a terrified guild of skilled Jinzhou seamstresses who were eager to comply with her every request.

The seamstresses asked her to pick a color. She chose brown, largely because brown dyes were the cheapest, made with tannins easily found in tree bark, shells, and acorn cups. But brown was also fitting. The Southern Army's first uniforms had been dirt from a riverbed. When the Snail Goddess Nüwa had created the first humans, she had lovingly crafted the aristocracy from the finest red clay, lost patience, and hastily shaped the rest from mud. At Sinegard, they'd called her a mud-skinned commoner so often the insult felt now like a familiar call to arms.

Let them think of us as dirt, Rin thought. She *was* dirt. Her army was dirt. But dirt was common, ubiquitous, patient, and necessary. The soil gave life to the country. And the earth always reclaimed what it was owed.

"Great Tortoise," Kitay said. "You'd think this was a Warlord's palace."

They stood in the main council room of Jinzhou's city hall, a vast chamber with high ceilings, elaborately carved stone walls, and ten-foot-long calligraphic tapestries hanging at every corner. Long shelves gilded each wall, displaying an array of antique vases, swords, medals, and armor dating back as far as the Red Emperor. Miraculously, it had all survived the earthquakes.

Rin felt deliciously guilty as she perused the room and its treasures. She felt like a naughty child rummaging through her parents' wardrobe. She couldn't shake the sense that she shouldn't be in here, that none of this belonged to her.

It does, she reminded herself. *You conquered them. You razed this place. You won.*

They'd sell it all, of course. They'd come here to find treasures they could turn to silver through Moag's trading routes. As she ran her fingers over a silk fan, Rin fleetingly imagined herself wielding it, dressed in ornate silks of the kind Daji used to wear, carried through adoring crowds on a gilded palanquin.

She pushed the image away. Empresses carried fans. Generals carried swords.

"Look," Kitay said. "Someone certainly thought highly of themselves."

The magistrate's chair at the end of the room was laughably ornate, a throne better fit for an emperor than a city official.

"I wonder how he made it through any meetings," Rin said. The chair was nailed to a raised dais about half a foot off the floor. "You'd have to crane your neck just to look at anyone."

Kitay snorted. "Perhaps he was just very short."

Curious, Rin climbed up and settled into the chair. Contrary to expectations, the seat had actually been built for someone much taller than her. Her feet swung childishly from the edge, nowhere close to scraping the floor. Still, she couldn't help feeling a small thrill of excitement as she looked out over the gilded chamber and the long council table at whose head she sat. She imagined the seats filled with people: soldiers, advisers, and city officials all listening attentively to her bidding.

Was this how it felt, day by day, to rule? Was this how Nezha felt seated within Arlong's cerulean halls, halfway across the country?

She knew very well how total, dominating power tasted. But as she sat on the conquered throne, gazing down at the empty seats below, she understood for the first time the delicious authority that went with it. This was not a taste she had inherited from Altan, because Altan had only ever concerned himself with destructive retribution. Altan had never dreamed of seizing a throne.

But Rin could burn, *was* burning, much more brightly than Altan ever had.

Small wonder Nezha had chosen his Republic over her. She'd have done the same in a heartbeat.

Enjoy your Republic, she thought, fingers curling against the cold armrest. *Enjoy it while it lasts, Young Marshal. Take a good look at your splendor, and remember well how it feels. Because I am coming to burn it all down beneath you.*

CHAPTER 26

In the *Principles of War*, the strategist Sunzi wrote at length about a concept he named *shi*, which from Old Nikara translated vaguely into "energy," "influence," or "strategic advantage." *Shi* was water rushing so quickly downstream it could dislodge stones from riverbeds. *Shi* was the devastation of boulders tumbling down a steep mountain slope. *Shi* dictated that energy, when present, accumulated and amplified itself.

Rin's victory at Jinzhou was the push that sent the first rock rolling.

Things became so easy after that. Nezha didn't have the troops to defend his outlying territories, so he rapidly retreated southeast, back behind the Qinling and Daba Mountains that served as Arlong's natural defenses. Assaulted on two fronts, he made the only strategic decision he could—to center his defenses in Dragon Province, leaving the rest of the Republic to fend for itself.

On their way through Ram Province, Rin's troops came across nothing but scorched fields and abandoned villages—evidence of civilians ordered to pack their things overnight and retreat into the mountains or back behind Republican lines. Anything the refugees couldn't take, they had left out in the sun to spoil.

On many occasions, the Southern Army stumbled upon piles and piles of animal carcasses, flies buzzing over split-open pigs whose meat might have been good just two or three days ago.

There was a classic principle of Nikara warfare: when facing enemy invasion, clear the countryside and erect high walls. When things looked dire, Nikara leaders destroyed rural settlements and moved food, people, and supplies behind walled cities to prevent them from becoming enemy assets. What couldn't be moved was burned, poisoned, or buried. It was the oldest practice of Nikara military tradition, and amplified the suffering of innocents. Someone wants to conquer you, someone else wants to prevent you from turning into an asset, and you get fucked from both sides.

From the Mugenese, such extravagant waste would have been an act of spiteful defiance. But from Nezha, who had provinces to rule and subjects to protect, this was the ultimate sign of weakness. It meant his Hesperian allies were abandoning him. It meant he knew he couldn't stop the southerners from marching on Dragon Province; he could only try to slow them down.

But the Southern Army had *shi*. It could not be slowed. Rin's troops were running high on victory. They had sharper swords now, better armor, and more food than they could eat. They were fighting with more skill and energy than they ever had before. They carved through the countryside like a knife through tofu. More often than not, villages surrendered without their having to lift a finger; some villagers even readily enlisted, happy for the chance at steady coin and two square meals a day.

The reversal of fortunes was astonishing. Months ago, Rin had led a desperate march into mountains, had gambled the lives of thousands on the barest chance of survival. Now she marched on the offensive, and Nezha had lost almost everything that made her fear him. He was a boy king, limping by with the support of a recalcitrant ally that, judging from the quiet skies, had strongly reconsidered its commitments. Meanwhile, Rin had an army swelling in confidence, experience, and supplies. Above all, she had shamans.

And they were performing marvelously. After Dulin's near breakdown at Jinzhou, Rin hadn't expected them to last so long. She'd thought she might get a few weeks' use from them at most before they inevitably died in battle or she had to kill them. She'd been particularly concerned about Lianhua, who regularly sank into daylong catatonic trances after her shifts on triage duty. This frightened Pipaji so much that she soon grew terrified of calling her own god, and had to be coaxed into participating in the next few battles.

But all three were getting more stable over time. Aside from a brief episode when Dulin was struck in the shoulder by an arrow and accidentally prompted an earthquake that split the battlefield with a ten-foot ravine, he never lost control again. Lianhua's trances decreased to once a week, and then ceased completely. Pipaji managed to overcome her nerves; three weeks after Jinzhou, she infiltrated a village posing as a refugee and took out its entire defensive line that night by slipping through their ranks, brushing her fingers against every patch of exposed skin.

They all learned to cope in their own ways. Dulin started meditating at night, sitting cross-legged on the dirt for hours on end. Lianhua sang to herself while she worked to keep herself grounded, going through a wide array of folk ballads and ditties in an impressively lovely soprano. Pipaji began disappearing from camp every evening shortly after dinner, and rarely came back until after dusk.

One night Rin, slightly worried, followed her out of camp. She was relieved to discover that all Pipaji did was stand still in the forest, surrounded by trees with no other human beings in sight, and breathe.

"You're not very good at hiding," Pipaji said after a while.

Rin stepped into the clearing. "I didn't want to disturb you."

"It's all right." Pipaji looked somewhat embarrassed. "I don't ever stay out here for very long. I just like to go where it's quiet. Where there's nobody I can hurt. It's, um, relaxing."

Rin felt an odd twinge in her chest. "That's prudent."

"You can stay if you want."

Rin lifted her eyebrows, somewhat touched. "Thank you."

For a moment they stood side by side, listening to the katydids shriek. It was, Rin agreed, oddly relaxing.

"You don't get to go back to normal," Pipaji said abruptly.

"Hmm?"

"I noticed your eyes. They're always red. Our eyes go back to normal. Yours don't. Why?"

"Because I'm too far gone," Rin said. She was only partly lying. "I can't shut it out anymore."

"Then what brings you back?" Pipaji demanded. "Why haven't you lost it like—like the rest of them?"

Rin considered telling her about the anchor bond. But what was the point? That option would never be possible for Pipaji—revealing it would only be cruel. And the fewer people who knew about Kitay, the better.

She liked Pipaji, but she wasn't going to trust the girl with her life.

"I've struck a deal with my god," she said after a pause. "And it's learned to stay put."

"You didn't tell us about that."

"Because it's the least likely outcome," Rin said. "You knew how this would end. There's no point giving you hope."

Her words came out flat and cold. She couldn't think of anything reassuring to say, and she suspected Pipaji didn't want to hear it. All her recruits had known this could only end two ways for them: death, or the Chuluu Korikh. She'd warned them many times over; she'd made sure they understood that volunteering was a death sentence.

"I'm not going to survive this war," Pipaji said after a long silence.

"You don't know that," Rin said.

Pipaji shook her head. "I'm not strong enough. You'll kill me. You'll need to kill me."

Rin gave her a pitying look. What good would lying do?

"Do you want me to say I'm sorry?"

"No." Pipaji snorted. "We knew what we signed up for."

And that was all it took to assuage Rin's conscience. She hadn't done anything wrong if they'd chosen this themselves. Dulin, Lianhua, and Pipaji were still here because they'd decided it was worth it. They'd foreseen and accepted their deaths. She'd offered them weapons, the only weapons strong enough to alter their miserable world, and they'd taken them. These were the choices war produced.

Several weeks later they occupied a small port town on the Western Murui at the border between Ram and Hare province, and made camp as they awaited an old friend.

"Well, look at you." Chiang Moag, Pirate Queen of Ankhiluun, stepped off the gangplank and strode down the pier with a broad smile on her face. "Look what you've made of yourself."

"Hello, Moag," Rin said. They regarded each other for a moment. Then, because Moag hadn't yet tried to stick a knife in her back, Rin waved down the twenty hidden archers who had been waiting to put an arrow through her head.

"Cute," Moag said when she saw them disperse.

"Learned that from you," Rin said. "I'm never quite sure what side you're on."

Moag snorted. "Oh, let's call this what it is. The Republic is done for. That pretty little boy they've got on Arlong's throne couldn't manage even a village without his father's help. I know where to throw in my lot."

She sounded convincing, but Rin knew better than to take her words at face value. Moag was, and always would be, a liability. True, she'd granted Rin safe haven in Ankhiluun after her escape from Arlong, but she hadn't lifted a finger to help since Rin left for the south. This entire war Moag had remained hidden in Ankhiluun, bolstering her fleets against an anticipated Hesperian attack. Moag was hedging her bets, waiting to see if she'd be better off resisting the Republic or playing by its rules.

Momentum was on Rin's side right now. But should anything go wrong, Moag was just as likely to sell her out to Arlong. She'd done it before.

For now, Rin was willing to swallow that risk. She needed ammunition—all the fire powder, cannons, and missiles that she hadn't been able to loot. Mobile warfare tactics worked well enough on underdefended cities from which Nezha's troops had been hastily recalled. But she needed proper artillery to breach the dragon's lair.

"It's nice to see you in charge." Moag clapped a broad hand on Rin's shoulder. "What did I tell you? You were never meant to serve, much less beneath snakes like Vaisra. Women like us have no business putting our services for sale."

Rin laughed. "It's good to see you."

She meant it. She'd always respected the Pirate Queen's blunt, naked self-interest. Moag had risen from an escort to the ruler of Nikan's only free city through ruthless, brilliant pragmatism, and though Rin knew very well this meant Moag was loyal to no one, she still admired her for it.

"What do you have for me?" she asked.

"See for yourself." Moag stuck two fingers in her mouth and whistled to her crew. "Some old toys, some new ones. I think you'll like them."

Over the next hour, Moag's crew and Rin's troops together unloaded dozens of crates onto the riverbank. Moag unlocked one and kicked open the hatch, revealing coffins stacked in neat rows of four.

"Does this trick really work?" Rin asked.

"It does if you claim they're plague victims." Moag motioned to one of her crew. He pulled the nearest coffin out of the crate, jammed a crowbar under the lid, and pushed down until the lid popped open. A thick pile of fire powder glinted in the sunlight, fine and shiny. Rin had the absurd impulse to bathe in it.

"It's an old smuggler's trick," Moag said. "Shockingly effective. Everyone's prudent, but no one wants to die."

"Smart," Rin said, impressed.

"Save the coffins," Moag suggested. "They're good for firewood."

For the rest of the afternoon they traded coffins crammed with swords, shields, missiles, and fire powder for the riches Rin's troops had accumulated throughout Ram Province. All this happened outside on the riverbank. Rin didn't want to let Moag near her camp—the less intelligence Moag gleaned about her forces the better—and Moag didn't want to wander too far from her ships. The riverbank was a buffer that assuaged their mutual distrust.

Moag was thorough. She inspected every item in every trunk of jewelry, rubbing the larger pieces between her fingers to determine their value before nodding her permission for her soldiers to lug it back on board.

Rin watched the two lines walking in parallel, trading. There was a lovely symbolism to it. All the treasures of one bloated city, in exchange for enough cold steel and fire powder to bring down the rest.

"Now, then." Moag stood back as the final crate was unloaded from her skimmers. "There's the issue of payment."

Rin balked. "What are you talking about?"

Moag showed her the figures she'd been marking in a ledger. "I've just unloaded twice as much weaponry as this pays for."

"By what standards?" Rin asked. "Those prices are made up. Your whole pricing system is shot; we're the only ones buying right now. You'd hardly be able to cut a deal in Arlong."

"True," Moag said. "But city magistrates are always buying. And I'm sure there are plenty of local platoons looking to improve their defenses now that they all know what's coming their way."

"If you try that shit," Rin said very calmly, "I will kill you."

There followed a long pause. Rin couldn't read Moag's expression. Was she afraid? Furious? Deliberating whether to strike first?

Rin's eyes darted around the beach, mapping out the possible fallout. Her first move would be to incinerate Moag where she stood, but she had to hedge against the Black Lilies, any one of whom could take her out with a well-aimed poisonous hairpin. If she expanded her radius she could take the Lilies out, too, but they were intermingled with southern troops, almost certainly on purpose. If she killed Moag, then she'd have to suffer at least a dozen casualties.

Her fingers curled into a fist. She could absorb those losses; no one would fault her for it. But she had to strike first.

Then Moag burst out laughing, a full-throated, booming laugh that startled Rin.

"Tiger's tits." Moag clapped a hand on her shoulder, grinning. "When did you grow such a massive pair of balls?"

Rin, wildly relieved, forced her grimace into a smile.

"But I will be coming to collect," Moag continued. "Not immediately," she amended quickly, noticing Rin's scowl. "I want to see you succeed, little Speerly. I won't get in your way. But you'd best start thinking about how to scrounge up some profits from your empire."

"Profits?" Rin wrinkled her nose. "I'm not running a business here—"

"Correct. You're about to run a nation." A familiar look of patronizing pity crossed Moag's face, the look she'd always put on when she thought Rin was being particularly naive. "And nations need silver, girlie. War is costly. You've got to pay your soldiers somehow. Then you've got to pay back the masses whose homelands you've just wrecked. Where are they supposed to live? What are they going to eat? You need lumber to rebuild village settlements. You need grain to ward off the famine you're facing down, since I guarantee your crop yields this year will be shit. No one plows when there's a war going on. They're too busy being, you know, refugees."

"I . . ." Rin didn't know what to say. She had to admit those were real problems, problems she had to deal with eventually, but they seemed so far off that she'd never given them any thought. Those seemed like good problems to have, because by the time they became relevant, it would mean that she'd won. But what was the point of daydreaming about an empire when Nezha still ruled the southeast? "I haven't—"

"Ah, don't look so scared." Moag gave her shoulder a condescending pat. "You'll be sitting on a throne of riches soon enough. That's what I'm trying to tell you. The Consortium wants to be here for a reason. All those silks? Porcelains? Tungsten deposits? Antique vases? They want that shit, and they'll pay good money for it."

"But they're not going to trade with us," Rin said. "Are they? I mean, if we win, won't they just blockade us?"

"They will, on paper, refuse to trade with the Nikara Empire." Moag spread her hands in a magnanimous gesture. "But I've got ships aplenty, and I know a million ways to disguise the trade channels so it's not coming directly from you. You can always find a way to make a sale when there's demand. I'll take a cut, of course."

Rin was still confused. "But if it's Nikara goods they're buying, won't they know—"

"Of course they'll know," Moag said. She shook her head, casting again that pitying smile. "Everyone knows. But that's the business of statecraft. Nations rise and fall, but appetites remain the same. Trust me, Speerly—you'll be carting in Hesperian grain weeks after you boot them from your shores, so long as you're willing to send back some of Arlong's treasures in return. The world runs on trade. Send an envoy when you're ready to start."

The battles got harder as the Southern Army moved farther east. Rin had expected this. She was essentially knocking on Nezha's door now; they were only several months' march from Arlong. Now well-trained Republican troops occupied every major city in their path. Now Rin regularly encountered artillery formations armed with opium missiles, which forced her to get more and more creative with how and when she deployed shamans. In half her battles she didn't send in Pipaji or Dulin at all, relying instead on conventional military means to break the opposition. More often than not she was the only shaman in action, since she had a higher opium tolerance than the rest; she could withstand close to twenty minutes of smoke, during which she could do incalculable damage before she was forced to retreat.

The fighting turned vicious. The defenders weren't so quick to surrender anymore; more often they fought to the death, taking as many southerners with them as they could. Her casualty rates, once in the dozens, climbed to triple digits.

But Rin was also blessed by the fact that Nezha's troops were so fucking *slow*. They weren't mobile in the least. They were stationary defenders—they stuck behind city walls and protected them as best they could, but never did they attempt the roving strikes that might have put the Southern Army in real trouble.

"It's likely because they're weighed down by tons of Hesperian equipment," Kitay guessed. "Mounted arquebuses, multiple fire cannons, all that heavy stuff. They haven't got the transportation support to take it on the road, so they're always tethered to one place."

That turned Nezha's troops into sitting targets and offset the technology imbalance somewhat—Nezha's troops were committed to their trenches with their heavy machinery, while Rin's squadrons were quick and agile, always on the offensive. They were fighting like a turtle and a wolf—one retreating into its ever-shrinking shell, while the other paced its boundaries, waiting for the slightest weakness to strike.

That suited Rin just fine. After all, she, Kitay, and Nezha had all been taught since their first year at Sinegard that it was always, *always* better to be on the offensive.

Despite the increased resistance, week by week they continued to gain ground, while Nezha's territory crumbled.

Rin knew Nezha's losses weren't entirely his fault. He had inherited a Republic fractured and riddled with resentment toward his father, as well as a massive, unwieldy army that was tired of fighting a civil war they'd been promised would end quickly. His inner circle was getting smaller and smaller, reduced now to a Hesperian attaché who did little more than make snide comments about how Nezha was on his way to losing a country, and a handful of Vaisra's old advisers who resented that he wasn't his father. She heard rumors that since Mount Tianshan, he'd already had to quash two attempted coups, and although he'd swiftly jailed the perpetrators, his dissenters had only increased.

Most importantly, he was losing the support of the countryside.

Most of the Nikara elite—aristocrats, provincial officials, and city bureaucrats—remained loyal to Arlong. But the villagers had no entrenched interests in the Republic. They hadn't benefited financially from Nezha's new trade policies, and now that they'd tasted life under Hesperian occupation, they threw their support behind the only other alternative.

The upshot of this was that as Rin moved south, she stumbled into a remarkable intelligence network. In the countryside, everyone was tangentially connected to everyone else. Market gossip became a hub for crucial information. It didn't matter that none of her new sources were privy to high-level conversations, or that none of them had ever seen a map of troop placements. They saw its evidence with their own eyes.

Three columns crossed this river two nights ago, they told her. *We saw wagons of fire powder moving east this morning.*

They are building temporary bridges across the river at these two junctions.

Much of this ground-level, eyewitness intelligence was useless. The villagers weren't trained spies, they didn't draw accurate maps, and they often embellished their stories for dramatic effect. But the sheer volume of information made up for it; once Rin had reports from at least three different sources, she and Kitay could piece them together into a mostly accurate composite image of where Nezha had arranged his defenses, and where he intended to strike next.

And that, again, confirmed what Rin had believed since the

start of her campaign—that Nikan's southerners were weak but many, and that united, they could topple empires.

"Nezha can't be doing this on purpose," Kitay said one evening after yet another city in Hare Province had tumbled into southern hands with barely so much as a whimper. "It's like he's not even trying."

Rin yawned. "Maybe it's the best he can do."

He shot her a wary look. "Don't get cocky."

"Yeah, yeah." She knew she couldn't really take credit for their victory. They both knew that their ongoing streak of wins was in large part because Nezha simply had not committed as many troops or resources as they had.

But *why*?

They had to assume at this point that Nezha's dominant strategy was to hole up in Arlong and concentrate his defenses there. But surely he knew better than to put all his eggs in one basket. Arlong was blessed with a bevy of natural defenses, but defaulting to a siege mentality this early screamed of either desperation or insanity.

"He must be confident about something," Kitay mused. "Otherwise the only possible explanation for all this is that he's gone batshit crazy. He's got to have something up his sleeve."

Rin frowned. "More dirigibles, you think?" But that didn't seem likely. If Nezha had increased Hesperian aid, he would have subjected them to air raids already, while they were still on open, distant terrain, instead of near his prized capital. "Is he wagering everything on the Dragon? Some new military technology that's more lethal than shamanism?"

"Or some military technology that can counteract shamanism," Kitay said.

Rin shot him a sharp look. He'd said it too quickly—it wasn't a guess. "Do you know something?"

"I, ah, I'm not sure."

"Did Nezha say something?" she demanded. "In the New City, when Petra was—I mean—did he—"

"He didn't know." Kitay tugged uncomfortably at a lock of hair. "Petra never told him anything. He went through her—her tests. The Hesperians lent him weapons. That was the deal they offered him, and he took it. They didn't think he had the right to know what they were researching."

"He could have been lying."

"Maybe. But I've seen Nezha lying. That wasn't it. That was just despair."

"But there's nothing Petra could invent," Rin insisted. "They've got nothing. Their theology is wrong. Their Maker doesn't exist. If they had some anti-shamanic tool, they would have used it to protect their fleet, but they didn't. All they have is conventional weapons—fire powder and opium—and we know how to counteract those. Right?"

Kitay looked unconvinced. "As far as we know."

She crossed her arms, frustrated. "Pick a side, Kitay. You just said there's no proof—"

"There's no proof either way. I'm just floating the possibility, because we have to consider it. You know that unless Nezha has something like this up his sleeve, his strategy so far has been utterly irrational. And we can't proceed assuming the worst of him."

"Then what? You want to divert from Arlong?"

Kitay mulled that over for a moment. "No. I don't think we change our overall strategy. We keep gaining ground. We keep bolstering our resources. Based on the information we have, we take Arlong on schedule. But I'm saying we need to be cautious."

"We're always cautious."

He gave her a tired look. "You know what I mean."

They left it at that. There was nothing else to discuss; without further proof, there was nothing they could do.

Privately, Rin thought Kitay was being paranoid.

What if Nezha didn't have some secret weapon? What if Nezha was just destined to lose? She couldn't shake the feeling that maybe, just maybe, the end to this story was a foregone conclusion. After all, the last several months had made it clear that she couldn't be defeated. Battle by battle, victory by victory, she became more and more convinced of the fact that she'd been chosen by fate to rule the Empire. What else explained her streak of incredible, implausible victories and escapes? She had survived Speer. Golyn Niis. Shiro's laboratory. She'd taken an army through the long march. She'd emerged victorious from Mount Tianshan. She'd outwitted and outlasted the Mugenese, the Trifecta, and Vaisra. And now she was about to conquer Nezha.

Of course, she couldn't leave everything to the fates. She couldn't stop meticulously preparing for every battle just because she hadn't yet lost a single one. Nikara history was crammed with fools who imagined themselves kings. When their luck bled out, they died like anyone else.

That was why she never voiced this feeling out loud to Kitay. She knew what he would say. *Come on, Rin. You're losing your grip on reality. The gods don't choose their champions. That's not how this works.*

And while she understood that in the rational part of her mind, she still knew *something* had changed when she'd come back down from Mount Tianshan, when she'd survived an explosion that killed the greatest figures in Nikara history and nearly wiped out the Hesperian fleet. The tides of history had shifted. She had never before believed in fate, but this she came to know with more and more certainty as each day passed: the script of the world was now wholly, inalterably colored by a brilliant crimson streak.

Rin's favorite part by far of the southeastern campaign was the Southern Army's slow acquisition and mastery of Hesperian military technology. She made a game of it—the standing rule was double portions of dinner to the squadron that returned from active engagement with the largest haul of functioning Hesperian equipment.

Most of the pieces they retrieved were minor improvements on equipment they already had—more accurate compasses, sturdier splints for the physicians, more durable axles for their wagons. Often they found contraptions they had no idea what to do with—little lamps without wicks that they didn't know how to light, ticking orbs that resembled clocks but whose arms corresponded to inexplicable letters and numbers, and whirring mini-dirigibles that Rin assumed were messenger crafts, which she couldn't fly. She felt stupid, turning the devices over and over in her fingers, unable to find the controls to make them start. Kitay fared slightly better—he finally determined that the lamps were activated with a series of taps—but even he grew frustrated with machines that seemed to run purely on magic.

Three miles out from Bobai, a recently abandoned Republican holdout, they found under a thin layer of soil a hastily buried crate of functioning arquebuses.

"Fuck me," Kitay murmured when they pried the lid off the crate. "These are almost brand-new."

Rin lifted an arquebus from the top of the pile and weighed it in her hand. She'd never held one before; she hadn't dared. The steel was icy cool to the touch. It was heavier than she imagined—she found a new respect for Hesperian soldiers who lugged these running into battle.

She glanced at Kitay, whose jaw hung open as he knelt down to examine the weapons. She knew what he was thinking.

These changed everything.

They'd made it this far with minimal ranged capabilities. There were only several dozen archers in the Southern Army, and their ranks weren't growing. It took weeks for a novice soldier to learn to properly fire an arrow, and months if not years for them to fire with decent accuracy. Archery required tremendous arm strength, particularly if arrows were meant to pierce armor.

The next best thing they had to arrows were fire lances, a recent Republican invention Kitay had heard about during his stay in the New City, then reverse engineered. Those were tubes made of sixteen layers of thin wrapped paper, a little longer than two feet, stuffed with willow charcoal, sulfur, saltpeter, and shards of iron. The lances could shoot flames nearly ten feet when lit, but they still required a ready fire source to activate, and they backfired easily, often exploding in the hands of their wielders.

But arquebuses required less arm strength than bows, and they were more reliable than fire lances. How long would it take to train troops to shoot? Weeks? Days, perhaps, if they devoted their time to nothing else? If she could get just twenty to thirty soldiers who were halfway proficient with the arquebus, that would open up a host of new strategies they'd only dreamed of.

"Think you can figure out how to use these?" she asked Kitay.

He chuckled, brushing his fingers over the metal tubes. "Give me until sunset."

Kitay took only the afternoon before he called her over into a clearing, empty except for the dozen dissembled arquebuses scattered around the grass. Pale little notches dotted the trunks of every tree in sight.

"It's actually quite simple." He pointed at various parts of the arquebus as he spoke. "I thought I was going to have to interrogate some Hesperian prisoners, but the design really revealed its own function. Very clever invention. It's basically a cannon in miniature—you set off some fire powder inside the barrel, and the force of the explosion sends the lead ball ricocheting out."

"How does the firing mechanism work?" Rin asked. "Do they have to light a spark every time?"

This seemed inconvenient to her, as well as implausible; the Hesperians seemed to fire at will without fumbling for flint.

"No, they don't," said Kitay. "They've done something clever with the match. It's already a burning fuse—you can light it before you're out on the field. Then when you're ready to shoot, you squeeze this lever here, and it brings the match down into the powder. Click, boom." He reached for an intact arquebus. "Here, I've loaded that one. Want to give it a try?"

She waved her stump at him. "Not sure if I can."

"I'll aim for you." He stood behind her and wrapped his arms around her torso, pointing the barrel at a thick tree across the clearing. "Ready when you are."

She curled her fingers around metal latch. "I just squeeze this?"

"Yup. Make sure you plant your feet, there'll be a kickback against your shoulder. Remember, it's a miniature cannon explosion. And give it a hard yank, it's quite resistant—prevents accidental firing."

She bent her knees as he demonstrated, took a deep breath, and pulled the trigger.

A bang split the clearing. The gun jerked backward at her chest and she flinched, but Kitay's firm grip kept it from slamming into her ribs. Smoke poured out of the muzzle. She turned her head away, coughing.

"That's one disadvantage," Kitay said after the smoke had cleared. "Takes a while to see whether you've actually hit anything."

Rin strode toward a tree on the opposite end of the clearing, where smoke unfurled into the air like little dragons. The pellet had struck true, burrowing deep into the center of the trunk. She stuck her finger into the groove. It sank into wood up to her third knuckle, until she couldn't dig her finger in any farther, and even then she couldn't feel the pellet.

"Holy fucking shit," she said.

"I know," Kitay said. "I've tried firing on armor, too. We've seen what they do to flesh, but these things penetrate *steel*."

"Fuck. How long does that take to reload?"

"It's taking me about half a minute now," he said. "It'll be faster with training."

So that meant three, perhaps four, shots per minute. That was nothing near what an archer like Venka could manage in the same time span, but the arquebus's superior lethality more than compensated.

"How many of your shots end up anywhere close to the target?" she asked.

He gave a sheepish shrug. "Eh. One in six hit the trunk. That should improve."

"And how many of those bullets did we find?"

"Three boxes. About two hundred bullets in each."

She frowned. "Kitay."

He sighed. "I know. We're going to run out."

She took a moment to do the math in her head. Thirty soldiers on arquebuses firing at an ambitious rate of three shots per minute would run out of ammunition in less than—

"Six to seven minutes," said Kitay. "We're out in six to seven minutes."

"I was getting there."

"Course you were, I just figured I'd speed things up. Yes, that is the problem." He rubbed his chin. "There were armories in that town we passed through last week. We could make some casts, melt some scrap metal down . . ."

"What scrap metal?" Rin asked. They were short on swords as it was, and they both knew it was folly to trade swords for bullets when most of their troops were far better in close-range combat.

"Then we've got to obtain it somehow," Kitay said. "Or steal ammunition. But that'll be tough—they've been pretty good about guarding their weapons so far, and those arquebuses were a rare find—"

"Hold on." An idea had just struck her. "Master Irjah gave us a puzzle like this once. Almost *exactly* like this."

"What are you talking about?"

"Don't you remember? What do you do when you need your enemy's ammunition?" She nudged his elbow. "Come on."

He shook his head. "Rin, that worked for *arrows*."

"So what? Same principle."

"Steel pellets are different," he insisted. "They distort upon impact; you can't just collect them and shove them right back into the barrel."

"So we'll melt them down," she countered. "Why is this so implausible? The Hesperians love firing on things. It'll be easy enough to bait them, we just need to give them any reason to shoot. And we're about to hit a tributary, which means—"

"It won't work," he interrupted. "Come on. They've got better spyglasses than we do. Straw targets will be too obvious, they'll know they're decoys."

"That's easy," she said. "We'll just use the real thing."

And so, three days later, they found themselves fastening corpses to the mast and railings of an opium skimmer. The key, Rin learned, was a combination of nails and twine. Ropes would have been ideal, but they were too visible to the naked eye. Nails she could pound through bare flesh, and easily conceal the protrusions under layers of clothing. Anyone who stared long enough through a spyglass could see these were clearly corpses, but Rin hoped the Republican artillerymen would be too trigger-happy for that to matter.

When they'd populated the upper deck with enough corpses to make it look manned, they sent it floating down the river with a sole helmsman whose job was to keep it from crashing onto the bank. They'd chosen a wide, fast-moving stretch of water, with a current quick enough to pull the skimmer out of Republican range before anyone tried to board it.

"Gross." Rin wiped her hand on her tunic as she watched the skimmer drift out of view. "This smell isn't coming out for days, is it?"

"Just as well," Kitay said. "We still have to cut the bullets out."

When at last they neared the southern border of Hare Province, they found a messenger waiting with a letter from Venka. She and Cholang had been sending regular updates throughout the campaign. They'd swept through the north easily enough, as predicted. They hadn't had much to do; Nezha seemed to have pulled his troops in from the east and north alike, concentrating them in a last stand in Dragon Province. So far Venka's missives had involved happy updates of townships captured, shipments of historical artifacts she'd looted in magistrates' estates, and the occasional crate of armor from Tiger Province's famed blacksmiths.

As both divisions of the Southern Army moved closer to the center, Venka's correspondence had come back faster and faster. Now Venka and Cholang were merely a week's ride away—close enough to converge on Arlong in a joint attack.

"This is from six days ago." The messenger handed Rin the scroll. "She wants a quick response."

"Understood," Rin said. "Wait outside."

The messenger gave a curt nod and left the command tent. Rin checked that he was out of hearing range, then ripped the scroll open with her teeth.

> Change of plans. Don't move yet on Arlong—my scouts say he's taking forces north to meet us between the mountains. Rendezvous at Dragab? Please confirm as soon you can; we'd rather not walk alone into a massacre.

"Dragab?" Rin asked. "Where's that?"

"Little outpost south of Xuzhou." Kitay had been reading over her shoulder. "And Xuzhou is, I assume, where the Republic intends to meet us."

"But that's . . ." Rin trailed off, trying to work through her mental map of Southern and Republican troop placements. This didn't track. All this time they had assumed Nezha would keep his forces in Arlong city proper, where the Red Cliffs and canals offered him the clearest advantage. "Why would he push north?"

"I can guess three reasons," Kitay said. "One, Xuzhou's situated over a narrow mountain channel, which restricts the fighting terrain to the opposite cliffsides and the wide ravine beneath. Two, it's monsoon season, and the water locks into the pass when the rains get heavy. And three, it's on our only route to Arlong."

"That's not true," she said. "We could cut around it, there are forest passes—"

"Yes, with roads so bumpy we won't be able to move any of our heavy artillery, and then we'll still have to scale down mountain faces that leave us wide open for their archers. Nezha knows we're coming through for him. He intends to choke us off in the mountains, where your shamans can't strike with discrimination, which forces the battle into a conventional bloodbath."

"So this isn't some last, desperate feint," Rin said. "It's an invitation."

Then why on earth should the Southern Army accept?

Even as the question rose to her lips, the answer became obvious. They should take Xuzhou as their next battleground, purely because it wasn't Arlong.

Nezha's power amplified the closer he was to sources of water. Under the Red Cliffs, where the Murui filtered into canals that surrounded every inch of Arlong, he'd be nearly unstoppable. He'd be right on top of the Dragon's grotto. Xuzhou was their last, and best, chance to fight him while separating him from his god.

Rin saw the grim press of Kitay's mouth, and knew that he'd realized the same. Xuzhou might be Nezha's dominant strategy, but it was theirs, too.

He nodded to the scroll. "Shall we give him what he wants?"

Rin hated that phrasing. This choice was frustrating. Unanticipated. She didn't like meeting their opponent on a terrain of his choosing, under the least favorable strategic conditions possible.

And yet, deep in her gut, she felt a hot coil of excitement.

Until now, this had not been a true war, only a series of skirmishes against cowards in retreat. Every win so far had meant nothing except as instrumental fuel for this moment, when at last they'd meet true resistance. This was the final test. Rin wanted to go up against Nezha's best-prepared strategy and see who came out on top.

"Why not?" she said at last. "Nezha's finally putting his pieces on the board. So let's play."

She stepped outside the tent to summon the messenger. He extended his hand, expecting a written reply, but she shook her head. "I'll be brief. Tell Venka to route to Dragab quick as she can. We'll be waiting."

CHAPTER 27

"I see you found some seamstresses." Venka's eyes roved over the Southern Army's neat brown uniforms as she dismounted from her horse to clasp Rin's hand in greeting. "Do I get one?"

"Of course," Rin said. "It's waiting in the tent."

"General's stripe and everything?"

"Is this your way of asking for a promotion?" Kitay asked.

"I've just handed you the north," said Venka. "That's half a fucking country, mind you. I think the title General Sring is a little overdue, don't you?"

"Honestly," said Rin, "I thought you'd just take the title for yourself."

"Honestly," said Venka, "I did."

They grinned at each other.

Venka and Cholang's troops filed into the southern camp at Dragab, falling eagerly on the prepared meals by the campfires. They'd emerged from their northern expedition with close to their original numbers—an impressive achievement, given that the Dog Province's militia had historically only waged battle against underequipped raiders from the Hinterlands. They also came bearing gifts—wagon upon wagon of spare armor, swords, and shields carted down from the forges in Tiger Province.

After Venka and Cholang had eaten, they joined Rin and Kitay on the floor of the command tent with a map spread between them to piece together their joint intelligence.

"It's an odd play." Venka marked Republican columns in blue ink along the eastern end of the Xuzhou ravine. "I really don't know why he's not just committing all his defenses to Arlong, especially if he can control the fucking river."

"Agreed," Kitay said. "But we think that's the point. He wants to take the Phoenix out of the equation."

"Why, just because we'll be fighting in close quarters?" Cholang asked.

"And because of the rain," Rin said. "He can call the rain, can make it fall as hard or as thick as he likes. Bit hard to sustain a flame when the sky keeps putting it out."

They all regarded the map for a few seconds in silence.

The battle for Xuzhou had become a game of warring tactics, a puzzle that Rin had to admit was highly entertaining. It felt like the sort of exam question she might receive from Master Irjah. Xuzhou was the field of engagement. The limiting conditions were known: The rain disadvantaged them both by damping down fire and fire powder alike. Nezha had superior numbers, better artillery capabilities, and fresher troops due to a shorter march. Nezha had the rain. But Rin had shamans Nezha didn't know about, and she could get to Xuzhou first.

Given the circumstances, piece together a winning strategy.

After a moment, Venka sighed. "What's this coming down to, then? Pure attrition? Are we just going to slug it out in the mud?"

None of them wanted that. No good commander ever left an outcome to the chances that sheer, mindless friction produced. The brunt of the fighting might very well come down to swords, spears, and shields, but they had to find some gambit, some hidden advantage that Nezha hadn't thought of.

Suddenly Kitay began to chuckle.

"What?" Rin asked. She didn't follow; she didn't know what

he'd seen that she hadn't. But that didn't matter. Kitay had solved it, and that was all she needed.

"This is very smart," he said. "You've got to give Nezha credit, really. He's reduced the number of factors at play until the only vectors that matter are the ones where he holds the advantage. He's swept almost all the chess players off the board."

"But?" Rin pressed.

"But he's forgotten one thing." He tapped his forehead. "I've always thrashed him at chess."

Xuzhou was a city of tombs. The Red Emperor had designed it to be an imperial graveyard, the final resting place for his most beloved generals, advisers, wives, and concubines. He'd commissioned the most skilled sculptors, architects, and gardeners across his territories to build grand monuments to his regime, and over the decades, what had begun as a single cemetery sprawled into a memorial the size of a city. Xuzhou became a place with the sole economy of death—its inhabitants were artisans employed to sweep the tombs, light incense, play ritual concerts to tame vengeful ghosts, and craft intricate mansions, clothes, and furniture out of paper to be burned as offerings so that the deceased might receive them in the afterlife. Even after the Red Emperor's regime collapsed, the caretakers remained employed, their salaries paid by one ruler or another out of reverence to the dead.

"Can you imagine such an old civilization built all this?" Kitay ran his hands across remarkably well-preserved limestone as they walked through the central cemetery, staking out vantage points for their artillery units. "They didn't have anything like modern tools. I mean, they barely even had *math*."

"Then how'd they manage it?" Venka asked.

"Sheer human labor. When you can't figure something out, you just throw bodies at it." Kitay pointed to the far end of the graveyard, where a forty-foot sculpture of the Red Emperor loomed over the ravine. "There are bones in that statue. Actually, there are probably bones in all these statues. The Red Emperor believed that human souls kept buildings structurally sound forever, so when the laborers were done chiseling his face into stone, he had them bound up and hurled into the hollow centers."

Rin shuddered. "I thought he wasn't religious."

"He wasn't a shaman. Still superstitious as fuck." Kitay gestured to the monuments surrounding them. "Imagine you're living in a land of beasts and Speerlies. Why wouldn't you believe in spells?"

Rin craned her head up at the Red Emperor. His face had been weathered by time, but had retained its structural integrity well enough that she could still make out his features. He looked the same way he did on all the replicas she'd ever seen of his official portrait—a severe, humorless man whose expression displayed no kindness. Rin supposed he'd had to be cruel. A man who intended to stitch the disparate, warring factions of Nikan into a united empire had to have a ruthless, iron will. He couldn't bend or break. He couldn't compromise; he had to mold the world to his vision.

His first wife stood at the opposite end of the graveyard. The Winter Empress was famously beautiful and famously sad. She'd been born with such impossible, heavenly beauty that the Red Emperor had kidnapped her as a mere child and deposited her in his court. There, her constant weeping only heightened her beauty because it made her eyebrows arch and her lips purse in such an enticing manner that the Red Emperor would watch as she cried, fascinated and aroused.

According to the stories, she looked so beautiful when she was in pain that no one realized she was wasting away from a heart disease until one day she collapsed in the garden, fingers clawing futilely at her snow-white chest. In the old stories, that counted as romance.

But Rin recognized the stone face across the graveyard. And that wasn't, *couldn't* be, the Winter Empress.

"That's Tearza," she murmured, amazed.

"The Speerly queen?" Venka wrinkled her nose. "What are you talking about?"

Rin pointed. "Look around her neck. See that necklace? That's a Speerly necklace."

She'd seen that crescent moon pendant before in her dreams. She'd seen it hanging on Altan's neck. She knew she couldn't have imagined it; those visions were branded into her mind.

Why would the Red Emperor cast Tearza as his Empress?

Was it true, then, that they'd been lovers?

But all the tales said he'd tried to kill her. He'd sent assassins after her since the moment they met. He'd tried many times on the battlefield to take her head. He had been so afraid of her that he ensconced himself in an island hideout surrounded by water. When she'd died, he'd made her island his colony and her people his slaves.

Yet, Rin supposed, lovers could still inflict that kind of violence on each other. Hadn't Riga loved Daji? Hadn't Jiang loved Tseveri?

Hadn't Nezha once loved her?

"If that's Mai'rinnen Tearza," Kitay said, "that's a history no one's ever written."

"Only because the Red Emperor wrote her out of history," Rin said. "Wrote her out so cleanly that no one even recognized her face."

She had to respect the man. When you conquered as totally and completely as he had, you could alter the course of everything. You could determine the stories that people told about you for generations.

When they sing about me, she decided, *Nezha won't warrant even a mention.*

Under her direction, the Southern Army finished preparing the city for Nezha's arrival. They hid cannons behind every statue. They dug trenches and tunnels. They placed their sandbags around their forts. They staked out target points for Dulin, identifying weak points in the stone that could bring entire structures down on the Republican Army.

Then they hunkered down to wait.

Rainfall started that evening and continued steadily through the night, fat droplets hammering down in unrelenting sheets that turned the ground beneath their feet to such slippery mud that they had to prop their carts up on boulders so their wheels wouldn't get stuck overnight. Rin hoped the heavy downpour might drain the clouds empty by morning, but the pattering only intensified as the hours drew on. At dawn, the gray shroud over Xuzhou showed no sign of thinning.

Rin tried to snatch a bit of sleep, but the rain battering against her tent made it impossible. She gave up and waited out the night sitting outside, keeping watch over the graveyard beneath Tearza's statue.

Nezha had been right to attack in monsoon season. Her fire would do very little today aside from keeping her warm. She'd tested it throughout the night, sending arcs of flame across the night sky. They all fizzled away in seconds. She could still incinerate anyone within her immediate proximity, but that didn't help in a ranged battle. Cannons and arquebuses wouldn't be half as effective in this weather; the fuses would take forever to light. Both sides had been largely reduced to brutal, primitive, and familiar weapons—swords, arrows, and spears.

The winner today would be determined by sheer tactical proficiency. And Rin, despite herself, couldn't wait to see what Nezha had come up with.

The sun crept higher in the sky. Rin's troops were awake, armed, and ready, but there was still no word from the sentries. They waited another hour in tense anticipation. Then, suddenly, the rain intensified from a loud patter to a violent roar.

It might have been an accident of nature, but Rin doubted it. The timing was too abrupt. Someone was hauling that rain down from the heavens.

"He's here." She stood up and waved to her officers. "Ready the columns."

Seconds later, her sentries caught on to what she already knew, and a series of horns resounded across the tombstones.

The Republican Army appeared at the other end of the ravine, fanning out beneath the Red Emperor's feet.

Rin scanned the front lines with her spyglass until she spotted Nezha marching at the fore. He was dressed in a strange hybrid fashion; his chest was clad in the familiar blue cloth and lamellar plating of the Dragon Army, but his arms and legs were wrapped in some armor made of overlapping metal plates. It looked obstructively heavy. His shoulders, usually so arrogantly squared, seemed to sag.

"What's that around his wrists?" Kitay asked.

Rin squinted into her spyglass. She could just barely make out golden circlets around both of Nezha's wrists. They served no function she could discern—they didn't seem a part of his armor, and she couldn't imagine how they might be used as weapons.

She shifted the spyglass down. Another pair of golden circlets was visible over his boots. "Did he have those in Arabak?"

"Not that I remember," Kitay said. "But I remember seeing these odd scars once, right around—"

"He's seen us," Rin said abruptly.

Nezha had taken out a spyglass, too. He was looking right back at them.

She was struck by the symmetry of the scene. They could have been a painting—two opposing factions lined under statues that may as well have been their patron gods. Tearza and the Red Emperor, Speerly against conqueror, the newest participants in a centuries-old conflict that had never died, but had only continued to reverberate through history.

Until now. Until one of them ended it, for better or for worse.

Nezha raised a hand.

Rin tensed. Blood roared in her ears; the familiar, addictive rush of adrenaline thrummed through her body.

So this was how it began. No pleasantries, no obligatory attempt at negotiation; just battle. Nezha brought his hand down and his troops began charging down the ravine, feet thundering against the mud.

Rin turned to Commander Miragha. "Send in the turtles."

Throughout Nikara history, the traditional way to deal with arrow fire had been sending in shielded front lines to absorb the blow. Dozens of guaranteed fatalities bought time for melee combatants to breach the enemy lines. But Rin didn't have the dozens of warm bodies to spare.

Enter the turtles. These were one of Kitay's recent inventions. Inspired by the thickly armored turtle boats in the Republican Fleet, he'd designed small cart-mounted vehicles that could survive heavy fire of almost any kind. He hadn't had the time nor resources to construct anything sophisticated, so he'd cobbled the turtles together from wooden tables, water-soaked cotton quilts, and scavenged plates of Hesperian armor that, combined, kept out most flying projectiles.

One by one they rolled out from behind the tombstones into the ravine. As if on cue, Nezha's archers launched their opening volleys, and arrows dotted the surfaces of the turtles until they looked like roving hedgehogs.

"They look so stupid," Rin muttered.

"Shut up," Kitay said. "They're working."

Republican missiles landed two lucky hits, launching turtles into the air like spinning balls of fire. Undaunted, the other armored vehicles barreled forward. A symphony of whistling sounds filled the air as the Southern Army returned the Republic's fire. This was largely for show—most of their projectiles skidded ineffectively off the Republic's metal shields—but the volleys forced the Republican artillery to duck, creating a reprieve for the advancing turtles. Venka's contingent, stationed with long-distance crossbows on a protruding ledge near the middle of the ravine, landed the most hits, picking off Nezha's cannon operators with well-placed bolts.

Over the din of the rain, Rin could just barely make out a distinct, low rumble echoing across the ravine. She bent low, placed her hand to the shuddering ground, and smiled.

Dulin was right on time.

They'd determined during training that he couldn't summon earthquakes outside a ten-yard radius, which meant he couldn't meaningfully affect fighting conditions inside the ravine unless they threw him into the melee. Rin couldn't keep him there for long. The turtles weren't invincible—half had been reduced to smoldering wrecks, obliterated by a concentrated round of missiles.

But Dulin didn't need to last the entire battle. He only needed to take out the Republic's upper-level artillery stations. He was so close now, even as his marked turtle vehicle stuttered to a halt, barraged by bolts and arrows.

Come on.

The cliffs began to vibrate. Rin tilted her spyglass up at the artillery stations. Stones slid like powder off the cliffside, cascading over one line of crossbows. The ledge shifted and collapsed, sending Republican troops tumbling dozens of feet into the ravine.

Nearly there, just finish it . . .

A rocket exploded right in front of Dulin's turtle, flipping the vehicle backward into the air.

Rin let out a wordless screech.

Kitay seized her arm. "It's fine, he's fine, look—"

He was right. The cliffs were still quaking, the artillery stations buried in rubble beneath. Dulin was still alive, still channeling the Tortoise. Three armored vehicles clustered protectively around the wreck of Dulin's turtle, shielding it from the next barrage of bullets. Through her spyglass, Rin saw Dulin climb out from beneath the overturned craft and limp toward the nearest turtle. Soldiers popped out of the hatch to drag him into the armored belly. Then the cart reversed course and started retreating back behind Rin's waiting infantry.

Nezha's troops didn't pursue him. Like everyone else, Nezha was preoccupied with the melee inside the ravine, which—as predicted—had now turned into an utter clusterfuck. No one could aim properly under the rain. Arrows forced off course by the weather buried themselves uselessly in the dirt or ricocheted off the ravine walls. Occasionally someone managed to keep a flame alight long enough to light a fuse, but the battlefield was now too muddled to land a clear hit. Cannonballs, mortar shells, and fire rockets hurtled haphazardly into allies and enemies alike. The silver lining was that Nezha's wheeled arquebuses had become useless, bogged down in thick mud, their range limited only to the midsection of the ravine.

The remaining four turtles continued their advance toward him, followed by a press of the Southern Army's infantry. They wouldn't get far. Nezha's front line was armed with halberds, extended straight outward in an impaling welcome.

But the turtles weren't intended to breach the lines. They only needed to get close enough to toss their pipe bombs. Each squadron had set out with a lit coal shielded inside an iron tin. Ten feet from Nezha's front lines, they lit the bomb fuses and tossed them out the carts' top hatches.

Several seconds passed. Rin tensed. Then Nezha's front lines blew apart like ripped paper, and Rin's infantry surged through.

The battle had now turned into a conventional bloodbath. Swords, halberds, and shields clashed in a frenetic crush of bodies. It should have been a massacre—Nezha's troops were better trained and better armed—but the rain and mud had made it impossible for anyone to see, which allowed Rin's peasant infantry to last much longer than they should have.

But they didn't need to last forever. Just long enough.

Rin felt a sudden, bizarre sense of detachment as she watched the carnage playing out from the far side of the ravine. *None of this seems real.* Yes, she knew the costs were real—she knew that below her feet, real bodies were bleeding and breaking as a consequence of orders she'd given, that real lives were being snuffed out in the rain while she waited out the timetable of her plan.

But the adrenaline, that mad rush of energy that accompanied the irrepressible fear of death, was missing. Here she stood, watching from an angle so safe that Kitay was standing right next to her. None of those missiles could reach her. None of those swords could touch her. Her only true opponent was Nezha, and he hadn't entered the fray, either. Like her, he waited from his vantage point, calmly observing the chaos playing out below.

This wasn't really a fight. This wasn't one of those bare-knuckled, bruising scuffles they'd been so fond of at school. This battle was, at its core, a contest of their ideas. Nezha had gambled on the environment—the rain and ravine. Rin had placed her hopes on wild, distracting gambits.

They'd learn soon who had placed the better bet.

An arrow thudded into the ground ten feet away. Rin glanced down, jerked from her reverie. The arrow shaft was wrapped with red ribbon—Venka's signal: *Your turn.*

Kitay noticed it, too.

"Turtle's ready behind the third column," he said, lowering his spyglass. "Quickly, before he notices."

Rin sprinted down into the ravine. A last turtle cart awaited her near the front lines, already manned by waiting troops. They grasped her by the arms and hauled her into the center of the cart, where she crouched down, arms folded over her knees. Two soldiers set off at a run, pushing the cart downhill until it gained momentum.

Rin braced herself in the cramped, dark interior, jolting from side to side as the cart careened over bumpy terrain. She heard loud thuds as arrows assailed the sides of the cart. The tip of a spear slammed through the wall in front of her, wedged between a chink in the armor plating.

She hugged her knees tighter. *Almost there.*

Everything up until now—Dulin's avalanches, the initial charge of turtle carts, the pipe bombs, and the infantry rush—had been a distraction. Rin knew she couldn't win a battle of attrition against Nezha's ranks; she'd just put up the front of trying.

Nezha had chosen this graveyard, in this weather, to neutralize the Phoenix. The bloodbath happening below only mattered because the rain kept Rin from igniting everyone in a blue uniform.

But what did you do when nature presented your greatest disadvantage?

How did you shut out nature itself?

The turtle cart jerked to a halt. Rin peeked out through the top hatch. When she squinted, she could just make out thin black ropes stretched taut over the top of the ravine, and a massive tarp meant for a battleship slowly unfurling from one side of the cliffs to the other.

Her troops, who knew to watch for the tarp's unfolding, were already retreating, shields locked behind them. The Republican soldiers seemed confused. Some half-heartedly gave chase, and some fell back, as if sensing some impending disaster.

Within seconds, the tarp reached the other end of the pass, secured from both sides by Venka's squadrons. Rain hammered hard against the canvas, but nothing penetrated the pass. Suddenly the middle patch of the ravine was gloriously, miraculously dry.

Rin climbed out of the turtle and reached into her mind for the waiting god. *Your turn.*

The Phoenix surged forth, warm and familiar. *Finally.*

She flung her arms up. Flames burst into the pass, a crescent arc roaring outward at Nezha's forces.

His front lines charred instantly. She advanced unobstructed, picking her way over bodies sizzling black under glowing armor. Her flames shimmered around her, forming a shield of unimaginable heat. Arrows disintegrated in the air before they reached her. Nezha's mounted arquebuses and cannons glowed bright, twisting and crumpling beyond use. The Southern Army advanced behind her, bowstrings taut, cannons loaded, fire lances aimed forward and ready to launch.

She only had minutes. She kept her fire concentrated low inside the ravine, but at this heat, the tarp would burn from sheer proximity, which meant she had to end this fast.

She could make out Nezha's figure through the wall of orange—alone and unguarded, shouting orders to his men as they fled. He had not retreated ahead of his troops; he was waiting until the last of his ranks reached safe ground. He'd refused to abandon his army.

Always so noble. Always so stupid.

She had him. She'd won this game of ideas, she had him in sight and in range, and this time she would not falter.

"*Nezha!*" she screamed.

She wanted to see his face.

He turned around. They stood close enough now that she could make out every detail on his lovely, wretched, cracked-porcelain face. His expression twisted as he met her eyes—not in fear, but in a wary, exhausted sorrow.

Did he realize he was about to die?

In her daydreams, whenever she'd fantasized about the moment that she would truly, finally kill him, he had always burned. But he stood just out of range of the tarp, so iron and steel would have to do. And if his body still kept stitching itself together, then she would take him apart piece by piece and burn them down to ash until not even the Dragon could put him back together.

She nodded to her waiting army, signaled with a hand. "Fire."

She pulled her flames back inside her and knelt. A great rip echoed through the ravine as projectiles of every type surged over her head.

Nezha raised his arms. The air rippled around him, then appeared to coalesce. Time diluted; arrows, missiles, and cannonballs hung arrested in midair, unable to budge forward. It took Rin a moment to realize that the projectiles had been trapped inside a barrier—a wall of clear water.

Again, she slashed a hand through the air. "Fire!"

Another volley of arrows shrieked over the ravine, but she knew before she even gave the command that it would make no difference. Nezha's shield held firm. Her troops shot another round, then another, but everything they hurled at Nezha was swallowed into the barrier.

Fuck. Rin wanted to scream. *We're just dumping weapons into the river.*

She'd known he could control the rain. She'd watched him do it at Tikany—had felt it pummeling against her like a thousand fists as he called it down harder and harder. But she hadn't known he could manipulate it at such a massive scale, that he could pull all the water out of the sky to construct barriers more impenetrable than steel.

She hadn't imagined his link to his god might now rival her own.

Nezha used to fear the Dragon more than he feared his enemies. He used to call his god only when forced to with his back against the wall, and every time he'd done so, it had looked like torture.

But now, he and the water moved like one.

This means nothing, she thought. Nezha could erect all the shields he wanted. She'd simply evaporate them.

"Get back," she ordered her troops. Once they'd retreated ten yards she pulled another parabola of flame into the ravine and brought its heat to the highest possible intensity, sinking deeper and deeper into the Phoenix's reverie until her world turned red. Heat baked the air. Above, the tarp sizzled and dissipated to ash.

Rin pushed the parabola forward. Two walls met at the center of the pass—blue and red, Phoenix and Dragon. Any normal body of water should have long since dissipated. This divine heat could have evaporated a lake.

Still the barrier held firm.

Burn, Rin prayed frantically. *What are you doing, burn—*

The Phoenix stunned her with a reply. *The Dragon is too strong. We can't.*

Her flames shrank back into her body. Rin glared at Nezha through the water. He grinned back, smug. His army had completed their retreat. Her troops could still pursue them overland, but how would they get past Nezha?

Then it all struck Rin with devastating clarity.

Nezha had never intended to make a stand at Xuzhou. Sending his men to the ravine had been a ploy, an opportunity to find out the extent of Rin's new capabilities, both shamanic and conventional, with minimal loss of his own forces. He hadn't come to fight, he'd come to embarrass her.

He'd pitted his god against hers. And he'd *won*.

Nezha lowered his arms. The barrier crashed down, splashing hard against the rocks. The clouds resumed their heavy downpour. Rin spat out a mouthful of water, face burning.

Nezha gave her a small, taunting wave.

He was alone, but Rin knew better than to pursue. She knew the threat on his mind, could predict exactly what he would do if her troops surged forward.

Just try. See what the rain does then.

Though it felt like ripping her heart out to say it, she turned back to the Southern Army and gave the only order she could. "Fall back."

They hesitated, their eyes darting confusedly to the clearly vulnerable Nezha.

"*Fall back*," she snapped.

This time they obeyed. Sparks of humiliated rage poured off her shoulders as she followed them in retreat, steaming the water from her armor in a thick, choking mist. *Fuck.*

She'd had him.

She'd *had* him.

She hadn't felt this sort of petty rage, this sheer *indignation*, since Sinegard. This wasn't about troops, this was about pride. In that moment they were schoolchildren again, pummeling each other in the ring, and he'd just laughed in her face.

CHAPTER 28

"What just happened?" Cholang demanded. "What *was* that?"

"He's got a god." Rin paced back and forth before the general staff, cheeks flushed with humiliation. They were supposed to be celebrating. She'd promised them resounding victory, not this embarrassing stalemate. "The Dragon of Arlong, the ruler of the seas. I've never seen him pull rain into a shield like that. He must have gotten stronger. Must have—must have practiced."

She kept her voice low so it wouldn't carry. Outside the tent, the Southern Army waited in baffled suspense, their disappointment tinged with a mounting fear.

She knew whispers about Nezha were spreading throughout the troops. *The gods favor the Young Marshal*, they said. *The Republic called down the heavens, and they've granted them a power to rival our own.*

"Then why are we just sitting around?" Venka asked. "We were thrashing them, we should have given chase—"

"If we give chase, we'll drown," Rin snapped.

Xuzhou lay only miles north of the Western Murui. Any follow-up strike would be futile. Nezha had certainly positioned himself along the riverbanks, and as soon as their troops attempted a crossing he'd wrap the rapids around them like a fist and drag them to the Murui's muddy depths.

Rin remembered vividly how it felt to drown. But this time Nezha wouldn't save her. This time, he might pull her to the bottom of the river himself, holding her still as she thrashed until her lungs collapsed.

I can't beat him.

She had to face that stark, immutable fact. The Phoenix had made that abundantly clear. Right now she could not engage Nezha one-on-one and win. It didn't matter how many soldiers she had; it didn't matter that she now controlled twice as much territory as he did. If they met again on the battlefield, he could easily kill her in a thousand different ways, because in the end, the sea and its dark, swallowing depths would always conquer fire.

And she knew Nezha would only get stronger the closer she marched to Arlong. He'd created a shield thick enough to ward off bullets with mere rainwater. It terrified her to imagine what he might do in a river so vast it looked like an ocean.

Days ago, she'd held every strategic advantage. How had her momentum vanished so abruptly?

If the entire leadership weren't watching her, she would have screamed.

"There's no way around this," Kitay said quietly. "We've got to heed Chaghan's advice. Back to the original plan."

Rin met his eyes. Silent understanding sparked between them, and instantly the pieces of the obvious, inevitable strategy fell into place.

It terrified her. But they had no other choice. They had only one path forward, and now it was a matter of working through the logistics.

"We'll have to stick to land routes as long as we can," she said.

"Right," he said. "Get over the river. Head straight down the mountains to the capital."

"And when we've reached the Red Cliffs—"

"We'll find the grotto. Kill it at the source."

Yes. This was it. She'd been stupid to think that she might win this campaign without touching Arlong, when that was the locus of power all along.

Nezha fell if Arlong fell. Nezha died if the Dragon died. Nothing short of that would do.

"I don't understand." Venka glanced between them. "What are we trying to do?"

"We're going to the Nine Curves Grotto," Rin breathed. "And we're going to kill a dragon."

Rin ordered everyone out of the tent but Kitay.

They both knew, without saying it out loud, that what came next had to be delicately and discreetly planned. There were many roads to Arlong, but only one route that got her army there intact. Altan had once taught her that amateurs obsessed over strategy, and professionals obsessed over logistics. The logistics involved now meant the difference between dozens of casualties and thousands, and they could not be leaked.

Rin waited until the footsteps outside the tent had faded into silence to speak. "You know what we've got to do."

Kitay nodded. "You want a decoy."

"I'm thinking several. All pursuing separate crossings, with no knowledge of the other crossings, just the rendezvous point."

That was the only way this could work. Nezha controlled the entire river, which meant he had every advantage except one. He didn't know where or how Rin would cross it.

Meanwhile, Rin's problem was how to move a large column over the river at a point that Nezha wouldn't anticipate. She wasn't working with a fast, tiny strike force anymore; she couldn't pull off the kind of surprise ambushes she used to.

Moreover, she had to assume Nezha had spies within her ranks. Perhaps not in her inner circle, but certainly from the officer ranks down. That was inevitable in war—she had to plan every operation with the assumption that something would be leaked. The question was whether she could limit how much they knew. If she could trust Cholang and Venka, then she could break up a plan into pieces to give her generals limited, but sufficient, information.

"We split this army into seven parts," she said. "Nezha could get lucky with a random pick if we split into just two or three. Seven makes guessing much harder."

"The consequence, of course, is that you send at least a seventh of your army to certain death," said Kitay.

She paused, then nodded. They'd have to stomach that. They had to accept that they wouldn't only lose troops—they'd lose good officers, too, because a clear imbalance in power distribution would appear all too suspicious.

There was no way around it. They had to absorb the risk, and hope that the other six squadrons made it across to rendezvous outside Arlong.

"Let's assume the worst," Kitay continued. "Assume Nezha realizes we've got to set up decoys, and he splits his forces accordingly. Suppose you end up with only three squadrons at the rendezvous. How do you distribute those along Arlong's forces?"

"We don't have to conquer Arlong," Rin said. "We just have to poison the grotto. And you don't need six squadrons for that, you just need one."

"Fine." He nodded grimly. "So let's figure out how to get the one."

For the next three hours they hashed out an itinerary over the most detailed maps they could find. One squadron, led by Venka, would cross over the Sage's Ford. That was where Nezha would expect them to go—it was the shallowest crossing, the one that didn't involve bridge-building equipment. But the obviousness of that strategy, combined with the fact that Rin was visibly absent, should be enough to deter Nezha from striking hardest at Venka. They would dispatch three other squadrons to wide bridges, and one to a narrow ford crossing, and one to a stretch along the Murui where there was no crossing at all.

During the long march, Kitay had come up with an ingenious

design for a self-supporting bridge that could be assembled in minutes from portable wooden crossbeams. They hadn't used it in the mountains for want of lumber, but now they had plenty. If the bridge didn't exist, they'd build it.

"And where do we cross?" Kitay asked.

"Anywhere." Rin nudged the pieces. "Does it matter? It's a one-in-seven chance no matter where we go."

He shook his head. "One in seven is too high. There must be some way to reduce it to zero."

"There's not." She understood his urge for perfectionism, knew he'd be anxious unless he resolved every last variable, but she also knew better than to underestimate Nezha a second time. They could make their chances pretty good by avoiding the bulk of the Republican defense line, assuming their intelligence was accurate, but otherwise one in seven would have to be good enough.

"We'll take the narrow bridge at Nüwa's Waist," she decided. "Our squadron won't have to move any heavy artillery, so the width constraints won't matter."

"Then how do you want to cross?" he asked.

"What are you talking about? There's a bridge."

"But suppose they blow up the bridge in advance," he said. "Or suppose they've got soldiers stationed all around it. How do we get around that?"

These questions were rhetorical, Rin realized. Kitay leaned back, watching her with a familiar, anticipatory grin.

"You are not sending me up in a kite," she said.

He beamed. "I'm thinking something bigger."

"No," she said immediately. "You've never gotten that thing up in the air. And I'm not dying in a Hesperian death trap."

His grin widened. "Come on, Rin. Trust me. I gave you wings once."

"Yes, and that's how I got this scar!"

He reached over and patted her on the shoulder. "Then it's a good thing you've never cared much about looking pretty."

∞

Six squadrons dispersed the next morning to designated crossing points spread out over a ten-mile radius. Most had a good chance of making it across. Kitay had sent crews out to decoy crossing points the night before to chop haphazardly at nearby bamboo groves. Bamboo made good material for temporary bridges or fording walkways. Nezha's scouts would see the cut forests and, hopefully, anticipate bridge crossings that would never happen.

Rin, Dulin, and Pipaji, accompanied by just enough troops to drag the dirigible along in three carts, headed straight south.

Five miles from their camp outside Xuzhou was a shallow stretch of river called Nüwa's Waist, named for the way it curved sharply to the east. The bridge had indeed been dismantled, but the water there was only about knee-deep. Despite the swollen, monsoon-drenched rapids, well-prepared troops with flotation bags could wade across without being swept away.

It was a boring plan. Good enough not to arouse suspicion, but also not optimal. They weren't going to take it.

They detached from a decoy crew at Nüwa's Waist and continued marching two miles farther south, where the river was wider and faster. Earlier that morning, Kitay had dismantled his dirigible and loaded the parts into three wagons. They spent two hours on the riverbanks reconstructing it according to his careful instructions. Rin felt every second ticking by like an internal clock as they worked, nervously watching the opposite bank for Republican troops. But Kitay took his sweet time, fiddling with every bolt and yanking at every rope until he was satisfied.

"All right." He stood back, dusting the oil off his hands. "Safe enough. Everyone in."

The shamans stood back, staring at the basket with considerable hesitation.

"There's no way that thing actually flies," Dulin muttered.

"Of course they fly," Pipaji said. "You've seen them fly."

"I've seen the *good* ones fly," Dulin pointed out. "That thing's a fucking mess."

Rin had to admit Kitay's repairs did not give her much confidence. The airship's original balloon had ripped badly in the explosion at Tianshan. He'd patched it up with cowhide so that, fully inflated, it looked like a hideous, half-flayed animal.

"Hurry up," Kitay said, annoyed.

Rin swallowed her doubts and stepped into the basket. "Come on, kids. It's a short trip."

They didn't need a smooth, seamless flight. They just needed to get up in the air. If they crashed, at least they'd crash on the other side.

Reluctantly, Pipaji and Dulin followed. Kitay took a seat in the steering chamber and yanked at several levers. The engine roared to life, then maintained a deafening, ground-shaking hum. From a distance, the engine noise had always sounded like bees. Up close, Rin didn't hear the drone so much as she *felt* it, vibrating through every bone in her body.

Kitay twisted around, waved his hands over his head, and mouthed, *Hold on.*

The balloon inflated with a whoosh above their heads. The carriage tilted hard to the right, lurched off the ground, then wobbled in the air as Kitay worked frantically to stabilize their flight. Rin clutched the handrail and tried not to vomit.

"We're fine!" Kitay shouted over the engine.

"Guys?" Pipaji pointed over the side of the carriage. "We've got company."

Something shot past her head as she spoke. The rope by her arm snapped, ends frayed by an invisible arrow. Pipaji flinched back, shrieking.

"Get down," Rin ordered. That was redundant—everyone had already dropped to the carriage floor, arms over their heads as bullets whizzed above them.

Rin crawled to the far edge of the basket and pressed her eye against a slit in the carriage. She saw a mass of blue uniforms racing toward the riverbanks, arquebuses pointed to the sky.

Fuck. Nezha must have deployed troops along every stretch of the river once he'd realized the Southern Army had split into parts. And their aircraft was now visible from miles off, a clear target hanging plump in the air.

Another round of fire rocked the basket. Someone screamed in pain. Rin glanced over her shoulder to see one of her soldiers clutching his leg, his foot a bloody mess below the ankle.

"Use the cannons!" Kitay shouted, wrestling at the levers. He was managing to steer, but badly—the dirigible veered sharply east, wrenching them closer to both the opposite shore and the ambush. "They're loaded!"

"I don't know how!" Rin screamed back. But she ducked down beside him and fumbled at the cannons regardless. *Ingenious*, she thought, dazed. The handles let her swerve the gun mouths nearly 360 degrees, aiming at anything except herself.

Squinting, she aimed one cannon as best she could toward the ground platoon and funneled a stream of fire into the barrel.

The blowback flung her against the wall of the carriage. She scrambled to her knees, clambered forth, and grabbed the handle of the second cannon. Same process. This time she knew to drop down before the blowback could hit her. She couldn't see the fallout, not from where she was crouched, but the ensuing crash and screams promised good results.

The carriage lurched to the left. Rin careened into Kitay's side.

"The balloon," Kitay gasped. He'd given up with the levers. "They've pierced it, we're falling—"

She opened her mouth to respond just as they tilted again, veering hard in the other direction.

"Get out," Kitay said sharply.

She understood. Together they scrambled out of the steering chamber into the main carriage. They had no hope of flying this thing anymore; they just had to hold steady until they got near enough to the ground. Closer, *closer*—

Rin jumped from the basket, landing knees bent, hoping to distribute the impact across her body. It didn't work. Pain shocked through both her ankles, so intense that she doubled over for several seconds, screaming wordlessly, before she caught a grip on herself. "Kitay—"

"Right here." He clambered to his knees, coughing. Scorch marks streaked through his wiry hair. He pointed at something behind her. "Take care of—"

Rin reached out with her palm. Fire exploded out, arced around them in a parabola, and pushed forth twenty, then thirty yards. Rin forced as much fury as she could into that inferno, made it wickedly, devastatingly hot. If anyone in the Republican ambush had survived the airship cannons, they were ashes now.

"Enough." Kitay put a hand on her arm. "That's enough."

Rin called the flame back in.

Pipaji and Dulin climbed out of the basket, coughing. Pipaji moved with a limp, hopping along with her arm slung over Dulin's shoulder, but neither looked seriously wounded. A handful of soldiers filtered out of the dirigible behind them.

Rin loosed a sigh of relief. They hadn't been too high up before they'd crashed. This could have been so much worse.

"General?" Pipaji pointed at the wreck behind her. "There—there's someone..."

Only one of the soldiers hadn't made it out. He lay pinned under the side of the engine. He was still conscious—he groaned, face twisting in anguish. His legs were a ruin under the mass of warped steel.

Rin recognized him. He was one of Qinen's friends, one of the young, stubble-chinned men who had unhesitatingly followed her all the way from Leiyang to Mount Tianshan.

Ashamed, she realized she couldn't remember his name.

Together the soldiers strained against the side of the carriage, but nobody could move it. And what was the point? It had crushed more than half of the soldier's body. Rin could see fragments of his hip bone littered across the scorched earth. They couldn't possibly get him to Lianhua in time. There was no recovery from this.

"Please," said the soldier.

"I understand," Rin said, and knelt down to slit his throat.

Once she would have hesitated; now she didn't even blink. His agony was so obvious, and death so necessary. She jerked her knife through his jugular, waited several seconds for the blood to run its course, then pulled the soldier's eyes shut.

She stood up. Dulin's eyes were huge. Pipaji had a hand clamped over her mouth.

"Let's go," Rin said curtly. "Time to kill a dragon."

CHAPTER 29

From the wreckage of the dirigible, it was a quick three-mile march through the mountainside to the edge of the cliffs that sealed in Arlong like an oyster shell. When at last they pushed through the wall of thick forest, the great, wide Murui river lay on their horizon, stretching on without end as if it were the ocean. Before them lay Arlong's famous Red Cliffs, glinting in the noon sun like freshly spilled blood.

Rin halted at the ledge, searching the opposite wall until she found a string of characters, carved at a slant into the rock face so that they were only visible when the light caught them just so.

Nothing lasts.

Those were the famous words, written in near-indecipherable Old Nikara, carved into the Red Cliffs by the last minister loyal to the Red Emperor just before his enemies stormed the capital and hung his flayed body above the palace doors.

Nothing lasts. The world does not exist. Nezha and Kitay had come up with those conflicting translations. They were both wrong, and they were both right. Their translations were two sides of the same truth—that the universe was a waking dream, a fragile and mutable thing, a blur of colors shaped by the unpredictable whims of divinity.

The last time Rin had been here, a year that felt like a lifetime ago, she'd been blinded by loyalty and love. She'd been soaring between these cliffs on wings borne by fire, fighting on Yin Vaisra's behalf for a Republic founded on a lie. She'd been fighting to save Nezha's life.

Past the narrow channel, she could just barely make out the silhouette of the capital city. She fished her spyglass from her pocket and examined the city perimeter for a moment, until she glimpsed movement near each of its gates—her squadrons, moving in like chess pieces falling neatly into formation. From what she could see, at least four of the decoys had made it past the Murui. Venka's column, to her relief, was among them—as Rin watched, they marched steadily down the slopes from the northeast. She saw no sign of the last two squadrons, but she couldn't worry about that now. In minutes, the ground invasion of Arlong would commence.

That part of the assault was just noise. The four columns encircling Arlong were armed with the flashiest projectiles in their arsenal—double-mounted missiles, massive short-range cannons, and repurposed firecrackers stuffed with shrapnel. These were meant to capture Nezha's attention, to fool him into thinking the overground assault was a more significant effort than it was. Rin knew, based purely on the numbers, that she couldn't win a sustained ground battle, nor a protracted siege. Not when Nezha had been laying his defenses for weeks; not when all the Republic's last tricks and weapons lay hidden behind those walls.

But they didn't have to win, they only had to make a racket.

"Good luck," Kitay said. He would stay behind atop the Red Cliffs—close enough to witness everything through his spyglass, but far enough that he'd remain well out of harm's way. He squeezed her wrist. "Don't do anything stupid."

"Stay safe," Rin responded.

She forced her voice to remain casual. Brusque. No time to get emotional now. They already knew this might fail; they'd said their goodbyes last night.

Kitay gave her a mocking salute. "Give Nezha my regards."

A round of cannon fire punctuated his words from across the channel. Venka's smoke signals flared bright against the gray sky. The final invasion had begun. While Arlong erupted in explosions, Rin and her shamans descended the cliffside to finish things once and for all.

Rin had been worried that the grotto might be difficult to find. All she had to go on were fragments remembered from one of the most painful conversations she'd ever had, echoing through her mind in Nezha's low, tortured voice. *There's a grotto about a mile out from the entrance to this channel, this underwater crystal cave.*

But once she was down in the shadow of the Red Cliffs, wading through the same shallows where Nezha and his siblings had played so long ago, she realized the path to the Dragon was obvious. Only one side of the channel was lined with cave mouths. And if she wanted to find the Dragon's lair, all she had to do was follow the jewels.

They lay embedded in the river floor, glinting and sparkling underneath the gentle waves. The treasures piled up higher the closer they drew to the caves—jade-studded goblets, gilded breastplates, sapphire necklaces, and golden circlets, littered against a dazzling array of silver ingots. Small wonder Nezha and his brother had once ventured foolhardily into the grotto. It wouldn't have mattered how many times they'd been warned to stay away. What small child could resist this allure?

Rin could sense she was close. She could feel the power emanating from the grotto; the air felt thick with energy, laced with a constant, inaudible crackle, so very similar to the atmosphere she'd felt on Mount Tianshan.

The boundary between the mortals and the divine here was extraordinarily thin.

Rin paused for a moment, struck with the oddest sense that she'd been here before.

Right outside the grotto's entrance, the jewels gave way to

bones. They were startlingly pretty, lighting up the water with their own faintly green luminescence. This was no product of rot and erosion. Someone—*something*—had constructed this pathway, had lovingly peeled the flesh off its collected corpses and arranged the bones in a neat, glowing invitation.

"Great Tortoise," Dulin muttered. "Let's just blow this whole place out of the water."

Rin shook her head. "We're too far out."

They hadn't even seen the Dragon. They needed to draw much closer—if they lit their missiles now, they'd only alert Nezha's sentries. "Hold your fire until we see it move."

She strode boldly forward, trying to ignore the ridged bones beneath her boots. She opened her palm as she passed into the dark interior, but her flames only illuminated a few feet into the cave. The darkness beyond seemed to swallow it whole. Rin traced her fingers along the ridges in the wall for something to guide her, then yanked her hand back when she realized what they were. Her stomach churned.

The walls were lined with faces—beautiful, symmetrical faces of every size and shape; of grown men and little girls; faces without hair, without eyes, and without expression. Rot had not touched the pristine, bloodless skin. These heads hung in a space carved outside of time, now and forever.

Rin shuddered.

The ocean likes to keep its treasures. The ocean doesn't destroy. The ocean collects.

Once upon a time, Nezha had walked hand-in-hand with his little brother toward this grotto. He'd ignored the countless warnings because Mingzha had begged so hard, and because Nezha could refuse Mingzha nothing. He hadn't known the danger, and no one had stopped him. Of course no one had stopped him—because Vaisra had let him go, had deliberately sent him in, because he'd known that one day, he'd need the monster that Nezha would become.

Rin realized now why the grotto felt so familiar. This wasn't like Mount Tianshan at all. The Heavenly Temple was a place of lightness, clarity, and air. This place bore a heavier history. This place was tainted with a mortal stain, was suffused with pain and sorrow, was a testament to what happened when mortals dared to wrestle with the gods.

She'd felt divinity like this only once before, an eternity ago, on the worst day of her life.

Right then, she could have been standing in the temple on Speer.

"General!"

A burst of shouts echoed from the cave mouth. Rin spun around. Her soldiers pointed across the river, where a small, sleek sampan flew over the water toward them. That speed couldn't be achieved with sails or paddle wheels.

Nezha was on that boat.

"Now," Rin ordered Dulin.

He knelt and pressed his hands against the grotto floor. Vibrations rolled under Rin's feet, echoing down the cave's unfathomable depths. Dust and water streamed from the cave roof, coating them all in dirt.

But the rumbling did not crescendo to an earth-shattering quake. The grotto's interior did not collapse.

"What are you doing?" Rin hissed. "Bury that thing."

A vein protruded from Dulin's temple. "I can't."

The sampan was already halfway across the river; it'd reach them in seconds. *Conventional means, then.* Rin nodded to her troops.

"Fire."

They obliged, hefting their rocket lances. They aimed; she sent a flame snaking out to light the fuses. Eight lances tipped with powerful explosives flew screeching into the cave mouth. She couldn't see how far they went, but a moment later, she heard a muffled boom and, beneath that, a low, rumbling groan that sounded almost human.

Then the river surged, and Nezha was upon them.

∞

Rin crouched, bracing for his opening strike. It didn't come.

Nezha stepped off the side of the sampan, moving as casually as if he'd just arrived for teatime. He'd come alone. His feet didn't sink when they touched the water, but trod flatly over the river's surface as if it were marble.

He didn't pull a shield around him as he drew closer. He didn't need to. He was confident here in his domain, protected by endless water on all sides. He could ward off any attack she might attempt without trying.

She knew very well she remained standing only because he was curious.

"Hello, Rin," he said. "What do you think you're doing here?"

"Why don't you ask yourself?" She nodded toward Arlong. "City's burning."

"I noticed. So why aren't you there?"

"Thought they could manage without me."

Her eyes flitted toward Pipaji, who stood hunched inconspicuously behind Dulin. Her eyes were closed, lips moving silently as she sank into a trance. A small black cloud formed around her ankles, gave a tentative pulse, then began to stretch toward Nezha like tendrils of smoke unfurling underwater.

Good girl. Rin just needed to buy her several seconds of time.

"Tell me," Nezha said. "What did you think you'd do, once you found the grotto?"

"I'd think of something," Rin said. "I always do."

Nezha hadn't even glanced at Pipaji. His eyes were locked on Rin's. He approached slowly, fingers stroking the hilt of his sword. *He's gloating*, Rin realized. He thought he'd blown her plan wide open. He thought he'd won.

He shouldn't be so careless.

The inky tendrils reached the water under Nezha's feet.

Rin sucked in a sharp breath.

Nezha flinched and stumbled backward. The poison followed

him, racing up his legs and under his clothes. Black lines emerged from beneath his collars and sleeves. Where they touched his golden circlets, they hissed.

Pipaji made an inhuman growling noise. Her eyes shone dark violet, and her mouth was twisted into a cruel sneer that Rin had never seen on her face.

"Shatter," she whispered.

But Nezha didn't fall. He was clearly in great pain—he convulsed where he stood, the lines of poison writhing around his body like a horde of black snakes. But his skin didn't wither; his limbs didn't rot and corrode. Pipaji's victims usually succumbed in seconds. But something under his skin repelled the dark streaks, repairing their corrosion.

Pipaji glanced down at her fingertips, puzzled, as if checking that they were still black.

Nezha stopped writhing. He straightened up, rubbing at his neck. The black had already faded from his skin.

"Ah, Rin." He sighed theatrically. "That would have worked, too. But you showed your hand too early."

He made a fist and brought it down in a savage slash. A column of water rose behind Pipaji and smashed her into the river. Pipaji, sputtering, tried to rise to her feet. But the water rose and fell, slamming her again and again to her knees.

Pipaji shrieked. The black in her fingers stretched up through her arms. More indigo clouds blossomed underwater, racing toward Nezha like sea creatures. Nezha made a cupping motion. The water beneath Pipaji's feet shot up, flinging her several feet back. This time she lay still. The dark streaks disappeared.

"That's the best you could come up with?" Nezha sneered. "You came after me with a *little girl*?"

Rin couldn't speak. Panic fogged her mind. There was nothing she could say, nothing she could do—even the Phoenix was terrified, reluctant to lend its flames, already anticipating a losing battle.

Nezha stretched his fingers toward Pipaji. Rin thought the girl had died—part of her *hoped* she'd just died—but Pipaji was alive and conscious, and she screamed as a mass of water lifted her up, encircled her waist, then crept up her shoulders.

"Stop!" she shrilled. "Stop, please, mercy—"

The river closed over her face. Her screams cut to nothing. Nezha raised his arm to the sky. Pipaji hung high over the river, suspended inside a towering column of water. She thrashed wildly, trying to swim her way out, but the water just bulged to accommodate her flailing. Dulin drew his sword and hacked wildly at the pillar like one might a tree, but Nezha twisted his fingers, and the water wrenched Dulin's blade from his grasp.

Pipaji's mouth contorted in desperation. Rin could read her lips. *Help me.*

Without another thought, Rin pulled fire into her hand and lunged.

Nezha flicked his wrist. A wave rose before her and crashed, knocking her flat on her back. Nezha sighed and shook his head.

"That's all?"

Horror squeezed her chest as she rose. So easy. This was *so easy* for him.

"Now you." Nezha directed a fist at the charging Dulin.

Dulin never stood a chance. Rin didn't see what Nezha did. She was still clambering to her feet, blinking water from her eyes. All she felt was a hard tug, like a temporary current, then a crash of water. When she finally straightened up, Dulin was gone.

"Here's the thing about the ocean." Nezha turned back toward Pipaji. "If you swim down deep enough, the pressure can kill you."

Ever so casually, he squeezed his fist. Pipaji's eyes bulged. Nezha made a throwing motion. The water pillar flung Pipaji to the side like a rag doll. She landed facedown, limp, in the shallows. She floated, but did not stir.

Rin rolled onto her side and sent a jet of fire roaring at Nezha's face. He waved a hand. Water shot up to diffuse the flames. But that bought Rin a few precious seconds, which she used to regain her footing, crouch, and leap.

She had to get him on the ground. Ranged attacks wouldn't work; his shields were too strong. Once again, her only hope was a blow at close quarters. For the briefest moment, as she barreled into his side, the gods didn't matter—it was only the two of them, mortal and human, rolling and twisting in the river. He kneed her in the thigh. She groped around his face, trying to gouge out his eyes. His hands found a grip around her neck and squeezed.

Water crashed over them and forced them down, holding them beneath the surface. Rin kicked and choked to no avail. Nezha's fingers tightened on her neck, thumbs crushing her larynx.

Help me. Rin cast her thoughts wildly toward the Phoenix. *Help me.*

She heard the god's reply like a muted, distant echo. *The Dragon is too strong. We cannot—*

She clung at their connection. *Yanked* at it. *I don't care.*

Heat surged through her veins. She forced her mouth onto Nezha's. Flames erupted underwater, and the river exploded around them. Nezha's grip broke loose. She saw bubbles roiling over his skin, searing pink marks across his face.

Rin broke the surface, gasping. The world seemed swathed in black fog. She sucked in several hoarse, deep breaths. Her vision cleared, and from the corner of her eye she saw Nezha standing up.

She crouched, flames sparking around her, ready for a second round.

But Nezha wasn't looking at her. He struggled upright, his clothes ripped and burned beneath his armor, his face shining red with quickly disappearing blisters. His eyes, wide with horror, were fixed on something behind her.

She turned.

Deep within the grotto, something moved.

Nezha gave a low moan of terror. "Rin, what have you *done?*"

She had no response. She was rooted to the floor with sheer terror, unable to do anything but watch in fascinated horror as the Dragon of Arlong emerged from its lair.

It moved slowly, ponderously. She struggled to take in its shape; it was so massive she couldn't grasp its outline, only the scale of it. When it reared its head, it cast them all—Rin, Nezha, and her troops—in its mountainous shadow.

Dragons in Nikara myth were elegant creatures, wise, sophisticated lords of rivers and rain. But the Dragon was nothing like the sleek cerulean serpents that hung in paintings around the palace in Arlong. It looked vaguely like a snake, thick and undulating, its dark, bulbous body ending in a ridged, bumpy head. It was the underbelly of the ocean come alive.

The Dragon collects pretty things. Was it because the sea absorbed anything it touched? Because it was so vast and so unfathomably dark that it sought whatever ornament it could find to give it shape?

The Dragon tilted its massive head and roared—a sound felt rather than heard, a vibration that seemed capable of shattering the world.

"Hold your ground," Rin told her troops, trying her best to keep her voice level. She wasn't scared. *She wasn't scared*—if she acknowledged she was scared, then she'd go to pieces. "Stay calm, aim for its eyes—"

The Dragon surged. To the troops' great credit, they never faltered. They held their weapons high and useless until the very end.

It was over in seconds. There was a flash of movement, a split second of screams, and then a rapid retreat. Rin didn't see its jaws move. All she saw were discarded weapons, red streaks spreading over the surface, and scraps of armor floating on the bobbing waves.

The Dragon reared back, its head cocked to the side, examining its remaining prey.

Nezha swept his arms up. The river surged into a barrier between him and the Dragon, a blue wall stretching nearly twenty feet into the sky. The Dragon moved like a flicking whip. Something huge and dark crashed through the water. The barrier dissolved, ripped through like a flimsy sheet of paper.

Let me, urged the Phoenix. Its voice rang louder in her mind than she'd ever heard it, momentarily drowning her own thoughts. *Give me control.*

Rin hesitated. An objection half formed. *Kitay—*

The boy will be no barrier, said the Phoenix. *If you will it.*

Rin's eyes flickered toward the Dragon. What choice did she have?

I will it.

The Phoenix took full rein. Flames poured from her eyes, nose, and mouth. The world exploded into red; she could perceive nothing else. She couldn't tell if Nezha was safe, or if he'd been burned alive by their mere proximity. She couldn't have stopped it if he was. She had no agency now, no control—she was not calling the fire; she was merely its conduit—a ragged, unresisting gate through which it roared into the material realm.

The Phoenix, racing free, howled.

She reeled, overwhelmed by the double vision of the spiritual plane layered onto the material world. She saw pulsing divine energies, vermilion red against cerulean blue. The river bubbled and steamed. Scalded fish bobbed to the surface. Something flashed in her mind, then the river and grottoes disappeared from her sight.

All she could see now was a vast black plain, and two forces darting and dueling within it.

She couldn't feel Kitay. In that moment, he seemed so distant that they might not have been anchored at all.

Hello again, little bird. The Dragon's voice was a rumbling groan, deep, yawning, and suffocating. It sounded how drowning felt. *You are persistent.*

The Phoenix lunged. The Dragon reared back.

Rin struggled to make sense of the colliding gods. She couldn't follow their duel; this battle was happening on planes far too complex for her mind to process. She could see only hints of it; great explosions of sound and color in unimaginable shades and registers as forces of fire and water tangled, two forces strong enough to bring down the world, each balanced only by the other.

How can you win? she thought frantically. The gods were not personalities; they were fundamental forces of creation, constituent elements of existence itself. What did it mean for one to conquer another?

Over the din, she thought she heard Nezha screaming.

Then the heat inside her crescendoed, burning so white-hot she was afraid she'd evaporated. The Phoenix seemed to have gained the upper hand—bursts of crimson dominated the spirit plane now, and Rin could vaguely make out a great funnel of fire surrounding the Dragon's dark form.

Had they done it? Had they *won*? Surely nothing, no man or god, could survive that onslaught. But when it was over—when her flames died away, when the material world reappeared in her vision, when her body became hers and she staggered and tripped in the shallow water, struggling to breathe, she saw that she was still in the great beast's shadow.

Her fire had done nothing to the Dragon at all.

The Phoenix was silent. Rin felt the god recede from her mind, a spot of heat fleeing like a dying star, growing colder and more distant until it was gone.

Then she was alone. Helpless.

The Dragon cocked its head, as if to ask, *What now?*

Rin tried to stand and failed. Her legs were logs in the water; they would not obey. She scooted back, numb fingers fighting to keep hold of her sword. But it was such a tiny, fragile thing. What scrap of metal could even scratch that creature?

The Dragon drew itself to its full height, darkening the entire river with its shadow. When it surged forth, all she could do was close her eyes.

She felt the impact later, an earth-shaking crash that left her ears ringing. But she wasn't dead. She wasn't even hurt. She opened her eyes, confused, then glanced up. A great shield of water stood above her. Beside her stood Nezha, hands stretched to the sky.

His mouth was moving. Several seconds passed before his shouts became audible through her ringing ears.

"—you fucking *idiot*—what were you—"

"I thought I could kill it," she murmured, still dazed. "I thought . . . I really thought—"

"Do you know what you've done?"

He nodded toward the city. Rin followed his gaze. Then she understood that the only reason that either of them was still alive was because the Dragon was preoccupied with a far greater prize.

Massive waves rose ponderously from the river and surged, unnaturally high and unnaturally slowly, down the channel. The gray clouds darkened, thickening within seconds into an impending storm. From this distance, Arlong looked so flimsy. A tiny sand castle, so fragile, so *temporary*, in the shadow of the risen depths.

"Help me up," Rin whispered. "I almost did it, I can try again—"

"You can't. You're too weak." Nezha spoke without inflection or spite. It wasn't an insult, it was simple fact. As he watched the dark form moving beneath the surface toward the city, his scarred face set in resolve. He dropped the water barrier—it was hardly necessary now—and began striding toward the Dragon.

Rin reached instinctively for his hand, then drew back, confused by herself. "What are you—"

"Keep down," he said. "And when you get the chance, run."

She was too stunned to do anything but nod. She couldn't get past how bizarre this was; how they had suddenly stopped trying to kill each other; how they were, of all things, fighting again on the same side. She couldn't fathom why Nezha had saved her. Nor could she understand the way her heart twisted as she watched him walk forth, arms spread and vulnerable, offering himself to the beast.

She remembered that stance. She remembered watching a long time ago as Altan walked toward a frothing Suni, unafraid and unarmed, speaking calmly as if chatting with an old friend. As if the god in Suni's mind, strange and capricious, would not dare to break his neck.

Nezha wasn't trying to fight the Dragon. He was trying to tame it.

"Mingzha." He shouted the word over and over, waving his arms to get the Dragon's attention.

It took Rin a moment to remember what that meant—Yin Mingzha, Nezha's little brother, the fourth heir to the House of Yin, and the first of Vaisra's sons to die.

The Dragon paused, then rose up out of the water, its head cocked back toward Nezha.

"Do you remember?" Nezha shouted. "You ate Mingzha. You were so hungry, you didn't keep him for your cave. But you wanted me. You've always wanted me, haven't you?"

Astonishingly, the Dragon lowered its head, dipping low until its eyes were level with Nezha's. Nezha reached out as if to stroke its nose. The Dragon did not stir. Rin clamped her hand over her mouth, terrified beyond words.

He looked so *small*.

"I'll go," Nezha said. "We'll go into that grotto. You don't have to be alone anymore. But you have to stop. Leave this city alone."

The Dragon remained very still. Then, ever so slowly, the waters began to recede.

The Dragon made a slight motion toward Nezha that seemed bizarrely affectionate. Rin stared, mouth agape, as Nezha pressed his hand against the Dragon's side.

I'll go.

With that one gesture, he'd prevented hundreds of thousands of deaths. He'd tamed a god that she'd woken, he'd prevented a massacre that would have been her fault, and he'd thrown her this victory.

"Nezha," she whispered, "what the *fuck*?"

Too late, she heard a faint and distinctive drone.

The aircraft emerged over the side of the cliff and dove, fast and low, straight over the grotto. It was much smaller than the bomber dirigibles that had pursued Rin through the mountains; its cockpit seemed large enough for only one person. Stranger still was its underbelly—extending from the bottom of its basket where its cannon should have been was a long, glinting wire that branched into several curved points like a reaching claw.

Rin glanced to Nezha. He stood stock-still, eyes wide in horror. But the Hesperians were his allies. What did he have to fear?

She pulled fire into her hand, deliberating whether to attack. Before, she wouldn't have hesitated. But if the dirigible had come to fight the Dragon . . .

The dirigible veered sharply toward her. *That answers that.* She aimed her palm at the cockpit. But before she could pull her fire forth, a thin line of lightning, lovely and absurd, arced through the blue sky. A second later, she saw a blinding white light. Then nothing.

She wasn't hurt. She felt no pain. She was still standing; she could hear and move and feel. Though her vision blurred for a moment, it returned after several blinks. But something had shifted about the world. It seemed, somehow, stripped of its life and luster—its colors were drained, blues and greens muted into shades of gray, and its sounds reduced to sandpapery scratches.

The Phoenix went quiet.

No—the Phoenix *disappeared.*

Rin strained in her mind, flailing desperately through the void to pull the god through Kitay's mind into hers, but she grasped at nothing. There was no void. There was no gate. The Pantheon was not drifting beyond her reach, it simply *wasn't there.*

Then she screamed.

She was in the Chuluu Korikh again. She was drowning in air, sealed and suffocating, imprisoned this time not in stone but in her own heavy, mortal body, pounding helplessly against the walls of her own mind, and that was such unbearable torture that she barely registered the lightning still coursing through her body, making her teeth chatter and singeing her hair.

You are nothing but an agent of Chaos. Sister Petra's voice rose unbidden to her mind—that cold, clinical voice speaking with assured confidence that until today had never seemed justified. *You are not shamans, you are the miserable and corrupted. And I will find a way to contain you.*

She'd found it.

Child. Rin heard the Phoenix's voice. Impossible. And yet the fire returned; a warm heat surged over her body, cradling her, protecting her.

The lightning now landed on Nezha.

He stood with his back to her, arms splayed out like he was being crucified, twitching and jerking as crackling brightness ricocheted across his body. Sparks arced back and forth from his golden circlets, which seemed to amplify the electricity before it burrowed deep into his flesh.

The bolts thickened, doubled, and intensified. Harsh, ragged sobs escaped Nezha's throat. The Dragon, too, seemed racked with pain. It was performing the oddest dance, head jerking and body writhing, flailing back and forth through the air in a way that would have been funny if it weren't so horrific.

Rin's mouth filled with bile.

Focus, child, the Phoenix urged. *Strike now.*

Rin's glance darted between the Dragon and the dirigible.

She knew she had one chance to attack—but which target? Nezha had saved her from the dirigible; the dirigible was saving her from the Dragon. Who was her enemy now?

She raised her left hand. The dirigible darted backward several yards, as if sensing her intentions. She opened her palm and aimed a thick stream of flame at its balloon, forcing it faster and higher, hoping desperately that she had the range.

A ripping noise shattered the sky. The dirigible balloon glowed orange for an instant, burst, then vanished. The basket hurtled toward the cliffs; the lightning disappeared.

Nezha crumpled.

Rin's first instinct was to rush toward him. She took two steps, then caught herself, utterly bewildered. Why would she help him? Because he'd just saved her? But that was his mistake, not hers—she shouldn't bother, she should just let him die—

Shouldn't she?

The water turned icy cold around her knees. She felt a wave of exhausted dread.

But the Dragon did not attack. Incredibly, it seemed frightened into submission. It turned its head toward the grotto and slithered back into the dark. Suddenly the air was not so heavy. The gray clouds disappeared, and sunlight was again visible against the glinting waves. Gravity took hold over the river once again, and the suspended waters dropped with a resounding crash.

I must get to shore.

The thought ran like a mantra several times through Rin's mind before it finally registered into action. Swaying and stumbling like a drunkard, she made her way to the riverbank. She felt detached, distant, as if someone else were clumsily controlling her body while her mind raced with questions.

What had just happened? What had Nezha just done? Was that a surrender?

Had she *won*?

But none of her dreams of victory had looked anything like this.

She heard a faint, pitiful gurgle. She turned. Pipaji lay farther down the sands, curled into a fetal position. Her face was barely above water; Rin didn't know how she hadn't drowned. But her narrow shoulders rose and fell, and her fingers scratched tiny, desperate patterns in the mud as she whimpered.

Rin hastened to her side.

"Oh, gods." She propped Pipaji up in her arms and slammed her fist against the girl's narrow back, trying to force the water from her lungs. "Pipaji? Can you hear me?"

Water dribbled from Pipaji's mouth—just a little trickle at first, and then her shoulders heaved and a stinking torrent of river water and bile spewed from her mouth. Pipaji gagged and slumped weakly against Rin's chest, breathing in shallow, desperate hitches.

"Hold on." Rin slung Pipaji's right arm around her shoulder

and pulled her to her feet. The positioning was awkward, but Pipaji was so thin and light that Rin found it surprisingly easy to drag them both forward, one step at a time. "Just hold on, you're going to be fine, we'll just get you to Lianhua."

They'd made it ten steps up the shore when Rin heard a vicious fit of coughing. She twisted her head over her shoulder. Nezha was doubled over on his knees in the shallows, shoulders heaving.

She halted.

He was only several yards away. He was so close she could make out every detail on his face—his chalk-white pallor, his red-rimmed eyes, the faded scars on porcelain-pale skin. She couldn't remember the last time they'd stood so close without trying to kill each other.

For a moment, they merely looked at each other, taking stock of one another, staring as if they were strangers.

Rin's gaze dropped to the golden circlets around his wrists. Her stomach twisted as she realized what they were. Not jewelry. Conductors. They hadn't attracted the lightning by accident. They'd been *designed* for it.

Then it dawned on her, what Nezha must have gone through in the year since she'd left Arlong. After Rin escaped, Petra had needed a shaman upon whom to experiment.

After the Cike were killed, that left only one in the Republic.

The skin around his wrists and ankles was badly discolored, mottled shades of bruised purple and angry red. The sight made her chest tighten. She'd seen Nezha's body stitch itself together from wounds that should have killed instantly. She'd seen his skin smooth itself over from burns that had turned it black. She'd thought the Dragon's powers could heal anything. But they couldn't heal this.

Rin had once been so absolutely sure the Pantheon constituted the whole of creation. That there was no higher power, and that the Hesperian religion, their Divine Architect, was nothing more than a convenient story.

Now she wasn't so sure.

Slowly, miserably, Nezha stood and wiped the back of his mouth with his hand. It came away bloody. "Is she alive?"

Rin was so bewildered that his words didn't process. Nezha nodded at Pipaji and repeated the question. "Is she alive?"

"I—I don't know," Rin said, startled into a response. "She—I'll try."

"I didn't want to . . ." Nezha coughed again. His chin glistened red. "It wasn't her fault."

Rin opened her mouth to respond, but nothing came out.

The problem wasn't that she had nothing to say. It was that she had too much, and she didn't know where to begin, because everything that came to mind seemed so utterly inadequate.

"You should have killed me," she said at last.

He gave her a long look. She couldn't read his face; what she thought she saw confused her. "But I never wanted you dead."

"Then *why?*"

Those two words weren't enough. Nothing she could think to say was enough. The gulf between them was too vast now, and the thousand questions on her mind all seemed too shallow, too frivolous to have the slightest chance of bridging it.

"Duty," he said. "You couldn't understand."

She had nothing to say to that.

He watched her in silence, his sword dangling uselessly at his side. His face spasmed, as if he, too, was struggling with thoughts he could never say out loud.

It would be so easy to kill him. He could barely stand. His god had just fled, shuddering from some greater power that she hadn't even known existed. If she'd carved him open right then, the wounds likely wouldn't heal.

But she couldn't make the flame come. That required rage, and she couldn't even summon the faintest memory of anger. She couldn't curse, or shout, or do any of the million things she'd imagined she might do if she had the chance to confront him like this.

How many chances, asked Altan, *are you going to throw away?*

At least one more, she thought, and ignored his jeering laughter.

If she could remember how to hate Nezha, she would have killed him. But instead, she turned her back and let him make his retreat while she made hers.

CHAPTER 30

Pipaji was dying.

Her condition deteriorated rapidly in the half hour it took for Rin to drag her toward her main forces in the city and flag down soldiers to find and fetch Lianhua. By the time Rin had her laid out on a dry tarp on the beach, her pulse had grown so faint that Rin almost thought she'd already died, until she lifted Pipaji's eyelids and saw her twitching eyeballs flickering dangerously between brown and black.

She'd tried giving the girl opium. She always kept a packet in her back pocket, and she'd started carrying double ever since she began sending the shamans into battle. It didn't work. Pipaji obediently inhaled the smoke, but her whimpering didn't stop, and the purple veins protruding grotesquely from her skin only grew thicker.

The god was taking control.

Great Tortoise. Rin stared down at Pipaji's white face, trying not to panic. Shamans who lost their minds to the gods couldn't be killed. They were trapped inside bodies turned divine, sentenced to live until the world stopped turning.

Rin couldn't sentence Pipaji to that.

But that meant she had to kill her, while her eyes were still flickering back to brown, while she still clung to a shred of mortality.

Rin reached a shaking hand toward Pipaji's throat.

"I have opium!" Lianhua shouted as she rushed down the beach. She halted over Pipaji, panting. "Do you—"

"I've tried it," Rin said. "Didn't work. She's losing it, she's on the edge—the pain's not helping, she's hurt on the inside, Nezha did something to her and I can't see but I think there's bleeding on the inside and I need you to—*don't touch.*"

Lianhua, now kneeling over Pipaji, jerked her hands back.

"Touch her over her clothes," Rin said. "And watch the sand. Be careful. She's not in control."

Lianhua nodded. To her great credit she didn't seem afraid, just focused. She exhaled, closed her eyes, and spread her fingers over Pipaji's torso. A soft glow illuminated Pipaji's drenched uniform.

Pipaji's eyelids fluttered. Rin held her breath.

Maybe this wasn't the end. Maybe the pain was the only problem; maybe she'd come back to them.

"Pipaji? *Pipaji!*"

Rin glanced up and cursed under her breath. The little sister—Jiuto—was racing down the beach, screaming.

Who had let her out here? Rin could have throttled someone.

"Get back." As Jiuto approached, Rin whipped out an arm to bar her from her sister. Jiuto was tiny, but she was scared and hysterical; she wriggled ferociously from Rin's grasp and dropped to her knees beside her sister.

"Don't—" Rin shouted.

But Jiuto had already pushed Lianhua aside. She flung herself over her sister, sobbing. "Pipaji!"

Just as Rin and Lianhua reached to drag Jiuto away, Pipaji lifted her head. "Don't."

Her eyes shot open. They were their normal, lovely brown.

Rin hesitated, left hand clutching the neck of Jiuto's shirt.

"It's okay." Pipaji reached her arms up, stroking her sister's hair. "Jiuto, calm down. I'm okay."

Jiuto's sobs instantly subsided to frightened hiccups. Pipaji rubbed her hand in circles against her sister's back, whispering a stream of comfort into her ear.

Rin shot Lianhua a glance. "Is she—"

Lianhua sat frozen, hands outstretched. "I'm not sure. I fixed the rib, but the rest—I mean, there's something . . ."

Pipaji met Rin's gaze over Jiuto's shoulder. Her face was pinched in discomfort. "They're so loud."

Rin's heart sank. "Who's being loud?"

"They're screaming," Pipaji murmured. Her eyes darkened. "They're so . . . oh."

"Focus on us," Rin said urgently. "On your sister—"

"I can't." Pipaji's hands, still wrapped around Jiuto's shoulders, started to twitch. They curved into claws, scratching at the air. "She's *in* there, she's . . ."

"Get her away," Rin ordered Lianhua.

Lianhua understood immediately. She wrapped her arms around Jiuto's waist and pulled. Jiuto struggled, wailing, but Lianhua didn't let go. She dragged Jiuto away from the beach and up toward the forest, until finally Jiuto's wails faded into the distance.

"Stay with me," Rin told Pipaji. "Pipaji, *listen to my voice*—"

Pipaji didn't respond.

Rin didn't know what to do. She wanted to wrap her arms around Pipaji and comfort her, but she was afraid to touch. A great purple cloud blossomed around Pipaji's collarbones, stretching up to her neck, turning her entire visage a bright, smooth violet. Pipaji's back arched. She choked wordlessly, struggling against some invisible force.

Rin skirted backward, suddenly terrified.

Pipaji turned her head toward Rin. The movement looked horrifically unnatural, as if her limbs were being yanked this way and that by unseen puppet strings.

"Please," she said. Her eyes flickered the faintest brown. "While I'm here."

Rin held her gaze, stricken.

Death or the Chuluu Korikh. Five simple, devastating words. Rin had known them from the start. There were only two possible fates for the Cike: death or immurement. A commander made sure it was the first. *A commander culls.*

"I need you to focus." Rin spoke with a calm she did not feel. She could not relinquish her responsibility; she had to do this. At this point, it was a mercy. "You still have to fight it. You can't poison me."

"I won't," Pipaji whispered.

"Thank you." Rin reached out, cupped the side of Pipaji's head with her left hand, pressed one knee against Pipaji's shoulder for leverage, and wrenched.

The crack was louder than she'd expected. Rin shook out her fingers, focusing on the pain so she wouldn't have to look at Pipaji's glassy eyes. She'd never broken a neck before. She'd been taught the method in theory; she'd practiced plenty of times on dummies at Sinegard. But until now, she hadn't realized how much force it really took to make a spine snap.

Then it was over.

Rin entered the city on foot. No one announced her presence; no musicians or dancers followed in her wake. Barely anyone noticed her; the city was too consumed with its own collapse. In her exhaustion, all she perceived was a great flurry of movement; of burned and bloody bodies carried into the city on stretchers; of crowds streaming out of Arlong's gates dragging along sacks spilling with clothing, heirlooms, and silver; of bodies packed in teetering hordes atop the remnants of Arlong's fleet, escaping in the few ships that hadn't been sunk in the Dragon's wrath.

Vaguely she understood that she had won.

Arlong was destroyed. The Hesperians had fled. Nezha and his government had made a hasty retreat out the channel. Rin learned these facts over the next hour, had them repeated to her over and over again by ecstatic officers, but she was drifting about in a fugue state, so tired and confused that she thought they were joking.

For how could this be called a victory?

She knew what victory felt like. Victory was when she scoured enemy troops from the field with a divine blaze, and her men rallied around her, screaming as they took back what was rightfully theirs. Victory felt deserved. *Just*.

But this felt like cheating—like her opponent had tripped and she'd been declared the winner by accident, which made this outcome a slippery, precarious thing, a victory that could be torn away at any time for any reason.

"I don't understand," she kept saying to Kitay. "What happened?"

"It's over," he told her. "The city's ours."

"But how?"

He responded patiently, the same way he had all afternoon. "The Dragon destroyed the city. And then you banished the Dragon."

"But I didn't do that." She gazed out at the flooded canals. "I didn't do anything."

All she'd done was poke a beast she couldn't handle. All she'd done was lie flat on her ass, scared out of her wits, while Nezha and a Hesperian pilot fought a battle of lightning that she didn't understand. She'd meddled in forces she couldn't control. She'd nearly sunk the entire city, nearly drowned every person in this valley, all because she'd thought she could wake the Dragon and win.

"Maybe he's seen what they're like," Kitay guessed, after she'd told him all that transpired in the river. It made absolutely no sense that Nezha would have just given up, had just retreated when he could have killed Rin and stopped the Dragon in one fell swoop. "The Hesperians, I mean. And maybe he doesn't want to let go of the only forces that can stop them."

"Seems like a belated realization," Rin muttered.

"Maybe it was self-preservation. Maybe things were getting worse."

"Maybe," she said, unconvinced. "What do you think he'll do now?"

"I don't know. But we've got a more pressing issue at hand." Kitay nodded to the palace gates. "We just deposed the ruler of half this country. Now you've got to present yourself as his replacement."

There were troops to address. Speeches to make. A city to occupy, and a country to claim.

Rin shuddered with exhaustion. She didn't feel like a ruler; she barely felt like the victor. She couldn't think of anything she wanted less right now than to face a crowd and pretend.

"Tomorrow," she said. "Give me today. There's something I have to do."

In Tikany there was a little graveyard hidden deep in the forest, concealed so well behind thickets of poplar trees and bamboo groves that the men never found it by accident. But every woman in Tikany knew its location. They'd visited it with their mothers, their mothers-in-law, their grandmothers, or their sisters. Or they'd made the trip alone, pale-faced and crying while they hugged their wretched loads to their chests.

It was the graveyard of babies. Infant girls smothered in ash at birth because their fathers only wanted sons. Little boys who'd died too early and left their mothers grief-stricken and terrified of being replaced by younger, more fertile wives. The messy products of miscarriages and late-term abortions.

Arlong, Rin assumed, had an equivalent. Every city needed a place to hide the shameful deaths of its children.

Venka knew where it was. "Half a mile past the evacuation cliffs," she said. "Turn north when you can see the channel. There's a footpath in the grass. Takes a while to see it, but once you've got it in sight, it'll take you all the way."

"Will you come with me?" Rin asked.

"You're fucking kidding me," Venka said. "I'm never going back there again."

So at sunset, Rin wrapped the jar containing Pipaji's ashes inside several layers of linen, shoved it in a bag, and set out for the cliffs with a shovel strapped to her back.

Venka was right—once she knew what she was looking for, the hidden path was clear as day. Nothing marked the graves, but the tall grass grew in curious whorls, twisting and spiraling as if avoiding the once-loved bones in the soil beneath.

Rin surveyed the clearing. How many bodies had been buried here, over how many decades? How far did she have to walk until her fingers wouldn't lodge into tiny bones when she pushed them into the dirt?

Her fingers kept trembling. She glanced around, made sure that she was alone, then sat down and pulled a pipe out of her pocket. She didn't take enough opium to knock herself unconscious—just enough to get her hand steady so she could firmly grip the shovel.

"It's not easy, is it?"

She saw Altan in the corner of her gaze, following her down the rows of unmarked graves. His shape lingered only if she looked elsewhere; if she focused where she thought he stood, he disappeared.

"They were like children," she said. "I didn't—I didn't want..."

"You never want to hurt them." Altan sounded gentler than she'd ever heard him—gentler than she'd ever permitted his memory to be. "But you have to. You have to put them through hell, because that's the only way anyone else will survive."

"I would have spared them if I could have."

For once, he didn't jeer. He just sounded sad. "Me too."

Finally she found a spot where the soil looked undisturbed and the grass grew straight. She put the linen-wrapped jar on the ground, clenched the shovel tight, and began to dig while Altan watched silently from the shade. Several long minutes trickled by. Despite the evening chill, sweat beaded on the back of her neck.

The ground was rocky and stiff, and the shovel kept wobbling out of her grasp. Eventually she found a perilous equilibrium, using her hand to guide the shovel and her foot to wedge it farther into the ground.

"I think I understand you now," she said after a long silence.

"Oh?" Altan cocked his head. "What do you understand?"

"Why you pushed me so hard. Why you hurt me. I wasn't a person to you, I was a weapon, and you needed me to work."

"You can still love your weapons," Altan said. "You can beat them into shape and then watch them destroy themselves and know that it was all fully necessary, but that doesn't mean you can't love them, too."

She didn't need to dig quite so long or so hard—nobody was ever going to come disturb these graves—but something about the difficult, repetitive motion soothed her, even as the ache in her shoulder grew worse and worse. It felt like penance.

At last, when the hole stretched so deep that the dying sunlight couldn't hit the bottom, when the soil went from brown and rocky to a soft and sludgy clay, she stopped and carefully lowered Pipaji's ashes into the grave.

She wished she could have buried Dulin, too. But she'd scoured the channel for hours, and she hadn't even been able to find a shred of his uniform.

"Does it ever get easier?" she asked.

"What? Sending people to their deaths?" Altan sighed. "You wish. It'll never stop hurting. They'll think that you don't care. That you're a ruthless monster in single-minded pursuit of victory. But you do care. You love your shamans like your own family, and a knife twists in your heart every time you watch one of them die. But you have to do it. You've got to make the choices no one else can. It's death or the Chuluu Korikh. Commanders cull."

"I didn't want it to be me," she said. "I'm not strong enough."

"No."

"It should have been you."

"It should have been me," he agreed. "But you're the one who got out. So see this through to the end, kid. That's the least you owe to the dead."

Kitay stood waiting for her at the bottom of the cliffs, holding a bundle of incense sticks in one hand and a jug of sorghum wine in the other.

"What's all this?" she asked.

"Qingmingjie," he said. "We have to keep vigil."

Qingmingjie. The Tomb-Sweeping Festival. The night when the hungry ghosts of the restless dead walked the world of the living and demanded their due. She'd seen others celebrating it in Tikany, but she'd never participated in the rituals herself. She'd never had anyone to mourn.

"That's not for two weeks," she said.

"That's not the point. We have to keep vigil."

"Do we have to?"

"Thousands of people died to win you this war. It wasn't just your shamans. It was soldiers whose names you never even learned. You're going to honor them. You're going to keep vigil."

She was so tired she almost simply walked away.

What did ritual matter? The dead couldn't hurt her. She wanted to be finished with them; she'd done enough penance today.

But then she saw the look on Kitay's face and knew she could not refuse him this. She followed him quietly down to the valley.

The field of corpses was so quiet at night that she might never have known a battle had been fought on these grounds. Mere hours ago it was a site of shouting, of detonations, of clashing steel and smoke. And now the show was over, the puppet strings were cut, and everyone lay in silent repose.

"It's so odd," she murmured. "I wasn't even here."

She hadn't commanded this battle. She hadn't witnessed how it had played out, didn't know which side breached first, didn't know how it would have gone if the Dragon had not raised the Murui. She'd been occupied with an entirely different fight, too busy in the realm of gods and lightning to remember that a conventional battle was even happening, until its aftermath was laid out before her eyes.

"What now?" she asked.

"I'm not sure." Kitay lifted the incense sticks half-heartedly, as if he'd just realized what an inconsequential gesture this was. They couldn't begin to count the bodies in the valley. All the incense in the world could not repay this sacrifice.

"In Tikany we burn paper," she said. "Paper money. Paper houses. Sometimes paper wives, if they were young men who died before they were married." She broke off. She didn't have a point. She was babbling, afraid of the silence.

"I don't think it's the paper that's important," Kitay said. "I think we just need to . . ."

His voice trailed away. His eyes widened, focused on something just over her shoulder. Too late she heard it as well, the crunch of footsteps over burned grass and bone.

When she turned, she saw only one silhouette against the dark.

Nezha had come alone. Unarmed.

He always looked so different in the moonlight. His skin shone paler, his features looked softer, resembling less the harsh visage of his father and more the lovely fragility of his mother. He looked younger. He looked like the boy she'd known at school.

Rin wondered briefly if he'd come back to die.

Kitay broke the silence. "We brought wine."

Nezha held out a hand. Kitay passed him the bottle as he approached. Nezha didn't bother to sniff for poison; he just tossed back a mouthful and swallowed hard.

That gesture confirmed the spell—the suspension of reality all three of them wanted. The unwritten rules hung in the air, reinforced by every passing moment that blood wasn't spilled. No one would lift a weapon. No one would fight or flee. Just this night, just this moment, they had entered a liminal space where their past and their future did not matter, where they could be the children they used to be.

Nezha held out a bundle of incense. "Do you have a light?"

Somehow they found themselves sitting in a silent triangle, shrouded in thick, scented smoke. The wine bottle lay between them, empty. Nezha had drunk almost all of it, Kitay the rest. Kitay had been the first to reach out with his fingers, and then all three of them were holding hands, Nezha and Rin on either side of Kitay, and it felt and looked absolutely, terribly wrong and still Rin never wanted to let go.

Was this how Daji, Jiang, and Riga had once felt? What were they like at the height of their empire? Did they love one another so fiercely, so desperately?

They must have. No matter how much they despised one another later, so much that they'd precipitated their own deaths, they must have loved one another once.

She tilted her face up at the low crimson moon. The dead were supposed to talk to the living on Qingmingjie. They were supposed to come through the moon like it was a door, transfixed by the fragrance of incense and the sound of firecrackers. But when she gazed out over the battlefield, all she saw were corpses.

She wondered what she would say if she could reach her dead.

She would tell Pipaji and Dulin that they had done well.

She would tell Suni, Baji, and Ramsa that she was sorry.

She would tell Altan that he was right.

She would tell Master Jiang thank you.

And she would promise them all that she would make their sacrifice worth it. Because that was what the dead were for her—necessary sacrifices, chess pieces lost to advance her position, tradeoffs that, if she were given the chance, she would make all over again.

She didn't know how long they sat there. It could have been minutes. It could have been hours. It felt like a moment carved out of time, a refuge from the inexorable progress of history.

"I wish things had been different," Nezha said.

Rin and Kitay both tensed. He was breaking the rules. They

couldn't maintain this fragile fantasy, this indulgence of nostalgia, if he broke the rules.

"They could have been different." Kitay's voice was hard. "But you had to go and be a fucking prick."

"Your Republic is dead," Rin said. "And if we see you tomorrow, then so are you."

No one had anything to say after that.

There would be no truce or negotiation tonight. Tonight was a borrowed grace, innocent of the future. They sat in miserable and desperate silence, wishing and regretting while the bloody moon traced its ponderous path across the sky. When the sun came up, Rin and Kitay got up, shook the ache from their bones, and trudged back toward the city. Nezha walked in the other direction. They didn't care to watch where he went.

They marched back to Arlong, eyes fixed forward on the half-drowned city whose ruins shone in the glimmering light of dawn.

They'd won their war. Now they had a country to rule.

CHAPTER 31

Arlong had fallen immediately upon Nezha's retreat. That morning, the Southern Army swept through the city streets just as the Hesperians and the Republic finished their final evacuations. They found a confused, uneven city—half its districts were still populated with Nikara civilians with nowhere else to go, and the other half had become hollow ghost towns. The barracks and residential complexes that once housed Hesperian soldiers had been abandoned. Inside the wrecked shipyards, large hangars that must have been used to house dirigibles now stood empty, their floors littered with spare tools and leftover parts.

"I'll permit plunder to a reasonable extent," Rin told her officers. "Take whatever you want. But be civilized—no brawling over spoils, and keep to the affluent neighborhoods. Leave the poorest districts alone. Target the Hesperian quarters first—they won't have been able to take everything. Weapons, trinkets, and clothes are fair game. But food supplies come back to the palace for central redistribution."

"How should we deal with armed resistance?" asked Commander Miragha.

"Avoid bloodshed if possible," Kitay said. "Capture over

kill—we want their intelligence. Bring all soldiers to the dungeons and keep the Hesperians and Republican soldiers apart."

The Republican soldiers who hadn't managed to escape on the ships were desperately trying to pass themselves off as civilians. The streets were strewn with discarded uniforms; an hour into the occupation, Rin received a report of an entire squadron of naked men begging for secondhand civilian clothes so that they might disguise their identities. She laughed for a good five minutes, then ordered the men to be rounded up in chains and made to stand naked on the dais outside the palace for the rest of the day.

"Good for morale," she told Kitay when he protested.

"It's excessive," he said.

"It's exactly the right amount of public humiliation. A secret underground resistance might have credibility with the civilians." She pointed at the shivering men. "*They* certainly won't."

He didn't have a rebuttal.

While her troops continued their takeover of the streets, Rin made her way to the Red Cliffs to watch the last of the evacuation ships hurrying out of the narrow channel.

She remembered the day, nearly a year ago now, when she first saw the Hesperian fleet arrive on Nikara shores. How relieved she'd been then. How grateful. The white sails had represented hope and survival. Divine intervention.

But they hadn't come until the Republic had nearly bled itself out. They could have ended the whole civil war in minutes from the very beginning. They could have saved the entire country months of starvation and bloodshed. But they'd waited out the unnecessary tragedy until the very end, when they could simply step in and call themselves the heroes.

They were nowhere near so pompous in their departure.

"Bloody cowards," Venka said. "You're just going to let them go?"

"Dunno," Rin said. "Could be fun to sink all those ships in the harbor."

Kitay sighed. "Rin."

"I'm serious," she said.

"Occupying a city is one thing," he said. "Setting civilians on fire is quite another."

"But it'd be so funny." She was only half joking. She felt a thrill of dark, vindictive glee as she watched the mangled, escaping fleet. If she wanted to, she could turn every ship in that channel to ash. She had that power.

"Please, Rin." Kitay shot her a wary look. "Don't be an idiot. Right now the Hesperians are retreating because they're exhausted, they've expended everything on a war on a continent that they don't care for. They gambled on the wrong faction and lost. Right now, they're just licking their wounds. But if you send flames after *fleeing women and children*, they really just might reconsider."

"Spoilsport," said Venka.

Rin sighed. "I so hate when you're right."

So she let the ships sail undisturbed out of the harbor. She'd let the Hesperians think, for now, that her new regime bore them no ill will. That her priorities lay within Nikan's boundaries. She'd let them think they were safe.

And then, when they'd been lulled into complacency, when they'd become convinced that perhaps those dirty, stupid, inferior Nikara didn't pose such a great threat after all—that was when she would strike.

Rin's next task was to occupy the palace.

The place was in shambles. The grand painted doors had been left hanging ajar, hallways strewn with shattered vases that had fallen out of hastily packed wagons. The vast hall in the palace center had been stripped of almost all its furnishings; only the wall tapestries remained, too heavy and unwieldy to pull down and carry away.

The Yin family portrait hung at the far end of the chamber. Rin stood beneath it for a moment, gazing at the faces of the family that had imagined they might rule the Empire.

Whoever had woven this had rendered the Yins with impressive accuracy. Standing together, their similarities were even more pronounced. They all had the same high cheekbones, arched eyebrows, and sculpted, angular jaws. None of them smiled—not even the children, who gazed over the empty hall with identically haughty, contemptuous expressions.

At first Rin mistook Jinzha for Nezha, but then realized that the youths standing to their father's right must be the firstborn twins—Jinzha and Muzha. Nezha was by himself, somber and forlorn, to his father's left. This tapestry must have been completed years ago—he was represented here as a small child, barely rising to his father's waist. To the far right stood Lady Yin Saikhara, cradling a baby in her arms. That had to be Mingzha—Nezha's dead baby brother, the one lost to the Dragon.

What a beautiful family, destroyed in only the span of a year. Jinzha was captured and ground into dumpling stuffing at Lake Boyang. The charred remnants of Vaisra's body lay indistinguishable from the burned wreckage of his fleet. Muzha had reportedly drowned in the Dragon's attack on Arlong. And Nezha was broken and defeated, a slave to his Hesperian masters.

Rin wished, with a pulse of vicious hatred, she could have ended the lineage herself.

But the Lady Saikhara had escaped her justice. She'd flung herself off the highest tower of the palace when she saw the banners of southern troops marching into the city. Her fragile bones smashed like porcelain against the execution grounds outside the palace, and she joined a long tradition of noblewomen who had died along with their dynasties.

Rin learned from reports that Arlong's residents had come to hate Saikhara in the final days. It was no great secret that the House of Yin had profited greatly from the civil war, even as it impoverished entire populations just on its border. Nezha's sister, Muzha, had become rich acting as the go-between for Hesperian traders and the powerful merchant cronies that crowded the Republican court.

When Lady Saikhara had come back from her grand publicity tour in Hesperia, it had been revealed that she and Muzha had dumped huge swaths of Nikara goods into waiting Hesperian markets while everyone else was hoarding food and buying in a panic from rapidly inflating markets.

Popular opinion had called for Nezha to sanction his mother and sister, but he did nothing except remove them from his cabinet. So Nezha's moniker had gone from the Young Marshal to the Filial Fool, while his mother was titled the Whore of the West. In the past week, the streets had been calling so loudly for her punishment that if the Southern Army hadn't stormed Arlong's gates then she might very well have been torn apart by the mobs regardless.

"You'd think she would have gotten out with the Hesperians," Kitay said as they stood on the second-floor balcony, watching as servants scrubbed Saikhara's blood from the steps. Her body lay several feet away, wrapped unceremoniously in a spare canvas sheet. Rin planned to weigh it down with rocks and toss it into the harbor for the fish. "I thought they loved her."

"I think they left her behind," Rin said. "I think they had to save their own skins."

They would have done it. The Hesperians, facing an overwhelming tide of public hatred, wouldn't have dared trying to ferret the despised Saikhara out of the city.

It didn't matter that Lady Saikhara spoke fluent Hesperian, that she worshipped their Maker, or that she'd been masquerading as a Hesperian woman for half her life. In the end she was still Nikara, still one of the inferior race, and the Hesperians only looked out for their own.

The adjacent hallways were crammed with riches that put those in Jinzhou to shame. Rin had walked through those corridors a dozen times before, always on her way to Vaisra's office, though she'd never dared to pause and peruse. Back then, their mere proximity had filled her with awe; those artifacts were shining evidence of a historical elite that she had, somehow, been invited to join.

Walking through the hallways felt very different now that she knew everything displayed on the walls belonged to her.

"Look." Kitay stopped before a very old, very shiny helmet. "It says this belonged to the Red Emperor."

"There's no way."

"Read the placard."

The helmet did look old enough. Rin could see little jade stones embedded into the forehead. She reached into the case, plucked the helmet out, and tried it on. It was uncomfortably cold, obstructively heavy. Quickly she pulled it off. "I don't know how anyone managed to fight wearing this."

"It's ceremonial, probably," Kitay said. "I doubt he actually wore it into battle. This place is loaded with his stuff—look, there's his breastplate, and that's his old tea set."

His fingers hovered over the relics, as if he was too awed to touch them. But Rin, glancing about the hall, was struck with a deep sense of pity. The Red Emperor was the greatest man in Nikara history, a man so famous that every child in the Empire knew his name by the time they could speak. The myths about him could and did fill up entire bookshelves. He'd united the country for the very first time; he'd brought fire and bloodshed on a scale the land had never witnessed before; and he'd built cities that remained intellectual, cultural, and commercial centers of the Empire.

And now, a millennium later, all that remained were his helmet, his breastplate, and a tea set.

His dynasty had not even survived a generation. Upon his death his sons had immediately fallen upon each other, and after the centuries of bloodshed that followed, the Empire was split under a provincial system that the Red Emperor had not designed nor intended. His bloodline was lost, his heirs extinguished within the first twenty years of the civil war they started. If his line persisted, no one recognized it.

He was king for a day. For a brief moment, he stood in the center of the universe. And for what?

He should have married Tearza, Rin thought. He was a fool to make the shamans his enemies. He should have leashed them to his regime. He should have put a Speerly on the throne, and then his Empire would have lasted for an eternity. By now their heirs would have conquered the world.

"This one has your name on it," Kitay called from farther down the hall.

"What?"

"Look." He pointed. It was the sword—the twin of the one she'd lost in the water during the battle at the Red Cliffs, the second one crafted from Altan's melted-down trident.

They'd kept it as a trophy. *Speerly mineral*, read the placard, *last wielded by Fang Runin.*

Rin drew the sword out of its case and blew the dust off the blade. She'd thought it had sunk to the bottom of the river forever.

Her placard was so small. There were no further details, no reports of her exploits, just her name and the weapon's make. She snorted. That was just like Vaisra. If he'd had his way, then she would only ever have remained a footnote in history.

When they build museums to my regime, Vaisra, I won't even give you a plaque.

Nearly half the artifacts were missing from their cases. They looked recently pilfered, likely by Republican leadership; dust hadn't had time to settle in the outlines they left behind. Rin couldn't tell by reading the plaques why some had been stolen and some were left behind; the missing items were valuables of all types from all eras, and appeared to have been packed away at random.

One empty case stood on a prominent display—a shelf protruding from the wall, rimmed with golden edges to draw the viewer's attention.

Rin picked up the plaque.

Imperial Seal of the Red Emperor.

She nearly dropped it. *Incredible.* She'd learned about this seal at school. When the Red Emperor died, he'd declared that his seal could only pass, along with the mandate of heaven, to the next rightful ruler of the Empire. It was promptly stolen the morning after his funeral. In the centuries after, the seal changed hands between princes, generals, clever concubines, and assassins, followed wherever it went by a trail of blood. Three hundred years later it finally dropped off the historical record, though provincial Warlords still claimed occasionally to have it locked in their private vaults.

So the House of Yin had kept it all along.

Of course Nezha had taken it with him. Rin found that hilarious. He'd lost the country, but he'd taken the ruler's mandate.

Keep it, asshole, she thought. Nezha could have the seal, and every other shiny piece of junk his staff had loaded into their wagons. It didn't matter that those treasures were hallmarks of Nikara history. That history didn't matter to Rin. It was a record of slavery, oppression, misrule, and corruption. She wanted no heirlooms of her predecessors. She did not carry their legacy. She intended to build something new.

Vaisra's throne remained at the end of the hall, too heavy to be carted away.

Rin felt very small as she approached it. It was much grander than the throne she'd sat on at Jinzhou. This was a proper emperor's throne—a high-backed, ornamented chair on a multi-stair dais. An intricate map of the Empire was inked in black ridges across the entire marble floor. Sitting atop that throne, one surveyed the world.

Kitay nodded at the seat. "Gonna give it a try?"

"No," Rin said. "That's not for me."

She knew as she stood in this dark, cold palace that she could never make this place hers. She'd never feel comfortable here; this place was haunted by the ghosts of the House of Yin. And that was just as well. The seat at Arlong had never ruled the entire Empire. It was the home of traitors and imposters, pretenders to the throne doomed to fail. She would not be the latest imposter to rule from the Dragon Province.

This was only a temporary base from which she would solidify her hold on the rest of the country.

The palace interior suddenly felt icy cold. *We have so much work to do,* Rin thought. The task before her seemed so monumental it did not quite seem real. She'd ripped the world apart, had inflicted one great tear that stretched from Mount Tianshan to the Nine Curves Grotto. And now she had to stitch it back together.

Had to restore order in the provinces. Had to clear the corpses off the streets. Had to put food on people's tables. Had to return this country, which had fallen apart in every way conceivable, to normal.

Oh, *gods*. She swayed on her feet, suddenly dizzy. *Where do we even start?*

A knock sounded against the great hall's heavy doors, echoing through the vast, dark space.

Rin blinked, struck from her reverie. "Come in."

A young officer stepped through the doors. He was one of Cholang's staff. Rin could remember his face—she'd seen it before in the command tent—but not his name. "Commander Miragha sent me to tell you we've found it."

"Where?" Rin asked sharply.

"The far end of the Hesperian quarters. We have it surrounded, but haven't moved in yet. No one's going in or out. They're waiting on your orders."

"Good." Rin had to pause for a moment before she could move. She couldn't tell if the woozy rush in her limbs was a product of excitement or fatigue. When she took a step, it felt as if she were floating through air. "I'll go now."

She shrugged off Kitay's concerned glance as she followed the officer out of the palace. They'd already concluded this debate. He knew what she intended. They agreed on what was necessary.

There was no room to hesitate. It was time for a reckoning.

The last time Rin had been near Arlong's Hesperian quarter, she'd killed a man by burning off his testicles. Her clearest memories of this place were seeped in fear and panic—were of frantically dragging a body to a sampan, paddling out toward the harbor, and weighing the corpse down with rocks before anyone saw her and shot her full of bullets.

But then, all her memories involving the Hesperians were laced with fear. Even though they'd first come to Arlong as Vaisra's allies, and even though for half a year they'd nominally fought on the same side, Rin could only associate the Hesperians with alien superiority: forceful, groping hands; steel instruments; and cold indifference.

Sister Petra's laboratory occupied a square one-story building opposite the barracks. Rin's troops surrounded the perimeter, armed and waiting. Commander Miragha saluted Rin as she approached.

"It's locked from the inside," she reported. "Someone's definitely in there."

"Have you communicated with them?" Rin asked.

"We shouted for them to come out, but they didn't respond. Heard a bit of banging about—whoever is in there, they're bracing for a fight."

Rin knew most of the missionaries had already fled the city. She'd seen their slate-gray cloaks on the first boats out of the harbor, easily identified even from across the channel. The Gray Company were revered like royalty in the west; the remaining Hesperian troops would have personally escorted them out of the city.

That meant whoever was barricaded in the laboratory had remained there on purpose.

Outside the door, four of Miragha's men stood ready around an iron-plated, wheeled battering ram the size of a small tent.

"That looks like overkill," Rin said.

"We only bring our best," Miragha said. "Ready whenever you are."

"Hold on." Rin scanned the soldiers until she found one holding a halberd. "Give me that."

She wrapped a discarded Hesperian flag around the blade,

knotted it tightly, and set the tip ablaze. She handed it back to the soldier. "You go in first. Let her think you're me."

He looked alarmed. "But—General, then—"

"You'll be fine," Rin said sternly. The arc of lightning, whatever it was, had not done lasting physical damage to her or Nezha. Against someone who wasn't a shaman, it ought to have no effect at all. "Just prepare for a shock."

She was impressed when he did not argue. He held the flaming halberd firm and gave her a curt, obedient nod.

"Do it," Rin told Miragha.

Miragha gave the order. Her soldiers dragged the battering ram back several yards, then pushed it running against the door.

The wooden door smashed inward upon impact. The soldier with the halberd burst through, waving the torch about the dim interior, but nothing happened. The room was empty. When Rin walked inside, all she saw were toppled chairs and bare tables—and a trap door in the corner.

She pointed. "Down there."

The soldier with the halberd descended first, Rin following several steps behind. The makeshift torch seemed a plausible imitation; its flame flickered and curved like something alive, casting distorted shadows against the wall.

Lightning immediately arced through the dark. The soldier yelped and dropped the halberd. In the brief, bright flash, Rin glimpsed a silhouette across the room—a crouched figure behind something the shape of a mounted cannon. That was enough. Flames burst from her palm and roared across the room. She heard a high mechanical whine, then saw an explosion of sparks, ricocheting across the room like a thunderstorm concentrated inside a jar.

The cannon-like device exploded. The lightning disappeared. When the smoke cleared, Rin's flames, dancing steadily around her arms and shoulders as a makeshift lamp, illuminated a mass of scattered metallic parts and a limp form curled up in the corner.

Too easy, Rin thought as she crossed the room. If a soldier had designed this ambush, they wouldn't have been so trigger-happy with the lightning. They would have known they would only get one chance; they would have waited until they'd established a clear line of fire at Rin.

But Sister Petra Ignatius was a scholar, not a soldier.

Rin pushed at Petra's ribs with her foot, shoving her over onto her back. "If you wanted an audience, you could have just asked."

Petra cringed under her boot. A thin trickle of blood ran down the left side of her face where shrapnel had sliced her temple, and bright red burn marks scorched her hands and neck, but she looked otherwise unharmed. Her eyes were open. She was conscious. She could talk.

Rin turned to the stairs, where Miragha waited with her troops. "Leave us."

Miragha hesitated. "You sure?"

"She's unarmed," Rin said. "Post two troops to guard the exits and dispatch the rest back to the city center."

"Yes, General." Miragha followed her men back up through the trap door. The single column of sunlight winked out as they lowered the door closed behind them.

Then Rin and Petra were alone in the dim, fire-lit basement.

"Was that all you had?" Rin dragged a chair out from Petra's work table and sat down. "An amateur's ambush?"

Petra moaned softly as she drew herself to a sitting position.

"What is this?" Rin demanded. She snatched one of the machine's broken fragments from the ground. The metal was spun in a tight coil, cold to the touch. "What does this do?"

Petra responded with wary silence. She tilted her head back against the wall, her stone-gray eyes roving up and down Rin's form as if sizing up a wild animal.

Fine, thought Rin. Then she'd just have to resort to torture. She'd never done that before—she'd only ever watched Altan extract information with well-placed, sadistic bursts of flame—but the basic principles seemed simple enough. She knew how to hurt.

Then, absurdly, Petra began to laugh.

"As if you'd ever understand." She raised an arm to wipe the blood from her eyes. "What, did you imagine you might devise a countermeasure? The theory behind my machines is centuries beyond your grasp. I could show you every component, every draft of my designs, and you still wouldn't understand. You don't have the *brains*."

She rose to her feet. Rin tensed, prepared to strike. But Petra only stumbled to the chair opposite her and sat down, hands folded primly in her lap in some sick imitation of a teacher lecturing a student.

"It terrifies you, doesn't it?" she sneered. "That your gods are nothing?"

Burn her, said the Phoenix. *Make her scream.*

Rin pushed away the impulse. She had this one chance to get information. She'd get her revenge later.

She held the metal coil out again and repeated the question. "What does this do?"

"Didn't you feel it?" Petra's bloody lips split in a grin. For the first time since Rin had met her, she saw a manic glint in the Gray Sister's eyes, a crack in her inhumanly calm facade. "It silences your god. It *nullifies*."

"That's not possible," Rin objected, despite herself. "The gods are fundamental forces; they made this world, they can't just be cut off by some piece of metal, that's not—"

"Listen to you," Petra crooned. "Clinging to your pagan babble, even now. Your gods are nothing but a delusion. A chaotic rot in your brains that has plagued your country for centuries. But I've found the cure. I fixed that boy, and I'll fix you, too."

She was gloating now. She didn't mind explaining—she *wanted* to explain, because even now, she wanted to wave her superiority in Rin's face. Torture wouldn't be necessary, Rin realized. Petra was going to tell her everything she wanted, because she knew she was about to die, and gloating was all that she had left.

"The principle was quite simple. In Hesperia, we have shock therapies for souls who have lost their grip on reality. The electricity calms their madness. It banishes Chaos from their brains. And once I realized that your shamanism was just madness of the extreme sort, the solution was so easy. Chaos was worming through your minds into the material world. So all I had to do was *shut it off*."

She leaned forward. Blood had dripped again into her left eye, but she just blinked without wiping it away. "How does it feel? To know that your gods are nothing before the Divine Architect? We tamed the Dragon. We tamed your so-called Phoenix. Without your shamans, your army is an untrained, backward mass of idiot peasants that will never, *ever*—"

"Conquer Arlong?" Rin interrupted. She shouldn't have burst out; she should have just let Petra keep talking, but she couldn't stand the *fucking condescension*. "The Republic's finished. Your people fled the harbor the first chance they got. You've lost."

Petra barked out a laugh. "And you think you've *won*? The Gray Company's network spans the world. We have eyes on every continent. And those pieces of trash"—she kicked at a bent shard of metal at her feet—"were only prototypes. When I understood what made Yin Nezha bleed, I sent my notes to the Gray Towers. They'll have perfected my designs by now. The next time you encounter one will be the last.

"The Architect works in mysterious ways. Sometimes he moves slowly. Sometimes he makes sacrifices." Petra took a rattling breath, coughed, then sighed. "But the world marches inevitably, inexorably toward order. This is his intent. The Gray Company is greater than you could ever imagine, and we now have the weapons to burn Chaos out of the world. You kill me and you accomplish nothing. Your world as you know it will end."

Rin remained silent.

Petra meant to provoke. She wanted Rin to lose control, to explode and rage, all to prove her point that in the end, Speerlies were no better than animals. During those weeks on the northern expedition, Petra had always maintained such a cool placidity when she made Rin moan and thrash and howl, the condescending control of a woman who believed she was superior in every way.

But this time Rin was in control. She would not squander it.

She had meant to burn Petra alive. When Miragha's messenger arrived in the palace, Rin had seen an immediate, fantastical vision of Petra screaming and writhing on the floor, begging for mercy as flames corroded her pale white flesh.

But all that now seemed so trite, so easy. Petra deserved no mundane death. Mere bodily torture wouldn't satisfy. Rin had just been struck by a far better idea, something so deliciously cruel that part of her was astonished, amazed by her own creativity.

"I'm not going to kill you," she said with as much calm as she could muster. "You don't deserve that."

For the first time, fear flickered across Petra's face.

"Get up," Rin ordered. "Get on the table."

Petra remained in her chair, body tensing as if trying to decide whether to run or resist.

"*Get on the table.*" Rin let the flames around her shoulders jump higher, resembling wings for an instant before they flared out toward Petra. "Or I will char every part of your body. I'll do it slowly, and I'll start with your throat so I don't have to hear you scream."

Trembling, Petra stood up, climbed onto the examination table, and lay down.

Rin reached over the side of the table for the straps. Her left hand fumbled with the buckles, but she managed to loop them through the metal rings on the sides of the table and yank them tight. Petra lay still all the while. Rin could see the veins protruding from her jaw where she clenched it tight, trying to conceal her fear. But when Rin pulled the straps around Petra's waist, pinning her arms to her sides, a keening whimper escaped the sister's throat.

"Calm down." Rin gave her cheek a patronizing pat. Somehow, that felt better than a slap. "It'll be over soon."

A year ago Petra had strapped her naked to a table and lectured her on the inferiority of her mind, the shortcomings of her body, and the genetically determined backwardness of her race. In the months since then, she'd likely done the same to Nezha. She'd probably stood where Rin stood now, watching impassively as lightning arced through his body, taking meticulous notes while her subject contorted in pain. She'd probably lectured him, too, on why this was the Divine Architect's intention. Why these humiliations and violations were necessary for the slow, holy march toward civilization and order.

Now it was Rin's turn to proselytize.

"Remember that time you drew my blood?" She smoothed Petra's hair back with her fingers. "You filled entire jars with it. You didn't need that much; you told me so yourself. You just wanted to punish me. You were angry because you wanted proof of Chaos, but I couldn't show you the gods."

A pungent smell filled the air. Rin glanced down and saw a damp spot spreading through Petra's robes. She'd soiled herself.

"Don't be scared." Rin reached into her back pocket and withdrew a sachet of poppy seeds. "I'm giving you what you want. I'm going to show you the gods."

She pulled the sachet open with her teeth, tipped it into her palm, and clamped it over Petra's mouth.

A soldier might have been able to resist—might have held their breath, bit Rin's palm hard enough to draw blood, or concealed the seeds under their tongue and spat them out the moment they broke free. But Petra didn't know how to struggle. The Gray Company were untouchable in Hesperia; she'd never had the need. She wriggled pathetically under Rin's grasp, but couldn't break free; Rin jammed her stump over her nose, restricting her air flow, until at last she had no choice but to open her mouth and gasp.

Rin saw her throat bob. Then, several long minutes later, she saw her eyes flutter closed as the drug seeped through her bloodstream.

"Good girl." She removed her palm—empty, good—and wiped it against her pant leg. "Now we wait."

She wasn't sure this would work. Petra could not even conceive of the Pantheon's existence, much less how to get there. And Rin was not Chaghan; she could not flit back and forth between planes, dragging souls along like a shepherd.

But she could call upon the gods, and hers was the god of vengeance.

She dragged a chair next to the table, sat down, and closed her eyes.

The Phoenix answered immediately. It sounded amused. *Really, little one?*

Bring her to me, Rin thought. *And take us to your brethren.*

The Phoenix cackled. *Whatever you wish.*

Darkness rushed in around her. The workroom faded away. She felt herself hurtling into the void, spiraling through the bridge in her mind like an arrow shot straight into the heavens.

"Where are we?" Petra's presence lashed out, panicked. "What is this?"

Rin could sense her fear like a tidal wave, an ongoing flood of horrified, uprooted alienation. This was the same emotion Rin had felt in the New City dialed to the extreme: the jarring realization that the world was not what she thought it was, that everything she believed, everything she had faith in, was wrong.

Petra wasn't just scared, she was falling apart.

"It's divinity," Rin told her gleefully. "Look around."

Suddenly the Pantheon was visible, a circle of plinths surrounding them like spectators around a stage. They crept closer, cruel and curious, one and sixty-three entities entranced by the presence of a soul that refused to acknowledge their presence.

"These are the forces that make up our world," said Rin. "They have no intent. They have no agenda, and they do not tend toward order. They want nothing more than to be what they are. And they don't care."

Petra uttered something low and fearful, some repetitive chant in a language that sounded almost like Hesperian but not quite.

A curse? A prayer? Whatever it was, the Pantheon did not care, because the Pantheon, unlike the Maker, was real.

"Take me back," pleaded Petra. She'd lost all dignity; she'd lost all faith. Without her Maker she was stripped to a lost and terrified core, flailing wildly for something to cling to. "Take me—"

The gods pressed in.

Sound did not quite exist in the plane of spirit. What Rin perceived as words were transmitted thoughts, all equal in volume despite distance or intensity. She knew this in abstract. She knew that here, one could not really scream.

But the sheer intensity of Petra's desperation came close.

"Bring me back down," Rin told the Phoenix. "I'm finished here."

She landed back in her body with a jolt. She opened her eyes.

Sister Petra lay still on the table. Her eyes were wide open. Her pupils darted fretfully about, tracking nothing. Rin watched her for a long while, wondering if she might find her way back to her body, but the only movement she made was the occasional tremor in her shoulders. A choked murmur escaped her throat.

Rin prodded Petra's shoulder. "What was that?"

Drool trickled from the side of her mouth. Petra gurgled something incomprehensible, then fell silent.

"Congratulations." Rin patted her head. "You've finally found religion."

CHAPTER 32

Safely ensconced in a heavily guarded house behind the barracks, Rin slept better that night than any night she could remember in years. She didn't need laudanum to knock herself unconscious. She didn't wake up multiple times in the night, sweaty and shivering, straining to hear a dirigible attack she'd only imagined. She didn't see Altan, didn't see the Cike, didn't see Speer. The moment she lay down she slid into a deep, dreamless sleep, and didn't awake until warm rays of sunlight crept over her face.

She was twenty-one years old and it was the first night she could remember that she could close her eyes without fearing for her life.

In the morning she stood up, combed the tangles out of her hair with her fingers, and stared at herself in front of the mirror. She worked at the muscles in her face until she looked composed. Assured. Ready. Leaders couldn't display doubt. When she walked out that door, she was their general.

And then what? asked Altan's voice. *Their Empress? Their President? Their Queen?* Rin didn't know. She and Kitay had never discussed what kind of regime they might replace the Republic with. This whole time, they had—rather naively, she now realized—assumed that once they won, life in the Empire could go back to normal.

But there was no normal. In the span of a year they had smashed apart everything that was *normal*. Now there were no Warlords, no Empresses, and no Presidents. Just a great, big, beautiful, and shattered country, held together by common awe of a single god.

She was just General Fang for now, she decided. She didn't have a kingdom to rule yet. Not until the Hesperians had been decisively defeated.

She walked out of the house. Five guards stood waiting outside her door, ready to escort her across the city. When they reached the palace, she had to stop and remind herself that she wasn't dreaming. Ever since the start of the campaign from Ruijin, she'd spent so long thinking about what would happen if she were in charge that it seemed unreal that she was truly standing here, about to seize the levers of power.

Never mind that she had been in here only yesterday, pulling artifacts off the walls like she owned the place—because she *did* own the place. Yesterday was about a takeover, about eradicating the last traces of Republican authority. Today was the first day of the rest of Nikara history.

"You good?" Kitay asked.

"Yeah," she breathed. "Just—trying not to forget this."

She stepped over the threshold. Blood rushed to her head. She felt buoyant, weightless. The scales of everything had shifted. The decrees she wrote in that palace would ripple across the country. The rules she conceived would become law.

Overnight, she had become as close to a god as a mortal could be.

I've reached behind the canvas, she thought. *And now I hold the brush.*

Rin ran her administration not from the grand, empty great hall—that room was too cavernous, too intimidating—but from Vaisra's smaller war office, which was furnished with only a single spare table and several uncomfortable hard-backed chairs. She couldn't have sat on the palace throne—it was too grand, too dauntingly official. She wasn't ready to play the role of Empress yet. But she felt comfortable in this cramped, undecorated chamber. She'd fought campaigns from this room before; it felt like the most natural thing in the world to do so again. Sitting at this table with Kitay to her right and Venka to her left, she didn't feel like such an imposter. This was just a much nicer version of her tent.

This is not right, said a small voice in the back of her mind. *This is insane.*

But what in the past two years had not been insane? She had leveled a country. She'd destroyed the Trifecta. She'd commanded an army. She'd become, for all intents and purposes, a living god.

If she could do that, why could she not run a country?

The first thing on their agenda that morning was deciding what to do about Nezha. Rin's scouts reported that he'd fled the country along with his closest officers and advisers, all packed into every last merchant skimmer and fishing dinghy that the Republic could scrounge together.

"Where have they gone?" Rin asked. "Ankhiluun? Moag won't put him up."

Kitay lowered the last page of the dispatch. "A little farther east."

"Not the longbow island," she said. "The air there is still poison."

He gave her an odd look. "Rin, he's on Speer."

She couldn't stop herself; she flinched.

So Nezha had taken refuge on the Dead Island.

It made sense. He couldn't go all the way to Hesperia; that was as good as a surrender. But he must have known that he wasn't safe anywhere on the mainland. If he wanted to stay alive, he needed to put an ocean between them.

"That's cute," she said with as much calm as she could manage. She saw them both watching her; she couldn't let them think she was rattled. Nezha had certainly chosen Speer to aggravate her. She could just hear the taunts in his voice. *You might have everything, but I have your home. I have the last piece of territory that you don't control.*

And she did feel a flicker of irritation, a sharp jolt of humiliation in her back where once he'd twisted a blade. But that was all she felt—annoyance. No fear, no panic. Escaping to Speer was an annoying move, but it was also the ultimate sign of weakness. Nezha had no cards left. He'd lost his capital and his fleet. He ruled a Republic in name only, and he'd been relegated to a cursed, desiccated island where nothing lived and where hardly anything grew. All he could do was taunt.

Moreover, according to dispatches, he'd lost the faith of his allies. The Hesperians didn't listen to him anymore. The Consortium had chosen to cut their losses.

"He's not received any reinforcements since Arlong fell," Venka read. "And the Hesperians stripped his authority to command ground troops. He's only got Nikara infantry at his disposal now, and a third of those numbers deserted after Arlong." She glanced up from the report. "Incredible. You think the Consortium's finished?"

"Perhaps for now—" Kitay began, at the same moment that Rin said, "Absolutely not."

"They've withdrawn all their forces," Kitay said.

"They'll come back," Rin said.

"Perhaps in a few months," Kitay said. "But I think they've suffered more losses than they—"

"Doesn't matter," Rin said. "They'll be back as soon as they possibly can. Could be days, could be weeks. But they're going to hit back, hard, and we've got to be prepared. I told you what Petra said. They don't merely think we're just—just obstacles to trade. We're not inconveniences to them. They think we're an existential threat. And they won't stop until we're dust."

She looked around the table. "We're not done fighting. You all understand this, don't you? They didn't request an armistice. They haven't sent diplomats. We don't have a peace, we've only got a reprieve, and we don't know how long it'll last. We can't just sit around and wait for it. We've got to strike first."

If Rin had her way, the rest of the day would have been occupied with military remobilization. She wanted to open the ranks for enlistment. She wanted to set up training camps in the fields to plunder Arlong for Hesperian military technology and get her troops learning how to use it.

But her first priority had to be civil reconstruction. For armies were fueled by cities, and the city was on the verge of falling apart.

They upturned Arlong in a flurry of restoration. Work teams deployed to the beaches to run rescue operations on the settlements the Dragon had flooded. Triage centers opened across the city to treat civilians who had been injured in the battle and subsequent occupation. Lines formed before the public kitchens and stretched around the canals, intimidating crowds composed of thousands upon thousands of people whom she was now responsible for feeding.

Governance required a wholly different set of skills from commanding an army, very few of which Rin possessed. She didn't know the first thing about civil administration, yet suddenly a million mundane tasks demanded her immediate attention. Relocation for civilians whose homes were underwater. Law enforcement against looting and pillaging. Finding caretakers for children whose parents were dead or missing. It was going to be a gargantuan task just to restore the city to a minimal level of functionality, and its difficulty was compounded by the fact that the public officers normally responsible for keeping the city running were either dead, imprisoned, or had fled with Nezha to Speer.

Rin was astonished they got anything done. She certainly couldn't have gotten through that first morning without Kitay, who seemed undaunted by the impossibility of their mission, who calmly summoned staff and designated responsibilities like he knew exactly where everything was and what needed to be done.

Still, that morning did not quite seem real. It felt like a dream. It was *absurd*, the fact that the three of them were running a city. Her mind kept ricocheting between the wildly arrogant conviction that this was fine, they were managing, and doing a better job of it than any of Arlong's corrupt leadership ever had; and the crippling fear that they weren't qualified for this at all because they were just *soldiers*, just kids who hadn't even graduated from Sinegard, and so wholly unprepared for the task of ruling that the city was going to collapse around them any minute. Despite Kitay's astounding competency, their problems only kept stacking up. The moment they resolved one issue, they received reports of a dozen more. It felt as if they were trying to plug a dam with their fingertips while water kept bursting forth around them. If they strayed off focus for even one minute, Rin feared, they'd drown.

By midmorning she wanted to curl up and cry, *I don't want this, I can't do this*; wanted to hand off her responsibilities to an adult.

But you waged this war, Altan reminded her. *You wanted to be in charge. And now you are. Don't fuck it up.*

But every time she got her thoughts back in order, she remembered that it wasn't just Arlong at stake—it was the country.

And Arlong's problems paled in comparison to what was going on across Nikan. The Republic had been holding together worse than she'd thought. Grain deficiencies plagued every province. The livestock trade was nearly nonexistent; it had been wrecked by the Mugenese invasion, and the following civil war had afforded it no space to recover. Fish, a staple in the southeast, was in short supply since Daji had poisoned the rivers a year ago. Rates of infectious diseases were skyrocketing. Almost every part of the country was suffering epidemics of typhus, malaria, dysentery, and—in a remote village in Rat Province—unprecedented cases of leprosy. These diseases affected rural populations on a cyclical schedule, but the tumult of war had uprooted entire communities and forced masses of people—many of whom had never been in contact with one another before—into smaller, cramped spaces. Infections had exploded as a result. Hesperian medicine had helped, to some extent. That wasn't available anymore.

Then there were the normal by-products of war. Mass displacement. Rampant banditry. Trade routes were no longer safe; entire economies had ceased to function. The normal flow of goods, that crucial circulation that kept the Empire running, had broken down and would require months, if not years, to restore.

Rin wouldn't have known about half of these issues if she hadn't learned about them from Nezha's private papers—a stack of neat, startlingly comprehensive accounts of every plea for government assistance over the last six months, kept fastidiously in elegant, oddly feminine handwriting. Despite herself, Rin found them immensely helpful. She spent hours poring over the scrolls, marking down his reflections and suggested solutions. They displayed the thoughts of someone trained for statesmanship since he could read. A distressing number of his proposals were better than anything she or Kitay could have thought of.

"I can't believe he left all this behind," she said. "They're not that heavy. He could have done a lot more harm by taking them with him. You think they're sabotage?"

Kitay looked unconvinced. "Maybe."

No, they both knew that wasn't true. The notes were too detailed, too clearly compiled over months of difficult rule, to be staged overnight. And too many of Nezha's warnings—the importance of dam reconstruction, of vigilant canal traffic management—had turned out to be salient.

"Or," Kitay ventured, "he's trying to help you out. Or at least, he's trying to keep the city's disasters to a minimum."

Rin hated that explanation. She didn't want to credit Nezha with that generosity. It painted a different picture of Nezha—not as the vicious, opportunistic bootlicker to the Hesperians that she'd been rallying against this entire campaign, but as a leader genuinely trying his best. It made her think of the tired boy in the cell. The frightened boy in the river.

It made it so much harder to fixate on planning his death.

"It doesn't matter," she said curtly. "Nezha couldn't hold on to his city, let alone a country. These are our problems now. Pass me that page."

They were deep into the afternoon before they broke for a midday meal, and only then because Kitay's stomach began rumbling so loudly the distraction became unbearable. Rin had been so absorbed in Nezha's documents, she'd forgotten she was hungry until a junior officer set plates of steamed scallion buns, boiled fish with chilis, and braised cabbage before them. Then she was ravenous.

"Hold on," Kitay said, just as Rin reached for a bun. "Who cooked this?"

"Palace staff," said the officer who'd brought it in.

"They're still working the kitchens?" Venka asked.

"You said to keep all palace staff in their positions if they wished to defect," said the officer. "We're quite sure the food is safe. We had guards watching when they prepared it."

Rin stared at the array of dishes, amazed. It hadn't really hit her, not until then, that she ruled Nikan. *She ruled Nikan*, which meant all the privileges along with the responsibilities. She had an entire palace staff waiting on her. She'd never have to cook her own meals again.

But Kitay didn't look quite as delighted. Just as she lifted a morsel of fish to her mouth, he slapped the chopsticks from her hand. "Don't eat that."

"But he said—"

"I don't care what he said." He dropped his voice so the officer couldn't overhear. "You don't know who cooked this. You don't know how it got here. And we certainly didn't request lunch, which means either this kitchen staff had a remarkably quick change of heart, or someone had a vested interested in feeding us."

"General?" The officer shifted from foot to foot. "Is there something you—"

"Bring us an animal," Kitay told him.

"Sir?"

"A dog, ideally, or a cat. The first pet you can find should do. Be quick."

The officer returned twenty-five minutes later with a small, fluffy white creature with perky ears, head drooping under the weight of an ornate collar of gold and jade. This breed, Rin thought, must have been very popular with Nikara aristocracy; it resembled very much the pups she'd once seen at Kitay's estate.

Kitay seemed to have noticed this, too; he winced as the officers set the dog on the floor.

"The servants said this used to belong to the Lady Saikhara," said the guard. "They call it Binbin."

"Good gods," Venka muttered. "Don't tell us its name."

It was over quickly. The dog set eagerly at the boiled fish, but it had barely swallowed two bites before it stepped back and began to whine piteously.

Kitay started forward, but Rin held him back. "It could bite."

They remained in their seats, watching as the dog slumped to the floor, sides heaving. Its stubby front paws scrabbled at its bloated stomach, as if trying to scratch out some parasite gnawing at its innards. Gradually its movements grew weak, then listless. It whimpered once and fell silent. It seemed to take an eternity for it to stop twitching.

Rin felt a violent wave of nausea. She was no longer remotely hungry.

"Arrest the kitchen staff," Kitay ordered calmly. "Detain them in separate rooms and keep them isolated until we've time to interrogate them."

"Yes, sir."

The officer left. The door slammed shut. Kitay turned to Venka. "It could've been—"

"I know," Venka said curtly. "I'm on it."

She stood up, plucked her bow off the table, and left the room—

presumably to see whether the officer would carry out his orders or flee.

She and Kitay sat in stunned silence. Kitay's temporary calm had evaporated—he was staring at the dishes, blinking very rapidly, mouth half-open as if unsure what to say. Rin, too, felt lost in a fog of panic. The betrayal had been so sudden, so unexpected, her overriding thought was fury at her sheer *stupidity*, for accepting food from the kitchens without even stopping to think.

Someone was trying to kill her. Someone was trying to kill her in the most obvious way possible, and they'd almost succeeded.

She realized then that she could never feel safe in her own office again.

The door creaked open.

Rin jumped. "What is it?"

It was a messenger. He hesitated, taking in their distressed faces, and then tentatively lifted a scroll in Rin's direction. "There's, ah, a missive."

"From who?" Kitay asked.

"It's sealed with the House of—"

"Bring it here," Rin said curtly. "Then get out."

The moment the door swung closed, she ripped the scroll open with her teeth. She didn't know why her heart was hammering so loudly, why she still felt a surge of fearful anticipation even though Nezha had *lost*, had fled, had retreated so far out into the ocean that he couldn't possibly threaten her here.

Calm down, she told herself. *This is nothing. He has nothing. Just a formality from a defeated foe.*

Hello, Rin. Hope you're enjoying the palace. Did you take my old rooms?

You'll have realized by now, I think, that this country is in deep shit. Let me guess, Kitay's been going through agricultural reports all morning. He's probably losing his mind over the inconsistencies. Here's a hint—the smarter magistrates always underreport their crop yields to get more subsidies. Or they might really just be starving. Hard to know, huh?

"That patronizing shit," Rin muttered.

"Hold on." Kitay was already on the second page. He skimmed the bottom, blinked, and then handed it to her. "Keep reading."

The kitchen staff are good, but you'll find that several are quite loyal to my family. I hope you didn't eat the lunch.

Rin's mouth went dry. He couldn't know that. How did he know that?

Don't punish them all. It'll either be the head cook, Hairui, or his assistant. The others don't have a backbone. I mean, knowing you, you've probably had them all thrown in prison. But at least let Minmin and Little Xing back in the kitchens. They make excellent steamed buns. And you like those, don't you?

She lowered the letter. She suddenly found it hard to breathe; the walls seemed to constrict around her, the air deprived of oxygen.
Someone's spying on us.

"Nezha's not on Speer," she said. "He's *here*."

"He can't be," Kitay said. "Our scouts saw him leaving—"

"That means nothing. He could have snuck back. He controls the fucking water, Kitay, you don't think he could have traveled up the river in one night? He's *watching us*—"

"There's no place for him to go," Kitay said. "That'd be suicide. Come on, Rin—what, do you think he's crouched in a shack somewhere in the city? Peeking out at you from behind corners?"

"He knows about the granaries." Her pitch shot up several octaves. "He knows about the fucking *cooks*! Pray tell, Kitay, how the *fuck* would he know that unless he—"

"Because it's the easiest guess in the world," Kitay said. "And he knows about the granaries because those were the same problems that he's been dealing with for months. Up until we arrived, feeding this country was *his* problem. He doesn't have eyes over your shoulder, he's just trying to rattle you. Don't let him win."

Rin shot him an incredulous look. "I think you're giving quite a lot of credit to his capabilities for conjecture."

"And I think you're massively overestimating how much Nezha wants to die," Kitay said. "He's not hiding in the city. That's certain suicide. He's got scouts, yes, but we're in his fucking capital—of course people are going to report to him."

"Then he'll *know*—"

"So he'll know. We've just got to operate assuming Nezha has a good idea of what we're planning. That's inevitable with regimes in power—you can't keep your operations secret for long, there are too many people involved. In the end, it won't matter. We've got too many advantages. You just can't squander them by freaking the fuck out."

She forced herself to take several deep, shaky breaths. Gradually, her pulse slowed. The darkness creeping at the edges of her vision faded away. She squeezed her eyes shut, trying to organize her thoughts, trying to take stock of the problem.

She knew she had enemies in Arlong. She'd known that from the start. She'd had no choice but to ask many of the former administrative personnel to stay on in their roles, simply because she had no qualified staff who could fill their positions. She didn't know how to run a country, so she'd had to employ Republicans who did. They'd all nominally defected to her regime, of course, but how many of them were secretly plotting against her? How many was Nezha still in correspondence with? How many tiny traps had he left in his wake?

Her breathing quickened. The panic returned; her vision ebbed black. She felt a low, creeping dread, a prickling under her skin as if a million ants were crawling over her body.

It didn't go away. It persisted throughout the afternoon, even after they'd interrogated the kitchen staff and executed the cook in charge. It intensified into a flurry of symptoms: a debilitating fatigue; a throbbing headache that developed as her eyes grew strained, darting around for shadows where they didn't exist.

The palace didn't seem such an empty playground anymore. It seemed a house of infinite darkness, crowded with thousands of enemies that she couldn't see or anticipate.

"I know," Kitay said, every time she voiced her fears. "I'm scared, too. But that's ruling, Rin. There's always someone who doesn't want you on the throne. But we've just got to keep going. We can't let go of the reins. There's no one else."

The days stretched on. Slowly, incredibly, the business of city administration stopped feeling like a fever dream and started feeling more like a familiar duty as they fell into a routine—they woke an hour before sunrise, sifted through intelligence reports during the early hours of the morning, spent the afternoon checking in on reconstruction projects they'd set underway, and put out fires as they arose throughout the day.

They hadn't brought Arlong back to normal. Not even close. Most of the civilian population was still displaced, camping out in makeshift shacks on the same grounds where once Vaisra had corralled all the southern refugees. Food shortages were a persistent problem. The communal kitchens always ran out of food long before everyone in the line was served. There simply weren't enough rations, and Rin didn't have a clue where they could extract more on short notice. Their best hope was to wait for Moag's missives and hope she could convert boatloads of Nikara antiques into smuggled Hesperian grain.

But somehow, as days turned into weeks, their hold on the city seemed to stabilize. The civil administration, comprising southern soldiers with no experience and Republican officials who had to be guarded at all times, became semifunctional and self-sustaining. Some semblance of order had been restored to the city. Fights and riots no longer broke out on the streets. All Republican soldiers who hadn't fled had either stopped trying to cause trouble or had been caught and locked in prison. Arlong had not quite welcomed the south with open arms, but it seemed to have reluctantly accepted its new government.

Those seemed like tentative signs of progress. Or that was, at least, the lie Rin and Kitay told themselves, to avoid facing the crushing pressure of the fact that they were children, unprepared and unqualified, juggling a towering edifice that could collapse at any minute.

Rin, Kitay, and Venka always holed up in the war room long past sunset. As the moon crept across the sky, they went from slouching at the table to sitting on the floor to lying by the hearth, swigging at bottles of sorghum wine recovered from Vaisra's private cellars, all pretense of work forgotten.

All three of them had started drinking religiously. It felt like a compulsion; by the end of the day, alcohol seemed as necessary as eating or drinking water. It was the only thing that took the edge off the debilitating stress that pounded their temples. In those hours, they lurched to the opposite of anxiety. They became temporary, private megalomaniacs. They fantasized about everything they would change about the Empire once they'd gotten it into their order. The future was full of sandcastles, flimsy prospects to be destroyed and rebuilt at will.

"We'll ban child marriage," Rin declared. "We'll make matchmaking illegal until all parties are at least sixteen. We'll make education mandatory. And we'll need an officers' school, obviously—"

"You're going to reinstate Sinegard?" Venka asked.

"Not at Sinegard," Kitay said. "That place has too much history. We'll build a new school, somewhere down south. And we'll revamp the whole curriculum—more emphasis on Strategy and Linguistics, less focus on Combat . . ."

"You can't get rid of Combat," Venka said.

"We can get rid of Combat the way Jun taught it," Rin said.

"Martial arts don't belong on the battlefield, they belong on an opera stage. We have to teach a curriculum geared for modern warfare. Artillery—arquebuses, cannons, the whole gamut."

"I want a dirigible division," Venka said.

"We'll get you one," Kitay vowed.

"I want a dozen. All equipped with state-of-the-art cannons."

"Whatever you like."

As the night drew on, their ideas always went from bold to wishful to simply absurd. Kitay wanted to issue a standardized set of abacuses because pea-size beads, apparently, made better clacking noises. Venka wanted to ban intricate, heavy hair ornaments required by women of aristocracy on the grounds that they strained the neck, as well as the black, double-flapped headwear favored by northern bureaucrats on the grounds that they were ugly.

Those last few proposals were trivial, so obviously not worth their time. But it still thrilled them, tossing out ideas as if they had the power to speak them into being. And then remembering that they *did*, they fucking did, because they owned this country now and everyone had to do what they said.

"I want free tuition at all the scholars' academies," Rin said.

"I want the punishment for forced sexual intercourse to be castration," Venka said.

"I want multiple copies made of every ancient text in the archives that will be disseminated to each of the top universities to prevent knowledge decay," Kitay said.

And they could have it all. Because fuck it—they were in charge now; absurd as it was, they sat on the throne at Arlong, and what they said was *law*.

"I am the force of creation," Rin murmured as she stared at the ceiling and watched it spin. Vaisra's sorghum wine burned sweet and sour on her tongue; she wanted to swig more of it, just to feel her insides blaze. "I am the end and the beginning. The world is a painting and I hold the brush. I am a god."

∞

But morning always came and, along with the stabbing headaches of the previous night's indulgences, returned the exhaustion, exasperation, and mounting despair that came with trying to repair a country that had spent the majority of its history at war.

Every bit of progress they made in Arlong, it seemed, was constantly being undone by bad news from the rest of the country. Bandit attacks were rampant. Epidemics were getting worse. Power vacuums had sprung up throughout the southeastern provinces Rin's army had conquered, and since she didn't have enough troops to deploy nationwide to cement her regime, a dozen pockets of local rebellion were forming that she'd later have to put down.

The biggest emergency was food. They were arguing about food in the war room. Dwindling grain was the subject of every missive they received from outlying cities, was the cause of almost every riot Rin's troops had to quell. Until now Arlong had been fed by regular shipments of Hesperian supplies, and now those were gone.

Even Kitay couldn't find a solution. No amount of juggling resources, diplomacy, or clever reorganization could mask the fact that the grain stores simply were not there.

Moag, who had been Rin's best option, sent back a brief letter quashing their hopes.

No can do, little Speerly, she wrote. *Can't get you that much grain in such a short time frame. And Arlong's treasures aren't trading for much on the market right now. First of all, they're hard to get past the embargo when they're so obviously Nikara; second, Yin family artifacts have gone down quite a bit in value. I'm sure you can see why. Keep looking, I'm sure you'll find something they want.*

The perverse upside to the impending famine was that enlistment numbers shot up, since army recruits were the only ones guaranteed to receive two full rations a day. But then, of course, once this became widespread knowledge, fights and protests started breaking out around the barracks over this perceived injustice.

This, Rin thought, was a dreadfully apt metaphor for her frustrations with the city. For why *shouldn't* the army receive priority? The strength of their defenses was critical, now more than ever—why couldn't anyone else see that?

Every endless meeting, every redundant conversation they had about how to feed the city felt much more frustrating because Rin couldn't shake the feeling that this was all a mere distraction. That she was wasting her time trying to restore a broken country back to functionality, when what clearly should have been prioritized was driving her victory home.

She was so close to the end, she could nearly taste it.

One more campaign. One more battle. Then she'd be the only one left, sitting on her throne in the south, set up to remake this broken country to her liking.

But this wasn't about her personal ambitions. This was about the threat, the ever-looming threat that no one else seemed to realize was so much more frightening than famine.

The Hesperians were coming back.

Why wouldn't they? And why wouldn't they strike *now*, when they knew Rin's incipient regime was on such shaky ground? If Rin led the Hesperians, she would call for additional airships and launch a counterstrike as soon as she could, before the Nikara could rebuild their army.

Rin didn't have artillery forces capable of taking down dirigibles. She had only half of her original numbers, now that Cholang and his troops had retreated home to Dog Province. She had no other offensive shamans; the Trifecta were gone, Dulin and Pipaji were dead. She didn't have anything but fire with which to stop the west, and she didn't know if she alone was enough.

In her dreams she saw the dirigibles again, a buzzing horde that blotted out the sky, more than she could count. They descended in full force on Nikara shores, circling the air above her. She saw the faces of their pilots: uniformly pale, demonic blue eyes laughing at her as they trained their cannons in her direction.

And before she could lift her arms to the sky, they opened fire. The world erupted in scattered dirt and orange flame, and for all her bravado, all she could do was kneel on the ground, wrap her arms around her head, and hope that death came quickly.

"Rin." Kitay shook her by the shoulders. "*Wake up.*"

She tasted blood in her mouth. Had she bitten her tongue? She turned to the side, spat, and winced at the crimson splatter on her sheets.

"What?" she asked, suddenly afraid. "Was there—"

"Nothing's happened," he said. He pulled down his lip. Angry scars dotted the inside of his mouth. "But you're hurting me."

"Gods." She felt a twist of guilt. "I'm sorry."

"It's fine." Kitay rubbed at his cheek and yawned. "Just—try to go back to sleep."

It struck her then how incredibly tired he looked, how shrunken and diminished, so wholly different from the confident, authoritative persona he acquired during the daytime.

That scared her. It seemed like physical evidence that everything was, after all, a farce. That they were pretenders to the throne, playing at competency, while their victory slipped from their fingers.

The Empire was fracturing. Their people were starving. The Hesperians were going to return, and they had nothing with which to stop them.

She reached for his fingers. "Kitay."

He squeezed her hand in his. He looked so young. He looked so scared. "I know."

Worst of all, the letters did not stop.

They were relentless. Nezha, apparently, was trying to wage psychological warfare through a sheer barrage of scrolls. They appeared outside her quarters. They found their way into her intelligence reports. They kept showing up with her meals. Rin had changed the kitchen staff so many times that the quality of food was now decidedly poor, but each day at noon a scroll invariably appeared tucked underneath her porridge bowl.

One morning a letter showed up on her pillow, and Rin immediately launched a manhunt in an attempt to find the messenger. But a thorough search of the entire barracks revealed no leads. Eventually she stopped trying to root out suspected couriers—that would have required replacing nearly her entire staff—and started venting by ripping up and burning Nezha's scrolls instead.

But only after she read them. She always had to read them first. She really should have just burned them without looking—she knew that reading them just meant she was playing into his game. But she couldn't help it. She had to know what he knew.

She could never quite pin down their tone. Sometimes they were mocking and patronizing—he knew she had no aptitude for governance, and he was clearly relishing this fact. But sometimes they were genuinely helpful.

> Lao Ho's a good man to supervise regional taxation if you haven't thrown him in prison yet. And tell Kitay that as much as he wants to reorganize the labeling system for the old annals in the library, we've kept them that way for a reason. The first numerals stand for relative importance, not scroll size. Don't let him get confused.

He alternated constantly between writing taunts and delivering pieces of accurate, important information. Rin couldn't grasp what was going on in his mind. Was he just playing games? If so, it was working—the taunts redoubled her frustrations, made her furious that their mistakes were so visible they were obvious all the way across the strait; the pieces of advice were even more torturous, because she never knew whether to take them at face value, and spent so much time second-guessing his tips, trying to discover his underlying motives, that she got less done than if she'd never read them at all.

He always ended his letters with the same offer. *Come to the negotiating table. The Hesperians always produce grain at a surplus—they've got machines doing the planting for them. They have food aid to spare. Just make a few concessions and you've got it.*

It never sounded the slightest bit more attractive. The more missives she received, the more condescending they became.

Keep your grain, she wanted to write back. *I'd rather choke than let you feed me. I'd rather starve to death than take anything from your hands.*

But she bit down the impulse. If she sent Nezha any response, then he'd know she'd been reading his letters.

But he must have known anyways. Every missive was terrifyingly omniscient. He identified so clearly the same issues they were struggling with that he might have been standing over their shoulders in the war room. She knew he was trying to make her paranoid, but it *worked*. She didn't feel safe in her own room anymore. She couldn't get any rest—she and Kitay had to start sleeping in shifts again, guarding each other in the same bed, otherwise she was too overcome with anxiety to even close her eyes. She could hardly focus anywhere she went; her eyes were too busy darting about, watching for spies or assassins. She started spending each day holed up in the war room because it was the only place where she felt safe, with the only window three floors up, and its single door guarded by a dozen handpicked soldiers.

"You need to stop reading those," Venka said.

Rin was staring at the latest missive, glaring at the characters until they felt seared into her eyelids, as if she could decipher Nezha's intent if she stared at them long enough.

"Put that down, Rin. He's just fucking with you."

"No, he's not." Rin pointed. "Look. He knows we tried getting contraband grain from Moag. He *knows*—"

"Of course he knows," Venka said. "That's an obvious guess; what else are we going to try? You're only letting him win when you read those. He's just messing with you because he's exiled on an island in bum-fuck nowhere and can't do anything except squeal for attention—"

"*Squeal for attention.*" Rin lowered the scroll. "That's an interesting phrase."

There was an awkward silence. Kitay glanced up from a stack of trade reports, brows lifted.

Venka blinked. "Sorry?"

For a moment Rin just stared at her, expression blank, while her mind spun to catch up to the conclusion she'd just formed.

No cards left to play. She'd just read those words in Nezha's handwriting—they'd caught her eye because it had been such a specific phrasing. *I'm sure you think I'm just squealing for attention, but take a look at the ledgers and you'll know I'm right.* It hadn't been in any of Nezha's previous letters; she would have remembered it. And Venka hadn't yet read the one she was holding in her hand, unless—

Unless.

The room seemed to dim. Rin narrowed her eyes. "How did you know that Nezha was going to make a stand at Xuzhou?"

Venka's throat pulsed. "What do you mean?"

"Answer the question."

"We intercepted their messengers, I told you—"

"You're very good at that," Rin said.

She saw the muscles in Venka's face working, as if she couldn't decide whether to smile and accept the compliment. She looked scared. Did that mean she was lying? It had to—what other reason did she have to be afraid?

"Answer this." Rin stood up. "How do you think Nezha knew we were trying to reach the Trifecta?"

Venka's mouth worked soundlessly for a moment. "I don't understand."

"I think you do." Rin took a step toward her. Her ears were ringing. Her voice dropped low. "Do you know how many people knew about that plan? Five. Me, Kitay, Master Jiang, the Vipress, and you."

Venka stepped back. "I don't know what—"

"Rin," Kitay interrupted. "Don't do this. Let's talk—"

Rin ignored him. "I have another question." She wouldn't give Venka a chance to collect her thoughts, to spin together a cover. She wanted to launch all her suspicions at once, to build a mounting case from every angle until Venka cracked from the pressure. "Why didn't you tell us Nezha was going to bomb Tikany?"

Venka shot her an incredulous look. "How the fuck would I have known about that?"

"You made us think that we were safe once we'd taken the Beehive," Rin said. "You told me Nezha was nowhere close to launching a southern strike. You said he was ill."

"Because he *was*!" Venka's voice rose several octaves in pitch. "Everyone was gossiping about it, I wouldn't make that up—"

Kitay grasped Rin's elbow. "That's *enough*—"

Rin shook her arm from his grasp. "And yet two weeks later he was in Tikany, miraculously cured. Answer this, Venka: Why did they leave you alive in the Anvil? The Southern Army was under siege for months, but you came out just fine. Why?"

Venka's cheeks went a pale, furious white. "This is bullshit."

"Answer the question."

"You think I'm a spy? *Me?*"

"Why did you leave Arlong that night?" Rin pressed.

Venka threw her hands up. "*What* night?"

"In Arlong. The night we escaped. We all had reasons to go, we were all running for our lives, except you. No one was coming after you. So why did you leave?"

"Are you fucking kidding me?" Venka snapped. "I left for *you*."

"And why would you do that?" Rin pressed. This was all so obvious now; the pieces fit so well. Venka's sudden change of heart, the implausibility of her motivations—the contradictions were so glaring, she was amazed she hadn't seen it before. "You never liked me. You *hated* me at Sinegard; you thought I was dirt-skinned trash. You think all the south are dirt-skinned trash. What changed your mind?"

"This is fucking unbelievable," Venka spat.

"No, what's unbelievable is a Sinegardian aristocrat deciding to throw her lot in with southern rebels. How long has it been? Were you reporting to Nezha from the start?"

Kitay slammed a fist against the desk. "Rin, shut the fuck up."

Rin was so startled by his vehemence that, despite herself, she fell silent.

"You're exhausted." Kitay grabbed the scroll from her hand and began ferociously ripping it to tiny, then tinier shreds. "You're not reading these anymore. You're giving Nezha exactly what he wants—"

"Or it could be I've just found his mole," Rin said.

"Don't be ridiculous," he snapped.

"You read that scroll, Kitay, you saw those words—"

"It's a fucking turn of phrase—" Venka started.

"It's a turn of phrase that only *you* used." Rin jabbed a finger at her. "Because you wrote these, didn't you? You've been drafting them all this time, laughing at us, watching us sweat—"

"You're fucking crazy," Venka said.

"Oh, I'm sure that's what you want me to think," Rin snarled. "You and Nezha both—"

Something shifted suddenly in Venka's face. "Get down."

Then she flung herself at Rin, arms reaching for her waist as if to pin her to the ground.

Rin hadn't processed what she'd heard. She saw Venka advancing and her vision went red, locked into the fight response that had so far kept her alive, and instead of twisting and ducking to the ground, she grabbed Venka by the shoulders and brought her knee up against her thigh instead.

Afterward, she'd torture herself wondering whether it was her fault. She'd run through the list of all the things she should have done. Should have realized Venka's last words were a warning, not a threat. Should have noticed Venka was unarmed, and that her hands weren't going for Rin's head and neck, the way they would have if Venka truly meant to hurt her. Should have seen that Venka's face was contorted in fear, not anger.

Should have understood that Venka was trying to save her life.

But in that moment, she was so convinced that Venka was the traitor, that Venka was *attacking* her, that she didn't notice the crossbow bolt in Venka's neck until they'd both collapsed to the floor. Until after she'd already burned ridges into Venka's shoulders. Until she realized that Venka was twitching, but she wasn't getting up.

Too late, she noticed the figure in the window.

Another bolt shrieked through the air. Rin watched its path, helpless and terrified, but it missed Kitay by a yard. He dove under the table; the bolt buried its head in the doorframe.

Rin flung her palm at the window. Flames roared; the glass exploded. Through the blaze, she saw the dark-clothed figure tumbling through the air.

She wriggled out from under Venka's body and ran toward the window. The assassin lay in a crumpled heap three floors below. He wasn't stirring. Rin didn't care. She pointed down, and a stream of flame shot toward the ground, licking hungrily around the corpse.

She thickened the flame, made it burn as hot as she was capable, until she couldn't see the body anymore, just thick, roiling waves of orange under shimmering air. She didn't want to preserve the assassin's body. She knew who had sent him: either Nezha or the Gray Company or the two acting in tandem. There was no mystery to solve here; she'd learn nothing from interrogation. It might have been prudent to try, but in that moment, all she wanted was to watch something burn.

CHAPTER 33

The next morning the Southern Army departed for Tikany.

Rin couldn't rule from Dragon Province. That should have been evident from the start—it wasn't her hometown, she didn't know the city's inner workings, and she had no local supporters. In Arlong, she was a foreign upstart working against centuries of anti-southern discrimination. Venka's death was just the final straw—proof that if Rin wanted to cement her rule, she had to do it from home.

A small crowd of civilians gathered in the valley to watch as the columns marched past. Rin couldn't tell from their grim expressions if they were sending the Southern Army off with respect, if they were simply glad to see their backs, or if they were scared she was carrying off all their food.

She'd left behind a minimal force—just three hundred troops, the most she was willing to spare—to maintain occupation of the city. They'd likely fail. Arlong might collapse under the strain of its myriad resource shortages; its civilians might emigrate en masse, or they might overthrow the southern troops in internal revolt. It didn't matter. Arlong was no great loss. One day the city would be well and properly hers, purged of dissenters, stripped of its treasures, and transformed into a tame, obedient resource hub for her regime.

But first, she had to reclaim the south.

Rin kept her mind trained on Tikany, on going home, and tried not to think about how much their departure stank of failure.

She and Kitay spent much of the journey in silence. There was little to talk about. By the fourth day, they'd exhausted all discussion of what resources they had, what troop numbers they were now working with, what kind of foundation they'd have to build in Tikany to train a fighting force capable of taking on the west. Anything else at this point lapsed into useless conjecture.

They couldn't talk about Venka. They'd tried, but no words came out when they opened their mouths, nothing but a heavy, reproachful silence. Kitay thought Venka's death exonerated her. Rin was still convinced Venka might have been the informant, but any number of alternatives were possible. Venka was not the only one with access to the information Nezha kept hinting at. Some junior officer could easily have been passing intelligence to the Republic throughout their march. The scrolls had stopped appearing since Venka's death, but that might have simply been because they'd left Arlong. Venka remained an open question, a traitor and ally both at once, which was the only way Rin could bear to remember her.

She didn't want to know the truth. She didn't want to even wonder. She simply couldn't think about Venka for too long because then her chest throbbed from a twisting, invisible knife, and her lungs seized like she was being held underwater. Venka's confused, reproachful face kept resurfacing in her mind, but if she let it linger, then she started to drown, and the only way to make those feelings stop was to burn instead.

It was much easier to focus on the rage. Through all her confused grief, the one thought that burned clear was that this fight was not over. Hesperia wanted her dead; Hesperia was coming for her.

She no longer dreamed of Nezha's death. That grudge seemed so petty now, and the thought of his broken body brought her no satisfaction. She'd had the chance to break him, and she hadn't taken it.

No, Nezha wasn't the enemy, just one of its many puppets. Rin had realized now that her war wasn't civil, it was global. And if she wanted peace—true, lasting peace—then she had to bring down the west.

Two weeks out, the road to Tikany became a mosaic of human suffering.

Rin didn't know what she'd expected when she passed into the south. Perhaps not the joyful shouts of the liberated—she wasn't that naive. She knew she'd assumed responsibility for a broken country, wrecked in every way by years of constant warfare. She knew mass displacement, crop failure, famine, and banditry were problems that she'd have to deal with eventually, but she'd slotted them to the back of her mind, deprioritized against the far more urgent problem of the impending Hesperian attack.

They were far harder to ignore when they stared her in the face.

The Southern Army had just crossed over the border to Rooster Province when supplicants began coming out to meet them on the roadside. It seemed word had spread through the village networks about Rin's return, and as the marching column wound into the southern heartland, large crowds started appearing on every stretch of the road.

But Rin found no welcome parties on her journey. Instead she was witness to the consequences of her civil war.

Her first encounter with starvation shocked her. She had seen bodies in almost every state of destruction—burned, dismembered, dissected, bloated. But she had never in her life witnessed famine this severe. The bodies that approached her wagon—*living* bodies, she realized in shock—were stretched and distorted, more like a child's confused sketch of human anatomy than any human bodies she'd ever encountered. Their hands and feet were swollen like grapefruits, bloated extremities hanging implausibly from stick-thin limbs. Many of them appeared unable to walk; instead they crawled and rolled toward Rin's wagon in a slow, horrific advance that made Rin burn with shame.

"Stop," she ordered the driver.

Warily he regarded the approaching crowd. "General . . ."

"I said *stop*."

He reined the horses to a halt. Rin climbed out of the wagon.

The starving civilians began to cluster toward her. She felt a momentary thrill of fear—there were so many of them, and their faces were so unnaturally hollow, so caked with dirt that they looked like monsters—but quickly pushed it away. These weren't monsters, these were her people. They'd suffered because of her war. They needed her help.

"Here," she said, pulling a piece of hard jerky from her pocket.

In retrospect she should have realized how stupid it was to offer food to a horde of starving people when clearly she didn't have enough to go around.

She wasn't thinking. She'd seen miserable, gnawing hunger, and she'd wanted to alleviate it. She didn't expect that they'd begin stampeding, pulling one another to the ground, bare feet crushing frail limbs as they surged forth. In an instant, dozens of hands reached toward her, and she was so startled she dropped the jerky and stumbled back.

They fell on the food like sharks.

Terrified, and ashamed by her terror, Rin clambered back on the wagon.

Without asking, the driver urged the horses forward. The wagon lurched into a speedy pace. The starving bodies did not follow.

Heart pounding, Rin hugged her knees to her chest and swallowed down the urge to vomit.

She felt Kitay's eyes on her. She couldn't bear to meet them. But he was merciful, and said nothing. When they stopped for dinner that night, the food tasted like ashes.

∞

The roadside parties became a daily sight as they drew closer to Tikany. It didn't matter that the wagons never stopped, never distributed rations to pleading hands because their own supplies were running so short. They had just enough bags of grain and rice to keep the army alive for three more months; they could spare nothing out of charity. The soldiers learned to march with their eyes trained forward as if they hadn't seen and hadn't heard. But still the crowds persisted, arms stretched out, murmuring pleas in breathy whispers because they didn't have the energy to shout.

The children were the hardest to look at because their bodies were the most distorted. Their bellies were so swollen they looked pregnant, while every other part of them had shriveled to the width of reeds. Their heads bobbled on their thin necks like wooden toys Rin used to see at market. The only other parts of them that did not shrink were their eyes. Their beseeching, sorrowful eyes protruded from shrunken skulls, as if, with their limbs whittled away, they had been reduced to those desperate gazes.

Gradually, through interview after interview with those starving civilians who could still muster the energy to talk, Rin and Kitay learned the full picture of how bad famine had grown in the south.

It wasn't just a lean year. There simply wasn't any food at all. Fresh meat had been the first to disappear, then spices and salts. The grain lasted several months, and then the starving villagers had turned to any sort of nutrients at all—chaff, tree bark, insects, carrion, roots, and wild grasses. Some had resorted to scooping the green scum off pond surfaces for the protein in algae. Some were cultivating plankton in vats of their own urine.

The worst part was that she couldn't chalk this up to enemy cruelty. Those grotesque bodies weren't the product of torture. The famine wasn't the fault of Federation troops—they had slashed and burned on their march south, but not at the scale necessary to cause starvation this bad. This hadn't been caused by the Republicans or the Hesperians. This was just the shitty, shitty result of ongoing civil war, of what happened when the whole country was upended in lost labor and mass migration because nowhere was safe.

Everyone was just trying their best to stay alive, which meant no one planted crops. Six months later, no one had a shred to eat.

And Rin had nothing to give them.

She could tell from their resentful glares that they knew she was holding resources back. She made herself look away. It wasn't hard to steel her gaze against misery; it didn't take any special emotional fortitude. All it took was repeated, hopeless exposure.

She'd witnessed this kind of desperation before. She remembered sailing slowly up the Murui River to Lusan on Vaisra's warship, the *Seagrim*, observing from the railings as crowds of displaced refugees stood on soggy banks where their flooded villages once lay, watching the Dragon Warlord—the rich, powerful, affluent Dragon Warlord—sail by without tossing them so much as a silver. She'd been astounded by Vaisra's callousness back then.

Yet Nezha had defended it. *Silver won't help them*, he'd told her. *There's nothing they can buy with it. The best thing we can do for those refugees is to keep our eyes on Lusan and kill the woman who brokered the war that put them there.*

Back then that logic had seemed so cold and distant, so clinical compared to the real evidence of suffering before her face.

But now, as Rin occupied the position Vaisra once held, she understood his reasoning. Deep-seated problems couldn't be fixed with temporary solutions. She couldn't let every skeletal child distract her when the final cause of their suffering was so obvious, was still lurking out there.

She consoled herself and her troops by reminding them that wouldn't go on for much longer. She'd fix this, soon; she'd fix everything soon. She reminded herself of that every time she saw another hollow, bony face, which was the only way she could face the dying southerners and not empty out everything in their supply wagons on the spot.

They only had to hold on for a little longer.

This became a mantra, the only thing capable of strengthening her resolve. Only a little longer, and she'd finish this war. She'd subdue the west. And then they'd have all the sacks of golden, glorious grain they wanted. They'd have so much to eat they would fucking choke.

"Rin." Kitay nudged her shoulder.

She stirred. "Hmm?"

It was midday but she'd fallen asleep, lulled by the rhythmic bouncing of the wagon. They'd been marching for four weeks, now into the final stretch, and the bleak monotony, silent hours, and restricted diet had her eyes fluttering shut whenever she wasn't on watch duty.

"Look." He pointed. "Out there."

She sat up, rubbed her eyes, and squinted.

Rows and rows of scarlet emerged on the horizon. She thought it a trick of the light at first, but then they drew closer and it became apparent that the brilliant red sheen that covered the fields was not a reflection of the setting sun but a rich hue that came from the blossoms themselves.

Poppy flowers were blooming all around Tikany.

Her mouth fell open. "What the—"

"Shit," Kitay said. "Holy shit."

She jumped out of the wagon and began to sprint.

She reached the fields in minutes. The flowers stood taller than any flowers she'd ever seen; they nearly came up to her waist. She took a flower in her hand, closed her eyes, inhaled deeply.

A heady thrill flooded her senses.

She still had this. Nothing else mattered. Venka's betrayal, her enemies in Arlong, the violence dissolving the country—none of that mattered. Everything else could crumble and she still had this, because *this* Moag could trade. Moag had told her, months ago, that this was exactly the kind of liquid gold she needed to acquire Hesperian resources.

These fields were worth ten times as much as all the treasures in Arlong. These fields were going to save her country.

She sank to her knees, pressed a palm to her forehead, and laughed.

"I don't understand." Kitay joined her by her side. "Who..."

"They listened," she murmured. "They knew."

She seized him by the hand and led him toward the flat, humble outline of the village on the horizon.

A crowd was forming near the gates. They'd seen her coming; they'd come out to welcome her.

"I'm here," she told them. And then, because they could not have possibly heard her from this distance, she sent a flare into the air: a massive, undulating phoenix, wings unfolding slowly against the shimmering blue sky, to prove that she was back.

Tikany, against all odds, had survived. Despite the famine and firebombs, many of its residents had stayed, largely because there was nowhere else for them to go. Over months it had become the center of its own beehive as residents from smaller, decimated villages came with their homes and livelihoods loaded up on carts to settle in one of the lean-to shacks that now formed the bulk of the township. Famine had not hit Tikany as hard as it had other parts of the Empire—during their occupation, the Mugenese had stockpiled an astonishing amount of rice, which Tikany's survivors had judiciously rationed out over the months.

Rin learned from the de facto village leadership that the decision to plant opium had been made in the wake of Nezha's firebombing. Grain did not grow well in Rooster Province, but opium flowers did, and poppy in these quantities, in a country where everyone needed respite from pain, was worth its weight in gold.

They'd known she'd come back. They'd known she would need leverage. Tikany, the least likely of places, had kept its faith, had invested its future in Rin's victory.

Now she stood facing the assembled villagers in the town square, the several thousand thin faces who had handed her the keys to the final stage of her war, and she loved them so much that she could cry.

"This war is ours to win," she said.

She gazed over the sea of faces, gauging their reaction. Her throat felt dry. She coughed, but a lump remained, sitting heavy on her prepared words.

"The Young Marshal has fled, of all places, to the Dead Island," she said. "He knows he isn't safe anywhere on Nikara soil. The Consortium have lost their faith in the Republic, and they are inches from pulling away entirely. All we need is to make our final drive. We just—we just need to last a little longer."

She swallowed involuntarily, then coughed. Her words floated, awkward and hesitant, over dry air.

She was nervous. Why was she so nervous? This was nothing new; she had rallied gathered ranks before. She'd screamed invectives against Vaisra and the Republic while thousands cheered. She'd whipped a crowd up to such frenzy once that they'd torn a man apart, and the words had come so easily then.

But the air in Tikany felt different, not charged with the exhilarating thrill of battle, of *hate*, but dead with exhaustion.

She blinked. This couldn't be right. She was in her hometown, speaking to troops who had followed her to hell and back and villagers who had turned the fields scarlet for her. For *her*. They thought her divine. They adored her. She'd razed the Mugenese for them; she'd conquered Arlong for them.

But then why did she feel like a fraud?

She coughed again. Tried to inject some force into her words. "This war—"

Someone in the crowd shouted over her. "I thought we won the war."

She broke off, stunned.

No one had ever interrupted her before.

Her eyes roved over the square. She couldn't find the source of the voice. It could have belonged to any one of these faces; they all looked equally unsympathetic, equally resentful.

They looked like they *agreed*.

She felt a hot burst of impatience. Did they not understand the threat? Hadn't they been here when Nezha dropped a hundred tons of explosives on unarmed, celebrating civilians?

"There is no armistice," she said. "The Hesperians are still trying to kill me. They watch from the skies, waiting to see us fail, hoping for an opportunity to take us down in one fell swoop. What happens next is the great test of the Nikara nation. If we seize this chance, then we seize our future. The Hesperians are weak, they're unprepared, and they're reeling from what we did at Arlong. I just need you behind me for this final stretch—"

"Fuck the Hesperians!" Another shout, a different voice. "Feed us first!"

A good leader, Rin knew, did not respond to the crowd. A leader was above hecklers—answering shouted questions only granted them legitimacy they did not deserve.

She cast about for the sentence where she'd left off, trying to resume her train of thought. "This opium will fuel—"

She never finished her sentence. A din erupted from the back of the crowd. At first she thought it was another bout of heckling, but then she heard the clang of steel, and then a second round of shouting that escalated and spread.

"Get down." Kitay grasped her wrist to pull her down from the stage. She resisted just for a moment, bewildered as she faced the crowd, but they weren't paying attention to her anymore. They'd all turned toward the source of the commotion, which rippled out like ink dropped in water, an unfurling cloud of chaos that dragged in everyone in the vicinity.

He yanked harder. "You need to get out of here."

"Hold on." Her palm was hot, ready to funnel flame, though she had no clue what she meant to do. Who did she aim at? The crowd? Her own *people*? "I can—"

"There's nothing you can do." He hustled her away from the riot. People were screaming now. Rin glanced over her shoulder and saw weapons flashing through the air, bodies falling, spear shafts and sword hilts smashing against unprotected flesh. "Not now."

"What the fuck is wrong with them?" Rin demanded.

They'd retreated to the general's headquarters, where she'd be safe and out of sight, out of earshot while her troops finished reimposing order in the square. Her shock had worn off. Now she was simply pissed, *furious* that her own people would act like such a brainless, petulant mob.

"They're exhausted," Kitay said quietly. "They're hungry. They thought this war was over, and that you'd come home to bring them the spoils. They didn't think you were going to drag them into another one."

"Why does everyone think this war is over?" Rin's fingers clawed in frustration. "Am I the only one with eyes?"

Was this how mothers felt when their children threw tantrums? The sheer fucking *ingratitude*. She had walked through hell and back for them, and they had the nerve to stand there, to *complain* and demand things that she couldn't spare.

"The Hesperians were right," she snapped. "They're fucking sheep. All of them."

No wonder Petra thought the Nikara were inferior. Rin saw it now. No wonder the Trifecta had ruled like they did, with abundant blood and ruthless iron. How else did you stoke the masses, except through fear?

How could the Nikara be so shortsighted? Their stomachs weren't the only things at stake. They were on the edge of something so much greater than a full dinner if they'd just *think*, if they'd just rally for one more push. But they didn't understand. How could she make them understand?

"They're not sheep. They're ordinary people, Rin, and they're tired of suffering. They just want this to be over."

"So do I! I'm offering them that chance! What do they want us to do?" she demanded. "Hang up our swords, throw down our shields, and wait for them to kill us in our beds? Tell me, Kitay, are they honestly *so stupid* they think the Hesperians will just turn around and leave us alone?"

"Try to understand," he said gently. "It's hard to prioritize the enemy that you can't see."

She scoffed. "If that's how they feel, then they don't deserve to live."

She shouldn't have said that. She knew as soon as the words left her mouth that she was wrong. She'd spoken not in anger, but from panic, from icy, gut-twisting fear.

Everything was falling apart.

Tikany was supposed to be the bastion of her resistance, the base from which she launched her final assault on the west. Symbolically, geographically, Tikany and its people were *hers*. She'd been raised on this dirt. She'd returned and liberated her hometown. She'd defended them first from the Mugenese, and then from the Republic. Now, when she most needed their support, they wanted to fucking riot.

Either they fear you, or they love you, Daji had told her. *But the one thing you can't stomach is for them to disrespect you. Then you've got nothing. Then you've lost.*

No. No. She pressed her palm against her temple, trying to slow her breathing. This was only a setback; she hadn't lost yet. She tried to remind herself of the assets she still held—she had Moag; she had the opium fields; she had a massive reserve of troops from across the Empire, even if they still needed training. She had the financial resources of the entire country; she just needed to extract them. And she had a *god*, for fuck's sake, the most powerful god left in the Nikara Empire.

So why did she feel like she was on the verge of defeat?

Her troops were starving, her support base hated her, her ranks were plagued with spies she could not see, and Nezha was taunting her at every turn, twisting his knife where it hurt the most. Her regime, that frail edifice they'd built at Arlong, was crumbling in every corner and she didn't have enough strength to hold it all together.

"General?"

She whipped around. "What?"

The aide looked terrified. His mouth worked several times, but no sound came out.

"Spit it out," Rin snapped.

His wide eyes blinked. His throat bobbed. When at last he spoke, his voice was such a timid croak that Rin made him repeat himself twice before she finally heard him.

"It's the fields, General. They're burning."

It took Rin several long seconds to register that she was not dreaming, that the red clouds in the distance, glowing so brightly against the moonless sky they seemed surreal, were not an illusion.

The opium fields were on fire.

The blaze grew as she watched, expanding outward at a terrifying rate. In seconds it could encompass the entirety of the fields. And all Rin could do was stand there, eyes wide, struggling to comprehend what she saw before her—the destruction of her only trump card.

Dimly she heard Kitay issuing orders, calling for evacuation from the shacks nearest the fields. From the corners of her eyes she saw a flurry of movement around her as troops sprang into action, forming lines from the wells to pass buckets of water to the fields.

She couldn't move. Her feet felt rooted, trapped in place. And even if she could—what could she possibly do? One more bucket of water wouldn't help. All the fucking buckets in Tikany wouldn't help. The blaze had ripped through more than half the fields now; the water did little more than sizzle into steam that unfurled, joining the great clouds of smoke that now billowed over the horizon.

She couldn't call her god to stop this. The Phoenix could only start fires. It couldn't put them out.

She knew these fields hadn't caught fire by accident. No, accidental wildfires spread outward from a single source, but this fire had several—at least three initial points of burn whose ranges gradually converged as the fire spread wider and wider.

Nezha had done this, too.

This was sabotage, and the perpetrators were long gone, disappeared into the dark.

You led them here, said Altan's voice. *You brought them in your caravan because you couldn't root out the spies, and you showed them exactly where they needed to strike.*

The wave of despair hit so wrenchingly deep that it almost felt funny. Because of course, of fucking *course*, at the end of the line, when everything whittled down to a single hope, she'd lose that, too. This wasn't a surprise, this was just the culmination of a series of failures that had begun the moment she occupied Arlong, and then spiraled when she hadn't noticed; a sudden, unpredicted reversal of the rolling ball of fortune that had won her the south.

She couldn't stop this. She couldn't fix this.

All she could do was watch. And some sick, desperate part of her wanted to watch, found some perverse glee in staring as the flowers withered and crumpled into ash, because she wanted to see how far the hopelessness would go, and because the destruction felt good—the wanton erasure of life and hope felt *good*, even if the hope going up in smoke was her own.

"You have to talk to the Republic," Kitay said.

They were alone, just the two of them inside the office, all their aides and guards banished out of earshot. Everyone was clamoring for answers; they wanted orders and assurances, and Rin had nothing to give them. The burned fields were the final blow. Now Rin had no plan, no recourse, and nothing to offer her men. She and Kitay had to solve this, and they could not leave the room until they did.

But to her disbelief, the first suggestion he made was surrender.

The way he said it made it sound like a foregone conclusion. As if he knew this to be true, had known months ago, and was only now bothering to let her in on it.

"No," she said. "Never."

"Rin, come on—"

"This is what they want."

"Of course it's what they want! Nezha's offering food aid. He's been offering that from the start. We have to take it."

"Are you working with them?" she demanded.

He recoiled. "No—what are you—"

"I knew it. I fucking *knew it*." That explained everything—why he'd bogged her down with mindless, exhausting tasks at Arlong, why he'd kept detracting from the military front, why he'd kept willfully ignoring the clear threat of Nezha's constant letters. "First Venka, now you? Is that what this is?"

"Rin, that's—"

"Don't call me crazy."

"You *are* being crazy," he snapped. "You're acting like a maniac. Shut up for a moment and face the fucking facts." She opened her mouth to retort but he shouted over her, hand splayed in front of her face as if she were a misbehaving child. "We're dealing with famine—not something cyclical, not something we can weather out, but the worst famine in recent history. There's no grain left in the entire fucking country because Daji poisoned half the south, the entire heartland was too busy fleeing for their lives to till the fields, our rivers are flooded, and we've had an unnaturally cold and dry winter that's shortened the growing season for crops, which has made things doubly difficult for anyone who even tried planting."

His breathing grew shaky as he spoke; his words spilled out at such a frantic rate that she could barely understand him. "No irrigation or flood control projects. No one's been maintaining or supervising the granaries, so if any existed, they've been plundered empty by now. We've got no leverage, no backup options, no money, nothing—"

"So we fight for it," she said. "We *beat* them, and then we take what we want—"

"That's insane."

"Insane? Insane is giving them what they want. We can't stop here, we can't just let everything go, we can't let them win—"

"*Shut up!*" he shouted. "Can you even hear yourself?"

"Can *you*? You want to give up!"

"It's not what I want," he said. "It's the only option that we have. People are starving. *Our* people. Those corpses on the roadside? Pretty soon that's going to be the entire country, unless you learn to swallow your pride."

She almost screamed.

This wasn't how it was supposed to work.

She'd won. She'd fucking won, she'd razed Nezha's city, she'd obliterated her enemies, she'd conquered the Nikara south, she'd *won*, so why, *why* were they talking like they'd already been defeated?

Suddenly her rage dissipated. She couldn't be furious with Kitay; yelling at him wouldn't change the facts.

"They can't do this to me," she said dully. "I was supposed to win."

"You *did* win," he said sadly. "This entire country is yours. Just please don't throw it away with your pride."

"But we were going to rebuild this world," she said. The words sounded plaintive as she said them, a childish fantasy, but that was how she felt, that was what she really believed—because otherwise, what the fuck was this all for? "We were going to be free. We were going to *make* them free—"

"And you can still do that," he insisted. "Look at what we've done. Where we are. We've built an entire nation, Rin. We don't have to let it collapse."

"But they're going to come after us—"

"I promise you they won't." He took her face in his hands. "Look at me. Nezha's defeated. There's no fight left in him. What he wants is what we all want, which is to stop killing our own people.

"We're about to have the world we fought for. Can't you see it? It's so close, it's just over the horizon. We'll have an independent south, we'll have a world free from war, and all you have to do is *say the word*."

But that wasn't the world she'd fought for, Rin thought. The world she'd fought for was one where she, and only she, was in charge.

"We told them they were free," she said miserably. "We won. We *won*. And you want us to go back to the foreigners and bow."

"Cooperation isn't bowing."

She scoffed. "It's close enough."

"It's a long march to liberation," he said. "And it's not so easy as burning our enemies. We won our war, Rin. We were the righteous river of blood. But ideological purity is a battle cry, it's not the stable foundation for a unified country. A nation means nothing if it can't provide for the people in it. You have to act for their sake. Sometimes you've got to bend the knee, Rin. Sometimes, at least, you've got to pretend."

No, that's where he was wrong. Rin *could not bow*. Tearza bowed. Hanelai bowed. And look what that got them: quick, brutal deaths and complete erasure from a history that should have been theirs to write. Their fault was that they were *weak*, they trusted the men they loved, and they didn't have the guts to do what was necessary.

Tearza should have killed the Red Emperor. Hanelai should have murdered Jiang when she'd had the chance. But they couldn't hurt the people they loved.

But Rin could kill anything.

She could unshackle this country. She could succeed where everyone else had failed, because she alone was willing to pay the price.

She'd thought Kitay understood the necessary sacrifice, too. She'd thought that he, if anyone, knew what victory required.

But if she was wrong—if he was too weak to see this revolution through—then she'd have to do it alone.

"Rin?"

She blinked at him. "What?"

"Tell me you see it, too." He squeezed her shoulders. "Please, Rin. Tell me you get it."

He sounded so desperate.

She looked into his eyes, and she couldn't recognize the person she saw there.

This was not Kitay. This was someone weak, gullible, and corrupted.

She'd lost him. When had he become her enemy? She hadn't seen it happening, yet now it was obvious. He might have been turned against her at Arabak. He might have been planning his eventual betrayal ever since they'd left Arlong. He might have been working against her this entire time, holding her back, stopping her from burning as brightly as she could. He might have been on Nezha's side all along.

The only thing she knew for certain was that Kitay was no longer hers. And if she couldn't win him back, then she'd have to do the rest of this by herself.

"Please, Rin," he urged. "*Please.*"

She hesitated, carefully weighing her words before she answered. She had to be clever about this. She couldn't let him know that she'd seen through him.

What was a plausible lie? She couldn't simply agree. He'd know she was faking it; she'd never conceded a point so easily.

She had to feign vulnerability. She had to make him believe this was a hard choice for her—that she'd broken, just like he wanted her to.

"I'm just . . ." She let her voice tremble. She widened her eyes, so that Kitay would think she was terrified rather than capricious. Kitay would believe that. Kitay had always wanted to see the best in people, damn him, and that meant he would fucking fall for anything. "I'm scared I can't come back from this."

He pulled her close against him. She managed not to flinch against his embrace.

"You can come back. I'll bring you back. We're in this together, we're linked . . ."

She started to cry. That, she didn't have to fake.

"All right," she whispered. "All right."

"Thank you."

He squeezed her tight. She returned his embrace, pressing her head against his chest while her mind raced, wondering where she went from here.

If she couldn't count on her people and she couldn't count on Kitay, then she'd have to finish things herself. She had the only ally she needed—a god that could bury countries. And if Kitay tried to deny her that, then she'd just have to break him.

She knew she could do it. She'd always known she could, since the day they knelt before the Sorqan Sira and melded their souls together. She could have erased him then. She almost had; she was just that much stronger. She'd held herself back because she loved him.

And she still loved him. She'd never stop. But that didn't matter.

You've abandoned me, she thought as he wept with relief into her shoulder. *You thought you could fool me, but I know your soul. And if you're not with me, you'll burn, too.*

CHAPTER 34

Nezha would meet them alone in three weeks on Speer. No guards, no delegates, no troops lying in wait, and no Hesperians. Rin and Kitay would represent Nikan, and Nezha would speak for the Republic and the Consortium both. If Rin caught even a glimpse of anyone else on the island, the cease-fire was off.

Those were the terms she demanded in the first and only response to Nezha's letters. She was stunned when he and the Consortium agreed without question.

But then, the Hesperians could not understand the power that lay in the sands of the Dead Island. They thought Nikara superstitions were the products of feeble, uncivilized minds, that her command of fire was nothing more than an outburst of Chaos. They couldn't know that Speer was suffused with history and blood, with the power of thousands of vengeful deceased who haunted its every corner.

There are places in the world where the boundaries between the gods and mortals are thin, Chaghan had once told her. Where reality blurs, where the gods very nearly materialize.

The Speerlies had made their home in such a place, right on the edge of mortality and madness, and the Phoenix had both punished and blessed them in turn.

The Dead Island's legacy ran through Rin's blood. Now it called her home to finish what she'd started, to see her revenge through to the end. When she returned to that island, she'd be in the Phoenix's holy domain, one step closer to divinity.

She'd destroyed a nation from that island once before. She wouldn't hesitate to do it again.

They crossed the channel in a small fisherman's dinghy. Rin sat with her knees pulled up to her chest, shivering against the ocean breeze while Kitay fussed with the sails. Neither of them spoke. There was nothing more to be said. Everything had been spilled the night the fields in Tikany burned, and now what lay between them was a quiet, exhausted resignation. There was no point in commiseration or reassurance. Rin knew what happened next and Kitay thought he did; now there was only the wait.

When the Dead Island emerged on the horizon, a gray, ashy mound that at first seemed indistinguishable from the mist, Kitay reached over and rubbed his thumb over her wrist.

"It'll be all right," he murmured. "We'll fix this."

She gave him a tight smile, twisted around to face the island, and said nothing.

Nezha was waiting on the beach when their vessel approached the shallows. He didn't appear to be armed, but that didn't matter. Neither of them was far from their army. Rin had troops waiting in ships off the coast of Snake Province, spyglasses trained on the horizon for the first sign of her beacon. She could only assume that Nezha's reinforcements were doing the same.

No, she was counting on it.

"Scared?" she inquired as she stepped onto the sand.

He gave her a hollow smile. "You know I can't die."

"We're trying to broker a peace here." Kitay dropped an anchor off the side of the dinghy, then followed Rin onto the shore. "Let's not start off with death threats, shall we?"

"Fair enough." Nezha gestured farther up the beach, where

Rin saw he'd prepared three chairs and a square tea table covered in ink, brushes, and blank parchment. "After you."

They crossed the length of the beach in silence.

Rin couldn't help but take quick, furtive glances at Nezha as she walked beside him.

He looked wrecked. He still carried himself like a general. His shoulders never slumped; his voice never wavered. Yet every part of him seemed diminished, stretched thin and whittled down. His scarred mouth, once twisted on one side into a jeering grin, now seemed trapped in a painful rictus.

She'd expected him to jeer at her, to gloat over their capitulation, but he didn't seem at all like he was enjoying this. He looked exhausted. He looked like someone waiting to die.

They pulled their chairs out and sat. Rin nearly laughed when the first thing Nezha did was politely, meticulously pour each of them a full, steaming cup of tea. It lent such an air of ceremony, of *normalcy*, to negotiations made possible by an ocean of blood.

Neither she nor Kitay touched their cups. Nezha drained his in a single swallow.

"Well, then." He reached for an ink brush and held it lightly over the parchment. "Where shall we start?"

"Tell us their final terms," Rin said.

Nezha faltered for a moment. He'd expected more of a dance. "You mean—"

"Lay it all out," she said. "List every last thing it'll take to get the Hesperians off our back. We're not here to bandy words. Just tell us how much it'll cost."

"As you wish." He cleared his throat. He had no papers to consult; he knew by heart what the Hesperians wanted. "The Consortium is willing to withdraw their forces, commit to a signed armistice, and provide enough shipments of grain, dried meat, and starches to tide the entire country over to the next harvest."

"Great Tortoise," Kitay breathed. "Thank—"

Rin spoke over him. "And in return?"

"First, full amnesty for all soldiers and leadership involved with the Republic," Nezha said. "That benefits you, too. You need people to keep the country running. Let them go back home with their safety guaranteed, and they'll work for you. I'll vouch for that. Second, the Consortium wants designated treaty ports—at least one in each province that borders the ocean. Third, they'd like their missionary privileges back. The Gray Order conduct proselytization with immunity, and anyone who lays a finger on them gets extradited to Hesperia for punishment."

"And what about me?" she pressed.

He held out his arms. Golden circlets gleamed bright around pale skin rubbed painfully raw. Up close, it was clear they were fitted perfectly to the width of his wrists. She didn't know how he ever took them off, or even if he could. "You'll put these on. You'll never call the Phoenix again. You'll never pass on your knowledge of how shamanism works in any form to anyone alive, and you'll cooperate with hunting down everyone in Nikan who is even suspected to know about the Pantheon. You can walk free in the south—even rule it, if you like—so long as you make yourself available."

"Available in what ways?" Kitay asked.

Nezha swallowed. "In the same ways I was."

A heavy silence descended on the table. Nezha wouldn't meet their eyes. But neither did his gaze drop—he stared straight forward, shoulders still squared, meeting their pity with silent defiance as they stared at his circlets.

"Why?" Rin asked at last. She couldn't keep her voice from breaking. The sight of the circlets was suddenly too much to bear. She wanted to rip them off his wrists, to cover them with his sleeves—anything to make them disappear. "Nezha, why the *fuck*—"

"Because they had all the power," he said quietly. "Because they still do."

She shook her head, astonished. "Have you no pride?"

"It's not about pride." He withdrew his arms. "It's about sacrifice. I chose the Hesperians because I recognize that they aren't just decades but *centuries* ahead of us in every way that matters, and if they decide to work with us, we could use their knowledge to make life better for millions of people. Despite the cost."

"The costs are where we differ," she said coldly.

"You've only seen one side of them, Rin. You've seen them at their very worst, but you also stand for everything they can't abide. But what if you didn't? I know they are condescending, I know they don't think we're human, I know—" His throat pulsed. He coughed. "I know the depths of their cruelty. But they were willing to cooperate with me. They're getting this close to respecting me. And if I just had *that*—"

"What's it going to take?" Kitay asked abruptly. "For them to respect you?"

Nezha didn't hesitate. "Your deaths."

There was no malice in his voice. That wasn't a threat, just a simple statement of fact. Nezha had not been able to deliver Rin's corpse, despite having ample opportunity to kill her, and for that he'd given up a nation.

Kitay gave a slight nod, as if he'd fully expected that answer. "And what's it going to take for them to respect *us*?"

"They'll never respect you," Nezha said tonelessly. "They will never see you as anything more than subhuman. They will work warily with you because they're afraid of you, but you'll always have to stay on edge. You'll always have to grovel to get what you want. My father's Republic was the only regime they would ever have willingly supported, and they still wouldn't ever have really trusted me unless I delivered your heads."

Rin snorted. "So there's the impasse."

"Come on. You know that's not what I'm here for." He pressed his fingers against his temples. "You won, Rin. Fair and square. I'm not angling for the throne. I'm just trying to make this less painful for everyone involved."

"You seem so certain that I'll be an awful ruler."

"It's not an insult. I just think you have no interest in ruling at all. You don't care about statecraft. You're not an administrator, you're a soldier."

"I'm a general," she corrected.

"You're a general who's conclusively wiped everyone else off the map," he said. "You won, all right? You beat me. But your role—that role, at least, is over. You've got no wars left to fight."

"You know that's not true."

"It *can* be true," he insisted. "This isn't what Hesperia wants. This war continues if you bring it to them. But if you work with them, if you let them believe you're not a threat, they won't treat you like one. If you make concessions, if you stay in their good graces—"

"That's bullshit," she snapped. "I've heard that logic before. Su Daji initiated the Third Poppy War because she thought losing half the country was better than losing it all. And what happened then, Nezha? How'd you get that scar on your face? How'd we get to Golyn Niis?"

"What you're doing," Nezha said quietly, "will be worse than a thousand Golyn Niises."

"Not if we win."

He gave her a wary look. "This is a peace negotiation."

"It's not," she said softly. "You know it's not."

His eyes narrowed. "Rin—"

She pushed her chair back and stood up. Enough of these pretensions. She hadn't come to sign a peace treaty, and neither had he.

"Where is the fleet?" she asked.

He tensed. "I don't know what you mean."

"Call them out." She let flames roll down her shoulders. "That's what I came for. Not this charade."

Kitay stood up. "Rin, what are you doing?"

She ignored him. "Call them out, Nezha. I know they're hiding. I won't ask again."

Nezha's expression went slack. He exchanged a bewildered glance with Kitay, and the sheer patronization of that gesture made her flames jump twice as high.

"Fine," she said. "I'll do it myself."

Then she turned toward the ocean and unleashed a brilliant flare into the sky.

A fleet of dirigibles immediately emerged over the horizon.

I was right. She felt a hot wave of satisfaction. The Hesperians hadn't been bold enough to conceal their airships on Speer—smart of them, for she would have decimated them otherwise—but they'd kept them waiting all along the coast of Snake Province.

So much for Nezha's cease-fire. This confirmed everything she'd suspected. The Hesperians weren't interested in peace, and neither was she. Both just wanted to finish this. They'd come for an ambush, and she'd just called their bluff.

Nezha stood up. "Rin, they're not—"

"Liar," she snarled. "They're *right there*."

"They're backup," he said. "In case—"

"In case what?" she demanded. "In case you couldn't get the job done? You wanted to end this, so let's end this. Let's answer this question once and for all. Let's pit their god against mine. Let's see which one is real."

Her beacon surged higher, a pillar so searingly bright it cast an orange hue over the entire shore. The fleet surged forth. They were already halfway across the channel; they'd be over Speer in seconds.

Rin watched the horizon and waited.

She and Kitay had determined her maximum radius a long time ago. Since they had been anchored, it had always been fifty yards in any direction. She could never push farther without Kitay collapsing, without losing access to the Phoenix.

But now she was on Speer. Everything changed on Speer.

When the first of the airships drew close enough that she could see its cannons, she swept it out of the sky. The cannons never fired; it plummeted straight into the ocean like a rock.

The rest of the fleet advanced, undaunted.

Keep coming, she thought, exhilarated. *I'll smite you all.*

This was it. This was the moment she rewrote history. The Hesperian fleet would crowd the sky like storm clouds, and she'd destroy it in minutes. This would be more than a crushing victory. It would be a display of force—an undeniable, irrefutable display of divine authority.

Then the Hesperians she permitted to survive would flee, this time for good. They would never return to the eastern hemisphere. They would never dare threaten her people. And when she demanded gold and grain, they wouldn't dare say no.

This was what Speer had always been capable of, what Queen Mai'rinnen Tearza had been too afraid to do. The last Speerly queen let her homeland become an island of slaves because she thought unleashing the Phoenix might burn down the world. She could have had everything, but she didn't have the *will*.

Rin would not make that same mistake.

"I didn't want this." Dimly, over the roar of the flames, she heard Kitay pleading to Nezha. "That's not what she—"

"Stop her," Nezha said.

"I can't."

Nezha stood, pushing his chair to the ground. Rin grinned. When he lunged, she was ready. She'd seen the bulge under his shirt where he'd concealed a knife. She knew that when he had the initiative, he favored a right-handed strike to the upper torso. She twisted to the side. His blade met empty air. When he tried tackling her, she mirrored his momentum and rolled with him to the ground.

Subduing him was so easy.

It should have been a struggle. Nezha had all the advantages in hand-to-hand combat—he was just taller and heavier, his limbs were longer, and every time they'd ever brawled, unless she pulled a gimmick, he'd always managed to pin her through sheer brute force.

But something was wrong.

That formidable skill wasn't there. Strength, speed—both gone. His strikes were stiff and sluggish. She couldn't see proof of any wounds, yet he winced with every motion, as if invisible knives were digging into his flesh.

And he wasn't calling the Dragon.

Why wasn't he calling the Dragon?

If Nezha had demanded more of her focus she would have noticed the way his golden circlets rang eerily every time he moved, darkening the skin around his wrists and ankles. But her mind was not on Nezha. He was just an obstacle, a great, blockish object that she needed out of the way. In that moment, Nezha was an afterthought.

Her mind was on the sky; her focus was on the fleet.

Was this how Jiang had always felt on the battlefield, when he'd felled columns with little more than a thought? The difference in scale was inconceivable. This wasn't fighting. There was no struggle involved in this, no effort. She was simply writing reality. She was *painting*. She pointed, and balloons incinerated. She clenched her fist, and carriages exploded.

Her vision lurched, sharpened, *expanded*. When she'd sunk the Federation she'd been underground, alone inside a stone temple, and yet when she'd awakened the dormant volcano it had felt like she was floating right above the archipelago, keenly aware of the million sleeping souls beneath her, flaring like match heads, only to go suddenly, irreversibly dark.

Now, again, she saw the material world—such a flimsy thing, so fragile and temporary—through the eyes of a god. She saw the airships in such close detail she could have been standing under them. She saw the smooth texture of the airship balloons. Time dilated as she watched the fire ignite around them, ripping through whatever gas filled their interiors that was so *delicious* to the flame—

"Rin, *stop*!" She saw Nezha's mouth moving seconds before she realized he was yelling. He wasn't even really fighting anymore—he certainly couldn't be trying, because his blows hardly landed, and his parries were sluggish.

She jerked her knee into his side, clamped her left hand against his shoulder, and pushed him hard to the ground.

His head slammed against the corner of the table. He slumped sideways, mouth agape. He didn't get up.

She turned back to the fleet.

The beach faded from her sight. She saw what the fire saw—not bodies or ships but simply *shapes*, all equal, all simply kindling for the pyres of her worship. And she knew the Phoenix was pleased because its screeching laughter grew louder and louder, its presence intensifying until their minds felt as if they were one, as, from one end of the horizon to the other, she methodically wrecked the fleet—

Until it went silent.

The shock sent her reeling.

The sky seemed very blue and bright; the airships so far away. She was just a girl again, without fire. The Phoenix was gone, and when she reached to find it she met only a mute, indifferent wall.

She whirled on Kitay. "What have you—"

He was barely managing to stand, clutching the table for support. His face had turned a deathly gray. Sweat dripped from his temples, and his knees buckled so hard she was sure he was about to collapse.

"You can't," he whispered.

"Kitay—"

"Not without my help. Not without my permission. That was our deal."

She gaped at him, astonished. He'd cut her off. The *traitor*, he'd fucking *cut her off*.

Kitay was her back door, her bridge, her single channel to the Phoenix. Since the moment they'd been anchored he'd always kept it open, had let her abuse his mind to funnel as much fire as she desired. He'd never closed it off. She'd almost forgotten that he *could*.

"I didn't think I could, either," he said. "I thought I couldn't deny you anything. But I can, I always could, I'd just never really tried."

"Kitay . . ."

"Stop this," he ordered. A spasm rippled through his body and he lurched forward, wincing, but caught himself on the edge of the table before he fell. "Or you'll never call the fire again."

No. No, this wasn't how this ended. She hadn't come this far to be thwarted by Kitay's idiotic scruples. He didn't get to withhold her power like a condescending parent, dangling her toys just out of reach.

She saw the defiance in his eyes, and her heart shattered.

You, too?

She didn't attack first. If Kitay hadn't taken the first blow, she might not have had the will to strike him. Despite his betrayal he was still *Kitay*—her best friend, her anchor, the person she loved most in the world and the one person she'd sworn to always protect.

But he did take the blow.

He lunged forward, fists aimed at her face, and once he did, it was like a glass pane had shattered. Then there was nothing holding her back, no sentiment, no pangs of guilt when she redirected her fury toward him.

She'd never fought Kitay before.

She realized this as they wrestled to the ground—a dim, floating observation that was really quite amazing, for almost everyone in her class at Sinegard had fought everyone else at some point. She'd sparred against Venka and Nezha plenty of times. Her first year, she'd tried so hard to kill Nezha that she'd nearly succeeded.

But she'd never once touched Kitay. Not even in practice. The few times they were paired against each other they found excuses to seek different partners, because neither of them could stand the thought of trying to hurt the other, not even for pretend.

She hadn't realized how strong he was. Kitay in her mind was a scholar, a strategist. Kitay hadn't seen combat since Vaisra's northern expedition. He always waited out battles from a distance, kept safe by an entire squadron.

She'd forgotten that he, too, had been trained as a soldier. And he'd been very, very good at it.

Kitay was not as strong as Nezha, nor as fast as her. But he struck with crisp, deadly precision. His attacks landed with maximal force concentrated to the thinnest point of impact—the knife edge of his hand, the point of his knuckle, the protruding cap of his knee. He chose his targets carefully. He knew her body better than anyone; he knew the spots where she hurt the most—her amputated wrist, the scars along her back, her twice-cracked ribs. And he attacked them with brutal precision.

She was losing. She was getting exhausted, slowed by the accumulated hurts of a dozen direct blows. He'd maintained the offensive from the start. She was flailing to even parry; she wouldn't last another minute.

"Give up," he panted. "Give up, Rin, it's over."

"Fuck you," she snarled, and flung her right fist toward his eye.

In her fury she forgot that fist did not exist, that she would not meet the sharp bones of his face with curled knuckles but the stump of her wrist, sore and vulnerable and protected only by a thin, irritated layer of skin.

The pain was white-hot, debilitating. She howled.

Kitay staggered back, out of her range, and picked Nezha's knife up from the ground.

She flinched back, arms flung up instinctively to protect her chest. But he hadn't pointed the blade at her.

Fuck.

She lunged and caught his wrist just as he plunged the blade toward his chest. She wasn't strong enough; the tip burrowed under his skin and slid down, slicing a gash across his ribs. They struggled against each other, her pulling with all her might while he pushed the knife against himself, the sharp blade trembling just an inch from his chest.

She wasn't going to win.

She couldn't overpower him. He was stronger. He had both his hands.

But she didn't have to physically defeat him—she only needed to break his will. And she knew one unspoken fact for a certainty, one truth that had underlined their bond since the day she'd met him.

Her will was so much stronger than his. It always had been.

She acted. He followed. Like two hands on a sword's blade, she determined the direction and he provided the force; she was the visionary, and he was her willing executioner. He'd always enforced what she wanted. He would not defy her now.

She focused all her thoughts toward the Phoenix, railing against the fragile barrier of Kitay's mind.

I know you're there, she prayed to the silence. *I know you're with me.*

"Give up," Kitay said. But sweat was dripping down his forehead; his teeth were clenched with strain. "You can't."

Rin shut her eyes and redoubled her efforts, grasping around the void until she found a tiny filament, the barest hint of divine presence. That was enough.

Break him, she told the Phoenix.

She heard a shattering sound in her mind, a porcelain cup dashed against stone.

She saw a flash of red. The beach disappeared.

They were alone in the plane of spirit, standing on opposite sides of a great circle, both of them naked and fully revealed. It was all there, laid out between them. All their shared fury, vindictiveness, bloodlust, and guilt. Her cruelty. His complicity. Her desperation. His regret.

She saw him across the circle and knew that if she wanted to subdue him, all she had to do was think it. She'd nearly done it before—the instant they were anchored, in the first moments after she'd reestablished her bond with the Phoenix, she'd nearly erased him. She could rip the god's power through his mind like he was nothing more than a flimsy net.

He knew it, too. She felt his resignation, his wretched surrender.

Surrender, not agreement. They were enemies now—and she could bend his will, but she'd never again have his heart.

Yet something—sentiment, heartbreak—compelled her to try.

"Kitay, please—"

"Don't," he said. "Just—go ahead. But don't."

His body went limp. The spirit world disappeared. Rin came to her senses just as Kitay slumped to the ground, falling heavily against her arms. Then, somehow, she was kneeling above him with her hand on his neck, her thumb resting against the bulge of his throat.

Their eyes met. She felt a shock of horror.

She recognized the way he was looking at her. It was how she'd once looked at Altan. It was the way she'd seen Daji look at Riga—that look of wretched, desperate, and reproachful loyalty.

It said, *Do it.*

Take what you want, it said. *I'll hate you for it. But I'll love you forever. I can't help but love you.*

Ruin me, ruin us, and I'll let you.

She almost took that for permission.

But if she did, if she broke through his soul and took everything she wanted . . .

She'd never stop. There would be no limits to her power. She'd never stop using him, ripping his mind open and setting it on fire every hour and minute and second, because she would always need the fire. If she did this then her war would extend across the world and her enemies would multiply—there would always be someone else, someone like Petra trying to banish her god and crush her nation, or someone like Nezha trying to foment rebellion from within.

And unless she killed every single one of them, she would never be safe and her revolution would never succeed, and so she'd have to keep going until she reduced the rest of the world to ashes, until she was the last one standing.

Until she was alone.

Was that peace? Was that liberation?

She could see her victories. She could see the burned wreckage of Hesperian shores. She could see herself at the center of a conflagration that consumed the world, scorched it, cleansed it, ate away its rotted foundations—

But she couldn't see where it ended.

She couldn't see where the pain stopped—not for the world, and not for Kitay.

"You're hurting me," he whispered.

It was like being doused in ice water. Repulsed, she gave a sharp sob and jerked her hand away from his neck.

The humming above crescendoed to a deafening roar.

Too late, Rin glanced up. Lightning enveloped her body, a dozen painless arcs of light a thousand times brighter than the sun. The Phoenix went silent. So did the rage; so did the crimson visions of a world on fire. The lightning vanished her divinity, and all that it left behind was utter horror at what she'd nearly done.

Kitay moaned, touched two fingers to his temple, and went limp. Rin clutched him against her chest and rocked back and forth, dazed.

"Rin," croaked Nezha.

She twisted around. He was sitting up. Blood dribbled down the side of his head, and his eyes were bleary, unfocused. He stared at the electricity dancing across Rin's body, mouth agape. He rose slowly, but she knew he wasn't going to attack. He was the furthest thing from a threat at that moment—he just looked like a young boy, scared and confused, utterly at a loss for what to do.

There's nothing he can do, Rin realized. Neither Nezha nor Kitay could determine what happened next. They weren't strong enough.

This choice had to be hers.

She saw it in a flash of utter clarity. She knew what she had to do. The only path, the only way forward.

And what a familiar path it was. It was so obvious now. The world was a dream of the gods, and the gods dreamed in sequences, in symmetry, in patterns. History repeated itself, and she was only the latest iteration of the same scene in a tapestry that had been spun long before her birth.

So many others had stood on this precipice before her.

Mai'rinnen Tearza, the Speerly queen who chose to die rather than bind herself to a king she hated.

Altan Trengsin, the boy who burned too bright, who became his own funeral pyre.

Jiang Ziya, the Dragon Emperor's blade, the monster, the murderer, her mentor, her savior.

Hanelai, who fled to her death before she knelt.

They'd wielded unprecedented power, unimaginable and unmatchable power capable of rewriting the script of history. And they'd written themselves out.

Now here they were again: three people—children, really; too young and inexperienced for the roles they'd inherited—holding the fate of Nikan in their hands. And Rin was poised to acquire the empire Riga had wanted, if only she could be just as cruel.

But what kind of emperor would Riga have been? And how much worse would she be?

Oh, but history moved in such vicious circles.

She could see the future and its shape was already drawn, predetermined by patterns that had been set in motion before she was born—patterns of cruelty and dehumanization and oppression and trauma that had pulled her right back into the place where the Trifecta had once stood. And if she did this, if she broke Kitay like Riga would have broken Jiang, she would only re-create those patterns—because there *would* be resistance, there would be blood, and the only way she could eliminate that possibility was by burning down the world.

Yet a single decision could escape the current, could push history off its course.

It's a long march to liberation, Kitay had said.

Sometimes you've got to bend the knee.

Sometimes, at least, you've got to pretend.

She finally understood what that meant.

She knew what she had to do next. It wasn't about surrender. It was about the long game. It was about survival.

She stood up, reached for Nezha's hand, and curled his fingers around the handle of the knife.

He stiffened. "What are you—"

"Get their respect," she said. "Tell them you killed me. Tell them everything they want to hear. Say whatever you need to to get them to trust you."

"Rin—"

"It's the only way forward."

He understood what she meant him to do. His eyes widened in alarm, and he tried to wrench his hand away, but she clenched his fingers tight.

"Nezha—"

"You can't do this for me," he said. "I won't let you."

"It's not for you. It's not a favor. It's the cruelest thing I could do."

She meant it.

Dying was easy. Living was so much harder—that was the most important lesson Altan had ever taught her.

She glanced down at Kitay.

He was awake, his face set in resolve. He gave her a grim nod. That was all she had to see. That was permission.

She couldn't release him. Neither of them knew how. But she knew, as clearly as if he'd said it out loud, that he intended to follow her to the end. Their fates were tied, weighed down by the same culpability.

"Come, now." She linked her fingers around Nezha's. Closed both his hands around the cold, cold hilt as lightning arced around them, between them. Brought the blade round to the front. "Properly this time."

"Rin." Nezha looked so scared. It was a funny thing, how fear made him look so much younger, how it rounded his eyes and erased the cruel grimace of his sneer so that he looked, just for an instant, like the boy she'd first met at Sinegard. "Rin, don't—"

"Fix this," she ordered.

Nezha's fingers went slack in hers. She tightened her grip; she had enough resolve for the both of them. As the dirigibles descended toward Speer, she brought Nezha's hand up to her chest and plunged the blade into her heart.

EPILOGUE

She was so small.

Nezha couldn't register the choking gurgles in her throat, the glassy panic in her eyes, or the warmth of her blood as it spilled down his hands. He couldn't, or he would shatter. As Rin bled out over the sand, the only thought running through his mind was that she was so small, so light, so fragile in his arms.

Then the twitching stopped, and she was gone.

Kitay lay still beside him. He knew Kitay was gone, too—that Kitay had died a bloodless death the moment he plunged the blade into Rin's heart, because Rin and Kitay were bonded in a way that he could never understand, and there was no world where Rin died and Kitay remained alive. Because Kitay—the third party, the in-between, the weight that tipped the scale—had chosen to follow Rin into the afterlife and to leave Nezha behind. Alone.

Alone, and shouldering the immense burden of their legacy.

He couldn't move. He could hardly breathe. As he stared down at the tiny body in his arms—so limp and lifeless, so utterly unlike the vicious human hurricane he knew as Fang Runin—all he could do was tremble.

You bitch, he thought. *You fucking bitch.*

He realized dimly that he ought to be glad she was dead. He should have been fucking *delighted*. And rationally, intellectually, he was. Rin was a monster, a murderer, a destroyer of worlds. Nothing but blood and ashes ever trailed in her wake. The world was a better, safer, and more peaceful place without her in it. He believed that. He had to believe that.

And yet.

And yet, when he looked at that broken body, all he wanted to do was howl.

Why? He wanted to scream at her. He wanted to shake her, throttle her, until she answered. *Rin, what the fuck?*

But he knew why.

He knew exactly what choice she'd made and what she'd intended. And that made everything—hating her, loving her, *surviving* her—so much harder.

Fix this.

He tilted his head back. His knees shook from a wave of exhaustion washing over his limbs, and he took a deep, rattling breath as he contemplated the monumental task before him.

Fix this? *Fix this?* What did he have left to work with? She'd broken *everything*.

But theirs had always been a broken country. It had never been unified, not truly; it had only ever been held tightly together by steel and blood, a facade of internal unity, while factions always threatened to split from within. Rin had forced those tensions to the surface, and then to their breaking point. She'd forced the Nikara to confront the greatest lie it had ever told about itself—that there had ever been a united Nikara Empire at all.

And yet, she'd laid a foundation for him. She'd burned away all that was rotten and corrupt. He didn't have to reform the Warlord system because she'd destroyed it for him. He didn't have to face backlash from the crumpling system of feudal aristocracy, because she'd already wrecked it. She'd wiped clear the maps of the past. She'd hurled the pieces off the board.

She was a goddess. She was a monster. She'd nearly destroyed this country.

And then she'd given it one last, gasping chance to live.

He knew she hadn't done this for him. No, she'd done him no great mercy. She'd known that his future—the future she'd just assigned him—was full of horrors. They both knew that Nikan's only path forward was through Hesperia—through a cruel, supercilious, exploitative entity that would certainly try to remold and reshape them, until the only vestiges of Nikara culture that remained lay buried in the past.

But Nikan had survived occupation before. If Nezha played his cards right—if he bent where he needed to, if he lashed back at just the right time—then they might survive occupation again.

He didn't know how he'd weather what came next, but he had to try.

He owed it to her to try.

Nezha lowered Rin's body to the ground, stood up, squared his shoulders, and awaited the coming of the fleet.

DRAMATIS PERSONAE

THE SOUTHERN COALITION AND ITS ALLIES

Fang Runin: a war orphan from Rooster Province, former commander of the Cike, the last living Speerly
Chen Kitay: the son of the former Imperial defense minister, heir to the House of Chen, Rin's anchor
Sring Venka: an archer from Sinegard, daughter of the former Imperial finance minister
Liu Gurubai: the Monkey Warlord, a brilliant politician
Ma Lien: bandit chief, member of the southern leadership
Liu Dai: member of the southern leadership, Gurubai's longtime ally
Yang Souji: resistance leader from Rooster Province, commands the Iron Wolves
Quan Cholang: the young, newly appointed Dog Warlord
Chiang Moag: Pirate Queen of Ankhiluun, aka the Stone Bitch and the Lying Widow

THE HOUSE OF YIN

Yin Vaisra: the Dragon Warlord and leader of the Nikara Republic
Yin Saikhara: the Lady of Arlong and the wife of Yin Vaisra
*Yin Jinzha: the oldest son of the Dragon Warlord and the grand marshal of the Republican Army, killed by Su Daji
Yin Muzha: Jinzha's twin sister, Vaisra's only daughter
Yin Nezha: the second son of the Dragon Warlord
*Yin Mingzha: the third son of the Dragon Warlord, killed by the Dragon of Arlong as a child

THE TRIFECTA

Su Daji: formerly the Empress of Nikan, aka the Vipress, calls on the Snail Goddess of Creation Nüwa

Jiang Ziya: the Gatekeeper, calls on the beasts of the Emperor's Menagerie

Yin Riga: the Dragon Emperor, presumed dead since the end of the Second Poppy War

THE HESPERIANS

General Josephus Tarcquet: the leader of the Hesperian troops in Nikan

Sister Petra Ignatius: a representative of the Gray Company (the Hesperian religious order) in Nikan, one of the most brilliant religious scholars of her generation

THE CIKE

***Altan Trengsin:** a Speerly, formerly the commander of the Cike

***Ramsa:** a former prisoner at Baghra, munitions expert

***Baji:** a shaman who calls on the Boar God

***Suni:** a shaman who calls on the Monkey God

Chaghan Suren: a shaman of the Naimad clan and the twin brother of Qara

***Qara Suren:** a sharpshooter, speaker to birds, and the twin sister of Chaghan

***Aratsha:** a shaman who calls on a river god

*Deceased

ACKNOWLEDGMENTS

Four years, three books, and countless memories. We started this journey when I was nineteen and now, at twenty-three, I can't quite believe that we actually did it. Rin's story, and this chapter of my publishing career, are finished. I've got a lot of people to thank for getting me here.

I'm so grateful to the team at Harper Voyager who've done such a fantastic job publishing these books—David Pomerico, Natasha Bardon, Mireya Chiriboga, Jack Renninson, Pamela Jaffee, and Angela Craft. Jung Shan Ink keeps dazzling me with the loveliest illustrations a writer could ask for. Hannah Bowman, the best and sharpest agent in the business, had faith in what this trilogy could be from the start, even when I didn't. Havis Dawson, Joanne Fallert, and the rest of the team at Liza Dawson Associates have continued to bring my books to the rest of the world. Thank you all for seeing me through to the end.

To all my teachers, mentors, and professors: Jeanne Cavelos, Kij Johnson, Ken Liu, Fonda Lee, Mary Robinette Kowal, Adam Mortara, Howard Spendelow, Carol Benedict, John McNeill, James Millward, Hans van de Ven, Heather Inwood, and Aaron Timmons—thank you for guiding me to become a person who can, in the way I think, write, and treat others, be a little bit more like you.

To friends and family who helped me feel like a real human being and encouraged me to keep writing until the very last page: Mom, Dad, James, Grace, Jack-Jack, Tiffany, Ben, Christine, Chris, Coco, Farah, Josh, Linden, and Pablo—thank you for your constant love and support.

To the Marshfam and beyond: Joani, Martin, Kobi, Kevin, Nancy, Katie, Aksha, Sarah, Julius, Taylor, Noam, Ben, Rhea, and David—thank you for lighting up my life, and for giving me two years in England full of laughter, home-cooked creations, and board games.

To Magdalene College, Cambridge, and University College, Oxford: thank you for being such magical places to write, and places I was lucky to call home.

To the Vaults & Garden Café: more characters were killed under your roof than you will ever know. Thanks for the scones.

And to Bennett, who's been on this ride from the start: I can't wait to see where we go next, together.

FIRE AND WATER LOOK SO LOVELY TOGETHER.
IT'S A PITY THEY DESTROY EACH OTHER BY NATURE.

A BONUS SHORT STORY ABOUT YIN NEZHA, AND
HOW HE BECAME RIN'S FOE, THEN FRIEND, THEN FOE

THE

DROWNING

FAITH

"Who is the true god?" asks Sister Petra Ignatius.

Nezha knows what she wants him to say. He knows how this game is played; that it's not about the truth or debate but about the submission, and if he just utters the right words then she'll stop. But this is where he draws the line. He has conceded everything else—his body, his pride, his dignity. The soul of his country. But he can't concede the truth.

He's seen the gods. He's touched them.

He's fought them.

"Who is the true god?"

Pain. Pain so bad he doesn't know how much more he can endure. Nezha stopped associating pain with death long ago, since pain can't kill or maim him because he'll always come back. He wishes he wouldn't; that his body wouldn't always stitch itself back together no matter how viciously it was rendered apart. He wishes pain bad enough would mean things were coming to an end. But he's known for a while now he will always live through it; that he will always heal, survive, and return to suffer more.

That's infinitely worse.

"Who is the true god?"

The Maker. The Watchmaker, the Divine Architect, the one who pieced together this universe like a well-crafted machine. A singular, rational, entity; the end point of the cosmos; all that is and ever will be. Say it.

"Who is the true god?"

The true god is their god. Say it, and this stops.

It makes no sense that they waste so much time every day on this same, nonsensical conversation. There's no utilitarian reason for this. This doesn't advance Petra's research, it hinders it. It distracts from it.

But he knows why she does it. Petra is a scientist, but she's also a disciple. A zealot. For all her talk of rationalism, of the scientific process, she is a believer at heart. All the Hesperians are. What lies at the heart of her faith is not reason but dogma. And fear, dogma's ever-present companion. She *needs* her Maker to be real. She *needs* to be right. She can't imagine a world where she's not.

But Nezha won't lie.

"Who is the true god?"

"Chaos," he says.

That's the closest the Hesperians will ever come to understanding the Pantheon. They'll never grasp the depths of it; the terrifying swirl of forces that constitute all that is. Their minds can't handle its incoherence; the fact that the sixty-four gods do not will and do not care. They can't fathom a world without intention. The only word they might accept is *chaos*.

But Nezha knows divinity. It's fathomless. It is not something that can be measured or studied; can't be described through meticulously constructed logic. The forces that dreamed up this world are the opposite of rational. Divinity isn't knowable. It's the Dragon in the grotto. It's the Dragon inside him. It's the three madmen who united a nation and tore themselves apart. It's pain, eternity, and terror. It's endless, all-consuming fire.

It's *her*.

He's lost.

He can't fucking believe he's lost. This match should have ended in thirty seconds with Rin on the ground, flat on her back and moaning, but somehow it's Nezha who is on the floor, face pressed against the dirt. He can't breathe. He can't move—every time he tries, she digs her elbow harder into his neck.

Dimly, he registers she's still hitting him, pummeling her fist into the back of his head over and over, even though he's clearly down for the count with no way of defending himself. It's cruel—

No, that's not cruelty. It's prudence. She's making sure he won't get up.

Smart, he thinks. It's what he'd do.

She keeps going. Nezha's gone completely limp, but she doesn't care. She grasps a handful of his hair, yanks his head back, and slams his face again into the floor.

It hurts. He's stunned by how much it hurts. Nezha's cuts and scrapes usually heal themselves so quickly he barely has time to register the pain, but it's going to take several minutes at least for his face to reconstruct itself. He feels his nose break. He feels his teeth split through his lip.

Shit, he thinks when the blows don't stop. *Holy shit*.

Whatever power the Dragon has here is gone. Startled away by something—her? No, it must be something else—but Nezha can't think straight. Right now he can't even see. The world is a haze of black, red flashes bursting in his vision every time she grinds his face into the dirt.

She's going to kill him. She might actually kill him.

Now he's scared.

All these years trying to find a way to kill himself, and here's someone who might actually finish the job. And somehow, paradoxically, this is the most he's ever wanted to be alive. This is the first time in an eternity he doesn't feel like he's drowning.

"Break," someone says, and the pressure gives.

Heavy footsteps in the ring. They're stopping the match; they're pulling Rin off him. Nezha drops his head against the ground and moans.

"I'm sending you to Ankhiluun," says Vaisra.

Nezha's only been home for several days, just back from a stint in a Federation war camp that felt like a living hell, yet these are the first words his father utters upon their reunion.

But what did he expect?

A hug?

"Why Ankhiluun?" Nezha winces. It still hurts to speak. His muscles pull at barely healed wounds, a web of bright red scars that should have disappeared by now. But some wounds, it appears, are beyond even the Dragon's reach. Some wounds are too vicious, too unnatural.

"I need you to pick up an old classmate. It's delicate."

Nezha frowns. "Did they find Kitay?"

"Better," says Vaisra. "Moag found the Speerly."

You're shitting me, Nezha almost says, but doesn't, because his father doesn't appreciate swearing.

"You'll have to be careful. Moag can't know how badly we need her. Will she come back with you?"

"Of course she will," says Nezha. "We're friends."

He's suddenly ridiculously excited. Rin is in Ankhiluun. Rin is *alive*. He'd never feared for a day she was dead, because creatures like Rin are impossible to kill. And the rumors from the coast had been getting too loud to ignore. They'd made their way as far north as the Federation camp by Ankhiluun, where the soldiers were just starting to figure out that they'd lost the war, and that perhaps there was no home to return to.

No, he's always known Rin would make it out intact. *She*, however, thinks he's dead.

He imagines the look on her face when she sees him, hale and hearty and alive. Suddenly he can't wait to set sail.

Yes, it's worth it. Risky, maybe, to trick a Speerly into thinking she's been kidnapped. In retrospect, he probably shouldn't have fired on her ship. Probably that was coming on a bit strong. But it was so worth it.

"You're dead." She looks like she's about to faint. "I saw you die."

He'd rehearsed something about being glad to see her, but right now he just wants to get a jab in. "And you were always supposed to be the clever one."

"*What the fuck?*" she screams, and it's all Nezha can do not to throw his head back and laugh.

"Democracy." She spits the word like she's tried it for the first time and has decided she doesn't like the taste. She shakes her head. "You really believe all this shit?"

"Of course I do," he says, confused.

"That's cute."

"Come on, Rin. We're trying to build something new here."

"'We're trying to build something new here,'" she mimics, then goes back to sharpening her trident.

He gives up. She doesn't want a good-faith debate, she wants to provoke him. He wonders sometimes if Rin even cares what she's fighting for, so long as she gets to fight.

She likes to joke about his republic; his and his father's. She likes to call it his presumed inheritance. She thinks this is a war about ambition; for personal gain. She doesn't understand he doesn't want to rule. He doesn't want power. He doesn't want a kingdom.

But it's never mattered what he wanted. *Your life is not your own.* This lesson has been drilled into him from childhood. His life belongs to the people. His role in the future of the nation was determined before his birth.

"Our structure of government is the worst thing about this empire," he insists. "It's what's held us back for centuries. Democracy is the only way forward."

"It certainly seems like what's best for the House of Yin," she said. "What do you do when they vote for someone else?"

"Then there's a peaceful transition of power."

"Oh, *that's* likely."

He can't refute her cynicism. Rin thinks everyone's out for themselves. Duty is not a concept she understands, because she is beholden to no one. She's tied to nothing. There's no weight sinking her down. She has her secrets, her painful memories, but she doesn't drown in them. She ignores them, shoves them aside, sets them on fire.

Nezha wonders what it's like to be that reckless, that free.

"Come on," she says. "Be honest. It makes no difference to me if you're just swapping one emperor for another."

"But that's precisely it," he says. "The imperial system has to change. One person can't rule the entire nation. Government must be decentralized."

"See, that's why I don't believe you."

"Why not?"

"Because you're about to be the ones in power," she says. "And because you never decentralize power once you've got it. I wouldn't."

"Well, we all know *you* wouldn't."

She gives him a look. "That's not my cynicism, Nezha. That's human nature."

Yin Jinzha is dead, and the House of Yin mourns.

Vaisra is alone in the great hall when Nezha's permitted in. The Lady Saikhara is not present. Confined to her rooms, they say. They say she's gone mad, catatonic, unable to say anything but the name of her favorite son.

She hasn't asked for Nezha. When Mingzha died, she did not so much as look in his direction for up to a year. Nezha's mother loves him, but it's a strained, wretched love, one stained by the ever-lingering suspicion that the person who came back from the grotto was not really her son.

Vaisra sits stooped atop his throne, hunched over, shoulders still bent from the injuries he sustained at Lusan. He looks aged twenty years by grief.

Nezha wants to rush to his father, to throw his hands around his shoulders. But habit, and propriety, keep them apart.

"I'm sorry," he says. "I know it should have been me."

Vaisra doesn't hesitate. "It should have been you."

A great silence stretches between them.

"How is Mother?" Nezha asks.

"She's with Sister Petra," Vaisra says. "She finds more comfort from her...priests."

Nezha dares to ask. "Is that prudent?"

"It doesn't matter. Let her seek solace where she can find it, the poor woman. Three sons she gave me." Vaisra sighs. "Three."

What goes unsaid: that only one remains.

What also goes unsaid: the wrong one.

"I'll kill her," Nezha vows. He doesn't have to feign his vehemence. He hates Su Daji, hates her for what she's done to this country, to his family. Never has he been so convinced of the righteousness of their cause. "I'll destroy the Empress for what she did to us. I'll deliver you her head, Father, I promise—"

"Don't." Vaisra only shakes his head. "You don't have the strength."

Rin or the Hesperians. Rin or military aid. Rin or victory. Only now has Nezha come to accept this. There is no future where Rin and the Republic coexist, because everything about her is antithetical to what they are trying to accomplish. There's no space for Rin in the world they're trying to build, and the unavoidable truth of this kills him.

He loves her.

Of this he's certain.

He loves her laugh; that sharp, sudden sound; the cynical laugh that always comes too quick, like it's ripped out of her. He loves her quick, confident grin. He loves her resilience, her bravery, even her impulsiveness.

She's everything he's not: unbound, reckless, free. He's never known anyone like her.

She terrifies him, and he loves her so much it hurts.

In all of his worst nightmares, she's dying. She's fading away in his arms, helpless and whimpering, while hot, dark blood spills over his fingers.

This, he tells her.

He doesn't tell her that his hand holds the blade.

"You can't beat that thing," Nezha says. "You have no idea what you're up against."

She scoffs. "I think I have some idea."

"Not about this." It scares him that she sounds so cavalier. It scares him that they're even having this conversation. Rin is so brave, but she's stupid—so stupid—and he doesn't know how to make her understand. There's so much she won't understand. "You will never ask me about this again."

She shrugs. "Fine."

They lapse into silence.

Rin leans back, trailing her fingers through the water. Flames dance up and down her wrists, skim capriciously over the gentle waves. She's showing off, he knows. She loves this. She's never been able to do this before, never been able to exert this much control, but ever since she got her fire back, she's wielded it as comfortably as a limb—a force inextricable from her very being. She can't stop calling it. She's besotted with what she can do.

He can't take his eyes off her. She's the most magnificent thing he's ever seen.

"Can I ask another question now?" he says.

"Go ahead."

"Did you mean it when you said we should raise an army of shamans?"

He's encouraged by the fact that she seems startled by the suggestion. "When did I say that?"

"New Year's," he says cautiously. "Back on the campaign, when we were sitting in the snow."

She wrinkles her nose. "Why not? It'd be marvelous. We'd never lose."

He tries to keep his voice calm. He tries not to give anything away. "You understand that's precisely what the Hesperians are terrified of."

"For good reason. It'd fuck them up, wouldn't it?"

Nezha swallows. This is a test, and Rin is failing, and his heart is breaking. But he needs to continue the show.

"Did you know Tarcquet is seeking a moratorium on all shamanic activity?"

She frowns. "What does that mean?"

"It means you promise never to call on your powers again, and you'll be punished if you do. We report every living shaman in the Empire. And we destroy all written knowledge of shamanism so it can't be passed down."

"Very funny."

"I'm not joking," he insists. "You'd have to cooperate. If you never call the fire again, you'll be safe."

He wants to tell her everything. He wants to lay out the stakes for her—either she cooperates with the Hesperians, or she dies. They're building a glorious new world here, a world where she and her gods have no place.

If Rin knows the stakes, then she'll say whatever she needs to. That, or she'll strike first. And if she strikes first, then he's dead.

Her next answer is her only chance. Nezha needs to know where her heart lies.

But that was never a question, was it?

"Fat chance," she sneers. "I've just gotten the fire back. I don't intend to give it up."

Please, Rin. Please, for once, don't be brave. Be smart.

"And if they tried to force you?" he whispers. He can barely get the words out.

"Then good fucking luck," she says blithely—so cruel, so disdainful—and trails her flames through the water.

And he feels like he's choking then, sinking below waves where nothing can reach.

He wants to feel like he has a choice. That if he does this, at least this is *his* doing. But he knows that's not true. They are, both of them, bound by forces far behind their making: vicious paths that put them in this spot, across each other, never on the same side. Their visions of the future don't include each other. There is no compromise or neutrality. Only her way.

Or his.

It doesn't matter that he loves her. It doesn't matter. It's never mattered.

What matters is what she is, and what she'll do.

Oh, he thinks. *But history moves in such cruel circles.*

He moves to sit down beside her. He reaches for her back. He needs to find the wound that's already open; the place where his blade will sink effortlessly into flesh.

She flinches, alarmed. "What are you doing?"

"Where's your injury? Here?"

"That hurts." But she's not moving. Either she's too drunk, or she trusts him, or both.

"Good."

She gasps.

"Don't try to speak," Nezha murmurs, because it'll kill him if she does.

Because his resolve is only so strong, and if she utters another word then he'll be lost.

"Sir."

Nezha glances up. "Yes?"

The aide steps in. From the look on his face, Nezha can tell he's been standing there for a while. This isn't the first time he's spoken.

He's finding it harder to concentrate these days. His thoughts are slow, his body exhausted. He thought he could do it all—lead an army, unite his base, please his father, please the Hesperians. But he's whittled down to the bone. If this has been a test of his mettle, then he's failed.

He finds his attention slipping in the council room. He tires easily in training. Every time he leaves the laboratory, it takes his body longer and longer to recover.

He needs this war to end quickly, because he's not sure how long he can last.

"There's news." The aide looks uncertain. It's important then. Bad news—or very good news?

Nezha rallies his focus. "Did they—"

"She's in Rooster Province, sir," the aide blurts out. They can't say her name in his presence. He's never made this a rule. But for some reason, none of them dares.

"Then tell them," Nezha says softly, "to mobilize."

At last. The moment he's been waiting for, the confrontation that will finally put an end to this long, bloody war.

He shudders at the thought. Her face across the battlefield. Her flames, scorching the air. Her fist against his face. That lovely, familiar pain.

They've been going back and forth, he and Rin, for what feels like a lifetime. But it's got to come to an end. All the rest—all the scheming, the minor skirmishes, all the political infighting—means nothing. The future of the Republic hinges on one outcome only: her death. Nezha knows what he's meant to do, what Vaisra expects. It's the role he was born for.

There's no time to waste. They must move now, before Rin again disappears off the map. It takes the dirigible sixteen hours to traverse the country, but just six to get from Arlong to Tikany. In six hours he'll be face-to-face with Rin. In six hours they'll see, at last, which of them has the will to finish things off.

She's the only divine thing he's ever believed in. The only creature in this vast, cruel land who could kill him. And sometimes, in his loveliest dreams, he imagines she does.

ABOUT THE AUTHOR

R. F. Kuang lives in New Haven, Connecticut, where she is pursuing a PhD in East Asian Languages and Literatures at Yale University.

READ MORE FROM
R. F. KUANG

THE POPPY WAR
BOOK 1 OF THE POPPY WAR

A brilliantly imaginative talent makes her exciting debut with this epic historical military fantasy, inspired by the bloody history of China's twentieth century and filled with treachery and magic, in the tradition of Ken Liu's *The Grace of Kings* and N. K. Jemisin's Inheritance Trilogy.

THE DRAGON REPUBLIC
BOOK 2 OF THE POPPY WAR

Rin's story continues in this acclaimed sequel to *The Poppy War*—an epic fantasy combining the history of twentieth-century China with a gripping world of gods and monsters.

The war is over.

The war has just begun.

DISCOVER GREAT AUTHORS, EXCLUSIVE OFFERS, AND MORE AT HC.COM.

AVAILABLE WHEREVER BOOKS ARE SOLD

PRAISE FOR **THE POPPY WAR**

"A thrilling, action-packed fantasy of gods and mythology.... The ambitious heroine's rise from poverty to ruthless military commander makes for a gripping read, and I eagerly await the next installment."
—Julie C. Dao, author of *Forest of a Thousand Lanterns*

"A blistering, powerful epic of war and revenge that will captivate you to the bitter end."
—Kameron Hurley, author of *The Stars Are Legion*

"I have no doubt this will end up being the best fantasy debut of the year. ... I have absolutely no doubt that [Kuang's] name will be up there with the likes of Robin Hobb and N.K. Jemisin."
—BookNest

"The best fantasy debut of 2018.... This year's Potter."
—Wired

"The 'year's best debut' buzz around this one was warranted; it really is that good."
— B&N Sci-fi and Fantasy Blog

"Debut novelist Kuang creates an ambitious fantasy reimagining of Asian history populated by martial artists, philosopher-generals, and gods.... This is a strong and dramatic launch to Kuang's career."
—*Publishers Weekly*

"The book starts as an epic bildungsroman, and just when you think it can't get any darker, it does.... Kuang pulls from East Asian history, including the brutality of the Second Sino-Japanese war, to weave a wholly unique experience."
—*Washington Post*

"[*The Poppy War* is a] strikingly grim military fantasy that summons readers into an East Asian–inspired world of battles, opium, gods, and monsters. Fans of Ken Liu's *The Grace of Kings* will snap this one up."
—*Library Journal* (starred review)

"This isn't just another magical, fantasy world with artificially fabricated stakes. Rin's journey and the war against the Federation feel incredibly urgent and powerful.... R.F. Kuang is one of the most exciting new authors I've had the privilege of reading."
—the Roarbots

"I can safely say that this will be the finest debut of 2018 and I'd be surprised if it isn't one of the top 3 books of the year full stop. Spectacular, masterclass, brilliant, awesome. . . . Simply put, R.F. Kuang's *The Poppy War* is a towering achievement of modern fantasy."
—Fantasy Book Review

"The narrative is an impactful, impressive symphony of words that grant life to this incredible morality tale. Setting the stage for an epic fantasy is an understandably enormous undertaking, but Kuang does an exceptional job of world and character building."
—RT Book Reviews (4 1/2 stars, top pick)

"Kuang ambitiously begins a trilogy that doesn't shy away from the darkest sides of her characters, wrapped in a confectionery of high-fantasy pulp. . . . The future of Rin in this world may appear quite dark, but that of the series seems bright indeed."
—*Daily News* (New York)

"A young woman's determination and drive to succeed and excel at any cost runs into the horrors of war, conflict and ancient, suppressed forces in R. F. Kuang's excellent debut novel, *The Poppy War*."
—*The Skiffy and Fanty Show*

"[*The Poppy War*] feels entirely immersive and rich in a way that kind of sucks you in. . . . It's a treasure trove."
—Utopia State of Mind

THE POPPY WAR

R. F. KUANG

An Imprint of HarperCollinsPublishers

This is a work of fiction. Names, characters, places, and incidents are products of the author's imagination or are used fictitiously and are not to be construed as real. Any resemblance to actual events, locales, organizations, or persons, living or dead, is entirely coincidental.

P.S.™ is a trademark of HarperCollins Publishers.

THE POPPY WAR. Copyright © 2018 by Rebecca Kuang. All rights reserved. Printed in the United States of America. No part of this book may be used or reproduced in any manner whatsoever without written permission except in the case of brief quotations embodied in critical articles and reviews. For information, address HarperCollins Publishers, 195 Broadway, New York, NY 10007.

HarperCollins books may be purchased for educational, business, or sales promotional use. For information, please email the Special Markets Department at SPsales@harpercollins.com.

Harper Voyager and design are trademarks of HarperCollins Publishers LLC.

A hardcover edition of this book was published in 2018 by Harper Voyager, an imprint of HarperCollins Publishers.

FIRST HARPER VOYAGER PAPERBACK EDITION PUBLISHED 2019.

Designed by Paula Russell Szafranski
Interior art © by Mariyana Lozanova/Shutterstock, Inc.
Map by Eric Gunther and copyright © 2017 Springer Cartographics

Library of Congress Cataloging-in-Publication Data has been applied for.

ISBN 978-0-06-266258-3

25 26 27 28 29 LBC 42 41 40 39 38

This is for Iris

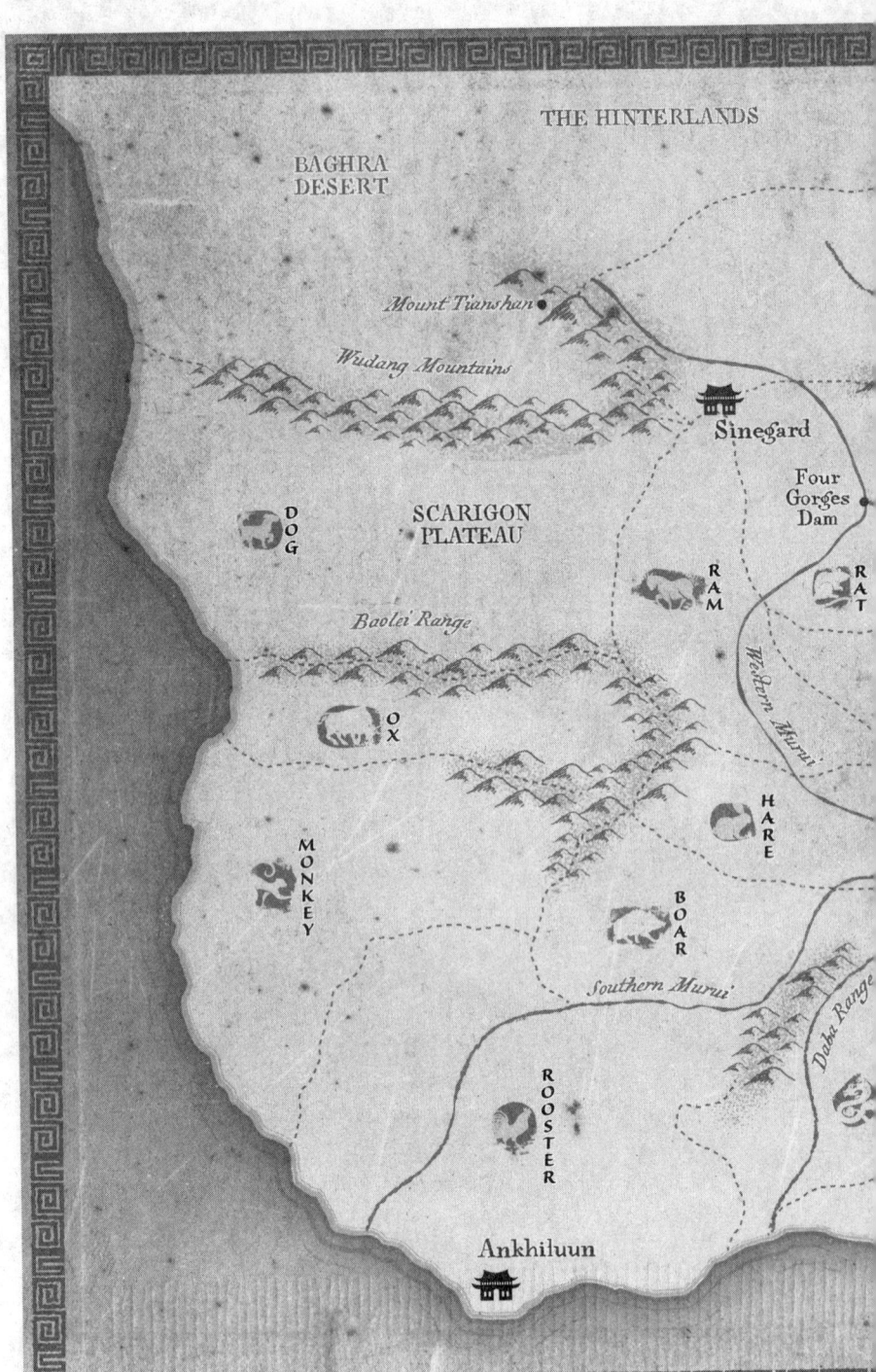

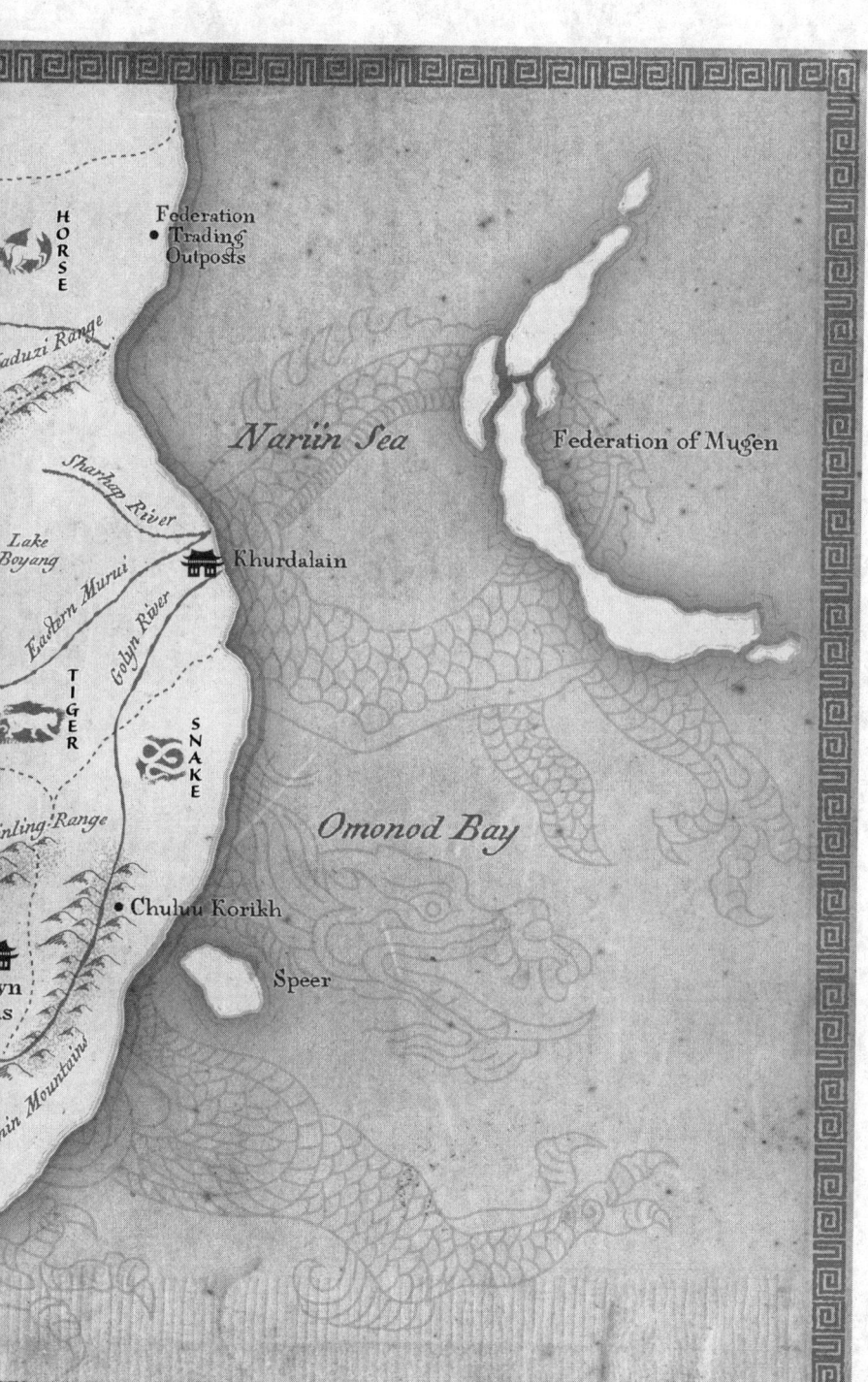

PART I

CHAPTER 1

"Take your clothes off."

Rin blinked. "What?"

The proctor glanced up from his booklet. "Cheating prevention protocol." He gestured across the room to a female proctor. "Go with her, if you must."

Rin crossed her arms tightly across her chest and walked toward the second proctor. She was led behind a screen, patted thoroughly to make sure she hadn't packed test materials up any orifices, and then handed a formless blue sack.

"Put this on," said the proctor.

"Is this really necessary?" Rin's teeth chattered as she stripped. The exam smock was too large for her; the sleeves draped over her hands so that she had to roll them up several times.

"Yes." The proctor motioned for her to sit down on a bench. "Last year twelve students were caught with papers sewn into the linings of their shirts. We take precautions. Open your mouth."

Rin obliged.

The proctor prodded her tongue with a slim rod. "No discoloration, that's good. Eyes wide open."

"Why would anyone drug themselves *before* a test?" Rin asked as the proctor stretched her eyelids. The proctor didn't respond.

Satisfied, she waved Rin down the hallway where other prospective students waited in a straggly line. Their hands were empty, faces uniformly tight with anxiety. They had brought no materials to the test—pens could be hollowed out to contain scrolls with answers written on them.

"Hands out where we can see them," ordered the male proctor, walking to the front of the line. "Sleeves must remain rolled up past the elbow. From this point forward, you do not speak to one another. If you have to urinate, raise your hand. We have a bucket in the back of the room."

"What if I have to shit?" a boy asked.

The proctor gave him a long look.

"It's a twelve-hour test," the boy said defensively.

The proctor shrugged. "Try to be quiet."

Rin had been too nervous to eat anything that morning. Even the thought of food made her nauseated. Her bladder and intestines were empty. Only her mind was full, crammed with an insane number of mathematical formulas and poems and treatises and historical dates to be spilled out on the test booklet. She was ready.

The examination room fit a hundred students. The desks were arranged in neat rows of ten. On each desk sat a heavy exam booklet, an inkwell, and a writing brush.

Most of the other provinces of Nikan had to section off entire town halls to accommodate the thousands of students who attempted the exam each year. But Tikany township in Rooster Province was a village of farmers and peasants. Tikany's families needed hands to work the fields more than they did university-educated brats. Tikany only ever used the one classroom.

Rin filed into the room along with the other students and took her assigned seat. She wondered how the examinees looked from above: neat squares of black hair, uniform blue smocks, and brown wooden tables. She imagined them multiplied across identical classrooms throughout the country right now, all watching the water clock with nervous anticipation.

Rin's teeth chattered madly in a staccato that she thought everyone could surely hear, and it wasn't just from the cold. She clamped her jaw shut, but the shuddering just spread down her limbs to her hands and knees. The writing brush shook in her grasp, dribbling black droplets across the table.

She tightened her grip and wrote her full name across the booklet's cover page. *Fang Runin.*

She wasn't the only one who was nervous. Already there were sounds of retching over the bucket in the back of the room.

She squeezed her wrist, fingers closing over pale burn scars, and inhaled. *Focus.*

In the corner, a water clock rang softly.

"Begin," said the examiner.

A hundred test booklets were opened with a flapping noise, like a flock of sparrows taking off at once.

Two years ago, on the day Tikany's magistracy had arbitrarily estimated to be her fourteenth birthday, Rin's foster parents had summoned her into their chambers.

This rarely happened. The Fangs liked to ignore Rin until they had a task for her, and then they spoke to her the way they would command a dog. *Lock up the store. Hang up the laundry. Take this packet of opium to the neighbors and don't leave until you've scalped them for twice what we paid for it.*

A woman Rin had never seen before sat perched on the guest's chair. Her face was completely dusted over with what looked like white rice flour, punctuated with caked-up dabs of color on her lips and eyelids. She wore a bright lilac dress dyed with a plum-flower pattern, cut in a fashion that might have suited a girl half her age. Her squat figure squeezed over the sides like a bag of grain.

"Is this the girl?" the woman asked. "Hm. She's a little dark—the inspector won't be too bothered, but it'll drive your price down a bit."

Rin had a sudden, horrifying suspicion of what was happening. "Who are you?" she demanded.

"Sit down, Rin," said Uncle Fang.

He reached out with a leathery hand to maneuver her into a chair. Rin immediately turned to flee. Auntie Fang seized her arm and dragged her back. A brief struggle ensued, in which Auntie Fang overpowered Rin and jerked her toward the chair.

"I won't go to a brothel!" Rin yelled.

"She's not from the brothel, you idiot," Auntie Fang snapped. "Sit down. Show some respect to Matchmaker Liew."

Matchmaker Liew looked unfazed, as if her line of work often involved accusations of sex trafficking.

"You're about to be a very lucky girl, sweet," she said. Her voice was bright and falsely saccharine. "Would you like to hear why?"

Rin clutched the edge of her chair and stared at Matchmaker Liew's red lips. "No."

Matchmaker Liew's smile tightened. "Aren't you a dear."

It turned out that after a long and arduous search, Matchmaker Liew had found a man in Tikany willing to marry Rin. He was a wealthy merchant who made a living importing pig's ears and shark fins. He was twice divorced and three times her age.

"Isn't that wonderful?" Matchmaker Liew beamed.

Rin bolted for the door. She hadn't made it two steps before Auntie Fang's hand shot out and seized her wrist.

Rin knew what came next. She braced herself for the blow, for the kicks to her ribs where bruises wouldn't show, but Auntie Fang only dragged her back toward her chair.

"You will *behave*," she whispered, and her clenched teeth promised punishment to come. But not now, not in front of Matchmaker Liew.

Auntie Fang liked to keep her cruelty private.

Matchmaker Liew blinked, oblivious. "Don't be scared, sweet. This is exciting!"

Rin felt dizzy. She twisted around to face her foster parents, fighting to keep her voice level. "I thought you needed me at the shop." Somehow, it was the only thing she could think to say.

"Kesegi can run the shop," Auntie Fang said.

"Kesegi is *eight*."

"He'll grow up soon enough." Auntie Fang's eyes glittered. "And your prospective husband happens to be the village import inspector."

Rin understood then. The Fangs were making a simple trade: one foster orphan in exchange for a near monopoly over Tikany's black market in opium.

Uncle Fang took a long draught from his pipe and exhaled, filling the room with thick, cloying smoke. "He's a rich man. You'll be happy."

No, the *Fangs* would be happy. They'd get to import opium in bulk without bleeding money for bribes. But Rin kept her mouth clamped shut—further argument would only bring pain. It was clear that the Fangs would have her married if they had to drag her to the bridal bed themselves.

They had never wanted Rin. They'd taken her in as an infant only because the Empress's mandate after the Second Poppy War forced households with fewer than three children to adopt war orphans who otherwise would have become thieves and beggars.

Since infanticide was frowned upon in Tikany, the Fangs had put Rin to use as a shopgirl and opium runner since she was old enough to count. Still, for all the free labor she provided, the cost of Rin's keep and feed was more than the Fangs cared to bear. Now was their chance to get rid of the financial burden she posed.

This merchant could afford to feed and clothe Rin for the rest of her life, Matchmaker Liew explained. All she had to do was serve him tenderly like a good wife and give him babies and take care of his household (which, as Matchmaker Liew pointed out, had not one but *two* indoor washrooms). It was a much better deal than a war orphan like Rin, with no family or connections, could otherwise hope to secure.

A husband for Rin, money for the matchmaker, and drugs for the Fangs.

"Wow," Rin said faintly. The floor seemed to wobble beneath her feet. "That's great. Really great. Terrific."

Matchmaker Liew beamed again.

Rin concealed her panic, fought to keep her breathing even until the matchmaker had been ushered out. She bowed low to the Fangs and, like a filial foster daughter, expressed her thanks for the pains they had gone through to secure her such a stable future.

She returned to the store. She worked silently until dark, took orders, filed inventory, and marked new orders in the ledger.

The thing about inventory was that one had to be very careful with how one wrote the numbers. So simple to make a nine look like an eight. Easier still to make a one look like a seven . . .

Long after the sun disappeared, Rin closed the shop and locked the door behind her.

Then she shoved a packet of stolen opium under her shirt and ran.

"Rin?" A small, wizened man opened the library door and peeked out at her. "Great Tortoise! What are you doing out here? It's pouring."

"I came to return a book," she said, holding out a waterproof satchel. "Also, I'm getting married."

"Oh. Oh! What? Come in."

Tutor Feyrik taught a tuition-free evening class to the peasant children of Tikany, who otherwise would have grown up illiterate. Rin trusted him above anyone else, and she understood his weaknesses better than anyone else.

That made him the linchpin in her escape plan.

"The vase is gone," she observed as she glanced around the cramped library.

Tutor Feyrik lit a small flame in the fireplace and dragged two cushions in front of it. He motioned for her to sit down. "Bad call. Bad night overall, really."

Tutor Feyrik had an unfortunate adoration for Divisions, an immensely popular game played in Tikany's gambling dens. It wouldn't have been so dangerous if he were better at it.

"That makes no sense," said Tutor Feyrik after Rin recounted to him the matchmaker's tidings. "Why would the Fangs marry you off? Aren't you their best source of unpaid labor?"

"Yes, but they think I'll be more useful in the import inspector's bed."

Tutor Feyrik looked revolted. "Your folks are assholes."

"So you'll do it," she said hopefully. "You'll help."

He sighed. "My dear girl, if your family had let you study with me when you were younger, we might have considered this . . . I *told* the Fangs then, I *told* her you might have potential. But at this stage, you're speaking of the impossible."

"But—"

He held up a hand. "More than twenty thousand students take the Keju each year, and hardly three thousand enter the academies. Of those, barely a handful test in from Tikany. You'd be competing against wealthy children—merchants' children, nobles' children—who have been studying for this their entire lives."

"But I've taken classes with you, too. How hard can it be?"

He chuckled at that. "You can read. You can use an abacus. That's not the kind of preparation it takes to pass the Keju. The Keju tests for a deep knowledge of history, advanced mathematics, logic, and the Classics . . ."

"The Four Noble Subjects, I know," she said impatiently. "But I'm a fast reader. I know more characters than most of the adults in this village. Certainly more than the Fangs. I can keep up with your students if you just let me try. I don't even have to attend recitation. I just need books."

"Reading books is one thing," Tutor Feyrik said. "Preparing for the Keju is a different endeavor entirely. My Keju students spend their whole lives studying for it; nine hours a day, seven days a week. You spend more time than that working in the shop."

"I can study at the shop," she protested.

"Don't you have actual responsibilities?"

"I'm good at, uh, multitasking."

He eyed her skeptically for a moment, then shook his head. "You'd only have two years. It can't be done."

"But I don't have any other options," she said shrilly.

In Tikany, an unmarried girl like Rin was worth less than a gay rooster. She could spend her life as a foot servant in some rich household—if she found the right people to bribe. Otherwise her options were some combination of prostitution and begging.

She was being dramatic, but not hyperbolic. She could leave town, probably with enough stolen opium to buy herself a caravan ticket to any other province . . . but where to? She had no friends or family; no one to come to her aid if she was robbed or kidnapped. She had no marketable skills. She had never left Tikany; she didn't know the first thing about survival in the city.

And if they caught her with that much opium on her person . . . Opium possession was a capital offense in the Empire. She'd be dragged into the town square and publicly beheaded as the latest casualty in the Empress's futile war on drugs.

She had only this option. She had to sway Tutor Feyrik.

She held up the book she had come to return. "This is Mengzi. *Reflections on Statecraft*. I've only had this for three days, right?"

"Yes," he said without checking his ledger.

She handed it to him. "Read me a passage. Any will do."

Tutor Feyrik still looked skeptical, but flipped to the middle of the book to humor her. "The feeling of commiseration is the principle of . . ."

"Benevolence," she finished. "The feeling of shame and dislike is the principle of righteousness. The feeling of modesty and complaisance is the principle of . . . the principle of, uh, propriety. And the feeling of approving and disapproving is the principle of knowledge."

He raised an eyebrow. "And what does that mean?"

"No clue," she admitted. "Honestly, I don't understand Mengzi at all. I just memorized him."

He flipped toward the end of the book, selected another passage, and read: "Order is present in the earthly kingdom when all beings understand their place. All beings understand their place when they fulfill the roles set out for them. The fish does not attempt to fly. The polecat does not attempt to swim. Only when each being respects the heavenly order may there be peace." He shut the book and looked up. "How about this passage? Do you understand what it means?"

She knew what Tutor Feyrik was trying to tell her.

The Nikara believed in strictly defined social roles, a rigid hierarchy that all were locked into at birth. Everything had its own place under heaven. Princelings became Warlords, cadets became soldiers, and orphan shopgirls from Tikany should be content with remaining orphan shopgirls from Tikany. The Keju was a purportedly meritocratic institution, but only the wealthy class ever had the money to afford the tutors their children needed to actually pass.

Well, fuck the heavenly order of things. If getting married to a gross old man was her preordained role on this earth, then Rin was determined to rewrite it.

"It means I'm very good at memorizing long passages of gibberish," she said.

Tutor Feyrik was silent for a moment. "You don't have an eidetic memory," he said finally. "I taught you to read. I would have known."

"I don't," she acknowledged. "But I'm stubborn, I study hard, and I really don't want to be married. It took me three days to memorize Mengzi. It was a short book, so I'll probably need a full week for the longer texts. But how many texts are on the Keju list? Twenty? Thirty?"

"Twenty-seven."

"Then I'll memorize them all. Every single one. That's all you need to pass the Keju. The other subjects aren't that hard; it's the Classics that trip people up. You told me that yourself."

Tutor Feyrik's eyes were narrowing now, his expression no longer skeptical but calculated. She knew that look. It was the look he got when he was trying to predict his returns at Divisions.

In Nikan, a tutor's success was tied to his reputation for Keju results. You attracted clients if your students made it into an academy. More students meant more money, and to an indebted gambler like Tutor Feyrik, each new student counted. If Rin tested into an academy, an ensuing influx of students could get Tutor Feyrik out of some nasty debts.

"Enrollment's been slow this year, hasn't it?" she pressed.

He grimaced. "It's a drought year. Of course admission is slow. Not many families want to pay tuition when their children barely have a chance to pass regardless."

"But I can pass," she said. "And when I do, you'll have a student who tested into an academy. What do you think that'll do for enrollment?"

He shook his head. "Rin, I couldn't take your tuition money in good faith."

That posed a second problem. She steeled her nerve and looked him in the eye. "That's okay. I can't pay tuition."

He balked visibly.

"I don't make anything at the store," Rin said before he could speak. "The inventory isn't mine. I don't get any wages. I need you to help me to study for the Keju at no cost, and twice as fast as you train your other students."

Tutor Feyrik began to shake his head again. "My dear girl, I can't—this is—"

Time to play her last card. Rin pulled her leather satchel out from under her chair and plunked it on the table. It hit the wood with a solid, satisfying smack.

Tutor Feyrik's eyes followed her eagerly as she slipped a hand into the satchel and drew out one heavy, sweet-smelling packet. Then another. And then another.

"This is six tael worth of premium opium," she said calmly. Six tael was half of what Tutor Feyrik might earn in an entire year.

"You stole this from the Fangs," he said uneasily.

She shrugged. "Smuggling's a difficult business. The Fangs know the risk. Packages go missing all the time. They can hardly report it to the magistrate."

He twiddled his long whiskers. "I don't want to get on the Fangs' bad side."

He had good reason to fear. People in Tikany didn't cross Auntie Fang—not if they cared about their personal safety. She was patient and unpredictable as a snake. She might let faults go unacknowledged for years, and then strike with a well-placed poisonous pellet.

But Rin had covered her tracks.

"One of her shipments was confiscated by port authorities last week," Rin said. "And she hasn't had time to do inventory yet. I've just marked these packets as lost. She can't trace them."

"They could still beat you."

"Not so badly." Rin forced a shrug. "They can't marry off damaged merchandise."

Tutor Feyrik was staring at the satchel with obvious greed.

"Deal," he said finally, and grasped for the opium.

She snatched it out of his reach. "Four conditions. One, you teach me. Two, you teach me for free. Three, you don't smoke when you're teaching me. And four, if you tell anyone where you got this, I'll let your creditors know where to find you."

Tutor Feyrik glared at her for a long moment, and then nodded.

She cleared her throat. "Also, I want to keep this book."

He gave her a wry smile.

"You *would* make a terrible prostitute. No charm."

"No," said Auntie Fang. "We need you in the shop."

"I'll study at night," Rin said. "Or during off-hours."

Auntie Fang's face pinched together as she scrubbed at the frying wok. Everything about Auntie Fang was raw: her expression, an open display of impatience and irritation; her fingers, red from hours of cleaning and laundering; her voice, hoarse from screaming at Rin; at her son, Kesegi; at her hired smugglers; at Uncle Fang, lying inert in his smoke-filled room.

"What did you promise him?" she demanded suspiciously.

Rin stiffened. "Nothing."

Auntie Fang abruptly slammed the wok onto the counter. Rin flinched, suddenly terrified that her theft had been discovered.

"What is so wrong with getting married?" Auntie Fang demanded. "I married your uncle when I was younger than you are now. Every other girl in this village will get married by her sixteenth birthday. Do you think you're so much better than them?"

Rin was so relieved that she had to remember to look properly chastised. "No. I mean, I don't."

"Do you think it will be so bad?" Auntie Fang's voice became dangerously quiet. "What is it, really? Are you afraid of sharing his bed?"

Rin hadn't even considered that, but now the very thought of it made her throat close up.

Auntie Fang's lip curled in amusement. "The first night is the worst, I'll give you that. Keep a wad of cotton in your mouth so you don't bite your tongue. Do not cry out, unless he wants you to. Keep your head down and do as he says—become his mute little household slave until he trusts you. But once he does? You start plying him with opium—just a little bit at first, though I doubt he's never smoked before. Then you give him more and more every day. Do it at night right after he's finished with you, so he always associates it with pleasure and power.

"Give him more and more until he is fully dependent on it, and on you. Let it destroy his body and mind. You'll be more or less married to a breathing corpse, yes, but you will have his riches, his estates, and his power." Auntie Fang tilted her head. "Then will it hurt you so much to share his bed?"

Rin wanted to vomit. "But I . . ."

"Is it the children you're afraid of?" Auntie Fang cocked her head. "There are ways to kill them in the womb. You work in the apothecary. You know that. But you'll want to give him at least one son. Cement your position as his first wife, so he can't fritter his assets on a concubine."

"But I don't want that," Rin choked out. *I don't want to be like you.*

"And who cares what you want?" Auntie Fang asked softly. "You are a *war orphan*. You have no parents, no standing, and no connections. You're lucky the inspector doesn't care that you're not pretty, only that you're young. This is the best I can do for you. There will be no more chances."

"But the Keju—"

"*But the Keju*," Auntie Fang mimicked. "When did you get so deluded? You think *you're* going to an academy?"

"I do think so." Rin straightened her back, tried to inject confidence into her words. *Calm down. You still have leverage.* "And you'll let me. Because one day, the authorities might start asking where the opium's coming from."

Auntie Fang examined her for a long moment. "Do you want to die?" she asked.

Rin knew that wasn't an empty threat. Auntie Fang was more than willing to tie up her loose ends. Rin had watched her do it before. She'd spent most of her life trying to make sure *she* never became a loose end.

But now she could fight back.

"If I go missing, then Tutor Feyrik will tell the authorities precisely what happened to me," she said loudly. "And he'll tell your son what you've done."

"Kesegi won't care," Auntie Fang scoffed.

"I raised Kesegi. He loves me," Rin said. "And you love him. You don't want him to know what you do. That's why you don't send him to the shop. And why you make me keep him in our room when you go out to meet your smugglers."

That did it. Auntie Fang stared at her, mouth agape, nostrils flaring.

"Let me at least try," Rin begged. "It can't hurt you to let me study. If I pass, then you'll at least be rid of me—and if I fail, you still have a bride."

Auntie Fang grabbed at the wok. Rin tensed instinctively, but Auntie Fang only resumed scrubbing it with a vengeance.

"You study in the shop, and I'll throw you out on the streets,"

Auntie Fang said. "I don't need this getting back to the inspector."

"Deal," Rin lied through her teeth.

Auntie Fang snorted. "And what happens if you get in? Who's going to pay your tuition, your dear, impoverished tutor?"

Rin hesitated. She'd been hoping the Fangs might give her the dowry money as tuition, but she could see now that had been an idiotic hope.

"Tuition at Sinegard is free," she pointed out.

Auntie Fang laughed out loud. "Sinegard! You think you're going to test into Sinegard?"

Rin lifted her chin. "I could."

The military academy at Sinegard was the most prestigious institution in the Empire, a training ground for future generals and statesmen. It rarely recruited from the rural south, if ever.

"You *are* deluded." Auntie Fang snorted again. "Fine—study if you like, if that makes you happy. By all means, take the Keju. But when you fail, you *will* marry that inspector. And you will be grateful."

That night, cradling a stolen candle on the floor of the cramped bedroom that she shared with Kesegi, Rin cracked open her first Keju primer.

The Keju tested the Four Noble Subjects: history, mathematics, logic, and the Classics. The imperial bureaucracy in Sinegard considered these subjects integral to the development of a scholar and a statesman. Rin had to learn them all by her sixteenth birthday.

She set a tight schedule for herself: she was to finish at least two books every week, and to rotate between two subjects each day. Each night after she had closed up shop, she ran to Tutor Feyrik's house before returning home, arms laden with more books.

History was the easiest to learn. Nikan's history was a highly entertaining saga of constant warfare. The Empire had been formed a millennium ago under the mighty sword of the merciless Red Emperor, who destroyed the monastic orders scattered across the continent and created a unified state of unprecedented size. It was the first time the Nikara people had ever conceived of themselves as a single nation. The Red Emperor standardized the Nikara language, issued a uniform set of weights and measurements, and built a system of roads that connected his sprawling territory.

But the newly conceived Nikara Empire did not survive the Red Emperor's death. His many heirs turned the country into a bloody mess during the Era of Warring States that followed, which divided Nikan into twelve rival provinces.

Since then, the massive country had been reunified, conquered, exploited, shattered, and then unified again. Nikan had in turn been at war with the khans of the northern Hinterlands and the tall westerners from across the great sea. Both times Nikan had proven itself too massive to suffer foreign occupation for very long.

Of all Nikan's attempted conquerors, the Federation of Mugen had come the closest. The island country had attacked Nikan at a time when domestic turmoil between the provinces was at its peak. It took two Poppy Wars and fifty years of bloody occupation for Nikan to win back its independence.

The Empress Su Daji, the last living member of the troika who had seized control of the state during the Second Poppy War, now ruled over a land of twelve provinces that had never quite managed to achieve the same unity that the Red Emperor had imposed.

The Nikara Empire had proven itself historically unconquerable. But it was also unstable and disunited, and the current spell of peace held no promise of durability.

If there was one thing Rin had learned about her country's history, it was that the only permanent thing about the Nikara Empire was war.

The second subject, mathematics, was a slog. It wasn't overly challenging but tedious and tiresome. The Keju did not filter for genius mathematicians but rather for students who could keep up things such as the country's finances and balance books. Rin had been doing accounting for the Fangs since she could add. She was naturally apt at juggling large sums in her head. She still had to bring herself up to speed on the more abstract trigonometric theorems, which she assumed mattered for naval battles, but she found that learning those was pleasantly straightforward.

The third section, logic, was entirely foreign to her. The Keju posed logic riddles as open-ended questions. She flipped open a sample exam for practice. The first question read: "A scholar traveling a well-trodden road passes a pear tree. The tree is laden with fruit so heavy that the branches bend over with its weight. Yet he does not pick the fruit. Why?"

Because it's not his pear tree, Rin thought immediately. *Because the owner might be Auntie Fang and break his head open with a shovel.* But those responses were either moral or contingent. The answer to the riddle had to be contained within the question itself. There must be some fallacy, some contradiction in the given scenario.

Rin had to think for a long while before she came up with the answer: *If a tree by a well-traveled road has this much fruit, then there must be something wrong with the fruit.*

The more she practiced, the more she came to see the questions as games. Cracking them was very rewarding. Rin drew diagrams in the dirt, studied the structures of syllogisms, and memorized the more common logical fallacies. Within months, she could answer these kinds of questions in mere seconds.

Her worst subject by far was Classics. It was the exception to her rotating schedule. She had to study Classics every day.

This section of the Keju required students to recite, analyze, and compare texts of a predetermined canon of twenty-seven books. These books were written not in the modern script but in the Old Nikara language, which was notorious for unpredictable grammar patterns and tricky pronunciations. The books contained poems, philosophical treatises, and essays on statecraft written by the legendary scholars of Nikan's past. They were meant to shape the moral character of the nation's future statesmen. And they were, without exception, hopelessly confusing.

Unlike with logic and mathematics, Rin could not reason her way out of Classics. Classics required a knowledge base that most students had been slowly building since they could read. In two years, Rin had to simulate more than five years of constant study.

To that end, she achieved extraordinary feats of rote memorization.

She recited backward while walking along the edges of the old defensive walls that encircled Tikany. She recited at double speed while hopping across posts over the lake. She mumbled to herself in the store, snapping in irritation whenever customers asked for her help. She would not let herself sleep unless she had recited that day's lessons without error. She woke up chanting classical analects, which terrified Kesegi, who thought she had been possessed by ghosts. And in a way, she had been—she dreamed of ancient poems by long-dead voices and woke up shaking from nightmares where she'd gotten them wrong.

"The Way of Heaven operates unceasingly, and leaves no accumulation of its influence in any particular place, so that all things are brought to perfection by it . . . so does the Way operate, and all under the sky turn to them, and all within the seas submit to them."

Rin put down Zhuangzi's *Annals* and scowled. Not only did she have no idea what Zhuangzi was writing about, she also couldn't see why he had insisted on writing in the most irritatingly verbose manner possible.

She understood very little of what she read. Even the scholars of Yuelu Mountain had trouble understanding the Classics; she could hardly be expected to glean their meaning on her own. And because she didn't have the time or the training to delve deep into the texts—and since she could think of no useful mnemonics, no shortcuts to learning the Classics—she simply had to learn them word by word and hope that would be enough.

She walked everywhere with a book. She studied as she ate. When she tired, she conjured up images for herself, telling herself the story of the worst possible future.

You walk up the aisle in a dress that doesn't fit you. You're trembling. He's waiting at the other end. He looks at you like you're a juicy, fattened pig, a marbled slab of meat for his purchase. He spreads saliva over his dry lips. He doesn't look away from you throughout the entire banquet. When it's over, he carries you to his bedroom. He pushes you onto the sheets.

She shuddered. Squeezed her eyes shut. Reopened them and found her place on the page.

By Rin's fifteenth birthday she held a vast quantity of ancient Nikara literature in her head, and could recite the majority of it. But she was still making mistakes: missing words, switching up complex clauses, mixing up the order of the stanzas.

This was good enough, she knew, to test into a teacher's college or a medical academy. She suspected she might even test into the scholars' institute at Yuelu Mountain, where the most brilliant minds in Nikan produced stunning works of literature and pondered the mysteries of the natural world.

But she could not afford any of those academies. She *had* to test into Sinegard. She had to test into the highest-scoring percentage of students not just in the village, but in the entire country. Otherwise, her two years of study would be wasted.

She had to make her memory perfect.

She stopped sleeping.

Her eyes became bloodshot, swollen. Her head swam from days of cramming. When she visited Tutor Feyrik at his home one night to pick up a new set of books, her gaze was desperate, unfocused. She stared past him as he spoke. His words drifted over her head like clouds; she barely registered his presence.

"Rin. Look at me."

She inhaled sharply and willed her eyes to focus on his fuzzy form.

"How are you holding up?" he asked.

"I can't do it," she whispered. "I only have two more months, and I can't do it. Everything is spilling out of my head as quickly as I put it in, and—" Her chest rose and fell very quickly.

"Oh, Rin."

Words spilled from her mouth. She spoke without thinking. "What happens if I don't pass? What if I get married after all? I guess I could kill him. Smother him in his sleep, you know? Would I inherit his fortune? That would be fine, wouldn't it?" She began to laugh hysterically. Tears rolled down her cheeks. "It's easier than doping him up. No one would ever *know*."

Tutor Feyrik rose quickly and pulled out a stool. "Sit down, child."

Rin trembled. "I can't. I still have to get through Fuzi's *Analects* before tomorrow."

"Runin. Sit."

She sank onto the stool.

Tutor Feyrik sat down opposite her and took her hands in his. "I'll tell you a story," he said. "Once, not too long ago, there lived a scholar from a very poor family. He was too weak to work long hours in the fields, and his only chance of providing for his parents in their old age was to win a government position so that he might receive a robust stipend. To do this, he had to matriculate at an academy. With the last of his earnings, the scholar bought a set of textbooks and registered for the Keju. He was very tired, because he toiled in the fields all day and could only study at night."

Rin's eyes fluttered shut. Her shoulders heaved, and she suppressed a yawn.

Tutor Feyrik snapped his fingers in front of her eyes. "The scholar had to find a way to stay awake. So he pinned the end of his braid to the ceiling, so that every time he drooped forward, his hair would yank at his scalp and the pain would awaken him." Tutor Feyrik smiled sympathetically. "You're almost there, Rin. Just a little further. Please do not commit spousal homicide."

But she had stopped listening.

"The pain made him focus," she said.

"That's not really what I was trying to—"

"The pain made him focus," she repeated.

Pain could make *her* focus.

So Rin kept a candle by her books, dripping hot wax on her arm if she nodded off. Her eyes would water in pain, she would wipe her tears away, and she would resume her studies.

The day she took the exam, her arms were covered with burn scars.

Afterward, Tutor Feyrik asked her how the test went. She couldn't tell him. Days later, she couldn't remember those horrible, draining hours. They were a gap in her memory. When she tried to recall how she'd answered a particular question, her brain seized up and did not let her relive it.

She didn't want to relive it. She never wanted to think about it again.

Seven days until the scores were out. Every booklet in the province had to be checked, double-checked, and triple-checked.

For Rin, those days were unbearable. She hardly slept. For the past two years she had filled her days with frantic studying. Now she had nothing to do—her future was out of her hands, and knowing that made her feel far worse.

She drove everyone else mad with her fretting. She made mistakes at the shop. She created a mess out of inventory. She snapped at Kesegi and fought with the Fangs more than she should have.

More than once she considered stealing another pack of opium and smoking it. She had heard of women in the village committing suicide by swallowing opium nuggets whole. In the dark hours of the night, she considered that, too.

Everything hung in suspended animation. She felt as if she were drifting, her whole existence reduced to a single score.

She thought about making contingency plans, preparations to escape the village in case she hadn't tested out after all. But her mind refused to linger on the subject. She could not possibly conceive of life after the Keju because there might not be a life after the Keju.

Rin grew so desperate that for the first time in her life, she prayed.

The Fangs were far from religious. They visited the village temple sporadically at best, mostly to exchange packets of opium behind the golden altar.

They were hardly alone in their lack of religious devotion. Once the monastic orders had exerted even greater influence on the country than the Warlords did now, but then the Red Emperor had come crashing through the continent with his glorious quest for unification, leaving slaughtered monks and empty temples in his wake.

The monastic orders were gone now, but the gods remained: numerous deities that represented every category from sweeping themes of love and warfare to the mundane concerns of kitchens and households. Somewhere, those traditions were kept alive by devout worshippers who had gone into hiding, but most villagers in Tikany frequented the temples only out of ritualistic habit. No one truly believed—at least, no one who dared admit it. To the Nikara, gods were only relics of the past: subjects of myths and legends, but no more.

But Rin wasn't taking any chances. She stole out of the shop early one afternoon and brought an offering of dumplings and stuffed lotus root to the plinths of the Four Gods.

The temple was very quiet. At midday, she was the only one inside. Four statues gazed mutely at her through their painted eyes. Rin hesitated before them. She was not entirely certain which one she ought to pray to.

She knew their names, of course—the White Tiger, the Black Tortoise, the Azure Dragon, and the Vermilion Bird. And she knew that they represented the four cardinal directions, but they formed only a small subset of the vast pantheon of deities that were worshipped in Nikan. This temple also bore shrines to smaller guardian gods, whose likenesses hung on scrolls draped over the walls.

So many gods. Which was the god of test scores? Which was the god of unmarried shopgirls who wished to stay that way?

She decided to simply pray to all of them.

"If you exist, if you're up there, help me. Give me a way out of this shithole. Or if you can't do that, give the import inspector a heart attack."

She looked around the empty temple. What came next? She had always imagined that praying involved more than just speaking out loud. She spied several unused incense sticks lying by the altar. She lit the end of one of them by dipping it in the brazier, and then waved it experimentally in the air.

Was she supposed to hold the smoke to the gods? Or should she smoke the stick herself? She had just held the burned end to her nose when a temple custodian strode out from behind the altar.

They blinked at each other.

Slowly Rin removed the incense stick from her nostril.

"Hello," she said. "I'm praying."

"Please leave," he said.

Exam results were to be posted at noon outside the examination hall.

Rin closed up shop early and went downtown with Tutor Feyrik half an hour in advance. A large crowd had already gathered around the post, so they found a shady corner a hundred meters away and waited.

So many people had accumulated by the hall that Rin couldn't see when the scrolls were posted, but she knew because suddenly everyone was shouting, and the crowd was rushing forward, pressing Rin and Tutor Feyrik tightly into the fold.

Her heart beat so fast she could hardly breathe. She couldn't see anything except the backs of the people before her. She thought she might vomit.

When they finally got to the front, it took Rin a long time to find her name. She scanned the lower half of the scroll, hardly daring to breathe. Surely she hadn't scored well enough to make the top ten.

She didn't see *Fang Runin* anywhere.

Only when she looked at Tutor Feyrik and saw that he was crying did she realize what had happened.

Her name was at the very top of the scroll. She hadn't placed in the top ten. She'd placed at the top of the entire village. The entire *province*.

She had bribed a teacher. She had stolen opium. She had burned herself, lied to her foster parents, abandoned her responsibilities at the store, and broken a marriage deal.

And she was going to Sinegard.

CHAPTER 2

The last time Tikany had sent a student to Sinegard, the town magistrate threw a festival that lasted three days. Servants had passed baskets of red bean cakes and jugs of rice wine out in the streets. The scholar, the magistrate's nephew, had set off for the capital to the cheers of intoxicated peasants.

This year, Tikany's nobility felt reasonably embarrassed that an orphan shopgirl had snagged the only spot at Sinegard. Several anonymous inquiries were sent to the testing center. When Rin showed up at the town hall to enroll, she was detained for an hour while the proctors tried to extract a cheating confession from her.

"You're right," she said. "I got the answers from the exam administrator. I seduced him with my nubile young body. You caught me."

The proctors didn't believe a girl with no formal schooling could have passed the Keju.

She showed them her burn scars.

"I have nothing to tell you," she said, "because I didn't cheat. And you have no proof that I did. I studied for this exam. I mutilated myself. I read until my eyes burned. You can't scare me into a confession, because I'm telling the truth."

"Consider the consequences," snapped the female proctor. "Do you understand how serious this is? We can void your score and have you jailed for what you've done. You'll be dead before you're done paying off your fines. But if you confess now, we can make this go away."

"No, *you* consider the consequences," Rin snapped. "If you decide my score is void, that means this simple *shopgirl* was clever enough to bypass your famous anticheating protocols. And that means you're shit at your job. And I bet the magistrate will be just thrilled to let you take the blame for whatever cheating did or didn't happen."

A week later she was cleared of all charges. Officially, Tikany's magistrate announced that the scores had been a "mistake." He did not label Rin a cheater, but neither did he validate her score. The proctors asked Rin to keep her departure under wraps, threatening clumsily to detain her in Tikany if she did not comply.

Rin knew that was a bluff. Acceptance to Sinegard Academy was the equivalent of an imperial summons, and obstruction of any kind—even by provincial authorities—was tantamount to treason. That was why the Fangs, too, could not prevent her from leaving—no matter how badly they wanted to force her marriage.

Rin didn't need validation from Tikany; not from its magistrate, not from the nobles. She was leaving, she had a way out, and that was all that mattered.

Forms were filled out, letters were mailed. Rin was registered to matriculate at Sinegard on the first of the next month.

Farewell to the Fangs was an understandably understated affair. No one felt like pretending they were especially sad to be rid of the other.

Only Rin's foster brother, Kesegi, displayed any real disappointment.

"Don't go," he whined, clinging to her traveling cloak.

Rin knelt down and squeezed Kesegi hard.

"I would have left you anyway," she said. "If not for Sinegard, then to a husband's house."

Kesegi wouldn't let go. He spoke in a pathetic mumble. "Don't leave me with *her*."

Rin's stomach clenched. "You'll be all right," she murmured in Kesegi's ear. "You're a boy. And you're her son."

"But it's not fair."

"It's life, Kesegi."

Kesegi began to whimper, but Rin extracted herself from his viselike embrace and stood up. He tried to cling to her waist, but she pushed him away with more force than she had intended. Kesegi stumbled backward, stunned, and then opened his mouth to wail loudly.

Rin turned away from his tear-stricken face and pretended to be preoccupied with fastening the straps of her travel bag.

"Oh, shut your mouth." Auntie Fang grabbed Kesegi by the ear and pinched hard until his crying ceased. She glowered at Rin, standing in the doorway in her simple traveling clothes. In the late summer Rin wore a light cotton tunic and twice-mended sandals. She carried her only other set of clothing in a patched-up satchel slung over her shoulder. In that satchel Rin had also packed the Mengzi tome, a set of writing brushes that were a gift from Tutor Feyrik, and a small money pouch. That satchel held all of her possessions in the world.

Auntie Fang's lip curled. "Sinegard will eat you alive."

"I'll take my chances," Rin said.

To Rin's great relief, the magistrate's office supplied her with two tael as transportation fare—the magistrate had been compelled by Rin's imperial summons to cover her travel costs. With a tael and a half, Rin and Tutor Feyrik managed to buy two places on a caravan wagon traveling north to the capital.

"In the days of the Red Emperor, an unaccompanied bride carrying her dowry could travel from the southernmost tip of Rooster Province to the northernmost peaks of the Wudang Mountains." Tutor Feyrik couldn't help lecturing as they boarded the wagon. "These days, a lone soldier wouldn't make it two miles."

The Red Emperor's guards hadn't patrolled the mountains of Nikan in a long time. To travel alone over the Empire's vast roads was a good way to get robbed, murdered, or eaten. Sometimes all three—and sometimes not in that order.

"Your fare is going toward more than a seat on the wagon," the caravan leader said as he pocketed their coins. "It's paying for your bodyguards. Our men are the best in their business. If we run into the Opera, we'll scare them right off."

The Red Junk Opera was a religious cult of bandits and outlaws famous for their attempts on the Empress's life after the Second Poppy War. It had faded to myth by now, but remained vividly alive in the Nikara imagination.

"The Opera?" Tutor Feyrik scratched his beard absentmindedly. "I haven't heard that name for years. They're still out and about?"

"They've quieted down in the last decade, but I've heard a few rumors about sightings in the Kukhonin range. If our luck holds, though, we won't see hide or hair of them." The caravan leader slapped his belt. "I would go load up your things. I want to head out before this day gets any hotter."

Their caravan spent three weeks on the road, crawling north at what seemed to Rin an infuriatingly slow pace. Tutor Feyrik spent the trip regaling her with tales of his adventures in Sinegard decades ago, but his dazzling descriptions of the city only made her wild with impatience.

"The capital is nestled at the base of the Wudang range. The palace and the academy are both built into the mountainside, but the rest of the city lies in the valley below. Sometimes, on misty days, you'll look over the edge and it'll seem like you're standing higher than the clouds themselves. The capital's market alone is larger than all of Tikany. You could lose yourself in that market . . . you will see musicians playing on gourd pipes, street vendors who can fry pancake batter in the shape of your name, master calligraphers who will paint fans before your eyes for just two coppers.

"Speaking of. We'll want to exchange these at some point."

Tutor Feyrik patted the pocket where he kept the last of their travel money.

"They don't take taels and coppers in the north?" Rin asked.

Tutor Feyrik chuckled. "You really have never left Tikany, have you? There are probably twenty kinds of currency being circulated in this Empire—tortoise shells, cowry shells, gold, silver, copper ingots . . . all the provinces have their own currencies because they don't trust the imperial bureaucracy with monetary supply, and the bigger provinces have two or three. The only thing everyone takes is standard Sinegardian silver coins."

"How many can we get with this?" Rin asked.

"Not many," Tutor Feyrik said. "But exchange rates will get worse the closer we get to the city. We'd best do it before we're out of Rooster Province."

Tutor Feyrik was also full of warnings about the capital. "Keep your money in your front pocket at all times. The thieves in Sinegard are daring and desperate. I once caught a child with his hand in my pocket. He fought for my coin, even after I'd caught him in the act. Everyone will try to sell you things. When you hear solicitors, keep your eyes forward and pretend you haven't heard them, or they'll hound you the entire way down the street. They're paid to bother you. Stay away from cheap liquor. If a man is offering sorghum wine for less than an ingot for a jug, it's not real alcohol."

Rin was appalled. "How could you fake alcohol?"

"By mixing sorghum wine with methanol."

"Methanol?"

"Wood spirits. It's poisonous stuff; in large doses it'll make you go blind." Tutor Feyrik rubbed his beard. "While you're at it, stay away from the street vendors' soy sauce, too. Some places use human hair to simulate the acids in soy sauce at a lower cost. I hear hair has also found its way into bread and noodle dough. Hmm . . . for that matter, you're best off staying away from street food entirely. They sell you breakfast pancakes for two coppers apiece, but they fry them in gutter oil."

"*Gutter oil?*"

"Oil that's been scooped off the street. The big restaurants toss their cooking oil into the gutter. The street food vendors siphon it up and reuse it."

Rin's stomach turned.

Tutor Feyrik reached out and yanked on one of Rin's tight braids. "You'll want to find someone to cut these off for you before you get to the Academy."

Rin touched her hair protectively. "Sinegardian women don't grow their hair out?"

"The women in Sinegard are so vain about their hair that they'll imbibe raw eggs to maintain its gloss. This isn't about aesthetics. I don't want someone yanking you into the alleys. No one would hear from you until you turned up in a brothel months later."

Rin looked reluctantly down at her braids. She was too dark-skinned and scrawny to be considered any great beauty, but she had always felt that her long, thick hair was one of her better assets. "Do I have to?"

"They'll probably make you shear your hair at the Academy anyway," said Tutor Feyrik. "And they'll charge you for it. Sinegardian barbers aren't cheap." He rubbed his beard as he thought up more warnings. "Beware of fake currency. You can tell a silver's not an imperial silver if it lands Red Emperor–side up ten throws in a row. If you see someone lying down with no visible injuries, don't help them up. They'll say you pushed them, take you to court, and sue you for the clothes off your back. And stay away from the gambling houses." Tutor Feyrik's tone turned sour. "Their people don't mess around."

Rin was starting to understand why he had left Sinegard.

But nothing Tutor Feyrik said could dampen her excitement. If anything, it made her even more impatient to arrive. She would not be an outsider in the capital. She would not be eating street food or living in the city slums. She did not have to fight for scraps or scrounge together coins for a meal. She had already secured a position for herself. She was a student of the most prestigious academy in all of the Empire. Surely that insulated her from the city's dangers.

That night she cut off her braids by herself with a rusty knife she'd borrowed from one of the caravan guards. She jerked the blade as close to her ears as she dared, sawing back and forth until her hair gave way. It took longer than she had imagined. When she was done, she stared for a minute at the two thick ropes of hair that lay in her lap.

She had thought she might keep them, but now she could not see any sentimental value in doing so. They were just clumps of dead hair. She wouldn't even be able to sell them for much up north—Sinegardian hair was famously thin and silky, and no one wanted the coarse tresses of a peasant from Tikany. Instead, she hurled them out the side of the wagon and watched them fall behind on the dusty road.

Their party arrived in the capital just as Rin was starting to go mad from boredom.

She could see Sinegard's famous East Gate from miles off—an imposing gray wall topped by a three-tiered pagoda, emblazoned with a dedication to the Red Emperor: *Eternal Strength, Eternal Harmony.*

Ironic, Rin thought, for a country that had been at war more often than it had been at peace.

Just as they approached the rounded doors below, their caravan came to an abrupt halt.

Rin waited. Nothing happened.

After twenty minutes had passed, Tutor Feyrik leaned out of their wagon and caught the attention of a caravan guide. "What's going on?"

"Federation contingent up ahead," the guide said. "They're here about some border dispute. They're getting their weapons checked at the gate—it'll be a few more minutes."

Rin sat up straight. "Those are Federation soldiers?"

She'd never seen Mugenese soldiers in person—at the end of the Second Poppy War, all Mugenese nationals had been forced out of their occupied areas and either sent home or relocated to limited diplomatic and trading offices on the mainland. To those Nikara born after occupation, they were the specters of modern history—always lingering in the borderlands, an ever-present threat whose face was unknown.

Tutor Feyrik's hand shot out and grabbed her wrist before she could hop out of the wagon. "Get back here."

"But I want to see!"

"No, you don't." He gripped her by the shoulders. "You *never* want to see Federation soldiers. If you cross them—if they even think you've *looked* at them funny—they can and will hurt you. They still have diplomatic immunity. They don't give a shit. Do you understand?"

"We *won* the war," she scoffed. "The occupation's over."

"We *barely* won the war." He shoved her back into a sitting position. "And there's a reason why all your instructors at Sinegard care only about winning the next one."

Someone shouted a command at the front of the caravan. Rin felt a lurch; then the wagons began to move again. She leaned over the side of their wagon, trying to catch a glimpse up ahead, but all she could see was a blue uniform disappearing through the heavy doors.

And then, at last, they were through the gates.

The downtown marketplace was an assault on the senses. Rin had never seen so many people or *things* in one place at one time. She was quickly overwhelmed by the deafening clamor of buyers haggling with sellers over prices, the bright colors of flowery skeins of silk splayed out on grand display boards, and the cloyingly pungent odors of durian and peppercorn drifting up from vendors' portable grills.

"The women here are so *white*," Rin marveled. "Like the girls in wall paintings."

The skin tones she observed from the caravan had moved up

the color gradient the farther north they drove. She knew that the people of the northern provinces were industrialists and businessmen. They were citizens of class and means; they didn't labor in the fields like Tikany's farmers did. But she hadn't expected the differences to be this pronounced.

"They're pale as their corpses will be," Tutor Feyrik said dismissively. "They're terrified of the sun." He grumbled in irritation as a pair of women with day parasols strolled past him, accidentally whacking him in the face.

Rin discovered quickly that Sinegard had the unique ability to make newcomers feel as unwelcome as possible.

Tutor Feyrik had been right—everyone in Sinegard wanted money. Vendors screamed at them persistently from all directions. Before Rin had even stepped off the wagon, a porter ran up to them and offered to carry their luggage—two pathetically light travel bags—for the small fee of eight imperial silvers.

Rin balked; that was almost a quarter of what they'd paid for a spot on the caravan.

"I'll carry it," she stammered, jerking her travel bag away from the porter's clawing fingers. "Really, I don't need—let go!"

They escaped the porter only to be assaulted by a crowd, each person offering a different menial service.

"Rickshaw? Do you need a rickshaw?"

"Little girl, are you lost?"

"No, we're just trying to find the school—"

"I'll take you there, very low fee, five ingots, only five ingots—"

"Get lost," snapped Tutor Feyrik. "We don't need your services."

The hawkers slunk back into the marketplace.

Even the spoken language of the capital made Rin uncomfortable. Sinegardian Nikara was a grating dialect, brisk and curt no matter the content. Tutor Feyrik asked three different strangers for directions to the campus before one gave a response that he understood.

"Didn't you live here?" Rin asked.

"Not since the occupation," Tutor Feyrik grumbled. "It's easy to lose a language when you never speak it."

Rin supposed that was fair. She herself found the dialect nearly indecipherable; every word, it seemed, had to be shortened, with a curt *r* noise added to the end. In Tikany, speech was slow and rolling. The southerners drew out their vowels, rolled their words over their tongues like sweet rice congee. In Sinegard, it seemed no one had time to finish his words.

Even with directions, the city itself was no more navigable than its dialect. Sinegard was the oldest city in the country, and its architecture bore evidence of the multiple shifts in power in Nikan over the centuries. Buildings were either of new construction or were falling into decay, emblems of regimes that had long ago fallen out of power. In the eastern districts stood the spiraling towers of the old Hinterlander invaders from the north. To the west, blocklike compounds stood wedged narrowly next to one another, a holdover from Federation occupation during the Poppy Wars. It was a tableau of a country with many rulers, represented in a single city.

"Do you know where we're going?" Rin asked after several minutes of walking uphill.

"Only vaguely." Tutor Feyrik was sweating profusely. "It's become a labyrinth since I was here. How much money have we got left?"

Rin dug out her coin pouch and counted. "A string and a half of silvers."

"That should more than cover what we need." Tutor Feyrik mopped at his brow with his cloak. "Why don't we treat ourselves to a ride?"

He stepped out onto the dusty street and raised an arm. Almost immediately a rickshaw runner swerved across the road and halted jerkily in front of them.

"Where to?" panted the runner.

"The Academy," said Tutor Feyrik. He tossed their bags into the back and climbed into the seat. Rin grasped the sides and was about to pull herself in when she heard a sharp cry behind her. Startled, she turned around.

A child lay sprawled in the center of the road. Several paces ahead, a horse-drawn carriage had veered off course.

"You just hit that kid!" Rin screamed. "Hey, *stop*!"

The driver yanked the horse's reins. The wagon screeched to a halt. The passenger craned his neck out of the carriage and caught sight of the child feebly stirring in the street.

The child stood up, miraculously alive. Blood trickled down in tiny rivulets from the top of his forehead. He touched two fingers to his head and glanced down, dazed.

The passenger leaned forward and uttered a harsh command to the driver that Rin didn't understand.

The wagon turned slowly. For an absurd moment Rin thought the driver was going to offer the child a lift. Then she heard the crack of a whip.

The child stumbled and tried to run.

Rin shrieked over the sound of clomping hooves.

Tutor Feyrik reached toward the gaping rickshaw runner and tapped him on the shoulder. "Go. *Go!*"

The runner sped up, dragged them faster and faster over the rutted streets until the exclamations of bystanders died away behind them.

"The driver was smart," said Tutor Feyrik as they wobbled over the bumpy road. "You cripple a child, you pay a disabilities fine for their entire life. But if you kill them, you pay the funeral fee once. And that's only if you're caught. If you hit someone, better make sure they're dead."

Rin clung to the side of the carriage and tried not to vomit.

Sinegard the city was smothering, confusing, and frightening.

But Sinegard Academy was beautiful beyond description.

Their rickshaw driver dropped them at the base of the mountains at the edge of the city. Rin let Tutor Feyrik handle the luggage and ran up to the school gates, breathless.

She'd been imagining for weeks now what it would be like to ascend the steps to the Academy. The entire country knew how Sinegard Academy looked; the school's likeness was painted on wall scrolls throughout Nikan.

Those scrolls didn't come close to capturing the campus in reality. A winding stone pathway curved around the mountain, spiraling upward into a complex of pagodas built on successively higher tiers. At the highest tier stood a shrine, on the tower of which perched a stone dragon, the symbol of the Red Emperor. A glimmering waterfall hung like a skein of silk beside the shrine.

The Academy looked like a palace for the gods. This was a place out of legend. This was her home for the next five years.

Rin was speechless.

Rin and Tutor Feyrik were given a tour of the grounds by an older student who introduced himself as Tobi. Tobi was tall, bald-headed, and clad in a black tunic with a red armband. He wore a dedicatedly bored sneer to indicate he would rather have been doing anything else.

They were joined by a slender, attractive woman who initially mistook Tutor Feyrik for a porter and then apologized without embarrassment. Her son was a fine-featured boy who would have been very pretty if he hadn't had such a resentful expression on his face.

"The Academy is built on the grounds of an old monastery." Tobi motioned for them to follow him up the stone steps to the first tier. "The temples and praying grounds were converted to classrooms once the Red Emperor united the tribes of Nikan. First-year students have sweeping duty, so you'll get familiar with the grounds soon enough. Come on, try to keep up."

Even Tobi's lack of enthusiasm couldn't detract from the Academy's beauty, but he did his best. He walked the stone steps in a rapid, practiced manner, not bothering to check whether his guests were keeping pace. Rin was left behind to help the wheezing Tutor Feyrik up the perilously narrow stairs.

There were seven tiers to the Academy. Each curve of the stone pathway brought into view a new complex of buildings and training grounds, embedded in lush foliage that had clearly been carefully cultivated for centuries. A rushing brook sliced down the mountainside, cleaving the campus neatly in two.

"The library is over there. Mess hall is this way. New students live at the lowest tier. Up there are the masters' quarters." Tobi pointed very rapidly to several stone buildings that all looked alike.

"What about that?" Rin asked, pointing to an important-looking building by the brook.

Tobi's lip curled up. "That's the outhouse, kid."

The handsome boy snickered. Cheeks burning, Rin pretended to be very fascinated by the view from the terrace.

"Where are you from, anyway?" Tobi asked in a not-very-friendly tone.

"Rooster Province," Rin muttered.

"Ah. The south." Tobi sounded like something made sense to him now. "I guess multistory buildings are a new concept to you, but try not to get too overwhelmed."

After Rin's registration papers had been checked and filed, Tutor Feyrik had no reason to stay. They said their goodbyes outside the school gates.

"I understand if you're scared," Tutor Feyrik said.

Rin swallowed down the massive lump in her throat and clenched her teeth. Her head buzzed; she knew a dam of tears would break out from under her eyes if she didn't suppress it.

"I'm not scared," she insisted.

He smiled gently. "Of course you're not."

Her face crumpled, and she rushed forward to embrace him. She buried her face in his tunic so that no one could see her crying. Tutor Feyrik patted her on the shoulder.

She had made it all the way across the country to a place she had spent years dreaming of, only to discover a hostile, confusing city that despised southerners. She had no home in Tikany or Sinegard. Everywhere she traveled, everywhere she escaped to, she was just a war orphan who was not supposed to be there.

She felt so terribly alone.

"I don't want you to go," she said.

Tutor Feyrik's smile fell. "Oh, Rin."

"I hate it here," she blurted suddenly. "I *hate* this city. The way they talk—that stupid apprentice—it's like they don't think I should be here."

"Of course they don't," said Tutor Feyrik. "You're a war orphan. You're a southerner. You weren't supposed to pass the Keju. The Warlords like to claim that the Keju makes Nikan a meritocracy, but the system is designed to keep the poor and illiterate in their place. You're offending them with your very presence."

He grasped her by the shoulders and bent slightly so that they were eye to eye. "Rin, listen. Sinegard is a cruel city. The Academy will be worse. You will be studying with children of Warlords. Children who have been training in martial arts since before they could even walk. They'll make you an outsider, because you're not like them. That's *okay*. Don't let any of that discourage you. No matter what they say, *you deserve to be here*. Do you understand?"

She nodded.

"Your first day of classes will be like a punch to the gut," Tutor Feyrik continued. "Your second day, probably even worse. You'll find your courses harder than studying for the Keju ever was. But if anyone can survive here, it's you. Don't forget what you did to get here."

He straightened up. "And don't ever come back to the south. You're better than that."

As Tutor Feyrik disappeared down the path, Rin pinched the bridge of her nose, willing the hot feeling behind her eyes to go away. She could not let her new classmates see her cry.

She was alone in a city without a friend, where she barely spoke the language, at a school that she now wasn't sure she wanted to attend.

He leads you down the aisle. He's old and fat, and he smells like sweat. He looks at you and he licks his lips . . .

She shuddered, squeezed her eyes shut, and opened them again.

So Sinegard was frightening and unfamiliar. It didn't matter. She didn't have anywhere else to go.

She squared her shoulders and walked back through the school gates.

This was better. No matter what, this was a thousand times better than Tikany.

"And then she asked if the outhouse was a classroom," said a voice from farther down in the line for registration. "You should have seen her clothes."

Rin's neck prickled. It was the boy from the tour.

She turned around.

He really was pretty, impossibly so, with large, almond-shaped eyes and a sculpted mouth that looked good even twisted into a sneer. His skin was a shade of porcelain white that any Sinegardian woman would have murdered for, and his silky hair was almost as long as Rin's had been.

He caught her eye and smirked, continuing loudly as if he hadn't seen her. "And her teacher, you know, I bet he's one of those doddering failures who can't get a job in the city so they spend their lives trying to scrape a living from local magistrates. I thought he might die on the way up the mountain, he was wheezing so loud."

Rin had dealt with verbal abuse from the Fangs for years. Hearing insults from this boy hardly fazed her. But slandering Tutor Feyrik, the man who had delivered her from Tikany, who had saved her from a miserable future in a forced marriage . . . that was unforgivable.

Rin took two steps toward the boy and punched him in the face.

Her fist connected with his eye socket with a pleasant popping noise. The boy staggered backward into the students behind him, nearly toppling to the ground.

"You *bitch*!" he screeched. He righted himself and rushed at her. She shrank back, fists raised.

"Stop!" A dark-robed apprentice appeared between them, arms flung out to keep them apart. When the boy struggled forward anyway, the apprentice quickly grabbed his extended arm by the wrist and twisted it behind his back.

The boy stumbled, immobilized.

"Don't you know the rules?" The apprentice's voice was low, calm, and controlled. "No fighting."

The boy said nothing, mouth twisted into a sullen sneer. Rin fought the sudden urge to cry.

"Names?" the apprentice demanded.

"Fang Runin," she said quickly, terrified. Were they in trouble? Would she be expelled?

The boy struggled in vain against the apprentice's hold.

The apprentice tightened his grip. "Name?" he asked again.

"Yin Nezha," the boy spat.

"Yin?" The apprentice let him go. "And what is the well-bred heir to the House of Yin doing brawling in a hallway?"

"She punched me in the face!" Nezha screeched. A nasty bruise was already blossoming around his left eye, a bright splotch of purple against porcelain skin.

The apprentice raised an eyebrow at Rin. "And why would you do that?"

"He insulted my teacher," she said.

"Oh? Well, that's different." The apprentice looked amused. "Weren't you taught not to insult teachers? That's taboo."

"I'll kill you," Nezha snarled at Rin. "I will fucking *kill* you."

"Aw, shut it." The apprentice feigned a yawn. "You're at a military academy. You'll have plenty of opportunities to kill each other throughout this year. But save it until after orientation, won't you?"

CHAPTER 3

Rin and Nezha were the last ones to the main hall—a converted temple on the third tier of the mountain. Though the hall was not particularly large, its spare, dim interior gave an illusion of great space, making those inside feel smaller than they were. Rin supposed this was the intended effect when one was in the presence of both gods and teachers.

The class of first-years, no more than fifty in total, sat kneeling in rows of ten. They twisted their hands in their laps, blinking and looking around in silent anxiety. The apprentices sat in rows around them, chatting casually with one another. Their laughter sounded louder than normal, as if they were trying to make the first-years feel uncomfortable on purpose.

Moments after Rin sat down, the front doors swung open and a tiny woman, shorter even than the smallest first-year, strode into the hall. She walked with a soldier's gait—perfectly erect, precise, and controlled.

Five men and one woman, all wearing dark brown robes, followed her inside. They formed a row behind her at the front of the room and stood with hands folded into their sleeves. The apprentices fell silent and rose to their feet, hands clasped behind them and heads tilted forward in a slight bow. Rin and the other first-years took their cue and hastily scrambled to their feet.

The woman gazed out at them for a moment, then gestured for them to sit.

"Welcome to Sinegard. I am Jima Lain. I am grand master of this school, commander of the Sinegardian Reserve Forces, and former commander of the Nikara Imperial Militia." Jima's voice cut through the room like a blade, precise and chilly.

Jima indicated the six people arrayed behind her. "These are the masters of Sinegard. They will be your instructors during your first year, and will ultimately decide whether to take you on as their apprentices following your end-of-year Trials."

The masters were a solemn crowd, each more imposing than the last. None of them smiled. Each wore a belt of a different color—red, blue, purple, green, and orange.

Except one. The man to Jima's left wore no belt at all. His robe, too, was different—no embroidery at the edges, no insignia of the Red Emperor stitched over his right breast. He was dressed as if he'd forgotten orientation was happening and had thrown on a formless brown cloak at the last minute.

This master's hair was the pure white of Tutor Feyrik's beard, but he was nowhere near as old. His face was curiously unlined but not youthful; it was impossible to tell his age. As Jima spoke, he dug his little finger around in his ear canal, and then brought his finger up to his eyes to examine the discharge.

He glanced up suddenly, caught Rin staring at him, and smirked. She hastily looked away.

"You all are here because you achieved the highest Keju scores in the country," said Jima, spreading her hands magnanimously. "You have beaten thousands of other pupils for the honor of studying here. Congratulations."

The first-years cast awkward glances at one another, uncertain of whether they should be applauding themselves. A few tentative claps sounded across the room.

Jima smirked. "Next year a fifth of you will be gone."

The silence then was acute.

"Sinegard does not have the time nor resources to train every child who dreams of glory in the military. Even illiterate farmers can become soldiers. But we do not train soldiers here. We train *generals*. We train the people who hold the future of the Empire in their hands. So, should I decide you are no longer worth our time, you will be asked to leave.

"You'll notice that you were not given a choice of a field of study. We do not believe this choice should be left in the hands of the students. After your first year, you will be evaluated for proficiency in each of the subject tracks we teach here: Combat, Strategy, History, Weaponry, Linguistics, and Medicine."

"And Lore," interrupted the white-haired master.

Jima's left eye twitched. "And Lore. If, in your end-of-year Trials, you are found worthy of one track of study, you will be approved to continue at Sinegard. You will then attain the rank of apprentice."

Jima gestured to the older students surrounding them. Rin saw now that the apprentices' armbands matched the masters' belts in color.

"If no master sees fit to take you on as an apprentice, you will be asked to leave the Academy. The first-year retention rate is usually eighty percent. Look around you. This means that this time next year, two people in your row will be gone."

Rin glanced around her, fighting a rising swell of panic. She had thought testing into Sinegard was a guarantee of a home for at least the next five years, if not a stable career afterward.

She hadn't realized she might be sent home in months.

"We cull out of necessity, not cruelty. Our task is to train only the elite—the best of the best. We don't have time to waste on dilettantes. Take a good look at your classmates. They will become your closest friends, but also your greatest rivals. You are competing against each other to remain at this academy. We believe it is through that competition that those with talent will make themselves known. And those without will be sent home. If you deserve it, you will be present next year as an apprentice. If you aren't . . . well then, you should never have been sent here in the first place." Jima seemed to look directly at Rin.

"Lastly, I will give a warning. I do not tolerate drugs on this campus. If you have even so much as a whiff of opium on you, if you are caught within ten *paces* of an illegal substance, you will be dragged out of the Academy and thrown into the Baghra prison."

Jima fixed them with a last, stern look and then dismissed them with a wave of her hand. "Good luck."

Raban, the apprentice who had broken up Rin and Nezha's fight, led them out of the main hall to the dormitories on the lowest tier.

"You're first-years, so you'll have sweeping duties starting next week," Raban said, walking backward to address them. He had a kind and soothing voice, the sort of tone Rin had heard village physicians adopt before amputating limbs. "First bell rings at sunrise; classes begin half an hour after that. Be in the mess hall before then or you miss breakfast."

The boys were housed in the largest building on campus, a three-story structure that looked like it had been built long after the Academy grounds were seized from the monks. The women's quarters were tiny in contrast, a spare one-story building that used to be a single meditation room.

Rin expected the dorm to be uncomfortably cramped, but only two other bunks showed signs of habitation.

"Three girls in one year is actually a record high," Raban said before he left them to settle in. "The masters were shocked."

Alone in the dorm, the three girls warily sized one another up.

"I'm Niang," offered the girl to Rin's left. She had a round, friendly face, and she spoke with a lilting accent that belied her northern heritage, though it was nowhere as indecipherable as the Sinegardian dialect. "I'm from the Hare Province."

"Pleased," the other girl drawled. She was inspecting her bedsheets. She rubbed the thin off-white material between her fingers, made a disgusted face, and then let the fabric drop. "Venka," she said begrudgingly. "Dragon Province, but I grew up in the capital."

Venka was an archetypical Sinegardian beauty; she was pretty in a pale way, and slim as a willow branch. Rin felt coarse and unsophisticated standing next to her.

She realized both were watching her expectantly.

"Runin," she said. "Rin for short."

"*Runin.*" Venka mangled the name with her Sinegardian accent, rolled the syllables through her mouth like some bad-tasting morsel. "What kind of name is *that*?"

"It's southern," Rin said. "I'm from Rooster Province."

"That's why your skin's so dark," Venka said, lip curling. "Brown as cow manure."

Rin's nostrils flared. "I went out in the sun once. You should try it sometime."

Just as Tutor Feyrik had warned, classes escalated quickly. Martial arts training commenced in the second-tier courtyard immediately after sunrise the next day.

"What's this?" Master Jun, the red-belted Combat instructor, regarded their huddled class with a disgusted expression. "Line up. I want straight rows. Stop clumping together like frightened hens."

Jun possessed a pair of fantastically thick black eyebrows that almost met in the middle of his forehead. They rested on his swarthy face like a thundercloud over a permanent scowl.

"Backs straight." Jun's voice matched his face: gruff and unforgiving. "Eyes forward. Arms behind your backs."

Rin strained to mirror the stances of her classmates in front of her. Her left thigh prickled, but she didn't dare scratch it. Too late, she realized she had to pee.

Jun paced to the front of the courtyard, satisfied that they were standing as uncomfortably as possible. He stopped in front of Nezha. "What happened to your face?"

Nezha had developed a truly spectacular bruise over his left eye, a bright splotch of violet on his otherwise flawless mien.

"Got in a fight," Nezha mumbled.

"When?"

"Last night."

"You're lucky," Jun said. "If it had been any later, I would have expelled you."

He raised his voice to address the class. "The first and most important rule of my class is this: do not fight irresponsibly. The techniques you are learning are lethal in application. If improperly performed, they will cause serious injury to yourself or your training partner. If you fight irresponsibly, I will suspend you from my class and lobby to have you expelled from Sinegard. Am I understood?"

"Yes, sir," they answered.

Nezha twisted his head over his shoulder and shot Rin a look of pure venom. She pretended not to see.

"Who's had martial arts training before?" Jun asked. "Show of hands."

Nearly the entire class raised their arms. Rin glanced around the courtyard, feeling a swell of panic. Had so many of them trained before the Academy? *Where* had they trained? How far ahead of her were they? What if she couldn't keep up?

Jun pointed to Venka. "How many years?"

"Twelve," said Venka. "I trained in the Gentle Fist style."

Rin's eyes widened. That meant Venka had been training almost since she could walk.

Jun pointed to a wooden dummy. "Backward crescent kick. Take the head off."

Take the head off? Rin looked doubtfully at the dummy. Its head and torso had been carved from the same piece of wood. The head hadn't been screwed on; it was solidly connected to the torso.

Venka, however, seemed entirely unperturbed. She positioned her feet, squinted at the dummy, and then whipped her back leg around in a twist that brought her foot high up over her head. Her heel cut through the air in a lovely, precise arc.

Her foot connected with the dummy's head and lobbed it off, sent it flying clean across the courtyard. The head clattered against the corner wall and rolled to one side.

Rin's jaw fell open.

Jun nodded curtly in approval and dismissed Venka. She returned to her place in the ranks, looking pleased.

"How did she do that?" Jun asked.

Magic, Rin thought.

Jun stopped in front of Niang. "You. You look bewildered. How do you think she did that?"

Niang blinked nervously. "*Ki?*"

"What is *ki*?"

Niang blushed. "Um. Inner energy. Spiritual energy?"

"Spiritual energy," Master Jun repeated. He snorted. "Village nonsense. Those who elevate *ki* to the level of mystery or the supernatural do a great disservice to martial arts. *Ki* is nothing but plain energy. The same energy that flows through your lungs and blood vessels. The same energy that moves rivers downstream and causes the wind to blow."

He pointed up to the bell tower on the fifth tier. "Two servicemen installed a newly smelted bell last year. Alone, they never would have lifted the bell all that distance. But with cleverly placed ropes, two men of average build managed to lift something many times their weight.

"The principle works in reverse for martial arts. You have a limited quantity of energy in your body. No amount of training will allow you to accomplish superhuman feats. But given the right discipline, knowing where to strike and when . . ." Jun slammed his fist out at the dummy's torso. It splintered, forming a perfect radius of cracks around his hand.

He pulled his arm away. The dummy torso shattered into pieces that clattered to the ground. "You can do what average humans *think* impossible. Martial arts is about action and reaction. Angles and trigonometry. The right amount of force applied at the proper vector. Your muscles contract and exert force, and that force is dispelled through to the target. If you build muscle mass, you can exert greater force. If you practice good technique, your force disperses with greater concentration and higher effectiveness. Martial arts is no more complicated than pure physics. If that confuses you, then simply take the advice of the grand masters. Don't ask questions. Just obey."

History was a lesson in humility. Stooped, balding Master Yim began expounding on Nikan's military embarrassments before they had even finished filing into the classroom.

"In the last century, the Empire has fought five wars," Yim said. "And we've lost every single one of them. This is why we call this past century the Age of Humiliation."

"Upbeat," muttered a wiry-haired kid in the front.

If Yim heard him, he didn't acknowledge it. He pointed to a large parchment map of the eastern hemisphere. "This country used to span half the continent under the Red Emperor. The Old Nikara Empire was the birthplace of modern civilization. The center of the world. All inventions originated from Old Nikan; among them the lodestone, the parchment press, and the blast furnace. Nikara delegates brought culture and methods of good governance to the islands of Mugen in the east and to Speer in the south.

"But empires fall. The old empire fell victim to its own splendor. Flush with victories of expansion in the north, the Warlords began fighting among themselves. The Red Emperor's death set off a series of succession battles with no clear resolution. And so Nikan split into the Twelve Provinces, each headed by one Warlord. For most of recent history, the Warlords have been preoccupied with fighting each other. Until—"

"The Poppy Wars," said the wiry-haired kid.

"Yes. The Poppy Wars." Yim pointed to a country on Nikan's

border, a tiny island shaped like a longbow. "Without warning, Nikan's little brother to the east, its old tributary nation, turned its dagger on the very country that had given it civilization. The rest you know, surely."

Niang raised her hand. "Why did relations sour between Nikan and Mugen? The Federation was a peaceful tributary in the days of the Red Emperor. What happened? What did they want from us?"

"Relations were never peaceful," Yim corrected. "And are not to this day. Mugen has always wanted more, even when it was a tributary. The Federation is an ambitious, rapidly growing country with a bulging population on a tiny island. Imagine you're a highly militaristic country with more people than your land can sustain, and nowhere to expand. Imagine that your rulers have propagated an ideology that they are gods, and that you have a divine right to extend your empire across the eastern hemisphere. Suddenly the sprawling landmass right across the Nariin Sea looks like a prime target, doesn't it?"

He turned back to the map. "The First Poppy War was a disaster. The fractured Empire could never stand up against well-trained Federation troops, who had been drilling for decades for this enterprise. So here's a puzzle for you. How did we win the Second Poppy War?"

A boy named Han raised his hand. "The Trifecta?"

Muted snickers sounded around the classroom. The Trifecta—the Vipress, the Dragon Emperor, and the Gatekeeper—were three heroic soldiers who had unified the Empire against the Federation. They were real—the woman known as the Vipress still sat on the throne at Sinegard—but their legendary martial arts abilities were the subject of children's tales. Rin had grown up hearing stories about how the Trifecta had single-handedly flattened entire Federation battalions, leveraging storms and floods with their supernatural powers. But even she thought it sounded ridiculous in a lecture about history.

"Don't laugh. The Trifecta were important—without their political machinations, we might never have rallied the Twelve Provinces," said Yim. "But that's not the answer I'm looking for."

Rin raised her hand. She had memorized this answer from Tutor Feyrik's history primers. "We razed the heartland. Pursued a strategy of slash and burn. When the Federation army marched too far inland, their supply lines ran out and they couldn't feed their armies."

Yim acknowledged this answer with a shrug. "Good answer, but false. That's just propaganda they put in the countryside textbooks. The slash-and-burn strategy hurt the rural countryside more than it hurt Mugen. Anyone else?"

It was the wiry-haired boy in the front who got it right. "We won because we lost Speer."

Yim nodded. "Stand up. Explain."

The boy shoved his hair back and stood. "We won the war because losing Speer made Hesperia intervene. And, uh, Hesperia's naval abilities were vastly superior to Mugen's. They won the war over the ocean theater, and Nikan got looped into the subsequent peace treaty. The victory wasn't really ours at all."

"Correct," Yim said.

The boy sat, looking immensely relieved.

"Nikan did not win the Second Poppy War," Yim reiterated. "The Federation is gone because we were so pathetic that the great naval powers to the west felt bad for us. We did such a terrible job defending our country that it took *genocide* for Hesperia to intervene. While Nikara forces were tied up on the northern front, a fleet of Federation ships razed the Dead Island overnight. Every man, woman, and child on Speer was butchered, and their bodies burned. An entire race, gone in a day."

Their class was silent. They had grown up hearing stories about the destruction of Speer, a tiny island that punctuated the ocean between the Nariin Sea and Omonod Bay like a teardrop, lying just beside Snake Province. It had been the Empire's only remaining tributary state, conquered and annexed at the height of the

Red Emperor's reign. It held a fraught place in Nikan's history, a glaring example of the massive failure of the disunited army under the Warlords' regime.

Rin had always wondered whether the loss of Speer was purely an accident. If any other province had been destroyed the way Speer had, the Nikara Empire wouldn't have stopped with a peace treaty. They would have fought until the Federation of Mugen was in pieces.

But the Speerlies weren't really Nikara at all. Tall and brown-skinned, they were an island people who had always been ethnically separate from the Nikara mainlanders. They spoke their own language, wrote in their own script, and practiced their own religion. They had joined the Imperial Militia only at the Red Emperor's sword point.

This all pointed to strained relations between the Nikara and the Speerlies all the way up through the Second Poppy War. So, Rin thought, if any Nikara territory had to be sacrificed, Speer was the obvious choice.

"We have survived the last century through nothing more than sheer luck and the charity of the west," said Yim. "But even with Hesperia's help, Nikan only barely managed to drive out the Federation invaders. Under pressure from Hesperia, the Federation signed the Non-Aggression Pact at the end of the Second Poppy War, and Nikan has retained its independence since. The Federation has been relegated to trading outposts on the edge of the Horse Province, and for the past nearly two decades, they've more or less behaved.

"But the Mugenese grow restless, and Hesperia has never been good about keeping its promises. The heroes of the Trifecta have been reduced to one; the Emperor is dead, the Gatekeeper is lost, and only the Empress remains on the throne. Perhaps worse, we have no Speerly soldiers." Yim paused. "Our best fighting force is gone. Nikan no longer possesses the assets that helped us survive the Second Poppy War. Hesperia cannot be relied upon to save us again. If the past centuries have taught us anything, it is that

Nikan's enemies never rest. But this time when they come, we intend to be ready."

The noontime bell marked lunch.

Food was served from giant cauldrons lined up by the far wall—congee, fish stew, and loaves of rice flour buns—distributed by cooks who seemed wholly indifferent to their jobs.

The students were given portions just large enough to sate their growling stomachs, but not so much that they felt fully satisfied. Students who tried to pass through the line again were sent back to their tables empty-handed.

To Rin, the prospect of regular meals was more than generous—she'd frequently gone without dinner in the Fang household. But her classmates complained to Raban about the single portions.

"Jima's philosophy is that hunger is good. It'll keep you light, focused," explained Raban.

"It'll keep us miserable," Nezha grumbled.

Rin rolled her eyes but kept her mouth shut. They sat crammed in two rows of twenty-five along the wooden table near the end of the mess hall. The other tables were occupied by the apprentices, but not even Nezha had the nerve to attempt to sit among them.

Rin found herself crammed between Niang and the wiry-haired boy who had spoken up in History class.

"I'm Kitay," he introduced himself, once he'd finished inhaling his stew.

He was one year her junior and looked it—scrawny, freckled, with enormous ears. He also happened to have achieved the highest Keju score in Sinegard Municipality, by far the most competitive testing region, which was especially impressive for someone who had taken it a year early. He had a photographic memory, he wanted to study Strategy under Master Irjah once he got past the Trials, and didn't she think Jun was kind of an asshole?

"Yes. And I'm Runin. Rin," she said, once he let her get a word in.

"Oh, you're the one Nezha hates."

Rin supposed there were worse reputations to have. In any case, Kitay didn't seem to hold it against her. "What's his problem, anyway?" she asked.

"His father is the Dragon Warlord and his aunts have been concubines to the throne for generations. You'd be a prick too if your family was both rich *and* attractive."

"Do you know him?" Rin asked.

"We grew up together. Me, Nezha, and Venka. Shared the same tutor. I thought they'd be nicer to me once we were all at the Academy." Kitay shrugged, glancing at the far end of the table, where Nezha and Venka appeared to be holding court. "Guess I thought wrong."

Rin wasn't surprised that Nezha had cut Kitay out of his social circle. There was no way Nezha would have stuck around anyone half as witty as Kitay—there were too many opportunities for Kitay to upstage him. "What'd you do to offend him?"

Kitay pulled a face. "Nothing, except beat him on the exam. Nezha's prickly about his ego. Why, what did you do?"

"I gave him that black eye," she admitted.

Kitay raised an eyebrow. "Nice."

Lore was scheduled for after lunch, and then Linguistics. Rin had been looking forward to Lore all day. But the apprentices who led them to the class looked like they were trying not to laugh. They climbed the winding steps to the fifth tier, higher up than any of their other classes. Finally they stopped at an enclosed garden.

"What are we doing here?" Nezha asked.

"This is your classroom," said one of the apprentices. They glanced at each other, grinned, and then left. After five minutes, the cause of their amusement became clear. The Lore Master didn't show. Ten minutes passed. Then twenty.

The class milled around the garden awkwardly, trying to figure out what they were supposed to do.

"We've been pranked," suggested Han. "They led us to the wrong place."

"What do they grow in here, anyway?" Nezha pulled a flower down to his nose and sniffed it. "Gross."

Rin took a closer look at the flowers, then her eyes widened. She'd seen those petals before.

Nezha recognized it at the same moment that she did.

"Shit," he said. "That's a poppy plant."

Their class reacted like a startled nest of dormice. They scurried hastily away from the poppy plant as if mere proximity would get them high.

Rin fought the absurd urge to burst out laughing. Here on the other side of the country was at least one thing she was familiar with.

"We're going to be expelled," Venka wailed.

"Don't be stupid, it's not *our* poppy plant," Kitay said.

Venka flapped her hands around her face. "But Jima said if we were even within ten paces of—"

"It's not like they can expel the entire class," Kitay said. "I bet he's testing us. Seeing if we really want to learn."

"Or testing us to see how we'll react around illegal drugs!" Venka shrilled.

"Oh, calm down," Rin said. "You can't get high just by touching it."

Venka did not calm down. "But Jima didn't say she had to catch us high, she said—"

"I don't think it's a real class," Nezha interrupted. "I bet the apprentices are just having their bit of fun."

Kitay looked doubtful. "It's on our schedule. And we saw the Lore Master, he was at orientation."

"Then where were his apprentices?" Nezha shot back. "What color was his belt? Why don't you see anyone walking around with *Lore* stitched into their armbands? This is stupid."

Nezha stalked out through the gates. Encouraged, the rest of the class followed him out, one by one. Finally Rin and Kitay were the only ones left in the garden.

Rin sat down and leaned back on her elbows, admiring the

variety of plants in the garden. Aside from the blood-red poppy flowers, there were tiny cacti with pink and yellow blossoms, fluorescent mushrooms glowing faintly in the dark corners under shelves, and leafy green bushes that emitted a tealike odor.

"This isn't a garden," she said. "This is a drug farm."

Now she *really* wanted to meet the Lore Master.

Kitay sat down next to her. "You know, the great shamans of legend used to ingest drugs before battle. Gave them magical powers, so the stories say." He smiled. "You think that's what the Lore Master teaches?"

"Honestly?" Rin picked at the grass. "I think he just comes in here to get high."

CHAPTER 4

Classes only escalated in difficulty as the weeks progressed. Their mornings were devoted to Combat, Medicine, History, and Strategy. On most days Rin's head was reeling by noon, crammed with names of theorems she'd never heard and titles of books she needed to finish by the end of the week.

Combat class kept their bodies exhausted along with their minds. Jun put them through a torturous series of calisthenics—they regularly ran up the Academy stairs and back down, did handstands in the courtyard for hours on end, and cycled through basic martial arts forms with bags of bricks hanging from their arms. Every week Jun took them to a lake at the bottom of the mountain and had them swim the entire length.

Rin and a handful of other students had never been taught to swim. Jun demonstrated the proper form exactly once. After that, it was up to them not to drown.

Their homework was heavy and clearly meant to push the first-years right up against their limits. So when the Weapons Master, Sonnen, taught them the correct proportions of saltpeter, sulfur, and charcoal necessary to mix the incendiary fire powder that powered war rockets, he also had them create their own impromptu missiles. And when the Medicine Master, Enro, assigned them to learn the names of all the bones in the human body, she also expected them to know the most common patterns of breakage and how to identify them.

It was Strategy, though, taught by Master Irjah, that was their hardest course. Their first day of class he distributed a thick tome—Sunzi's *Principles of War*—and announced that they were to have it memorized by the end of the week.

"This thing is massive!" Han complained. "How are we supposed to do the rest of our homework?"

"Altan Trengsin learned it in a night," said Irjah.

The class exchanged exasperated looks. The masters had been singing the praises of Altan Trengsin since the start of the term. Rin gathered he was some kind of genius, apparently the most brilliant student to come through Sinegard in decades.

Han looked as irritated as she felt. "Okay, but we're not Altan."

"Then try to be," said Irjah. "Class dismissed."

Rin settled into a routine of constant study and very little sleep; their course schedules left the first-years with no time to do anything else.

Autumn had just started to bite at Sinegard. A cold gust of wind accompanied them as they raced up the steps one morning. It rustled through the trees in a thunderous crescendo. The pupils had not yet received their thicker winter robes, and their teeth chattered in unison as they huddled together under a large mimosa tree at the far end of the second-tier courtyard.

Despite the cold, Jun refused to move Combat class indoors before the snowfall made it impossible to hold outside. He was a brutal teacher who seemed to delight in their discomfort.

"Pain is good for you," he said as he forced them to crouch in low, torturous endurance stances. "The martial artists of old used to hold this position for an hour straight before training."

"The martial artists of old must have had amazing thighs," Kitay gasped.

Their morning calisthenics were still miserable, but at least they had finally moved past fundamentals to their first weapon-based arts: staff techniques.

Jun had just assumed his position at the fore of the courtyard when a loud shuffle sounded above his head. A smattering of leaves fell down right over where he stood.

Everyone glanced up.

Perched high up on a thick branch of the mimosa tree stood their long-absent Lore Master.

He wielded a large pair of gardening shears, cheerfully clipping leaves at random while singing an off-key melody loudly to himself.

After hearing a few words of the song, Rin recognized it as "The Gatekeeper's Touches." Rin knew it from her many trips delivering opium to Tikany's whorehouses—it was an obscene ditty bordering on erotica. The Lore Master butchered the tune, but he sang it aloud with wild abandon.

"I can't touch you there, miss / else you'll perish from the bliss . . ."

Niang shook with suppressed giggles. Kitay's jaw hung wide open as he stared at the tree.

"Jiang, I've got a class," Jun snapped.

"So teach your class," said Master Jiang. "Leave me alone."

"We need the courtyard."

"You don't need *all* of the courtyard. You don't need this tree," Jiang said petulantly.

Jun whipped his iron staff through the air several times and slammed it against the base of the tree. The trunk actually shook from the impact. There was the crackling noise of deadweight dropping through several layers of dry mimosa leaves.

Master Jiang landed in a crumpled heap on the stone floor.

Rin's first thought was that he wasn't wearing a shirt. Her second thought was that he must be dead.

But Jiang simply rolled to a sitting position, shook out his left leg, and brushed his white hair back past his shoulders. "That was rude," he said dreamily as blood trickled down his left temple.

"Must you bumble around like a lackwit?" Jun snapped.

"Must you interrupt my morning gardening session?" Jiang responded.

"You're not doing any gardening," Jun said. "You are here purely to annoy me."

"I think you're flattering yourself."

Jun slammed his staff on the ground, making Jiang jump in surprise. "*Out!*"

Jiang adopted a dramatically wounded expression and hauled himself up to his feet. He flounced out of the garden, swaying his hips like a whorehouse dancer. "*If for me your heart aches / I'll lick you like a mooncake . . .*"

"You're right," Kitay whispered to Rin. "He *has* been getting high."

"Attention!" Jun shouted at the gawking class. He still had a mimosa leaf stuck in his hair. It quivered every time he spoke.

The class hastily lined up in two rows before him, staves at the ready.

"When I give the signal, you will repeat the following sequence." He demonstrated with his staff as he spoke. "Forward. Back. Upper left parry. Return. Upper right parry. Return. Lower left parry. Return. Lower right parry. Return. Spin, pass through the back, return. Understood?"

They nodded mutely. No one dared admit that they had missed nearly the entire sequence. Jun's demonstrations were usually rapid, but he had moved faster just now than any of them could follow.

"Well then." Jun slammed his staff against the floor. "Begin."

It was a fiasco. They moved with no rhythm or purpose. Nezha blazed through the sequence at twice the speed of the rest of the class, but he was one of the only students who was able to do it at all. The rest of them either omitted half the sequence or badly mangled the directions.

"Ow!"

Kitay, parrying where he should have turned, hit Rin in the

back. She jerked forward, knocking Venka in the head by accident.

"Stop!" Jun shouted.

Their flailing subsided.

"I'm going to tell you a story about the great strategist Sunzi." Jun paced along their ranks, breathing heavily. "When Sunzi finished writing his great treatise, *Principles of War*, he submitted the chapters to the Red Emperor. The Emperor decided to test Sunzi's wisdom by having him train a group of people with no military experience: the Emperor's concubines. Sunzi agreed and assembled the women outside the palace gates. He told them: 'When I say, "Eyes front," you will look straight ahead. When I say, "Left turn," you will face your left. When I say, "Right turn," you must face your right. When I say, "About turn," you must turn one hundred and eighty degrees. Is that clear?' The women nodded. Sunzi then gave the signal, 'Right turn.' But the women only burst out laughing."

Jun paused in front of Niang, whose face was pinched in trepidation.

"Sunzi told the Emperor, 'If words of command are not clear and distinct, if orders are not thoroughly understood, then the general is to blame.' So he turned to the concubines and repeated his instructions. 'Right turn,' he commanded. Again, the women fell about laughing."

Jun swiveled his head slowly, making eye contact with each one of them. "This time, Sunzi told the Emperor, 'If words of command are not clear, then the general is to blame. But if words of command are clear, but orders are not executed, then the troop leaders are to blame.' Then he selected the two most senior concubines in the group and had them beheaded."

Niang's eyes looked like they were going to pop out of her head.

Jun stalked back to the front of the courtyard and raised his staff. While they watched, terrified, Jun repeated the sequence, slowly this time, calling out the moves as he performed them. "Was that clear?"

They nodded.

He slammed his staff against the floor. "Then begin."

They drilled. They were flawless.

Combat was a soul-sucking, spirit-crushing ordeal, but there was at least the fun of nightly practice sessions. These were guided drill periods supervised by two of Jun's apprentices, Kureel and Jeeha. The apprentices were somewhat lazy teachers, and disproportionately enthused at the prospect of inflicting as much pain as possible on imagined opponents. As such, drill periods usually bordered on disaster, with Jeeha and Kureel milling around, shouting bits of advice while the pupils sparred against one another.

"Unless you've got a weapon, don't aim for the face." Jeeha guided Venka's hand down so her extended knife hand strike would land on Nezha's throat rather than his nose. "Aside from the nose, the face is practically all made of bone. You'll only bruise your hand. The neck's a better target. With enough force, you could fatally collapse the windpipe. At the very least, you'll give him breathing trouble."

Kureel knelt down next to Kitay and Han, who were rolling around the ground in mutual headlocks. "Biting is an excellent technique if you're in a tight spot."

A moment later, Han shrieked in pain.

A handful of first-years clustered around a wooden dummy as Jeeha demonstrated a proper knife hand strike. "Nikara monks used to believe this point was a major *ki* center." Jeeha indicated a spot under the dummy's stomach and punched it dramatically.

Rin took the bait to speed things along. "Is it?"

"Nah. No such thing as *ki* centers. But this area below the rib cage has a ton of necessary organs that are exposed. Also, it's where your diaphragm is. *Hah!*" Jeeha slammed his fist into the dummy. "That should immobilize any opponent for a good few seconds. Gives you time to scratch out their eyes."

"That seems vulgar," said Rin.

Jeeha shrugged. "We aren't here to be sophisticated. We're here to fuck people up."

"I'll show you all one last blow," Kureel announced as the session drew to a close. "This is the only kick you'll ever need, really. A kick to bring down the most powerful warriors."

Jeeha blinked in confusion. He turned his head to ask her what she meant. And Kureel raised her knee and jammed the ball of her foot into Jeeha's groin.

Mandatory drill sessions lasted for only two hours, but the first-years began staying in the studio to practice their forms long after the period had ended. The only problem was that the students with previous training seized this chance to show off. Nezha performed a series of twirling leaps in the center of the room, attempting spinning kicks that became progressively more flamboyant. A small ring of his classmates gathered around to watch.

"Admiring our prince?" Kitay strolled across the room to stand next to Rin.

"I fail to see how this would be useful in battle," Rin said. Nezha was now spinning a full 540 degrees in the air before kicking. It looked very pretty, but also very pointless.

"Oh, it's not. A lot of old arts are like that—cool to watch, practically useless. The lineages were adapted for stage opera, not combat, and then adapted back. That's where the Red Junk Opera got their name, you know. The founding members were martial artists posing as street performers to get closer to their targets. You should read the history of inherited arts sometime, it's fascinating."

"Is there anything you haven't read about?" Rin asked. Kitay seemed to have an encyclopedic knowledge of almost every topic. That day over lunch he had given Rin a lecture on how fish-gutting techniques differed across provinces.

"I have a soft spot for martial arts," said Kitay. "Anyway, it's depressing when you see people who can't tell the difference between self-defense and performance art."

Nezha landed, crouched impressively, after a particularly high leap. Several of their classmates, absurdly, began to clap.

Nezha straightened up, ignoring the applause, and caught Rin's eye. "*That's* what family arts are," he said, wiping the sweat off his forehead.

"I'm sure you'll be the terror of the school," said Rin. "You can dance for donations. I'll toss you an ingot."

A sneer twisted Nezha's face. "You're just jealous you have no inherited arts."

"I'm glad I don't, if they all look as absurd as yours."

"The House of Yin innovated the most powerful kicking-based technique in the Empire," Nezha snapped. "Let's see how you'd like being on the receiving end."

"I think I'd be fine," Rin said. "Though it would be a dazzling visual spectacle."

"At least I'm not an artless *peasant*," Nezha spat. "You've never done martial arts before in your life. You only know one kick."

"And you keep calling me a peasant. It's like you only know one insult."

"Duel me, then," Nezha said. "Fight to incapacitation for ten seconds or first blood. Right here, right now."

"You're on," Rin started to say, but Kitay slapped a hand over her mouth.

"Oh, no. Oh, no, no." Kitay yanked Rin back. "You heard Jun, you shouldn't—"

But Rin shrugged Kitay off. "Jun's not here, is he?"

Nezha grinned nastily. "Venka! Get over here!"

Venka broke off her conversation with Niang at the other end of the room and flounced over, flushed at Nezha's summons.

"Referee us," Nezha said, not taking his eyes off Rin.

Venka folded her hands behind her back, imitating Master Jun, and lifted her chin. "Begin."

The rest of their class had now formed a circle around Nezha and Rin. Rin was too angry to notice their stares. She had eyes only for Nezha. He began moving around her, darting back and forth with quick, elegant movements.

Kitay was right, Rin thought. Nezha really did look like he was performing stage opera. He didn't seem particularly lethal then, just foolish.

She narrowed her eyes and crouched low, following Nezha's movements carefully.

There. A clear opening. Rin raised a leg and kicked out, hard.

Her leg caught Nezha in midair with a satisfying *whoomph*.

Nezha uttered an unnatural shriek and clutched his crotch, whimpering.

The entire studio fell silent as all heads swiveled in their direction.

Nezha clambered to his feet, scarlet-faced. "You—how *dare* you—"

"Just as you said." Rin dipped her head into a mocking bow. "I only know one kick."

Humiliating Nezha felt good, but the political repercussions were immediate and brutal. It didn't take long for their class to form alliances. Nezha, mortally offended, made it clear that associating with Rin meant social alienation. He pointedly refused to speak to her or acknowledge her existence, unless it was to make snide comments about her accent. One by one the members of their class, terrified of receiving the same treatment, followed suit.

Kitay was the one exception. He had grown up on Nezha's bad side, he told Rin, and it wasn't about to start bothering him now.

"Besides," he said, "that look on his face? Priceless."

Rin was grateful for Kitay's loyalty, but was amazed by how cruel the other students could be. There was apparently no end of things about Rin to be mocked: her dark skin, her lack of status, her country accent. It was annoying, but Rin was able to brush the taunts off—until her classmates started snickering every time she talked.

"Is my accent so obvious?" she asked Kitay.

"It's getting better," he said. "Just try rolling the ends of your words more. Shorten your vowels. And add the *r* sound where it doesn't exist. That's a good rule of thumb."

"*Ar. Arrr.*" Rin gagged. "Why do Sinegardians have to sound like they're chewing cud?"

"Power dictates acceptability," Kitay mused. "If the capital had been built in Tikany, I'm sure we'd be running around dark as wood bark."

In the following days Nezha didn't utter a single word to her, because he didn't have to. His adoring followers wasted no opportunity to mock Rin. Nezha's manipulations turned out to be brilliant—once he established that Rin was the prime target, he could just sit back and watch.

Venka, who was obsessively attached to Nezha, actively snubbed Rin whenever she had the chance. Niang was better; she wouldn't associate with Rin in public, but she at least spoke to her in the privacy of their dorm.

"You could try apologizing," Niang whispered one night after Venka had gone to sleep.

Apologizing was the last thing Rin had in mind. She wasn't about to concede defeat by massaging Nezha's ego. "It was his idea to duel," she snapped. "It's not my fault he got what he was asking for."

"Doesn't matter," Niang said. "Just say you're sorry, and then he'll forget about you. Nezha just likes to be respected."

"For *what*?" Rin demanded. "He hasn't done anything to earn my respect. All he's done is act high and mighty, like being from Sinegard makes him *so* special."

"Apologizing won't help," interjected Venka, who apparently hadn't been asleep after all. "And being from Sinegard *does* make us special. Nezha and I"—it was always *Nezha and I* with Venka—"have trained for the Academy since we could walk. It's in our blood. It's our destiny. But you? You're *nothing*. You're just some tramp from the south. You shouldn't even be here."

Rin sat up straight in her bed, suddenly hot with anger. "I took the same test as you, Venka. I have every right to be at this school."

"You're just here to fill up the quota," Venka retorted. "I mean, the Keju has to *seem* fair."

Annoying as Venka was, Rin scarcely had the time or energy to pay much attention to her. They stopped snapping at each other after several days, but only because they were too exhausted to speak. When training sessions ended for the week, they straggled back to the dormitory, muscles aching so much they could barely walk. Without a word, they shed their uniforms and collapsed on their bunks.

They awoke almost immediately to a rapping at their door.

"Get up," said Raban when Rin yanked the door open.

"What the—"

Raban peered over her shoulder at Venka and Niang, who were whining incoherently from their bunks. "You too. Hurry up."

"What's the matter?" Rin mumbled grumpily, rubbing at her eyes. "We've got sweeping duty in six hours."

"Just come."

Still complaining, the girls wriggled into their tunics and met Raban outside, where the boys had already assembled.

"If this is some sort of first-year hazing thing, can I have permission to go back to bed?" asked Kitay. "Consider me bullied and intimidated, just let me sleep."

"Shut up. Follow me." Without another word, Raban took off toward the forest.

They were forced to jog to keep up with him. At first Rin thought he was taking them deep into the mountainside forest, but it was only a shortcut; after a minute they emerged in front of the main training hall. It was lit up from within, and they could hear loud voices from inside.

"More class?" asked Kitay. "Great Tortoise, I'm going on strike."

"This isn't class." For some reason, Raban sounded very excited. "Get inside."

Despite the audible shouting, the hall was empty. Their class bumbled around in groggy confusion until Raban motioned for them to follow him down the stairs to the basement floor. The basement was filled with apprentices crowded around the center of the room. Whatever stood at the center of attention, it sounded extremely exciting. Rin craned to get a glimpse over the apprentices' heads but could see nothing but bodies.

"First-years coming through," Raban yelled, leading their little group into the packed crowd. Through vigorous use of elbows, Raban carved them a path through the apprentices.

The spectacle at the center was two circular pits dug deep into the ground, each at least three meters in diameter and two meters deep. The pits stood adjacent to one another, and were ringed with waist-high metal bars to keep spectators from falling in. One pit was empty. Master Sonnen stood in the center of the other, arms folded across his broad chest.

"Sonnen always referees," Raban said. "He gets the short straw because he's the youngest."

"Referees what?" Kitay asked.

Raban grinned widely.

The basement door opened. Even more apprentices began to stream inside, filling the already cramped hall to the brim. The press of bodies forced the first-years perilously close to the edges of the rings. Rin clenched the rail to keep from falling in.

"What's going on?" Kitay asked as the apprentices jostled for positions closer to the rings. There were so many people in the room now that apprentices in the back had brought stools on which to stand.

"Altan's up tonight," Raban said. "Nobody wants to miss Altan."

It must have been the twelfth time that week Rin had heard that name. The whole Academy seemed obsessed with him. Fifth-year student Altan Trengsin was associated with every school record, was every master's favorite student, the exception to every rule. He had now become a running joke within their class.

Can you piss over the wall into town?

Altan can.

A tall, lithe figure suddenly dropped into Master Sonnen's ring without bothering to use the rope ladder. As his opponent scrambled down, the figure stretched his arms behind his back, head tilted up toward the ceiling. His eyes caught the reflection of the lamplight above.

They were crimson.

"Great Tortoise," said Kitay. "That's a real Speerly."

Rin peered inside the pit. Kitay was right; Altan didn't look close to Nikara. His skin was several shades darker than any of the other students'; a darker hue, even, than Rin's. But where Rin's sun-browned skin made her look coarse and unsophisticated, Altan's skin gave him a unique, regal air. His hair was the color of wet ink, closer to violet than black. His face was angular, expressionless, and startlingly handsome. And those eyes—scarlet, blazing red.

"I thought the Speerlies were dead," said Rin.

"*Mostly* dead," said Raban. "Altan's the last one."

"I am Bo Kobin, apprentice to Master Jun Loran," announced his opponent. "I challenge Altan Trengsin to a fight to incapacitation."

Kobin had to be twice Altan's weight and several inches taller, yet Rin suspected this would not be a particularly close fight.

Altan shrugged noncommittally.

Sonnen looked bored. "Well, go on," he said.

The apprentices fell into their opening stances.

"What, no introduction?" Kitay asked.

Raban looked amused. "Altan doesn't need an introduction."

Rin wrinkled her nose. "He's a little full of himself, isn't he?"

"Altan Trengsin," Kitay mused. "Is Altan the clan name?"

"Trengsin. The Speerlies put clan names last," Raban explained hastily. He pointed to the ring. "Shush, you'll miss it."

They already had.

She hadn't heard Altan move, hadn't even seen the scuffle begin. But when she looked back down at the ring, she saw Kobin pinned against the ground, one arm twisted unnaturally behind his back. Altan knelt above him, slowly increasing the pressure on Kobin's arm. He looked impassive, detached, almost lackadaisical.

Rin clenched at the railing. "When did—when did he—"

"He's Altan Trengsin," Raban said, as if this were explanation enough.

"Yield," Kobin shouted. "*Yield*, damn it!"

"Break," said Sonnen, yawning. "Altan wins. Next."

Altan released Kobin and offered him a hand. Kobin let Altan hoist him to his feet, then shook Altan's hand once he stood up. Kobin took his defeat with good grace. There was no shame, it seemed, in being defeated by Altan Trengsin in less than three seconds.

"That's it?" Rin asked.

"It's not over," Raban said. "Altan got a lot of challengers tonight."

The next contender was Kureel.

Raban frowned, shaking his head. "She shouldn't have been given permission for this match."

Rin found this appraisal unfair. Kureel, who was one of Jun's prized Combat apprentices, had a reputation for viciousness. Kureel and Altan appeared matched in height and strength; surely she could hold her own.

"Begin."

Kureel charged Altan immediately.

"Great Tortoise," Rin murmured. She had trouble following as Kureel and Altan began trading blows in close combat. They matched multiple strikes and parries per second, dodging and ducking around each other like dance partners.

A minute passed. Kureel flagged visibly. Her blows became sloppy, overextended. Droplets of sweat flew from her forehead every time she moved. But Altan was unfazed, still moving with that same feline grace he had possessed since the beginning of the match.

"He's playing with her," said Raban.

Rin couldn't take her eyes off Altan. His movements were dancelike, hypnotic. Every action bespoke sheer *power*—not the hulking muscle that Kobin had embodied, but a compact energy, as if at every moment Altan were a tightly coiled spring about to go off.

"He'll end it soon," Raban predicted.

It was ultimately a game of cat and mouse. Altan had never been evenly matched with Kureel. He fought on another level entirely. He had acted the part of her mirror to humor her at first, and then to tire her out. Kureel's movements slowed with every passing second. And, mockingly, Altan too slowed down his pace to match Kureel's rhythm. Finally Kureel lunged desperately forward, trying to score a hit on Altan's midriff. Instead of blocking it, Altan jumped aside, ran up against the dirt wall of the ring, rebounded off the other side, and twisted in the air. His foot caught Kureel in the side of the head. She snapped backward.

She was unconscious before Altan landed behind her, crouched like a cat.

"Tiger's tits," said Kitay.

"Tiger's tits," Raban agreed.

Two orange-banded Medicine apprentices jumped immediately into the pit to lift Kureel out. A stretcher was already waiting by the side of the ring. Altan hung in the center of the pit, arms folded, waiting calmly for them to finish. Even as they carried Kureel out of the basement, another student climbed down the rope ladder.

"Three challengers in one night," Kitay said. "Is that normal?"

"Altan fights a lot," said Raban. "Everyone wants to be the one who takes him down."

"Has that ever happened?" Rin asked.

Raban just laughed.

The third challenger turned his shaved head up to the lamplight, and Rin realized with a start that it was Tobi—the apprentice from the tour.

Good, Rin thought. *I hope Altan destroys him.*

Tobi introduced himself loudly, whipping up yells from his Combat classmates. Altan picked at his sleeve and again said nothing. He might have rolled his eyes, but in the dim light Rin couldn't be sure.

"Begin," Sonnen said.

Tobi flexed his arms and sank back into a low crouch. Rather than forming fists with his hands, he curled his knobby fingers tightly as if wrapping them around an invisible ball.

Altan tilted his head as if to say, *Well, come on.*

The match quickly lost its elegance. It was a knockdown, bloody-knuckled, no-holds-barred struggle. It was heavy-handed and abrupt, and full of brute, animalistic force. Nothing was off-limits. Tobi clawed furiously at Altan's eyes. Altan ducked his head and slammed an elbow into Tobi's chest.

Tobi staggered back, wheezing for air. Altan backhanded him across the head as if disciplining a child. Tobi tumbled to the floor, then rebounded with a complicated flipping motion and barreled forward. Altan raised his fists in anticipation, but Tobi threw himself at Altan's waist, pushing both of them back to the ground.

Altan slammed backward onto the dirt floor. Tobi pulled his right arm back and drove his clawed fingers into Altan's stomach. Altan's mouth opened in the shape of a soundless scream. Tobi dug his fingers in deeper and twisted. Rin could see veins protruding from his lower arm. His face warped into an wolf's snarl.

Altan convulsed under Tobi's grip and coughed. Blood sprayed from his mouth.

Rin's stomach roiled.

"Shit," Kitay kept saying. "Shit, shit, shit."

"That's Tiger Claws," said Raban. "Tobi's signature technique. Inherited arts. Altan won't be able to shit properly for a week."

Sonnen leaned forward. "All right, break—"

But then Altan wrapped his free hand around Tobi's neck and

jammed Tobi's face down into his own forehead. Once. Twice. Tobi's grip went slack.

Altan flung Tobi off and lunged forward. Half a second later their positions were reversed; Tobi lay inert on the ground as Altan kneeled atop him, hands pressed firmly around his neck. Tobi tapped frantically at Altan's arm.

Altan flung Tobi away from him in disdain. He glanced at Master Sonnen as if awaiting further instructions.

Sonnen shrugged. "That's the match."

Rin let out a breath she hadn't known she was holding.

The Medicine apprentices jumped into the ring and hauled Tobi up. He moaned. Blood streamed from his nose.

Altan hung back, leaning against the dirt wall. He looked bored, disinterested, as if his stomach weren't twisted into a sickening knot, as if he had never been touched at all. Blood dripped down his chin. Rin watched, partly in fascination and partly in horror, as Altan's tongue snaked out and licked the blood from his upper lip.

Altan closed his eyes for a long time, and then tilted his head up and exhaled slowly through his mouth.

Raban grinned when he saw their expressions. "Make sense now?"

"That was—" Kitay flapped his hands. "How? *How?*"

"Doesn't he feel pain?" Rin demanded. "He's not human."

"He's not," said Raban. "He's a Speerly."

The next day at lunch, all any of the first-years could talk about was Altan.

The entire class had fallen in love with him, to some extent, but Kitay especially was besotted with him. "The way he *moves*, it's just—" Kitay waved his arms in the air, at a loss for words.

"He doesn't talk much, does he?" Han said. "Wouldn't even introduce himself. Prick."

"He doesn't need to introduce himself," Kitay scoffed. "Everyone knows who he is."

"Strong and mysterious," Venka said dreamily. She and Niang giggled.

"Maybe he doesn't know how to talk," Nezha suggested. "You know how the Speerlies were. Wild and bloodthirsty. Hardly knew what to do with themselves unless they'd been given orders."

"The Speerlies weren't idiots," Niang protested.

"They were primitive. Scarcely more intelligent than children," Nezha insisted. "I heard that they're more closely related to monkeys than human beings. Their brains are smaller. Did you know they didn't even have a written language before the Red Emperor? They're good at fighting, but not much else."

Several of their classmates nodded as if this made sense, but Rin found it hard to believe that someone who fought with such graceful precision as Altan could possibly have the cognitive ability of a monkey.

Since arriving in Sinegard, she'd come to learn what it was like to be presumed stupid because of the shade of her skin. It rankled her. She wondered if Altan suffered the same.

"You heard wrong. Altan's not stupid," Raban said. "Best student in our class. Possibly in the entire Academy. Irjah says he's never had such a brilliant apprentice."

"I heard he's a shoo-in for command when he graduates," said Han.

"*I* heard he's doped up," Nezha said. He was clearly unused to not being the center of attention; he seemed determined to undermine Altan's credibility in any way possible. "He's on opium. You can see it in his eyes, they're bloodshot all the time."

"He's got red eyes because he's *Speerly*, you idiot," Kitay said. "All the Speerlies had crimson eyes."

"No, they didn't," said Niang. "Only the warriors."

"Well, Altan's *clearly* a warrior. And his eyes are red in the iris," Kitay said. "Not the veins. He's not an addict."

Nezha's lip curled. "Spend a lot of time staring at Altan's eyes, do you?"

Kitay blushed.

"You haven't heard the other apprentices talk," Nezha continued smugly, like he was privy to special information that they weren't. "Altan *is* an addict. *I* heard Irjah gives him poppy every time he wins. That's why he fights so hard. Opium addicts will do anything."

"That's absurd," said Rin. "You have no idea what you're talking about."

She knew what addiction looked like. Opium smokers were yellowed, useless sacks of flesh. They did not fight like Altan did. They did not *move* like Altan did. They were not perfect, lethal animals of graceful beauty.

Great Tortoise, she realized. *I'm just as obsessed with him myself.*

"Six months after the Non-Aggression Pact was signed, Empress Su Daji formally banned the possession and use of all psychoactive substances within Nikan's borders, and instituted a series of harshly retributive punishments in an attempt to wipe out illegal drug use. Of course, black markets in opium continue to thrive in many provinces, provoking debates over the efficiency of such policies." Master Yim looked up at his class. They were invariably twitching, scratching in their booklets, or staring out the window. "Am I lecturing to a graveyard?"

Kitay raised his hand. "Can we talk about Speer?"

"What?" Yim furrowed his brow. "Speer doesn't have anything to do with what we're . . . Ah." He sighed. "You've just met Trengsin, haven't you?"

"He was awesome," Han said fervently to nods of agreement.

Yim looked exasperated. "Every year," he muttered. "*Every year.* Fine." He tossed his lecture notes aside. "You want to talk about Speer, we'll talk about Speer."

The class was now paying rapt attention. Yim rolled his eyes as he shuffled through a thick stack of maps in his desk drawer.

"Why was Speer bombed?" Kitay asked with impatience.

"First things first," said Yim. He flipped through several sheets of parchment until he found what he was looking for: a wrinkly map of Speer and the southern Nikan border. "I don't tolerate hasty historiography," he said as he tacked it up on the board. "We'll start with appropriate political context. Speer became a Nikara colony during the Red Emperor's reign. Who can tell me about Speer's annexation?"

Rin thought that *annexation* was a light way to put it. The truth was hardly so clinical. Centuries ago the Red Emperor had taken the island by storm and forced the Speerlies into military service, turning the island warriors into the most feared contingent in the Militia until the Second Poppy War wiped them out.

Nezha raised his hand. "Speer was annexed under Mai'rinnen Tearza, the last warrior queen of Speer. The Old Nikara Empire asked her to give up her throne and pay tribute to Sinegard. Tearza agreed, mostly because she was in love with the Red Emperor or something, but she was opposed by the Speerly Council. Legend has it Tearza stabbed herself in desperation, and that final act convinced the Speerly Council of her passion for Nikan."

The room was silent for a moment.

"That," Kitay mumbled, "is the dumbest story I've ever heard."

"Why would she kill herself?" Rin asked out loud. "Wouldn't she have been more useful alive to argue her case?"

Nezha shrugged. "Reasons why women shouldn't be in charge of small islands."

This provoked a hubbub of responses. Yim silenced them with a raised hand. "It was not that simple. Legend, of course, has blurred the facts. The tale of Tearza and the Red Emperor is a love story, not a historical anecdote."

Venka raised her hand. "I heard the Red Emperor betrayed her. He promised he wouldn't invade Speer, but went back on his word."

Yim shrugged. "It's a popular theory. The Red Emperor was famed for his ruthlessness; a betrayal of that sort would not have been out of character. The truth is, we don't know *why* Tearza died, or if anyone killed her. We know only that she did die,

Speer's tradition of warrior monarchs was discontinued, and the isle became annexed to the Empire until the Second Poppy War.

"Now, economically, Speer hardly pulled its weight as a colony. The island exported almost nothing of use to the Empire but soldiers. There is evidence that the Speerlies may not even have been aware of agriculture. Before the civilizing influence of the Red Emperor's envoys, the Speerlies were a primitive people who practiced vulgar and barbaric rituals. They had very little to offer culturally or technologically—in fact, they seemed centuries behind the rest of the world. Militarily, however, the Speerlies were worth their weight in gold."

Rin raised her hand. "Were the Speerlies really fire shamans?"

Muted snickers sounded around the classroom, and Rin immediately regretted speaking.

Yim looked amazed. "They still believe in shamans down in Tikany?"

Rin's cheeks felt hot. She had grown up hearing stories upon stories about Speer. Everyone in Tikany was morbidly obsessed with the Empire's frenzied warrior force and their supposed supernatural abilities. Rin knew better than to take the stories for the truth, but she'd still been curious.

But she had spoken without thinking. Of course the myths that had enthralled her in Tikany only sounded backward and provincial here in the capital.

"No—I mean, I don't—" Rin stammered. "It's just something I read, I was just wondering . . ."

"Don't mind her," Nezha said. "Tikany still thinks we lost the Poppy Wars."

More snickers. Nezha leaned back, smug.

"But the Speerlies had *some* weird abilities, right?" Kitay swiftly came to Rin's defense. "Why else would Mugen target Speer?"

"Because it's a convenient target," Nezha said. "Smack-dab between the Federation archipelago and Snake Province. Why not?"

"That makes no sense." Kitay shook his head. "From what I've read, Speer was an island of little to no strategic value. It's not even useful as a naval base—the Federation would be better off sailing directly over the narrow strait to Khurdalain. Mugen would only have cared about Speer if the Speerlies could do something that terrified them."

"The Speerlies *were* terrifying," Nezha said. "Primitive, drug-loving freaks. Who *wouldn't* want them gone?"

Rin couldn't believe Nezha could be so terribly crass in describing a tragic massacre, and was amazed when Yim nodded in agreement. "The Speerlies were a barbaric, war-obsessed race," he said. "They trained their children for battle as soon as they could walk. For centuries, they subsisted by regularly raiding Nikara coastal villages, because they had no agriculture of their own. Now, the rumors of shamanism probably have more to do with their religion. Historians believe they had bizarre rituals in which they pledged themselves to their god—the Vermilion Phoenix of the South. But that was only ever a ritual. Not a martial ability."

"The Speerly affinity for fire is well documented, though," said Kitay. "I've read the war reports. There are more than a few generals, Nikara and Federation alike, who thought the Speerlies could manipulate fire at will."

"All myths," Yim said dismissively. "The Speerly ability to manipulate fire was a ruse used to terrify their enemies. It probably originated from their use of flaming weapons in nighttime raids. But most scholars today agree that the Speerly battle prowess is entirely a product of their social conditioning and harsh environment."

"So why couldn't our army copy them?" Rin asked. "If the Speerly warriors were really so powerful, why couldn't we emulate their tactics? Why'd we have to enslave them?"

"Speer was a tributary. Not a slave colony," Yim said impatiently. "And we *could* re-create their training programs, but again, their methods were barbaric. The way Jun tells it, you're struggling with general training enough as it is. You'd hardly want to undergo the Speerly regimen."

"What about Altan?" Kitay pressed. "He didn't grow up on Speer, he was trained at Sinegard—"

"Have you ever seen Altan summon fire at will?"

"Of course not, but—"

"Has the very sight of him addled your minds?" Yim demanded. "Let me be perfectly clear. There are no shamans. There are no more Speerlies. Altan is human just like the rest of you. He possesses no magic, no divine ability. He fights well because he's been training since he could walk. Altan is the last scion of a dead race. If the Speerlies prayed to their god, it clearly didn't save them."

Their obsession with Altan wasn't entirely wasted in their lessons, though. After witnessing the apprentices' matches, the first-years redoubled their efforts in Jun's class. They wanted to become graceful, lethal fighters like Altan. But Jun remained a meticulous coach. He refused to teach them the flashy techniques they'd seen in the ring until they had thoroughly mastered their fundamentals.

"If you attempted Tobi's Tiger Claws now, you couldn't kill a rabbit," he sneered. "You'd just as quickly break your own fingers. It'll be months before you can channel the *ki* that sort of technique requires."

At least he had finally bored of drilling them in formation. Their class was now handling their staves with reasonable competence—at least, the accidental injuries were minimal. Near the end of class one day, Jun lined them up in rows and ordered them to spar.

"*Responsibly*," he emphasized. "Half speed if you must. I have no patience for idiotic injuries. Drill on the strikes and parries that you've practiced in the form."

Rin found herself standing across from Nezha. Of course she was. He shot her a nasty smile.

She wondered, briefly, how they could possibly finish the match without harming each other.

"On my count," said Jun. "One, two—"

Nezha launched himself forward.

The force behind his blow stunned her. She barely got her staff up over her head in time to block a swing that would have knocked her out cold—the impact sent tremors through her arms.

But Nezha continued to advance, ignoring Jun's instructions completely. He swung his staff with savage abandon, but also with startlingly good aim. Rin wielded her weapon clumsily; the staff was still awkward in her arms, nothing like the spinning blur in Nezha's hands. She could barely keep her grip on it; twice it almost spun out of her grasp. Nezha landed far more hits than she blocked. The first two—elbow strike, upper thigh strike—hurt. Then Nezha landed so many that she couldn't feel them anymore.

She had been wrong about him. He had been showing off earlier, but his command of martial arts was prodigious and real. Last time they'd fought, he'd gotten cocky. Her lucky blow had been a fluke.

He was not being cocky now.

His staff connected with her kneecap with a sickening crunch. Rin's eyes bulged. She crumpled to the ground.

Nezha wasn't even bothering with his staff anymore. He kicked at her while she was still down, each blow more vicious than the last.

"That's the difference between you and me," muttered Nezha. "I've trained for this my entire life. You don't get to just stroll in here and embarrass me. You understand? You're *nothing*."

He's going to kill me. He's actually going to kill me.

Enough with the staff. She couldn't defend herself with a weapon she didn't know how to use. She dropped the staff and lunged upward to tackle Nezha around the waist. Nezha dropped his staff and tripped over backward. She landed on top of him. He swung at her face; she forced a palm into his nose. They pummeled furiously at each other, a chaotic tangle of limbs.

Then something yanked hard at her collar, cutting off her airflow. Jun pried them apart in an impressive display of strength, held them suspended in the air for a minute, then flung them both to the ground.

"What part of *block and parry* was unclear?" he growled.

"She started it," Nezha said quickly. He rolled to a sitting position and pointed at Rin. "She dropped her—"

"I know what I saw," Jun snapped. "And I saw you rolling around the floor like imbeciles. If I enjoyed training animals, I would be in the Cike. Shall I put in a word?"

Nezha cast his eyes down. "No, sir."

"Put your weapon away and leave my class. You're suspended for a week."

"Yes, sir." Nezha rose to his feet, tossed his staff at the weapons rack, and stalked off.

Jun then turned his attention to Rin. Blood dripped down her face, streaming from her nose, trickling down her forehead. She wiped clumsily at her chin, too nervous to meet Jun's eyes.

He loomed above her. "You. Get up."

She struggled to her feet. Her knee screamed in protest.

"Get that pathetic look off your face. You won't receive any sympathy from me."

She didn't expect his sympathy. But neither was she expecting what came next.

"That was the most miserable display I've seen from a student since I left the Militia," Jun said. "Your fundamentals are horrific. You move like a paraplegic. What did I just witness? Have you been asleep for the past month?"

He moved too fast. I couldn't keep up. I don't have years of training like he does. Even as the words came to her mind, they sounded like the pathetic excuses they were. She opened her mouth and closed it, too stunned to respond.

"I hate students like you," Jun continued relentlessly. The sounds of staves clashing against one another had long died away. The entire class was listening. "You skip into Sinegard from your little village, thinking that this is it—you've made it, you're going to make Mommy and Daddy proud. Maybe you were the smartest kid in your village. Maybe you were the best test taker your tutor has ever seen! But guess what? It takes more than memorizing a few Classics to be a martial artist.

"Every year we get someone like you, some country bumpkin who thinks that just because they were good at taking some *test*, they deserve my time and attention. Understand this, southerner. The exam proves nothing. Discipline and competence—those are the *only* things that matter at this school. That boy"—Jun jerked his thumb in the direction Nezha had gone—"may be an ass, but he has the makings of a commander in him. You, on the other hand, are just peasant trash."

The entire class was staring at her now. Kitay's eyes were wide with sympathy. Even Venka looked stunned.

Rin's ears rang, drowning out Jun's words. She felt so small. She felt as if she might crumble into dust. *Don't let me cry.* Her eyes throbbed from the pressure of forcing back her tears. *Please don't let me cry.*

"I do not tolerate troublemakers in my class," Jun said. "I do not have the happy privilege to expel you, but as Combat Master I can do this: From now on you are banned from the practice facilities. You do not touch the weapons rack. You do not train in the studio during off-hours. You do not set foot in here while I am teaching a class. You do not ask older students to teach you. I don't need you causing any more trouble in my studio. Now get out of my sight."

CHAPTER 5

Rin stumbled out the courtyard door. Jun's words echoed over and over in her head. She was suddenly dizzy; her legs wobbled and her vision went temporarily black. She slid down against the stone wall, hugging her knees to her chest while blood pumped furiously in her ears.

Then the pressure in her chest bubbled up and she cried for the first time since orientation, sobbing with her face pressed into her hands so that no one could hear.

She cried from the pain. She cried from the embarrassment. But mostly she cried because those two long years of studying for the Keju hadn't meant a thing. She was years behind her peers at Sinegard. She had no martial arts experience, much less an inherited art—even one that looked as stupid as Nezha's. She hadn't trained since childhood, like Venka. She wasn't brilliant, didn't have an eidetic memory like Kitay.

And the worst thing was, now she had no way to make up for it. Without Jun's tutelage, frustrating though it was, Rin knew she didn't have a chance of making it past the Trials. No master would choose to take on an apprentice who couldn't fight. Sinegard was primarily a *military* academy. If she couldn't hold her own on the battlefield, then what was the point?

Jun's punishment was as good as an expulsion. She was done. It was over. She'd be back in Tikany within a year.

But Nezha attacked first.

The more she considered this, the faster her despair crystallized into anger. Nezha had tried to *kill* her. She had acted only in self-defense. Why had she been thrown out of the class, when Nezha had gotten off with little more than a slap on the wrist?

But it was so clear why. Nezha was a Sinegardian noble, the son of a Warlord, and she was a country girl with no connections and no status. Expelling Nezha would have been troublesome and politically contentious. He mattered. She did not.

No—they couldn't just do this to her. They might think they could sweep her away like rubbish, but she didn't have to lie down and take it. She had come from nothing. She wasn't going back to nothing.

The courtyard doors opened as class let out. Her classmates hurried past her, pretending they didn't see her. Only Kitay hung behind.

"Jun will come around," he said.

Rin took his proffered hand and stood up in silence. She wiped at her face with her sleeve and sniffed.

"I mean it," Kitay said. He placed a hand on her shoulder. "He only suspended Nezha for a week."

She shrugged his hand off violently, still wiping furiously at her eyes. "That's because Nezha was born with a gold ingot in his mouth. Nezha got off because his father's got half the faculty here by their balls. Nezha's from Sinegard, so Nezha's *special*, Nezha *belongs* here."

"Come on, you belong here too, you passed the Keju—"

"The Keju doesn't mean anything," Rin said scathingly. "The Keju is a ruse to keep uneducated peasants right where they've always been. You slip past the Keju, they'll find a way to expel you anyway. The Keju keeps the lower classes sedated. It keeps us dreaming. It's not a ladder for mobility; it's a way to keep people like me exactly where they were born. The Keju is a drug."

"Rin, that's not true."

"It *is*!" She slammed her fist against the wall. "But they're not going to get rid of me like this. Not this easily. I won't let them. I *won't*."

She swayed suddenly. Her vision pulsed black and then cleared.

"Great Tortoise," said Kitay. "Are you all right?"

She whirled on him. "What are you talking about?"

"You're sweating."

Sweating? She wasn't sweating. "I'm fine," she said. Her voice sounded inordinately loud; it rang in her ears. Was she shouting?

"Rin, calm down."

"I'm calm! I'm extremely calm!"

She was far from fucking calm. She wanted to hit something. She wanted to scream at someone. Anger pulsed through her like a wave of heat.

Then her stomach erupted with a pain like she had been stabbed. She gasped sharply and clutched at her midriff. She felt as if someone were sliding a jagged stone through her innards.

Kitay grasped at her shoulders. "Rin? *Rin?*"

She felt the sudden urge to vomit. Had Nezha's blows given her internal damage?

Oh, fantastic, she thought. *Now you're humiliated and injured, too. Wait until they watch you limp into class; Nezha's going to love that.*

She shoved Kitay away. "I don't need— Leave me alone!"

"But you're—"

"I'm *fine*!"

Rin awoke that night to a deeply confusing sticky sensation.

Her sleeping pants felt cold, the way her pants had felt when she'd been little and peed in her sleep. But her legs were too sticky to be covered in urine. Heart pounding, she scrambled out of her bunk and lit a lamp with shaking fingers.

She glanced down at herself and almost shrieked out loud. The soft candlelight illuminated pools of crimson everywhere. She was covered in an enormous amount of blood.

She fought to still her panic, to force her drowsy mind to think rationally. She felt no acute pain, only a deep discomfort and great irritation. She hadn't been stabbed. She hadn't somehow ejected all of her inner organs. A fresh flow of blood trickled down her leg that moment, and she traced it to the source with soaked fingers.

Then she was just confused.

Going back to sleep was out of the question. She wiped herself off with the parts of the sheet that weren't soaked in blood, jammed a piece of cloth between her legs, and ran out of the dormitory to get to the infirmary before the rest of the campus woke.

Rin reached the infirmary in a sweaty, bloody mess, halfway to a nervous breakdown. The physician on call took one look at her and called his female assistant over. "One of those situations," he said.

"Of course." The assistant looked like she was trying hard not to laugh. Rin did not see anything remotely funny about the situation.

The assistant took Rin behind a curtain, handed her a change of clothes and a towel, and then sat her down with a detailed diagram of the female body.

It was a testament, perhaps, to the lack of sexual education in Tikany that Rin didn't learn about menstruation until that morning. Over the next fifteen minutes, the physician's assistant explained in detail the changes going on in Rin's body, pointing to various places on the diagram and making some very vivid gestures with her hands.

"So you're not dying, sweetheart, your body is just shedding your uterine lining."

Rin's jaw had been hanging open for a solid minute.

"What the *fuck*?"

She returned to the bunks with a deeply uncomfortable girdle strapped under her pants and a sock filled with heated uncooked rice grains. She placed the sock on her lower torso to dull the aching pain, but the cramping was so bad that she couldn't crawl out of bed before classes started.

"Do you want me to get someone?" Niang asked.

"No," Rin mumbled. "I'm fine. Just go."

She lay in bed for the entire day, despairing at all the class she was missing.

I'll be all right. She chanted it over and over to herself so that she wouldn't panic. One missed day couldn't hurt. Pupils got sick all the time. Kitay would lend her his notes if she asked. Surely she could catch up.

But this was going to happen every month. Every gods-damned month her uterus would tear itself to pieces, send flashes of rage through her entire body, and make her bloated, clumsy, lightheaded, and worst of all, weak. No wonder women rarely remained at Sinegard.

She needed to fix this problem.

If only it weren't so deeply embarrassing. She needed help. Venka seemed like someone who would have already begun menstruating. But Rin would have died rather than ask her how she'd managed it. Instead, she mumbled her questions to Kureel one night after she was sure Niang and Venka had gone to sleep.

Kureel laughed out loud in the darkness. "Just wear the girdle to class. You'll be fine. You get used to the cramping."

"But how often do I have to change it? What if it leaks in class? What if it gets on my uniform? What if someone *sees*?"

"Calm down," said Kureel. "The first time is hard, but you'll adapt to it. Keep track of your cycle, then you'll know when it's coming on."

This wasn't what Rin wanted to hear. "There's no way to just stop it forever?"

"Not unless you cut out your womb," Kureel scoffed, then paused at the look on Rin's face. "I was kidding. That's not actually possible."

"It's possible." Arda, who was a Medicine apprentice, interrupted them quietly. "There's a procedure they offer at the infirmary. At your age, it wouldn't even require open surgery. They'll give you a concoction. It'll stop the process pretty much indefinitely."

"Seriously?" Hope flared in Rin's chest. She looked between the two apprentices. "Well, what's stopping you from taking it?"

They both looked at her incredulously.

"It destroys your womb," Arda said finally. "Basically kills one of your inner organs. You won't be able to have children after."

"And it hurts like a bitch," Kureel said. "It's not worth it."

But I don't want children, Rin thought. *I want to stay here.*

If that procedure could stop her menstruating, if it could help her remain at Sinegard, it was worth it.

Once her bleeding stopped, Rin went back to the infirmary and told the physician what she wanted. He did not argue with her; in fact, he seemed pleased.

"I've been trying to convince the girls here to do this for years," he said. "None of them listen. Small wonder so few of you make it past your first year. They should make this mandatory."

He made her wait while he disappeared into the back room, mixing together the requisite medicines. Ten minutes later he returned with a steaming cup.

"Drink this."

Rin took the cup. It was dark porcelain, so she couldn't tell the color of the liquid inside. She wondered if she should feel anything. This was significant, wasn't it? There would be no children for her. No one would agree to marry her after this. Shouldn't that matter?

No. No, of course not. If she'd wanted to grow fat with squealing brats, she would have stayed in Tikany. She had come to Sinegard to escape that future. Why hesitate now?

She searched herself for any twinge of regret. Nothing. She felt absolutely nothing, just as she had felt nothing the day she left Tikany, watching the dusty town recede forever into the distance.

"It'll hurt," the physician warned. "Much worse than it hurt when you were menstruating. Your womb will self-destruct over the next few hours. After this, it will stop fulfilling its function. When your body has matured fully, you can get a surgery to have your womb removed altogether, but this should solve your problem in the interim. You'll be out of class for at least a week after this. But afterward, you'll be free forever. Now, I'm required to ask you one more time if you're certain this is what you want."

"I'm certain." Rin didn't want to think it over any more. She held her breath and lifted the mug to her mouth, wincing at the taste.

The physician had added honey to mask the bitterness, but the sweetness only made it more horrible. It tasted the way that opium smelled. She had to swallow many times before she drained the entire mug. When she finished, her stomach felt numb and weirdly sated, bloated and rubbery. After a few minutes an odd prickling feeling tingled at the base of her torso, like someone was poking her with tiny needles from inside.

"Get back to your room before it starts to hurt," the physician advised. "I'll tell the masters you're ill. The nurse will check on you tonight. You won't want to eat, but I'll have one of your classmates bring you some food just in case."

Rin thanked him and ran with a wobbling gait back to her quarters, clutching her abdomen. The prickling had turned into an acute pain spreading across her lower stomach. She felt as if she had swallowed a knife and it was twisting in a slow circle inside her.

Somehow she made it back to her bed.

Pain is just a message, she told herself. She could choose to ignore it. She could . . . she could . . .

It was terrible. She whimpered aloud.

She did not sleep so much as lie in a fevered daze. She turned deliriously on the sheets, dreaming of unborn, misshapen infants, of Tobi digging his five claws into her stomach.

"Rin. Rin?"

Someone hovered over her. It was Niang, bearing a wooden bowl.

"I brought you some winter melon soup." Niang knelt down beside Rin and held the bowl to her face.

Rin took one whiff of the soup. Her stomach seized painfully.

"I'm good," she said weakly.

"There's also this sedative." Niang pushed a cup toward her. "The physician said it's safe for you to take it now if you want to, but you don't have to."

"Are you joking? Give me that." Rin grabbed the cup and guzzled it down. Immediately her head began to swim. The room became delightfully fuzzy. The stabbing in her abdomen disappeared. Then something rose up in the back of her throat. Rin lunged to the side of the bed and vomited into the basin she had set there. Blood splattered the porcelain.

She glanced down at the basin with a deranged satisfaction. *Better to get the blood out this way*, she thought, *all at once, rather than slowly, every month, for years*.

While she continued to retch, she heard the door to the dormitory open.

Someone walked inside and paused in front of her. "You're insane," said Venka.

Rin glared up at her, blood dripping from her mouth, and smiled.

Rin spent four delirious days in bed before she could return to class. When she did drag herself out of bed, against both Niang's and the physician's recommendations, she found she was hopelessly behind.

She had missed an entire unit on Mugini verb conjugations in Linguistics, the chapter on the demise of the Red Emperor in History, Sunzi's analysis of geographical forecasting in Strategy, and the finer points of setting a splint in Medicine. She expected no lenience from the masters and received none.

The masters treated her like missing class was her fault, and it was. She had no excuses; she could only accept the consequences.

She flubbed questions every time a master called on her. She scored at the bottom of every exam. She didn't complain. For the entire week, she endured the masters' condescension in silence.

Oddly, she didn't feel discouraged, but rather as if a veil had been lifted. Her first few weeks at Sinegard had been like a dream. Dazzled by the magnificence of the city and the Academy, she had allowed herself to drift.

She had now been painfully reminded that her place here was not permanent.

The Keju had meant nothing. The Keju had tested her ability to recite poems like a parrot. Why had she ever imagined that might have prepared her for a school like Sinegard?

But if the Keju had taught her anything, it was that pain was the price of success.

And she hadn't burned herself in a long time.

She had grown content at the Academy. She had grown lazy. She had lost sight of what was at stake. She had needed to be reminded that she was nothing—that she could be sent back home at a moment's notice. That as miserable she was at Sinegard, what awaited her in Tikany was much, much worse.

He looks at you and licks his lips. He brings you to the bed. He forces a hand between your legs. You scream, but no one hears you.

She would stay. She would stay at Sinegard even if it killed her.

She threw herself into her studies. Classes became like warfare, each interaction a battle. With every raised hand and every homework assignment, she competed against Nezha and Venka and every other Sinegardian. She had to prove that she deserved to be kept on, that she merited further training.

She had needed failure to remind her that she wasn't like the Sinegardians—she hadn't grown up speaking casual Hesperian, wasn't familiar with the command structure of the Imperial Militia, didn't know the political relationships between the Twelve Warlords like the back of her hand. The Sinegardians had this knowledge ingrained from childhood. She would have to develop it.

Every waking hour that she didn't spend in class, she spent in the archives. She read the assigned texts out loud to herself; wrapping her tongue around the unfamiliar Sinegardian dialect until she had eradicated all hints of her southern drawl.

She began to burn herself again. She found release in the pain; it was comforting, familiar. It was a trade-off she was well used to. Success required sacrifice. Sacrifice meant pain. Pain meant success.

She stopped sleeping. She sat in the front row so that there was no way she could doze off. Her head ached constantly. She always wanted to vomit. She stopped eating.

She made herself miserable. But then, all of her options led to misery. She could run away. She could get on a boat and escape to another city. She could run drugs for another opium smuggler. She could, if it came down to it, return to Tikany, marry, and hope no one found out that she couldn't have children until it was too late.

But the misery she felt now was a good misery. This misery she reveled in, because she had chosen it for herself.

One month later, Rin tested at the top of one of Jima's frequent Linguistics exams. She beat Nezha's score by two points. When Jima announced the top five scores, Rin jerked upright, happily shocked.

She had spent the entire night cramming Hesperian verb tenses, which were infinitely confusing. Modern Hesperian was a language that followed neither rhyme nor reason. Its rules were close to pure randomness, its pronunciation guides haphazard and riddled with exceptions.

She couldn't reason through Hesperian, so she memorized it, the way she memorized everything she didn't understand.

"Good," Jima said crisply when she handed Rin's exam scroll back to her.

Rin was startled at how good "good" made her feel.

She found that she was fueled by praise from her masters. Praise meant that she had finally, *finally* received validation that she was not nothing. She could be brilliant, could be worth someone's attention. She adored praise—craved it, needed it, and realized she found relief only when she finally had it.

She realized, too, that she felt about praise the way that addicts felt about opium. Each time she received a fresh infusion of flattery, she could think only about how to get more of it. Achievement was a high. Failure was worse than withdrawal. Good test scores brought only momentary relief and temporary pride—she basked in her grace period of several hours before she began to panic about her next test.

She craved praise so deeply that she felt it in her bones. And just like an addict, she did whatever she could to get it.

In the following weeks, Rin clawed her way up from the bottom of the ranks to become one of the top students in each class. She competed regularly with Nezha and Venka for the highest marks in nearly every subject. In Linguistics, she was second now only to Kitay.

She particularly enjoyed Strategy.

Gray-whiskered Master Irjah was the first teacher she'd ever had who didn't rely principally on rote memorization as a learning method. He made the students solve logical syllogisms. He made them define concepts they had taken for granted, concepts like *advantage* and *victory* and *war*. He forced them to be precise and accurate in their answers. He rejected responses that were phrased vaguely or could have multiple interpretations. He stretched their minds, shattered their preconceptions of logic, and then pieced them back together.

He gave praise only sparingly, but when he did, he made sure that everyone in the class heard. Rin craved his approval more than anything.

Now that they had finished analyzing Sunzi's *Principles of War*, Irjah spent the second half of class lobbing hypothetical military situations at them, challenging them to think their way out of various quagmires. Sometimes these simulations involved only questions of logistics ("Calculate how much time and how many supplies you need to move a force of this size across this strait"). Other times he drew up maps for them, indicating with symbols how many troops they had to work with, and forced them to come up with a battle plan.

"You are stuck behind this river," said Irjah. "Your troops stand in a prime position for a ranged assault, but your main column has run out of arrows. What do you do?"

Most of their class suggested raids on the enemy's weapons carriages. Venka wanted to abandon the ranged idea entirely and pursue a direct frontal assault. Nezha suggested they commission the nearby farmers to mass-produce arrows in one night.

"Gather scarecrows from the nearby farmers," said Kitay.

Nezha snorted. "What?"

"Let him talk," said Irjah.

"Dress them in spare uniforms, stick them in a boat, and send them downriver," Kitay continued, ignoring him. "This area is a mountainous region notorious for heavy precipitation. We can assume it has rained recently, so there should be fog. That makes it difficult for the enemy forces to see the river clearly. Their archers will mistake the scarecrows for soldiers, and shoot until they resemble pincushions. We will then send our men downstream and have them collect the arrows. We use our enemy's arrows to kill our enemies."

Kitay won that one.

Another day Irjah presented them with a map of the Wudang mountain region marked with two red crosses to indicate two Federation battalions surrounding the Nikara army from both ends of the valley.

"You're trapped in this valley. The villagers have mostly evacuated, but the Federation general holds a school full of children hostage. He says he will set the children free if your battalion surrenders. You have no guarantee he will honor the terms. How do you respond?"

They stared at the map for many minutes. Their troops had no advantage, no easy way out.

Even Kitay was puzzled. "Try an assault on the left flank?" he suggested. "Evacuate the children while they're preoccupied with a small guerrilla force?"

"They're on higher ground," said Irjah. "They'll shoot you down before you get the chance to draw your weapons."

"Light the valley on fire," Venka tried. "Distract them with the smoke?"

"Good way to burn yourselves to death." Irjah snorted. "Remember, you do not have the high ground."

Rin raised her hand. "Cut around the second army and get onto the dam. Break the dam. Flood the valley. Let everyone inside drown."

Her classmates turned to stare at her in horror.

"Leave the children," she added. "There's no way to save them."

Nezha laughed out loud. "We're trying to *win* this simulation, idiot."

Irjah motioned for Nezha to be silent. "Runin. Please elaborate."

"It's not a victory either way," said Rin. "But if the costs are so high, I would throw all my tiles in. This way they die, and we lose half our troops but no more. Sunzi writes that no battle takes place in isolation. This is just one small move in the grand scheme of the war. The numbers you've given us indicate that these Federation battalions are massive. I'm guessing they constitute a large percentage of the entire Federation army. So if we give up some of our own troops, we lessen their advantage in all subsequent battles."

"You'd rather kill your own people than let the opponent's army walk away?" Irjah asked.

"Killing isn't the same as letting die," Rin objected.

"They're casualties nonetheless."

Rin shook her head. "You don't let an enemy walk away if they'll certainly be a threat to you later. You get rid of them. If they're that far inland, they know the lay of almost the entire country. They have a geographical advantage. This is our one chance to take out the enemy's greatest fighting force."

"Sunzi said to always give the enemy a way out," Irjah said.

Rin privately thought that this was one of Sunzi's stupider principles, but hastily pulled together a counterargument. "But Sunzi didn't mean to *let* them take that way out. The enemy just has to think the situation is less dire than it is, so they don't grow desperate and do stupid and mutually destructive things." Rin pondered for a moment. "I suppose they could try to swim."

"She's talking about decimating entire villages!" Venka protested. "You can't just break a dam like that. Dams take years to rebuild. The entire river delta will flood, not just that valley. You're talking about famine. Dysentery. You'll mess with the agriculture of the entire region, create a whole host of problems that mean decades of suffering down the line—"

"Problems that can be solved," Rin maintained stubbornly. "What was your solution, to let the Federation walk free into the heartland? Fat lot of good the agricultural regions will do you when your whole country's been occupied. You would offer up the whole country to them on a platter."

"Enough, enough." Irjah slammed the table to silence them. "Nobody wins this one. You're dismissed for today. Runin, I want to have a word. My office."

"Where did you come by this solution?" Irjah held up a booklet.

Rin recognized her scrawling handwriting at the top.

Last week Irjah had assigned them to write essay responses to another simulated quagmire—a counterfactual scenario where the Militia had lost popular support for a war of resistance against the Federation. They couldn't rely on peasants to supply soldiers with food or animal feed, could not use peasant homes as lodging without forceful entry. In fact, outbreaks of rebellion in rural areas added several layers of complication to coordinating troop movements.

Rin's solution had been to burn down one of the minor island villages.

The twist was that the island in question belonged to the Empire.

"The first day of Yim's class we talked about how losing Speer ended the Second Poppy War," she said.

Irjah frowned. "You based this essay on the Speerly Massacre?"

She nodded. "Losing Speer during the Second Poppy War pushed Hesperia over the edge—made them uncomfortable enough that they didn't want Mugen expanding farther into the continent. I thought the destruction of another minor island might do the same for the Nikara population, convince them that the real enemy was Mugen. Remind them what the threat was."

"Surely Militia troops attacking a province of the Empire would send the wrong message," Irjah objected.

"They wouldn't *know* it was Militia troops," she said. "We would pose as a Federation squadron. I suppose I should have been clearer about that in the essay. Better still if Mugen just went ahead and attacked the island for us, but you can't leave these things to chance."

He nodded slowly as he perused her essay. "Crude. Crude, but clever. Do you think that's what happened?"

It took her a moment to understand his question. "In this simulation, or during the Poppy Wars?"

"The Poppy Wars." Irjah tilted his head, watching her carefully.

"I'm not entirely sure that's not what happened," Rin said. "There's some evidence that the attack on Speer was allowed to succeed."

Irjah's expression betrayed nothing, but his fingers tapped thoughtfully against his wooden desk. "Explain."

"I find it very difficult to believe that the strongest fighting force in the Militia could have been annihilated so easily. That, and the island was suspiciously poorly defended."

"What are you suggesting?"

"Well, I'm not certain, but it seems as if—I mean, maybe someone on the inside—a Nikara general, or someone else who was privy to certain information—knew about the attack on Speer but didn't alert anyone."

"Now why would we have wanted to lose Speer?" Irjah asked quietly.

She took a moment to formulate a coherent argument. "Maybe they knew Hesperia wouldn't stand for it. Maybe they wanted to generate popular support to distract from the Red Junk movement. Maybe because we needed a sacrifice, and Speer was expendable in a way other regions weren't. We couldn't let any Nikara die. But Speerlies? Why not?"

She had been grasping at straws when she had started to speak, but the moment she said it, her answer sounded startlingly plausible to her.

Irjah looked deeply uncomfortable. "You must understand that this is a very awkward part of Nikan's history," he said. "The way that the Speerlies were treated was . . . regrettable. They were used and exploited by the Empire for centuries. Their warriors were regarded as little more than vicious dogs. Savages. Until Altan came to study at Sinegard, I don't believe anyone really thought the Speerlies were capable of sophisticated thought. Nikan does not like to speak of Speer, and for good reason."

"Yes, sir. It was just a theory."

"Anyhow." Irjah leaned back in his chair. "That isn't all I wanted to discuss. Your strategy in the valley worked for the purposes of the exercise, but no competent ruler would ever give those orders. Do you know why?"

She contemplated in silence for a minute. "I confused tactics with grand strategy," she said finally.

Irjah nodded. "Elaborate."

"The *tactic* would have worked. We might have even won the war. But no ruler would have chosen that option, because the country would have fallen apart afterward. My tactic doesn't grant the possibility of peace."

"Why is that?" Irjah pressed.

"Venka was right about destroying the agricultural heartland. Nikan would suffer famine for years. Rebellions like the Red Junk Opera would spring up everywhere. People would think it was the Empress's fault that they were starving. If we used my strategy, what would happen next is probably a civil war."

"Good," said Irjah. He raised his eyebrows. "Very good. You know, you are astoundingly bright."

Rin tried to conceal her delight, though she felt a flutter of warmth spread across her body.

"Should you perform well in the Trials," Irjah continued, "you might do well as a Strategy apprentice."

Under any other circumstances his words would have thrilled her. Rin managed a resigned smile. "I'm not sure I'll make it that far, sir."

His brow crinkled. "Why's that?"

"Master Jun kicked me out of his class. I probably won't pass the Trials."

"How on earth did that happen?" Irjah demanded.

She recounted her last, disastrous class with Jun without bothering to edit the story. "He let Nezha off with a suspension, but told me not to come back."

"Ah." Irjah frowned. "Jun didn't punish you because you were brawling. Tobi and Altan did far worse than that their first year. He punished you because he's a purist about the school—he thinks any student who isn't descended from a Warlord isn't worth his time. But never mind what Jun thinks. You're clever, you'll pick up whatever techniques they covered this month without much trouble."

Rin shook her head. "It won't make much difference. He's not letting me back in."

"*What?*" Irjah looked outraged. "That's absurd. Does Jima know?"

"Jima can't intervene in a Combat matter. Or won't. I've asked." Rin stood up. "Thanks for your time, sir. If I make it past the Trials, I'd be honored to study with you."

"You'll find a way," Irjah said. His eyes twinkled. "Sunzi would."

Rin hadn't been completely forthcoming with Irjah. He was right—she *would* find a way.

Starting with the fact that she hadn't given up on martial arts.

Jun had banned her from his class, but he hadn't banned her from the library. The stacks at Sinegard contained a wealth of martial arts instruction tomes, the largest collection in all the Empire. Rin had within reach the secrets of most inherited arts, excepting those tightly guarded techniques like the House of Yin's.

In the course of her research Rin discovered that existing martial arts literature was hugely comprehensive and dauntingly complex. She learned that martial arts revolved largely around lineage: different forms belonged to different families, similar techniques taught and improved upon by pupils who had shared the same master. More often than not, schools became torn by rivalries or schisms, so techniques splintered and developed independently of others.

The history was deeply enjoyable, almost more entertaining than novels. But practicing the techniques turned out to be devilishly hard. Most tomes were too dense to serve as useful manuals. A majority assumed that the student was reading the book along with a master who could demonstrate the techniques in real life. Others expounded for pages about a certain school's breathing techniques and philosophy of fighting, but only sporadically mentioned things like kicking and punching.

"I don't want to read about the balance in the universe," Rin grumbled, tossing aside what seemed like the hundredth text she'd tried. "I want to know how to beat people up."

She attempted asking the apprentices for help.

"Sorry," Kureel said without meeting her eyes. "Jun said that teaching first-years outside of the practice rooms was against the rules."

Rin doubted this was a real rule, but she should have known better than to ask one of Jun's apprentices.

Asking Arda was also not an option; she spent all her time in the infirmary with Enro and never returned to the bunks before midnight.

Rin was going to have to teach herself.

A month and a half in, she finally found a gold mine of information in the texts of Ha Seejin, quartermaster under the Red Emperor. Seejin's manuals were wonderfully illustrated, filled with detailed descriptions and clearly labeled diagrams.

Rin perused the pages gleefully. This was it. This was what she needed.

"You can't take this one out," said the apprentice at the front desk.

"Why not?"

"It's from the restricted shelves," said the apprentice, as if this were obvious. "First-years don't get access to those."

"Oh. Sorry. I'll take it back."

Rin walked to the back end of the library. She glanced furtively about to make sure no one was watching. She stuffed the tome down her shirt. Then she turned around and walked back out.

Alone in the courtyard, book in hand, Rin learned. She learned to shape the air with her fists, to imagine a great spinning ball in her arms to guide the shape of her movements. She learned to root her legs against the ground so she couldn't be tipped over, not even by opponents twice her weight. She learned to form fists with her thumb on the outside, to always keep her guard up around her face, and to shift her balance quickly and smoothly.

She became very good at punching stationary objects.

She attended the matches at the rings regularly. She arrived in the basement early and secured a place by the railing so that she didn't miss a single kick or throw. She hoped that by watching the apprentices fight, she could absorb their techniques.

This actually helped—to some extent. By closely examining the apprentices' movements, Rin learned to identify the right place and time for various techniques. When to kick, when to dodge, when to roll madly on the floor to avoid—wait, no, that was an accident, Jeeha had simply tripped. Rin didn't have muscle memory of sparring against another person, so she had to hold these contingencies in her head. But vicarious sparring was better than nothing.

She also attended the matches to watch Altan.

She would have been lying to herself if she didn't admit that she derived great aesthetic pleasure from staring at him. With his lithe, muscled form and chiseled jawline, Altan was undeniably handsome.

But he was also the paragon of good technique. Altan did everything that the Seejin text recommended. He never let his guard down, never allowed an opening, never let his attention slip. He never telegraphed his next move, didn't bounce erratically or go flat on his heels to advertise to his opponent when he was going to kick. He always attacked from angles, never from the front.

Rin had initially conceived of Altan as simply a good, strong fighter. Now she could see that he was, in every sense, a genius. His fighting technique was a study in trigonometry, a beautiful composition of trajectories and rebounded forces. He won consistently because he had perfect control of distance and torque. He had the mathematics of fighting down to a science.

He fought more often than not. Throughout the semester his challengers only grew in number—it seemed every single one of Jun's apprentices wanted to have a go at him.

Rin watched Altan fight twenty-three matches before the end of the fall. He never lost.

CHAPTER 6

Winter descended on Sinegard with a vengeance. The students enjoyed one last pleasant day of autumn sun, and woke the next morning to find that a cold sheet of snow had fallen over the Academy. The snow was lovely to observe for all of two serene minutes. Then it became nothing but a pain in the ass.

The entire campus turned into a risk zone for broken limbs—the streams froze over; the stairways became slushy and treacherous. Outdoor classes moved indoors. The first-years were assigned to scatter salt across the stone walkways at regular intervals to melt the snow, but the slippery paths sent a regular stream of students to the infirmary regardless.

As far as Lore went, the icy weather was the last straw for most of the class, who had been intermittently frequenting the garden in hopes that Jiang might make an appearance. But waiting around in a drug garden for a never-present teacher was one thing; waiting in freezing cold temperatures was another.

In the months since the semester began, Jiang hadn't shown up once to class. Students occasionally spotted him around campus doing inexcusably rude things. He had in turn flipped Nezha's lunch tray out of his hands and walked away whistling, petted

Kitay on the head while making a pigeon-like cooing noise, and tried to snip Venka's hair off with garden shears.

Whenever a student managed to pin him down to ask about his course, Jiang made a loud farting noise with his mouth and elbow and skirted away.

Rin alone continued to frequent the Lore garden, but only because it was a convenient place to train. Now that first-years avoided the garden out of spite, it was the one place where she was guaranteed to be alone.

She was grateful that no one could see her fumbling through the Seejin text. She had picked up the fundamentals with little trouble, but discovered that even just the second form was devilishly hard to put together.

Seejin was fond of rapidly twisting footwork. Here the diagrams failed her. The models' feet in the drawings were positioned in completely different angles from picture to picture. Seejin wrote that if a fighter could extricate himself from any awkward placement, no matter how close he was to falling, he would have achieved perfect balance and therefore the advantage in most combat positions.

It sounded good in theory. In practice, it meant a lot of falling over.

Seejin recommended pupils practice the first form on an elevated surface, preferably a thick tree branch or the top of a wall. Against her better judgment, Rin climbed to the middle of the large willow tree overhanging the garden and positioned her feet hesitantly against the bark.

Despite Jiang's absence throughout the semester, the garden remained impeccably well kept. It was a kaleidoscope of garishly bright colors, similar in color scheme to the decorations outside Tikany's whorehouses. Despite the cold, the violet and scarlet poppy flowers had remained in full blossom, their leaves trimmed in tidy rows. The cacti, which were twice the size they had been at the start of term, had been moved into a new set of clay pots painted in eerie patterns of black and burnt orange. Underneath the shelves, the luminescent mushrooms still pulsed with a faintly disturbing glow, like tiny fairy lamps.

Rin imagined that an opium addict could pass entire days in here. She wondered if that was what Jiang did.

Poised precariously on the willow tree, struggling to stand up straight against the harsh wind, Rin held the book in one hand, mumbling instructions out loud while she positioned her feet accordingly.

"Right foot out, pointing straight forward. Left foot back, perpendicular to the straight line of the right foot. Shift weight forward, lift left foot . . ."

She could see why Seejin thought this might be good balance practice. She also saw why Seejin strongly recommended against attempting the exercise alone. She wobbled perilously several times, and regained her balance only after a few heart-stopping seconds of frantic windmilling. *Calm down. Focus. Right foot up, bring it around . . .*

Master Jiang walked around the corner, loudly whistling "The Gatekeeper's Touches."

Rin's right foot slid out from beneath her. She teetered off the edge of the branch, dropped the book, and would have plummeted to the stone floor if her left ankle hadn't snagged in the crook of two dividing branches.

She jolted to a halt with her face inches from the ground and gasped out loud in relief.

Jiang stared down silently at her. She gazed back, head thundering while the blood rushed down into her temples. The last notes of his song dwindled and faded away in the howling wind.

"Hello there," he said finally. His voice matched his demeanor: placid, disengaged, and idyllically curious. In any other context, it might have been soothing.

Rin struggled ungracefully to haul herself upward.

"Are you all right?" he asked.

"I'm stuck," she mumbled.

"Mmm. Appears so."

He clearly wasn't going to help her down. Rin wriggled her ankle out of the branch, tumbled to the floor, and landed in a painful heap at Jiang's feet. Cheeks burning, she clambered to her feet and brushed the snow off her uniform.

"Elegant," Jiang remarked.

He tilted his head very far to the left, studying her intently as if she were a particularly fascinating specimen. Up close, Jiang looked even more bizarre than Rin had first thought. His face was a riddle; it was neither lined with age nor flushed with youth but rather invulnerable to time, like a smooth stone. His eyes were a pale blue color she had never seen on anyone in the Empire.

"Bit daring, aren't you?" He sounded like he was suppressing laughter. "Do you often dangle from trees?"

"You startled me, sir."

"Hmmph." He puffed air through his cheeks like a little child. "You're Irjah's pet pupil, aren't you?"

Her cheeks flushed. "I—I mean, I don't . . ."

"You *are*." He scratched his chin and scooped her book off the ground, riffling through its pages with a mild curiosity. "Dusky little peasant prodigy, you. He can't stop raving about you."

She shuffled her feet, wondering where this was going. Had that been a compliment? Was she supposed to thank him? She tucked a lock of hair back behind her ear. "Um."

"Oh, don't pretend to be bashful. You love it." Jiang glanced casually down at the book and gazed back up at her. "What are you doing with a Seejin text?"

"I found it in the archives."

"Oh. I take that back. You're not daring. You're just stupid."

When Rin looked confused, Jiang explained: "Jun explicitly forbade Seejin until at least your second year."

She hadn't heard this rule. No wonder the apprentice hadn't let her sign the book out of the archives. "Jun expelled me from his class. I wasn't informed."

"Jun expelled you," Jiang repeated slowly. She couldn't tell if he was amused or not. "What on earth did you do to him?"

"Um. Tackled another student during sparring, sort of. He started it," she added quickly. "The other student, I mean."

Jiang looked impressed. "Stupid *and* hotheaded."

His eyes wandered over to the plants on the shelf behind her. He walked around her, lifted a poppy flower up to his nose, and sniffed experimentally. He made a face. He dug around in the deep pockets of his robes, fished out a pair of shears, then clipped the stem and tossed the broken end into a pile in the corner of a garden.

Rin began to inch toward the gate. Perhaps if she left now, Jiang would forget about the book. "I'm sorry if I shouldn't be in here—"

"Oh, you're not sorry. You're just annoyed I interrupted your training session, and you're hoping I'll leave without mentioning your stolen book." Jiang snipped another stem off the poppy plant. "You're a plucky one, you know that? Got banned from Jun's class, so you thought you'd teach yourself *Seejin*."

He made several syncopated wheezing noises. It took Rin a moment to realize he was laughing.

"What's so funny?" she demanded. "Sir, if you're going to report me, I just want to say—"

"Oh, I'm not going to *report* you. What fun would that be?" He was still chuckling. "Were you really trying to learn Seejin from a book? Do you have a death wish?"

"It's not that hard," she said defensively. "I just followed the pictures."

He turned back toward her; his expression was one of amused disbelief. He opened the book, riffled through the pages with a practiced hand, and then stopped on the page detailing the first form. He brandished the book at her. "That one. Do that."

Rin obliged.

It was a tricky form, full of shifting movements and ball change steps. She squeezed her eyes shut as she moved. She couldn't concentrate in full sight of those luminous mushrooms, those bizarrely pulsing cacti.

When she opened her eyes, Jiang had stopped laughing.

"You're nowhere near ready for Seejin," he said. He slammed the book shut with one hand. "Jun was right. At your level you shouldn't even be *touching* this text."

Rin fought a wave of panic. If she couldn't even use the Seejin text, she might as well leave for Tikany right now. She had found no other books that were half as useful or as clear.

"You might benefit from some animal-based fundamentals," Jiang continued. "Yinmen's work. He was Seejin's predecessor. Have you heard of him?"

She glanced up at him in confusion. "I've looked for those. Those scrolls are incomplete."

"Of course you won't be learning from *scrolls*," Jiang said impatiently. "We'll discuss this in class tomorrow."

"Class? You haven't been here all semester!"

Jiang shrugged. "I find it difficult to bother myself with first-years I don't find particularly interesting."

Rin thought this was just irresponsible teaching, but she wanted to keep Jiang talking. Here he was in a rare moment of lucidity, offering to teach her martial arts that she couldn't learn by herself. She was half-afraid that if she said the wrong thing, she would send him running off like a startled hare.

"So am I interesting?" she asked slowly.

"You're a walking disaster," Jiang said bluntly. "You're training with arcane techniques at a rate that will lead to inevitable injury, and not the kind you recover from. You've misinterpreted Seejin's texts so badly that I believe you've come up with a new art form all by yourself."

Rin scowled. "Then why are you helping me?"

"To spite Jun, mostly." Jiang scratched his chin. "I hate the man. Did you know he petitioned to have me fired last week?"

Rin was mostly surprised that Jun hadn't tried that sooner.

"Also, anyone this obstinate deserves some attention, if only to make sure you don't become a walking hazard to everyone around you," Jiang continued. "You know, your footwork is remarkable."

She flushed. "Really?"

"Placement is perfect. Beautiful angles." He cocked his head. "Of course, everything you're doing is useless."

She scowled. "Well, if you're not going to teach me, then—"

"I didn't say that. You've done a good job working only with the text," Jiang acknowledged. "A better job than many apprentices would have done. It's your upper body strength that's the problem. Namely, you have none." He grabbed for her wrist and pulled her arm up as if he were examining a mannequin. "So skinny. Weren't you a farmhand or something?"

"Not everyone from the south is a farmer," she snapped. "I was a shopgirl."

"Hm. No heavy labor, then. Pampered. You're useless."

She crossed her arms against her chest. "I wasn't *pampered*—"

"Yeah, yeah." He held up a hand to cut her off. "It doesn't matter. Here's the thing: all the technique in the world won't do you any good if you don't have the strength to back it up. You don't need Seejin, kid. You need *ki*. You need muscle."

"So what do you want me to do? Calisthenics?"

He stood still, contemplative, for a long moment. Then he beamed. "No. I have a better idea. Be at the campus gates for class tomorrow."

Before she could respond, he strolled out of the garden.

"Wow." Raban set down his chopsticks. "He must really like you."

"He called me stupid and hotheaded," Rin said. "And then he told me to be on time for class."

"He *definitely* likes you," Raban said. "Jiang's never uttered anything nice to anyone in my year. He mostly yells at us to stay away from his daffodils. He told Kureel that her braids made her look like snakes were growing out of the back of her head."

"I heard he got drunk on rice wine last week and pissed into Jun's window," Kitay chipped in. "He sounds *awesome*."

"How long has Jiang been here?" Rin asked. The Lore Master seemed amazingly young, at most half of Jun's age. She couldn't believe the other masters would put up with such aggravating behavior from someone who was clearly their junior.

"Not sure. He was here when I was a first-year, but that doesn't mean much. I heard he came from the Night Castle twenty years ago."

"Jiang was *Cike*?"

Among the divisions of the Militia, only the Cike bore an ill reputation. They were a division of soldiers holed up in the Night Castle, far up the Wudang mountain range, whose sole task was to carry out assassinations for the Empress. The Cike fought without honor. They respected no rules of combat, and they were notorious for their brutality. They operated in the darkness; they did the Empress's dirty work and received no recognition afterward. Most apprentices would have quit the service rather than join the Cike.

Rin had a hard time reconciling her image of the whimsical Lore Master with that of a hardened assassin.

"Well, that's just the rumor. None of the masters will say anything about him. I get the feeling that Jiang's considered a bit of an embarrassment to the school." Raban rubbed the back of his head. "The apprentices love to gossip, though. Every class plays the 'Who is Jiang?' guessing game. My class was convinced that he was the founder of the Red Junk Opera. The truth's been stretched so many times that the only thing certain is that we know absolutely nothing about him."

"Surely he's had apprentices before," said Rin.

"Jiang is the *Lore Master*," Raban said slowly, as if talking to a child. "Nobody pledges Lore."

"Because Jiang won't take any students?"

"Because Lore is a bloody joke," said Raban. "Every other track at Sinegard prepares you for a government position or for command in the Militia. But Lore is . . . I don't know, Lore's odd. I think it was originally meant to be a study of the Hinterlanders, to see if there's any substance to their witch-magic rituals, but everyone lost interest pretty quickly. I know Yim and Sonnen have both petitioned Jima to have the class canceled, but it's still offered every year. I'm not sure why."

"Surely there have been Lore students in the past," said Kitay. "What have they said?"

Raban shrugged. "It's a new discipline—the others have been taught since the Red Emperor founded this school, but Lore's only been around for two decades or so—and no one's stuck with the course all the way through. I hear that a couple years ago some suckers took the bait, but they dropped out of Sinegard and were never heard from again. No one in their right mind now would pledge Lore. Altan was the exception, but nobody ever knows what's going on in Altan's head."

"I thought Altan pledged Strategy," said Kitay.

"Altan could have pledged whatever he wanted. For some reason he was hell-bent on Lore, but then Jiang changed his mind and Altan had to settle for Irjah instead."

This was news to Rin. "Does that happen often—students choosing the master?"

"Very rarely. Most of us are relieved to get one bid; it's an especially impressive student who gets two."

"How many bids did Altan get?"

"Six. Seven if you include Lore, but Jiang withdrew his bid at the last minute." Raban gave her a knowing look. "Why so curious about Altan?"

"Just wondering," Rin said quickly.

"Taken a shine to our crimson-eyed hero, huh? You wouldn't be the first." Raban grinned. "Just be careful. Altan's not too kind to admirers."

"What's he like?" She couldn't help but ask. "As a person, I mean."

Raban shrugged. "We haven't had classes together since our

first year. I don't know him well. I don't think anyone really does. He mostly keeps to himself. He's quiet. Trains alone and doesn't really have friends."

"Sounds like someone we know." Kitay jabbed an elbow at Rin. She bristled. "Shut up. I have friends."

"You have *a* friend," Kitay said. "Singular."

Rin pushed at Kitay's arm. "But Altan's so *good*," she said. "At everything. Everyone adores him."

Raban shrugged. "Altan's more or less a god on this campus. Doesn't mean he's happy."

Once the conversation had derailed to Altan, Rin forgot half the questions she had meant to ask about Jiang. She and Kitay prodded Raban for anecdotes about Altan until dinner break ended. That night, she tried asking Kureel and Arda, but neither of them could confirm anything substantial.

"I see Jiang in the infirmary sometimes," said Arda. "Enro keeps a walled-off bed just for him. He stays for a day or two every other month and then leaves. Maybe he's sick with something. Or maybe he just really likes the smell of disinfectant, I can't tell. Enro caught him trying to get high off medicine fumes once."

"Jun doesn't like him," said Kureel. "Not hard to see why. What kind of master *acts* like that? Especially at Sinegard?" Her face twisted with disapproval. "I think he's a disgrace to the Academy. Why're you asking?"

"No reason," said Rin. "Just curious."

Kureel shrugged. "Every class falls for it at first. Everyone thinks there's more to Jiang than there is, that Lore is a real subject worth learning. But there's nothing there. Jiang's a joke. You're wasting your time."

But the Lore Master was real. Jiang was a faculty member of the Academy, even if all he did was wander around and annoy the other masters. No one else could have gotten away with provoking Jun like Jiang did on a regular basis. So if Jiang didn't bother teaching, what was he doing at Sinegard?

Rin was slightly amazed when she saw Jiang waiting at the campus gates the next afternoon. She wouldn't have put it past him to simply forget. She opened her mouth to ask where they were going, but he simply waved at her to follow him.

She assumed that she was just going to have to get used to being led around by Jiang with no clear explanation.

They had hardly started down the path before they ran into Jun, returning from city patrol with a group of his apprentices.

"Ah. The lackwit and the peasant." Jun slowed to a stop. His apprentices looked somewhat wary, as if they'd seen this exchange before. "And where are you going on this fine afternoon?"

"None of your business, Loran," Jiang said breezily. He tried to skirt around Jun, but Jun stepped into his path.

"A master leaving the grounds alone with a student. I wonder what they'll say." Jun narrowed his eyes.

"Probably that a master of his rank and standing could do much better than dicking around with female students," Jiang replied cheerfully, looking directly at Jun's apprentices. Kureel looked outraged.

Jun scowled. "She doesn't have permission to leave the grounds. She needs written approval from Jima."

Jiang stretched out his right arm and shoved his sleeve up to the elbow. At first Rin thought that he might punch Jun, but Jiang simply raised his elbow to his mouth and made a loud farting noise.

"That's not written approval." Jun looked unimpressed. Rin suspected he had seen this display many times before.

"I'm Lore Master," Jiang said. "That comes with privileges."

"Privileges like never teaching class?"

Jiang lifted his chin and said self-importantly, "I have taught her class the crushing sensation of disappointment and the even more important lesson that they do not matter as much as they think they do."

"You have taught her class and every class before it that Lore is a joke and the Lore Master is a bumbling idiot."

"Tell Jima to fire me, then." Jiang waggled his eyebrows. "I know you've tried."

Jun raised his eyes to the sky in an expression of eternal suffering. Rin suspected that this was only a small part of an argument that had been going on for years.

"I'm reporting this to Jima," Jun warned.

"Jima has better things to waste her time on. As long as I bring little Runin back in time for dinner, I doubt she'll care. In the meantime, stop blocking the road."

Jiang snapped his fingers and motioned for Rin to follow. Rin clamped her mouth shut and tripped down the path behind him.

"Why does he hate you so much?" Rin asked as they climbed down the mountain pass toward the city.

Jiang shrugged. "They tell me I killed half the men under his command during the Second War. He's still bitter about it."

"Well, did you?" Rin felt like she was obligated to ask.

He shrugged again. "Haven't the faintest clue."

Rin had no idea how to respond to this, and Jiang did not elaborate.

"So tell me about your class," Jiang said after a while. "Same crowd of entitled brats?"

"I don't know them very well," Rin admitted. "They're all . . . I mean . . ."

"Smarter? Better trained? More important than you?"

"Nezha's the son of the Dragon Warlord," Rin blurted out. "How am I supposed to compete with that? Venka's father is the finance minister. Kitay's father is defense minister, or something like that. Niang's family are physicians to the Hare Warlord."

Jiang snorted. "Typical."

"Typical?"

"Sinegard likes to collect the Warlords' broods as much as it can. Keeps them under the Empire's careful watch."

"What for?" she asked.

"Leverage. Indoctrination. This generation of Warlords hate each other too much to coordinate on anything of national importance, and the imperial bureaucracy has too little local authority to force them. Just look at the state of the Imperial Navy."

"We have a navy?" Rin asked.

"Exactly." Jiang snorted. "We used to. Anyhow, Daji's hoping that Sinegard will forge a generation of leaders who like each other—and better, who will obey the throne."

"She really struck gold with me, then," Rin muttered.

Jiang shot her a sideways grin. "What, you're not going to be a good soldier to the Empire?"

"I will," Rin said hastily. "I just don't think most of my classmates like me very much. Or ever will."

"Well, that's because you're a dark little peasant brat who can't pronounce your *r*'s," Jiang said breezily. He made a turn into a narrow corridor. "This way."

He led her into the meatpacking district, where the streets were cramped and crowded and smelled overwhelmingly like blood. Rin gagged and clamped a hand over her nose as they walked. Butcher shops lined the alleyways, built so close they were almost on top of one another in crooked rows like jagged teeth. After twenty minutes of twists and turns, they stopped at a little shack at the end of a block. Jiang rapped thrice on the rickety wooden door.

"*What?*" screeched a voice from within. Rin jumped.

"It's me," Jiang called back, unfazed. "Your favorite person in the whole wide world."

There was the noise of clattering metal from inside. After a moment, a wizened little lady in a purple smock opened the door. She greeted Jiang with a curt nod but squinted suspiciously at Rin.

"This is the Widow Maung," Jiang said. "She sells me things."

"Drugs," clarified the Widow Maung. "I am his drug dealer."

"She means ginseng, and roots and such," Jiang said. "For my health."

The Widow Maung rolled her eyes.

Rin watched the exchange, fascinated.

"The Widow Maung has a problem," Jiang continued cheerfully.

The Widow Maung cleared her throat and spat a thick wad of phlegm into the dirt next to where Jiang stood. "I do not have a problem. You are making up this problem for reasons unbeknownst to me."

"Regardless," Jiang said, maintaining his idyllic smile, "the Widow Maung has graciously allowed you to help her in resolving her problem. Madam, would you bring out the animal?"

The Widow Maung disappeared into the back of the shop. Jiang motioned for Rin to follow him inside. Rin heard a loud squealing sound from behind the wall. Moments later, the Widow Maung returned with a squirming animal clutched in her arms. She plopped it on the counter before them.

"Here's a pig," Jiang said.

"That is a pig," Rin agreed.

The pig in question was a tiny thing, no longer than Rin's forearm. Its skin was spotted black and pink. The way its snout curved up made it look like it was grinning. It was oddly cute.

Rin scratched it behind the ears and it nuzzled her forearm affectionately.

"I named it Sunzi," Jiang said happily.

The Widow Maung looked like she couldn't wait for Jiang to leave.

Jiang hastened to explain. "The Widow Maung needs little Sunzi watered every day. The problem is Sunzi requires a very special sort of water."

"Sunzi could drink sewage water and be fine," the Widow Maung clarified. "You're just making things up for this training exercise."

"Can we just do it like we rehearsed?" Jiang demanded. It was the first time Rin had seen anyone actually get to him. "You're killing the mood."

"Is that something you're often told?" the Widow Maung inquired.

Jiang snorted, amused, and clapped Rin on the back. "Here's the situation. The Widow Maung needs Sunzi to drink this very special sort of water. Fortunately, this fresh, crystal-clear water can be found in a stream at the top of the mountain. The catch is getting Sunzi up the mountain. This is where you come in."

"You're *joking*," Rin said.

Jiang beamed. "Every day you will run into town to visit the Widow Maung. You will lug this adorable piglet up the mountain and let him drink. Then you will bring him back and return to the Academy. Understood?"

"It's a two-hour trip up the mountain and back!"

"It's a two-hour trip *now*," Jiang said cheerfully. "It'll be longer once this little guy starts growing."

"But I have class," she protested.

"Better get up early, then," said Jiang. "It's not like you have Combat in the morning anyway. Remember? Someone got expelled?"

"But—"

"Someone," Jiang drawled, "does not want very much to stay at Sinegard."

The Widow Maung snorted loudly.

Glowering, Rin gathered up Sunzi the piglet in her arms and tried not to wrinkle her nose at the smell.

"Guess I'll be seeing a lot of you," she grumbled.

Sunzi squirmed and nuzzled into the crook of her arm.

Every day over the next four months, Rin rose before the sun came up, ran as fast as she could down the mountain pass and into the meatpacking district to fetch Sunzi, strapped the piglet to her back, and ran back up the mountain. She took the long way up, routing around Sinegard so that none of her classmates would see her running around with a squealing pig.

She was often late to Medicine.

"Where the hell have you been? And why do you smell like *swine*?" Kitay wrinkled his nose as she slid into the seat next to him.

"I've been carrying a pig up a mountain," she said. "Obeying the whims of a madman. Finding a way out."

It was desperate behavior, but she had fallen on desperate times. Rin was now relying on the campus madman to keep her spot at Sinegard. She began to sit in the back of the room so that nobody could smell the traces of Sunzi on her when she returned from the Widow Maung's butcher shop.

From the way everyone kept their distance, she wasn't sure it mattered.

Jiang did more than make her carry the pig. In an astonishing streak of reliability, he stood waiting for her in the garden every day at class time.

"You know, animal-based martial arts weren't developed for combat," he said. "They were first created to promote health and longevity. The Frolics of the Five Animals"—he held up the Yinmen scroll that Rin had spent so long looking for—"is actually a system of exercises to promote blood circulation and delay the inconveniences of old age. It wasn't until later that these forms were adapted for fighting."

"So why am I learning them?"

"Because Jun's curriculum skips the Frolics entirely. Jun teaches a simplified version of watered-down martial arts adapted purely to human biomechanics. But it leaves out far too much. It whittles away centuries of lineage and refinement all for the sake of military efficiency. Jun can teach you how to be a decent soldier. But I can teach you the key to the universe," Jiang said grandly, before bumping his head on a low-hanging branch.

Training with Jiang was nothing like training with Jun. There were obvious hierarchies to Jun's lesson plans, a clear progression from basic techniques to advanced.

But Jiang taught Rin every random thing that came to his deeply unpredictable mind. He would revisit a lesson if he found it particularly interesting; if not, he pretended like it had never happened. Occasionally he would go on long tirades without provocation.

"There are five principal elements present in the universe—get that look off your face, it's not as absurd as it sounds. The masters of old used to believe that all things were made of fire, water, air, earth, and metal. Obviously, modern science has proven that false. Still, it's a useful mnemonic for understanding the different types of energy.

"Fire: the heat in your blood in the midst of a fight, the kinetic energy that makes your heart beat faster." Jiang tapped his chest. "Water: the flowing of force from your muscles to your target, from the earth up through your waist, into your arms. Air: the breath you draw that keeps you alive. Earth: how you stay rooted to the ground, how you derive energy from the way you position yourself against the floor. And metal, for the weapons you wield. A good martial artist will possess all five of these in balance. If you can control each of these with equal skill, you will be unstoppable."

"How do I know if I've got control of them?"

He scratched a spot behind his ears. "Good question. I'm not actually sure."

Asking Jiang for clarification was inevitably infuriating. His answers were always bizarrely worded and absurdly phrased. Some didn't make sense until days later; some never did. If she asked him to explain, he changed the subject. If she let his more absurd comments slide ("Your water element is off balance!"), he poked and prodded about why she wasn't asking more questions.

He spoke oddly, always a little too quickly or a little too slowly, with strange pauses between his words. He laughed in two ways; one laugh was off-kilter—nervous, high-pitched, and obviously forced—the other great and deep and booming. The first kind she heard constantly; the second was rare, and startling when it burst forth. He rarely met her gaze, but rather focused always at a spot on her brow between her eyes.

Jiang moved through the world like he didn't belong there. He acted as if he came from a country of near-humans, people who acted almost exactly like Nikara but not quite, and his behavior was that of a confused visitor who had stopped bothering with trying to imitate those around him. He didn't belong—not simply in Sinegard, but in the very idea of a physical earth. He acted like the rules of nature did not apply to him.

Perhaps they didn't.

One day they went to the highest tier of the Academy, up past the masters' lodges. The single building on this tier was a tall, spiraling pagoda, nine stories stacked elegantly on top of one another. Rin had never been inside.

She recalled from that tour so many months ago that Sinegard Academy had been built on the grounds of an old monastery. The pagoda on the highest tier could have still been a temple. Old stone trenches for burning incense sat outside the pagoda entrance. Guarding either side of the door were two large cylinders mounted on tall rods to let them spin. When she looked closer, Rin saw Old Nikara characters carved into the sides.

"What do these do?" she asked, idly spinning one cylinder.

"They're prayer wheels. But we don't have time to get into that today," Jiang said. He gestured for her to follow him. "In here."

Rin expected that the nine stories of the pagoda would be proper floors connected by flights of stairs, but the interior was merely a winding staircase that led to the very top, an empty cylinder of air in the middle. A solitary beam of sunlight shone in from a square opening in the ceiling, illuminating dust motes floating through the air. A series of musty paintings had been hung on the sides of the staircase. They looked like they hadn't been cleaned in decades.

"This is where the statues to the Four Gods used to stand," said Jiang, pointing up into the dark void.

"Where are they now?"

He shrugged. "The Red Emperor had most religious imagery stripped and looted when he took over Sinegard. Most of it's been melted down into jewelry. But that doesn't matter." He beckoned for Rin to follow him up the staircase.

He lectured as they climbed. "Martial arts came to the Empire by way of a warrior named Bodhidharma from the southeastern continent. When Bodhidharma found the Empire during his travels of the world, he journeyed to a monastery and demanded entry, but the head abbot refused him entrance. So Bodhidharma sat his ass in a nearby cave and faced the wall for nine years, listening to the ants scream."

"Listening to *what*?"

"The ants scream, Runin. Keep up."

She muttered something unrepeatable. Jiang ignored her.

"Legend has it that the intensity of his gaze bored a hole into the cave wall. The monks were either so moved by his religious commitment or so seriously impressed that anyone could be so obstinate that they finally let him into their temple." Jiang paused in front of a painting depicting a dark-skinned warrior and a group of pale men in robes. "That's Bodhidharma there in the center."

"That guy on the left has blood spurting out of a stump," Rin observed.

"Yeah. Legend also has it that one monk was so impressed with his commitment that he cut off his hand in sympathy."

Rin recalled the myth of Mai'rinnen Tearza committing suicide for the sake of Speer's unification with the mainland. Martial arts history seemed to be riddled with people making pointless sacrifices.

"Anyhow. The monks at the temple were interested in what Bodhidharma had to say, but because of their sedentary lives and poor diets, they were weak as shit. Scrawnier than you, even. Kept falling asleep during his lectures. Bodhidharma found this somewhat annoying, so he devised three sets of exercises to improve their health. Now, these monks were in constant physical danger from outlaws and robbers, but were also forbidden by their religious code to carry weapons, so they modified many of the exercises to form a system of weaponless self-defense."

Jiang stopped before another painting. It depicted a row of monks lined up on a wall, frozen in identical stances.

Rin was amazed. "That's—"

"Seejin's first form. Yeah." Jiang nodded in approval. "Bodhidharma warned the monks that martial arts was about the refinement of the individual. Martial arts used well would produce a wise commander, a man who could see clearly through fog and understand the will of the gods. The martial arts in their conception were not meant solely as military tools."

Rin struggled to envision the techniques Jun had taught their class as purely health exercises. "But there had to be an evolution in the arts."

"Correct." Jiang waited for her to ask the question he wanted to hear.

She obliged. "When did the arts become adapted for mass military use?"

Jiang bobbed his head, pleased. "Shortly before the days of the Red Emperor, the Empire was invaded by the horsemen from the Hinterlands to the north. The occupation force introduced a number of repressive measures to control the indigenous population, which included forbidding the Nikara to carry weapons."

Jiang stopped again before a painting depicting a horde of Hinterlander hunters riding upon massive steeds. Their faces were twisted into wild, barbaric scowls. They held bows that were longer than their torsos. At the bottom of the painting, Nikara monks were shown cowering in fear or strewn about in various states of dismemberment.

"The temples that were once havens of nonviolence became instead a sanctuary for anti-Northerner rebels and a center for revolutionary planning and training. Soldiers and sympathizers would don monks' robes and shave their heads, but train for war within the temple grounds. In sacred spaces like these, they plotted the overthrow of their oppressors."

"And health exercises would hardly have helped them," Rin said. "The martial techniques had to be adapted."

Jiang nodded again. "Exactly. The arts then taught in the temple required the progressive mastery of hundreds of long, intricate forms. These could take decades to master. The leaders of the rebellion, thankfully, realized that this approach was unsuitable to the rapid development of a fighting force."

Jiang turned around to face her. They had reached the top of the pagoda. "And so modern martial arts were developed: a system based on human biomechanics rather than the movements of animals. The enormous variety of techniques, some of which were only marginally useful to a soldier, were distilled into an essential core of forms that could be taught to a soldier in five years rather than fifty. This is the basis of what you are taught at Sinegard. This is the common core that is taught to the Imperial Militia. This is what your classmates are learning." He grinned. "I am showing you how to beat it."

Jiang was an effective if unconventional combat instructor. He made her hold her kicks up in the air for long minutes until her leg trembled. He made her duck as he hurled projectiles at her off the weapons rack. He made her do the same exercise blindfolded, and then admitted later that he just thought it would be funny.

"You're a real asshole," she said. "You know that, right?"

Once Jiang was pleased with her fundamentals, they began to spar. They sparred every day, for hours at a time. They sparred bare-fisted and with weapons; sometimes she was bare-fisted while he bore a weapon.

"Your state of mind is just as important as the state of your body," Jiang lectured. "In the confusion of a fight, your mind must be still and steady as a rock. You must be grounded in your center, able to see and control everything. Each of the five elements must be in balance. Too much fire, and you'll lash out recklessly. Too much air and you'll fight skittishly, always on the defensive. Too much earth, and—are you even listening?"

She was not. It was hard to concentrate while Jiang jabbed an unguarded halberd at her, forcing her to dance around to avoid sudden impalement.

By and large, Jiang's metaphors meant little to her, but she learned quickly to avoid injury. And perhaps that was his point. She developed muscle memory. She learned that there were only so many permutations to the way a human body could move, only so many attack combinations that worked, that she could reasonably expect from her opponent. She learned to react automatically to these. She learned to predict Jiang's moves seconds in advance, to read from the tilt of his torso and the flicker of his eyes what he was about to do next.

He pushed her relentlessly. He fought the hardest when she was exhausted. When she fell, he attacked her as soon as she'd gotten back on her feet. She learned to stay constantly on guard, to react to the slightest movements in her peripheral vision.

The day came when she angled her hip against his just so, forced his weight to the side and jammed all her force at an angle that hurled him over her right shoulder.

Jiang skidded across the stone floor and bumped against the garden wall, which shook the shelves so that a potted cactus came perilously close to shattering on the ground.

Jiang lay there for a moment, dazed. Then he looked up, met her eyes, and grinned.

Rin's last day with Sunzi was the hardest.

Sunzi was no longer an adorable piglet but an absurdly fat monster that smelled heinously bad. It wasn't remotely cute. Any affection Rin had felt for those trusting brown eyes was negated by the animal's massive girth.

Carrying Sunzi up the mountain was torture. Sunzi no longer

fit in any sort of sling or basket. Rin had to drape it over her shoulders, grasping it by its two front legs.

She could hardly move as fast as she had when Sunzi could still be cradled in her arms, but she had to, unless she wanted to go without breakfast—or worse, miss class. She rose earlier. She ran faster. She staggered up the mountain, gasping for air with every step. Sunzi lay against her back with its snout resting over one of her shoulders, basking in the morning sun while Rin's muscles screamed with resentment. When she reached Sunzi's drinking area, she let the pig drop to the ground and collapsed.

"Drink, you glutton," she grumbled as Sunzi frolicked in the stream. "I can't wait until the day they carve you up and eat you."

On her way down the mountain, the sun began to beat down in earnest, eliciting rivulets of sweat all over Rin's body despite the winter cold. She limped through the meatpacking district to the Widow Maung's cottage and deposited Sunzi gracelessly on the floor.

It rolled over, squealed loudly and ran in a circle, chasing its own tail.

The Widow Maung came out to the front carrying a bucket of slops.

"I'll be back tomorrow," Rin panted.

The Widow Maung shook her head. "There won't be a tomorrow. Not for this one, anyway." She rubbed Sunzi's snout. "This one's going to the butcher tonight."

Rin blinked. "What? So soon?"

"Sunzi's already reached his peak weight." The Widow Maung slapped Sunzi's sides. "Look at that girth. None of my pigs have ever grown so heavy. Perhaps your crazy teacher was right about the mountain water. Maybe I should send all my pigs up there."

Rin rather hoped that she didn't. Chest still heaving, she bowed low to the widow. "Thank you for letting me carry your pig."

The Widow Maung harrumphed. "Academy freaks," she muttered under her breath, and began to lead Sunzi back to the sty. "Come on, you. Let's get you ready for the butcher."

Oink? Sunzi looked imploringly at Rin.

"Don't look at me," Rin said. "It's the end of the road for you."

She couldn't help but feel a stab of guilt; the longer she looked at Sunzi, the more she was reminded of its piglet form. She tore her eyes away from its dull, naive gaze and headed back up the mountain.

"Already?" Jiang looked surprised when Rin reported Sunzi's fate. He was sitting on the far wall of the garden, swinging his legs over the edge like an energetic child. "Ah, I had high hopes for that pig. But in the end, swine are swine. How do you feel?"

"I'm devastated," Rin said. "Sunzi and I were finally starting to understand each other."

"No, you sod. Your *arms*. Your core. Your legs. How do they feel?"

She frowned and swung her arms about. "Sore?"

Jiang jumped off the wall and walked toward her. "I'm going to hit you," he announced.

"Wait, what?"

She dug her heels into the ground and only managed to get her elbows up right before he slammed a fist at her face.

The force of his punch was enormous—harder than he'd ever hit her. She knew she should have deflected the blow at an angle, sent the *ki* dispersing into the air where it would dispel harmlessly. But she was too startled to do anything but block it head-on. She barely remembered to crouch so that the *ki* behind his punch channeled harmlessly through her body and into the ground.

A crack like a thunderbolt echoed beneath her.

Rin jumped back, stunned. The stone under her feet had splintered under the force of the dispelled energy. One long crack ran between her feet to the edge of the stone block.

They both stared down at it. The crack continued to splinter the stone floor, crawling all the way to the far end of the garden, where it stopped at the base of the willow tree.

Jiang threw his head back and laughed.

It was a high, wild laugh. He laughed like his lungs were bellows. He laughed like he was nothing human. He spread his arms out and windmilled them in the air, and danced with giddy abandon.

"You darling child," he said, spinning toward her. "You brilliant child."

Rin's face split into a grin.

Fuck it, she thought, and leaped up to embrace him.

He picked her up and swung her through the air, around and around among the kaleidoscopically colorful mushrooms.

They sat together under the willow tree, staring serenely at the poppy plants. The wind was still today. Snow continued to fall lightly over the garden, but the first inklings of spring had arrived. The furious winter winds had gone to blow elsewhere; the air felt settled, for once. Peaceful.

"No more training today," Jiang said. "You rest. Sometimes you must loose the string to let the arrow fly."

Rin rolled her eyes.

"You have to pledge Lore," Jiang continued excitedly. "No one—*no one*, not even Altan, picked things up this fast."

Rin suddenly felt very awkward. How was she to tell him the only reason she wanted to learn combat was so she could get through the Trials and study with Irjah?

Jiang hated lies. Rin decided she might as well be straightforward. "I'd been thinking about pledging Strategy," she said hesitantly. "Irjah said he might bid for me."

He waved his hand. "Irjah can't teach you anything you couldn't learn by yourself. Strategy's a limited subject. Spend enough time in the field with Sunzi's *Principles* by your bed, and you'll pick up everything you need to win a campaign."

"But . . ."

"Who are the gods? Where do they reside? Why do they do what they do? These are the fundamental questions of Lore. I can teach you more than *ki* manipulation. I can show you the pathway to the gods. I can make you a shaman."

Gods and shamans? It was often difficult to tell when Jiang was joking and when he wasn't, but he seemed genuinely convinced that he could talk to heavenly powers.

She swallowed. "Sir . . ."

"This is *important*," Jiang insisted. "Please, Rin. This is a dying art. The Red Emperor almost succeeded in killing it. If you don't learn it, if no one learns it, then it disappears for good."

The sudden desperation in his voice made her intensely uncomfortable.

She twisted a blade of grass between her fingers. Certainly she was curious about Lore, but she knew better than to throw away four years of training under Irjah to chase a subject that the other masters had long ago lost faith in. She hadn't come to Sinegard to pursue stories on a whim, especially stories that were disdained by everyone else in the capital.

She was admittedly fascinated by myths and legends, and the way that Jiang made them sound almost real. But she was more interested in making it past the Trials. And an apprenticeship with Irjah opened doors at the Militia. It all but guaranteed an officer position *and* her choice of division. Irjah had contacts with each of the Twelve Warlords, and his protégées always found esteemed placements.

She could lead troops of her own within a year of graduating. She could be a nationally renowned commander within five. She couldn't throw that away on a mere fancy.

"Sir, I just want to learn to be a good soldier," she said.

Jiang's face fell.

"You and the rest of this school," he said.

CHAPTER 7

Jiang did not appear in the garden the next day, or the day after. Rin went to the garden faithfully in the hope that he would return, but she knew, deep down, that Jiang was done with teaching her.

One week later she saw him in the mess hall. She abruptly put her bowl down and made a beeline toward him. She had no clue what he might say, but knew that she needed to at least talk to him. She would apologize, promise to study with him even if she became Irjah's apprentice, or say *something* . . .

Before she could corner him he upended his tray over a startled apprentice's head and dashed out the kitchen door.

"Great Tortoise," said Kitay. "What did you *do* to him?"

"I don't know," she said.

Jiang was unpredictable and fragile, like an easily startled wild animal, and she hadn't realized how precious his attention was until she had scared him away.

After that, he acted as if he didn't even know her. She continued to see brief glimpses of him around campus, just as everyone did, but he refused to acknowledge her.

She should have tried harder to patch things up with him. She should have actively sought him out and admitted her mistake, nebulous though it was.

But she found it less and less of a priority as the term came to an end, and the competition between the first-years reached a frenzied peak.

Throughout the year, the possibility of being culled from Sinegard had hung like a sword over their heads. Now that threat was imminent. In two weeks they would undergo the series of exams that constituted the Trials.

Raban relayed the rules to them. The Trials would be administered and observed by the entire faculty. Depending on their performance, the masters would submit bids for apprenticeship. If a student received no bids, he or she would leave the Academy in disgrace.

Enro exempted all students who were not intent on pledging Medicine from her exam, but the other subjects—Linguistics, History, Strategy, Combat, and Weaponry—were mandatory. There was, of course, no scheduled exam for Lore.

"Irjah, Jima, Yim, and Sonnen give oral exams," said Raban. "You'll be questioned in front of a panel of the masters. They'll take turns interrogating you, and if you mess up, that's the end of your session for that subject. The more questions you answer, the more you get to prove how much you know. So study hard—and speak carefully."

Jun did not conduct an oral exam. The Combat exam consisted of the Tournament.

This would take course over the two days of exams. The first-years would duel in the rings using the same rules that the apprentices used in their matches. They would compete in three preliminary rounds determined by random draws, and based on their win-loss ratios, eight would advance to elimination rounds. Those eight would be placed in a randomized bracket and fight one another until the final round.

Reaching the eliminations in the Tournament was no guarantee of gaining a sponsor, and losing early was not a guarantee of expulsion. But those students who advanced further in the tournament had more chances to show the masters how well they fought. And the winner of the Tournament always received a bid.

"Altan won his year," Raban said. "Kureel won hers. You'll notice they both landed the two most prestigious apprenticeships at Sinegard. There's no actual prize for winning, but the masters like placing bets. Get your ass kicked, and no master will want to take you on."

"I want to pledge Medicine, but we've got to memorize so many extra texts on top of the readings we've done so far, and if I do I won't have time study for History . . . Do you think I should pledge History? Do you think Yim likes me enough?" Niang flapped her hands in the air, agitated. "My brother said I shouldn't rely on getting a Medicine apprenticeship; there are four of us taking Enro's exam and she only ever picks three, so maybe I won't get it . . ."

"Enough, Niang," Venka snapped. "You've been talking about this for days."

"What do you want to pledge?" Niang persisted.

"Combat. And that's the last time we're talking about it," Venka said shrilly. Rin suspected that if Niang said another word, Venka might scream.

But Rin couldn't blame Niang. Or Venka, really. The first-years gossiped obsessively about apprenticeships, and it was both understandable *and* grating. Rin had learned about the hierarchy of masters through eavesdropping on conversations in the mess hall: bids from Jun and Irjah were ideal for apprentices who wanted command positions in the Militia, Jima rarely chose apprentices unless they were nobility destined to become court diplomats, and Enro's bid mattered only to the few of them who wanted to be military physicians.

"Training under Irjah would be nice," said Kitay. "Of course, Jun's apprentices have their pick of divisions, but Irjah can get me into the Second."

"The Rat Province's division?" Rin wrinkled her nose. "Why?"

Kitay shrugged. "They're Army Intelligence. I would *love* to serve in Army Intelligence."

Jun was out of the question for Rin, though she too hoped Irjah might take her. But she knew Irjah wouldn't place a bid unless she proved she had the martial arts to back up her Strategy prowess. A strategist who couldn't fight had no place in the Militia. How could she draw up battle plans if she'd never been on the front lines? If she didn't know what real combat was like?

For her, it all came down to the Tournament.

As for the apprentices, it was apparently the most exciting thing to happen on campus all year. They began speculating wildly about who might win and who would beat whom—and they didn't try very hard to keep the betting books secret from the first-years. Word spread quickly about who the front-runners were.

Most of the money backed the Sinegardians. Venka and Han were solid contenders for the semifinals. Nohai, a massive kid from a fishing island in Snake Province, was widely backed to reach the quarterfinals. Kitay had his fair share of supporters, although this was largely because he had demonstrated a talent for dodging so well that most of his sparring opponents grew frustrated and got sloppy after several long minutes.

Oddly, a number of apprentices put decent money on Rin. Once word got out that she had been training privately with Jiang, the apprentices took an inordinate degree of interest in her. It helped that she was nipping at Kitay's heels in every other one of their classes.

The clear front-runner in their year, however, was Nezha.

"Jun says he's the best to come through his class since Altan," Kitay said, jabbing vehemently at his food. "Won't shut up about him. You should have seen him take out Nohai yesterday. He's a *menace.*"

Nezha, who had been a pretty, slender child at the start of the year, had since packed on an absurd amount of muscle. He'd cut short his stupidly long hair in favor of a clipped military cut similar to Altan's. Unlike the rest of them, he already looked like he belonged in a Militia uniform.

He had also garnered a reputation for striking first and thinking later. He had injured eight sparring partners over the course of the term, all in increasingly severe "accidents."

But of course Jun had never punished him—not as severely as he deserved, anyhow. Why would something so mundane as rules apply to the son of the Dragon Warlord?

As the date of the exams loomed closer, the library became oppressively silent. The only sound among the stacks was the furious scribbling of brushes on paper as the first-years tried to commit an entire year's lessons to memory. Most study groups had disbanded, since any advantage given to a study partner was potentially a lost spot in the ranks.

But Kitay, who didn't need to study, obliged Rin purely out of boredom.

"Sunzi's Eighteenth Mandate." Kitay didn't bother looking at the texts. He had memorized the entirety of *Principles of War* on his first read-through. Rin would have killed for that talent.

Rin squinted her eyes in concentration. She knew she looked stupid, but her head was swimming again, and squinting was the only way to make it stop. She felt very cold and hot all at once. She hadn't slept in three days. All she wanted was to collapse on her bunk, but another hour of cramming was worth more than an hour of sleep.

"It's not one of the Seven Considerations . . . wait, is it? No, okay: always modify plans according to circumstances . . . ?"

Kitay shook his head. "That's the Seventeenth Mandate."

Rin cursed out loud and rubbed her fists against her forehead.

"I wonder how you people do it," Kitay mused. "You know, actually having to try to remember things. Your lives sound so difficult."

"I will murder you with this ink brush," Rin grumbled.

"Sunzi's appendix is all about why soft ends make for bad weapons. Didn't you do the extra reading?"

"Quiet!" Venka snapped from the opposite desk.

Kitay dipped his head out of Venka's sight and cracked a grin at Rin. "Here's a hint," he whispered. "Menda in the temple."

Rin gritted her teeth and squeezed her eyes shut. *Oh. Of course.* "All warfare is based on deception."

In preparation for the Tournament, their entire class had taken Sunzi's Eighteenth Mandate to heart. The pupils stopped using the open practice rooms during common hours. Anyone with an inherited art suddenly stopped bragging about it. Even Nezha had ceased to hold his nightly performances in the studio.

"This happens every year," Raban had said. "It's a bit silly, to be honest. As if martial artists your age ever have anything worth stealing."

Silly or not, their class freaked out in earnest. Everyone was accused of having a hidden weapon up his or her sleeve; whoever had never displayed an inherited art was alleged to be harboring one in secret.

Niang confided to Rin one night that Kitay was actually the heir to the long-forgotten Fist of the North Wind, an art that allowed the user to incapacitate opponents by touching a few choice pressure points.

"I might have had a hand in spreading that story," Kitay admitted when Rin asked him about it. "Sunzi would call it psychological warfare."

She snorted. "Sunzi would call it horseshit."

The first-years weren't allowed to train after curfew, so the preparation period turned into a contest of who could find the most creative way of sneaking past the masters. The apprentices, of course, began vigilantly patrolling the campus after curfew to catch students who had stolen outside to train. Nohai reported that he'd stumbled across a sheet detailing points for such captures in the boys' dormitory.

"It's almost like they're enjoying this," Rin muttered.

"Of course they enjoy it," said Kitay. "They get to watch us suffer through the same things they did. This time next year we'll be equally obnoxious."

Displaying a stunning lack of sympathy, the apprentices had also taken advantage of the first-years' anxiety to establish a flourishing market in "study aids." Rin laughed when Niang returned to the dormitory with what Niang thought was willow bark aged a hundred years.

"That's a ginger root," Rin said with a snicker. She weighed the wrinkled root in her hand. "I mean, I suppose it's good in tea."

"How do you know?" Niang looked dismayed. "I paid twenty coppers for that!"

"We dug up ginger roots all the time in our garden back at home," Rin said. "Put them in the sun and you can sell them to old men looking for a virility cure. Does absolutely nothing, but it makes them feel better. We'd also sell wheat flour and call it rhino's horn. I'll bet you the apprentices have been selling barley flour, too."

Venka, whom Rin had seen stowing a vial of powder under her pillow a few nights before, coughed and looked away.

The apprentices also sold information to first-years. Most sold bogus test answers; others offered lists of purported exam questions that seemed highly plausible but obviously wouldn't be confirmed until after the Trials. Worst, though, were the apprentices who posed as sellers to root out the first-years who were willing to cheat.

Menda, a boy from the Horse Province, had agreed to meet with an apprentice after hours in the temple on the fourth tier to purchase a list of Jima's exam questions. Rin didn't know how the apprentice had managed the timing, but Jima had been meditating in said temple that very night.

Menda was noticeably absent from campus the next day.

Meals became silent and reserved affairs. Everyone ate with a book held before his or her nose. If any students ventured to strike up a conversation, the rest of the table quickly and violently shushed them. In short, they made themselves miserable.

"Sometimes I think this is as bad as the Speer Massacre," Kitay said cheerfully. "And then I think—nah. Nothing is as bad as the casual genocide of an entire race! But this is pretty bad."

"Kitay, *please* shut up."

Rin continued to train alone in the garden. She never saw Jiang anymore, but that was just as well; masters were banned from training the students for the Tournament, although Rin suspected Nezha was still receiving instruction from Jun.

One day she heard footsteps as she approached the garden gate. Someone was inside.

At first she hoped it might be Jiang, but when she opened the door she saw a lean, graceful figure with indigo-black hair.

It took her a moment to process what she'd stumbled upon.

Altan. She'd interrupted Altan Trengsin in his practice.

He wielded a three-pronged trident—no, he didn't just *wield* it, he held it intimately, curved it through the air like a ribbon. It was both an extension of his arm and a dance partner.

She should have turned to go, found somewhere else to train, but she couldn't help her curiosity. She couldn't look away. From a distance, he was extraordinarily beautiful. Up close, he was hypnotizing.

He turned at the sound of her footsteps, saw her, and stopped.

"I'm so sorry," she stammered. "I didn't know you were—"

"It's a school garden," he said neutrally. "Don't leave on my account."

His voice was more somber than she had anticipated. She had imagined a harsh, barking tone to match his brutal movements in the ring, but Altan's voice was surprisingly melodious, soft and deep.

His pupils were oddly constricted. Rin couldn't tell if it was simply the light in the garden, but his eyes didn't seem red then. Rather, they looked brown, like hers.

"I've never seen that form before," Rin uttered.

Altan raised an eyebrow. She immediately regretted opening

her mouth. Why had she said that? Why did she *exist*? She wanted to crumble into ashes and scatter away into the air.

But Altan just looked surprised, not irritated. "Stick around Jiang long enough, and you'll learn plenty of arcane forms." He shifted his weight to his back leg and brought his arms in a flowing motion around to the other side of his torso.

Rin's cheeks burned. She felt very clumsy and vast, like she was taking up space that belonged to Altan, even though she was on the other end of the garden. "Master Jiang didn't say anyone else liked to come here."

"Jiang likes to forget about a lot of things." He tilted his head at her. "You must be quite the student, if Jiang's taken an interest in you."

Was that bitterness in his voice, or was she imagining things?

She remembered then that Jiang had withdrawn his bid for Altan, right after Altan had declared he wanted to pledge Lore. She wondered what had happened, and if it still bothered Altan. She wondered if she'd annoyed him by bringing Jiang up.

"I stole a book from the library," she managed. "He thought that was funny."

Why was she still talking? Why was she still here?

The corner of Altan's mouth quirked up in a terribly attractive grin, which set her heart beating erratically. "What a rebel."

She flushed, but Altan just turned away and completed the form.

"Don't let me stop you from training," he said.

"No, I—I came here to think. But if you're here—"

"I'm sorry. I can leave."

"No, it's okay." She didn't know what she was saying. "I was going to—I mean, I'll just . . . bye."

She quickly backed out of the garden. Altan didn't say anything else.

Once she had closed the garden gates behind her, Rin buried her face in her hands and groaned.

* * *

"Is there ever a place for meekness in battle?" Irjah asked. This was the seventh question he had posed to her.

Rin was on a streak. Seven was the maximum number of questions any master could ask, and if she nailed this one, she would ace Irjah's exam. And she knew the answer—it was lifted directly from Sunzi's Twenty-Second Mandate.

She lifted her chin and responded in a loud, clear voice. "Yes, but only for the purposes of deception. Sunzi writes that if your opponent is of choleric temper, you should seek to irritate him. Pretend to be weak so that he grows arrogant. The good tactician plays with his enemy like a cat plays with a mouse. Feign weakness and immobility, and then pounce on him."

The seven masters each marked small notes into their scrolls. Rin bounced slightly on her heels, waiting for them to continue.

"Good. No further questions." Irjah nodded and gestured at his colleagues. "Master Yim?"

Yim pushed his chair back and rose slowly. He consulted his scroll for a moment, and then gazed at Rin over the top of his spectacles. "Why did we win the Second Poppy War?"

Rin sucked in a breath. She had not prepared for this question. It was so basic she'd thought she didn't need to. Yim had asked it on the first day of class, and the answer was a logical fallacy. There was no "why," because Nikan hadn't won the Second Poppy War. The Republic of Hesperia had, and Nikan had simply ridden the foreigners' coattails to a victory treaty.

She considered answering the question directly, but then thought she might try a more original response. She had only one shot at an answer. She wanted to impress the masters.

"Because we gave up Speer," she said.

Irjah jerked his head up from his scroll.

Yim raised an eyebrow. "Do you mean because we *lost* Speer?"

"No. I mean it was a strategic decision to sacrifice the island so that the Hesperian parliament might decide to intervene. I think the command in Sinegard knew the attack was going to happen and didn't warn the Speerlies."

"I was *at* Speer," Jun interrupted. "This is amusing historiography at best, slander at worst."

"No, you weren't," Rin said before she could stop herself.

Jun looked amazed. "Excuse me?"

All seven masters were watching her intently now. Rin remembered too late that Irjah had disliked this theory. And that Jun *hated* her.

But it was too late to stop. She weighed the costs in her head. The masters rewarded bravery and creativity. If she backed off, it would be a sign of uncertainty. She had begun digging this hole for herself. She might as well finish.

She took a deep breath. "You can't have been at Speer. I read the reports. None of the regular Militia were there the night the island was attacked. The first troops didn't arrive until sunrise, after the Federation had left. After the Speerlies had all been killed."

Jun's face darkened to the color of an overripe plum. "You dare accuse—"

"She's not accusing anyone of anything," Jiang interrupted serenely. It was the first time he'd spoken since the start of her exam. Rin glanced at him in surprise, but Jiang just scratched his ear, not even looking at her. "She's merely attempting a clever answer to an otherwise inane question. Honestly, Yim, this one has gotten pretty old."

Yim shrugged. "Fair enough. No further questions. Master Jiang?"

All the masters twitched in irritation. From what Rin understood, Jiang was present only as a formality. He never gave an exam; he mostly just made fun of the students when they tripped over their answers.

Jiang gazed levelly into Rin's eyes.

She swallowed, feeling the unsettling sensation of his searching gaze. It was like she was as transparent as a puddle of rainwater.

"Who is imprisoned in the Chuluu Korikh?" he asked.

She blinked. Not once in the four months that he had trained her had Jiang ever mentioned the Chuluu Korikh. Neither had

Master Yim or Irjah, or even Jima. *Chuluu Korikh* wasn't medical terminology, wasn't a reference to a famous battle, wasn't some linguistic term of art. It could be a deeply loaded phrase. It could also be gibberish.

Either Jiang was posing a riddle, or he just wanted to throw her off.

But she didn't want to admit defeat. She didn't want to look clueless in front of Irjah. Jiang had asked her a question, and Jiang never asked questions during the Trials. The masters were expecting an interesting answer now; she couldn't disappoint them.

What was the cleverest way to say *I don't know*?

The Chuluu Korikh. She'd studied Old Nikara with Jima for long enough now that she could gloss this as *stone mountain* in the ancient dialect, but that didn't give her any clues. None of Nikan's major prisons were built under mountains; they were either out in the Baghra Desert or in the dungeons of the Empress's palace.

And Jiang hadn't asked what the Chuluu Korikh *was*. He'd asked who was imprisoned there.

What kind of prisoner couldn't be held in the Baghra Desert?

She pondered this until she had an unsatisfying answer to an unsatisfying question.

"Unnatural criminals," she said slowly, "who have committed unnatural crimes?"

Jun snorted audibly. Jima and Yim looked uncomfortable.

Jiang gave a minuscule shrug.

"Fine," he said. "That's all I have."

Oral exams concluded by midmorning on the third day. The pupils were sent to lunch, which no one ate, and then herded to the rings for the commencement of the Tournament.

Rin drew Han for her first opponent.

When it was her turn to fight she climbed down the rope ladder and looked up. The masters stood in a row before the rails. Irjah gave her a slight nod, a tiny gesture that filled her with determination. Jun folded his arms over his chest. Jiang picked at his fingernails.

Rin had not fought any of her classmates since her expulsion from Combat. She had not even watched them fight. The only person she had ever sparred against was Jiang, and she had no clue if he was a good approximation of how her classmates might fight.

She was entering this Tournament blind.

She squared her shoulders and took a deep breath, willing herself to at least appear calm.

Han, on the other hand, looked very disconcerted. His eyes darted across her body and then back up to her face as if she were some wild animal he had never seen before, as if he didn't know quite what to make of her.

He's scared, she realized.

He must have heard the rumors that she had studied with Jiang. He didn't know what to believe about her. Didn't know what to expect.

What was more, Rin was the underdog in this match. No one expected her to fight well. But Han had trained with Jun all year. Han was a Sinegardian. Han *had* to win, or he wouldn't be able to face his peers after.

Sunzi wrote that one must always identify and exploit the enemy's weaknesses. Han's weakness was psychological. The stakes were much, much higher for him, and that made him insecure. That made him beatable.

"What, you've never seen a girl before?" Rin asked.

Han blushed furiously.

Good. She made him nervous. She grinned widely, baring teeth. "Lucky you," she said. "You get to be my first."

"You don't have a chance," Han blustered. "You don't know any martial arts."

She merely smiled and slouched back into Seejin's fourth opening stance. She bent her back leg, preparing herself to spring, and raised her fists to guard her face.

"Don't I?"

Han's face clouded with doubt. He had recognized her posture as deliberate and practiced—not at all the stance of someone who had no martial arts training.

Rin rushed him as soon as Sonnen signaled them to begin.

Han played defensive from the start. He made the mistake of giving her the forward momentum, and he never recovered. From the outset, Rin controlled every part of the bout. She attacked, he reacted. She led him in the dance, she decided when to let him parry, and she decided where they would go. She fought methodically, purely from muscle memory. She was efficient. She played his moves against him and confused him.

And Han's attacks fell into such predictable patterns—if one of his kicks missed, he would back up and attempt it again, and again, until she forced him to change direction.

Finally he let his guard down, let her get in close. She jammed her elbow hard into his nose. She felt a satisfying crack. Han dropped to the floor like a puppet whose strings had been cut.

Rin knew she hadn't hurt him that badly. Jiang had punched her in the nose at least twice. Han was more stunned than injured. He could have gotten up. He didn't.

"Break," ordered Sonnen.

Rin wiped the sweat off her forehead and glanced up at the railing.

There was silence above the ring. Her classmates looked like they had on the first day of class—startled and bewildered. Nezha looked dumbfounded.

Then Kitay began to clap. He was the only one.

She fought two more matches that day. They were both variations on her match with Han—pattern recognition, confusion, finishing blow. She won both of them.

Over the span of a day Rin went from the underdog to a leading contender. All those months spent lugging that stupid pig around had given her better endurance than her classmates. Those long, frustrating hours with the Seejin forms had given her impeccable footwork.

The rest of the class had learned their fundamentals from Jun. They moved the same way, sank into the same default patterns when nervous. But Rin didn't. Her best advantage was her unpredictability. She fought like nothing they had been expecting, she threw them off rhythm, and so she continued to win.

At the end of the first day, Rin and six others, including Nezha and Venka, advanced undefeated into elimination rounds. Kitay had ended the first day with a 2–1 record but advanced on good technique.

The quarterfinals were scheduled for the second day. Sonnen drew up a randomized bracket and hung it on a scroll outside the main hall for all to see. The pairings placed Rin against Venka first thing in the morning.

Venka had trained in martial arts for years, and it showed. She was all rapid strikes and slick, impeccable footwork. She fought with a savage viciousness. Her technique was precise to the centimeter, her timing perfect. She was just as fast as Rin, perhaps faster.

The one advantage Rin had was that Venka had never fought with an injury.

"She's sparred plenty of times," said Kitay. "But nobody is actually willing to hit her. Everyone's always stopped before the punch lands. Even Nezha. I'll bet you none of her home tutors were willing to hit her, either. They would have been fired immediately, if not thrown in jail."

"You're kidding," Rin said.

"I know *I've* never hit her."

Rin rubbed a fist into her palm. "Maybe it'll be good for her, then."

Still, injuring Venka was no easy task. More by sheer luck than anything, Rin managed to land a blow early on in the match. Venka, underestimating Rin's speed, had brought her guard back up too slowly after an attempted left hook. Rin took the opening and whipped a backhand through at Venka's nose.

Bone broke under Rin's fist with an audible crack.

Venka immediately retreated. One hand flew to her face, groping around her swelling nose. She glanced down at her blood-covered fingers and then back up at Rin. Her nostrils flared. Her cheeks turned a ghastly white.

"Problem?" Rin asked.

The look Venka gave her was pure murder.

"You shouldn't even be here," she snarled.

"Tell that to your nose," Rin said.

Venka was visibly unhinged. Her pretty sneer was gone, her hair messy, her face bloodied, her eyes wild and unfocused. She was on edge, off rhythm. She attempted several more wild blows until Rin caught her with a solid roundhouse kick to the side of her head.

Venka sprawled to the side and stayed on the ground. Her chest heaved rapidly up and down. Rin couldn't tell if she was crying or panting.

She didn't really care.

The applause as Rin emerged from the ring was scattered at best. The audience had been rooting for Venka. Venka was supposed to be in the finals.

Rin didn't care about that, either. She was used to this by now.

And Venka wasn't the victory she wanted.

Nezha tore his way through the other side of the bracket with ruthless efficiency. His fights were always scheduled in the other ring concurrently with Rin's, and they invariably ended earlier. Rin never saw Nezha in action. She only saw his opponents carried out on stretchers.

Alone among Nezha's opponents, Kitay emerged from his bout unharmed. He had lasted a minute and a half before surrendering.

There were rumors Nezha would be disqualified for intentional maiming, but Rin knew better than to hope. The faculty wanted to see the heir to the House of Yin in the finals. As far as Rin knew, Nezha could kill someone without repercussion. Jun, certainly, would allow it.

No one was surprised when Rin and Nezha both won their semifinals rounds. Finals were postponed until after dinner so that the apprentices could also come and watch.

Nezha disappeared somewhere halfway through dinner. He was likely getting private coaching from Jun. Rin briefly considered reporting it to get Nezha disqualified, but knew that would be a hollow victory. She wanted to see this through to the finish.

She picked at her food. She knew she needed energy, but the thought of eating made her want to vomit.

Halfway through the break, Raban approached her table. He was sweating hard, as if he had just run all the way up from the lower tier.

She thought he was going to congratulate her on making it to finals, but all he said was "You should surrender."

"You're joking," Rin responded. "I'm going to win this thing."

"Look, Rin—you haven't seen any of Nezha's fights."

"I've been a little preoccupied with my own."

"Then you don't know what he's capable of. I just dealt with his semifinals opponent in the infirmary. Nohai." Raban looked deeply rattled. "They're not sure if he's going to be able to walk again. Nezha shattered his kneecap."

"Seems like Nohai's problem." Rin didn't want to hear about Nezha's victories. She was feeling queasy enough as it was. The only way she could go through with the finals was if she convinced herself that Nezha was beatable.

"I know he hates you," Raban continued. "He could cripple you for life."

"He's just a kid." Rin scoffed with a confidence she didn't feel.

"*You're* just a kid!" Raban sounded agitated. "I don't care how good you think you are. Nezha's got six inches and twenty pounds of muscle on you, and I swear he wants to kill you."

"He has weaknesses," she said stubbornly. That had to be true. Didn't it?

"Does it matter? What does this Tournament mean to you anyway?" Raban asked. "There's no way you're getting culled now. Every master is going to submit a bid for you. Why do you have to win?"

Raban was right. At this point Irjah would have no qualms about bidding for her. Rin's position at Sinegard was safe.

But it wasn't about bids now, it was about pride. It was about power. If she surrendered to Nezha, he would hold it over her for the rest of their time at the Academy. No—he'd hold it over her for life.

"Because I can," she said. "Because he thought he could get rid of me. Because I want to break his stupid face."

The basement hall was silent as Rin and Nezha climbed into the ring. The air was thick with anticipation, a voyeuristic bloodlust. Months of hateful rivalry were coming to a head, and everyone wanted to watch the fallout of their collision.

Both Jun and Irjah wore deliberately neutral expressions, giving nothing away. Jiang was absent.

Nezha and Rin bowed shortly, never taking their eyes off each other, and both immediately backed away.

Nezha kept his gaze trained intently on Rin's, almond eyes narrowed in a tight focus. His lips were pressed in concentration. There were no jeers, no taunts. Not even a snarl.

Nezha was taking her seriously, Rin realized. He took her as an equal.

For some reason, this made her fiercely proud. They stared at each other, daring each other to break eye contact first.

"Begin," said Sonnen.

She leaped at him immediately. Her right leg lashed out again and again, forcing him back in retreat.

Kitay had spent all of lunch helping her strategize. She knew Nezha could be blindingly fast. Once he got momentum, he wouldn't stop until his opponent was incapacitated or dead.

Rin needed to overwhelm him from the beginning. She needed to constantly put him on the defensive, because to be on the defensive against Nezha was certain defeat.

The problem was that he was terribly strong. He didn't possess the brute force of Kobin, or even Kureel, but he was so precise in his movements that it didn't matter. He channeled his *ki* with a brilliant precision, built it up and then released it through the smallest pressure point to create the maximum impact.

Unlike Venka, Nezha could absorb losses and continue. She bruised him once or twice. He adapted and hit her back. And his blows *hurt*.

They were two minutes in. Rin had now lasted longer than any of Nezha's previous opponents, and something had become clear to her: He *wasn't* invincible. The techniques that had seemed impossibly difficult to her before now were transparently beatable. When Nezha kicked, his movements were wide and obvious like a boar's. His kicks held terrifying power, but only if they landed.

Rin made sure they never landed.

There was no way she would let him maim her. But she was not here merely to survive. She was here to win.

Exploding Dragon. Crouching Tiger. Extended Crane. She cycled through the movements in Seejin's Frolics as they were needed. The movements she'd practiced so many times before, linked together one after another in that damned form, snapped automatically into play.

But if Nezha was baffled by Rin's fighting style, he didn't show it. He remained calm and concentrated, attacking with methodical efficiency.

They were now four minutes in. Rin felt her lungs seizing, trying to pump oxygen into her fatigued body. But she knew that if she was tired, so was Nezha.

"He gets desperate when he's tired," Kitay had said. "And he's the most dangerous when he's desperate."

Nezha was getting desperate.

There was no control to his *ki* anymore. He threw punch after punch in her direction. He didn't care about the maiming rule. If he got her on the ground, he would kill her.

Nezha swept a low kick at the back of her knees. Rin made a frantic call and let him connect, sinking backward, pretending she'd lost her balance. He moved in immediately, looming over her. She grounded herself against the floor and kicked up.

She nailed him directly in his solar plexus with more force than she'd ever kicked with before—she could *feel* the air forced out of his lungs. She flipped up off the ground, and was astonished to find Nezha still reeling backward, gasping for air.

She flung herself forward and punched wildly at his head.

He dropped to the floor.

Shocked murmurs swept through the audience.

Rin circled Nezha, hoping he wouldn't get up, but knowing he would. She wanted to end it. Slam her heel into the back of his head. But the masters cared about honor. If she hit Nezha while he was down, she'd be sent packing from Sinegard in minutes.

Never mind that if he did the same, she doubted anyone would bat an eye.

Four seconds passed. Nezha raised a shaking hand and slammed it into the ground. He dragged himself forward. His forehead was bleeding, dripping scarlet into his eyes. He blinked it away and glared up at her.

His eyes screamed murder.

"Continue," said Sonnen.

Rin circled Nezha warily. He crouched like an animal, like a wounded wolf rising on its haunches.

The next time she threw a punch he grabbed her arm and pulled her in close. Her breath hitched. He raked his nails across her face and down to her collarbone.

She jerked her arm out of his grasp and cycled backward in rapid retreat. She felt a sharp sting under her left eye, across her neck. Nezha had drawn blood.

"Watch yourself, Yin," Sonnen warned.

Both of them ignored him. *Like a warning would make any difference*, Rin thought. The next time Nezha lunged at her she pulled him to the floor with her. They rolled around in the dirt, each attempting to pin the other and failing.

He punched madly in the air, flinging blows haphazardly at her face.

She dodged the first one. He swung his fist back in reverse and caught her with a backhand that left her gasping. The lower half of her face went numb.

He'd slapped her.

He'd *slapped* her.

A kick she could take. A knife hand strike she could absorb. But that slap had a savage intimacy. An undertone of superiority.

Something in Rin broke.

She couldn't breathe. Black tinged the edges of her vision— black, and then scarlet. An awful rage filled her, consumed her thoughts entirely. She needed revenge like she needed to breathe. She wanted Nezha to *hurt*. She wanted Nezha *punished*.

She lashed back, fingers curled into claws. He let go of her to jump back, but she followed him, redoubling her frenzied attacks. She wasn't as fast as he was. He retaliated, and she was too slow to block, and he hit her on the thigh, on the arm, but her body wouldn't register the damage. Pain was a message she was ignoring, to be felt later.

No—pain led to success.

He struck her face one, twice, thrice. He beat her like an animal and yet she kept fighting.

"What is *wrong* with you?" he hissed.

More important was what was wrong with *him*. Fear. She could see it in his eyes.

He had her backed against the wall, hands around her neck, but she grabbed his shoulders, jammed her knee up into his rib cage, and rammed an elbow into the back of his head. He collapsed forward to the ground, wheezing. She flung herself down and ground her elbow into his lower back. Nezha cried out, arched his back in agony.

Rin pinned Nezha's left arm to the floor with her foot and held his neck down with her right elbow. When he struggled, she slammed her fist into the back of his head and ground his face against the dirt until it was clear that he wouldn't get up.

"Break," said Sonnen, but she barely heard him. Blood thundered in her ears to a rhythm like war drums. Her vision was filtered through a red lens that registered only enemy targets.

She grasped a handful of Nezha's hair in her hand and yanked his head up again to slam into the floor.

"*Break!*"

Sonnen's arms were around her neck, restraining her, dragging her off Nezha's limp form.

She staggered away from Sonnen. Her body was burning up, feverish. She reeled, suddenly dizzy. She felt full to bursting with heat; she had to dispel it, force it out somewhere or she'd surely die, but the only place to put it was in the bodies of everyone else around her—

Something deep inside her rational mind screamed.

Raban reached for her as she climbed up out of the ring. "Rin, what—"

She shoved his hand away.

"Move," she panted. "Move."

But the masters crowded around her, a hubbub of voices—hands reaching, mouths moving. Their presence was suffocating. She felt if she screamed she could disintegrate them entirely, *wanted* to disintegrate them—but the very small part of her that was still rational reined it in, sent her reeling for the exit instead.

Miraculously they cleared a path for her. She pushed her way through the crowd of apprentices and ran to the stairwell. She barreled up the stairs, burst out the door of the main hall into the cold open air, and sucked in a great breath.

It wasn't enough. She was still burning.

Ignoring the shouts of the masters behind her, she set off at a run.

Jiang was in the first place she looked, the Lore garden. He was sitting cross-legged, eyes closed, still as the stone he sat upon.

She lurched through the garden gates, gripping at the doorpost. The world swirled sideways. Everything looked red: the trees, the stones, Jiang most of all. He flared in front of her like a torch.

He opened his eyes to the sound of her crashing through the gate. "Rin?"

She had forgotten how to speak. The flames within her licked out toward Jiang, sensed his presence like a fire sensed kindling and *yearned* to consume him.

She became convinced that if she didn't kill him, she might explode.

She moved to attack him. He scrambled to his feet, dodged her outstretched hands, and then upended her with a deft throw. She landed on her back. He pinned her to the ground with his arms.

"You're burning," he said in amazement.

"Help me," she gasped. "*Help*."

He leaned forward and cupped her head in his hands.

"Look at me."

She obeyed with great difficulty. His face swam before her.

"Great Tortoise," he murmured, and let go of her.

His eyes rolled up in the back of his head and he began uttering indecipherable noises, syllables that didn't resemble any language she knew.

He opened his eyes and pressed the palm of his hand to her forehead.

His hand felt like ice. The searing cold flooded from his palm to her forehead and into the rest of her body, through the same rivulets the flame was coursing through; arresting the fire, stilling it in her veins. She felt as if she'd been doused in a freezing bath.

She writhed on the floor, breathing in shock, trembling as the fire left her blood.

Then everything was still.

Jiang's face was the first thing she saw when she regained consciousness. His clothes looked rumpled. There were deep circles under his eyes, as if he hadn't slept in days. How long had she been asleep? Had he been here the entire time?

She raised her head. She was lying in a bunk in the infirmary, but she wasn't injured, as far as she could tell.

"How do you feel?" Jiang asked quietly.

"Bruised, but okay." She sat up slowly and winced. Her mouth felt like it was filled with cotton. She coughed and rubbed at her throat, frowning. "What happened?"

Jiang offered her a cup of water that had been sitting beside her bunk. She took it gratefully. The water sluiced down her dry throat with the most wonderful sensation.

"Congratulations," Jiang said. "You're this year's champion."

His tone did not sound congratulatory at all.

Rin felt none of the exhilaration that she should have, anyway. She couldn't even relish her victory over Nezha. She didn't feel the least bit proud, just scared and confused.

"What did I do?" she whispered.

"You have stumbled upon something that you're not ready for," said Jiang. He sounded agitated. "I never should have taught you the Five Frolics. From this point forward you're just going to be a danger to yourself and everyone around you."

"Not if you help me," she said. "Not if you teach me otherwise."

"I thought you just wanted to be a good soldier."

"I do," she said.

But more than that, she wanted power.

She had no idea what had happened in the ring; she would be foolish not to feel terrified by it, and yet she had never felt power like it. In that instant, she had felt as if she could defeat anyone. Kill anything.

She wanted that power again. She wanted what Jiang could teach her.

"I was ungrateful that day in the garden," she said, choosing her words carefully. If she spoke too obsequiously then it would scare Jiang off. But if she didn't apologize, then Jiang might think that she hadn't learned anything since they'd last spoken. "I wasn't thinking. I apologize."

She watched his eyes apprehensively, looking for that telltale distant expression that indicated that she had lost him.

Jiang's features did not soften, but neither did he get up to leave. "No. It was my fault. I didn't realize how much like Altan you are."

Rin jerked her head up at the mention of Altan.

"He won in his year, you know," Jiang said flatly. "He fought Tobi in the finals. It was a grudge match, just like your match with Nezha. Altan *hated* Tobi. Tobi made some jabs about Speer their first week of school, and Altan never forgave him. But he wasn't like you; he didn't squabble with Tobi throughout the year like a pecking hen. Altan swallowed his anger and concealed it under a mask of indifference until, at the very end, in front of an audience that included six Warlords and the Empress herself, he unleashed a power so potent that it took Sonnen, Jun, and myself to restrain him. By the time the smoke cleared, Tobi was so badly injured that Enro didn't sleep for five days while she watched over him."

"I'm not like that," she said. She hadn't beaten Nezha that badly. Had she? It was hard to remember through that fog of anger. "I'm not—I'm not like Altan."

"You are precisely the same." Jiang shook his head. "You're too reckless. You hold grudges, you cultivate your rage and let it explode, and you're careless about what you're taught. Training you would be a mistake."

Rin's gut plummeted. She was suddenly afraid that she might go mad; she had been given a tantalizing taste of incredible power, but was this the end of the road?

"So that's why you withdrew your bid for Altan?" she asked. "Why you refused to teach him?"

Jiang looked puzzled.

"I didn't withdraw my bid," he said. "I *insisted* they put him under my watch. Altan was a Speerly, already predisposed to rage and disaster. I knew I was the only one who could help him."

"But the apprentices said—"

"The apprentices don't know shit," Jiang snapped. "I asked Jima to let me train him. But the Empress intervened. She knew the military value of a Speerly warrior, she was so *excited* . . . in the end, national interests superseded the sanity of one boy. They put him under Irjah's tutelage, and honed his rage like a weapon, instead of teaching him to control it. You've seen him in the ring. You know what he's like."

Jiang leaned forward. "But *you*. The Empress doesn't know about you." He muttered to himself more than he spoke to her. "You're not safe, but you will be . . . They won't intervene, not this time . . ."

She watched Jiang's face, not daring to hope. "So does that mean—"

He stood up. "I will take you on as an apprentice. I hope I will not come to regret it."

He extended a hand toward her. She reached up and grasped it.

Of the original fifty students who matriculated at Sinegard at the start of the term, thirty-five received bids for apprenticeship. The masters sent their scrolls to the office in the main hall to be picked up by the students.

Those students who received no scrolls were asked to hand in their uniforms and make arrangements to leave the Academy immediately.

Most students received one scroll only. Niang, to her delight, joined two other students in the Medicine track. Nezha and Venka pledged Combat.

Kitay, convinced he'd lost his bids the moment he surrendered to Nezha, tugged at his hair so frantically the entire way to the front office that Rin was half-afraid he'd go bald.

"It was a stupid thing," Kitay said. "Cowardly. No one's surrendered uninjured in the last two decades. Nobody's going to want to sponsor me now."

Up until the Tournament he'd been expecting bids from Jima, Jun, and Irjah. But only one scroll was waiting for him at the registrar.

Kitay unfurled it. His face split into a grin. "Irjah thinks surrendering was brilliant. I'm pledging Strategy!"

The registrar handed two scrolls to Rin. Without opening them, she knew they were from Irjah and Jiang. She could choose between Strategy and Lore.

She pledged Lore.

CHAPTER 8

Sinegard Academy gave students four days off from studies to celebrate the Summer Festival. The next term would begin as soon as they returned.

Most students took this as a chance to visit their families. But Rin didn't have time to travel all the way back to Tikany, nor did she want to. She had planned on spending the break at the Academy, until Kitay invited her to stay at his estate.

"Unless you don't want to," Kitay said nervously. "I mean, if you already have plans—"

"I have no plans," Rin said. "I'd love to."

She packed for her excursion into the city the next morning. This took mere seconds—she had very few personal belongings. She carefully folded two sets of school tunics into her old travel satchel, and hoped Kitay would not find it rude if she wore her uniform during the festival. She had no other clothing; she'd gotten rid of her old southerner's tunics the first chance she got.

"I'll get a rickshaw," Rin offered as she met Kitay at the school gates.

Kitay looked puzzled. "Why do we need a rickshaw?"

Rin frowned. "Then how are we getting there?"

Kitay opened his mouth to reply just as a massive horse-drawn carriage pulled up by the gates. The driver, a portly man in robes of rich gold and burgundy, hopped off the coachman's seat and bowed deeply in Kitay's direction. "Master Chen."

He blinked at Rin, as if trying to decide whether to bow to her as well, and then managed a perfunctory head dip.

"Thanks, Merchi." Kitay handed their bags to the servant and helped Rin into the carriage.

"Comfortable?"

"Very."

From their vantage point in the carriage, they could see almost all the city nested in the valley below: the spiraling pagodas of the administrative district rising through a faint blanket of mist, white houses built into the valley slopes with curved tiled roofs, and the winding stone walls of the alleyways leading downtown.

From the shaded interior of the carriage, Rin felt insulated from the dirty city streets. She felt clean. For the first time since she had arrived in Sinegard, she felt as if she belonged here. She leaned against the side and enjoyed the warm summer breeze against her face. She had not rested like this in a long time.

"We will discuss what happened to you in detail when you return," Jiang had told her. "But your mind has just suffered a very particular trauma. The best thing you can do for yourself now is rest. Let the experience germinate. Let your mind heal."

Kitay, tactfully, did not ask her what had happened. Rin was grateful for it.

Merchi drove them at a brisk pace down the mountain pass. They continued on the main city road for an hour and then turned left onto the isolated road that led into the Jade District.

When Rin had arrived in Sinegard a year ago, she and Tutor Feyrik had traveled through the working-class district, where the inns were cheap and gambling houses stood around every corner. Her daily trips to see the Widow Maung had led her through the loudest, dirtiest, and smelliest parts of the city. What she'd seen of Sinegard so far was no different from Tikany—it was just noisier and more cramped.

Now, riding in the Chen family's carriage, she saw how splendid Sinegard could be. The roads of the Jade District were freshly paved, and glistened like they had been scrubbed clean that very morning. Rin saw no wooden shacks, no evident dumping grounds for chamber pots. She saw no grumpy housewives steaming breads and dumplings on outdoor grills, too poor to afford indoor stoves. She saw no beggars.

She found the stillness unsettling. Tikany was always bustling with activity—drifters collecting trash to repackage and sell; old men sitting on stoops outside, smoking or playing mahjong; little children wearing jumpers that exposed their butt cheeks, wandering around the streets followed by squatting grandparents ready to catch them when they toppled over.

She saw none of that here. The Jade District was composed of pristine barriers and walled-off gardens. Aside from their carriage, the roads were empty.

Merchi stopped the carriage before the gates of a massive compound. They swung ponderously open, revealing four long rectangular buildings arranged in a square, enclosing an enormous garden pavilion. Several dogs rushed them at the entrance, tiny white things whose paws were as immaculately clean as the tiled path they walked on.

Kitay gave a shout, climbed out of the carriage, and knelt down. His dogs leaped on him, tails wagging with delirious delight.

"This one's the Dragon Emperor." He tickled a dog under its chin. "They're all named after the great rulers."

"Which one's the Red Emperor?" Rin asked.

"The one that's going to pee on your foot if you don't move."

The estate's housekeeper was a short, plump woman with freckled, leathery skin named Lan. She spoke with a friendly, girlish voice that was at odds with her wrinkled face. Her Sinegardian accent was so strong that even after several months' practice with the heavily accented Widow Maung, Rin still could only barely decipher it.

"What do you want to eat? I'll cook you anything you want. I know the culinary styles of all twelve provinces. Except the Monkey Province. Too spicy. It's not good for you. I also don't do stinky tofu. My only constraint is what's on the market, but I can get just about anything at the import store. Any favorite recipes? Lobster? Or water chestnuts? You name it, I'll cook it."

Rin, who was accustomed to eating the uninspired slop of the Academy canteen, was at a loss for a response. How was she to explain she simply didn't have the repertoire of meals that Lan demanded? Back in Tikany, the Fangs were fond of a dish named "whatever," which was quite literally made of whatever scraps were left at the shop—usually fried eggs and glass noodles.

"I want Seven Treasure Soup," Kitay intervened, leaving Rin to wonder what on earth that was. "And Lion's Head."

Rin blinked. "What?"

Kitay looked amused. "Oh, you'll see."

"You could act less like a dazed peasant, you know," Kitay said as Lan laid out a spread of quail, quail eggs, shark fin soup served in turtle's shell, and pig's intestines before them. "It's just food."

But "just food" was rice porridge. Maybe some vegetables. A piece of fish, pork, or chicken whenever they could get it.

Nothing on the table was "just" anything.

Seven Treasure Soup turned out to be a deliciously sweet congee-based concoction of red dates, honeyed chestnuts, lotus seeds, and four other ingredients that Rin could not identify. Lion's Head, she discovered with some relief, was not actually a lion's head, but rather a ball of meat mixed with flour and boiled amid strips of white tofu.

"Kitay, I *am* a dazed peasant." Rin tried fruitlessly to pick up a quail egg with her chopsticks. Finally she gave up and used her fingers. "You eat like this? All the time?"

Kitay blushed. "You get used to it. I had a hard time our first week at school. The Academy canteen was *awful*."

It was hard not to feel jealous of Kitay. His private washroom was bigger than the cramped bedroom Rin had shared with Kesegi. His estate's library rivaled the stacks at Sinegard. Everything Kitay owned was replaceable; if he got mud on his shoes, he threw them away. If his shirt ripped, he got a new one—a newly *made* shirt, tailored to his precise height and girth.

Kitay had spent his childhood in luxurious comfort, with nothing better to do than study for the Keju. For him, testing into Sinegard had been a pleasant surprise; a confirmation of something he'd always known was his destiny.

"Where's your father?" Rin asked. Kitay's father was the defense minister to the Empress herself. She was privately relieved she wouldn't have to converse with him yet—the thought itself was terrifying—but she couldn't help feeling curious about the man. Would he be an older version of Kitay—wiry-haired, just as brilliant, and exponentially more powerful?

Kitay made a face. "Defense meetings. You wouldn't know it, but the whole city is on high security alert. The entire City Guard will be on duty all this week. We don't need another Opera incident."

"I thought the Red Junk Opera was dead," said Rin.

"*Mostly* dead. You can't kill a movement. Somewhere out there, some religious lunatics are intent on killing the Empress." Kitay speared a chunk of tofu. "Father's going to be at the palace until the parade is over. He's directly responsible for the Empress's safety. If anything goes wrong, Father's head is on the line."

"Isn't he worried?"

"Not really. He's done this for decades; he'll be all right. Besides, the Empress is a martial artist herself; she's hardly an easy target." Kitay launched into a series of anecdotes his father had told him about serving in the palace, about hilarious encounters with the Empress and the Twelve Warlords, about court gossip and provincial politics.

Rin listened in amazement. What was it like to grow up knowing that your father served at the right hand of the Empress? What a difference an accident of birth made. In another world she might have grown up at an estate like this, with all of her desires within reach. In another world, she might have been born into power.

Rin spent the night in a massive suite she had all to herself. She hadn't slept so long or so well since she came to Sinegard. It was as if her body had shut down after weeks of abuse. She awoke feeling better and clearer-minded than she had in months.

After a lackadaisical breakfast of sweet congee and spiced goose eggs, Kitay and Rin wandered downtown to the marketplace.

Rin hadn't set foot downtown since arriving to Sinegard with Tutor Feyrik a year prior. The Widow Maung lived on the other side of the city, and her strict academic schedule had left her with no time to explore Sinegard on her own.

She had thought the market was overwhelming last year. Now, at peak activity during the Summer Festival, it seemed like the city had exploded. Pop-up vendor carts were parked everywhere, crammed into the alleyways so tightly that shoppers had to navigate the market in a cramped, single-file line. But the *sights*. Oh, the sights. Rin saw rows upon rows of pearl necklaces and jade bracelets. Stands of smooth egg-sized rocks that displayed characters, sometimes entire poems, only if you dipped them in water. Stations where calligraphy masters wrote names on giant, lovely fans, wielding their black ink brushes with the care and bravado of swordsmen.

"What do these do?" Rin stopped in front of a rack bearing tiny wooden statues of fat little boys. The boys' tunics were yanked down, exposing their penises. She couldn't believe anything this obscene was on sale.

"Oh, those are my favorite," Kitay said.

By way of explanation, the vendor picked up a teapot and poured water over the statues. The clay darkened as the statues turned wet. Water began spurting out of the penises like sprays of urine.

Rin laughed. "How much are these?"

"Four silvers for one. I'll give you two for seven."

Rin blanched. All she had was a single string of imperial silvers and a handful of copper coins left over from the money Tutor Feyrik had helped her exchange. She had never had to spend money at the Academy, and hadn't considered how expensive things might be in Sinegard when she wasn't living on the Academy's coin.

"Do you want it?" Kitay asked.

Rin waved her hands wildly. "No, I'm good, I can't really . . ."

Understanding dawned on Kitay's face. "My gift." He handed a string of silvers to the merchant. "One urinating statue for my easily entertained friend."

Rin blushed. "Kitay, I can't."

"It costs nothing."

"It costs a lot to me," she said.

Kitay placed the statue in her hand. "If you say one more thing about money, I'm leaving you to get lost."

The market was so massive that Rin was reluctant to stray too far from the entrance; if she became lost in those winding pathways, how would she ever find her way out? But Kitay navigated the market with the ease of a seasoned connoisseur, pointing out which shops he liked and which he didn't.

Kitay's Sinegard was full of wonders, completely accessible, and crammed with things that belonged to him. Kitay's Sinegard wasn't terrifying, because Kitay had money. If he tripped, half the shop owners on the street would help him up, hoping for a handsome tip. If his pocket were cut, he'd go home and get another purse. Kitay could afford to be victimized by the city because he had room to fail.

Rin couldn't. She had to remind herself that, despite Kitay's absurd generosity, none of this was hers. Her only ticket into this city was through the Academy, and she'd have to work hard to keep it.

At night the marketplace lit up with lanterns, one for each vendor. Together the lanterns looked like a horde of fireflies, casting unnatural shadows on everything their light touched.

"Have you ever seen shadow puppetry?" Kitay stopped in front of a large canvas tent. A line of children stood at the entrance doling out copper shells for entrance. "I mean, it's for little kids, but . . ."

"Great Tortoise." Rin's eyes widened. In Tikany, they told *stories* about shadow puppetry. She fished the change out of her pocket. "I got this."

The tent was packed with rows of children. Kitay and Rin filed into the back, trying to pretend they weren't at least five years older than the rest of the audience. At the front, a massive silk screen hung from the top of the tent, illuminated from behind with soft yellow light.

"I tell you now about the rebirth of this nation."

The puppeteer spoke from a box beside the screen, so that even his silhouette was invisible. His voice filled the cramped tent, deep and smooth and resonant. "This is the tale of the salvation and reunion of Nikan. This is the story of the Trifecta, the three warriors of legend."

The light behind the screen dimmed and then flared a bright scarlet hue.

"The Warrior." The first shadow appeared on the screen: the silhouette of a man with a massive sword almost as tall as he was. He was heavily armored, with spiked pads protruding out from his shoulders. The plume on his helmet furled into the air above him.

"The Vipress." The slender form of a woman appeared next to the Warrior. Her head tilted coquettishly to one side; her left arm bent as if she wielded something behind her back. A fan, perhaps. Or a dagger.

"And the Gatekeeper." The Gatekeeper was the thinnest of the three, a stooped figure wrapped in robes. By his side crawled a large tortoise.

The scarlet hue of the screen faded away to a soft yellow that pulsed slowly like a heartbeat. The shadows of the Trifecta grew larger and then disappeared. A silhouette of a mountainous land appeared in their place. And the puppeteer began his story in earnest.

"Sixty-five years ago, in the wake of the First Poppy War, the people of Nikan suffered under the weight of their Federation oppressors. Nikan lay sick, feverish under the clouds of the poppy drug." Translucent ribbons drifted up from the profile of the countryside, giving the illusion of smoke. "The people starved. Mothers sold their infants for a pound of meat, for a bolt of cloth. Fathers killed their children rather than watch them suffer. Yes, that's right. Children just like you!

"The Nikara thought the gods had abandoned them, for how else could the barbarians from the east have wreaked such destruction upon them?"

The screen turned the same sickly yellow pallor as the cheeks of poppy addicts. A line of Nikara peasants knelt with their heads bent to the floor, as if weeping.

"The people found no protection in the Warlords. The rulers of the Twelve Provinces, once powerful, were now weak and disorganized. Preoccupied with ancient grudges, they wasted time and soldiers fighting against each other rather than uniting to drive out the invaders from Mugen. They squandered gold on drink and women. They breathed the poppy drug like air. They taxed their provinces at exorbitant rates, and gave nothing back. Even when the Federation destroyed their villages and raped their women, the Warlords did nothing. They could do nothing.

"The people prayed for heroes. They prayed for twenty years. And finally, the gods sent them."

A silhouette of three children, hand in hand, appeared on the lower left corner of the screen. The child in the center stood taller than the rest. The one on his right had long, flowing hair. The third child, standing a little removed from the other two, had his profile turned away toward the end of the screen, as if he was looking at something the other two could not see.

"The gods did not send these heroes from the skies. Rather they chose three children—war orphans, peasants whose parents had been killed in village raids. They were born of the humblest origins. But they were meant to walk with the gods."

The child in the center strode purposefully to the middle of the screen. The other two followed him at a distance, like he was their leader. The limbs of the shadows moved so smoothly there might have been little men in costume behind the screen, not puppets made of paper and string. Rin marveled at the technique involved, even as she was further absorbed into the story.

"When their village burned, the three children formed a pact to seek revenge against the Federation and liberate their country from the invaders, so that no more children would suffer as they had.

"They trained for many years with the monks of the Wudang temple. By the time they matured, their martial arts skills were prodigious, and they rivaled in skill fully grown men who had been training for decades. At the end of their apprenticeship, they journeyed to the top of the highest peak in all of the land: Mount Tianshan."

A massive mountain came into view. It took up almost the entire screen; the shadows of the three heroes were minuscule beside it. But as they walked toward the mountain, the peak grew smaller and smaller, flatter and flatter, until the heroes stood on flat ground at the very top.

"There are seven thousand steps that lead up to the peak of Mount Tianshan. And at the very top, far up so high that the strongest eagle could not circle the peak, lies a temple. From that temple, the three heroes walked into the heavens and entered the Pantheon, the home of the gods."

The three heroes now approached a gate similar to those that guarded the entrance to the Academy. The doors were twice the heroes' height, decorated with intricately curling patterns of butterflies and tigers, and guarded by a great tortoise that bowed its head low as it let them pass.

"The first hero, strongest among his companions, was summoned by the Dragon Lord. The hero stood a head taller than his friends. His back was broad, his arms like tree trunks. He had been deemed by the gods to be the leader of the three.

"'If I am to command the armies of Nikan, I must have a great blade,' he said, and knelt at the feet of the Dragon Lord. The Dragon Lord bade him stand, and bestowed upon him a massive sword. Thus he became the Warrior."

The Warrior's figure swung the huge sword in a great arc above his head and brought it smashing downward. Sparks of red and gold light emitted from the ground where the sword struck.

"The second hero was a girl among the two men. She walked past the Dragon Lord, the Tiger Lord, and the Lion Lord, for they were gods of war and therefore gods of men. She said: 'I am a woman, and women need different weapons than men. The woman's place is not in the thick of battle. The woman's battlefield is in deception and seduction.' And she knelt before the plinth of the Snail Goddess Nüwa. The Goddess Nüwa was pleased by her words, and made the second hero as deadly as a serpent, as bewitching as the most hypnotic of snakes. Thus was born the Vipress."

A great serpent slithered out from under the Vipress's dress and undulated about her body, coiling upward to rest on her shoulders. The audience applauded the graceful trick of puppetry.

"The third hero was the humblest among his peers. Weak and sickly, he had never been able to train to the extent of his two friends. But he was loyal and unswerving in his devotion to the gods. He did not beg a favor from any deity in the Pantheon, for he knew he was not worthy. Instead he knelt before the humble tortoise who had let them in.

"'I ask only for the strength to protect my friends and the courage to protect my country,' he said. The tortoise replied, 'You will be given this and more. Take the chain of keys from around my neck. From this day forth you are the Gatekeeper. You have the means to unlock the menagerie of the gods, inside which are kept beasts of every kind, both creatures of beauty and monsters vanquished by heroes long past. You will command them as you see fit.'"

The Gatekeeper's shadow raised his robed hands slowly, and from his back unfurled many shadows of different shapes and sizes. Dragons. Demons. Beasts. They enveloped the Gatekeeper like a shroud of darkness.

"When they came back down the mountain, the monks who had once trained them realized the three had surpassed in skill even the oldest master at the temple. Word spread, and martial artists across the land bowed down to the prodigious skill of the three heroes. The Trifecta's reputation grew. Now that their names were known in all of the Twelve Provinces, the Trifecta sent out word to each of the Warlords to invite them to a great banquet at the base of Mount Tianshan."

Twelve figures, each representing a different province, appeared on the screen. Each wore a helmet with a plume shaped like the province he hailed from: Rooster, Ox, Hare, Monkey, and on and on.

"The Warlords, who were full of pride, were each furious that the other eleven had been invited. Each had thought that he alone had been summoned by the Trifecta. Plotting was what the Warlords did best, and immediately they set about planning to get revenge on the Trifecta."

The screen beamed an eerie, misty purple. The shadows of the Warlords dipped their heads toward one another over their bowls as if conducting nefarious negotiations.

"But halfway through their meal, they found they could not move. The Vipress had poisoned their drinks with a numbing agent, and the Warlords had drunk many bowls of the sorghum wine. As they lay incapacitated in their seats, the Warrior stood on the table before them. He announced: 'Today I declare myself the Emperor of Nikan. If you oppose me, I will cut you down and your lands will become mine. But if you pledge to serve me as an ally, to fight as a general under my banner, I will reward you with status and power. Never again will you fight to defend your borders from another Warlord. Never again will you struggle for domination. All will be equal under me, and I will be the greatest leader this kingdom has seen since the Red Emperor.'"

The shadow of the Warrior raised his sword to the sky. Lightning erupted from the sword point, a symbol of a blessing from the heavens themselves.

"When the Warlords regained control of their limbs, each and every one of them agreed to serve the new Dragon Emperor. And so Nikan was united without the shedding of a single drop of blood. For the first time in centuries, the Warlords fought under the same banner, rallying to the Trifecta. And for the first time in recent history, Nikan presented a united front against the Federation invaders. At long last, we drove out the oppressors. And the Empire, again, became free."

The mountainous silhouette of the country returned again, only this time the land was filled with spiraling pagodas, with temples and many villages. It was a country freed from invaders. It was a country blessed by the gods.

"Today we celebrate the unity of the Twelve Provinces," said the puppeteer. "We celebrate the Trifecta. And we pay homage to the gods who have gifted them."

The children burst into applause.

Kitay was frowning when they exited the tent. "I never realized how horrible that story was," he said quietly. "When you're little, you think the Trifecta were being so clever, but really this is just a story of poison and coercion. Nikara politics as usual."

"I don't know anything about Nikara politics," said Rin.

"I do." Kitay made a face. "Father's told me everything that happens at the palace. It's just the same as the puppeteer said. The Warlords are always at each other's throats, vying for the Empress's attention. It's pathetic."

"What do you mean?"

Kitay looked anxious. "You know how the Warlords were so busy fighting each other that they let Mugen wreck the country during the Poppy Wars? Father's convinced that's happening again. Remember what Yim said the first day of class? He was right. Mugen isn't just sitting quietly on that island. My father thinks it's only a matter of time before they attack again, and he's worried the Warlords aren't taking the threat seriously enough."

The Empire's fragmentation seemed to be a concern of every master at the Academy. Although the Militia was technically under the Empress's control, its twelve divisions drew soldiers largely from their home provinces and lay under the direct command of the provincial Warlords. And provincial relations had never been good—Rin had not realized how deep-seated northern contempt for the south was until she arrived in Sinegard.

But Rin didn't want to talk about politics. This break was the first time in a long time that she was able to let herself relax, and she didn't want to dwell on matters like some impending war that she could do nothing to stop. She was still dazed by the visual spectacle of the shadow puppetry, and she wished Kitay would leave the serious matters be.

"I liked the part about the Pantheon," she said after a while.

"Of course you did. It's the only part that's pure fiction."

"Is it, though?" Rin asked. "Who's to say the Trifecta weren't shamans?"

"The Trifecta were martial artists. Politicians. Immensely talented soldiers, sure, but the part about shamanism is just exaggeration," said Kitay. "The Nikara love embellishing war stories, you know that."

"But where did the stories come from?" Rin persisted. "The Trifecta's powers are terribly specific for a kid's tale. If their powers were only myth, then how come that myth is always the same? We heard about the Trifecta all the way in Tikany. Across the provinces, the story has never changed. They're always the Gatekeeper, the Warrior, and the Vipress."

Kitay shrugged. "Some poet got creative, and those characters caught on. It's not that hard to believe. More credible than the existence of shamans, anyhow."

"But there have been shamans before," said Rin. "Back before the Red Emperor conquered Nikan."

"There's no conclusive proof. There are just anecdotes."

"The Red Emperor's scribes kept track of foreign imports down to the last banana cluster," Rin objected. "They were hardly likely to exaggerate about their enemies."

Kitay looked skeptical. "Sure, but none of that means the Trifecta were actually shamans. The Dragon Emperor's dead, and no one's seen or heard of the Gatekeeper since the Second Poppy War."

"Maybe he's just in hiding. Maybe he's still out there, waiting for the next invasion. Or—maybe—what if the Cike are shamans?" The idea had just occurred to Rin. "That's why we don't know anything about them. Maybe they're the only shamans left—"

"The Cike are just killers," Kitay scoffed. "They stab, kill, and poison. They don't call down gods."

"As far as you know," Rin said.

"You're really hung up on this idea of shamans, aren't you?" Kitay asked. "It's just a kid's story, Rin."

"The Red Emperor's scribes wouldn't have kept extensive documentation of a kid's story."

Kitay sighed. "Is that why you pledged Lore? You think you can become a shaman? You think you can summon gods?"

"I don't believe in gods," said Rin. "But I believe in power. And I believe the shamans had some source of power that the rest of us don't know how to access, and I believe it's still possible to learn."

Kitay shook his head. "I'll tell you what shamans are. At some point in time some martial artists were really powerful, and the more battles they won, the more stories spread. They probably encouraged those stories, too, thinking it'd scare their enemies. I wouldn't be surprised if the Empress made up those stories about the Trifecta being shamans herself. It'd certainly help her hold on power. She needs it now, more than ever. The Warlords are getting restless—I bet we're barely years from a coup. But if she's really the Vipress, then how come she hasn't just summoned giant snakes to subdue the Warlords to her will?"

Rin couldn't think of a glaring counterargument to this theory, so she conceded with silence. Debating with Kitay became pointless after a while. He was so convinced of his own rationality, of his encyclopedic knowledge of most things, that he had difficulty conceiving of gaps in his understanding.

"I notice the puppeteer glossed over how we actually *won* the Second Poppy War," Rin said after a while. "You know. Speer. Butchery. Thousands dead in a single night."

"Well, it was a kid's story after all," said Kitay. "And genocide is a little depressing."

Rin and Kitay spent the next two days lazing around, indulging in every act of sloth they hadn't been able to at the Academy. They played chess. They lounged in the garden, stared idly at the clouds, and gossiped about their classmates.

"Niang's pretty cute," Kitay said. "So is Venka."

"Venka's been obsessed with Nezha since we got there," Rin said. "Even I could see that."

Kitay waggled his eyebrows. "One might say *you've* been obsessed with Nezha."

"Don't be disgusting."

"You *are*. You're always asking me about him."

"Because I'm curious," Rin said. "Sunzi says to know your enemy."

"Fuck Sunzi. You just think he's pretty."

Rin tossed the chessboard at his head.

At Kitay's insistence, Lan cooked them spicy peppercorn hot pot, and delicious though it was, Rin had the singular experience of weeping while eating. She spent most of the next day squatting over the toilet with a burning rectum.

"You think this is how the Speerlies felt?" Kitay asked. "What if burning diarrhea is the price of lifelong devotion to the Phoenix?"

"The Phoenix is a vengeful god," Rin groaned.

They sampled all the wines in Kitay's father's liquor closet and got wonderfully, dizzyingly drunk.

"Nezha and I spent most of our childhood raiding this closet. Try this one." Kitay passed her a small ceramic bottle. "White sorghum wine. Fifty percent alcohol."

Rin swallowed hard. It slid down her throat with a marvelous burn.

"This is liquid fire," she said. "This is the sun in a bottle. This is the drink of a Speerly."

Kitay snickered.

"You wanna know how they brew this?" he asked. "The secret ingredient is urine."

She spat the wine out.

Kitay laughed. "They just use alkaline powder now. But the tale goes that a disgruntled official pissed all over one of the Red Emperor's distilleries. Probably the best accidental discovery of the Red Emperor's era."

Rin rolled over onto her stomach to look sideways at him. "Why aren't you at Yuelu Mountain? You should be a scholar. A sage. You know so much about everything."

Kitay could expound for hours on any given subject, and yet showed little interest in their studies. He had breezed through the Trials because his eidetic memory made studying unnecessary, but he had surrendered to Nezha the moment the Tournament took a dangerous turn. Kitay was brilliant, but he didn't belong at Sinegard.

"I wanted to," Kitay admitted. "But I'm my father's only son. And my father's the defense minister. So what choice do I have?"

She fiddled with the bottle. "You're an only child, then?"

Kitay shook his head. "Older sister. Kinata. She's at Yuelu now—studying geomancy, or something like that."

"*Geomancy?*"

"The artful placement of buildings and things." Kitay waved his hands in the air. "It's all aesthetics. Supposedly it's important, if your greatest aspiration is to marry someone important."

"You haven't read every book about it?"

"I only read about the interesting things." Kitay rolled over onto his stomach. "You? Any siblings?"

"None," she said. Then she frowned. "Yes, actually. I don't know why I said that. I have a brother—well, foster brother. Kesegi. He's ten. *Was.* He's eleven now, I guess."

"Do you miss him?"

Rin hugged her knees to her chest. She didn't like the way her stomach suddenly felt. "No. I mean—I don't know. He was so little when I left. I used to take care of him. I guess I'm glad that I don't have to do that anymore."

Kitay raised an eyebrow. "Have you written to him?"

"No." She hesitated. "I don't know why. I guess I assumed the Fangs didn't want to hear from me. Or maybe that he'd be better off if he just forgot about me."

She had wanted to at least write Tutor Feyrik in the beginning, but things had been so awful at the Academy that she couldn't bear to tell him about it. Then, as time passed, and as her schoolwork became more exhausting, it had become so painful to think about home that she'd just stopped.

"You didn't like it at home, huh?" Kitay asked.

"I don't like thinking about it," she mumbled.

She never wanted to think about Tikany. She wanted to pretend that she'd never lived there—no, that it had never existed. Because if she could just erase her past, then she could write herself into whoever she wanted to be in the present. Student. Scholar. Soldier. Anything except who she used to be.

The Summer Festival culminated in a parade in Sinegard's city center.

Rin arrived at the grounds with the members of the House of Chen—Kitay's father and willowy mother, his two uncles and their wives, and his older sister. Rin had forgotten how important Kitay's father actually was until she saw the entire clan decked out in their house colors of burgundy and gold.

Kitay suddenly grabbed Rin's elbow. "Don't look to your left. Pretend like you're talking to me."

"But I *am* talking to you." Rin immediately looked to her left.

And saw Nezha, standing in a crowd of people wearing gowns of silver and cerulean. A massive dragon was embroidered across the back of his robe, the emblem of the House of Yin.

"Oh." She jerked her head away. "Can we go stand over there?"

"Yes, let's."

Once they were safely ensconced behind Kitay's rotund second uncle, Rin peered out to gawk at the members of the House of Yin. She found herself staring at two older versions of Nezha, one male and one female. Both were well into their twenties and unfairly attractive. Nezha's entire family, in fact, looked like they belonged on wall paintings—they appeared more like idealized versions of humans than actual people.

"Nezha's father isn't there," said Kitay. "That's interesting."

"Why?"

"He's the Dragon Warlord," said Kitay. "One of the Twelve."

"Maybe he's sick," said Rin. "Maybe he hates parades as much as you do."

"I'm here, though, aren't I?" Kitay fussed with his sleeves. "You don't just *miss* the Summer Parade. It's a display of unity of all the Twelve Provinces. One year my father broke his leg the day before and he still made it, doped up on sedatives the entire time. If the head of the House of Yin hasn't come, that means something."

"Maybe he's embarrassed," Rin said. "Furious that his son lost the Tournament. He's too ashamed to show his face."

Kitay cracked a smile.

A bugle sounded through the thin morning air, followed by a servant shouting for all members of the procession to fall into order.

Kitay turned to Rin. "So, I don't know if you can . . ."

"No, it's fine," she said. Of course she wouldn't be riding with the House of Chen. Rin was not in Kitay's family; she had no business being in the procession. She spared him the embarrassment of bringing it up. "I'll watch you from the marketplace."

After a good deal of squeezing and elbowing, Rin escaped the crowd and found a spot on top of a fruit stand where she could get a good view of the parade without being crushed to death in the horde of Sinegardians who had gathered downtown. As long as the thatched straw roof did not suddenly cave in, the fruit stand owner need never know.

The parade began with an homage to the Heavenly Menagerie, the roster of mythical creatures that were held by legend to exist in the era of the Red Emperor. Giant dragons and lions snaked through the crowd, undulating up and down on poles controlled by dancers hidden within. Firecrackers popped in rhythm as they moved, like coordinated bursts of thunder. Next came a massive scarlet effigy on tall poles that had been set carefully aflame: the Vermilion Phoenix of the South.

Rin watched the Phoenix curiously. According to her history books, this was the god whom the Speerlies had venerated above all others. In fact, Speer had never worshipped the massive pantheon of gods that the Nikara did. The Speerlies had only ever worshipped their Phoenix.

The creature following the Phoenix resembled nothing Rin had ever seen before. It bore the head of a lion, antlers like a deer's, and the body of a four-legged creature; a tiger, perhaps, but its feet ended in hooves. It wove quietly through the parade; its puppeteers beat no drums, sang no chants, rang no bells to announce its coming.

Rin puzzled over the creature until she matched it with a description she had heard in stories told in Tikany. It was a kirin, the noblest of earthly beasts. Kirins walked the lands of Nikan only when a great leader had passed away, and then only in times of great peril.

Then the procession turned to the illustrious houses, and Rin quickly lost interest. Aside from seeing Kitay's moping face, there was nothing fun about watching palanquin after palanquin of important people dressed in their house colors.

The sun shone at full force overhead. Sweat dripped down Rin's temples. She wished she had something to drink. She shielded her face with her sleeve, waiting for the parade to end so she could find Kitay.

Then the crowd around her began screaming, and Rin realized with a start that borne on a palanquin of golden silk, surrounded by a platoon of both musicians and bodyguards, the Empress had arrived.

The Empress was flawed in many ways.

Her face was not perfectly symmetrical. Her eyebrows were finely arched, one slightly above the other, which gave her an expression of constant disdain. Even her mouth was uneven; one side of her mouth curved higher than the other.

And yet she was without question the most beautiful woman Rin had ever seen.

It was not enough to describe her hair, which was darker than the night and glossier than butterfly wings. Or her skin, which was paler and smoother than any Sinegardian could have wished for. Or her lips, which were the color of blood, as if she had just been sucking at a cherry. All of these things could have applied to normal women in the abstract, might even have been remarkable on their own. But on the Empress they were simple inevitabilities, casual truths.

Venka would have paled in comparison.

Youth, Rin thought, was an amplification of beauty. It was a filter; it could mask what one was lacking, enhance even the most average features. But beauty without youth was dangerous. The Empress's beauty did not require the soft fullness of young lips, the rosy red of young cheeks, the tenderness of young skin. This beauty cut deep, like a sharpened crystal. This beauty was immortal.

Afterward, Rin could not have described what the Empress

had been wearing. She could not recall whether or not the Empress spoke, or if the Empress waved in her direction. She could not remember anything the Empress did at all.

She would only remember those eyes, deep pools of black, eyes that made her feel as if she were suffocating, just like Master Jiang's did, but if this was drowning then Rin didn't want air, didn't need it so long as she could keep gazing into those glittering obsidian wells.

She couldn't look away. She couldn't even *imagine* looking away.

As the Empress's palanquin moved out of sight, Rin felt an odd pang in her heart.

She would have torn apart kingdoms for this woman. She would have followed her to the gates of hell and back. This was her ruler. This was whom she was meant to serve.

CHAPTER 9

"Fang Runin of Tikany, Rooster Province," Rin said. "Second-year apprentice."

The office clerk stamped the Academy's crest in the space next to her name on the registration scroll, and then handed her three sets of black apprentice tunics. "What track?"

"Lore," Rin said. "Under Master Jiang Ziya."

The clerk consulted the scroll again. "You sure?"

"Pretty sure," Rin said, though her pulse quickened. Had something happened?

"I'll be right back," the clerk said, and disappeared into the back office.

Rin waited by the desk, growing more and more anxious as the minutes passed. Had Jiang left the Academy? Been fired? Suffered a nervous breakdown? Been arrested for opium possession off campus? For opium possession *on* campus?

She thought suddenly of the day she had enrolled for Sinegard, when the proctors had tried to detain her for cheating. Had Nezha's family filed a complaint against her for costing their heir the championship? Was that even possible?

Finally the clerk returned with a sheepish look on his face.

"I'm sorry," he said. "But it's been so long since anyone's

pledged Lore. We're not sure what color your armband is supposed to be."

In the end they took leftover cloth from the first-years' uniforms and fashioned her a white armband.

Classes began the next day. After pledging, Rin still spent half her time with the other masters. As she was the only one in her track, she studied Strategy and Linguistics along with Irjah's apprentices. She found to her dismay that though she hadn't pledged Medicine, second-years still had to suffer a mandatory emergency triage class under Enro. History had been replaced with Foreign Relations under Master Yim. Jun still wouldn't allow her to train under him, but she was eligible to study weapons-based combat with Sonnen.

Finally her morning classes ended, and Rin was left with half the day to spend with Jiang. She ran up the steps toward the Lore garden. Time to meet with her master. Time to get answers.

"Describe to me what we are studying," said Jiang. "What is Lore?"

Rin blinked. She'd rather been hoping that he would tell her.

Rin had tried many times over the break to rationalize to herself why she'd chosen to study Lore, only to find herself uttering vague, circular truisms.

It came down to an intuition. A truth she knew for herself but couldn't prove to anyone else. She was studying Lore because she knew Jiang had tapped into some other source of power, something real and mystifying. Because she had tapped into that same source the day of the Tournament. Because she had been consumed by fire, had seen the world turned red, had lost control of herself and been saved by the man whom everyone else at the school deemed insane.

She had seen the other side of the veil, and now her curiosity was so great she would go mad unless she understood what had happened.

That didn't mean she had the faintest inkling of what she was doing.

"Weird things," she said. "We're studying very weird things."

Jiang raised an eyebrow. "How articulate."

"I don't know," she said. "I'm just here because I wanted to study with you. Because of what happened during the Trials. I don't actually know what I'm getting into."

"Oh, you do." Jiang lifted his index finger and touched the tip to a spot on her forehead precisely between her eyes, the spot from which he'd stilled the fire inside her. "Deep in your subconscious mind, you know the truth of things."

"I wanted to—"

"You want to know what happened to you during the Tournament." Jiang cocked his head to the side. "Here is what happened: you called a god, and the god answered."

Rin made a face. Again with the gods? She had been hoping for answers throughout the entire break, had thought that Jiang might make things clear once she returned, but she was now more confused than ever.

Jiang lifted a hand before she could protest. "You don't know what any of this means yet. You don't know if you'll ever replicate what happened in the ring. But you do know that if you don't get answers now, the hunger will consume you and your mind will crack. You've glimpsed the other side and you can't rest until you fill in the blanks. Yes?"

"Yes."

"What happened to you was common in the era before the Red Emperor, back when Nikara shamans didn't know what they were doing. If this had continued, you would have gone mad. But I am here to make sure that doesn't happen. I'm going to keep you sane."

Rin wondered how someone who regularly strolled through campus without clothes on could say that with a straight face.

And she wondered what it said about her that she trusted him.

* * *

Understanding came, like all things with Jiang, in infuriatingly small increments. As Rin had learned before the Trials, Jiang's preferred method of instruction was to do first and explain later, if ever. She learned early on that if she asked the wrong question, she wouldn't get the answer she wanted. "The fact that you're asking," Jiang would say, "is evidence that you're not ready to know."

She learned to shut up and simply follow his lead.

He carefully laid out a foundation for her, though at first his demands seemed menial and pointless. He made her transcribe her history textbook into Old Nikara and back. He made her spend a chilly fall afternoon squatting over the stream catching minnows with her bare hands. He demanded she complete all assignments for every class using her nondominant left hand, so that her essays took twice as long to finish and looked like a child had written them. He made her live by twenty-five-hour days for an entire month. He made her go nocturnal for an entire two weeks, so that all she ever saw was the night sky and an eerily quiet Sinegard, and he was wholly unsympathetic when she complained about missing her other classes. He made her see how long she could go without sleeping. He made her see how long she could go without waking up.

She swallowed her skepticism, took a leap of faith, and chose to follow his instructions, hoping that enlightenment might be on the other side. Yet she did not leap blindly, because she knew what was at the other end. Daily, she saw the proof of enlightenment before her.

Because Jiang did things that no human should be able to do.

The first time, he made the leaves at his feet spin without moving a muscle.

She thought it was a trick of the wind.

And then he did it again, and then a third time, just to prove he had utter control over it.

"Shit," she said, and then repeated, "Shit. Shit. Shit. How. How?"

"Easily," he said.

She gaped at him. "This is—this isn't martial arts, it's . . ."

"It's what?" he pressed.

"It's supernatural."

He looked smug. "Supernatural is a word for anything that doesn't fit your present understanding of the world. I need you to suspend your disbelief. I need you to simply accept that these things are possible."

"I'm supposed to take it as true that you're a *god*?"

"Don't be silly. I am not a god," he said. "I am a mortal who has woken up, and there is power in awareness."

He made the wind howl at his command. He made trees rustle by pointing at them. He made water ripple without touching it, and could cause shadows to twist and screech with a whispered word.

She realized that Jiang showed her these things because she would not have believed them if he'd merely told her they were possible. He was building up a background of possibilities for her, a web of new concepts. How did you explain to a child the idea of gravity, until they knew what it meant to fall?

Some truths could be learned through memorization, like history textbooks or grammar lessons. Some had to be ingrained slowly, had to become true because they were an inevitable part of the pattern of all things.

Power dictates acceptability, Kitay had once told her. Did the same apply to the fabric of the natural world?

Jiang reconfigured Rin's perception of what was real. Through demonstrations of impossible acts, he recalibrated the way she approached the material universe.

It was easier because she was so willing to believe. She fit these challenges to her conceptions of reality into her mind without too much trauma from adjustment. The traumatic event had already occurred. She had felt herself consumed by fire. She had known what it meant to burn. She hadn't imagined it. It had happened.

She learned to resist denying what Jiang showed her because it didn't square with her previous notions of how things worked. She learned to stop being shocked.

Her experience during the Tournament had torn a great, jagged hole through her understanding of the world, and she waited for Jiang to fill it in for her.

Sometimes, if she bordered on asking the right question, he sent her to the library to find the answer herself.

When she asked him where Lore had been practiced before, he sent her on a wild goose chase after all that was odd and cryptic. He made her read texts on the ancient dream walkers of the southern islands and their plant spirit healing practices. He made her write detailed reports about village shamans of the Hinterlands to the north, about how they fell into trances and journeyed as spirits in the bodies of eagles. He had her pore over decades of testimony from southern Nikara villagers who claimed to be clairvoyant.

"How would you describe all of these people?" he inquired.

"Oddities. People with abilities, or people who were pretending to have abilities." Other than that, Rin saw no way that these groups of people were linked. "How would you describe them?"

"I would call them shamans," he said. "Those who commune with the gods."

When she asked him what he meant by the gods, he made her study religion. Not just Nikara religion—all religions of the world, every religion that had been practiced since the dawn of time.

"What does anyone mean by gods?" he asked. "Why do we have gods? What purpose does a god serve in a society? Vex these issues. Find these answers for me."

In a week, she produced what she thought was a brilliant report on the difference between Nikara and Hesperian religious traditions. She proudly recounted her conclusions to Jiang in the Lore garden.

The Hesperians had only one church. They believed in one divine entity: a Holy Maker, separate from and above all mortal affairs, wrought in the image of a man. Rin argued that this god, this Maker, was a means by which Hesperia's government maintained order. The priests of the Order of the Holy Maker held no political office but exerted more cultural control than the Hesperian central government did. Since Hesperia was a large country without warlords who had absolute power over each of its states, rule of law had to be enforced by propagation of the myth of moral codes.

The Empire, in contrast, was a country of what Rin labeled superstitious atheists. Of course, Nikan had its gods in abundance. But like the Fangs, the majority of Nikara were religious only when it suited them. The Empire's wandering monks constituted a small minority of the population, mere curators of the past, rather than part of any institution with real power.

Gods in Nikan were the heroes of myths, tokens of culture, icons to be acknowledged during important life events like weddings, births, or deaths. They were personifications of emotions that the Nikara themselves felt. But no one actually believed that you would have bad luck for the rest of the year if you forgot to light incense to the Azure Dragon. No one really thought that you could keep your loved ones safe by praying to the Great Tortoise.

The Nikara practiced these rituals regardless, went through the motions because there was comfort in doing so, because it was a way for them to express their anxieties about the ebbs and flows of their fortunes.

"And so religion is merely a social construct in both the east and west," Rin concluded. "The difference lies in its utility."

Jiang had been listening attentively throughout her presentation. When she finished, he blew air out of his cheeks like a child and rubbed at his temples. "So you think Nikara religion is simply superstition?"

"Nikara religion is too haphazard to hold any degree of truth," Rin said. "You have the four cardinal gods—the Dragon, the Tiger, the Tortoise, and the Phoenix. Then you have local household gods, village guardian gods, animal gods, gods of rivers, gods of mountains . . ." She counted them off on her fingers.

"How could all of them exist in the same space? How could the spiritual realm be, with all these gods vying for dominance? The best explanation is that when we say 'god' in Nikan, we mean a story. Nothing more."

"So you have no faith in the gods?" Jiang asked.

"I believe in the gods as much as the next Nikara does," she replied. "I believe in gods as a cultural reference. As metaphors. As things we refer to keep us safe because we can't do anything else, as manifestations of our neuroses. But not as things that I truly trust are real. Not as things that hold actual consequence for the universe."

She said this with a straight face, but she was exaggerating.

Because she knew that something was real. She knew that on some level, there was more to the cosmos than what she encountered in the material world. She was not truly such a skeptic as she pretended to be.

But the best way to get Jiang to explain anything was by taking radical positions, because when she argued from the extremes, he made his best arguments in response.

He hadn't yet taken the bait, so she continued: "If there is a divine creator, some ultimate moral authority, then why do bad things happen to good people? And why would this deity create people at all, since people are such imperfect beings?"

"But if nothing is divine, why do we ascribe godlike status to mythological figures?" Jiang countered. "Why bow to the Great Tortoise? The Snail Goddess Nüwa? Why burn incense to the heavenly pantheon? Believing in any religion involves sacrifice. Why would any poor, penniless Nikara farmer knowingly make sacrifices to entities he knew were just myths? Who does that benefit? How did these practices originate?"

"I don't know," admitted Rin.

"Then find out. Find out the nature of the cosmos."

Rin thought it was somewhat unreasonable to ask her to puzzle out what philosophers and theologians had been trying to answer for millennia, but she returned to the library.

And came back with more questions still. "But how does the existence or nonexistence of the gods affect me? Why does it matter how the universe came to be?"

"Because you're part of it. Because you exist. And unless you want to only ever be a tiny modicum of existence that doesn't understand its relation to the grander web of things, you will explore."

"Why should I?"

"Because I know you want power." He tapped her forehead again. "But how can you borrow power from the gods when you don't understand what they are?"

Under Jiang's orders, Rin spent more time in the library than most fifth-year apprentices. He assigned her to write essays on a daily basis, the prompt always derived from a topic they had arrived at after hours of conversation. He made her draw connections between texts of different disciplines, texts that were written centuries apart, and texts written in different languages.

"How do Seejin's theories of transmitting *ki* through human air passages relate to the Speerly practice of inhaling the ash of the deceased?"

"How has the roster of Nikara gods changed over time, and how did this reflect the eminence of different Warlords at different points in history?"

"When did the Federation begin worshipping their sovereign as a divine entity, and why?"

"How does the doctrine of separation of church and state affect Hesperian politics? Why is this doctrine ironic?"

He tore apart her mind and pieced it back together, decided he didn't like the order, tore it apart again. He strained her mental capacity just as Irjah did. But Irjah stretched Rin's mind within known parameters. His assignments simply made Rin more nimble within the spaces she was already familiar with. Jiang forced her mind to expand outward into entirely new dimensions.

He did, in essence, the mental equivalent of making her carry a pig up a mountain.

She obeyed on every count, and wondered what alternative worldview he was trying to make her piece together. She wondered what he was trying to teach her, other than that none of her notions of how the world worked were true.

Meditation was the worst.

Jiang announced in the third month of the term that henceforth Rin would spend an hour each day meditating with him. Rin half hoped he would forget this stipulation, the same way he occasionally forgot what year it was, or what his name was.

But of all the rules Jiang imposed on her, he chose this one to observe faithfully.

"You will sit still for one hour, every morning, in the garden, without exception."

She did. She hated it.

"Press your tongue against the roof of your mouth. Feel your spine elongate. Feel the spaces between your vertebrae. *Wake up!*"

Rin inhaled sharply and jerked out of her slump. Jiang's voice, always so quiet and soothing, had been putting her to sleep.

The spot above her left eyebrow twitched. She fidgeted. Jiang would scold her if she scratched it. She raised her brow as high as it could go instead. The itching intensified.

"Sit still," Jiang said.

"My back hurts," Rin complained.

"That's because you're not sitting up straight."

"I think it's cramped from sparring."

"I think you're full of shit."

Five minutes passed in silence. Rin twisted her back to one side, then the other. Something popped. She winced.

She was painfully bored. She counted her teeth with her tongue. She counted again starting from the opposite direction. She shifted her weight from one butt cheek to the other. She felt an intense urge to get up, move, jump around, anything.

She peeked one eye open and found Master Jiang staring directly back at her.

"Sit. *Still*."

She swallowed her protest and obeyed.

Meditation felt like a massive waste of time to Rin, who was used to years of stress and constant studying. It felt wrong to be sitting so still, to have nothing occupying her mind. She could barely stand three minutes of this torture, let alone sixty. She was so terrified of the thought of not thinking that she wasn't able to accomplish it because she kept thinking about not thinking.

Jiang, on the other hand, could meditate indefinitely. He became like a statue, serene and tranquil. He seemed like air, like he might fade away if she didn't concentrate enough on him. He seemed like he'd simply left his body behind and gone somewhere else.

A fly settled on her nose. Rin sneezed violently.

"Start the time over," Jiang said placidly.

"Damn it!"

When spring returned to Sinegard, when the weather was warm enough that Rin could stop bundling up in her thick winter robes, Jiang took her on a hiking trip into the nearby Wudang mountain range. They walked for two hours in silence, until noon, when Jiang chose to stop at a sunny alcove that overlooked the entire valley below.

"The subject of today's lesson will be plants." He sat down, pulled off his satchel, and emptied the contents onto the grass. Out spilled an assortment of plants and powders, the severed arm of a cactus, several bright red poppy flowers with pods still attached, and a handful of sun-dried mushrooms.

"Are we getting high?" Rin said. "Oh, wow. We're getting high, aren't we?"

"*I'm* getting high," said Jiang. "You're watching."

He lectured as he crushed the poppy seeds in a small stone bowl with a pestle. "None of these plants are native to Sinegard. These mushrooms were cultivated in the forests of the Hare Province. You won't find them anywhere else; they do well only in tropical climates. This cactus grows best in the Baghra Desert between our northern border and the Hinterlands. This powder is derived from a bush found only in the rain forests of the southern hemisphere. The bush grows small orange fruit that are tasteless and sticky. But the drug is made from the dried, shredded root of the plant."

"And possession of all of these in Sinegard is a capital offense," Rin said, because she felt one of them might as well mention that.

"Ah. The law." Jiang sniffed at an unidentified leaf and then tossed it away. "So inconvenient. So irrelevant." He looked suddenly at her. "Why does Nikan frown upon drug use?"

He did this often: hurled questions at her that she hadn't prepared answers to. If she spoke too quickly or made a hasty generalization, he challenged it, backed her up into an argumentative corner until she spelled out exactly what she meant and justified it rigorously.

Rin had enough practice by now to reason carefully before uttering a response. "Because use of psychedelics is associated with blown minds, wasted potential, and social chaos. Because drug addicts can give very little to society. Because it is an ongoing plague on our country left by the dear Federation."

Jiang nodded slowly. "Well put. Do you agree?"

Rin shrugged. She had seen enough of the opium dens of Tikany to know the effects of addiction. She understood why the laws were so harsh. "I agree now," she said carefully. "But I suppose I'll change my mind after you've had your say."

Jiang's mouth quirked into a lopsided grin. "It is the nature of all things to have a dual purpose," he said. "You've seen what poppy does to the common man. And given what you know of addiction, your conclusions are reasonable. Opium makes wise men stupid. It destroys local economies and weakens entire countries."

He weighed another handful of poppy seeds in his palm. "But something so destructive inherently and simultaneously has marvelous potential. The poppy flower, more than anything, displays the duality of hallucinogens. You know poppy by three names. In its most common form, as opium nuggets smoked from a pipe, poppy makes you useless. It numbs you and closes you off to the world. Then there is the madly addictive heroin, which is extracted as a powder from the sap of the flower. But the seeds? These seeds are a shaman's dream. These seeds, used with the proper mental preparation, give you access to the entire universe contained within your mind."

He put the poppy seeds down and gestured to the array of psychedelics before him. "Shamans across continents have used plants to alter their states of consciousness for centuries. The medicine men of the Hinterlands used this flower to fly upward like an arrow to enter into communion with the gods. This one will put you into a trance where you might enter the Pantheon."

Rin's eyes widened. Here it was. Slowly the lines began to connect. She was finally beginning to understand the purpose of the last six months of research and meditation. So far she had been pursuing two separate lines of inquiry—the shamans and their abilities; the gods and the nature of the universe.

Now, with the introduction of psychedelic plants, Jiang drew these threads into one unified theory, a theory of spiritual connection through psychedelics to the dream world where the gods might reside.

The separate concepts in her mind flung connections at one another, like a web suddenly grown overnight. The formative background Jiang had been laying suddenly made total, utter sense.

She had an outline, but the picture hadn't fully developed. Something didn't square.

"Contained within my mind?" Rin repeated carefully.

Jiang glanced sideways at her. "Do you know what the word *entheogen* means?"

She shook her head.

"It means the generation of the god within," he said. He reached out and tapped her forehead in that same place. "The merging of god and person."

"But we aren't gods," she said. She had spent the past week in the library trying to trace Nikara theology to its roots. Nikara religious mythology was full of encounters between the mortal and divine, but nowhere in her research had anyone mentioned anything about god-creation. "Shamans communicate with gods. They don't create gods."

"What's the difference between a god within and a god outside? What is the difference between the universe contained in your mind and the universe external?" Jiang tapped both of her temples. "Wasn't that the basis of your criticism of Hesperia's theological hierarchy? That the idea of a divine creator separate from us and ruling over us made no sense?"

"Yes, but . . ." She trailed off, trying to make sense of what she wanted to say. "I didn't mean that we are gods, I meant that . . ." She wasn't sure what she meant. She looked at Jiang in supplication.

For once, he gave her the easy answer. "You must conflate these concepts. The god outside you. The god within. Once you understand that these are one and the same, once you can hold both concepts in your head and know them to be true, you'll be a shaman."

"But it can't be so simple," Rin stammered. Her mind was still reeling. She struggled to formulate her thoughts. "If this is . . . then . . . then why doesn't everyone do this? Why doesn't anyone in the opium houses stumble upon the gods?"

"Because they don't know what they're looking for. The Nikara don't believe in their deities, remember?"

"Fine," Rin said, refusing to rise to the bait of having her own words thrown in her face. "But why not?" She had thought the Nikara religious skepticism was reasonable, but not when people like Jiang could do the things they did. "Why aren't there more believers?"

"Once there were," Jiang said, and she was surprised at how bitter he sounded. "Once there were monasteries upon monasteries. Then the Red Emperor in his quest for unification came and burned them down. Shamans lost their power. The monks—the ones with real power, anyhow—died or disappeared."

"Where are they now?"

"Hidden," he said. "Forgotten. In recent history, only the nomadic clans of the Hinterlands and the tribes of Speer had anyone who could commune with the gods. This is no coincidence. The national quest to modernize and mobilize entails a faith in one's ability to control world order, and when that happens, you lose your connection with the gods. When man begins to think that he is responsible for writing the script of the world, he forgets the forces that dream up our reality. Once, this academy was a monastery. Now it is a military training ground. You'll find this same pattern has repeated itself in all the great powers of this world that have entered a so-called civilized age. Mugen doesn't have shamans. Hesperia doesn't have shamans. They worship men whom they believe are gods, not gods themselves."

"What about Nikara superstition?" Rin asked. "I mean—in Sinegard, obviously, where people are educated, religion's defunct, but what about the little villages? What about folk religion?"

"The Nikara believe in icons, not gods," said Jiang. "They don't understand what they're worshipping. They've prioritized ritual over theology. Sixty-four gods of equal standing? How convenient, and how absurd. Religion cannot be packaged so cleanly. The gods are not so neatly organized."

"But I don't understand," she said. "Why have the shamans disappeared? Wouldn't the Red Emperor be all the more powerful for having shamans in his army?"

"No. In fact, the opposite is true. The creation of empire requires conformity and uniform obedience. It requires teachings that can be mass-produced across the entire country. The Militia is a bureaucratic entity that is purely interested in results. What I teach is impossible to duplicate to a class of fifty, much less a division of thousands. The Militia is composed almost entirely of people like Jun, who think that things matter only if they are getting results *immediately*, results that can be duplicated and reused. But shamanism is and always has been an imprecise art. How could it be anything else? It is about the most fundamental truths about each and every one of us, how we relate to the phenomenon of existence. Of course it is imprecise. If we understood it completely, then we would be gods."

Rin was unconvinced. "But surely *some* teachings could be spread."

"You overestimate the Empire. Think of martial arts. Why were you able to defeat your classmates in the trial? Because they learned a version that is watered down, distilled and packaged for convenience. The same is true of their religion."

"But they can't have forgotten completely," Rin said. "This class still exists."

"This class is a joke," said Jiang.

"I don't think it's a joke."

"You, and no one else," said Jiang. "Even Jima doubts the value of this course, but she can't bring herself to abolish it. On some level, Nikara has never given up hope that it can find its shamans again."

"But it has them," she said. "I'll bring shamanism back to this world."

She glanced hopefully toward him, but Jiang sat frozen, staring over the edge of the cliff as if his mind were somewhere far away. He looked very sad then.

"The age of the gods is over," he said finally. "The Nikara may speak of shamans in their legends, but they cannot abide the prospect of the supernatural. To them, we are madmen." He swallowed. "We are not madmen. But how can we convince anyone of this, when the rest of the world believes it so? Once an empire has become convinced of its worldview, anything that evidences the contrary must be erased. The Hinterlanders were banished to the north, cursed and suspected of witchcraft. The Speerlies were marginalized, enslaved, thrown into battle like wild dogs, and ultimately sacrificed."

"Then we'll teach them," she said. "We'll make them remember."

"No one else would have the patience to learn what I have taught you. It's merely our job to remember. I have searched for years for an apprentice, and only you have ever understood the truth of the world."

Rin felt a pang of disappointment at those words; not for herself but for the Empire. It was difficult to know that she lived in a world where humans had once freely spoken to the gods but no longer did.

How could an entire nation simply forget about gods that might grant unimaginable power?

Easily, that's how.

The world was simpler when all that existed was what you could perceive in front of you. Easier to forget the underlying forces that constructed the dream. Easier to believe that reality existed only on one plane. Rin had believed that up until this very moment, and her mind still struggled to readjust.

But she knew the truth now, and that gave her power.

Rin stared silently out over the valley below, still grappling to absorb the magnitude of what she had just learned. Meanwhile Jiang packed the powders into a pipe, lit it up, and took a long, deep draught.

His eyes fluttered closed. A serene smile spread over his face.

"Up we go," he said.

The thing about watching someone get high was that if you weren't getting high yourself, things got very boring very soon. Rin prodded Jiang after a few minutes, and when he didn't stir, she went back down the mountain by herself.

If Rin had thought Jiang might let her start using hallucinogens to meditate, she was wrong. He made her help out in the garden, had her watering the cacti and cultivating the mushrooms, but forbade her to try any plants until he gave her permission.

"Without the right mental preparation, psychedelics won't do anything for you," he said. "You'll just become terribly annoying for a while."

Rin had accepted this initially, but it had now been weeks. "When am I going to be mentally prepared, then?"

"When you can sit still for five minutes without opening your eyes," he said.

"I can sit still! I've been sitting still for nearly a year! That's all I've been doing!"

Jiang brandished his garden shears at her. "Don't take that tone with me."

She slammed her tray of cacti clippings on the shelf. "I know there are things you're not teaching me. I know you're keeping me behind on purpose. I just don't understand why."

"Because you worry me," said Jiang said. "You have an aptitude for Lore like no one I've ever met, not even Altan. But you're impatient. You're careless. And you skimp on meditating."

She *had* been skimping on meditating. She was supposed to keep a meditation log, to document each time she made it to the end of an hour successfully. But as coursework from her other classes piled up, Rin had neglected her daily requisite period of doing nothing.

"I don't see the point," she said. "If it's focus that you want, I can give you focus. I can concentrate on anything. But to empty my mind? To be devoid of all thought? All sense of self? What good does that serve?"

"It serves to sever you from the material world," Jiang answered. "How do you expect to reach the spirit realm when you're obsessing over the things in front of you? I know why it's hard for you. You like beating your classmates. You like harboring your old grudges. It feels good to hate, doesn't it? Up until now you've been storing your anger up and using it as fuel. But unless you learn to let it go, you are never going to find your way to the gods."

"So give me a psychedelic," she suggested. "*Make* me let it go."

"Now you're being rash. I'm not letting you meddle in things that you barely understand yet. It's too dangerous."

"How dangerous could it be to just sit still?"

Jiang stood up straight. The hand holding the shears dropped to his side. "This isn't some fairy story where you wave your hand and ask the gods for three wishes. We are not fucking around here. These are forces that could break you."

"Nothing's going to happen to me," she snapped. "Nothing's been happening to me for months. You keep going on about seeing the gods, but all that happens when I meditate is that I get bored, my nose itches, and every second takes an eternity."

She reached for the poppy flowers.

He slapped her hand away. "You're not ready. You're not even *close* to ready."

Rin flushed. "They're just *drugs*—"

"Just drugs? Just *drugs*?" Jiang's voice rose in pitch. "I'm going to issue you a warning. And I'm only going to do it once. You're not the first student to pledge Lore, you know. Oh, Sinegard's been trying to produce a shaman for years. But you want to know why no one takes this class seriously?"

"Because you keep farting in faculty meetings?"

He didn't even laugh at that, which meant this was more serious than she'd thought.

Jiang, in fact, looked pained.

"We've tried," he said. "Ten years ago. I had four students just as brilliant as you, without Altan's rage or your impatience. I taught them to meditate, I taught them about the Pantheon, but those apprentices only had one thing on their minds, which was to call on the gods and siphon their power. Do you know what happened to them?"

"They called the gods and became great warriors?" Rin said hopefully.

Jiang fixed her with his pale, suffocating gaze. "They all went mad. Every single one. Two were calm enough to be locked in an asylum for the rest of their lives. The other two were a danger to themselves and others around them. The Empress had them sent to Baghra."

She stared at him. She had no idea what to say to that.

"I have met spirits unable to find their bodies again," said

Jiang. He looked very old then. "I have met men who are only halfway to the spirit realm, caught between our world and the next. What does that mean? It means don't. Fuck. Around." He tapped her forehead with each word. "If you don't want that brilliant little mind of yours to shatter, you'll do as I say."

The only time Rin felt fully grounded was during her other classes. These were proceeding at twice the rate as they had her first year, and though Rin barely managed to keep up given the absurd course load Jiang had already assigned her, it was nice to study things that made sense for a change.

Rin had always felt like an outsider among her classmates, but as the year carried on, she began to feel as if she inhabited an entirely separate world from them. She was steadily growing further and further away from the world where things functioned as they should, where reality was not constantly in flux, where she thought she knew the shape and nature of things instead of being constantly reminded that really she knew nothing at all.

"Seriously," Kitay asked over lunch one day. "What are you learning?"

Kitay, like everyone else in her class, thought that Lore was a course in religious history, a smorgasbord of anthropology and folk mythology. She hadn't bothered to correct them. Easier to spread a believable lie than to convince them of the truth.

"That none of my beliefs about the world were true," Rin answered dreamily. "That reality is malleable. That hidden connections exist in every living object. That the whole of the world is merely a thought, a butterfly's dream."

"Rin?"

"Yes?"

"Your elbow is in my porridge."

She blinked. "Oh. Sorry."

Kitay slid his bowl farther away from her arm. "They talk about you, you know. The other apprentices."

Rin folded her arms. "And what do they say?"

He paused. "You can probably catch the drift. It's not, uh, good."

Had she expected anything else? She rolled her eyes. "They don't like me. Big surprise."

"It's not that," Kitay said. "They're *scared* of you."

"Because I won the Tournament?"

"Because you stormed in here from a rural township no one's ever heard of, then threw away one of the school's most prestigious bids to study with the academy madman. They can't figure you out. They don't know what you're trying to do." Kitay cocked his head at her. "What *are* you trying to do?"

She hesitated. She knew that look on Kitay's face. He'd been wearing it more often of late, as her own studies grew more and more distant from topics that she could easily explain to a layman. Kitay hated not having full access to information, and she hated keeping things from him. But how was she supposed to articulate the point of studying Lore to him, when often she could barely justify it to herself?

"Something happened to me that day in the ring," she said finally. "I'm trying to figure out what."

She'd braced herself to deal with Kitay's clinical skepticism, but he only nodded. "And you think Jiang has the answers?"

She exhaled. "If he doesn't, nobody does."

"You've heard the rumors, though—"

"The madmen. The dropouts. The prisoners at Baghra," she said. Everyone had their own horror story about Jiang's previous apprentices. "I know. Trust me, I know."

Kitay gave her a long, searching look. Finally he nodded toward her untouched bowl of porridge. She'd been cramming for one of Jima's exams; she'd forgotten to eat.

"Just take care of yourself," he said.

Second-years were granted eligibility to fight in the ring.

Now that Altan had graduated, the star of the matches turned out to be Nezha, who was rapidly becoming an even more formidable fighter under Jun's brutal training. Within a month he was challenging students two or three years his senior; by their second spring he was the undefeated champion of the rings.

Rin had been eager to enter the matches, but one conversation with Jiang had put an end to her aspirations.

"You don't fight," he said one day as they were balancing on posts above the stream.

She immediately splashed into the water.

"*What?*" she sputtered once she climbed out.

"The matches are only for apprentices whose masters have consented."

"Then consent!"

Jiang dipped a toe into the water and pulled it back out gingerly. "Nah."

"But I *want* to fight!"

"Interesting, but irrelevant."

"But—"

"No buts. I'm your master. You don't question my orders, you obey them."

"I'll obey orders that make sense to me," she retorted as she teetered wildly on a post.

Jiang snorted. "The matches aren't about winning, they're about demonstrating new techniques. What are you going to do, light up in front of the entire student body?"

She didn't push the point further.

Aside from the matches, which Rin attended regularly, she rarely saw her roommates; Niang was always working overtime with Enro, and Venka spent her waking hours either on patrol with the City Guard or training with Nezha.

Kitay began studying with her in the women's dormitory, but only because it was the one place on campus always guaranteed to be empty. The newest class of first-years had no women, and Kureel and Arda had left the Academy at the end of Rin's first year. Both had been offered prestigious positions as junior officers, in the Third and Eighth Divisions respectively.

Altan, too, was gone. But no one knew which division he had joined. Rin had expected it to be the talk of campus. But Altan had vanished as if he'd never been at Sinegard. The legend of Altan Trengsin had already begun to fade within their class, and when the next group of first-years came to Sinegard, none of them even knew who Altan was.

As the months passed, Rin found that one unexpected benefit of being the only apprentice who had pledged Lore was that she was no longer in direct competition with the rest of her classmates.

By no means did they become friendly. But Rin stopped hearing jokes about her accent, Venka stopped wrinkling her nose every time they were both in the women's dormitory, and one by one the other Sinegardians grew accustomed to, if not enthusiastic about, her presence.

Nezha was the sole exception.

They shared every class except Combat and Lore. They each did their best to utterly ignore the other's existence. Many of their advanced classes were so small that this often became incredibly awkward, but Rin supposed cold disengagement was better than active bullying.

Still, she paid attention to Nezha. How could she not? He was clearly the star of the class—inferior to Kitay perhaps in only Strategy and Linguistics, but otherwise Nezha had essentially become the new Altan of the school. The masters adored him; the incoming class of pupils thought he was a god.

"He's not that special," she grumbled to Kitay. "He didn't even win his year's Tournament. Do any of them know that?"

"Sure they do." Kitay, not looking up from his language homework, spoke with the patient exasperation of someone who'd had this conversation many times before.

"Then why don't they worship *me*?" Rin complained.

"Because you don't fight in the ring." Kitay filled in a final blank on his chart of Hesperian verb conjugations. "And also because you're weird and not as pretty."

In general, however, the childish infighting within their class had disappeared. It was partly because they were simply getting older, partly because the stress of the Trials had disappeared—apprentices were secure in their enrollment so long as they kept their grades up—and partly because their coursework had gotten so difficult they couldn't be bothered with petty rivalries.

But near the end of their second year, the class began to split again—this time along provincial and political lines.

The proximate cause was a diplomatic crisis with Federation troops on the border of Horse Province. An outpost brawl between Mugenese traders and Nikara laborers had turned deadly. The Mugenese had sent in armed policemen to kill the instigators. The border patrol of the Horse Province responded in kind.

Master Irjah was summoned immediately to the Empress's diplomatic party, which meant Strategy was canceled for two weeks. The students didn't know that, though, until they found the hastily scrawled note Irjah had left behind.

"'Don't know when I'll be back. Open fire from both sides. Four civilians dead.'" Niang read Irjah's note aloud. "Gods. That's war, isn't it?"

"Not necessarily." Kitay was the only one who seemed utterly calm. "There are skirmishes all the time."

"But there were casualties—"

"There are always casualties," said Kitay. "This has been going on for nearly two decades. We hate them, they hate us, a handful of people die because of it."

"Nikara citizens are dead!" Niang exclaimed.

"Sure, but the Empress isn't going to do anything about it."

"There's nothing she *can* do," Han interrupted. "Horse Province doesn't have enough troops to hold a front—our population's too small, there's no one to recruit from. The real problem is that some Warlords don't know how to put national interest first."

"You don't know what you're talking about," Nezha said.

"What I know is that my father's men are dying on the border," said Han. The sudden venom in his voice surprised Rin. "Meanwhile, your father's sitting pretty in his little palace, turning a blind eye because he's kept nice and safe between two buffer provinces."

Before anyone could move, Nezha's hand shot toward the back of Han's neck and slammed his face into the desk.

The classroom fell silent.

Han looked up, too stunned to retaliate. His nose had broken with an audible crack; blood streamed freely down his chin.

Nezha released Han's neck. "Shut up about my father."

Han spat out something that looked like a fragment of a tooth. "Your father's a fucking coward."

"I said *shut up*—"

"You have the biggest surplus of troops in the Empire and you won't deploy them," Han said. "Why, Nezha? Planning to use them for something else?"

Nezha's eyes flashed. "You want me to break your neck?"

"The Mugenese aren't going to invade," Kitay interrupted quickly. "They'll make noise on the Horse Province border, sure, but they won't commit ground troops. They don't want to make Hesperia angry—"

"The Hesperians don't give a shit," said Han. "They haven't bothered with the eastern hemisphere for years. No ambassadors, no diplomats—"

"Because of the armistice," Kitay said. "They think they don't need to. But if the Federation tips the balance, they'll have to intervene. And Mugen's leadership knows that."

"They also know we have no coordinated frontier defense and no navy," Han snapped. "Don't be delusional."

"A ground invasion is not rational for them," Kitay insisted. "The armistice benefits them. They don't want to bleed thousands of men in the Empire's heartland. There will be no war."

"Sure." Han crossed his arms. "What are we training for, then?"

The second crisis came two months later. Several border cities in Horse Province had begun to boycott Mugenese goods. The Mugenese governor-generals responded by methodically closing, looting, then burning down any Nikara businesses located on the Mugenese side of the border.

When the news broke, Han abruptly departed the Academy to join his father's battalion. Jima threatened permanent expulsion if he left without permission; Han responded by tossing his armband onto her desk.

The third crisis was the death of the Federation's emperor. Nikara spies reported that the crown prince Ryohai was lined up to succeed to the throne, news that deeply unsettled every master at the academy. Prince Ryohai—young, hotheaded, and violently nationalist—was a leading member of Mugen's war party.

"He's been calling for a ground invasion for years," Irjah explained to the class. "Now he has his chance to actually do it."

The next six weeks were terribly tense. Even Kitay had stopped arguing that Mugen would do nothing. Several students, most from the outer north, put in requests for a home leave. They were denied without exception. A few left regardless, but most obeyed Jima's command—if it came down to a war, then some affiliation with Sinegard was better than none.

The new Emperor Ryohai did not declare a ground invasion. The Empress sent a diplomatic party to the longbow island, and by all accounts was politely received by Mugen's new administration. The crisis passed. But a cloud of anxiety hung over the academy still—and nothing could not erase the growing fear that their class might be the first to graduate into a war.

The one person seemingly uninterested in news of Federation politics was Jiang. If asked about Mugen, he grimaced and waved the subject away; if pressed, he squeezed his eyes shut, shook his head, and sang out loud like a little child.

"But you *fought* the Federation!" Rin exclaimed. "How can you not care?"

"I don't remember that," Jiang said.

"How can you not remember that?" she demanded. "You were in the Second Poppy War—all of you were!"

"That's what they tell me," Jiang said.

"So then—"

"So I don't remember," Jiang said loudly, and his voice took on a fragile, tremulous tone that made Rin realize she had better drop the subject or risk sending him on a weeklong spell of absence or erratic behavior.

But as long as she didn't bring up the Federation, Jiang continued to conduct their lessons in the same meandering, lackadaisical manner. It had taken Rin until the end of her first year of apprenticeship to learn to meditate for an hour without moving; once she could do that, Jiang had demanded that she meditate for five. This took her nearly another year. When she finally managed it, Jiang gave her a small opaque flask, the kind used to store sorghum wine, and instructed her to take it to the top of the mountain.

"There's a cave near the peak. You'll know it when you see it. Drink down that flask, then start meditating."

"What's in it?"

Jiang examined his fingernails. "Bits and things."

"For how long?"

"As long as it takes. Days. Weeks. Months. I can't tell you before you start."

Rin told her other masters that she would be absent from class for an indefinite period of time. By now they had resigned themselves to Jiang's nonsense; they waved her off and told her to try not to be gone for more than a year. She hoped they were joking.

Jiang did not accompany her to the top. He bade her farewell from the highest tier of the campus. "Here's a cloak in case you get cold. There's not much up there in terms of rain shelter. I'll see you on the other side."

It rained the entire morning. Rin hiked miserably, wiping mud off her shoes every few steps. When she reached the cave, she was shivering so hard that she almost dropped the flask.

She glanced around the muddy interior. She wanted to build a fire to warm herself, but couldn't find any material for kindling that wasn't soaked through. She huddled into the far end of the cave, as far away from the rain as she could get, and assumed a cross-legged stance. Then she closed her eyes.

She thought of the warrior Bodhidharma, meditating for years while listening to the ants scream. She suspected that the ants wouldn't be the only ones screaming when she was done.

The contents of the flask turned out to be a slightly bitter tea. She thought it might be a hallucinogen distilled in liquid, but hours passed and her mind was as clear as ever.

Night fell. She meditated in darkness.

At first it was horribly difficult.

She couldn't sit still. She was hungry after six hours. All she thought about was her stomach. But after a while the hunger was so overwhelming that she couldn't think about it anymore, because she couldn't remember a time when she hadn't been this hungry.

On the second day she felt dizzy. She was woozy with hunger, so starved that she couldn't feel her stomach. Did she even have a stomach? What was a stomach?

On the third day her head was delightfully light. She was just air, just breath, just a breathing organ. A fan. A flute. In, out, in, out, and on and on.

On the fifth day things moved too fast, too slow, or not at all. She felt infuriated by the slow passage of time. Her brain was racing in a way that wouldn't calm; she felt as if her heartbeat must now be faster than a hummingbird's. How had she not dissolved? How had she not vibrated into nothingness?

On the seventh day she tipped into the void. Her body became very still; so still that she forgot she had one. Her left finger itched and she was amazed at the sensation. She didn't scratch it, but observed the itch as if from the outside and marveled that after a very long time, it went away by itself.

She learned how breath moved through her body as if through an empty house. Learned how to stack her vertebrae one by one on top of each other so her spine formed a perfectly straight line, an unobstructed channel.

But her still body became heavy, and as it became heavy it became easier and easier to discard it, and to drift upward, weightless, into that place she could glimpse only from behind closed eyelids.

On the ninth day she suffered a geometric assault of lines and shapes without form or color, without regard to any aesthetic value except randomness.

You stupid shapes, she thought over and over again like a mantra. *You stupid fucking shapes.*

On the thirteenth day she had a horrible sensation of being trapped, as if buried within stone, as if covered in mud. She was so light, so weightless, but she had nowhere to go; she rebounded around inside this bizarre vessel called a body like a caught firefly.

On the fifteenth day she became convinced that her consciousness had expanded to encompass the totality of life on the planet—the germination of the smallest flower to the eventual death of the largest tree. She saw an endless process of energy transfer, growing and dying, and she was part of every stage of it.

She saw bursts of color and animals that probably didn't exist. She did not see visions, precisely, because visions would have been far more vivid and concrete. But nor were the apparitions merely thoughts. They were like dreams, an uncertain plane of realness somewhere in between, and it was only by washing out every other thought from her mind that she could perceive them clearly.

She stopped counting the days. She had traveled somewhere beyond time; a place where a year and a minute felt the same. What was the difference between finite and infinite? There was being and nonbeing and that was it. Time was not real.

The apparitions became solid. Either she was dreaming, or she had transcended somewhere, but when she took a step forward, her foot touched cold stone. She looked around and saw that she stood in a tiled room no larger than a washroom. There were no doors.

A form appeared before her, dressed in strange garb. At first she thought it was Altan, but the figure's face was softer, its crimson eyes rounder and kinder.

"They said you'd come," said the figure. The voice was a woman's, deep and sad. "The gods have known you'd come."

Rin was at a loss for words. Something about the Woman was deeply familiar, and it wasn't just her resemblance to Altan. The shape of her face, the clothes she wore . . . they sparked memories Rin didn't know she had, of sands and water and open skies.

"You will be asked to do what I refused to do," said the Woman. "You will be offered power beyond your imagination. But I warn you, little warrior. The price of power is pain. The Pantheon controls the fabric of the universe. To deviate from their premeditated order you must give them something in return. And for the gifts of the Phoenix, you will pay the most. The Phoenix wants suffering. The Phoenix wants blood."

"I have blood in abundance," Rin answered. She had no idea what possessed her to say it, but she continued. "I can give the Phoenix what it desires, if the Phoenix gives me power."

The Woman's tone grew agitated. "The Phoenix doesn't *give*. Not permanently. The Phoenix takes, and takes, and takes . . . Fire is insatiable, alone among the elements . . . it will devour you until you are nothing . . ."

"I'm not afraid of fire," said Rin.

"*You* should *be*," hissed the Woman. She glided slowly toward Rin; she didn't move her legs, didn't quite walk, but simply appeared larger and closer with every passing moment—

Rin couldn't breathe. She didn't feel the least bit calm; this was nothing like the peace she was supposed to have achieved, this was terrible . . . She suddenly heard a cacophony of screams echoing around her ears, and then the Woman was screaming and shrieking, writhing in the air like a tortured dancer, even as she reached out and seized Rin's arm . . .

. . . Images spun around Rin, brown-skinned bodies dancing around a campfire, mouths open in grotesque leers, shouting words in a language that sounded like something she'd heard in a dream she no longer remembered... The campfire flared and the bodies fell back, burned, charred, disintegrating to nothing but glistening white bones, and Rin thought that was the end of it—death ended things—but the bones jumped back up and continued to dance... One of the skeletons looked at her with its bare, toothy smile, and beckoned with a fleshless hand:

"From ashes we came and to ashes we return..."

The Woman's grip around Rin's shoulders tightened; she leaned forward and whispered fiercely in Rin's ear: "Go back."

But Rin was enticed by the fire... she looked past the bones into the flames, which were furling upward like something alive, taking the shape of a living god, an animal, a bird...

The bird lowered its head at them.

The Woman burst into flame.

Then Rin was floating upward again, flying like an arrow at the sky to the realm of the gods.

When she opened her eyes, Jiang was crouched in front of her, watching her intently with his pale eyes. "What did you see?"

She took a deep breath. Tried to orient herself to possessing a body again. She felt so clumsy and heavy, like a puppet formed badly out of wet clay.

"A great circular room," she said hesitantly, squinting to remember her final vision. She did not know if she was having trouble finding the words, or if it was simply her mouth that refused to obey. Every order she gave her body seemed to happen only after a delay. "It was arranged like a set of trigrams, but with thirty-two points splitting into sixty-four. And creatures on pedestals all around the circle."

"Plinths," Jiang corrected.

"You're right. Plinths."

"You saw the Pantheon," he said. "You found the gods."

"I suppose." Her voice trailed off. She felt somewhat confused. *Had* she found the gods? Or had she only imagined those sixty-four deities, spinning about her like glass beads?

"You seem skeptical," he said.

"I was tired," she answered. "I don't know if it was real, or . . . I mean, I could have just been dreaming." How were her visions any different from her imagination? Had she seen those things only because she wanted to?

"Dreaming?" Jiang tilted his head. "Have you ever seen anything like the Pantheon before? In a diagram? Or a painting?"

She frowned. "No, but—"

"The plinths. Were you expecting those?"

"No," she said, "but I've seen plinths before, and the Pantheon wouldn't have been too difficult to conjure from my imagination."

"But why that particular dream? Why would your sleeping mind have chosen to extract those images from your memory compared to any other images? Why not a horse, or a field of jasmine flowers, or Master Jun riding buck naked on the back of a tiger?"

Rin blinked. "Is that something you dream about?"

"Answer the question," he said.

"I don't know," she said, frustrated. "Why do people dream what they dream?"

But he was smiling, as if that was precisely what he'd wanted to hear. "Why indeed?"

She had no response to that. She stared blankly out at the mouth of the cave, mulling these thoughts in her mind, and realized that she had awoken in more ways than one.

Her map of the world, her understanding of reality, had shifted. She could see the outlines, even if she didn't know how to fill in the blanks. She knew the gods existed and that they spoke, and that was enough.

It had taken a long time, but she finally had a vocabulary for what they were learning now. Shamans: those who communed with the gods. The gods: forces of nature, entities as real and yet ephemeral as wind and fire themselves, things inherent to the existence of the universe.

When Hesperians wrote of "God," they wrote of the supernatural.

When Jiang talked of "gods," he talked of the eminently natural.

To commune with the gods was to walk the dream world, the world of spirit. It was to relinquish that which she was and become one with the fundamental state of things. The space in limbo where matter and actions were not yet determined, the fluctuating darkness where the physical world had not yet been dreamed into existence.

The gods were simply those beings that inhabited that space, forces of creation and destruction, love and hatred, nurturing and neglect, light and dark, cold and warm . . . they opposed one another and complemented one another; they were fundamental truths.

They were the elements that constituted the universe itself.

She saw now that reality was a facade; a dream conjured by the undulating forces beneath a thin surface. And by meditating, by ingesting the hallucinogen, by forgetting her connection to the material world, she was able to wake up.

"I understand the truth of things," she murmured. "I know what it means to exist."

He smiled. "It's wonderful, isn't it?"

She understood, then, that Jiang was very far from mad.

He might, in fact, be the sanest person she had ever met.

A thought occurred to her. "So what happens when we die?"

Jiang raised an eyebrow. "I think you can answer that."

She mulled over this for a moment. "We go back to the world of spirit. We—we leave the illusion. We wake up."

Jiang nodded. "We don't *die* so much as we return to the void. We dissolve. We lose our ego. We change from being just one thing to becoming everything. Most of us, at least."

She opened her mouth to ask what he meant by that, but Jiang reached out and poked her in the forehead. "How do you feel?"

"Incredible," she said. She felt more clearheaded than she had in months, as if all this time she'd been trying to peer through a fog and it had suddenly disappeared. She was ecstatic; she'd solved the puzzle, she knew the source of her power, and now all that remained was to learn to siphon it out at will. "So what now?"

"Now we've solved your problem," said Jiang. "Now you know how you are connected to a greater web of cosmological forces. Sometimes martial artists who are particularly attuned to the world will find themselves overwhelmed by one of those forces. They suffer an imbalance—an affinity to one god over the others. This happened to you in the ring. But now you know where that flame came from, and when it happens to you again, you can journey to the Pantheon to find its balance. Now you're cured."

Rin jerked her head toward her master.

Cured?

Cured?

Jiang looked pleased, relieved, and serene, but Rin only felt confused. She hadn't studied Lore so that she could still the flames. Yes, the fire had felt awful, but it had also felt powerful. *She* had felt *powerful*.

She wanted to learn to channel it, not to suppress it.

"Problem?" Jiang asked.

"I . . . I don't . . ." She bit down on her lip before the words tumbled out of her mouth. Jiang was violently averse to any discussion of warfare; if she kept asking about military use, then he might drop her again the way he had before the Trials. He already thought she was too impulsive, too reckless and impatient; she knew how easily she might scare him off.

Never mind. If Jiang wasn't going to teach her to call the power, then she'd figure it out for herself.

"So what's the point of this?" she asked. "Just to feel good?"

"The point? What point? You're enlightened. You have a better understanding of the cosmos than most theologians alive!" Jiang waved his hands around his head. "Do you have any idea what you can do with this knowledge? The Hinterlanders have been interpreting the future for years, reading the cracks in a tortoise shell to divine events to come. They can fix illnesses of the body by healing the spirit. They can speak to plants, cure diseases of the mind..."

Rin wondered why the Hinterlanders would achieve all of this and not militarize their abilities, but she held her tongue. "So how long will that take?"

"It makes no sense to speak of this in measurements of years," said Jiang. "The Hinterlanders don't allow interpretation of divinations until one has been training for at least five. Shamanic training is a process that lasts across your lifetime."

She couldn't accept that, though. She wanted power, and she wanted it now—especially if they were on the verge of a war with the Mugenese.

Jiang was watching her curiously.

Be careful, she reminded herself. She still had too much to learn from Jiang. She'd have to play along.

"Anything else?" he asked after a while.

She thought of the Speerly Woman's admonitions. She thought of the Phoenix, and of fire and pain.

"No," she said. "Nothing else."

PART II

CHAPTER 10

The *Emperor Ryohai* had now patrolled the eastern Nikara border in the Nariin Sea for twelve nights. The *Ryohai* was a lightly built ship, an elegant Federation model designed for slicing quickly through choppy waters. It carried few soldiers; its deck wasn't large enough to hold a battalion. It wasn't doing reconnaissance. No courier birds circled the flagless masthead; no spies left the ship under the cover of the ocean mist.

The only thing the *Ryohai* did was flit fretfully around the shoreline, pacing back and forth over still waters like an anxious housewife. Waiting for something. Someone.

The crew spent their days in silence. The *Ryohai* carried only a skeleton crew: the captain, a few deckhands, and a small contingent from the Federation Armed Forces. It bore one esteemed guest: General Gin Seiryu, grand marshal of the Armed Forces and esteemed adviser to Emperor Ryohai himself. And it bore one visitor, one Nikara who had lurked in the shadows of the hold since the *Ryohai* had crossed into the waters of the Nariin Sea.

Cike commander Tyr was good at being invisible. In this state, he did not need to eat or sleep. Absorbed in the shadow, shrouded in darkness, he hardly needed to breathe.

He found the passing days irksome only due to boredom, but he had maintained longer vigils than this one. He had waited a week in the bedroom closet of the Dragon Warlord. He had spent an entire month ensconced under the floorboards beneath the feet of the leaders of the Republic of Hesperia.

Now he waited for the men aboard the *Ryohai* to reveal their purpose.

Tyr had been surprised when he received orders from Sinegard to infiltrate a Federation ship. For years the Cike had operated only within the Empire, killing off dissidents the Empress found particularly troublesome. The Empress did not send the Cike overseas—not since her disastrous attempt to assassinate the young Emperor Ryohai, which had ended with two dead operatives and another driven so mad he had to be carted off, screaming, to a plinth in the stone prison.

But Tyr's duty was not to question but to obey. He crouched inside the shadow, unperceived by all. He waited.

It was a still, windless night. It was a night heavy with secrets.

It had been a night like this one, so many decades ago, when the moon was full and resplendent in the sky, that Tyr's master had first taken him deep into the underground tunnels where light would never touch. His master had guided him around one winding turn after another, spinning him about in the darkness so that he could not keep a map in his head of the underground labyrinth.

When they'd reached the heart of the spider's web, Tyr's master had abandoned him within. *Find your way out*, he had ordered Tyr. *If the goddess takes you, she will guide you. If she does not, you will perish.*

Tyr had never resented his master for leaving him in the darkness. Such was how things must be. Still, his fear had been real and urgent. He had lingered in the airless tunnels for days in a panic. First had come the thirst. Then the hunger. When he tripped over objects in the darkness, objects that clattered and echoed about him, he knew they were bones.

How many apprentices had been sent into the same underground maze? How many had emerged?

Only one in Tyr's generation. Tyr's shamanic line remained pure and strong through the proven ability of its successors, and only a survivor could be instilled with the gifts of the goddess to pass down to the next generation. The fact that Tyr was given this chance meant that every apprentice before him had tried and failed, and died.

Tyr had been so scared then.

He was not scared now.

Now, aboard the ship, the darkness took him once more, just as it had thirty years ago. Tyr was swathed in it, an unborn infant in his mother's womb. To pray to his goddess was to regress to that primordial state before infancy, when the world was quiet. Nothing could see him. Nothing could harm him.

The schooner made its way across the midnight sea, sailing skittishly, like a little child doing something that it shouldn't. The tiny boat wasn't a part of the Nikara fleet. All identifying marks had been clumsily chipped off its hull.

But it sailed from the direction of the Nikara shore. Either the schooner had taken a very long and convoluted route to meet with the *Ryohai* in order to fool an assassin that the *Ryohai* didn't know it had on board, or it was a Nikara vessel.

Tyr crouched behind the masthead, spyglass trained on the schooner's deck.

When he stepped out of the darkness, he experienced a sudden vertigo. This happened more and more often now, whenever he had waited in shadows for too long. It became harder to walk in the world of the material, to detach himself from his goddess.

Careful, he warned himself, *or you won't be able to come back.*

He knew what would happen then. He would become a spouting, unstoppable conduit for the gods, a gate to the spirit realm without a lock. He would be a foaming, useless, seizing vessel, and someone would cart him off to the Chuluu Korikh, where he couldn't do any harm. Someone would register his name in the Wheels and watch him sink into the stone prison the way he'd imprisoned so many of his own subordinates.

He remembered his first visit to the Chuluu Korikh, when he had immured his own master in the mountain. Stood before him, face-to-face, as the stone walls closed around his master's mien: Eyes closed. Sleeping but not dead.

The day would come soon when he would go mad if he left, and madder still if he didn't. But that was the fate that awaited the men and women of the Cike. To be an Empress's assassin meant early death or madness, or both.

Tyr had thought he might still have one or two more decades, as his master had before he'd relinquished the goddess to Tyr. He thought he still had a solid period of time to train an initiate and teach them to walk the void. But he was following his goddess's timeline, and he had no say in when she would ultimately call him back.

I should have chosen an apprentice. I should have chosen one of my people.

Five years ago he'd thought he might choose the Seer of the Cike, that thin child from the Hinterlands. But Chaghan was so frail and bizarre, even for his people. Chaghan would have commanded like a demon. He would have achieved utter obedience from his underlings, but only because he would have taken away their free will. Chaghan would have shattered minds.

Tyr's new lieutenant, the boy sent to him from the Academy, made a far better candidate. The boy was already slated to command the Cike when the time came that Tyr was no longer fit to lead.

But the boy already had a god of his own. And the gods were selfish.

The schooner halted under the *Ryohai*'s shadow. A solitary cloaked figure climbed into a rowboat and crossed the narrow distance between the two ships.

The *Ryohai*'s captain ordered ropes to be lowered. He and half the crew stood on the main deck, waiting for the Nikara contingent to come aboard.

Two deckhands helped the cloaked figure onto the deck.

She pulled the dark hood off her head and shook out a mass of long, shimmering hair. Hair like obsidian. Skin of a mineral whiteness that shone like the moon itself. Lips like freshly spilled blood.

The Empress Su Daji was on this ship.

Tyr was so surprised he nearly stumbled out of the shadows.

Why was she here? His first thought was absurdly petty—did she not trust him to take care of this on his own?

Something had to have gone wrong. Was she here of her own volition? Had the Federation compelled her to come?

Or had his own orders changed?

Tyr's mind raced frantically, wondering how to react. He could act now, kill the soldiers before they could hurt the Empress. But Daji knew he was here—she would have signaled him if she wanted the Federation men dead.

He was to wait, then—wait and watch what Daji's play was.

"Your Highness." General Gin Seiryu was a massive soldier, a giant among men. He towered over the Empress. "You have been long in coming. The Emperor Ryohai grows impatient with you."

"I am not Ryohai's dog to command." Daji's voice resounded across the ship—cool and clear as ice, sharp as knives.

A circle of soldiers formed around Daji, closing her in with the general. But Daji stood tall, chin raised, betraying no fear.

"But you *will* be summoned," the general said harshly. "The Emperor Ryohai grows irritated with your dallying. Your advantages are dwindling. You hold precious few cards, and this you know. You should be glad the Emperor has deigned to speak to you at all."

Daji's lip curled. "His Excellency is certainly gracious."

"Enough of this banter. Speak your piece."

"All in due time," Daji said calmly. "But first, another matter to attend to."

And she looked directly into the shadows where Tyr stood. "Good. You're here."

Tyr took that for his signal.

Knives raised, he rushed from the shadows—only to stumble to his knees as Daji arrested him with her gaze.

He choked, unable to speak. His limbs were numb, frozen; it was all he could do to remain upright. Daji had the power of hypnosis, he knew, but never had she used it on *him*.

All thoughts were pushed from his mind. All he could think about were her eyes. They were at first large, luminous and black; and then they were yellow like a snake's, with narrow pupils that drew him in like a mother grasping at her baby, like a cruel imitation of his own goddess.

And like his goddess, she was so beautiful. So very beautiful.

Transfixed, Tyr lowered his knives.

Visions danced before him. Her great yellow eyes pulsed in his gaze; suddenly gigantic, they filled his entire field of sight to the periphery, drew him into her world.

He saw shapes without names. He saw colors beyond description. He saw faceless women dancing through vermilion and cobalt, bodies curved like the silk ribbons they spun in their hands. Then, as her prey was entranced, the Vipress slammed down into him with her fangs and flooded him with poison.

The psychospiritual assault was devastating and immediate.

She shattered Tyr's world like glass, like he existed in a mirror and she had dashed it against a sharp corner, and he was arrested in the moment of breaking so that it was not over in seconds but took place over eons. Somewhere a shriek began and grew higher and higher in pitch, and did not stop. The Vipress's eyes turned a colorless white that bored into his vision and turned everything into pain. Tyr sought refuge in the shadows, but his goddess was nowhere, and those hypnotic eyes were everywhere. Everywhere he turned, the eyes looked upon him; the great Snake hissed, her gaze trained on him, boring into him, paralyzing him—

Tyr called out for his goddess again, but still she was silent, she had been driven away by a power that was infinitely stronger than darkness itself.

Su Daji had channeled something older than the Empire. Something as old as time.

Tyr's world ceased to spin. He and the Empress drifted alone together in the eye of the hurricane of colors, stabilized only by her generosity. He took a form again, and so did she; no longer a viper but a goddess in the shape of Su Daji, the woman.

"Do not resent me for this. There are forces at play you could not possibly understand, against which your life is irrelevant." Although she appeared mortal, her voice came from everywhere, originated within him, vibrated in his bones. It was the only thing that existed, until she relented and let him speak.

"Why are you doing this?" Tyr whispered.

"Prey do not question the motives of the predator," hissed the thing that was not Su Daji. "The dead do not question the living. Mortals do not challenge the gods."

"I killed for you," Tyr said. "I would have done anything for you."

"I know," she said, and stroked his face. She spoke with a casual sorrow, and for an instant she sounded like the Empress again. The colors dimmed. "You were fools."

She pushed him off the ship.

The pain of drowning, Tyr realized, came in the struggle. But he could not struggle. He was every part of him paralyzed, unable to blink even to shut his eyes against the stinging assault of salt water.

Tyr could do nothing then but die.

He sank back into the darkness. Back into the deep, where sounds could not be heard, sights could not be seen, where nothing could be felt, where nothing lived.

Back into the soft stillness of the womb.
Back to his mother. Back to his goddess.

The death of a shaman did not go unnoticed in the world of spirit. The shattering of Tyr sent a psychospiritual shock wave across the realm of things unknown.

It was felt far away in the peaks of the Wudang Mountains, where the Night Castle stood hidden from the world. It was felt by the Seer of the Bizarre Children, the lost son of the last true khan of the Hinterlands.

The pale Seer traversed the spirit plane as easily as passing through a door, and when he looked for his commander he saw only darkness and the shattered outline of what had once been human. He saw, on the horizon of things yet to come, a land covered in smoke and fire. He saw a battalion of ships crossing the narrow strait. He saw the beginning of a war.

"What do you see?" asked Altan Trengsin.

The white-haired Seer tilted his head to the sky, exposing long, jagged scars running down the sides of his pale neck. He uttered a harsh, cackling laugh.

"He's gone," he said. "He's really gone."

Altan's fingers tightened on the Seer's shoulder.

The Seer's eyes flew open. Behind thin eyelids there was nothing but white. No pupils, no irises, no spot of color. Only a pale mountain landscape, like freshly fallen snow, like nothingness itself. "There has been a Hexagram."

"*Tell me*," Altan said.

The Seer turned to face him. "I see the truth of three things. One: we stand on the verge of war."

"This we've known," Altan said, but the Seer cut him off.

"Two: we have an enemy whom we love."

Altan stiffened.

"Three: Tyr is lost."

Altan swallowed hard. "What does that mean?"

The Seer took his hand. Brought it to his lips and kissed it.

"I have seen the end of things," he said. "The shape of the world has changed. The gods now walk in men as they have not for a long, long time. Tyr will not return. The Bizarre Children answer to you now, and you alone."

Altan exhaled slowly. He felt a tremendous sense of both grief and relief. He had no commander. No. He *was* the commander.

Tyr cannot stop me now, he thought.

Tyr's death was felt by the Gatekeeper himself, who had lingered all these years, not quite dead but not quite alive, ensconced in the shell of a mortal but not mortal himself.

The Gatekeeper was broken and confused, and he had forgotten much of who he was, but one thing he would never forget was the stain of the Vipress's venom.

The Gatekeeper felt her ancient power dissipate into the void that both separated them and brought them together. And he raised his head to the sky and knew that an enemy had returned.

It was felt by the young apprentice at Sinegard who meditated alone when her classmates slept. Who frowned at the disturbance she felt acutely but did not understand.

Who wondered, as she constantly did, what would happen if she disobeyed her master, swallowed the poppy seed, and traversed to commune again with the gods.

If she did more than commune. If she pulled one back down with her.

For although she was forbidden from calling the Phoenix, that did not stop the Phoenix from calling upon her.

Soon, whispered the Phoenix in her sleep. *Soon you will call on me for my power, and when the time comes, you will not be able to resist. Soon you will ignore the warnings of the Woman and the Gatekeeper and fall into my fiery embrace.*

I can make you great. I can make you a legend.

She tried to resist.

She tried to empty her mind, like Jiang had taught her; she tried to clear the anger and the fire from her head.

She found that she couldn't.

She found that she didn't want to.

On the first day of the seventh month, another border skirmish erupted, between the Eighteenth Battalion of the Federation Armed Forces and the Nikara patrol in Horse Province bordering the Hinterlands to the north. After six hours of combat, the parties reached a cease-fire. They passed the night in an uneasy truce.

On the second day, a Federation soldier did not report for morning patrol. After a thorough search of the camp, the Federation general at the border city of Muriden demanded the Nikara general open the gates of his camp to be searched.

The Nikara general refused.

On the third day, Emperor Ryohai of the Federation of Mugen issued by courier pigeon a formal demand to the Empress Su Daji for the return of his soldier at Muriden.

The Empress called the Twelve Warlords to her throne at Sinegard and deliberated for seventy-two hours.

On the sixth day, the Empress formally replied that Ryohai could go fuck himself.

On the seventh day, the Federation of Mugen declared war on the Empire of Nikan. Across the longbow island, women wept tears of joy and purchased likenesses of Emperor Ryohai to hang in their homes, men enlisted to serve in the reserve forces, and children ran in the streets screaming with the celebratory bloodlust of a nation at war.

On the eighth day, a battalion of Federation soldiers landed at the port of Muriden and decimated the city. When resisted by province Militia, they ordered that all the males in Muriden, children and babies included, be rounded up and shot.

The women were spared only by the Federation army's haste to move inland. The battalion looted the villages as it went, seized grain and transport animals for their own. What they could not take with them, they killed. They needed no supply lines. They took from the land as they traveled. They marched across the heartland on a warpath to the capital.

On the thirteenth day, a courier eagle reached the office of Jima Lain at the Academy. It read simply:

Horse Province has fallen. Mugen comes for Sinegard.

"It's sort of exciting, really," Kitay said.

"Yes," said Rin. "We're about to be invaded by our centuries-old enemy after they breached a peace treaty that has maintained a fragile geopolitical stability for two decades. So very exciting."

"At least now we know we have job security," said Kitay. "Everyone wants more soldiers."

"Could you be a little less glib about this?"

"Could you be less depressing?"

"Could we move a bit faster?" asked the magistrate.

Rin and Kitay glanced at each other.

Both of them would rather have been doing anything other than aiding the civilian evacuation effort. Since Sinegard was too far north for comfort, the Empire's bureaucracy was moving to a wartime capital in the city of Golyn Niis to the south.

By the time the Federation battalion arrived, Sinegard would be nothing but a ghost city. A city of soldiers. In theory, this meant that Rin and Kitay had the incredibly important job of ensuring that the central leadership of the Empire survived even if the capital didn't.

In practice, this meant dealing with very fat, very annoying city bureaucrats.

Kitay tried to hoist the last crate up into the wagon and promptly staggered under the weight. "What's in this?" he demanded, wobbling as he tried to balance the crate on his hip.

Rin hastily reached down and helped Kitay ease the crate up onto the wagon, which was already teetering from the weight of the magistrate's many possessions.

"My teapots," said the magistrate. "See how I marked the side? Careful not to let it tilt."

"Your teapots," Kitay repeated incredulously. "Your *teapots* are a priority right now."

"They *were* a gift to my father from the Dragon Emperor, may his soul rest in peace." The magistrate surveyed the top-heavy wagon. "Oh, that reminds me—don't forget the vase on the patio."

He looked imploringly at Rin.

She was dazed from the afternoon heat, exhausted from hours of packing the magistrate's entire estate into several ill-prepared moving vehicles. She noticed in her stupor that the magistrate's jowls quivered hilariously when he spoke. Under different circumstances she might have pointed that out to Kitay. Under different circumstances, Kitay might have laughed.

The magistrate gestured again to the vase. "Be careful with that, will you? It's as old as the Red Emperor. You might want to strap it down to the back of the wagon."

Rin stared at him in disbelief.

"Sir?" Kitay asked.

The magistrate turned to look at him. "What?"

With a grunt, Kitay raised the crate over his head and flung it to the ground. It landed on the dirt with a hard thud, not the tremendous crash Rin had rather been hoping for. The wooden lid of the crate popped off. Out rolled several very nice porcelain teapots, glazed with a lovely flower pattern. Despite their tumble, they looked unbroken.

Then Kitay took to them with a slab of wood.

When he was done smashing them, he pushed his wiry curls out of his face and whirled on the sweating magistrate, who cringed in his seat as if afraid Kitay might start smashing at him, too.

"We are at *war*," Kitay said. "And you are being evacuated because for *gods know what reason*, you've been deemed important to this country's survival. So do your job. Reassure your people. Help us maintain order. *Do not pack your fucking teapots.*"

* * *

Within days, the Academy was transformed from a campus to a military encampment. The grounds were overrun with green-clad soldiers from the Eighth Division of the nearby Ram Province, and the students were absorbed into their number.

The Militia soldiers were a stoic, curt crowd. They took on the Academy students begrudgingly, all the while making it very clear that they thought the students had no place in the war.

"It's a superiority issue," Kitay speculated later. "Most of the soldiers were never at Sinegard. It's like being told to work with someone who in three years would have been your superior officer, even though you have a decade of combat experience on them."

"They don't have combat experience, either," said Rin. "We've fought no wars in the last two decades. They know less of what they're doing than we do."

Kitay couldn't argue with that.

At least the arrival of the Eighth Division meant the return of Raban, who was tasked with evacuating the first-year students out of the city, along with the civilians.

"But I want to fight!" protested a student who barely came up to Rin's shoulder.

"Fat lot of good you'll do," Raban answered.

The first-year stuck out his chin. "Sinegard is my home. I'll defend it. I'm not a little kid, I don't have to be herded out like all those terrified women and children."

"You *are* defending Sinegard. You're protecting its inhabitants. All those women and children? You're in charge of their safety. Your job is to make sure they get to the mountain pass. That's quite a serious task." Raban caught Rin's eye as he shepherded the first-years out of the main gate.

"I'm scared some of the younger ones are going to sneak back in," he told her quietly.

"You've got to admire them," said Rin. "Their city's about to be invaded and their first thought is to defend it."

"They're being stupid," said Raban. He spoke with none of

his usual patience. He looked exhausted. "This is not the time for heroism. This is war. If they stay, they're dead."

Escape plans were made for the students. In case the city fell, they were to flee down the little-known ravine on the other side of the valley to join the rest of the civilians in a mountain hideout where they couldn't be reached by the Federation battalions. This plan did not include the masters.

"Jima doesn't think we can win," said Kitay. "She and the faculty are going to go down with the school."

"Jima's just being cautious," said Raban, trying to lift their spirits. "Sunzi said to plan for every contingency, right?"

"Sunzi also said that when you cross a river, you should burn the bridges so that your army can't entertain thoughts of retreating," said Kitay. "This sounds a lot like retreating to me."

"Prudence is different from cowardice," said Raban. "And besides, Sunzi also wrote that you should never attack a cornered foe. They'll fight harder than any man thinks possible. Because a cornered enemy has nothing to lose."

The days seemed to both stretch for an eternity and disappear before anything could get done. Rin had the uncomfortable sense that they were just waiting around for the enemy to land on their front porch. At the same time she felt frantically underprepared, as if battle preparations were not being done quickly enough.

"I wonder what a Federation soldier looks like," Kitay said as they descended the mountain to pick up sharpened weapons from the armory.

"They have arms and legs, I'm guessing. Maybe even a head."

"No, I mean, what do they *look* like?" Kitay asked. "Like Nikara? All of the Federation came from the eastern continent. They're not like Hesperians, so they must look *somewhat* normal."

Rin couldn't see why this was relevant. "Does it matter?"

"Don't you want to see the face of the enemy?" Kitay asked.

"No, I don't," she said. "Because then I might think they're human. And they're not human. We're talking about the people who gave opium to toddlers the last time they invaded. The people who massacred Speer."

"Maybe they're more human than we realize," said Kitay. "Has anyone ever stopped to ask what the Federation want? Why is it that they must fight us?"

"Because they're crammed on that tiny island and they think Nikan should be *theirs*. Because they fought us before and they almost won," Rin said curtly. "What does it matter? They're coming, and we're staying, and at the end of the day whoever is alive is the side that wins. War doesn't determine who's right. War determines who remains."

All classes at Sinegard ceased to meet. The masters resumed positions they had retired from decades ago. Irjah took over strategic command of the Sinegardian Reserve Forces. Enro and her apprentices returned to the city's central hospital to set up a triage center. Jima assumed martial command over the city, a position she shared with the Ram Warlord. This involved, in parts, shouting at city officials and at obstinate squadron leaders.

The outlook was grim. The Eighth Division was three thousand men strong, hardly enough to take on the reported invading force of ten thousand. The Ram Warlord had sent for reinforcements from the Third Division, which was returning from patrol up north by the Hinterlands, but the Third was unlikely to arrive before the Federation did.

Jiang was rarely available. He was always either in Jima's office going over contingency plans with Irjah, or not on campus at all. When Rin finally managed to track him down, he seemed harried and impatient. She had to run to keep up with him on his way down the steps.

"We're putting lessons on hiatus," he said. "I'm sure you've noticed there's no time for that now. I can't devote the time to train you properly."

He made to brush past her, but she grabbed his sleeve. "Master,

I wanted to ask—what if we called the gods? I mean, against the Federation?"

"What are you *talking* about?" He seemed faintly aghast. "Now is hardly the time for this."

"Surely there are battle applications to what we've been studying," she pressed.

"We've been studying how to consult the gods," he said. "Not how to bring them back down to earth."

"But they could help us fight!"

"What? No. *No.*" He flapped his hands, growing visibly agitated as he spoke. "Have you not listened to a word I've said these past two years? I *told* you, the gods are not weapons you can just dust off and use. The gods won't be summoned into battle."

"That's not true," she said. "I've read the reports from the Red Emperor's crusades. I know the monks summoned gods against him. And the tribes of the Hinterlands—"

"The Hinterlanders consult the gods for healing. They seek guidance and enlightenment," Jiang interrupted. "They do not call the gods down onto earth, because they know better. Every war we've fought with the aid of the gods, we've won at a terrible consequence. There is a price. There is always a price."

"Then what's the *point*?" she snapped. "Why learn Lore at all?"

His expression then was terrible. He looked as he had that day Sunzi the pig was slaughtered, when she told him she wanted to pledge Strategy. He looked wounded. Betrayed.

"The point of every lesson does not have to be to destroy," he said. "I taught you Lore to help you find balance. I taught you so that you would understand how the universe is more than what we perceive. I didn't teach you so that you could weaponize it."

"The gods—"

"The gods will not be used at our beck and call. The gods are so far out of our realm of understanding that any attempt to weaponize them can only end in disaster."

"What about the Phoenix?"

Jiang stopped walking. "Oh, no. Oh, no, no, no."

"The god of the Speerlies," said Rin. "Each time it has been called, it has answered. If we could just . . ."

Jiang looked pained. "You know what happened to the Speerlies."

"But they were channeling fire long before the Second Poppy War! They practiced shamanism for centuries! The *power*—"

"The power would consume you," Jiang said harshly. "That's what fire *does*. Why do you think the Speerlies never won back their freedom? You'd think a race like that wouldn't have remained subordinate for long. They would have conquered all of Nikan, if their power were sustainable. How come they never revolted against the Empire? The fire *killed* them, Rin, just as it empowered them. It drove them mad, it robbed them of their ability to think for themselves, until all they knew to do was fight and destroy as they had been ordered. The Speerlies were obsessed with their own power, and as long as the Emperor gave them free license to run rampant with their bloodlust, there was very little they cared about. The Speerlies were collectively deluded. They called the fire, yes, but they are hardly worth emulating. The Red Emperor was cruel and ruthless, but even he had the good sense never to train shamans in his Militia, outside of the Speerlies. Treating the gods as weapons only ever spells death."

"We're at *war*! We might die anyway. So maybe calling the gods gives us a fighting chance. What's the worst that could happen?"

"You're so young," he said softly. "You have no idea."

After that, Rin saw neither hide nor hair of Jiang on campus at all. Rin knew he was deliberately avoiding her, as he had before her Trials, as he did whenever he didn't want to have a conversation. She found this incredibly frustrating.

You're so young.

That was even more frustrating.

She wasn't so young that she didn't know her country was at war. Not so young that she hadn't been tasked to defend it.

Children ceased to be children when you put a sword in their hands. When you taught them to fight a war, then you armed them and put them on the front lines, they were not children anymore. They were soldiers.

Sinegard's time was running out. Scouts reported daily that the Federation force was almost on their doorstep.

Rin couldn't sleep, though she desperately needed to. Each time she closed her eyes, anxiety crushed her like an avalanche. During the day her head swam with exhaustion and her eyes burned, yet she could not calm herself enough to rest. She tried meditating, but terror plagued her mind; her heart raced and her breath contracted with fear.

At night, when she lay alone in the darkness, she heard over and over the call of the Phoenix. It plagued her dreams, whispered seductively to her from the other realm. The temptation was so great that it nearly drove her mad.

I will keep you sane, Jiang had promised.

But he had not kept her sane. He had shown her a great power, a tantalizingly wonderful power strong enough to protect her city and country, and then he had forbidden her from accessing it.

Rin obeyed, because he was her master, and the allegiance between master and apprentice still meant something, even in times of war.

But that didn't stop her from going into his garden when she knew he was not on campus, and shoving several handfuls of poppy seeds in her front pocket.

CHAPTER 11

When the main column of the Federation Armed Forces marched on Sinegard, they did not attempt to conceal their arrival. They did not need to. Sinegard knew already that they were coming, and the terror the Federation inflicted gave them a far greater strategic advantage than the element of surprise. They advanced in three columns, marching from every direction but the west, where Sinegard was backed by the Wudang Mountains. They forged forward with massive crimson banners flying overhead, illuminated by raised torches.

For Ryohai, the banners read. *For the Emperor.*

In his *Principles of War*, the great military theorist Sunzi had warned against attacking an enemy that occupied the higher ground. The target above held the advantage of surveillance and would not need to tire out their troops by climbing uphill.

The Federation invasion strategy was a giant *fuck you* to Sunzi.

To storm Sinegard from higher ground would have required a detour up the Wudang Mountains, which would have delayed the Federation assault by almost an entire week. The Federation would not give Sinegard a week. The Federation had the weapons and the numbers to take Sinegard from below.

From her vantage point high on the southern city wall, Rin watched the Federation force approach like a great fiery snake winding its way through the valley, encircling Sinegard to crush and swallow it. She saw it coming, and she trembled.

I want to hide. I want someone to tell me I'm going to be safe, that this is just a joke, a bad dream.

In that moment she realized that all this time she had been playing at being a soldier, playing at bravery.

But now, on the eve of the battle, she could not pretend anymore.

Fear bubbled in the back of her throat, so thick and tangible that she almost choked on it. Fear made her fingers tremble violently so that she almost dropped her sword. Fear made her forget how to breathe. She had to force air into her lungs, close her eyes, and count to herself as she inhaled and exhaled. Fear made her dizzy and nauseated, made her want to vomit over the side of the wall.

It's just a physiological reaction, she told herself. *It's just in your mind. You can control it. You can make it go away.*

They had gone over this in training. They had been warned about this feeling. They were taught to control their fear, turn it to their advantage; use their adrenaline to remain alert, to ward off fatigue.

But a few days of training could not negate what her body instinctively felt, which was the imminent truth that she was going to bleed, she was going to hurt, and she was most likely going to die.

When had she last been this scared? Had she felt this paralysis, this numbing dread before she stepped into the ring with Nezha two years ago? No, she had been angry then, and proud. She had thought she was invincible. She had been looking forward to the fight, anticipating the bloodlust.

That felt stupid now. *So*, so stupid. War was not a game, where one fought for honor and admiration, where masters would keep her from sustaining any real harm.

War was a nightmare.

She wanted to cry. She wanted to scream and hide behind someone, behind one of the soldiers, wanted to whimper, *I am scared, I want to wake up from this dream, please save me.*

But no one was coming for her. No one was going to save her. There was no waking up.

"Are you all right?" Kitay asked.

"No," she said, trembling. Her voice was a frightened squeak. "I'm scared. Kitay, we're going to die."

"No, we're not," Kitay said fiercely. "We're going to win, and we are going to *live*."

"You've done the math, too." They were outnumbered three to one. "Victory is not possible."

"You have to believe it is." Kitay's fingers were clenched so tightly around his sword hilt that they had turned white. "The Third will get here in time. You have to tell yourself that's true."

Rin swallowed hard and nodded. *You were not trained to snivel and cower*, she told herself. The girl from Tikany, the escaped bride who had never seen a city, would have been scared. The girl from Tikany was gone. She was a third-year apprentice of the Academy at Sinegard, she was a soldier of the Eighth Division, and she was trained to fight.

And she was not alone. She had poppy seeds in her pocket. She had a god on her side.

"Tell me when," Kitay said. He was poised with his sword over the rope that constrained a booby trap they had set to defend the outer perimeter. Kitay had designed this trap; he would unleash it just as soon as the enemy was within range.

They were so close she could see the firelight flickering over their faces.

Kitay's hand trembled.

"Not yet," she whispered.

The first of the Federation battalion crossed the boundary.

"Now."

Kitay slashed at the rope.

A rolling avalanche of logs was freed from its breaking point, pulled down by gravity to bowl straight through the main advancing force. The logs rolled chaotically, shattered limbs and crushed bone with a noise like thunder that went on and on. For a moment the rumbling of carnage was so great Rin thought they might have won the battle before it started, might have seriously crippled the advancing force. Kitay whooped hysterically over the clamor, clutching Rin to keep from falling over as the gates themselves shook.

But when the roar of the logs died down, the invaders continued to advance into Sinegard to the steady beat of war drums.

A tier above Rin and Kitay, standing at the highest precipices of the South Gate, the archers loosed a round of arrows. Most clattered uselessly against raised shields. Some found their way through the cracks, embedded their heads in the unguarded fleshy parts of soldiers' necks. But the heavily armored Federation soldiers simply marched over the bodies of their fallen comrades, continuing their relentless assault toward the city gates.

The squadron leader shouted for another round of arrows.

It was close to pointless. There were far more soldiers than there were arrows. Sinegard's outer defense was flimsy at best. Each of Kitay's booby traps had been sprung, and though all but one went off beautifully, they were not enough to even dent the enemy ranks.

There was nothing to do but wait. Wait until the gate was broken, until there was a tremendous crash. Then the signal gongs were ringing, screaming to all who didn't already know that the Federation had breached the walls. The Federation was in Sinegard.

They marched to the cacophony of cannon fire and rockets, bombarding Sinegard's outer defenses with their siege breakers.

The gate buckled and broke under the strain.

They poured through like a swarm of ants, like a cloud of hornets; unstoppable and infinite, overwhelming in number.

We can't win. Rin stood in a daze of despair, sword hanging by her side. What difference would it make if she fought back? It might stay her death sentence by a few seconds, maybe minutes, but at the end of the night she would be dead, her body broken and bloody on the ground, and nothing would matter . . .

This battle wasn't like the ones in the legends, where numbers didn't matter, where a handful of warriors like the Trifecta could flatten an entire legion. It didn't matter how good their techniques were, it mattered how the numbers balanced.

And the Sinegardians were so badly outnumbered.

Rin's heart sank as she watched the armored troops advance into the city, rows and columns stretching into infinity.

I'm going to die here, she realized. *They're going to slaughter all of us.*

"Rin!"

Kitay shoved her hard; she stumbled against stones as an axe embedded itself in the wall where her head had been.

Its wielder jerked the axe out of the wall and swung it again toward them, but this time Rin blocked it with her sword. The impact sent adrenaline coursing through her blood.

Fear was impossible to eradicate. But so was the will to survive.

Rin ducked under the soldier's arm and jammed her sword up through the soft groove beneath his chin, unprotected by the helmet. She cut through fat and sinew, felt the tip of her sword pierce directly through his tongue and move up past his nose to where his brain was. His carotid artery exploded over the length of steel. Blood wet her hand to the elbow. He jerked a little and fell toward her.

He's dead, she thought numbly. *I've killed him.*

For all her combat training, Rin had never thought about what it would be like to actually take someone's life. To sever an artery, not just feign doing so. To break a body so badly that all functions ceased, that the animation was stilled forever.

They were taught to incapacitate at the Academy. They were trained to fight against their friends. They operated within the masters' strict rules, monitored closely to avoid injury. For all their talk and theory, they had not been trained to truly kill.

Rin thought she might feel the life leave her victim's body. She thought she might register his death with thoughts more significant than *One down, ten thousand to go*. She thought she'd feel *something*.

She registered nothing. Just a temporary shock, then the grim realization that she needed do this again, and again, and again.

She extricated her weapon from the soldier's jaw just as another swung a sword over her head. She rammed her sword up, blocked the blow. And parried. And thrust. And spilled blood again.

It wasn't any easier the second time.

It seemed as if the world were filled with Federation soldiers. They all looked the same—identical helmets, identical armor. *Cut one down and here comes another.*

Within the melee Rin didn't have time to think. She fought by reflex. Every action demanded a reaction. She couldn't see Kitay anymore; he had disappeared into the sea of bodies, an ocean of clashing metal and torches.

Fighting the Federation was wholly different from fighting in the ring. She didn't have melee practice. The enemy came from every angle, not just one, and defeating one opponent didn't bring you any closer to winning the battle.

The Federation did not have martial arts. Their movements were blocky, studied. Their patterns were predictable. But they had practice with formations, with group combat. They moved as if they had a hive mind; coordinated actions produced by years of drilling. They were better trained. They were better equipped.

The Federation didn't fight a graceful fight. They fought a brutal one. And they didn't fear death. If they were hurt, they fell, and their comrades advanced over their dead bodies. They were relentless. There were *so many of them*.

I am going to die.

Unless. Unless.

The poppy seeds in her pocket screamed for her to swallow them. She could take them now. She could go to the Pantheon and call a god down. What did Jiang's warnings matter, when they were all going to die regardless?

She had seen the face of the Phoenix. She knew what power was at her fingertips, if only she asked.

I can make you fearless. I can make you a legend.

She did not want to be a legend, but she wanted to stay alive. She wanted more than anything to live, consequences be damned, and if calling the Phoenix would do that for her, then so be it. Jiang's warning meant nothing to her now, not while her countrymen and classmates were hacked to pieces beside her, not while she didn't know if each second was going to be her last. If she was going to die, she would not die like this—small, weak, and helpless.

She had a link to a god.

She would die a shaman.

Heart hammering, she ducked behind a gated corner; for the few seconds in which nobody saw her, she jammed her hand into her pocket and dug the seeds out. She brought them to her mouth.

She hesitated.

If she swallowed the seeds but it didn't work, she would certainly die. She could not fight drugged, dazed, and hallucinating.

A horn blasted through the air. She jerked her head up. It was a distress signal, coming from the East Gate.

But the South Gate had no troops to spare. Everywhere was a crisis zone. They were outnumbered three to one; if they lost half their troops to the East Gate, then they may as well let the Federation stroll into the city unchecked.

But Rin's squadron had been ordered to rally if they heard the distress call. She froze, uncertain, seeds uneaten in her palm. Well, she couldn't swallow them *now*—the drug needed time to take effect, and then she would be in limbo indefinitely while she probed her way to the Pantheon. And even if she could still her thoughts long enough to call the gods, she didn't know that they would answer.

Should she stay here, hidden, and try to call a god, or should she go to the aid of her comrades?

"Go!" Her squadron leader shouted to her over the din of battle. "Go to the gate!"

She ran.

The South Gate had been a melee. But the East Gate was a slaughter zone.

The Nikara soldiers were down. Rin raced toward their posts, but her hope died the closer she got. She couldn't see anyone in Nikara armor still fighting. The Federation soldiers were just pouring through the gate, completely unopposed.

It was obvious now that the Federation forces had made the East Gate their main target. They had stationed three times as many troops there, had set up sophisticated siege weaponry outside the city walls. Trebuchets launched flaming pieces of debris into the unresponsive sentry towers.

She saw Niang slumped in a corner, crouched over a limp body in a Militia uniform. As Rin passed, Niang lifted her face, streaked with tears and blood. The body was Raban's.

Rin felt as if she'd been stabbed in the gut. *No—not Raban, no . . .*

Something slammed against her back. She whipped around. Two Federation soldiers had crept up behind her. The first raised his sword again and slashed down. She ducked around the path of his blade and lashed out with her sword.

Metal met sinew. She was blinded by the blood streaming into her eyes; she couldn't see what she was cutting, only felt a great tension and then release, and then the Federation soldier was at her knees howling in pain.

She stabbed downward without thinking. The howling stopped.

Then his comrade slammed his shield into her sword arm. Rin cried out and dropped her sword. The soldier kicked it away and smashed his shield at Rin's rib cage, then pulled his sword back to deliver the finishing blow while she was down.

His sword arm faltered, then dropped. The soldier made a startled gurgling noise as he stared in disbelief at the blade protruding from his stomach.

He fell forward and lay still.

Nezha met Rin's eyes, and then wrenched his sword out of the soldier's back. With his other hand he flung a spare weapon at her.

She pulled it from the air. Her fingers closed with familiarity around the hilt. A wave of relief shot through her. She had a weapon.

"Thanks," she said.

"On your left," he responded.

Without thinking they sank into a formation; back to back, fighting while covering each other's blind spots. They made a startlingly good team. Rin covered for Nezha's overstretched attacks; Nezha guarded Rin's lower corners. They were each intimately familiar with the other's weaknesses: Rin knew Nezha was slow to bring his guard back up after missed blows; Nezha parried from above while Rin ducked in low for close-quarters attacks.

It wasn't as if she could read his mind. She had simply spent so much time observing him that she knew exactly how he was going to attack. They were like a well-oiled machine. They were a spontaneously coordinated dance. They weren't two parts of a whole, not quite, but they came close.

If they hadn't spent so much time hating each other, Rin thought, they might have trained together.

Backs to each other, swords at the enemy, they fought with savage desperation. They fought better than men twice their age. They drew on each other's strengths; as long as Nezha was fighting, wasn't flagging, Rin didn't feel fatigued, either. Because she wasn't just fighting to keep herself alive now, she was fighting with a partner. They fought so well that they half-convinced themselves they might emerge intact. The onslaught was, in fact, thinning.

"They're retreating," Nezha said in disbelief.

Rin's chest flooded with hope for one short, blissful moment, until she realized that Nezha was wrong. The soldiers weren't backing away from them. They were making way for their general.

The general stood a head taller than the tallest man Rin had ever seen. His limbs were like tree trunks, his armor made of enough metal to coat three smaller men. He sat astride a warhorse as massive as he was; a monstrous creature, decked in steel. His face was hidden behind a metal helmet that covered all but his eyes.

"What is this?" His voice sounded with an unnatural reverberation, as if the very ground shook when he spoke. "Why have you stopped?"

He brought his warhorse to a halt before Rin and Nezha.

"Two puppies," he said, his voice low in amusement. "Two Nikara puppies, holding an entire gate by themselves. Has Sinegard fallen so low that the city must be defended by children?"

Nezha was trembling. Rin was too scared to tremble.

"Watch closely," the general said to his soldiers. "This is how we deal with Nikara scum."

Rin reached out and grasped Nezha's wrist.

Nezha nodded curtly in response to her unspoken question.

Together?

Together.

The general reared his monstrous horse back and charged them.

There was nothing they could do now. In that moment, Rin could only squeeze her eyes shut and wait for the end.

It didn't come.

A deafening *clang* shattered the air—the sound of metal against metal. The air itself shook with the unnatural vibration of a great force stopped in its tracks.

When Rin realized she hadn't been cut in half or trampled to death, she opened her eyes.

"What the fuck," Nezha said.

Jiang stood before them, his white hair hanging still in the air as if he had been struck by lightning. His feet did not touch the ground. Both his arms were flung out, blocking the tremendous force of the general's halberd with his own iron staff.

The general tried to force Jiang's staff out of the way, and his arms trembled with a mighty pressure, but Jiang did not look like he was exerting any force at all. The air crackled unnaturally, like a prolonged rumble of thunder. The Federation soldiers fell back, as if they could sense an impending explosion.

"Jiang Ziya," said the general. "So you live after all."

"Do I know you?" Jiang asked.

The general responded with another massive swing of his halberd. Jiang waved his staff and blocked the blow as effortlessly as if he were swatting away a fly. He dispelled the force of the blow into the air and the ground below them. The paving stones shuddered from the impact, nearly knocking Rin and Nezha off their feet.

"Call off your men."

Though Jiang spoke calmly, his voice echoed as if he had shouted. He appeared to have grown taller; not larger, but extended somehow, just as his shadow was extended against the wall behind them. No longer willowy and fidgety, Jiang seemed an entirely different person—someone younger, someone infinitely more powerful.

Rin stared at him in awe. The man before her was not the doddering, eccentric embarrassment of the Academy. This man was a soldier.

This man was a shaman.

When Jiang spoke again, his voice contained the echo of itself; he spoke in two pitches, one normal and one far lower, as if his shadow shouted back everything he said at double the volume. "Call off your men, or I will summon into existence things that should not be in this world."

Nezha grabbed at Rin's arm. His eyes were wide. "*Look.*"

The air behind Jiang was warping, shimmering, turning darker than the night itself. Jiang's eyes had rolled up into the back of his head. He chanted loudly, singing in that unfamiliar language that Rin had heard him use only once before.

"You are *Sealed*!" the general bellowed. But he backed rapidly away from the void and clutched his halberd close.

"Am I now?" Jiang spread his arms.

Behind him sounded a keening wail, too high-pitched for any beast known to man.

Something was coming through the darkness.

Beyond the void, Rin saw silhouettes that should exist only in puppetry, outlines of beasts that belonged to story. A three-headed lion. A nine-tailed vixen. A mass of serpents tangled into one another, its multitude of heads snapping and biting in every direction.

"Rin. Nezha." Jiang didn't turn around to look at them. "*Run.*"

Then Rin understood. Whatever was being summoned, Jiang couldn't control them. *The gods will not be called willingly into battle. The gods will always demand something in return.* He was doing precisely what he had forbidden her to do.

Nezha pulled Rin to her feet. Her left leg felt as if white-hot knives had been jammed into her kneecap. She cried out and staggered against him.

He steadied her. His eyes were wide with terror. There was no time to run.

Jiang convulsed in the air before them, and then lost control altogether. The void burst outward, ripping the fabric of the world, collapsing the gated wall around them. He slammed his staff into the air. A wave of force emitted from the site of contact and exploded outward in a visible ring. For a moment everything was still.

And then the east wall came down.

Rin moaned and rolled onto her side. She could barely see, barely feel. None of her senses worked; she was wrapped in a cocoon of darkness penetrated only by shards of pain. Her leg rubbed against something soft and human, and she reached for it. It was Nezha.

She groaned and forced her eyes open. Nezha lay slumped

against her, bleeding profusely from a cut on his forehead. His eyes were closed.

Rin sat up, wincing, and shook his shoulder. "Nezha?"

He stirred faintly. Relief washed over her.

"We have to get up—Nezha, come on, we have to—"

A shower of debris erupted in the far corner by the gate.

Something was buried there under the rubble. Something was alive.

She clung to Nezha's hand and watched the shifting rubble, hoping wildly it would be Jiang, that he would have survived whatever terror he had called and that he was all right, and he would be himself again, and he would save the—

The hand that clawed out from beneath the rubble was bloody, massive, and heavily armored.

Rin should have killed the general before he pulled himself out of the rubble. She should have taken Nezha and run. She should have done *something*.

But her limbs would not obey the commands that her brain sent; her nerves could not register anything but that same fear and despair. She lay paralyzed on the ground, heart slamming against her ribs.

The general staggered to his feet, took one lopsided step forward and then another. His helmet was gone. When he turned toward them, Rin's breath caught. Half of his face had been scraped away in the explosion, revealing an awful skeletal smile underneath peeling skin.

"Nikara *scum*," he snarled as he advanced. His foot caught against the limp form of one of his own soldiers. Without looking, he kicked it aside in disgust. His furious gaze remained fixed on Rin and Nezha. "I will *bury* you."

Nezha gave a low moan of terror.

Rin's arms were finally responding to her commands. She tried to haul Nezha up, but her own legs were weak with fear and she could not stand.

The general loomed over them. He raised his halberd.

Half-crazed with panic, Rin swung her sword upward in a great, wild arc. Her blade clattered uselessly against the general's armored torso.

The general closed his gauntleted fingers around her thin blade and wrenched it out of her hands. His fingers bent grooves into the steel.

Trembling, she let go of her sword. He dragged her up by the collar and flung her at what was left of the wall. Her head cracked against stone; her vision erupted in black, then spots of light, then a fuzzy nothing. She blinked slowly, and whatever vision was restored showed the general raising his halberd slowly over Nezha's limp form.

Rin opened her mouth to scream just as the general jammed the bladed tip into Nezha's stomach. Nezha made a high, keening noise. A second thrust silenced him.

Sobbing with fear, Rin scrabbled in her pocket for the poppy seeds. She seized a handful and brought them to her mouth, choked them down just as the general noticed she was still moving.

"No, you don't," he snarled, hauling her back up by the front of her robes. He dragged her close to his face, leering down at her with his horrific half-smile. "No more of that Nikara witchcraft. Even the gods won't inhabit dead vessels."

Rin shook madly in his grasp, tears leaking down her face as she choked for air. Her head throbbed where he'd slammed it against the stone. She felt as if she were floating, swimming in darkness, whether from the poppy seeds or her head injury, she didn't know. She was either dying or going to see the gods. Maybe both.

Please, she prayed. *Please come to me. I'll do anything.*

Then she tipped forward into the void; she was in that tunnel to the heavens again, spirited upward, hurtling at a tremendous speed to a place unknown. The edges of her vision turned black and then a familiar red, a sheet of crimson that spread across her entire field of vision like a glass lens.

In her mind's eye she saw the Woman appear before her. The Woman reached a hand toward her, but—

"*Get out of my way!*" Rin screamed. She didn't have time for a guardian, she didn't have time for warnings—she needed the gods, she needed *her* god.

To her shock, the Woman obeyed.

And then she was through the barrier, she was hurtling upward again, and she was in the throne room of the gods, the Pantheon.

All the plinths were empty except one.

She saw it then in all of its glorious fire. A great and terrible voice echoed in her mind. It echoed throughout the universe.

I can give you the power you seek.

She struggled wildly to breathe, but the general's grip only tightened around her neck.

I can give you the strength to topple empires. To burn your enemies until their bones are nothing but ash. All this I will give you and more. You know the trade. You know the terms.

"Anything," Rin whispered. "Anything at all."

Everything.

Something like a gust of wind blew through the chamber. She thought she heard something cackling.

Rin opened her eyes. She was not light-headed anymore. She reached up and clasped the general's wrists. She was deathly weak; her grasp should have been like a feather's touch. But the general howled. He dropped her, and when he raised his arms to strike her, she saw that both his wrists were a mottled, bubbling red.

She crouched, raised her elbows over her head to form a pathetic shield.

And a great sheet of flame erupted before her. The heat of it hit her in the face. The general stumbled backward.

"No . . ." His mouth opened wide in disbelief. He looked at her like he was seeing someone else. "Not you."

Rin struggled to her feet. Flames continued to pour out before her, flames she had no control over.

"You're *dead*!" the general shouted. "I killed you!"

She rose slowly, flames streaming from her hands, rivulets that ensconced them, gave no escape. The general howled in pain as the fire licked at his open wounds, the gaping holes on his face, all across his body.

"I watched you burn! I watched you all burn!"

"Not me," she whispered, and opened her hands toward him.

The fire billowed outward with a vengeance. She felt a tearing sensation, as if it were being ripped from her gut, from somewhere inside her. It coursed through her, not harming her but immobilizing her. It used her as a conduit. She controlled the flame no more than the wick of a candle might; it rallied to her and enveloped her.

In her mind's eye she saw the Phoenix, undulating from its plinth in the Pantheon. Watching. Laughing.

She couldn't see the general through the flame, only a silhouette, an outline of armor collapsing and folding in on itself, a kneeling pile of something that was less a man than it was a chunk of charred flesh, carbon, and metal.

"Stop," she whispered. *Please, make it stop.*

But the fire kept burning. The lump that had been the general staggered back and crumpled, a ball of flame that grew smaller and smaller and then was extinguished.

Her lips were dry, cracked; when she moved them, they bled. "Please, stop."

The fire roared louder and louder. She couldn't hear; she couldn't breathe through the heat. She sank to her knees, eyes squeezed shut, grabbing her face with her hands.

I'm begging you.

In her mind's eye she saw the Phoenix recoil, as if irritated. It opened its wings in a huge, fiery expanse and then folded them.

The way to the Pantheon shut.

Rin swayed and fell.

Time ceased to hold meaning. There was a battle around her and then there wasn't. Rin was enveloped in a silo of nothing, insulated from anything that happened around her. Nothing else existed, until it did.

"She's burning," she heard Niang say. "Feverish . . . I checked for poison in her wounds, but there's nothing."

It's not a fever, Rin wanted to say, *it's a god*. The water that Niang dripped on her forehead did nothing to quench the flames still coursing inside her.

She tried to ask for Jiang, but her mouth would not obey. She couldn't speak. She couldn't move.

She thought she could see, but she didn't know if she was dreaming, because when she opened her eyes next she saw a face so lovely she almost cried.

Arched eyebrows, a porcelain smoothness. Lips like blood.

The Empress?

But the Empress was far away, with the Third Division, still marching in from the north. They could not have arrived so soon, before daybreak.

Was it daybreak already? She thought she could see the first rays of the rising sun, the break of dawn on this long, horrible night.

"What do they call her?" the Empress demanded.

"Her"? Is the Empress talking about me?

"Runin." Irjah's voice. "Fang Runin."

"Runin," the Empress repeated. Her voice was like a plucked string on a table harp, sharp and penetrating and beautiful all at once. "Runin, look at me."

Rin felt the Empress's fingers on her cheeks. They were cool, like snow, like a winter breeze. She opened her eyes to the Empress, looked into those lovely eyes. How could anyone possess such beautiful eyes? They were nothing like a viper's eyes. They were not the eyes of a snake; they were wild and dark and strange, but beautiful, like a deer's.

And the *visions* . . . she saw a cloud of butterflies, silk sheets of ribbon fluttering in the wind. She saw a world that consisted only of beauty and color and rhythm. She would have done anything to stay trapped within that gaze.

The Empress inhaled sharply, and the visions fell away.

Her grasp on Rin's face tightened.

"I watched you burn," she said. "I thought I watched you die."

"I'm not dead," Rin tried to say, but her tongue was too heavy in her mouth and all she made was a gagging noise.

"Shhh." The Empress held an icy finger against her lips. "Don't speak. It's all right. I know what you are."

Then there was a cool press of lips against her forehead, the same coolness that Jiang had forced into her during her Trials, and the fire inside her died.

CHAPTER 12

When Rin was released from Enro's supervision, she was moved to the basement of the main hall, where the matches used to be held. She should have found this odd, but she was too dazed to think much about anything. She slept an inordinate amount. There was no clock in the basement, but often she dozed off to find that the sun had gone down. She had trouble staying awake for more than a few minutes. Food was brought to her, and each time she ate, she fell asleep again almost immediately.

Once, as she slept, she heard voices above her.

"This is inelegant," said the Empress.

"This is *inhumane*," said Irjah. "You're treating her like a common criminal. This girl might have won the battle for us."

"And she might yet burn down this city," said Jun. "We don't know what she's capable of."

"She's just a girl," said Irjah. "She'll be scared. Someone needs to tell her what's happening to her."

"We don't *know* what's happening to her," said Jun.

"It's obvious," the Empress said. "She's another Altan."

"So we'll let Tyr deal with her when he's here," said Jun.

"Tyr's coming all the way from the Night Castle," said Irjah. "You're going to keep her sedated for an entire week?"

"I'm certainly not going to let her wander the city," Jun answered. "You *saw* what the Gatekeeper did to the east wall. His Seal is breaking, Daji. He's a bigger threat than the Federation."

"Not anymore," the Empress said coolly. "The Gatekeeper's been dealt with."

When Rin ventured to open her eyes, she saw no one standing over her, and she only half remembered what had been said. After another indefinite spell of dreamless sleep she wasn't sure whether she had imagined the entire thing.

Eventually she came to her senses. But when she tried to leave the basement, she was forcibly restrained by three Third Division soldiers stationed outside the door.

"What's happening?" she demanded. She was still a bit dazed, but conscious enough to know this wasn't normal. "Why can't I go?"

"It's for your safety," one of them responded.

"What are you talking about? Who authorized this?"

"Our orders are to keep you here," the soldier said tersely. "If you try to force your way out, we will have to hurt you."

The soldier nearest her was already reaching for his weapon. Rin backed up. She understood there was no arguing her way out of this.

So she reverted to the most primitive of methods. She opened her mouth and screamed. She writhed on the floor. She beat at the soldiers with her fists and spat in their faces. She threatened to urinate in front of them. She shouted obscenities about their mothers. She shouted obscenities about their grandmothers.

This continued for hours.

Finally they acquiesced to her demand to see someone in charge. Unfortunately, they sent Master Jun.

"This isn't necessary," she said sulkily when he arrived. She had hastily rearranged her clothes so that it didn't look like she had just been rolling around in the dirt. "I'm not going to harm anyone."

Jun looked like the last thing he would do was believe her.

"You've just demonstrated an ability to spontaneously combust. You set fire to the eastern half of the city. Do you understand why we might not want you running around camp?"

Rin thought the combustion had been more deliberate than spontaneous, but she didn't think explaining *how* she'd done it would make her seem like any less of a threat.

"I want to see Jiang," she said.

Jun's expression was unreadable. He left without replying.

Once Rin got over the indignation of being locked up, she decided the best thing to do was wait. She was loyal to the Empress. She was a good soldier. The other masters at Sinegard would vouch for her, even if Jun wouldn't. So long as she kept her head, she had nothing to fear. She mused, absurdly, that if she was going to get in trouble for anything, it might be opium possession.

At least she wasn't being kept in isolation. Rin discovered that visitors could enter the basement freely. She just couldn't leave.

Niang visited often, but she wasn't much for conversation. When Niang smiled, it was forced. She moved listlessly. She didn't laugh when Rin tried to cheer her up. They passed hours sitting beside each other in silence, listening to each other breathe. Niang was stunned with grief, and Rin didn't know how to comfort her.

"I miss Raban too," she tried once, but that only made Niang tear up and leave.

Kitay, on the other hand, she grilled mercilessly for news. He visited as often as he could, but was constantly being called away for relief operations.

In bits and pieces, she learned what had happened in the aftermath of the battle.

The Federation had been on the verge of taking Sinegard when she had killed their general. That, combined with the timely arrival of the Empress and the Third Division, had turned the battle in their favor. The Federation had retreated in the interim. Kitay doubted they would soon return.

"Things ended pretty quick once the Third got here," he said. He cradled his arm in a sling, but assured Rin that it was only a minor sprain. "It had a lot to do with . . . well, you know. The Federation was spooked. I think they were afraid that we had more than one Speerly."

She sat up. "What?"

Kitay looked confused. "Well, isn't that what you are?"

A Speerly? *Her?*

"That's what they've been saying all over the city," said Kitay. Rin could sense his discomfort. Kitay's mind worked at twice the speed of a normal person's; his curiosity was insatiable. He needed to know what she had done, what she was, and why she hadn't told him.

But she didn't know what to tell him. She didn't know herself.

"What are they saying?" she asked.

"That you fell into a frenzied bloodlust. That you fought like you'd been possessed by a horde of demons. That the general cut you down over and over and stabbed you eighteen times and still you kept moving."

She held out her arms. "No stab wounds. That was just Nezha."

Kitay didn't laugh. "Is it true? You're locked down here, so it *must* be."

So Kitay didn't know about the fire. Rin considered telling him, but hesitated.

How would she explain shamanism to Kitay, who was so convinced of his own rationality? Kitay was the paragon of the modernist thought that Jiang despised. Kitay was an atheist, a skeptic, who couldn't accept challenges to his worldview. He would think her mad. And she was too exhausted to argue.

"I don't know what happened," she said. "It was all just a blur. And I don't know what I am. I was a war orphan. I could be from anywhere. I could be anyone."

Kitay looked unsatisfied. "Jun's convinced you're a Speerly."

But how could that be? Rin would have been an infant when Speer was attacked, and there was no way she would have survived if no one else had.

"But the Federation massacred the Speerlies," she said. "They left no survivors."

"Altan survived," Kitay said. "You survived."

The Academy students had suffered a far higher proportion of casualties than the soldiers of the Eighth Division. Barely half of their class had made it through, most of them with minor injuries. Fifteen of their classmates were dead. Five more were in critical condition in Enro's triage center, their lives hanging perilously in balance.

Nezha was among them.

"He's going through a third round of operations today," said Kitay. "They don't know if he's going to live. Even if he does, he might never fight again. They say the halberd pierced his torso all the way through. They say his spine is severed."

Rin had simply been relieved that Nezha wasn't dead. She hadn't considered that the alternative might be worse.

"I hope he dies," Kitay said suddenly.

She whirled on him, shocked, but Kitay continued, "If it's death or a lifetime as a cripple, I hope he gets off easy. Nezha couldn't live with himself if he couldn't fight."

Rin didn't know how to respond to that.

The Nikara's victory had bought them time, but it had not guaranteed them the city. Intelligence from the Second Division reported that Federation reinforcements were being sent across the narrow sea while the main invading forces waited for their rendezvous.

When the Federation attacked for a second time, the Nikara wouldn't be able to hold the city. Sinegard was being fully evacuated. The Imperial bureaucracy had been moved completely to the wartime capital of Golyn Niis, which meant Sinegard's security had been deprioritized.

"They're liquidating the Academy," Kitay said. "We've all been drafted into the Divisions. Niang's been sent to the Eleventh,

Venka to the Sixth in Golyn Niis. They're not sending Nezha anywhere until he . . . well, you know." He paused. "I got my orders for the Second yesterday. Junior officer."

It was the division Kitay had always dreamed of joining. Under different circumstances congratulations would have been in order. But now, celebration simply felt wrong. Rin tried anyway. "That's great. That's what you wanted, right?"

He shrugged. "They're desperate for soldiers. It's not a matter of prestige anymore; they've started drafting people right out of the countryside. But it'll be good to serve under Irjah. I'm shipping out tomorrow."

She placed a hand on his shoulder. "Take care of yourself."

"You too." Kitay sat back on his hands. "Any idea when they're going to let you out of here?"

"You know more than I do."

"No one's come in to talk to you?"

She shook her head. "Not since Jun. Have they found Jiang yet?"

Kitay gave her a sympathetic look, and she knew the answer before he spoke. It was the same answer he had given her for days.

Jiang was gone. Not dead—disappeared. No one had heard or seen anything since the end of the battle. The rubble of the east wall had been thoroughly searched for survivors, yet there was no sign of the Lore Master. There was no proof that he was dead, but nothing that gave hope that he was alive. He seemed to have vanished into the very void that he had called into being.

Once Kitay left with the Second Division for Golyn Niis, there was no one to keep Rin company. She passed her time sleeping. She wanted to sleep all the time now, especially after meals, and when she did it was a heavy and dreamless sleep. She wondered if her food and drink were drugged. Somehow, she was almost grateful for this. It was worse to be alone with her thoughts.

She wasn't safe, now that she had succeeded in calling a god. She didn't feel powerful. She was locked in a basement. Her own commanders didn't trust her. Half her friends were dying or dead, her master was lost to the void, and she was being contained for her own safety and the safety of everyone around her.

If this was what it meant to be a Speerly—if she even *was* a Speerly—Rin didn't know if it was worth it.

She slept, and when she couldn't force herself to sleep anymore, she curled into the corner and cried.

On the sixth day of her containment, Rin had just awoken when the door to the main hall opened. Irjah looked inside, checked to see that she was awake, and then quickly shut the door behind him.

"Master Irjah." Rin smoothed her rumpled tunic and stood.

"I'm General Irjah now," he said. He didn't seem particularly happy about it. "Casualties lead to promotions."

"General," she amended. "Apologies."

He shrugged and motioned for her to sit back down. "It hardly matters at this point. How are you doing?"

"Tired, sir," she said. She assumed a cross-legged position on the floor, because there were no stools in the basement.

After a moment's hesitation, Irjah sat on the floor as well.

"So." He placed his hands on his knees. "They're saying you're a Speerly."

"How much do you know?" she asked in a small voice. Did Irjah know she had called the fire? Did Irjah know what Jiang had taught her?

"I raised Altan after the Second War," said Irjah. "I know."

Rin felt a deep sense of relief. If Irjah knew what Altan was like, what Speerlies were capable of, then surely he could vouch for her, persuade the Militia that she wasn't dangerous—at least not to them.

"They've come to a decision about you," Irjah said.

"I didn't know I was up for debate," she answered, just to be difficult.

Irjah gave her a tired smile that did not reach his eyes. "You're going to get your transfer orders soon."

"Really?" She straightened up, suddenly excited. They were letting her out. *Finally.* "Sir, I was hoping I could join the Second with Kitay—"

Irjah cut her off. "You're not joining the Second. You're not joining any of the Twelve Divisions."

Her elation was replaced immediately by dread. She was suddenly aware of a faint buzzing noise in the air. "What do you mean?"

Irjah fiddled uncomfortably with his thumbs, and then said: "The Warlords have decided it best to send you to join the Cike."

For a moment she sat there looking dumbly at him.

The Cike? That infamous thirteenth division, the Empress's squad of assassins? The killers with no honor, no reputation, and no glory? The fighting force so vile, so nefarious, that the Militia preferred to pretend it didn't exist?

"Rin? Do you understand what I'm telling you?"

"The *Cike*?" Rin repeated.

"Yes."

"You're sending me to the freak squad?" Her voice cracked. She had a sudden urge to burst into tears. "The Bizarre Children?"

"The Cike is a division of the Militia just like the others," Irjah said hastily. His tone was artificially soothing. "They are a perfectly respectable contingent."

"They are losers and rejects! They—"

"They serve the Empress just as the army does."

"But I—" Rin swallowed hard. "I thought I was a good soldier."

Irjah's expression softened. "Oh, Rin. You *are*. You are an incredible soldier."

"So why can't I be in a real division?" She was acutely aware of how childish she sounded. But under the circumstances, she thought she deserved to act like a child.

"You know why," Irjah said quietly. "Speerlies have not fought with the Twelve Provinces since the last Poppy War. And before that, when they did, the cooperation was always . . . difficult."

Rin knew her history. She knew what Irjah alluded to. The last time the Speerlies had fought alongside the Militia, they had been regarded as barbaric oddities, much as the Cike was regarded now. The Speerlies raged and fought in their own camps; they were a walking hazard to everyone in their vicinity, friends and foe alike. They followed orders, but only vaguely; they were given targets and objectives, but good luck to the officer who tried any sophisticated maneuvers. "The Militia hates Speerlies."

"The Militia is afraid of Speerlies," Irjah corrected. "The Nikara have never been good at dealing with what they don't understand, and Speer has always made the Nikara uncomfortable. I expect you now know why."

"Yes, sir."

"*I* recommended you to the Cike. And I did it for you, child." Irjah fixed her with a level gaze. "The rivalry between the Warlords has never completely disappeared, even since their alliance under the Dragon Emperor. Though their soldiers might hate you, the Twelve Warlords would be very eager to get their hands on a Speerly. Whatever division you joined would gain an unfair advantage. And whatever division you didn't join might not like the shift in the balance of power. If I sent you to any one of the twelve divisions, you would be in very grave danger from the other eleven."

"I . . ." She hadn't considered this. "But there's already a Speerly in the Militia," she said. "What about Altan?"

Irjah's beard twitched. "Would you like to meet your commander?"

"*What?*" She blinked, not comprehending.

Irjah turned and called to someone behind the door, "Well, come on in."

The door opened. The man who walked through was tall and lithe; he did not wear a Militia uniform but a black tunic without any insignia. He carried a silver trident strapped across his back.

Rin swallowed, fighting a ridiculous urge to sweep her hair

behind her ears. She felt a familiar flush, a heat starting at the tops of her ears.

He had gained several scars since she'd last seen him, including two on his forearm and one that ran ragged across his face, from the lower right corner of his left eye down to his right jaw. His hair was no longer cropped tidily as it had been at school, but had grown unruly and wild, like he hadn't bothered with it in months.

"Hi," said Altan Trengsin. "What was that about losers and rejects?"

"How on earth did you survive the firebombs?"

Rin opened her mouth, but no words came out.

Altan. *Altan Trengsin.* She tried to form a coherent response, but all she could process was that her childhood hero was standing before her.

He knelt down in front of her.

"How do you exist?" he asked quietly. "I thought I was the only one left."

She finally found her voice. "I don't know. They never told me what happened to my parents. My foster parents didn't know."

"And you never suspected what you were?"

She shook her head. "Not until I . . . I mean, when I . . ."

She choked suddenly. The memories she had been suppressing flooded up in front of her: the shrieking Woman, the cackling Phoenix, the terrible heat ripping through her body, the way the general's armor bent and liquefied under the heat of the fire . . .

She lifted her hands to her face and found that they were trembling.

She hadn't been able to control it. She hadn't been able to turn it off. The flames had just kept pouring out of her without end; she might have burned Nezha, she might have burned Kitay, she might have turned all of Sinegard to ashes if the Phoenix hadn't heeded her prayer. And even when the flames did stop, the fire coursing inside her hadn't, not until the Empress kissed her forehead and made them die away.

I'm going crazy, she thought. *I have become everything that Jiang warned me against.*

"Hey. *Hey.*"

Cool fingers wrapped around her wrists. Gently, Altan pulled her hands away from her face.

She looked up and met his eyes. They were a shade of crimson brighter than poppy petals.

"It's okay," he said. "I know. I know what it's like. I'm going to help you."

"The Cike aren't so bad once you get to know them," he said as he led her out of the basement. "I mean, we kill people on orders, but on the whole we're quite nice."

"Are you all shamans?" she asked. She felt dizzy.

Altan shook his head. "Not all. We've got two who don't mess with the gods—a munitions expert and a physician. But the rest are. Tyr had the most training out of all of us before he came to the Cike—he grew up with a sect of monks that worshipped a goddess of darkness. The others were like you: dripping in power and shamanic potential, but confused. We take them to the Night Castle, train them, and set them loose on the Empress's enemies. Everybody wins."

Rin tried to find this reassuring. "Where do they come from?"

"All over. You'd be surprised how many places the old religions are still alive," said Altan. "Lots of hidden cults from across the provinces. Some contribute an initiate to the Cike every year in exchange for the Empress leaving them alone. It's not easy to find shamans in this country, not in this age, but the Empress procures them wherever she can. A lot of them come from the prison at Baghra—the Cike is their second chance."

"But you're not really Militia."

"No. We're assassins. In wartime, though, we function as the Thirteenth Division."

Rin wondered how many people Altan had killed. *Whom* he had killed. "What do you do in peacetime?"

"Peacetime?" He gave her a wry look. "There's no peacetime for the Cike. There's never a shortage of people the Empress wants dead."

Altan instructed her to pack her things and meet him at the gate. They were scheduled to march out that afternoon with the squadron of Officer Yenjen of the Fifth Division to the war front, where the rest of the Cike had gone a week prior.

All of Rin's belongings had been confiscated after the battle. She barely had time to pick up a new set of weapons from the armory before making her way across the city. The Fifth Division soldiers bore light traveling packs and two sets of weapons each. Rin had only a sword with a slightly dull blade and its accompanying sheath. She looked and felt woefully unprepared. She did not even have a second set of clothing. She suspected she would begin to smell very bad very soon.

"Where are we headed?" she asked as they began descending the mountain path.

"Khurdalain," Altan said. "Tiger Province. It'll be two weeks' march south until we get to the Western Murui River, and then we'll catch a ride down to the port."

Despite everything, Rin felt a thrill of excitement. Khurdalain was a coastal port city by the eastern Nariin Sea, a thriving center of international trade. It was the only city in the Empire that regularly dealt with foreigners; the Hesperians and Bolonians had established embassies there centuries ago. Even Federation merchants had once occupied the docks, until Khurdalain became a central theater of the Poppy Wars.

Khurdalain was a city that had seen two decades of warfare and survived. And now the Empress had established a front in Khurdalain once again to draw the Federation invaders into eastern and central Nikan.

Altan relayed the Empress's defense strategy to Rin as they marched.

Khurdalain was an ideal location to establish the initial front.

The Federation armored columns would have enjoyed a crushing advantage in the wide-open plains of northern Nikan, but Khurdalain abounded in rivers and creeks, which favored defensive operations.

Routing the Federation into Khurdalain would force them onto their weakest ground. The attack on Sinegard had been a bold attempt to separate the northern provinces from the southern. If the Federation generals could choose, they would almost certainly have cut directly into the Nikara heartland by marching directly south. But if Khurdalain was well defended, the Federation would be forced to change the north-to-south direction of their offensive to east-to-west. And Nikan would have room in the southwest to retreat and regroup should Khurdalain fall.

Ideally, the Militia would have attempted a pincer maneuver to squeeze the Federation from both sides, cutting them off from both their escape routes and supply lines. But the Militia was nowhere near competent or large enough for such an attempt. The Twelve Warlords had barely coordinated in time to rally to Sinegard's defense; now each was too preoccupied defending his own province independently to genuinely attempt joint military action.

"Why can't they just unite like they did during the Second War?" Rin asked.

"Because the Dragon Emperor is dead," said Altan. "He can't rally the Warlords to him this time, and the Empress can't command the same allegiance that he did. Oh, the Warlords will kowtow to Sinegard and swear vows of loyalty to the Empress's face, but when it comes to it, they'll put their own provinces first."

Holding Khurdalain would not be easy. The recent offensive at Sinegard had proven the Federation had clear military superiority in terms of mobility and weaponry. And Mugen held the advantage on the northern coastline; their troops were easily reinforced over the narrow sea; fresh troops and supplies were just a ship's journey away.

Khurdalain had little advantage in the way of defense structures.

It was an open port city, designed as an enclave for foreigners prior to the Poppy Wars. Nikan's best defense structures had been built along the lower river delta of the Western Murui, far south of Khurdalain. Compared to the heavily garrisoned wartime capital at Golyn Niis, Khurdalain was a sitting duck, arms flung open to welcome invaders.

But Khurdalain had to be defended. If Mugen advanced down the heartland and managed to take Golyn Niis, they could then easily turn east, chasing whatever remnants of the Militia were left onto the coast. And if they were trapped by the sea, the pitifully small Nikara fleet could not save them. So Khurdalain was the vital crux on which the fate of the rest of the country lay.

"We're the final front," said Altan. "If we fail, this country's lost." He clapped her on the shoulder. "Excited?"

CHAPTER 13

Clang.

Rin barely got her sword up in time to stop Altan's trident from slicing her face in half. She did her best to ground herself, to dispel the *ki* of the blow evenly across her body and into the dirt, but even so, her legs trembled from the impact.

She and Altan had been at this for hours, it seemed. Her arms ached; her lungs seized for air.

But Altan wasn't done. He shifted the trident, caught the blade of her sword between two prongs, and twisted hard. The pressure wrenched the sword out of Rin's hands and sent it clattering against the ground. Altan pressed the tip of his trident to her throat. She raised her arms hastily in surrender.

"You're reacting based on fear," Altan said. "You're not controlling this fight. You need to clear your mind and concentrate. Concentrate on *me*. Not my weapon."

"It's a bit hard when you're trying to jab my eyes out," she muttered, pushing his trident away from her face.

Altan lowered his weapon. "You're still hedging. You're resisting. You've got to let the Phoenix in. When you've called the god, when the god is walking in you, that's a state of ecstasy. It's a *ki* amplifier. You don't get tired. You're capable of extraordinary exertion. You don't feel pain. You have to sink into that state."

Rin could recall vividly the state of mind he wanted her to embrace. The burning feeling in her veins, the red lenses that shielded her vision. How other people became not people but targets. How she didn't need rest, only pain, pain to fuel the fire.

The only times Rin had consciously been in this state were during the Trials, and then again at Sinegard. Both times she had been furious, desperate.

She hadn't been able to rekindle the same state of mind since. She hadn't been that angry since. She had only been confused, agitated, and, like right now, exhausted.

"Learn to tame it," Altan said. "Learn to sink in and out of it. If you're focused only on your enemy's weapon, you'll always be on the defensive. Look past the weapon to your target. Focus on what you want to kill."

Altan was a much better teacher than Jiang. Jiang was frustratingly vague, absentminded, and deliberately obtuse. Jiang liked to dance around the answers, liked to make her circle around the truth like a starving vulture before he would give her a gratifying morsel of understanding.

But Altan wasted no time. He cut straight to the chase, gave her precisely the answers that she wanted. He understood her fears, and he knew what she was capable of.

Training with Altan was like training with an older brother. It was so bizarre for someone to tell her that they were the *same*—that his joints hyperextended like hers did, so she should turn out her foot in such a way. To have similarities with someone else, similarities that lay deep in their genes, was an overwhelmingly wonderful sensation.

With Altan she felt as if she *belonged*—not just to the same division or army, but to something deeper and older. She felt situated within an ancient web of lineage. She had a place. She was not a nameless war orphan; she was a Speerly.

At least, everyone seemed to think so. But despite everything, she couldn't shake the feeling that something was amiss. She couldn't call the god as easily as Altan could. Couldn't move with the same grace as he could. Was that heritage, or training?

"Were you always like this?" she asked.

Altan appeared to tense. "Like what?"

"Like . . . *you*." She gestured vaguely at him. "You're—you're not like the other students. Other soldiers. Could you always summon the fire? Could you always fight like you do?"

Altan's expression was unreadable. "I trained at Sinegard for a long time."

"But so did I!"

"You weren't trained like a Speerly. But you're a warrior, too. It's in your blood. I'll beat your heritage into you soon enough." Altan gestured to her with his trident. "Weapons up."

"Why a trident?" she asked when he finally let her take a break. "Why not a sword?" She hadn't seen any other soldier who didn't wield the standard Militia halberd and sword.

"Longer reach," he said. "Opponents don't come in close quarters when you're fighting inside a silo of fire."

She touched the prongs. The ends had been sharpened many times over; they were not shiny or smooth, but etched with the evidence of multiple battles. "Is that Speerly-made?"

It had to be. The trident was metal all the way through, not like Nikara weapons, which had wooden hilts. The trident was heavier, true, but Altan needed a weapon that wouldn't burn through when he touched it.

"It came from the island," he said. He poked her with the blunt end and gestured for her to pick up her sword. "Stop stalling. Come on, get up. Again."

She threw her arms down in exhaustion. "Can't we just get high?" she asked. She didn't see how relentless physical training got her any closer to calling the Phoenix at all.

"No, we can't just get high," Altan said. He poked her again. "Lazy. That kind of thinking is a rookie mistake. Anyone can swallow some seeds and reach the Pantheon. That part's easy. But forming a link with the god, channeling its power to your will and calling it back down—that takes discipline. Unless you've had practice honing your mind, it's too easy for you to lose control. Think of it as a dam. The gods are sources of potential energy, like water flowing downhill. The drug is like the gate—it opens the way to let the gods through. But if your gate is too large, or flimsily constructed, then power rushes through unobstructed. The god ignores your will. Chaos ensues. Unless you want to burn down your own allies, you have to remember why you called the Phoenix. You've got to direct its power."

"It's like a prayer," she said.

Altan nodded. "It's exactly like a prayer. All prayer is simply repetition—a imposition of your demands upon the gods. The difference between shamans and everyone else is that our prayers actually work. Didn't Jiang teach you this?"

Jiang had taught her the opposite of that. Jiang had asked her to clear her mind in meditation, to forget her own ego; to forget that she was a being separate from the universe. Jiang had taught her to erase her own will. Altan was asking her to impose her will on the gods.

"He only ever taught me to access the gods. Not to pull them back to our world."

Altan looked amazed. "Then how did you call the Phoenix at Sinegard?"

"I wasn't supposed to," she said. "Jiang warned me not to. He said the gods weren't meant to be weaponized. Only consulted. He was teaching me to calm myself, to find my connection to the larger cosmos and correct my imbalance, or . . . or whatever," she finished lamely.

It was becoming apparent how little Jiang had really taught her. He hadn't prepared her for this war at all. He had only tried to restrain her from wielding the power that she now knew she could access.

"That's useless." Altan looked disdainful. "Jiang was a scholar.

I am a soldier. He was concerned with theology; I am concerned with how to destroy." He opened his fist, turned it outward, and a small ring of fire danced over the lines of his palm. With his other hand he extended his trident. The flame raced from the ends of his fingers, danced across his shoulders, and licked all the way out to the trident's three prongs.

She marveled at the utter command Altan held over the fire, the way he shaped it like a sculptor might shape clay, how he bent it to his will with the slightest movement of his fingers. When she had summoned the Phoenix, the fire had poured out of her in an uncontrolled flood. But Altan controlled it like an extension of his own self.

"Jiang was right to be cautious," he said. "The gods are unpredictable. The gods are dangerous. And there's no one who understands them, not fully. But we at the Night Castle have practiced the weaponization of the gods to an art. We have come closer to understanding the gods than the old monks ever did. We have developed the power to rewrite the fabric of this world. If we don't use it, then what's the point?"

After two weeks of hard marching, four days of sailing, and another three days' march, they reached Khurdalain's city gates shortly before nightfall. When they emerged from the tree line toward the main road, Rin glimpsed the ocean for the first time.

She stopped walking.

Sinegard and Tikany were both landlocked regions. Rin had seen rivers and lakes, but never such a large body of water as this. She gaped openmouthed at that great expanse of blue, stretching on farther than she could see, farther than she could imagine.

Altan halted beside her. He glanced down at her dumbfounded expression, and he smiled. "Never seen the ocean before?"

She couldn't look away. She felt like she had the first day she had glimpsed Sinegard in all of its splendor, like she had been dropped into a fantastical world where the stories she'd heard were somehow true.

"I saw paintings," she said. "I read descriptions. In Tikany the merchants would ride up from the coast and tell us about their adventures at sea. But this—I never dreamed *anything* could look like this."

Altan took her hand and pointed it out toward the ocean. "The Federation of Mugen lies just across the narrow strait. If you climb the Kukhoni range, you can just glimpse it. And if you take a ship south of there, down close by Golyn Niis and into Snake Province, you'll get to Speer."

She couldn't possibly see it from where they stood, but still she stared out over the shimmering water, imagining a small, lonely island in the South Nikan Sea. Speer had spent decades in isolation before the great continental powers tore the island apart in the struggle between them.

"What's it like?"

"Speer? Speer was beautiful." Altan's voice was soft, wistful. "They call it the Dead Island now, but all I can remember of it is green. On one side of the island you could see the shore of the Nikara Empire; on the other was boundless water, a limitless horizon. We would take boats out and sail into that ocean without knowing what we would find; journeys into the endless dark to seek out the other side of the world. The Speerlies divided the night sky into sixty-four houses of constellations, one for each god. And as long as you could find the southern star of the Phoenix, you could always find your way back to Speer."

Rin wondered what the Dead Island was like now. When Mugen destroyed Speer, had they destroyed the villages as well? Or did the huts and lodges still stand, ghost towns waiting for inhabitants who would never return?

"Why did you leave?" she asked.

She realized then that she knew very little about Altan. His survival was a mystery to her, just as her very existence was a mystery to everyone else.

He must have been very young when he came to Nikan, a refugee of the war that killed his people. He couldn't have been older than four or five. Who had spirited him off that island? Why only him?

And why her?

But Altan didn't answer. He stared silently at the darkening sky for a long moment and then turned back toward the path.

"Come on," he said, and reached for her arm. "We're going to fall behind."

Officer Yenjen raised a Nikara flag outside the city walls, and then ordered his squadron to take cover behind the trees until they received a response. After a half hour's wait, a slight girl, dressed head to toe in black, peeked out from the city gate. She motioned frantically for the party to hurry up and get inside, then quickly shut the gate once they were through.

"Your division is waiting in the old fishing district. That's north of here. Follow the main road," she instructed Officer Yenjen. Then she turned and saluted her commander. "Trengsin."

"Qara."

"That's our Speerly?"

"That's her."

Qara tilted her head as she sized Rin up. She was a tiny woman—girl, really—reaching only to Rin's shoulder. Her hair hung past her waist in a thick, dark braid. Her features were oddly elongated, not quite Nikara but not quite anything that Rin could put her finger on.

A massive hunting falcon sat perched on her left shoulder, tilting its head at Rin with a disdainful expression. Its eyes and Qara's were an identical shade of gold.

"How are our people?"

"Fine," said Qara. "Well. Mostly fine."

"When's your brother back?"

Qara's falcon stretched its head up and then hunched back down, feathers raised as if unsettled. Qara reached up and stroked the bird's neck.

"When he's back," she said.

Yenjen and his squadron had already disappeared down the winding alleys of the city. Qara motioned for Rin and Altan to follow her up a set of stairs adjacent to the city walls.

"Where is she from?" Rin muttered to Altan.

"She's a Hinterlander," Altan said, and grabbed her arm just as she stumbled against the rickety stairs. "Don't trip."

Qara led them up a high walkway that spanned over the first few blocks of Khurdalain. Once at the top, Rin turned and got her first good look at the port city.

Khurdalain could have been a foreign city uprooted at the foundations and dropped straight onto the other side of the world. It was a chimera of multiple architectural styles, a bizarre amalgamation of building types from different countries spanning continents. Rin saw churches of the kind she'd seen only sketches of in history textbooks, the proof of former Bolonian occupation. She saw buildings with spiraling columns, buildings with elegant monochrome towers with deep grooves etched in their sides instead of the sloping pagodas native to Sinegard. Sinegard was the beacon of the Nikara Empire, but Khurdalain was Nikan's window to the rest of the world.

Qara led them across the walkway and onto a flat rooftop. They covered another block by running over the level-topped houses, built in the style of old Hesperia, and then dropped down to walk on the street when the buildings became too far apart. Between the gaps of the buildings, Rin could see the dying sun reflected in the ocean.

"This used to be a Hesperian settlement," said Qara, pointing out over the wharf. The long strip was a waterfront boulevard, ringed with blocky storefronts. The walkway was built of thick wooden planks soggy from seawater. Everything in Khurdalain smelled faintly of the sea; the breeze itself was laced with a salty ocean tang. "That ring of buildings over there—the ones with those terraced roofs—those used to be the Bolonian consulates."

"What happened?" Rin asked.

"The Dragon Emperor happened," said Qara. "Don't you know your history?"

The Dragon Emperor had expelled the foreigners from Nikan in the days of turmoil following the Second Poppy War, but Rin knew that a scattering of Hesperians still remained—missionaries intent on spreading the word of their Holy Maker.

"Are there still any Hesperians in the city?" she asked hopefully. She had never seen a Hesperian. Foreigners in Nikan were not permitted to travel as far north as Sinegard; they were restricted to trading at a handful of port cities, of which Khurdalain was the largest. She wondered if Hesperians were really pale-skinned and covered with fur, if their hair was really carrot red.

"A couple hundred," Altan said, but Qara shook her head.

"Not anymore. They've cleared out since the attack on Sinegard. Their government sent a ship for them. Nearly tipped over, they were trying to cram so many people in. There are one or two of their missionaries left, and a few foreign ministers. They're documenting what they see, sending it to their governments back at home. But that's it."

Rin remembered what Kitay had said about calling on Hesperia for aid, and snorted. "They think that's helping?"

"They're Hesperians," said Qara. "They always think they're helping."

The old section of Khurdalain—the Nikara quarter—was set in low-rise buildings embedded inside a grid of alleyways, intersected by a webbed system of canals, so narrow that even a cart would have a hard time getting through. It made sense that the Nikara army had set up base in this part of the city. Even if the Federation knew vaguely where they were, their overwhelming numbers would be no advantage in these crooked, tunneling streets.

Architecture aside, Rin imagined that under normal circumstances, Khurdalain might be a louder, dirtier version of Sinegard. Before occupation, this place must have been a bustling hub of exchange, more exciting even than the Sinegardian downtown markets. But Khurdalain under siege was quiet and muted, almost sullenly so. She saw no civilians as they walked; they either had already evacuated or were heeding the warnings of the Militia, keeping their heads down and staying away from where Federation soldiers might see them.

Qara briefed them on the combat situation as they walked. "We've been under siege for almost a month now. We've got Federation encampments on three sides, all except the one you came from. Worst is that they've been steadily encroaching into urban areas. Khurdalain has high walls, but they have trebuchets."

"How much of the city have they taken?" Altan asked.

"Only a narrow strip of beach by the sea, and half of the foreign quarter. We could take back the Bolonian embassies, but the Fifth Division won't cooperate."

"Won't cooperate?"

Qara scowled. "We're having some, ah, difficulties with integration. That new general of theirs doesn't help. Jun Loran."

Altan looked as dismayed as Rin felt. "Jun's here?"

"Shipped in three days ago."

Rin shuddered. At least she wasn't serving directly under him. "Isn't the Fifth from Tiger Province? Why isn't the Tiger Warlord in command?"

"The Tiger Warlord is a three-year-old kid whose steward is a politician with no military experience. Jun has resumed command of his province's army. The Ram and Ox Warlords are here too, with their provincial divisions, but they've been squabbling with each other over supplies more than they've been fighting the Federation. And no one can figure out an attack plan that doesn't put civilian areas in the line of fire."

"What are the civilians still doing here?" Rin asked. It seemed to her that the Militia's job would be a lot easier if civilian protection were not a priority. "Why haven't they evacuated, like the Sinegardians?"

"Because Khurdalain is not a city that you can easily leave," said Qara. "Most of the people here make their living from fishing or in the factories. There's no agriculture out here. If they move further inland, they have nothing. Most of the peasants moved here to escape rural squalor in the first place. If we ask them to leave, they'll starve. The people are determined to stay, and we'll just have to make sure they stay alive."

Qara's falcon cocked its head suddenly, as if it heard something. When she walked forward several paces Rin could hear it, too: raised voices coming from behind the general's compound.

"Cike!"

Rin cringed. She would recognize that voice anywhere.

General Jun Loran stormed down the alley toward them, purple-faced with fury.

"Ow-*ow*!"

By his side, Jun dragged a scrawny boy by the ear, jerking him along with brutal tugs. The boy wore an eyepatch over his left eye, and his right eye watered in pain as he tottered along behind Jun.

Altan stopped short. "Tiger's tits."

"Ramsa," Qara swore under her breath. Rin couldn't tell if it was a name or a curse in Qara's language.

"You." Jun stopped in front of Qara. "Where is your commander?"

Altan stepped forward. "That'd be me."

"*Trengsin?*" Jun regarded Altan with open disbelief. "You're joking. Where's Tyr?"

A spasm of irritation flickered across Altan's face. "Tyr is dead."

"*What?*"

Altan crossed his arms. "No one bothered to tell you?"

Jun ignored the jibe. "He's dead? How?"

"Occupational hazard," Altan said, which Rin suspected meant that he didn't have a clue.

"So they put the Cike in the hands of a child," Jun muttered. "Incredible."

Altan looked between Jun and the boy, who was still bent over by Jun's side, whimpering in pain. "What's this about?"

"My men caught him elbows-deep in their munitions stores," Jun said. "Third time this week."

"I thought it was *our* munitions wagon!" the boy protested.

"You don't have a munitions wagon," Jun snapped. "We established that the first two times."

Qara sighed and rubbed her forehead with the palm of her hand.

"I wouldn't have to steal if they'd just *share*," the boy said plaintively, appealing to Altan. His voice was thin and reedy, and his good eye was huge in his thin face. "I can't do my job if I don't have fire powder."

"If your men are lacking equipment, you might have thought to bring it from the Night Castle."

"We used up all ours at the embassy," the boy grumbled. "Remember?"

Jun jerked the boy's ear downward, and the boy howled in pain.

Altan reached behind his back for his trident. "Let go, Jun."

Jun glanced at the trident, and the side of his mouth quirked up. "Are you threatening me?"

Altan did not extend his weapon—to point his blade at a commander of another division would be the highest treason—but he didn't take his hand off the shaft. Rin thought she saw fire flicker momentarily across his fingertips. "I'm making a request."

Jun took one step back, but did not let go of the boy. "Your men do not have access to Fifth Division supplies."

"And disciplining him is my prerogative, not yours," said Altan. "Unhand him. *Now*, Jun."

Jun made a disgusted noise and let go of the boy, who skirted away quickly and scampered over to Altan's side, rubbing the side of his head with a rueful expression.

"Last time they hung me up by my ankles in the town square," the boy complained. He sounded like a child tattling on a classmate to a teacher.

Altan looked outraged.

"Would you treat the First or Eighth like this?" he demanded.

"The First and Eighth have better sense than to root around in the Fifth's equipment," Jun snapped. "Your men have been causing nothing but trouble since they got here."

"We've been doing our damn job!" the boy burst out. "*You're* the ones hiding behind walls like bloody cowards."

"Quiet, Ramsa," Altan snapped.

Jun barked out a short, derisive laugh. "You are a squad of ten. Do not overestimate your value to this Militia."

"Be that as it may, we serve the Empress just as you do," Altan said. "We left the Night Castle to be your reinforcements. So you'll treat my men with respect, or the Empress will hear of it."

"Of course. You're the Empress's special brats," Jun drawled. "*Reinforcements*. What a *joke*."

He shot a last disdainful look at Altan and stalked off. He pretended not to see Rin.

"So that's been the last week," Qara said with a sigh.

"I thought you said everything was fine," Altan said.

"I exaggerated."

Ramsa peered up at his commander. "Hi, Trengsin," he said cheerfully. "Glad you're back."

Altan pressed his hands against his face and then tilted his head up, inhaling deeply. His arms dropped. He sighed. "Where's my office?"

"Down that alley to the left," said Ramsa. "Cleared out the old customs office. You'll like it. We brought your maps."

"Thanks," Altan said. "Where are the Warlords stationed?"

"The old government complex around the corner. They've been holding councils on the regular. They don't really invite us, on account of, well. You know." Ramsa trailed off, suddenly looking very guilty.

Altan shot Qara a questioning look.

"Ramsa blew up half the foreign quarter at the docks," she reported. "Didn't give the Warlords advance warning."

"I blew up *one building*."

"It was a big building," Qara said flatly. "The Fifth still had two men inside."

"Well, did they survive?" Altan asked.

Qara stared at him in disbelief. "*Ramsa detonated a building on them.*"

"I take it you lot have done nothing useful while I've been gone, then," Altan said.

"We set up fortifications!" Ramsa said.

"Of the defense line?" Altan asked hopefully.

"No, just around your office. And our barracks. Warlords won't let us near the defense line anymore."

Altan looked deeply aggravated. "I need to go get that squared up. The government complex is down that way?"

"Yeah."

"Fine." Altan cast a distracted look at Rin. "Qara, she'll need equipment. Get her geared up and moved in. Ramsa, come with me."

"Are you Altan's lieutenant?" Rin asked as Qara led her down another winding set of alleyways.

"Not me. My brother," Qara said. She quickened her pace, ducked under a round gate embedded in a wall, and waited for Rin to follow her through. "I'm filling in until he's back. You'll stay here with me."

She pulled Rin down yet another stairwell that led to a damp underground room. It was a tiny chamber, barely the size of the Academy outhouse. A draft blew in from the cellar opening. Rin rubbed her arms and shivered.

"We get the women's barracks all to ourselves," Qara said. "Lucky us."

Rin glanced about the room. The walls were packed dirt, not brick, which meant no insulation. A single mat had been unfurled in the corner, surrounded by a bundle of Qara's things. Rin supposed she'd have to get her own blanket unless she wanted to sleep among the cockroaches. "There aren't any women in the divisions?"

"We don't share barracks with the divisions." Qara fumbled in a bag near her mat, pulled out a bundle of clothing, and tossed it at Rin. "You should probably change out of that Academy uniform. I'll take your old things. Enki wants old linens for bandages."

Rin quickly wriggled out of her travel-worn Academy tunic, pulled on the uniform, then handed her old clothes to Qara. Her new uniform was a nondescript black tunic. Unlike the Militia uniforms, it bore no insignia of the Red Emperor over her left breast. The Cike uniforms were designed to have no identifying marks at all.

"Armband, too." Qara's hand was outstretched, expectant.

Rin touched her white armband, feeling self-conscious. She hadn't taken it off since the battle, even though she was no longer officially Jiang's apprentice. "Do I have to?" She'd seen plenty of academy armbands among the soldiers in Yenjen's squadron, even though they looked well past academy age. Officers from Sinegard often wore those armbands for years after they graduated as a mark of pride.

Qara folded her arms. "This isn't the Academy. Your apprentice affiliation doesn't matter here."

"I know that—" Rin began to say, but Qara cut her off.

"You don't understand. This is not the Militia, this is the Cike. We were all sent here because we were deemed fit to kill, but unfit for a division. Most of us didn't go to Sinegard, and the ones who did don't have great memories of the place. Nobody here cares who your master was, and advertising it won't earn you any goodwill. Forget about approval or rankings or glory, or whatever bullshit you were angling for at Sinegard. You are *Cike*. By default, you don't get a good reputation."

"I don't care about my reputation—" Rin protested, but again Qara cut her off.

"No, you listen to me. You're not at school anymore. You aren't competing with anyone; you're not trying to get good marks. You live with us, you fight with us, you die with us. From now on, your utmost loyalty is to the Cike and the Empire. You want an illustrious career, you should have joined the divisions. But you didn't, which means something's wrong with you, which means you're stuck with us. Understand?"

"I didn't ask to come here," Rin snapped defensively. "I didn't have a choice."

"None of us did," Qara said curtly. "Try to keep up."

Rin tried to keep a map of the base in her head as they walked, a mental picture of the labyrinth that was Khurdalain, but she gave up after the fifteenth turn. She half suspected Qara was taking a deliberately convoluted route to wherever they were going.

"How do you guys get anywhere?" she asked.

"Memorize the routes," Qara responded. "The harder we are to find, the better. And if you want to find Enki, just follow the whining."

Rin was about to ask what this meant when she heard another set of raised voices from around the corner.

"Please," begged a male voice. "Please, it hurts so much."

"Look, I sympathize, I really do," said a second, much deeper voice. "But frankly it's not my problem, so I don't care."

"It's just a few seeds!"

Rin and Qara rounded the corner. The voices belonged to a slight, dark-skinned man and a hapless-looking soldier with an insignia that marked him as a private of the Fifth. The soldier's right arm ended in a bloody stub at the elbow.

Rin cringed at the sight; she could almost see the gangrene through the poor bandaging. No wonder he was begging for poppy.

"It's just a few seeds to you, and the next poor chap who asks, and the next after that," said Enki. "Eventually I'm all out of seeds, and my division hasn't got anything to fight with. Then the next time *your* division's backed up in a corner, *my* division can't do their jobs and save your sorry asses. They are a priority. You are not. Understand?"

The soldier spat on Enki's doorstep. "*Freaks.*"

He brushed past Enki and backed out into the alleyway, casting dark glances at Rin and Qara as he passed them.

"I need to move shop," Enki complained to Qara as she shut the door behind her. Inside was a small, crowded room filled with the bitter smell of medicinal herbs. "This is no condition to store materials in. I need somewhere dry."

"Move closer to the division barracks and you'll have a thousand soldiers on your doorstep demanding a quick fix," said Qara.

"Hm. You think Altan would let me move into the back closet?"

"I think Altan likes having his closet to himself."

"You're probably right. Who's this?" Enki examined Rin from head to toe, as if looking for signs of injury. His voice was truly lovely, rich and velvety. Simply listening to him made Rin feel sleepy. "What's ailing you?"

"She's the Speerly, Enki."

"Oh! I'd forgotten." Enki rubbed the back of his shaved head. "How did *you* slip through Mugen's fingers?"

"I don't know," said Rin. "I only just found out myself."

Enki nodded slowly, still studying Rin as if she were a particularly fascinating specimen. He wore a carefully neutral expression that gave nothing away. "But of course. You had no idea."

"She'll need equipment," said Qara.

"Sure, no problem." Enki disappeared into a closet built into the back of the room. They listened to him bustling around for a moment, and then he reappeared with a tray of dried plants. "Any of these work for you?"

Rin had never seen so many different kinds of psychedelics in one place. There were more drug varieties here than in Jiang's entire garden. Jiang would have been delighted.

She brushed her fingers along the opium pods, the shriveled mushrooms, and the muddy white powders.

"What difference does it make?" she asked.

"It's really a matter of preference," said Enki. "These drugs will all get you nice and tripped up, but the key is to find a mixture that lets you summon the gods without getting so stoned that you can't wield your weapon. The stronger hallucinogens will shoot you right up to the Pantheon, but you'll lose all perception of the material world. Fat lot of good summoning a god will do you if you can't see an arrow right in front of your face. The weaker drugs require a bit more focus to get in the right mind state, but they leave you with more of your bodily faculties. If you've had meditation training, then I'd stick with more moderate strains if you can."

Rin didn't think that a siege was a great time to experiment, so she decided to settle for the familiar. She found the poppy seed variety that she had stolen from Jiang's garden among Enki's collection. She reached out to grab a handful, but Enki pulled the tray back out of her reach.

"No you don't." Enki brought a scale out from under the counter and began measuring precise amounts into little pouches. "You come to me for doses, which I will document. The amount you receive is calibrated to your body weight. You're not big; you definitely won't need as much as the others. Use it sparingly, and only when ordered. A shaman who's addicted is better off dead."

Rin hadn't considered that. "Does that happen often?"

"In this line of work?" Enki said. "It's almost inevitable."

The Militia's food rations made the Academy canteen look like a veritable restaurant in comparison. Rin stood in line for half an hour and received a measly bowl of rice gruel. She swirled her spoon around the gray, watery soup, and several uncooked lumps drifted up to the surface.

She looked around the mess hall for black uniforms, and found a few of her contingent clustered at one long table at the end of the hall. They sat far away from the other soldiers. The two tables closest to them were empty.

"This is our Speerly," Qara announced when Rin sat down.

The Cike looked up at Rin with a mixture of apprehension and wary interest. Qara, Ramsa, and Enki sat with a man she didn't recognize, all four of them garbed in pitch-black uniforms without any insignia or armband. Rin was struck by how young they all were. None looked older than Enki, and even he didn't look like he'd seen a full four zodiac cycles. Most appeared to be in their late twenties. Ramsa barely looked fifteen.

It was no surprise that they had no problem with a commander of Altan's age, or that they were called the Bizarre Children. Rin wondered if they were recruited young, or if they simply died before they had the chance to grow older.

"Welcome to the freak squad," said the man next to her. "I'm Baji."

Baji was a thickly built mercenary type with a loud booming voice. Despite his considerable girth he was somewhat handsome, in a coarse, dark sort of way. He looked like one of the Fangs' opium smugglers. Strapped to his back was a huge nine-pointed rake. It looked amazingly heavy. Rin wondered at the strength it took to wield it.

"Admiring this?" Baji patted the rake. The pointed ends were crusted over with something suspiciously brown. "Nine prongs. One of a kind. You won't find its make anywhere else."

Because no smithy would create a weapon so outlandish, Rin thought. *And because farmers have no use for lethally sharp rakes.* "Seems impractical."

"That's what *I* said," Ramsa butted in. "What are you, a potato farmer?"

Baji directed his spoon at the boy. "Shut your mouth or I swear to heaven I will put nine perfectly spaced holes in the side of your head."

Rin lifted a spoonful of rice gruel to her mouth and tried not to picture what Baji had just described. Her eyes landed on a barrel placed right behind Baji's seat. The water inside was oddly clouded, and the surface erupted in occasional ripples, as if a fish were swimming around inside.

"What's that in the barrel?" she asked.

"That's the Friar." Baji twisted around in his seat and rapped his knuckles against the wooden rim. "Hey, Aratsha! Come say hello to the Speerly!"

For a second the barrel did nothing. Rin wondered whether Baji was entirely in his right mind. She had heard rumors that Cike operatives were crazy, that they had been sent to the Night Castle when they lost their sanity.

Then the water began rising out of the barrel, as if falling in reverse, and solidified into a shape that looked vaguely like a man. Two bulbous orbs that might have been eyes widened as they swiveled in Rin's direction. Something that looked vaguely like a mouth moved. "Oh! You cut your hair."

Rin was too busy gaping to respond.

Baji made an impatient noise. "No, you dolt, this is the new one. From *Sinegard*," he emphasized.

"Oh, really?" The water blob made a gesture that seemed like a bow. Vibrations rippled through his entire form when he spoke. "Well, you should have said so. Careful, you'll catch a moth in your mouth."

Rin's jaw shut with a click. "What happened to you?" she finally managed.

"What are you talking about?" The watery figure sounded alarmed. He dipped his head, as if examining his torso.

"No, I mean—" Rin stammered. "What—why do you—"

"Aratsha prefers to spend his time in this guise if he can help it," Baji interjected. "You don't want to see his human form. Very grisly."

"Like you're such a visual delight." Aratsha snorted.

"Sometimes we let him out into the river when we need a drinking source poisoned," Baji said.

"I am quite handy with poisons," Aratsha acknowledged.

"Are you? I thought you just fouled things up with your general presence."

"Don't be rude, Baji. You're the one who can't be bothered to clean his weapon."

Baji dipped his rake threateningly over the barrel. "Shall I clean it off in you? What part of you is this, anyway? Your leg? Your—"

Aratsha yelped and collapsed back into the barrel. Within seconds the water was very still. It could have been a barrel of rainwater.

"He's a weird one," Baji said cheerfully, turning back to Rin. "He's an initiate of a minor river god. Far more committed to his religion than the rest of us."

"Which god do you summon?"

"The god of pigs."

"What?"

"I summon the fighting spirit of a very angry boar. Come off it. Not all gods are as glorious as yours, sweetheart. I picked the first one I saw. The masters were disappointed."

The masters? Had Baji gone to Sinegard? Rin remembered Jiang had told her there had been Lore students before her, students who had gone mad, but they were supposed to be in mental asylums or Baghra. They were too unstable, they had been locked up for their own good. "So that means—"

"It means I smash things very well, sweetheart." Baji drained his bowl, tilted his head back, and belched. His expression made it clear he didn't want to discuss it further.

"Will you slide down?" A very slight young man with a whispery goatee walked over to their table with a heaping bowl of lotus root and slid into the seat on the other side of Rin.

"Unegen can turn into a fox," Baji said by way of introduction.

"Turn into—?"

"My god lets me shift shapes," Unegen said. "And yours lets you spit fire. Not a big deal." He spooned a heap of steamed lotus into his mouth, swallowed, grimaced, and then belched. "I don't think the cook's even trying anymore. How are we low on salt? We're next to an ocean."

"You can't just pour seawater on food," interjected Ramsa. "There's a sanitation process."

"How hard can it be? We're soldiers, not barbarians." Unegen leaned down the table, tapping to get Qara's attention. "Where's your other half?"

Qara looked irritated. "Out."

"Well, when's he back?"

"When he's back," Qara said testily. "Chaghan comes and goes on his own schedule. You know that."

"As long as his schedule accommodates the fact that we're, you know, fighting a war," said Baji. "He could at least hurry."

Qara snorted. "You two don't even like Chaghan. What do you want him back for?"

"We've been eating rice gruel for days. It's about time we had some dessert up here." Baji smiled, displaying sharp incisors. "I'm talking sugar."

"I thought Chaghan was getting something for Altan," Rin said, confused.

"Sure," said Unegen. "Doesn't mean he can't stop at a bakery on the way back."

"Is he at least close?" Baji asked.

"I'm not my brother's homing pigeon," Qara grumbled. "We'll know where he is when he's back."

"Can't you two just, you know, do that thing?" Unegen tapped his temples.

Qara made a face. "We're anchor twins, not mirror-wells."

"Oh, you can't do mirror-wells?"

"Nobody can do mirror-wells," Qara snapped. "Not anymore."

Unegen looked at Rin over the table and winked, as if winding Qara up was something he and Baji regularly did for fun.

"Oh, leave Qara alone."

Rin twisted around in her seat to see Altan. He walked up to them, looking over her head. "Someone needs to patrol the outer perimeter. Baji, it's your turn."

"Oh, I can't," Baji said.

"Why not?"

"I'm eating."

Altan rolled his eyes. "*Baji*."

"Send Ramsa," Baji whined. "He hasn't been out since—"

Bang. The door to the mess hall slammed open. All heads whipped toward the far end of the room, where a figure garbed in the black robes of the Cike was staggering through the doorway. The division soldiers standing by the exit hastily skirted away, clearing a path for the massive stranger.

Only the Cike were unfazed.

"Suni's back," Unegen said. "Took him long enough."

Suni was a giant man with a boyish face. A thick golden dusting of hair covered his arms and legs, more hair than Rin had ever seen on a man. He walked with an odd lope, like an ape's walk, like he'd rather be swinging through a tree instead of moving ponderously over land. His arms were almost thicker than Rin's entire torso; he looked as if he could crush her head in like a walnut if he wanted to.

He made a beeline toward the Cike.

"Great Tortoise," Rin muttered under her breath. "What is he?"

"Suni's mom fucked a monkey," Ramsa said happily.

"Shut up, Ramsa. Suni channels the Monkey God," Unegen reported. "Makes you glad he's on our side, doesn't it?"

Rin wasn't sure that made her any less scared of him, but Suni was already at their table.

"How'd it go?" Unegen asked cheerfully. "Did they see you?"

Suni didn't seem to hear Unegen. He cocked his head, as if sniffing at them. His temples were caked with dried blood. His tousled hair and vacant stare made him appear more animal than human, like some wild beast that couldn't decide whether to attack or flee.

Rin tensed. Something was wrong.

"It's so loud," Suni said. His voice was a low growl, gritty and guttural.

The smile slid off Unegen's face. "What?"

"They keep shouting."

"Who keeps shouting?"

Suni's eyes darted around the table. They were wild and unfocused. Rin tensed a split second before Suni leaped over the table at them. He slammed his arm into Unegen's neck, pinning him to the floor. Unegen choked, batted frantically at Suni's hulking torso.

Rin jumped to the side, lifting up her chair as a weapon just as Qara grabbed for her longbow.

Suni was grappling furiously with Unegen on the floor. There was a popping noise and then a little red fox was where Unegen had been before. It almost slithered out of Suni's grip, but Suni tightened his hold and seized the fox by the throat.

"Altan!" Qara shouted.

Altan hurtled over the fallen table, pushing Rin out of the way. He jumped onto Suni just before Suni could wrench Unegen's neck. Startled, Suni lashed out with his left arm, catching Altan in the shoulder. Altan ignored the blow and slapped Suni hard across the face.

Suni roared and let go of Unegen. The fox wriggled away and scampered toward Qara's feet, where he collapsed, sides heaving for air.

Suni and Altan were now wrestling on the floor, each trying to pin the other. Altan looked tiny against the massive Suni, who had to be twice his weight. Suni got a hold around Altan's shoulders, but Altan gripped Suni's face and squeezed his fingers toward his eyes.

Suni howled and flung Altan away from him. For a moment Altan looked like a limp puppet, tossed in the air, but he landed upright, tensed like a cat, just as Suni charged him again.

The Cike had formed a ring around Suni. Qara held an arrow fitted to her bow, ready to pierce Suni through the forehead. Baji held his rake at the ready, but Suni and Altan were rolling around so wildly he couldn't get a clean blow in. Rin's fingers closed tightly around the hilt of her sword.

Altan landed a solid kick to Suni's sternum. A crack echoed through the room. Suni tottered back, stunned. Altan rose to a low crouch, standing between Suni and the rest of the Cike.

"Get back," Altan said softly.

"They're so loud," Suni said. He didn't sound angry. He sounded scared. "*They're so loud!*"

"I said get *back*!"

Baji and Unegen retreated reluctantly. But Qara remained where she was, keeping her arrow trained at Suni's head.

"They're being so loud," said Suni. "I can't understand what they're saying."

"I can tell you everything you need to know," Altan said quietly. "Just put your arms down, Suni, can you do that for me?"

"I'm scared," Suni whimpered.

"We don't point arrows at our friends," Altan snapped without moving his head.

Qara lowered her longbow. Her arms shook visibly.

Altan walked slowly toward Suni, arms spread out in supplication. "It's me. It's just me."

"Are you going to help me?" Suni asked. His voice didn't match his demeanor. He sounded like a little child—terrified, helpless.

"Only if you let me," Altan answered.

Suni dropped his arms.

Rin's sword trembled in her hands. She was certain that Suni would snap Altan's neck.

"They're so loud," Suni said. "They keep telling me to do things, I don't know who to listen to . . ."

"Listen to me," said Altan. "Just me."

With brisk, short steps, he closed the gap between himself and Suni.

Suni tensed. Qara's hands flew to her longbow again; Rin crouched to spring forward.

Suni's massive hand closed around Altan's. He took a deep breath. Altan touched his forehead gently and brought Suni's forehead down to his own.

"It's okay," he whispered. "You're fine. You're Suni and you belong to the Cike. You don't have to listen to any voices. You just have to listen to me."

Eyes closed, Suni nodded. His heavy breathing subsided. A lopsided grin broke out over his face. When he opened his eyes, the wildness had left them.

"Hi, Trengsin," he said. "Good to have you back."

Altan exhaled slowly, then nodded and clapped Suni on the shoulder.

CHAPTER 14

"So much of a siege is sitting around on your ass," Ramsa complained. "You know how much actual fighting there's been since the Federation started landing on the beach in droves? None. We're just scouting each other out, testing the limits, playing chicken."

Ramsa had recruited Rin to help him fortify the back alleys of the intersection by the wharf.

They were slowly transforming the streets of Khurdalain into defense lines. Each evacuated house became a fort; each intersection became a trap of barbed wire. They had spent the morning methodically knocking holes through walls to link the labyrinth of lanes into a navigable transportation system to which only the Nikara had the map. Now they were filling bags with sand to pad the gaps in the walls against Federation bombardments.

"I thought you blew up an embassy building," said Rin.

"That was one time," Ramsa snapped. "More action than anyone's attempted since we got here, anyhow."

"You mean the Federation hasn't attacked yet?"

"They've launched exploratory parties to sniff out the borders. No major troop movements yet."

"And they've been at it this long? *Why?*"

"Because Khurdalain's better fortified than Sinegard. Khurdalain withstood the first two Poppy Wars, and it sure as hell is going to make it through a third." Ramsa bent down. "Pass me that bag."

She hauled it up, and he hoisted it to the top of the fortification with a grunt.

Rin couldn't help liking the scrawny urchin, who reminded her of a younger Kitay, if Kitay had been a one-eyed pyromaniac with an unfortunate adoration for explosions. She wondered how long he'd had been with the Cike. He looked impossibly young. How did a child end up on the front lines of a war?

"You've got a Sinegardian accent," she noticed.

Ramsa nodded. "Lived there for a while. My family were alchemists for the Militia base in the capital. Oversaw fire powder production."

"So what are you doing here?"

"You mean with the Cike?" Ramsa shrugged. "Long story. Father got wrapped up in some political stuff, ended up turning on the Empress. Extremists, you know. Could have been the Opera, but I'll never be sure. Anyways, he tried to detonate a rocket over the palace and ended up blowing up our factory instead." He pointed to his eyepatch. "Burned my eyeball right out. Daji's guards lopped the heads off everyone remotely involved. Public execution and everything."

Rin blinked, mostly stunned by Ramsa's breezy delivery. "Then what about you?"

"I got off easy. Father never told me much about his plans, so after they realized I didn't know anything, they just tossed me into Baghra. I think they thought killing a kid might make them look bad."

"*Baghra?*"

Ramsa nodded cheerfully. "Worst two years of my life. Near the tail end, the Empress paid me a visit and said she'd let me out if I worked on munitions for the Cike."

"And you just said yes?"

"Do you know what Baghra is like? By then, I was just about ready to do anything," said Ramsa. "Baji was in Baghra, too. Just ask him."

"What was he there for?"

Ramsa shrugged. "Who knows? He won't say. He was only there for a few months, though. But let's face it—even Khurdalain is so much better than a cell in Baghra. And the work here is *awesome*."

Rin gave him a sideways look. Ramsa sounded disturbingly chipper about his situation.

She decided to change the subject. "What was that about in the mess hall?"

"What do you mean?"

"The—uh . . ." She flailed her arms around. "The monkey man."

"Huh? Oh, that's just Suni. Does that maybe every other day. I think he just likes the attention. Altan's pretty good with him; Tyr used to just lock him up for hours until he'd calmed down." Ramsa handed her another bag. "Don't let Suni scare you. He's really pretty nice when he's not being a terror. It's just that god fucking with his head."

"So you're not a shaman?" she asked.

Ramsa shook his head quickly. "I don't mess with that shit. It screws you up. You saw Suni in there. My only god is science. Combine six parts sulfur, six parts saltpeter, and one part birthwort herb, and you've got fire powder. Formulaic. Dependable. Doesn't change. I understand the appeal, I really do, but I like having my mind to myself."

Three days passed before Rin spoke with Altan again. He spent a good deal of his time tied up in meetings with the Warlords, trying to patch up relations with the military leadership before they deteriorated any further. She would see him darting back to his office in between meetings, looking haggard and pissed. Finally, he sent Qara to summon her.

"Hey. I'm about to call a meeting. Wanted to check in on you first." Altan didn't look at her as he spoke; he was busy scrawling something on a map covering his desk. "I'm sorry it couldn't be earlier, I've been dealing with bureaucratic bullshit."

"That's all right." She fidgeted with her hands. He looked exhausted. "What are the Warlords like?"

"They're nearly useless." Altan made a disgusted noise. "The Ox Warlord's a slimy politician, and the Ram Warlord is an insecure fool who'll bend whichever way the wind blows. Jun's got them both by the ear, and the only thing they all agree on is that they hate the Cike. Means we don't get supplies, reinforcements, or intelligence, and they wouldn't let us into the mess hall if they had their way. It's a stupid way to fight a war."

"I'm sorry you have to put up with that."

"It's not your problem." He looked up from his map. "So what do you think of your division?"

"They're weird," she said.

"Oh?"

"None of them seem to realize we're in a war zone," she rephrased. Every regular division soldier she'd encountered was grim-faced, exhausted, but the way the Cike spoke and behaved made them seem like fidgety children—bored rather than scared, off-kilter and out of touch.

"They're killers by profession," Altan said. "They're desensitized to danger—everyone but Unegen, anyway; he's skittish about everything. But the rest can act like they don't understand what everyone's so freaked out about."

"Is that why the Militia hates them?"

"The Militia hates us because we have unlimited access to psychedelics, we can do what they can't, and they don't understand why. It is very difficult to justify how the Cike behave to people who don't believe in shamans," Altan said.

Rin could sympathize with the Militia. Suni's fits of rage were frequent and public. Qara mumbled to her birds in full view of the other soldiers. And once word had gotten out about Enki's veritable apothecary of hallucinogens, it spread like wildfire; the division soldiers couldn't understand why only the Cike should have access to morphine.

"So why don't you just try to tell them?" she asked. "How shamanism works, I mean."

"Because that's such an easy conversation to have? But trust me. They'll see soon enough." Altan tapped his map. "They're treating you all right, though? Made any friends?"

"I like Ramsa," she offered.

"He's a charmer. Like a new puppy. You think he's adorable until he pisses on the furniture."

"Did he?"

"No. But he did take a shit in Baji's pillow once. Don't get on his bad side." Altan grimaced.

"How old is he?" Rin had to ask.

"At least twelve. Probably no older than fifteen." Altan shrugged. "Baji's got this theory that he's actually a forty-year-old who doesn't age, because we've never seen him get any taller, but he's not nearly mature enough."

"And you put him into war zones?"

"Ramsa puts himself into war zones," Altan said. "You just try to stop him. Have you met the rest? No problems?"

"No problems," she said hastily. "Everything's fine, it's just . . ."

"They're not Sinegard graduates," he finished for her. "There's no routine. No discipline. Nothing you're used to. Am I right?"

She nodded.

"You can't think of them as just the Thirteenth Division. You can't command them like ground troops. They're like chess pieces, right? Only they're mismatched and overpowered. Baji's the most competent, and probably should be the commander, but he gets distracted by anything with legs. Unegen's good for intelligence gathering, but he's scared of his own shadow. Bad in open combat. Aratsha's useless unless you're right beside a body of water. You always want Suni in a firefight, but he's got no subtlety, so you can't assign him to anything else. Qara's the best archer I've seen and probably the most useful of the lot, but she's mediocre in hand-to-hand. And Chaghan's a walking psychospiritual bomb, but only when he's here." Altan threw his hands up. "Put that all together and try to formulate a strategy."

Rin glanced down at the markings on his map. "But you've thought of something?"

"I think so." A grin quirked over his face. "Why don't we go call the rest of them?"

Ramsa arrived first. He smelled suspiciously of fire powder, though Rin couldn't imagine where he'd gotten more. Baji and Unegen showed up minutes later, hoisting Aratsha's barrel between them. Qara appeared with Enki, heatedly discussing something in Qara's language. When they saw the others, they quickly fell silent. Suni came in last, and Rin was privately relieved when he took a seat at the opposite end of the room.

Altan's office had only the one chair, so they sat on the floor in a circle like a ring of schoolchildren. Aratsha bobbed conspicuously in the corner, towering over them like some grotesque watery plant.

"Gang's together again," Ramsa said happily.

"Sans Chaghan," said Baji. "When's he back? Qara? Estimated location?"

Qara glowered at him.

"Never mind," said Baji.

"We're all here? Good." Altan walked into the office carrying a rolled-up map in one hand. He unfurled it over his desk, then pinned it up against the far wall. The crucial landmarks of the city had been marked in red and black ink, dotted over with circles of varying size.

"Here's our position in Khurdalain," he said. He pointed to the black circles. "This is us." Then to the red ones. "This is Mugen."

The maps reminded Rin of a game of wikki, the chess variation Irjah had taught them to play in their third-year Strategy class. Wikki play did not involve direct confrontation, but rather dominance through strategic encirclement. Both the Nikara and the Federation had as of yet avoided direct clash, instead filling empty spaces on the complicated network of canals that was Khurdalain to establish a relative advantage. The opposing forces held each other in a fragile equilibrium, gradually raising the stakes as reinforcements flocked to the city from both sides.

"The wharf now stands as the main line of defense. We insulate the civilian quarters against Federation encampments on the beach. They haven't attempted a press farther inland because all three divisions are concentrated right on the mouth of the Sharhap River. But that balance only holds so long as they're uncertain about our numbers. We're not sure how good their intelligence is, but we're guessing they're aware that we'd be pretty evenly matched in an open field. After Sinegard, the Federation forces don't want to risk direct confrontation. They don't want to bleed forces before their inland campaign. They'll only attack when they have the sure numbers advantage."

Altan indicated on the map where he had circled an area to the north of where they were stationed.

"In three days, the Federation will bring in a fleet to supplement the troops at the Sharhap River. Their warship will unload twelve sampans bearing men, supplies, and fire powder off the coast. Qara's birds have seen them sailing over the narrow strait. At their current speed, we predict they will land after sunset of the third day," Altan announced. "I want to sink them."

"And I want to sleep with the Empress." Baji looked around. "Sorry, I thought we were voicing our fantasies."

Altan looked unamused.

"Look at your own map," Baji insisted. "The Sharhap is swarming with Jun's men. You can't attack the Federation without escalation. This forces their hand. And the Warlords won't get on board—they're not ready, they want to wait for the Seventh to get here."

"They're not landing at the Sharhap," Altan responded. "They're docking at the Murui. Far away from the fishing wharf.

The civilians stay away from Murui; the flat shore means that there's a broad intertidal zone and a fast-running tide. Which means there's no fixed coastline. They'll have difficulty unloading. And the terrain beyond the beaches is nonideal for them; it's crisscrossed by rivers and creeks, and there are hardly any good roads."

Baji looked confused. "Then why the hell are they docking there?"

Altan looked smug. "For precisely the same reasons that the First and Eighth are amassing troops by Sharhap. Sharhap's the obvious landing spot. The Federation don't think anyone will be guarding Murui. But they weren't counting on, you know, talking birds."

"Nice one," Unegen said.

"Thank you." Qara looked smug.

"The coast at Murui leads into a tight latticework of irrigation channels by a rice paddy. We will draw the boats as far as possible inland, and Aratsha will ground them by reversing the currents to cut off an escape route."

They looked to Aratsha.

"You can do that?" Baji asked.

The watery blob that was Aratsha's head bobbed from side to side. "A fleet that size? Not easily. I can give you thirty minutes. One hour, tops."

"That's more than enough," said Altan. "If we can get them bunched together, they'll catch fire in seconds. But we need to corral them into the narrow strait. Ramsa. Can you create a diversion?"

Ramsa tossed something round in a sack across the table to Altan.

Altan caught it, opened it, and made a face. "What *is* this?"

"It's the Bone-Burning Fire Oil Magic Bomb," Ramsa said. "New model."

"Cool." Suni leaned toward the bag. "What's in it?"

"Tung oil, sal ammoniac, scallion juice, and feces." Ramsa rattled off the ingredients with relish.

Altan looked faintly alarmed. "*Whose* feces?"

"That's not important," Ramsa said hastily. "This can knock birds out of the sky from fifty feet away. I can plant some bamboo rockets for you, too, but you'll have trouble igniting in this humidity."

Altan raised an eyebrow.

"Right." Ramsa chuckled. "I love Speerlies."

"Aratsha will reverse the currents to trap them," Altan continued. "Suni, Baji, Rin, and I will defend from the shore. They'll have reduced visibility from the combination of smoke and fog, so they'll think we're a larger squad than we are."

"What happens if they try to storm the shore?" Unegen asked.

"They can't," said Altan. "It's marshland. They'll sink into the bog. At nighttime it'll be impossible for them to find solid land. We will defend those crucial points in teams of two. Qara and Unegen will detach supply boats from the back of the van and drag them back to the main channel. Whatever we can't take, we'll burn."

"One problem," Ramsa said. "I'm out of fire powder. The Warlords aren't sharing."

"I'll deal with the Warlords," Altan said. "You just keep making those shit bombs."

The great military strategist Sunzi wrote that fire should be used on a dry night, when flames might spread with the smallest provocation. Fire should be used when one was upwind, so that the wind would carry its brother element, smoke, into the enemy encampment. Fire should be used on a clear night, when there was no chance for rainfall to quench the flames.

Fire should not be used on a night like this, when the humid winds from the beach would prevent it from spreading, when stealth was of utmost importance but any torchlight would give them away.

But tonight they were not using regular fire. They needed nothing so rudimentary as kindling and oil. They didn't need torches. They had Speerlies.

Rin crouched among the reeds beside Altan, eyes fixed on the darkening sky as she awaited Qara's signal. They pressed flat against the mud bank, stomachs on the ground. Water seeped through her thin tunic from the moist mud, and the peat emitted such a rank odor of rotten eggs that breathing through her mouth only made her want to gag.

On the opposite bank she could just see Suni and Baji crawl up against the river and drop down among the reeds. Between them, they held the only two strips of solid land in the paddy; two slender pieces of dry peat that reached into the marsh like fingers.

The thick fog that might have dampened regular kindling now gave them the advantage. It would be a boon to the Federation as they made their amphibious landing, but it would also serve to conceal the Cike and to exaggerate their numbers.

"How did you know there would be a fog?" she whispered to Altan.

"There's a fog every time it rains. This is the wet cycle for the rice paddies. Qara's birds have been keeping track of cloud movements for the past week," Altan said. "We know the marsh inside out."

Altan's attention to detail was remarkable. The Cike operated with a system of signals and cues that Rin would never have been able to decipher had she not been drilled relentlessly the day before. When Qara's falcon flew overhead, that had been the signal for Aratsha to begin his subtle manipulation of the river currents. Half an hour before that, an owl had flown low over the river, signaling Baji and Suni to ingest a handful of colorful fungi. The drug's reaction time was timed precisely to the estimated arrival of the fleet.

Amateurs obsess over strategy, Irjah had once told their class. *Professionals obsess over logistics.*

Rin had choked down a bagful of poppy seeds when she saw Qara's first signal; they stuck thickly to her throat, settled lightly in her stomach. She felt the effects when she stood; she was just high enough that her head felt light but not so woozy that she couldn't wield a sword.

Altan had ingested nothing. Altan, for some reason, did not seem to need any drugs to summon the Phoenix. He called the fire as casually as one might whistle. It was an extension of him that he could manipulate with no concentration at all.

A faint rustle overhead. Rin could barely make out the silhouette of Qara's eagle, passing over for the second time to alert them to the arrival of the Federation. She heard a gentle sloshing noise coming from the channel.

Rin squinted at the river and saw not a fleet of boats but a line of Federation soldiers, implausibly walking in the river that reached up to their shoulders. They carried wooden planks high over their heads.

She realized that they were engineers. They were going to use those planks to create bridges for the incoming fleet to roll supplies onto dry land. *Smart*, she thought. The engineers each held a waterproof lamp high over the murky channel, casting an eerie glow over the canal.

Altan motioned for Suni and Baji to crouch deeper to the ground so they wouldn't be visible over the reeds. The long grass tickled Rin's earlobes, but she didn't move.

Then, far down by the mouth of the channel, Rin saw the dim flicker of a lantern signal. At first she could see only the boat at the fore.

Then the full fleet emerged from the mist.

Rin counted under her breath. The fleet was twelve boats—sleek, well-constructed river sampans—packed with eight men each, sitting in a straight line with trunks of equipment stacked in high piles at the center of each boat.

The fleet paused at a fork in the river. The Federation had two choices; one channel took them to a wide bay where they could unload with relative ease, and the other took them on a detour into the salt marsh labyrinth where the Cike lay in waiting.

The Cike needed to force the fleet to the left.

Altan lifted an arm and flicked his hand out as if releasing a whip. Tendrils of flame licked out from his hands, streaking in either direction like glowing snakes. Rin heard a short sizzling noise as the flame raced through the reeds.

Then, with a high-pitched whistling noise, the first of Ramsa's rockets erupted into the night sky.

Ramsa had rigged the marsh so that each rocket's ignition would light the next sequentially, granting several seconds of delay between explosions. They set the marsh ablaze with a horrifically pungent stink that overwhelmed even the sulfurous odor of the peat.

"Tiger's tits," Altan muttered. "He wasn't joking about the feces."

The explosions continued, a chain reaction of fire powder to simulate the noise and devastation of an army that didn't exist. Bamboo bombs at the far end of the river erupted with what sounded like thunderclaps. A succession of smaller fire rockets exploded with resonant booms and enormous pillars of smoke; these did not catch fire, but served to confuse the Federation soldiers and obstruct their vision, so their boats could not see where they were going.

The explosions goaded the Federation soldiers directly into the dead zone created by Aratsha. When the first flare went up, the Federation boats swerved rapidly away from the source of the explosions. The boats collided with one another, snarled together and crammed in the narrow creek as the fleet moved clumsily forward. The tall rice fields, unharvested since the siege had begun, forced the boats to clump together.

Realizing his mistake, the Federation captain ordered his men to reverse direction, but panicked shouts echoed across the boats as the ships realized they could not move.

The Federation was locked in.

Time for the real attack.

As fire rockets continued to shoot toward the Federation fleet, a series of flaming arrows screamed through the night sky and thudded into the cargo trunks. The volley of arrows came so rapidly that it seemed as if an entire squadron were concealed in the marshes, firing from different directions, but Rin knew that it was only Qara, safely ensconced on the opposite bank, firing with the blinding speed of a trained huntress from the Hinterlands.

Next Qara took out the engineers. She punctured the forehead of every other man, tidily collapsing the man-made bridge with a surreal neatness.

Assaulted from all sides by enemy fire, the Federation fleet began to burn.

The Federation soldiers abandoned their flaming boats in a panic. They leaped for the bank, only to be bogged down in the muddy marsh. Men slipped and fell in paddy water that came up to their waists, filling up their heavy armor. Then, at a whisper from Altan, the reeds along the shore also burst into flame, surrounding the Federation like a death trap.

Even so, some made it to the opposite bank. A throng of soldiers—ten, twenty—clambered onto dry land—only to run into Suni and Baji.

Rin wondered how Suni and Baji intended to hold the entire strip of peat alone. They were only two, and from what she knew of their shamanic abilities, they couldn't control a far-ranging element the way Altan or Aratsha could. Surely they were outnumbered.

She shouldn't have worried.

They barreled through the soldiers like boulders crashing through a wheat field.

In the dim light of Ramsa's flares, Suni and Baji were a flurry of motion that evoked the flashing combat of a shadow puppetry show.

They were so much the opposite of Altan. Altan fought with the practiced grace of a martial artist. Altan moved like a ribbon of smoke, like a dancer. But Baji and Suni were a study in brutality, paragons of sheer and untempered force. They utilized none of the economical forms of Seejin. Their only guiding principle was to smash everything in their vicinity—which they did with abandon, knocking men back off the shore as quickly as they clambered on.

A Sinegard-trained martial artist was worth four Militia men. But Suni and Baji were each worth at least ten.

Baji cut through bodies like a canteen cook chopping through vegetables. His absurd nine-pointed rake, unwieldy in the hands of any other soldier, became a death machine in Baji's grip. He snagged sword blades between the nine prongs, locking three or four blades together before wrenching them out of his opponents' grasps.

His god had given him no apparent transformations, but he fought with a berserker's rage, truly a wild boar in a bloodthirsty frenzy.

Suni fought with no weapon at all. Already massive, he seemed to have grown to the size of a small giant, stretching up to well over ten feet. It shouldn't have been possible for Suni to disarm men with steel swords as he did, but he was simply so terribly strong that his opponents were like children in comparison.

As Rin watched, Suni grasped the heads of the two closest soldiers and smashed them against each other. They burst like ripe cantaloupes. Blood and brain matter splashed out, drenching Suni's entire torso, but he hardly paused to wipe the gore from his face as he turned to smash his fist into another soldier's head.

Fur had sprouted from his arms and back that seemed to serve as an organic shield, repelling metal. A soldier jammed his spear into Suni's back from behind, but the blade simply clattered off to the side. Suni turned around and bent slightly, placed his arms around the soldier's head, and tore it clean off his body with such ease that he might have been twisting the lid off a jar.

When he turned back to the marsh, Rin caught a glimpse of his eyes in the firelight. They were black all the way through.

She shuddered. Those were the eyes of a beast. Whatever was fighting on the shore, that wasn't Suni. That was some ancient entity, malevolent and gleeful, ecstatic to be given free rein to break men's bodies like toys.

"The other bank! Get to the other bank!"

A clump of soldiers broke off from the jammed fleet and approached Altan and Rin's shore in a desperate swarm.

"We're up, kiddo," Altan said, and emerged from the reeds, trident spinning in his grasp.

Rin scampered to her feet, then swayed when the effects of the poppy hit her like a club to the side of the head. She stumbled. She knew she was in a dangerous place. Unless she called the god, the poppy would only make her useless in battle, high and disoriented. But when she reached inside herself for the fire, she grasped nothing.

She tried chanting in the old Speerly language. Altan had taught her the incantation. She didn't understand the words; Altan barely understood them himself, but that didn't matter. What mattered were the harsh sounds, the repetition of incantations that sounded like spitting. The language of Speer was primal, guttural, and savage. It sounded like a curse. It sounded like a condemnation.

Still, it slowed her mind, brought her to the center of her swirling thoughts, and established a direct connection to the Pantheon above.

But she didn't feel herself tipping forward into the void. She heard no whooshing sound in her ears. She was not journeying upward. She reached inside herself, searching for the link to the Phoenix and . . . nothing. She felt nothing.

Something soared through the air and embedded itself in the mud by Rin's feet. She examined it with great difficulty, as if she were looking through a hazy fog. Finally, her drugged mind identified it as an arrow.

The Federation was shooting back.

She was faintly aware of Baji shouting at her from across the channel. She tried to shake away the distractions and direct her mind inward, but panic bubbled up in her chest. She couldn't concentrate. She focused on everything at once: Qara's birds, the incoming soldiers, the bodies getting closer and closer to the shore.

Across the bay she heard an unearthly scream. Suni emitted a series of high-pitched shrieks like a deranged monkey, beat his fists against his chest, and howled up at the night sky.

Beside him Baji threw his head back and boomed out a laugh, and that, too, sounded unnatural. He was too gleeful, more delighted than anyone in the midst of such carnage had the right to be. And Rin realized that this wasn't Baji laughing, this was the god in him that read spilled blood as worship.

Baji lifted his foot and shoved the soldiers squarely into the water, toppling them over like dominoes; he sent them sprawling into the river, where they flailed and struggled against the soggy marsh.

Who controlled whom? Was it the soldier who had called the god, or the god in the body of the soldier?

She didn't want to be possessed. She wanted to remain free.

But the cognitive dissonance clashed in her head. Three sets of countervailing orders competed for priority in her mind—Jiang's mandate to empty her mind, Altan's insistence that she hone her anger as a razor blade, and her own fear of letting the fire rip through her again, because once it began she didn't know how to stop it.

But she couldn't just *stand* there.

Come on, come on . . . She reached for the flames and grasped nothing. She was stuck halfway to the Pantheon and halfway in the material world, unable to fully grasp either. She had lost all sense of balance; she was disoriented, navigating her body as if remotely from very far away.

Something cold and clammy grasped at her ankles. Rin jumped back just as a soldier hauled himself out of the water. He sucked in air with hoarse gasps; he must have held his breath the entire length of the channel.

He saw her, yelled, and fell backward.

All she could register was how *young* he looked. He was not a hardened, trained soldier. This might have been his first combat engagement. He hadn't even thought to draw his weapon.

She advanced on him slowly, walking as if in a dream. Her sword hand felt foreign to her; it was someone else's arm that brought the blade down, it was someone else's foot that kicked the soldier down by his shoulder—

He was faster than she thought; he swept out and kicked her kneecap, knocking her into the mud. Before she could react, he climbed over her, pinning her down with both knees.

She looked up. Their eyes met.

Naked fear was written across his face, round and soft like a child's. He was barely taller than her. He couldn't have been older than Ramsa.

He fumbled with his knife, had to adjust it against his stomach to get a proper grip before he brought it down—

Three metal prongs sprouted from above his collarbone, puncturing the place where his windpipe met his lungs. Blood bubbled from the corners of the soldier's mouth. He splashed backward into the marsh.

"Are you all right?" Altan asked.

Before them the soldier flailed and gurgled pitifully. Altan had aimed two inches above his heart, robbed him of the mercy of an instant death and sentenced him to drown in his own blood.

Rin nodded mutely, scrabbling in the mud for her sword.

"Stay down," he said. "And get back."

He pushed her behind him with more force than necessary. She stumbled against the reeds, then looked up just in time to see Altan light up like a torch.

The effect was like a match struck to oil. Flames burst out of his chest, poured off his bare shoulders and back in streaming rivulets; surrounding him, protecting him. He was a living torch. His fire took the shape of a pair of massive wings that unfurled magnificently about him. Steam rose from the water in a five-foot radius from where Altan stood.

She had to shield her eyes from him.

This was a fully grown Speerly. This was a god in a man.

Altan repelled the soldiers like a wave. They scrambled backward, preferring to take their chances on their burning boats rather than take on this terrifying apparition.

Altan advanced on them, and the flesh sloughed off their bodies.

She could not bear the sight of him and yet she could not tear her eyes away.

Rin wondered if this was how she had burned at Sinegard.

But surely in that moment, with the flames ripping out of every orifice, she had not been so wonderfully graceful. When Altan moved, his fiery wings swirled and dipped as a reflection of him, sweeping indiscriminately across the flotilla and setting things freshly aflame.

It made sense, she thought wildly, that the Cike became living manifestations of their gods.

When Jiang had taught her to access the Pantheon, he had only ever taught her to kneel before the deities.

But the Cike pulled them down with them back into the world of mortals, and when they did, they were destructive and chaotic and terrible. When the shamans of the Cike prayed, they were not requesting that the gods do things for them so much as they were begging the gods to act *through* them; when they opened their minds to the heavens they became vessels for their chosen deities to inhabit.

The more Altan moved, the brighter he burned, as if the Phoenix itself were slowly burning through him to breach the divide between the world of dreaming and the material world. Any arrows that flew in his direction were rendered useless by roiling flames, flung to the side to sizzle dully in the marshy waters.

Rin was half-afraid that Altan would burn away altogether, until there was nothing but the fire.

In that moment she found it impossible to believe that the Speerlies could have been massacred. What a marvel the Speerly army must have been. A full regiment of warriors who burned with the same glory as Altan . . . how had anyone ever killed that race off? One Speerly was a terror; a thousand should have been unstoppable. They should have been able to burn down the world.

Whatever weaponry they had used then, the Federation soldiers were not so powerful now. Their fleet was at every possible disadvantage: trapped on all sides, with fire to their backs, a muddy marsh under their feet, and veritable gods guarding the only strips of solid land in sight.

The jammed boats had begun to burn in earnest; the crates of uniforms, blankets, and medicine smoldered and crackled, emitting thick streams of smoke that cloaked the marsh in an impenetrable shroud. The soldiers on the boats doubled over, choking, and the ones who huddled uncertainly in the shallow water began to scream, for the water had begun to boil under the heat of the blazing inferno.

It was utter carnage. It was beautiful.

Altan's plan had been brilliant in conception. Under normal circumstances, a squad of eight could not hope to stand a chance against such massive odds. But Altan had chosen a battlefield where every single one of the Federation advantages was negated by their surroundings, and the Cike's advantages were amplified.

What it came down to was that the smallest division of the Militia had brought down an entire fleet.

Altan didn't break balance when he strode onto the boat at the fore. He adjusted to the tilting floor so gracefully he might have been walking on solid ground. While the Federation soldiers flailed and reeled away, he flashed his trident out and out again, eliciting blood and silencing cries each time.

They clambered and fell before him like worshippers. He cut them down like reeds.

They splashed into the water, and the screams became louder. Rin saw them boil to death before her very eyes, skin scalded bubbling red like crab shells, and then bursting; cooked inside and out, eyes bulging in their death throes.

She had fought at Sinegard; she had incinerated a general with her own flames, but in that moment she could barely comprehend the casual destruction that Altan wrought. He fought on a scale that should not be human.

Only the captain of the fleet did not scream, did not jump into the water to escape him, but stood as erect and proud as if he were back on his ship, not in the burning wreckage of his fleet.

The captain withdrew his sword slowly and held it out before him.

He could not possibly defeat Altan in combat, but Rin found it strangely honorable that he was going to try.

The captain's lips moved rapidly, as if he was muttering an incantation to the darkness. Rin half wondered whether the captain was a shaman himself, but when she parsed out his frantic Mugini she realized he was praying.

"I am nothing to the glory that is the Emperor. By his favor I am made clean. By his grace I am given purpose. It is an honor to serve. It is an honor to live. It is an honor to die. For Ryohai. For Ryohai. For—"

Altan stepped lightly across the charred helm. Flames licked around his legs, engulfed him, but they could not hurt him.

The captain lifted his sword to his neck.

Altan lunged forward at the last moment, suddenly aware of what the captain meant to do, but he was too far to reach.

The captain drew the blade to the side in a sharp sawing motion. His eyes met Altan's, and a moment before the life dimmed from them, Rin thought she saw a glimmer of victory. Then his corpse slumped into the bog.

When Aratsha's power gave out, the wreckage that drifted back out into the Nariin Sea was a smoldering mess of charred boats, useless supplies, and broken men.

Altan called for a retreat before the Federation soldiers could regroup. Far more soldiers had escaped than they had killed, but their aim had never been to destroy the army. Sinking the supplies was enough.

Not all of the supplies, though. In the confusion of the melee, Unegen and Qara had detached two boats from the rear and hidden them in an inland canal. They boarded these now, and Aratsha spirited them through the narrow canals of Khurdalain into a downtown nook not far from the wharf.

Ramsa ran up to them when they returned.

"Did it work?" he demanded. "Did the flares work?"

"Lit up like a charm. Nice work, kid," Altan said.

Ramsa gave a hoot of victory. Altan clapped him on the shoulder, and Ramsa beamed widely. Rin could read it clearly on Ramsa's face: he adored Altan like an older brother.

It was hard not to feel the same. Altan was so solemnly competent, so casually brilliant, that all she wanted was to please him. He was strict in his command, sparing with his praise, but when he gave it, it felt wonderful. She wanted it, craved it like something tangible.

Next time. Next time she wouldn't be deadweight. She would learn to channel that anger at will, even if she risked losing herself to it.

They celebrated that night with a sack of sugar pillaged from one of the stolen boats. The mess hall was locked and they had nothing to sprinkle the sugar on, so they ate it straight by the spoonful. Once Rin would have found this disgusting; now she shoved great heaps of it into her mouth when the spoon and sack came around to her place in the circle.

Upon Ramsa's insistence, Altan acquiesced to lighting a roaring bonfire for them out in an empty field.

"We're not worried about being seen?" Rin asked.

"We're well behind Nikara lines. It's fine. Just don't throw anything on it," he said. "You can't experiment with pyrotechnics so close to civilians."

Ramsa blew air out of his cheeks. "Whatever you say, Trengsin."

Altan gave him an exasperated look. "I mean it this time."

"You suck the fun out of everything," Ramsa grumbled as Altan stepped away from the fire.

"You're not staying?" Baji asked.

Altan shook his head. "Need to brief the Warlords. I'll be back in a few hours. You go on and celebrate. I'm very pleased with your performance today."

"'*I'm very pleased with your performance today*,'" Baji mimicked when Altan had left. "Someone tell him to get that stick out of his butt."

Ramsa leaned back on his elbows and nudged Rin with his foot. "Was he this insufferable at the Academy?"

"I don't know," she said. "I didn't know him well at Sinegard."

"I bet he's always been like this. Old man in a young man's body. You think he ever smiles?"

"Only once a year," said Baji. "Accidentally, in his sleep."

"Come on," Unegen said, though he was also smiling. "He's a good commander."

"He *is* a good commander," Suni agreed. "Better than Tyr."

Suni's gentle voice surprised Rin. When he was free of his god, Suni was remarkably quiet, almost timid, and he spoke only after ponderous deliberation.

Rin watched him sitting calmly before the fire. His broad features were relaxed and placid; he seemed utterly at ease with himself. She wondered when he would next lose control and fall prey to that screaming voice in his mind. He was so terrifyingly strong—he had broken men apart in his hands like eggs. He killed so well and so efficiently.

He could have killed Altan. Three nights ago in the mess hall Suni could have broken Altan's neck as easily as he would wring a chicken's. The thought made her dry-mouthed with fear.

And she wondered at how Altan had known this and had crossed the distance to Suni anyway, had placed his life completely in the hands of his subordinate.

Baji had somehow extracted a bottle of sorghum spirits from

one of the many warehouses of Khurdalain. They passed it around the circle. They had just scored a major combat victory; they could afford to be off guard for just one night.

"Hey, Rin." Ramsa rolled onto his stomach and propped his chin up on his hands.

"Yeah?"

"Does this mean the Speerlies aren't extinct after all?" he inquired. "Are you and Altan going to make babies and repopulate the Speerly race?"

Qara snorted loudly. Unegen spat out a mouthful of sorghum wine.

Rin turned bright red. "Not likely," she said.

"Why not? You don't like Altan?"

The cheeky little shit. "No, I mean I can't," she said. "I can't have children."

"Why not?" Ramsa pressed.

"I had my womb destroyed at the Academy," she said. She hugged her knees up to her chest. "It was, um, interfering with my training."

Ramsa looked so bewildered then that Rin burst out laughing. Qara snickered into her canteen.

"*What?*" Ramsa asked, indignant.

"I'll tell you one day," Baji promised. He'd imbibed twice as much wine as the rest of them; he was already slurring his words together. "When your balls have dropped."

"My balls *have* dropped."

"When your voice drops, then."

They passed the bottle around in silence for a moment. Now that the frenzy at the marsh was over, the Cike seemed diminished somehow, like they had been animated only by the presence of their gods, and now in the gods' absence they were empty, shells that lacked vitality.

They seemed eminently human—vulnerable and breakable.

"So you're the last of your kind," said Suni after a short silence. "That's sad."

"I guess." Rin poked a stick at the fire. She still didn't feel quite acclimated to her new identity. She had no memories of Speer, no real attachments to it. The only time she felt like being a Speerly meant something was when she was with Altan. "Everything about Speer is sad."

"It's that idiot queen's fault," said Unegen. "They never would have died off if Tearza hadn't stabbed herself."

"She didn't stab herself," said Ramsa. "She burned to death. Imploded from inside. Boom." He spread his fingers in the air.

"Why *did* she kill herself?" Rin asked. "I never understood that story."

"In the version I heard, she was in love with the Red Emperor," said Baji. "He comes to her island, and she's immediately besotted with him. He turns around and threatens to invade the island if Speer doesn't become a tributary state. And she's so distraught at his betrayal that she flees to her temple and kills herself."

Rin wrinkled her nose. Every version she heard of the myth made Tearza seem more and more stupid.

"It is not a love story." Qara spoke up from her corner for the first time. Their eyes flickered toward her with mild surprise.

"That myth is Nikara propaganda," she continued flatly. "The story of Tearza was modeled on the myth of Han Ping, because the story makes for a better telling than the truth."

"And what is the truth?" asked Rin.

"You don't know?" Qara fixed Rin with a somber gaze. "Speerlies especially ought to know."

"Obviously I don't. So how would you tell it?"

"I would tell it not as a love story, but as a story of gods and humans." Qara's voice dropped to such a low volume that the Cike had to lean in to hear her. "They say Tearza could have called the Phoenix and saved the isle. They say that if Tearza had summoned the flames, Nikan never would have been able to annex Speer. They say that if she wanted to, Tearza could have summoned such a power that the Red Emperor and his armies would not have dared set foot on Speer, not for a thousand years."

Qara paused. She did not take her eyes off Rin.

"And then?" Rin pressed.

"Tearza refused," Qara said. "She said the independence of Speer did not warrant the sacrifice the Phoenix demanded. The Phoenix declared that Tearza had broken her vows as the ruler of Speer, and so it punished her for it."

Rin was quiet for a moment. Then she asked, "Do you think she was right?"

Qara shrugged. "I think Tearza was wise. *And* I think that she was a bad ruler. Shamans should know when to resist the power of the gods. That is wisdom. But rulers should do everything in their power to save their country. That is responsibility. If you hold the fate of the country in your hands, if you have accepted your obligation to your people, then your life ceases to be your own. Once you accept the title of ruler, your choices are made for you. In those days, to rule Speer meant serving the Phoenix. Speer used to be a proud race. A free people. When Tearza killed herself, the Speerlies became little more than the Emperor's mad dogs. Tearza has the blood of Speer on her hands. Tearza deserved what she got."

When Altan returned from reporting to the Warlords, most of the Cike had drifted off to sleep. Rin remained awake, staring at the flickering bonfire.

"Hey," he said, and sat down next to her. He smelled of smoke.

She drew her knees up to her chest and tilted her head sideways to look at him. "How'd they take it?"

Altan smiled. It was the first time she'd seen him smile since they came to Khurdalain. "They couldn't believe it. How are you doing?"

"Embarrassed," she said frankly, "and still a little high."

He leaned back and crossed his arms. His smile disappeared. "What happened?"

"Couldn't concentrate," she said. *Got scared. Held off. Did everything you told me not to do.*

Altan looked faintly puzzled, and more than a little disappointed.

"I'm sorry," she said in a small voice.

"No, it's my fault." His voice was carefully neutral. "I threw you into combat before you were ready. At the Night Castle, you would have trained for months before we put you in the field."

This was meant to make her feel better, but Rin only felt ashamed.

"I couldn't clear my mind," she said.

"Then don't," Altan said. "Open-minded meditation is for monks. It only gets you to the Pantheon, it doesn't bring the god back down with you. You don't need to open your mind to all sixty-four deities. You only need our god. You only need the fire."

"But Jiang said that was dangerous."

Though Rin thought she saw a spasm of impatience flicker across Altan's face, his tone remained carefully neutral. "Because Jiang *feared*, and so he held you back. Were you acting under his orders when you called the Phoenix at Sinegard?"

"No," she admitted, "but—"

"Have you *ever* successfully called a god under Jiang's instruction? Did Jiang even teach you how? I'll bet he did the opposite. I'll bet he wanted you to shut them out."

"He was trying to protect me," she protested, though she wasn't sure why. After all, it was precisely what had frustrated her about Jiang. But somehow, after what she'd done at Sinegard, Jiang's caution made more sense. "He warned that I might . . . that the consequences . . ."

"Great danger is always associated with great power. The difference between the great and the mediocre is that the great are willing to take that risk." Altan's face twisted into a scowl. "Jiang was a coward, scared of what he had unlocked. Jiang was a doddering fool who didn't realize what talents he had. What talents *you* have."

"He was still my master," she said, feeling an instinctive urge to defend him.

"He's not your master anymore. You don't have a master. You have a commander." Altan put a hand on her shoulder. "The easiest shortcut to the state is anger. Build on your anger. Don't *ever* let go of that anger. Rage gives you power. Caution does not."

Rin wanted to believe him. She was in awe of the extent of Altan's power. And she knew that, if she allowed it, the same power could be her own.

And yet, Jiang's warnings echoed in the back of her mind.

I have met spirits unable to find their bodies again. I have met men who are only halfway to the spirit realm, caught between our world and the next.

Was that the price of power? For her mind to shatter, like Suni's clearly had? Would she become neurotically paranoid, like Unegen?

But Altan's mind hadn't shattered. Among the Cike, Altan used his abilities most recklessly. Baji and Suni needed hallucinogens to call their gods, but the fire was never more than a whisper away for Altan. He seemed to always be in that state of rage he wanted Rin to cultivate. And yet he never lost control. He gave an incredible illusion of sanity and stability, whatever was going on below his dispassionate mask.

Who is imprisoned in the Chuluu Korikh?
Unnatural criminals, who have committed unnatural crimes.

She suspected she knew now what Jiang's question had meant.

She didn't want to admit that she was scared. Scared of being in a state where she had little control of herself, less still of the fires pouring out of her. Scared of being consumed by the fire, becoming a conduit that demanded more and more sacrifice for her god.

"The last time I did it, I couldn't stop," she said. "I had to beg it. I don't—I don't know how to control myself when I've called the Phoenix."

"Think of it like a candle," he said. "Difficult to light. Only this is even more difficult to extinguish, and if you're not careful, you'll burn yourself."

But that didn't help at all—she'd *tried* lighting the candle, yet nothing had happened. So what would happen if she finally figured that out, only to be unable to extinguish the flames? "Then how do *you* do it? How do you make it stop?"

Altan leaned back away from the flames.

"I don't," he said.

CHAPTER 15

The Ram and Ox Warlords quickly realigned to Altan's side once they realized the Cike had accomplished what the First, Fifth, and Eighth Divisions together had not even attempted. They disseminated the news through the ranks in a way that made it seem that they were jointly responsible for the feat.

Khurdalain's citizens threw a victory parade to raise morale and collect supplies for the soldiers. Civilians donated food and clothing to the barracks. When the Warlords paraded through the streets, they were met with wide applause that they were only too happy to accept.

The civilians assumed the marsh victory had been achieved through a massive joint assault. Altan did nothing to correct them.

"Lying fart-bags," Ramsa complained. "They're stealing your credit."

"Let them," said Altan. "If it means they'll work with me, let them say anything they want."

Altan had needed that victory. In a cohort of generals who had survived the Poppy Wars, Altan was the youngest commander by decades. The battle at the marsh had given him much-needed credibility in the eyes of the Militia, and more important, in the eyes of the Warlords. They treated him now with deference instead of condescension, consulted him in their war councils, and not only listened to Cike intelligence but acted on it.

Only Jun offered no congratulations.

"You've left a thousand starving enemy soldiers in the wetlands with no supplies and no food," Jun said slowly.

"Yes," Altan said. "Isn't that a good thing?"

"You idiot," said Jun. He paced about the office, circled back, then slammed his hands on Altan's desk. "You *idiot*. Do you realize what you've done?"

"Secured a victory," Altan said, "which is more than you've managed in the weeks you've been here. Their supply ship has turned all the way back to the longbow island to restock. We've set their plans back at least two weeks."

"You've invited retaliation," Jun snapped. "Those soldiers are cold, wet, and hungry. Maybe they didn't care much about this war when they crossed the narrow strait, but now they're angry. They're pissed, they're humiliated, and more than anything they desperately need supplies. You've raised the stakes for them."

"The stakes were already high," Altan said.

"Yes, and now you've dragged pride into it. Do you know how much reputation matters to Federation commanders? We needed time for fortifications, but you've doubled their timetables. What, did you think they would just turn tail and go home? You want to know what they'll do next? They're going to come for us."

But when the Federation did come, it was with a white flag and a plea for a cease-fire.

When Qara's birds spotted the incoming Federation delegation, she sent Rin to alert Altan with the news. Thrilled, Rin barged past Jun's aides to force her way into the office of the Ram Warlord.

"Three Federation delegates," she reported. "They brought a wagon."

"Shoot them," Jun suggested immediately.

"They're carrying a white flag," Rin said.

"A strategic gambit. Shoot them," Jun repeated, and his junior officers nodded their assent.

The Ox Warlord held up a hand. He was a tremendously large man, two heads taller than Jun and thrice again his girth. His weapon of choice was a double-bladed battle-axe that was the size of Rin's torso, which he kept on the table in front of him, stroking the blade obsessively. "They could be coming under peace."

"Or they could be coming to poison our water supply, or to assassinate any one of us," Jun snapped. "Do you really think we've won this war so easily?"

"They're bearing a white flag," the Ox Warlord said slowly, as if speaking to a child.

The Ram Warlord said nothing. His wide-set eyes darted nervously between Jun and the Ox Warlord. Rin could see what Ramsa had meant; the Ram Warlord seemed like a child waiting to be told what to do.

"A white flag doesn't mean anything to them," Jun insisted. "This is a ruse. How many false treaties did they sign during the Poppy Wars?"

"Would you take a gamble on peace?" the Ox Warlord challenged.

"I wouldn't gamble with any of these citizens' lives."

"It's not your cease-fire to refuse," the Ram Warlord pointed out.

Jun and the Ox Warlord both glared at him, and the Ram Warlord stammered in his haste to explain. "I mean, we ought to let the boy handle it. The marsh victory was his doing. They're surrendering to him."

All eyes turned to Altan.

Rin was amazed at the subtle interdivisional politics at play. The Ram Warlord was shrewder than she'd guessed. His suggestion was a clever way of absolving responsibility. If negotiations went sour, then blame would fall on Altan's shoulders. And if they went well, then the Ram Warlord still came out on top for his magnanimity.

Altan hesitated, clearly torn between his better judgment and desire to see the full extent of his victory at Khurdalain. Rin could see the hope reflected clearly on his face. If the Federation surrender was genuine, then he would be single-handedly responsible for winning this war. He would be the youngest commander ever to have achieved a military victory on this scale.

"Shoot them," Jun repeated. "We don't need a peace negotiation. Our forces are tied now; if the assault on the wharf goes well, we can push them back indefinitely until the Seventh gets here."

But Altan shook his head. "If we reject their surrender, then this war goes on until one party has decimated the other. Khurdalain can't hold out that long. If there's a chance we can end this war now, we need to take it."

The Federation delegates who met them in the town square bore no weapons and wore no armor. They dressed in light, form-fitting blue uniforms designed to make it clear that they concealed no weapons in their sleeves.

The head delegate, whose uniform stripes indicated his higher rank, stepped forward when he saw them.

"Do you speak our language?" He spoke in a halting and outdated Nikara dialect, complete with a bad approximation of a Sinegardian accent.

The Warlords hesitated, but Altan cut in, "I do."

"Good," the delegate responded in Mugini. "Then we may proceed without misunderstanding."

It was the first time Rin had gotten a good look at the Mugenese outside the chaos of a melee, and she was disappointed by how very similar they looked to the Nikara. The slant of their eyes and the shape of their mouths were nowhere near as pronounced as the textbooks reported. Their hair was the same pitch-black as Nezha's, their skin as pale as any northerner's.

In fact, they looked more like Sinegardians than Rin and Altan did.

Aside from their language, which was more clipped and rapid than Sinegardian Nikara, they were virtually indistinguishable from the Nikara themselves.

It disturbed her that the Federation soldiers so closely resembled her own people. She would have preferred a faceless, monstrous enemy, or one that was entirely foreign, like the pale-haired Hesperians across the sea.

"What are your terms?" Jun asked.

"Our general requests a cease-fire for the next forty-eight hours while we meet to negotiate conditions of surrender," said the head delegate. He indicated the wagon. "We know your city has been unable to import spices since the fighting began. We bring an offering of salt and sugar. A gesture of our goodwill." The delegate placed his hand on the lid of the closest chest. "May I?"

Altan gave a nod of permission. The delegates pulled up the lids, displaying heaps of white and caramel crystals that glistened in the afternoon sun.

"Eat it," suggested Jun.

The delegate cocked his head. "Pardon?"

"Taste the sugar," Jun said. "So we know you're not trying to poison us."

"That would be a terribly inefficient way of conducting warfare," said the delegate.

"Even so."

Shrugging, the delegate obliged Jun's request. His throat bobbed as he swallowed. "Not poison."

Jun licked his finger, stuck it in the chest of sugar, and tipped it into his mouth. He swilled it around in his mouth, and seemed disappointed when he couldn't detect traces of any other material.

"Only sugar," said the delegate.

"Excellent," the Ox Warlord said. "Bring these to the mess hall."

"No," said Altan quickly. "Leave it out here. We'll distribute this in the town square. A small amount for every household."

He met the Ox Warlord's eyes with a level gaze, and Rin realized why he'd said it. If the rations were brought to the mess hall, the divisions would immediately fight over distribution of resources. Altan had tied the Warlords' hands by designating the rations for the people.

In any case, a trickle of Khurdalaini civilians had already begun to gather around the wagon in curiosity. Salt and sugar had been sorely missed since the siege began. Rin suspected that if the Warlords confiscated the trunks for military use, the people would riot.

The Ox Warlord shrugged. "Whatever you say, kid."

Altan looked warily about the square. Given the ranks of Militia soldiers present, a large crowd of civilians had deemed it safe to form around the three delegates. Rin saw such open hostility in their eyes that she didn't doubt they would tear the Mugenese apart if the Militia didn't intervene.

"We will continue this negotiation in a private office," Altan suggested. "Away from the people."

The delegate inclined his head. "As you like."

"The Emperor Ryohai is impressed with the resistance at Khurdalain," said the delegate. His tone was clipped and courteous, despite his words. "Your people have fought well. The Emperor Ryohai would like to extend his compliments to the people of Khurdalain, who have proven themselves a stronger breed than the rest of this land of sniveling cowards."

Jun translated to the Warlords. The Ox Warlord rolled his eyes.

"Let's skip ahead to the part where you surrender," said Altan.

The delegate raised an eyebrow. "Alas, the Emperor Ryohai has no intentions of abandoning his designs on the Nikara continent. Expansion onto the continent is the divine right of the glorious Federation of Mugen. Your provincial government is weak and fragile. Your technology is centuries behind that of the west. Your isolation has set you behind while the rest of the world develops.

Your demise was only a matter of time. This landmass belongs to a country that can propel it into the next century."

"Did you come here just to insult us?" Jun demanded. "Not a wise way to surrender."

The delegate's lip curled. "We came only to *discuss* surrender. The Emperor Ryohai has no desire to punish the people of Khurdalain. He admires their fighting spirit. He says that your resilience has proven worthy of the Federation. He adds also that the people of Khurdalain would make excellent subjects to the Federation crown."

"Ah," said Jun. "This is *that* kind of negotiation."

"We do not want to destroy this town," said the delegate. "This is an important port. A hub of international trade. If Khurdalain lays down its arms, then the Emperor Ryohai will consider this city a territory of the Federation, and we will not lay a finger on a single man, woman, or child. All citizens will be pardoned, on the condition that they swear allegiance to the Emperor Ryohai."

"Pause," said Altan. "You're asking us to surrender to *you*?"

The delegate inclined his head. "These are generous terms. We know how Khurdalain struggles under occupation. Your people are starving. Your supplies will only last you a few more months. When we break the siege, we will take the open battle to the streets, and then your people will die in droves. You can avoid that. Let the Federation fleet through, and the Emperor will reward you. We shall permit you to live."

"Incredible," muttered Jun. "Absolutely incredible."

Altan crossed his arms. "Tell your generals that if you turn your fleets back and evacuate the shore now, we will let *you* live."

The delegate merely regarded him with an idle curiosity. "You must be the Speerly from the marsh."

"I am." Altan said. "And I'll be the one who accepts your surrender."

The corners of the head delegate's mouth turned up. "But of course," he said smoothly. "Only a child would assume a war could end so quickly, or so bloodlessly."

"That child speaks for all of us," Jun cut in, voice steely. He spoke in Nikara. "Take your conditions and tell the Emperor Ryohai that Khurdalain will never bow to the longbow island."

"In that case," said the delegate, "every last man, woman, and child in Khurdalain shall die."

"Tall words from a man who's just had his fleet burned to bits," Jun sneered.

The delegate answered in flat, emotionless Nikara. "The marsh defeat has set us back several weeks. But we have been preparing for this war for two decades. Our training schools far outstrip your pathetic Sinegard Academy. We have studied the western techniques of warfare while you have spent these twenty years indulging in your isolation. The Nikara Empire belongs to the past. We will raze your country to the ground."

The Ox Warlord reached for his axe. "Or I can take your head off right now."

The delegate looked supremely unconcerned. "Kill me if you like. On the longbow island, we are taught that our lives are meaningless. I am only one in a horde of millions. I will die, and I will be reincarnated again in the Emperor Ryohai's service. But for you, heretics who do not bow to the divine throne, death will be final."

Altan stood up. His face had turned pale with fury. "You are trapped on a narrow strip of land. You are outnumbered. We took your supplies. We burned your boats. We sank your munitions. Your men have met the wrath of a Speerly, and they burned."

"Oh, Speerlies are not so difficult to kill," the delegate said. "We managed it once. We'll do it again."

The office doors burst open. Ramsa ran inside, wild-eyed.

"That's saltpeter!" he shrieked. "That's not salt, it's *saltpeter*."

The office fell silent.

The Warlords looked at Ramsa as if they couldn't comprehend what he was saying. Altan's mouth opened in confusion.

Then the delegate threw his head back and laughed with the abandon of a man who knew he was about to die.

"Remember," he said. "You could have saved Khurdalain."

Rin and Altan stood up at the same time.

She had barely reached for her sword when a blast split the air like a thunderbolt.

One moment she was standing behind Altan and the next she was on the floor, dazed, with such a ferocious ringing in her ears that it drowned out any other sound.

She lifted her hand to her face and it came away bloody.

As if to compensate for her hearing, her vision became exceedingly bright; the blurred sights were like images on a shadow puppet screen, occurring both too fast and too slow for her to comprehend. She perceived movements as if from inside a drug-induced fever dream, but this was no dream; her senses simply refused to comply with the perception of what had happened.

She saw the walls of the office shudder and then lean so far to the side she was sure that the building would collapse with them in it, and then right themselves.

She saw Ramsa tackle Altan to the ground.

She saw Altan stagger to his feet, reaching for his trident.

She saw the Ox Warlord swing his axe through the air.

She saw Altan shouting "No, *no!*"—before the Ox Warlord decapitated the delegate.

The delegate's head rolled to a stop by the doorway, eyes open and glassy, and Rin thought she saw it smile.

Strong arms grasped her by the shoulders and hauled her to her feet. Altan spun her around to face him, eyes darting around her form as if checking for injuries.

His mouth moved, but no sound came through. She shook her head frantically and pointed to her ears.

He mouthed the words. *"Are you all right?"*

She examined her body. Somehow all four limbs were working, and she couldn't even feel the pain where she bled from a head wound. She nodded.

Altan let her go and knelt down before Ramsa, who was curled in a ball on the ground, pale and trembling.

On the other side of the room General Jun and the Ram Warlord hauled themselves to their feet. They were both unharmed; the blast had blown them over but had not injured them. The Warlords' quarters were far enough from the center of the town that the explosion only shook them.

Even Ramsa seemed like he would be fine. His eyes were glassy and he wobbled when Altan pulled him to his feet, but he was nodding and talking, and looked otherwise uninjured.

Rin exhaled in relief.

They were all right. It hadn't worked. They were all right.

And then she remembered the civilians.

Odd how the rest of her senses were amplified when she couldn't hear.

Khurdalain looked like the Academy in the first days of winter. She squinted; at first she thought her eyesight had blurred as well, and then she realized that a fine powder hung in the air. It clouded everything like some bizarre mix of fog and snowfall, a blanket of innocence that mixed in with the blood, that obscured the full extent of the explosion.

The square had been flattened, shop fronts and residential complexes collapsed, debris strewn out in oddly symmetrical lines from the radius of the blast, as if they stood inside a giant's footprint.

Farther out from the blast site, the buildings were not flattened but blown open; they tilted at bizarre angles, entire walls torn away. There was a strangely intimate perversity to how their insides were revealed, displaying private bedrooms and washrooms to the outside.

Men and women had been thrown against the walls of buildings. They remained frozen there with a kind of ghastly adhesion, pinned like preserved butterflies. The intense pressure from the bombs had torn off their clothes; they hung naked like a grotesque display of the human form.

The stench of charcoal, blood, and burned flesh was so heavy that Rin could taste it on her tongue. Even worse was the sickening sweet undercurrent of caramelized sugar wafting through the air.

She did not know how long she stood there staring. She was incited to movement only when jostled by a pair of soldiers rushing past her with a stretcher, reminding her that she had a job to do.

Find the survivors. Help the survivors.

She made her way down the street, but her sense of balance seemed to have disappeared completely along with her hearing. She lurched from side to side when she tried to walk, and so she traversed the street by clinging to furniture like a drunkard.

To her left she saw a group of soldiers hauling a pair of children out from a pile of debris. She couldn't believe they had survived, it seemed impossible so close to the blast epicenter—but the little boy they lifted from the wreckage was moving, wailing and struggling but moving nonetheless. His sister was not so fortunate; her leg was mangled, crushed by the foundations of the house. She clung to the soldier's arms, white-faced, too racked with pain to cry.

"Help me! *Help me!*"

A tinny voice made it through the roaring in her ears, like someone shouting from across a great field, but it was the only sound she could hear.

She looked up and saw a man clinging desperately to the remains of a wall with one hand.

The floor of the building had been blown out right beneath him. It was a five-story inn; without its fourth wall it looked like one of the porcelain dollhouses that Rin had seen in the market, the kind that swung wide open to reveal its contents.

The floors tilted down toward the gap; the inn's furniture and its other occupants had already slid out, forming a grotesque pile of shattered chairs and bodies.

A small crowd had gathered under the teetering inn to watch the man.

"*Help*," he moaned. "Someone, help . . ."

Rin felt like a spectator, like this was a show, like the man was the only thing in the world that mattered, yet she couldn't think of anything to do; the building had been blown apart; it looked minutes from collapsing in on itself, and the man was too high up to reach from the rooftops of any surrounding buildings.

All she could do was stand there in awe with her mouth hanging slackly open, watching as the man struggled in vain to hoist himself up.

She felt so utterly, entirely useless. Even if she could call the Phoenix then, summoning fire now would not save this man from dying.

Because all the Cike knew how to do was destroy. For all their powers, for all their gods, they couldn't protect their people. Couldn't reverse time. Couldn't bring back the dead.

They had won that battle on the marsh, but they were powerless in the face of the consequences.

Altan shouted something, and he might have been calling for a sheet to break the man's fall, because moments later Rin saw several soldiers come running back down into the square with a cloth.

But before they could reach the end of the street, the inn teetered perilously. Rin thought it might crash all the way to the ground, flattening the man underneath it, but the wooden planks dipped downward and came to a jarring halt.

The man was now only four floors up. He flung his other hand up at the roof in an attempt to secure a better hold. Perhaps he was emboldened by his closeness to the ground. For a moment Rin thought he might make it—but then his hand slipped against the shattered glass and he fell back, the downward rebound pulling him off the roof entirely.

He seemed to hang in the air for a moment before he fell.

The crowd scrambled backward.

Rin turned away, grateful that she could not hear his body break on the ground.

* * *

The city settled into a tense silence.

Every soldier was dispatched to Khurdalain's defenses in anticipation of a ground assault. Rin held her post on the outer wall for hours, eyes trained on the perimeter. If the Federation was going to attempt to breach the walls, certainly it would be now.

But evening fell, and no attack came.

"They can't possibly be afraid," Rin murmured, then winced. Her hearing had finally come back, though a high-pitched ringing still sounded constantly in her ears.

Ramsa shook his head. "They're playing the long game. They'll keep trying to weaken us. Get us scared, hungry, and tired."

Eventually the defensive line relaxed. If the Federation launched a midnight invasion, the city alarm system would bring the troops back to the walls; in the meantime, there was more pressing work to do.

It felt brutally ironic that civilians had been dancing on this street only hours ago, celebrating what they'd thought would be a Federation surrender. Khurdalain had expected to win this war. Khurdalain had thought that things were going back to normal.

But Khurdalain was resilient. Khurdalain had survived two Poppy Wars. Khurdalain knew how to deal with devastation.

The civilians quietly combed through the wreckage for their loved ones, and when so many hours had passed that the only bodies that were recovered were those of the dead, they built them a funeral bier, lit it on fire, and pushed it out to the sea. They did this with a sad, practiced efficiency.

The medical squads of all three divisions jointly created a triage center in the city center. For the rest of the day civilians straggled in, amateur tourniquets tied clumsily around severed limbs—crushed ankles, hands shattered to the stump.

Rin had a year's worth of instruction in field medicine under Enro, so Enki put her to work tying off new tourniquets for those bleeding in line as they waited for medical attention.

Her first patient was a young woman, not much older than Rin was. She held out her arm, wrapped in what looked like an old dress.

Rin unwrapped the blood-soaked bundle and hissed involuntarily at the damage. She could see bone all the way up to the elbow. That entire hand would have to go.

The girl waited patiently as Rin assessed the damage, eyes glassy, as if she'd long ago resigned herself to her new disability.

Rin pulled a strip of linen out of a pot of boiling water and wrapped it around the upper arm, looped one end around a stick, and twisted to tighten the binding. The girl moaned with pain, but gritted her teeth and glared straight forward.

"They'll probably take the hand off. This will keep you from losing any more blood, and it'll make it easier for them to amputate." Rin fastened the knot and stepped back. "I'm sorry."

"I knew we should have left," the girl said. The way she spoke, Rin wasn't sure that she was talking to her. "I knew we should have left the moment those ships landed on the shore."

"Why didn't you?" Rin asked.

The girl glared at her. Her eyes were hollow, accusatory. "You think we had anywhere to go?"

Rin fixed her eyes on the ground and moved on to the next patient.

CHAPTER 16

Hours later Rin finally received permission to leave the triage center. She stumbled back toward the Cike's quarters, hollow-eyed and light-headed from sleep deprivation. Once she checked in with Altan, she intended to collapse in her bunk and sleep until someone forced her out to report for duty.

"Enki finally let you off?"

She glanced over her shoulder.

Unegen and Baji rounded the corner, coming back from patrol. They joined her as she walked down the eerily empty streets. The Warlords had imposed martial law on the city; civilians had a strict curfew now, no longer allowed to venture beyond their block without Militia permission.

"I'm to be back in six hours," she said. "You?"

"Nonstop patrol until something more interesting happens," said Unegen. "Did Enki get the casualty count?"

"Six hundred dead," she said. "A thousand wounded. Fifty division soldiers. The rest civilians."

"Shit," Unegen muttered.

"Yeah," she said listlessly.

"The Warlords are just sitting on their hands," Baji complained. "The bombs scared the wits out of them. Fucking useless.

Don't they see? We can't just absorb the attack. We've got to strike back."

"Strike back?" Rin repeated. The very idea sounded halfhearted, disrespectful, and pointless. All she wanted to do was curl up in a ball and hold her hands over her ears and pretend nothing was happening. Leave this war to someone else.

"What are we supposed to do?" Unegen was saying. "The Warlords won't attack, and we'll get slaughtered on the open field ourselves."

"We can't just wait for the Seventh, they'll take weeks—"

They approached headquarters just as Qara stepped out of Altan's office. She closed the door delicately behind her, noticed them, and her face froze.

Baji and Unegen stopped walking. The heavy silence that transpired seemed to contain some unspoken message that everyone but Rin understood.

"It's like that, huh?" Unegen asked.

"It's worse," said Qara.

"What's going on?" Rin asked. "Is he in there?"

Qara looked warily at her. For some reason she smelled overwhelmingly of smoke. Her expression was unreadable. Rin might have seen tear tracks glistening on her cheek, or it might have been a trick of the lamplight.

"He's indisposed," Qara said.

The Federation's retaliation did not end with the bombing.

Two days after the downtown explosions, the Federation sent bilingual agents to negotiate with starving fishermen in the town of Zhabei, just south of Khurdalain, and told them the Mugenese would clear their boats from the dock if the fishermen collected all the stray cats and dogs in the town for them.

Only starving civilians would have obeyed such a bizarre order. The fishermen were desperate, and they handed over every last stray animal they could find without question.

The Federation soldiers tied kindling to the animals' tails and lit them on fire. Then they set them loose in Zhabei.

The ensuing flames burned for three days before rainfall finally extinguished them. When the smoke cleared, nothing remained of Zhabei but ashes.

Thousands of civilians were left homeless overnight, and the refugee problem in Khurdalain became unmanageable. The men, women, and children of Zhabei crammed into the shrinking parts of the city that were not yet under Federation occupation. Poor hygiene, lack of clean water, and an outbreak of cholera made the civilian districts a nightmare.

Popular sentiment turned against the Militia. The First, Fifth, and Eighth Divisions attempted to maintain martial rule, only to meet open defiance and riots.

The Warlords, desperately needing a scapegoat, publicly blamed their reversals of fortune on Altan. It helped them that the bombing shattered his credibility as a commander. He had won his first combat victory, only to have it ripped from him and turned into a tragic defeat, an example of the consequences of acting without thinking.

When Altan finally emerged from his office, he seemed to take it in stride. No one made mention of his absence; the Cike seemed to collectively pretend that nothing had happened at all. He showed no signs of insecurity—if anything, his behavior become almost manic.

"So we're back where we started," he said, pacing rapidly about his office. "Fine. We'll fight back. Next time we'll be thorough. Next time we'll win."

He planned far more operations than they could ever feasibly carry out. But the Cike were not historically soldiers, they were assassins. The battle at the marsh had been an unprecedented feat of teamwork for them; they were trained to take out crucial targets, not entire battalions. Yet assassinations did not go far in winning wars. The Federation was not like a snake, to be vanquished by cutting off the head. If a general was killed in his camp, a colonel was immediately promoted in his place. For the Cike to go about their business as usual, conducting one assassination after another, would have been a slow and inefficient way of waging a war.

So Altan used his soldiers like a guerrilla strike force instead. They stole supplies, waged hit-and-run attacks, and caused as much disruption as they could in enemy camps.

"I want the entire intersection sealed off," Altan declared, drawing a large circle on the map. "Sandbags. Barbed wire. We need to minimize all points of entry within the next twenty-four hours. I want this warehouse back."

"We can't do that," Baji said uneasily.

"Why not?" Altan snapped. A vein pulsed in his neck; dark circles ringed his eyes. Rin didn't think he had slept in days.

"Because they've got a thousand men right in that circle. It's impossible."

Altan examined the map. "For normal soldiers, maybe. But we have *gods*. They can't defeat us on an open field."

"They can if there are a thousand of them." Baji stood up, pushing his chair back with a screech. "The confidence is touching, Trengsin, but this is a suicide mission."

"I'm not being—"

"We have *eight soldiers*. Qara and Unegen haven't slept in days, Suni is one bad trip away from the Stone Mountain, and Ramsa still hasn't gotten his wits back from that explosion. Maybe we could do this with Chaghan, but I suppose wherever you've sent him matters more—"

The brush snapped in Altan's hand. "Are you contradicting me?"

"I'm pointing out your delusions." Baji pushed his chair to the side and slung his rake over his back. "You're a good commander, Trengsin, and I'll take the risks I'm asked to take, but I'll only obey commands that make some fucking sense. This doesn't even come close."

He stormed out of the office.

Even the operations that they did execute had a fatalistic, desperate air to them. For every bomb they planted, for every camp they set fire to, Rin suspected they were only annoying disturbances to the Federation. Though Qara and Unegen delivered valuable intelligence, the Fifth refused to act on it. And all the disruption Suni, Baji, and Ramsa together could create was only a drop in a bucket compared to the massive encampment that grew steadily larger as more and more ships unloaded troops on the coast.

The Cike were stretched to their limit, especially Rin. Each moment not spent on an operation was spent on patrol. And when she was off duty, she trained with Altan.

But those sessions had come to a standstill. She made rapid progress with her sword, disarming Altan almost as often as he disarmed her, but she came no closer to calling the Phoenix than she had on the marsh.

"I don't understand," Altan said. "You've done this before. You did this at Sinegard. What's stopping you?"

Rin knew what the problem was, though she couldn't admit it.

She was afraid.

Afraid that the power would consume her. Afraid she might rip a hole into the void, like Jiang had, and that she would disappear into the very power that she had called. Despite what Altan had told her, she could not just ignore two years of Jiang's teachings.

And as if she could sense her fear, the Speerly Woman became more and more vivid each time Rin meditated. Rin could see details now she hadn't seen before; cracks in her skin like she had been smashed apart and then put back together, burn scars where piece met piece.

"Don't give in," the Woman said. "You've been so brave . . . but it takes more bravery to resist the power. That boy couldn't do it, and you are so close to giving in . . . but that's what it wants, that's precisely what it's planned."

"Gods don't want anything," said Rin. "They're just forces. Powers to be tapped. How can it be wrong to use what exists in nature?"

"Not this god," said the Woman. "The nature of this god is to destroy. The nature of this god is to be greedy, to never be satisfied with what he has consumed. Be careful . . ."

Light streamed through the cracks in the Speerly Woman, as if she were being illuminated from within. Her face twisted in pain and then she disappeared, shattering the space in the void.

As downtown warfare took a greater toll on civilian life, the city was permeated with an atmosphere of intense suspicion. Two weeks after the saltpeter explosion, six Nikara farmers were sentenced to death by Jun's men for spying on behalf of the Federation. Likely they had been promised safe passage out of the besieged city if they provided valuable snippets of information. That, or they simply needed to feed themselves. Either way, thousands of fishermen, women, and children watched with a mixture of glee and disgust as Jun took their heads off in public, spiked them on poles, and placed them on display along the tall outer walls.

The vigilante justice the civilians inflicted on one another was greater—and more vicious—than anything the Militia could enforce. When rumors abounded that the Federation was planning to poison the central city water supply, armed bands of men with clubs stalked the streets, stopping and searching individuals at random. Anyone with a powdery substance was beaten severely. In the end, division soldiers had to intervene to save a group of merchants delivering herbs to the hospital from being torn apart by a crowd.

As the weeks dragged on, Altan's shoulders became stooped, his face lined and haggard. His eyes were now permanently ringed with shadows. He hardly slept; he stopped working far later than any of them and was up earlier. He took his rest in short, fretful shifts, if at all.

He spent many hours frantically pacing the walled fortifications himself, watching the horizon for any sign of Federation movement, as if willing the next assault to happen so that he could fight the entire Federation army by himself.

Once when Rin walked into his office to submit an intelligence report, she found him asleep on his desk. His cheek had ink on it; it was pressed against war plans that he had been deliberating over for hours. His shoulders were slumped on the wooden surface. In sleep, the tense lines that normally arrested his face were gone, bringing his age down at least five years.

She always forgot how young he was.

He looked so vulnerable.

He smelled like smoke.

She couldn't help herself. She stretched out a hand and touched him tentatively on the shoulder.

He sat up immediately. One hand flew instinctively to a dagger at his waist, the other shot out in front of him, igniting instantaneously. Rin took a quick step backward.

Altan took several panicked breaths before he saw Rin.

"It's just me," she said.

His chest rose and fell, and then his breathing slowed. She thought she had seen fear in his eyes, but then he swallowed and an impassive mask slid over his face.

His pupils were oddly constricted.

"I don't know," he said after a long moment. "I don't know what I'm doing."

Nobody does, she wanted to say, but she was interrupted by the loud ringing of a signal gong.

Someone was at the gates.

Qara was already standing sentry over the west wall when they climbed the stairs.

"They're here," she said simply before Altan could ask.

Rin leaned over the wall to see an army riding slowly up to the gates. It had to be a force of no less than two thousand. She was anxious at first, until she saw that they were clad in Nikara armor. At the front of the column flew a Nikara banner, the symbol of the Red Emperor above the emblems of the Twelve Warlords.

Reinforcements.

Rin refused to allow herself to hope. It couldn't be.

"Possibly it's a trap," said Altan.

But Rin was looking past the flag at a face in the ranks—a boy, a beautiful boy with the palest skin and lovely almond eyes, walking on his own two legs as if his spine had never been severed. As if he had never been impaled on a general's halberd.

As if he could sense her gaze, Nezha looked up.

Their eyes met under the moonlight. Rin's heart leaped.

The Dragon Warlord had responded to the call. The Seventh Division was here.

"That's not a trap," she said.

CHAPTER 17

"You're really all better?"

"Near enough," said Nezha. "They sent me down with the next shipment of soldiers as soon as I could walk."

The Seventh Division had brought with them three thousand fresh troops and wagons of badly needed supplies from farther inland—bandages, medicine, sacks of rice and spices. It was the best thing to happen at Khurdalain in weeks.

"Three months," she marveled. "And Kitay said you were never going to walk again."

"He exaggerated," he said. "I got lucky. The blade went right in between my stomach and my kidney. Didn't puncture anything on its way out. Hurt like hell, but it healed cleanly. Scar's ugly, though. Do you want to see?"

"Keep your shirt on," she said hastily. "Still, three months? That's amazing."

Nezha looked away, gazing over the quiet stretch of city under the wall that they'd been assigned to patrol. He hesitated, as if trying to decide whether or not to say something, but then abruptly changed the subject. "So. Screaming at rocks. Is that, like, normal behavior here?"

"That's just Suni." Rin broke a wheat bun in half and offered a piece to Nezha. They had increased bread rations to twice a week, and it was worth savoring. "Ignore him."

He took it, chewed, and made a face. Even in wartime, Nezha had a way of acting as if he'd expected better luxuries. "It's a little hard to ignore when he's yelling right outside your tent."

"I'll ask Suni to avoid your particular tent."

"Would you?"

Snideness aside, Rin was deeply grateful for Nezha's presence. As much as they had hated each other at the Academy, Rin found comfort in having someone else from her class here on the other side of the country, so far away from Sinegard. It was good to have someone who could sympathize, in some way, with what she was going through.

It helped that Nezha had stopped acting like he had a stick up his ass. War brought out the worst in some people; with Nezha, though, it had transformed him, stripping away his snobby pretensions. It seemed petty now to maintain her old grudge. It was difficult to dislike someone who had saved her life.

And she didn't want to admit it, but Nezha was a welcome relief from Altan, who had taken lately to hurling objects across the room at the slightest hint of disobedience. Rin found herself wondering why they hadn't become friends sooner.

"You know they think your contingent is a freak show, right?" Nezha said.

But then, of course, he would say things like that. Rin bristled. They *were* freaks. But they were *her* freaks. Only the Cike got to speak about the Cike like that. "They're the best damn soldiers in this army."

Nezha raised an eyebrow. "Didn't one of you blow up the foreign embassy?"

"That was an accident."

"And didn't that big hairy one choke out your commander in the mess hall?"

"All right, Suni's pretty weird—but the rest of us are perfectly—"

"Perfectly normal?" Nezha laughed out loud. "Really? Your

people just casually ingest drugs, mumble to animals, and scream through the night?"

"Side effect of battle prowess," she said, forcing levity into her voice.

Nezha looked unconvinced. "Sounds like battle prowess is the side effect of the madness."

Rin didn't want to think about that. It was a horrifying prospect, and she knew it was more than just a rumor. But the more terrified she became, the less likely she'd be able to summon the Phoenix, and the angrier Altan would become.

"Why aren't your eyes red?" Nezha asked abruptly.

"What?"

He reached out and touched a spot on her temple, beside her left eye. "Altan's irises are red. I thought Speerly eyes were red."

"I don't know," she said, suddenly confused. She had never once considered it—Altan had never brought it up. "My eyes have always been brown."

"Maybe you're not a Speerly."

"Maybe."

"But they were red before." Nezha looked puzzled. "At Sinegard. When you killed the general."

"You weren't even conscious," she said. "You had a spear in your stomach."

Nezha arched an eyebrow. "I know what I saw."

Footsteps sounded behind them. Rin jumped, although she had no reason to feel guilty. She was only keeping watch; she wasn't barred from idle small talk.

"There you are," said Enki.

Nezha swiftly stood. "I'll go."

She glanced up at him, confused. "No, you don't have to—"

"He should go," said Enki.

Nezha gave Enki a stiff nod and disappeared briskly around the corner of the wall.

Enki waited a few moments until the sound of Nezha's footsteps pattering down the stairs died away. Then he glanced down at Rin, mouth pressed in a solemn line. "You didn't tell me the Dragon Warlord's brat was a shaman."

Rin frowned. "What are you talking about?"

"The insignia." Enki gestured around to his upper back, where Nezha wore his family crest across his uniform. "That's a dragon mark."

"That's just his crest," said Rin.

"Wasn't he injured at Sinegard?" Enki inquired.

"Yes." Rin wondered how Enki had known. Then again, Nezha was the son of the Dragon Warlord; his personal life was public knowledge among the Militia.

"How badly was he hurt?"

"I don't know," Rin said. "I was half-unconscious myself when it happened. The general stabbed him—twice, stomach wounds, probably—why does that matter?" She was confused by Nezha's rapid recovery herself, but she didn't see why Enki was interrogating her about it. "They missed his vitals," she added, though that sounded implausible as soon as the words left her mouth.

"Two stomach wounds," Enki repeated. "Two wounds from a highly experienced Federation general who was not likely to miss. And he's up and walking in months?"

"You know, considering that one of us literally lives in a *barrel*, Nezha getting lucky is not that absurd."

Enki looked unconvinced. "Your friend is hiding something."

"Ask him yourself, then," Rin said irritably. "Did you need something?"

Enki was frowning, contemplative, but he nodded. "Altan wants to see you. His office. Now."

Altan's office was a mess.

Books and brushes littered the floor. Maps were strewn haphazardly across his desk, city plans tacked up over every inch of wall. They were covered in Altan's jagged, messy scrawl, outlining diagrams of strategies that made no sense to anyone but Altan. He had circled some critical regions so hard that they looked like he had etched them into the wall with a knifepoint.

Altan was sitting alone at his desk when Rin entered. His eyes were ringed with such a prominent indigo that they looked like bruises.

"You summoned me?" she asked.

Altan set his pen down. "You're spending too much time with the Dragon Warlord's brat."

Rin bristled. "What's *that* supposed to mean?"

"It means I won't allow it," said Altan. "Nezha's one of Jun's people. You know better than to trust him."

Rin opened her mouth and then closed it, trying to figure out whether Altan was being serious. Finally she said, "Nezha's not in the Fifth. Jun can't give him orders."

"Jun was his master," Altan said. "I've seen his armband. He pledged Combat. He's loyal to Jun; he'll tell him anything . . ."

Rin stared at him in disbelief. "Nezha's just my *friend*."

"No one is ever your friend. Not when you're Cike. He's spying on us."

"*Spying* on us?" Rin repeated. "Altan, we're in the same army."

Altan stood up and slammed his hands down on the table.

Rin flinched back.

"*We are* not *in the same army*. We are the Cike. We're the Bizarre Children. We're the force that shouldn't exist, and Jun wants us to fail. He wants *me* to fail," he said. "They all do."

"The other divisions aren't our enemy," Rin said quietly.

Altan paced around the room, arms twitching involuntarily, glaring at his maps as if he could will into formation armies that didn't exist. He looked quite deranged.

"Everyone is our enemy," he said. He seemed to be talking to himself more than he was talking to her. "Everyone wants us dead, gone . . . but I won't go out like this . . ."

Rin swallowed. "Altan—"

He jerked his head toward her. "Can you call the fire yet?"

Rin felt a twinge of guilt. Try as she might, she still couldn't access the god, could not call it back like she had in Sinegard.

Before she could respond, though, Altan made a noise of disgust. "Never mind. Of course you can't. You still think you're playing a game. You think you're still at school."

"I do *not*."

He crossed the room toward her, grasped her shoulders, and shook her so hard that she gasped out loud. But he only pulled her closer until they were face-to-face, eye to eye. His irises were a furious crimson.

"How hard could it be?" he demanded. His grip tightened, fingers digging painfully into her collarbone. "Tell me, *why* is this so hard for you? It's not like this is new to you; you've done it before, why can't you do it now?"

"Altan, you're hurting me."

His grip only tightened. "You could at least fucking *try*—"

"I've tried!" she exploded. "It's not easy, all right? I can't just . . . I'm not *you*."

"Are you a toddler?" Altan said, as if curious. He didn't shout, but his voice took on a strangled monotone, carefully controlled and deadly quiet. That was how she knew he was furious. "Or are you, perhaps, an idiot masquerading as a soldier? You said you needed time. I have allotted you months. On Speer, you would have been disowned by now. Your family would have hurled you into the ocean for the sheer *embarrassment*."

"I'm sorry," Rin whispered, then immediately regretted it. Altan didn't want her apology. He wanted her humiliation. He wanted her to burn in shame, to feel so miserable with herself that she couldn't bear it.

And she did. How was it that he could make her feel so small? She felt more useless than she had at Sinegard when Jun had humiliated her before everyone. This was worse. This was a thousand times worse, because unlike Jun, Altan mattered to her. Altan was a Speerly, Altan was her *commander*. She needed his approval like she needed air.

He pushed her violently away from him.

Rin fought the urge to touch her collarbone, where she knew she would soon have two bruises left by Altan's thumbs, perfectly formed dents like teardrops. She swallowed hard, averted her eyes, and said nothing.

"You call yourself a Sinegard-trained soldier?" Altan's voice had sunk to barely more than a whisper, and it was worse than if he were shouting. She *wished* he were shouting. Anything would be better than this cold evisceration. "You're no soldier. You're deadweight. Until you can call the fire, you're fucking *useless* to me. You're here because you're purportedly a Speerly. So far I have seen no proof that you are. Fix this. Prove your worth. Do your fucking job or get out."

She saved her tears for after she was out of the office. Her eyes were still red when she entered the mess hall.

"Have you been *crying*?" Nezha demanded as he sat down across from her.

"Go away," she mumbled.

He didn't go away. "Tell me what happened."

Rin bit her lower lip. She wasn't supposed to speak to Nezha. It would have been a double betrayal to complain to him about Altan.

"Was it Altan? Did he say something?"

She looked away pointedly.

"Wait. What's that?" Nezha reached for her collarbone.

She slapped his hand away and yanked at her uniform.

"You're just going to sit there and take it?" Nezha asked in disbelief. "I remember a girl who punched me in the face for uttering an ill word about her teacher."

"Altan's different," Rin said.

"Not so different that he gets to talk to you like that," Nezha said. His eyes slid over her collarbone. "It *was* Altan. Tiger's tits. They're saying he's gone mad in the Fifth, but I never thought he'd actually resort to *this*."

"You don't get to talk," Rin snapped. Why did Nezha think he could now take on the role of confidant? "You made fun of me for years at Sinegard. You didn't say a kind word to me until Mugen was at our doorstep."

To his credit, Nezha actually looked guilty. "Rin, I'm—"

She cut him off before he could get a word in. "I was the war orphan from the south, and you were the rich kid from Sinegard, and you tormented me. You made Sinegard a living hell, Nezha."

It felt good to say it out loud. It felt good to see Nezha's stricken expression. They had skirted around this since Nezha had arrived, had acted as if they had always been friends at the Academy, because theirs had been such a childish feud compared to the very real battles they were fighting now. But if he wanted to malign her commander, then she would remind him exactly whom he was talking to.

Nezha slammed a hand on the table, just as Altan had, but this time she didn't flinch.

"You weren't the only victim!" he said. "The first day we met you punched me. Then you kicked me in the balls. Then you tackled me in class. In front of Jun. In front of *everyone*. How do you think that felt? How fucking embarrassing do you think that was? Look, I'm sorry, all right? I'm really sorry." The remorse in Nezha's voice sounded genuine. "But I saved your life. Doesn't that make us at least a little square?"

Square? *Square*? She had to laugh. "You almost got me expelled!"

"And you almost killed me," he said.

That shut her up.

"I was scared of you," Nezha continued. "And I lashed out. I was stupid. I was a spoiled brat. I was a real pain in the ass. I thought I was better than you, and I'm not. I'm sorry."

Rin was too stunned to come up with a response, so she turned away. "I'm not supposed to be talking to you," she said stiffly to the wall.

"Fine," Nezha snapped. "Sorry I tried. I'll leave you alone, then."

He grabbed his plate, stood up, and walked briskly away. She let him.

Night watch was lonely and boring without Nezha. All of the Cike had watch duty on rotation, but at that moment Rin was convinced Altan had placed her there as punishment. What was the point of staring down at a coastline where nothing ever happened? If another fleet did show up, Qara's birds would see it days in advance.

Rin twisted her fingers irritably together as she huddled against the wall, trying to warm herself. *Stupid*, she thought, glaring at her hands. Probably she wouldn't feel so cold if she could just summon a bit of flame.

Everything felt awful. The mere thought of both Altan and Nezha made her cringe. She knew vaguely that she'd fucked up, that she'd probably done something that she shouldn't have, but she couldn't reason a way out of this dilemma. She wasn't even sure precisely what the matter *was*, only that both were furious with her.

She heard then a droning noise; so faint at first she thought she was imagining it. But then it increased quickly in volume, like a fast-approaching swarm of bees. The noise reached a peak and clarified into human shouts. She squinted; the commotion wasn't coming from the coastline but from the downtown districts behind her. She jumped down from her perch and ran to look down the other side. A flood of civilians streamed into the alleyways, a frantic stampede of bodies. She searched the crowd and saw Qara and Unegen emerging from their barracks. She scaled down the wall and wove through the flood of bodies, pushing against the crowd to reach them.

"What's going on?" She grabbed Unegen's arm. "Why are they running?"

"No clue," Unegen said. "Find the others."

A civilian—an old woman—tried to push past Rin but stumbled. Rin knelt to help her, but the woman had already picked herself up, scurrying along faster than Rin had ever seen an old person move. Men, women, and children streamed around her, some barefoot, some only half-dressed, wearing identical expressions of terror in their frenzy to flee out the city gates.

"What the hell is going on?" Baji, bleary-eyed and shirtless, pushed through the crowd toward them. "Great Tortoise. Are we evacuating now?"

Something bumped into Rin's knee. She looked down and saw a small child—tiny, half Kesegi's age. He wasn't wearing any pants. He groped blindly at her shin, bawling loudly. He must have lost his parents in the confusion. She reached down and picked him up, the same way she used to hold Kesegi when he cried.

As she searched through the mob for anyone who looked like they were missing a child, she saw three great spouts of flame appear in the air, in the shape of three small dragons flying upward at the sky. It had to be Altan's signal.

Through the noise Rin heard his hoarse yell, "Cike, to me!"

She placed the child in the arms the first civilian she saw and fought her way through the masses to where Altan stood. Jun was there, too, surrounded by about ten of his men. Nezha stood among them. He didn't meet her eyes.

Altan looked more openly furious than she had ever seen him. "I *warned* you not to evacuate without giving notice."

"This isn't me," said Jun. "They're running from something."

"From what?"

"Damned if I know," Jun snapped.

Altan heaved a great sigh of impatience, reached into the horde of bodies, and pulled someone out at random. It was a young woman, a little older than Rin, wearing nothing but a nightgown. She screeched loudly in protest, then clamped her jaw shut when she saw their Militia uniforms.

"What's going on?" Altan demanded. "What are you all running from?"

"A chimei," she said, out of breath and terrified. "There's a chimei downtown, near the town square . . ."

A chimei? The name was vaguely familiar. Rin thought back to where she had last seen it—somewhere in the library, perhaps, in one of the absurd tomes Jiang had made her read when conducting a thorough investigation on every piece of arcane knowledge known to mankind. She thought it might be a beast, some mythological creature with bizarre abilities.

"Really," Jun said skeptically. "How do you know it's a chimei?"

The girl looked him straight in the eyes. "Because it's tearing the faces off corpses," she said in a wavering voice. "I saw the bodies, I saw . . ." She broke off.

"What does it look like?" Altan asked.

The woman shivered. "I didn't get a close look, but I think . . . it looked like a great four-legged beast. Large as a horse, arms like a monkey's."

"A beast," Altan repeated. "Anything else?"

"Its fur was black, and its eyes . . ." She swallowed.

"Its eyes were what?" Jun pressed.

The woman flinched. "Like *his*," she said, and pointed to Altan. "Red like blood. Bright as flame."

Altan released the young woman back into the crowd, and she immediately disappeared into the fleeing mass.

The two commanders faced each other.

"We need to send someone in," Altan said. "Someone has to kill that beast."

"Yes," Jun agreed immediately. "My people are tied up with crowd control, but I can gather a squadron."

"We don't need a squadron. One of my people should be fine. We can't dispatch everyone. Mugen could use this chance to attack our base. This could be a diversion."

"I'll go," Rin volunteered immediately.

Altan frowned at her. "You know how to handle a chimei?"

She didn't know. She'd only just remembered what a chimei *was*—and that was only from Academy readings that she barely remembered. But she was sure that was more than anyone else in the divisions or the Cike knew, because no one else had been forced to read arcane bestiaries at Sinegard. And she wasn't about to admit incompetence to Altan in front of Jun. She could handle this task. She *had* to.

"As well as anyone else does, sir. I've read the bestiaries."

Altan considered for a short moment, then nodded curtly. "Go against the grain of the crowd. Keep to the alleys."

"I'll go, too," Nezha volunteered.

"That's not necessary," Altan said immediately.

But Jun said, "She should take a Militia man. Just in case."

Altan glared at Jun, and she realized what this was about. Jun wanted someone to accompany her, just in case she saw something that Altan didn't report to Jun.

Rin couldn't believe that division politics were at play even now.

Altan looked like he wanted to argue. But there was no time. He shoved past Nezha toward the crowd and seized a torch from a passing civilian.

"Hey! I need that!"

"Shut up," Altan said, and pushed the civilian away. He handed the torch to Rin and pulled her into a side alley where she could avoid the traffic. "*Go.*"

Rin and Nezha couldn't reach downtown by fighting the stampede of bodies. But the buildings in their district had low, flat roofs that were easy to climb onto. Rin and Nezha ran across them, their torches bobbing in the light. When they reached the end of the block, they dropped down into an alley and crossed another block in silence.

Finally Nezha asked, "What's a chimei?"

"You heard the woman," Rin said curtly. "Great beast. Red eyes."

"I've never heard of it."

"Probably shouldn't have come along, then." She turned a corner.

"I read the bestiaries, too," Nezha said after he had caught up to her. "Nothing about a chimei."

"You didn't read the old texts. Archive basement," she said. "Red Emperor's era. It only gets a few mentions, but it's there. Sometimes it's depicted as a child with red eyes. Sometimes as a black shadow. It tears the faces off its victims but leaves the rest of the corpse intact."

"Creepy," Nezha said. "What's its deal with faces?"

"I'm not sure," Rin admitted. She searched her memory for anything else she could remember about chimeis. "The bestiaries didn't say. I think it collects them. The books claim that the chimei can imitate just about anyone—people you care about, people you could never hurt."

"Even people it hasn't killed?"

"Probably," she guessed. "It's been collecting faces for thousands of years. With that many facial features, you could approximate anyone."

"So what? How does that make it dangerous?"

She shot him a glance over her shoulder. "You'd be fine stabbing something with your mother's face?"

"I'd know it wasn't real."

"You'd know in the back of your mind it wasn't real. But could you do it in the moment? Look in your mother's eyes, listen to her begging, and put your knife to her throat?"

"If I knew there was no way it could be my mother," Nezha said. "The chimei sounds scary only if it catches you by surprise. But not if you *know*."

"I don't think it's that simple," said Rin. "This thing didn't just frighten one or two people. It scared off half the city. What's more, the bestiaries don't tell us how to kill it. There isn't a defeat of a chimei on record in history. We're fighting this one blind."

The streets in the middle of town were still—doors closed, wagons parked. What should have been a bustling marketplace was dusty and quiet.

But not empty.

Bodies were littered around the streets in various states.

Rin knelt down by the closest one and turned it over. The corpse was unmarked except for the head. The face had been chewed off in the most grotesque manner. The eye sockets were empty, the nose missing, lips torn clean off.

"You weren't kidding," Nezha said. He covered his mouth with a hand. "Tiger's tits. What happens when we find it?"

"Probably I'll kill it," she said. "You can help."

"You are obnoxiously overconfident in your combat abilities," said Nezha.

"I thrashed you at school. I'm frank about my combat abilities," she said. It helped if she talked big. It made the fear go away.

Several feet away, Nezha kicked another body over. It wore the dark blue uniform of the Federation Armed Forces. A five-pointed yellow star on his right breast identified him as an officer of rank.

"Poor guy," he said. "Someone didn't get the message."

Rin walked past Nezha and held her torch out over the bloody walkway. An entire squadron of slain Federation forces was littered across the cobblestones.

"I don't think the Federation sent it," she said slowly.

"Maybe they've kept it locked up all this time," Nezha suggested. "Maybe they didn't know what it could do."

"The Federation doesn't take chances like that," she said. "You saw how cautious they were with the trebuchets at Sinegard. They wouldn't unleash a beast they couldn't control."

"So it just came on its own? A monster that no one's seen in centuries decides to reappear in the one city under siege?"

Rin had a sinking suspicion of where the chimei had come from. She'd seen the monster before. She'd seen it in the illustrations of the Jade Emperor's menagerie.

I will summon into existence beings that should not be in this world.

When Jiang had opened that void at Sinegard, he had ripped a hole in the fabric between their world and the next. And now, with the Gatekeeper gone, demons were climbing through at will.

There is a price. There is always a price.
Now she could see what he meant.

She pushed the thoughts from her mind and knelt down to examine the corpses more closely. None of the soldiers had drawn their weapons. This made no sense. Surely they couldn't all have been caught off guard. If they'd been fighting a monstrous beast, they should have died with their swords drawn. There should be signs of a struggle.

"Where do you think—" she began to ask, but Nezha clamped a cold hand over her mouth.

"Listen," he whispered.

She could hear nothing. But then, across the market square from where they stood, a faint noise came from within an overturned wagon, the sound of something shaking. Then the shaking stilled, giving way to what sounded like high-pitched sobbing.

Rin walked closer with her torch held out to investigate.

"Are you mad?" Nezha grabbed her arm. "That could be the beast itself."

"So what are we going to do, run from it?" She shook him off and continued at a brisk pace toward the wagon.

Nezha hesitated, but she heard him following. When they reached the wagon, he met her eyes over the torchlight, and she nodded. She drew her sword, and together they yanked the cover off the wagon.

"Go away!"

The thing under the cover wasn't a beast. It was a tiny girl, no taller than Nezha's waist, curled up in the back end of the wagon. She wore a flimsy blood-covered dress. She shrieked when she saw them and buried her head in her knees. Her entire body convulsed with violent, terrified sobs. "Get away! Get away from me!"

"Put your sword down, you're scaring her!" Nezha stepped in front of Rin, blocking her from the little girl's view. He shifted his torch to his other hand and put a hand softly on the girl's shoulder. "Hey. Hey, it's okay. We're here to help you."

The girl sniffled. "Horrible monster . . ."

"I know. The monster isn't here. We've, uh, we've scared it away. We're not here to hurt you, I promise. Can you look at me?"

Slowly, the girl lifted her head and met Nezha's gaze. Her eyes were enormous, wide and scared, in her tear-streaked face.

As Rin looked over Nezha's shoulder into those eyes, she was struck with the oddest sensation, a fierce desire to protect the little girl at all costs. She felt it like a physical urge, a foreign maternal desire. She would die before letting any harm come to this innocent child.

"You're not a monster?" the girl whimpered.

Nezha stretched his arms out to her. "We're humans through and through," he said gently.

The girl leaned into his arms, and her sobs subsided.

Rin watched Nezha in amazement. He seemed to know exactly how to act around the child, adjusting his tone and his body language to be as comforting as possible.

Nezha handed Rin his torch with one arm and patted the girl on the head with the other. "Will you let me help you out of this thing?"

She nodded hesitantly and rose to her feet. Nezha grasped her waist, lifted her out of the broken wagon, and set her gently on the ground.

"There. You're all right. Can you walk?"

She nodded again and reached shakily for his hand. Nezha grasped it firmly, wrapped his slender fingers around her tiny hand. "Don't worry, I'm not going anywhere. Do you have a name?"

"Khudali," she whispered.

"Khudali. You're safe now," Nezha promised. "You're with us. And we're monster killers. But we need your help. Can you be brave for me?"

Khudali swallowed and nodded.

"Good girl. Now can you tell me what happened? Anything you remember."

Khudali took a deep breath and began to speak in a halting, trembling voice. "I was with my parents and my sister. We were just riding the wagon back home. The Militia told us not to be out too late so we wanted to get back in time, and then . . ." Khudali began to sob again.

"It's okay," Nezha said quickly. "We know the beast came. I just need you to give me any details you can. Anything that comes to mind."

Khudali nodded. "Everyone was screaming, but none of the soldiers did anything. And when it came near us, the Federation just watched. I hid inside the wagon. I didn't see its face."

"Did you see where it went?" Rin asked sharply.

Khudali flinched and shrank back behind Nezha.

"You're scaring her," Nezha said in a low voice, gesturing again for Rin to stand back. He turned back to Khudali. "Can you show me what direction it ran in?" he asked softly. "Where did it go?"

"I . . . I can't tell you how to get there. But I can take you," she said. "I remember what I saw."

She led them a few steps toward a corner of the alley, then paused.

"That's where it ate my brother," she said. "But then it disappeared."

"Hold on," said Nezha. "You said you came here with your sister."

Khudali looked up at Nezha, again with those wide, imploring eyes.

"I suppose I did," she said.

Then she smiled.

In one instant she was a tiny girl; the next, a long-limbed beast. Except for its face, it was entirely covered in coarse pitch-black fur. Its loping arms could have reached the ground, like Suni's, a monkey's arms. Its head was very small, still the head of Khudali, which made it all the more grotesque. It reached for Nezha with thick fingers and lifted him into the air by his collar.

Rin drew her sword and hacked at its legs, its arms, its torso. But the chimei's bristly fur was like a coat of iron needles, repelling her sword better than any shield could.

"Its face," she yelled. "Aim for the face!"

But Nezha wasn't moving. His hands dangled uselessly at his sides. He gazed into the chimei's tiny face, Khudali's face, entranced.

"What are you doing?" Rin screamed.

Slowly, the chimei turned its head to look down at her. It found her eyes.

Rin reeled and stumbled backward, choking.

When she gazed into those eyes, its entrancing eyes, the chimei's monstrous body melted away in her vision. She couldn't see the black hair, the beast's body, the rough torso matted with blood. Only the face.

It wasn't the face of a beast. It was the face of something beautiful. It was blurry for a moment, like it couldn't decide what it wanted to be, and then it turned into a face she hadn't seen in years.

Soft, mud-colored cheeks. Rumpled black hair. One baby tooth slightly larger than the rest, one baby tooth missing.

"Kesegi?" Rin uttered.

She dropped her torch. Kesegi smiled uncertainly.

"Do you recognize me?" he asked in his sweet little voice. "After all this time?"

Her heart broke. "Of *course* I recognize you."

Kesegi looked at her hopefully. Then he opened his mouth and screeched, and the screech wasn't anything human. The chimei rushed at her—Rin flung her hands up before her face—but something stopped it.

Nezha had broken free of its grasp; now he held on to its back, where he couldn't see its face. Nezha stabbed inward, but his knife clattered uselessly against the chimei's collarbone. He tried again, aiming for its face. Kesegi's face.

"No!" Rin screamed. "Kesegi, no—"

Nezha missed—his blade ricocheted off iron fur. He raised his weapon for a second blow, but Rin dashed forward and shoved her sword between Nezha's blade and the chimei.

She had to protect Kesegi, couldn't let Nezha kill him, not *Kesegi* . . . he was just a kid, so helpless, so little . . .

It had been three years since she'd left him. She had abandoned him with a pair of opium smugglers, while she left for Sinegard without sending so much as a letter for three years, three impossibly long years.

It seemed like so long ago. An entire lifetime.

So why was Kesegi still so small?

She reeled, mind fuzzy. Answering the question was like trying to see through a dense mist. She knew there was some reason why this didn't make sense, but she couldn't quite piece together what it was . . . only that there was something wrong with this Kesegi in front of her.

It wasn't *her* Kesegi.

It wasn't Kesegi at all.

She struggled to come to her senses, blinking rapidly like she was trying to clear away a fog. *It's the chimei, you idiot*, she told herself. *It's playing off your emotions. This is what it does. This is how it kills.*

And now that she remembered, she saw there was something wrong with Kesegi's face . . . his eyes were not soft and brown, but bright red, two glaring lanterns that demanded her gaze . . .

Howling, the chimei finally succeeded in flinging Nezha off its back. Nezha jerked through the air and crashed against the alley wall. His head thudded against the stone. He slid to the ground and did not stir.

The chimei bolted into the shadows and disappeared.

Rin ran toward Nezha's prone form.

"Shit, *shit* . . ." She pressed her hand to the back of his head. It came away sticky. She probed around, feeling for the contours of the cut, and was relieved to find it was fairly shallow—even light head wounds bled heavily. Nezha might be fine.

But where had the chimei gone . . . ?

She heard a rustling noise above her. She turned, too slowly.

The chimei jumped straight down to land on her back, seizing her shoulders with a horrifically strong grip. She wriggled ferociously, stabbing backward with her sword. But she attacked in vain; the chimei's fur was still an impenetrable shield, against which her blade could only scrape uselessly.

With one massive hand the chimei seized the blade and broke it. It made a disdainful noise and flung the pieces into the darkness. Then it encircled Rin's neck with its arms, clinging to her back like a child—a giant, monstrous child. Its arms pressed against her windpipe. Rin's eyes bulged. She couldn't breathe. She fell to her knees and clambered desperately over the dirt toward the dropped torch.

She felt the chimei's breath hot on her neck. It scratched at her face, pulled at her lips and nostrils the way a child might.

"Play with me," it insisted in Kesegi's voice. "Why won't you *play with me*?"

Can't breathe . . .

Rin's fingers found the torch. She seized it and jabbed it blindly upward.

The burning end smashed into the chimei's exposed face with a loud sizzle. The beast screeched and flung itself off Rin. It writhed in the dirt, limbs twitching at bizarre angles as it keened loudly in pain.

Rin screamed, too—her hair had caught fire. She pulled up her hood and rubbed the cloth over her head to smother the flames.

"Sister, please," the chimei gasped. In its agony it somehow managed to sound even more like Kesegi.

She crawled doggedly toward it, pointedly looking away from its eyes. She clutched the torch tightly in her right hand. She had to burn it again. Burning it seemed to be the only way to hurt it.

"*Rin.*"

This time it spoke in Altan's voice.

This time she couldn't stop herself from looking.

At first it only had Altan's face, and then it *was* Altan, lying sprawled on the ground, blood dripping from his temple. It had Altan's eyes. It had Altan's scar.

Raw, smoking, he snarled at her.

Staving off the chimei's attempts to claw off her face, she pinned it against the ground, jamming down its arms with her knees.

She had to burn its face off. The faces were the source of its power. The chimei had collected a mass of likenesses from every person it had killed, every face it had torn off. It sustained itself on human likenesses, and now it tried to obtain hers.

She forced the torch into its face.

The chimei screamed again. *Altan* screamed again.

She had never heard Altan scream, not in reality, but she was certain that it would have sounded like this.

"Please," sobbed Altan, his voice raw. *"Please, don't."*

Rin clenched her teeth and tightened her grip on the torch, pressed it harder against the chimei's head. The smell of burning flesh filled her nostrils. She choked; the smoke made her tear up but she did not stop. She tried to rip her gaze away, but the chimei's eyes were arresting. It held her eyes. It forced her to look.

"You can't kill me," Altan hissed. "You love me."

"I don't love you," Rin said. "And I can kill anything."

It was a terrifying power of the chimei's that the more it burned, the more it looked like Altan. Rin's heart slammed against her rib cage. *Close your mind. Block out your thoughts. Don't think. Don't think. Don't think. Don't . . .*

But she couldn't detach Altan's likeness from the chimei. They were one and the same. She loved it, she loved him, and he was going to kill her. Unless she killed him first.

But no, that didn't make sense . . .

She tried to focus again, to still her terror and regain her rationality, but this time what she concentrated on was not detaching Altan from the chimei but resolving to kill it no matter who she thought it was.

She was killing the chimei. She was killing Altan. Both were true. Both were necessary.

She didn't have the poppy seed, but she didn't need to call the Phoenix in this moment. She had the torch and she had the pain, and that was enough.

She smashed the blunt end of the torch into Altan's face. She smashed again, with a greater force than she knew she was capable of. Bone gave way to wood. His cheek caved in, creating a cavernous hole where flesh and bone should be.

"You're hurting me." Altan sounded shocked.

No, I'm killing you. She smashed it again and again and again. Once her arm started going, she couldn't stop. Altan's face became a mottled mess of fragmented bone and flesh. Brown skin turned bright red. His face lost shape altogether. She beat out those eyes, beat them bloody so she wouldn't have to look into them anymore. When he struggled, she turned the torch around and burned him in the wounds. Then he screamed.

Finally the chimei ceased its struggles beneath her. Its muscles stopped tensing, its legs stopped kicking. Rin lurched forward over its head, breathing heavily. She had burned through its face to the bone. Underneath the charred, smoking skin lay a tiny, pristine white skull.

Rin climbed off the corpse and sucked in a great, heaving breath. Then she vomited.

"I'm sorry," said Nezha when he awoke.

"Don't be," Rin said. She lay slumped against the wall beside him. The entire contents of her stomach were splattered on the sidewalk. "It's not your fault."

"It *is* my fault. You didn't freeze when you saw it."

"I *did* freeze. An entire squadron froze." Rin jerked her thumb back toward the Federation carcasses in the market square. "And you helped me snap out of it. Don't blame yourself."

"I was stupid. I should have known that little girl—"

"Neither of us knew," Rin said curtly.

Nezha said nothing.

"Do you have a sister?" she asked after a while.

"I used to have a brother," Nezha said. "A little brother. He died when we were young."

"Oh." Rin didn't know what to say to that. "Sorry."

Nezha pulled himself to a sitting position. "When the chimei was screaming at me it felt like—like it was my fault again."

Rin swallowed hard. "When I killed it, it felt like murder."

Nezha gave her a long look. "Who was it for you?"

Rin didn't answer that.

They limped back to the base together in silence, occasionally ducking around a dark corner to make sure they weren't being followed. They did so more out of habit than necessity. Rin guessed there wouldn't be any Federation soldiers in that part of the city for a while.

When they reached the junction that split the Cike headquarters and the Seventh Division's base, Nezha stopped and turned to face her.

Her heart skipped a beat.

He was so beautiful then, standing right in the space of the road where a beam of moonlight fell across his face, illuminating one side and casting long shadows on the other.

He looked like glazed porcelain, preserved glass. He was a sculptor's approximation of a person, not human himself. *He can't be real*, she thought. A boy made of flesh and bone could not be so painfully lovely, so free of any blemish or flaw.

"So. About earlier," he said.

Rin folded her arms tightly across her chest. "Not a good time."

Nezha laughed humorlessly. "We're fighting a war. There's never going to be a good time."

"Nezha . . ."

He put his hand on her arm. "I just wanted to say I'm sorry."

"You don't have to—"

"Yes, I do. I've been a real dick to you. And I had no right to talk about your commander like that. I'm sorry."

"I forgive you," she said cautiously, and found that she meant it.

Altan was waiting in his office when she returned to base. He opened the door even before she knocked.

"It's gone?"

"It's gone," Rin confirmed. She swallowed; her heart was still racing. "Sir."

He nodded curtly. "Good."

They regarded each other in silence for a moment. He was hidden in the shadow of the door. Rin couldn't see the expression on his face. She was glad of that. She couldn't face him right now. She couldn't look at him without seeing his face burning, breaking under her hands, dissolving into a pulpy mess of flesh and gore and sinew.

All thoughts of Nezha had been pushed out of her mind. How could that possibly matter right now?

She had just killed Altan.

What was that supposed to mean? What did it say that the chimei had thought she wouldn't be able to kill Altan, and that she had killed him anyway?

If she could do this, what couldn't she do?

Who couldn't she kill?

Maybe that was the kind of anger it took to call the Phoenix easily and regularly the way Altan did. Not just rage, not just fear, but a deep, burning resentment, fanned by a particularly cruel kind of abuse.

Maybe she'd learned something after all.

"Anything else?" Altan asked.

He took a step toward her. She flinched. He must have noticed it, and still he moved closer. "Something you want to tell me?"

"No, sir," she whispered. "There's nothing."

CHAPTER 18

"The riverbanks are clear," Rin said. "Small signs of activity on the northwestern corner, but nothing we haven't seen before. Probably just transporting more supplies to the far end of camp. I doubt they'll try today."

"Good," said Altan. He marked a point on his map, then set the brush down. He rubbed at his temples and paused like he'd forgotten what he was going to say.

Rin fidgeted with her sleeve.

They hadn't trained together in weeks. It was just as well. There was no time for training now. Months into the siege, the Nikara position in Khurdalain was dire. Even with the added reinforcements of the Seventh Division, the port city was perilously close to falling under Federation occupation. Three days before, the Fifth Division had lost a major town in the suburbs of Khurdalain that had served as a transportation center, exposing much of the eastern part of the city to the Federation.

Beyond that, they'd also lost a good deal of their imported supplies, which forced the army onto even poorer rations than they'd been subsisting on. They were surviving on rice gruel and yams now, two things that Baji declared he would never touch again after this war was over. As it was, they were more likely to chew down handfuls of raw rice than receive fully cooked meals from the mess hall.

Jun's frontline units were inching backward, and suffering heavy casualties while doing so. The Federation took stronghold after stronghold on the riverbank. The water of the creek had been red for days, forcing Jun to send out men to bring back barrels of water not contaminated by putrefied corpses.

Apart from downtown Khurdalain, the Nikara still occupied three crucial buildings on the wharf—two warehouses and a former Hesperian trading office—but their increasingly limited manpower was spread too thin to hold the buildings indefinitely.

At least they had shattered fantasies of an early Federation victory. They knew from intercepted missives that Mugen had expected to take Khurdalain within a week. But the siege had now stretched on for months. Rin realized in the abstract that the longer they fended Mugen off at Khurdalain, the more time Golyn Niis had to assemble defenses. They had already bought more time than they could have hoped for.

But that didn't make Khurdalain feel like any less of an utter defeat.

"One more thing," she said.

Altan nodded jerkily for her to continue.

She spoke quickly. "The Fifth wanted a meeting about the beach offensive. They want to move it up before they lose any more troops at the warehouse. The day after tomorrow at the latest."

Altan raised an eyebrow. "Why is the Fifth conveying a request through you?"

The request had actually been conveyed through Nezha, speaking on behalf of his father, the Dragon Warlord, whom Jun had approached because he didn't want to give Altan legitimacy by going to his headquarters. Rin found the interdivisional politics incredibly annoying, but could do nothing about it.

"Because at least one of them likes me. Sir."

Altan blinked. Rin immediately regretted speaking.

Before he could answer, a scream shattered the morning air.

* * *

Altan reached the top of the sentry tower first, but Rin was right behind him, her heart pounding furiously. Had there been an attack? But she saw no Federation soldiers in the vicinity, no arrows flying overhead . . .

Qara lay collapsed on the floor of the tower. She was alone. As they watched, she writhed against the stone floor, making low, tortured moans in the back of her throat. Her eyes had rolled back in her head. Her limbs seized uncontrollably.

Rin had never seen anyone react to a wound like this. Had Qara been poisoned? But why would the Federation target a sentry, and no one else? Rin and Altan instinctively crouched low, out of the line of potential fire, but there were no subsequent arrows, if there had even been a first. Except for Qara's twitching, they saw no disturbances at all.

Altan dropped to his knees. He grasped Qara by her shoulders, dragging her to a sitting position. "What's wrong? What's happened?"

"It *hurts* . . ."

Altan shook her hard. *"Answer me."*

Qara just moaned again. Rin was stunned by how roughly Altan treated her, despite her obvious agony. But, she realized belatedly, Qara had no visible injuries. There was no blood on the ground, or on her clothes.

Altan smacked Qara's face lightly to get her attention. "Is he back?"

Rin looked between them in confusion. Who was he talking about? Qara's brother?

Qara's face twisted in agony, but she managed to nod.

Altan cursed under his breath. "Is he hurt? Where is he?"

Chest heaving, Qara clenched the front of Altan's tunic. Her eyes were squeezed shut, as if she was concentrating on something.

"The east gate," she managed. "He's here."

* * *

By the time Rin had helped Qara down the stairs, Altan had disappeared from sight.

She looked up and saw archers of the Fifth Division standing frozen at the top of the wall, arrows fitted to their bows. Rin could hear clashing steel on the other side, but none of the soldiers were shooting.

Altan had to be on the other side. Were they afraid they might hit him? Or were they just unwilling to help?

She helped Qara to a sitting position by the nearest wall and made a mad dash up to the wall overlooking the east gate.

On the other side of the gate, an entire squadron of Federation soldiers clustered around Altan. He fought astride a horse, slashing his way through in a frenzied effort to get back to the gate. His arms moved faster than Rin's eyes could follow. His trident flashed once, twice in the noon sun, glistening with blood. Each time he wrenched it back out, a Federation soldier collapsed.

The crowd of soldiers thinned as soldier after soldier dropped, and finally Rin saw the reason why Altan had not summoned his flames. A young man was seated in front of him on the horse, sagging back against his arms. His face and chest were covered with blood. His skin had turned the same pallid white as his hair. For a moment Rin thought—*hoped*—that he was Jiang, but this man was shorter, visibly younger, and much thinner.

Altan was taking on the Federation soldiers as best he could, but they had backed him up against the gate.

Down below, Rin saw the Cike had gathered on the other side.

"Open the doors!" Baji shouted. "Let them back through!"

The soldiers exchanged reluctant looks and did nothing.

"What are you waiting for?" Qara shrieked.

"Jun's orders," one of them stammered. "We're not to open it at any cost—"

Rin looked back over the wall and saw another squadron of Federation reinforcements rapidly approaching. She leaned over the wall and waved her hands to get Baji's attention. "There are more coming!"

"Fuck it." Baji kicked one of the soldiers out of his way, jammed the butt of his rake into the stomach of another, and began cranking the gate open himself while Suni fended off the guards behind him.

The heavy doors inched ponderously open.

Standing directly behind the opening crack, Qara whipped arrow after arrow out of her quiver, firing them rapidly one after the next into the crowd of Federation soldiers. Under a hail of arrow fire, the Mugenese fell back long enough for Altan to squeeze through the blockade.

Baji cranked the gates the other way until they slammed shut.

Altan yanked on the reins, forcing his horse to a sudden stop.

Qara ran up to him, shouting in a language Rin didn't understand. Her tirade was interspersed with a variety of colorful Nikara invectives.

Altan held up a hand to silence her. He dismounted in one fluid movement, and then helped the young man down. The man staggered as his legs touched the ground; he slumped against the horse for support. Altan offered him a shoulder, but the man shook him off.

"Is he there?" Altan demanded. "Did you see him?"

Chest heaving, the man nodded.

"Do you have schematics?" Altan asked.

The man nodded again.

What were they talking about? Rin shot Unegen a questioning glance, but Unegen was equally nonplussed.

"Okay," Altan said. "Okay. So. You're an idiot."

Then he and Qara both began yelling at him.

"Are you *stupid*—"

"—could have been killed—"

"—sheer recklessness—"

"—don't care how powerful you think you are, how dare you—"

"Look," said the man, whose cheeks had gone as white as snow. He had begun to tremble. "I'm happy to discuss this, really, but I'm currently leaking life out three different wounds and I think I may pass out. Would you give me a moment?"

Altan, Qara, and the newcomer did not come out of Altan's office for the rest of that afternoon. Rin was sent to fetch Enki for medical attention, but was then told by Altan in no uncertain terms to get lost. She milled around the city, bored and unsettled and without orders. She wanted to ask one of the other operatives for some explanation of what had just happened, but Unegen and Baji were gone on a reconnaissance assignment and did not return until dinner.

"Who was that?" Rin asked as soon as they appeared in the mess hall.

"The man of dramatic entrance? He's Altan's lieutenant," said Unegen. He sat down on the bench across from her. He adopted a contemptuous, proud affectation. "The one and only Chaghan Suren of the Hinterlands."

"Took him long enough," Baji grumbled. "Where's he been, on vacation?"

"That was Qara's brother? Is that why . . ." Rin didn't know how to ask politely about Qara's seizure, but Baji read the puzzled look on her face.

"They're anchor twins. Some sort of . . . ah, some kind of spiritual link," said Baji. "Qara explained it to us once, but I forget the details. Long story short, they're bound together. Cut Chaghan and Qara bleeds. Kill Qara and Chaghan dies. Something like that."

This concept was not wholly new to Rin. She recalled that Jiang had discussed this kind of dependency before. She had read that shamans of the Hinterlands would sometimes anchor themselves to each other to enhance their abilities. But after seeing Qara on the floor like that, Rin didn't think it was an advantage but rather an awful vulnerability.

"Where's he been?"

"All over the place." Baji shrugged. "Altan sent him out of Khurdalain months ago, right around the time we got word they'd invaded Sinegard."

"But *why*? What was he doing?"

"He didn't tell us. Why don't you ask him yourself?" Baji nodded, his eyes fixed over her shoulder.

She turned around and jumped. Chaghan stood directly behind her; she hadn't even heard him approach.

For someone who had been bleeding out that morning, Chaghan looked remarkably well. His left arm was carefully bandaged up to his torso, but otherwise he seemed unhurt. Rin wondered exactly what Enki had done to heal him so quickly.

Up close, Chaghan's resemblance to Qara was obvious. He was taller than his sister, but they possessed the same slight, birdlike frame. His cheeks were high and hollow; his eyes embedded within deep sockets that cast a shadow over his pale gaze.

"May I join you?" he asked. The way he spoke made it sound like an order, not a question.

Unegen immediately shifted to make space. Chaghan circled the table and sat directly opposite Rin. He placed his elbows delicately on the surface, steepled his fingers together, and rested his chin on his fingertips.

"So you're the new Speerly," he said.

He reminded Rin very much of Jiang. It wasn't simply his white hair or his slender frame, but the way he looked at her, as if he saw straight through her, not looking at her at all but a place behind her. When he looked at her, Rin felt the unsettling sensation of being searched, as if he could see straight through her clothing.

She had never seen eyes like his. They were abnormally huge, dominating his otherwise narrow face. He had no pupils or irises.

She forced a facade of calm and picked up her spoon. "That's me."

The corner of his mouth twitched upward. "Altan said you were having performance issues."

Baji choked and coughed into his food.

Rin felt the heat rising in her cheeks. "*Excuse me?*"

Was that what Altan and Chaghan had spent the afternoon discussing? The idea of Altan talking about her shortcomings to this newcomer was deeply humiliating.

"Have you managed to call the Phoenix once since Sinegard?" Chaghan inquired.

I bet I could call it on you right now, you twit. Her fingers tightened around her spoon. "I've been working on it."

"Altan seems to think you're stuck in a rut."

Unegen looked like he dearly wished he were sitting anywhere else.

Rin gritted her teeth. "Well, he thought wrong."

Chaghan shot her a patronizing smile. "I can help, you know. I'm his Seer. This is what I'm good at. I traverse the world of spirit. I speak to the gods. I don't summon deities, but I know my way around the Pantheon better than anyone else. And if you're having issues, I can help you find your way back to your god."

"I'm not *having issues*," she snapped. "I was scared at the marsh. I am not now."

And that was the truth. She suspected she could call the Phoenix now, right in this mess hall, if Altan asked her to. If Altan would deign to talk to her beyond giving her orders. If Altan trusted her enough to give her an assignment above patrolling stretches of the city where nothing ever happened.

Chaghan raised an eyebrow. "Altan isn't so sure."

"Well, maybe Altan should get his head out of his ass," she snapped, then immediately regretted speaking. Disappointing Altan was one thing; complaining about it to his lieutenant was another.

No one at the table was bothering to pretend to eat anymore; Baji and Unegen both fidgeted like they couldn't wait to leave, looking around at everything except Rin and Chaghan.

But Chaghan only looked amused. "Oh, you think he's an asshole?"

Anger flared inside her. Her last remaining shreds of caution fled. "He's impatient, overdemanding, paranoid, and—"

"Look, everyone's on edge," Baji interrupted hastily. "We

shouldn't complain. Chaghan, there's no need to tell—I mean, look..."

Chaghan tapped his fingers against the table. "Baji. Unegen. I want a word with Rin."

He spoke so imperiously, so arrogantly, that Rin thought that surely Baji would tell Chaghan where he could shove it, but he and Unegen simply picked up their bowls and left the table. Amazed, she watched them walk to the other end of the room without so much as a word. Not even Altan commanded that kind of unquestioning subordination.

When the others were out of earshot, Chaghan leaned forward. "If you ever speak about Altan like that again," he said pleasantly, "I will have you killed."

Chaghan might have cowed Baji and Unegen, but Rin was too angry to be afraid of him. "Go ahead and try," she snapped. "It's not like we have soldiers to spare."

Chaghan's mouth quirked into a grin. "Altan did say you were difficult."

She gave him a wary look. "Altan's not wrong."

"So you don't respect him."

"I respect him," she said. "I just—he's been..." *Different. Paranoid. Not the commander I thought I knew.*

What she didn't want to admit was that Altan was scaring her.

But Chaghan looked surprisingly sympathetic. "You must understand. Altan is new to command. He's trying to figure out what he's doing just as much as you are. He's scared."

He was scared? Rin almost laughed. Altan's attempted operations had grown so much in scale over the past two weeks that it felt as if he were trying to take on the entire Federation by himself. "Altan doesn't know what *scared* means."

"Altan is perhaps the most powerful martial artist in Nikan right now. Maybe the world," said Chaghan. "But for all that, most of his life he was just good at following orders. Tyr's death was a shock to us. Altan wasn't ready to take over. Command is difficult for him. He doesn't know how to make peace with the

Warlords. He's overextended. He's trying to fight an entire war with a squad of ten. And he's going to lose."

"You don't think we can hold Khurdalain?"

"I think we were never meant to hold Khurdalain," said Chaghan. "I think Khurdalain was a sacrifice for time paid in blood. Altan is going to lose because Khurdalain is not winnable, and when he does, it's going to break him."

"Altan won't break," she said. Altan was the strongest fighter she'd ever seen. Altan *couldn't* break.

"Altan is more fragile than you think," said Chaghan. "He's cracking under the weight of command, can't you see? This is new territory for him, and he's flailing, because he's utterly dependent on victory."

Rin rolled her eyes. "The entire country's dependent on our victory."

Chaghan shook his head. "That's not what I mean. Altan is used to *winning*. His entire life he's been put on a pedestal. He was the last Speerly, a national rarity. Best student at the Academy. Tyr's favorite in the Cike. He's been fed a steady stream of constant affirmation for being very good at destroying things, but he won't get any praise here, especially not when his own soldiers are openly insubordinate."

"I'm not being—"

"Oh, come now, Rin. You're being a little bitch, is what you're doing, all because Altan won't pet you on the head and say you're doing a great job."

She stood up and slammed her hands on the table. "Look, asshole, I don't need you to tell me what to do."

"And yet, as your lieutenant, that is precisely my job." Chaghan glanced lazily up at her, and his expression was so smug that Rin trembled from the effort of not smashing his face into the table. "Your duty is to obey. My duty is to see that you stop fucking up. So I would suggest you get your shit together, learn to call the damn fire, and give Altan one less thing to worry about. Am I clear?"

CHAPTER 19

"So who's the newcomer?" Nezha asked casually.

Rin wasn't sure if she could discuss Chaghan without kicking something, which would be bad, especially since they were supposed to be hiding. But they had been staking out the barricade for what seemed like hours, and she was getting bored.

"He's Altan's lieutenant."

"How come I've never seen him before?"

"He's been away," she said.

A hail of arrows whizzed above them. Nezha ducked back below the barricade.

The Seventh Division had launched a joint assault with the Cike against the embassies by the wharf in an attempt to cut the main Federation encampment in two. In theory if they could hold the old Hesperian quarters, they could then divide the enemy forces and cut off their access to the docks. They had sent two regiments: one attacking perpendicular to the river and the other snaking around to the wharf from the direction of the canals.

But they had to move past five heavily defended intersections to get to the wharf, and those had turned into five separate bloodbaths. The Federation hadn't met them out on the open field because they didn't need to; safely ensconced behind the walls of the buildings they held on the wharf, they responded to the Nikara onslaught by embedding themselves on rooftops and shooting from windows on the upper floors of the embassy buildings.

The Seventh Division's only option was to throw their infantry en masse against the Federation's fortified position. They had to gamble that the press of Nikara bodies would be enough to force the Federation out. It had turned into a contest of flesh against steel, and the Militia was determined to break the Federation upon their bodies.

"You mean, you have no clue," Nezha said as a fire rocket exploded over his head.

"I mean, you have no business asking."

She didn't know if Nezha was fishing for information for his father, or if he was just trying to make small talk. She supposed it didn't matter. Chaghan's presence was hardly a secret, especially after Altan's dramatic rescue outside the east gate. Perhaps because of that, though, the Militia seemed even more spooked by him than they were by the rest of the Cike combined.

Several paces down, Suni lit one of Ramsa's specialty bombs and hurled it over the barricade.

They ducked back down and plugged up their ears until a now-familiar acrid, sulfuric smell filled their nostrils.

The arrow fire stopped.

"Is that *shit*?" Nezha demanded.

"Don't ask," Rin said. In the temporary lull granted by Ramsa's dung bomb they moved past the barricade and stormed down the street to reach the next of the five intersections.

"I heard he's creepy," Nezha continued. "I heard he's from the Hinterlands."

"Qara's from the Hinterlands, too. So what?"

"So I've heard he's unnatural," Nezha said.

Rin snorted. "It's the Cike. We're *all* unnatural."

A massive explosion rolled through the air in front of them, followed by a series of bursts of fire.

Altan.

He was leading the charge. His roiling flames, combined with Ramsa's many fire powder spectacles, created a number of large fires that drastically improved their nighttime visibility.

Altan had broken through to the next intersection. The Nikara continued their surge forward.

"But he can do things that Speerlies can't," Nezha said as they pressed on. "They say he can read the future. Shatter minds. My father says that even the Warlords know of him, did you know that? It makes you wonder. If Altan's got a lieutenant who's so powerful that he scares the Warlords, why is he sending him away from Khurdalain? What are they planning?"

"I'm not spying on my own division for you," Rin said.

"I didn't ask you to," Nezha said delicately. "I'm just saying you might want to keep an open mind."

"And you might want to keep your nose out of my division's matters."

But Nezha had stopped listening; he stared over Rin's shoulder at something farther along the wharf, where the first line of Nikara soldiers was pressing. "What is *that*?"

Rin craned her neck to see what he was looking at. Then she squinted in confusion.

An odd greenish-yellow fog had begun wending its way over the blockade toward the two division squadrons in front of them.

As if in a dream, the fighting stopped. The foremost squadron ceased moving, lowering their weapons with an almost hypnotic fascination as the cloud reached the wall, paused, gathered itself like a wave, and then ponderously lapped over into the dugouts.

Then the screaming began.

"Retreat," shouted a squadron officer. "*Retreat!*"

The Militia reversed direction immediately, commencing a disorganized stampede away from the gas. They abandoned their hard-won stations along the wharf in a frenzy to get away from the gas.

Rin coughed and glanced over her shoulder as she ran. Most of the soldiers who hadn't escaped the gas lay gasping and twitching on the ground, clawing at their faces as if their own throats were attacking them. Others lay quite still.

An arrowhead lashed across her cheek and embedded itself in the ground before her. The side of her mouth exploded in pain; she cupped a hand against it and continued running. The Federation soldiers were firing from behind the poisonous fog, they were going to pick them off one by one . . .

The forest line loomed up before her. She would be fine once she could take cover behind the foliage. Rin ducked her head and sprinted for the trees. Only a hundred yards . . . fifty . . . twenty . . .

Behind her she heard a strangled cry. She twisted her head to look and tripped over a rock, just as another arrow whistled over her head. Blood streamed from her cheek into her eyes. Rin wiped it furiously off and rolled over flat against the ground.

The source of the cry was Nezha. He was crawling furiously forward, but the gas had caught up to him. He met her eyes through the fog. He might have lifted one hand toward her.

She watched in horror, mouth open in a silent scream, as the gas enveloped him.

Through the gas, she saw forms advancing. Federation soldiers. They wore bulky contraptions over their heads, masks that concealed their necks and faces. They seemed unaffected by the gas.

One of them lifted a bulky gloved hand and pointed where Nezha lay.

Without thinking, Rin took a deep breath of air and rushed into the fog.

It burned her skin as soon as she touched it.

She clenched her teeth and forged ahead through the pain—but she'd hardly gone ten paces when someone grabbed her by the shoulder and yanked her back out of the gas zone. She struggled furiously to escape their grip.

Altan didn't let go.

"Back off!" She elbowed him in the face. Altan stumbled and grabbed at his nose. Rin tried to duck past him, but Altan wrenched her backward by her wrist.

"What are you doing?" he demanded.

"They've got Nezha!" she screamed.

"I don't care." He pushed her in the direction of the tree line. "Retreat."

"You're leaving one of our men to die!"

"He's not one of our men, he's one of the Seventh's men. *Go*."

"I won't leave my friend behind!"

"You will do as I command."

"But *Nezha*—"

"I'm not sorry about this," Altan said, and jammed a fist into her solar plexus.

Stunned, paralyzed, she sank to her knees.

She heard Altan shout out an order, and then someone picked her up and slung her over their shoulders as if she were a child. She beat and screamed as the soldier began jogging in the direction of the barracks. From the soldier's back, she thought she could see the masked Federation soldiers dragging Nezha away.

The gas attack created the precisely the effect that the Federation intended. The sugar bomb had been devastating—the gas attack was monstrous. Khurdalain erupted into a state of terror. Though the gas itself dissipated within an hour, rumors of it spread quickly. The fog was an invisible enemy, one that killed indiscriminately. There was no hiding from the fumes. Civilians began fleeing the city en masse, no longer confident in the Militia's ability to protect them. Panic enveloped the streets.

Jun's soldiers had shouted themselves hoarse in the alleys, trying to convince civilians they would be safer behind city walls. But the people weren't listening. They felt trapped. The narrow, winding roads of Khurdalain meant certain death in case of another gas attack.

While the city collapsed into chaos, the commanders commenced an emergency meeting in the nearest headquarters. The Cike crammed into the Ram Warlord's office along with the Warlords and their junior officers. Rin leaned against the corner of the wall, listening dully as the commanders argued over their immediate strategy.

Only one of Jun's soldiers on the beach had survived the attack. He had been posted in the back, and had dropped his weapon and run as soon as he saw his comrades choking.

"It was like breathing fire," he reported. "Like red-hot needles were piercing my lungs. I thought I was being strangled by some invisible demon . . . my throat closed up, I couldn't breathe . . ." He shuddered.

Rin listened, and resented him for not being Nezha.

It was only fifty yards. I could have saved him. I could have dragged us both out.

"We need to evacuate downtown right now," Jun said. He was remarkably calm for a man who had just lost more than a hundred men to a poisonous fog. "My men will—"

"Your men will do crowd control. The civilians are going to trample themselves trying to get out of the city, and it'll be easy for Mugen to pick them off if they're not corralled out in an orderly fashion," Altan said.

Amazingly, Jun didn't argue.

"We'll pack up headquarters and move it farther back into the Sihang warehouse," Altan continued. "We can dump the prisoner in the basement."

Rin jerked her head up. "What prisoner?"

She was faintly aware that she should not be talking, that as an unranked soldier of the Cike she was not technically a part of this meeting and was certainly acting out of line. But she was too grief-stricken and exhausted to care.

Unegen leaned down and murmured into her ear, "One of the Federation soldiers got caught in their own gas. Altan took his mask and pulled him out."

Rin blinked in disbelief.

"You went back in?" she asked. Her voice rang very loudly in her ears. "You had a mask?"

Altan shot her an irritated look. "This is not the time," he said.

She clambered to her feet. "You let one of our people die?"

"You and I can discuss this later."

She understood, in the abstract, the strategic boon of taking a Federation prisoner; the last Federation soldiers who had been captured spying across the bank had promptly been torn apart by furious civilians. And yet . . .

"You are *unbelievable*," Rin said.

"We will see to headquarters evacuation," Altan said loudly over her. "We'll regroup in the warehouse."

Jun nodded curtly, then muttered something to his officers. They saluted him and left the headquarters at a run.

At the same time, Altan issued orders to the Cike.

"Qara, Unegen, Ramsa: secure us a safe route to the warehouse and guide Jun's officers there. Baji and Suni, help Enki pack up shop. The rest of you resume positions in case of another gas attack." He paused at the door. "Rin. You stay."

She hung back as the rest of them exited the office. Unegen cast her a nervous look on his way out.

Altan waited until they were alone, and then he closed the door. He crossed the room and stood so that there was very little distance between them.

"You do not contradict me," he said quietly.

Rin crossed her arms. "Ever, or just in front of Jun?"

Altan didn't rise to the bait. "You will answer to me as a soldier to her commander."

"Or what? You'll have Suni drag me out of your office?"

"You're out of line." Altan's voice dropped to a dangerously low volume.

"And you let my friend die," Rin answered. "He was lying there and you *left him there*."

"You couldn't have extracted him."

"Yes, I could have," she seethed. "And even if I couldn't have—you might have, you might have saved my *friend* instead of dragging out some Federation soldier who deserved to die in there—"

"Prisoners of war have greater strategic importance than individual soldiers," Altan said calmly.

"That is such bullshit," she snarled.

Altan didn't answer. He took two steps forward and struck her across the face.

None of her guards were up. She took the full force of his hit with no preparation. His blow was so powerful that her head snapped to the side. The sudden impact made her knees buckle, jerked her to the ground. She raised a hand to her cheek, stunned. Her fingers came away bloody; he'd reopened her arrow wound.

Slowly she looked up at Altan. Her ears rang.

Altan's scarlet gaze met hers, and the naked rage on his face stunned her.

"How *dare* you," he said. His voice was overly loud, distorted through her thundering ears. "You misunderstand the nature of our relationship. I am not your friend. I am not your brother, though kin we may be. I am your commander. You do not argue with my orders. You follow them without question. You obey me, or you leave this Militia."

His voice held the same double timbre that Jiang's voice had held when he opened the void at Sinegard. Altan's eyes burned red—no, they were not red, they were the color of fire itself. Flames blazed behind him, flames whiter and hotter than any fire she'd ever been able to summon. She was immune to her own fire, but not his; it burned in her face, choking her, forcing her backward.

The ringing in her ears reached a crescendo.

He doesn't get to do this to you, said a voice in Rin's head. *He doesn't get to terrorize you*. She had not come this far to crouch like this in fear. Not to Altan. Not to anyone.

She stood up, even as she reached somewhere inside herself—somewhere spiteful and dark and horrible—and opened the channel to the entity she already knew was waiting for her summons. The room pitched forward as if viewed through a long scarlet prism. The familiar burn was back in her veins, the burn that demanded blood and ashes.

Through the red haze she thought she saw Altan's eyes widen in surprise. She squared her shoulders. Flames flared from her shoulders and back, flames that mirrored Altan's.

She took a step toward him.

A loud crackling noise filled the room. She felt an immense pressure. She trembled under the weight of it. She heard a bird's laughter. She heard a god's amused sigh.

You children, murmured the Phoenix. *You absurd, ridiculous children.* My *children.*

Altan looked stunned.

But just as her flames resisted his, she began to feel uncomfortably hot again, felt his fire begin to burn her. Rin's fire was an incendiary flash, an impulsive flare of anger. Altan's fire drew as its source an unending hate. It was a deep, slow burn. She could almost taste it, the venomous intent, the ancient misery, and it horrified her.

How could one person hate so much?

What had *happened* to him?

She could not maintain her fire anymore. Altan's flames burned hotter than hers. They had fought a contest of wills and she had lost.

She struggled for another moment and then her flames shrank back into her as quickly as they'd sprung out. Altan's fire dimmed a moment after hers did.

This is it, Rin thought. *I've crossed the line. This is the end.*

But Altan didn't look furious. He didn't look like he was about to execute her.

No—he looked *pleased*.

"So that's what it takes," he said.

She felt drained, as if the fire had burned up something inside her. She couldn't even feel anger. She could barely stand.

"Fuck you," she said. "*Fuck you.*"

"Get to your post, soldier," said Altan.

She left his office, slamming the door shut behind her.

Fuck me.

CHAPTER 20

"There you are."

She found Chaghan over the north wall. He stood with his arms crossed, watching as civilians poured out of Khurdalain's dense streets like ants fleeing a collapsed hill. They straggled through the city gates with their worldly possessions packed onto wagons, strapped to the sides of oxen or horses, slung across their shoulders on poles meant for carrying water, or simply dragged along in sacks. They had chosen to take their chances in the open country rather than to stay another day in the doomed city.

The Militia was remaining in Khurdalain—it was still a strategic base that needed to be held—but they would be protecting nothing but empty buildings from here on out.

"Khurdalain's done for," Chaghan said, leaning against the wall. "Militia included. There'll be no supplies after this. No hospital. No food. Soldiers fight battles, but civilians keep armies alive. Lose the resource well, and you've lost the war."

"I need to talk to you," she said.

He turned to face her, and she suppressed a shudder at the sight of those eyes without pupils. His gaze seemed to rest on the scarlet palm print on her cheek. His lips pressed together in a thin line, as if he knew exactly how the mark had gotten there.

"Lovers' spat?" he drawled.

"Difference of opinion."

"Shouldn't have harped on about that boy," he tutted. "Altan doesn't tolerate shit like that. He's not very patient."

"He's not *human*," she said, recalling the horrible anger behind Altan's power. She'd thought she understood Altan. She'd thought she had reached the man behind the command title. But she realized now that she didn't know him at all. The Altan she'd known—at least, the Altan in her mind—would have done anything for his troops. He wouldn't have left someone in the gas to die. "He—I don't know *what* he is."

"But Altan was never allowed to be human," Chaghan said, and his voice was uncharacteristically gentle. "Since childhood, he's been regarded as a Militia asset. Your masters at the Academy fed him opium for attacking his classmates and trained him like a dog for this war. Now he's been shouldered with the most difficult command position that exists in the Militia, and you wonder why he's not going to trouble himself with your little boy toy?"

Rin almost hit Chaghan for that, but she restrained herself with a twitch and set her jaw. "I'm not here to talk about Altan."

"Then why, pray tell, are you here?"

"I need you to show me what you can do," she said.

"I do a lot of things, sweetheart."

She bristled. "I need you to take me to the gods."

Chaghan looked smug. "I thought you didn't have a problem calling the gods."

"I can't do it as easily as Altan can."

"But you *can* do it."

Her fingers curled into fists by her sides. "I want to do what Altan can do."

Chaghan raised an eyebrow.

She took a deep breath. Chaghan didn't need to know what had happened in the office. "I've been trying for months now. I think I've got it, I'm not sure, but there's something . . . someone that's blocking me."

Chaghan assumed a mildly curious expression, tilting his head in a manner painfully reminiscent of Jiang. "You're being haunted?"

"It's a woman."

"Really."

"Come with me," she said. "I'll show you."

"Why now?" He crossed his arms over his chest. "What happened?"

She didn't answer his question. "I need to do what he can do," she said flatly. "I need to call the same power that he can."

"And you didn't bother with me before because . . ."

"You weren't fucking here!"

"And when I returned?"

"I was obeying the warnings of my master."

Chaghan sounded like he was gloating. "Those warnings no longer apply?"

She set her jaw. "I've realized that masters inevitably let you down."

He nodded slowly, though his expression gave nothing away. "And if I can't get rid of this . . . ghost?"

"Then at least you'll understand." She held out her hands. "*Please*."

That supplication was enough. Chaghan gave a slight nod, and then beckoned her to sit down beside him. While she watched, he unpacked his knapsack and spread it out on the stone floor. An impressive supply of psychedelics was packed inside, tucked neatly into more than twenty little pockets.

"This is not derived from the poppy plant," he said as he mixed powders into a glass vial. "This drug is something far more potent. A small overdose will cause blindness. More than that and you will be dead in minutes. Do you trust me?"

"No. But that's irrelevant."

Chuckling softly, Chaghan gave the vial a shake. He dumped the mixture into his palm, licked his index finger, and dipped it lightly in the drug so that the tip of his finger was covered by a light smattering of fine blue dust.

"Open your mouth," he said.

She pushed down a swell of hesitation and obliged.

Chaghan pressed the tip of his finger against her tongue.

She closed her eyes. Felt the psychedelics seep into her saliva.

The onset was immediate and crushing, like a dark wave of ocean water had suddenly slammed on top of her. Her nervous system broke down completely; she lost the ability to sit up and crumpled at Chaghan's feet.

She was at his mercy now, completely and utterly vulnerable before him. *He could kill me right now*, she thought dully. She didn't know why it was the first thought that sprang to her mind. *He could get rid of me now, if he wanted to.*

But Chaghan only knelt down beside her, grasped her face by her cheeks, and pressed his forehead against hers. His eyes were open very, very wide. She stared into them, fascinated; they were a pale expanse, a window into a snowy landscape, and she was traversing through them . . .

And then they were hurtling upward.

She hadn't known what she had expected. Not once in two years of training had Jiang guided her into the spirit realm. It had always been her mind alone, her soul alone in the void, journeying up toward the gods.

With Chaghan, she felt as if a piece of her had been ripped away, was clutched in the palm of his hand, being taken somewhere of his choosing. She was immaterial, without body or form, but Chaghan was not; Chaghan remained as solid and real as before, perhaps even more so. In the material world, he was gaunt and emaciated, but in the realm of spirit he was solid and present . . .

She understood, now, why Chaghan and Qara had to be two halves of a whole. Qara was grounded, material, fully made of earth. To call them anchor twins was a misnomer—*she* alone was the anchor to her ethereal brother, who belonged more in the realm of spirit than he did in a world of flesh and blood.

The route to the Pantheon was familiar by now, and so was the gate. Once again the Woman materialized in front of her. But something was different this time; this time the Woman was less like a ghost and more like a corpse; half her face was torn away, revealing bone underneath, and her warrior's garb had burned away from her body.

The Woman stretched a hand out toward Rin in supplication.

"It'll eat you alive," she said. "The fire will consume you. To find our god is to find hell on earth, little warrior. You will burn and burn and never find peace."

"How curious," said Chaghan. "Who are you?"

The Woman whirled on him.

"You know who I am," she said. "I am the guardian. I am the Traitor and the Damned. I am redemption. I am the girl's last chance for salvation."

"I see," Chaghan murmured. "So this is where you've been hiding."

"What are you talking about?" Rin demanded. "Who is she?"

But Chaghan spoke past her, directly to the woman. "You should have been immured in the Chuluu Korikh."

"The Chuluu Korikh can't hold me," hissed the Woman. "I am a Speerly. My ashes are free." She reached out and stroked Rin's damaged cheek like a mother caressing her child. "You don't want me gone. You need me."

Rin shuddered at her touch. "I need my god. I need power, and I need fire."

"If you call it now, you will bring down hell on earth," the Woman warned.

"Khurdalain is hell on earth," said Rin. She saw Nezha screaming in the fog, and her voice wavered.

"You don't know what true suffering is," the Woman insisted angrily.

Rin curled her fingers into fists at her sides, suddenly pissed off. True suffering? She had seen her friends stabbed with halberds, shot full of arrows, cut down with swords, burned to death in poisonous fog. She had seen Sinegard go up in flames. She had seen Khurdalain occupied by Federation invaders almost overnight.

"I have seen more than my fair share of suffering," she hissed.

"I'm trying to save you, little one. Why can't you see that?"

"What about Altan?" Rin challenged. "Why haven't you ever tried to stop him?"

The Woman tilted her head. "Is that what this is about? Are you jealous of what he can do?"

Rin opened her mouth, but nothing came out. No. Yes. Did it matter? If she had been as strong as Altan, he wouldn't have been able to restrain her.

If she were as strong as Altan, she could have saved Nezha.

"That boy is beyond redemption," said the Woman. "That boy is broken like the rest. But you, *you* are still pure. You can still be saved."

"I don't want to be saved!" Rin shrieked. "I want power! I want Altan's power! I want to be the most powerful shaman there ever was, so that there is no one I can't save!"

"That power can burn down the world," the Woman said sadly. "That power will destroy everything you've ever loved. You will defeat your enemy, and the victory will turn to ashes in your mouth."

Chaghan had finally regained his composure.

"You have no right to remain here," he said. His voice trembled slightly as he spoke, but he raised one thin hand toward the Woman in a banishing gesture. "You belong to the realm of the dead. Return to the dead."

"Do not try," sneered the Woman. "You cannot banish me. In my time I have bested shamans far more powerful than you."

"There are no shamans more powerful than me," said Chaghan, and he began to chant in his own language, the harshly guttural language Jiang had once spoken, the language Rin recognized now as the speech of the Hinterlands.

His eyes glowed golden.

The Woman started to shake, as if standing over an earthquake, and then suddenly she burst into flames. The fire lit her face from within, like a glowing coal, like an ember about to explode.

She shattered.

Chaghan took Rin's wrist and *tugged*. She became immaterial again, rushing headlong into the space where things were not real. She did not choose where they went; she could only concentrate on staying whole, staying *herself*, until Chaghan stopped and she could regain her bearings without losing herself entirely.

This was not the Pantheon.

She glanced around, confused. They were in a dimly lit room the size of Altan's office, with a low, curved ceiling that forced them to crouch where they stood. Everywhere she looked, small tiles had been arranged in mosaics, depicting scenes she did not recognize or understand. A fisherman bearing a net full of armored warriors. A young boy encircled by a dragon. A woman with long hair weeping over a broken sword and two bodies. In the room's center stood a great hexagonal altar, engraved with sixty-four intricate characters of Old Nikara calligraphy.

"Where are we?" Rin asked.

"A safe place of my choosing," Chaghan said. He looked visibly rattled. "She was much stronger than I expected. I took us to the first place I thought of. This is a Divinatory. Here we can ask questions about your Woman. Come to the altar."

She looked about in wonder as she followed him, running her fingers over the carefully designed tiles. "Is this part of the Pantheon?"

"No."

"Then is this place real?"

"It's real in your mind," said Chaghan. "That's as real as anything gets."

"Jiang never taught me about this."

"That's because you Nikara are so *primitive*," said Chaghan. "You still think there's a strict binary between the material world and the Pantheon. You think calling the gods is like summoning a dog from the yard into the house. But you can't conceive of the dream world as a physical place. The gods are painters. Your material world is a canvas. And this Divinatory is an angle from which we can see the colors on the palette. This isn't really a *place*, it's a *perspective*. But you're interpreting it as a room because your human mind can't process anything else."

"What about this altar? The mosaics? Who built them?"

"No one did. You still don't understand. They're mental constructions so that you can comprehend concepts that are already written. To the Talwu, this room looks completely different."

"The Talwu?"

Chaghan tilted his chin toward something in front of them.

"You're back so soon," spoke a cool, alien voice.

In the dim light, Rin had not noticed the creature standing behind the hexagonal altar. It walked around the circle at a steady pace and sank into a deep bow before Chaghan. It looked like nothing Rin had ever seen; it was similar to a tiger, but its hair grew two feet long. It had a woman's face, a lion's feet, a pig's teeth, and a very long tail that might have belonged to a monkey.

"She is a goddess. Guardian of the Hexagrams," Chaghan said to Rin as he sank into an equally deep bow. He pulled her down to the floor with him.

The Talwu dipped her head toward Chaghan. "The time of asking has expired for you. But *you* . . ." She looked at Rin. "You have never asked a question of me. You may proceed."

"What is this place?" Rin asked Chaghan. "What can it—*she*—tell me?"

"The Divinatory keeps the Hexagrams," he answered. "The Hexagrams are sixty-four different combinations of lines broken and unbroken." He indicated the calligraphy at the sides of the altar, and Rin saw that each character indeed was made up of six lines. "Ask the Talwu your question, cast a Hexagram, and it will read the lines for you."

"It can tell me the future?"

"No one can divine the future," said Chaghan. "It is always

shifting, always dependent on individual choices. But the Talwu can tell you the forces at play. The underlying shape of things. The color of events to pass. The future is a pattern dependent on the movements of the present, but the Talwu can read the currents for you, just as a seasoned sailor can read the ocean. You need only present a question."

Rin was beginning to see the reason why Chaghan commanded the fear that he did. He was just like Jiang—unthreatening and eccentric, until one understood what deep power lay behind his frail facade.

How would Jiang pose a question? She contemplated the wording of her inquiry for a moment. Then she stepped toward the Talwu.

"What does the Phoenix want me to know?"

The Talwu almost smiled.

"Cast the coins six times."

Three coins suddenly appeared, stacked on the hexagonal altar. They were not coins of the Nikara Empire; they were too large, cut into a hexagonal shape rather than the round taels and ingots Rin was familiar with. She picked them up and weighed them in her palm. They were heavier than they looked. On the front side of each was etched the unmistakable profile of the Red Emperor; on the back were inscribed characters of Old Nikara that she could not decipher.

"Each throw of the coins will determine one line in the Hexagram," said Chaghan. "These lines are patterns written into the universe. They are ancient combinations, descriptions of shapes that were long before either of us was born. They will not make sense to you. But the Talwu will read them, and I will interpret."

"Why must *you* interpret?"

"Because I am a Seer. This is what I'm trained to do," said Chaghan. "We Hinterlanders do not call the gods down as you do. We go *to* them. Our shamans spend hours in trances, learning the secrets of the cosmos. I have spent more time in the Pantheon than I have in your world. I have deciphered enough Hexagrams now to know how they describe the shape of our world. And if you try to interpret for yourself, you'll just get confused. Let me help you."

"Fine." Rin flung the three coins out onto the hexagonal altar.

All three coins landed tails up.

"*The first line, undivided,*" read the Talwu. "*One is ready to move, but his footprints run crisscross.*"

"What does that mean?" Rin asked.

Chaghan shook his head. "Any number of things. The lines each assume shades of meaning depending on the others. Finish the Hexagram."

She tossed the coins again. All heads.

"*The second line, divided,*" read the Talwu. "*The subject ascends to his place in the sun. There will be supreme good fortune.*"

"That's good, isn't it?" Rin asked.

"Depends on whose fortune it is," said Chaghan. "The subject is not necessarily you."

Her third toss saw one head, two tails.

"*The third line, divided. The end of the day has come. The net has been cast on the setting sun. This spells misfortune.*"

Rin felt a sudden chill. The end of an era, the setting sun on a country . . . she hardly needed Chaghan to interpret that for her.

"We're not going to win this war, are we?" she asked the Talwu.

"I only read the Hexagrams," said the Talwu. "I confirm and deny nothing."

"It's the net I'm concerned about. It's a trap," said Chaghan. "We've missed something. Something's been laid out for us, but we can't see it."

Chaghan's words confused Rin as much as the line itself did, but Chaghan commanded her to throw the coins again. Two tails, one head.

"*The fourth line, undivided,*" read the Talwu. "*The subject comes, abrupt with fire, with death, to be rejected by all. As if an exit; as if an entry. As though burning; as though dying; as though discarded.*"

"That one is quite clear," said Chaghan, although Rin had more questions about that line than the others. She opened her mouth, but he shook his head. "Throw the coins again."

The Talwu looked down. "*The fifth line, divided. The subject is with tears flowing in torrents, groaning in sorrow.*"

Chaghan looked stricken. "Truly?"

"The Hexagrams do not lie," the Talwu said. Her voice was devoid of emotion. "The only lies are in the interpretation."

Chaghan's hand shook suddenly. The wooden beads of his bracelet clattered, echoing in the silent room. Rin shot him a concerned look, but he only shook his head and motioned for her to finish. Arms heavy with dread, Rin cast the coins a sixth and final time.

"*A leader abandons their people,*" read the Talwu. "*A ruler begins a campaign. One sees great joy in decapitating enemies. This signifies evil.*"

Chaghan's pale eyes were open very, very wide.

"You have cast the Twenty-Sixth Hexagram. The Net," announced the Talwu. "There is a clinging, and a conflict. Things will come to pass that exist only side by side. Misfortune and victory. Liberation and death."

"But the Phoenix . . . the Woman . . ." Rin had not received any of the answers she wanted. The Talwu hadn't helped her at all; it had only warned of even worse things to come, things she didn't have the power to prevent.

The Talwu lifted a clawed hand. "Your time of asking is up. Return in a lunar month, and you may cast another Hexagram."

Before Rin could speak, Chaghan knelt forward hastily and dragged Rin down beside him.

"Thank you, Enlightened One," he said, and to Rin he murmured, "Say nothing."

The room dissolved as she sank to her knees, and with an icy jolt, like she had been doused in cold water, Rin found herself shoved back into her material body.

She took a deep breath. She opened her eyes.

Beside her, Chaghan drew himself up to a sitting position. His pale eyes were huge, deep in their shadowed sockets. His gaze seemed to be focused still on something very far away, something entirely not in this world. Slowly, he returned to himself, and when he finally registered Rin's presence, his expression became one of deep anxiety.

"We must get Altan," he said.

If Altan was surprised when Chaghan barged into the Sihang warehouse with Rin in tow, he didn't show it. He looked too exhausted for anything to faze him at all.

"Summon the Cike," said Chaghan. "We need to leave this city."

"On what information?" Altan asked.

"There was a Hexagram."

"I thought you didn't get another question for a month."

"It wasn't mine," said Chaghan. "It was hers."

Altan didn't even glance at Rin. "We can't leave Khurdalain. They need us now more than ever. We're about to lose the city. If the Federation gets through us, they enter the heartland. We are the final front."

"You are fighting a battle the Federation does not need to win," said Chaghan. "The Hexagrams spoke of a great victory, and great destruction. Khurdalain has only been a frustration for both sides. There is one other city that Mugen wants right now."

"That's impossible," said Altan. "They cannot march to Golyn Niis so soon from the coast. The Golyn River route is too narrow to move troop columns. They would have to find the mountain pass."

Chaghan raised his eyebrows. "I'll bet you they've found it."

"All right. Fine." Altan stood up. "I believe you. Let's go."

"Just like that?" Rin asked. "No due diligence?"

Altan walked out of the room and headed down the hallway at a brisk stride. They scurried to keep up with him. He descended the steps of the warehouse until he stood before the basement cellar where the Federation prisoner was kept.

"What are you doing?" Rin asked.

"Due diligence," Altan said, and yanked the door open.

The cellar smelled strongly of defecation.

The prisoner had been shackled to a post in the corner of the room, hands and feet bound, a cloth jammed into his mouth. He was unconscious when they entered the room; he didn't stir when Altan slammed the door shut, or when Altan crossed the room to kneel down beside him.

He had been beaten; one eye was swollen a violent shade of purple, and blood was crusted around a broken nose. But the worst damage had been inflicted by the gas: what skin was not purple had blistered into an angry red rash, so that his face did not look human at all but rather like a frightening combobulation of colors. Rin found a savage satisfaction in seeing the prisoners' features as burned and disfigured as they were.

Altan touched two fingers to an open wound on the prisoner's cheek and gave a small, sharp jab.

"Wake up," he said in fluent Mugini. "How are you feeling?"

With a groan, the prisoner slowly opened his swollen eyes. When he saw Altan, he hacked and spat out a gob of spit at Altan's feet.

"Wrong answer," said Altan, and dug his nail into the cut.

The prisoner screamed loudly. Altan let go.

"What do you want?" the prisoner demanded. His Mugini was coarse and slurred, a far cry from the polished accent Rin had studied at Sinegard. It took her a moment to decipher his dialect.

"It occurs to me that Khurdalain was never the main target," Altan said casually, resting back on his haunches. "Perhaps you would like to tell us what is."

The prisoner smiled an awful, bloody-faced smile that twisted his burn scars. "*Khurdalain*," he repeated, rolling the Nikara word through his mouth like a wad of phlegm. "Who would want to capture this shit hole?"

"Never mind," said Altan. "Where is the main offensive going?"

The prisoner glowered up at him and snorted.

Altan raised a hand and slapped the prisoner on the blistered side of his face. Rin winced. By targeting the prisoner's sore, open wounds, Altan was making him hurt worse and more acutely than any heavy-handed blows could.

"Where is the other offensive?" Altan repeated.

The prisoner spat blood at Altan's feet.

"*Answer me!*" Altan shouted.

Rin jumped.

The prisoner raised his head. "Nikara swine," he sneered.

Altan grabbed the prisoner by a fistful of hair in the back of his head. He slammed his other fist into the prisoner's already bruised eye. Again. And again. Blood flew across the room, splashed against the dirt floor.

"Stop," Rin squeaked.

Altan turned around.

"Leave the room or shut up," he said.

"At this rate he'll pass out," she responded, her heart hammering. "And we don't have time to revive him."

Altan stared at her for a wild-eyed moment. Then he nodded curtly and turned back to the prisoner.

"Sit up."

The prisoner muttered something none of them could understand.

Altan kicked him in the ribs. "*Sit up!*"

The prisoner spat another gob of blood on Altan's boots. His head lolled to the side. Altan wiped his toe on the ground with deliberate slowness, then knelt down in front of the prisoner. He stuck two fingers under the prisoner's chin and tilted his face up to his own in a gesture that was almost intimate.

"Hey, I'm talking to you," he said. "Hey. Wake up."

He slapped the prisoner's cheeks until the prisoner's eyes fluttered back open.

"I have nothing to say to you," the prisoner sneered.

"You will," Altan said. His voice dropped in pitch, a sharp contrast from his previous shouts. "Do you know what a Speerly is?"

The prisoner's eyes furrowed together in confusion. "What?"

"Surely you know," Altan said softly. His voice became a low, velvety purr. "Surely you've heard tales of us. Surely the island hasn't forgotten. You must have been a child when your people massacred Speer, no? Did you know they did it overnight? Killed every single man, woman, and child."

Sweat beaded at the prisoner's temples, dripping down to mingle with fresh rivulets of blood. Altan snapped his fingers before the prisoner's eyes. "Can you see this? Can you see my fingers? Yes or no."

"Yes," the prisoner said hoarsely.

Altan tilted his head. "They say your people were terrified of the Speerlies. That the generals gave orders that not one single Speerly child should survive, because they were so terrified of what we might become. Do you know why?"

The prisoner stared blankly forward.

Altan snapped again. His thumb and index finger burst into flames.

"This is why," he said.

The prisoner's eyes bulged with terror.

Altan brought his hand close to the prisoner's face, so that the edge of the flame licked threateningly at the gas blisters.

"I will burn you piece by piece," said Altan. His tone was so soft that he could have been speaking to a lover. "I will start with the bottoms of your feet. I will feed you one bit of pain at a time, so you will never lose consciousness. Your wounds will cauterize as soon as they manifest, so you won't die from blood loss. When your feet are charred, coated entirely in black, I'll move on to your fingers. I'll make them drop off one by one. I will line up the charcoal stubs in a string to hang around your neck. When I've finished with your extremities, I'll move on to your testicles. I will singe them so slowly you will go insane from the agony. *Then* you'll sing."

The prisoner's eyes twitched madly, but still he shook his head.

Altan's tone softened even further. "It doesn't have to be like this. Your division let us take you. You don't owe them anything." His voice became soothing and hypnotic, almost gentle. "The others wanted to have you put to death, you know. Publicly executed before the civilians. They would have had you torn apart. An eye for an eye." Altan's voice was so lovely. He could be so beautiful, so charismatic, when he wanted to be. "But I'm not like the others. I'm reasonable. I don't want to hurt you. I just want your cooperation."

The soldier's throat bobbed. His eyes darted across Altan's face; he was hopelessly confused, trying to get a read and concluding nothing. Altan wore two masks at the same time, feigned two contrasting entities, and the prisoner did not know which to expect or pander to.

"Tell me, and I can have you released," Altan said gently. "Tell me, and I'll let you go."

The prisoner maintained his silence.

"No?" Altan searched the prisoner's face. "All right." His flames doubled in intensity, shooting sparks through the air.

The prisoner shrieked. "Golyn Niis!"

Altan kept the flames held perilously close to the prisoner's eyes. "Elaborate."

"We never needed to take Khurdalain," spat the prisoner. "The goal was always Golyn Niis. All your best divisions came flocking to the coast as soon as this war started. Idiots. We never even wanted this beach town."

"But the fleet," said Altan. "Khurdalain has been your point of entry for every offensive. You can't get to Golyn Niis without going through Khurdalain."

"There was another fleet," hissed the prisoner. "There have been many fleets, sailing south of this pathetic city. They found the mountain pass. You poor idiots, did you think you could keep that a secret? They're cutting straight toward Golyn Niis itself. Your war capital will burn, our Armed Forces are cutting directly across your heartland, and you're still holed up here in this pathetic excuse for a city."

Altan drew his hand back.

Rin flinched instinctively, expecting him to lash out again.

But Altan only extinguished his flame and patted the prisoner condescendingly on the head. "Good boy," he said in a low whisper. "Thank you."

He nodded to Rin and Chaghan, indicating they were about to leave.

"Wait," the prisoner said hastily. "You said you'd let me go."

Altan tilted his face up to the ceiling and sighed. A thin trickle of sweat ran from the bone under his ear down his neck.

"Sure," he said. "I'll let you go."

He whipped his hand across the prisoner's neck. A spray of blood flew outward.

The prisoner bore an astonished expression. He made a last startled, choked noise. Then his eyes drooped closed and his head slumped forward. The smell of cooked meat and burned blood filled the air.

Rin tasted bile in the back of her throat. It was a long while before she remembered how to breathe.

Altan rose to his feet. The veins at his neck protruded in the dim light. He took a deep breath and then exhaled slowly, like an opium smoker, like a man who had just filled his lungs with a drug. He turned toward them. His eyes glowed bright red in the darkness. His eyes were nothing human.

"Fine," he said to his lieutenant. "You were right."

Chaghan hadn't moved throughout the entire interrogation.

"I'm rarely wrong," said Chaghan.

PART III

CHAPTER 21

Baji yawned loudly, winced, and pulled his neck far to the side. A series of cracks punctuated the still morning air. There was no room to lie down in the river sampan, so sleep had to be acquired in short, fitful bursts, bent over in cramp-inducing positions. He blinked blearily for a minute, and then reached across the narrow boat with his foot to nudge Rin's leg.

"I can take watch now."

"I'm fine," Rin said. She sat huddled with her hands shoved into her armpits, slumped forward so that her head rested on her knees. She stared blankly out at the running water.

"You really should get some sleep."

"Can't."

"You should try."

"I've tried," Rin said shortly.

Rin could not silence the Talwu's voice in her head. She had heard the Hexagram uttered only once, but she was unlikely to forget a single word. It had been seared into her mind, and no matter how many times she revisited it, she could not interpret it in a way that did not leave her feeling sick with dread.

Abrupt with fire, with death . . . as though burning; as though dying ... the subject is with tears flowing in torrents ... great joy in decapitating enemies ...

She used to think divination was a pale science, a vague approximation if valuable at all. But the Talwu's words were anything but vague. There was only one possible fate for Golyn Niis.

You have cast the Twenty-Sixth Hexagram. The Net. Chaghan had said the net meant a trap had been laid. But had the trap been laid for Golyn Niis? Had it already been sprung, or were they heading straight toward their deaths?

"You're going to wear yourself out. Fretting won't make these boats run any faster." Baji pulled his head to the side until he heard another satisfying crack. "And it won't make the dead come back to life."

They raced up the Golyn River, making absurd time in a journey that should have taken a month on horseback. Aratsha ferried them along the river at blinding speed. Still, it took them a week to travel the length of the Golyn River to the lush delta where Golyn Niis had been built.

Rin glanced up to look at the boat at the very fore, where Altan sat. He rode beside Chaghan; their heads were tilted together, speaking in low tones as usual. They had been like this since they had left Khurdalain. Chaghan and Qara may have been linked as anchor twins, but it was Altan whom Chaghan seemed bonded to.

"Why isn't Chaghan commander?" she asked.

Baji looked confused. "What do you mean?"

"I don't understand why Chaghan obeys Altan," she said. Against the Woman, he had proclaimed himself the most powerful shaman in existence. She believed it. Chaghan navigated the spirit world like he belonged there, as if he were a god himself. The Cike didn't hesitate to talk back to Altan, but she had never seen any of them dare to so much as contradict Chaghan. Altan commanded their loyalty, but Chaghan enjoyed their fear.

"He was slated to be commander after Tyr," said Baji. "Got shunted to the side after Altan showed up, though."

"And he was fine with that?" Rin couldn't imagine someone like Chaghan relinquishing authority peacefully.

"Of course not. Nearly spit fire when Tyr started favoring the golden boy from Sinegard over him."

"So then why—"

"Why's he happy serving under Altan? He wasn't, at first. He bitched about it for a straight week, until Altan finally got fed up. He asked Tyr for permission for a duel and got it. He took Chaghan out into the valleys for three days."

"What happened?"

Baji snorted. "What happens when anyone fights Trengsin? When Chaghan got back, all that pretty white hair was singed black and he was obeying Altan like a whipped dog. Our friend from the Hinterlands might shatter minds, but he couldn't touch Trengsin. No one can."

Rin dropped her head back onto her knees and closed her eyes against the light from the rising sun. She hadn't slept—hadn't truly rested—since they'd left Khurdalain. But her body couldn't sustain itself any longer. She was so tired . . .

Their boat jolted in the water. Rin snapped up to a sitting position. They had bumped straight into the boat in front of them.

"Something's in the water," Ramsa shouted from the fore.

Rin looked over the side and squinted at the river. The water was the same muddy brown, until she glanced upstream.

At first she thought it was a trick of the light, an illusion of the sun's rays. And then her boat reached an odd patch of colored water, and she draped her fingers over the edge. Then she yanked it back in horror.

They were riding through a river of blood.

Altan and Chaghan both jumped up with startled exclamations. Behind them, Unegen uttered a long, inhuman shriek.

"Oh gods," Baji said, over and over. "Oh gods, oh gods, oh gods."

Then the bodies began to float toward them.

Rin was paralyzed, stricken with an irrational fear that the bodies might be the enemy, that they would rise out of the water and attack them.

Their boat stopped moving completely. They were surrounded by corpses. Soldiers. Civilians. Men. Women. Children. They were uniformly bloated and discolored. Some of their faces were disfigured, slashed apart. Others were simply blank, resigned, bobbing listlessly in the crimson water as if they had never been living, breathing bodies.

Chaghan reached out to examine a young girl's blue lips. His own mouth was pursed dispassionately as if he were tracking a footprint, not touching a rubbery carcass. "These bodies have been in the river for days. Why haven't they drifted out to sea yet?"

"It's the Golyn Niis Dam," Unegen suggested. "It's blocking them up."

"But we're still miles out from the city . . ." Rin trailed off.

They fell silent.

Altan stood up at the head of his boat. "Get out. Start running."

The road to Golyn Niis was empty. Qara and Unegen scouted ahead but reported no sign of enemy combatants. Yet evidence of Federation presence was obvious everywhere they looked—trampled grass, abandoned campfires, rectangular patches in the dirt where tents had been erected. Rin felt sure that Federation soldiers were lying in wait for them, setting an ambush, but as they drew closer to the city, she realized that made no sense; the Federation wouldn't have known they were coming, and they wouldn't have set such an elaborate trap for such a small squadron.

She would have preferred an ambush. The silence was worse.

If Golyn Niis were still under siege, the Federation would be on guard. They would be prepared for skirmishes. They would have posted guards to make sure no reinforcements could reach the resistance inside.

There would *be* a resistance.

But the Federation seemed to have simply packed up and walked away. They hadn't even bothered to leave behind a skeleton patrol. Which meant that the Federation didn't care who came into Golyn Niis.

Which meant that whatever lay behind those city walls, it wasn't worth guarding.

When the Cike finally succeeded in dragging open the heavy gates, an appalling stink assaulted them like a slap to the face. Rin knew the smell. She had experienced it at Sinegard and Khurdalain. She knew what to expect now. It had been a fool's hope to expect anything different, but still she could not fully register the sight that awaited them when they passed through the barrier.

All of them stood still at the gates, unwilling to take one step farther inside.

For a long time none of them could speak.

Then Ramsa fell to his knees and began to cackle with laughter.

"Khurdalain," he gasped. "We were all so obsessed with holding *Khurdalain*."

He doubled over, sides shaking with mirth, and beat his fists against the dirt.

Rin envied him.

Golyn Niis was a city of corpses.

The bodies had been arranged deliberately, as if the Federation had wanted to leave a greeting message for the next people to walk into the city. The destruction possessed a strange artfulness, a sadistic symmetry. Corpses were piled in neat, even rows, forming pyramids of ten, then nine, then eight. Corpses were stacked against the wall. Corpses were placed across the street in tidy lines. Corpses were arranged as far as the eye could see.

Nothing human moved. The only sounds in the city were wind rustling through debris, the buzzing of flies, and the squawking of carrion birds.

Rin's eyes watered. The stench was overwhelming. She looked to Altan, but his face was a mask. He marched them stoically down the main street into the city center, as if he was determined to witness the full extent of the destruction.

They marched in silence.

The Federation handiwork became more elaborate the deeper they traveled into the city. Close to the city square, the Federation had arrayed the corpses in states of incredible desecration, grotesque positions that defied human imagination. Corpses nailed to boards. Corpses hung by their tongues from hooks. Corpses dismembered in every possible way; headless, limbless, displaying mutilations that must have been performed while the victim was still alive. Fingers removed, then stacked in a small pile beside stubby hands. An entire line of castrated men, severed penises placed delicately on their slack-jawed mouths.

One sees great joy in decapitating enemies.

There were so many beheadings. Heads stacked up in neat little piles, not yet so rotted that they had become skulls, but no longer resembling human faces. Whatever heads retained enough flesh to form expressions wore identical looks of terrible dullness, as if they had never been alive.

As though burning; as though dying.

Perhaps due to some initial desire for sanitation, or mere curiosity, the Federation had tried to ignite several corpse pyramids. But they had given up before the job was finished. Perhaps they did not want to waste the oil. Perhaps the stink became unbearable. The bodies were grotesque, half-charred spectacles; hair had turned to ash, and the top layers of skin had turned a crinkling black, but the worst part was that there was something beneath the ashes that looked identifiably human.

The subject is with tears flowing in torrents, groaning in sorrow.

In the square they found bizarrely short skeletons—not corpses, but skeletons gleaming pristine white. They looked at first like children's bones, but upon closer examination, Enki identified them as adult torsos. He bent down and touched the dirt where one skeleton was fixed to the ground. The top half of the body had been stripped clean so the bones glistened in the sunlight, while the lower half remained intact in the dirt.

"They were buried," he said, disgusted. "They were buried up to the waist and set upon by dogs."

Rin could not understand how the Federation had found so many different ways to inflict suffering. But each corner they turned revealed another instance in the string of horrors, barbarian savagery matched only by inventiveness. A family, arms still around each other, impaled upon the same spear. Babies lying at the bottoms of vats, their skin a horrible shade of crimson, floating in the water in which they'd boiled to death.

In the hours that had passed, the only living creatures they encountered were dogs unnaturally fattened by feeding on corpses. Dogs, and vultures.

"Orders?" Unegen finally asked Altan.

They looked to their commander.

Altan hadn't spoken since they had walked through the city gates. His skin had turned a ghostly shade of gray. He might have been ill. He was sweating profusely, his left arm trembling. When they reached another pile of charred corpses, he convulsed, sank to his knees, and could not keep walking.

This was not Altan's first genocide.

This is Speer again, Rin thought. Altan must have been imagining the massacre of Speer in his mind, imagining the way his people were slaughtered overnight like cattle.

After a long time Chaghan extended his hand to Altan.

Altan grasped it and rose to his feet. He swallowed, closed his eyes. A mask of detachment spread across his expression once more with a curious ripple, like a facade of indifference had formed a seal over the surface of his face, locking any vulnerabilities within.

"Spread out," Altan ordered. His voice was impossibly level. "Find any survivors."

Surrounded by death, spreading out was the last thing any of them wanted to do.

Suni opened his mouth to protest. "But the Federation—"

"The Federation isn't here. They've been marching inland for a steady week. Our people are dead. Find me survivors."

They found evidence of a last desperate battle near the southern gate. The victors were clear. The Militia corpses had been given the same deliberate treatment as the carcasses of the civilians. Corpses had been stacked in the middle of the square, neat little piles with bodies arranged carefully on top of one another.

Rin saw the broken flag of the Militia lying on the ground, burned and smeared with blood. The flag bearer's hand was detached at the wrist; the rest of his body lay several feet away, eyes blank and unseeing.

The flag bore the dragon crest of the Red Emperor, the symbol of the Nikara Empire. In the lower left corner was stitched the number two in Old Nikara calligraphy. It was the insignia of the Second Division.

Rin's heart skipped a beat.

Kitay's division.

Rin dropped to her knees and touched the flag. A barking noise sounded from behind a pile of corpses. She looked up just as a dark, flea-matted mongrel came running at her. It was the size of a small wolf. Its gut was grotesquely round, like it had been gorging for days.

It dashed past Rin toward the flag bearer's corpse, sniffing hopefully.

Rin watched it rooting around, salivating eagerly, and something inside her snapped.

"*Get away!*" she shrieked, kicking out at the dog.

Any Sinegardian animal would have slunk away in fear. But this dog had lost all fear of human beings. This dog had lived amid a juicy feast of carnage for too long. Perhaps it assumed that she, too, was close to death. Perhaps it thought fresh meat would taste better than rotting flesh.

It snarled and lunged at her.

Rin was caught off guard by the dog's tremendous weight; it knocked her to the ground. It slobbered from open jaws as it lunged for her artery, but she raised her arms in defense and it sank its teeth into her left forearm instead. She screamed out loud, but the dog did not let go; with her right arm she reached for her sword, unsheathed it, and shoved it upward.

Her sword found its way through the dog's ribs. The dog's jaws went slack.

She stabbed again. The dog fell off her.

She jumped to her feet and jammed her sword down, piercing the dog's side. It was in its death throes now. She stabbed it again, this time in the neck. A spray of blood exploded outward, coating her face with its warm wetness. She was using her sword like a dagger now, bringing her arm down again and again just to feel bones and muscle give way to metal, just to hurt and *break* something . . .

"Rin!"

Someone grabbed her sword arm. She whirled on him, but Suni pulled her arms behind her back and held her tightly, so that she could not move until her sobbing had subsided.

"You're lucky it didn't get your sword arm," said Enki. "Keep this on for a week. See me if it starts to smell."

Rin flexed her arm. Enki had bound the dog bite tightly with a poultice that stung like she had stuck her arm in a hornet's nest.

"It's good for you," he said when she grimaced. "It'll prevent infection. We don't need you to go frothing mad."

"I think I'd like to go frothing mad," said Rin. "I'd like to lose my head. I think I'd be happier."

"Don't talk like that," Enki said sternly. "You have work to do."

But was it really work, what they were doing? Or were they deluding themselves that by finding the survivors, they could atone for the simple truth that they were too late?

She continued her miserable work of combing through the empty streets, upending debris, searching homes whose doors had been smashed in. After hours of looking she stopped hoping to find Kitay alive, and started to hope she wouldn't find his corpse during her patrols, because the sight of him flayed, dismembered, jammed into a wheelbarrow with a pile of other corpses, half-burned, would be worse than never finding him at all.

She walked Golyn Niis alone in a daze, trying to both see and not see. In time she found herself inured to the smell, and eventually the sight of bodies was not a shock, just another array of faces to be scanned for someone she knew.

All the while she called Kitay's name. She screamed it every time she saw a hint of motion, anything that could be alive: a cat disappearing into an alley, a pack of crows taking off suddenly, startled by the return of humans who weren't dead or dying. She screamed it for days.

And then from the ruins, so faintly she thought it was an echo, she heard her name in response.

"Remember that time I said the Trials were as bad as Speer?" Kitay asked. "I was wrong. This is as bad as Speer. This is worse than Speer."

It wasn't remotely funny, and neither of them laughed.

Rin's eyes and throat were sore from weeping. She had been clutching Kitay's hand for hours, fingers wound tightly around his, and she never wanted to let go. They sat side by side in a hastily constructed shelter half a mile outside the city, the only place they could escape the stench of death that permeated Golyn Niis. Kitay's survival was nothing short of a miracle. He and a small band of soldiers from the Second Division had hidden for days under the bodies of their slain comrades, too afraid to venture out in case the Federation patrols should return.

When it looked like they could sneak away from the killing fields, they hid in the demolished slums of the eastern side of the city. They had pulled a cellar door away and filled the open space with bricks, so from the outside it just looked like a wall. That was why the Cike hadn't seen them on their first pass through the city.

Only a handful of Kitay's squadron was still alive. He didn't know if the city contained any more survivors.

"Have you seen Nezha?" Kitay finally asked. "I heard he was being shipped to Khurdalain."

Rin opened her mouth to respond, but a horrible prickling feeling spread from the bridge of her nose to under her eyes, and then she was choking under wild, heaving sobs, and she couldn't form any words at all.

Kitay said nothing, just held his arms out in wordless sympathy. She collapsed into them. It was absurd that he should be comforting her, that she should be the one crying, after all that Kitay had survived. But Kitay was numb; for Kitay the suffering had been normalized, and he couldn't grieve any more than he already had. He was still holding her when Qara ducked into the tent.

"You're Chen Kitay?" She wasn't really asking, she just needed to say something to break the silence.

"Yes."

"You were with the Second Division when . . . ?" Qara trailed off.

Kitay nodded.

"We need you to brief us. Can you walk?"

Under the open sky, in front of a silent audience of Altan and the twins, Kitay recounted in a halting voice the massacre at Golyn Niis.

"The city's defense was doomed from the start," Kitay said. "We thought we still had weeks. But you could have given us months, and the same thing would have happened."

Golyn Niis had been defended by an amalgamation of the Second, Ninth, and Eleventh Divisions. In this case, greater numbers did not mean greater strength. Perhaps even worse than in Khurdalain, the soldiers of the different provinces felt little sense of cohesion or purpose. The commanding officers were rivals, paranoid with distrust, unwilling to share intelligence.

"Irjah begged the Warlords over and over again to put aside their differences. He couldn't make them see reason." Kitay swallowed. "The first two skirmishes went badly. They took us by surprise. They surrounded the city from the southeast. We hadn't been expecting them so early. We didn't think they had found the mountain pass. But they came at night, and they . . . they captured Irjah. They flayed him alive over the city wall so that everyone could see. That broke our resistance. Most of the soldiers wanted to flee after that.

"After Irjah was dead, the Ninth and Eleventh surrendered en masse. I don't blame them. They were outnumbered, and they thought they'd get off easier if they didn't resist. Thought maybe it'd be better to become prisoners than to die." Kitay shuddered violently. "They were so wrong. The Federation general took their surrender with all the usual etiquette. Confiscated their arms, corralled the soldiers into prison camps. The next morning they were marched up the mountain and beheaded. There were a lot of deserters from the Second after that. A couple of us stayed to fight. It was pointless, but . . . it was better than surrendering. We couldn't dishonor Irjah. Not like that."

"Wait," Chaghan interrupted. "Did they take the Empress?"

"The Empress fled," Kitay said. "She took twenty of her guards and stole out of the city the night after Irjah died."

Qara and Chaghan made synchronous noises of disbelief, but Kitay shook his head warily. "Who can blame her? It was that or let those monsters get their hands on her, and who knows what they would have done to her . . ."

Chaghan did not look convinced.

"Pathetic," he spat, and Rin agreed with him. The idea that the Empress had fled from a city while her people were burned, killed, murdered, raped went against everything Rin had been taught about warfare. A general did not abandon his soldiers. An Empress did not abandon her people.

Again, the Talwu's words rang true.

A leader abandons their people. A ruler begins a campaign. . . . Joy in decapitating enemies. This signifies evil.

Was there any other way to interpret the Hexagram, in the face of the evidence of destruction before them? Rin had been torturing herself with the Talwu's words, trying to construe them in any way that didn't point to the massacre at Golyn Niis, but she had been deluding herself. The Talwu had told them exactly what to expect.

She should have known that when the Empress had abandoned the Nikara, then all truly was lost.

But the Empress was not the only one who had abandoned Golyn Niis. The entire army had surrendered the city. Within a week Golyn Niis had more or less been delivered to the Federation on the platter, and the entirety of its half million people subjected to the whims of the invading forces.

Those whims turned out to have little to do with the city itself. Instead, the Federation simply wanted to squeeze Golyn Niis for whatever resources they could find in preparation for a deeper march inland. They sacked the marketplace, rounded up the livestock, and demanded that families bring out their stores of rice and grain. Whatever couldn't be loaded up on their supply wagons, they burned or left out to spoil.

Then they disposed of the people.

"They decided that beheadings took too long, so they started doing things more efficiently," said Kitay. "They started with gas. You should probably know this, actually; they've got this thing, this weapon that emits yellow-green fog—"

"I know," Altan said. "We saw the same thing in Khurdalain."

"They took out practically the entire Second Division in one night," said Kitay. "Some of us put up a last stand near the south gate. When the gas cleared, nothing was alive. I went there afterward to find survivors. At first I didn't know what I was looking at. All over the ground, you could see animals. Mice, rats, rodents of every kind. So many of them. They'd crawled out of their holes to die. When the Militia was gone, nothing stood between the soldiers and our people. The Federation had fun. They made it a sport. They threw babies in the air to see if they could cleave them in half before they hit the ground. They had contests to see how many civilians they could round up and decapitate in an hour. They raced to see who could stack bodies the fastest." Kitay's voice cracked. "Could I have some water?"

Qara wordlessly handed him her canteen.

"How did Mugen become like this?" Chaghan asked wonderingly. "What did you ever do to make them hate you so much?"

"It's not anything we did," said Altan. His left hand, Rin noticed, was shaking again. "It's how the Federation soldiers were trained. When you believe your life means nothing except for your usefulness to your Emperor, the lives of your enemies mean even less."

"The Federation soldiers don't feel anything." Kitay nodded in agreement. "They don't think of themselves as people. They are parts of a machine. They do as they are commanded, and the only time they feel joy is when reveling in another person's suffering. There is no reasoning with them. There is no attempting to understand them. They are accustomed to propagating such grotesque evil that they cannot properly be called human." Kitay's voice trembled.

"When they were cutting my squadron down, I looked into the eyes of one of them. I thought I could make him recognize me as a fellow man. As a person, not just an opponent. And he stared back at me, and I realized I couldn't connect with him at all. There was nothing human in those eyes."

Once the survivors began to realize that the Militia had arrived, they emerged from their hiding holes in miserable, straggling groups.

The few survivors of Golyn Niis had been driven deep into the city, hiding in disguised shelters like Kitay or locked up in makeshift prisons and then forgotten when the Federation soldiers decided to continue their march inland. After discovering two or three such holding rooms, Altan ordered them—Cike and civilians alike—to carefully search the city.

No one disagreed with the order. They all knew, Rin suspected, that it would be horrible to die alone, chained to walls when their captors had long since departed.

"I guess we're saving people for once," Baji said. "Feels nice."

Altan himself led a squad to take on the nearly impossible task of clearing away the bodies. He claimed it was to ward against rot and disease, but Rin suspected it was because he wanted to give them a proper funeral—and because there was so little else that he could do for the city.

They had no time to dig mass graves on the scale necessary before the stench of rotting bodies became unbearable. So they stacked the corpses into large pyres, great bonfires of bodies that burned constantly. Golyn Niis turned from a city of corpses to a city of ash.

But the sheer number of the dead was staggering. The corpses Altan burned barely made a dent in the piles of rotting bodies inside the city walls. Rin didn't think it was possible to truly cleanse Golyn Niis unless they burned the entire city to the ground.

Eventually they might have to. But not while there could still be survivors.

Rin was outside the city walls trying to find a fresh source of water that wasn't spoiled with blood when Kitay pulled her aside and reported that they had found Venka. She had been kept in a "relaxation house," which was likely the only reason why the Federation had let a division soldier live. Kitay did not elaborate on what a "relaxation house" was, but he didn't need to.

Rin could hardly recognize Venka when she went to see her that night. Her lovely hair was shorn short, as if someone had hacked at it with a knife. Her lively eyes were now dull and glassy. Both her arms had been broken at the wrist. She wore them in slings. Rin saw the angle at which Venka's arms had been twisted, and knew there was only one way they could have gotten like that.

Venka hardly stirred when Rin entered her room. Only when Rin closed the door did she flinch.

"Hi," Rin said in a small voice.

Venka looked up dully and said nothing.

"I thought you'd want someone to talk to," said Rin, though the words sounded hollow and insufficient even as they left her mouth.

Venka glared at her.

Rin struggled for words. She could think of no questions that were not inane. *Are you all right?* Of course Venka was not all right. *How did you survive?* By having the body of a woman. *What happened to you?* But she already knew.

"Did you know they called us public toilets?" Venka asked suddenly.

Rin stopped two paces from the door. Comprehension dawned on her, and her blood turned to ice. "*What?*"

"They thought I couldn't understand Mugini," Venka said with a horrifying attempt at a chuckle. "That's what they called me, when they were in me."

"Venka . . ."

"Do you know how badly it hurt? They were in me, they were in me for hours and they wouldn't stop. I blacked out over and over but every time I awoke they were still going, a different man would be on top of me, or maybe the same man . . . they were all the same after a while. It was a nightmare, and I couldn't wake up."

Rin's mouth filled with the taste of bile. "I'm so sorry—" she tried, but Venka didn't seem to hear her.

"I'm not the worst," Venka said. "I fought back. I was trouble. So they saved me for last. They wanted to break me first. They made me watch. I saw women disemboweled. I saw the soldiers slice off their breasts. I saw them nail women alive to walls. I saw them mutilate young girls, when they had tired of their mothers. If their vaginas were too small, they cut them open to make it easier to rape them." Venka's voice rose in pitch. "There was a pregnant woman in the house with us. She was seven months to term. Eight. At first the soldiers let her live so she'd take care of us. Wash us. Feed us. She was the only kind face in that house. They didn't touch her because she was pregnant, not at first. Then one day the general decided he'd had enough of the other girls. He came for her. You'd think she'd have learned by then, after watching what the soldiers did to us. You'd think she would know there wasn't any point in resisting."

Rin didn't want to hear any more. She wanted to bury her head under her arms and block everything out. But Venka continued, as if now that she had started her testimony she couldn't stop. "She kicked and dragged. And then she slapped him. The general howled and grabbed at her stomach. Not with his knife. With his fingers. His nails. He knocked her down and he tore and tore." Venka turned her head away. "And he pulled out her stomach, and her intestines, and then finally the baby . . . and the baby was still moving. We saw everything from the hallway."

Rin stopped breathing.

"I was glad," Venka said. "Glad that she was dead, before the general ripped her baby in half the way you'd split an orange." Underneath her slings, Venka's fingers clenched and spasmed. "He made me mop it up."

"Gods. Venka." Rin couldn't look her in the eye. "I'm so sorry."

"*Don't pity me!*" Venka shrieked suddenly. She made a movement as if trying to reach for Rin's arm, as if she had forgotten that her arms were broken. She stood up and walked toward Rin so that they were face-to-face, nose to nose.

Her expression was as unhinged as it had been that day when they fought in the ring.

"I don't need your pity. I need you to kill them for me. You *have* to kill them for me," Venka hissed. "Swear it. Swear on your blood that you will *burn them*."

"Venka, I can't . . ."

"I know you can." Venka's voice climbed in pitch. "I heard what they said about you. You have to burn them. Whatever it takes. Swear it on your life. Swear it. Swear it for me."

Her eyes were like shattered glass.

It took all of Rin's courage to meet her gaze.

"I swear."

* * *

Rin left Venka's room and set off at a run.

She couldn't breathe. She couldn't speak.

She needed Altan.

She didn't know why she thought that he would offer the relief she was looking for, but among them only Altan had gone through this once before. Altan had been on Speer when it burned, Altan had seen his people killed . . . Altan, surely, could tell her that the Earth might keep on turning, that the sun would continue to rise and set, that the existence of such abominable evil, such disregard for human life did not mean the entire world was shrouded in darkness. Altan, surely, could tell her they still had something worth fighting for.

"In the library," Suni told her, pointing to an ancient-looking tower two blocks past the city gates.

The door to the library was closed, and nobody responded when she knocked.

Rin turned the handle slowly and peered within.

The great inner chamber was filled with lamps, yet none were lit. The only light came from the moonbeams shining in through tall glass windows. The room was filled with a sickly sweet smoke that tugged at her memory, so thick and cloying that Rin nearly choked.

In a corner among stacks of books, Altan was sprawled, legs out and head tilted listlessly. His shirt was off.

Her breath hitched in her throat.

His chest was a crisscross of scars. Many were jagged battle wounds. Others were startlingly neat, symmetrical and clean as if carved deliberately into his skin.

A pipe lay in his hand. As she watched, he brought it to his lips and inhaled deeply, crimson eyes rolling upward as he did so. He let the smoke fill his lungs and then exhaled slowly with a low, satisfied sigh.

"Altan?" she said quietly.

He didn't seem to hear her at first. Rin crossed the room and slowly knelt down next to him. The smell was nauseatingly familiar:

opium nuggets, sweet like rotted fruit. It gave her memories of Tikany, of living corpses wasting away in drug dens.

Finally, Altan looked in her direction. His face twisted into a droll, uninterested smile, and even in the ruins of Golyn Niis, even in this city of corpses, Rin thought that the sight of Altan then was the most terrible thing she'd ever seen.

CHAPTER 22

"You knew?" Rin asked.

"We all did," Ramsa murmured. He touched her shoulder tentatively, attempting a comforting gesture, but it didn't help. "He tries to hide it. Doesn't do a very good job."

Rin moaned and pressed her forehead into her knees. She could hardly see through her tears. It hurt to inhale now; it felt like her rib cage was being crushed, like the despair was pressing against her chest, weighing her down so that she could barely breathe.

This had to be the end. Their wartime capital had fallen, her friends were dead or broken, and Altan . . .

"*Why?*" she wailed. "Doesn't he know what it *does* to you?"

"He knows." Ramsa let his hand drop. He twisted his fingers in his lap. "I don't think he can help it."

Rin knew that was true, but she couldn't accept it.

She knew the horrors of opium addiction. She'd seen the Fangs' clientele—promising young scholars, well-to-do merchants, talented men—whose lives had been ruined by opium nuggets. She'd seen proud government officials reduced in the span of months to shriveled, penniless men begging in the streets to fund their next fix.

But she couldn't reconcile those images with her commander.

Altan was invincible. Altan was the best martial artist in the country. Altan wasn't—Altan *couldn't be*—

"He's supposed to be our commander," she said hoarsely. "How can he fight when he—when he's like *that*?"

"We cover for him," Ramsa said quietly. "He never used to do it more than once a month."

All those times he'd smelled like smoke. All those times he'd been missing when she tried to find him.

He'd just been sprawled in his office, sucking in and out, glassy and empty and *gone*.

"It's disgusting," she said. "It's—it's *pathetic*."

"Don't say that," Ramsa said sharply. He curled his fingers into a fist. "Take that back."

"He's our commander! He has a duty to us! How could he—"

But Ramsa cut her off. "I don't know how Altan survived that island. But I do know whatever happened to him is unimaginable. You didn't know you were a Speerly until months ago. But Altan lost everyone in his life overnight. You don't get over that kind of pain. So it's what he needs. So it's a vulnerability. I won't judge him. I don't dare, because I don't have the right. And neither do you."

After two weeks of sifting through rubble, breaking into locked basements, and relocating corpses, the Cike found fewer than a thousand survivors in the city that had once been home to half a million. Too many days had passed. They gave up hope of finding any more.

For the first time since the start of the war, the Cike had no operations planned.

"What are we waiting around for?" Baji asked several times a day.

"Orders," Qara always answered.

But no commands were forthcoming. Altan was usually absent, sometimes disappearing for entire days. When he was present, he was in no state to give orders. Chaghan took over smoothly, assigned the Cike routine duties in the interim. Most of them were told to keep watch. They all knew that the enemy was already moving inland to finish what they had started, and that there was nothing in Golyn Niis to guard but ruins, but still they obeyed.

Rin sat over the gate, clutching a spear to keep herself upright as she watched the path leading to the city. She had the twilight watch, which was just as well, because she could not sleep if she tried. Each time she closed her eyes she saw blood. Dried blood in the streets. Blood in the Golyn River. Corpses on hooks. Infants in barrels.

She couldn't eat, either. The blandest foods still tasted like carcasses. Only once did they have meat; Baji caught two rabbits in the woods, flayed them, and staked them on a narrow piece of wood to roast. When Rin smelled them, she dry-heaved for several long minutes. She could not dissociate the rabbits' flesh from the charred flesh of bodies in the square. She could not walk Golyn Niis without imagining the deaths in the moment of the execution. She could not see the hundreds of decapitated heads on poles without seeing the soldier who had walked down the row of kneeling prisoners, methodically bringing his sword down again and again as if reaping corn. She could not pass the babies in their barrel graves without hearing their uncomprehending screams.

The entire time, her own mind screamed the unanswerable question: *Why?*

The cruelty could not register for her. Bloodlust, she understood. Bloodlust, she was guilty of. She had lost herself in battle, too; she had gone further than she should have, she had hurt others when she should have stopped.

But this—viciousness on this scale, wanton slaughter of this magnitude, against innocents who hadn't even lifted a finger in self-defense, *this* she could not imagine doing.

They surrendered, she wanted to scream at her disappeared enemy. *They dropped their weapons. They posed no threat to you. Why did you have to do this?*

A rational explanation eluded her.

Because the answer could not be rational. It was not founded in military strategy. It was not because of a shortage of food rations, or because of the risk of insurgency or backlash. It was, simply, what happened when one race decided that the other was insignificant.

The Federation had massacred Golyn Niis for the simple reason that they did not think of the Nikara as *human*. And if your opponent was not human, if your opponent was a cockroach, what did it matter how many of them you killed? What was the difference between crushing an ant and setting an anthill on fire? Why shouldn't you pull wings off insects for your own enjoyment? The bug might feel pain, but what did that matter to you?

If you were the victim, what could you say to make your tormentor recognize you as human? How did you get your enemy to recognize you at all?

And why should an oppressor care?

Warfare was about absolutes. Us or them. Victory or defeat. There was no middle way. There was no mercy. No surrender.

This was the same logic, Rin realized, that had justified the destruction of Speer. To the Federation, to wipe out an entire race overnight was not an atrocity at all. Only a necessity.

"You're insane."

Rin's head jerked up. She had sunk into another exhausted daze. She blinked twice and squinted out into the darkness until the source of the voice shifted from amorphous shadows to two recognizable forms.

Altan and Chaghan stood underneath the gate, Chaghan with his arms tightly crossed, Altan slouched against the wall. Heart hammering, Rin ducked under the low wall so they wouldn't see her if they looked up.

"What if it wasn't just us?" Altan asked in a low, eager voice. Rin was stunned; Altan sounded alert, alive, like he hadn't been in days. "What if there were more of us?"

"Not this again," said Chaghan.

"What if there were *thousands* of the Cike, soldiers as powerful as you and me, soldiers who could call the gods?"

"Altan . . ."

"What if I could raise an entire army of shamans?"

Rin's eyes widened. An *army*?

Chaghan made a choking noise that might have been a laugh. "How do you propose to do that?"

"You know precisely how," said Altan. "You know why I sent you to the mountain."

"You said you only wanted the Gatekeeper." Chaghan's voice grew agitated. "You didn't say you wanted to release every madman in there."

"They're not madmen—"

"They are not men at all! By now they are demigods! They are like bolts of lightning, like hurricanes of spiritual power. If I'd known what you were planning, I wouldn't have—"

"Bullshit, Chaghan. You knew *exactly* what I was planning."

"We were supposed to release the Gatekeeper *together*." Chaghan sounded wounded.

"And we will. Just as we'll release everyone else. Feylen. Huleinin. All of them."

"*Feylen?* After what he tried to do? You don't know what you're saying. You are speaking of atrocities."

"Atrocities?" Altan asked coolly. "You've seen the bodies here, and you accuse *me* of atrocities?"

Chaghan's voice rose steadily in pitch. "What Mugen has done is *human* cruelty. But humans alone are only capable of so much destruction. The beings locked inside the Chuluu Korikh are capable of ruin on a different scale altogether."

Altan barked out a laugh. "Do you have *eyes*? Do you see what they've done to Golyn Niis? A ruler should do anything necessary to protect their people. I will not be Tearza, Chaghan. *I will not let them kill us off like dogs.*"

Rin heard a scuffling noise. Feet shuffling against dry leaves.

Limbs brushing against limbs. Were they *fighting*? Hardly daring to breathe, Rin peeked out from over the wall.

Chaghan grasped Altan by the collar with both hands, pulling him down so that they were face-to-face. Altan was half a foot taller than Chaghan, could have snapped him in half with ease, and yet he did not lift a hand in defense.

Rin stared at them in disbelief. Nobody touched Altan like that.

"This isn't *Speer* again," Chaghan hissed. His face was so close to Altan's that their noses almost touched. "Even Tearza wouldn't unleash her god to save one island. But you are sentencing thousands of people to death."

"I'm trying to *win* this war—"

"What for? Look around, Trengsin! No one is going to pat you on the back and tell you good job. There's no one *left*. This country is going to shit, and no one cares—"

"The Empress cares," said Altan. "I sent a falcon, she approved my plan—"

"Who cares what your Empress says?" Chaghan screamed. His hands shook wildly. "*Fuck* your Empress! Your Empress fled!"

"She's one of us," Altan said. "You know she is. If we have her, and we have the Gatekeeper, then we can lead this army—"

"No one can lead that army." Chaghan let go of Altan's collar. "Those people in the mountain are not like you. They're not like Suni. You can't control them, and you're not going to try. I won't let you."

Chaghan raised his hands to push Altan again, but Altan grabbed them this time, seized his wrists and lowered them easily. He did not let them go. "Do you really think you can stop me?"

"This isn't you," Chaghan said. "This is about Speer. This is about your revenge. That's all you Speerlies do, you hate and burn and destroy without consequence. Tearza was the only one of you with any foresight. Maybe the Federation was right about you, maybe it was best they burned down your island—"

"How dare you," Altan said, his voice so quiet Rin pressed herself against the wall as if she could somehow get closer and make sure she was hearing right. Altan's fingers tightened around Chaghan's wrists. "You've crossed the line."

"I'm your Seer," Chaghan said. "I give you counsel, whether you want to hear it or not."

"The Seer does not command," Altan said. "The Seer does not *disobey*. I have no place for a disloyal lieutenant. If you won't help me, then I'll send you away. Go north. Go to the dam. Take your sister and do as we planned."

"Altan, listen to reason," Chaghan pleaded. "You don't have to do this."

"Do as I command," Altan said curtly. "Go, or leave the Cike."

Rin sank back behind the wall, heart hammering.

She abandoned her post as soon as she heard Altan's footsteps fading into the distance. Once she could no longer see his form from the gate, she darted down the steps and raced out onto the open road. She caught Chaghan and Qara as they were saddling a recovered gelding.

"Let's go," Chaghan told his sister when he saw Rin approaching, but Rin grabbed the reins before Qara could prod the horse forward.

"Where are you going?" she demanded.

"Away," Chaghan said tersely. "Please let go."

"I need to talk to you."

"We have orders to leave."

"I overheard you with Altan."

Qara muttered something in her own language.

Chaghan scowled. "Have you ever been able to mind your own business?"

Rin tightened her grip on the reins. "What army is he talking about? Why won't you help him?"

Chaghan's eyes narrowed. "You have no idea what you're getting into."

"So tell me. Who is Feylen?" Rin continued loudly. "Who is Huleinin? What did he mean, he'll release the Gatekeeper?"

"Altan is going to burn down Nikan. I will not be responsible."

"*Burn down Nikan?*" Rin repeated. "How—"

"Your commander has gone mad," Chaghan said bluntly. "That is as much as you need to know. And you know the worst part? I think he's meant to do this all along. I've been blind. This is what he's wanted since the Federation marched on Sinegard."

"And you're just going to let him?"

Chaghan recoiled violently, as if he'd been slapped. Rin had a fear that he might yank on the reins and ride away, but Chaghan merely sat there, mouth slightly open.

She had never seen Chaghan speechless before. It scared her.

She wouldn't have expected Chaghan to shrink from cruelty. Chaghan, alone among the Cike, had never displayed an ounce of fear about his power, about losing control. Chaghan reveled in his abilities. He relished them.

What could be so unthinkable that it horrified even Chaghan?

Without taking his eyes off Rin, Chaghan reached down, grasped the reins, and swung himself off the horse. She took two steps backward as he walked toward her. He stopped much closer to her than she would have liked. He studied her in silence for a long moment.

"Do you understand the source of Altan's power?" he asked finally.

Rin frowned. "He's a Speerly. It's obvious."

"Even the average Speerly was not half as powerful as Altan is," said Chaghan. "Have you ever asked yourself why Altan alone among Speerlies survived? Why he was allowed to live when the rest of his kin were burned and dismembered?"

Rin shook her head.

"After the First Poppy War, the Federation became obsessed with your people," said Chaghan. "They couldn't believe their Armed Forces had been bested by this tiny island nation. That's what spurred their interest in shamanism. There has never been a Federation shaman. The Federation needed to know how the Speerlies got their powers. When they occupied the Snake Province, they built a research base opposite the island and spent the decades in between the Poppy Wars kidnapping Speerlies, experimenting on them, trying to figure out what made them special. Altan was one of those experiments."

Rin's chest felt very tight. She dreaded what might come next, but Chaghan continued, his voice as flat and emotionless as if he were reciting history lessons. "By the time the Hesperians liberated the facilities, Altan had spent half his life in a lab. The Federation scientists drugged him daily to keep him sedated. They starved him. They tortured him to make him comply. He wasn't the only Speerly they took, but he was the only one who survived. Do you know how?"

Rin shook her head. "I . . ."

Chaghan continued, ruthless. "Did you know they strapped him down and made him watch as they took the others apart to find out what made them tick? What are Speerlies made of? The Federation was determined to find out. Did you know they kept them alive as long as they could, even when they had peeled their flesh away from their rib cages, so they could see how their muscles moved while they were splayed out like rabbits?"

"He never told me," Rin whispered.

"And he never would have." Chaghan said. "Altan likes to suffer in silence. Altan likes to let his hatred fester, likes to incubate it as long as he can. Now do you understand the source of his power? It is not because he is a Speerly. It is nothing genetic. Altan is so powerful because he hates so deeply and so thoroughly that it constitutes every part of his being. Your Phoenix is the god of fire, but it is also the god of rage. Of vengeance. Altan doesn't need opium to call the Phoenix because the Phoenix is always alive inside him. You asked me why I wouldn't stop him. Now you understand. You can't stop an avenger. You can't reason with a madman. You think I am running, and I admit to you that I am afraid. I am afraid of what he might do in his quest for vengeance. And I am afraid that he is right."

* * *

When she found Altan, lying in that same corner of the ancient library he had been last time, she said nothing. She crossed the moonlit room and took the pipe from his languid fingers. She sat down cross-legged, leaning against the shelves of ancient scrolls. Then she took a long draught herself. The effect took a long while to set in, but when it did, she wondered why she had ever meditated at all.

She understood, now, why Altan needed opium.

Small wonder he was addicted. Smoking the pipe had to be the only time that he was not consumed with his misery, with scars that would never heal. The haze induced by the smoke was the only time that he could feel nothing, the only time that he could forget.

"How are you doing?" Altan mumbled.

"I hate them," she said. "I hate them so much. I hate them so much it hurts. I hate them with every drop of my blood. I hate them with every bone in my body."

Altan blew out a long stream of smoke. He didn't look like a human so much as he did a simple vessel for the fumes, an inanimate extension of the pipe.

"It doesn't stop hurting," he said.

She sucked in another deep breath of the wonderful sweetness.

"I understand now," she said.

"Do you?"

"I'm sorry about before."

Her words were vague, but Altan seemed to know what she meant. He took the pipe back from her and inhaled again, and that was acknowledgment enough.

It was a long while before he spoke again.

"I am about to do something terrible," he said. "And you will have a choice. You can choose to come with me to the prison under the stone. I believe you know what I intend to do there."

"Yes." She knew, without asking, what was imprisoned in the Chuluu Korikh.

Unnatural criminals, who have committed unnatural crimes.

If she went with him, she would help him to unleash monsters. Monsters worse than the chimei. Monsters worse than anything in the Emperor's Menagerie—because these monsters were not beasts, mindless things that could be leashed and controlled, but warriors. Shamans. The gods walking in humans, with no regard for the mortal world.

"Or you can stay in Golyn Niis. You can fight with the remnants of the Nikara army and you can try to win this war without the help of the gods. You can remain Jiang's good girl, you can heed his warnings, and you can shy away from the power that you know you have." He extended his hand to her. "But I need your help. I need another Speerly."

She glanced down at his slender brown fingers.

If she helped him free this army, would that make her a monster? Would they be guilty of everything Chaghan had accused them of?

Perhaps. But what else did they have to lose? The invaders who had already pumped her country full of opium and left it to rot had returned to finish the job.

She reached for his hand, curled her fingers around his. The sensation of his skin under hers was a feeling unlike anything she had dared to imagine. Alone in the library, with only the ancient scrolls of Old Nikan to bear witness, she pledged her allegiance.

"I'm with you," she said.

CHAPTER 23

THE CHULUU KORIKH

From *The Seejin Classification of Deities*, compiled in the Annals of the Red Emperor, recorded by Vachir Mogoi, High Historian of Sinegard

Long before the days of the Red Emperor, this country was not yet a great empire, but a sparse land populated by a small scattering of tribes. These tribesmen were horse-riding nomads from the north, who had been cast out of the Hinterlands by the hordes of the great khan. Now they struggled to survive in this strange, warm land.

They were ignorant of many things: the cycles of the rain, the tides of the Murui River, the variations of soil. They knew not how to plow the land or to sow seeds so they could grow food instead of hunt for it. They needed guidance. They needed the gods.

But the deities of the Pantheon were yet reluctant to grant their aid to mankind.

"Men are selfish and petty," argued Erlang Shen, Grand Marshal of the Heavenly Forces. "Their life spans are so short that they give no thought to the future of the land. If we lend them aid, they will drain this earth and squabble among themselves. There will be no peace."

"But they are suffering now." Erlang Shen's twin sister, the beautiful Sanshengmu, led the opposing faction. "We have the power to help them. Why do we withhold it?"

"You are blind, sister," said Erlang Shen. "You think too highly of mortals. They give nothing to the universe, and the universe owes them nothing in return. If they cannot survive, then let them die."

He issued a heavenly order forbidding any entity in the Pantheon from interfering with mortal matters. But Sanshengmu, always the gentler of the two, was convinced that her brother was too quick to judge mankind. She hatched a plan to descend to Earth in secret, in hopes of proving to the Pantheon that men were worthy of help from the gods. However, Erlang Shen was alerted to Sanshengmu's plot at the last moment, and he gave chase. In her haste to escape from her brother, Sanshengmu landed badly on Earth.

She lay on the road for three days. Her mortal guise was of a woman of uncommon beauty. In those times, that was a dangerous thing to be.

The first man who found her, a soldier, raped her and left her for dead.

The second man, a merchant, took her clothes but left her behind, as she would have been too heavy for his wagon.

The third man was a hunter. When he saw Sanshengmu he took off his cloak and wrapped her in it. Then he carried her back to his tent.

"Why are you helping me?" Sanshengmu asked. "You are a human. You live only to prey upon each other. You have no compassion. All you do is satisfy your own greed."

"Not all humans," said the hunter. "Not me."

By the time they reached his tent, Sanshengmu had fallen in love.

She married the hunter. She taught the men of the hunter's

tribe many things: how to chant at the sky for rain, how to read the patterns of the weather in the cracked shell of a tortoise, how to burn incense to appease the deities of agriculture in return for a bountiful harvest.

The hunter's tribe flourished and spread across the fertile land of Nikan. Word spread of the living goddess who had come to Earth. Sanshengmu's worshippers increased in number across the country. The men of Nikan lit incense and built statues in her honor, the first divine entity they had ever known of.

And in time, she bore the hunter a child.

From his throne in the heavens, Erlang Shen watched, and grew enraged.

When Sanshengmu's son reached his first birthday, Erlang Shen journeyed down to the world of man. He set fire to the banquet tent, driving out the guests in a panicked terror. He impaled the hunter with his great three-pronged spear and killed him. He took Sanshengmu's son and hurled him off the side of a mountain. Then he grasped his horrified sister by the neck and lifted her in the air.

"You cannot kill me," choked Sanshengmu. "You are bound to me. We are two halves of one whole. You cannot survive my death."

"No," acknowledged Erlang Shen. "But I can imprison you. Since you love the world of men so much, I will build for you an earthly prison, where you will pass an eternity. This will be your punishment for daring to love a mortal."

As he spoke, a great mountain formed in the air. He flung his twin sister away from him, and the mountain sank on top of her, an unbreakable prison of stone. Sanshengmu tried and tried to escape, but inside her prison, she could not access her magic.

She languished in that stone prison for years. And every moment was torture to the goddess, who had once flown free through the heavens.

There are many stories about Sanshengmu. There are stories of her son, the Lotus Warrior, and how he was the first shaman to walk Nikan, a liaison between gods and men. There are stories of his war against his uncle, Erlang Shen, in order to free his mother.

There are stories, too, about the Chuluu Korikh. There are stories of the monkey king, the arrogant shaman who was locked for five thousand years within by the Jade Emperor as punishment for his impudence. One could say that this was the beginning of the age of stories, because that was the beginning of the age of shamans.

Much is true. Much more is not.

But one thing can be said to be fact. To this day, of all the places on this Earth, only the Chuluu Korikh may contain a god.

"Are you finally going to tell me where you're headed?" Kitay asked. "Or did you call me here just to say goodbye?"

Rin was packing her equipment into traveling bags, deliberately avoiding eye contact with Kitay. She had avoided him the past week while she and Altan planned their journey.

Altan had forbidden her to speak of it to anyone outside the Cike. He and Rin would travel to the Chuluu Korikh alone. But if they succeeded, Rin wanted Kitay to know what was coming. She wanted him to know when to flee.

"We're leaving as soon as the gelding is ready," she said. Chaghan and Qara had departed Golyn Niis on the only halfway decent horse that the Federation hadn't taken with them. It had taken days to find another gelding that wasn't diseased or dying, and days more to nurture it back to a state fit for travel.

"Can I ask where to?" Kitay asked. He tried not to display his annoyance, but she knew him too well to overlook it; irritation was written across his face. Kitay was not used to missing information; she knew he resented her for it.

She hesitated, and then said, "The Kukhonin range."

"*Kukhonin?*" Kitay repeated.

"Two days' ride south from here." She rummaged around in her bag to avoid looking at him. She had packed an enormous amount of poppy seed, everything from Enki's stores that she could hold. Of course, none of it would be useful inside the Chuluu Korikh itself, but once they left the mountain, once they had freed every shaman inside . . .

"I know where the Kukhonin range is," Kitay said impatiently. "I want to know why you're riding in the opposite direction from Mugen's main column."

You have to tell him. Rin could not see a way of warning Kitay without divulging part of Altan's plan. Otherwise he would insist on finding out for himself, and his curiosity would spell the death of him. She set the bag down, straightened up, and met Kitay's eyes.

"Altan wants to raise an army."

Kitay made a noise of disbelief. "Come again?"

"It's . . . they're . . . You wouldn't understand if I told you." How was she to explain this to him? Kitay had never studied Lore. Kitay had never truly believed in the gods, not even after the battle at Sinegard. Kitay thought that shamanism was a metaphor for arcane martial arts, that Rin and Altan's abilities were sleights of hand and parlor tricks. Kitay did not know what lay in the Pantheon. Kitay did not understand the danger they were about to unleash.

"Just—look, I'm trying to warn you—"

"No, you're trying to deceive me. You don't get to deceive me," Kitay said very loudly. "I have seen cities burning. I have seen you do what mortals should not be able to do. I have seen you raise fire. I think I have the right to know. Try me."

"Fine."

She told him.

Amazingly, he believed her.

"This sounds like a plan where many things could go wrong," said Kitay when she finished. "How does Altan even know this army will fight for him?"

"They're Nikara," said Rin. "They have to. They've fought for the Empire before."

"The same Empire that had them buried alive in the first place?"

"Not buried alive," she said. "Immured."

"Oh, sorry," Kitay amended, "*immured*. Enclosed in stone in some magic mountain, because they became so powerful that a fucking *mountain* was the only thing that could stop them tearing apart entire villages. *This* is the army you're just going to set loose on the country. *This* is what you think is going to save Nikan. Who came up with this, you or your opium-addled commander? Because this sure as hell isn't the kind of plan you come up with sober, I can tell you that."

Rin crossed her arms tightly against her chest. Kitay wasn't saying anything she hadn't already considered. What could anyone predict about maddened souls who had been entombed for years? The shamans of the Chuluu Korikh might do nothing. They might destroy half the country out of spite.

But Altan was certain they would fight for him.

They have no right to begrudge the Empress, Altan had said. *All shamans know the risks when they journey to the gods. Everyone in the Cike knows that at the end of the line, they are destined for the Stone Mountain.*

And the alternative was the extermination of every Nikara alive. The massacre of Golyn Niis made it obvious that the Federation did not want to take any prisoners. They wanted the massive piece of land that was the Nikara Empire. They were not interested in cohabitation with its former occupants. She knew the risks, and she had weighed them and concluded that she didn't care. She had thrown her lot in with Altan, for better or worse.

"You can't change my mind," she said. "I'm telling you this as a favor. When we come out of that mountain, I don't know how much control we'll have, only that we'll be powerful. Do not try to stop us. Do not try to join us. When we come, you should flee."

* * *

"The rendezvous point will be at the base of the Kukhonin Mountains," Altan told the assembled Cike. "If we don't meet you there in seven days' time, assume we were killed. Do not go inside the mountain yourselves. Wait for a bird from Qara and do as the message commands. Chaghan is commander in my stead."

"Where *is* Chaghan?" Unegen ventured to ask.

"With Qara." Altan's face betrayed nothing. "They've gone north on my orders. You'll know when they're back."

"When will that be?"

"When they've done their job."

Rin waited by their horse, watched Altan speaking with a self-assured aura that she had not seen since Sinegard. Altan, as he presented himself now, was not that broken boy with the opium pipe. He was not the despairing Speerly reliving the genocide of his people. He was not a victim. Altan was different now than he had been even in Khurdalain. He was no longer frustrated, pacing around his office like a cornered animal, no longer constrained under Jun's thumb. Altan had orders now, a mission, a singular purpose. He didn't have to hold back anymore. He had been let off his leash. Altan was going to take his anger to a final, terrible conclusion.

She had no doubts they would succeed. She just didn't know if the country would survive his plan.

"Good luck," said Enki. "Say hi to Feylen for us."

"Great guy," Unegen said wistfully. "Until, you know, he tried to flatten everything in a twenty-mile radius."

"Don't exaggerate," said Ramsa. "It was only ten."

They rode as fast as the old gelding would allow. At midday they passed a boulder with two lines etched into its side. She would have missed it if Altan had not pointed it out.

"Chaghan's work," said Altan. "Proof that the way is safe."

"You sent Chaghan here?"

"Yes. Before we left the Night Castle for Khurdalain."

"Why?"

"Chaghan and I . . . Chaghan had a theory," said Altan. "About the Trifecta. Before Sinegard, when he realized Tyr had died, he'd seen something on the spirit horizon. He thought he'd seen the Gatekeeper. He saw the same disturbance a week later, and then it disappeared. He thought the Gatekeeper must have intentionally closed himself in the Chuluu Korikh. We thought we might extract him, find out the truth—maybe discover the truth behind the Trifecta, see what's happened to the Gatekeeper and the Emperor, find out what the Empress did to them. Chaghan didn't know I wanted to free anyone else."

"You lied to him."

Altan shrugged. "Chaghan believes what he wants to believe."

"Chaghan also . . . He said . . ." She trailed off, unsure of how to phrase her question.

"What?" Altan demanded.

"He said they trained you like a dog. At Sinegard."

Altan laughed drily. "He phrased it like that, did he?"

"He said they fed you opium."

Altan stiffened.

"They trained soldiers at Sinegard," he said. "With me, they did their job."

They might have done their job too well, Rin thought. Like the Cike, the masters at Sinegard had conjured a more frightening power than they were equipped to handle. They'd done more than train a Speerly. They'd created an avenger.

Altan was a commander who would burn down the world to destroy his enemy.

This should have bothered her. Three years ago, if she had known what she knew about Altan now, she would have run in the opposite direction.

But now, she had seen and suffered too much. The Empire didn't need someone reasonable. It needed someone mad enough to try to save it.

They stopped riding when it became too dark to see the path in front of them. They had ventured onto a trail so lightly trodden it could hardly be called a road, and their horse could have easily cut its hooves on a jagged rock or sent them tumbling into a ravine. Their gelding staggered when they dismounted. Altan poured out a pan of water for it, but only after Rin's prodding did it begin to halfheartedly drink.

"He'll die if we ride him any harder," Rin said. She knew very little about horses, but she could tell when an animal was on the verge of collapse. One of the military steeds at Khurdalain, perhaps, could have easily made the trip, but this horse was a miserable pack animal—an old beast so thin its ribs showed through its matted coat.

"We just need him for one more day," said Altan. "He can die after."

Rin fed the gelding a handful of oats from their pack. Meanwhile Altan built their camp with austere, methodical efficiency. He collected fallen pine needles and dry leaves to insulate against the cold. He formed a frame out of broken tree limbs and draped a spare cloak over it to shield against overnight snowfall. He pulled from his pack dry kindling and oil, quickly dug a pit, and arranged the flammables inside. He extended his hand. A flare caught immediately. Casually, as if he were doing nothing harder than waving a fan, Altan increased the volume of the flame until they were sitting before a roaring bonfire.

Rin held her hands out, let the heat seep through into her bones. She hadn't noticed how cold she'd become over the day; she realized she hadn't been able to feel her toes until now.

"Are you warm?" Altan asked.

She nodded quickly. "Thanks."

He watched her in silence for a moment. She felt the heat of his gaze on her, and tried not to flush. She was not used to receiving Altan's full attention; he had been distracted with Chaghan ever since Khurdalain, ever since their falling-out. But things were reversed now. Chaghan had abandoned Altan, and Rin stood by his side. She felt a thrill of vindictive joy when she considered this. Suddenly guilty, she tried to quash it down.

"You've been to the mountain before?"

"Only once," Altan said. "A year ago. I helped Tyr bring Feylen in."

"Feylen's the one who went crazy?"

"They all go crazy, in the end," he said. "The Cike die in battle, or they get immured. Most commanders assume their title when they've disposed of their old master. If Tyr hadn't died, I probably would have locked him in myself. It's always a pain when it happens."

"Why aren't they just killed?" she asked.

"You can't kill a shaman who's been fully possessed," said Altan. "When that happens, the shaman isn't human anymore. They're not mortal. They're vessels of the divine. You can behead them, stab them, hang them, but the body will keep moving. You dismember the body, and still the pieces will skitter to rejoin the others. The best you can do is bind them, incapacitate them, and overpower them until you get them into the mountain."

Rin imagined herself bound and blindfolded, dragged involuntarily along this same mountain path into an eternal stone prison. She shuddered. She could understand this sort of cruelty from the Federation, but from her own commander?

"And you're all right with that?"

"Of course I'm not all right with that," he snapped. "But it's the job. It's *my* job. I'm supposed to bring the Cike to the mountain when they've become unfit to serve. The Cike controls itself. The Cike is the Empire's way of eliminating the threat of rogue shamans."

Altan twisted his fingers together. "Every Cike commander is charged with two things: to obey the will of the Empress, and to cull the force when it's time. Jun was right. There's no place for the Cike in modern warfare. We're too small. We can't achieve anything a well-trained Militia force couldn't. Fire powder, cannons, and steel—these things win wars, not a handful of shamans. The only unique role of the Cike is to do what no other military force can do. We can subdue ourselves, which is the only reason why we're allowed to exist."

Rin thought of Suni—poor, gentle, and horrifically strong Suni, who was so clearly unstable. How long before he would meet the same fate that had befallen Feylen? When would Suni's madness outweigh his usefulness to the Empire?

"But I won't be like the commanders of before," Altan said. His fingers clenched to form fists. "I won't turn from my people because they've drawn more power than they should have. How is that fair? Suni and Baji were sent to the Baghra desert because Jiang got scared of them. That's what he does—erases his mistakes, runs from them. But Tyr trained them instead, gave them back a shred of rationality. So there must be a way of taming the gods. The Feylen that I knew would not kill his own people. There must be a way to bring him back from madness. There *has* to be."

He spoke with such conviction. He looked so sure, so absolutely sure that he could control this sleeping army the same way he had calmed Suni in that mess hall, had brought him back to the world of mortals with nothing more than whispers and words.

She forced herself to believe him, because the alternative was too terrible to comprehend.

They reached the Chuluu Korikh on the afternoon of the second day, hours earlier than they had planned. Altan was pleased at this; he was pleased at everything today, forging ahead with an ecstatic, giddy energy. He acted as if he had waited years for this day. For all Rin knew, he had.

When the terrain became too treacherous to keep riding, they dismounted and let the animal go. The gelding strode away with a grievous air to find somewhere to die.

They hiked for the better part of the afternoon. The ice and snow thickened the higher up they climbed. Rin was reminded of the treacherously icy stairs at Sinegard, how one misstep could mean a shattered spine. But here, no first-years had scattered salt across the ice to make the ground safe. If they slipped now, they were guaranteed a quick, icy death.

Altan used his trident as a staff, stabbing at the ground in front of him before he stepped forward. Rin followed gingerly in the path he had marked as safe. She suggested that they simply melt the ice with Speerly fire. Altan tried it. It took too long.

The sky had just begun to darken when Altan paused before a stretch of wall.

"Wait. This is it."

Rin froze in her steps, teeth chattering madly. She glanced around. She could see no marker, no indication that this was the special entrance. But Altan sounded certain.

He backtracked several steps and then began scrubbing at the mountainside, wiping off snow to get at the smooth stone face underneath. He grumbled with exasperation and pressed a flaming hand against the rock. The fire gradually melted a clean circle in the ice with Altan's hand at its center.

Rin could now see a crevice carved into the rock. It had been barely visible under a thick coat of snow and ice. A traveler could have walked past it twenty times and never seen it.

"Tyr said to stop when we reached the crag that looked like an eagle's beak," Altan said. He gestured toward the precipice they stood upon. It did, in fact, look like the profile of one of Qara's birds. "I almost forgot."

Rin dug two strips of dry cloth out of her travel sack, dribbled a vial of oil over them, and busied herself with wrapping the heads of a couple of wooden sticks. "You've never been inside?"

"Tyr had me wait outside," said Altan. He stood back from the entrance. He had cleanly melted the ice away from the stone face, revealing a circular door embedded in the side of the mountain. "The only person alive who's ever been inside is Chaghan. I've no idea how he got this door open. You ready?"

Rin yanked the last cloth knot tight with her teeth and nodded.

Altan turned around, braced his back against the stone door, bent his legs, and pushed. His face strained with the effort.

For a second nothing happened. Then, with a ponderous screech, the rock slid at an angle into its stone bed.

When the rock ground to a halt, Rin and Altan stood before the great maw of darkness. The tunnel was so black inside it seemed to swallow the sunlight whole. Glancing into the dark interior, Rin felt a sense of dread that had nothing to do with the darkness. Inside this mountain, there was no calling the Phoenix. They would have no access to the Pantheon. No way to call the power.

"Last chance to turn back," said Altan.

She scoffed, handed him a torch, and strode forward.

Rin had barely made it ten feet in when she took one step too wide. The dark passageway turned out to be perilously narrow. She felt something crumble under her foot, and scrambled back against the wall. She held her torch out over the precipice and was immediately overcome with a horrible sense of vertigo. There was no visible bottom to the abyss; it dropped away into nothing.

"It's hollow all the way down," said Altan, standing close behind her. He put a hand on her shoulder. "Stick to me. Watch your feet. Chaghan said we'd reach a wider platform in about twenty paces."

She pressed herself against the cliff wall and let Altan squeeze past her, following him gingerly down the steps.

"What else did Chaghan say?"

"That we would find this." Altan held out his torch.

A lone pulley lift hung in the middle of the mountain. Rin held her torch out as far as it would go, and the light illuminated something black and shiny on the platform surface.

"That's oil. This is a lamp," Rin realized. She drew her arm back.

"Careful," Altan hissed just as Rin flung her torch out onto the lift.

The ancient oil blazed immediately to life. Fire snaked through the darkness across predetermined oil patterns in a hypnotizing sequence, revealing several similar pulley lamps hanging at various heights. Only after several long minutes was the entire mountain illuminated, revealing an intricate architecture to the stone prison. Below the passageway where they stood, Rin could see circles upon circles of plinths, extending down as far as the light reached. Around and around the inside of the mountain went a spiraling pathway that led to countless stone tombs.

The pattern was oddly familiar. Rin had seen this before.

It was a stone version of the Pantheon in miniature, multiplied in a spiraling helix. It was a perverse Pantheon, for the gods were not alive here but arrested in suspended animation.

Rin felt a sudden burst of panic. She took a deep breath, trying to dispel the feeling, but the overwhelming sense of suffocation only grew.

"I feel it, too," Altan said quietly. "It's the mountain. We've been sealed off."

Back in Tikany, Rin had once fallen out of a tree and hit her head so hard against the ground that she lost her hearing temporarily. She'd seen Kesegi shouting at her, gesturing at his throat, but nothing had come through. It was the same here. Something was missing. She had been denied access to something.

She could not imagine what it was like to be trapped here for years, decades upon decades, unable to die but unable to leave the material world. This was a place that did not allow dreaming. This was a place of never-ending nightmares.

What a horrible fate to be entombed here.

Rin's fingers brushed against something round. Under the pressure of her touch, it shifted and began to turn. She shone her torch on it and signaled for Altan's attention.

"Look."

It was a stone cylinder. Rin was reminded of the prayer wheels in front of the pagoda at the Academy. But this cylinder was much larger, rising up to her shoulder. Rin held the torch up to the stone and examined it closely. Deep grooves had been cut into its sides. She placed a hand on one side and dug her heels into the dirt, pushed hard.

With a screech that sounded like a scream, the wheel began to turn.

The grooves were words. No—names. Names upon names, each one followed by a string of numbers. It was a record. A registry of every soul that had been sealed inside the Chuluu Korikh.

There must have been a hundred names carved into that wheel.

Altan held the torch up to her right. "It's not the only one."

She looked up and saw that the fire illuminated another record wheel.

Then another. Then another.

They stretched through the entire first tier of the Stone Mountain.

Thousands and thousands of names. Names dating past the reign of the Dragon Emperor. Names dating past the Red Emperor himself.

Rin almost staggered at the significance.

There were people here who had not been conscious since the birth of the Nikara Empire.

"The investiture of the gods," said Altan. He was trembling. "The sheer power in this mountain . . . no one could stop them, not even the Federation . . ."

And not even us, Rin thought.

If they woke the Chuluu Korikh, they would have an army of madmen, of primordial spigots of psychic energy. This was an army they would not be able to control. This was an army that could raze the world.

Rin traced her fingers against the first record wheel, the one closest to the entrance.

At the top, in very careful, deliberate writing, was the most recent entry.

She recognized that handwriting.

"I found him," she said.

"Who, the Gatekeeper?" Altan looked confused.

"It's him," she said. "*Of course* it's him."

She ran her fingers over the engraved stone, and a deep flood of relief shot through her.

Jiang Ziya.

She had found him, finally found him. Her master was sealed inside one of these plinths. She grabbed the torch back from Altan and started at a run down the steps. Whispers echoed past her as she ran. She thought she could sense things coming through from the other side, the things that had been whispering through the void Jiang summoned at Sinegard.

She felt in the air an overwhelming *want*.

They must have immured the shamans starting at the bottom of the prison. Jiang could not be far from where they stood. Rin ran faster, felt the stone scrape under her feet. Up before her, her torch illuminated a plinth carved in the image of a stooped gatekeeper. She came to a sudden halt.

This had to be Jiang.

Altan caught up to her. "Don't just take off like that."

"He's here," she said, shining her torch up at the plinth. "He's in there."

"Move," said Altan.

She had barely stepped out of the way when Altan slammed the end of his trident into the plinth.

When the rubble cleared, Jiang's serene form was revealed under a layer of crumbling dust. He lay perfectly still against the rock, the sides of his mouth curved faintly upward as if he found something deeply amusing. He might have been sleeping.

He opened his eyes, looked them up and down, and blinked. "You might have knocked first."

Rin stepped toward him. "Master?"

Jiang tilted his head sideways. "Have you gotten taller?"

"We're here to rescue you," said Rin, although the words

sounded stupid as soon as she uttered them. No one could have forced Jiang into the mountain. He must have wanted to be there.

But she didn't care why he had come here; she had found him, she had released him, she had his attention now. "We need your help. *Please*."

Jiang stepped forward out of the stone and shook his limbs as if working out the kinks. He brushed the dust meticulously off his robes. Then he uttered mildly, "You should not be here. It's not your time."

"You don't understand—"

"And you do not listen." He was not smiling anymore. "The Seal is breaking. I can feel it—it's almost gone. If I leave this mountain, all sorts of terrible things will come into your world."

"So it's true," Altan said. "You're the Gatekeeper."

Jiang looked irritated. "What did I just say about not listening?"

But Altan was flushed with excitement. "You are the most powerful shaman in Nikara history! You can unlock this entire mountain! You could command this army!"

"*That's* your plan?" Jiang gaped at him as if in disbelief that anyone could be this stupid. "Are you mad?"

"We . . ." Altan faltered, then regained his composure. "I'm not—"

Jiang buried his face in his palm, like an exasperated schoolteacher. "The boy wants to set everyone in this mountain free. The boy wants to unleash the contents of the Chuluu Korikh on the world."

"It's that, or let Nikan fall," Altan snapped.

"Then let it."

"*What?*"

"You don't know what the Federation is capable of," Rin said. "You didn't see what they did to Golyn Niis."

"I saw more than you think," said Jiang. "But this is not the way. This path leads only to darkness."

"How can there be more darkness?" she screamed in frustration. Her voice echoed off the cavernous walls. "How can things possibly get worse than this? Even you took the risks, you opened the void . . ."

"That was my mistake," Jiang said regretfully, like a child who had been chastened. "I never should have done that. I should have let them take Sinegard."

"Don't you dare," Rin hissed. "You opened the void, you let the beasts through, and you ran and hid here to let us deal with the consequences. When are you going to stop hiding? When are you going to stop being such a damn *coward*? What are you running from?"

Jiang looked pained. "It's easy to be brave. Harder to know when not to fight. I've learned that lesson."

"Master, *please* . . ."

"If you unleash this on Mugen, you will ensure that this war will continue for generations," said Jiang. "You will do more than burn entire provinces to the ground. You will rip apart the very fabric of the universe. These are not men entombed in this mountain; these are gods. They will treat the material world as a plaything. They will shape nature according to their will. They will level mountains and redraw rivers. They will turn the mortal world into the same chaotic flow of primal forces that constitutes the Pantheon. But in the Pantheon, the gods are balanced. Life and death, light and dark—each of the sixty-four entities has its opposite. Bring the gods into your world, and that balance will shatter. You will turn your world to ash, and only demons will live in the rubble."

When Jiang finished speaking, the silence rang heavily in the darkness.

"I can control them," said Altan, though even to Rin he sounded hesitant, like a boy insisting to himself that he could fly. "There are men in those bodies. The gods can't run free. I've done it with my people. Suni should have been locked up here years ago, but I've tamed him, I can talk them back from the madness—"

"You *are* mad." Jiang's voice was almost a whisper, containing as much awe as disbelief. "You're blinded by your own desire for vengeance. Why are you doing this?" He reached out and grasped Altan's shoulder. "For the Empire? For love of the country? Which is it, Trengsin? What story have you told yourself?"

"I want to save Nikan," Altan insisted. He repeated in a strained voice, as if trying to convince himself, "I want to save Nikan."

"No, you don't," said Jiang. "You want to raze Mugen."

"They're the same thing!"

"There is a world of difference between them, and the fact that you don't see that is why you can't do this. Your patriotism is a farce. You dress up your crusade with moral arguments, when in truth you would let millions die if it means you get your so-called justice. That's what will happen if you open the Chuluu Korikh, you know," said Jiang. "It won't be just Mugen that pays to sate your need for retribution, but anyone unlucky enough to be caught in this storm of insanity. Chaos does not discriminate, Trengsin, and that's why this prison was designed to never be unlocked." He sighed. "But of course, you don't care."

Altan could not have looked more shocked if Jiang had struck him across the face.

"You have not cared about anything for a very long time," Jiang continued. He regarded Altan with pity. "You are broken. You're hardly yourself anymore."

"I'm trying to save my country," Altan reiterated hollowly. "And you're a coward."

"I am terrified," Jiang acknowledged. "But only because I'm starting to remember who I once was. Don't go down that path. Your country is ash. You can't bring it back with blood."

Altan gaped at him, unable to respond.

Jiang tilted his head to the side. "Irjah knew, didn't he?"

Altan blinked rapidly. He looked terrified. "What? Irjah didn't—Irjah never—"

"Oh, he knew." Jiang sighed. "He must have known. Daji would have told him—Daji saw what I didn't, Daji would have made sure Irjah knew how to keep you tame."

Rin looked between them, confused. The blood had drained

from Altan's face; his features twisted with rage. "How dare you—you dare allege—"

"It's my fault," Jiang said. "I should have tried harder to help you."

Altan's voice cracked. "I didn't need to be *helped*."

"You needed it more than anything," Jiang said sadly. "I'm so sorry. I should have fought to save you. You were a scared little boy, and they turned you into a weapon. And now . . . now you're lost. But not *her*. She can still be saved. Don't burn her with yourself."

They both looked to her then.

Rin glanced between them. So this was her choice. The paths before her were clear. Altan or Jiang. Commander or master. Victory and revenge, or . . . or whatever Jiang had promised her.

But what had he ever promised her? Only wisdom. Only understanding. Enlightenment. But those meant only further warnings, petty excuses to hold her back from exercising a power that she knew she could access . . .

"I taught you better than this." Jiang put a hand on her shoulder. He sounded as if he were pleading. "Didn't I? Rin?"

He could have helped them. He could have stopped the massacre at Golyn Niis. He could have saved Nezha.

But Jiang had hidden. His country had needed him, and he had fled to ensconce himself here, without any regard for those he left behind.

He had abandoned her.

He hadn't even said goodbye.

But Altan . . . Altan had not given up on her.

Altan had verbally abused her and hit her, but he had faith in her power. Altan had only ever wanted to make her stronger.

"I'm sorry, sir," she said. "But I have my orders."

Jiang exhaled, and his hand fell away from her shoulder. As always under his gaze, she felt as if she were suffocating, as if he could see through to every part of her. He weighed her with those pale eyes then, and she failed him.

And even though she had made her choice, she couldn't bear his disappointment. She looked away.

"No, I am sorry," Jiang said. "I'm so sorry. I tried to warn you."

He stepped backward over the ruins of his plinth. He closed his eyes.

"Master, please—"

He began to chant. At his feet the broken stone began to move as if liquid, assuming again the form of a smooth, unbroken plinth that built slowly from the ground up.

Rin ran forward. "*Master!*"

But Jiang was still, silent. Then the stone covered his face completely.

"He's wrong."

Altan's voice trembled, whether from fear or naked rage, she didn't know. "That isn't why—I'm not . . . We don't need him. We'll wake the others. They'll fight for me. And you—you'll fight for me, won't you? Rin?"

"Of course I will," she whispered, but Altan was already bashing at the next plinth with his trident, slamming the metal down over and over with naked desperation.

"Wake up," he shouted, voice cracking. "Wake up, come on . . ."

The shaman in the plinth had to be Feylen, the mad and murderous one. That should have posed a deterrent, but Altan certainly didn't seem to care as he slammed his trident down again into the thin stone veneer that lay over Feylen's face.

The rocks came crumbling down, and the second shaman woke.

Rin held her torch out hesitantly. When she saw the figure inside she cringed in revulsion.

Feylen was barely recognizable as human. Jiang had only just immured himself; his body was still passably that of a man, displaying no signs of decay. But Feylen . . . Feylen's body was a dead one, grayed and hardened after months of entombment without nourishment or oxygen. He had not decayed, but he had petrified.

Blue veins protruded against ash-gray skin. Rin doubted any blood still flowed through those veins.

Feylen's build was slender, thin and stooped, and his face looked like it might have been pleasant once. But now his skin was pulled taut over his cheekbones, eyes sunken in deep craters in his skull.

And then he opened his eyes, and Rin's breath hitched in her throat.

Feylen's eyes glowed brilliantly in the darkness, an unnerving blue like two fragments of the sky.

"It's me," Altan said. "Trengsin." She could hear the way he fought to keep his voice level. "Do you remember me?"

"We remember voices," Feylen said slowly. His voice was scratchy from months without use; it sounded like a steel blade dragged against the ancient stone of the mountain. He cocked his head at an unnatural angle, as if trying to tip maggots out of his ear. "We remember fire. And we remember you, Trengsin. We remember your hand across our mouth and your other hand at our throat."

The way Feylen spoke made Rin clench the hilt of her sword with fear. He didn't speak like a man who had fought by Altan's side.

He referred to himself as *we*.

Altan seemed to have realized this, too. "Do you remember who you are?"

Feylen frowned at this as if he had forgotten. He pondered a long time before he rasped out, "We are a spirit of the wind. We may take the body of a dragon or the body of a man. We rule the skies of this world. We carry the four winds in a bag and we fly as our whims take us."

"You're Feylen of the Cike. You serve the Empress, and you served under Tyr's command. I need your help," Altan said. "I need you to fight for me again."

"To . . . fight?"

"There's a war," Altan said, "and we need the power of the gods."

"The power of the gods," Feylen drawled slowly. Then he laughed.

It wasn't a human laugh. It was a high-pitched echo that sounded off the mountain walls like the shrieking of bats.

"We fought for you the first time," he said. "We fought for the Empire. For your thrice-damned Empress. What did that get us? A slap on the back, and a trip to this mountain."

"You did try to send the Night Castle tumbling down a cliff," Altan pointed out.

"We were confused. We didn't know where we were." Feylen sounded rueful. "But no one helped us . . . no one calmed us. No, instead you helped put us in here. When Tyr subdued us, you held the rope. You dragged us here like cattle. And he stood there and watched the stone close across our face."

"That wasn't my decision," Altan said. "Tyr thought—"

"Tyr got *scared*. The man asked for our power, and backed off when it became too much."

Altan swallowed. "I didn't want this for you."

"You promised us you wouldn't hurt us. I thought you cared about us. We were scared. We were vulnerable. And you bound us in the night, you subdued us with your flames . . . can you imagine the pain? The terror? All we ever did was fight for you, and you repaid us with eternal torture."

"We put you to sleep," Altan said. "We gave you rest."

"Rest? Do you think this is rest?" Feylen hissed. "Do you have any idea what this mountain is like? Try stepping into that stone, see if you can last even an hour. Gods were not meant to be contained, least of all us. We are the *wind*. We blow in each and every direction. We obey no master. Do you know what torment this is? Do you know what the *boredom* is like?"

He stepped forward and opened his hands out toward Altan.

Rin tensed, but nothing happened.

Perhaps the god Feylen had summoned was capable of immense power. Perhaps he could have leveled villages, might have ripped Altan apart under normal circumstances. But they were inside the mountain. Whatever Feylen was capable of, whatever he would have done, the gods had no power here.

"I know how terrible it must be to be cut off from the Pantheon," said Altan. "But if you fight for me, if you promise to contain yourself, then you never have to suffer that again."

"We have become divine," said Feylen. "Do you think we care what happens to mortals?"

"I don't need you to care about mortals," said Altan. "I need you to remember *me*. I need the power of your god, but I need more the man inside. I need the person in control. I know you're in there, Feylen."

"In control? You speak to us of *control*?" Feylen gnashed his teeth when he spoke, like every word was a curse. "We cannot be controlled like pack animals for your use. You're in over your head, little Speerly. You've brought down forces you don't understand into your pathetic little material world, and your world would be infinitely more interesting if someone *smashed it up for a bit*."

The color drained from Altan's face.

"Rin, get back," he said quietly.

Jiang was right. Chaghan had been right. An entire army of these creatures would have spelled the end of the world.

She had never felt so *wrong*.

We can't let this thing leave the mountain.

The same thought seemed to strike Feylen at precisely that moment. He looked between them and the stream of light two tiers up, through which they could just hear the wind howling outside, and he smiled crookedly.

"Ah," he said. "Left it wide open, haven't you?"

His luminous eyes came alive with malicious glee, and he regarded the exit with the yearning of a drowning man desperate to come up for air.

"Feylen, please." Altan stretched out a hand, and his voice was quiet when he spoke to Feylen, as if he thought he could calm him the way he had calmed Suni.

"You cannot threaten us. We can rip you apart," sneered Feylen.

"I know you can," said Altan. "But I trust that you won't. I'm trusting the person inside."

"You are a fool to think me human."

"Me," said Altan. "You said *me*."

Feylen's face spasmed. The blue light dimmed from his eyes. His features morphed just so slightly; the sneer disappeared, and his mouth worked as if trying to decide what commands to obey.

Altan lifted his trident out to the side, far away from Feylen. Then, with a slow deliberateness, he flung the weapon away from him. It clattered against the wall, echoed in the silence of the mountain.

Feylen stared at the weapon in wide-eyed disbelief.

"I'm trusting you with my life," said Altan. "I know you're in there, Feylen."

Slowly, he stretched his hand out again.

And Feylen grasped it.

The contact sent tremors through Feylen's body. When he looked up, he had that same terrified expression she'd seen in Suni. His eyes were wide, dark and imploring, like a child seeking a protector; a lost soul desperately seeking an anchor back to the mortal world.

"Altan?" he whispered.

"I'm here." Altan walked forward. As before, he approached the god without fear, despite full knowledge of what it could do to him.

"I can't die," Feylen whispered. His voice contained none of that grating quality now; it was tremulous, so vulnerable there was no doubt that this Feylen was human. "It's awful, Trengsin. Why can't I die? I should never have summoned that god . . . Our minds are meant to be our own, not shared with these *things* . . . I do not live here in this mountain . . . but *I can't die*."

Rin felt sick.

Jiang was right. The gods had no place in their world. No wonder the Speerlies had driven themselves mad. No wonder Jiang was so terrified of pulling the gods down into the mortal realm.

The Pantheon was where they belonged; the Pantheon was where they should stay. This was a power mankind never should have meddled with.

What were they thinking? They should leave, now, while Feylen was still under control; they should pull the stone door closed so that he could never escape.

But Altan showed none of her fear. Altan had his soldier back.

"I can't let you die yet," Altan said. "I need you to fight for me. Can you do that?"

Feylen had not let go of Altan's arm; he drew him closer, as if into an embrace. He leaned in and brushed his lips against Altan's ear, and whispered so that Rin could barely hear what he said: "Kill yourself, Trengsin. Die while you still can."

His eyes met Rin's over Altan's shoulder. They glinted a bright blue.

"*Altan!*" Rin screamed.

And Feylen wrenched his commander across the plinth and flung him toward the abyss.

It was not a strong throw. Feylen's muscles were atrophied from months of disuse; he moved clumsily, like newborn fawn, a god tottering about in a mortal body.

But Altan careened wildly over the side, flailing in the air for balance, and Feylen pushed past him and scrambled up the stone steps toward the exit. His face was wild with a gleeful malice, ecstatic.

Rin threw herself across the stone; she landed stomach-first on floor, arms extended, and the next thing she felt was terrible pain as Altan's fingers closed around her wrist just before he plunged into the darkness.

His weight wrenched her arm down. She cried out in agony as her elbow slammed against stone.

But then Altan's other arm shot up from the darkness. She strained down. Their fingers clasped together.

Rocks clattered off the edge of the precipice, falling away into the abyss, but Altan hung steady by both of her arms. They slid forward and for one sick moment she feared his weight might pull the both of them over the edge, but then her foot caught in a groove and they came to a stop.

"I've got you," she panted.

"Let go," Altan said.

"What?"

"I'm going to swing myself up," he said. "Let my left arm go."

She obeyed.

Altan kicked himself to the side to generate momentum and then threw his other hand up to grasp the edge. She lay straining against the floor, legs digging into the stone to keep herself from sliding forward while he pulled himself over the edge of the precipice. He slammed one arm over the top and dug his elbow into the floor. Grunting, he hauled his legs over the edge in a single fluid movement.

Sobbing with relief, Rin helped him to his feet, but he brushed her off.

"Feylen," he hissed, and set out at an uneven sprint up the stone pathway.

Rin followed him, but it was pointless. When they ran, the only footsteps they could hear were their own, because Feylen had long disappeared out the mouth of the Chuluu Korikh.

They'd given him free rein in the world.

But Altan had overpowered him once. Surely they could do so again. They *had* to.

They stumbled out the stone door and skidded to a halt before a wall of steel.

Federation soldiers thronged the mountainside.

Their general barked a command and the soldiers pressed forward with their shields linked to create a barrier, backing Rin and Altan inside the stone mountain.

She caught Altan's stricken expression for a brief moment before he was buried beneath a crowd of armor and swords.

She had no time to wonder why the Federation soldiers were

there or how they had known to arrive; all questions disappeared from her mind with the immediacy of combat. The fighting instinct took over—the world became a matter of blades and parries, just another melee—

Yet even as she drew her sword she knew it was hopeless.

The Federation had chosen precisely the right place to kill a Speerly.

Altan and Rin had no advantage in here. The Phoenix could not reach them through the thick walls of stone. Swallowing the poppy would be useless. They might pray to their god, but no one would answer.

A pair of gauntleted arms reached around Rin from behind, pinning her arms to her sides. From the corner of her eye she saw Altan backed against the wall, no fewer than five blades at his neck.

He might have been the best martial artist in Nikan. But without his fire, without his trident, he was still only one man.

Rin jammed her elbow into her captor's stomach, wriggled free, and whipped her sword outward at the nearest soldier. Their blades clashed; she landed a lucky, wild swing. He tumbled, yelling, into the abyss with her sword embedded in his knee. Rin made a grab for her weapon, but it was too late.

The next soldier swung wide overhead. She ducked into close quarters, reaching for the knife in her belt.

The soldier cracked the hilt of his blade down on her shoulder and sent her sprawling across the floor. She fumbled blindly against the rock.

Then someone slammed a shield against the back of her head.

CHAPTER 24

She woke in darkness. She was lying on a flat, swaying surface—a wagon? A ship? Though she was certain her eyes were open, she could see nothing. Had she been sealed inside something, or was it simply nighttime? She had no idea how much time had passed. She tried to move and discovered that she was bound: hands tied tightly behind her back, legs strapped together. She tried to sit up, and the muscles around her left shoulder screamed in pain. She choked back a whimper and lay down until the throbbing subsided.

Then she tried moving horizontally instead. Her legs were stiff; the one she lay on was numb from lack of blood flow, and when she shifted so that it would regain feeling, it hurt like a thousand needles were being slowly inserted into her foot. She could not move her legs separately so she writhed back and forth like a worm, inching about until her feet kicked against the sides of something. She pushed against it and writhed the other way.

She was sure now that she was in a wagon.

With great effort she pulled herself to a sitting position. The top of her head bumped against something scratchy. A canvas sheet. Or a tarp? Now that her eyes had adjusted, she could see that it was not dark outside after all; the wagon cover simply blocked out the sunlight.

She strained against the tarp until a crack of light flooded in through the side. Trembling with effort, she pressed her eye to the slit.

It took her a while to comprehend what she saw.

The road looked like something out of a dream. It was as if a great gust of wind had blown through a small city, turning households inside out, distributing the contents at random on the grass by the trail. A pair of ornate wooden chairs lay tipped over next to a set of woolen stockings. A dining table sat beside a carved chess set, jade pieces scattered across the dirt. Paintings. Toys. Entire trunks of clothing lay open by the roadside. She saw a wedding dress. A matching set of silken sleepwear.

It was a trail of fleeing villagers. Whatever Nikara had lived in this area, they had long gone, and they had flung things by the roadside as they became too heavy to carry. As desperation for survival outweighed their attachment to their possessions, the Nikara had dropped off their belongings one by one.

Was this Feylen's doing, or the Federation's? Rin's stomach curdled at the idea that she might be responsible for this. But if the Wind God had indeed caused this destruction, then he had long moved on. The air was calm when they rode, and no freak winds or tornadoes materialized to rip them to pieces.

Perhaps he was wreaking havoc on the world elsewhere. Perhaps he had fled north to bide his time, to heal and adjust to his long-awaited freedom. Who could predict the will of a god?

Had the Federation razed Tikany to the ground yet? Had the Fangs heard rumors of the advancing army early enough to run before the Federation tore their village apart? What about Kesegi?

She thought the Federation soldiers might loot the debris. But they were moving so fast that the officers yelled at their troops when they stopped to pick things up. Wherever they were going, they wanted to get there soon.

Among the abandoned chests and furniture, Rin saw a man sitting by the road. He slouched beside a bamboo carrying pole, the kind farmers used to balance buckets of water for irrigation. He had fashioned a large sign out of the back of a painting, on which he'd scrawled in messy calligraphy FIVE INGOTS.

"Two girls," he said in a slow chant. "Two girls, healthy girls, for sale."

Two toddlers peered out over the tops of the wooden buckets. They stared wonderingly at the passing soldiers. One noticed Rin peeking out from under the tarp, and she blinked her luminous eyes in uncomprehending curiosity. She lifted her tiny fingers and waved at them, just as a soldier shouted out in excitement.

Rin shrank back into the wagon. Tears leaked out the sides of her eyes. She couldn't breathe. She squeezed her eyes shut. She did not want to see what became of those girls.

"Rin?"

For the first time she noticed that Altan was curled up in the other corner of the wagon. She could barely see him under the darkness of the tarp. She inched clumsily toward him like a caterpillar.

"Where are we?" he asked.

"I can't tell," she said. "But we're nowhere near the Kukhonin range. We're traveling over flat roads."

"We're in a wagon?"

"I think so. I don't know how many of them there are."

"It doesn't matter. I'll get us out. I'm going to burn through these ropes," he announced. "Get back."

She wriggled to the other side of the wagon just as Altan ignited a small flame from his arms. His bonds caught fire at the edges, began slowly to blacken.

Smoke filled the wagon. Rin's eyes teared up; she could not stop herself from coughing. Minutes passed.

"Just a bit longer," Altan said.

The smoke curled off the rope in thick tendrils. Rin glanced about the tarp, panicked. If the smoke didn't escape out the sides, they might suffocate before Altan broke through his bonds. But if it did . . .

She heard shouting above her. The language was Mugini but the commands were too terse and abrupt for her to translate.

Someone yanked the tarp off.

Altan's flames exploded into full force, just as a soldier drenched him with an entire bucket full of water. A great sizzling noise filled the air.

Altan screamed.

Someone clamped a damp cloth over Rin's mouth. She kicked and struggled, holding her breath, but they jabbed something sharp into her bruised shoulder and she could not help inhaling sharply in pain. Then her nostrils filled with the sweet smell of gas.

Lights. Lights so bright they hurt like knives jabbing into her eyes. Rin tried to squirm away from the source, but nothing happened. For a moment she thrashed in vain, terrified that she'd been paralyzed, until she realized she was tied down with restraints. Strapped to some flat bed. Rin's peripheral vision was limited to the top half of the room. If she strained, she could just see Altan's head adjacent to hers.

Rin's eyes darted around in terror. Shelves filled the sides of the room. They brimmed with jars that contained feet, heads, organs, and fingers, all meticulously labeled. A massive glass chamber stood in the corner. Inside was the body of an adult man. Rin stared at him for a minute before she realized the man was long dead; it was only a corpse that was being preserved in chemicals, like pickled vegetables. His eyes were still frozen in an expression of horror; mouth wide in an underwater scream. The label at the top of the jar read in fine, neat handwriting: *Nikara Man, 32.*

The jars on the shelves were labeled similarly. *Liver, Nikara Child, 12. Lungs, Nikara Woman, 51.* She wondered dully if that was how she would end up, neatly parceled in this operating room. *Nikara Woman, 19.*

"I'm back." Altan had awoken beside her. His voice was a dry whisper. "I never thought I'd be back."

Rin's insides twisted with dread. "Where are we?"

"Please," Altan said. "Don't make me explain this to you."

She knew, then, exactly where they were.

Chaghan's words echoed in her mind.

After the First Poppy War, the Federation became obsessed with your people . . . They spent the decades in between the Poppy Wars kidnapping Speerlies, experimenting on them, trying to figure out what made them special.

The Federation soldiers had brought them to that same research facility that Altan had been abducted to as a child. The place that had left him with a crippling addiction to opium. The place that had been liberated by the Hesperians. The place that *should* have been destroyed after the Second Poppy War.

Snake Province must have fallen, she realized with a sinking feeling. The Federation had occupied more ground than she'd feared.

The Hesperians were long gone. The Federation was back. The monsters had returned to their lair.

"You know the worst part?" Altan said. "We're so close to home. To Speer. We're on the coastline. We're right by the sea. When they first brought us here, there weren't so many cells . . . they put us in a room with a window facing the water. I could see the constellations. Every night. I saw the star of the Phoenix and thought that if I could just slip away, I could swim and keep swimming and find my way back home."

Rin thought of a four-year-old Altan, locked in this place, staring out at the night sky while around him his friends were strapped down and dissected. She wanted to reach out and touch him, but no matter how hard she strained against those straps, she couldn't move. "Altan . . ."

"I thought someone would come and get us," he continued, and Rin didn't think he was talking to her anymore. He spoke like he was recounting a nightmare to the empty air. "Even when they killed the others, I thought that maybe . . . maybe my parents would still come for me. But when the Hesperian troops liberated me, they told me I could never go back. They told me there was nothing on the island but bones and ash."

He fell quiet.

Rin was at a loss for words. She felt like she needed to say something, something to rouse him, turn his attention to seeking a way out of this place, but anything that came to mind was laughably inadequate. What kind of consolation could she possibly give?

"Good! You're awake."

A high, tremulous voice interrupted her thoughts. Whoever it was spoke from directly behind her, out of her line of sight. Rin's eyes bulged and she strained against the straps.

"Oh, I'm sorry—but of course you cannot see me."

The owner of the voice moved to stand directly above her. He was a very thin white-haired man in a doctor's uniform. His beard was trimmed meticulously to a sharp point ending two inches below his chin. His dark eyes glittered with a bright intelligence.

"Is this better?" He smiled benignly, as if greeting an old friend. "I am Eyimchi Shiro, chief medical officer of this camp. You may call me Dr. Shiro."

He spoke Nikara, not Mugini. He had a very prim Sinegardian accent, as if he'd learned the language fifty years ago. His tone was stilted, artificially cheerful.

When Rin did not respond, the doctor shrugged and turned to the other table.

"Oh, Altan," he said. "I had no idea you'd be coming back. This is a wonderful surprise! I couldn't believe it when they told me. They said, 'Dr. Shiro, we've found a Speerly!' And I said, 'You've got to be joking! There are no more Speerlies!'" Shiro chuckled mildly.

Rin strained to see Altan's face. He was awake; his eyes were open, but he glared at the ceiling without looking at Shiro.

"They have been so scared of you, you know," Shiro continued cheerfully. "What do they call you? The monster of Nikan? The Phoenix incarnate? My countrymen love exaggerations, and they love you Nikara shamans even more. You are a myth, a legend! You are so special! Why do you act so sullen?"

Altan said nothing.

Shiro seemed to deflate slightly, but then he grinned and patted Altan on the cheek. "Of course. You must be tired. Do not worry. We will fix you up in just a moment. I have *just the thing* . . ."

He hummed happily as he bustled over to the corner of the operating room. He perused his shelves, plucking out various vials and instruments. Rin heard a popping noise, and then the sound of a candle being lit. She could not see what Shiro was doing with his hands until he returned to stand above Altan.

"Did you miss me?" he inquired.

Altan said nothing.

"Hm." Shiro lifted a syringe over Altan's face, tapping the glass so that both of them could see the liquid inside. "Did you miss this?"

Altan's eyes bulged.

Shiro held Altan's wrist down with a gentle touch, almost as a mother would caress her child. His skilled fingers prodded for a vein. With his other hand he brought the needle to Altan's arm and pushed.

Only then did Altan scream.

"Stop!" Rin shrieked. Spittle flew out the sides of her mouth. "*Stop it!*"

"My dear!" Shiro set the empty syringe down and rushed to her side. "Calm! Calm down! He will be fine."

"*You're killing him!*" She thrashed wildly against her bonds, but they held firm.

Tears leaked from her eyes. Shiro wiped them meticulously away, keeping his fingers out of reach of her gnashing teeth.

"Killing? Don't be dramatic. I just gave him some of his favorite medicine." Shiro tapped his temple and winked at her. "You know he enjoys it. You traveled with him, didn't you? This drug is not anything new to him. He will be fine in a few minutes."

They both looked to Altan. Altan's breathing had stabilized, but he certainly did not look fine.

"Why are you doing this?" Rin choked. She'd thought she

understood Federation cruelty by now. She had seen Golyn Niis. She'd seen the evidence of Mugenese scientists' handiwork. But to look this evil in the eye, to watch Shiro inflict such pain on Altan and *smile* about it . . . Rin could not comprehend it. "What do you *want* from us?"

Shiro sighed. "Is it not obvious?" He patted her cheek. "I want knowledge. Our work here will advance medical technology by decades. When else do you get such a good chance to do research? An endless supply of cadavers! Boundless opportunities for experimentation! I can answer every question I've ever had about the human body! I can devise ways to prevent death!"

Rin gaped at him in disbelief. "*You are cutting my people open.*"

"*Your* people?" Shiro snorted. "Don't degrade yourself. You're nothing like those pathetic Nikara. You Speerlies are so fascinating. Composed of such lovely material." Shiro fondly brushed the hair from Altan's sweaty forehead. "Such beautiful skin. Such fascinating eyes. The Empress doesn't know what she has."

He pressed two fingers against Rin's neck to take her pulse. She swallowed down the bile that rose up at his touch.

"I wonder if you might oblige me," he said gently. "Show me the fire. I know you can."

"*What?*"

"You Speerlies are so special," Shiro confided. His voice had taken on a low, husky tone. He spoke as if to an infant, or a lover. "So strong. So unique. They say you are a god's chosen people. What makes you this way?"

Hatred, Rin thought. *Hatred, and a history of suffering inflicted by people like you.*

"You know my country has never achieved feats of shamanism," Shiro said. "Do you have any idea why?"

"Because the gods wouldn't bother with scum like you," Rin spat.

Shiro brushed at the air, as if swatting the insult away. He must have heard so many Nikara curses by now that they meant nothing to him.

"We will do it like this," he said. "I will request you to show me the way to the gods. Each time you refuse, I will give him another injection of the drug. You know how he will feel it."

Altan made a low, guttural noise from his bed. His entire body tensed and spasmed.

Shiro murmured something into his ear and stroked Altan's forehead, as tenderly as a mother might comfort an ailing child.

Hours passed. Shiro posed his questions about shamanism to Rin again and again, but she maintained a stony front. She would not reveal the secrets behind the Pantheon. She would not place yet another weapon in Mugen's hands.

Instead she cursed and spat, called him a monster, called him every vile thing she could think of. Jima hadn't taught them to curse in Mugini, but Shiro caught the gist.

"Come now," Shiro said dismissively. "It's not like you've never seen this before."

She paused, spittle dripping from her mouth. "I don't know what you mean."

Shiro touched his fingers to Altan's neck to feel his pulse, pulled his eyelids back and pursed his lips as if confirming something. "His tolerance is astounding. Inhuman. He's been smoking opium for years."

"Because of what *you* did to him," she screeched.

"And afterward? After he was liberated?" Shiro sounded like a disappointed teacher. "They had the last Speerly in their hands, and they never tried to wean him off the drug? It's obvious—someone's been feeding it to him for years. Clever of them. Oh, don't look at me like that. The Federation weren't the first to use opium to control a population. The Nikara originated this technique."

"What are you *talking* about?"

"They didn't teach you?" Shiro looked amused. "But of course. Of course they wouldn't. Nikan likes to scrub out all that is embarrassing about its past."

He crossed the room to stand over her, brushing his fingers along the shelves as he walked. "How do you think the Red Emperor kept the Speerlies on their leash? Use your head, my dear. When Speer lost its independence, the Red Emperor sent crates of opium over to the Speerlies as an offering. A gift, from the colonizing state to the tributary. This was deliberate. Previously the Speerlies had only ever ingested their local bark in their ceremonies. They were used to such mild hallucinogens that to them, smoking opium was like drinking wood alcohol. When they tried it, they immediately became addicted. They did anything they could to get more of it. They were slaves to the opium just as much as they were slaves to the Emperor."

Rin's mind reeled. She could not think of any response.

She wanted to call Shiro a liar. She wanted to scream at him to stop. But it made sense.

It made so much sense.

"So you see, our countries are not so different after all," Shiro said smugly. "The only difference is that we revere shamans, we desire to learn from them, while your Empire is terrified and paranoid about the power it possesses. Your Empire has culled you and exploited you and made you eliminate each other. I will unleash you. I will grant you freedom to call the god as you have never been allowed to before."

"If you give me freedom," she snarled, "the first thing I will do is burn you alive."

Her connection to the Phoenix was the last advantage she had. The Federation had raped and burned her country. The Federation had destroyed her school and killed her friends. By now they had mostly likely razed her hometown to the ground. Only the Pantheon remained sacred, the one thing in the universe that Mugen still had no access to.

Rin had been tortured, bound, beaten, and starved, but her

mind was her own. Her god was her own. She would die before she betrayed it.

Eventually, Shiro grew bored of her. He summoned the guards to drag the prisoners into a cell. "I will see you both tomorrow," he said cheerfully. "And we will try this again."

Rin spat on his coat as the guards marched her out. Another guard followed with Altan's inert form thrown over his shoulder like an animal carcass.

One guard chained Rin's leg to the wall and slammed the cell door shut on them. Beside her Altan jerked and moaned, muttering incoherently under his breath. Rin cradled his head in her lap and kept a miserable vigil over her fallen commander.

Altan did not come to his senses for hours. Many times he cried out, spoke words in the Speerly language that she didn't understand.

Then he moaned her name. "*Rin*."

"I'm here," she said, stroking his forehead.

"Did he hurt you?" he demanded.

She choked back a sob. "No. No—he wanted me to talk, teach him about the Pantheon. I didn't, but he said he'd just keep hurting you . . ."

"It's not the drug that hurts," he said. "It's when it wears off."

Then, with a sickening pang in her stomach, she understood.

Altan was not lapsing when he smoked opium. No—smoking opium was the only time when he was not in pain. He had lived his entire life in perpetual pain, always longing to have another dose.

She had never understood how horrendously difficult it was to be Altan Trengsin, to live under the strain of a furious god constantly screaming for destruction in the back of his mind, while an indifferent narcotic deity whispered promises in his blood.

That's why the Speerlies became addicted to opium so easily, she realized. Not because they needed it for their fire. Because for some of them, it was the only time they could get away from their horrible god.

Deep down, she had known this, had suspected this ever since she'd learned that Altan didn't need drugs like the rest of the Cike did, that Altan's eyes were perpetually bright like poppy flowers.

Altan should have been locked into the Chuluu Korikh himself a long time ago.

But she hadn't wanted to believe, because she needed to trust that her commander was sane.

Because without Altan, what was she?

In the hours that followed, when the drug seeped out of his bloodstream, Altan suffered. He sweated. He writhed. He seized so violently that Rin had to restrain him to keep him from hurting himself. He screamed. He begged for Shiro to come back. He begged for Rin to help him die.

"You can't," she said, panicking. "We have to escape here. We have to get out."

His eyes were blank, defeated. "Resistance here means suffering, Rin. There is no escape. There is no future. The best you can hope for is that Shiro gets bored and grants you a painless death."

She almost did it then.

She wanted to end his misery. She couldn't see him tortured like this anymore, couldn't watch the man she had admired since she set eyes on him reduced to *this*.

She found herself kneeling over his inert torso, hands around his neck. All she had to do was put pressure into her arms. Force the air out of his throat. Choke the life out of him.

He would hardly feel it. He could hardly feel anything anymore.

Even as her fingers grasped his skin, he did not resist. He wanted it to end.

She had done this once before. She had killed the likeness of him in the guise of the chimei.

But Altan had been fighting then. Then, Altan had been a threat. He was not a threat now, only the tragic, glaring proof that her heroes inevitably let her down.

Altan Trengsin was not invincible after all.

He had been so good at following orders. They told him to jump and he flew. They told him to fight and he *destroyed*.

But here at the end, without a purpose and without a ruler, Altan Trengsin was broken.

Rin's fingers tensed, but then she trembled and pushed his limp form violently away from her.

"How are my darling Speerlies doing? Ready for another round?"

Shiro approached their cell, beaming. He was coming from the lab at the opposite end of the hallway. He held several round metallic containers in his arms.

They didn't respond.

"Would you like to know what those canisters are for?" Shiro asked. His voice remained artificially bright. "Any guesses? Here's a hint. It's a weapon."

Rin glowered at the doctor. Altan stared at the floor.

Shiro continued, unfazed. "It's the plague, children. Surely you know what the plague does? First your nose begins to run, and then great welts start growing on your arms, your legs, between your legs . . . you die from shock when the wounds rupture, or from your own poisoned blood. It takes quite a long time to die down, once it's caught on. But perhaps that was before your time. Nikan has been plague free for a while now, hasn't it?"

Shiro tapped the metal bars. "It took us a devilishly long time to figure out how it spread. Fleas, can you believe that? Fleas, that latch onto rats, and then spread their little plague particles over everything they touch. Of course, now that we know how it spreads, it's only a hop step to turning it into a weapon. Obviously it will not do to have the weapon run around without control—we *do* plan to inhabit your country one day—but when released in some densely populated areas, with the right critical mass . . . well, this war will be over much sooner than we anticipated, won't it?"

Shiro leaned forward, head resting against the bars. "You have nothing to fight for anymore," he said quietly. "Your country is lost. Why do you hold your silence? You have an easy way out of this place. Just cooperate with me. Tell me how you summon the fire."

"I'll die first," Rin spat.

"What are you defending?" Shiro asked. "You owe Nikan nothing. What were you to them? What were the Speerlies to them, ever? Freaks! Outcasts!"

Rin stood up. "We fight for the Empress," she said. "I'm a Militia soldier until the day I die."

"The Empress?" Shiro looked faintly puzzled. "Have you really not figured it out?"

"Figured *what* out?" Rin snapped, even as Altan silently mouthed *no*.

But she had taken the bait, she had risen to the doctor's provocation, and she could tell from the way Shiro's eyes gleamed that he had been waiting for this moment.

"Have you even asked how we knew you were at the Chuluu Korikh?" Shiro asked. "Who must have given us that information? Who was the *only other person* who knew of that wonderful mountain?"

Rin gaped at him, openmouthed, while the truth pieced itself together in her mind. She could see Altan puzzling it out, too. His eyes widened as he came to the same realization that she did.

"No," said Altan. "You're lying."

"Your precious Empress betrayed you," Shiro said with relish. "You were a trade."

"That's impossible," said Altan. "We served her. We *killed* for her."

"Your Empress gave you up, you and your precious band of shamans. You were *sold*, my dear Speerlies, just like Speer was sold. Just like your Empire was sold."

"*You're lying!*"

Altan flung himself at the bars. Fire ignited across his body, flared out in tentacles that almost reached the guards. Altan continued to scream, and the fire licked wider and wider, and although the metal did not melt, Rin thought she saw the bars begin to bend.

Shiro shouted a command in Mugini.

Three guards rushed to the cell. As one worked to unlock the gate, another sloshed a bucket of water over Altan. Once he was doused, the third rushed in to pull Altan's arms back behind his head while the first jammed a needle into his neck. Altan jerked and dropped to the floor.

The guards turned to Rin.

Rin thought she saw Shiro's mouth moving, yelling, "No, not her," before she, too, felt the needle sink into her neck.

The rush she felt was nothing like poppy seeds.

With poppy seeds, she still had to concentrate on clearing her mind. With poppy seeds it took conscious effort to ascend to the Pantheon.

Heroin was nowhere near as subtle. Heroin evicted her from her own body so that she had no choice but to seek refuge in the realm of spirit.

And she realized, with a fierce joy, that in attempting to sedate her, Shiro's guards had set her *free*.

She found Altan in the other realm. She *felt* him. She knew the pattern of him as well as she knew her own.

She had not always known the shape of him. She had loved the version of him she'd constructed for herself. She had admired him. She had idolized him. She had adored an idea of him, an archetype, a version of him that was invulnerable.

But now she knew the truth, she knew the realness of Altan and his vulnerabilities and most of all his *pain* . . . and still she loved him.

She had mirrored herself against him, molded herself after him; one Speerly after another. She had emulated his cruelty, his hatred, and his vulnerability. She knew him, finally knew all of him, and that was how she found him.

Altan?

Rin.

She could feel him all around her; a hard edge, a deeply wounded aura, and yet a comforting presence.

Altan's form appeared before her as if he stood across a very large field. He walked, or floated, toward her. Space and distance did not exist in this realm, not really, but her mind had to interpret it as such for her to orient herself.

She did not have to read the anguish in his eyes. She felt it. Altan did not keep his spirit closed off, the way Chaghan did; he was an open book, available for her to peruse, as if he were offering himself up for her to try to understand.

She understood. She understood his pain and his misery, and she understood why all he wanted to do now was die.

But she had no patience for it.

Rin had given up the luxury of fear a long, long time ago. She had wanted to give up so many times. It would have been easier. It would have been painless.

But throughout everything, the one thing she had held on to was her anger, and she knew one truth: She would not die like this. She would not die without vengeance.

"They killed our people," she said. "They sold us. Since Tearza, Speer has been a pawn in the Empire's geopolitical chess game. We were disposable. We were tools. Tell me that doesn't make you furious."

He looked exhausted. "I am sick with fury," he said. "And I am sick knowing that there is nothing I can do."

"You've blinded yourself. You're a *Speerly*. You have power," she said. "You have the anger of all of Speer. Show me how to use it. *Give it to me.*"

"You'll die."

"Then I will die on my feet," she said. "I will die with flames in my hand and fury in my heart. I will die fighting for the legacy of my people, rather than on Shiro's operating table, drugged and wasted. I will not die a coward. And neither will you. Altan, look at me. We are not like Jiang. We are not like *Tearza*."

Altan lifted his head then.

"Mai'rinnen Tearza," he whispered. "The queen who abandoned her people."

"Would you abandon them?" she pressed. "You heard what Shiro said. The Empress didn't just sell us out. She sold the entire Cike. Shiro won't stop until he has every Nikara shaman locked up in this hellhole. When you are gone, who will protect them? Who will protect Ramsa? Suni? *Chaghan?*"

She felt it from him then—a stab of defiance. A flicker of resolve.

That was all she needed.

"The Phoenix isn't only the god of fire," he said. "It is the god of revenge. And there is a power, born of centuries of festering hatred, that only a Speerly can access. I have tapped into it many times, but never in full. It would consume you. It would burn at you until there was nothing left."

"Give it to me," she said immediately, hungrily.

"I can't," he said. "It's not mine to give. That power belongs to the Speerlies."

"Then take me to them," Rin demanded.

And so he took her back.

In the realm of dreams, time ceased to hold meaning. Altan took her back centuries. He took her back into the only spaces where their ancestors still existed, in ancient memory.

Being led by Altan was not the same as being led by Chaghan. Chaghan was a sure guide, more native to the spirit world than the world of the living. With Chaghan, she had felt as if she were being dragged along, and that if she didn't obey, Chaghan would have shattered her mind. But with Altan . . . Altan did not feel even like a separate presence. Rather, he and she made two parts of a much greater whole. They were two small instances of the grand, ancient entity of all that was Speer, hurtling through the world of spirit to rejoin their kind.

When space and time again became tangible concepts to her,

Rin perceived that they were at a campfire. She saw drums, she heard people chanting and singing, and she knew that song, she had been taught that song when she was a little girl, she could not believe she had ever forgotten that song . . . all Speerlies could sing that song before their fifth birthday.

No—not her. Rin had never learned that song. This was not her recollection; she was living inside the remembrance of a Speerly who had lived many, many years ago. This was a shared memory. This was an illusion.

So was this dance. And so, too, was the man who held her by the fire. He danced with her, spinning her about in great arcs, then pulling her back against his warm chest. He could not be Altan, and yet he had Altan's face, and she was certain that she had always known him.

She had never been taught to dance, but somehow she knew the steps.

The night sky was lit up with stars like little torches. A million tiny campfires scattered across the darkness. A thousand Isles of Speer, a thousand fireside dances.

Years ago Jiang had told her that the spirits of the dead dissolved back into the void. But not the spirits of Speer. The Speerlies refused to let go of their illusions, refused to forget about the material world, because Speer's shamans couldn't be at peace until they got their vengeance.

She saw faces in the shadow. She saw a sad-looking woman who looked like her, sitting beside an old man wearing a crescent pendant around his neck. Rin tried to look closer but their faces were blurred, those of people she only half remembered.

"Is this what it was like?" she asked out loud.

The voices of the ghosts answered as one. *This was the golden age of Speer. This was Speer before Tearza. Before the massacre.*

She could have wept at the beauty of it.

There was no madness here. Only fires and dances.

"We could stay here," Altan said. "We could stay here forever. We wouldn't have to go back."

In that moment it was all she wanted.

Their bodies would waste away and become nothing. Shiro would deposit their corpses into a waste chamber and incinerate them. Then, when the last part of them had been given to the Phoenix, once their ashes were scattered in the winds, they would be free.

"We could," she agreed. "We could be lost to history. But you'd never do that, would you?"

"They wouldn't take us now," he said. "Do you feel them? Can you feel their anger?"

She could. The ghosts of Speer were so sad, but they were also furious.

"This is why we are strong. We draw our strength from centuries and centuries of unforgotten injustices. Our task—our very reason for being—is to make those deaths mean something. After us, there will be no Speer. Only a memory."

She had thought she understood Altan's power, but only now did she realize the *depth* of it. The weight of it. He was burdened with the legacy of a million souls forgotten by history, vengeful souls screaming for justice.

The ghosts of Speer were chanting now, a deep and sorrowful song in the language she was born too late to understand, but connected to her very bones. The ghosts spoke to them for an eternity. Years passed. No time passed at all. Their ancestors imparted all that they knew of Speer, all that had ever been remembered of their people. They instilled in her centuries of history and culture and religion.

They told her what she had to do.

"Our god is an angry god," said the woman who looked like Rin. "It will not let this injustice rest. It demands vengeance."

"You must go to the isle," said the old man with the crescent pendant. "You must go to the temple. Find the Pantheon. Call the Phoenix, and wake the ancient fault lines on which Speer lies. The Phoenix will only answer to you. It has to."

The man and woman faded back into the blur of brown faces.

The ghosts of Speer began to sing as one, mouths moving in unison.

Rin could not determine the meaning of the song from the words, but she felt it. It was a song of vengeance. It was a horrible song. It was a wonderful song.

The ghosts gave Rin their blessing, and it made the rush from the heroin feel like a feathery touch in comparison.

She had been granted a power beyond imagination.

She had the strength of their ancestors. She held within her every Speerly who had died on that terrible day, and every Speerly who had ever lived on the Dead Island.

They were the Phoenix's chosen people. The Phoenix thrived on anger, and Rin possessed that in abundance.

She reached for Altan. They were of one mind and one purpose.

They forced their way back into the world of the living.

Their eyes flared open at the same time.

One of Shiro's assistants had been bending over them, back on the table in Shiro's laboratory. The flames roiling from their bodies immolated him immediately, catching his hair and clothes so that when he reeled away from them, screaming, every bit of him was on fire.

Flames licked out in every direction. They caught the chemicals in the laboratory and combusted, shattering glass. They caught the alcohol used to sterilize wounds and spread rapidly on the fumes. The jar in the corner bearing the pickled man trembled from the heat and exploded, spilling its vile contents out onto the floor. The fumes of the embalming fluid caught fire, too, lighting up the room in an earnest blaze.

The lab assistant ran into the hallway, screaming for Shiro to save him.

Rin writhed and twisted where she lay. The straps keeping her down could not bear the heat of the flame at such a close angle. They snapped and she fell off the table, picked herself up, and turned just as Shiro rushed into the room clutching a reloading crossbow.

He shifted his aim from Altan to Rin and back again.

Rin tensed, but Shiro did not pull the trigger—whether out of inexperience or reluctance, Rin did not know.

"Beautiful," he marveled in a low voice. The fire reflected in his hungry eyes, and for a moment made him seem as if he, too, possessed the scarlet eyes of the Speerlies.

"*Shiro!*" Altan roared.

The doctor did not move as Altan advanced. Rather he lowered his crossbow, held his arms out to Altan as if welcoming a son into his embrace.

Altan grabbed his tormentor by the face. And squeezed. Flames poured from his hands, white-hot flames, surrounding the doctor's head like a crown. First Altan's hands left fingerprints of black against around Shiro's temples, and then the heat burned through bone and Altan's fingers bored holes through Shiro's skull. Shiro's eyes bulged. His arms twitched madly. He dropped the crossbow.

Altan pressed Shiro's skull between his hands. Shiro's head split open with a wet crack.

The twitching stopped.

Altan dropped the body and stepped away from it. He turned to Rin. His eyes burned a brighter red than they ever had before.

"Okay," he said. "Now we run."

Rin scooped the crossbow off the ground and followed Altan out of the operating room.

"Where's the exit?"

"No clue," Altan said. "Look for light."

They ran for their lives, turning corners at random. The research facility was a massive complex, far larger than Rin had imagined. As they ran, Rin saw that the hallway containing their cells was only one corridor in the mazelike interior; they passed empty barracks, many operating tables, and storage rooms stacked with canisters of gas.

Alarm bells sounded across the entire complex, alerting the soldiers to the breach.

Finally they found an exit: a side door in an empty corridor. It was boarded shut, but Altan pushed Rin aside and then kicked it down. She jumped out and helped him climb through.

"Over there!"

A Federation patrol group caught sight of them and raced in their direction.

Altan grabbed the crossbow from Rin and aimed it at the patrol group. Three soldiers dropped to the ground, but the others advanced over their comrades' dead bodies.

The crossbow made a hollow clicking noise.

"Shit," Altan said.

The patrol group drew closer.

Rin and Altan were starved, weakened, still half-drugged. And yet they fought, back to back. They moved as perfect complements to each other. They achieved a better synchronization than Rin had even with Nezha, for Nezha knew how she moved only by observing her. Altan didn't have to—Altan knew by *instinct* who she was, how she would fight, because they were the same. They were two parts of a whole. They were Speerlies.

They dispatched the patrol of five, only to see another squadron of twenty approach them from the side of the building.

"Well, we can't kill all of them," said Altan.

Rin wasn't sure about that. They kept running anyway.

Her feet were scraped raw from the cobbled floor. Altan gripped her arm as they ran, dragging her forward.

The cobblestones became sand, then wooden planks. They were at a port. They were by the sea.

They needed to get to the water, to the sea. Needed to swim across the narrow strait. Speer was so close . . .

You must go to the isle. You must go to the temple.

They reached the end of the pier. And stopped.

The night was lit up with torches.

* * *

It seemed as if the entire Federation army had assembled by the docks—Mugenese soldiers behind the pier, Mugenese ships in the water. There were hundreds of them. They were hundreds against two. The odds were not simply bad, they were insurmountable.

Rin felt a sensation of crushing despair. She couldn't breathe under the weight of it. This was where it ended. This was Speer's last stand.

Altan hadn't let go of her arm. Blood dripped from his eyes, blood dropped from his mouth.

"Look." He pointed. "Do you see that star? That's the constellation of the Phoenix."

She raised her head.

"Take it as your guide," he said. "Speer is southeast of here. It'll be a long swim."

"What are you talking about?" she demanded. "We'll swim together. You'll guide me."

His hand closed around her fingers. He held them tight for a moment and then let go.

"No," he said. "I'll finish my duty."

Panic twisted her insides.

"Altan, no."

She couldn't stop the onslaught of hot tears, but Altan wasn't looking at her. He was gazing out at the assembled army.

"Tearza didn't save our people," he said. "I couldn't save our people. But this comes close."

"Altan, please . . ."

"It will be harder for you," Altan said. "You'll have to live with the consequences. But you're brave . . . you're the bravest person I've ever met."

"Don't leave me," she begged.

He leaned forward and grasped her face in both hands.

She thought for a bizarre moment that he was going to kiss her. He didn't. He pressed his forehead against hers for a long time.

She closed her eyes. She drank in the sensation of her skin against his. She seared it into her memory.

"You're so much stronger than I am," said Altan. Then he let her go.

She shook her head frantically. "No, I'm not, it's *you*, I need *you*—"

"Someone's got to destroy that research facility, Rin."

He stepped away from her. Arms stretched forward, he walked toward the fleet.

"No," Rin begged. "*No!*"

Altan took off at a run.

A hail of arrows erupted from the Federation force.

At the same moment Altan lit up like a torch.

He called the Phoenix and the Phoenix came; enveloping him, embracing him, loving him, bringing him back into the fold.

Altan was a silhouette in the light, a shadow of a man. She thought she saw him look back toward her. She thought she saw him smile.

She thought she heard a bird's cackle.

Rin saw in the flames the image of Mai'rinnen Tearza. She was weeping.

The fire doesn't give, the fire takes, and takes, and takes.

Rin screamed a wordless scream. Her voice was lost in the fire.

A great column of flame erupted from the site of Altan's immolation.

A wave of heat rolled out in every direction, bowling over the Federation soldiers like they were straw. It hit Rin like a punch to the gut, and she pitched backward into the inky black water.

CHAPTER 25

She swam for hours. Days. An eternity. She remembered only the beginning, the initial shock as her body slammed into the water, how she thought she had died because she could not make her body obey, and because her skin prickled where it hit the water as if she had been flayed alive. If she craned her head she could see the research base burning. It was a beautiful burn, crimson and gold licking up in tendrils to the softly dark sky.

At first Rin swam the way she had been trained to at the Academy—a stroke with a minimized profile so her arms would not exit the water. The Federation archers would shoot her dead in the water if they saw her, if there were any left alive . . . Then the fatigue set in, and she simply moved her limbs to keep afloat, to keep drifting, without any consideration for technique. Her strokes became mechanical, automated, and formless.

Even the water had warmed from the heat of Altan's conflagration. It felt like a bath, like a soft bed. She drifted, and thought it might be nice to drown. The ocean floor would be quiet. Nothing would hurt. There would be no Phoenix, no war, nothing at all, only silence . . . In those warm, dark depths she would feel no loss at all . . .

But the sight of Altan walking to his death was seared into

her memory; it burned at the forefront of her thoughts, more raw and painful than the salt water seeping into her open wounds. He commanded her from the grave, whispering orders even now . . . She did not know if she merely hallucinated his voice, or if he was truly with her, guiding her.

Keep swimming, follow the wings, don't stop, don't give up, keep moving . . .

She trained her eyes on the constellation of the Phoenix. *Southeast. You must swim to the southeast.*

The stars became torches, and the torches became fire, and she thought she saw her god. "I feel you," said the Phoenix, undulating before her. "I sense your sacrifice, your pain, and I want it, bring it to me . . . you are close, so close."

Rin reached a shaking hand toward the god, but then something jolted in her mind, something primal and terrified.

Stay away, screamed the Woman. *Stay far away from here.*

No, Rin thought. *You can't keep me away. I'm coming.*

She floated senselessly in the black water; arms and legs spread-eagled to remain afloat. She wavered in and out of reality. Her spirit went flying. She lost all sense of direction; she had no destination. She went wherever she was pulled, as if by a magnetic power, as if by an entity beyond her control.

She saw visions.

She saw a storm cloud that looked like a man gathering over the mountains, with four cyclones branching off like limbs, and when she stared at the source, two intelligent spots of cerulean peered back at her—too bright to be natural, too malicious to be anything but a god.

She saw a great dam with four gorges, the largest structure she had ever seen. She saw water gushing in every direction, flooding the plains. She saw Chaghan and Qara standing somewhere high, watching the fragments of the broken dam stream into the shifting river mouth.

She brushed against them, wondering, and Chaghan jerked his head up.

"Altan?" Chaghan asked hopefully.

Qara looked to her brother. "What is it?"

Chaghan ignored his sister, gazing around as if he could see Rin. But his pale eyes went straight through her. He was looking for something that no longer existed.

"Altan, are you there?"

She tried to say something, but no sound came out. She didn't have a mouth. She didn't have a body. Scared, she flitted away, and then the void was pulling her through again so that she couldn't have gone back if she'd tried.

She flew through the present to the past.

She saw a great temple, a temple built of stone and blood.

She saw a familiar woman, tall and magnificent, brown-skinned and long-limbed. She wore a crown of scarlet feathers and ash-colored beads. She was weeping.

"I won't," said the woman. "I will not sacrifice the world for the sake of this island."

The Phoenix shrieked with a fury so great that Rin trembled under its naked rage.

"I will not be defied. I will smite those who have broken their promises. And *you* . . . you have broken the greatest vow of all," hissed the god. "I condemn you. You will never know peace."

The woman screamed, collapsed to her knees, and clutched at something within her, as if trying to claw her very heart out. She glowed from inside like a burning coal; light poured through her eyes, her mouth, until cracks appeared in her skin and she shattered like rock.

Rin would have screamed, too, if she had a mouth.

The Phoenix turned its attention to her, just as the void dragged her away again.

She hurtled through time and space.

She saw a shock of white hair, and then everything stood still.

The Gatekeeper hung in a vacuum, frozen in a state of suspended animation, a place next to nowhere and on the way to everywhere.

"Why did you abandon us?" she cried. "You could have helped us. You could have saved us."

His eyes shot open and found her.

She did not know how long he stared at her. His eyes bored into the back of her soul, searched through all of her. And she stared back. She stared back, and what was she saw nearly broke her.

Jiang was no mortal. He was something old, something ancient, something very, very powerful. And yet at the same time he was her teacher, he was that frail and ageless man whom she knew as human.

He reached out for her and she almost touched him, but her fingers glided through his and touched nothing, and she thought with a sickening fright that she was drifting away again. But he uttered a word, and she hung still.

Then their fingers met, and she had a body again, and she could feel, feel his hands cup her cheeks and his forehead press against hers. She felt it acutely when he grasped her shoulders and shook her, hard.

"Wake up," he said. "You're going to drown."

She hauled herself out of the water onto hot sand.

She took a breath, and her throat burned as if she had drunk a gallon of peppercorn sauce. She whimpered and swallowed, and it felt like a fistful of rocks was trying to scrape its way down her esophagus. She curled into herself, rolled over, hauled herself to her feet, and attempted a step forward.

Something crunched under her foot. She lurched forward and tripped onto the ground. Dazed, she glanced around. Her ankle had wedged inside something. She wiggled her foot and lifted it up.

She dragged a skull out of the sand.

She had stepped inside a dead man's jaw.

She shrieked and fell backward. Her vision pulsed black. Her eyes were open but they had shut down, refusing all sensory input. Bright flashes of light swam before her eyes. Her fingers scrabbled through the sand. It was full of hard little objects. She lifted them out and brought them to her eyes, squinting until her vision returned.

They weren't pebbles.

Little bits of white stuck up in the sand everywhere she looked. Bones. Bones, everywhere.

She was kneeling in a massive graveyard.

She trembled so hard the sand beneath her vibrated. She doubled over onto her knees and gagged. Her stomach was so shrunken that with every dry heave, she felt as if she had been stabbed with a knife.

Get out of the target line. Was that Altan's voice echoing in her head, or her own thoughts? The voice was harsh, commanding. She obeyed. *You are visible against white sand. Take cover in the trees.*

She dragged herself across the sand, heaving every time her fingers rolled over a skull. She shook with tearless sobs, too dehydrated to cry.

Go to the temple. You'll find the way. All paths lead to the temple.

Paths? What paths? Whatever walkways had once existed had long ago been reclaimed by the island. She knelt there, staring stupidly at the foliage.

You're not looking hard enough.

She crawled up and down the tree line on her hands and knees, trying to find any indication of something that might have been a trail. Her fingers found a flat rock, the size of her head, just visible under a veneer of grass. Then another. And another.

She hauled herself to her feet and stumbled along the path, holding the surrounding trees for support. The rocks were hard and jagged, and they cut her feet so that she left bloody footprints as she walked.

Her head swam; she had been so long without food or drink that she hardly remembered she had a body anymore. She saw, or imagined, grotesque animals, animals that should not exist. Birds with two heads. Rodents with many tails. Spiders with a thousand eyes.

She continued following the path until she felt as if she'd walked the length of the entire island. *All paths lead to the temple*, the ancestors had told her. But when she came to the clearing at the center, she found only ruins among the sand. She saw shattered rocks engraved in a calligraphy she could not read, a stone entrance that led nowhere.

The Federation must have torn down the temple twenty years ago. It must have been the first thing they did, after they had butchered the Speerlies. The Federation had to destroy the Speerlies' place of worship. They had to remove their source of power, to ruin and smash it so completely so that no one on Speer could seek the Phoenix for help.

Rin ran through the ruins, searching for a door, some remnant of the holy area, but she found nothing. Nothing was there.

She sank to the ground, too numb to move. No. Not like this. Not after all she had been through. She had almost begun to cry when she felt the sand giving way under her hands. It was sliding. Falling somewhere.

She laughed suddenly. She laughed so hard that she gasped in pain. She fell over on her side and clutched her stomach, shrieking with relief.

The temple was underground.

She fashioned herself a torch from a stick of dry wood and held it before her as she descended the stairs of the temple. She climbed down for a long time. The air became cool and dry. She rounded a corner and could no longer see sunlight. She found it difficult to breathe.

She thought of the Chuluu Korikh, and her head reeled. She had to lean against the stone and took several heaving breaths before her panic subsided. This was not the prison under the stone. She was not walking away from her god. No—she was getting closer.

The inner chamber was entirely devoid of sound. She could hear none of the ocean, not the rustling of wind or sounds of wildlife above. But silent though it was, the temple was the opposite of the Chuluu Korikh. The silence in the temple was lucid, enhancing. It helped her focus. She could almost see her way upward, as if the path to the gods were as mundane as the dirt on which she trod.

The wall formed a circle, just like the Pantheon, but she saw only one plinth.

The Speerlies needed only one.

The entire room was a shrine to the Phoenix. Its likeness had been carved in stone in the far wall, a bas-relief thrice her size. The bird's head was turned sideways, its profile etched into the chamber. Its eye was huge, wild, and mad. Fear struck her as she looked into that eye. It seemed furious. It seemed alive.

Rin's hands moved instinctively to her belt, but she didn't have poppy with her. She realized she didn't need it, the same way that Altan had never needed it. Her very presence inside the temple placed her halfway to the gods already. She entered the trance simply by gazing into the furious eyes of the Phoenix.

Her spirit flew up until it was stopped.

When she saw the Woman, this time she spoke first.

"Not this again," Rin said. "You can't stop me. You know where I stand."

"I warn you one more time," said the ghost of Mai'rinnen Tearza. "Do not give yourself to the Phoenix."

"Shut up and let me through," Rin said. Starved and dehydrated, she had no patience for warnings.

Tearza touched her cheek. Her expression was desperate. "To give your soul to the Phoenix is to enter hell. It consumes you. You will burn eternally."

"I'm already in hell," Rin said hoarsely. "And I don't care."

Tearza's face twisted in grief. "Blood of my blood. Daughter of mine. Do not go down this path."

"I'm *not going* down your path. You did nothing," said Rin. "You were too scared to do what you needed to do. You sold our people. You acted from cowardice."

"Not cowardice," Tearza said. "I acted from a higher principle."

"You acted from selfishness!" Rin screamed. "If you hadn't given up Speer, our people might still be alive right now!"

"If I hadn't given up Speer, the world would be burning down," said Tearza. "When I was young, I thought that I would have done it. I sat where you sit now. I came to this temple and prayed to our god. And the Phoenix came to me, too, for I was his chosen ruler. But I realized what I was about to do, and I turned the fire on myself. I burned away my body, my power, and Speer's hope for freedom. I gave my country to the Red Emperor. And I maintained peace."

"How is death and slavery *peace*?" Rin spat. "I have lost my friends and my country. I have lost everything I care about. I don't want peace, I want revenge."

"Revenge will only bring you pain."

"What do you know?" Rin sneered. "Do you think you brought peace? You left your people to become slaves. You let the Red Emperor exploit and abuse and mistreat them for a millennium. You set Speer on a path that made centuries of suffering inevitable. If you hadn't been such a fucking coward, I wouldn't have to do this. And Altan would still be alive."

Mai'rinnen Tearza's eyes blazed red, but Rin moved first. A wall of flame erupted between them. Tearza's spirit dissolved in the fire.

And then she was before her god.

The Phoenix was so much more beautiful up close, and so much more terrible. As she watched, it unfurled its great wings behind her back and spread them. They stretched to the ends of the room. The Phoenix tilted its head to the side and fixed her with its ember eyes. Rin saw entire civilizations rise and fall in those eyes. She saw cities built from the ground up, then burning, then crumbling into ash.

"I've been waiting for you for a long time," said her god.

"I would have come sooner," said Rin. "But I was warned against you. My master . . ."

"Your master was a coward. But not your commander."

"You know what Altan did," Rin said in a low whisper. "You have him forever now."

"The boy could never have done what you are able to do," said the Phoenix. "The boy was broken in body and spirit. The boy was a coward."

"But he called you—"

"And I answered. I gave him what he wanted."

Altan had won. Altan had achieved in death what he couldn't do in life because Altan, Rin suspected, had been tired of living. He couldn't wage the protracted war of vengeance that the Phoenix demanded, so he'd sought a martyr's death and gotten it.

It's harder to keep living.

"And what do *you* want from me?" the Phoenix inquired.

"I want an end to the Federation."

"How do you intend to achieve that?"

She glowered at the god. The Phoenix was playing with her, forcing her to spell out her demand. Forcing her to specify exactly what abomination she wanted to commit.

Rin forced the last parts of what was human out of her soul and gave way to her hatred. Hating was so easy. It filled a hole inside her. It let her feel something again. It felt so good.

"Total victory," she said. "It's what you want, isn't it?"

"What I want?" The Phoenix sounded amused. "The gods do not *want* anything. The gods merely exist. We cannot help what we are; we are pure essence, pure element. You humans inflict everything on yourselves, and then blame us afterward. Every calamity has been man-made. We do not force you to do anything. We have only ever helped."

"This is my destiny," Rin said with conviction. "I'm the last Speerly. I have to do this. It is written."

"Nothing is written," said the Phoenix. "You humans always think you're destined for things, for tragedy or for greatness.

Destiny is a myth. Destiny is the *only* myth. The gods choose nothing. You *chose*. You chose to take the exam. You chose to come to Sinegard. You chose to pledge Lore, you chose to study the paths of the gods, and you chose to follow your commander's demands over your master's warnings. At every critical juncture you were given an option; you were given a way out. Yet you picked precisely the roads that led you here. You are at this temple, kneeling before me, only because you wanted to be. And you know that should you give the command, I will call something terrible. I will wreak a disaster to destroy the island of Mugen completely, as thoroughly as Speer was destroyed. By your choice, many will die."

"Many more will live," Rin said, and she was nearly certain that it was true. And even if it wasn't, she was willing to take that gamble. She knew she would bear full responsibility for the murders she was about to commit, bear the weight of them for as long as she lived.

But it was worth it.

For the sake of her vengeance, it was worth it. This was divine retribution for what the Federation had wreaked on her people. This was her justice.

"They aren't people," she whispered. "They're animals. I want you to make them burn. Every last one."

"And what will you give me in return?" inquired the Phoenix. "The price to alter the fabric of the world is steep."

What did a god, especially the Phoenix, want? What did any god ever want?

"I can give you worship," she promised. "I can give you an unending flow of blood."

The Phoenix inclined its head. Its want was tangible, as great as her hatred. The Phoenix could not help what it craved; it was an agent of destruction, and it needed an avatar. Rin could give it one.

Don't, cried the ghost of Mai'rinnen Tearza.

"Do it," Rin whispered.

"Your will is mine," said the Phoenix.

For one moment, glorious air rushed into the chamber, sweet air, filling her lungs.

Then she burned. The pain was immediate and intense. There was no time for her to even gasp. It was as if a roaring wall of flame had attacked every part of her at once, forcing her onto her knees and then onto the floor when her knees buckled.

She writhed and contorted at the base of the carving, clawing at the floor, trying to find some grounding against the pain. It was relentless, however, consuming her in waves of greater and greater intensity. She would have screamed, but she couldn't force air into her seizing throat.

It seemed to last for an eternity. Rin cried and whimpered, silently begging the impassive figure looming over her . . . anything, death even, would be better than this; she just wanted it to stop.

But death wasn't coming; she wasn't dying, she wasn't hurt, even; she could see no change in her body even though it felt as if she were being consumed by fire . . . no, she was whole, but something was burning inside. Something was disappearing.

Then Rin felt herself jerked back by a force infinitely greater than she was; her head flung back, arms stretched out to the sides. She had become a conduit. An open door without a gatekeeper. The power came not from her but from the terrible source on the other side; she was merely the portal that let it into this world. She erupted in a column of flame. The fire filled the temple, gushed out the doors and into the night where many miles away Federation children lay sleeping in their beds.

The whole world was on fire.

She had not just altered the fabric of the universe, had not simply rewritten the script. She had *torn* it, ripped a great gaping hole in the cloth of reality, and set fire to it with the ravenous rage of an uncontrollable god.

Once, the fabric had contained the stories of millions of lives— the lives of every man, woman, and child on the longbow island—

civilians who had gone to bed easy, knowing that what their soldiers did across the narrow sea was a far-off dream, fulfilling the promise of their Emperor of some great destiny that they had been conditioned to believe in since birth.

In an instant, the script had written their stories to the end.

At one point in time those people existed.

And then they didn't.

Because nothing was written. The Phoenix had told Rin that, and the Phoenix had *shown* Rin that.

And now the unrealized futures of millions were scorched out of existence, like a sky full of stars suddenly darkened.

She could not abide the terrible guilt of it, so she closed her mind off to the reality. She burned away the part of her that would have felt remorse for those deaths, because if she felt them, if she felt each and every single one of them, it would have torn her apart. The lives were so many that she ceased to acknowledge them for what they were.

Those weren't lives.

She thought of the pathetic little noise a candle wick made when she licked her fingers and pinched it. She thought of incense sticks fizzling out when they had burned to the end. She thought of the flies that she had crushed under her finger.

Those weren't lives.

The death of one soldier was a tragedy, because she could imagine the pain he felt at the very end: the hopes he had, the finest details like the way he put on his uniform, whether he had a family, whether he had kids whom he told he would see right after he came back from the war. His life was an entire world constructed around him, and the passing of that was a tragedy.

But she could not possibly multiply that by thousands. That kind of thinking did not compute. The scale was unimaginable. So she didn't bother to try.

The part of her that was capable of considering that no longer worked.

Those weren't lives.
They were numbers.
They were a necessary subtraction.

Hours later, it seemed, the pain slowly subsided. Rin drew breath in great, hoarse gasps. Air had never tasted so sweet. She uncurled herself from the fetal position she'd withdrawn into and slowly pulled herself up, clutching at the carving for support.

She tried to stand. Her legs trembled. Flames erupted wherever her hands touched stone. She lit sparks every time she moved. Whatever gift the Phoenix had given her, she couldn't control it, couldn't contain it or use it in discrete bits. It was a flood of divine fire pouring straight from the heavens, and she barely functioned as the channel. She could hardly keep from dissolving into the flames herself.

The fire was everywhere: in her eyes, streaming from her nostrils and mouth. A burning sensation consumed her throat and she opened her mouth to scream. The fire burst out of her mouth, on and on, a blazing ball in the air before her.

Somehow she dragged herself out of the temple. Then she collapsed into the sand.

CHAPTER 26

When Rin woke inside yet another unfamiliar room, she was seized with a panic so great that she could not breathe. Not this again. No. She had been caught again, she was back in Mugen's clutches, and they were going to cut her to pieces and splay her out like a rabbit . . .

But when she flung her arms outward, no restraints kept them down. And when she tried to sit up, nothing stopped her. She was bound by no chains. The weight she felt on her chest was a thin blanket, not a strap.

She was lying on a bed. Not tied down to an operating table. Not shackled to a floor.

It was only a bed.

She curled in on herself, clutched her knees to her chest, and rocked back and forth until her breathing slowed and she had calmed enough to take stock of her surroundings.

The room was small, dark, and windowless. Wooden floors. Wooden ceiling, wooden walls. The floor moved beneath her, tilting back and forth gently, the way a mother rocked an infant. She thought at first that she had been drugged again, for what else could explain the way the room shifted rhythmically even when she lay still?

It took her a while to realize that she might be out at sea.

She flexed her limbs gingerly, and a fresh wave of pain rolled over her. She tried it again, and it hurt less this time. Amazingly, none of her limbs were broken. She was all of herself. She was whole, intact.

She rolled to her side and gingerly placed her bare feet on the cool floor. She took a deep breath and tried to stand, but her legs gave out under her and she immediately collapsed against the small bed. She had never been out on open sea before. She was suddenly nauseated, and although her stomach was empty, she dry-heaved over the side of the bed for several minutes before she finally got a grip on herself.

Her stained, tattered shift was gone. Someone had dressed her in a clean set of black robes. She thought the cloth felt oddly familiar, until she examined the fabric and realized she had worn robes like this before. They were Cike robes.

For the first time, the possibility struck her that she was not on enemy ground.

Hoping against hope, not daring to wish, Rin slid off the bed and found the strength to stand. She approached the door. Her arm trembled as she tried the handle.

It swung free.

She walked up the first staircase she saw and climbed onto a wooden deck, and when she saw the open sky above her, purple in the evening light, she could have cried.

"She awakens!"

She turned her head, dazed. She knew that voice.

Ramsa waved to her from the other end of the deck. He held a mop in one hand, a bucket in the other. He smiled widely at her, dropped the mop, and started at a run toward her.

The sight of him was so unexpected that for a long moment Rin stood still, staring at him in confusion. Then she walked tentatively toward him, hand outstretched. It had been so long since she had seen any of the Cike that she was half-convinced that

Ramsa was an illusion, some terrible trick conjured by Shiro to torture her.

She would have welcomed the mirage anyway, if she could at least hold on to *something*.

But he was real—no sooner had he reached her than Ramsa knocked her hand aside and wrapped his skinny arms around her in a tight embrace. And as she pressed her face into his thin shoulder, every part of him felt and looked so real: his bony frame, the warmth of his skin, the scarring around his eyepatch. He was solid. He was *there*.

She was not dreaming.

Ramsa broke away and stared at her eyes, frowning. "Shit," he said. "*Shit*."

"What?"

"Your eyes," he said.

"What about them?"

"They look like Altan's."

At the sound of that name she began to cry in earnest.

"Hey. Hey, now," Ramsa said, patting her awkwardly on the head. "It's all right. You're safe."

"How did you . . . *where*?" She choked out incoherent questions in between her sobs.

"Well, we're several miles out from the southern coast," said Ramsa. "Aratsha has been navigating for us. We think it's best if we stay off the shore for a while. Things are getting messy on the mainland."

"'We' . . . ?" Rin repeated with bated breath. *Could it be?*

Ramsa nodded, grinning broadly. "We're all here. Everyone else is belowdecks. Well—except the twins, but they'll join us in a few days."

"How?" Rin demanded. The Cike hadn't known what happened at the Chuluu Korikh. They couldn't have known what happened in the research facility. How could they have known to come to Speer?

"We waited at the rendezvous point like Altan commanded," Ramsa explained. "When you didn't show, we knew something had happened. Unegen tracked the Federation soldiers all the way to that . . . that place. We staked the whole thing out, sent Unegen in to try to figure out a way to grab you, but then . . ." Ramsa trailed off. "Well. You know."

"That was Altan," Rin said. She felt a fresh pang of grief the moment she said it, and her face crumpled.

"We saw," Ramsa said softly. "We figured that was him."

"He saved me."

"Yeah."

Ramsa hesitated. "So he's definitely . . ."

She began to sob.

"Fuck," Ramsa said quietly. "Chaghan's . . . someone's going to have to tell Chaghan."

"Where is he?"

"Close. Qara sent us a message with a raven but it didn't say much, except that they're coming. We'll rendezvous with them soon. She'll know how to find us."

She looked up at him. "How did you find *me*?"

"After a lot of corpse digging." Ramsa shot her a thin smile. "We searched the rubble for survivors for two days. Nothing. Then your friend had the idea to sail to the island, and that's where we stumbled upon you. You were lying on a sheet of glass, Rin. Sand all around you, and you were on a sheet of clear crystal. It was something like a story. A fairy tale."

Not a fairy tale, she thought. She had burned so hot that she had melted down the sand around her. That was no story. It was a nightmare.

"How long have I been out?"

"About three days. We put you up in the captain's cabin."

Three days? How long had she been without food? Her legs nearly gave way under her then, and she hastily shifted to lean against the rail. Her head felt very, very light. She turned to face the sea. The spray of ocean mist felt wonderful against her face. She lost herself for a minute, basked in lingering rays of the sun, until she remembered herself.

In a small voice she asked, "What did I do?"

Ramsa's smile slid off his face.

He looked uneasy, trying to decide upon words, but then another familiar voice spoke from behind her.

"We were rather hoping you'd tell us."

And then there was Kitay.

Lovely, wonderful Kitay. Amazingly unharmed Kitay.

There was a hard glint to his eyes that she had never seen in him before. He looked as if he had aged five years. He looked like his father. He was like a sword that had been sharpened, metal that had been tempered.

"You're okay," she whispered.

"I made them take me along after you left with Altan," Kitay said with a wry smile. "They took some convincing."

"Good thing he did, too," said Ramsa. "It was his idea to search the island."

"And I was right," said Kitay. "I've never been so glad to be right." He rushed forward and hugged Rin tightly. "You didn't give up on me at Golyn Niis. I couldn't give up on you."

All Rin wanted to do was stand forever in that embrace. She wanted to forget everything, to forget the war, to forget her gods. It was enough to simply *be*, to know that her friends were alive and that the entire world was not so dark after all.

But she could not remain inside this happy delusion.

More powerful than her desire to forget was her desire to know. What had the Phoenix done? What, precisely, had she accomplished in the temple?

"I need to know what I did," she said. "Right now."

Ramsa looked uncomfortable. There was something he wasn't telling her. "Why don't you come back belowdecks?" he suggested, shooting Kitay a glance. "Everyone else is in the mess. It's probably best if we talk about this together."

Rin began to follow him, but Kitay reached for her wrist. He leveled a grim look at Ramsa.

"Actually," said Kitay, "I'd rather talk to her alone."

Ramsa shot Rin a confused glance, but she hesitantly nodded her assent.

"Sure." Ramsa backed away. "We'll be belowdecks when you're ready."

Kitay remained silent until Ramsa had walked out of earshot. Rin watched his expression but couldn't tell what he was thinking. What was wrong with him? Why didn't he look happier to see her? She thought she might go mad from anxiety if he didn't say something.

"So it's true," he said finally. "You can really call gods."

His eyes hadn't left her face. She wished she had a mirror, so that she could see her own crimson eyes.

"What is it? What are you not telling me?"

"Do you really have no idea?" Kitay whispered.

She shrank from him, suddenly fearful. She had some idea. She had more than an idea. But she needed confirmation.

"I don't know what you're talking about," she said.

"Come with me," Kitay said. She followed him the length of the deck until they stood on the other side of the ship.

Then he pointed out to the horizon.

"There."

Far out over the water sprouted the most unnatural-looking cloud Rin had ever seen. It was a massive, dense plume of ash, spreading over the earth like a flood. It looked like a thundercloud, but it was erupting upward from a dark landmass, not concentrated in the sky. Great rolls of gray and black smoke billowed out, like a slow-growing mushroom. Illuminated from behind by red rays of the setting sun, it looked like it was bleeding bright rivulets of blood into the ocean.

It looked like something alive, like a vengeful smoke giant arisen from the depths of the ocean. It was somehow beautiful, the way that the Empress was beautiful: lovely and terrible all at once. Rin could not tear her eyes away.

"What is that? What happened?"

"I didn't see it happen," said Kitay. "I only felt it. Even miles away from the shore, I felt it. A great trembling under my feet. A sudden jolt, and then everything was still. When we went outside, the sky was pitch-black. The ash blotted out the sun for days. This is the first sunset I've seen since we found you."

Rin's insides curdled. That small, dark landmass, there in the distance . . . that was Mugen?

"What is it?" she asked in a small voice. "The cloud?"

"Pyroclastic flows. Ash clouds. Do you remember the old fire mountain eruptions we studied in Yim's class?" Kitay asked.

She nodded.

"That's what happened. The landmass under the island was stable for millennia, and then it erupted without warning. I've spent days trying to puzzle out how it happened, Rin. Trying to imagine how it must have felt for the people on the island. I'll bet most of the population was incinerated in their homes. The survivors wouldn't have lasted much longer. The whole island is trapped in a firestorm of poisonous vapors and molten debris," said Kitay. His voice was oddly flat. "We couldn't get nearer if we tried. We would choke. The ship would burn from the heat a mile off."

"So Mugen is gone?" Rin breathed. "They're all dead?"

"If they aren't, they will be soon," said Kitay. "I've imagined it so many times. I've pieced things together from what we studied. The fire mountain would have emitted an avalanche of hot ash and volcanic gas. It would have swallowed their country whole. If they didn't burn to death, they choked. If they didn't choke to death, they were buried under rubble. And if all of that didn't kill them, then they'll starve to death, because sure as hell nothing is going to grow on that island now, because the ash would have decimated the island agriculture. When the lava dries, the island will be a solid tomb."

Rin stared out at the plume of ash, watched the smoke yet unfurling, bit by bit, like an eternally burning furnace.

The Federation of Mugen had become, in some perverse way, like the Chuluu Korikh. The island across the narrow strait had turned into a stone mountain of its own. The citizens of the Federation were prisoners arrested in suspended animation, never to reawaken.

Had she really destroyed that island? She felt a swell of panicked confusion. Impossible. It couldn't be. That kind of natural disaster could not have been her doing. This was a freak coincidence. An accident.

Had she truly done this?

But she had *felt* it, precisely at the moment of eruption. She had triggered it. She had willed it into being. She had felt each one of those lives wink out of existence. She had felt the Phoenix's exhilaration, experienced vicariously its frenzied bloodlust.

She had destroyed an entire country with the power of her anger. She had done to Mugen what the Federation did to Speer.

"The Dead Island was dangerously close to that ash cloud," Kitay said finally. "It's a miracle you're alive."

"No, it's not," she said. "It's the will of the gods."

Kitay looked as if he was struggling with his words. Rin watched him, confused. Why wasn't Kitay relieved to see her? Why did he look as if something terrible had happened? She had survived! She was okay! She had made it out of the temple!

"I need to know what you did," he said finally. "Did you will that?"

She trembled without knowing why, and then nodded. What was the point in lying to Kitay now? What was the point in lying to anyone? They all knew what she was capable of. And, she realized, she *wanted* them to know.

"Was that your will?" Kitay demanded.

"I told you," she whispered. "I went to my god. I told it what I wanted."

He looked aghast.

"You're saying—so your god, it—it made you do this?"

"My god didn't *make* me do anything," she said. "The gods can't make our choices for us. They can only offer their power, and we can wield it. And I did, and this is what I chose." She swallowed. "I don't regret it."

But Kitay's face had drained of color. "You just killed thousands of innocent people."

"They *tortured* me! They killed Altan!"

"You did to Mugen the same thing that they did to Speer."

"They deserved it!"

"How could anyone deserve that?" Kitay yelled. "*How*, Rin?"

She was amazed. How could he be angry with her now? Did he have *any idea* what she had been through?

"You don't know what they did," she said in a low whisper. "What they were planning. They were going to kill us all. They don't care about human lives. They—"

"They're monsters! I know! I was at Golyn Niis! I lay amid the corpses for days! But *you*—" Kitay swallowed, choking on his words. "You turned around and did the exact same thing. Civilians. Innocents. Children, Rin. You just buried an *entire country* and you don't feel a *thing*."

"*They were monsters!*" Rin shrieked. "*They were not human!*"

Kitay opened his mouth. No sound came out. He closed it. When he finally spoke again, it sounded as if he was close to tears.

"Have you ever considered," he said slowly, "that that was exactly what they thought of us?"

They glared at each other, breathing heavily. Blood thundered in Rin's ears.

How dare he? How *dare* he stand there like this and accuse her of atrocities? He had not seen the inside of that laboratory, he had not known how Shiro had planned to wipe out every Nikara alive . . . he had not seen Altan walk off that dock and light up like a human torch.

She had achieved revenge for her people. She had *saved* the Empire. Kitay would not judge her for it. She wouldn't let him.

"Get out of my way," she snapped. "I need to go find my people."

Kitay looked exhausted. "What for, Rin?"

"We have work to do," she said tightly. "This isn't over."

"Are you serious? Have you listened to anything I've said? Mugen's *finished*!" Kitay shouted.

"Not Mugen," she said. "Mugen is not the final enemy."

"What are you talking about?"

"I want a war against the Empress."

"The *Empress*?" Kitay looked dumbfounded.

"Su Daji betrayed our location to the Federation," she said. "That's why they found us, they knew we'd be at the Chuluu Korikh—"

"That's insane," said Kitay.

"But they said it! The Mugenese, they said—"

Kitay stared at her. "And it never occurred to you that they had good incentive to lie?"

"Not about that. They knew who we were. Where we'd be. Only she knew that." Her breathing quickened. The anger had returned. "I need to know why she did it. And then I need to punish her for it. I need to make her *suffer*."

"Are you listening to yourself? Does it matter who sold who?" Kitay grasped her by her shoulders and shook her hard. "Look around you. Look at what's happened to this world. All of our friends are *dead*. Nezha. Raban. Irjah. Altan." Rin flinched at each name, but Kitay continued, relentless. "Our entire *world* has been torn apart, and you still want to go to war?"

"War's already here. A traitor sits on the throne of the Empire," she said stubbornly. "I will see her burn."

Kitay let go of her arm, and the expression on his face stunned her.

He looked at her as if looking at a stranger. He looked scared of her.

"I don't know what happened to you in that temple," he said. "But you are not Fang Runin."

* * *

Kitay left her on the deck. He did not seek her out again.

Rin saw the Cike in the galley belowdecks, but she did not join them. She was too drained, exhausted. She went back to her cabin and locked herself inside.

She thought—hoped, really—that Kitay would seek her out, but he didn't. When she cried, there was no one to comfort her. She choked on her tears and buried her face in the mattress. She stifled her screams in the hard straw padding, then decided she didn't care who heard her, and screamed out loud into the dark.

Baji came to the door, bearing a tray of food. She refused it.

An hour later Enki forced his way into her quarters. He enjoined her to eat. Again she refused. He argued she wouldn't do any of them any favors by starving to death.

She agreed to eat if he would give her opium.

"I don't think that's such a good idea," Enki said, looking over Rin's gaunt face, her tangled, matted hair.

"It's not that," she said. "I don't need seeds. I need the smoke."

"I can make you a sleeping draught."

"I don't need to sleep," she insisted. "I need to *feel nothing*."

Because the Phoenix had not left her when she crawled out of that temple. The Phoenix spoke to her even now, a constant presence in her mind, hungry and frenzied. It had been ecstatic, out there on the deck. It had seen the cloud of ash and read it as worship.

Rin could not separate her thoughts from the Phoenix's desire. She could resist it, in which case she thought she'd go mad. Or she could embrace it and love it.

If Jiang could see me now, she realized, *he would have me locked in the Chuluu Korikh.*

That was, after all, where she belonged.

Jiang would say that self-immurement was the noble thing to do.

No fucking way, she thought.

She would never step voluntarily into the Chuluu Korikh, not while the Empress Su Daji walked this earth. Not while Feylen ran free.

She was the only one powerful enough to stop them, because she had now attained a power that Altan had only ever dreamed of.

She saw now that the Phoenix was right: Altan *had* been weak. Altan, despite how hard he tried, could only ever have been weak. He was crippled by those years spent in captivity. He did not choose his anger freely; it was inflicted on him, blow after blow, torture after torture, until he reacted precisely the way an injured wolf might, rising up to bite the hand that hit him.

Altan's anger was wild and undirected; he was a walking vessel for the Phoenix. He never had any choice in his quest for vengeance. Altan could not negotiate with the god like she did.

She was sane, she was convinced of it. She was whole. She had lost much, yes, but she still had her own mind. She made her decisions. She *chose* to accept the Phoenix. She chose to let it invade her mind.

But if she wanted her thoughts to herself, then she had to think nothing at all. If she wanted a reprieve from the Phoenix's bloodlust, she needed the pipe.

She mused out loud to the darkness as she sucked in that sickly sweet drug.

In, out. In, out.

I have become something wonderful, she thought. *I have become something terrible.*

Was she now a goddess or a monster?

Perhaps neither. Perhaps both.

Rin was curled up on her bed when the twins finally boarded the ship. She did not know they had even arrived until they appeared at her cabin door unannounced.

"So you made it," Chaghan said.

She sat up. They had caught her in a rare state, a sober state. She had not touched the pipe for hours, but only because she had been asleep.

Qara dashed inside and embraced her.

Rin accepted the embrace, eyes wide in shock. Qara had always been so reticent. So distant. She lifted her arm awkwardly, trying to decide if she should pat Qara on the shoulder.

But Qara drew back just as abruptly.

"You're burning," she said.

"I can't turn it off," Rin said. "It's with me. It's always with me."

Qara touched Rin's shoulders softly. She gave her a knowing look, a pitying look. "You went to the temple."

"I did it," Rin said. "That cloud of ash. That was me."

"I know," Qara said. "We felt it."

"Feylen," she said abruptly. "Feylen's out, Feylen escaped, we tried to stop him but—"

"We know," said Chaghan. "We felt that, too."

He stood stiffly at the doorway. He looked as if he were choking on something.

"Where's Altan?" he finally asked.

She said nothing. She just sat there, matching his gaze.

Chaghan blinked and made a noise like an animal that had been kicked.

"That's not possible," he said very quietly.

"He's dead, Chaghan," Rin said. She felt very tired. "Give it up. He's gone."

"But I would have felt it. I would have *felt* him go," he insisted.

"That's what we all think," she said flatly.

"You're lying."

"Why would I? I was there. I saw it happen."

Chaghan abruptly stalked out of the room and slammed the door behind him.

Qara glanced down at Rin. She didn't wear her normal irate expression then. She just looked sad.

"You understand," she said.

Rin more than understood.

"What did you do? What happened?" she asked Qara finally.

"We won the war in the north," said Qara, twisting her hands in her lap. "We followed orders."

Altan's last, desperate operation had involved not one but two prongs. To the south, he had taken Rin to open the Chuluu Korikh. And to the north, he sent the twins.

They had flooded the Murui River. That river delta Rin had seen from the spirit realm was the Four Gorges Dam, the largest set of levees that held the Murui back from inundating all four surrounding provinces with river water. Altan had ordered the breaking of the levees to divert the river south into an older channel, cutting off the Federation supply route to the south.

It was almost exactly like a battle plan Rin had suggested in Strategy class in her first year. She remembered Venka's objections. *You can't just break a dam like that. Dams take years to rebuild. The entire river delta will flood, not just that valley. You're talking about famine. Dysentery.*

Rin drew her knees to her chest. "I suppose there's no point asking if you evacuated the countryside first."

Qara laughed without smiling. "Did *you*?"

Qara's words hit her like a blow. There was no reasoning through what she had done. It had happened. It was a decision that had been ripped out of her. And she had . . . and she had . . .

She began to quiver. "What have I done, Qara?"

Until now the sheer scale of the atrocity had not computed for her, not really. The number of lives lost, the enormity of what she had invoked—it was an abstract concept, an unreal impossibility.

Was it *worth* it? Was it enough to atone for Golyn Niis? For Speer?

How could she compare the lives lost? One genocide against another—how did they balance on the scale of justice? And who was she, to imagine that she could make that comparison?

She seized Qara's wrist. "What have I *done*?"

"The same thing that we did," said Qara. "We won a war."

"No, I *killed* . . ." Rin choked. She couldn't finish saying it.

But Qara suddenly looked angry. "What do you want from me? Do you want forgiveness? I can't give you that."

"I just . . ."

"Would you like to compare death tolls?" she asked sharply. "Would you like to argue about whose guilt is greater? You created an eruption, and we caused a flood. Entire villages, drowned in an instant. Flattened. You destroyed the enemy. *We killed the Nikara.*"

Rin could only stare at her.

Qara wrenched her arm out of Rin's grip. "Get that look off your face. We made our decisions, and we survived with our country intact. Worth it is worth it."

"But we *murdered*—"

"*We won a war!*" Qara shouted. "We avenged him, Rin. He's gone, but avenged."

When Rin didn't respond, Qara seized her by both shoulders. Her fingers dug painfully into her flesh.

"This is what you have to tell yourself," Qara said fiercely. "You have to believe that it was necessary. That it stopped something worse. And even if it wasn't, it's the lie we'll tell ourselves, starting today and every day afterward. You made your choice. There's nothing you can do about it now. It's over."

That was what Rin had told herself on the island. It was what she had told herself when talking to Kitay.

And later, in the dead of night, when she couldn't sleep for the nightmares and had to reach for her pipe, she would do as Qara said and keep telling herself what was done was done. But Qara was wrong about one thing:

It was not over. It couldn't be over—because Federation troops were still on the mainland, scattered throughout the south; because even Chaghan and Qara hadn't managed to drown them all. And now they had no leader to obey and no home to return to, which made them desperate, unpredictable . . . and dangerous.

And somewhere on the mainland sat an Empress on a makeshift throne, taking refuge in a new wartime capital because Sinegard had been destroyed by a conflict she'd invented. Perhaps by now she had heard the longbow island was gone. Was she distressed to lose an ally? Relieved to be freed from an enemy? Perhaps she had already taken credit for a victory she hadn't planned; perhaps she was using it to cement her hold on power.

Mugen was gone, but the Cike's enemies had multiplied. And they were rogue agents now, no longer loyal to the crown that had sold them.

Nothing was over.

The Cike had never before acknowledged the passing of their commander. By nature of their occupation, a change in leadership was an unavoidably messy affair. Past Cike commanders had either gone frothing mad and had to be dragged into the Chuluu Korikh against their will, or been killed on assignment and never come back.

Few had died with such grace as Altan Trengsin.

They said their goodbyes at sunrise. The entire contingent gathered on the front deck, solemn in their black robes. The ritual was no Nikara ceremony. It was a Speerly ceremony.

Qara spoke for all of them. She conducted the ceremony, because Chaghan, the Seer, refused to. Because Chaghan could not.

"The Speerlies used to burn the dead," she said. "They believed that their bodies were only temporary. *From ash we come, and to ash we return*. To the Speerlies, death was not an end but only a great reunion. Altan has left us to go home. Altan has returned to Speer."

Qara cast her arms over the waters. She began to chant, not in the language of the Speerlies but in the rhythmic language of the Hinterlands. Her birds circled overhead in silent tribute. And the wind itself seemed to cease, the rocking of the waves halted, as if the very universe stood still for the loss of Altan.

The Cike stood in a line, all in their identical black uniforms, watching Qara wordlessly. Ramsa's arms were folded tightly over his narrow chest, shoulders hunched as if he could withdraw into himself. Baji silently put a hand on his shoulder.

Rin and Chaghan stood at the back of the deck, removed from the rest of their division.

Kitay was nowhere to be seen.

"We should have his ashes," Chaghan said bitterly.

"His ashes are already in the sea," Rin said.

Chaghan glared at her. His eyes were red with grief, bloodshot. His pale skin was pulled over his high cheekbones so tightly that he looked even more skeletal than he usually did. He appeared as if he had not eaten in days. He appeared as if he might blow away with the wind.

Rin wondered how long it would take for him to stop blaming her in his mind for Altan's death.

"I guess he gave as good as he got," Chaghan said, nodding toward the ashen mess that was the Federation of Mugen. "Trengsin got his revenge in the end."

"No, he didn't."

Chaghan stiffened. "Explain."

"Mugen didn't betray him," she said. "Mugen didn't draw him to that mountain. Mugen didn't sell Speer. The Empress did."

"Su Daji?" Chaghan said incredulously. "Why? What would she have to gain?"

"I don't know. I intend to find out."

"*Tenega*," Chaghan swore. He looked as if he had just realized something. He crossed his thin arms against his chest, muttering in his own language. "But of course."

"What?"

"You drew the Hexagram of the Net," he said. "The Net signifies traps, betrayals. The wires of your capture were laid out ahead of you. She must have sent a missive to the Federation the minute Altan got it in his head to go to that damned mountain. *One is ready to move, but his footprints run crisscross.* You two were pawns in someone else's game this entire time."

"We were not *pawns*," Rin snapped. "And don't act like you saw this coming." She felt a sudden flash of anger then—at Chaghan's lecturing tone, his retrospective musing, as if he'd seen it all, like he'd expected this to happen, like he'd known better than Altan all along. "Your Hexagrams only make sense in hindsight and give no guidance when they're cast. Your Hexagrams are fucking useless."

Chaghan stiffened. "My Hexagrams are not useless. I see the shape of the world. I understand the changing nature of reality. I have read countless Hexagrams for the Cike's commanders—"

She snorted. "And in all the Hexagrams you read for Altan, you never foresaw that he might die?"

To her surprise, Chaghan flinched.

She knew it wasn't fair, to hurl accusations when Altan's death was hardly Chaghan's fault, but she needed to lash out, needed to blame it on someone other than herself.

She couldn't stand Chaghan with his attitude that he knew better, that he'd foreseen this tragedy, because he *hadn't*. She and Altan had gone to the mountain blind, and he had let them.

"I told you," Chaghan said. "The Hexagrams can't foresee the future. They're portraits of the world as it is, descriptions of the forces at hand. The gods of the Pantheon represent sixty-four fundamental forces, and the Hexagrams reflect their undulations."

"And none of those undulations screamed, *Don't go to this mountain, you'll be killed*?"

"I *did* warn him," Chaghan said quietly.

"You could have tried harder," Rin said bitterly, even though she knew that, too, was an unfair accusation, and that she was saying it only to hurt Chaghan. "You could have told him he was about to die."

"All of Altan's Hexagrams spoke of death," said Chaghan. "I didn't expect that this time it would mark his own."

She laughed out loud. "Aren't you supposed to be a Seer? Do you ever see *anything* useful?"

"I saw Golyn Niis, didn't I?" Chaghan snapped.

But the moment those words left his mouth he made a choking noise, and his features twisted with grief.

Rin didn't say what they were both thinking—that maybe if they hadn't gone to Golyn Niis, Altan wouldn't have died.

She wished they had just fought the war out at Khurdalain. She wished they had abandoned the Empire completely and escaped back to the Night Castle, let the Federation ravage the countryside while they waited out the turmoil in the mountains, safe and insulated and *alive*.

Chaghan looked so miserable that Rin's anger dissipated. Chaghan had, after all, tried to stop Altan. He'd failed. Neither of them could have talked Altan out of his frenzied death drive.

There was no way Chaghan could have predicted Altan's future because the future was not written. Altan made his choices; at Khurdalain, at Golyn Niis, and finally on that pier, and neither of them could have stopped him.

"I should have known," Chaghan said finally. "*We have an enemy whom we love.*"

"What?"

"I read it in Altan's Hexagram. Months ago."

"It meant the Empress," she said.

"Perhaps," he said, and turned his gaze out to the sea.

They watched Qara's falcons in silence. The birds flew in great circles overhead, as if they were guides, as if they could lead a spirit toward the heavens.

Rin thought of the parade from so long ago, of the puppets of the animals of the Emperor's Menagerie. Of the majestic kirin, that noble lion-headed beast, which appeared in the skies upon the death of a great leader.

Would a kirin appear for Altan?

Did he deserve one?

She found that she could not answer.

"The Empress should be the least of your concerns," said Chaghan after a while. "Feylen's getting stronger. And he always was powerful. Almost more so than Altan."

Rin thought of that storm cloud she'd seen over the mountains. Those malicious blue eyes. "What does he want?"

"Who knows? The God of the Four Winds is one of the most mercurial entities of the Pantheon. His moods are entirely unpredictable. He will become a gentle breeze one day, and rip apart entire villages the next. He will sink ships and topple cities. He might be the end of this country."

Chaghan spoke lightly, casually, as if he couldn't care less if Nikan was destroyed the very next day. Rin had expected blame and accusation, but she heard none; only detachment, as if the Hinterlander held no stake in Nikan's affairs now that Altan was gone. Maybe he didn't.

"We'll stop him," Rin said.

Chaghan gave an indifferent shrug. "Good luck. It'll take all of you."

"Then will you command us?"

Chaghan shook his head "It couldn't be me. Even back when I was Tyr's lieutenant, I knew it could never be me. I was Altan's Seer, but I was never slated to be a commander."

"Why not?"

"A foreigner in charge of the Empire's most lethal division? Not likely." Chaghan folded his arms across his chest. "No, Altan named his successor before we left for Golyn Niis."

Rin jerked her head up. That was news. "Who?"

Chaghan looked like he couldn't believe she had asked.

"It's you," he said, as if it were obvious.

Rin felt like he had punched her in the solar plexus.

Altan had named her as his successor. Entrusted his legacy to her. He had written and signed the order in blood before they had even left Khurdalain.

"I am the commander of the Cike," she said, and then had to repeat the words to herself before their meaning sank in. She held a status equivalent to the generals of the Warlords. She had the power to order the Cike to do as she wished. "*I command the Cike.*"

Chaghan looked sideways at her. His expression was grim. "You are going to paint the world in Altan's blood, aren't you?"

"I'm going to find and kill everyone responsible," said Rin. "You cannot stop me."

Chaghan laughed a dry, cutting laugh. "Oh, I'm not going to stop you."

He held out his hand.

She grasped it, and the drowned land and the ash-choked sky bore witness to the pact between Seer and Speerly.

They had come to an understanding, she and Chaghan. They were no longer opposed, vying for Altan's favor. They were allies, now, bound by the mutual atrocities they had committed.

They had a god to kill. A world to reshape. An Empress to overthrow.

They were bound by the blood they had spilled. They were bound by their suffering. They were bound by what had happened to them.

No.

This had not *happened* to her.

We do not force you to do anything, the Phoenix had whispered, and it had spoken the truth. The Phoenix, for all its power, could not compel Tearza to obey it. And it could not have compelled Rin, because she had agreed wholeheartedly to the bargain.

Jiang was wrong. She was not dabbling in forces she could not control, for the gods were not dangerous. The gods had no power at all, except what she gave them. The gods could affect the universe only through humans like her. Her destiny had not been written in the stars, or in the registers of the Pantheon. She had made her choices fully and autonomously. And though she called upon the gods to aid her in battle, they were her tools from beginning to end.

She was no victim of destiny. She was the last Speerly, commander of the Cike, and a shaman who called the gods to do her bidding.

And she would call the gods to do such terrible things.

ACKNOWLEDGMENTS

Hannah Bowman is an incredible agent, editor, and advocate. Without her, more characters would have lived. The team at Liza Dawson Associates has been wonderful to me. David Pomerico and Natasha Bardon are sharp, insightful editors who made this manuscript infinitely better. Laura Cherkas is an eagle-eyed copyeditor, who caught far too many continuity errors. Thank you all for giving me a chance.

Jeanne Cavelos, my personal Gandalf, transformed me from a person who liked to write into a person who is a writer. I hope Elijahcorn is treating you well. Kij Johnson is a genius, and I want to be just like her when I grow up. Barbara Webb is ridiculously cool. (I hope Ethan and Nick find happiness.) My office-hour chats with Dr. John Glavin always inspired and motivated me. Thank you all for encouraging me to try harder and write better.

My Odyssey 2016 class put me in actual, physical pain. I miss you all! It's been very hard to talk to you ever since you gained omnipotence, Bob. To the Binobos—Huw, Jae, Jake, Marlee, Greg, Becca, Caitlin—thanks for the laughs, the happy-hour margaritas, and multiple *Pacific Rim* viewings. Bennett: Look! The word *Scargon* finally made it into a book. One day his story will be told. PS: I love you. The Tomatoes—Farah Naz, Linden,

Pablo, Richard, Jeremy, Josh—are my shining stars, my lifelines, and my best friends. Thank you all for being there for me.

Finally, to Mom and Dad: I love you very much. I can never repay you for the sacrifices you've made to give me the life that I have, but I can try to make you proud. Immigrants, we get the job done.

About the author
2 Meet R. F. Kuang

Read on
3 A Note from the Author

About the book
5 Reading Group Discussion Questions

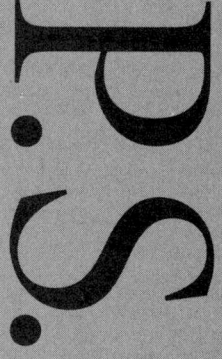

Insights,
Interviews
& More...

About the author

Meet R. F. Kuang

R. F. KUANG studies modern Chinese history. She has a BA from Georgetown University and is currently a graduate student in the United Kingdom on a Marshall Scholarship. *The Poppy War* is her debut novel.

A Note from the Author

Since *The Poppy War* came out, many readers have emailed me asking for nonfiction resources on the Rape of Nanjing, Sino-Japanese relations, and the history of World War II in China. As a graduate student of this very subject, I'm delighted that *The Poppy War* has stoked such an interest in China's wartime history. I also happen to have many, many nonfiction recommendations (largely because I've been forced to read them for class!), some of which I'll list here as an accompanying reading guide. I've tried to choose books that would be most engaging and accessible to lay readers approaching this history for the first time.

Iris Chang's gorgeously written and bestselling *The Rape of Nanking: The Forgotten Holocaust of World War II* was one of the first books that brought the (then rather neglected) history of the Nanjing Massacre to the attention of Western readers. Almost every scene from the chapters of Golyn Niis came from Chang's account of the Nanjing Massacre. Very little was made up—most of what you see truly happened.

Descriptions of the battle at Khurdalain, particularly the bombing scene and the challenges of urban warfare, were based largely on accounts from the Battle of Shanghai in 1937. Peter Harmsen's *Shanghai 1937: Stalingrad on the Yangtze* is a riveting account of those first few weeks of the war. On the topic of sexual assault, abuse, and slavery by the Japanese military, look into Yoshimi Yoshiaki's *Comfort Women: Sexual Slavery in the Japanese Military During World War II* and ▶

A Note from the Author
(continued)

George Hicks's *The Comfort Women: Japan's Brutal Regime of Enforced Prostitution in the Second World War.*

For broader, comprehensive histories of China's War of Resistance against Japan, I highly recommend Rana Mitter's *Forgotten Ally: China's World War II, 1937–1945* and Hans van de Ven's *China at War: Triumph and Tragedy in the Emergence of the New China.* Readers who are fascinated by military particularities and don't mind a bit more of a challenge will enjoy *The Battle for China: Essays on the Military History of the Sino-Japanese War of 1937–1945,* edited by Mark Peattie, Edward Drea, and Hans van de Ven. I particularly enjoyed the essay on Japanese air tactics and was disappointed I didn't get to discuss them in *The Poppy War.*

I wrote *The Poppy War* after several long discussions with my Chinese grandparents about their experiences during World War II. The last few years—from publishing *The Poppy War* to finishing my master's thesis on the complicated remembrance to the Rape of Nanjing to starting my MPhil in Chinese studies at Cambridge—have been a long, often painful process of excavating both familial and national history to understand where I—we—come from. It's a history that isn't often taught in American classrooms, and which often isn't known even to members of the Chinese diaspora. I hope my work does a little bit to change that. Thank you for reading.

Reading Group Discussion Questions

1. R. F. Kuang's academic background is evident throughout the novel. Do you see any connection between modern Chinese history and the world and system that Kuang creates?

2. *The Art of War* by Sun Tzu appears often (in a slightly different form) in *The Poppy War*—how does this text interact with the book? How does *The Art of War* influence the society's political climate as one of its core principles? What is the significance of the Nikara military's inability to follow through on those principles?

3. What track would you pledge as a student of Sinegard?

4. There are several great relationships at play in this book: Rin and Jiang, Rin and Kitay, Rin and Nezha, and Rin and Altan. How do these relationships affect Rin? How do the relationships change and grow? Is one person in the relationship more powerful than the other?

5. Human connection is a huge theme in this novel. After graduating Sinegard, Rin—being an outsider in many ways—finally finds a place where she belongs. How does ▶

Reading Group Discussion Questions
(continued)

her previous experience of exclusion affect the relationship with her found family? What does Rin gain by being part of this group? Or would it be safe to say she is *never* part of a group?

6. Who would you say has the most control in the book? How do control and power play together in this novel?

7. There are many underlying sociopolitical themes at play in *The Poppy War*, including race and colorism. What challenges does Rin experience being darker skinned than most of the children in her society? How does it affect her experiences? How does it affect your reading of the book?

8. Do you agree with Tearza's decision? Or do you agree with Rin's decision to obtain power from the Phoenix, even though it comes at a terrible cost? What would you have done in this situation?

9. Where do you hope the story goes in book two, *The Dragon Republic*?

Praise for *The Dragon Republic*

"[Rin's] story's refreshing, shocking, and there's some sort of invisible phoenix fire god controlling everything. Behold the horizons of fantasy expand."
—*Wired*

"R. F. Kuang's sophomore novel continues an enthralling saga from one of fantasy's exciting new voices."
—*Paste* magazine (Best Book of August 2019)

"This stunning sequel to *The Poppy War* is an epic journey of vengeance, friendship, and power. . . . Kuang has created a young woman torn by her connections to friends and family, searching for love and belonging, and given power beyond her imagining. Her story is unforgettable."
—*Library Journal* (starred review)

"Kuang brings brilliance to this invigorating and complex military fantasy sequel to *The Poppy War*."
—*Publishers Weekly*

"Kuang's descriptive storytelling reveals the grueling psychological and material cost of war on combatants and those they are supposed to protect. Fans of epic military fantasy will be eager for the next volume."
—*Booklist* (starred review)

"Kuang does a wonderful job of showing the effects of that pain in the initial period of this book, as well as the impact of addiction and PTSD. Rin seems destined to find war wherever she goes, and Kuang is fantastic at putting us in Rin's head to witness her internal conflict."
—*BookPage*

"It's not a sequel readers will want to miss."
—Culturess

"*The Dragon Republic* is straight up incredible. . . . It's big, bold, beautiful, and badass."
—Fantasy Hive

"*The Dragon Republic* is a brilliantly unputdownable sequel that deflects the infamous middle book syndrome with brutal precision. With *The Dragon Republic*, Kuang has proven that her debut wasn't a one-hit wonder, further establishing herself as the new rising queen of fantasy."
—Novel Notions

"A sequel born of flames and emerging not unscathed, but anew. Enter *The Dragon Republic*." —Utopia State of Mind

Praise for *The Poppy War*

"A thrilling, action-packed fantasy of gods and mythology. . . . The ambitious heroine's rise from poverty to ruthless military commander makes for a gripping read, and I eagerly await the next installment."
—Julie C. Dao, author of *Forest of a Thousand Lanterns*

"A blistering, powerful epic of war and revenge that will captivate you to the bitter end." —Kameron Hurley, author of *The Stars Are Legion*

"I have no doubt this will end up being the best fantasy debut of the year. . . . I have absolutely no doubt that [Kuang's] name will be up there with the likes of Robin Hobb and N.K. Jemisin." —Booknest

"The best fantasy debut of 2018. . . . This year's Potter." —*Wired*

"The 'year's best debut' buzz around this one was warranted; it really is that good." —B&N Sci-fi and Fantasy Blog

"Debut novelist Kuang creates an ambitious fantasy reimagining of Asian history populated by martial artists, philosopher-generals, and gods. . . . This is a strong and dramatic launch to Kuang's career."
—*Publishers Weekly*

"The book starts as an epic bildungsroman, and just when you think it can't get any darker, it does. . . . Kuang pulls from East Asian history, including the brutality of the Second Sino-Japanese war, to weave a wholly unique experience." —*Washington Post*

"[*The Poppy War* is] strikingly grim military fantasy that summons readers into an East Asian–inspired world of battles, opium, gods, and monsters. Fans of Ken Liu's *The Grace of Kings* will snap this one up."
—*Library Journal* (starred review)

"This isn't just another magical, fantasy world with artificially fabricated stakes. Rin's journey and the war against the Federation feel incredibly urgent and powerful. . . . R. F. Kuang is one of the most exciting new authors I've had the privilege of reading."

—The Roarbots

"I can safely say that this will be the finest debut of 2018 and I'd be surprised if it isn't one of the top 3 books of the year full stop. Spectacular, masterclass, brilliant, awesome. . . Simply put, R. F. Kuang's *The Poppy War* is a towering achievement of modern fantasy."

—Fantasy Book Review

"The narrative is an impactful, impressive symphony of words that grant life to this incredible morality tale. Setting the stage for an epic fantasy is an understandably enormous undertaking, but Kuang does an exceptional job of world and character building."

—RT Book Reviews (4 1/2 stars, Top Pick!)

"Kuang ambitiously begins a trilogy that doesn't shy away from the darkest sides of her characters, wrapped in a confectionery of high-fantasy pulp. . . . The future of Rin in this world may appear quite dark, but that of the series seems bright indeed."

—*Daily News* (New York)

"A young woman's determination and drive to succeed and excel at any cost runs into the horrors of war, conflict and ancient, suppressed forces in R. F. Kuang's excellent debut novel, *The Poppy War*."

—*The Skiffy and Fanty Show*

"*The Poppy War* feels entirely immersive and rich in a way that kind of sucks you in. . . . It's a treasure trove."   —Utopia State of Mind

Also by R. F. Kuang

The Poppy War

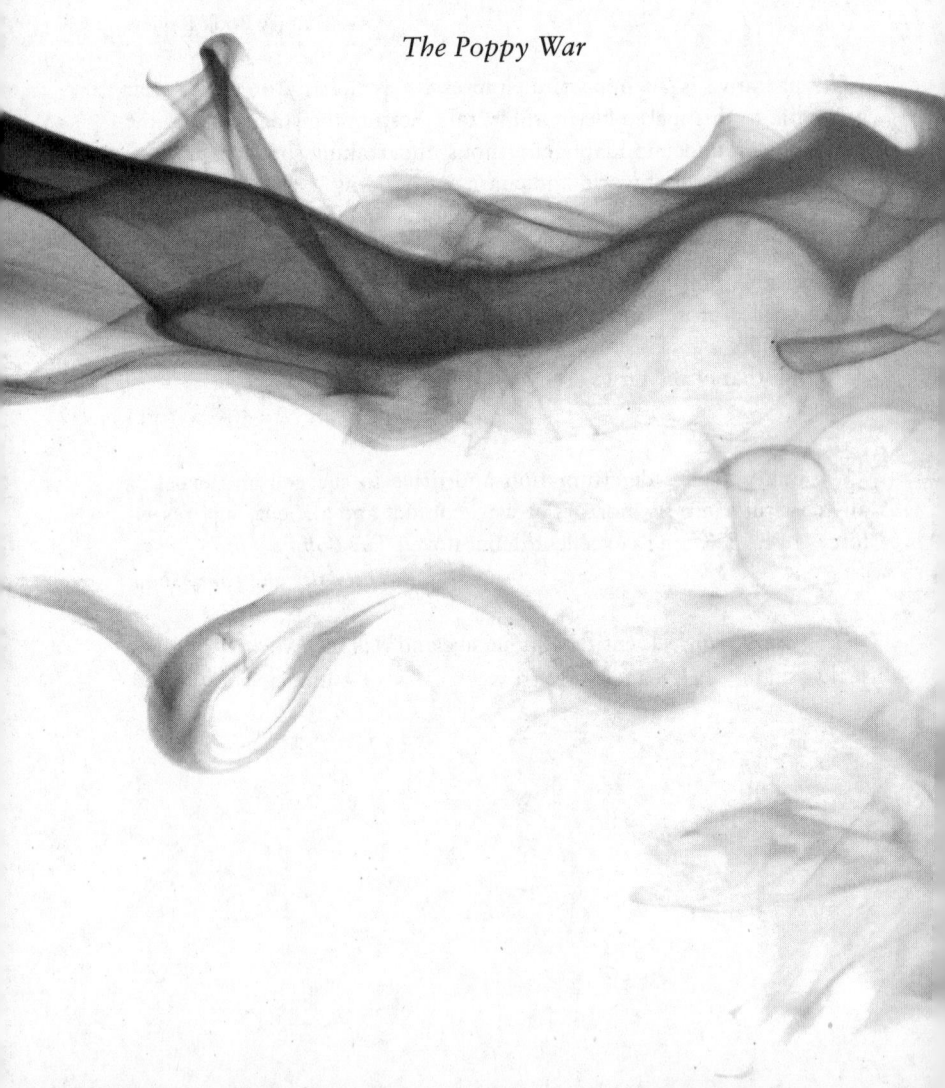

THE
DRAGON
REPUBLIC

THE POPPY WAR, BOOK TWO

R. F. KUANG

HARPER Voyager
An Imprint of HarperCollins*Publishers*

This is a work of fiction. Names, characters, places, and incidents are products of the author's imagination or are used fictitiously and are not to be construed as real. Any resemblance to actual events, locales, organizations, or persons, living or dead, is entirely coincidental.

THE DRAGON REPUBLIC. Copyright © 2019 by Rebecca Kuang. All rights reserved. Printed in the United States of America. No part of this book may be used or reproduced in any manner whatsoever without written permission except in the case of brief quotations embodied in critical articles and reviews. For information, address HarperCollins Publishers, 195 Broadway, New York, NY 10007.

HarperCollins books may be purchased for educational, business, or sales promotional use. For information, please email the Special Markets Department at SPsales@harpercollins.com.

Harper Voyager and design are trademarks of HarperCollins Publishers LLC.

A hardcover edition of this book was published in 2019 by Harper Voyager, an imprint of HarperCollins Publishers.

FIRST HARPER VOYAGER PAPERBACK EDITION PUBLISHED IN 2020.

Designed by Paula Russell Szafranski

Frontispiece © Jannarong / Shutterstock

Maps by Eric Gunther and copyright © 2017 Springer Cartographics

Library of Congress Cataloging-in-Publication Data has been applied for.

ISBN 978-0-06-266260-6

25 26 27 28 29 LBC 28 27 26 25 24

To

匡为华

匡萌芽

冯海潮

钟辉英

杜华

冯宝兰

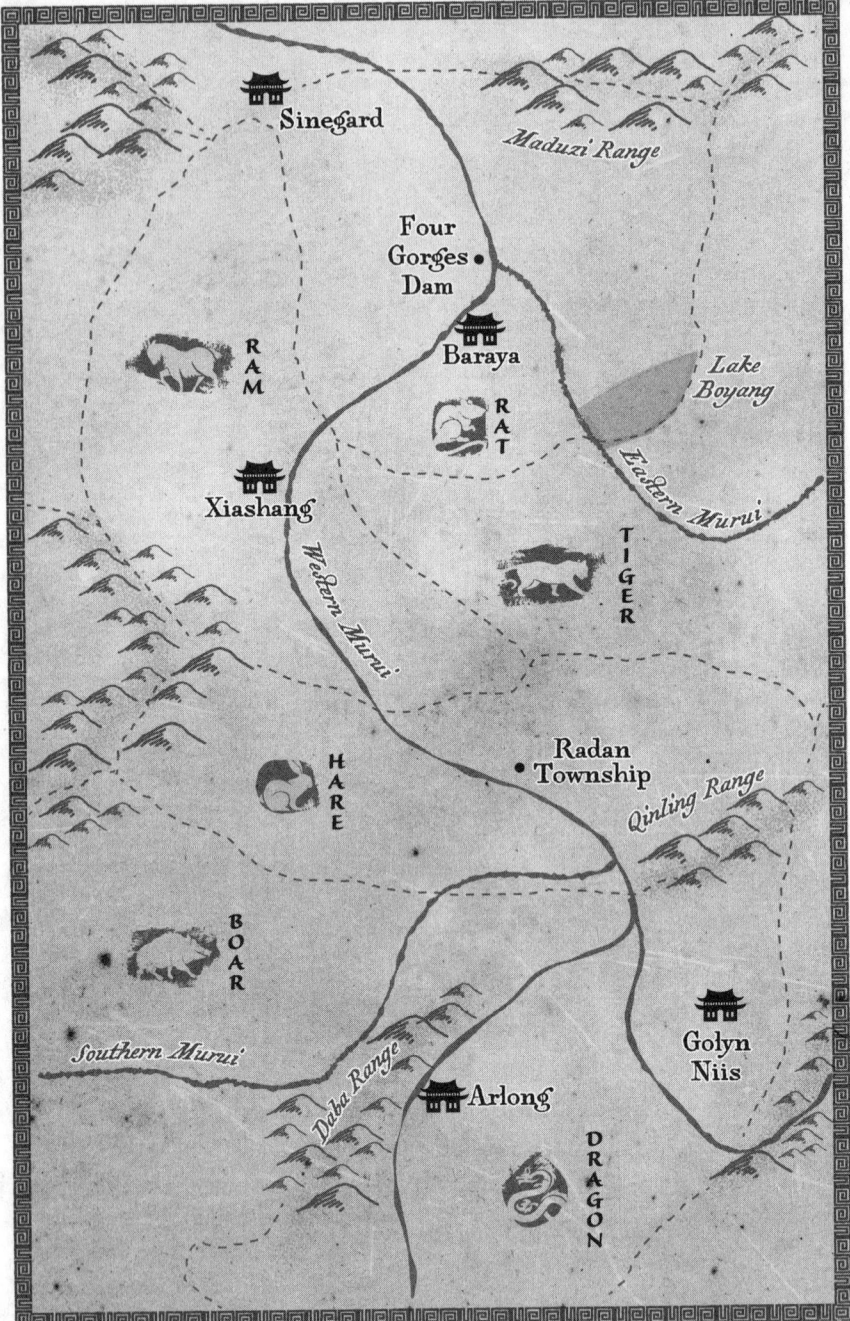

ARLONG, EIGHT YEARS PRIOR

"Come on," Mingzha begged. "Please, I want to see."

Nezha seized his brother by his chubby wrist and pulled him back from the shallows. "We're not allowed to go past the lily pads."

"But don't you want to know?" Mingzha whined.

Nezha hesitated. He, too, wanted to see what lay in the caves around the bend. The grottoes of the Nine Curves River had been mysteries to the Yin children since they were born. They'd grown up with warnings of dark, dormant evils concealed behind the cave mouths; of monsters that lurked inside, eager for foolish children to stumble into their jaws.

That alone would have been enough to entice the Yin children, all of whom were adventurous to a fault. But they'd heard rumors of great treasures, too; of underwater piles of pearls, jade, and gold. Nezha's Classics tutor had once told him that every piece of jewelry lost in the water inevitably wound up in those river grottoes. And sometimes, on a clear day, Nezha thought he could see the glimmer of sunlight on sparkling metal in the cave mouths from the window of his room.

He'd desperately wanted to explore those caves for years—and today would be the day to do it, when everyone was too busy to pay attention. But it was his responsibility to protect Mingzha. He'd never been trusted to watch his brother alone before; until today he'd always been too young. But this week Father was in the capital, Jinzha was at the Academy, Muzha was abroad at the Gray Towers in Hesperia, and the rest of the palace was so frazzled over Mother's sudden illness that the servants had hastily passed Mingzha into Nezha's arms and told them both to keep out of trouble. Nezha wanted to prove he was up to the task.

"Mingzha!"

His brother had wandered back into the shallows. Nezha cursed and dashed into the water behind him. How could a six-year-old move so quickly?

"Come *on*," Mingzha pleaded when Nezha grabbed him by the waist.

"We can't," Nezha said. "We'll get in trouble."

"Mother's been in bed all week. She won't find out." Mingzha twisted around in Nezha's grip and shot him an impish smile. "I won't tell. The servants won't tell. Will you?"

"You're a little demon," Nezha said.

"I just want to see the entrance." Mingzha beamed hopefully at him. "We don't have to go in. *Please?*"

Nezha relented. "We'll just go around the bend. We can look at the cave mouths from a distance. And then we're turning back, do you understand?"

Mingzha shouted with delight and splashed into the water. Nezha followed, stooping down to grab his brother's hand.

No one had ever been able to deny Mingzha anything. Who could? He was so fat and happy, a bouncing ball of giggles and delight, the absolute treasure of the palace. Father adored him. Jinzha and Muzha played with him whenever he wanted, and they never told him to get lost the way Jinzha had done so often to Nezha.

Mother doted on him most of all—perhaps because her other sons were destined to be soldiers, but she could keep Mingzha all to herself. She dressed him in finely embroidered silks and adorned him with so many lucky amulets of gold and jade that Mingzha clinked everywhere he walked, weighed down with the burden of good fortune. The palace servants liked to joke that they could always hear Mingzha before they saw him. Nezha wanted to make Mingzha stop to remove his jewelry now, worried it might drag him down under waves that already came up to his chest, but Mingzha charged forward like he was weightless.

"We're stopping here," Nezha said.

They'd gotten closer to the grottoes than they had ever been in their lives. The cave mouths were so dark inside that Nezha couldn't see more than two feet past the entrances, but their walls looked beautifully smooth, glimmering with a million different colors like fish scales.

"Look." Mingzha pointed at something in the water. "It's Father's cloak."

Nezha frowned. "What's Father's cloak doing at the bottom of the river?"

Yet the heavy garment lying half-buried in the sand was undeniably Yin Vaisra's. Nezha could see the crest of the dragon embroidered in silver thread against the rich cerulean-blue dye that only members of the House of Yin were permitted to wear.

Mingzha pointed to the closest grotto. "It came from in there."

An inexplicable, chilly dread crept through Nezha's veins. "Mingzha, get away from there."

"Why?" Mingzha, stubborn and fearless, waded closer to the cave.

The water began to ripple.

Nezha reached out to pull his brother back. "Mingzha, wait—"

Something enormous burst out of the water.

Nezha saw a huge dark shape—something muscled and coiled like a serpent—before a massive wave rose above him and slammed him facedown into the water.

The river shouldn't have been deep. The water had only come up to Nezha's waist and Mingzha's shoulders, had only been getting shallower the closer they moved to the grotto. But when

Nezha opened his eyes underwater, the surface seemed miles away, and the bottom of the grotto seemed as vast as the palace of Arlong itself.

He saw a pale green light shining from the grotto floor. He saw faces, beautiful, but eyeless. Human faces embedded in the sand and coral, and an endless mosaic studded with silver coins, porcelain vases, and golden ingots—a bed of treasures that stretched on and on into the grotto as far as the light went.

He saw a blink of movement, dark against the light, that disappeared as quickly as it came.

Something was wrong with the water here. Something had stretched and altered its dimensions. What should have been shallow and bright was deep; deep, dark, and terribly, hypnotically quiet.

Through the silence Nezha heard the faint sound of his brother screaming.

He kicked frantically for the surface. It seemed miles away.

When at last he emerged from the water, the shallows were mere shallows again.

Nezha wiped the river water from his eyes, gasping. "Mingzha?"

His brother was gone. Crimson streaks stained the river. Some of the streaks were solid, lumpy masses. Nezha knew what they were.

"*Mingzha?*"

The waters were quiet. Nezha stumbled to his knees and retched. Vomit mixed into bloodstained water.

He heard a clink against the rocks.

He looked down and saw a golden anklet.

Then he saw a dark shape rising before the grottoes, and heard a voice that came from nowhere and vibrated his very bones.

"Hello, little one."

Nezha screamed.

PART I

CHAPTER 1

Dawn saw the *Petrel* sail through swirling mist into the port city of Adlaga. Shattered by a storm of Federation soldiers during the Third Poppy War, port security still hadn't recovered and was almost nonexistent—especially for a supply ship flying Militia colors. The *Petrel* glided past Adlaga's port officers with little trouble and made berth as close to the city walls as it could get.

Rin propped herself up on the prow, trying to conceal the twitching in her limbs and to ignore the throbbing pain in her temples. She wanted opium terribly and couldn't have it. Today she needed her mind alert. Functioning. Sober.

The *Petrel* bumped against the dock. The Cike gathered on the upper deck, watching the gray skies with tense anticipation as the minutes trickled past.

Ramsa drummed his foot against the deck. "It's been an hour."

"Patience," Chaghan said.

"Could be that Unegen's run off," Baji said.

"He hasn't run off," Rin said. "He said he needed until noon."

"He'd also be the first to seize this chance to be rid of us," Baji said.

He had a point. Unegen, already the most skittish by far

among the Cike, had been complaining for days about their impending mission. Rin had sent him ahead overland to scope out their target in Adlaga. But the rendezvous window was quickly closing and Unegen hadn't shown.

"Unegen wouldn't dare," Rin said, and winced when the effort of speaking sent little stabs through the base of her skull. "He knows I'd hunt him down and skin him alive."

"Mm," Ramsa said. "Fox fur. I'd like a new scarf."

Rin turned her eyes back to the city. Adlaga made an odd corpse of a township, half-alive and half-destroyed. One side had emerged from the war intact; the other had been bombed so thoroughly that she could see building foundations poking up from blackened grass. The split appeared so even that half houses existed on the line: one side blackened and exposed, the other somehow teetering and groaning against the ocean winds, yet still standing.

Rin found it hard to imagine that anyone still lived in the township. If the Federation had been as thorough here as they'd been at Golyn Niis, then all that should be left were corpses.

At last a raven emerged from the blackened ruins. It circled the ship twice, then dove straight toward the *Petrel* as if locked on a target. Qara lifted a padded arm into the air. The raven pulled out of its dive and wrapped its talons around her wrist.

Qara ran the back of her index finger over the bird's head and down its spine. The raven ruffled its feathers as she brought its beak to her ear. Several seconds passed. Qara stood still with her eyes shut, listening intently to something the rest of them couldn't hear.

"Unegen's pinned Yuanfu," Qara said. "City hall, two hours."

"Guess you're not getting that scarf," Baji told Ramsa.

Chaghan yanked a sack out from under the deck and emptied its contents onto the planks. "Everyone get dressed."

Ramsa had come up with the idea to disguise themselves in stolen Militia uniforms. Uniforms were the one thing Moag hadn't been able to sell them, but they weren't hard to find. Rotting corpses lay in messy piles by the roadside in every abandoned coastal town, and it took only two trips to scavenge enough clothes that weren't burned or covered in blood.

Rin had to roll up the arms and legs of her uniform. Corpses of her stature were difficult to come by. She suppressed the urge to vomit as she laced on her boots. She'd pulled the shirt off a body wedged inside a half-burned funeral pyre, and three washes still couldn't conceal the smell of charred flesh under salty ocean water.

Ramsa, draped absurdly in a uniform three times his size, gave her a salute. "How do I look?"

She bent down to tie her boot laces. "Why are you wearing that?"

"Rin, please—"

"You're not coming."

"But I want to—"

"*You are not coming*," she repeated. Ramsa was a munitions genius, but he was also short, scrawny, and utterly worthless in a melee. She wasn't losing her only fire powder engineer because he didn't know how to wield a sword. "Don't make me tie you to the mast."

"Come on," Ramsa whined. "We've been on this ship for weeks, and I'm so fucking seasick just walking around makes me want to vomit—"

"Tough." Rin yanked a belt through the loops around her waist.

Ramsa pulled a handful of rockets from his pocket. "Will you set these off, then?"

Rin gave him a stern look. "I don't think you understand that we're not trying to blow Adlaga up."

"Oh, no, you just want to topple the local government, that's so much better."

"With minimal civilian casualties, which means we don't

need you." Rin reached out and tapped at the lone barrel leaning against the mast. "Aratsha, will you watch him? Make sure he doesn't get off the ship."

A blurry face, grotesquely transparent, emerged from the water. Aratsha spent most of his time in the water, spiriting the Cike's ships along to wherever they needed to go, and when he wasn't calling down his god he preferred to rest in his barrel. Rin had never seen his original human form. She wasn't sure he had one anymore.

Bubbles floated from Aratsha's mouth as he spoke. "If I must."

"Good luck," Ramsa muttered. "As if I couldn't outrun a fucking barrel."

Aratsha tilted his head at him. "Please be reminded that I could drown you in seconds."

Ramsa opened his mouth to retort, but Chaghan spoke over him. "Everyone take your pick." Steel clattered as he dumped out a chest of Militia weapons onto the deck. Baji, complaining loudly, traded his conspicuous nine-pointed rake for a standard infantry sword. Suni scooped up an Imperial halberd, but Rin knew the weapon was purely for show. Suni's specialty was bashing heads in with his shield-sized hands. He didn't need anything else.

Rin fastened a curved pirate scimitar to her waist. It wasn't Militia standard, but Militia swords were too heavy for her to wield. Moag's blacksmiths had fashioned her something lighter. She wasn't yet used to the grip, but she also doubted the day would end in a sword fight.

If things got so bad that she needed to get involved, then it would end in fire.

"Let's reiterate." Chaghan's pale eyes roved over the assembled Cike. "This is surgical. We have a single target. This is an assassination, not a battle. You will harm no civilians."

He looked pointedly at Rin.

She crossed her arms. "I know."

"Not even by accident."

"I *know*."

"Come off it," Baji said. "Since when did you get so high and mighty about casualties?"

"We've done enough harm to your people," said Chaghan.

"*You* did enough harm," Baji said. "I didn't break those dams."

Qara flinched at that, but Chaghan acted as if he hadn't heard a word. "We're finished hurting civilians. Am I understood?"

Rin jerked out a shrug. Chaghan liked to play commander, and she was rarely in a state to be bothered. He could boss them around all he liked. All she cared about was that they got this job done.

Three months. Twenty-nine targets, all killed without error. One more head in a sack, and then they'd be sailing north to assassinate their very last mark—the Empress Su Daji.

Rin felt a flush creep up her neck at the thought. Her palms grew dangerously hot.

Not now. Not yet. She took a deep breath. Then another one, more desperate, when the heat only extended through her torso.

Baji clamped a hand on her shoulder. "You all right?"

She exhaled slowly. Made herself count backward from ten, and then up to forty-nine by odd numbers, and then back down by prime numbers. Altan had taught her that trick, and it mostly worked, at least when she took care not to think about Altan when she did it. The fever flush receded. "I'm fine."

"And you're sober?" Baji asked.

"*Yes*," she said stiffly.

Baji didn't take his hand off her shoulder. "You're sure? Because—"

"I've *got this*," she snapped. "Let's go gut this bastard."

Three months ago, after the Cike had first sailed out from the Isle of Speer, they'd faced a bit of a dilemma.

Namely, they had nowhere to go.

They knew they couldn't return to the mainland. Ramsa had pointed out, quite astutely, that if the Empress had been willing to sell the Cike out to Federation scientists, then she wouldn't be happy to see them alive and free. A quick, furtive supply trip to a tiny coastal city in Snake Province confirmed their suspicions. All of their faces were plastered on the village post boards. They'd been named as war criminals. Bounties were out for their arrest—five hundred Imperial silvers dead, six hundred alive.

They'd stolen as many crates of provisions as they could and hurried out of Snake Province before anyone saw them.

Back in Omonod Bay, they'd debated their options. The only thing they could all agree on was that they needed to kill the Empress Su Daji—the Vipress, the last of the Trifecta, and the traitor who had sold her nation to the Federation.

But they were nine people—eight, without Kitay—against the most powerful woman in the Empire and the combined forces of the Imperial Militia. They'd had few supplies, only the weapons they carried on their backs and a stolen skimmer so banged up that they spent half their time bailing water out of the lower decks.

So they'd sailed down south, past Snake Province into Rooster territory, tracing the coastline until they reached the port city Ankhiluun. There they had come into the employ of the Pirate Queen Moag.

Rin had never met anyone she respected as much as she did Moag—the Stone Bitch, the Lying Widow, and the ruthless ruler of Ankhiluun. She was a consort-turned-pirate who went from Lady to Queen when she murdered her husband, and she'd been running Ankhiluun as an illegal enclave of foreign trade for years. She'd skirmished with the Trifecta during the Second Poppy War, and she'd been fending off the Empress's scouts ever since.

She was more than happy to help the Cike rid her of Daji for good.

In return, she demanded thirty heads. The Cike had returned twenty-nine. Most had been low-level smugglers, captains, and mercenaries. Moag's primary income stream came from contraband opium imports, and she liked to keep her eye out for opium dealers who didn't play by her rules—or at least line her pockets.

The thirtieth mark would be harder. Today Rin and the Cike intended to topple Adlaga's local government.

Moag had been trying to break into the Adlaga market for years. The little coastal city didn't offer much, but its civilians, many with lingering addictions to opiates since the days of Federation occupation, would gladly spend their life savings on Ankhiluuni imports. Adlaga had held out against Moag's aggressive opium trade for the past two decades only because of a particularly vigilant city magistrate, Yang Yuanfu, and his administration.

Moag wanted Yang Yuanfu dead. The Cike specialized in assassination. They were a matchmaker's dream.

Three months. Twenty-nine heads. Just one more job and they'd have silver, ships, and enough soldiers to distract the Imperial Guard long enough for Rin to march up to Daji and wrap flaming fingers around her throat.

If port security was lax, wall defense was nonexistent. The Cike passed through Adlaga's walls with no interference—which wasn't hard to do, considering the Federation had blown great holes all across the boundary and none of them were guarded.

Unegen met them behind the gates.

"We picked a good day for murder," he said as he guided them into the alleyway. "Yuanfu's due in the city square at noon for a war commemoration ceremony. He'll be out in broad daylight, and we can pick him off from the alleys without showing our faces."

Unlike Aratsha, Unegen preferred his human form when he wasn't calling down the shape-shifting powers of the fox spirit. But Rin had always sensed something distinctly vulpine in the way he carried himself. Unegen was both crafty and easily startled; his narrow eyes were always darting from side to side, tracking all of his possible escape routes.

"So we've got what, two hours?" Rin asked.

"A little over. There's a warehouse a few blocks down from

here that's fairly empty," he said. "We can hunker down to wait in there. Then, ah, we split pretty easily if things go south."

Rin turned toward the Cike, considering.

"We'll take the corners of the square when Yuanfu shows up," she decided. "Suni in the southwest. Baji northwest, and I'll take the northeast."

"Diversions?" Baji asked.

"No." Normally diversions were a fantastic idea, and Rin loved assigning Suni to wreak as much havoc as possible while she or Baji darted in to slit their target's throat, but during a public ceremony the risk to civilians was too great. "We'll let Qara take the first shot. The rest of us clear a path back to the ship if they put up resistance."

"Are we still trying to pretend we're normal mercenaries?" Suni asked.

"Might as well," Rin said. They'd done a decent job so far of concealing the extent of their abilities, or at least silencing anyone who would spread rumors. Daji didn't know the Cike were coming for her. The longer she believed them dead, the better. "We're dealing with a better opponent than usual, though, so do what you need to. At the end of the day, we want a head in a bag."

She took a breath and ran the plan once more through her mind, considering.

This would work. This was going to be fine.

Strategizing with the Cike was like playing a chess game in which she had several massively overpowered, unpredictable, and bizarre pieces. Aratsha commanded the waters. Suni and Baji were berserkers, capable of leveling entire squadrons without breaking a sweat. Unegen could transform into a fox. Qara not only communed with birds, she could shoot out a peacock's eye from a hundred meters away. And Chaghan . . . she wasn't quite sure what Chaghan did, other than irritate her at every possible turn, but he seemed capable of making people lose their minds.

All of them combined against a single township official and his guards seemed like overkill.

But Yang Yuanfu was used to assassination attempts. You had to be, if you were one of the few uncorrupt officials left in the Empire. He shielded himself with a squadron of the most battle-hardy men in the province wherever he went.

Rin knew, based on Moag's reports, that Yang Yuanfu had survived at least thirteen assassination attempts over the past fifteen years. His guards were well accustomed to treachery. To get past them, you'd need fighters of unnatural ability. You needed overkill.

Once inside the warehouse, the Cike had nothing to do but wait. Unegen kept watch by the slats in the wall, twitching continuously. Chaghan and Qara sat with their backs against the wall, silent. Suni and Baji stood slouched, arms crossed casually as if simply waiting for their dinners.

Rin paced the room, focusing on her breathing and trying to ignore the twinges of pain in her temples.

She counted thirty hours since she'd ingested any opium. That was longer than she'd gone for weeks. She twisted her hands together as she walked, trying to force the twitching to go away.

It didn't help. It didn't stop the headache, either.

Fuck.

At first she'd thought she only needed the opium for the grief. She thought she would smoke it for the relief, until the memories of Speer and Altan dulled to a faint ache, until she could function without the suffocating guilt of what she'd done.

She thought *guilt* must be the word for it. The irrational feeling, not the moral concept. Because she'd told herself she wasn't sorry, that the Mugenese deserved what they got and that she was never looking back. Except the memory loomed like a gaping chasm in her mind where she'd tossed in every human feeling that threatened her.

But the abyss kept calling for her to look in. To fall inside.

And the Phoenix didn't want to let her forget. The Phoenix wanted her to gloat about it. The Phoenix lived on rage, and rage was intricately tied to the past. So the Phoenix needed to claw apart the open wounds in her mind and set fire to them, day after day, because that gave her memories and those memories fueled the rage.

Without opium the visions flashed constantly through Rin's mind's eye, often more vivid than her surrounding reality.

Sometimes they were of Altan. More times they weren't. The Phoenix was a conduit to generations of memories. Thousands upon thousands of Speerlies had prayed to the god in their grief and desperation. And the god had collected their suffering, stored it, and turned it into flames.

The memories could also be deceptively calm. Sometimes Rin saw brown-skinned children running up and down a pristine white beach. She saw flames burning higher on the shore—not funeral pyres, not flames of destruction, but campfires. Bonfires. Hearth fires, warm and sustaining.

And sometimes she saw the Speerlies, enough of them to fill a thriving village. She was always amazed by how *many* of them there were, an entire race of people that sometimes she feared she'd only dreamed up. If the Phoenix lingered, then Rin could even catch fragments of conversations in a language she almost understood, could see glimpses of faces that she almost recognized.

They weren't the ferocious beasts of Nikara lore. They weren't the mindless warriors the Red Emperor had needed them to be and every subsequent regime had forced them to be. They loved and laughed and cried around their fires. They were *people*.

But every time, before Rin could sink into the memory of a heritage she didn't have, she saw on the fading horizon boats sailing in from the Federation naval base on the mainland.

What happened next was a haze of colors, accumulated perspectives that shifted too fast for Rin to follow. Shouts, screams, movement. Rows and rows of Speerlies lined up on the beach, weapons in hand.

But it was never enough. To the Federation, they must have

seemed savages, using sticks to fight gods, and the booms of cannon fire lit up the village as quickly as if someone had held a light to kindling.

Gas pellets launched from the tower ships with terribly innocent popping noises. Where they hit the ground they expelled huge, thick clouds of acrid yellow smoke.

Women fell. Children twitched. The warrior ranks broke. The gas did not kill immediately; its inventors were not so kind.

Then the butchering began. The Federation fired continuously and indiscriminately. Mugenese crossbows could shoot three bolts at a time, unleashing an unceasing barrage of metal that ripped open necks, skulls, limbs, hearts.

Spilled blood traced marble patterns into white sand. Bodies lay still where they fell. At dawn, the Federation generals marched to the shore, boots treading indifferently over crushed bodies, advancing to slam their flag into the bloodstained sand.

"We've got a problem," Baji said.

Rin snapped back to attention. "What?"

"Take a look."

She heard the sudden sound of jangling bells—a happy sound, utterly out of place in this ruined city. She pressed her face to a gap in the warehouse slats. A cloth dragon bobbed up and down through the crowd, held up on tent poles by dancers below. Dancers waving streamers and ribbons followed behind, accompanied by musicians and government officials lifted on bright red sedan chairs. Behind them was the crowd.

"You said it was a small ceremony," Rin said. "Not a fucking parade."

"It was quiet just an hour ago," Unegen insisted.

"And now the whole township's clustering in that square." Baji squinted through the slats. "Are we still going by that 'no civilian casualties' rule?"

"Yes," Chaghan said before Rin could answer.

"You're no fun," Baji said.

"Crowds make targeted assassinations easier," Chaghan said. "It's a better opportunity to get in close. Make your hit without being spotted, then filter out before his guards have time to react."

Rin opened her mouth to say *That's still a lot of witnesses*, but the withdrawal cramps hit her first. A wave of pain tore through her muscles; it started in her gut and flared out, so sudden that for a moment the world turned black, and all she could do was clutch her chest, gasping.

"Are you all right?" Baji asked.

A wave of bile rose up in her throat before she could respond. She heaved. A second swell of nausea racked her gut. Then a third.

Baji put a hand on her shoulder. "Rin?"

"I'm *fine*," she insisted for what seemed like the thousandth time.

She wasn't fine. Her head was throbbing again, and this time the pain was accompanied by a nausea that seized her rib cage and didn't let go until she was doubled over on her knees, whimpering.

Vomit splattered the floor.

"Change of plans," Chaghan said. "Rin, get back to the ship."

She wiped her mouth. "No."

"I'm telling you you're not in any state to be useful."

"And I'm your commander," she said. "So shut up and do as I say."

Chaghan's eyes narrowed. The warehouse fell silent.

Rin had been wrestling Chaghan for control over the Cike for months. He questioned her decisions at every turn; he took every chance he could to make it very clear that he thought Altan had made a stupid decision naming her commander.

And Rin knew, in all fairness, he was right.

She was dreadful at leadership. Most of her attack plans over the past three months had boiled down to "everyone attack at once and see if we come out all right on the other side."

But command ability aside, she had to be here. Had to see Adlaga through. Since they'd left Speer her withdrawals had only been getting worse and worse. She'd been mostly functional during their first few missions for Moag. Then the endless killings, the screams, and the flashbacks to the battlefield kept setting her anger off again and again until she was spending more hours of the day high than she did sober, and even when she *was* sober she felt like she was still teetering on the brink of madness because the fucking Phoenix never shut up.

She needed to pull herself back from the precipice. If she couldn't do this basic, simple task; couldn't kill some township official who wasn't even a shaman, then she would hardly be able to stand up to the Empress.

And she couldn't lose her chance at revenge. Revenge was the only thing she had.

"Don't you jeopardize this," Chaghan said.

"Don't you patronize me," she retorted.

Chaghan sighed and turned to Unegen. "Can you watch her? I'll give you laudanum."

"I thought I was supposed to return to the ship," Unegen said.

"Change of plans."

"Fine." Unegen twitched out a shrug. "If I have to."

"Come on," Rin said. "I don't need a wet nurse."

"You'll wait in the corner of the crowd," Chaghan ordered, ignoring her. "You won't leave Unegen's side. You'll both act as reinforcements, and barring that, you will be the last resort."

She scowled. "Chaghan—"

"The *last resort*," he repeated. "You've killed enough innocents."

The hour came. The Cike dissipated, darting out of the warehouse to join the moving crowd one by one.

Rin and Unegen blended into Adlaga's masses easily enough. The main streets were packed with civilians, all caught up in their own miseries, and so many noises and sights came from all directions that Rin, unsure of where to look, couldn't help but feel a constant state of mild panic.

A wildly discordant mash of gongs and war drums drowned out the lute music from the front of the parade. Merchants hawked their wares every time they turned a corner, screaming prices with the sort of urgency that she associated with evacuation warnings. Celebratory red confetti littered the streets, tossed out in handfuls by children and entertainers, a snowfall of red paper flecks that covered every surface.

"How do they have the funds for this?" Rin muttered. "The Federation left them starving."

"Aid from Sinegard," Unegen guessed. "End-of-war celebration funds. Keeps them happy, keeps them loyal."

Rin saw food everywhere she looked. Huge cubes of watermelon on sticks. Red bean buns. Stalls selling soup dumplings dripping with soy sauce and lotus seed tarts lined the streets. Merchants flipped egg cakes with deft movements, and the crackle of oil under any other circumstances would make her hungry, but now the pungent smells only made her stomach turn.

It seemed both unfair and impossible that there could be such an abundance of food. Just days ago they had sailed past people who were drowning their babies in river mud because that was a quicker and more merciful death than letting them slowly starve.

If all this came from Sinegard, then that meant the Imperial bureaucracy had possessed food stores like this the entire time. Why had they withheld it during the war?

If the people of Adlaga were asking that same question, they didn't show it. Everyone looked so *happy*. Faces relaxed in simple relief because the war was over, the Empire was victorious, and they were safe.

And that made Rin furious.

She'd always had trouble with anger, she knew that. At Sinegard she'd constantly acted in furious, impulsive bursts and dealt with the consequences later. But now the anger was permanent, an unspeakable fury imposed upon her that she could neither contain nor control.

But she also didn't want to make it stop. The anger was a shield. The anger helped her to keep from remembering what she'd done.

Because as long as she was *angry*, then it was okay—she'd acted within reason. She was afraid that if she stopped being angry, she might crack apart.

She tried to distract herself by scanning the crowd for Yang Yuanfu and his guards. Tried to focus on the task at hand.

Her god wouldn't let her.

Kill them, encouraged the Phoenix. *They don't deserve their happiness. They didn't fight.*

She had a sudden vision of the marketplace on fire. She shook her head frantically, trying to tune out the Phoenix's voice. "No, stop . . ."

Make them burn.

Heat flared up in her palms. Her gut twisted. No—not here, not now. She squeezed her eyes shut.

Turn them to ash.

Her heartbeat began to quicken; her vision narrowed to a pinprick and expanded again. She felt feverish. The crowd suddenly seemed full of enemies. In one instant everyone was a blue-uniformed Federation soldier, bearing weapons; and in another they were civilians once again. She took a deep, choking breath, trying to force air into her lungs, eyes squeezed shut while she willed the red haze to go away once more.

This time it wouldn't.

The laughter, the music, the smiling faces standing around her all made her want to scream.

How dare they live when Altan was dead? It seemed horrifically unfair that life could keep on going and these people could be celebrating a war that they hadn't won for themselves, when they hadn't suffered for it . . .

The heat in her hands intensified.

Unegen seized her by the shoulder. "I thought you had your shit under control."

She jumped and spun around. "*I do!*" she hissed. Too loud. The people around her backed away from her.

Unegen pulled her toward the edge of the crowd, into the safety of the shadows under Adlaga's ruins. "You're drawing attention."

"I'm *fine*, Unegen, just let go—"

He didn't. "You need to calm down."

"I know—"

"No. I mean *right now*." He nodded over her shoulder. "She's here."

Rin turned.

And there sat the Empress, borne like a bride on a palanquin of red silk.

CHAPTER 2

The last time Rin had encountered the Empress Su Daji, she had been burning with fever, too delirious to see anything but Daji's face—lovely, hypnotic, with skin like porcelain and eyes like moth's wings.

The Empress was just as arresting as ever. Everyone Rin knew had emerged from the Mugenese invasion looking a decade older, jaded and scarred, but the Empress was as pale, ageless, and unmarked as ever, as if she existed on some transcendent plane untouchable by mortals.

Rin's breath quickened.

Daji wasn't supposed to be here.

It wasn't supposed to happen like this.

Images of Daji's body flashed through her mind. Head cracked against white marble. Pale neck sliced open. Body charred to nothing—but she wouldn't have burned immediately. Rin wanted to do it slowly, wanted to relish it.

A slow cheer went up through the crowd.

The Empress leaned out through the curtains and raised a hand so white it nearly glimmered in the sunlight. She smiled.

"We are victorious," she called out. "We have survived."

Anger flared inside Rin, so thick she almost choked on it. She felt like her body was covered with ant bites that she couldn't scratch at—a kind of frustration bubbling inside her, just begging her to let it explode.

How could the Empress be alive? The sheer contradiction infuriated her, the fact that Altan and Master Irjah and so many others were dead and Daji looked like she'd never even been wounded. She was the head of a nation that had bled millions to a senseless invasion—an invasion *she'd* invited—and she looked like she'd just arrived for a banquet.

Rin barged forward.

Unegen immediately dragged her back. "What are you doing?"

"What do you think?" Rin wrenched her arms out of his grip. "I'm going to get her. Go rally the others, I'll need backup—"

"Are you crazy?"

"She's *right there*! We'll never get a shot this good again!"

"Then let Qara do it."

"Qara doesn't have a clear shot," Rin hissed. Qara's station in the ruined bell towers was too high up. She couldn't get an arrow through—not past the carriage windows, not past this crowd. Inside the palanquin Daji was shielded on all sides; shots from the front would be blocked by the guards standing right before her.

And Rin was more concerned that Qara *wouldn't* shoot. She'd certainly seen the Empress by now, but she might be afraid to fire into a crowd of civilians, or to give away the Cike's location before any of them had a clear shot. Qara might have decided to be prudent.

Rin didn't care for prudence. The universe had delivered her this chance. She could end this all in minutes.

The Phoenix strained at her consciousness, eager and impatient. *Come now, child . . . Let me . . .*

She dug her fingernails into her palms. *Not yet.*

Too much distance separated her from the Empress. If she lit up now, everyone in the square was dead.

She wished desperately that she had better control over the fire. Or any control at all. But the Phoenix was antithetical to control.

The Phoenix wanted a roaring, chaotic blaze, consuming everything around her as far as the eye could see.

And when she called the god she couldn't tell her own desire apart from the Phoenix's; its desire, and her desire, was a death drive that demanded more to feed its fire.

She tried to think of something else, anything other than rage and revenge. But when she looked at the Empress, all she saw were flames.

Daji looked up. Her eyes locked on to Rin's. She lifted a hand and waved.

Rin froze. She couldn't look away. Daji's eyes became windows became memories became smoke, fire, corpses, and bones, and Rin felt herself falling, falling into a black ocean where all she could see was Altan as a human beacon igniting himself on a pier.

Daji's lips curved into a cruel smile.

Then the firecrackers set off behind Rin without warning—*pop-pop-pop*—and Rin's heart almost burst out of her chest.

Suddenly she was shrieking, hands pressed to her ears while her entire body shook.

"It's fireworks!" Unegen hissed. He dragged her wrists away from her head. "Just fireworks."

But that didn't mean anything—she *knew* they were fireworks, but that was a rational thought, and rational thoughts didn't matter when she shut her eyes and saw with every blast of sound explosions bursting behind her eyelids, flailing limbs, screaming children—

She saw a man dangling from the floorboards of a building that had been rent apart, trying to hold on with slippery fingers to slanting wooden planks to not fall into the flaming spears of timber below. She saw men and women plastered to the walls, dusted over with faint white powder so she might have thought they were statues if she couldn't see the dark shadow of blood in an outline all around them—

Too many people. She was trapped by too many people. She sank to her knees, face buried in her hands. The last time she'd been inside a crowd of people like this they'd been stampeding away from the horror of the inner city of Khurdalain—her eyes shot up and darted around, searching for escape routes, and found none, just unending walls of bodies packed together.

Too much. Too many sights, the information—her mind collapsed in on itself; bursts and flickers of fire emitted from her shoulders and exploded in the air above her, which just made her tremble harder.

And there were still *so many people*—they were crammed together, a teeming mass of outstretched arms, a nameless and faceless entity that wanted to tear her apart—

Thousands, hundreds of thousands—and you wiped them out of existence, you burned them in their beds—

"Rin, *stop*!" Unegen shouted.

It didn't matter, though. The crowd had formed a wide berth around her. Mothers dragged their children back. Veterans pointed and exclaimed.

She looked down. Smoke furled out from every part of her.

Daji's litter had disappeared. She'd been spirited to safety, no doubt; Rin's presence had been a glaring warning beacon. A line of Imperial guards pushed through the crowded street toward them, shields raised, spears pointed directly at Rin.

"Oh, fuck," Unegen said.

Rin backed away unsteadily, palms held out before her as if they belonged to a stranger. Someone else's fingers sparking with fire. Someone else's will dragging the Phoenix into this world.

Burn them.

Fire pulsed inside her. She could feel the veins straining behind her eyes. The pressure shot little stabs of pain behind her head, made her vision burst and pop.

Kill them.

The guard captain shouted an order. The Militia stormed her. Then her defensive instincts kicked in, and she lost all self-control. She heard a deafening silence in her mind, then a high, keening noise, the victorious cackle of a god that knew it had won.

When she finally looked at Unegen she didn't see a man, she saw a charred corpse, a white skeleton glistening over flesh sloughing away; she saw him decompose to ash within seconds and she was struck by how *clean* that ash was; so infinitely preferable to the complicated mess of bones and flesh that made him up now . . .

"Stop it!"

She heard not a scream, but a whimpering beg. For a split second Unegen's face flickered through the ash.

She was killing him. She knew she was killing him, and she couldn't stop.

She couldn't even move her own limbs. She stood immobile, fire roaring out of her extremities, holding her still like she'd been encased in stone.

Burn him, said the Phoenix.

"No, stop—"

This is what you want.

It wasn't what she wanted. But it wouldn't stop. Why would the Phoenix's gift include any inkling of control? It was an appetite that only strengthened; the fire consumed and wanted to consume more, and Mai'rinnen Tearza had warned her about this once but she hadn't listened and now Unegen was going to die. . . .

Something heavy clamped over her mouth. She tasted laudanum. Thick, sweet, and cloying. Panic and relief warred in her head as she choked and struggled, but Chaghan just squeezed the soaked cloth harder over her face as her chest heaved.

The ground swooped under her feet. She loosed a muffled shriek.

"Breathe," Chaghan ordered. "Shut up. Just breathe."

She choked against the sick and familiar smell; Enki had made this for her so many times. She fought not to struggle; pushed down her natural instincts—she had ordered them to do this, this was *supposed* to happen.

That didn't make it any easier to take.

Her legs buckled beneath her. Her shoulders sagged. She swooned into Chaghan's side.

He dragged her upright, slung her arm over his shoulder, and helped her toward the stairs. Smoke billowed in their path; the heat didn't affect Rin, but she could see Chaghan's hair curling, crinkling black at the edges.

"*Fuck*," he muttered under his breath.

"Where's Unegen?" she mumbled.

"He's fine, he'll be fine. . . ."

She wanted to insist on seeing him, but her tongue felt too heavy to form words. Her knees gave way entirely, but she didn't feel herself fall. The sedative worked its way through her bloodstream, and the world was a light and airy place, a fairy's domain. She heard someone yell. She felt someone lift her and place her on the bottom of the sampan.

She managed a last look over her shoulder.

On the horizon, the entire port town was lit up like a beacon—lamps illuminated on every deck, bells and smoke signals going up in the glowing air.

Every Imperial sentry could see that warning.

Rin had learned the standard Militia codes. She knew what those signals meant. They'd announced a manhunt for traitors to the throne.

"Congratulations," Chaghan said. "You've brought the entire Militia down on our backs."

"What are we going to—" Her tongue lolled heavy in her mouth. She'd lost the capacity to form words.

He put a hand on her shoulder and shoved. "Get down."

She tumbled gracelessly into the space under the seats. She opened her eyes wide to see the wooden base of the boat inches from her nose, so close she could count the grains. The lines along the wood swirled into ink images, which she tilted into, and then the ink assumed colors and became a world of red and black and orange.

The chasm opened. That was the only time it could—when she was high out of her mind, too out of control to stay away from the one thing she refused to let herself think about.

She was flying over the longbow island, she was watching the fire mountain erupt, streams of molten lava pouring over the peak, rushing in rivulets toward the cities below.

She saw the lives crushed out, burned and flattened and transformed to smoke in an instant. And it was so easy, like blowing out a candle, like crushing a moth under her finger; she wanted it and it happened; she had willed it like a god.

As long as she remembered it from that detached, bird's-eye view, she felt no guilt. She felt rather remotely curious, as if she had set an anthill on fire, as if she had impaled a beetle on a knife tip.

There was no guilt in killing insects, only the lovely, childish curiosity of seeing them writhe in their dying throes.

This wasn't a memory or a vision; this was an illusion she had conjured for herself, the illusion she returned to every time she lost control and they sedated her.

She wanted to see it—she *needed* to dance at the edge of this memory that she did not have, skirting between the godlike cold indifference of a murderer and the crippling guilt of the deed. She played with her guilt the way a child holds his palm to a candle flame, daring to venture just close enough to feel the stabbing licks of pain.

It was mental self-flagellation, the equivalent of digging a nail into an open sore. She knew the answer, of course, she just couldn't admit it to anyone—that at the moment she sank the island, the moment she became a murderer, she had wanted it.

"Is she all right?" Ramsa's voice. "Why is she laughing?"

Chaghan's voice. "She'll be fine."

Yes, Rin wanted to shout, yes, she was fine; just dreaming, just caught between this world and the next, just enraptured by the illusions of what she had done. She rolled around on the bottom of the sampan and giggled until the laughter turned to loud, harsh sobs, and then she cried until she couldn't see anymore.

CHAPTER 3

"Wake up."

Someone pinched her arm, hard. Rin bolted upright. Her right hand reached to a belt that wasn't there for a knife that was in the other room, and her left hand slammed blindly sideways into—

"Fuck!" Chaghan shouted.

She focused with difficulty on his face. He backed up, hands held out before her to show that he held no weapons, just a washcloth.

Rin's fingers moved frantically over her neck and wrists. She knew she wasn't tied down, she *knew*, but still she had to check.

Chaghan rubbed ruefully at his rapidly bruising cheek.

Rin didn't apologize for hitting him. He knew better than that. All of them knew better than that. They knew not to touch her without asking. Not to approach her from behind. Not to make sudden movements or sounds around her unless they wanted to end up a stick of charcoal floating to the bottom of Omonod Bay.

"How long have I been out?" She gagged. Her mouth tasted like something had died in it; her tongue was as dry as if she had spent hours licking at a wooden board.

"Couple of days," Chaghan said. "Good job getting out of bed."

"*Days?*"

He shrugged. "Messed up the dosage, I think. At least it didn't kill you."

Rin rubbed at dry eyes. Bits of hardened mucus came off the sides of her eyes in clumps. She caught a glimpse of her face in her bedside mirror. Her pupils weren't red—they took a while to adjust back every time she'd been on any kind of opiates—but the whites of her eyes were bloodshot, full of angry veins thick and sprawling like cobwebs.

Memories seeped slowly into the forefront of her mind, fighting through the fog of laudanum to sort themselves out. She squeezed her eyes shut, trying to separate what had happened from what she'd dreamed. A sick feeling pooled in her gut as slowly, her thoughts formed into questions. "Where's Unegen . . . ?"

"You burned over half his body. Nearly killed him." Chaghan's clipped tone spared her no sympathy. "We couldn't bring him with us, so Enki stayed behind to look after him. And they're, ah, not coming back."

Rin blinked several times, trying to make the world around her less blurry. Her head swam, disorienting her terribly every time she moved. "What? Why?"

"Because they've left the Cike."

That took several seconds to sink in.

"But—but they *can't*." Panic rose in her chest, thick and constricting. Enki was their only physician, and Unegen their best spy. Without them the Cike were reduced to six.

She couldn't kill the Empress with six people.

"You really can't blame them," Chaghan said.

"But they're *sworn*!"

"They swore to Tyr. They were sworn to Altan. They have no obligation to an incompetent like you." Chaghan cocked his head. "I suppose I don't have to tell you that Daji got away."

Rin glared at him. "I thought you were on my side."

"I said I'd help you kill Su Daji," he said. "I didn't say I'd hold your hand while you threatened the lives of everyone on this ship."

"But the others—" A sudden fear seized her. "They're still with me, aren't they? They're loyal?"

"It's nothing to do with loyalty," he said. "They are terrified."

"Of me?"

"You really can't see past yourself, can you?" Chaghan's lip curled. "They're terrified of themselves. It's very lonely to be a shaman in this Empire, especially when you don't know when you're going to lose your mind."

"I know. I understand that."

"You don't understand *anything*. They aren't afraid of going mad. They *know* they will. They know that soon they will become like Feylen. Prisoners inside their own bodies. And when that day comes, they want to be around the only other people who could put an end to it. *That's* why they're still here."

The Cike culls the Cike, Altan had once told her. *The Cike takes care of its own.*

That meant they defended one another. It also meant they protected the world from one another. The Cike were like children playing at acrobatics, perched precariously against one another, relying on the rest to stop them from hurtling into the abyss.

"Your duty as commander is to protect them," Chaghan said. "They are with you because they are scared, and they don't know where else they can go. But you're endangering them with every stupid decision you make and your utter lack of control."

Rin moaned, clutching her head between her hands. Every word was like a knife to her eardrums. She knew she'd fucked up, but Chaghan seemed to take inordinate delight in rubbing it in. "Just leave me alone."

"No. Get out of bed and stop being such a brat."

"Chaghan, please—"

"You're a fucking mess."

"I know that."

"Yes, you've known that since Speer, but you're not getting better, you're getting worse. You're trying to fix everything with opium and it's destroying you."

"I *know*," she whispered. "I just—it's always *there*, it's screaming in my mind—"

"Then control it."

"I *can't*."

"Why not?" He made a noise of disgust. "Altan did."

"But I'm not Altan." She couldn't hold back her tears. "Is that what you wanted to tell me? I'm not as strong as him, I'm not as smart as him, I can't do what he could do—"

He laughed harshly. "Oh, that much is clear."

"*You* take command then. You act like you're in charge already, why don't you just take the post? I don't fucking care."

"Because Altan named you commander," he said simply. "And between us, at least I know how to respect his legacy."

That shut her up.

He leaned forward. "That burden's on you. So you will learn to control yourself, and you will start protecting them."

"But what if that's not possible?" she asked.

His pale eyes didn't blink. "Frankly? Then you should kill yourself."

Rin had no idea how to respond to that.

"If you think you can't beat it, then you should die," Chaghan said. "Because it will corrode you. It will turn your body into a conduit, and it will burn down everything until it's not just civilians, not just Unegen, but everyone around you, everything you've ever loved or cared about.

"And once you've turned your world to ash, you'll *wish* you could die."

She found the others in the mess once she finally recovered the physical coordination to make her way down the passageway without tripping.

"What is this?" Ramsa spat something onto the table. "Bird droppings?"

"Goji berries," Baji said. "You don't like them in porridge?"

"They've got mold on them."

"Everything's got mold on them."

"But I thought we were getting new supplies," Ramsa whined.

"With what money?" Suni asked.

"We are the *Cike*!" Ramsa exclaimed. "We could have stolen something!"

"Well, it's not like—" Baji broke off as he saw Rin standing in the doorway. Ramsa and Suni followed his gaze. They fell silent.

She stared back at them, utterly lost for words. She'd thought she knew what she was going to say to them. Now she only wanted to cry.

"Rise and shine," Ramsa said finally. He kicked a chair out for her. "Hungry? You look horrific."

She blinked at him. Her words came out in a hoarse whisper. "I just wanted to say . . ."

"Don't," said Baji.

"But I just—"

"*Don't*," Baji said. "I know it's hard. You'll get it eventually. Altan did."

Suni nodded in silent agreement.

Rin's urge to cry grew stronger.

"Have a seat," Ramsa said gently. "Eat something."

She shuffled to the counter and tried clumsily to fill a bowl. Porridge slopped out of the ladle onto the deck. She walked toward the table, but the floor kept shifting under her feet. She collapsed into the chair, breathing hard.

No one commented.

She glanced out the porthole. They were moving startlingly fast over choppy waters. The shoreline was nowhere in sight. A wave rolled under the planks, and she stifled the attendant swell of nausea.

"Did we at least get Yang Yuanfu?" she asked after a pause.

Baji nodded. "Suni took him out during the commotion. Bashed his head against the wall and flung his body into the ocean while his guards were too busy with Daji to fend us off. I guess the diversion tactic worked after all. We were going to tell you, but you were, ah, incapacitated."

"High out of your mind," Ramsa supplied. "Giggling at the floor."

"I get it," Rin said. "And we're heading back to Ankhiluun now?"

"As fast as we can. We've got the entire Imperial Guard chasing us, but I doubt they'll follow us into Moag's territory."

"Makes sense," Rin murmured. She worked her spoon through the porridge. Ramsa was right about the mold. The greenish-black blotches were so large that they almost rendered the entire thing inedible. Her stomach roiled. She pushed the bowl away.

The others sat around the table, fidgeting, blinking, and making eye contact with everything except her.

"I heard Enki and Unegen left," she said.

The statement was met with blank stares and shrugs.

She took a deep breath. "So I suppose—what I wanted to say was—"

Baji interrupted before she could continue. "We're not going anywhere."

"But you—"

"I don't like being lied to. And I especially hate being sold. Daji has what's coming for her. I'm seeing this through to the end, little Speerly. You don't have to worry about desertion from me."

Rin glanced around the table. "Then what about the rest of you?"

"Altan deserved better than he got," Suni said simply, as if that much sufficed.

"But you don't have to stay here." Rin turned to Ramsa. Young, innocent, tiny, brilliant, and dangerous Ramsa. She wanted to make sure he'd remain with her, and knew it'd be selfish to ask. "I mean, you shouldn't."

Ramsa scraped at the bottom of his bowl. He seemed thoroughly disinterested in the conversation. "I think going anywhere else would get a little boring."

"But you're just a kid."

"Fuck off." He dug around his mouth with his little finger,

picking at something stuck behind his back molars. "You've got to understand that we're killers. You spend your life doing one thing, it's very hard to stop."

"That, and our only other option is the prison at Baghra," Baji said.

Ramsa nodded. "I hated Baghra."

Rin remembered that none of the Cike had good track records with Nikara law enforcement. Or with civilized society, for that matter.

Aratsha hailed from a tiny village in Snake Province where the villagers worshipped a local river god that purportedly protected them from floods. Aratsha, a novice initiate to the river god's cult, became the first shaman in generations who succeeded in doing what his predecessors had claimed. He drowned two little girls by accident in the process. He was about to be stoned to death by the same villagers who praised his fraudulent teachers when Tyr, the Cike's former commander, recruited him to the Night Castle.

Ramsa came from a family of alchemists who'd produced fire powder for the Militia until an accidental explosion near the palace had killed his parents, cost him an eye, and landed him in the notorious prison at Baghra for alleged conspiracy to assassinate the Empress, until Tyr pulled him out of his cell to engineer weapons for the Cike instead.

Rin didn't know much about Baji or Suni. She knew they had both been students at Sinegard once, members of Lore classes of years past. She knew they'd been expelled when things went terribly wrong. She knew they'd both spent time at Baghra. Neither of them would volunteer much else.

The twins Chaghan and Qara were equally mysterious. They weren't from the Empire. They spoke Nikara with a lilting Hinterlander accent. But when asked about home, they offered only the vaguest utterances. *Home is very far away. Home is at the Night Castle.*

Rin understood what they were trying to say. They, like the others, simply had no other place to go.

"What's the matter?" Baji asked. "Sounds like you want us gone."

"It's not that," Rin said. "I just—I can't make it go away. I'm scared."

"Of what?"

"I'm scared I'll hurt you. Adlaga won't be the end. I can't make the Phoenix go away and I can't make it stop and—"

"Because you're new to this," Baji interrupted. He sounded so kind. How could he be so kind? "We've all been there. They want to use your body all the time. And you think you're on the brink of madness, you think that this moment is going to be when you finally snap, but it's not."

"How do you know that?"

"Because it gets easier every time. Eventually you learn to exist on the precipice of insanity."

"But I can't promise I won't—"

"You won't. And we'll go after Daji again. And we'll keep doing it, over and over, as many times as it takes, until she's dead. Tyr didn't give up on us. We're not giving up on you. This is why the Cike exists."

She stared at him, stricken. She didn't deserve this, whatever this was. It wasn't friendship. She didn't deserve that. It wasn't loyalty, either. She deserved that even less. But it was camaraderie, a bond formed by a common betrayal. The Empress had sold them to the Federation for a silver and a song, and none of them could rest until the rivers ran red with Daji's blood.

"I don't know what to say."

"Then just shut up and stop being a little bitch about it." Ramsa pushed her bowl back in front of her. "Eat your porridge. Mold is nutritious."

Night fell over Omonod Bay. The *Petrel* spirited down the coast under the cover of darkness, buoyed by a shamanic force so powerful that within hours it had lost its Imperial pursuers. The Cike spread out—Qara and Chaghan to their cabin, where they spent almost all of their time, secluded from the others; Suni and Ramsa onto the front deck for night watch, and Baji to his hammock in the main sleeping quarters.

Rin locked herself inside her cabin to wage a mental battle with a god.

She didn't have much time. The laudanum had nearly worn off. She wedged a chair under the doorknob, sat down on the floor, squeezed her head between her knees, and waited to hear the voice of a god.

She waited to return to the state in which the Phoenix wanted utter command and shouted down her thoughts until she obeyed.

This time she would shout back.

She placed a small hunting knife beside her knee. She pressed her eyes shut. She felt the last of the laudanum pass through her bloodstream, and the numb, foggy cloud left her mind. She felt the curdling clench in her stomach and gut that never disappeared. She felt, along with the terrifying possibility of sobriety, *awareness*.

She always came back to the same moment, months ago, when she'd been on her hands and knees in that temple on the Isle of Speer. The Phoenix relished that moment because to the god it was the height of destructive power. And it kept bringing her back because it wanted her to believe that the only way to reconcile herself with that horror was to finish the job.

It wanted her to burn up this ship. To kill everyone around her. Then to find her way to land, and start burning that down, too; like a small flame igniting the corner of a sheet of paper, she was to make her way inland and burn down everything in her path until nothing was left except a blank slate of ash.

And then she would be clean.

She heard a symphony of screams, voices both collective and individual, Speerly or Mugini voices—it never mattered because wordless agony didn't have a language.

She could not bear how they were numbers and not numbers all at once, and the line kept blurring and it was awful because as long as they were numbers it wasn't so bad but if they were *lives*, then the multiplication was unbearable—

Then the screaming solidified into Altan.

His face splintered apart along cracks of skin turned charcoal, eyes burning orange, black tears opening streaks across his face, fire tearing him open from the inside—and she couldn't do anything about it.

"I'm sorry," she whispered. "I'm sorry, I'm sorry, I *tried* . . ."

"It should have been you," he said. His lips blistered, crackled, fell away to reveal bone. "You should have died. You should have gone up in flames." His face became ash became a skull, pressed against hers; bony fingers around her neck. "It should have been you."

Then she couldn't tell if her thoughts were his or her own, only that they were so loud they drowned out everything in her mind.

I want you to hurt.

I want you to die.

I want you to burn.

"No!" She slammed her blade into her thigh. The pain was only a temporary respite, a blinding whiteness that drove out everything in her mind, and then the fire would be back.

She'd failed.

And she'd failed last time, too, and the time before that. She'd failed every time she tried. At this point she didn't know why she did it, except to torture herself with the knowledge that she could not control the fire raging in her mind.

The cut joined a line of open wounds on her arms and legs that she'd sliced open weeks before—and kept sliced open—because even though it was only temporary, pain was still the only option other than opium that she could think of.

And then she couldn't think anymore.

The motions were automatic now, and it all came so easily—rolling the opium nugget between her palms, the spark of the first flicker of flame, and then the smell of crystallized candy concealing something rotten.

The nice thing about opium was that once she'd inhaled it, everything stopped mattering; and for hours at a time, carved out into her world, she could stop dealing with the responsibility of existence.

She sucked in.

The flames receded. The memories disappeared. The world stopped hurting her, and even the frustration of surrender faded to a dull nothing. And the only thing that remained was the sweet, sweet smoke.

CHAPTER 4

"Did you know that Ankhiluun has a special government office dedicated to figuring out how much weight the city can sustain?" Ramsa asked brightly.

He was the only one of them who could navigate the Floating City with ease. He hopped ahead, effortlessly navigating the narrow footbridges that lined the sludgy canals, while the rest inched warily along the wobbly planks.

"And how much weight is that?" Baji asked, humoring him.

"I think they're approaching maximum capacity," Ramsa said. "Someone's got to do something about the population, or Ankhiluun's going to start sinking."

"You could send them inland," Baji said. "Bet we've lost a couple hundred thousand people in the last few months."

"Or just have them fight another war. Good way to kill people off." Ramsa skipped off toward the next bridge.

Rin followed clumsily behind, blinking blearily under the unforgiving southern sun.

She hadn't left her cabin on the ship for days. She'd taken the smallest possible daily dose of opium that worked to keep her mind quiet while leaving her functional. But even that amount fucked so badly with her sense of balance that she had to cling to Baji's arm as they walked inland.

Rin hated Ankhiluun. She hated the salty, tangy ocean odor that followed her wherever she went; she hated the city's sheer loudness, the pirates and merchants screaming at each other in Ankhiluuni pidgin, an unintelligible mix of Nikara and western languages. She hated that the Floating City teetered over open water, roiling back and forth with each incoming wave, so that even standing still, she felt like she was about to fall.

She wouldn't have come here except out of utter necessity. Ankhiluun was the single place in the Empire where she was close to safe. And it was home to the only people who would sell her weapons.

And opium.

At the end of the First Poppy War, the Republic of Hesperia sat down with delegates from the Federation of Mugen to sign a treaty that established two neutral zones on the Nikara coastline. The first was at the international port of Khurdalain. The second was at the floating city of Ankhiluun.

Back then Ankhiluun had been a humble port—just a smattering of nondescript one-story buildings without basements because the flimsy coastal sands couldn't support any larger architecture.

Then the Trifecta won the Second Poppy War, and the Dragon Emperor bombed half the Hesperian fleet to smithereens in the South Nikan Sea.

In the absence of foreigners, Ankhiluun flourished. The locals occupied the half-destroyed ships like ocean parasites, linking them together to form the Floating City. Now Ankhiluun extended precariously from the coastline like an overreaching spider, a series of wooden planks that formed a web of walkways between the myriad ships anchored to shore.

Ankhiluun was the juncture through which poppy in all its forms entered the Empire. Moag's opium clippers sailed in from the western hemisphere and deposited their cargo in giant, empty husks of ships that served as repositories, from which long, thin smuggling boats picked it up and poured through branches of tributaries spreading out from the Murui River, steadily infusing the Empire's bloodstream like seeping poison.

Ankhiluun meant cheap, abundant opium, and that meant glorious, peaceful oblivion—hours upon hours when she didn't have to think about or remember anything at all.

And that, above all, was why Rin hated Ankhiluun. It made her so terribly afraid. The more time she spent here, locked alone in her cabin while she drifted on Moag's drugs, the less she felt able to leave.

"Odd," said Baji. "You'd think we'd get more of a welcome."

To get to the city center, they'd passed floating markets, garbage piles strewn along the canals, and rows of distinctive Ankhiluuni bars that had no benches or chairs—only ropes strung across walls where patrons could hang drunk by their armpits.

But they had been walking for more than half an hour now. They were well within the heart of the city, in full view of its residents, and no one had intercepted them.

Moag had to know they were back. Moag knew *everything* that happened in the Floating City.

"That's just how Moag likes to play power politics." Rin stopped walking to catch her breath. The shifting planks made her want to vomit. "She doesn't seek us out. We have to go to her."

Getting an audience with Chiang Moag was no easy affair. The Pirate Queen surrounded herself with so many layers of security that no one knew where she was at any given time. Only the Black Lilies, her cohort of spies and assistants, could be counted upon to get word directly to her, and the Lilies could only be found at a gaudy pleasure barge floating in the center of the city's main canal.

Rin looked up, shielding her eyes from the sun. "There."

The *Black Orchid* wasn't so much a ship as it was a floating three-story mansion. Garishly colorful lanterns hung from its sloped pagoda roofs, and bawdy, energetic music drifted constantly from its papered windows. Each day starting at noon, the *Black Orchid* crawled up and down the still canal, picking up patrons who rowed out to its decks in bright red sampans.

Rin dug around in her pockets. "Anyone got a copper?"

"I do." Baji tossed a coin toward the sampan boatman, who guided his vessel toward the shore to ferry the Cike onto the pleasure barge.

A handful of Lilies, perched lightly on the second-story railing, waved insouciantly at them as they approached. Baji whistled back.

"Stop that," Rin muttered.

"Why?" Baji asked. "It makes them happy. Look, they're smiling."

"No, it makes them think you're an easy target."

The Lilies were Moag's private army of terribly attractive women, all with breasts the size of pears and waists so narrow they looked in danger of snapping in half. They were trained martial artists, linguists, and uniformly the most obnoxious group of women Rin had ever met.

A Lily stopped them at the top of the gangplank, her tiny hand stretched out as if she could physically stop them from boarding. "You don't have an appointment."

She was clearly a new girl. She couldn't have been older than fifteen. Her face bore only small dabs of lipstick, her breasts were just little buds poking through her shirt, and she didn't seem to realize she was standing in front of a handful of the most dangerous people in the Empire.

"I'm Fang Runin," said Rin.

The girl blinked. "Who?"

Rin heard Ramsa turn his snicker into a cough.

"*Fang Runin*," she repeated. "I don't need an appointment."

"Oh, love, that's not how it works here." The girl tapped slim fingers against her impossibly narrow waist. "You've got to make an appointment, and we're booked up days in advance." She peered over Rin's shoulder at Baji, Suni, and Ramsa. "Also, it's extra for groups larger than four. The girls don't like it when you share."

Rin reached for her blade. "Look here, you little shit—"

"*Back up.*" Suddenly the girl was holding a fistful of needles she must have concealed in her sleeve. Their tips were purple with poison. "No one touches a Lily."

Rin fought the sudden urge to slap the girl across her face. "If you don't move aside this *second*, I'll shove this blade so far up your—"

"Well, this is a surprise." The silk sheets over the main doors rustled, and a voluptuous figure emerged on deck. Rin stifled a groan.

It was Sarana, a Black Lily of the highest distinction and Moag's personal favorite. She'd been Moag's go-between with the Cike since they landed at Ankhiluun three months ago. She possessed an unbearably sharp tongue, an obsession with sexual innuendo, and—according to Baji—the most perfect breasts south of the Murui.

Rin hated her.

"Fancy seeing you here." Sarana approached, cocking her head to the side. "We thought you weren't interested in women."

She had a way of shimmying when she spoke, accentuating each word with a shake of her hips. Baji made a choking noise. Ramsa was staring unabashedly at Sarana's chest.

"I need to see Moag," Rin said.

"Moag's busy," Sarana replied.

"I think Moag knows better than to keep me waiting."

Sarana raised her finely drawn eyebrows. "She also doesn't like to be disrespected."

"Must I be blunt?" Rin snapped. "Unless you want this boat going up in flames, you go get your mistress and tell her I want an audience."

Sarana feigned a yawn. "Be nice to me, Speerly. Else I'll tattle."

"I could sink your barge in minutes."

"And Moag would have you shot full of arrows before you

could even get off the boat." Sarana gave her a dismissive wave. "Get going, Speerly. We'll send for you when Moag is ready."

Rin saw red.

The fucking *nerve*.

Sarana might have thought it an insult, but Rin *was* a Speerly. She'd single-handedly won the Third Poppy War. She'd sunk a fucking *country*. She hadn't come this far just to banter with some stupid Lily whore.

Her hands shot out and grabbed Sarana by the collar. Sarana moved for her hairpiece, which was no doubt poisoned, but Rin slammed her against the wall, wedged one elbow against her throat, and pinned her right wrist down with the other.

She leaned forward to press her lips against Sarana's ear. "Maybe you think you're safe now. Maybe I'll just turn and walk away. You'll brag to the other bitches how you scared the Speerly off! Lucky you! Then one night, when you've turned off the lanterns and rolled up the gangplank, you'll smell smoke in your quarters. You'll run out onto the deck, but by then the flames will be burning so hot you can't see two feet in front of you. You'll know it's me, but you'll never be able to tell Moag, because a sheet of fire will burn all your pretty skin off, and the last thing you'll see before you leap off the ship into boiling-hot water is my laughing face." Rin dug her elbow deeper into Sarana's pale throat. "Don't *fuck with me*, Sarana."

Sarana patted frantically at Rin's wrists.

Rin tilted her head. "What was that?"

Sarana's voice was a strangled whisper. "Moag . . . might make an exception."

Rin let go. Sarana collapsed back against the wall, frantically fanning her face.

The red haze ebbed from the edges of Rin's vision. She closed a fist and opened it, let loose a long breath, and wiped her palm against her tunic. "That's more like it."

"We're here," Sarana announced.

Rin reached up to remove the blindfold from her face. Sarana had made her come alone—the others were more than happy to stay on the pleasure barge—and her naked vulnerability had kept her twitching and sweating during their entire journey through the canals.

At first she saw nothing but darkness. Then her eyes adjusted to the dim lights, and she saw that the room was lit up with tiny, flickering fire lamps. She saw no windows, no glints of sunshine. She couldn't tell whether they were in a ship or in a building; whether nighttime had fallen or if the room was simply sealed so well that no outside light could get in. The air indoors was much cooler than outside. She thought she could still feel the rocking sea beneath her legs, but only faintly, and she couldn't tell if it was real or imagined.

Wherever she was, the building was massive. A grounded warship? A warehouse?

She saw blocky furniture with curved legs that surely had to be of foreign origin; they didn't carve tables like that in the Empire. Along the walls hung portraits, though they couldn't have been of Nikara men; the subjects were pale-skinned, angry-looking, and all wearing absurdly shaped white wigs. A massive table, large enough to seat twenty, occupied the center of the room.

On the other side, flanked by a squadron of Lily archers, sat the Pirate Queen herself.

"Runin." Moag's voice was a gravelly drawl, deep and oddly compelling. "Always a pleasure."

In the streets of Ankhiluun, they called Moag the Stone Widow. She was a tall, broad-shouldered woman, more handsome than pretty. They said she was a prostitute from the bay who'd married one of Ankhiluun's many pirate captains. Then he died under circumstances that were never properly examined, and Moag rose steadily through the ranks of Ankhiluun's pirate hierarchy and consolidated a fleet of unprecedented strength. She was the first to ever unite the pirate factions of Ankhiluun under one flag. Until her reign, the disparate bandits of Ankhiluun had been at war with one another in the same way the twelve provinces of Nikan had been at war since the death of the Red Emperor. In a way, she had managed to do what Daji never could. She'd convinced disparate factions of soldiers to serve a single cause—herself.

"I don't think you've ever been to my private office." Moag gestured around the room. "Nice place, isn't it? The Hesperians were unbearably annoying, but they knew how to decorate."

"What happened to the original owners?" Rin asked.

"Depends. I assume the Hesperian Navy taught their sailors how to swim." Moag pointed to the chair opposite her. "Sit."

"No, thanks." Rin couldn't bear sitting in chairs anymore. She hated the way that tables blocked her legs—if she jumped or tried to run, her knees would slam against the wood, costing her precious escape time.

"Have it your way, then." Moag cocked her head to the side. "I heard Adlaga didn't go well."

"Got derailed," Rin said. "Had a surprise encounter with Daji."

"Oh, I know," Moag said. "The whole coastline knows about it. You know how Sinegard has spun this, right? You're the rogue Speerly, traitor to the crown. Your Mugenese captors drove you mad, and now you're a threat to everyone you come across. The bounty on your head has been raised to six thousand Imperial silvers. Double if you're alive."

"That's nice," Rin said.

"You don't seem concerned."

"They're not wrong about anything." Rin leaned forward. "Look, Yang Yuanfu is dead. We couldn't bring back his head, but your scouts will confirm everything as soon as they can get to Adlaga. It's time to pay up."

Moag ignored that, resting her chin on her fingertips. "I don't get it. Why go to all this trouble?"

"Moag, come on—"

Moag lifted a hand to cut her off. "Talk me through this. You have power beyond what most people could dream of. You could do anything you want. Become a warlord. Become a pirate. Hell, captain one of my ships if you want to. Why keep picking this fight?"

"Because Daji started this war," Rin said. "Because she killed my friends. Because she remains on the throne and she shouldn't. Because *someone* has to kill her, and I'd rather it be me."

"But *why*?" Moag pressed. "No one hates our Empress as much as I do. But understand this, little girl: you're not going to find allies. Revolution is fine in theory. But nobody wants to die."

"I'm not asking anyone else to risk it. Just give *me* weapons."

"And if you fail? You don't think the Militia will track where your supplies came from?"

"I killed thirty men for you," Rin snapped. "You owe me any supplies I want; those were the terms. You can't just—"

"What can't I do?" Moag leaned forward, ringed fingers circling the hilt of her dagger. She looked deeply amused. "You think I *owe* you? By what contract? Under what laws? What will you do, take me to court?"

Rin blinked. "But you said—"

"'But you said,'" Moag mocked in a high-pitched voice. "People say things they don't mean all the time, little Speerly."

"But we had an agreement!" Rin raised her voice, but her words came out plaintive, not dominant. She sounded childish even to her own ears.

Several Lilies began to titter into their fans.

Rin's hands tightened into fists. The residual opium kept her from erupting into fire, but still a haze of scarlet entered her vision.

She took a deep breath. *Calm.*

Murdering Moag might feel good in the moment, but she doubted even she could get out of Ankhiluun alive.

"You know, for someone of your pedigree, you're incredibly stupid," Moag said. "Speerly abilities, Sinegard education, Militia service, and you still don't understand the way the world works. If you want to get things done, you need brute force. I need you, and I'm the only one who can pay you, which means you need me. Complain all you want. You're not going anywhere."

"But you're *not* paying me." Rin couldn't help it. "So fuck you."

Eleven arrowheads pointed to her forehead before she could move.

"*Stand down*," Sarana hissed.

"Don't be so dramatic." Moag examined her lacquered nails. "I'm trying to help you, you know. You're young. You've got a whole life ahead of you. Why waste it on revenge?"

"I need to get to the capital," Rin insisted stubbornly. "And if you won't give me supplies, then I'll go elsewhere."

Moag sighed theatrically, pressed her fingers against her temples, and then folded her arms on the table. "I propose a compromise. One more job, and then I'll give you everything you want. Will that work?"

"What, I'm supposed to trust you now?"

"What choice do you have?"

Rin chewed on that. "What kind of job?"

"How do you feel about naval battles?"

"Hate them." Rin didn't like being over open water. She'd only agreed to jobs on land so far, and Moag knew that. Around the ocean, she was too easily incapacitated.

Fire and water didn't mix.

"I'm sure a healthy reward would change your mind." Moag rummaged in her desk, pulled out a charcoal rendering of a ship and slid it across the table. "This is the *Heron*. Standard opium skimmer. Red sails, Ankhiluuni flag, unless the captain's changed it. He's been coming up short in the books for months."

Rin stared at her. "You want me to kill someone based on accounting errors?"

"He's keeping more than his fair share of his profits. He's been very clever about it, too. Got an accountant to fudge the numbers so that it took me weeks to detect. But we keep triple copies of everything. The numbers don't lie. I want you to sink his ship."

Rin considered the rendering. She recognized the ship build.

Moag had at least a dozen skimmers just like it sitting in Ankhiluun's harbor. "Is he still in the city?"

"No. But he's scheduled to return to port in a few days. He thinks I don't know what he's done."

"Then why don't you get rid of him yourself?"

"Under regular circumstances I would," said Moag. "But then I'd have to give him the pirate's justice."

"Since when does Ankhiluun care about *justice*?"

"The fact that we're independent from the Empire doesn't make us an anarchy, dear. We'd hold a trial. It's standard procedure with embezzlement cases. But I don't want to give him a fair trial. He's well-liked, he has too many friends in this city, and punishment by my hand would certainly provoke retaliation. I'm not in the mood for politics. I want him blown out of the water."

"No prisoners?"

Moag grinned. "Not a high priority."

"Then I'll need to borrow a skimmer."

Moag's smile widened. "Do this for me and you can keep the skimmer."

This wasn't optimal. Rin needed a ship with Militia colors, not a smuggling vessel, and Moag might still withhold the weapons and money. No—she had to take it for granted Moag would cheat her, some way or another.

But she had no leverage. Moag had the ships, she had the soldiers, so she could dictate the terms. All Rin had was the ability to kill people, and no one better to sell it to.

She had no better options. She was strategically backed into a corner, and she couldn't think her way out.

But she knew someone who could.

"There's something else I want," she said. "Kitay's address."

"Kitay?" Moag narrowed her eyes. Rin could watch the thoughts spinning in her head, trying to determine if it was a liability, if it was worth the charity.

"We're friends," Rin said as smoothly as she could. "We were classmates. I care about him. That's all it is."

"And you're only asking about him now?"

"We're not going to flee the city, if that's what you're worried about."

"Oh, you'd never manage that." Moag gave her a pitying look. "But he asked me not to tell you where to find him."

Rin supposed she shouldn't have been surprised. It still stung.

"Doesn't matter," she said. "I still want the address."

"I gave him my word I'd keep it a secret."

"Your word means nothing, you old hag." Rin couldn't suppress her impatience. "Right now you're just dithering for the fun of it."

Moag laughed. "Fair enough. He's in the old foreign district. A safe house at the very end of the walkway. You'll see Red Junk Fleet symbols on the doorposts. I've posted a guard there, but I'll tell them to stand down if they see you. Shall I let him know you're coming?"

"Please don't," Rin said. "I'll surprise him."

The old foreign district was still and silent, a rare oasis of calm in the never-ending cacophony that comprised Ankhiluun. Half these houses were abandoned—no one had lived here since the Hesperians left, and the remaining buildings were used only to store inventory. The bright lights that littered the rest of Ankhiluun were absent. This place lay uncomfortably far from the open central square, where Moag's guards had easy access.

Rin didn't like that.

But Kitay had to be safe. Tactically, it would be a terrible idea to let him get hurt. He was a remarkable reserve of knowledge. He read everything and forgot nothing. He was best kept alive as an asset, and Moag had surely realized it since she'd put him under house arrest.

The lone house at the end of the road floated a little ways off from the rest of the bobbing street, tethered only by two long chains and a hazardous floating walkway made of badly spaced planks.

Rin stepped gingerly over the planks, then rapped on the wooden door. No response.

She tried the handle. It didn't even have a lock—she couldn't see a keyhole. They'd made it impossible for Kitay to keep visitors out.

She pushed the door open.

The first thing she noticed was the mess—a sprawl of yellowing books, maps, and ledgers that littered every visible surface. She blinked around in the dim lamplight until she finally saw Kitay sitting in the corner with a thick tome over his lap, nearly buried under stacks of leather-bound books.

"I've already eaten," he said without looking up. "Come back in the morning."

She cleared her throat. "Kitay."

He looked up. His eyes widened.

"Hello," she said.

Slowly he set his books to the side.

"Can I come in?" she asked.

Kitay stared at her for a long moment before waving her inside. "Fine."

She shut the door behind her. He made no move to get up, so she picked her way through the papers toward him, taking care not to step on any pages. Kitay had always hated when anyone disturbed his carefully arranged messes. During exam season at Sinegard, he'd thrown temper tantrums whenever someone moved his inkwells.

The room was so cramped that the only empty space was a patch of floor against the wall right beside him. Taking care not to touch him, she slid down, crossed her legs, and placed her hands on her knees.

For a moment they simply stared at each other.

Rin wanted desperately to reach out and touch his face. He looked weak, and far too thin. He had healed some since Golyn Niis, but even now his collarbone protruded to a frightening degree, and his wrists looked so fragile she might snap them with one hand. He had grown his hair out in a long, curly mess that he'd bunched up at the back of his head, which pulled at the edges of his face and made his cheekbones stick out more than they already did.

He didn't remotely resemble the boy she'd met at Sinegard.

The difference was in his eyes. They used to be so bright, lit up with a feverish curiosity about everything. Now they were just dull and blank.

"Can I stay?" she asked.

"I let you in, didn't I?"

"You told Moag to keep your address from me."

"Oh." He blinked. "Yes. I did do that."

He wouldn't meet her eyes. She knew him well enough to know that this meant he was furious with her, but after all these months, she still didn't know precisely why.

No—she did, she just wouldn't admit that she was wrong about it. The one time they'd fought about it, *really* fought about it, he'd slammed the door shut on her and hadn't spoken to her until they reached dry land.

She hadn't let herself think about it since. It went into the chasm, just like every other memory that made her start craving her pipe.

"How are you doing?" she asked.

"I'm under house arrest. How do you think I'm doing?"

She looked around at the papers splayed out across the table. They littered the floor, pinned down with inkwells.

Her eyes landed on the ledger he'd been scribbling in. "She's kept you busy, at least?"

"'Busy' is a word for it." He slammed the ledger shut. "I'm working for one of the Empire's most wanted criminals, and she's got me doing her *taxes*."

"Ankhiluun doesn't pay taxes."

"Not taxes to the Empire. To Moag." Kitay twirled the ink brush in his fingers. "Moag's running a massive crime ring with a taxation scheme that's just as complicated as any city bureaucracy's. But the record-keeping system they've been using so far, it's . . ." He waved his hands in the air. "Whoever designed this didn't understand how numbers work."

What a brilliant move on Moag's part, Rin thought. Kitay had the mental dexterity of twenty scholars combined. He could add impossibly large sums without blinking, and he had a mind for strategy that had rivaled Master Irjah's. He might be grumpy under house arrest, but he couldn't resist a puzzle when presented with one. The ledgers may as well have been a bucket of toys.

"Are they treating you all right?" she asked.

"Well enough. I get two meals a day. Sometimes more, if I've been good."

"You look thin."

"The food's not very good."

He still wouldn't look at her. She ventured to place a hand on his arm. "I'm sorry Moag's kept you here."

He jerked away. "Wasn't your decision. I'd do the same if I'd taken myself prisoner."

"Moag's really not so bad. She treats her people well."

"And she uses violence and extortion to run a massively illegal city that has been lying to Sinegard for twenty years," said Kitay. "I'm worried you're starting to lose your sense of scale here, Rin."

She rankled at that. "Her people are still better off than the Empress's subjects."

"The Empress's subjects would be fine if her generals weren't running around trying to commit treason."

"Why are you so loyal to Sinegard?" Rin demanded. "It's not like the Empress has done anything for you."

"My family has served the crown at Sinegard for ten generations," said Kitay. "And no, I'm not helping you with your personal vendetta just because you think the Empress got your stupid commander killed. So you can stop pretending to be my friend, Rin, because I know that's all you came for."

"I don't just *think* that," she said. "I know it. And I know the Empress invited the Federation onto Nikara land. She wanted this war, she started the invasion, and everything you saw at Golyn Niis was Daji's fault."

"False accusations."

"I heard it from Shiro's mouth!"

"And Shiro didn't have any motivation to lie to you?"

"Daji doesn't have any motivation to lie to *you*?"

"She's the Empress," Kitay said. "The Empress doesn't betray her own. Do you understand how absurd this is? There's literally no political advantage—"

"You should want this!" she yelled. She wanted to shake him, hit him, do anything to make that maddening blankness in his face go away. "Why don't you want this? Why aren't you furious? Didn't you see Golyn Niis?"

He stiffened. "I want you to leave."

"Kitay, please—"

"*Now.*"

"I'm your friend!"

"No, you're not. Fang Runin was my friend. I'm not sure who you are, but I don't want anything to do with you."

"Why do you keep saying that? What did I ever do to you?"

"How about what you did to *them*?" He grabbed for her hand. She was so surprised that she let him. He slammed her palm over the lamp beside him, forced it down directly over the fire. She yelped from the sudden pain—a thousand tiny needles, pressing deeper and deeper into her palm.

"Have you ever been burned before?" he whispered.

For the first time Rin noticed little burn scars dotting his palms and forearms. Some were recent. Some looked inflicted yesterday.

The pain intensified.

"Shit!" She kicked out. She missed Kitay but hit the lamp. Oil spilled over the papers. The fire whooshed up. For a second she saw Kitay's face illuminated in the flame, absolutely terrified, and then he yanked a blanket off the floor and threw it over the fire.

The room went dark.

"What the hell was that?" she screamed.

She didn't raise her fists, but Kitay flinched away as if she had—his shoulder hit the wall, and then he curled toward the ground with his head buried under his arms, raw sobs shaking his thin frame.

"I'm sorry," he whispered. "I don't know what . . ."

The throbbing pain in her hand made her breathless, almost light-headed. Almost as good as it felt when she got high. If she thought about it too hard she would start crying, and if she started crying it might tear her apart, so she tried laughing instead, and that turned into tortured hiccups that shook her entire frame.

"Why?" she finally managed.

"I was trying to see what it was like," he said.

"For who?"

"How *they* felt. In the moment that it happened. In their very last seconds. I wanted to know how they felt when it ended."

"It doesn't feel like anything," she said. A wave of agony shot up her arm again, and she slammed her fist against the floor in an attempt to numb out the pain. She clenched her teeth until it passed.

"Altan told me about it once," she said. "After a bit you're not able to breathe. And then you're gasping so hard you can't feel it hurt anymore. You don't die from the burning, you die from lack of air. You choke, Kitay. That's how it ends."

CHAPTER 5

"Try some ginger rock," Ramsa suggested.

Rin gagged and spat until she was sure her stomach would expel nothing else, and then pulled her head back over the side of the ship. Remnants of her breakfast, a phlegmy, eggy mess, floated in the green waves below.

She took the shards of candy from Ramsa's palm and chewed while fighting the urge to dry-heave. For all their weeks at sea, she'd still never gotten used to the constant sensation that the ground was swirling beneath her feet.

"Expect some choppier waves today," Baji said. "Monsoon season is kicking up in the Omonod. We'll want to avoid going upwind if this keeps up, but as long as we have the shore as a breakwater we should be all right."

He was the only one of them who had any real nautical experience—he'd worked on a transport ship as part of his labor sentence shortly before he'd been sent to Baghra—and he flaunted it obnoxiously.

"Oh, shut up," Ramsa said. "It's not like you do any real steering."

"I'm the navigator!"

"*Aratsha*'s the navigator. You just like the way you look standing at the helm."

Rin was grateful that they didn't have to do much maneuvering themselves. It meant they didn't have to bother with a crew of Moag's hired help. They needed only the six of them to sail up and down South Nikan Sea, doing minimal ship maintenance while blessed Aratsha trailed alongside the hull, guiding the ship wherever they needed to go.

Moag had lent them an opium skimmer named *Caracel*, a sleek and skinny vessel that somehow packed six cannons on each side. They didn't have the numbers to man each cannon, but Ramsa had devised a clever workaround. He'd connected all twelve fuses with the same strip of twine, which meant he could set them all off at once.

But that was only the last resort. Rin didn't intend to win this skirmish with cannons. If Moag didn't want survivors, then Rin only had to get close enough to board.

She folded her arms on the railing and rested her chin on them, staring down at the empty water. Sailing was far less interesting than staking out enemy camps. Battlefields were endlessly entertaining. The ocean was just lonely. She'd spent the morning watching the monotonous gray horizon, trying to keep her eyes open. Moag hadn't been certain when her tax-evading captain would sail back to port. It could be any time from now to past midnight.

Rin didn't understand how the sailors could stand the terrible lack of orientation at sea. To her, every stretch of the ocean looked the same. Without the coast to anchor her, one horizon was indistinguishable from the next. She could read star charts if she tried, but to her naked eye, each patch of greenish blue meant the same thing.

They could be anywhere in Omonod Bay. Somewhere out there lay the Isle of Speer. Somewhere out there was the Federation.

Moag had once offered to take her back to Mugen to survey the damage, but Rin had refused. She knew what she would find there. Millions of bodies encased within hardened rock, charred skeletons frozen in their last living acts.

How would they be positioned? Mothers reaching for their children? Husbands wrapping their arms around their wives? Maybe their hands would be stretched out toward the sea, as if they could escape the deadly thick sulfurous clouds rumbling down the mountainside if they could just get to the water.

She had imagined this too many times, had painted a far more vivid image of it in her mind than reality was likely to be. When she closed her eyes she saw Mugen and she saw Speer; the two islands blurred together in her mind, because in all cases the narrative was the same: children going up in flames, the skin sloughing off their bodies in large black patches, revealing glistening bone underneath.

They burned for someone else's war, someone else's wrongs; someone they had never met had made the decision they should die, so in their last moments they would have had no idea why their skin was scorching off.

Rin blinked and shook her head to clear it. She kept slipping into daydreams. She'd taken a small dose of laudanum last night after her singed palm hurt so much she couldn't sleep, which in retrospect was an awful idea because laudanum exhausted her more than opium did and wasn't half as fun.

She examined her hand. Her skin was puffy and furiously red, even though she'd soaked it in aloe for hours. She couldn't make a fist without wincing. She was grateful she'd only burned her left hand, not her sword hand. She cringed at the thought of grasping a hilt against the tender skin.

She moved her thumbnail over the center of her palm and dug it hard into the open wound. Pain lanced through her arm, bringing tears to her eyes. But it woke her up.

"Shouldn't have taken that laudanum," said Chaghan.

She jerked upright. "I'm awake."

He joined her by the railing. "Sure you are."

Rin shot him an irritated glare, wondering how much effort it would take to toss him overboard. Not very much, she guessed. Chaghan was so terribly frail. She could do it. They wouldn't miss him. Probably.

"You see those rock formations?" Baji, who must have sensed an impending screaming match, edged his way in between them. He pointed toward a series of cliffs on the distant Ankhiluuni shore. "What do they look like to you?"

Rin squinted. "A man?"

Baji nodded. "A drowned man. If you sail to shore during sunset, it looks like he's swallowing the sun. That's how you know you've found Ankhiluun."

"How many times have you been here?" Rin asked.

"Plenty. Came down here with Altan once, two years ago."

"For what?"

"Tyr wanted us to kill Moag."

Rin snorted. "Well, you failed."

"To be fair, it was the *only* time Altan ever failed."

"Oh, I'm sure," she said. "Wonderful Altan. Perfect Altan. Best commander you've ever had. Did everything right."

"Excepting the Chuluu Korikh," Ramsa piped up. "You could call that a disaster of monumental proportions."

"To be fair, Altan used to make some really good tactical decisions." Baji rubbed his chin. "Before, you know, that string of really bad ones."

Ramsa whistled. "Lost his mind near the end, he did."

"Went a little crazy, yeah."

"Shut up about Altan," said Chaghan.

"It's a pity how the best ones snap," Baji continued, ignoring him. "Like Feylen. Huleinin, too. And you remember how Altan started sleepwalking at Khurdalain? I swear, one night I was walking back from taking a piss and he—"

"I said *shut up*!" Chaghan slammed both hands against the railing.

Rin felt a noticeable chill sweep over the deck; goose bumps were forming on her arms. There was a stillness in the air, like the space between lightning and thunder. Chaghan's bone-white hair had begun to curl up at the edges.

His face didn't match his aura. He looked like he might cry.

Baji lifted his palms up. "All right. Tiger's tits. I'm sorry."

"You do not have the right," Chaghan hissed. He pointed a finger at Rin. "*Especially* you."

She bristled. "What's that supposed to mean?"

"You're the reason why—"

"Why *what*?" she asked loudly. "Go on, say it."

"Guys. *Guys*." Ramsa wedged his way between them. "Great Tortoise, lighten up. Altan's dead. All right? Dead. And fighting about it won't bring him back."

"Look at this." Baji handed Rin his spyglass, directing her attention to a black point just visible on the horizon. "Does that look like a Red Junk ship to you?"

Rin squinted into the eyepiece.

Moag's Red Junk fleet comprised distinctive opium skimmers, built narrow for enough speed to outrun other pirates and the Imperial Navy, possessing deep hulls to transport huge amounts of opium and distinctive battened sails that resembled carp fins. On the open seas they disguised all identifying marks, but when they docked in the South Nikan Sea, they flew the crimson flag of Ankhiluun.

But this ship was a bulky creation, large and squat, much rounder than an opium skimmer. It had white sails instead of red, and no flag in sight. As Rin watched, the ship cut a ridiculously sharp turn in the water toward them that should have been impossible without a shaman's help.

"That's not Moag's," she said.

"That doesn't make it an enemy ship," said Ramsa. He peered out at the ship with a spyglass of his own. "Could be a friendly."

Baji snorted. "We're fugitives working for a pirate lord. Do you think we have a lot of friends right now?"

"Fair enough." Ramsa slammed the spyglass shut and shoved it in his pocket.

"Just open fire," Chaghan suggested.

Baji shot him an incredulous look. "Look, I don't know how much time you've spent at sea, but when you see a foreign warship with no identifying marks and no indication of whether or not it's brought a support fleet, the response is usually not to *just open fire*."

"Why not?" Chaghan asked. "You said it yourself. It can't be a friendly."

"Doesn't mean it's looking for a fight."

Ramsa's head swiveled back and forth between Chaghan and Baji as they spoke. He looked like a very confused baby bird.

"Hold fire," Rin told him hastily. "At least until we know who they are."

The ship was close enough now that she could just make out an etching of characters on the sides of the ship. *Cormorant*. She'd been over the list of Red Junk ships harbored at Ankhiluun. This wasn't one of them.

"Are you seeing this?" Ramsa was peering through his spyglass again. "What the hell is this?"

"What?" Rin couldn't tell what was bothering Ramsa. She couldn't see any armored troops. Or crew of any uniform, for that matter.

Then she realized that was precisely what was wrong.

She couldn't see anyone on board at all.

No one stood at the helm. No one manned the oars. The *Cormorant* was close enough now that they could all see its empty decks.

"That's impossible," said Ramsa. "How are they propelling it?"

Rin leaned over the side of the ship and yelled. "Aratsha! Hard right turn."

Aratsha obeyed, reversing their direction faster than any oared ship would be able to. But the foreign ship veered about immediately to follow their course, cutting an absurdly precise turn. The ship was fast, too—even though the *Caracel* had Aratsha propelling it along, the *Cormorant* had no trouble following their pace.

Seconds later it had almost caught up. It was pulling in parallel. Whoever was on it intended to board.

"That's a ghost ship," Ramsa whimpered.

"Don't be stupid," Baji said.

"They've got a shaman, then. Chaghan's right, we should fire."

They looked helplessly at Rin to confirm the order. She opened her mouth just as a boom split the air, and the *Caracel* shook under their feet.

"You still think it's not hostile?" Chaghan asked.

"Fire," she said.

Ramsa ran belowdecks to light the fuse. Moments later a series of booms rocked the *Caracel* as their starboard-side cannons went off one by one. Blazing metal balls skimmed over the water, scorching bright orange trails behind them—but instead of blowing holes into the sides of the *Cormorant*, they only bounced off metal plating. The warship barely shook from the impact.

Meanwhile the *Caracel* lurched alarmingly to starboard. Rin peeked over the edge—they'd taken damage to their hull, and though she knew nearly nothing about ships, that didn't look survivable.

She cursed under her breath. They'd have to row one of the lifeboats back to shore. If the *Cormorant* didn't dispose of them first.

She could hear Ramsa's footsteps moving frantically around belowdecks, trying to reload. Arrows sailed over her head, courtesy of Qara, but they thudded ineffectively into the sides of the warship. Qara had no target—the warship had no crew on deck, no archers. Whoever it was didn't need archers when they had a row of cannons so powerful they could likely blow the *Caracel* out of the water in minutes.

"Get closer!" Rin shouted. They were outgunned, outmaneuvered. The only chance they had at winning was to board that ship and smoke it out. "Aratsha! Put me on that ship!"

But they weren't moving. The *Caracel* bobbed listlessly in the water.

"*Aratsha!*"

No response. Rin climbed on the railing and bent to look overboard. She saw an odd stream of black, like a smoke cloud unfurling underwater. Blood? But Aratsha didn't bleed, not when he was in his watery form. And the cloud looked too dark to be blood.

No. It looked like ink.

A projectile shrieked overhead. She ducked. The salvo landed in the water in front of her. Another burst of black emanated from the site of impact.

It *was* ink.

They were firing the pellets into the water. This was intentional. Their attackers knew the Cike had a water shaman, and they had blinded Aratsha on purpose because *they knew what he was.*

Rin's chest tightened. This was no random attack. The warship had targeted them, had prepared for what they could do. This was a calculated ambush planned well in advance.

Moag had sold them out.

Another series of missiles whistled through the air, this time headed for the deck. Rin crouched down, braced for the explosion, but the impact didn't come. She opened her eyes. A delayed explosive?

But no fiery explosion rocked the boat. Instead a cloud of black smoke shot out of the projectiles, unfurling outward with a terrifying rapidity. Rin didn't bother trying to run. The smoke covered the entire deck within seconds.

It wasn't just a smokescreen, it was an asphyxiate—she tried to suck in air but nothing went through; it was like her throat had closed up, as if someone had pinned her to the wall by the neck. She staggered back, gagging. She could taste something in the air—something sickly sweet and terribly familiar.

Opium.

They know what we are. They know what makes us weak.

Suni and Baji dropped to their knees, utterly subdued. Wherever Qara was, she'd stopped shooting. Rin could just make out Ramsa's and Chaghan's limp forms through the smoke. Only she remained standing, coughing violently, clutching feebly at her throat.

She had smoked opium so many times, the phases of the high were familiar to her by now. It was only a matter of time.

First there was the dizzying sensation of floating, accompanied by an irrational euphoria.

Then the numbness that felt almost as good.

Then nothing.

Rin's arms stung like she'd plunged them inside a beehive. Her mouth tasted like charcoal. She tried to conjure up enough spit to wet her throat and barely managed a repellent lump of phlegm. She forced her eyes open. The sudden attack of light made them water; she had to blink several times before she could look up.

She was tied to a mast, her arms stretched above her. She wiggled her fingers. She couldn't feel them. Her legs were also bound, tied so tightly that she couldn't even bend them.

"She awakens." Baji's voice.

She strained her neck but couldn't see him. When she swiveled her head around she suffered a sudden attack of vertigo. Even tied down, she felt like she was floating. Looking up or down gave her the terrible sensation of falling. She squeezed her eyes shut. "Baji? Where are you?"

"Behind you," he said. "Other side of the . . . the mast."

His words came out in a barely intelligible drawl.

"The others?" she asked.

"All here," Ramsa piped up from her other side. "Aratsha's in that barrel."

Rin sat up straight. "Wait, could he—"

"No go. They sealed the lid. Good thing he doesn't need to breathe." Ramsa must have been wiggling his arms, straining the rope, because she felt her bindings tighten painfully around her own wrists.

"Stop that," she said.

"Sorry."

"Whose ship is this?" she asked.

"They won't tell us," Baji said.

"They? Who are *they*?"

"We don't know. Nikara, I'm assuming, but they won't talk to us." Baji raised his voice to shout at a guard who must have been standing behind her, because Rin couldn't see anyone. "Hey, you! You Nikara?"

No response.

"Told you," said Baji.

"Maybe they're mutes," Ramsa said. "All of them."

"Don't be a fucking idiot," Baji said.

"They could be! You don't know!"

That wasn't remotely funny, but Ramsa devolved into a fit of giggles, leaning forward so that the ropes strained painfully against all of their arms.

"Can you all shut up?" Chaghan's voice. It came from several feet away.

Rin peeked her eyes open for a split second, just long enough to take in the sight of Chaghan, Qara, and Suni bound to the mast opposite her.

Chaghan was slumped against his sister. Suni was still unconscious, head drooped forward. A thick pool of saliva had collected beneath his open mouth.

"Why, hello," said Ramsa. "Good to see you, too."

"Shut your damn mouth," Chaghan grumbled, before he devolved into a string of curses that ended with "Damned Nikara swine."

"Are you high?" Ramsa let out a shrill cackle. "Tiger's tits, Chaghan's high—"

"I'm . . . not . . ."

"Quick, someone ask him if he's always constipated or his face just looks that way."

"At least I've got both eyes," Chaghan snapped.

"Oh, '*I've got both eyes*.' Nice one. At least I'm not so skinny a pigeon could knock me over—"

"Shut up," Rin hissed. She opened her eyes again, trying to take stock of their surroundings. All she could see was the ocean receding behind them. "Ramsa. What do you see?"

"Just the ship's side. Little bit of ocean."

"Baji?"

Silence. Had he fallen asleep again?

"*Baji!*" she shouted.

"Hmm? What?"

"What can you see?"

"Uh. My feet. A bulkhead. The sky."

"No, you idiot—where are we headed?"

"How the fuck should I know—wait. There's a dot. Yeah, that's a dot. An island, I think?"

Rin's heartbeat quickened. Speer? Mugen? But both were a several-weeks journey away; they couldn't be anywhere close. And she didn't remember any islands near Ankhiluun. The old Hesperian naval bases, maybe? But those were long abandoned. If the Hesperians had come back, Nikara foreign relations had changed drastically since she'd last checked.

"Are you sure?" she asked.

"Not really. Hold on." Baji was silent for a moment. "Great Tortoise. That's a nice ship."

"What do you mean, that's a *nice ship*?"

"I mean, if that ship were a person, I would fuck that ship," said Baji.

Rin suspected Baji wouldn't be much help until the opium wore off. But then their vessel took a sharp turn to port, putting Rin in full view of what turned out to be, indeed, a *very* nice ship. They had sailed into the shadow of the largest war vessel she had ever seen: a monstrous, multidecked war junk, with several layers of catapults and portholes, and a massive trebuchet mounted on top of a deck tower.

Rin had studied naval warfare at Sinegard, though never in depth. The Imperial Navy's own fleet had fallen into disrepair, and the only people sent to naval posts were the bottom-feeders of each class. Still, they'd learned enough about naval crafts that Rin knew this was no Imperial ship.

The Nikara couldn't build vessels like this. It had to be a foreign battleship.

Her mind pored sluggishly over possibilities. The Hesperians hadn't taken sides in the Third Poppy War—but if they had, then they would have allied with the Empire, which meant . . .

But then she heard the crew shouting commands to each other, and they were in fluent Nikara. "*Halt. Ready to board.*"

What Nikara general had access to a Hesperian ship?

Rin heard shouting, the sound of groaning wood, and heavy footsteps moving about the deck. She strained harder against the ropes, but all that did was chafe at her wrists; her skin stung like it had been scraped raw.

"What's happening?" she screamed. "Who are you?"

She heard someone order a salute formation, which meant they were being boarded by someone of higher rank. A Warlord? A *Hesperian*?

"I think we're about to be handed off," Baji said. "It was nice knowing you all. Except you, Chaghan. You're weird."

"Fuck you," Chaghan said.

"Wait, I've still got a whale bone in my back pocket," said Ramsa. "Rin, you could try igniting just a little bit, burn through the ropes and then I'll get it out—"

Ramsa droned on, but Rin barely heard what he was saying.

A man had just walked into her field of vision. A general, judging from his uniform. He wore a half mask over his face—a Sinegardian opera mask of cerulean-blue ceramic. But it was his tall, lean build that caught her gaze, and his gait: confident, arrogant, like he expected everyone around him to bow before him.

She knew that stride.

"Suni can handle the main guard, and I'll commandeer the cannons, implode the ship or something—"

"Ramsa," Rin said in a strangled voice. "*Shut. Up.*"

The general crossed the deck and paused in front of them.

"Why are they bound?" he asked.

Rin stiffened. She knew that voice.

One of the crew hastened over. "Sir, we were warned not to let their hands out of sight."

"These are our people. Not prisoners. Unbind them."

"Sir, but they—"

"I don't enjoy repeating myself."

It had to be him. She'd only ever met one person who could convey so much disdain in so few words.

"You've bound them so tight their limbs will suffer blood loss," the general said. "If you deliver them damaged to my father, he will be very, *very* angry."

"Sir, I don't think you understand the nature of the threat—"

"Oh, I understand. We were classmates. Weren't we, Rin?"

The general knelt down before her and pulled off his mask.

Rin flinched.

The boy she remembered was so beautiful. Skin like porcelain, features finer than any sculptor could carve, delicately arched eyebrows that conveyed precisely that mixture of condescension and vulnerability that Nikara poets had been trying to describe for centuries.

Nezha wasn't beautiful anymore.

The left side of his face was still perfect, somehow; still smooth like the glaze on fine ceramic. But the right side . . . the right side was mottled with scars, crisscrossing over his cheek like the plates of a tortoise shell.

Those were not natural scars. They looked nothing like the burn scars Rin had seen on bodies destroyed by gas. Nezha's face should have been twisted and deformed, if not utterly blackened. But his skin remained as pale as ever. His porcelain face had not darkened, but rather looked like glass that had been shattered and glued back together. Those oddly geometric scars could have been drawn over his skin with a fine brush.

His mouth was pulled into a permanent sneer toward the left

side of his face, revealing teeth, a mask of condescension that he couldn't ever take off.

When Rin looked into his eyes, she saw noxious yellow fumes rolling over withering grass. She heard shrieks that dwindled into chokes. And she heard someone screaming her name, over and over and over.

She found it harder and harder to breathe. A buzzing noise filled her ears, and black spots clouded the sides of her vision like ink drops on wet parchment.

"You're dead," she said. "I saw you die."

Nezha looked amused. "And you were always supposed to be the clever one."

CHAPTER 6

"*What the fuck?*" she screamed.

"Hello to you, too," said Nezha. "I thought you'd be happy to see me."

She couldn't do anything but stare at him. It seemed impossible, unthinkable, that he was really alive, standing before her, speaking, *breathing*.

"Captain," Nezha called. "The ropes."

Rin felt the pressure around her wrists tighten briefly, then disappear. Her arms dropped to her sides. Blood rushed back into her extremities, sending a million shocks of lightning through her fingers. She rubbed her wrists and winced when skin came off in her hands.

"Can you stand?" Nezha asked.

She managed a nod. He pulled her to her feet. She took a step forward, and a dizzying spell of vertigo slammed into her like a wave.

"Steady." Nezha caught her arm just as she lurched toward him. She righted herself. "Don't touch me."

"I know you're confused. But it'll—"

"I said *don't touch me*."

He backed away, hands out. "It'll all make sense in a minute. You're safe. Just trust me."

"Trust you?" she repeated. "You bombed my ship!"

"Well, it's not technically your ship."

"You could have killed us!" she shrieked. Her brain still felt terribly sluggish, but this fact struck her as very, very important. "You fired opium onto my ship!"

"Would you rather we fired real missiles? We were trying not to hurt you."

"Your men bound us to the mast for hours!"

"Because they didn't want to die!" Nezha lowered his voice. "Look, I'm sorry it came to that. We needed to get you out of Ankhiluun. We weren't trying to hurt you."

His placating tone only made her angrier. She wasn't a fucking child; he couldn't calm her with soothing whispers. "You let me think you were dead."

"What did you want, a letter? It's not like it was terribly easy to track you down, either."

"A letter would have been better than *bombing my ship*!"

"Are you ever going to let that go?"

"It's a rather large thing to let go!"

"I will explain everything if you come with me," he said. "Can you walk? Please? My father's waiting for us."

"Your father?" she repeated dumbly.

"Come on, Rin. You know who my father is."

She blinked at him. Then it hit her.

Oh.

Either she'd been hit by a massive stroke of fortune, or she was about to die.

"Just me?" she asked.

Nezha's eyes flickered toward the Cike, lingering briefly on Chaghan. "I was told you're the commander now?"

She hesitated. She hadn't been acting much like a commander. But the title was hers, even if in name only. "Yes."

"Then just you."

"I'm not going without my men."

"I'm afraid I can't allow that."

She stuck her chin out. "Sucks, then."

"Do you seriously think any of them are in a state for an audience with a Warlord?" Nezha gestured toward the Cike. Suni was still asleep, the puddle of drool widening under his mouth. Chaghan stared open-mouthed at the sky, fascinated, and Ramsa had his eyes squeezed shut, giggling at nothing in particular.

It was the first time Rin had ever been glad she'd developed such a high tolerance for opium.

"I need your word you won't hurt them," she said.

Nezha looked offended. "Please. You're not prisoners."

"Then what are we?"

"Mercenaries," he said delicately. "Think of it that way. You're mercenaries out of a job, and my father has a very generous offer for your consideration."

"What if we don't like it?"

"I really think you will." Nezha motioned for Rin to follow him down the deck, but she remained where she stood.

"Feed my men while we're gone, then. A hot meal, not leftovers."

"Rin, come on—"

"Give them baths, too. And then take them to their own quarters. Not the brig. Those are my terms. Also, Ramsa doesn't like fish."

"He's been operating out of the coast and he doesn't like *fish*?"

"He's picky."

Nezha muttered something to the captain, who adopted a face like he'd been forced to sniff curdled milk.

"Done," Nezha said. "Now will you come?"

She took a step and stumbled. Nezha extended his arm toward her. She let him help her to the edge of the ship.

"Thanks, Commander," Ramsa called behind them. "Try not to die."

The Hesperian warship *Seagrim* loomed huge over their rowboat, swallowing them completely in its shadow. Rin couldn't help but stare in awe at its sheer scale. She could have fit half of Tikany on that warship, temple included.

How did a monstrosity like that stay afloat? And how did it move? She couldn't see any oars. The *Seagrim* appeared to be just like the *Cormorant*, a ghost vessel with no visible crew.

"Don't tell me you've got a shaman powering that thing," she said.

"If only. No, that's a paddle-wheel boat."

"What's that?"

He grinned. "Have you heard the legend of the Old Sage of Arlong?"

She rolled her eyes. "Who's that, your grandfather?"

"Great-grandfather. The legend goes, the old sage was staring at a water wheel watering the fields and thought about reversing the circumstances; if he moved the wheel, then the water must move. Fairly obvious principle, isn't it? Incredible how long it took for someone to apply it to ships.

"See, the old Imperial ships were idiotically designed. Propelled by sculls from the top deck. Problem with that is if your rowers get shot out, you're dead in the water. But the paddle-wheel pushers are on the bottom deck. Entirely enclosed by the hull, totally protected from enemy artillery. A bit of an improvement from old models, eh?"

Nezha seemed to enjoy talking about ships. Rin heard a distinct note of pride in his voice as he pointed out the ridges at the bottom of the warship. "You see those? They're concealing the paddle wheels."

She couldn't help but stare at his face while he talked. Up close his scars weren't so unsettling, but rather oddly compelling. She wondered if it hurt him to talk.

"What is it?" Nezha asked. He touched his cheek. "Ugly, isn't it? I can put the mask back on, if it's bothering you."

"It's not that," she said hastily.

"What, then?"

She blinked again. "I just . . . I'm sorry."

He frowned. "For what?"

She stared at him, searching for evidence of sarcasm, but his expression was open, concerned.

"It's my fault," she said.

He stopped rowing. "It's not your fault."

"Yes, it was." She swallowed. "I could have pulled you out. I heard you calling my name. You *saw* me."

"I don't remember that."

"Yes, you do. Stop lying."

"Rin. Don't do this." Nezha stopped rowing to reach out and grasp her hand. "It wasn't your fault. I don't blame you."

"You should."

"I don't."

"I could have pulled you out," she said again. "I wanted to, I was going to, but Altan wouldn't let me, and—"

"So blame Altan," Nezha said in a hard voice, and resumed rowing. "The Federation was never going to kill me. The Mugenese like to keep prisoners. Someone figured out I was a warlord's son, so they kept me for ransom. They thought they might leverage me into a surrender from Dragon Province."

"How'd you escape?"

"I didn't. I was in the camp when word got out that Emperor Ryohai was dead. The soldiers who had captured me arranged to trade me back to my father in exchange for a safe exit from the country."

"Did they get it?" she asked.

He grimaced. "They got *an* exit."

When they reached the hull of the warship, Nezha hooked four ropes to the ends of the rowboat and whistled at the sky. Seconds later the boat began to rock as sailors hoisted them up.

The main deck hadn't been visible from the rowboat, but now Rin saw that soldiers were posted at every corner of the ship. They were Nikara in their features—they must have been from Dragon Province, but Rin noticed they did not wear Militia uniforms.

The Seventh Division soldiers she had met at Khurdalain wore green Militia gear with the insignia of a dragon stitched into their armbands. But these soldiers were decked out in dark blue, with a silver dragon pattern visible over their chests.

"This way." Nezha led her down the stairs to the second deck and down the passageway until they stopped before a set of wooden doors guarded by a tall, spare man holding a blue-ribboned halberd.

"Captain Eriden." Nezha stopped and saluted, though according to uniform he should have been the higher rank.

"General." Captain Eriden looked like a man who'd never smiled in his life. Deep frown lines seemed permanently etched into his gaunt, spare face. He dipped his head to Nezha, then turned to Rin. "Hold out your arms."

"That's not necessary," said Nezha.

"With all due respect, sir, you are not the one sworn to guard your father's life," Eriden said. "Hold out your arms."

Rin obeyed. "You're not going to find anything."

Normally she kept daggers in her boots and inner shirt, but she could feel their absence; the *Cormorant*'s crew must have removed them already.

"Still have to check." Eriden peered inside her sleeves. "I'm to warn you that if you dare to so much as point a chopstick in the Dragon Warlord's direction, then you'll be shot full of crossbow bolts faster than you can breathe." His hands moved up her shirt. "Do not forget we also have your men as hostages."

Rin shot Nezha an accusing glare. "You said we weren't hostages."

"They aren't," Nezha said. He turned to Eriden, eyes hard. "They *aren't*. They're our guests, Captain."

"Call them whatever you like." Eriden shrugged. "But try anything funny and they're dead."

Rin shifted so that he could feel the small of her back for weapons. "Wasn't planning on it."

Finished, Eriden wiped his hands off on his uniform, turned, and grasped the door handles. "In that case, I'm to extend you a welcome on behalf of the Dragon Warlord."

"Fang Runin, isn't it? Welcome to the *Seagrim*."

For a moment Rin could only gape. She couldn't look at the Dragon Warlord and not see Nezha. Yin Vaisra was a grown version of his son without scars. He possessed all the infuriating beauty of the House of Yin—pale skin, black hair without a single streak of gray, and fine features that looked like they had been carved from marble—cold, arrogant, and imposing.

She'd heard endless gossip about the Dragon Warlord during her years at Sinegard. He ruled the richest province in the Empire by far. He'd single-handedly led the defense of the Red Cliffs in the Second Poppy War, had obliterated a Federation fleet with only a small cluster of Nikara fishing boats. He'd been chafing under Daji's rule for years. When he'd failed to appear at the Empress's summer parade for the third consecutive year, the apprentices had speculated so loudly that he was planning open treason that Nezha had lost his cool and sent one of them to the infirmary.

"Rin is fine." Her words came out sounding frail and tiny, swallowed up by the vast gilded room.

"A vulgar diminutive," Vaisra declared. Even his voice was a deeper version of Nezha's, a hard drawl that seemed permanently coated in condescension. "They're fond of those in the south. But I shall call you Runin. Please, sit down."

She cast a fleeting glance at the oak table between them. It had a low surface, and the high-backed chairs looked terribly heavy. If she sat, her knees would be trapped. "I'll stand."

Vaisra raised an eyebrow. "Have I made you uncomfortable?"

"You bombed my ship," Rin said. "So yes, a little."

"My dear girl, if I wanted you dead, your body would be at the bottom of Omonod Bay."

"Then why isn't it?"

"Because we need you." Vaisra drew out his own chair and sat, gesturing to Nezha to do the same. "It hasn't been easy to find you, you know. We've been sailing down the coast of the Snake Province for weeks now. We even checked Mugen."

He said it like he'd meant to startle her, and it worked. She couldn't help but flinch. He watched her, waiting.

She took the bait. "What did you find?"

"Just a few fringe islands. Of course, they had no clue of your whereabouts, but we stayed a week or so to make sure. People will say anything under torture."

Her fingers tightened into fists. "They're still *alive*?"

She felt like someone had taken a bar to her rib cage. She knew Federation soldiers remained on the mainland, but not that *civilians* were still alive. She'd thought she had put a permanent end to the country.

What if she hadn't? The great strategist Sunzi cautioned to always finish off an enemy in case they came back stronger. What would happen when Federation civilians regrouped? What if she still had a war to fight?

"Their invasion is over," Vaisra reassured her. "You made certain of that. The main islands have been destroyed. Emperor Ryohai and his advisers are dead. A few cities on the edges of the archipelago remain standing, but the Federation has erupted into frothy madness, like ants pouring out of a hill once you've killed the queen. Some of them are sailing off the islands in droves, seeking refuge on Nikara shores, but . . . well. We're getting rid of them as they come."

"How?"

"The usual way." His lips twitched into a smile. "Why don't you sit?"

Reluctantly, she drew the chair out as far from the table as she could and sat at the very edge, knees locked together.

"There," Vaisra said. "Now we're friends."

Rin decided to be blunt. "Are you here to take me back to the capital?"

"Don't be stupid."

"Then what do you want from me?"

"Your services."

"I'm not murdering anyone for you."

"Dream a little bigger, my dear." Vaisra leaned forward. "I want to overthrow the Empire. I'd like you to help."

The room fell silent. Rin studied Vaisra's face, waiting for him to burst into laughter. But he looked so terribly sincere—and so did Nezha—that she couldn't help but cackle.

"Is something funny?" Vaisra asked.

"Are you mad?"

"'Visionary,' I think, is the word you want. The Empire is on the verge of falling apart. A revolution is the only alternative to decades of civil warfare, and someone has to start the ball rolling."

"And you'd bet on your odds against the Militia?" Rin laughed again. "You're one province against eleven. It'll be a massacre."

"Don't be so certain," Vaisra said. "The provinces are angry. They're hurting. And for the first time since any of the Warlords can remember, the specter of the Federation has disappeared. Fear used to be a unifying force. Now the cracks in the foundation grow day by day. Do you know how many local insurrections have erupted in the past month? Daji is doing everything she can to keep the Empire united, but the institution is a sinking ship that's rotted at the core. It may drift for a while, but eventually it will be dashed to pieces against the rocks."

"And you think you can destroy it and build a new one."

"Isn't that precisely what you want?"

"Killing one woman is not the same thing as overthrowing a regime."

"But you can't evaluate those events in a vacuum," said Vaisra. "What do you think happens if you succeed? Who steps into Daji's shoes? And whoever that person is, do you trust them to rule the Twelve Provinces? To be any kinder to people like you than Daji was?"

Rin hadn't thought that far. She had never bothered to think much about life after she'd killed Daji. Once she'd gotten Altan's revenge, she wasn't sure that she even wanted to keep living.

"It doesn't matter to me," she said.

"Then think of it this way," Vaisra said. "I can give you a chance to take your revenge with the full support of an army of thousands."

"Would I have to take orders?" she asked.

"Rin—" Nezha started.

"Would I have to take orders?"

"Yes," Vaisra said. "Of course."

"Then you can fuck off."

Vaisra looked confused. "All soldiers take orders."

"I'm not a soldier anymore," she said. "I put in my time, I gave the Empire my loyalty, and that got me strapped to a table in a Mugenese research lab. I'm done taking orders."

"We are not the Empire."

She shrugged. "You want to be."

"You little fool." Vaisra slammed his hand against the table. Rin flinched. "Look outside yourself for a moment. This isn't just about you, it's about the future of our people."

"*Your* people," she said. "I'm a Speerly."

"You are a scared little girl reacting from anger and loss in the most shortsighted way possible. All you want is to get your revenge. But you could be so much more. *Do* so much more. *Listen to me.* You could change history."

"Haven't I changed history enough?" Rin whispered.

She didn't care about anyone's visions for the future. She'd stopped wanting to be great, to carve out her place in history, a long time ago. She'd since learned the cost.

And she didn't know how to say that she was just so *tired*.

All she wanted was to get Altan's revenge. She wanted to put a blade in Daji's heart.

And then she wanted to disappear.

"Your people died not because of Daji but because of this Empire," Vaisra said. "The provinces have become weak, isolated, technologically inept. Compared to the Federation, compared to Hesperia, we are not just decades but centuries behind. And the problem isn't our people, it's their rulers. The twelve-province system is an antiquated, inefficient yoke dragging the Nikara behind. Imagine a country that was truly united. Imagine an army whose factions weren't constantly at war with one another. Who could possibly defeat us?"

Vaisra's eyes glimmered as he spread his hands across the table. "I am going to transform the Empire into a republic—a great republic, founded on the individual freedom of men. Instead of Warlords, we would have elected officials. Instead of an Empress, we would have a parliament, overseen by an elected president. I would make it impossible for a single person like Su Daji to bring ruin upon this realm. What do you think of that?"

A lovely speech, Rin thought, if Vaisra had been talking to someone more gullible.

Maybe the Empire did need a new government. Maybe a democracy would usher in peace and stability. But Vaisra had failed to realize that she simply did not care.

"I just finished fighting one war," she said. "I'm not terribly interested in fighting another."

"So what is your strategy? To roam up and down the coastline, killing off the only officials who have been brave enough to keep opium outside their borders?" Vaisra made a noise of disgust. "If that's your goal, you're just as bad as the Mugenese."

She bristled. "I'll kill Daji eventually."

"And how, pray tell?"

"I don't have to tell *you*—"

"By renting a pirate ship?" he mocked. "By entering into losing negotiations with a pirate queen?"

"Moag was *going* to give us supplies." Rin felt the blood rushing to her face. "And we would have had the money, too, until you assholes showed up—"

"You're so terribly naive. Don't you get it? Moag was always going to sell you out. Did you think she would pass up that bounty on your heads? You're lucky our offer was better."

"Moag wouldn't," Rin said. "Moag knows my value."

"You're assuming Moag is rational. And she is, until it comes to great sums of money. You can buy her off with any amount of silver, and that I have in abundance." Vaisra shook his head like a disappointed teacher. "Don't you get it? Moag only flourishes while Daji is on the throne, because Daji's isolationist policies create Ankhiluun's competitive advantage. Moag only benefits as long as she operates outside the law, while the rest of the country is in such deep shit that it's more profitable to operate inside her boundaries than without. Once trade becomes legitimized, she's out of an empire. Which means the very last thing she wants is for you to succeed."

Rin opened her mouth, realized she had nothing to say, and closed it. For the first time, she did not have a counterargument.

"Please, Rin," Nezha interjected. "Be honest with yourself. You can't fight a war on your own. You are *six people*. The Vipress is guarded by a corps of elite soldiers that you've never gone up against. And that's not to mention her own martial arts skills, which you know nothing about."

"And you no longer have the advantage of surprise," said Vaisra. "Daji knows you are coming for her, which means you need a way to get closer to her. You need *me*."

He gestured to the walls around them. "Look at this ship. This is the very best that Hesperian naval technology can offer. Twelve cannons lined on every side."

Rin rolled her eyes. "Congratulations?"

"I have ten more ships like it."

That gave her pause.

Vaisra leaned forward. "Now you get it. You're a smart girl; you can run the calculations yourself. The Empire does not have a functioning navy. I do. We will control this Empire's waterways. The war will be over in six months *at worst*."

Rin tapped her fingers against the table, considering. *Could they win this war? And what if they did?*

She couldn't help but balance the possibilities—she'd been trained too well at Sinegard not to.

If what Vaisra said was true, then she had to admit this *was* the perfect time to launch a coup. The Militia at present was fragmented and weak. The provinces had been decimated by Federation battalions. And they might switch sides quickly, once they learned the truth about Daji's deception.

The benefits of joining an army were also obvious. She'd never have to worry about her supplies. She'd have access to intelligence she couldn't get on her own. She'd have free transportation to wherever she wanted to go.

And yet.

"What happens if I say no?" she asked. "Are you going to compel me into service? Make me your own Speerly slave?"

Vaisra didn't take the bait. "The Republic will be founded on freedom of choice. If you refuse to join, then we can't make you."

"Then maybe I'll leave," she said, mostly to see how he would respond. "I'll go into hiding. I'll bide my time. Get stronger."

"You could do that." Vaisra sounded bored, like he knew she was just pulling objections out of her ass. "Or you could fight for me and get the revenge you want. This isn't hard, Runin. And you're not really considering saying no. You're just pretending to think because you like being a little brat."

Rin glared at him.

It was such a rational option. She *hated* that it was a rational option. And she hated more that Vaisra knew that, and knew she'd arrive at the same conclusion, and was now simply mocking her until her mind caught up to his.

"I have more money and resources at my disposal than anyone in this empire," Vaisra said. "Weapons, men, information—anything you need, you can get it from me. Work for me and you will want for nothing."

"I'm not putting my life in your hands," she said. The last time she had pledged her loyalty to someone, she'd been betrayed. Altan had died.

"I will never lie to you," said Vaisra.

"Everybody lies to me."

Vaisra shrugged. "Then don't trust me. Act purely in your own interest. But I think you'll find it clear soon enough that you don't have many other options."

Rin's temples throbbed. She rubbed her eyes, trying desperately to think through all the possibilities. There had to be a catch. She knew better than to take offers like this at face value. She'd learned her lesson from Moag—never trust someone who holds all the cards.

She had to buy herself some time. "I can't make a decision without speaking to my people."

"Do as you like," Vaisra said. "But have an answer for me by dawn."

"Or what?" she asked.

"Or you'll have to find your own way back to shore," he said. "And it's a long swim."

"Just to clarify, the Dragon Warlord does *not* want to kill us?" Ramsa asked.

"No," said Rin. "He wants us in his army."

He wrinkled his nose. "But why? The Federation's gone."

"Exactly that. He thinks it's his opportunity to overthrow the Empire."

"That's actually clever," Baji said. "Think about it. Rob the house while it's on fire, or however the saying goes."

"I don't think that's a real saying," Ramsa said.

"It's a little more noble than that," said Rin. "He wants to build a republic instead. Overthrow the Warlord system. Construct a parliament, appoint elected officials, restructure how governance works across the Empire."

Baji chuckled. "Democracy? Really?"

"It's worked for the Hesperians," said Qara.

"Has it?" Baji asked. "Hasn't the western continent been at war for the past decade?"

"The question isn't whether democracy could work," Rin said. "That doesn't matter. The question is whether we enlist."

"This could be a trap," Ramsa pointed out. "He could be bringing you to Daji."

"He could have just killed us when we were drugged, then. We're dangerous passengers to have on board. It wouldn't be worth the risk unless Vaisra really did think he could convince us to join him."

"So?" Ramsa asked. "Can he convince us?"

"I don't know," Rin admitted. "Maybe."

The more she thought about it, the more it seemed like a good idea. She wanted Vaisra's ships. His weapons, his soldiers, his power.

But if things went south, if Vaisra hurt the Cike, then this fell on her shoulders. And she couldn't let the Cike down again.

"There's still a benefit to going it on our own," said Baji. "Means we don't have to take orders."

Rin shook her head. "We're still six people. You can't assassinate a head of state with six people."

Never mind that she'd been perfectly willing to try just a few hours ago.

"And what if he betrays us?" Aratsha asked.

Baji shrugged. "We could always just cut our losses and defect. Run back to Ankhiluun."

"We can't run back to Ankhiluun," Rin said.

"Why not?"

She told them about Moag's ploy. "She'd have sold us to Daji if Vaisra hadn't offered her something better. He sank our ship because he wanted her to think that we'd died."

"So it's Vaisra or nothing," Ramsa said. "That's just fantastic."

"Is this Yin Vaisra really so bad?" Suni asked. "He's just one man."

"That's true," said Baji. "He can't be any scarier than the other Warlords. The Ox and Ram Warlords weren't anything special. It's nepotism and inbreeding all around."

"Oh, so like how you were produced," said Ramsa.

"Listen, you little bitch—"

"Join them," Chaghan said. His voice was hardly louder than a whisper, but the cabin fell silent. It was the first time he had spoken all evening.

"You're debating this like you get to decide," he said. "You don't. You really think Vaisra's going to let you go if you say no? He's too smart for that. He's just told you his intentions to commit treason. He'll have you killed if there's even the slightest risk you'd go to anyone else." He gave Rin a grim look. "Face it, Speerly. It's join up or die."

"You're gloating," Rin accused.

"I would never," said Nezha. He'd been beaming the entire way down the passageway, showing her around the warship like some ebullient tour guide. "But glad to have you on board."

"Shut up."

"Can't I be happy? I've missed you." Nezha stopped before a room on the first deck. "After you."

"What's this?"

"Your new quarters." He opened the door for her. "Look, it locks from the inside four different ways. Thought you'd like that."

She did like it. The room was twice as large as her quarters on her old ship, and the bed was a proper *bed*, not a cot with lice-ridden sheets. She stepped inside. "I have this all to myself?"

"I told you." Nezha sounded smug. "The Dragon Army has its benefits."

"Ah, that's what you call yourselves?"

"Technically it's the Army of the Republic. Nonprovincial, and all that."

"You'd need allies for that."

"We're working on it."

She turned toward the porthole. Even in the darkness she could see how fast the *Seagrim* was moving, slicing through black waves at speeds faster than Aratsha had ever been capable of. By morning Moag and her fleet would be dozens of miles behind them.

But Rin couldn't leave Ankhiluun like this. Not yet. She had one more thing to retrieve.

"You said Moag thinks we're dead?" she asked.

"I'd be surprised if she didn't. We even tossed some charred corpses in the water."

"Whose bodies?"

Nezha stretched his arms over his head. "Does it matter?"

"I suppose not." The sun had just set over the water. Soon the Ankhiluuni pirate patrol would begin to make its rounds around the coast. "Do you have a smaller boat? One that can sneak past Moag's ships?"

"Of course," he scoffed. "Why, do you need to go back?"

"*I* don't," she said. "But you've forgotten someone."

By all accounts Kitay's audience with Vaisra was an unmitigated disaster. Captain Eriden wouldn't let Rin onto the second deck, so she was unable to eavesdrop, but about an hour after they brought Kitay on board, she saw Nezha and two soldiers dragging him to the lower level. She ran down the passageway to catch up.

"—and I don't care if you're pissed, you can't *throw food* at the *Dragon Warlord*," said Nezha.

Kitay's face was purple with anger. If he was at all relieved to see Nezha alive, he didn't show it. "Your men tried to blow up my house!"

"They tend to do that," Rin said.

"We had to make it look like you'd died," Nezha said.

"I was still in it!" Kitay cried. "And so were my ledgers!"

Nezha looked amazed. "Who gives a shit about your ledgers?"

"I was doing the city's taxes."

"*What?*"

Kitay stuck his lower lip out. "And I was almost done."

"What the fuck?" Nezha blinked. "I don't—Rin, you talk some sense into this idiot."

"I'm the idiot?" Kitay demanded. "*Me? You're* the ones who think it'd be a good idea to start a bloody civil war—"

"Because the Empire needs one," Nezha insisted. "Daji's the reason why the Federation invaded; she's the reason why Golyn Niis—"

"You were not at Golyn Niis," Kitay snarled. "*Don't* talk to me about Golyn Niis."

"Fine—I'm sorry—but shouldn't that justify a regime change? She's hamstrung the Militia, she's fucked our foreign relations, she's not fit to rule—"

"You have no proof of that."

"We do have proof." Nezha stopped walking. "Look at your scars. Look at *me*. The proof's written on our skin."

"I don't care," Kitay said. "I don't give a shit what your politics are, I want to go home."

"And do what?" Nezha asked. "And fight for *whom*? There's a war coming, Kitay, and when it's here, there will be no such thing as neutrality."

"That's not true. I shall seclude myself and live the virtuous life of a scholarly hermit," Kitay said stiffly.

"Stop," Rin said. "Nezha's right. Now you're just being stubborn."

He rolled his eyes at her. "Of course you're in on this madness. What did I expect?"

"Maybe it's madness," she said. "But it's better than fighting for the Militia. Come on, Kitay. You know you can't go back to the status quo."

She could see it in Kitay's eyes, how badly he wanted to resolve the contradiction between loyalty and justice—because Kitay, poor, upright, moral Kitay, always so concerned with doing what was right, couldn't reconcile himself to the fact that a military coup might be justified.

He flung his hands in the air. "Even so, you think I'm in a position to join your republic? My father is the Imperial *defense minister.*"

"Then he's serving the wrong ruler," said Nezha.

"You don't understand! My entire family is at the heart of the capital. They could use them against me—my mother, my sister—"

"We could extract them," Nezha said.

"Oh, like you extracted me? Very nice, I'm sure they'll *love* getting abducted in the middle of the night while their house burns down."

"Calm down," Rin said. "They'd still be alive. You wouldn't have to worry."

"Like you'd know how it feels," Kitay snapped. "The closest thing you had to a family was a suicidal maniac who got himself killed on a mission almost as stupid as this one."

She could tell he knew he'd crossed the line, even as he said it. Nezha looked stunned. Kitay blinked rapidly, refusing to meet her eyes. Rin hoped for a moment that he might cave, that he'd apologize, but he simply looked away.

She felt a pang in her chest. The Kitay she knew would have apologized.

A long silence followed. Nezha stared at the wall, Kitay at the floor, and neither of them dared to meet Rin's eyes.

Finally Kitay held out his hands, as if waiting for someone to bind them. "Best get me down to the brig," he said. "Don't want your prisoners running around on deck."

CHAPTER 7

When Rin returned to her private quarters, she locked the door carefully from the inside, sliding all four bolts into place, and propped a chair against the door for good measure. Then she lay back on her bed. She closed her eyes and tried to relax, to make herself internalize a brief sense of security. She was safe. She was with allies. No one was coming for her.

Sleep didn't come. Something was missing.

It took her a moment to realize what it was. She was searching for that rocking feeling of the bed shifting over water, and it wasn't there. The *Seagrim* was such a massive warship that its decks mimicked solid land. For once, she was on stable ground.

This was what she wanted, wasn't it? She had a place to be and a place to go. She wasn't drifting anymore, wasn't desperately scrambling to put together plans she knew would likely fail.

She stared up at the ceiling, trying to will her racing heartbeat to slow down. But she couldn't shake the feeling that something was wrong—a deep-seated discomfort that wasn't just the absence of rolling waves.

It began with a prickling feeling in her fingertips. Then a flush of heat started in her palms and crept up her arms to her chest.

The headache began a minute after that, searing flashes of pain that made her grind her teeth.

And then fire started burning at the back of her eyelids.

She saw Speer and she saw the Federation. She saw ashes and bones blurred and melted into one, one lone figure striding toward her, slender and handsome, trident in hand.

"You stupid cunt," Altan whispered. He reached forward. His hands made a necklace around her throat.

Her eyes flew open. She sat up and breathed in and out, deep and slow and desperate breaths, trying to quell her sudden swell of panic.

Then she realized what was wrong.

She had no access to opium on this ship.

No. Calm. Stay calm.

Once upon a time at Sinegard, back when Master Jiang had been trying to help her shut her mind to the Phoenix, he'd taught her techniques to clear her thoughts and disappear into a void that imitated nonexistence. He'd taught her how to think like she was dead.

She had shunned his lessons then. She tried to recall them now. She forced her mind through the mantras he'd made her repeat for hours. *Nothingness. I am nothing. I do not exist. I feel nothing, I regret nothing . . . I am sand, I am dust, I am ash.*

It didn't work. Surges of panic kept breaking the calm. The prickling in her fingers intensified into twisting knives. She was on fire, every part of her burned excruciatingly, and Altan's voice echoed from everywhere.

It should have been you.

She ran to the door, kicked the chair away, undid the locks, and ran barefoot out into the passageway. Stabs of pain pricked the backs of her eyes, made her vision spark and flash.

She squinted, struggling to see in the dim light. Nezha had said his cabin was at the end of the passage . . . so this one, it had to be . . . She banged frantically against the door until it opened and he appeared in the gap.

"Rin? What are you—"

She grabbed his shirt. "Where's your physician?"

His eyebrows flew up. "Are you hurt?"

"*Where?*"

"First deck, third door to the right, but—"

She didn't wait for him to finish before she started sprinting toward the stairs. She heard him running after her but she didn't care; all that mattered was that she get some opium, or laudanum, or whatever was on board.

But the physician wouldn't let her into his office. He blocked the entrance with his body, one hand against the doorframe, the other clenched on the door handle.

"Dragon Warlord's orders." He sounded like he'd been expecting her. "I'm not to give you anything."

"But I need—the pain, I can't stand it, I need—"

He started to close the door. "You'll have to do without."

She jammed her foot in the door. "Just a little," she begged. She didn't care how pathetic she sounded, she just needed something. Anything. "*Please.*"

"I have my orders," he said. "Nothing I can do."

"Damn it!" she screamed. The physician flinched and slammed the door shut, but she was already running in the opposite direction, feet pounding as she neared the stairs.

She had to get to the top deck, away from everyone. She could feel the pricks of malicious memory pressing like shards of glass into her mind; bits and pieces of suppressed recollections that swam vividly before her eyes—corpses at Golyn Niis, corpses in the research facility, corpses at Speer, and the soldiers, all with Shiro's face, jeering and pointing and *laughing*, and that made her so furious, made the rage build and build—

"Rin!"

Nezha had caught up with her. His hand grasped her shoulder. "What the hell—"

She whirled around. "Where's your father?"

"I think he's meeting with his admirals," he stammered. "But I wouldn't—"

She pushed past him. Nezha reached for her arm, but she ducked away and raced through the passageway and down the stairs to Vaisra's office. She jiggled the handles—locked—then kicked furiously at the doors until they swung open from inside.

Vaisra didn't look remotely surprised to see her.

"Gentlemen," he said, "we'll need some privacy, please."

The men inside vacated their seats without a word. None of them looked at her. Vaisra pulled the doors shut, locked them, and turned around. "What can I do for you?"

"You told the physician not to give me opium," Rin said.

"That is correct."

Her voice trembled. "Look, asshole, *I need my*—"

"Oh, no, Runin." Vaisra lifted a finger and wagged it, as if chiding a small child. "I should have mentioned. A last condition of your enlistment. I do not tolerate opium addicts in my army."

"I'm not an addict, I just . . ." A fresh wave of pain racked her head and she broke off, wincing.

"You're no good to me high. I need you alert. I need someone capable of infiltrating the Autumn Palace and killing the Empress, not some opium-riddled sack of shit."

"You don't get it," she said. "If you don't drug me, I will incinerate everyone on this ship."

He shrugged. "Then we'll throw you overboard."

She could only stare at him. This made no sense to her. How could he remain so infuriatingly calm? Why wasn't he caving in, cowering in terror? This wasn't how it was supposed to work—she was supposed to threaten him and he was supposed to do what she wanted, that was always how it worked—

Why hadn't she scared him?

Desperate, she resorted to begging. "You don't know how much this hurts. It's in my mind—the god is always in my mind, and it *hurts* . . ."

"It's not the god." Vaisra stood up and crossed the room toward her. "It's the anger. And it's your fear. You've seen battle for the first time, and your nerves can't shut down. You're frightened all the time. You think everyone's out to get you, and you *want* them to be out to get you because then that'll give you an excuse to hurt them. That's not a Speerly problem, it's a universal experience of soldiers. And you can't cure it with opium. There's no running from it."

"Then what—?"

He put his hands on her shoulders. "You face it. You accept that it's your reality now. You fight it."

Couldn't he understand that she'd tried? Did he think it was easy? "No," she said. "I need—"

He cocked his head to the side. "What do you mean, 'no'?"

Rin's tongue felt terribly heavy in her mouth. Sweat broke out over her body; she could see it beading on her hands.

He raised his voice. "Are you contradicting my orders?"

She took a shuddering breath. "I—I can't. Fight it."

"Ah, Runin. You don't understand. You're my soldier now. You follow orders. I tell you to jump, you ask how high."

"But I *can't*," she repeated, frustrated.

Vaisra lifted his left hand, briefly examined his knuckles, and then slammed the back of his hand across her face.

She stumbled backward, more from the shock than the force. Her face registered no pain, only an intense sting, like she'd walked straight into a bolt of lightning. She touched a finger to her lip. It came away bloody.

"You hit me," she said, dazed.

He grasped her chin tightly in his fingers and forced her to look up at him. She was too stunned to feel any rage. She wasn't angry, she was only afraid. No one dared to touch her like this. No one had for a long time.

No one since Altan.

"I've broken in Speerlies before." Vaisra traced a thumb across her cheek. "You're not the first. Sallow skin. Sunken eyes. You're smoking your life away. Anyone could smell it on you. Do you know why the Speerlies died young? It wasn't their penchant for constant warfare, and it wasn't their god. They were smoking themselves to death. Right now I wouldn't give you six months."

He dug his nails into her skin so hard that she gasped. "That ends now. You're cut off. You can smoke yourself to death after you've done what I need you for. But only after."

Rin stared at him in shock. The pain was starting to seep in, first a little sting and then a great throbbing bruise across her entire face. A sob rose up in her throat. "But it hurts so much . . ."

"Oh, Runin. Poor little Runin." He smoothed her hair out of her eyes and leaned in close. "*Fuck* your pain. What you're dealing with is nothing that a little discipline can't solve. You're capable of blocking out the Phoenix. Your mind can build up its own defenses, and you just haven't done it because you're using the opium as a safe way out."

"Because I need—"

"You need *discipline*." Vaisra forced her head up farther. "You must concentrate. Fortify your mind. I know you hear the screaming. Learn to live with it. Altan did."

Rin could taste blood staining her teeth when she spoke. "I'm not Altan."

"Then learn to be," he said.

So Rin suffered alone in her quarters, with the door bolted shut, guarded from the outside by three soldiers, at her own request.

She couldn't bear lying on her bed. The sheets scratched at her skin and exacerbated the terrible prickling that had spread across her body. She wound up curled on the floor with her head between her knees, rocking back and forth, biting her knuckles to keep from screaming. Her whole body cramped and shivered, racked with wave after wave of what felt like someone stamping slowly on each of her internal organs.

The ship's physician had refused to give her any sedatives on the grounds that she would just trade her opium addiction for a milder substance, so she had nothing to silence her mind, nothing to quell the visions that flashed through her eyes every time she closed them, a combination of the Phoenix's never-ending visual tour of horrors and her own opioid-driven hallucinations.

And, of course, Altan. Her visions always came back to Altan. Sometimes he was burning on the pier; sometimes he was strapped to an operating table, groaning in pain, and sometimes he wasn't injured at all, but those visions hurt the most, because then he would be talking to her—

Her cheek still burned from the force of Vaisra's blow, but in her visions it was Altan who struck her, smiling cruelly as she stared stupidly up at him.

"You hit me," she said.

"I had to," he answered. "*Someone* had to. You deserved it."

Did she deserve it? She didn't know. The only version of the truth that mattered was Altan's, and in her visions, Altan thought she deserved to die.

"You're a failure," he said.

"You can't come close to what I did," he said.

"It should have been you," he said.

And under everything, the unspoken command: *Avenge me, avenge me, avenge me* . . .

Sometimes, fleetingly, the visions became a terribly twisted fantasy where Altan was not hurting her. A version where he loved her instead, and his strikes were caresses. But they were fundamentally irreconcilable because Altan's nature was the same as the fire that had devoured him: if he didn't burn everyone around him, then he wasn't himself.

Sleep came finally through sheer exhaustion, but then only in short, fitful bursts; every time she nodded off she awoke screaming, and it was only by biting her knuckles and pressing herself into the corner that she could remain quiet throughout the night.

"Fuck you, Vaisra," she whispered. "Fuck. Fuck. *Fuck*."

But she couldn't hate Vaisra, not really. It may have just been the sheer exhaustion; she was so racked with fear, grief, and rage that it was a trial to feel anything more. But she knew she needed this. She'd known for months she was killing herself and that she didn't have the self-control to stop, that the only person who might have stopped her was dead.

She needed someone who was capable of controlling her like no one since Altan could. She hated to admit it, but she knew that in Vaisra she might have found a savior.

Daytime was worse. Sunlight was a constant hammer on Rin's skull. But if she stayed cooped up in her quarters any longer, she would lose her mind, so Nezha accompanied her outside, keeping a tight grip on her arm while they walked along the top deck.

"How are you doing?" he asked.

It was a stupid question, asked more to break the silence than anything, because it should have been *obvious* how she was doing: she hadn't slept, she was trembling uncontrollably from both exhaustion and withdrawal, and eventually, she hoped, she would reach the point where she simply fell unconscious.

"Talk to me," she said.

"About what?"

"Anything. Literally anything else."

So he started telling her court stories in a low murmur that wouldn't give her a headache; trivial tales of gossip about who was fucking this Warlord's wife, who had really fathered that Warlord's son.

Rin watched him while he spoke. If she focused on the most minute details of his face, it distracted her from the pain, just for a little bit. The way his left eye opened just slightly wider than his right now. The way his eyebrows arched. The way his scars curled over his right cheek to resemble a poppy flower.

He was so much taller than she was. She had to crane her head to look up at him. When had he gotten so tall? At Sinegard they had been about the same height, nearly the same build, until their second year, when he'd started bulking up at a ridiculous pace. But then, at Sinegard they had just been *children*, stupid, naive, playing at war games that they had never seriously believed would become their reality.

Rin turned her gaze to the river. The *Seagrim* had moved inland, was traveling upstream on the Murui now. It moved upriver at a snail's pace as the men at the paddle boards wheeled furiously to push the ship through the sludgy mud.

She squinted at the banks. She wasn't sure if she was just hallucinating, but the closer they got, the more clearly she could make out little shapes moving in the distance, like ants crawling up logs.

"Are those people?" she asked.

They were. She could see them clearly now—men and women stooped beneath the sacks they carried over their shoulders, young children staggering barefoot along the riverside, and little babies strapped in bamboo baskets to their parents' backs.

"Where are they going?"

Nezha looked faintly surprised that she had even asked. "They're refugees."

"From where?"

"Everywhere. Golyn Niis wasn't the only city the Federation sacked. They destroyed the whole countryside. The entire time we were holding that pointless siege at Khurdalain they were marching southward, setting villages ablaze after they'd ripped them apart for supplies."

Rin was still hung up on the first thing he'd said. "So Golyn Niis wasn't . . ."

"No. Not even close."

She couldn't even fathom the death count this implied. How many people had lived in Golyn Niis? She multiplied that by the provinces and came up with a number nearing a million.

And now, all across the country, the Nikara refugees were shuffling back to their homes. The tide of bodies that had flowed from the war-ravaged cities to the barren northwest had started to turn.

"'You asked how large my sorrow is,'" Nezha recited. Rin recognized the line—it was from a poem she'd studied a lifetime ago, a lament by an Emperor whose last words became exam material for future generations. "'And I answered, like a river in spring flowing east.'"

As they floated up the Murui, crowds of people lined the banks with their arms outstretched, screaming at the *Seagrim*.

"Please, just up to the edge of the province..."

"Take my girls, leave me but take the girls..."

"You have space! You have space, damn you..."

Nezha tugged gently at Rin's wrist. "Let's go belowdecks."

She shook her head. She wanted to see.

"Why can't someone send boats?" she asked. "Why can't we bring them home?"

"They're not going home, Rin. They're running."

Dread pooled in her stomach. "How many are still out there?"

"The Mugenese?" Nezha sighed. "They're not a single army. They're individual brigades. They're cold, hungry, frustrated, and they have nowhere to go. They're thieves and bandits now."

"How many?" she repeated.

"Enough."

She made a fist. "I thought I brought peace."

"You brought *victory*," he said. "This is what happens after. The Warlords can hardly keep control over their home provinces. Food shortages. Rampant crime—and it's not just the Federation bandits. The Nikara are at each other's throats. Scarcity will do that to you."

"So of course you think it's a good time to fight another war."

"Another war is inevitable. But maybe we can prevent the next big one. The Republic will have growing pains. But if we can fix the foundation—if we can institute structures that make the next invasion less likely and keep future generations safe—then we'll have succeeded."

Foundation. Growing pains. Future generations. Such abstract concepts, she thought; concepts that wouldn't compute for the average peasant. Who cared who sat on the throne at Sinegard when vast stretches of the Empire were underwater?

The children's cries suddenly seemed unbearable.

"Couldn't we give them something?" she asked. "Money? Don't you have stacks of silver?"

"So they could spend it where?" Nezha asked. "You could give them more ingots than you could count, but they've got nowhere to buy goods. There's no supply."

"Food, then?"

"We tried doing that. They just tear each other to pieces trying to get at it. It's not a pretty sight."

She rested her chin on her elbows. Behind them the flock of humans receded; ignored, irrelevant, betrayed.

"You want to hear a joke?" Nezha asked.

She shrugged.

"A Hesperian missionary once said the state of the average Nikara peasant is that of a man standing in a pond with water coming up to his chin," said Nezha. "The slightest ripple is enough to put him underwater."

Staring out over the Murui, Rin didn't find that the least bit funny.

That night she decided to drown herself.

It wasn't a premeditated decision so much as it was an act of sheer desperation. The pain had gotten so bad that she banged on the door to her room, begging for help, and then when the guards opened it she ducked past their arms and ran up the stairs and out the hatch to the main deck.

Guards ran after her, shouting for reinforcements, but she doubled her pace, bare heels slamming against the wood. Splinters lanced little shreds of pain through her skin—but that was *good* pain because it distracted her from her screaming mind, if only for half a second.

The railing of the prow came up to her chest. She gripped the edge and attempted to pull herself up, but her arms were weak—surprisingly weak, she didn't remember getting that weak—and she sagged against the side. She tried again, hoisted herself far enough that her upper body draped over the edge. She hung there facedown for a moment, staring at the dark waves trailing alongside the *Seagrim*.

A pair of arms grasped her around the waist. She kicked and flailed, but they only tightened as they dragged her back down. She twisted her neck around.

"*Suni?*"

He walked backward from the prow, carrying her by the waist like a little child.

"Let go," she panted. "Let me *go!*"

He put her down. She tried to break away but he grabbed her wrists, twisted her arms behind her back, and forced her down into a sitting position.

"Breathe," he ordered. "Just breathe."

She obeyed. The pain didn't subside. The screaming didn't quiet. She began to shake, but Suni didn't let go of her arms. "If you just keep breathing, I'll tell you a story."

"I don't want to hear a fucking story," she said, gasping.

"Don't want. Don't *think*. Just breathe." Suni's voice was quiet, soothing. "Have you heard the story of the Monkey King and the moon?"

"No," she whimpered.

"Then listen carefully." He relaxed his grip ever so slightly, just enough that her arms stopped hurting. "Once upon a time, the Monkey King caught his first glimpse of the Moon Goddess."

Rin shut her eyes and tried to focus on Suni's voice. She'd never heard Suni talk this much. He was always so quiet, drawn into himself, as if he were unused to being in full occupation of his own mind that he wanted to relish the experience as much as possible. She'd forgotten how gentle he could sound.

He continued. "The Moon Goddess had just ascended to the heavens, and she was still drifting so close to Earth that you could see her face on the surface. She was such a lovely thing."

Some old memory stirred in the back of her mind. She did know this story after all. They told it to children in Rooster Province during the Lunar Festival, every autumn when children ate moon cakes and solved riddles written on rice paper and floated lanterns in the sky.

"Then he fell in love," she whispered.

"That's right. The Monkey King was struck with the most terrible passion. He had to possess her, he thought, or he might die. So he sent his best soldiers to retrieve her from the ocean. But they failed, for the moon lived not in the ocean but in the sky, and they drowned."

"Why?" she asked.

"Why did they drown? Why did the moon kill them? Because they weren't climbing to the sky to find her, they were diving into the water toward her reflection. But it was a fucking illusion they were grasping, not the real thing." Suni's voice hardened. It didn't rise above a whisper, but he might as well have been shouting. "You spend your whole life chasing after some illusion you think is real, only to realize you're a damned fool, and that if you reach any further, you'll drown."

He let go of her arms.

Rin turned around to face him. "Suni . . ."

"Altan liked that story," he said. "I first heard it from him. He told it whenever he needed to calm me down. Said it would help if I thought of the Monkey King as just another person, someone gullible and foolish, and not a god."

"The Monkey King is a dick," she said.

"And the Moon Goddess is a bitch," he said. "She sat there in the sky and watched the monkeys drowning over her. What does that say about her?"

That made her laugh. For a moment they both looked up at the moon. It was half-full, hiding behind a wispy dark cloud. Rin could imagine she was a woman, coy and devious, waiting to entice foolish men to their deaths.

She placed her hand over Suni's. His hand was massive, rougher than wood bark, mottled with calluses. Her mind spun with a thousand unanswered questions.

Who made you like this?

And, more importantly, *Do you regret it?*

"You don't have to suffer alone, you know." Suni gave her one of his rare, slow smiles. "You're not the only one."

She would have smiled back, but then a wave of sickness hit her gut and she jerked her head down. Vomit splattered the deck.

Suni rubbed circles on her back while she spat blood-speckled phlegm on the planks. When she was done, he smoothed her vomit-covered hair out of her eyes as she sucked in air in great, racking sobs.

"You're so strong," he said. "Whatever you're seeing, whatever you're feeling, it's not as strong as you are."

But she didn't want to be strong. Because if she were strong then she would be sober, and if she were sober she would have to consider the consequences of her actions. Then she'd have to look into the chasm. Then the Federation of Mugen would stop being an amorphous blur, and her victims would stop being meaningless numbers. Then she would recognize one death, what it meant, and then another, and then another and another and—

And if she wanted to recognize it, then she would have to be something, *feel* something other than anger, but she was afraid that if she stopped being angry then she might shatter.

She started to cry.

Suni smoothed the hair back from her forehead. "Just breathe," he murmured. "Breathe for me. Can you do that? Breathe five times."

One. Two. Three.

He continued to rub her back. "You just have to make it through the next five seconds. Then the next five. Then on and on."

Four. Five.

And then another five. And those five, oddly enough, were just the littlest bit more bearable than the last.

"There you go," Suni said after maybe a dozen counts to five. His voice was so low it was hardly a whisper. "There, look, you've done it."

She breathed, and counted, and wondered how Suni knew exactly what to say.

She wondered if he had done this before with Altan.

"She'll be all right," Suni said.

Rin looked up to see who he was talking to, and saw Vaisra standing in the shadows.

It couldn't have taken him long to respond to the soldiers' calls. Had he been there the entire time, watching without speaking?

"I heard you came out to get some air," he said.

She wiped vomit off her cheek with the back of her hand. Vaisra's gaze flickered to her stained clothing and back to her face. She couldn't read his expression.

"I'll be okay," she whispered.

"Will you?"

"I'll take care of her," Suni said.

A brief pause. Vaisra gave Suni a curt nod.

After another moment Suni helped her up and walked her back to her cabin. He kept one arm around her shoulders, warm, solid, comforting. The ship rocked against a particularly violent wave, and she staggered into his side.

"I'm sorry," she said.

"Don't be sorry," Suni said. "And don't worry. I've got you."

Five days later the *Seagrim* sailed over a submerged town. At first when Rin saw the tops of buildings emerging from the river she thought they were driftwood, or rocks. Then they got close enough that she could see the curving roofs of drowned pagodas, thatched houses lying under the surface. An entire village peeked up at her through river silt.

Then she saw the bodies—half-eaten, bloated and discolored, all with empty sockets because the glutinous eyes had already been nibbled away. They blocked up the river, decomposing at such a rate that the crew had to sweep away the maggots that threatened to climb on board.

Sailors lined up at the prow to shift bodies aside with long poles to make way for the ship. The corpses started piling up on the river's sides. Every few hours sailors had to climb down and drag them into a pile before the *Seagrim* could move—a duty the crew drew lots for with dread.

"What happened here?" Rin asked. "Did the Murui run its banks?"

"No. Dam breach." Nezha looked pale with fury. "Daji had the dam destroyed to flood the Murui river valley."

That wasn't Daji. Rin knew whose handiwork this was.

But did no one else know?

"Did it work?" she asked.

"Sure. It took out the Federation contingents in the north. Holed them up long enough for the northern Divisions to make mincemeat out of them. But then the floodwaters caught several hundred villages, which makes several thousand people who don't have homes now." Nezha made a fist. "How does a ruler do this? To her own *people*?"

"How do you know it was her?" Rin asked cautiously.

"Who else could it be? Something that big had to be an order from above. Right?"

"Of course," she murmured. "Who else would it be?"

Rin found the twins sitting together at the stern of the ship. They were perched on the railing, staring down at the wreckage trailing behind them. When they saw Rin approaching, they both jumped down and turned around, regarding her warily, as if they knew exactly why she had come.

"So how does it feel?" Rin asked.

"I don't know what you're talking about," Chaghan said.

"You did it, too," she said gleefully. "It wasn't just me."

"Go back to sleep," he said.

"Thousands of people!" she crowed. "Drowned like ants! Are you proud?"

Qara turned her head away, but Chaghan lifted his chin indignantly. "I did what Altan ordered."

That made her screech with laughter. "Me too! I was just acting on orders! He said I had to get vengeance for the Speerlies, and so I did, so it's not my fault, because Altan *said*—"

"Shut up," Chaghan snapped. "Listen—Vaisra thinks that Daji ordered the opening of those dikes."

She was still giggling. "So does Nezha."

He looked alarmed. "What did you tell him?"

"Nothing, obviously. I'm not stupid."

"You can't tell anyone the truth," Qara cut in. "Nobody in the Dragon Republic can know."

Of course Rin understood that. She knew how dangerous it would be to give the Dragon Army a reason to turn on the Cike. But in that moment all she could think of was how terribly funny it was that she wasn't the only one with mass murder on her hands.

"Don't worry," she said. "I won't tell. I'll be the only monster. Just me."

The twins looked stricken, but she couldn't stop laughing. She wondered how it had felt, the moment before the wave hit. The civilians might have been making dinner, playing outside, putting their children to bed, telling stories, making love, before a crushing force of water swept over their homes, destroyed their villages, and snuffed out their lives.

This was what the balance of power looked like now. People like her waved a hand and millions were crushed within the confines of some elemental disaster, flung off the chessboard of the world like irrelevant pieces. People like her—shamans, all of them—were like children stomping around over entire cities as if they were mud castles, glass houses, fungible entities that could be targeted and demolished.

On the seventh morning after they'd left Ankhiluun, the pain receded.

She woke up without a fever. No headache. She took a hesitant step toward the door and was pleasantly surprised at how steady her feet felt on the floor, how the world didn't whirl and shift around her. She opened the door, wandered out onto the upper deck, and was stunned by how good the river spray felt on her face.

Her senses felt sharper. Colors seemed brighter. She could smell things she hadn't before. The world seemed to exist with a vibrancy that she hadn't been aware of.

And then she realized that *she had her mind to herself.*

The Phoenix wasn't gone. She felt the god lingering still at the forefront of her mind, whispering tales of destruction, trying to control her desires.

But this time she knew what *she* wanted.

And she wanted control.

She'd been victim to the god's urges because she'd been keeping her own mind weak, dousing away the flame with a temporary and unsustainable solution. But now her head was clear, her mind was present—and when the Phoenix screamed, she could shut it down.

She requested to see Vaisra. He sent for her within minutes.

He was alone in his office when she arrived.

"You're not afraid of me?" she asked.

"I trust you," he said.

"You shouldn't."

"Then I trust you more than you trust yourself." He was acting like an entirely different person. The harsh persona was gone. His voice sounded so gentle, so encouraging that she was suddenly reminded of Tutor Feyrik.

She hadn't thought about Tutor Feyrik in a long time.

She hadn't felt *safe* in a long time.

Vaisra leaned back in his chair. "Go on, then. Try calling the fire for me. Just a little bit."

She opened her hand and focused her eyes on her palm. She recalled the rage, felt the heat of it coil in the pit of her stomach. But this time it didn't come all at once in an uncontrollable torrent, but manifested as a slow, angry burn.

A small burst of flame erupted in her palm. And it was just the burst; no more, no less, though she could increase its size, or if she wanted to, force it even smaller.

She closed her eyes, breathing slowly; cautiously she raised the flame higher and higher, a single ribbon of fire swaying over her hand like a reed, until Vaisra commanded her, "Stop."

She closed her fist. The fire went out.

Only afterward did she realize how fast her heart was beating.

"Are you all right?" Vaisra asked.

She managed a nod.

A smile spread over his face. He looked more than pleased. He looked proud. "Do it again. Make it bigger. Brighter. Shape it for me."

She reeled. "I can't. I don't have that much control."

"You *can*. Don't think about the Phoenix. Look at me."

She met his eyes. His gaze was an anchor.

A fire sparked out of her fist. She shaped it with trembling hands until it took on the image of a dragon, coils undulating in the space between her and Vaisra, making the air shimmer with the heat of the blaze.

More, said the Phoenix. *Bigger. Higher.*

Its screams pushed at the edge of her mind. She tried to shut it down.

The fire didn't recede.

She started to shake. "No, I can't—I can't, you have to get out—"

"Don't think about it," Vaisra whispered. "*Look at me.*"

Slowly, so faintly she was afraid she was imagining it, the red behind her eyelids subsided.

The fire disappeared. She collapsed to her knees.

"Good girl," Vaisra said softly.

She wrapped her arms around herself, rocked back and forth on the floor, and tried to remember how to breathe.

"May I show you something?" Vaisra asked.

She looked up. He crossed the room to a cabinet, opened a drawer, and pulled out a cloth-covered parcel. She flinched when he jerked the cloth off, but all she saw underneath was the dull sheen of metal.

"What is it?" she asked.

But she already knew. She would recognize this weapon anywhere. She had spent hours gazing upon that steel, the metal etched with evidence of countless battles. It was metal all the way through, even at the hilt, which would normally be made of wood, because Speerlies needed weapons that wouldn't burn through when they held them.

Rin felt a sudden light-headedness that had nothing to do with opium withdrawal and everything to do with the sudden and terribly vivid memory of Altan Trengsin walking down the pier to his death.

A harsh sob rose in her throat. "Where did you get that?"

"My men recovered it from the Chuluu Korikh." Vaisra bent down and held the trident out before her. "I thought you might want to have it."

She blinked at him, uncomprehending. "You—why were you there?"

"You've got to stop thinking I know less than I do. We were looking for Altan. He would have been, ah, useful."

She snorted through her tears. "You think Altan would have joined you?"

"I think Altan wanted any opportunity to rebuild this Empire."

"Then you don't know anything about him."

"I knew his people," Vaisra said. "I led the soldiers that liberated him from the research facility, and I helped train him when he was old enough to fight. Altan would have fought for this Republic."

She shook her head. "No, Altan just wanted to make things burn."

She reached out, grasped the trident, and hefted it in her hands. It felt awkward in her fingers, too heavy at the front and oddly light near the back. Altan had been much taller than she, and the weapon seemed too long for her to wield comfortably.

It couldn't function like a sword. It was no good for lateral blows. This trident had to be wielded surgically. Killing strikes only.

She held it away from her. "I shouldn't have this."

"Why not?"

She barely got the words out, she was crying so hard. "Because I'm not him."

Because I should have died, and he should be alive and standing here.

"No, you're not." Vaisra continued to stroke her hair with one hand, though he'd already smoothed it behind her ears. The other hand closed over her fingers, pressing them harder around the cool metal. "You'll be better."

When Rin was sure she could stomach solid food without vomiting, she joined Nezha abovedeck for her first actual meal in more than a week.

"Don't choke." Nezha sounded amused.

She was too busy ripping apart a steamed bun to respond. She didn't know if the food on deck was ridiculously good, or if she was just so famished that it tasted like the best thing she'd ever eaten.

"It's a pretty day," he said while she swallowed.

She made a muffled noise in agreement. The first few days she hadn't been able to bear standing outside in the direct sunlight. Now that her eyes no longer burned, she could look out over the bright water without wincing.

"Kitay's still sulking?" she asked.

"He'll come around," Nezha said. "He's always been stubborn."

"That's putting it lightly."

"Have a little sympathy. Kitay never wanted to be a soldier. He spent half his time wishing he'd gone to Yuelu Mountain, not Sinegard. He's an academic at heart, not a fighter."

Rin remembered. All Kitay had ever wanted to do was be a

scholar, go to the academy at Yuelu Mountain, and study science, or astronomy, or whatever struck his fancy at the moment. But he was the only son of the defense minister to the Empress, so his fate had been carved out before he was even born.

"That's sad," she murmured. "You shouldn't have to be a soldier unless you want to."

Nezha rested his chin on his hand. "Did you want to?"

She hesitated.

Yes. No. She hadn't thought there was anything else for her. She hadn't thought it mattered if she wanted to.

"I used to be scared of war," she finally said. "Then I realized I was very good at it. And I'm not sure I'd be good at anything else."

Nezha nodded silently, gazing out at the river, pulling mindlessly at his steamed bun without eating it.

"How's your . . . uh . . ." Nezha gestured toward his temples.

"Good. I'm good."

For the first time she felt as if she had a handle on her anger. She could think. She could breathe. The Phoenix was still there, looming in the back of her mind, ready to burst into flame if she called it—but *only* if she called it.

She looked down to discover the steamed bun was gone. Her fingers were clutching nothing. Her stomach reacted to this by growling.

"Here," Nezha said. He handed her his somewhat mangled bun. "Have mine."

"You're not hungry?"

"I don't have much of an appetite right now. And you look emaciated."

"I'm not taking your food."

"Eat," he insisted.

She took a bite. It slid thickly down her throat and settled in her stomach with a wonderful heaviness. She hadn't been so full for such a long time.

"How's your face?" Nezha asked.

She touched her cheek. Sharp twinges of pain lanced through her lower face whenever she spoke. The bruise had blossomed while the opium seeped out of her system, as if one had to trade off with the other.

"It feels like it's just getting worse," she said.

"Nah. You'll be fine. Father doesn't hit hard enough to injure."

They sat awhile in silence. Rin watched fish jumping out of the water, leaping and flailing as if begging to be caught.

"And your face?" she asked. "Does it still hurt?"

In certain lights Nezha's scars looked like angry red lines someone had carved all over his face. In other lights they looked like a delicately painted crosshatch of brush ink.

"It hurt for a long time. Now I just can't feel anything."

"What if I touched you?" She was struck by the urge to run her thumb over his scars. To caress them.

"I wouldn't feel that, either." Nezha's fingers drifted to his cheek. "I suppose it scares people, though. Father makes me wear the mask whenever I'm around civilians."

"I thought you were just being vain."

Nezha smiled but didn't laugh. "That too."

Rin ripped large chunks from the steamed bun and barely chewed before swallowing.

Nezha reached out and touched her hair. "That's a good look on you. Nice to see your eyes again."

She'd shorn her hair close to her head. Not until she'd seen her discarded locks on the floor had she realized how disgusting it had become; the scraggly tendrils had grown out greasy and tangled, a nesting site for lice. Her hair was shorter than Nezha's now, close-cropped and clean. It made her feel like a student again.

"Has Kitay eaten anything?" she asked.

Nezha shifted uncomfortably. "No. Still hiding in his room. We don't keep it locked, but he won't come out."

She frowned. "If he's that furious, then why don't you let him go?"

"Because we'd rather have him on our side."

"Then why not just use him as leverage against his father? Trade him as a hostage?"

"Because Kitay's a resource," Nezha said frankly. "You know the way his mind works. It's not a secret. He knows most things and he remembers everything. He has a better grasp on strategy than anyone should. My father likes to keep his best pieces around for as long as he can. Besides, his father was at Sinegard before they abandoned it. There's no guarantee he's alive."

"Oh" was all she could say. She looked down and realized that she had finished Nezha's bun, too.

He laughed. "You think you can handle something more than bread?"

She nodded. He signaled for a servant, who disappeared into the cabin and reemerged a few minutes later with a bowl that smelled so good that a disgusting amount of saliva filled Rin's mouth.

"This is a delicacy near the coast," Nezha said. "We call it the wawa fish."

"Why?" she asked through a full mouth.

Nezha turned it over with his chopsticks, deftly separating the white flesh from the spine. "Because of the way it shrieks. Flails in the water crying like a baby with a rash. Sometimes the cooks boil them to death just for fun. Didn't you hear it in the galley?"

Rin's stomach turned. "I thought there might be a baby on board."

"Aren't they hilarious?" Nezha picked up a slice and put it in her bowl. "Try it. Father loves them."

CHAPTER 8

"If you have an open shot at Daji, take it." Captain Eriden jabbed the blunt end of his spear at Rin's head as he spoke. "Don't give her a chance to seduce you."

She ducked the first blow. The second whacked her on the nose. She shook off the pain, winced, and readjusted her stance. She narrowed her eyes at Eriden's legs, trying to predict his movements by watching only his lower body.

"She'll want to talk," Eriden said. "She always does, she thinks it's funny to watch her prey squirm before she kills it. Don't wait for her to say her piece. You'll be deathly curious because she'll make you, but you must attack before your chance is gone."

"I'm not an idiot," Rin panted.

Eriden directed another flurry of blows at her torso. Rin managed to block about half of them. The rest wrecked her.

He withdrew his spear, signaling a temporary reprieve. "You don't understand. The Vipress is no mere mortal. You've heard the stories. Her face is so dazzling that when she walks outside, the birds fall out of the sky and the fish swim up to the surface."

"It's just a face," she said.

"It is not *just a face*. I've seen Daji beguile and bewitch some of the most powerful and rational men I know. She brings them to their knees with just a few words. More often with just a look."

"Did she ever charm you?" Rin asked.

"She charmed everyone," Eriden said, but didn't elaborate. Rin could never get anything but blunt, literal answers from Eriden, who had the dour visage and personality of a corpse. "Be careful. And keep your gaze down."

Rin knew that. He'd been saying it for days. Daji's preferred weapon was her eyes—those snake's eyes that could ensnare a soul with a simple look, could trap the viewer into a vision of Daji's own choosing.

The solution was to never look her in the face. Eriden was training Rin to fight solely by watching her opponent's lower body.

This turned out to be particularly difficult when it came to hand-to-hand combat. So much depended on where the eyes darted, where the torso was pointed. All motion on oblique planes came from the upper body, but Eriden chided Rin every time her eyes strayed too far upward.

Eriden lunged forward without warning. Rin fared slightly better blocking the next sequence of attacks. She'd learned to watch not just the feet but the hip—often that pivoted first, set into motion the legs and feet. She parried a series of blows before a strong hit got through to her shoulder. It wasn't painful, but the shock nearly made her drop her trident.

Eriden signaled another pause.

While Rin doubled over to catch her breath, he drew a set of long needles out of his pocket. "The Empress is also partial to these."

He flung three of them toward her. Rin hopped hastily to the side and managed to get out of the needles' trajectory but landed badly on her ankle.

She winced. The needles kept coming.

She waved her trident madly in a circle, trying to knock them out of the air. It almost worked. Five clattered against the ground. One struck her on the upper thigh. She yanked it out. Eriden hadn't bothered to blunt the tips. *Asshole.*

"Daji likes her poison," Eriden said. "You're dead now."

"Thanks, I got that," Rin snapped.

She let the trident drop and bent over her knees, sucking in deep draughts of air. Her lungs were on fire. Where had her stamina gone? At Sinegard, she could have sparred for hours.

Right—up in a puff of opium smoke.

Eriden hadn't even broken a sweat. She didn't want to look weak by asking for another break, so she tried distracting him with questions. "How do you know so much about the Empress?"

"We fought by her side. The Dragon Province had some of the best-trained troops during the Second Poppy War. We were almost always with the Trifecta on the front lines."

"What were the Trifecta like?"

"Brutal. Dangerous." Eriden pointed his spear toward her. "Enough talk. You should—"

"But I have to know," she insisted. "Did Daji fight on the battlefield? Did you see her? What was she like?"

"Daji's not a warrior. She's a competent martial artist, they all were, but she's never relied on blunt force. Her powers are more subtle than the Gatekeeper's or the Dragon Emperor's were. She understands desire. She knows what drives men, and she takes their deepest desire and makes them believe that she is the only thing that can give it to them."

"But I'm a woman."

"All the same."

"But that can't make so much of a difference," Rin said, more to convince herself than anything. "That's just—that's *desire*. What is that next to hard power?"

"You think fire and steel can trump desire? Daji was always the strongest of the Trifecta."

"Stronger than the Dragon Emperor?" A memory resurfaced of a white-haired man floating above the ground, beastly shadows circling around him. "Stronger than the Gatekeeper?"

"Of course she was," Eriden said softly. "Why do you think she's the only one left?"

That gave Rin pause.

How *had* Daji become the sole ruler of Nikan? Everyone she'd asked told a different story. All that anyone in the Empire seemed to know for sure was that one day the Dragon Emperor died, the Gatekeeper disappeared, and Daji alone remained on the throne.

"Do you know what she did to them?" she asked.

"I'd give my arms to find out." Eriden tossed his spear to the side and drew his sword. "Let's see how you do with this."

His blade moved blindingly fast. Rin staggered backward, trying desperately to keep up. Several times her trident nearly slipped out of her hands. She gritted her teeth, frustrated.

It wasn't just that Altan's trident was too long, too unbalanced, clearly designed for a taller stature than hers. If that were the problem, she would have just swallowed her pride and swapped it for a sword.

It was her body. She knew the right motions and patterns, but her muscles simply could not keep up. Her limbs seemed to obey her mind only after a two-second lag.

Simply put, *she* didn't work. Months of lying prone in her room, breathing smoke in and out, had whittled her muscles away. Only now had she become aware of how weak, how painfully thin and easily tired she'd become.

"Focus." Eriden closed in. Rin's movements became increasingly desperate. She wasn't even trying to get a blow in herself; it took all her concentration to keep his blade away from her face.

She couldn't win a weapons match at this rate.

But she didn't have to use her trident for the kill. The trident was only useful as a ranged weapon—it kept her opponents at a far enough distance to protect her.

But *she* need only to get close enough to use the fire.

She narrowed her eyes, waiting.

There it was. Eriden struck for her hilt—a low, reaching blow. She let him flip the weapon out of her hands. Then she took advantage of the opening, darted into the space created by their interlocking weapons, and jammed her knee into Eriden's sternum.

He doubled over. She kicked in his knees, dropped down onto his chest, and splayed her palms out before his face.

She emitted the smallest hint of flame—just enough to make him feel the heat on his skin.

"Boom," she said. "You're dead now."

Eriden's mouth pressed into something that almost resembled a smile.

"How's she doing?"

Rin twisted to look over her shoulder.

Vaisra and Nezha emerged on the deck. Eriden pulled himself to a sitting position.

"She'll be ready," he said.

"She'll *be* ready?" Vaisra repeated.

"Give me a few days," Rin said, panting. "Still figuring this out. But I'll get there."

"Good," Vaisra said.

"You're bleeding." Nezha pointed to her thigh.

But she barely heard him. She was still looking at Vaisra, who was smiling more widely than she'd ever seen him. He looked pleased. Proud. And somehow, the jolt of satisfaction that gave her felt better than anything she'd smoked in months.

"You'll accompany the Dragon Warlord into the Autumn Palace for the noon summit," Eriden said. "Remember, you'll be presented as a war criminal. Do not act like he is your ally. Make sure to look afraid."

A dozen of Vaisra's generals and advisers were in the stateroom, seated around an array of detailed maps of the palace. Rin sat on Vaisra's right, sweating slightly from the constant attention. The entire plan centered on her, and she had no room to fail.

Eriden held up a pair of iron handcuffs. "You'll be bound and muzzled. I'd get used to the feel of these."

"That's no good," Rin said. "I can't burn through metal."

"They're not completely metal." Eriden slid the handcuffs across the table so that Rin could take a closer look. "The link in the middle is twine. It will burn through with minimal heat."

She fiddled with the handcuffs. "And Daji won't just have me killed? I mean—she'll know what I'm there to do; she saw me try at Adlaga."

"Oh, she'll likely suspect us of treachery the moment we dock in Lusan. We're not trying to ambush her. Daji likes to play with her food before she eats it. And she especially won't want to get rid of *you*. You're too interesting."

"Daji never strikes first," Vaisra said. "She'll want to milk you for as much information as she can, so she'll try to take you somewhere private to talk. Feign surprise at that. Then she'll likely make an offer nearly as tempting as mine."

"Which will be what?" Rin asked.

"Use your imagination. A place in her Imperial Guard. Free rein to scour the Empire of any remaining Federation troops. More glory and riches than you could possibly dream of. It'll all be a lie, of course. Daji has kept her throne for two decades by eliminating people before they become problems. Should you take a position in her court, you will simply be the latest on her long list of political assassinations."

"Or they'll find your body in the sewers minutes after you say yes," said Eriden.

Rin looked around the table. "Does no one else see the gaping flaw in this plan?"

"Pray tell," Vaisra said.

"Why don't I just kill her on sight? Before she opens her mouth? Why even take the risk of letting her talk?"

Vaisra and Eriden exchanged a glance. Eriden hesitated a moment, then spoke. "You, ah, won't be able to."

Rin blanched. "What does *that* mean?"

"We just went over this," Vaisra said. "Once Daji sees you,

she'll know you're there to kill her. And she'll very strongly suspect my own intentions. The only way to get you into the Autumn Palace and close enough to attack without putting the rest of us in danger is if you're sedated first."

"Sedated," Rin repeated.

"We'll have to give you a dose of opium while Daji's guards are watching," Vaisra said. "Enough to pacify you for an hour or two. But Daji doesn't know about your increased tolerance, which helps us. It'll wear off sooner than she expects."

Rin hated this plan. They were asking her to enter the Autumn Palace unarmed, high out of her mind, and completely unable to call the fire. But no matter how she turned it over in her mind, she couldn't find a loophole in the logic. She had to be defanged if she was to get close enough to get a hit.

She tried not to let her fear show as she spoke. "So am I—I mean, will I be alone?"

"We cannot bring a larger guard to the Autumn Palace without arousing Daji's suspicion. You will have hidden but minimal reinforcements. We can get soldiers in here, here, and here." Vaisra tapped at three points on a map of the palace. "But remember, our objective here is very limited. If we wanted an all-out war, we would have brought the armada up the Murui. We are only here to cut the head off the snake. The battles come after."

"So I'm the only one at risk," Rin said. "Nice."

"We will not abandon you. We will extract you if it goes badly, I promise. Successful or not, you'll use one of these escape routes to get out of the palace. Captain Eriden will have the *Seagrim* ready to depart Lusan in seconds if escape is necessary."

Rin peered down at the map. The Autumn Palace was hopelessly large, arranged like a maze within a conch shell, a spiraling complex of narrow corridors and dead ends, with twisting hallways and tunnels constructed in every direction.

The escape routes were marked with green lines. She narrowed her eyes, muttering to herself. A few more minutes and she'd have them memorized. She'd always been good at memorizing things, and now that she was off opium she was finding it easier and easier to focus on mental tasks.

She cringed at the thought of giving that up, even for an hour.

"You make this sound so easy," she said. "Why hasn't anyone tried to kill Daji before?"

"She's the Empress," said Vaisra, as if that were explanation enough.

"She's one woman whose sole talent is being very pretty," Rin said. "I don't understand."

"Because you're too young," Eriden said. "You weren't alive when the Trifecta were at the peak of their power. You don't know the fear. You couldn't trust anyone around you, even your own family. If you whispered a word of treason against Emperor Riga, then the Vipress and the Gatekeeper would be sure to have you destroyed. Not just imprisoned—obliterated."

Vaisra nodded. "In those years, entire families were ruined, executed, or exiled, and their lineages wiped from history. Daji oversaw this all without blinking an eye. There is a reason why the Warlords still bow down before her, and it's not just because she is *pretty*."

Something about Vaisra's expression gave Rin pause. Then she realized it was the first time she had ever seen him look scared.

She wondered what Daji had done to him.

Someone knocked on the door just then. She jumped in her seat.

"Come in," Vaisra called.

A junior officer poked his head in. "Nezha sent me to alert you. We've arrived."

Near the end of his reign, the Red Emperor built the Autumn Palace in the northern city of Lusan. It was never meant to be a capital or an administrative center; it was too far removed from the central provinces to properly govern. It served merely as a resort for his favorite concubines and their children, an escape for the days when Sinegard became so scorching hot that their skin threatened to darken within seconds of stepping outside.

Under the Empress Su Daji's regime, Lusan had been a place for court officials to harbor their wives and families safely away from the dangers at court, until it turned into the interim capital after Sinegard and then Golyn Niis were razed to the ground.

As the *Seagrim* sailed toward the city, the Murui narrowed to a thinner and thinner stream, which forced them to move at a slower and slower pace until they weren't sailing so much as crawling toward the Autumn Palace.

Rin could see the city walls from miles off. Lusan seemed to be lit from within by some unearthly afternoon glow. Everything was somehow golden; it was like the rest of the Empire had dulled to shades of black, white, and bloody red during the war, and Lusan had soaked up all the surrounding color, shining brighter than anything she had seen in months.

Close to the city walls Rin saw a woman walking down the riverbank with buckets of dye and heavy rolls of cloth strapped to her back. Rin knew the cloth was silk from the way it glimmered when it was unrolled, so soft that she could almost imagine the butterfly-wing texture on the backs of her fingers.

How could Lusan have silk? The rest of the country was garbed in unwashed, threadbare scraps. All along the Murui, Rin had seen naked children and babies wrapped in lily pads in some effort to preserve their dignity.

Farther downriver, fishing sampans glided up and down the winding waterways. Each boat carried several large birds—white creatures with massive beaks—hooked to the boats on strings.

Nezha had to explain to Rin what the birds were for. "They've got a string around their necks, see? The bird swallows the fish; the farmer pulls the fish out of the bird's neck. The bird goes in again, always hungry, always too dumb to realize that everything it catches goes into the fish basket and that all it'll ever get are slops."

Rin made a face. "That seems inefficient. Why not just use a net?"

"It is inefficient," Nezha agreed. "But they're not fishing for staples, they're hunting for delicacies. Sweetfish."

"Why?"

He shrugged.

Rin already knew the answer. Why *not* hunt for delicacies? Lusan was clearly untouched by the refugee crisis that had swept the rest of the country; it could afford to focus on luxury.

Perhaps it was the heat, or perhaps because Rin's nerves were already always on edge, but she felt angrier and angrier as they made for port. She hated this city, this land of pale and pampered women, men who were not soldiers but bureaucrats, and children who didn't know what fear felt like.

She simmered not with resentment so much as with a nameless fury at the idea that outside the confines of warfare, life could go on and *did* go on, that somehow, still, in pockets scattered throughout the Empire there were cities and cities of people who were dyeing silk and fishing for gourmet dinners, unaffected by the single issue that plagued a soldier's mind: when and where the next attack would come.

"I thought I wasn't a prisoner," said Kitay.

"You're not," said Nezha. "You're a guest."

"A guest who isn't allowed off the ship?"

"A guest whom we'd like to keep with us a little longer," Nezha said delicately. "Can you stop glaring at me like that?"

When the captain announced that they had anchored in Lusan, Kitay had ventured abovedeck for the first time in weeks. Rin had hoped he'd come up for some fresh air, but he was just following Nezha around the deck, intent on antagonizing him in any way possible.

Rin had tried several times to intercede. Kitay, however, seemed determined to pretend she didn't exist by ignoring her every time she spoke, so she turned her attention to the sights on the riverbank instead.

A mild crowd had gathered around the base of the *Seagrim*,

made up mostly of Imperial officials, Lusani merchants, and messengers from other Warlords. Rin surmised from what snatches of conversation she could hear from the top deck that they were all trying to get an audience with Vaisra. But Eriden and his men were stationed at the bottom of the gangplank, turning everyone away.

Vaisra had also issued strict orders that no one was to leave the ship. The soldiers and crewmen were to continue living on board as if they were still out on open water, and only a handful of Eriden's men had been permitted to enter Lusan to purchase fresh supplies. This, Nezha had explained, was to minimize the risk that someone might give away Rin's cover. Meanwhile, she was only allowed on deck if she wore a scarf to cover her face.

"You know you can't keep me here indefinitely," Kitay said loudly. "Someone's going to find out."

"Like who?" Nezha asked.

"My father."

"You think your father's in Lusan?"

"He's in the Empress's guard. He commands her security detail. There's no way she would have left him behind."

"She left everyone else behind," Nezha said.

Kitay crossed his arms. "Not my *father*."

Nezha caught Rin's eye. For the briefest moment he looked guilty, like he wanted to say something that he couldn't, but she couldn't imagine what.

"That's the commerce minister," Kitay said suddenly. "He'll know."

"What?"

Before either Nezha or Rin could register what he meant, Kitay broke into a run at the gangplank.

Nezha shouted for the closest soldiers to restrain him. They were too slow—Kitay dodged their arms, climbed onto the side of the ship, grabbed a rope, and lowered himself to the riverbank so quickly that he must have burned his hands raw.

Rin ran for the gangplank to intercept him, but Nezha held her back with one arm. "Don't."

"But he—"

Nezha just shook his head. "Let him."

They watched from a distance, silent, as Kitay ran up to the commerce minister and seized his arm, then doubled over, panting.

Rin could see them clearly from the deck. The minister recoiled for a moment, hands lifted as if to ward off this unfamiliar soldier, until he recognized Defense Minister Chen's son and his arms dropped.

Rin couldn't tell what they were saying. She could only see their mouths moving, the expressions on their faces.

She saw the minister place his hands on Kitay's shoulders.

She saw Kitay ask a question.

She saw the minister shake his head.

Then she saw Kitay collapse in on himself as if he had been speared in the gut, and she realized that Defense Minister Chen had not survived the Third Poppy War.

Kitay didn't struggle when Vaisra's men marched him back onto the boat. He was white-faced, tight-lipped, and his madly twitching eyes looked red at the rims.

Nezha tried to put a hand on Kitay's shoulder. Kitay shook him off and made straight for the Dragon Warlord. Blue-clad soldiers immediately moved to form a protective wall between them, but Kitay didn't reach for a weapon.

"I've decided something," he said.

Vaisra waved a hand. His guard dispersed. Then it was just the two of them facing each other: the regal Dragon Warlord and the furious, trembling boy.

"Yes?" Vaisra asked.

"I want a position," Kitay said.

"I thought you wanted to go home."

"Don't fuck with me," Kitay snapped. "I want a position. Give me a uniform. I won't wear this one anymore."

"I'll see where we can—"

Kitay cut him off again. "I'm not going to be a foot soldier."

"Kitay—"

"I want a seat at the table. Chief strategist."

"You're rather young for that," Vaisra said drily.

"No, I'm not. You made Nezha a general. And I've always been smarter than Nezha. You know I'm brilliant. I'm a fucking genius. Put me in charge of operations and you won't lose a single battle, I *swear*." Kitay's voice broke at the end. Rin saw his throat bob, saw the veins protruding from his jaw, and knew that he was holding back tears.

"I'll consider it," Vaisra said.

"You knew, didn't you?" Kitay demanded. "You've known for months."

Vaisra's expression softened. "I'm sorry. I didn't want to be the one to have to tell you. I know how much pain you must feel—"

"No. *No*, shut the fuck up, I don't want that." Kitay backed away. "I don't need your fake sympathy."

"Then what would you like from me?"

Kitay lifted his chin. "I want troops."

The Warlords' summit would not commence until after the victory parade, and that stretched over the next two days. For the most part Vaisra's soldiers did not participate. Several troops entered the city in civilian clothes, sketching out final details in their already extensive maps of the city in case anything had changed. But the majority of the crew remained on board, watching the festivities from afar.

Every now and then an armed delegation arrived aboard the *Seagrim*, faces shrouded under hoods to conceal their identities. Vaisra received them in his office, doors sealed, guards posted outside to discourage curious eavesdroppers. Rin assumed the visitors were the southern Warlords—the rulers of Boar, Rooster, and Monkey provinces.

Hours passed without news. Rin grew maddeningly bored. She'd been over the palace maps a thousand times, and she'd already trained so long with Eriden that day that her leg muscles screamed when she walked. She was just about to ask Nezha if they might explore Lusan in disguise when Vaisra summoned her to his office.

"I have a meeting with the Snake Warlord," he said. "On land. You're coming."

"As a guard?"

"No. As proof."

He didn't explain further, but she suspected she knew what he meant, so she simply picked up her trident, pulled her scarf up higher over her face until it concealed all but her eyes, and followed him toward the gangplank.

"Is the Snake Warlord an ally?" she asked.

"Ang Tsolin was my Strategy master at Sinegard. He could be anything from ally to enemy. Today, we'll simply treat him as an old friend."

"What should I say to him?"

"You'll remain silent. All he has to do is look at you."

Rin followed Vaisra across the riverbank until they reached a line of tents propped up at the city borders as if it were an invading army's. When they approached the periphery, a group of green-clad soldiers stopped them and demanded their weapons.

"Go on," Vaisra muttered when Rin hesitated to part with her trident.

"You trust him that much?"

"No. But I trust you won't need it."

The Snake Warlord came to meet them outside, where his aides had set up two chairs and a small table.

At first Rin mistook him for a servant. Ang Tsolin didn't look like a Warlord. He was an old man with a long and sad face, so slender he seemed frail. He wore the same forest-green Militia uniform as his men, but no symbols announced his rank, and no weapon hung at his hip.

"Old master." Vaisra dipped his head. "It's good to see you again."

Tsolin's eyes flickered toward the outline of the *Seagrim*, which was just visible down the river. "So you didn't take the bitch's offer, either?"

"It was rather unsubtle, even for her," Vaisra said. "Is anyone staying in the palace?"

"Chang En. Our old friend Jun Loran. None of the southern Warlords."

Vaisra arched an eyebrow. "They hadn't mentioned that. That's surprising."

"Is it? They're southern."

Vaisra settled back in his chair. "I suppose not. They've been touchy for years."

No one had brought a chair out for Rin, so she remained standing behind Vaisra, hands folded over her chest in imitation of the guards who flanked Tsolin. They looked unamused.

"You've certainly taken your time getting here," Tsolin said. "It's been a long camping trip for the rest of us."

"I was picking up something on the coast." Vaisra pointed toward Rin. "Do you know who she is?"

Rin lowered her scarf.

Tsolin glanced up. At first he seemed only confused as he examined her face, but then he must have taken in the dark hue of her skin, the red glint in her eyes, because his entire body tensed.

"She's wanted for quite a lot of silver," he said finally. "Something about an assassination attempt in Adlaga."

"It's a good thing I've never wanted for silver," said Vaisra.

Tsolin rose from his chair and walked toward Rin until only inches separated them. He was not so much taller than she was, but his gaze made her distinctly uncomfortable. She felt like a specimen under his careful examination.

"Hello," she said. "I'm Rin."

Tsolin ignored her. He made a humming noise under his breath and returned to his seat. "This is a very blunt display of force. You're just going to march her into the Autumn Palace?"

"She'll be properly bound. Drugged, too. Daji insisted on it."

"So Daji knows she's here."

"I thought that'd be prudent. I sent a messenger ahead."

"No wonder she's getting antsy, then," Tsolin said. "She's increased the palace guard threefold. The Warlords are talking. Whatever you're planning, she's ready for it."

"So it will help to have your support," Vaisra said.

Rin noticed that Vaisra dipped his head every time he spoke to Tsolin. In a subtle fashion, he was bowing continuously to his elder, displaying deference and respect.

But Tsolin seemed unresponsive to flattery. He sighed. "You've never been content with peace, have you?"

"And you refuse to acknowledge that war is the only option," said Vaisra. "Which would you prefer, Tsolin? The Empire can die a slow death over the next century, or we can set the country on the right path within the week if we're lucky."

"Within a few bloody years, you mean."

"Months, at the most."

"Don't you remember the last time someone went up against the Trifecta?" Tsolin asked. "Remember how the bodies littered the steps of the Heavenly Pass?"

"It won't be like that," Vaisra said.

"Why not?"

"Because we have her." Vaisra nodded toward Rin.

Tsolin looked wearily in Rin's direction.

"You poor child," he said. "I'm so sorry."

She blinked, unsure what that meant.

"And we have the advantage of time," Vaisra continued quickly. "The Militia is reeling from the Federation attack. They need to recuperate. They couldn't marshal their defenses fast enough."

"Yet under your best-case scenario, Daji still has the northern provinces," Tsolin said. "Horse and Tiger would never defect. She has Chang En and Jun. That's all you need."

"Jun knows not to fight battles he can't win."

"But he can and will win this one. Or did you think you would defeat everyone through a little intimidation?"

"This war could be over in days if I had your support," Vaisra said impatiently. "Together we'd control the coastline. I own the canals. You own the eastern shore. Combined, our fleets—"

Tsolin held up a hand. "My people have undergone three wars in their lifetime, each time with a different ruler. Now they might have their first chance at a lasting peace. And you want to bring a civil war to their doorsteps."

"There's a civil war coming, whether you admit it or not. I only hasten the inevitable."

"We will not survive the inevitable," Tsolin said. True sorrow laced his words. Rin could see it in his eyes; the man looked haunted. "We lost so many men at Golyn Niis, Vaisra. Boys. You know what our commanders made their soldiers do the evening before the siege? They wrote letters home to their families. Told them they loved them. Told them they wouldn't be coming home. And our generals chose the strongest and fastest soldiers to deliver the messages back home, because they knew it wasn't going to make a difference whether we had them at the wall."

He stood up. "My answer is no. We have yet to recover from the scars of the Poppy Wars. You can't ask us to bleed again."

Vaisra reached out and grabbed Tsolin's wrist before he could turn to go. "You're neutral then?"

"Vaisra—"

"Or against me? Shall I expect Daji's assassins at my door?"

Tsolin looked pained. "I know nothing. I help no one. Let's leave it at that, shall we?"

"We're just going to let him go?" Rin asked once they were out of Tsolin's earshot.

Vaisra's harsh laugh surprised her. "You think he's going to report us to the Empress?"

Rin thought this had seemed rather obvious. "It's clear he's not with us."

"He will be. He's revealed his threshold for going to war. Provincial danger. He'll pick a side quick enough if it means the difference between warfare and obliteration, so I will force his hand. I'll bring the fight to his province. He won't have a choice then, and I suspect he knows that."

Vaisra's stride grew faster and faster as they walked. Rin had to run to catch up.

"You're angry," she realized.

No, he was *furious*. She could see it in the icy glare in his eyes, in the stiffness of his gait. She'd spent too much of her childhood learning to tell when someone was in a dangerous mood.

Vaisra didn't respond.

She stopped walking. "The other Warlords. They said no, didn't they?"

Vaisra paused before he answered. "They're undecided. It's too early to tell."

"Will *they* betray you?"

"They don't know enough about my plans to do anything. All they can tell Daji is that I'm displeased with her, which she already knows. But I doubt they'll have the backbone to say even that." Vaisra's voice dripped with condescension. "They are like sheep. They will watch silently, waiting to see how the balance of power falls, and they will align with whoever can protect them. But we won't need them until then."

"But you needed Tsolin," she said.

"This will be significantly harder without Tsolin," he admitted. "He could have tipped the balance. It'll truly be a war now."

She couldn't help but ask, "Then are we going to lose?"

Vaisra regarded her in silence for a moment. Then he knelt down in front of her, put his hands on her shoulders, and looked up at her with an intensity that made Rin want to squirm.

"No," he said softly. "We have you."

"Vaisra—"

"You will be the spear that brings this empire down," he said sternly. "You will defeat Daji. You will set in motion this war, and then the southern Warlords will have no choice."

The intensity in his eyes made her desperately uncomfortable. "But what if I can't?"

"You will."

"But—"

"You will, because I ordered you to." His grip tightened on her shoulders. "You are my greatest weapon. Do not disappoint."

CHAPTER 9

Rin had imagined the Autumn Palace as composed of blocky, abstract shapes, the way it was represented on the maps. But the real Autumn Palace was a perfectly preserved sanctuary of beauty, a sight lifted straight out of an ink brush painting. Flowers bloomed everywhere. White plum blossoms and peach flowers laced the gardens; lily pads and lotus flowers dotted the ponds and waterways. The complex itself was an elegantly designed structure of ornamented ceremonial gates, massive marble pillars, and sprawling pavilions.

But for all that beauty, a stillness hung over the palace that made Rin deeply uncomfortable. The heat was oppressive. The roads looked as if they were swept clean hourly by unseen servants, but still Rin could hear the ubiquitous sound of buzzing flies, as if they detected something rotten in the air that no one could see.

It felt as if the palace hid something foul under its lovely exterior; beneath the smell of blooming lilacs, something was in the last stages of decay.

Perhaps she was imagining it. Perhaps the palace was truly beautiful, and she just hated it because it was a coward's resort.

This was a refuge, and the fact that anyone had hidden alive in the Autumn Palace while corpses rotted in Golyn Niis infuriated her.

Eriden nudged the small of her back with his spear. "Eyes down."

She hastily obeyed. She had come posing as Vaisra's prisoner—hands cuffed behind her back, mouth sealed behind an iron muzzle that clamped her lower jaw tightly upward. She could barely speak except in whispers.

She didn't have to remember to look scared. She was terrified. The thirty grams of opium circulating through her bloodstream did nothing to calm her down. It magnified her paranoia even as it kept her heart rate low and made her feel as if she were floating among clouds. Her mind was anxious and hyperactive but her body was slow and sluggish—the worst possible combination.

At sunrise Rin, Vaisra, and Captain Eriden had passed under the arched gateways of the nine concentric circles of the Autumn Palace. Servants patted them down for weapons at each gate. By the seventh gate, they had been groped so thoroughly that Rin was surprised they hadn't been asked to strip naked.

At the eighth gate an Imperial guard stopped her to check her pupils.

"She took a dose before the guards this morning," Vaisra said.

"Even so," said the guard. He reached for Rin's chin and tilted it up. "Eyes open, please."

Rin obliged and tried not to squirm as he pulled her eyelids apart.

Satisfied, the guard stepped back to let them through.

Rin followed Vaisra into the throne room, shoes echoing against a marble floor so smooth it looked like still water at the surface of a lake.

The inner chamber was a rich and ornate assault of decorations that blurred and swam in Rin's opium-blurred eyesight. She blinked and tried to focus. Intricately painted symbols covered every wall, stretching all the way up to the ceiling, where they coalesced in a circle.

It's the Pantheon, she realized. If she squinted, she could make out the gods she had come to recognize: the Monkey God, mischievous and cruel; the Phoenix, imposing and ravenous. . . .

That was odd. The Red Emperor had hated shamans. After he'd claimed his throne at Sinegard, he'd had the monks killed and their monasteries burned.

But maybe he hadn't hated the gods. Maybe he'd just hated that he couldn't access their power for himself.

The ninth gate led to the council room. The Empress's personal guard, a row of soldiers in gold-lined armor, blocked their path.

"No attendants," said the guard captain. "The Empress has decided that she does not want to crowd the council room with bodyguards."

A flicker of irritation crossed Vaisra's face. "The Empress might have told me this beforehand."

"The Empress sent a notice to everyone residing in the palace," the guard captain said smugly. "You declined her invitation."

Rin thought Vaisra might protest, but he only turned to Eriden and told him to wait outside. Eriden bowed and departed, leaving them without guards or weapons in the heart of the Autumn Palace.

But they were not entirely alone. At that moment the Cike were swimming through the underground waterways toward the city's heart. Aratsha had constructed air bubbles around their heads so they could swim for miles without needing to come up for air.

The Cike had used this as an infiltration method many times before. This time, they would deliver reinforcements if the coup went sour. Baji and Suni would take up posts directly outside the council room, poised to spring in and break Vaisra out if necessary. Qara would station herself at the highest pavilion outside the council room for ranged support. And Ramsa would squirrel himself away wherever he and his waterproof bag of combustible treasures could cause the most havoc.

Rin found a small degree of comfort in that. If they couldn't capture the Autumn Palace, at least they had a good chance of blowing it up.

Silence fell over the council room when Rin and Vaisra walked in.

The Warlords twisted in their seats to stare at her, their expressions ranging from surprise to curiosity to mild distaste. Their eyes roved over her body, lingered on her arms and legs, took stock of her height and build. They looked everywhere except at her eyes.

Rin shifted uncomfortably. They were sizing her up like a cow at market.

The Ox Warlord spoke first. Rin recognized him from Khurdalain; she was surprised that he was still alive. "This little girl held you up for weeks?"

Vaisra chuckled. "The searching ate my time, not the extraction. I found her stranded in Ankhiluun. Moag got to her first."

The Ox Warlord looked surprised. "The Pirate Queen? How did you wrestle her away?"

"I traded Moag for something she likes better," Vaisra said.

"Why would you bring her here alive?" demanded a man at the other end of the table.

Rin swiveled her head around and nearly jumped in surprise. She hadn't recognized Master Jun at first glance. His beard had grown much longer, and his hair was shot through with gray streaks that hadn't been there before the war. But she could find the same arrogance etched into the lines of her old Combat master's face, as well as his clear distaste for her.

He glared at Vaisra. "Treason deserves the death penalty. And she's far too dangerous to keep around."

"Don't be hasty," said the Horse Warlord. "She might be useful."

"*Useful?*" Jun echoed.

"She's the last of her kind. We'd be fools to throw a weapon like that away."

"Weapons are only useful if you can wield them," said the Ox Warlord. "I think you'd have a little trouble taming this beast."

"Where do you think she went wrong?" The Rooster Warlord leaned forward to get a better look at her.

Rin had privately been looking forward to meeting the Rooster Warlord, Gong Takha. They came from the same province. They spoke the same dialect, and his skin was nearly as dark as hers. Word on the *Seagrim* was that Takha was the closest to joining the Republic. But if provincial ties counted for anything, Takha didn't show it. He stared at her with the same sort of fearful curiosity one displayed toward a caged tiger.

"She's got a wild look in her eyes," he continued. "Do you think the Mugenese experiments did that to her?"

I'm in the room, Rin wanted to snap. *Stop talking about me like I'm not here.*

But Vaisra wanted her to be docile. Act stupid, he'd said. Don't come off as too intelligent.

"Nothing so complex," said Vaisra. "She was a Speerly straining against her leash. You remember how the Speerlies were."

"When my dogs go mad, I put them down," Jun said.

The Empress spoke from the doorway. "But little girls aren't dogs, Loran."

Rin froze.

Su Daji had traded her ceremonial robes for a green soldier's uniform. Her shoulder pads were inlaid with jade armor, and a longsword hung at her waist. It seemed like a message. She was not only the Empress, she was also grand marshal of the Nikara Imperial Militia. She'd conquered the Empire once by force. She'd do it again.

Rin fought to keep her breathing steady as Daji reached out and traced her fingertips over her muzzle.

"Careful," Jun said. "She bites."

"Oh, I'm sure." Daji's voice sounded languid, almost disinterested. "Did she put up a fight?"

"She tried," Vaisra said.

"I imagine there were casualties."

"Not as many as you would expect. She's weak. The drug's done her in."

"Of course." Daji's lip curled. "Speerlies have always had their predilections."

Her hand drifted upward to pat Rin gently on the head.

Rin's fingers curled into fists.

Calm, she reminded herself. The opium hadn't worn off yet. When she tried to call the fire, she felt only a numb, blocked sensation in the back of her mind.

Daji's eyes lingered on Rin for a long while. Rin froze, terrified that the Empress might take her aside now like Vaisra had warned. It was too early. If she were alone in a room with Daji, the best she could do was hurl some disoriented fists in her direction.

But Daji only smiled, shook her head, and turned toward the table. "We've much to get through. Shall we proceed?"

"What about the girl?" Jun asked. "She ought to be in a cell."

"I know." Daji shot Rin a poisonous smile. "But I like to watch her sweat."

The next two hours were the slowest of Rin's life.

Once the Warlords had exhausted their curiosity over her, they turned their attention to an enormous roster of problems economic, agricultural, and political. The Third Poppy War had wrecked nearly every province. Federation soldiers had destroyed most of the infrastructure in every major city they'd occupied, set fire to huge swaths of grain fields, and wiped out entire villages. Mass refugee movements had reshaped the human density of the country. This was the kind of disaster that would have taken miraculous effort from a unified central leadership to ameliorate, and the council of the twelve Warlords was anything but.

"Control your damn people," said the Ox Warlord. "I have thousands streaming into my border as we speak and we don't have a place for them."

"What are we supposed to do, create a border guard?" The Hare Warlord had a distinctly plaintive, grating voice that made Rin wince every time he spoke. "Half my province is flooded, we haven't got food stores to last the winter—"

"Neither do we," said the Ox Warlord. "Send them elsewhere or we'll all starve."

"We'd be willing to repatriate citizens from the Hare Province under a set quota," said the Dog Warlord. "But they'd have to display provincial registration papers."

"Registration papers?" the Hare Warlord echoed. "These people had their villages sacked and you're asking for *registration papers*? Right, like the first thing they grabbed when their village started going up in flames was—"

"We can't house everyone. My people are pressed for resources as is—"

"Your province is a steppe wasteland, you've got more than enough space."

"We have space; we don't have food. And who knows what your sort would bring in over the borders . . ."

Rin had a difficult time believing that this council, if one could call it that, was really how the Empire functioned. She knew how often the Warlords went to arms over resources, trade routes, and—occasionally—over the best recruits graduating from Sinegard. And she knew that the fractures had been deepening, had gotten worse in the aftermath of the Third Poppy War.

She just hadn't known it was *this* bad.

For hours the Warlords had bickered and squabbled over details so inane that Rin could not believe anyone could possibly care. And she had stood waiting in the corner, sweating through her chains, waiting for Daji to drop her front.

But the Empress seemed content to wait. Eriden was right—she clearly relished playing with her food before she ate it. She sat at the head of the table with a vaguely amused expression on her face. Every once in a while, she met Rin's eyes and winked.

What was Daji's endgame? Certainly she knew that the opium would wear off in Rin eventually. Why was she running out the clock?

Did Daji *want* this fight?

The sheer anxiety made Rin feel weak-kneed and light-headed. It took everything she had to remain standing.

"What about Tiger Province?" someone asked.

All eyes turned to the plump child sitting with his elbows up on the table. The young Tiger Warlord looked around with an expression equal parts bewildered and terrified, blinked twice, then peered over his shoulder for help.

His father had died at Khurdalain and now his steward and generals ruled the province in his stead, which meant that the power in Tiger Province really lay with Jun.

"We've done more than enough for this war," Jun said. "We bled at Khurdalain for months. We're thousands of men down. We need time to heal."

"Come on, Jun." A tall man sitting at the far end of the room spat a wad of phlegm on the table. "Tiger Province is full of arable land. Spread some of the goodness around."

Rin grimaced. This had to be the new Horse Warlord—the Wolf Meat General Chang En. She'd been briefed extensively on this one. Chang En was a former divisional commander who had escaped from a Federation prison camp near the start of the Third Poppy War, taken up the life of a bandit, and assumed rapid control of the upper region of the Horse Province while the former Horse Warlord and his army were busy defending Khurdalain.

They had eaten anything. Wolf meat. Corpses by the roadside. The rumor was that they had paid good money for live human babies.

Now the former Horse Warlord was dead, skinned alive by Federation troops. His heirs had been too weak or too young to challenge Chang En, so the bandit ruler had assumed de facto control of the province.

Chang En caught Rin's eye, bared his teeth, and slowly licked his upper lip with a thick, mottled black tongue.

She suppressed a shudder and looked away.

"Most of our arable land near the coastline has been destroyed by tsunamis or ash fall." Jun gave Rin a look of utter disgust. "The Speerly made sure of that."

Rin felt a twist of guilt. But it had been either that or extinction at Federation hands. She'd stopped debating that trade. She could function only if she believed that it had been worth it.

"You can't just keep foisting your refugees on me," Chang En said. "They're cramming the cities. We can't get a moment's rest without their whining in the streets, demanding free accommodations."

"Then put them to work," Jun said coldly. "Have them rebuild your roads and buildings. They'll earn their own keep."

"And how are we supposed to feed them? If they starve at the borders, that's your fault."

Rin noticed it was the northern Warlords—the Ox, Ram, Horse, and Dog Warlords—who did most of the talking. Tsolin sat with his fingers steepled under his chin, saying nothing. The southern Warlords, clustered near the back of the room, largely remained silent. They were the ones who had suffered the most damage, lost the most troops, and thus had the least leverage.

Throughout all of this Daji sat at the head of the table, observing, rarely speaking. She watched the others, one eyebrow arched just a bit higher than the other, as if she were supervising a group of children who had managed to continually disappoint her.

Another hour passed and they had resolved nothing, except for a halfhearted gesture by Tiger Province to allocate six thousand catties of food aid to the landlocked Ram Province in exchange for a thousand pounds of salt. In the grander scheme of things, with thousands of refugees dying of starvation daily, this was hardly a drop in the bucket.

"Why don't we take a recess?" The Empress stood up from the table. "We're not getting anywhere."

"We've barely resolved anything," said Tsolin.

"And the Empire won't collapse if we break for a meal. Cool your heads, gentlemen. Dare I suggest you consider the radical option of compromising with each other?" Daji turned toward Rin. "Meanwhile, I shall retire for a moment to my gardens. Runin, it's time for you to head off to your cell, don't you think?"

Rin stiffened. She couldn't help but shoot a panicked glance at Vaisra.

He stared forward without meeting her eyes, betraying nothing.

This was it. Rin squared her shoulders. She dipped her head in submission, and the Empress smiled.

Rin and the Empress exited not through the throne room but by a narrow corridor in the back. The servants' exit. As they walked Rin could hear the gurgling of the irrigation pipes beneath the floors.

Hours had passed since the council began. The Cike should be stationed within the palace by now, but that thought made her no less terrified. For now she was operating alone with the Empress.

But she still didn't have the fire.

"Are you exhausted yet?" Daji asked.

Rin didn't respond.

"I wanted you to watch the Warlords at their best. They're such a troublesome bunch, aren't they?"

Rin continued pretending she hadn't heard.

"You don't talk very much, do you?" Daji glanced over her shoulder at her. Her eyes slid down to the muzzle. "Oh, of course. Let's get this off you."

She placed her slim fingers on either side of the contraption and gently pulled it off. "Better?"

Rin kept her silence. *Don't engage her*, Vaisra had warned her. *Maintain constant vigilance and let her speak her piece.*

She only needed to buy herself a few more minutes. She could feel the opium wearing off. Her vision had gotten sharper, and her limbs responded without delay to her commands. She just needed

Daji to keep talking until the Phoenix responded to her call. Then she could turn the Autumn Palace to ash.

"Altan was the same," Daji mused. "You know, the first three years he was with us, we thought he was a mute."

Rin nearly tripped over a cobblestone. Daji continued walking as if she had noticed nothing. Rin followed behind, fighting to keep her calm.

"I was sorry to hear of his loss," Daji said. "He was a good commander. One of our very best."

And you killed him, you old bitch. Rin rubbed her fingers together, hoping for a spark, but still the channel to the Phoenix remained blocked.

Just a little longer.

Daji led her behind the building toward a patch of empty space near the servants' quarters.

"The Red Emperor built a series of tunnels in the Autumn Palace so that he could escape to and from any room if need be. Ruler of an entire empire, and he didn't feel safe in his own bed." Daji stopped beside a well and pushed hard at the cover, bracing her feet against the stone floor. The cover slid off with a loud screech. She straightened and brushed her hands on her uniform. "Follow me."

Rin crawled after Daji into the well, which had a set of narrow, spiraling steps built into its wall. Daji reached up and slid the stone closed over them, leaving them standing in pitch darkness. Icy fingers wrapped around Rin's hand. She jumped, but Daji only tightened her grip.

"It's easy to get lost if you've never been here before." Daji's voice echoed around the chamber. "Stay close."

Rin tried to keep count of how many turns they had taken—fifteen, sixteen—but soon enough she lost track of where they were, even in her carefully memorized mental map. How far were they from the council room? Would she have to ignite in the tunnels?

After several more minutes of walking, they resurfaced into a garden. The sudden burst of color was disorienting. Rin peered, blinking, at the resplendent array of lilies, chrysanthemums, and plum trees planted in clusters around rows upon rows of sculptures.

This wasn't the Imperial Garden—the layout of the walls didn't match. The Imperial Garden was shaped in a circle; this garden was erected inside a hexagon. This was a private courtyard.

This hadn't been on the map. Rin had no clue where she was.

Her eyes flickered frantically around her surroundings, seeking out possible exit routes, mapping out useful trajectories and planes of motion for the impending fight, making note of objects that could be weaponized if she couldn't get the fire back in time. Those saplings looked fragile—she might break a branch off for a club if she got desperate. Best if she could back Daji up against the far wall. If nothing else, she could use those loose cobblestones to smash the Empress's head in.

"Magnificent, isn't it?"

Rin realized Daji was waiting for her to say something.

If she engaged Daji in conversation, she'd be walking headfirst into a trap. Vaisra and Eriden had warned her many times how easily Daji would manipulate, could plant thoughts in her mind that weren't her own.

But Daji would grow bored of talking if Rin stayed silent. And Daji's interest in playing with her food was the only thing buying Rin time. Rin needed to keep the conversation going until she had the fire back.

"I guess," she said. "I'm not one for aesthetics."

"Of course you're not. You got your education at Sinegard. They're all crude utilitarians." Daji put her hands on Rin's shoulders and slowly turned her about the garden. "Tell me something. Does the palace look new to you?"

Rin glanced around the hexagon. Yes, it had to be new. The lustrous buildings of the Autumn Palace, though designed with the architecture of the Red Emperor, did not bear the stains of time. The stones were smooth and unscratched, the wooden posts gleaming with fresh paint.

"I suppose," she said. "Is it not?"

"Follow me." Daji walked toward a small gate built into the far wall, pushed it open, and motioned for Rin to follow her through.

The other side of the garden looked like it had been smashed under a giant's heel. The midsection of the opposite wall was in pieces, as if it had been blown apart by cannon fire. Statues were strewn across the overgrown grass, limbs shattered, lying at grotesque and awkward angles.

This wasn't natural decay. Wasn't the result of failure to keep the grounds. This had to be the deliberate action of an invading force.

"I thought the Federation never reached Lusan," Rin said.

"This wasn't the Federation," Daji said. "This wreckage has been here for over seventy years."

"Then who . . . ?"

"The Hesperians. History likes to focus on the Federation, but the masters at Sinegard always gloss over the first colonizers. No one remembers who started the First Poppy War." Daji nudged a statue's head with her foot. "One autumn day seventy years ago, a Hesperian admiral sailed up the Murui and blasted his way into Lusan. He pillaged the palace, razed it to the ground, poured oil over the wreckage, and danced in the ashes. By that evening the Autumn Palace had ceased to exist."

"Then why haven't you rebuilt the garden?" Rin's eyes darted around the grounds while she spoke. A rake lay in the grass about half a yard from her feet. After all these years it was certainly blunt and covered in rust, but Rin might still use it as a staff.

"So we have the reminder," Daji said. "To remember how we were humiliated. To remember that nothing good can come of dealing with the Hesperians."

Rin couldn't let her eyes linger on the rake. Daji would notice. She carefully reconstructed its position from memory. The sharp end was facing her. If she got close enough, she could kick it up into her grasp. Unless the grass had grown too long . . . but it was just grass; if she kicked hard it shouldn't be a problem . . .

"The Hesperians have always intended to come back," Daji said. "The Mugenese weakened this country using western silver. We remember the Federation as the face of the oppressor, but the Hesperians and Bolonians—the Consortium of western countries—are the ones with real power. They are who you ought to be afraid of."

Rin moved just slightly so her left leg was positioned close enough to kick the rake up. "Why are you telling me this?"

"Don't play dumb with me," Daji said sharply. "I know what Vaisra intends to do. I know he intends to go to war. I'm trying to show you that it's the wrong one."

Rin's pulse began to race. This was it—Daji knew her intentions, she needed to fight, it didn't matter if she didn't have the fire yet, she had to get to the rake—

"*Stop that*," Daji ordered.

Rin's limbs froze suddenly in place, muscles stiffening painfully as if the slightest movement might shatter them. She should be springing to fight. She should have at least crouched down. But somehow her body was arrested where she stood, as if she needed the Empress's permission to even breathe.

"We are not finished talking," said Daji.

"I'm finished listening," Rin hissed through clenched teeth.

"Relax. I haven't brought you here to kill you. You are an asset, one of the few I have left. It would be stupid to let you go." Daji stepped in front of her so that they stood face-to-face. Rin hastily averted her eyes. "You're fighting the wrong enemy, dear. Can't you see it?"

Sweat beaded on Rin's neck as she strained to break out of Daji's hold.

"What did Vaisra promise you? You must know you're being used. Is it worth it? Is it money? An estate? No . . . I don't think you could be swayed by material promises." Daji tapped her lacquered nails against painted lips. "No—don't tell me you *believe* him, do you? Did he say he'd bring you a democracy? And you fell for it?"

"He said he'd depose you," Rin whispered. "That's good enough for me."

"Do you really believe that?" Daji sighed. "What would you replace me with? The Nikara people aren't ready for democracy. They're sheep. They're crude, uneducated fools. They need to be told what to do, even if that means tyranny. If Vaisra takes this nation then he'll run it into the ground. The people don't know what to vote for. They don't even understand what it means to vote. And they certainly don't know what's good for them."

"Neither do you," Rin said. "You let them die in hordes. You invited the Mugenese in yourself and you traded them the Cike."

To her surprise, Daji laughed. "Is that what you believe? You can't trust everything you hear."

"Shiro had no reason to lie. I know what you did."

"You understand *nothing*. I have toiled for decades to keep this Empire intact. Do you think I wanted this war?"

"I think that at least half of this country was disposable to you."

"I made a calculated sacrifice. The last time the Federation invaded, the Warlords rallied under the Dragon Emperor. The Dragon Emperor is dead. And the Federation was readying itself for a third invasion. No matter what I did, they were going to attack, and we were nowhere near strong enough to resist them. So I brokered a peace. They could have slices of the east if they would let the heartland remain free."

"So we'd only be *partially* occupied." Rin scoffed. "That's what you call statecraft?"

"Occupied? Not for long. Sometimes the best offensive is false acquiescence. I had a plan. I would become close to Ryohai. I would gain his trust. I would lure him into a false sense of complacency. And then I would kill him. But in the meantime, while their forces were impenetrable, I would play along. I'd do what it took to keep this nation alive."

"Kept alive only to die at Mugenese hands."

Daji's voice hardened. "Don't be so naive. What do you do when you know that war is inevitable? Who do you save?"

"What did you think *we* were going to do?" Rin demanded. "Did you think we would just lie down and let them raze our lands?"

"Better to rule over a fragmented empire than none at all."

"You sentenced millions of us to death."

"I was trying to *save* you. Without me the violence would have been ten times as devastating—"

"Without you, we would at least have had a choice!"

"That would have been no choice. Do you think the Nikara are so altruistic? What if you asked a village to give up their homes so that thousands of others might live? Do you think they would do it? The Nikara are selfish. This entire country is selfish. *People* are selfish. The provinces have always been so *fucking* parochial, unable to see past their own narrow interests to pursue any kind of joint action. You heard those idiots in there. I let you watch for a reason. I can't work with those Warlords. Those fools don't listen."

At the end Daji's voice trembled—only just barely, and only for a second, but Rin heard it.

And for just that moment she saw through that facade of cool, confident beauty, and she saw Su Daji for what she might truly have been: not an invincible Empress, not a treacherous monster, but rather a woman who had been saddled with a country that she didn't know how to run.

She's weak, Rin realized. *She wishes she could control the Warlords, but she can't.*

Because if Daji could have persuaded the Warlords to follow her wishes, she would have done so. She would have done away with the Warlord system and replaced provincial leadership with branches of the Imperial government. But she had left the Warlords in place because even she was not strong enough to supplant them. She was one woman. She couldn't take on their combined armies. She was just barely clinging to power through the last vestiges of the legacy of the Second Poppy War.

But now that the Federation was gone, now that the Warlords no longer had reason to fear, it was very likely the provinces would realize they had no need for Daji.

Daji didn't sound like she was spinning lies. If anything, Rin thought it more likely that she was telling the truth.

But if so—then what? That didn't change things.

Daji had sold the Cike to the Federation. Daji was the reason why Altan was dead. Those were the only two things that mattered.

"This Empire is falling apart," Daji said urgently. "It's becoming weak, you've seen that. But what if we bent the Warlords to our will? Just imagine what you could do under my command." She cupped Rin's cheek in her hand, drew their faces close together. "There's so much you have to learn, and I can teach you."

Rin would have bitten Daji's fingers off if she could move her head. "There's nothing you can teach me."

"Don't be foolish. You need me. You've been feeling the pull, haven't you? It's consuming you. Your mind is not your own."

Rin flinched. "I don't—you're not—"

"You're scared to close your eyes," Daji murmured. "You crave the opium, because that's the only thing that makes your mind your own again. You're fighting your god at every moment. Every instant you're not incinerating everything around you, you're dying. But I can help you." Daji's voice was so soft, so tender, so gentle and reassuring that Rin wanted terribly to believe her. "I can give you your mind back."

"I have control of my mind," Rin said hoarsely.

"Liar. Who would have taught you? Altan? He was barely sane himself. You think I don't know what that's like? The first time we called the gods, I wanted to die. We all did. We thought we were going mad. We wanted to fling our bodies off Mount Tianshan to end it."

Rin couldn't stop herself from asking, "So what did you do?"

Daji touched an icy finger to Rin's lips. "Loyalty first. Then answers."

She snapped her fingers.

Suddenly Rin could move again; could breathe easily again. She hugged trembling arms around her torso.

"You don't have anyone else," Daji said. "You're the last Speerly. Altan is gone. Vaisra has no clue what you're suffering. Only I know how to help you."

Rin hesitated, considering.

She knew she could never trust Daji.

And yet.

Was it better to serve at the hand of a tyrant, to consolidate the Empire into the true dictatorship that it had always aspired to be? Or should she overthrow the Empire and take her chances on democracy?

No—that was a political question, and Rin had no interest in its answer.

She was interested only in her own survival. Altan had trusted the Empress. Altan was dead. She wouldn't make that same mistake.

She kicked out with her left foot. The rake slammed hard into her hand—the grass offered less resistance than she'd thought—and she sprang forward, spinning the rake in a forward loop.

But attacking Daji was like attacking air. The Empress dodged effortlessly, skirting so fast through the courtyard that Rin could barely track her movements.

"You think this is wise?" Daji didn't sound the least bit breathless. "You're a little girl armed with a stick."

You're a little girl armed with fire, said the Phoenix.

Finally.

Rin held the rake still so she could concentrate on pulling the flame out from inside her, gathering the searing heat in her palms just as something silver flashed past her face and pinged off the brick wall.

Needles. Daji hurled them at her fistfuls at a time, pulling them out from her sleeves in seemingly endless quantities. The fire dissipated. Rin swung the rake in a desperate circle in front of her, knocking the needles out of the air as fast as they came.

"You're slow. You're clumsy." Now Daji was on the attack, forcing Rin backward in a steady retreat. "You fight like you've never seen battle."

Rin struggled to keep her hands on the heavy rake. She couldn't concentrate enough to call the fire; she was too focused on warding off the needles. Panic clouded her senses. At this rate she'd exhaust herself on the defensive.

"Does it ever bother you?" whispered Daji. "That you are only a pale imitation of Altan?"

Rin's back slammed into the brick wall. She had nowhere left to run.

"Look at me." Daji's voice reverberated through the air, echoed over and over again in Rin's mind.

Rin squeezed her eyes shut. She had to call the fire now, she'd never get this chance again—but her mind was leaving her. The world was not quite going dark, but *shifting*. Everything suddenly seemed too bright, everything was the wrong color and the wrong shape and she couldn't tell the grass from the sky, or her hands from her own feet . . .

Daji's voice seemed to come from everywhere. "Look into my eyes."

Rin didn't remember opening her eyes. She didn't remember having the chance to even resist. All she knew was that one instant her eyes were closed and the next she was staring into two yellow orbs. At first they were golden all the way through, and then little black dots appeared that grew larger and larger until they encompassed Rin's field of vision.

The world had turned entirely dark. She was so cold. She heard howls and screams from far away, guttural noises that almost sounded like words but none she could comprehend.

This was the spirit plane. This was where she faced Daji's goddess.

But she was not alone.

Help me, Rin thought. *Help me, please.*

And the god answered. A wave of bright, warm heat flooded the plane. Flames surrounded her like protective wings.

"Nüwa, you old bitch," said the Phoenix.

A woman's voice, much deeper than Daji's, reverberated through the plane. "And you, snippy as always."

What was this creature? Rin strained to see the goddess's form, but the Phoenix's flames illuminated only a small corner of the psychospiritual space.

"You could never challenge me," said Nüwa. "I was there when the universe tore itself out of darkness. I mended the heavens when they split apart. I gave life to man."

Something stirred in the darkness.

The Phoenix shrieked as a snake's head sprang out and sank its fangs into its shoulder. The Phoenix reared its head, flames spinning out at nothing. Rin felt the god's pain just as acutely as if the snake had bitten her, like two red-hot blades had been jammed between her shoulder blades.

"What do you dream of?" Daji's voice now, overwhelming Rin's mind with every word. "Is this it?"

The world shifted again.

Bright colors. Rin was running across an island in a dress she'd never worn before, with a crescent moon necklace she'd seen only in her dreams, toward a village that didn't exist now except as a place of ash and bone. She ran across the sands of Speer as it was fifty years ago—full of life, full of people with dark skin like hers, who stood up and waved and smiled when they saw her.

"You could have that," Daji said. "You could have everything you wanted."

Rin believed, too, that Daji would be that kind, would let her remain in that illusion until she died.

"Or is this what you want?"

Speer disappeared. The world turned dark again. Rin couldn't see anything but a shadowy figure. But she knew that silhouette, that tall, lean build. She could never forget it. The memory of it was scorched in her mind from the last time she had seen him, walking down that pier. But this time he walked toward her. She was watching the moment of Altan's death in reverse. Time was unraveling. She could take it all back, she could have *him* back.

This couldn't possibly be just a dream. He was too solid—she could sense the mortal weight of him filling up the space around her; and when she touched his face it was solid and warm and bloody and *alive* . . .

"Just relax," he whispered. "Stop resisting."

"But it *hurts* . . ."

"It only hurts if you fight."

He kissed her and it felt like a punch. This wasn't what she wanted—this felt wrong, this was all wrong—his grip was too tight around her arms, he was clutching her against his chest like he wanted to crush her. He tasted like blood.

"That's not him."

Chaghan's voice. A split second later Rin felt him in her mind—a cold, harsh presence in blinding white, a shard of ice piercing the spiritual plane. She had never been so relieved to see him.

"It's an illusion." Chaghan's voice cleared her mind like a shower of cold water. "Get a grip on yourself."

The illusions dissipated. Altan faded into nothing. Then there were only the three of them, souls tethered to gods, hanging suspended in primordial darkness.

"What's this?" Nüwa's voice blended together with Daji's. "A Naimad?" Laughter rang across the plane. "Your people should know not to defy me. Did the Sorqan Sira teach you nothing?"

"I don't fear you," Chaghan said.

In the physical world he was a skeletal waif, so frail he seemed only a shadow of a person. But here he emanated raw power. His voice carried a ring of authority, a gravity that pulled Rin toward him. Right then, Chaghan could reach into the center of her mind and extract every thought she'd ever had as casually as if he were flipping through a book, and she would let him.

"You will go back, Nüwa." Chaghan raised his voice. "Return to the darkness. This world no longer belongs to you."

The darkness hissed in response. Rin braced herself for an impending attack. But Chaghan uttered an incantation in words she did not understand, words that pushed Nüwa's presence back so far that Rin could barely see the outlines of the snake anymore.

Bright lights flooded her vision. Wrenched down from the realm of the ethereal, Rin staggered at the sheer solidity, the physicality of the solid world.

Chaghan stood doubled over beside her, gasping.

Across the courtyard, Daji wiped the back of her mouth with her sleeve. She smiled. Her teeth were stained with blood.

"You are adorable," she said. "And here I thought the Ketreyids were only a fond memory."

"Stand back," Chaghan muttered to Rin.

"What are you—"

"Run on my word." Chaghan tossed a dark circular lump onto the ground. It rolled forward several paces and came to a rest at the Empress's feet. Rin heard a faint sizzling noise, followed by an awful, acrid, and terribly familiar smell.

Daji glanced down, puzzled.

"Go," Chaghan said, and they fled just as Ramsa's signature poop bomb detonated inside the Autumn Palace.

A series of explosions followed them as they ran, ongoing blasts that could not have possibly been triggered by the single bomb. Building after building collapsed around them, creating a wall of fire and debris from behind which no one could pursue them.

"Ramsa," Chaghan explained. "Kid doesn't cut corners."

He yanked her behind a low wall. They crouched down, hands clapped over their ears as the last of the buildings erupted mere yards away.

Rin wiped the dust from her eyes. "Daji's dead?"

"Something like that doesn't die so easily." Chaghan coughed and pounded at his chest with his fist. "She'll be after us soon.

We should go. There's a well a block down; Aratsha knows we're coming."

"What about Vaisra?"

Still coughing, Chaghan staggered to his feet. "Are you crazy?"

"He's still in there!"

"And he's likely dead. Daji's guards will have swarmed the council room by now."

"We don't know that."

"So what, you're going to go *check*?" Chaghan grabbed her shoulders and pinned her against the wall. "Listen to me. It's over. Your coup is finished. Daji's going to come for Dragon Province, and when she does, we're going to lose. Vaisra can't protect you. You need to run."

"And go where?" she asked. "And do what?"

What did Vaisra promise you? You must know you're being used.

Rin knew that. She'd always known that. But maybe she *needed* to be used. Maybe she needed someone to tell her when, and who, to fight. She needed someone to give her orders and a purpose.

Vaisra was the first person in a long, long time who had made her feel stable enough to see a point in staying alive. And if he died here, it was on her.

"Are you insane?" Chaghan shouted. "You want to live, you fucking hide."

"Then you hide. I'm fighting." Rin wrenched her wrists from his grasp and pushed him away. She used more force than she'd meant to; she'd forgotten he was so thin. He stumbled backward, tripped on a rock, and toppled to the ground.

"You're crazy," he said.

"We're all crazy," she muttered as she jumped over his sprawled form and set off at a run toward the council room.

Imperial guards had swarmed the council chamber, pressing steadily in against the two-man army that was Suni and Baji. The Warlords had scattered from their seats. The Hare Warlord huddled against the wall, the Rooster Warlord crouched quivering under the table, and the young Tiger Warlord was curled in a corner, head pressed between his knees as blades clashed inches from his head.

Rin faltered at the doors. She couldn't call the fire now. She didn't have enough control to target her flames. If she lit up the room, she'd kill everyone in it.

"Here!" Baji kicked a sword toward her. She scooped it up and jumped into the fray.

Vaisra wasn't dead. He fought at the center of the room, battling both Jun and the Wolf Meat General. For a second it seemed like he might hold them off. He wielded his blade with a ferocious strength and precision that was stunning to watch.

But he was still only one man.

"Watch out!" Rin screamed.

The Wolf Meat General tried to catch Vaisra off guard. Vaisra spun about and disarmed him with a savage kick to the knee. Chang En dropped to the ground, howling. Vaisra reeled back from the kick, trying to regain his balance, and Jun took the opening to push his blade through Vaisra's shoulder.

Baji barreled into Jun's side and tackled him to the ground. Rin ran forward to catch Vaisra just as he crumpled to the floor; blood spilled over her arms, hot and wet and slippery, and she was astounded by how *much* of it there was.

"Are you— Please, are you—"

She prodded frantically around his chest, trying to stanch the blood with her palm. She could barely see the wound, his torso was so slick with blood, but finally her fingers pressed against the entry point in his right shoulder. Not a vital spot.

She dared to hope. If they acted quickly he might still live. But first they had to get out.

"Suni!" she shrieked.

He appeared instantly at her side. She pushed Vaisra into his arms. "Take him."

Suni slung Vaisra over his shoulders the way one might carry a calf and elbowed his way toward the exit. Baji followed closely, guarding their rear.

Rin picked her way past Jun's limp form. She didn't know if he was dead or alive, but that didn't matter now. She ducked under a guard's arm and followed her men out, over the threshold and toward the closest well.

She leaned over the side and screamed Aratsha's name into the dark surface.

Nothing. There was no time to wait for Aratsha's response; he was there or he wasn't, and Daji's guards were feet away. All she could do was plunge into the water, hold her breath, and pray.

Aratsha answered.

Rin fought the urge to flail inside the pitch-black irrigation channels—that would only make it harder for Aratsha to propel her through the water—and instead focused on taking deep and measured breaths in the pocket of air that enveloped her head. Still, she couldn't ward off the clenching fear that the air would run out. Already she could feel the warmth of her own stale breath.

She broke the surface. She clawed her way up the riverbank and collapsed, chest heaving as she sucked in fresh air. Seconds later Suni exploded out of the water, depositing Vaisra on the shore before climbing up himself.

"What happened?" Nezha came running up to them, followed closely by Eriden and his guard. His eyes landed on his father. "Is he—"

"Alive," Rin said. "If we're quick."

Nezha turned to the two closest soldiers. "Get my father on the ship."

They hoisted Vaisra up between them and set off at a dash toward the *Seagrim*. Nezha pulled Rin to her feet. "What just—"

"No time." She spat out a mouthful of river water. "Have your crew weigh anchor. We've got to get out."

Nezha slung her arm over his shoulder and helped her stagger toward the ship. "It failed?"

"It worked." Rin stumbled into his side, trying to keep pace. "You wanted a war. We just started one."

The *Seagrim* had already begun pushing away from its berth. Crewmen at both ends hacked the ropes keeping the ship tethered to the dock, setting it free to drift with the current. Nezha and Rin jumped into one of the rowboats dangling by the hull. Inch by inch the boat began to rise.

Above, deckhands lowered the *Seagrim*'s sails and turned them toward the wind. Below, a loud grinding noise sounded as the paddle wheel began to churn rhythmically against the water, carrying them swiftly away from the capital.

CHAPTER 10

The *Seagrim*'s crew operated under a somber silence. Word had spread that Vaisra was badly injured. But no news emerged from the physician's office and no one dared intrude to ask.

Captain Eriden had issued only one order: to get the *Seagrim* far away from Lusan as quickly as possible. Any soldier not working a paddling shift was sent to the top deck to man the trebuchets and crossbows, ready to fire at first warning.

Rin paced back and forth by the stern. She didn't have a crossbow or a spyglass, and in her state she was more of a hindrance than an asset to deck defense—she was too jumpy to hold a weapon steady, too anxious to comprehend rapid orders. But she refused to go wait belowdecks. She had to know what was happening.

She kept looking down at her body to check that it was still there, was still working. It seemed impossible to her that she had escaped an encounter with the Vipress unscathed. The ship's physician had cursorily examined her for broken bones but found nothing. Aside from some bruising, she felt no serious pain. Yet she was convinced that something was deeply wrong with her; something deep, internal, a poison that had wrapped around her bones.

Chaghan, too, seemed badly shaken. He'd been silent, unresponsive until they pulled out of harbor, and then he had collapsed against Qara and sunk to the floor, knees drawn up against his chest in a miserable huddle while his sister bent over him, whispering words no one else could understand into his ear.

The crew, clearly unsettled, gave them a wide berth. Rin tried to ignore them until she heard gasping noises from the deck. At first she thought he was sobbing, but no—he was just trying to breathe, jagged gasps rocking his frail form.

She knelt down beside the twins. She wasn't sure whether she ought to try to touch Chaghan. "Are you all right?"

"I'm fine."

"Are you sure?"

Chaghan raised his head and took a deep, shuddering breath. His eyes were ringed with red. "She was—I've never . . . I never imagined anyone could be so . . ."

"What?"

He shook his head.

Qara answered for him. "*Stable.*" She whispered the word like it was a horrifying idea. "She shouldn't be so stable."

"What is she?" Rin asked. "What goddess is that?"

"She's old power," Chaghan said. "She's something that's been alive longer than the world itself. I thought she'd be weakened, now that the other two are gone, but she's . . . if that's the Vipress at her weakest . . ." He slammed a palm against the deck. "We were fools to try."

"She's not invincible," Rin said. "You beat her."

"No, I surprised her. And then for only an instant. I don't think things like that can be *beat*. We got lucky."

"Any longer and she would have had your minds," Qara said. "You'd be trapped forever in those illusions."

She'd turned just as pale as her brother. Rin wondered how much Qara had seen. Qara hadn't even been there, but Rin knew the twins were bonded by some odd Hinterlander magic. When

Chaghan bled, Qara hurt. If Chaghan was shaken by Daji, then Qara must have felt it back on the *Seagrim*, a psychic tremble that threatened to poison her soul.

"So we'll find some other way," Rin said. "She's still a mortal body, she's still—"

"She will squeeze your soul in her fist and turn you into a babbling idiot," Chaghan said. "I'm not trying to dissuade you. I know you'll fight her to the end. But I hope you realize you're going to go mad trying."

Then so be it. Rin wrapped her arms around her knees. "Did you see? In there, when she showed me?"

Chaghan gave her a pitying look. "I couldn't help it."

Qara looked away. She must have seen, too.

For some reason, in that moment Rin felt like it was the most important thing in the world for her to explain herself to the twins. She felt guilty, dirty, like she had been caught in a terrible lie. "It wasn't like that. With him. With Altan, I mean—"

"I know," Chaghan said.

She wiped at her eyes. "It was never like that. I mean—I think I wanted—but he never—"

"We know," Qara said. "Trust us, we know."

Rin was stunned when Chaghan reached out and put his arm around her shoulder. She would have cried, but she felt too raw inside, like she had been hollowed out with a carving knife.

Chaghan's arm rested at an odd angle over her back; his bony elbow joint dug painfully into her bone. After a while she shifted her right shoulder, and he withdrew his arm.

Hours passed before Nezha reemerged onto the deck.

Rin searched his face for clues. He looked wan but not grief-stricken, exhausted but not panicked, which meant . . .

She hastened to her feet. "Your father?"

"I think he'll pull through." He rubbed at his temples. "Dr. Sien finally kicked me out. Said to give Father some space."

"He's awake?"

"Sleeping for now. He was delirious for a bit, but Dr. Sien said that was a good sign. Meant he was talking."

She let loose a long breath. "I'm glad."

He sat down and rubbed his hands down his legs with a small sigh of relief. He must have been standing beside his father's bedside for hours.

"Watching something?" he asked her.

"I'm watching nothing." She squinted at the receding outline of Lusan. Only the highest pagoda towers of the palace were still visible. "That's what's bothering me. No one's coming after us."

She couldn't understand why the riverways were so calm, so silent. Why weren't arrows flying through the air? Why weren't they being pursued by Imperial vessels? Perhaps the Militia lay in wait at the gates at the province's edge. Perhaps they were sailing straight toward a trap.

But the gates were open, and no ships came chasing after them in the darkness.

"Who would they send?" Nezha asked. "They don't have a navy at the Autumn Palace."

"And no one in any of the provinces has one?"

"Ah." Nezha smiled. Why was he *smiling*? "You don't understand. We're not going back the same way. We're headed out to sea this time. Tsolin's ships patrol the Nariin coast."

"And Tsolin won't interfere?"

"No. Father's made him choose. He's not going to choose the Empire."

She couldn't understand his logic. "Because . . . ?"

"Because now there's going to be a war, whether Tsolin likes it or not. And he's not putting his money against Vaisra. So he'll let us through unharmed, and I'll bet that he'll be at our council table in under a month."

Rin was frankly amazed by the confidence with which the House of Yin seemed to manipulate people. "That's assuming he gets out of Lusan."

"If he hasn't made contingency plans for this I'll be shocked."

"Did you ask if he had?"

Nezha chuckled. "It's *Tsolin*. Asking would be an insult."

"Or, you know, a decent precaution."

"Oh, we're about to fight a civil war. You'll have plenty of chances to take precautions." His tone sounded ridiculously cavalier.

"You really think we can win this?" she asked.

"We'll be all right."

"How do you know?"

He grinned sideways at her. "Because we've got the best navy in the Empire. Because we have the most brilliant strategist Sinegard has ever seen. And because we've got you."

"Fuck off."

"I'm serious. You know you're a military asset worth your weight in silver, and if Kitay's on strategy, then that gives us excellent chances."

"Is Kitay—"

"He's fine. He's belowdecks. He's been chatting with the admirals; Father gave him full access to our intelligence files, and he's getting caught up."

"I guess he came around pretty quickly, then."

"We thought he might." Nezha's tone confirmed what she already suspected.

"You knew his father was dead."

He didn't bother denying it. "Father told me weeks ago. He said not to tell Kitay. Not until we'd reached Lusan, anyway."

"Why?"

"Because it would mean more if it didn't come from us. Because it would feel less to him like manipulation."

"So you let him think his father was alive for *weeks*?"

"We're not the ones who killed him, were we?" Nezha didn't look sorry in the slightest. "Look, Rin. My father is very good at cultivating talent. He knows people. He knows how to pull their strings. That doesn't mean he doesn't care about them."

"But I don't want to be lied to," she said.

He squeezed her hand. "I would never lie to you."

Rin wanted desperately to believe that.

"Excuse me," said Captain Eriden.

They turned around.

For once, Eriden did not look immaculately groomed, was not standing at perfect attention. The captain was wan and diminished, shoulders slouching, lines of worry etched across his face. He dipped his head toward them. "The Dragon Warlord would like to see you."

"I'll go right now," Nezha said.

"Not you," said Eriden. He nodded to Rin. "Just her."

Rin was surprised to find Vaisra sitting upright behind the table, wearing a fresh military uniform free of blood. When he breathed, he winced, but only slightly; otherwise he looked as if he had never been injured.

"They told me you dragged me out of the palace," he said.

She sat down across from him. "My men helped."

"And why would you do that?"

"I don't know," she said frankly. She was still trying to figure that out herself. She might have left him in the throne room. Alone, the Cike would have a better chance at survival—they didn't need to ally themselves with a province that had declared open war on the Empire.

But then what? Where did they go from here?

"Why are you still with us?" Vaisra asked. "We failed. And I thought you weren't interested in being a foot soldier."

"Why does it matter? Do you want me to leave?"

"I would prefer to know why people serve in my army. Some do it for silver. Some do it for the sheer thrill of battle. I don't think you are here for either."

He was right. But she didn't know how to answer. How could she explain to him why she'd stayed when she couldn't articulate it to herself?

All she knew was that it felt *good* to be part of Vaisra's army, to act on Vaisra's orders, to be Vaisra's weapon and tool.

If she wasn't making the decisions, then nothing could be her fault.

She couldn't put the Cike in danger if she didn't tell them what to do. And she couldn't be blamed for anyone she killed if she was acting on orders.

And she didn't just crave the simple absolution of responsibility. She craved *Vaisra*. She wanted his approval. Needed it. He provided her with structure, control, and direction that she hadn't had since Altan died, and it felt so terribly good.

Since she'd set the Phoenix on the longbow island she'd been lost, spinning in a void of guilt and anger, and for the first time in a long time, she didn't feel like she was drifting anymore.

She had a reason to live past revenge.

"I don't know what I'm supposed to do," she said finally. "Or who I'm supposed to be. Or where I came from, or—or . . ." She broke off, trying to make sense of the feelings swirling through her mind. "All I know is that I'm alone, I'm the only one left, and it's because of her."

Vaisra leaned forward. "Do you want to fight this war?"

"No. I mean—I don't—I *hate* war." She took a deep breath. "At least I think I should. Everyone is supposed to hate war, or there's something wrong with you. Right? But I'm a soldier. That's all I know how to be. So isn't that what I'm supposed to do? I mean, sometimes I think maybe I can stop, maybe I can just run away. But what I've seen—what I've done—I can't come back from that."

She looked at him beseechingly, desperate for him to disagree, but Vaisra only shook his head. "No. You can't."

"Is it true?" she asked in a small, scared voice. "What the Warlords said?"

"What did they say?" he asked gently.

"They said I'm like a dog. They said I'd be better off dead. Does everyone want me dead?"

Vaisra reached out and took her hands in his. His grip was soft. Tender, almost.

"No one else is going to say this to you. So listen closely, Runin. You have been blessed with immense power. Don't guilt yourself for using it. I won't permit it."

She couldn't hold the tears back anymore. Her voice broke. "I just wanted to—"

"Stop crying. You're better than that."

She choked back a sob.

His voice turned steely. "It doesn't matter what you want. Don't you understand that? You are the most powerful creature in this world right now. You have an ability that can begin or end wars. You could launch this Empire into a glorious new and united age, and you could also destroy us. What you don't get to do is remain neutral. When you have the power that you do, your life is not your own."

His fingers tightened around hers. "People will seek to use you or destroy you. If you want to live, you must pick a side. So do not shirk from war, child. Do not flinch from suffering. When you hear screaming, run toward it."

PART II

CHAPTER 11

Nezha pushed her door open. "You awake?"

"What's going on?" Rin yawned. It was still dark outside her porthole, but Nezha was dressed in full uniform. Behind him stood Kitay, looking half-asleep and very crabby.

"Come upstairs," said Nezha.

"He wants to show us the view," Kitay grumbled. "Get a move on so I can go back to sleep."

Rin followed them down the hall, hopping on one foot as she pulled her shoes on.

The *Seagrim* was blanketed in such a dense blue mist that they might have been sailing through clouds. Rin could not see the landmarks surrounding them until they were close enough for shapes to emerge through the fog. On her left, great cliffs guarded the narrow entrance to Arlong: a dark sliver of space inside the yawning stone wall. Against the light of the rising sun, the rock face glimmered a bright crimson.

Those were the famous Red Cliffs of the Dragon Province. The cliff walls were said to shine a brighter red with every failed invasion against the stronghold, painted with the blood of sailors whose ships had been dashed against those stones.

Rin could just make out massive characters etched into the

walls—words that she could see only if she tilted her head the right way and if the faint sunlight hit them just so. "What do those say?"

"Can't you read it?" Kitay asked. "It's just Old Nikara."

She tried not to roll her eyes. "Translate for me, then."

"You actually can't," Nezha said. "All of those characters have layers upon layers of meaning, and they don't obey modern Nikara grammar rules, so any translation must be imperfect and unfaithful."

Rin had to smile. Those were words recited straight from the Linguistics texts they'd both read at Sinegard, back when their biggest concern was the next week's grammar quiz. "So which translation do you think is right?"

"'Nothing lasts,'" said Nezha, at the same time that Kitay said, "'The world doesn't exist.'"

Kitay wrinkled his nose at Nezha. "'Nothing lasts'? What kind of translation is that?"

"The historically accurate one," Nezha said. "The last faithful minister of the Red Emperor carved those words into the cliffs. When the Red Emperor died, his empire fragmented into provinces. His sons and generals snapped up prize pieces of land like wolves. But the minister of the Dragon Province didn't pledge allegiance to any of the newly formed states."

"I assume that didn't end well," Rin said.

"It's as Father says: there's no such thing as neutrality in a civil war," Nezha said. "The Eight Princes came for the Dragon Province and tore Arlong apart. Thus the minister's epigram. Most think it's a nihilistic cry, a warning that nothing lasts. Not friendships, not loyalties, and certainly not empire. Which makes it consistent with your translation, Kitay, if you think about it. This world is ephemeral. Permanence is an illusion."

As they spoke, the *Seagrim* passed into a channel through the cliffs so narrow that Rin marveled that the warship did not breach its hull along the rocks. The ship must have been designed according to the exact specifications of the channel—and even then, it was a remarkable feat of navigation that they slipped through the walls without so much as scraping stone.

As they penetrated the passage, the cliffs themselves appeared to cleave open, revealing Arlong between them like a pearl hidden inside an oystershell. The city within was startlingly lush, all waterfalls and running streams and more green than Rin had ever seen in Tikany. On the other side of the channel, she could just trace the faint outlines of two mountain chains peeking over the mist: the Qinling Mountains to the east and the Daba range to the west.

"I used to climb up those cliffs all the time." Nezha pointed toward a steep set of stairs carved into the red walls that made Rin dizzy just looking at them. "You can see everything from up there—the ocean, the mountains, the entire province."

"So you could see attackers coming from every direction from miles off," Kitay said. "That's very useful."

Now Rin understood. This explained why Vaisra was so confident in his military base. Arlong might be the most impenetrable city in the Empire. The only way to invade was by sailing through a narrow channel or scaling a massive mountain range. Arlong was easy to defend and tremendously difficult to attack—the ideal wartime capital.

"We used to spend days on the beaches, too," said Nezha. "You can't see them from here, but there are coves hidden under the cliff walls if you know where to find them. In Arlong the riverbanks are so large that if you didn't know any better, you'd think you were on the ocean."

Rin shuddered at the thought. Tikany had been landlocked, and she couldn't imagine growing up this close to so much water. She would have felt so vulnerable. Anything could land on those shores. Pirates. Hesperians. The Federation.

Speer had been that vulnerable.

Nezha cast her a sideways look. "You don't like the ocean?"

She thought of Altan pitching backward into black water. She thought of a long, desperate swim and of nearly losing her mind. "I don't like the way it smells," she said.

"But it just smells like salt," he said.

"No. It smells like blood."

The moment the *Seagrim* dropped anchor, a group of soldiers escorted Vaisra off the ship and ensconced him inside a curtained sedan chair to be carted off to the palace. Rin had not seen Vaisra in more than a week, but she'd heard rumors his condition had worsened. She supposed the last thing he wanted was for word to spread.

"Should we be concerned?" she asked, watching as the chair made its way down the pier.

"He just needs some shoreside rest." Nezha's words didn't sound forced, which Rin took as a good sign. "He'll recover."

"In time to lead a campaign north, you think?" Kitay asked.

"Certainly. And if not Father, then my brother. Let's get you to the barracks." Nezha motioned toward the gangplank. "Come on. I'll introduce you to the ranks."

Arlong was an amphibious city composed of a series of interconnected islands scattered inside a wide swath of the Western Murui. Nezha led Rin, Kitay, and the Cike into one of the slim, ubiquitous sampans that navigated Arlong's interior. As Nezha guided their boat into the inner city, Rin swallowed down a wave of nausea. The city reminded her of Ankhiluun; it was far less shabby but just as disorienting in its reliance on waterways. She hated it. *What was so wrong with dry land?*

"No bridges?" she asked. "No roads?"

"No need. Whole islands linked by canals." Nezha stood at the stern, steering the sampan forward with gentle sweeps of the rudder. "It's arranged in a circular grid, like a conch shell."

"Your city looks like it's halfway to sinking," Rin said.

"That's on purpose. It's nearly impossible to launch a land invasion on Arlong." He guided the sampan around a corner. "This was the first capital of the Red Emperor. Back during his wars with the Speerlies, he surrounded himself with water. He never felt safe without it—he chose to build a city at Arlong for precisely that reason. Or so the myth goes."

"Why was he obsessed with water?"

"How else do you protect yourself from beings who control fire? He was terrified of Tearza and her army."

"I thought he was in love with Tearza," Rin said.

"He loved her *and* feared her," Nezha said. "They're not mutually exclusive."

Rin was glad when they finally pulled up to a solid sidewalk. She felt far more comfortable on land, where the floorboards wouldn't shift under her feet, where she was at no risk of tipping into the water.

But Nezha looked happier over water than she'd ever seen him. He controlled the rudder like it was a natural extension of his body, and he hopped lightly from the edge of the sampan to the walkway as if it were no more difficult than walking through a grassy field.

He led them into the heart of Arlong's military district. As they walked, Rin saw a series of tower ships, vessels that could carry entire villages, mounted with massive catapults and studded with rows and rows of iron cannons shaped like dragons' heads, mouths curled in vicious sneers, waiting to spit fire and iron.

"These ships are stupidly tall," she said.

"That's because they're designed to capture walled cities," Nezha said. "Naval warfare is a matter of collecting cities like gambling chips. Those structures are meant to overtop walls along major waterways. Strategically speaking, most provinces are just empty space. The major cities control economic and political levers, the transportation and communications routes. So control the city and you've controlled the province."

"I know that," she said, slightly irked that he thought she needed a primer on basic invasion strategy. "I'm just concerned about their maneuverability. How much agility do you get in shallow waters?"

"Not much, but that doesn't matter. Most naval warfare is still decided by hand-to-hand combat," Nezha explained. "The tower ships take down the walls. We go in and pick up the pieces."

Ramsa piped up from behind them, "I don't understand why we couldn't have taken this beautiful, giant fleet and blasted the shit out of the Autumn Palace."

"Because we were attempting a bloodless coup," Nezha said. "Father wanted to avoid a war if he could. Sending a massive fleet up to Lusan might have given the wrong message."

"So what I'm hearing is that it's all Rin's fault," said Ramsa. "Classic."

Nezha walked backward so that he could face them as he talked. He looked terribly smug as he gestured to the ships around them. "A few years ago we added crossbeams to increase structural integrity in the hulls. And we redesigned the rudders—they have more mobility now, so they can operate in a broader range of water depths . . ."

"And your rudder?" Kitay inquired. "Still plunging those depths?"

Nezha ignored him. "We've improved our anchors, too."

"How so?" Rin asked, mostly because she could tell he wanted to brag.

"The teeth. They're arranged circularly instead of in one direction. Means they hardly ever break."

Rin found this very funny. "Does that happen often?"

"You'd be surprised," Nezha said. "During the Second Poppy War we lost a crucial naval skirmish because the ship started drifting out to sea without its crew during a maelstrom. We've learned from that mistake."

He continued to elucidate newer innovations as they walked, gesturing with the pride of a newborn parent. "We started building the hulls with the broadest beam aft—makes it easier to steer at slow speeds. The junks have sails divided into horizontal panels by bamboo slats that make them more aerodynamic."

"You know a lot about ships," Rin said.

"I spent my childhood next door to a shipyard. It'd be embarrassing if I didn't."

Rin stopped walking, letting the others pass her until she and Nezha stood alone. She lowered her voice. "Be honest with me. How long have you been preparing for this war?"

He didn't miss a beat. Didn't even blink. "As long as I've been alive."

So Nezha had spent his entire childhood readying himself to betray the Empire. So he had known, when he came to Sinegard, that one day he would lead a fleet against his classmates.

"You've been a traitor since birth," she said.

"Depends on your perspective."

"But I was fighting for the Militia until now. We could have been enemies."

"I know." Nezha beamed. "Aren't you so glad we're not?"

The Dragon Army absorbed the Cike into its ranks with impressive efficiency. A young woman named Officer Sola received them at the barracks. She couldn't have been more than a few years older than Rin, and she wore the green armband that indicated she had graduated from Sinegard with a Strategy degree.

"You trained with Irjah?" Kitay asked.

Sola glanced at Kitay's own faded armband. "What division?"

"Second. I was with him at Golyn Niis."

"Ah." Sola's mouth pressed into a thin line. "How did he die?"

Skinned alive and hung over a city wall, Rin thought.

"With honor," Kitay said.

"He'd be proud of you," Sola said.

"Well, I'm quite sure he would have called us traitors."

"Irjah cared about justice," Sola said in a hard voice. "He would have been with us."

Within the hour Sola had assigned them to bunks in the barracks, given them a walking tour of the sprawling base that occupied three mini islands and the canals in between, and outfitted them with new uniforms. These were made of warmer, sturdier material than any Militia suits Rin had ever seen. The cloth base came with a set of lamellar armor made up of overlapping leather and metal plates so confusing that Sola had to demonstrate in detail what went where.

Sola didn't point them to any changing rooms, so Rin stripped down along with her men, pulled her new uniform on, and stretched her limbs out. She was amazed at the flexibility. The lamellar armor was far more sophisticated than the flimsy uniforms the Militia issued, and likely cost three times as much.

"We have better blacksmiths than they do up north." Sola passed Rin a chest plate. "Our armor's lighter. Deflects more."

"What should we do with these?" Ramsa held up a bundle of his old clothing.

Sola wrinkled her nose. "Burn them."

The barracks and armory were cleaner, larger, and better stocked than any Militia facility Rin had ever visited. Kitay rifled through the gleaming rows of swords and knives until he found a set that suited him; the rest of them turned in their weapons to the blacksmith for refurbishment.

"I was told you had a detonations expert in your squadron." Sola pulled the curtain aside to reveal the full store of the First Platoon's explosives. Stacks upon stacks of missiles, rockets, and fire lances were arranged neatly in pyramidal piles waiting in the cool darkness to be loaded onto warships.

Ramsa made a highly suggestive whimpering noise. He lifted a missile shaped like a dragon head out from the pile and turned it over in his hands. "Is this what I think it is?"

Sola nodded. "It's a two-stage rocket. The main vessel contains the booster. The rest detonates in midair. Gives it a little extra thrust."

"How'd you manage these?" Ramsa demanded. "I've been working on this for at least two years."

"And we've been working on it for five."

Ramsa pointed at another pile of explosives. "What do *those* do?"

"They're fin-mounted winged rockets." Sola sounded amused. "The fins are for guided flight. We see better accuracy with these than the two-stage rockets."

Someone with a bad sense of humor had carved the head to look like a fish with a droopy expression. Ramsa ran his fingers along the fins. "What kind of range do you get on these?"

"That depends," said Sola. "On a clear day, sixty miles. Rainy days, as far as you can get them."

Ramsa weighed the missile in his hands, looking so delighted that Rin suspected he might have gotten an erection. "Oh, we are going to have fun with these."

"Are you hungry?" Nezha knocked on the door frame.

Rin glanced up. She was alone in the barracks. Kitay had left to find the Dragon Province's archives, and the other Cike members' first priority had been finding the mess hall.

"Not very," she said.

"Good. Do you want to see something cool?"

"Is it another ship?" she asked.

"Yes. But you'll really like this one. Nice uniform, by the way."

She smacked his arm. "Eyes up, General."

"I'm just saying the colors look good on you. You make a good Dragon."

Rin heard the shipyard long before they reached it. Over the cacophonous din of screeches and hammering, they had to yell to hear each other. She had assumed what she saw in the harbor was a completed fleet, but apparently several more vessels were still under construction.

Her eyes landed immediately on the ship at the far end. It was still in its initial stages—only a skeleton thus far. But if she imagined the structure to be built around it, it was titanic. It seemed impossible that a thing like that could ever stay afloat, let alone get past the channel through the Red Cliffs.

"We're going to board *that* to the capital?" she asked.

"That one isn't ready. It keeps getting updated with plans from the west. It's Jinzha's pet project; he's a perfectionist about stuff like this."

"A pet project," she repeated. "Your siblings just build massive boats for their *pet projects*."

Nezha shook his head. "It was supposed to be finished in time for the northern campaign, whenever that gets off the ground. Now it'll be much longer. They've changed the design to a defensive warship. It's meant to guard Arlong now, not to lead the fleet."

"Why is it behind schedule?"

"Fire broke out in the shipyard overnight. Some idiot on watch kicked his lamp over. Set construction back by months. They had to import the timber from the Dog Province. Father had to get pretty creative with that—it's hard to ship in massive amounts of lumber and hide the fact that you're building a fleet. Took a few weeks of dealing with Moag's smugglers."

Rin could see blackened edges on some of the skeleton's outer boards. But the rest had been replaced with new timber, smoothed to a shine.

"The whole thing made a big stir in the city," Nezha said. "Some people kept saying it was a sign from the gods that the rebellion would fail."

"And Vaisra?"

"Father took it as a sign that he should go out and get himself a Speerly."

Instead of taking a river sampan back to the military barracks, Nezha led her down the stairs to the base of the pier, where Rin could still hear the noise of the shipyard over the water rushing gently against the posts that kept the pier up. At first she thought they had walked into a dead end, until Nezha stepped from the glassy sand and right onto the river.

"What the hell?"

After a second she realized he was standing not on the water, but rather on a large circular flap that almost matched the river's greenish-blue hue.

"Lily pads," Nezha said before she could ask. Arms spread for balance, he shifted his weight just so as the waves lifted the lily pad under his feet.

"Show-off," Rin said.

"You've never seen these before?"

"Yes, but only in wall scrolls." She grimaced at the pads. Her balance wasn't half as good as Nezha's, and she wasn't keen to fall into the river. "I didn't know they grew so large."

"They don't usually. These will only last a month or two before they sink. They grow naturally in the freshwater ponds up the mountain, but our botanists found a way to militarize them. You'll find them up and down the harbor. The better sailors don't need rowboats to get to their ships; they can just run across the lily pads."

"Calm down," she said. "They're just stepping stones."

"They're militarized lily pads. Isn't that great?"

"I think you just like using the word 'militarized.'"

Nezha opened his mouth to respond, but a voice from atop the pier cut him off.

"Had enough of playing tour guide?"

A man descended the steps toward them. He wore a blue soldier's uniform, and the black stripes on his left arm marked him as a general.

Nezha hastily hopped off the lily pads onto the wet sand and sank to one knee. "Brother. Good to see you again."

Rin realized in retrospect she should have knelt as well, but she was too busy staring at Nezha's brother. Yin Jinzha. She had seen him once, briefly, three years back at her first Summer Festival in Sinegard. Back then she'd thought that Jinzha and Nezha could have been twins, but upon closer inspection, their similarities were not really so pronounced. Jinzha was taller, more thickly built, and he carried himself with the air of a firstborn—a son who knew he was heir to his father's entire estate, while his younger siblings would be left to a fate of squabbling over the refuse.

"I heard you screwed up at the Autumn Palace." Jinzha's voice was deeper than Nezha's. More arrogant, if that was possible. It sounded oddly familiar to Rin, but she couldn't quite place it. "What happened?"

Nezha rose to his feet. "Hasn't Captain Eriden briefed you?"

"Eriden didn't see everything. Until Father recovers I'm the senior ranking general in Arlong, and I'd like to know the details."

It's Altan, Rin realized with a jolt. Jinzha spoke with a clipped, military precision that reminded her of Altan at his best. This was a man used to competence and immediate obedience.

"I don't have anything to add," Nezha said. "I was on the *Seagrim*."

Jinzha's lip curled. "Out of harm's way. Typical."

Rin expected Nezha to lash out at that, but he swallowed the barb with a nod. "How is Father?"

"Better now than last night. He'd been straining himself. Our physician didn't understand how he was still alive at first."

"But Father told me it was just a flesh wound."

"Did you even get a good look at him? That blade went nearly all the way through his shoulder bone. He's been lying to everyone. It's a wonder he's even conscious."

"Has he asked for me?" Nezha asked.

"Why would he?" Jinzha gave his brother a patronizing look. "I'll let you know when you're needed."

"Yes, sir." Nezha dipped his head and nodded. Rin watched this exchange, fascinated. She'd never seen anyone who could bully Nezha the way Nezha tended to bully everyone else.

"You're the Speerly." Jinzha looked suddenly at Rin, as if he had just remembered she was there.

"Yes." For some reason Rin's voice came out strangled, girlish. She cleared her throat. "That's me."

"Go on, then," Jinzha said. "Let's see it."

"What?"

"Show me what you can do," Jinzha said very slowly, as if talking to a small child. "Make it big."

Rin shot Nezha a confused look. "I don't understand."

"They say you can call fire," Jinzha said.

"Well, yes—"

"How much? How hot? To what degree? Does it come from your body, or can you summon it from other places? What does it take for you to trigger a volcano?" Jinzha spoke at such a terribly fast clip that Rin had trouble deciphering his curt Sinegardian accent. She hadn't struggled with that in years.

She blinked, feeling rather stupid, and when she spoke she stumbled over her words. "I mean, it just *happens*—"

"'It just happens,'" he mimicked. "What, like a sneeze? What help is that? Explain to me how to use you."

"I'm not someone for you to use."

"Fancy that. The soldier won't take orders."

"Rin's had a long journey," Nezha cut in hastily. "I'm sure she'd be happy to demonstrate for you in the morning, when she's had some rest . . ."

"Soldiers get tired, that's part of the job," Jinzha said. "Come on, Speerly. Show us what you've got."

Nezha placed a placating hand on Rin's arm. "Jinzha, really . . ."

Jinzha made a noise of disgust. "You should hear the way Father talks about them. Speerlies this, Speerlies that. I told him he'd be better off launching an invasion from Arlong, but no, he thought he could win a bloodless coup if he just had you. Look how that worked out."

"Rin's stronger than you can imagine," Nezha said.

"You know, if the Speerlies were so strong, you'd think they'd be less dead." Jinzha's lip curled. "Spent my whole childhood hearing about what a marvel your precious Altan was. Turns out he was just another dirt-skinned idiot who blew himself up for nothing."

Rin's vision flashed red. When she looked at Jinzha she didn't see flesh but a charred stump, ashes peeling off what used to be a man—she wanted him dying, dead, hurting. She wanted him to scream.

"You want to see what I can do?" she asked. Her voice sounded very distant, as if someone were speaking at her from very far away.

"Rin..." Nezha cautioned.

"No, fuck off." She shrugged his hand off her arm. "He wants to see what I can do."

"I don't think that's a good idea."

"Get back."

She turned her palms out toward Jinzha. It took nothing to summon the anger. It was already there, waiting, like water bursting forth from a dam—*I hate, I hate, I hate*—

Nothing happened.

Jinzha raised his eyebrows.

Rin felt a twinge of pain in her temples. She touched her finger to her eyes.

The twinge blossomed into a searing bolt of agony. She saw an explosion of colors branded behind her eyelids: reds and yellows, flames flickering over a burning village, the silhouettes of people writhing inside, a great mushroom cloud over the longbow island in miniature.

For a moment she saw a character she couldn't recognize, swimming into shape like a nest of snakes, lingering just in front of her eyes before it disappeared. She drifted in a moment between the world in her mind and the material world. She couldn't breathe, couldn't see...

She sagged to her knees. She felt Nezha's arms hoisting her up, heard him shouting for someone to help. She struggled to open her eyes. Jinzha stood above her, staring down with open contempt.

"Father was right," he said. "We should have tried to save the other one."

Chaghan slammed the door shut behind him. "What happened?"

"I don't know." Rin's fingers clenched and unclenched around the bedsheets while Chaghan unpacked his satchel beside her. Her voice trembled; she had spent the last half hour trying simply to breathe normally, but still her heart raced so furiously that she could barely hear her own thoughts. "I got careless. I was going to call the fire—just a bit, I didn't really want to hurt him, and then—"

Chaghan grabbed her wrists. "Why are you shaking?"

She hadn't realized she was. She couldn't stop her hands from trembling, but thinking about it only made her shake harder.

"He won't want me anymore," she whispered.

"Who?"

"Vaisra."

She was terrified. If she couldn't call the fire, then Vaisra had recruited a Speerly for nothing. Without the fire, she might be tossed away.

She'd been trying since she regained consciousness to call the fire, but the result was always the same—a searing pain in her temples, a burst of color, and flashes of visions she never wanted to see again. She couldn't tell what was wrong, only that the fire remained out of her reach, and without the fire she was nothing but useless.

Another tremor passed through her body.

"Just calm down," Chaghan said. He set the satchel on the floor and knelt beside her. "Focus on me. Look in my eyes."

She obeyed.

Chaghan's eyes, pale and without pupils or irises, were normally unsettling. But up close they were strangely alluring, two shards of a snowy landscape embedded in his thin face that drew her in like some hypnotized prey.

"What is wrong with me?" she whispered.

"I don't know. Why don't we find out?" Chaghan rummaged in his satchel, closed his fist around something, and offered her a handful of bright blue powder.

She recognized the drug. It was the ground-up dust of some dried northern fungus. She'd ingested it once before with Chaghan in Khurdalain, when she'd taken him to the immaterial realm where Mai'rinnen Tearza was haunting her.

Chaghan wanted to accompany her to the inner recesses of her mind, the point where her soul ascended to the plane of the gods.

"Afraid?" he asked when she hesitated.

Not afraid. Ashamed. Rin didn't *want* to bring Chaghan into her mind. She was scared of what he might see.

"Do you have to come?" she asked.

"You can't do it alone. I'm all you've got. You have to trust me."

"Will you promise to stop if I ask you to?"

Chaghan scoffed, reached for her hand, and pressed her finger into the powder. "We'll stop when I say we can stop."

"Chaghan."

He gave her a frank look. "Do you really have another option?"

The drug began to act almost from the moment it hit her tongue. Rin was surprised at how fast and clean the high was. Poppy seeds were so frustratingly slow, a gradual crawl into the realm of spirit that worked only if she concentrated, but this drug was like a kick through the door between this world and the next.

Chaghan grabbed her hand just before the infirmary faded from her vision. They departed the mortal plane in a swirl of colors. Then it was just the two of them in an expanse of black. Drifting. Searching.

Rin knew what she had to do. She homed in on her anger and created the link to the Phoenix that pulled their souls from the chasm of nothing toward the Pantheon. She could almost feel the Phoenix, the scorching heat of its divinity washing over her, could almost hear its malicious cackle—

Then something dimmed its presence, cut her off.

Something massive materialized before them. There was no way to describe it other than a giant word, slashed into empty space. Twelve strokes hung in the air, a great pictogram the shimmering hue of green-blue snakeskin, glinting in the unnatural brightness like freshly spilled blood.

"That's impossible," Chaghan said. "She shouldn't be able to do this."

The pictogram looked both entirely familiar and entirely foreign. Rin couldn't read it, though it had to be written in the Nikara script. It came close to resembling several characters she knew but deviated from all of them in significant ways.

This was something ancient, then. Something old; something that predated the Red Emperor. "What is this?"

"What does it look like?" Chaghan reached out an incorporeal hand as if to touch it, then hastily drew it back. "This is a Seal."

A Seal? The term sounded oddly familiar. Rin remembered fragments of a battle. A white-haired man floating in the air, lightning swirling around the tip of his staff, opening a void to a realm of things not mortal, things that didn't belong in their world.

You're Sealed.

Not anymore.

"Like the Gatekeeper?" she asked.

"The Gatekeeper was *Sealed*?" Chaghan sounded astonished. "Why didn't you tell me?"

"I had no idea!"

"But that would explain so much! That's why he's been lost, why he doesn't remember—"

"What are you talking about?"

"The Seal blocks your access to the world of spirit," Chaghan explained. "The Vipress left her venom inside you. That's what it's made of. It will keep you from accessing the Pantheon. And over time it will grow stronger and stronger, eating away at your mind until you lose even your memories associated with the Phoenix. It'll make you a shell of yourself."

"Please tell me you can get rid of it."

"I can try. You'll have to take me inside."

"Inside?"

"The Seal is also a gateway. Look." Chaghan pointed into the heart of the character, where the glimmering snake blood formed a swirling circle. When Rin focused on it, it did indeed seem to call to her, drawing her into some unknown dimension beyond. "Go inside. I'm betting that's where Daji's left the venom. It exists here in the form of memory. Daji's power dwells in desire; she's conjured the things that you want the most to prevent you from calling the fire."

"Venom. Memory. Desire." Very little of this was making sense to Rin. "Look—just tell me whatever the fuck I'm supposed to do with it."

"You destroy it however you can."

"Destroy *what*?"

"I think you'll know when you see it."

Rin didn't have to ask how to pass the gate. It pulled her in as soon as she approached it. The Seal seemed to fold in over them, growing larger and larger until it enveloped them. Swirls of blood drifted around her, undulating, as if trying to decide what shape to take, what illusion to create.

"She'll show you the future you want," Chaghan said.

But Rin didn't see how that could possibly work for her, because her greatest desires didn't exist in the future. They were all in the past. She wanted the last five years back. She wanted lazy days on the Academy campus. She wanted lackadaisical strolls in Jiang's garden, she wanted summer vacations at Kitay's estate, she wanted, she *wanted* . . .

She was on the sands of the Isle of Speer again—vibrant, beautiful Speer, lush and vivid like she had never seen it before. And there Altan was, healthy and whole, smiling like she had never really seen him smile.

"Hello," he said. "Are you ready to come home?"

"Kill him," Chaghan said urgently.

But hadn't she already? At Khurdalain she'd fought a beast with Altan's face, and she'd killed him then. Then at the research facility she'd let him walk out on the pier, let him sacrifice himself to save her.

She'd already killed Altan, over and over, and he kept coming back.

How could she harm him *now*? He looked so happy. So free

from pain. She knew so much more about him now, she knew what he had suffered, and she couldn't touch him. Not like this.

Altan drew closer. "What are you doing out here? Come with me."

She wanted to go with him more than anything. She didn't even know where he would take her, only that he would be there. Oblivion. Some dark paradise.

Altan extended his hand toward her. "*Come.*"

She steeled herself. "Stop this," she managed. "Chaghan, I can't—stop it—take me back—"

"Surely you're joking," Chaghan said. "You can't even do this?"

Altan took her fingers in his. "Let's go."

"*Stop it!*"

She wasn't sure *what* she did but she felt a burst of energy, saw the Seal contort and writhe around Chaghan, like a predator sniffing out some new and interesting prey, and saw his mouth open in some soundless scream of agony.

Then they weren't on Speer anymore.

This was nowhere she had ever seen.

They were somewhere high up on a mountain, cold and dark. A series of caves were carved into stone, all glowing with candle fire on the inside. And sitting on the ledge, shoulders touching, were two boys: one dark haired and one fair haired.

She was an outsider in this memory, but the moment she stepped closer her perspective shifted and she wasn't the voyeur anymore but the subject. She saw Altan's face up close, and she realized she was looking at him the way Chaghan once had.

Altan's face was entirely too close to hers. She could make out every last terrible and wonderful detail: the scar running up from his right cheek, the clumsy way his hair had been tied up, the dark lids over his crimson eyes.

Altan was awful. Altan was beautiful. And as she looked into his eyes she realized the feeling that overcame her was not love;

this was a total, paralyzing fear. This was the terror of a moth drawn to the flame.

She hadn't thought that anyone else felt that way. It was such a familiar feeling that she almost cried.

"I could kill you," said Altan, muttering the death threat like a love song, and when she-as-Chaghan struggled against him he pressed his body closer.

"So you could," Chaghan said, and that was such a familiar voice, the coy, level voice. She'd always marveled at how Chaghan could speak so casually to Altan. But Chaghan hadn't been joking, she realized, he'd been afraid; he had been constantly terrified every time he was around Altan. "So what?"

Altan's fingers closed over Chaghan's; too hot, too crushing, an attempt at human contact with absolute disregard for the object of his affection.

His lips brushed against Chaghan's ear. She shuddered involuntarily; she thought he might bite her, move his mouth lower against her neck and rip out her arteries.

She realized that Chaghan felt this fear often.

She realized that Chaghan probably enjoyed it.

"Don't," Chaghan said.

She didn't listen; she wanted to stay in this vision, had the sickening desire to watch it play out to its conclusion.

"That's *enough*."

A wave of darkness slammed down onto them, and when she opened her eyes she was back in the infirmary, sprawled on top of her bed. Chaghan sat bolt upright on the floor, eyes wide open, expression blank.

She grabbed him by the collar. "What was that?"

Chaghan stirred awake. His features settled into something like contempt. "Why don't you ask yourself?"

"You *hypocrite*," she said. "You're just as obsessed with him—"

"Are you sure that wasn't you?"

"Don't lie to me!" she shrieked. "I know what I saw, I know

what you were doing, I bet you only wanted to get in my mind because you wanted to see him from another angle—"

He flinched back.

She hadn't expected him to flinch. He looked so small. So *vulnerable*.

Somehow, that made her angrier.

She clenched his collar tighter. "He's dead. All right? Can't you get that in your fucking head?"

"Rin—"

"He's dead, he's gone, and we can't bring him back. And maybe he loved you, maybe he loved me, but that doesn't fucking matter anymore, does it? He's gone."

She thought he might hit her then.

But he just leaned forward, shoulders hunched over his knees, and pressed his face into his hands. When he spoke he sounded like he was on the verge of tears. "I thought I could catch him."

"*What?*"

"Sometimes before the dead pass on, they linger," he whispered. "Especially your kind. Anger depends on resentment, and your dead exist in resentment. And I think he's still out there, drifting between this world and the next, but each time I try all I get is fragments of memories, and as more time passes I can't even remember the beautiful things, and I thought maybe—with the venom—"

"You don't know how to fix me, do you?" she asked. "You never did."

Chaghan didn't answer.

She released his collar. "Get out."

He packed up his satchel and left without a word. She almost called him back, but she couldn't think of a single thing to say before he slammed the door.

Once Chaghan was gone, Rin shouted down the hallway until she got the attention of a physician, whom she berated until she obtained a sleeping draught in twice the recommended dosage. She swallowed that in two large gulps, crawled back onto her bed, and fell into the deepest sleep she'd had in a long time.

When she woke, the physician refused her another sleeping draught for another six hours. So she waited in fearful apprehension, anticipating a visit from Jinzha or Nezha or even Vaisra himself. She didn't know what to expect, only that it couldn't be anything good. Who had any use for a Speerly who couldn't summon fire?

But her only visitor was Captain Eriden, who instructed her that she was to continue acting as if she were in full command of her abilities. She was still Vaisra's trump card, Vaisra's hidden weapon, and she was still to appear at his side, even if only as a psychological weapon.

He didn't convey Vaisra's disappointment. He didn't have to. Vaisra's absence stung more than anything else.

She chugged down the next sleeping draught they gave her. The sun had set by the time she woke again. She was terribly hungry. She stood up, unlocked the door, and walked down the hallway, barefoot and groggy, with the vague intention of demanding food from the first person she saw.

"Well, fuck you, too!"

Rin stopped walking.

The voice came from a door near the end of the hallway. "What was I supposed to do? Hang myself like the women of Lü? I bet you'd like that."

Rin recognized that voice—shrill, petulant, and furious. She tiptoed down the hall and stood just beyond the door.

"The women of Lü preserved their dignity." A male voice this time, much older and deeper.

"And who put my dignity in my cunt?"

Rin caught her breath. Venka. It had to be.

"Would you prefer I were a lifeless corpse?" Venka screamed. "Would you prefer my spine were broken, my body crushed, just so long as nothing had gone between my legs?"

The male voice again. "I wish you had never been taken. You know that."

"You're not answering the question." A choked noise. Was Venka crying? "Look at me, Father. *Look at me*."

Venka's father said something in response, too softly for Rin to hear. A moment later the door slammed open. Rin ducked around the corner and froze until she heard the footsteps recede down the hall in the opposite direction.

She exhaled in relief. She considered for a moment, then walked toward the door. It was open, hanging slightly ajar. She placed her fingertips on the wooden panel and pushed.

It *was* Venka. She had shorn her hair off completely—and clearly some time ago, because it was starting to grow back in little dark patches. But her face was the same—ridiculously pretty, all sharp angles and piercing eyes.

"What the hell do you want?" Venka demanded. "Can I help you?"

"You were being loud," Rin said.

"Oh, I'm *so* sorry. Next time my father disowns me, I'll keep it down."

"You were disowned?"

"Well. Probably not. It's not like he's got other heirs to spare." Venka's eyes were red around the rims. "I wish he would, it's better than him trying to tell me what to do with my own body. When I was pregnant—"

"You're *pregnant*?"

"*Was*." Venka scowled. "No thanks to that fucking doctor. He kept saying that fucking cunt Saikhara didn't permit abortions."

"Saikhara?"

"Nezha's mother. She's got some funny ideas about religion. Grew up in Hesperia, did you know that? She worships their stupid fucking Maker. She doesn't just pretend for diplomatic reasons, she actually *believes* in that shit. And she runs around obeying everything he wrote in some little book, which apparently includes forcing women to bear the children of their rapists."

"So what did you do?"

Venka's throat pulsed. "Got creative."

"Ah."

They both stared at the floor for a minute. Venka broke the silence. "I mean, it only hurt a little bit. Not as bad as—you know."

"Yeah."

"That's what I thought about when I did it. Kept thinking about their piggy little faces, and then it wasn't difficult. And the Lady Saikhara can go fuck herself."

Rin sat down on the edge of her bed. It felt oddly good to be around Venka—angry, impatient, abrasive Venka. Venka gave voice to the raw anger that everyone else seemed to have patched over, and for that Rin was grateful.

"How are your arms?" she asked. Last time she'd seen Venka her arms were swathed in so many bandages that Rin wasn't sure if she'd lost use of them altogether. But her bandages were gone now, and her arms weren't dangling uselessly by her sides.

Venka flexed her fingers. "Right one's healed. Left one won't, ever. It was bent all funny, and I can't move three fingers on my left hand."

"Can you still shoot?"

"Works just as well as long as I can hold a bow. They had a glove designed for me. Keeps the three fingers bent back so I don't have to. I'd be just fine on the field with a little practice. Not like anyone believes me." Venka shifted in her bed. "But what are *you* doing here? Did Nezha win you over with his pretty words?"

Rin shifted. "Something like that."

Venka was looking at her with something that might have been jealousy. "So you're still a soldier. Lucky you."

"I'm not sure about that," Rin said.

"Why not?"

For a moment Rin considered telling Venka everything—about the Vipress, about the Seal, about what she had seen with Chaghan. But Venka didn't have the patience for details. Venka didn't care that much.

"I just—I can't do what I did anymore. Not like that." She hugged her chest with her arms. "I don't think I'll ever do that again."

Venka pointed to her eyes. "Is that what you've been crying about?"

"No—I just . . ." Rin took a shaky breath. "I don't know if I'm useful anymore."

Venka rolled her eyes. "Well, you can still hold a sword, can't you?"

CHAPTER 12

In the following week, three more provinces announced their independence from the Empire.

As Nezha predicted, the southern Warlords capitulated first. After all, the south had no reason to stay loyal to the Empire or Daji. The Third Poppy War had hit them the hardest. Their refugees were starving, their bandit epidemic had exploded, and the attack at the Autumn Palace had destroyed any chance that they might win concessions or promises of aid at the Lusan summit.

The southern Warlords notified Arlong of their intentions to secede through breathless delegates traveling over land if they were close enough, and by messenger pigeon if they weren't. Days later the Warlords themselves arrived at Arlong's gates.

"Rooster, Monkey, and Boar." Nezha counted the provinces off as they watched Eriden's guards escort the portly Boar Warlord into the palace. "Not bad."

"That puts us at four provinces to eight," Rin said. "Not incredible odds."

"Five to seven. And they're good generals." That was true. None of the southern Warlords had been born into their ranks; they'd all assumed them in the bloodbaths of the Second and Third Poppy Wars. "And Tsolin will come through."

"How are you so sure?"

"Tsolin knows how to pick sides. He'll show up eventually. Cheer up, this is about as good as we expected."

Rin had imagined that once the four-province alliance solidified, they would march on the north immediately. But politics quickly crushed her hopes for rapid action. The southern Warlords had not brought their armies with them to Arlong. Their military forces remained in their respective capitals, hedging their bets, watching before joining the fray. The south was playing a waiting game. By seceding they had insulated themselves from Vaisra's ire, but so long as they didn't commit troops against the Empire, there was still the chance that Daji would welcome them back with open arms, all sins forgiven.

Days passed. The order to ship out didn't come. The four-province alliance spent hours and hours debating strategy in an endless series of war councils. Rin, Nezha, and Kitay were all present at these; Nezha because he was a general, Kitay because he, in a bizarre turn of events, was now considered a competent strategist if not an especially well-liked one, and Rin purely because Vaisra wanted her there.

She suspected her purpose was to intimidate, to give some reassurance that if the island-destroying Speerly was alive and well in Arlong, then this war could not be so difficult to win.

She tried her best to act as if that weren't a lie.

"We need cross-division squadrons, or this alliance is just a suicide pact." General Hu, Vaisra's senior strategist, had long ago given up on masking his frustration. "The Republican Army has to act as a cohesive whole. The men can't think they're still squadrons of their old province."

"I'm not putting my men under the command of soldiers I've never met," said the Boar Warlord. Rin detested Cao Charouk; he seemed to do nothing but complain so fiercely about everything Vaisra's staff suggested that often she wondered why he'd come to Arlong at all. "And those squads won't function. You're asking men who have never met to fight together. They don't know the same command signals, they don't use the same codes, and they don't have time to learn."

"Well, you lot don't seem keen on attacking the north anytime soon, so I imagine they'll have months at the least," Kitay muttered.

Nezha made a choking noise that sounded like a laugh.

Charouk looked as if he would very much like to skewer Kitay on a flagpole if given the chance.

"We can't beat Daji fighting as four separate armies," General Hu said quickly. "Our scouts report she's assembling a coalition in the north as we speak."

"Doesn't matter if they don't have a fleet," said the Monkey Warlord, Liu Gurubai. He was the most cooperative among the southern Warlords; sharp-tongued and clever-eyed, he spent most meetings stroking his thick, dark whiskers while he played both sides at the table.

If they were dealing only with Gurubai, Rin thought, they might have moved north by now. The Monkey Warlord was cautious, but he at least responded to reason. The Boar and Rooster Warlords, however, seemed determined to hunker down in Arlong behind Vaisra's army. Gong Takha had passed the last few days sitting silent and sullen at the table while Charouk continually blustered his suspicion of everyone else in the room.

"But they will. Daji is now commissioning ships from civilian centers for a restored Imperial Navy. They're converting grain transport ships into war galleys, and they've constructed naval yards at multiple sites in Tiger Province." General Hu tapped on the map. "The longer we wait, the more time they have to prepare."

"Who's leading that fleet?" asked Gurubai.

"Chang En."

"That's surprising," Charouk said. "Not Jun?"

"Jun didn't want the job," said General Hu.

Charouk raised an eyebrow. "That'd be a first."

"It's wise on his part," said Vaisra. "No one wants to have to give Chang En orders. When his officers question him, they lose their heads."

"That's certainly a sign the Empire's on the decline," tutted Takha. "That man is wicked and wasteful."

The Wolf Meat General was notorious for his brutality. When Chang En had staged his coup against the previous Horse Warlord, his troops had split skulls in half and hung strings of the severed heads across the capital walls.

"Or it just means, you know, that all the good generals are dead," Jinzha drawled. He had been remarkably restrained in council so far, though Rin had been watching the contempt build on his face for hours.

"You would know," said Charouk. "Did your apprenticeship with him, didn't you?"

Jinzha bristled. "That was five years ago."

"Not so long for such a short career."

Jinzha opened his mouth to retort, but Vaisra cut him off with a raised hand. "If you're going to accuse my eldest son of treachery—"

"No one is accusing Jinzha of anything," said Charouk. "Again, Vaisra, we just don't think Jinzha is the right choice to lead your fleet."

"Your men couldn't be in better hands. Jinzha studied warcraft at Sinegard, he commanded troops in the Third Poppy War—"

"As did we all," said Gurubai. "Why not give one of our generals the job? Or why not one of us?"

"Because you three are too important to spare."

Even Rin couldn't help but cringe at that naked flattery. The southern Warlords exchanged wry looks. Gurubai made a show of rolling his eyes.

"All right, then because the men of the Dragon Province are not prepared to fight under anyone else," Vaisra said. "Believe it or not, I *am* trying to find the solution that best protects you."

"And yet it's *our* troops you want on the front lines," said Charouk.

"Dragon Province is committing more troops than any of you,

asshat," Rin snapped. She couldn't help it. She knew Vaisra had wanted her to simply observe, but she couldn't stand watching this mess of passivity and petty infighting. The Warlords were acting like children, squabbling as if someone else would win their war for them if they only procrastinated long enough.

Everyone stared at her as if she'd suddenly grown wings. When Vaisra didn't cut her off, she kept going. "It's been three fucking days. Why the fuck are we arguing about division makeup? The Empire is weak *now*. We need to send a force up north *now*."

"Then how about we just send you?" asked Takha. "You sank the longbow island, didn't you?"

Rin didn't miss a beat. "You want me to kill off half the country? My powers don't discriminate."

Takha looked to Vaisra. "What is she even doing here?"

"I'm the commander of the Cike," Rin said. "And I'm standing right in front of you."

"You're a little girl with no command experience and hardly a year of combat under your belt," Gurubai said. "Do not presume to tell us how to fight a war."

"I *won* the last war. You wouldn't even be standing here without me."

Vaisra placed a hand on her shoulder. "Runin, hush."

"But he—"

"*Silence*," he said sternly. "This discussion is beyond you. Let the generals talk."

Rin swallowed her protest.

The door creaked open. A palace aide poked his head in through the gap. "The Snake Warlord is here to see you, sir."

"Let him in," Vaisra said.

The aide stepped inside to hold the door open.

Ang Tsolin walked inside, unaccompanied and unarmed. Jinzha moved to his right to let Tsolin stand next to his father. Nezha shot Rin a smug look, as if to say *I told you so*.

Vaisra looked equally vindicated. "I'm glad to see you join us, Master."

Tsolin scowled. "You didn't have to sail through my fleet."

"Going the other way would have taken longer."

"They came for my family first."

"I assume you had the foresight to extricate them in time."

Tsolin folded his arms. "My wife and children will arrive tomorrow morning. I want them set up with your most secure accommodations. If I catch so much as a whiff of a spy in their quarters, I will turn over my entire fleet to the Empire's use."

Vaisra dipped his head. "Whatever you ask."

"Good." Tsolin bent forward to examine the maps. "These are all wrong."

"How so?" Jinzha asked.

"The Horse Province hasn't remained inactive. They're gathering their troops to the Yinshan base." Tsolin pointed to a spot just above Hare Province. "And Tiger Province is bringing their fleet toward the Autumn Palace. They're closing off your attack routes. You don't have much time."

"Then tell me what I ought to do," Vaisra said. Rin was amazed at how his tone could shift—once commanding, but now deferential and meek, a student seeking a teacher's aid.

Tsolin gave him a wary look. "Good men are dead because of you. I hope you know."

"Then they died for a good cause," Vaisra said. "I suspect you know that, too."

Tsolin didn't answer. He simply sat down, pulled the maps toward him, and began to examine the attack lines with the weary, practiced air of a man who had spent his entire life fighting wars.

As the days dragged on, despite the northern offensive's ongoing delay, Arlong itself continued to mobilize for war like a tightening spring. War preparations were integrated into almost every facet of civilian life. Steely-eyed children worked the furnaces at the armory and carried messages back and forth across the city. Their mothers produced immaculately stitched uniforms at an astonishing rate. In the mess hall, grandmothers stirred congee in giant vats while their grandchildren ferried bowls around to the soldiers.

Another week passed. The Warlords continued to shout at each other in the council room. Rin couldn't bear the constant waiting, so she took out her adrenaline with Nezha.

Sparring was a welcome exercise. The skirmish at Lusan had made it abundantly clear to her that she had been relying far too much on calling the fire. Her reflexes had flagged, her muscles had atrophied, and her stamina was pathetic.

So at least once every day, she and Nezha picked up their weapons and hiked up to empty clearings far up on the cliffs. She lost herself in the sheer, mindless physicality of their bouts. When they were sparring, her mind couldn't languish on any one thought for too long. She was too busy calculating angles, maneuvering steel on steel. The immediacy of the fight was its own kind of drug, one that could numb her to anything else she might accidentally feel.

Altan couldn't torture her if she couldn't think.

Blow by blow, bruise by bruise, she relearned the muscle memory that she had lost, and she relished it. Here she could channel the adrenaline and fear that kept her vibrating with anxiety on a daily basis.

The first few days left her wrecked and aching. The next few were better. She filled in her uniform. She lost her hollow, skeletal appearance. This was the only reason she was grateful for the council's slow deliberation—it gave her time to become the soldier she used to be.

Nezha was not a lenient sparring partner, and she didn't want him to be. The first time he held back out of fear of hurting her, she swept out a leg and knocked him to the ground.

He propped himself up on his stomach. "If you wanted to go for a tumble, you could have just asked."

"Don't be disgusting," she said.

Once she stopped losing hand-to-hand bouts in under thirty seconds, they moved on to padded weapons.

"I don't understand why you insist on using that thing," he said after he disarmed her of her trident for the third time. "It's clumsy as hell. Father's been telling me to get you to switch to a sword."

She knew what Vaisra wanted. She was tired of that argument.

"Reach matters more than maneuverability." She wedged her foot under the trident and kicked it up into her hands.

Nezha came at her from the right. "Reach?"

She parried. "When you summon fire, there's no one who's going to get close to you."

He hung back. "Not to state the obvious, but you can't really do that anymore."

She scowled at him. "I'll fix it."

"Suppose you don't?"

"Suppose you stop underestimating me?"

She didn't want to tell him that she'd been trying. That every night she climbed up to this same clearing where no one would see her, took a dose of Chaghan's stupid blue powder, approached the Seal, and tried to burn the ghost of Altan out of her mind.

It never worked. She could never bring herself to hurt him, not that wonderful version of Altan that she'd never known. When she tried to fight him, he grew angry. And then he reminded her why she'd always been terrified of him.

The worst part was that Altan seemed to be getting stronger every time. His eyes burned more vividly in the dark, his laughter rang louder, and several nights he'd nearly choked the breath from her before she got her senses back. It didn't matter that he was only a vision. Her fear made him more present than anything else.

"Look alive." Rin jabbed at Nezha's side, hoping to catch him off guard, but he whipped his blade out and parried just in time.

They sparred for a few more seconds, but she was quickly losing heart. Her trident suddenly seemed twice as heavy in her arms; she felt like she was fighting at a third her normal speed. Her footwork was sloppy, without form or technique, and her swings grew increasingly haphazard and unguarded.

"It's not the worst thing," Nezha said. He batted a wild blow away from his head. "Aren't you glad?"

She stiffened. "Why would I be *glad*?"

"I mean, I just thought . . ." He touched a hand to his temple. "Isn't it at least nice to have your mind back to yourself?"

She slammed the hilt of the trident down into the ground. "You think I'd lost my mind?"

Nezha rapidly backtracked. "No, I mean, I thought—I saw how you were hurting. That looked like torture. I thought you might be a little relieved."

"It's not a relief to be useless," she said.

She twirled the trident over her head, whipped it around to generate momentum. It wasn't a staff—and she should know better than to wield it with staff techniques—but she was angry now, she wasn't thinking, and her muscles settled into familiar but wrong patterns.

It showed. Nezha may as well have been sparring with a toddler. He sent the trident spinning out of her hands in seconds.

"I told you," he said. "No flexibility."

She snatched the trident up off the ground. "Still has longer reach than your sword."

"So what happens if I get in close?" Nezha twisted his blade between the trident's gaps and closed the distance between them. She tried to fend him off, but he was right—he was out of the trident's reach.

He raised a dagger to her chin with his other hand. She kicked savagely at his shin. He buckled to the ground.

"Bitch," he said.

"You deserved it."

"Fuck you." He rocked back and forth on the grass, clutching his leg. "Help me up."

"Let's take a break." She dropped the trident and sat down on the grass beside him. Her lung capacity hadn't returned. She was still tiring too quickly; she couldn't last more than two hours sparring, much less a full day in the field.

Nezha hadn't even broken a sweat. "You're much better with a sword. Please tell me you know that."

"Don't patronize me."

"That thing is useless! It's too heavy for you! But I've seen you with a sword, and—"

"I'll get used to it."

"I just think that you shouldn't make life-or-death choices based on sentimentality."

She glared at him. "What's *that* supposed to mean?"

He ripped a handful of grass from the ground. "Forget it."

"No, say it."

"Fine. You won't trade because it's *his* weapon, isn't it?"

Rin's stomach twisted. "That's idiotic."

"Oh, come on. You're always talking about Altan like he was some great hero. But he wasn't. I saw him at Khurdalain, and I saw the way he spoke to people—"

"And how did he speak to people?" she asked sharply.

"Like they were objects, and he owned them, and they didn't matter to him apart from how they could serve." His tone turned vicious. "Altan was a shitty person and a shittier commander, and he would have let me die, and you *know* that, and here you are, running around with his trident, babbling on about revenge for someone you should hate."

The trident suddenly felt terribly heavy in Rin's hands.

"That's not fair." She heard a faint buzzing in her ears. "He's dead— You can't— That's not fair."

"I know," Nezha said softly. The anger had left him as quickly as it had come. He sounded exhausted. He sat, shoulders slouched, mindlessly shredding blades of grass with his fingers. "I'm sorry. I don't know why I said that. I know how much you cared about him."

"I'm not talking about Altan," she said. "Not with you. Not now. Not ever."

"All right," he said. He gave her a look that she didn't understand, a look that might have been equal parts pity and disappointment, and that made her desperately uncomfortable. "All right."

. . .

Three days later the council finally came to a joint decision. At least, Vaisra and Tsolin came up with a solution short of immediate military action, and then argued the others into submission.

"We're going to starve them out," Vaisra announced. "The south is the agricultural breadbasket of the Empire. If the northern provinces won't secede, then we'll simply stop feeding them."

Takha balked. "You're asking us to reduce our exports by at least a third."

"So you'll bleed income for a year or two," said Vaisra. "And then your prices will jack up in the next year. The north is in no position to become agriculturally self-sufficient now. If you make this one-time sacrifice, that's likely the end of tariffs, too. Beggars have no leverage."

"What about the coastal routes?" Charouk asked.

Rin had to admit that was a fair point. The Western Murui and Golyn River weren't the only rivers that crossed into the northern provinces. Those provinces could easily smuggle food up the coastline by sending merchants down in the guise of southerners to buy up food stores. They had more than enough silver.

"Moag will cover them," said Vaisra.

Charouk looked amazed. "You're trusting the *Pirate Queen*?"

"It's in her best interest," Vaisra said. "For every blockade runner's ship she seizes, her fleet gets seventy percent of the profits. She'd be a fool to double-cross us."

"The north has other grain supplies, though," Gurubai pointed out. "Hare Province has arable land, for instance—"

"No, they don't." Jinzha looked smug. "Last year the Hare Province suffered a blight and ran out of seed grain. We sold them several boxes of high-yielding seed."

"I remember," said Tsolin. "If you were trying to curry favor, it didn't work."

Jinzha grinned nastily. "We weren't. We sold them damaged seeds, which lulled them into consuming their emergency stores.

If we cut off their external supply, a famine should hit in about six months."

For once, the Warlords seemed impressed. Rin saw reluctant nods around the table.

Only Kitay looked unhappy.

"Six months?" he echoed. "I thought we were trying to move out in the next month."

"They won't have felt the blockade by then," said Jinzha.

"It doesn't matter! It's only the threat of the blockade that matters, you don't need them to actually *starve*—"

"Why not?" Jinzha asked.

Kitay looked horrified. "Because then you'd be punishing thousands of innocent people. And because that's not what you told me when you asked me to do the figures—"

"It doesn't matter what you were told," Jinzha said. "Know your place."

Kitay kept talking. "Why starve them slowly? Why wait at all? If we mount an offensive right now, we can end this war before winter sets in. Any later and we'll be trapped up north when the rivers freeze."

General Hu laughed. "The boy presumes to know how to fight a campaign better than we do."

Kitay looked livid. "I actually read Sunzi, so yes."

"You're not the only Sinegard student at the table," said General Hu.

"Sure, but I got in during an era when acceptance actually took brains, so your opinion doesn't count."

"Vaisra!" General Hu shouted. "Discipline this boy!"

"'Discipline this boy,'" Kitay mimicked. "'Shut up the only person who has a halfway viable strategy, because my ego can't take the heat.'"

"Enough," Vaisra said. "You're out of line."

"This plan is out of line," Kitay retorted.

"You're dismissed," Vaisra said. "Stay out of sight until you're sent for."

For a brief, terrifying moment Rin thought Kitay might start mocking Vaisra, too, but he just threw his papers down onto the table, knocking over inkwells, and stalked toward the door.

"Keep throwing fits like that and Father won't have you at his councils anymore," Nezha said.

He and Rin had both followed Kitay out, which Rin thought was a rather dangerous move on Nezha's part, but Kitay was too angry to be grateful for the gesture.

"Keep ignoring me and we won't have a palace to hold councils *in*," Kitay snapped. "A blockade? A fucking *blockade*?"

"It's our best option for now," Nezha said. "We don't have the military capability to sail north alone, but we could just wait them out."

"But that could take years!" Kitay shouted. "And what happens in the meantime? You just let people die?"

"Threats have to be credible to work," Nezha said.

Kitay shot him a disdainful look. "You try dealing with a country with a famine crisis, then. You don't unite a country by starving innocent people to death."

"They're not going to starve—"

"No? They're going to eat wood bark? Leaves? Cow dung? I can think of a million strategies better than murder."

"Try being diplomatic, then," Nezha snapped. "You can't disrespect the old guard."

"Why not? The old guard has no clue what they're doing!" Kitay shouted. "They got their positions because they're good at factional maneuvering! They graduated from Sinegard, sure, but that was when the entire curriculum was just emergency basic training. They don't have a thorough grounding in military science or technology, and they've never bothered to learn, because they know they'll never lose their jobs!"

"I think you're underestimating some rather qualified men," Nezha said drily.

"No, your father is in a double bind," Kitay said. "No, wait, I've got it, here's what it is—the men he can trust aren't competent, but the men who are competent, he must keep on a taut leash, because they might calculate to defect."

"So what, he trusts you instead?"

"I'm the only one who knows what I'm doing."

"And you basically only joined up yesterday, so can you not act so startled that my father trusts you less than men who have served him for decades?"

Kitay stormed off, muttering under his breath. Rin suspected they wouldn't see him emerge from the library for days.

"Asshole," Nezha grumbled once Kitay was out of earshot.

"Don't look at me," Rin said. "I'm on his side."

She didn't care so much about the blockade. If the northern provinces were holding out, then starvation served them right. But she couldn't bear the idea that they were about to kick a hornet's nest—because then their only strategy would be to wait, hide, and hope the hornets didn't sting first.

She couldn't stand the uncertainty. She wanted to be on the attack.

"Innocent people *aren't* going to die," Nezha insisted, though he sounded more like he was trying to convince himself. "They'll surrender before it gets that bad. They'll have to."

"And if they don't?" she asked. "Then we attack?"

"We attack, or they starve," Nezha said. "Win-win."

Arlong's military operations turned inward. The army stopped preparing ships to sail out and focused on building up defense structures to make Arlong completely invulnerable to a Militia invasion.

A defensive war was starting to seem more and more likely. If the Republic didn't launch their northern assault now, then they'd be stuck at home until the next spring. They were more than halfway into autumn, and Rin remembered how vicious the Sinegardian winters were. As the days became colder, it would get harder to boil water and prepare hot food. Disease and frostbite would spread quickly through the camps. The troops would be miserable.

But the south would remain warm, hospitable, and ripe for the picking. The longer they waited, the more likely it was the Militia would sail downriver toward Arlong.

Rin didn't want to fight a defensive battle. Every great treatise on military strategy agreed that defensive battles were a nightmare. And Arlong, impenetrable as it was, would still take a heavy beating from the combined forces of the north. Surely Vaisra knew that, too; he was too competent to believe otherwise. But in meeting after meeting, he chastised Kitay for speaking up, appeased the Warlords, and did nothing close to inciting the alliance to action.

Rin was beginning to think that even independent action by Dragon Province would be better than nothing. But the orders did not come.

"Father's hands are tied," said Nezha, again and again.

Kitay remained holed up in the library, drawing up war plans that would never be used with increasing frustration.

"I knew joining up with you would be treason," he raged at Nezha. "I didn't think it would be *suicide*."

"The Warlords will come around," Nezha said.

"Fat chance. Charouk's a lazy pig who wants to hide behind Republican swords, Takha doesn't have the spine to do anything but hide behind Charouk, and Gurubai might be the smartest of the lot, but he's not sticking his neck out if the other two won't."

There has to be something else, Rin thought. *Something we don't know about.* There was no way Vaisra would just sit back and let winter come without taking the initiative. What was he waiting for?

For lack of better options, she put her blind faith in Vaisra. She sucked it up when her men asked her about the delay. She closed her ears to the rumors that Vaisra was considering a peace agreement with the Empress. She realized she couldn't influence policy, so she poured her focus into the only things she could control.

She sparred more bouts with Nezha. She stopped wielding her trident like a staff. She became familiar with the generals and lieutenants of the Republican Army. She did her best to integrate the Cike into the Dragon Province's military ecosystem, though both Baji and Ramsa rankled at the strict ban on alcohol. She learned the Republican Army's command codes, communications channels, and amphibious attack formations. She prepared herself for war, whenever it came.

Until the day came when gongs sounded frantically across the harbor, and messengers ran up the docks, and all of Arlong was alight with the news that ships were sailing into the Dragon Province. Great white ships from the west.

Then Rin understood what the stalling had been about.

Vaisra hadn't been pulling back from the northern expedition after all.

He'd been waiting for backup.

CHAPTER 13

Rin squeezed through the crowd behind Nezha, who made liberal use of elbows to get them to the front of the harbor. The dock was already thronged with curious civilians and soldiers alike, all angling to get a good look at the Hesperian ship. But no one was looking out at the harbor. All heads were tilted to the sky.

Three whale-sized crafts sailed through the clouds above. Each had a long, rectangular basket strapped to its underbelly, with cerulean flags sewn along the sides. Rin blinked several times as she stared.

How could structures so massive possibly stay aloft?

They looked absurd and utterly unnatural, as if some god were moving them through the sky at will. But it couldn't be the work of the gods. The Hesperians didn't believe in the Pantheon.

Was this the work of their Maker? The possibility made Rin shiver. She'd always been taught that the Hesperians' Holy Maker was a construct, a fiction to control an anxious population. The singular, anthropomorphized, all-powerful deity that the Hesperians believed in could not possibly explain the complexity of the universe. But if the Maker was real, then everything she knew about the sixty-four deities, about the Pantheon, was wrong.

What *if* her gods weren't the only ones in the universe? What if a higher power did exist—one that only the Hesperians had access to? Was that why they were so infinitely more advanced?

The sky filled with a sound like the drone of a million bees, amplified a hundred times over as the flying crafts drew closer.

Rin saw people standing at the edges of the hanging baskets. They looked like little toys from the ground. The flying whales began approaching the harbor to land, looming larger and larger in the sky until their shadows enveloped everyone who stood below. The people inside the baskets waved their arms over their heads. Their mouths opened wide—they were shouting something, but no one could hear them over the noise.

Nezha dragged Rin backward by the wrist.

"Back away," he shouted into her ear.

There followed a brief period of chaos while the city guard wrangled the crowd back from the landing area. One by one the flying crafts thudded to the ground. The entire harbor shook from the impact.

At last, the droning noise died away. The metal whales shriveled and slumped to the side as they deflated over the baskets. The air was silent.

Rin watched, waiting.

"Don't let your eyes pop out of your head," said Nezha. "They're just foreigners."

"Just foreigners to you. Exotic creatures to me."

"They didn't have missionaries down in Rooster Province?"

"Only on the coastlines." Hesperian missionaries had been banned from the Empire after the Second Poppy War. Several dared to continue visiting cities peripheral to Sinegard's control, but most kept their distance from rural places like Tikany. "All I've ever heard are stories."

"Like what?"

"The Hesperians are giants. They're covered in red fur. They boil infants and eat them in soup."

"You know that never happened, right?"

"They're pretty convinced of it where I come from."

Nezha chuckled. "Let's let bygones be bygones. They're coming now as friends."

The Empire had a troubled history with the Republic of Hesperia. During the First Poppy War, the Hesperians had offered military and economic aid to the Federation of Mugen. Once the Mugenese had obliterated any notion of Nikara sovereignty, the Hesperians had populated the coastal regions with missionaries and religious schools, intent on wiping out the local superstitious religions.

For a short time, the Hesperian missionaries had even outlawed temple visits. If any shamanic cults still existed after the Red Emperor's war on religion, the Hesperians drove them even further underground.

During the Second Poppy War, the Hesperians became the liberators. The Federation had committed too many atrocities for the Hesperians, who had always claimed that their occupation benefited the natives, to pretend neutrality was morally defensible. After Speer burned, the Hesperians sent their fleets to the Nariin Sea, joined forces with the Trifecta's troops, pushed the Federation all the way back to their longbow island, and orchestrated a peace agreement with the newly reformed Nikara Empire in Sinegard.

Then the Trifecta seized dictatorial control of the country and threw the foreigners out by the ship. Whatever Hesperians remained were smugglers and missionaries, hiding in international ports like Ankhiluun and Khurdalain, preaching their word to anyone who bothered to entertain them.

When the Third Poppy War began, those last Hesperians had sailed away on rescue ships so fast that by the time Rin's contingent had reached Khurdalain they might never have been there. As the war progressed, the Hesperians had been willful bystanders, watching aloof from across the great sea while Nikara citizens burned in their homes.

"They might have come a little earlier," Rin quipped.

"There's been a war ravishing the entire western continent for the past two decades," said Nezha. "They've been a bit distracted."

This was news to her. Until now, news of the western continent had been so utterly irrelevant to her it might not have existed. "Did they win?"

"You could say that. Millions are dead. Millions more are without home or country. But the Consortium states came out in power, so they consider that a victory. Although I don't—"

Rin grabbed his arm. "They're coming out."

Doors had opened at the sides of each basket. One by one the Hesperians filed out onto the dock.

Rin recoiled at the sight of them.

Their skin was terribly pale—not the flawless porcelain-white shade that Sinegardians prized, but more like the tint of a freshly gutted fish. And their hair looked all the wrong colors—garish shades of copper, gold, and bronze, nothing like the rich black of Nikara hair. Everything about them—their coloring, their features, their proportions—simply seemed *off*.

They didn't look like people; they looked like things out of horror stories. They might have been demon-possessed monsters conjured up for Nikara folk heroes to fight. And though Rin was too old for folktales, everything about these light-eyed creatures made her want to run.

"How's your Hesperian?" Nezha asked.

"Rusty," she admitted. "I hate that language."

They had all been forced to study several years of diplomatic Hesperian at Sinegard. Rules of pronunciation were haphazard at best and its grammar system was so riddled with exceptions it might not exist at all.

None of Rin's classmates had paid much attention to their Hesperian grammar lessons. They had all assumed that as the Federation was the primary threat, Mugini was more important to learn.

Rin supposed things would be very different now.

A column of Hesperian sailors, identical in their close-cropped hair and dark gray uniforms, walked out of the baskets and formed two neat lines in front of the crowd. Rin counted twenty of them.

She examined their faces but couldn't tell one apart from

the next. They all seemed to have the same lightly colored eyes, broad noses, and strong jaws. They were all men, and each held a strange-looking weapon across his chest. Rin couldn't determine the weapon's purpose. It looked like a series of tubes of different lengths, joined together near the back with something like a handle.

A final soldier emerged from the basket door. Rin assumed he was their general by his uniform, which bore multicolored ribbons on the left chest where the others' were bare. He struck Rin immediately as dangerous. He stood at least half a head taller than Vaisra, he sported a chest as wide as Baji's, and his weathered face was lined and intelligent.

Behind the general walked a row of hooded Hesperians clothed in gray cassocks.

"Who are they?" Rin asked Nezha. They couldn't be soldiers; they wore no armor and held no weapons.

"The Gray Company," he said. "Representatives of the Church of the Divine Architect."

"They're missionaries?"

"Missionaries who can speak for the central church. They're highly trained and educated. Think of them like graduates from the Sinegard Academy of religion."

"What, they went to priest school?"

"Sort of. They're scientists, too. In their religion, the scientists and priests are one and the same."

Rin was about to ask what that meant when a last figure emerged from the center basket. She was a woman, slender and petite, wearing a buttoned black coat with a high collar that covered her neck. She looked severe, alien, and elegant all at once. Her attire was certainly not Nikara, but her face was not Hesperian. She seemed oddly familiar.

"*Hello.*" Baji whistled behind Rin. "Who is that?"

"It's Lady Yin Saikhara," said Nezha.

"Is she married?" Baji asked.

Nezha shot him a disgusted look. "That's my *mother*."

That was why Rin recognized the woman's face. She had met the Lady of Dragon Province once, years ago, on her first day at Sinegard. Lady Saikhara had taken Rin's guardian Tutor Feyrik for a porter, and she had dismissed Rin entirely as southerner trash.

Perhaps the past four years had done wonders for Lady Saikhara's attitude, but Rin was strongly inclined to dislike her.

Lady Saikhara paused before the crowd, eyes roving the harbor as if surveying her kingdom. Her gaze landed on Rin. Her eyes narrowed—in recognition, Rin thought; perhaps Saikhara remembered Rin as well—but then she grasped the Hesperian general's arm and pointed, her face contorted into what looked like fear.

The general nodded and spoke an order. At once, all twenty Hesperian soldiers pointed their barrel tube weapons at Rin.

A hush fell over the crowd as the civilians hastily backed away.

Several cracks split the air. Rin dove to the ground by instinct. Eight holes dotted the dirt in front of her. She looked up.

The air smelled like smoke. Gray flumes unfurled from the tips of the barrel tubes.

"Oh, fuck," Nezha muttered under his breath.

The general shouted something that Rin couldn't understand, but she didn't have to translate what he'd said. There was no way to interpret this as anything but a threat.

She had two default responses to threats. And she couldn't run away, not in this crowd, so her only choice was to fight.

Two of the Hesperian soldiers came running toward her. She slammed her trident against the closest one's shins. He doubled over, just briefly. She jammed an elbow into the side of his head, grabbed him by the shoulders, and barreled forward, using him as a human shield to deter further fire.

It worked until something landed over Rin's shoulders. A fishing net. She flailed, trying to wriggle out, but it only tightened around her arms. Whoever held it yanked hard, knocking her off balance.

The Hesperian general loomed above her, his weapon pointed straight down at her face. Rin looked up the barrel. The smell of fire powder was so thick she nearly choked on it.

"Vaisra!" she shouted. "Help—"

Soldiers swarmed around her. Strong arms pinned her arms over her head; others grabbed her ankles, rendering her immobile. She heard the clank of steel next to her head. She twisted around and saw a wooden tray on the ground beside her, upon which lay a vast assortment of thin devices that looked like torture instruments.

She'd seen devices like that before.

Someone pulled her head back and jerked her mouth open. One of the Gray Company, a woman with skin like alabaster, knelt over her. She pressed something hard and metallic against Rin's tongue.

Rin bit at her fingers.

The woman snatched her hand away.

Rin struggled harder. Miraculously, the grips on her shoulders loosened. She flailed out and upturned the tray, scattering the instruments across the ground. For a single, desperate moment, she thought she might break free.

Then the general slammed the butt of his weapon into her head and Rin's vision exploded into stars that winked out into nothing.

"Oh, good," said Nezha. "You're awake."

Rin found herself lying on a stone floor. She scrambled to her feet. She was unbound. Good. Her hand jumped for a weapon that wasn't there, and when she couldn't find her trident she curled her hands into fists. "What—"

"That was a misunderstanding." Nezha grabbed her by the shoulders. "You're safe, we're alone. What happened out there was a mistake."

"A *mistake*?"

"They thought you were a threat. My mother told them to attack as soon as they reached land."

Rin's forehead throbbed. She touched her fingers to where she knew a massive bruise was forming. "Your mother is a real bitch, then."

"She often is, yes. But you're in no danger. Father is talking them down."

"And if he can't?"

"He will. They're not idiots." Nezha grabbed her hand. "Will you stop that?"

Rin had begun pacing back and forth in the small chamber like a caged animal, teeth chattering, rubbing her hands agitatedly up and down her arms. But she couldn't stand still; her mind was racing in panic, if she stopped moving she would start to shake uncontrollably.

"Why would they think I was a threat?" she demanded.

"It's, ah, a little complicated." Nezha paused. "I guess the simplest way to put it is that they want to study you."

"Study?"

"They know what you did to the longbow island. They know what you *can* do, and as the most powerful country on earth of course they're going to investigate it. Their proposed treaty terms, I think, were that they'd get to examine you in exchange for military aid. Mother put it in their heads that you weren't going to come quietly."

"So what, Vaisra's selling me for their aid?"

"It's not like that. My mother . . ." Nezha continued talking, but Rin wasn't listening. She scrutinized him, considering.

She had to get out of here. She had to rally the Cike and get them out of Arlong. Nezha was taller, heavier, and stronger than she was, but she could still take him—she'd go after his eyes and scars, gouge her fingernails into his skin and knee his balls repeatedly until he dropped his guard.

But she might still be trapped. The doors could be locked from the outside. And if she broke the door down, there could be—no, there certainly were guards outside. What about the window? She could tell from a glance they were on the second, maybe third story, but maybe she could scale down somehow, if she could manage to knock Nezha unconscious. She just needed a weapon—the chair legs might do, or a shard of porcelain.

She lunged for the flower vase.

"Don't." Nezha's hand shot out and gripped her wrist. She struggled to break free. He twisted her arm painfully behind her back, forced her to her knees, and pressed a knee against the small of her back. "Come on, Rin. Don't be stupid."

"Don't do this," she gasped. "Nezha, please, I can't stay here—"

"You're not allowed to leave the room."

"So now I'm a prisoner?"

"Rin, please—"

"Let me go!"

She tried to break free. His grip tightened. "You're not in any danger."

"So *let me go*!"

"You'll derail negotiations that have been years in the making—"

"Negotiations?" she screeched. "You think I give a fuck about negotiations? They want to dissect me!"

"And Father won't let that happen! You think he's about to give you up? You think *I'd* let that happen? I'd die before I let anyone hurt you, Rin, calm down—"

That did nothing to calm her down. Every second she was still felt like a vise tightening around her neck.

"My family has been planning this war for over a decade," Nezha said. "My mother has been pursuing this diplomatic mission for years. She was educated in Hesperia; she has strong ties to the west. As soon as the third war was over, Father sent her overseas to solidify Hesperian military support."

Rin barked out a laugh. "Well, then she cut a shitty deal."

"We won't take it. The Hesperians are greedy and malleable. They want resources only the Empire can offer. Father can talk them down. But we must not anger them. We *need* their weapons." Nezha let go of her arms when it was clear she'd stopped struggling. "You've been in the councils. We won't win this war without them."

Rin twisted around to face him. "You want whatever those barrel things are."

"They're called arquebuses. They're like hand cannons, except they're lighter than crossbows, they can penetrate wooden panels, and they shoot for longer distance."

"Oh, I'm sure Vaisra just wants crates and crates of them."

He gave her a frank look. "We need anything we can get our hands on."

"But suppose you win this war, and the Hesperians don't want to leave," she said. "Suppose it's the First Poppy War all over again."

"They have no interest in staying," he said dismissively. "They're done with that now. They've found their colonies too difficult to defend, and the war's weakened them too much to commit the kind of ground resources they could before. All they want is trade rights and permission to dump missionaries wherever they want. At the end of this war we'll make them leave our shores quickly enough."

"And if they don't want to go?"

"I expect we'll find a way," Nezha said. "Just as we have before. But at present, Father's going to choose the lesser of two evils. And so should you."

The doors opened. Captain Eriden walked inside.

"They're ready for you," he said.

"'They'?" Rin echoed.

"The Dragon Warlord is entertaining the Hesperian delegates in the great hall. They'd like to speak to you."

"No," Rin said.

"You'll be fine," Nezha said. "Just don't do anything stupid."

"We have very different ideas of what defines 'stupid,'" she said.

"The Dragon Warlord would prefer not to be kept waiting." Eriden motioned with a hand. Two of his guards strode forward and seized Rin by the arms. She managed a last, panicked glance over her shoulder at Nezha before they escorted her out the door.

The guards deposited Rin in the short walkway that led to the palace's great hall and shut the doors behind her.

She stepped hesitantly forward. She saw the Hesperians sitting in gilded chairs around the center table. Jinzha sat at his father's right hand. The southern Warlords had been relegated to the far end of the table, looking flustered and uncomfortable.

Rin could tell she'd walked into the middle of a heated argument. A thick tension crackled in the air, and all parties looked flustered, red-faced, and furious, as if they were about to come to blows.

She hung back in the hallway for a moment, concealed by the corner wall, and listened.

"The Consortium is still recovering from its own war," the Hesperian general was saying. Rin struggled to make sense of his speech at first, but gradually the language returned to her. She felt like a student again, sitting in the back of Jima's classroom, memorizing verb tenses. "We're in no mood to speculate."

"This isn't speculation," Vaisra said urgently. He spoke Hesperian like it was his native tongue. "We could take back this country in days, if you just—"

"Then do it yourselves," the general said. "We're here to do business, not alchemy. We are not interested in transforming frauds into kings."

Vaisra sat back. "So you're going to run my country like an experiment before you choose to intervene."

"A necessary experiment. We didn't come here to lend ships at your will, Vaisra. This is an investigation."

"Into what?"

"Whether the Nikara are ready for civilization. We do not distribute Hesperian aid lightly. We made that mistake before. The Mugenese seemed even more ready for advancement than you are. They had no factional infighting, and their governance was more sophisticated by far. Look how that turned out."

"If we're underdeveloped, it's because of years of foreign occupation," Vaisra said. "That's your fault, not ours."

The general shrugged, indifferent. "Even so."

Vaisra sounded exasperated. "Then what are you looking for?"

"Well, it would be cheating if we told you, wouldn't it?" The Hesperian general gave a thin smile. "But all of this is a moot point. Our primary objective here is the Speerly. She has purportedly leveled an entire country. We'd like to know how she did it."

"You can't have the Speerly," Vaisra said.

"Oh, I don't think you get to decide."

Rin strode into the room. "I'm right here."

"Runin." If Vaisra looked surprised, he quickly recovered. He stood up and gestured to the Hesperian general. "Please meet General Josephus Tarcquet."

Stupid name, Rin thought. A garbled collection of syllables that she could hardly pronounce.

Tarcquet rose to his feet. "I believe we owe you an apology. Lady Saikhara had us rather convinced that we were dealing with something like a wild animal. We didn't realize that you would be so . . . human."

Rin blinked at him. Was that really supposed to be an apology?

"Does she understand what I'm saying?" Tarcquet asked Vaisra in choppy, ugly Nikara.

"I understand Hesperian," Rin snapped. She deeply wished that she'd learned Hesperian curse words at Sinegard. She didn't have the full vocabulary range to express what she wanted to say, but she had enough. "I'm just not keen on dialoguing with fools who want me dead."

"Why are we even speaking to her?" Lady Saikhara burst out.

Her voice was high and brittle, as if she had just been crying. The pure venom in her glare startled Rin. This was more than contempt. This was a vicious, murderous hatred.

"She is an unholy abomination," Saikhara snarled. "She is a mark against the Maker, and she ought to be dragged off to the Gray Towers as soon as possible."

"We're not dragging anyone off." Vaisra sounded exasperated. "Runin, please, sit—"

"But you *promised*," Saikhara hissed at him. "You said they'd find a way to fix him—"

Vaisra grabbed at his wife's wrist. "Now is not the time."

Saikhara jerked her hand free and slammed a fist down on the table. Her cup toppled over, spilling hot tea across the embroidered cloth. "You swore to me. You said you'd make this right, that if I brought them back they'd find a way to fix him, you *promised*—"

"Silence, woman." Vaisra pointed to the door. "If you cannot calm yourself, then you will leave."

Saikhara shot Rin a tight-lipped look of fury, muttered something under her breath, and stormed out of the room.

A long silence hung over her absence. Tarcquet looked somewhat amused. Vaisra leaned back in his chair, took a draught of tea, then sighed. "You'll have to excuse my wife. She tends to be ill-tempered after travel."

"She's desperate for answers." A woman in a gray cassock, the one who had stood over Rin at the dock, laid her hand on Vaisra's. "We understand. We'd like to find a cure, too."

Rin shot her a curious look. The woman's Nikara sounded remarkably good—she could have been a native speaker if her tones weren't so oddly flat. Her hair was the color of wheat, straight and slick, braided into a serpent-like coil that rested just over her shoulder. Gray eyes like castle walls. Pale skin like paper, so thin that blue veins were visible beneath. Rin had the oddest urge to touch it, just to see if it felt human.

"She's a fascinating creature," said the woman. "It is rare you meet someone possessed by Chaos who yet remains so lucid. None of our Hesperian madmen have been so good at fooling their observers."

"I'm standing right in front of you," Rin said.

"I'd like to get her in an isolation chamber," the woman continued, as if Rin hadn't spoken. "We're close to developing instruments that can detect raw Chaos in sterile environments. If we could bring her back to the Gray Towers—"

"I'm not going anywhere with you," Rin said.

General Tarcquet stroked the arquebus that lay in front of him. "You wouldn't really have a choice, dear."

The woman lifted a hand. "Wait, Josephus. The Divine Architect values free thought. Voluntary cooperation is a sign that reason and order yet prevail in the mind. Will the girl come willingly?"

Rin stared at the two of them in disbelief. Did Vaisra possibly believe that she would say yes?

"You could even keep her on campaign for the time being," the woman said to Vaisra, as if they were discussing something no more pressing than dinner arrangements. "I would only require regular meetings, perhaps once a week. They would be minimally invasive."

"Define 'minimally,'" Vaisra said.

"I would only observe her, for the most part. I'd perhaps conduct a few experiments. Nothing that will affect her permanently, and certainly nothing that would affect her fighting ability. I'd just like to see how she reacts to various stimuli—"

A ringing noise grew louder and louder in Rin's ears. Everyone's voices became both slurred and magnified. The conversation proceeded, but she could decipher only fragments.

"—fascinating creature—"

"—prized soldier—"

"—tip the balance—"

She found herself swaying on her feet.

She saw in her mind's eye a face she hadn't let herself imagine for a long time. Dark, clever eyes. Narrow nose. Thin lips and a cruel, excited smile.

She saw Dr. Shiro.

She felt his hands moving over her, checking her restraints, making sure she couldn't move an inch from the bed he'd strapped her down on. She felt his fingers feeling around in her mouth, counting her teeth, moving down past her jaw to her neck to locate her artery.

She felt his hands holding her down as he pushed a needle into her vein.

She felt panic, fear, and rage all at once and she wanted to burn but she *couldn't*, and the heat and fire just bubbled up in her chest and built up inside her because the fucking Seal had gotten in the way, but the heat just kept building and Rin thought she might implode—

"Runin." Vaisra's voice cut through the fog.

She focused with difficulty on his face. "No," she whispered. "No, I can't—"

He got up from his seat. "This isn't the same as the Mugenese lab."

She backed away from him. "I don't care, I can't do this—"

"What are you debating?" demanded the Boar Warlord. "Hand her to them and be done with it."

"Quiet, Charouk." Vaisra drew Rin hastily into the corner of the room, far from where the Hesperians could hear. He lowered his voice. "They will force you either way. If you cooperate you will garner us sympathy."

"You're trading me for ships," she said.

"No one is trading you," he said. "I am asking you for a favor. Please, will you do this for me? You're in no danger. You're no monster, and they'll discover that soon enough."

And then she understood. The Hesperians wouldn't find anything. They *couldn't*, because Rin couldn't call the fire anymore. They could run all the experiments they liked, but they wouldn't find anything. Daji had ensured that there was nothing left to find.

"Runin, please," Vaisra murmured. "We don't have a choice."

He was right about that. The Hesperians had made it clear that they would study her by force if necessary. She could try to fight, but she wouldn't get very far.

Part of her wanted desperately to say no. To say fuck it, to take her chances and try her best to escape and run. Of course, they'd hunt her down, but she had the smallest chance of making it out alive.

But hers wasn't the only life at stake.

The fate of the Empire hung in the balance. If she truly wanted the Empress dead, then Hesperian airships and arquebuses were the best way to get it done. The only way she could generate their goodwill was if she went willingly into their arms.

When you hear screaming, Vaisra had told her, *run toward it.*

She'd failed at Lusan. She couldn't call the fire anymore. This might be the only way to atone for the colossal wrongs she'd committed. Her only chance to put things right.

Altan had died for liberation. She knew what he would say to her now.

Stop being so fucking selfish.

Rin steeled herself, took a breath, and nodded. "I'll do it."

"Thank you." Relief washed over Vaisra's face. He turned to the table. "She agrees."

"One hour," Rin said in her best Hesperian. "Once a week. No more. I'm free to go if I feel uncomfortable, and you don't touch me without my express permission."

General Tarcquet removed his hand from his arquebus. "Fair enough."

The Hesperians looked far too pleased. Rin's stomach twisted. Oh, gods. What had she agreed to?

"Excellent." The gray-eyed woman rose from her chair. "Come with me. We'll begin now."

The Hesperians had already occupied the entire block of buildings just west of the palace, furnished residences that Rin suspected Vaisra must have prepared long ago. Blue flags bearing an insignia that looked like the gears of a clock hung from the windows. The gray-eyed woman motioned for Rin to follow her into a small, windowless square room on the first floor of the center building.

"What do you call yourself?" asked the woman. "Fang Runin, they said?"

"Just Rin," Rin muttered, glancing around the room. It was bare except for two long, narrow stone tables that had recently been dragged there, judging from the skid marks on the stone floor. One table was empty. The other was covered with an array of instruments, some made of steel and some of wood, few of which Rin recognized or could guess the function of.

The Hesperians had been preparing this room since they got here.

A Hesperian soldier stood in the corner, arquebus slung over his shoulder. His eyes tracked Rin every time she moved. She made a face at him. He didn't react.

"You may call me Sister Petra," said the woman. "Why don't you come over here?"

She spoke truly excellent Nikara. Rin would have been impressed, but something felt off. Petra's sentences were perfectly smooth and fluent, perhaps more grammatically perfect than those of most native speakers, but her words came out sounding all wrong. The tones were just the slightest bit off, and she inflected everything with the same flat clip that made her sound utterly inhuman.

Petra picked a cup off the edge of the table and offered it to her. "Laudanum?"

Rin recoiled, surprised. "For what?"

"It might calm you down. I've been told you react badly to lab environments." Petra pursed her lips. "I know opiates dampen the phenomena you manifest, but for a first observation that won't matter. Today I'm interested only in baseline measurements."

Rin eyed the cup, considering. The last thing she wanted was to be off her guard for a full hour with the Hesperians. But she knew she had no choice but to comply with whatever Petra asked of her. She could reasonably expect that they wouldn't kill her. She had no control over the rest. The only thing she could control was her own discomfort.

She took the cup and emptied it.

"Excellent." Petra gestured to the bed. "Up there, please.

Rin took a deep breath and sat down at the edge.

One hour. That was it. All she had to do was survive the next sixty minutes.

Petra began by taking an endless series of measurements. With a notched string she recorded Rin's height, wingspan, and the length of her feet. She measured the circumference around Rin's waist, wrists, ankles, and thighs. Then with a smaller string she took a series of smaller measurements that seemed utterly pointless. The width of Rin's eyes. Their distance from her nose. The length of each one of her fingernails.

This went on forever. Rin managed not to flinch too hard from Petra's touch. The laudanum was working well; a lead weight had settled comfortably in her bloodstream and kept her numb, torpid, and docile.

Petra wrapped the string around the base of Rin's thumb. "Tell me about the first time you communed with, ah, this entity you claim to be your god. How would you describe the experience?"

Rin said nothing. She had to present her body for examination. That didn't mean she had to entertain small talk.

Petra repeated her question. Again Rin kept silent.

"You should know," Petra said as she put the tape measure away, "that verbal cooperation is a condition of our agreement."

Rin gave her a wary look. "What do you want from me?"

"Only your honest responses. I am not solely interested in the stock of your body. I'm curious about the possibilities for the redemption of your soul."

If Rin's mind had been working any faster she would have managed some clever retort. Instead she rolled her eyes.

"You seem confident our religion is false," Petra said.

"I know it's false." The laudanum had loosened Rin's tongue, and she found herself spilling the first thoughts that came to her mind. "I've seen evidence of my gods."

"Have you?"

"Yes, and I know that the universe is not the doing of a single man."

"A single man? Is that what you think we believe?" Petra tilted her head. "What do you know about our theology?"

"That it's stupid," Rin said, which was the extent of what she'd ever been taught.

They'd studied Hesperian religion—Makerism, they called it—briefly at Sinegard, back when none of them thought the Hesperians would return to the Empire's shores during their lifetime. None of them had taken their studies of Hesperian culture seriously, not even the instructors. Makerism was only ever a footnote. A joke. Those foolish westerners.

Rin remembered idyllic walks down the mountainside with Jiang during the first year of her apprenticeship, when he'd made her research differences between eastern and western religions and hypothesize the reasons they existed. She remembered sinking hours into this question at the library. She'd discovered that the vast and varied religions of the Empire tended to be polytheistic, disordered, and irregular, lacking consistency even across villages. But the Hesperians liked to invest their worship in a single entity, typically represented as a man.

"Why do you think that is?" Rin had asked Jiang.

"Hubris," he'd said. "They already like to think they are lords of the world. They'd like to think something in their own image created the universe."

The question that Rin had never entertained, of course, was how the Hesperians had become so vastly technologically advanced if their approach to religion was so laughably wrong. Until now, it had never been relevant.

Petra plucked a round metal device about the size of her palm off the table and held it in front of Rin. She clicked a button at the side, and its lid popped off. "Do you know what this is?"

It was a clock of some sort. She recognized Hesperian numbers, twelve in a circle, with two needles moving slowly in rotation. But Nikara clocks, powered by dripping water, were installations that took up entire corners of rooms. This thing was so small it could have fit in her pocket.

"Is it a timepiece?"

"Very good," Petra said. "Appreciate this design. See the intricate gears, perfectly shaped to form, that keep it ticking on its own. Now imagine that you found this on the ground. You don't know what it is. You don't know who put it there. What is your conclusion? Does it have a designer, or is it an accident of nature, like a rock?"

Rin's mind moved sluggishly around Petra's questions, but she knew the conclusion Petra wanted her to reach.

"There exists a creator," she said after a pause.

"Very good," Petra said again. "Now imagine the world as a clock. Consider the sea, the clouds, the skies, the stars, all working in perfect harmony to keep our world turning and breathing as it does. Think of the life cycles of forests and the animals that live in them. This is no accident. This could not have been forged through primordial chaos, as your theology tends to argue. This was deliberate creation by a greater entity, perfectly benevolent and rational.

"We call him our Divine Architect, or the Maker, as you know him. He seeks to create order and beauty. This isn't mad reasoning. It is the simplest possible explanation for the beauty and intricacy of the natural world."

Rin sat quietly, running those thoughts through her tired mind.

It did sound terribly attractive. She liked the thought that the natural world was fundamentally knowable and reducible to a set of objective principles imposed by a benevolent and rational deity. That was much neater and cleaner than what she knew of the sixty-four gods—chaotic creatures dreaming up an endless whirlpool of forces that created the subjective universe, where everything was constantly in flux and nothing was ever written. Easier to think that the natural world was a neat, objective, and static gift wrapped and delivered by an all-powerful architect.

There was only one gaping oversight.

"So why do things go badly?" Rin asked. "If this Maker set everything in motion, then—"

"Then why couldn't the Maker prevent death?" Petra supplied. "Why do things go wrong if they were designed according to plan?"

"Yes. How did you know?"

Petra gave her a small smile. "Don't look so surprised. That is the most common question of every new convert. Your answer is Chaos."

"Chaos," Rin repeated slowly. She'd heard Petra use this word at the council earlier. It was a Hesperian term; it had no Nikara equivalent. Despite herself, she asked, "What is Chaos?"

"It is the root of evil," Petra said. "Our Divine Architect is not omnipotent. He is powerful, yes, but he leads a constant struggle to fashion order out of a universe tending inevitably toward a state of dissolution and disorder. We call that force Chaos. Chaos is the antithesis of order, the cruel force trying constantly to undo the Architect's creations. Chaos is old age, disease, death, and war. Chaos manifests in the worst of mankind—evil, jealousy, greed, and treachery. It is our task to keep it at bay."

Petra closed the timepiece and placed it back on the table. Her fingers hovered over the instruments, deliberating, and then selected a device with what looked like two earpieces and a flat circle attached to a metal cord.

"We don't know how or when Chaos manifests," she said. "But it tends to pop up more often in places like yours—undeveloped, uncivilized, and barbaric. And cases like yours are the worst outbreaks of individual Chaos that the Company has ever seen."

"You mean shamanism," Rin said.

Petra turned back to face her. "You understand why the Gray Company must investigate. Creatures like you pose a terrible threat to earthly order."

She raised the flat circle up under Rin's shirt to her chest. It was icy cold. Rin couldn't help but flinch.

"Don't be scared," Petra said. "Don't you realize I'm trying to help you?"

"I don't understand," Rin murmured, "why you would even keep me alive."

"Fair question. Some think it would be easier simply to kill you. But then we would come no closer to understanding Chaos's evil. And it would only find another avatar to wreak its destruction. So against the Gray Company's better judgment, I am keeping you alive so that at last we may learn to fix it."

"Fix it," Rin repeated. "You think you can fix me."

"I *know* I can fix you."

There was a fanatic intensity to Petra's expression that made Rin deeply uncomfortable. Her gray eyes gleamed a metallic silver when she spoke. "I'm the smartest scholar of the Gray Company in generations. I've been lobbying to come study the Nikara for decades. I'm going to figure out what is plaguing your country."

She pressed the metal disc hard between Rin's breasts. "And then I'm going to drive it out of you."

At last the hour was over. Petra put her instruments back on the table and dismissed Rin from the examination room.

The last of the laudanum wore off just as Rin returned to the barracks. Every feeling that the drug had kept at bay—discomfort, anxiety, disgust, and utter terror—came flooding back to her all at once, a sickening rush so abrupt that it wrenched her to her knees.

She tried to get to the lavatory. She didn't make it two steps before she lurched over and vomited.

She couldn't help it. She hunched over the puddle of her sick and sobbed.

Petra's touch, which had seemed so light, so noninvasive under the effect of laudanum, now felt like a dark stain, like insects burrowing their way under Rin's skin no matter how hard she tried to claw them out. Her memories mixed together; confusing, indistinguishable. Petra's hands became Shiro's hands. Petra's room became Shiro's laboratory.

Worst of all was the violation, the *fucking* violation, and the sheer helplessness of knowing that her body was not hers and she had to sit still and take it, this time not because of any restraints, but due to the simple fact that she'd chosen to be there.

That was the only thing that kept her from packing her belongings and immediately leaving Arlong.

She needed to do this because she deserved this. This was, in some horrible way that made complete sense, atonement. She knew she was monstrous. She couldn't keep denying that. This was self-flagellation for what she'd become.

It should have been you, Altan had said.

She should have been the one who died.

This came close.

After she had cried so hard that the pain in her chest had faded to a dull ebb, she pulled herself to her feet and wiped the tears and mucus off her face. She stood in front of a mirror in the lavatory and waited to come out until the redness had faded from her eyes.

When the others asked her what had happened, she said nothing at all.

CHAPTER 14

War came in the water.

Rin awoke to shouting outside the barracks. She threw her uniform on in a panicked frenzy; blindly attempted to force her right foot into her left shoe before she gave up and ran out the door barefoot, trident in hand.

Outside, half-dressed soldiers ran around and into one another in a confused swarm of activity while commanders shouted contradicting orders. But nobody had weapons drawn, projectiles weren't flying through the air, and Rin couldn't hear the sound of cannon fire.

Finally she noticed that most of the troops were running toward the beachfront. She followed them.

At first she didn't understand what she was looking at. The water was dusted over with spots of white, as if a giant had blown dandelion puffs over the surface. Then she reached the edge of the pier and saw in closer detail the silver crescents hanging just beneath the surface. Those spots of white were the bloated underbellies of fish.

Not just fish. When she knelt by the water she saw puffy, discolored corpses of frogs, salamanders, and turtles. Something had killed every living thing in the water.

It had to be poison. Nothing else could kill so many animals so quickly. And that meant the poison had to be in the water—and all the canals in Arlong were interconnected—which meant that perhaps every drinking source in Arlong was now tainted . . .

But why would anyone from Dragon Province poison the water? For a minute Rin stood there stupidly, thinking, *assuming* that it must have been someone from within the province itself. She didn't want to consider the alternative, which was that the poison came from upriver, because that would mean . . .

"Rin! Fuck—*Rin*!"

Ramsa tugged at her arm. "You need to see this."

She ran with him to the end of the pier, where the Cike were huddled around a dark mass on the planks. A massive fish? A bundle of clothes? No—a man, she saw that now, but the figure was hardly human.

It stretched a pale, skeletal hand toward her. "Altan . . ."

Her breath caught in her throat. "*Aratsha?*"

She had never before seen him in his human form. He was an emaciated man, covered from head to toe in barnacles embedded in blue-white skin. The lower half of his face was concealed by a scraggly beard so littered with sea worms and small fish that it was difficult to parse out the human bits of him.

She tried to slide her arms beneath him to help him up, but pieces of him kept coming away in her hands. A clump of shells, a stick of bone, and then something crackly and powdery that crumbled to nothing in her fingers. She tried not to push him away in disgust. "Can you speak?"

Aratsha made a strangled noise. At first she thought he was choking on his own spit, but then frothy liquid the color of curdled milk bubbled out the sides of his mouth.

"Altan," he repeated.

"I'm not Altan." She reached for Aratsha's hand. Was that something she should do? It felt like something she should do. Something comforting and kind. Something a commander would do.

But Aratsha didn't seem to even notice. His skin had gone from bluish white to a horrible violet color in seconds. She could see his veins pulsing beneath, a sludgy, inky black.

"Ahh, Altan," said Aratsha. "I should have told you."

He smelled of seawater and rot. Rin wanted to vomit.

"What?" she whispered.

He peered up at her through milky eyes. They were filmy like the eyes of a fish at market, oddly unfocused, staring out at two sides like he'd spent so long in the water that he didn't know what to make of the things on land.

He murmured something under his breath, something too quiet and garbled for her to decipher. She thought she heard a whisper that sounded like "misery." Then Aratsha disintegrated in her hands, flesh bubbling into water, until all that was left was sand, shells, and a pearl necklace.

"Fuck," Ramsa said. "That's gross."

"Shut up," Baji said.

Suni wailed loudly and buried his head in his hands. No one comforted him.

Rin stared numbly at the necklace.

We should bury him, she thought. That was proper, wasn't it?

Should she be grieving? She couldn't feel grief. She kept waiting to feel something, but it never hit, and it never would. This was not an acute loss, not the kind that had left her catatonic after Altan's death. She had barely known Aratsha; she'd just given him orders and he had obeyed, without question, loyal to the Cike until the day he died.

No, what sickened her was that she felt *disappointed*, irritated that now that Aratsha was gone they didn't have a shaman who could control the river. All he'd ever been to her was an immensely useful chess piece, and now she couldn't use him anymore.

"What's going on?" Nezha asked, panting. He'd just arrived.

Rin stood up and brushed the sand off her hands. "We lost a man."

He looked down at the mess on the pier, visibly confused. "Who?"

"One of the Cike. Aratsha. He's always in the water. Whatever hit the fish must have hit him, too."

"Fuck," Nezha said. "Were they targeting him?"

"I don't think so," she said slowly. "That's a lot of trouble for one shaman."

This couldn't be about just one man. Fish were floating dead across the entire harbor. Whoever had poisoned Aratsha had meant to poison the entire river.

The Cike were not the target. The Dragon Province was.

Because yes, Su Daji was that crazy. Daji was a woman who had welcomed the Federation into her territory to keep her throne. She would easily poison the southern provinces, would readily sentence millions to starvation, to keep the rest of her empire intact.

"How many troops?" Vaisra demanded.

All of them were crammed into the office—Captain Eriden, the Warlords, the Hesperians, and a smattering of whatever ranked officers were available. Decorum did not matter. The room had turned into a din of frantic shouting. Everyone spoke at once.

"We haven't counted the men who haven't made it to the infirmary—"

"Is it in the aquifers?"

"We have to shut down the fish markets—"

Vaisra shouted over the noise. "*How many?*"

"Almost the entire First Brigade has been hospitalized," said one of the physicians. "The poison was meant to affect the wildlife. It's weaker on men."

"It's not fatal?"

"We don't think so. We're hoping to see full recovery in a few days."

"Is Daji insane?" General Hu asked. "This is suicide. This doesn't just affect us, it kills everything that the Murui touches."

"The north doesn't care," Vaisra said. "They're upstream."

"But that means they'd need a constant source of poison," said

Eriden. "They'd have to introduce the agent to the stream daily. And it can't be as far as the Autumn Palace, or they screw over their own allies."

"Hare Province?" Nezha suggested.

"That's impossible," Jinzha said. "Their army is pathetic; they barely have defense capabilities. They'd never strike first."

"If they're pathetic, then they'd do whatever Daji told them."

"Are we sure it's Daji?" Takha asked.

"Who else would it be?" Tsolin demanded. He turned to Vaisra. "This is the answer to your blockade. Daji's weakening you before she strikes. I wouldn't wait around to see what she does next."

Jinzha banged a fist on the table. "I *told you*, we should have sailed up a week ago."

"With whose troops?" Vaisra asked coolly.

Jinzha's cheeks turned a bright red. But Vaisra wasn't looking at his son. Rin realized his remarks were meant for General Tarcquet.

The Hesperians had been watching silently at the back of the room, expressions impassive, standing with their arms crossed and lips pursed like teachers observing a classroom of unruly students. Every so often Sister Petra would scratch something into the writing pad she carried around everywhere, her lips curled in amusement. Rin wanted to hit her.

"This neutralizes our blockade," Tsolin said. "We can't wait any longer."

"But water moves steadily out to sea," said Lady Saikhara. "You never step in the same stream twice. In a matter of days the poisonous agent should have washed out into Omonod Bay, and we'll be fine." She looked imploringly around the table for someone to agree. "Shouldn't it?"

"But it's not just the fish." Kitay's voice was a strangled whisper. He said it again, and this time the room fell quiet when he spoke. "It's not just the fish. It's the entire country. The Murui supplies tributaries to all of the major southern regions. We're talking about all agricultural irrigation channels. Rice paddies. The water doesn't stop flowing there; it stays, it lingers. We are talking about massive crop failure."

"But the granaries," Lady Saikhara said. "Every province has stockpiled grain for lean years, yes? We could requisition those."

"And leave the south to eat what?" Kitay countered. "You force the south to give up their grain stores, and you're going to start bleeding allies. We don't have food, we don't even have *water*—"

"We have water," Saikhara said. "We've tested the aquifers, they're untouched. The wells are fine."

"Fine," said Kitay. "Then you'll just starve to death."

"What about them?" Charouk jabbed a finger in Tarcquet's direction. "They can't send us food aid?"

Tarcquet raised an eyebrow and looked expectantly at Vaisra.

Vaisra sighed. "The Consortium will not make investments until they feel better assured of our chances at victory."

There was a pause. The entire council looked toward General Tarcquet. The Warlords wore uniform expressions of desperate, pathetic, pleading hope. Sister Petra continued to scratch at her writing pad.

Nezha broke the silence. He spoke in deliberate, unaccented Hesperian. "Millions of people are going to die, sir."

Tarcquet shrugged. "Then you'd better get this campaign started, hadn't you?"

The Empress's ploy had the effect of setting fire to an anthill. Arlong erupted in a frenzy of activity, finally triggering battle plans that had been in place for months.

A war over ideology had suddenly become a war of resources. Now that waiting out the Empire was clearly no longer an option, the southern Warlords had no choice but to donate their troops to Vaisra's northern campaign.

Executive orders went out to generals, then filtered down

through commanders to squadron leaders to soldiers. Within minutes Rin had orders to report to the Fourteenth Brigade on the *Swallow*, departing in two hours from Pier Three.

"Nice, you're in the first fleet," Nezha said. "With me."

"Joyous day." She stuffed a change of uniform into a bag and hoisted it over her shoulder.

He reached over to ruffle her hair. "Look alive, little soldier. You're finally getting what you wanted."

En route to the pier they dodged through a maze of wagons carrying hemp, jute, lime for caulking, tung oil, and sailing cloth. The entire city smelled and sounded like a shipyard; it echoed everywhere with the same faint, low groan, the noise of dozens of massive ships detaching their anchors, paddle wheels beginning to turn.

"Move!" A wagon driven by Hesperian soldiers narrowly missed running them over. Nezha pulled Rin to the side.

"Assholes," he muttered.

Rin's eyes followed the Hesperians to the warships. "I guess we'll finally get to see Tarcquet's golden troops in action."

"Actually, no. Tarcquet's only bringing a skeleton platoon. The rest are staying in Arlong."

"Then why are they even going?"

"Because they're here to observe. They want to know if we're capable of coming close to winning this war, and if we are, if we're capable of running this country effectively. Tarcquet told Father some babble about stages of human evolution last night, but I think they really just want to see if we're worth the trouble. Everything Jinzha does gets reported to Tarcquet. Everything Tarcquet sees goes back to the Consortium. And the Consortium decides when they want to lend their ships."

"We can't take this Empire without them, and they won't help us until we take the Empire." Rin made a face. "Those are the terms?"

"Not quite. They'll intervene before this war is over, once they're sure it isn't a lost cause. They're willing to tip the scales, but we have to prove first that we can pull our own weight."

"So just another fucking test," Rin said.

Nezha sighed. "More or less, yes."

The sheer arrogance, Rin thought. It must be nice, possessing all the power, so that you could approach geopolitics like a chess game, popping in curiously to observe which countries deserved your aid and which didn't.

"Is Petra coming with us?" she asked.

"No. She'll stay on Jinzha's ship." Nezha hesitated. "But, ah, Father told me to make it clear that your meetings resume as usual when we rejoin my brother's fleet."

"Even on campaign?"

"They're most interested in you on campaign. Petra promised it wouldn't be much. An hour every week, as agreed."

"It doesn't sound like much to you," Rin muttered. "You've never been someone's lab rat."

Three fleets were preparing to sail out from the Red Cliffs. The first, commanded by Jinzha, would go up the Murui through the center of Hare Province, the agricultural heartland of the north. The second fleet, led by Tsolin and General Hu, would race up the rugged coastline around Snake Province to destroy Tiger Province ships before they could be deployed inland to fend off the main vanguard.

Combined, they were to squeeze the northeastern provinces between the inland attack and the coast. Daji would be forced to fight an enemy on two fronts, and both over water—a terrain the Militia had never been comfortable with.

In terms of sheer manpower, the Republic was still outnumbered. The Militia had tens of thousands of men on the Republican Army. But if Vaisra's fleet did its job, and if the Hesperians kept their word, there was a good chance they might win this war.

"Guys! Wait!"

"Oh, shit," Nezha muttered.

Rin turned around to see Venka running barefoot down the pier toward them. She clutched a crossbow to her chest.

Nezha cleared his throat as Venka came to a halt in front of him. "Uh, Venka, this isn't a good time."

"Just take this," Venka panted. She passed the crossbow into Rin's hands. "I took it from my father's workshop. Latest model. Reloads automatically."

Nezha shot Rin an uncomfortable glance. "This isn't really—"

"Beautiful, isn't it?" Venka asked. She ran her fingers over the body. "See this? Intricate trigger latch mechanism. We finally figured out how to get it to work; this is just the prototype but I think it's ready—"

"We're boarding in minutes," Nezha interrupted. "What do you want?"

"Take me with you," Venka said bluntly.

Rin noticed Venka had a pack strapped to her back, but she didn't have a uniform.

"Absolutely not," Nezha said.

Venka's cheeks reddened. "Why not? I'm all better now."

"You can't even bend your left arm."

"She doesn't need to," Rin said. "Not if she's firing a crossbow."

"Are you insane?" Nezha demanded. "She can't run around with a crossbow that big; she'll be exhausted—"

"Then we'll mount it on the ship," Rin said. "And she'll be removed from the heat of the battle. She'll need protection between rounds to reload, so she'll be surrounded by a unit of archers. It'll be safe."

Venka looked triumphantly at Nezha. "What she said."

"*Safe?*" Nezha echoed, incredulous.

"Safer than the rest of us," Rin amended.

"But she's not done . . ." Nezha looked Venka up and down, hesitating, clearly at a loss for the right words. "You're not done, uh . . ."

"Healing?" Venka asked. "That's what you mean, isn't it?"

"Venka, please."

"How long did you think I'd need? I've been sitting on my ass for months. Come on, *please*, I'm ready."

Nezha looked helplessly at Rin, as if hoping she'd make the entire situation dissipate. But what did he expect her to say? Rin didn't even understand the problem.

"There has to be room on the ships," she said. "Let her go."

"That's not your call. She could die out there."

"Occupational hazard," Venka shot back. "We're soldiers."

"*You* are not a soldier."

"Why not? Because of Golyn Niis?" Venka barked out a laugh. "You think once you're raped you can't be a soldier?"

Nezha shifted uncomfortably. "That's not what I said."

"Yes, it is. Even if you won't say it, that's what you're thinking!" Venka's voice rose steadily in pitch. "You think that because they raped me, I'm never going to go back to normal."

Nezha reached for her shoulder. "Meimei. Come on."

Meimei. Little sister. Not by blood, but by virtue of the closeness of their families. He was trying to invoke his ritual concern for her to dissuade her from going. "What happened to you was horrible. Nobody blames you. Nobody here agrees with your father, or my mother—"

"I know that!" Venka shouted. "I don't give a shit about that!"

Nezha looked pained. "I can't protect you out there."

"And when have you *ever* protected me?" Venka slapped his hand away from her shoulder. "Do you know what I thought when I was in that house? I kept hoping someone might come for me, *I really thought someone was coming for me.* And where the fuck were you? *Nowhere.* So fuck you, Nezha. You can't keep me safe, so you might as well let me fight."

"Yes, I can," Nezha said. "I'm a general. Go back. Or I'll have someone drag you back."

Venka grabbed the crossbow back from Rin and pointed it at Nezha. A bolt whizzed out, narrowly missed Nezha's cheek, and embedded itself into a post several feet behind his head, where it quivered in the wood, humming loudly.

"You missed," Nezha said calmly.

Venka tossed the crossbow on the pier and spat at Nezha's feet. "I never miss."

Captain Salkhi of the *Swallow* stood waiting for the Cike at the base of the gangplank. She was a lean, petite woman with closely cropped hair, narrow eyes, and pinkish-brown skin—not the dusky tint of a southerner, but the tanned hue of a pale northerner who had spent too much time in the sun.

"I'm assuming I'm to treat you lot as I would any other soldiers," she said. "Can you handle ground operations?"

"We'll be fine," said Rin. "I'll walk you through their specialties."

"I'd appreciate that." Salkhi paused. "And what about you? Eriden told me about your, ah, problem."

"I've still got two arms and two legs."

"And she has a trident," Kitay said, walking up behind her. "Very helpful for catching fish."

Rin turned around, pleasantly surprised. "You're coming with us?"

"It's either your ship or Nezha's. And frankly, he and I have been getting on each other's nerves."

"That's mostly your fault," she said.

"Oh, it absolutely is," he said. "Don't care. Besides, I like you better. Aren't you flattered?"

That was about as close to a peace offering from Kitay as she was going to get. Rin grinned. Together they boarded the *Swallow*.

The vessel was no multidecked warship. This was a sleek, tiny model, similar in build to an opium skimmer. A single row of cannons armed it on each side, but no trebuchets mounted its decks. Rin, who had gotten used to the amenities of the *Seagrim*, found the *Swallow* uncomfortably cramped.

The *Swallow* belonged to the first fleet, one of seven light, fast skimmers capable of tight tactical maneuvers. They would sail ahead two weeks in advance while the heavier fleet commanded by Jinzha prepared to ship out.

During that time they would be cut off from the chain of command at Arlong.

That didn't matter. Their instructions were short and simple: find the source of the poison, destroy it, and punish every last man involved. Vaisra hadn't specified how. He'd left that up to the captains, which was why everyone wanted to get to them first.

CHAPTER 15

The *Swallow*'s crew planned to keep sailing upstream until they weren't surrounded by dead fish, or until the poison's source became apparent. The facility would have to be near a main river juncture, and close enough to the Murui that there would be no chance the poison would wash out to the ocean or get blocked up in a dead end. They traveled north up the Murui until they reached the border of Hare Province, where the river branched off into several tributaries.

Here the skimmers split up. The *Swallow* took the westernmost route, a lazy bending creek that trailed slowly through the province's interior heartland. They went cautiously with their flag stowed away, disguising themselves as a merchant ship to avoid Imperial suspicion.

Captain Salkhi kept a clean, tightly disciplined ship. The Fourteenth Brigade rotated shifts on deck, either watching the shoreline or paddling down below. The soldiers and crew accepted the Cike into their fold with wary indifference. If they had questions about what the shamans could or couldn't do, they kept them to themselves.

"Seen anything?" Rin joined Kitay at the starboard railing, legs aching after a long paddling shift. She should have gone to sleep, according to the schedule, but midmorning was the only time that their breaks overlapped.

She was relieved that she and Kitay were on friendly terms again. They hadn't returned to normal—she didn't know if they would ever return to normal—but at least Kitay didn't emanate cold judgment every time he looked at her.

"Not yet." He stood utterly still, eyes fixed on the water, as if he could trace a path to the chemical source through sheer force of will. He was angry. Rin could tell when he was angry—his cheeks went a pale white, he held himself too rigidly, and he went long periods without blinking. She was just glad that he wasn't angry with her.

"Look." She pointed. "I don't think this is the right tributary."

Dark shapes moved under the muggy green water. Which meant the river life was still alive and healthy, unaffected by poison.

Kitay leaned forward. "What's that?"

Rin followed his gaze but couldn't tell what he was looking at.

He pulled a netted pole from the bulkhead, scooped it into the water, and plucked out a small object. At first Rin thought he'd caught a fish, but when Kitay deposited it onto the deck she saw it was some kind of dark and leathery pouch, about the size of a pomelo, knotted tightly at the end so that it looked oddly like a breast.

Kitay pinched it up with two fingers.

"That's clever," he said. "Gross, but clever."

"What is it?"

"It's incredible. This has to be a Sinegard graduate's work. Or a Yuelu graduate. No one else is this smart." He held the object toward her. She recoiled. It smelled awful—a combination of rank animal odor and the sharp, acrid smell of poison that brought back memories of embalmed pig fetuses from her medical classes with Master Enro.

She wrinkled her nose. "Are you going to tell me what it is?"

"Pig's bladder." Kitay turned it over in his palm and gave it a shake. "Resistant to acid, at least to some degree. It's why the poison hasn't been diluted before it reached Arlong."

He rubbed the edge of the bladder between his fingers. "This stays intact so the agent doesn't dissolve into the water until it reaches downstream. It was meant to last several days, a week at most."

The bladder popped open under the pressure. Liquid spilled out onto Kitay's hand, making his skin hiss and pucker. A yellow cloud seeped into the air. The acrid odor intensified. Kitay cursed and flung the bladder back out over the side of the ship, then hastily wiped his skin against his uniform.

"Fuck." He examined his hand, which had developed a pale, angry rash.

Rin yanked him away from the gas cloud. To her relief, it dissipated in seconds. "Tiger's tits, are you—"

"I'm fine. It's not deep, I don't think." Kitay cradled his hand inside his elbow and winced. "Go get Salkhi. I think we're getting close."

Salkhi split the Fourteenth Brigade into squads of six that dispersed through the surrounding region for a ground expedition. The Cike found the poison source first. It was visible the moment they emerged from the tree line—a blocky, three-story building with bell towers at both ends, erected in the architectural style of the old Hesperian missions.

At the southern wall, a single pipe extended over the river—a channel meant to move waste and sewage into the water. Instead, it dispensed poisonous pods into the river with a mechanical regularity.

Someone, or something, was dropping them off from inside.

"This is it." Kitay motioned for the rest of the Cike to crouch low behind the bushes. "We've got to get someone in there."

"What about the guard?" Rin whispered.

"What guard? There's no one there."

He was right. The mission looked barely garrisoned. Rin could count the soldiers on one hand, and after half an hour of scoping the perimeter, they didn't find any others on patrol.

"That makes no sense," she said.

"Maybe they just don't have the men," Kitay said.

"Then why poke the dragon?" Baji asked. "If they don't have backup, that strike was idiotic. This whole town is dead."

"Maybe it's an ambush," Rin said.

Kitay looked unconvinced. "But they're not expecting us."

"It could be protocol. They might all just be hiding inside."

"That's not how you lay out defenses. You only do that if you're under siege."

"So you want us to attack a building with minimal intelligence? What if there's a platoon in there?"

Kitay pulled a flare rocket from his pocket. "I know a way to find out."

"Hold on," Ramsa said. "Captain Salkhi said not to engage."

"Fuck Salkhi," Kitay said with a violence that was utterly unlike him. Before Rin could stop him he lit the fuse, aimed, and loosed the flare toward the patch of woods behind the mission.

A bang rocked the forest. Several seconds later Rin heard shouts from inside the mission. Then a group of men armed with farming implements emerged from the doors and ran toward the explosion.

"There's your guard," Kitay said.

Rin hoisted her trident. "Oh, *fuck* you."

Kitay counted under his breath as he watched the men. "About fifteen. There are twenty-four of us." He glanced back at Baji and Suni. "Think you can keep them out of the mission until the others get here?"

"Don't insult us," Baji said. "Go."

Only two guards remained at the mission's doors. Kitay dispatched one with his crossbow. Rin grappled with the other for a few minutes until at last she disarmed him and slammed her trident into his throat. She wrenched it back out and he dropped.

The doors stood wide open before them. Rin peered into the dark interior. The smell of rotting corpses hit her like a wall, so thick and sharp that her eyes watered. She covered her mouth with her sleeve. "You coming?"

Thud.

She turned. Kitay stood over the second guard, crossbow pointed down, wiping flecks of blood off his chin with the back of his hand. He caught her staring at him.

"Just making sure," he said.

Inside they found a slaughterhouse.

Rin's eyes took a moment to adjust to the darkness. Then she saw pig carcasses everywhere she looked—tossed on the floor, piled up in the corners, splayed over tables, all sliced open with surgical precision.

"Tiger's tits," she muttered.

Someone had killed them all solely for their bladders. The sheer waste amazed her. So much rotting meat was piled on these floors, and refugees in the next province over were so thin their ribs pushed through their ragged garments.

"Found them," Kitay said.

She followed his line of sight across the room. A dozen open barrels stood lined up against the wall. They contained the poison in liquid form—a noxious yellow concoction that sent toxic fumes spiraling lazily into the air above them. Above the barrels were shelves and shelves of metal canisters. More than Rin could count.

Rin had seen those canisters before, stacked neatly on shelves just like these. She'd stared up at them for hours while Mugenese scientists strapped her to a bed and forced opiates into her veins.

Kitay's face had turned a greenish color. He knew that gas from Golyn Niis.

"I wouldn't touch that." A figure emerged from the stairwell opposite them. Kitay jerked his crossbow up. Rin crouched back, trident poised to throw as she squinted to make out the figure's face in the darkness.

The figure stepped into the light. "Took you long enough."

Kitay let his arms drop. "*Niang?*"

Rin wouldn't have recognized her. War had transformed

Niang. Even into their third year at Sinegard, Niang had always looked like a child—innocent, round-faced, and adorable. She'd never looked like she belonged at a military academy. Now she just looked like a soldier, scarred and hardened like the rest of them.

"Please tell me you're not behind this," said Kitay.

"What? The pods?" Niang traced her fingers over the edge of a barrel. Her hands were covered in angry red welts. "Clever design, wasn't it? I was hoping someone might notice."

As Niang moved farther into light, Rin saw that the welts hadn't just formed on her hands. Her neck and face were mottled red, as if her skin had been scraped raw with the flat side of a blade.

"Those canisters," Rin said. "They're from the Federation."

"Yes, they really saved us some labor, didn't they?" Niang chuckled. "They produced thousands of barrels of that stuff. The Hare Warlord wanted to use it to invade Arlong, but I was smarter about it. Put it into the water, I said. Starve them out. The really hard part was converting it from a gas into a liquid. That took me weeks."

Niang pulled a canister off the wall and weighed it in her hand, as if preparing to throw. "Think you could do better?"

Rin and Kitay flinched simultaneously.

Niang lowered her arm, snickering. "Kidding."

"Put that down," Kitay said quietly. His voice was taut, carefully controlled. "Let's talk. Let's just talk, Niang. I know someone put you up to this. You don't have to do this."

"I know that," Niang said. "I volunteered. Or did you think I'd sit back and let traitors divide the Empire?"

"You don't know what you're talking about," Rin said.

"I know enough." Niang lifted the canister higher. "I know you threatened to starve out the north so they'd bow to the Dragon Warlord. I know you're going to invade our provinces if you don't get your way."

"So your solution is to poison the entire south?" Kitay asked.

"You're one to talk," Niang snarled. "You made us starve. You sold us that blighted grain. How does it feel getting a taste of your own medicine?"

"The embargo was just a threat," Kitay said. "No one has to die."

"People *have* died!" Niang pointed a finger at Rin. "How many did she kill on that island?"

Rin blinked. "Who gives a fuck about the Federation?"

"There were Militia troops there, too. Thousands of them." Niang's voice trembled. "The Federation took prisoners of war, shipped them over to labor camps. They took my brothers. Did you give them a chance to get off the island?"

"I . . ." Rin cast Kitay a desperate look. "That's not true."

Was it true?

Surely someone would have told her if it were true.

Kitay wouldn't meet her eyes.

She swallowed. "Niang, I didn't know—"

"*You didn't know!*" Niang screamed. The canister swung perilously in her hand. "That makes it all better, doesn't it?"

Kitay held a palm out, crossbow lowered. "Niang, *please*, put that down."

Niang shook her head. "This is your fault. We just fought a war. Why couldn't you just leave us alone?"

"We don't want to kill you," Rin said. "Please—"

"How generous!" Niang lifted the canister over her head. "She doesn't want to kill me! The Republic will take pity on—"

"Fuck this," Kitay muttered. In one fluid movement he lifted his crossbow, aimed, and shot an arrow straight into Niang's left breast.

The thud echoed like a final heartbeat.

Niang's eyes bulged open. She tilted her head down, examined her chest as if idly curious. Her knees gave out beneath her. The canister slipped from her hand and rolled to a halt by the wall.

The canister's lid burst off with a pop. Yellow smoke streamed out from it, rapidly filling the far end of the room.

Kitay lowered his crossbow. "Let's go."

They ran. Rin glanced over her shoulder just as they passed the door. The gas was almost too thick to see clearly, but she couldn't mistake the sight of Niang, twitching and jerking in a shroud of acid eating ravenously into her skin. Red spots blooming mercilessly across her body, as if she were a paper doll dropped in a pool of ink.

Light rain misted the air over the *Swallow* as it drifted down the tributary to rejoin the main fleet.

The crew had argued briefly over what to do with the canisters. They couldn't just leave them in the mission, but none of them wanted to have the gas on board. Finally Ramsa had suggested that they destroy the mission with a controlled burn. This was purportedly to deter anyone from approaching it until Jinzha could send a squadron to retrieve any remaining canisters, but Rin suspected that Ramsa just wanted an excuse to blow something up.

So they'd drenched the place in oil, piled kindling on the roof and in the makeshift slaughterhouse, and then fired flaming crossbow bolts from the ship once they were a safe sailing distance away.

The building had caught fire immediately, a lovely conflagration that remained visible from miles away. The rain hadn't yet managed to smother all of the flame. Little bursts of red still burned at the base of the building and smoke stretched out to embrace the sky from the towers.

A crack of thunder split the sky. Seconds later the light drizzle turned into fat, hard drops that slammed loudly and relentlessly against the deck. Captain Salkhi ordered the crew to set out barrels to capture fresh water. Most of the crew descended to their cabins, but Rin sat down on the deck, pulled her knees up to her chest, and tilted her head back. Raindrops hit the back of her throat, wonderfully fresh and cool. She gargled the rainwater, let it splash over her face and clothes. She knew the poison hadn't tainted her or she would have seen its effects, but somehow she couldn't feel clean.

"I thought you hated water," Kitay said.

She looked up. He stood over her, a miserable, drenched mess. He still had his crossbow clenched in his hands.

"You all right?" she asked.

His eyes were dead things. "No."

"Sit with me."

He obeyed without a word. Only when he was next to her did she see how violently he was trembling.

"I'm sorry about Niang," she said.

He jerked out a shrug. "I'm not."

"I thought you liked her."

"I barely knew her."

"You *did* like her. I remember. You thought she was cute. You told me that at school."

"Yes, and then that bitch went and poisoned half the country."

He tilted his head upward. His eyes were red, and she couldn't tell his tears apart from the rain. He took a long, shuddering breath.

Then he broke.

"I can't keep doing this." The words spilled out of him between choked, sudden sobs. "I can't sleep. I can't go a second without seeing Golyn Niis. I close my eyes and I'm hiding behind that wall again and the screams don't stop because the killing goes on all night—"

Rin reached for his hand. "Kitay . . ."

"It's like I'm frozen in one moment. And no one knows it because everyone else has moved on except me, but to me everything that's happened since Golyn Niis is a dream, and I know it's not real because I'm still behind the wall. And the worst part—the worst part is that I don't know who's causing the screams. It was easier when only the Federation was evil. Now I can't figure out who's right or wrong, and I'm the *smart* one, I'm always supposed to have the right answer, but I don't."

She didn't know what she could possibly say to comfort him, so she curled her fingers around his and held them tight. "Me neither."

"What happened on that island?" he asked abruptly.

"You know what happened."

"No. You never told me." He straightened up. "Was it conscious? Did you think about what you were doing?"

"I don't remember," she said. "I try not to remember."

"Did you know you were killing them?" he pressed. "Or did you just . . ." His fingers clenched into a fist and then unclenched beneath hers.

"I just wanted it to be over," she said. "I wasn't thinking. I didn't want to hurt them, not really, I just wanted it to end."

"I didn't want to kill her. I just—I don't know why I—"

"I know."

"That wasn't me," he insisted, but she wasn't the one he needed to convince.

All she could do was squeeze his hand again. "I know."

Signals were sent, courses were reversed. Within a day the dispersed skimmers had fled hastily down the Murui to rejoin the main armada.

When Rin saw the Republican Fleet from the front it seemed deceptively small, ships arranged in a narrow formation. Then they approached from the side and the full menace of the flotilla was splayed out in front of her, a marvelous and breathtaking display of force. Compared to the warships, the *Swallow* was just a tiny thing, a baby bird returning to the flock.

Captain Salkhi lit several lanterns to signal their return, and the patrol ships at the fore signaled back their permission to break through the line. The *Swallow* slipped into the ranks. An hour later Jinzha boarded their ship. The crew assembled on deck to report.

"We've stopped the poison at the source, but there may be canisters left in the ruins," Salkhi told Jinzha. "You'll want to send a squadron up there to see if you can retrieve it."

"Were they producing it themselves?" Jinzha asked.

"That's unlikely," Salkhi said. "That wasn't a research facility, it was a makeshift slaughterhouse. It seems like that was just the distribution point."

"We think they got it from the Federation facility on the coast," said Rin. "The one where I was— The one they took me to."

Jinzha frowned. "That's all the way out in Snake Province. Why bring it here?"

"They couldn't have set it off in Snake Province," Kitay said. "The current takes the poison out to sea instead of to Arlong. So someone must have gone there recently, retrieved the canisters, and carted them over to Hare Province."

"I hope that's right," said Jinzha. "I don't want to entertain the alternative."

Because the alternative, of course, was terrifying—that they were fighting a war not only against the Empire, but also against the Federation. That the Federation had survived, and had retained its weapons, and was sending them to Vaisra's enemies.

"Did you take prisoners?" Jinzha asked.

Salkhi nodded. "Two guardsmen. They're in the brig. We'll turn them over for interrogation."

"There's no need for that." Jinzha waved a hand. "We know what we need to know. Bring them out to the beach."

"Your brother has a flair for public spectacle," Kitay told Nezha.

The screaming had been going on for more than an hour now. Rin had almost gotten used to it, though it made it difficult to stomach her dinner.

The Hare Province guardsmen were strung up against posts in the ground, beaten for good measure. Jinzha had stripped them, flayed them, then poured diluted poison from one of the pods into a flask and boiled it. Now it ran in rivulets down the guardsmen's skin, tracing a steaming, angrily red path over their cheeks, their collarbones, down toward their exposed genitals, while the Republican soldiers sat back on the beach and watched.

"This wasn't necessary," Nezha said. His dinner rations sat untouched beside him. "This is grotesque."

Kitay laughed, a flat, hollow noise. "Don't be naive."

"What's that supposed to mean?"

"This *is* necessary. The Republic's just taken a massive blow. Vaisra can't undo the poisoning of the river, or the fact that thousands of people are going to starve. But give a few men a little pain, do it in public, and it'll all be all right."

"Does it make it all right to you?" Rin asked.

Kitay shrugged. "They poisoned a fucking river."

Nezha wrapped his arms around his knees. "Salkhi says you were in there for a while."

Rin nodded. "We saw Niang. Meant to tell you that."

Nezha blinked, surprised. "And how is she?"

"Dead," said Kitay. He was still staring at the men on the posts.

Nezha watched him for a moment, then raised an eyebrow at Rin. She understood his question. She shook her head.

"I hadn't thought about fighting our own classmates," Nezha murmured after a pause. "Who else do we know in the north? Kureel, Arda . . ."

"My cousins," Kitay said without turning around. "Han. Tobi. Most of the rest of our class, if they're still alive."

"I suppose it's not easy going to war against friends," Nezha said.

"Yes, it is," Kitay said. "They have a choice. Niang made her choice. She just happened to be dead fucking wrong."

CHAPTER 16

The guardsmen had stopped twitching by sunset.

Jinzha ordered their bodies burned as a final display. But there was far less retributive pleasure in watching corpses burn compared to hearing men scream, and eventually the smell of cooked meat grew so pungent on the beach that the soldiers started migrating back toward their ships.

"Well, that was fun." Rin stood up and brushed the crumbs off her uniform. "Let's go back."

"You're going to sleep already?" Kitay asked.

"I'm not staying here," she said. "It reeks."

"Not so fast," Nezha said. "You're off the *Swallow*. You've been reassigned to the *Kingfisher*."

"Just her?" Kitay asked.

"No, all of you. Cike, too. Jinzha wants you for strategic consultation, and he thinks the Cike can do more damage from a warship. The *Swallow*'s not an attack boat."

Rin glanced toward the *Kingfisher*, where Hesperian soldiers and Gray Company were clearly visible on deck.

"Yes, that's intentional." Nezha inferred the question from the exasperated look on her face. "They wanted to keep a closer eye on you."

"I already let Petra prod me like an animal once a week," Rin said. "I don't want to see them when I'm trying to eat."

Nezha held his hands up. "Jinzha's orders. Nothing we can do."

Rin suspected Captain Salkhi had also requested a transfer on grounds of disobedience. Salkhi had been deeply frustrated that the Cike had stormed the mission without her command, and Baji hadn't helped things by pointing out that they wouldn't have needed the rest of her troops regardless. Rin's suspicion was confirmed when Jinzha took twenty minutes informing her and the Cike that they would follow his orders to the letter or find themselves tossed into the Murui.

"I don't care that my father thinks the sun shines out of your ass," he said. "You'll act like soldiers or you'll be punished as deserters."

"Asshole," Rin muttered as they left his office.

"He's absolutely awful," Kitay agreed. "It's a rare person who makes Nezha look like the pleasant sibling."

"I'm not saying I want him to drown in the Murui," Ramsa said, "but I want him to drown in the Murui."

With the fleet united, the Republic's northern expedition began in earnest. Jinzha set a direct course that cut straight through Hare Province, which was agriculturally rich and comparatively weak. They would pick off the low-hanging fruit and solidify their supply base before taking on the full force of the Militia.

Hesperians aside, Rin found that traveling on the *Kingfisher* was a marked improvement from the *Swallow*. At least a hundred yards long from bow to stern, the *Kingfisher* was the only turtle boat in the fleet, with a closed top deck wrapped over by wood paneling and steel plates that made it nearly immune to cannon fire. The *Kingfisher* functioned as more or less a floating piece of armor, and for good reason—it carried Jinzha, Admiral Molkoi, almost all of the fleet's senior strategists, and most of the Hesperian delegation.

Flanking the *Kingfisher* were a trio of sister galleys known as the Seahawks—warships with floating boards attached to the port and starboard sides shaped like a bird's wings. Two were affectionately named the *Lapwing* and the *Waxwing*. The *Griffon*, commanded by Nezha, sailed directly behind the *Kingfisher*.

The other two galleys guarded the pride and battering ram of the fleet—two massive tower ships that someone with a bad sense of humor had named the *Shrike* and the *Crake*. They were monstrously large and top-heavy, outfitted with two mounted trebuchets and four rows of crossbows each.

The fleet proceeded up the Murui in a phalanx formation, lined up to adjust to the narrowing breadth of the river. The smaller skimmers alternately ducked in between the warships or followed them in a straightforward line, like a trail of ducklings following their mother.

It was such a beauty of riverine warfare, Rin thought, that the troops never had to weary themselves with marching. They just had to wait to be ferried to the Empire's most important cities, which were all close to the water. Cities needed water to survive, just like bodies needed blood. So if they wanted to seize the Empire, they needed only to sail through its arteries.

At dawn the fleet reached the border of Radan township. Radan was one of Hare Province's larger economic centers, targeted by Jinzha because of its strategic location at the junction of two waterways, its possession of several well-stocked granaries, and the simple fact that it barely had a military.

Jinzha ordered an immediate invasion without negotiation.

"Is he afraid they'll refuse?" Rin asked Kitay.

"More likely he's afraid they'll surrender," Kitay said. "Jinzha needs this expedition to be based on fear."

"What, the tower ships aren't scary enough?"

"That's a bluff. This isn't about Radan, it's about the next battle. Radan needs to be used as an example."

"Of what?"

"What happens when you resist," Kitay said grimly. "I'd go get your trident. We're about to start."

The *Kingfisher* was fast approaching Radan's river gates. Rin lifted her spyglass to get a closer look at the township's hastily assembled fleet. It was a laughably pathetic amalgamation of outdated vessels, mostly single-mast creations with sails made of oiled silk. Radan's ships were merchant vessels and fishing boats with no firing capacity. They had clearly never been used for warfare.

The Cike alone could have taken the city, Rin thought. They were certainly eager for it. Suni and Baji had been pacing the deck for hours, impatient to finally see action. The two of them could have likely broken the outer defenses by themselves. But Jinzha had wanted to commit his full resources to breaking Radan. That wasn't strategy, it was showmanship.

Jinzha strode onto the deck, took one look at the Radan defense fleet, and yawned into his hand. "Admiral Molkoi."

The admiral dipped his head. "Yes, sir?"

"Blow those things out of the water."

The ensuing battle was so one-sided that it seemed impossible. It wasn't a fight, it was a comic tragedy.

Radan's men had rubbed their sails down with oil. It was standard practice for merchants, who wanted to keep their sails waterproof and immune to rot. It was not so clever against pyrotechnics.

The Seahawks fired a series of double-headed dragon missiles that exploded midair into a swarm of smaller explosives, which spread a penumbral shower of fire across the Radan fleet. The sails caught fire immediately. Entire sheets of blistering flame engulfed the pathetic armada, roaring so loudly that for an instant it was all anyone could hear.

Rin found it oddly pleasing to watch, the same way it was fun to kick down sandcastles just because she could.

"Tiger's tits," Ramsa said, perched on the prow while flickering flames reflected in his eyes. "It's like they weren't even trying."

Hundreds of men leaped overboard to escape the searing heat.

"Have the archers pick off anyone who gets out of the river," said Jinzha. "Let the rest burn."

The skirmish took less than an hour from start to finish. The *Kingfisher* sailed triumphantly through the blackened remains of Radan's fleet to anchor right at the town border. Ramsa marveled at how thoroughly the cannons had demolished the river gates, Baji complained that he hadn't gotten to do anything, and Rin tried not to look into the water.

Radan's fleet was destroyed and its gates in shambles. The remaining population of the township laid down their weapons and surrendered with little trouble. Jinzha's men poured into the city and evacuated all civilians from their residences to clear the way for plundering.

Women and children lined up in the streets, heads down, quivering with fear as the soldiers marched them out the gates and along the beach. There they huddled in terrified bundles, glassy eyes staring at the remains of Radan's fleet.

The Republican soldiers were careful not to harm the civilians. Jinzha had been very adamant that the civilians were not to be mistreated. "They are not prisoners, and they are not victims," he'd said. "Let's call them potential members of the Republic."

For potential citizens of the Republic, they looked well and truly terrified of their new government.

They had good reason to fear. Their sons and husbands had been lined up in rows along the shore, held at sword point. They were told their fates hadn't yet been decided, that the Republican leadership was debating overnight on whether or not to kill them.

Jinzha intended to let the civilians pass the night unsure of whether they would live until the sun rose.

In the morning, he would announce to the crowd that he had received orders from Arlong. The Dragon Warlord had meditated on their fates. He recognized that it was no fault of their own that they were misled into resistance by their corrupt leaders, seduced by an Empress who no longer served them. He realized this decision was not made by these honest, common people. He would be merciful.

He would put the decision in the hands of the people.

He would have them vote.

"What do you think they're doing?" Kitay asked.

"They're proselytizing," Rin said. "Spreading the good word of the Maker."

"Doesn't seem like fantastic timing."

"I suppose they have to take a captive audience when they can get it."

They sat cross-legged on the shore in the *Kingfisher*'s shadow, watching as the Gray Company's missionaries made their way through the clumps of huddled civilians. They were too far away for Rin to hear what they were saying, but every now and then she saw a missionary kneel down next to several miserable civilians, put his hands on their shoulders even as they flinched away, and speak what was unmistakably a prayer.

"I hope they're talking in Nikara," said Kitay. "Otherwise they'll sound ominous as hell."

"I don't think it matters if they are." Rin found it hard not to feel a sense of guilty pleasure watching the crowds shrinking from the missionaries, despite the Hesperians' best efforts.

Kitay passed her a stick of dried fish. "Hungry?"

"Thanks." She took the fish, worked her teeth around the tail, and jerked off a bite.

There was an art to eating the salted mayau fish that made up the majority of their rations. She had to chew it up just so to make it soft enough that she could extract the meat from around the bones and spit out the spindly things. Too little chewing and the bones lacerated her throat; too much and the fish lost all flavor.

Salted mayau was a clever army food. It took so long to eat that by the time Rin was finished, no matter how little she'd actually consumed, she felt full on salt and saliva.

"Have you seen their penises?" Kitay asked.

Rin nearly spat out her fish. "What?"

He gestured with his hands. "Hesperian men are supposed to be much, ah, bigger than Nikara men. Salkhi said so."

"How would Salkhi know?"

"How do you think?" Kitay waggled his eyebrows. "Admit it, you've thought about it."

She shuddered. "Not if you paid me."

"Have you seen General Tarcquet? He's massive. I bet he—"

"Don't be disgusting," she snapped. "They're horrible. And they smell awful. They're . . . I don't know, it's like something curdled."

"It's because they drink cow's milk, I think. All that dairy is screwing with their systems."

"I just thought they weren't showering."

"You're one to talk. Have you gotten a whiff of yourself recently?"

"Hold on." Rin pointed across the river. "Look over there."

Some of the civilian women had started screaming at a missionary. The missionary stepped hastily away, hands out in a nonthreatening position, but the women didn't stop shrieking until he'd retreated all the way down the beach.

Kitay gave a low whistle. "That's going well."

"I wonder what they're saying to them," Rin said.

"'Our Maker is great and powerful,'" he said pompously. "'Pray with us and you shall never go hungry again.'"

"'All wars will be stopped.'"

"'All enemies will fall down dead, smitten by the Maker's great hand.'"

"'Peace will cover the realm and the demon gods will be banished to hell.'" Rin hugged her knees to her chest as she watched the missionary stand on the beach, seeking out another cluster of civilians to terrify. "You'd think they'd just leave us well enough alone."

Hesperian religion wasn't new to the Empire. At the height of his reign, the Red Emperor had frequently received emissaries from the churches of the west. Scholars of the church took up residence in his court at Sinegard and entertained the Emperor with their astronomical predictions, star charts, and nifty inventions. Then the Red Emperor died, the coddled scholars were persecuted by jealous court officials, and the missionaries were expelled from the continent for centuries.

The Hesperians had made intermittent efforts to come back, of course. They'd almost succeeded during the first invasion. But now the common Nikara people remembered only the lies the Trifecta had spread about them after the Second Poppy War. They killed and ate infants. They lured young women to their convents to serve as sex slaves. They'd more or less become monsters in folklore. If the Gray Company hoped to win converts, they had their work cut out for them.

"They've got to try regardless," Kitay said. "I read it in their holy texts once. Their scholars argue that as the Divine Architect's blessed and chosen people, their obligation is to preach to every infidel they encounter."

"'Chosen'? What does that mean?"

"I don't know." Kitay nodded past Rin's shoulder. "Why don't you ask her?"

Rin twisted around.

Sister Petra was striding briskly down the shore toward them.

Rin swallowed her last bite of fish too quickly. It crawled painfully down her throat, each swallow a painful scratch of unsoftened bone.

Sister Petra met Rin's eyes and beckoned with a finger. *Come.* That was an order.

Kitay patted her shoulder as he stood up. "Have fun."

Rin reached for his sleeve. "Don't you dare leave me—"

"I'm not getting in the middle of this," he said. "I've seen what those arquebuses can do."

"Congratulations," Petra said as they returned to the *Kingfisher*. "I'm told this was a great victory."

"'Great' is a word for it," Rin said.

"And the fire did not come to you in battle? Chaos did not rear its head?"

Rin stopped walking. "Would you rather I had burned those people alive?"

"Sister Petra?" A missionary ran up from behind them. He looked startlingly young. He couldn't have been a day over sixteen. His face was open and babyish, and his wide blue eyes were lashed like a girl's.

"How do you say 'I'm from across the great sea'?" he asked. "I forgot."

"Like so." Petra pronounced the Nikara phrase with flawless accuracy.

"I'm from across the great sea." The boy looked delighted as he repeated the words. "Did I get it right? The tones?"

Rin realized with a start that he was looking at her.

"Sure," she said. "That was fine."

The boy beamed at her. "I love your language. It's so beautiful."

Rin blinked at him. What was wrong with him? Why did he look so happy?

"Brother Augus." Petra's voice was suddenly sharp. "What's in your pocket?"

Rin looked and saw a handful of wotou, the steamed cornmeal buns that along with mayau fish comprised most of the soldiers' meals, peeking out the side of Augus's pocket.

"Just my rations," he said quickly.

"And were you going to eat them?" Petra asked.

"Sure, I'm just taking a walk—"

"*Augus.*"

His face fell. "They said they were hungry."

"You're not allowed to feed them," Rin said flatly. Jinzha had made that order adamantly clear. The civilians were to go hungry for the night. When the Republic fed them in the morning, their terror would be transformed into goodwill.

"That's cruel," Augus said.

"That's war," Rin said. "And if you can't follow basic orders, then—"

Petra swiftly intervened. "Remember your training, Augus. We do not contradict our hosts. We are here to spread the good word. Not to undermine the Nikara."

"But they're starving," Augus said. "I wanted to comfort them—"

"Then comfort them with the Maker's teachings." Petra placed a hand on Augus's cheek. "Go."

Rin watched Augus dart back down the beach. "He shouldn't be on this campaign. He's too young."

Petra turned and gestured for Rin to follow her onto the *Kingfisher*. "Not so much younger than your soldiers."

"Our soldiers are trained."

"And so are our missionaries." Petra led Rin down to her quarters on the second deck. "The brothers and sisters of the Gray Company have dedicated their lives to spreading the word of the Divine Architect across Chaos-ridden lands. All of us have been trained at the company academies since we were very young."

"I'm sure it's easy to find barbarians to civilize."

"There are indeed many on this hemisphere that have not found their way to the Maker." Petra seemed to have missed Rin's sarcasm entirely. She motioned for Rin to sit down on the bed. "Would you like laudanum again?"

"Are you going to touch me again?"

"Yes."

At this rate Rin was going to run the risk of backsliding into her opium addiction. But this choice was between the demon she knew and the foreigner she didn't. She took the proffered cup.

"Your continent has been closed off to us for a long time," Petra said as Rin drank. "Some of our superiors argued that we should stop learning your languages. But I've always known we would come back. The Maker demands it."

Rin closed her eyes as the familiar numbing sensation of laudanum seeped through her bloodstream. "So, what, your missionaries are walking up and down that beach giving everyone long spiels about clocks?"

"One need not comprehend the true form of the Divine Architect to act according to his will. We know that barbarians must crawl before they walk. Heuristics will do for the unenlightened."

"You mean easy moral rules for people who are too dumb to understand why they matter."

"If you must be vulgar about it. I am confident that in time, at least some of the Nikara will gain true enlightenment. In a few generations, some of you may even be fit to join the Gray Company. But heuristics must first be developed for the lesser peoples—"

"Lesser peoples," Rin echoed. "What are *lesser peoples*?"

"You, of course," Petra said, utterly straight-faced, as if this were a simple matter of fact. "It's no fault of your own. The Nikara haven't evolved to our level yet. This is simple science; the proof is in your physiognomy. Look."

She pulled a stack of books onto the table and flipped them open for Rin to see.

Drawings of Nikara people covered every page. They were heavily annotated. Rin couldn't decipher the scrawling, flat Hesperian script, but several phrases popped out.

See eye fold—indicates lazy character.

Sallow skin. Malnutrition?

On the last page, Rin saw a heavily annotated drawing of herself that must have been done by Petra. Rin was glad that Petra's handwriting was far too small for her to decipher. She didn't want to read any conclusions about herself.

"Since your eyes are smaller, you see within a smaller periphery than we do." Petra pointed to the diagrams as she explained. "Your skin has a yellowish tint that indicates malnutrition or an unbalanced diet. Now see your skull shapes. Your brains, which we know to be an indicator of your rational capacity, are by nature smaller."

Rin looked at her in disbelief. "You think you're just naturally smarter than me?"

"I don't think that," Petra said. "I know it. The proof is all well-documented. The Nikara are a particularly herdlike nation. You listen well, but independent thought is difficult for you. You reach scientific conclusions centuries after we discover them." Petra shut the book. "But worry not. In time, all civilizations will become perfect in the eyes of the Maker. That is the Gray Company's task."

"You think we're stupid," Rin said, almost to herself. She had the ridiculous urge to laugh. Did the Hesperians really take themselves this seriously? They thought this was *science*? "You think we're all inferior to you."

"Look at those people on the beach," Petra said. "Look at your country, squabbling over the refuse of wars you've been fighting for centuries. Do they look evolved to you?"

"And what, your own wars just happen to be civilized? Millions of you died, didn't they?"

"They died because we were fighting the forces of Chaos. Our wars are not internal. They are crusaders' battles. But look back to your own history, and tell me that any of your internal wars were fought for anything other than naked greed, ambition, or sheer cruelty."

Rin didn't know whether it was the laudanum, or whether Petra was truly correct, but she hated that she didn't have an answer.

In the morning, the remaining men of Radan were walked at sword point to the town square and instructed to cast their votes by throwing tiles into burlap bags. They could pick from two tile colors: white for yes and black for no.

"What happens if they vote against?" Rin asked Nezha.

"They'll die," he said. "Well, most of them. If they fight."

"Don't you think that kind of misses the point?"

Nezha shrugged. "Everyone joins the Republic by their own free choice. We're just, well, tipping the scales a little bit."

The voting took place one man at a time and lasted just over an hour. Rather than counting the tiles, Jinzha dumped the bags out onto the ground so that everyone could see the colors. By an overwhelming majority, the village of Radan had elected to join the Republic.

"Good decision," he said. "Welcome to the future."

He ordered a single skimmer to remain behind with its crew to enforce martial law and collect a monthly grain tax until the war's end. The fleet would confiscate a seventh of the township's food stores, leaving just enough to tide Radan over through the winter.

Nezha looked both pleased and relieved as they departed on the Murui. "That's what you get when the people decide."

Kitay shook his head. "No, that's what you get when you've killed all the brave men and let the cowards vote."

The Republican Fleet's subsequent skirmishes were similarly easy to the point of overkill. More often than not they took over townships and villages without a fight. A few cities put up resistance, but never to any effect. Against the combined strength of Jinzha's Seahawks, resisters usually capitulated within half a day.

As they went north, Jinzha detached brigades, and then entire platoons, to rule over recently liberated territory. Other crews bled soldiers to man those empty ships, until several skimmers had to be grounded and left on shore because the fleet had been spread too thin.

Some of the villages they conquered didn't put up a resistance at all, but readily joined the Republic. They sent out volunteers in boats laden with food and supplies. Hastily stitched flags bearing the colors of Dragon Province flew over city walls in a welcoming gesture.

"Look at that." Kitay pointed. "Vaisra's flag. Not the flag of the Republic."

"Does the Republic even *have* a flag?" Rin asked.

"I'm not sure. It's curious that they think they're being conquered by Dragon Province, though."

On Kitay's advice, Jinzha placed the volunteer ships and sailors in the front of the fleet. He didn't trust Hare Province sailors to fight on their home territory, and he didn't want them in strategically crucial positions in case they defected. But the extra ships were, in the worst-case scenario, excellent bait. Several times Jinzha sent allied ships out first to lure townships into opening their gates before he stormed them with his warships.

For a while it seemed like they might take the entire north in one clean, unobstructed sweep. But their fortunes finally took a turn for the worse at the northern border of Hare Province when a massive thunderstorm forced them to make anchor in a river cove.

The storm wasn't so much dangerous as it was boring. River storms, unlike ocean storms, could just be waited out if they grounded ships. So for three days the troops holed up belowdecks, playing cards and telling stories while rain battered at the hull.

"In the north they still offer divine sacrifices to the wind." The *Kingfisher*'s first mate, a gaunt man who had been at sea longer than Jinzha had been alive, had become the favorite storyteller of the mess. "In the days before the Red Emperor, the Khan of the Hinterlands sent down a fleet to invade the Empire. But a magician summoned a wind god to create a typhoon to destroy the Khan's fleet, and the Khan's ships turned to splinters in the ocean."

"Why not sacrifice to the ocean?" asked a sailor.

"Because oceans don't create storms. This was a god of the wind. But wind is fickle and unpredictable, and the gods have never taken lightly to being summoned by the Nikara. The moment the Khan's fleet was destroyed, the wind god turned on the Nikara magician who had summoned him. He pulled the magician's village into the sky and dropped it down in a bloody rain of ripped houses, crushed livestock, and dismembered children."

Rin stood up and quietly left the mess.

The passageways belowdecks were eerily quiet. Absent was the constant grinding sound of men working the paddle wheels. The crew and soldiers were concentrated in the mess, if they weren't sleeping, and so the passage was empty except for her.

When she pressed her face to the porthole she saw the storm raging outside, the vicious waves swirling about the cove like eager hands reaching to rip the fleet apart. In the clouds she thought she saw two eyes—bright, cerulean, maliciously intelligent.

She shivered. She thought she heard laughter in the thunder. She thought she saw a hand reach from the skies.

Then she blinked, and the storm was just a storm.

She didn't want to be alone, so she ventured downstairs to the soldiers' cabins, where she knew she could find the Cike.

"Hello there." Baji waved her inside. "Nice of you to join."

She sat down cross-legged beside him. "What are you playing?"

Baji tossed a handful of dice into a cup. "Divisions. Ever played?"

Rin thought briefly back to Tutor Feyrik, the man who had gotten her to Sinegard, and his unfortunate addiction to the game. She smiled wistfully. "Just a bit."

Nominally, no gambling of any kind was permitted on the ships. Lady Yin Saikhara, since her pilgrimage to the west, had instituted strict rules about vices such as drinking, smoking, gambling, and consorting with prostitutes. Almost everyone ignored them. Vaisra never enforced them.

It turned out to be a rather vicious game. Ramsa kept accusing Baji of cheating. Baji was not cheating, but they discovered that Ramsa *was* when a handful of dice spilled out of his sleeve, at which point the game turned into a wrestling match that ended only when Ramsa bit Baji on the arm hard enough to draw blood.

"You mangy little brat," Baji cursed as he wrapped a linen around his elbow.

Ramsa grinned, displaying teeth stained red.

All of them were clearly bored, going stir-crazy while waiting out the storm. But Rin suspected that they were also itching for action. She'd cautioned them not to put their full abilities on display where Hesperian soldiers might be watching. Petra knew about one shaman; she didn't need to discover the rest.

Concealment had turned out to be fairly easy on campaign. Suni and Baji's abilities were freakish, yes, but not necessarily in the realm of the supernatural. In the chaos of a melee, they could pass themselves off as hypercompetent soldiers. It had worked so far. As far as Rin knew, the Hesperians suspected nothing. Suni and Baji might be getting frustrated holding themselves back, but at least they were free.

For once, Rin thought, she'd made some decent decisions as commander. She hadn't gotten them killed. The Republican troops treated them better than the Militia ever had. They were getting paid, they were as safe as they'd ever be, and that was as good as she could do for them.

"What are the Gray Company like?" Baji asked as he scooped the dice off the floor for a new game. "I heard that woman talks your ear off every time you're together."

"It's stupid," Rin muttered. "Religious lecturing."

"Load of hogwash?" Ramsa asked.

"I don't know," she admitted. "They might be right about some things."

She wished she could discard the Hesperian faith more easily, but so many parts of it made sense. She wanted to believe it. She wanted to see her catastrophic actions as a product of Chaos, an entropic mistake, and to believe that she could repent for them by reinforcing order in the Empire, reversing devastation the way one pieced together a broken teacup.

It made her feel better. It made every battle she'd fought since Adlaga feel like another step toward putting things right. It made her feel less like a killer.

"You know their Divine Architect doesn't exist," Baji said. "I mean, you understand why that's obvious, right?"

"I'm not sure," she said slowly. Certainly the Maker didn't exist on the same psychospiritual plane as the sixty-four gods of the Pantheon, but was that enough to discount the Hesperians' theory? What if the Pantheon was, in fact, a manifestation of Chaos? What if the Divine Architect truly existed on a higher plane, out of reach of anyone but his chosen and blessed people?

"I mean, look at their airships," she said. "Their arquebuses. If they're claiming religion made them advanced, they might be right about some things."

Baji opened his mouth to respond and promptly closed it. Rin looked up and saw a shock of white hair in the doorway.

No one spoke. The dice clattered loudly to the floor and stayed there.

Ramsa broke the silence. "Hi, Chaghan."

Rin hadn't spoken to Chaghan since Arlong. When the fleet had sailed, she'd partly hoped that Chaghan might just elect to stay on land. He was never one for the thick of battle, and after their falling-out she couldn't imagine why he'd stay with her. But the twins had remained with the Cike, and Rin had found herself crossing the room whenever she saw a hint of white hair.

Chaghan paused by the door, Qara close behind him.

"Having fun?" he asked.

"Sure," Baji said. "You want in?"

"No, thank you," Chaghan said. "But it's nice to see you're all having such a good time."

No one responded to that. Rin knew she was being mocked, she just didn't have the energy to get into it with Chaghan right now.

"Does it hurt?" Qara asked.

Rin blinked. "What?"

"When the gray-eyed one takes you to her cabin," Qara said. "Does it hurt?"

"Oh. It's—it's not so bad. It's just a lot of measurements."

Qara cast her what looked like a glance of sympathy, but Chaghan grabbed his sister by the arm and stormed out of the cabin before she could speak.

Ramsa gave a low whistle and began to pick the dice up off the floor.

Baji gave Rin a curious look. "What happened between you two?"

"Stupid shit," Rin muttered.

"Stupid shit about Altan?" Ramsa pressed.

"Why would you think it was about Altan?"

"Because with Chaghan, it's always about Altan." Ramsa tossed his dice into a cup and shook. "Honestly? I think Altan was Chaghan's only friend. He's still grieving. And there's nothing you can do to make that hurt less."

CHAPTER 17

The storm passed with minimal damage. One skimmer capsized—the force of the winds had ripped it from its anchor. Three men drowned. But the crew managed to salvage most of its supplies, and the drowned men had been only foot soldiers, so Jinzha wrote it off as a minor setback.

The moment the skies cleared, he gave the order to continue upriver toward Ram Province. It was one step closer to the military center of the Empire and, as Kitay anticipated, the first territory that would present a fighting challenge.

The Ram Warlord had holed up inside Xiashang, his capital, instead of mounting a border defense. This was why the Republic encountered little other than local volunteer militias throughout their destructive trek north. The Ram Warlord had chosen to bide his time and wait for Jinzha's troops to tire before fighting a defensive battle.

That should have been a losing strategy. The Republican Fleet was simply *bigger* than whatever force the Ram Warlord could have rounded up. They knew they could take Ram Province; it was only a matter of time.

The only wrinkle was that Xiashang had unexpectedly robust defenses. Thanks to Qara's birds, the Republican forces had a good layout map of the capital's defensive structures. Even the tower ships with their trebuchets would have a difficult time breaching those walls.

As such, Rin spent her next few evenings in the *Kingfisher*'s office, crammed around a table with Jinzha's leadership coterie.

"The walls are the problem. You can't blow through them." Kitay pointed to a ring he'd drawn around the walls of the city. "They're made of packed earth, three feet thick. You could try ramming them with cannonballs, but it'd just be a waste of good fire powder."

"What about a siege?" Jinzha asked. "We could force a surrender if they think we're willing to wait."

"You'd be a fool," said General Tarcquet.

Jinzha bristled visibly. The leadership exchanged awkward looks.

Tarcquet was always present at strategy councils, though he rarely spoke and never offered the assistance of his own troops. He'd made his role clear. He was there to judge their competence and quietly deride their mistakes, which made his input both irreproachable and grating.

"If this were my fleet I'd throw everything I have at those walls," Tarcquet said. "If you can't take a minor capital, you won't take the Empire."

"But this is not your fleet," Jinzha said. "It's mine."

Tarcquet's lip curled in contempt. "You are in command because your father thought you'd at least be smart enough to do whatever I told you."

Jinzha looked furious, but Tarcquet held up a hand before he could respond. "You can't pull off this bluff. They know you don't have the supplies or the time. You'll have to fold in weeks."

Despite herself, Rin agreed with Tarcquet's assessment. She'd studied this precise problem at Sinegard. Of all the successful defensive campaigns on military record, most were when cities had warded off invaders through protracted siege warfare. A siege turned a battle into a waiting game of who starved first. The Republican Fleet had the supplies to last for perhaps a month. It was unclear how long Xiashang could last. It would be foolish to wait and find out.

"They certainly don't have enough food for the entire city," Nezha said. "We made sure of that."

"Doesn't matter," Kitay said. "The Ram Warlord and his people will be fine. They'll just let the peasants starve; Tsung Ho has done that before."

"Do we try negotiating?" Nezha asked.

"Won't work—Tsung Ho hates Father," Jinzha said. "And he has no incentive to cooperate, because he'll just assume that under the Republican regime he'd be deposed sooner or later."

"A siege *might* work," said Admiral Molkoi. "Those walls are not so impenetrable. We'd just have to break them down at a choke point."

"I wouldn't," Kitay said. "That's what they'll be preparing for. If you're going to storm the city, you want the element of surprise. Some gimmick. Like a false peace proposal. But I don't think they'd fall for that; Tsung Ho is too smart."

A thought occurred to Rin. "What about Fuchai and Goujian?"

The men stared blankly at her.

"Fuchai and who?" Jinzha asked.

Only Kitay and Nezha looked like they understood. The tale of Fuchai and Goujian was a favorite story of Master Irjah's. They'd all been assigned to write term papers about it during their second year.

"Fuchai and Goujian were two generals during the Era of Warring States," Nezha explained. "Fuchai destroyed Goujian's home state, and then made Goujian his personal servant to humiliate him. Goujian performed the most degrading tasks to make Fuchai believe he bore him no ill will. One time when Fuchai fell sick, Goujian volunteered to taste his stool to tell how bad his illness was. It worked—ten years later, Fuchai set Goujian free. The first thing Goujian did was hire a beautiful concubine and send her to Fuchai's court in the guise of a gift."

"The concubine, of course, killed Fuchai," Kitay said.

Jinzha looked baffled. "You're saying I send the Ram Warlord a beautiful concubine."

"No," Rin said. "I'm saying you should eat shit."

Tarcquet barked out a laugh.

Jinzha reddened. "Excuse me?"

"The Ram Warlord thinks he holds all the cards," Rin said. "So initiate a negotiation. Humiliate yourself, present yourself as weaker than you are, and make him underestimate your forces."

"That won't tear down his walls," said Jinzha.

"But it *will* make him cocky. How does his behavior change if he's not anticipating an attack? If he instead thinks you're running away? Then we have an opening to exploit." Rin cast about wildly in her head for ideas. "You could get someone behind those walls. Open the gates from the inside."

"There's no way you manage that," Nezha said. "You'd need to get an entire platoon to fight through from the inside, and you can't hide that many men in one ship."

"I don't need an entire platoon," Rin said.

"No squadron is capable of that."

She crossed her arms. "I can think of one."

For once, Jinzha wasn't looking at her with disdain.

"Who do we send to negotiate with the Ram Warlord, then?" he asked.

Rin and Nezha both answered at once. "Kitay."

Kitay frowned. "Because I'm a good negotiator?"

"No." Nezha clapped him on the shoulder. "Because you'll be a really, really bad one."

"I was under the impression that I was receiving your grand marshal." The Ram Warlord lounged casually on his chair, tapping his fingers together as he appraised the Republican delegation with sharp, intelligent eyes.

"You'll be meeting with me," Kitay said. He spoke in a perfectly tremulous voice, obviously nervous and pretending not to be. "The Dragon Warlord is indisposed."

The Republican delegation was deliberately shabby. Kitay was guarded only by two infantry soldiers from the *Kingfisher*. His life had to seem cheap. Jinzha hadn't wanted to let Rin come, but she refused to stay behind while Kitay went to face the enemy.

Their delegations had met at a neutral stretch along the shore. The backdrop made the meeting seem more like a competitive fishing match than the site of a war negotiation. This move, Rin assumed, was designed to humiliate Kitay.

The Ram Warlord looked Kitay up and down and pursed his lips. "Vaisra can't be bothered, so he sends a little puppy to negotiate for him."

Kitay puffed himself up. "I'm not a puppy. I'm the son of Defense Minister Chen."

"Yes, I wondered why you looked familiar. You're a far cry from your old man, aren't you?"

Kitay cleared his throat. "Jinzha sent me here with proposed terms for a truce."

"A truce should be settled between leaders. Jinzha does not even afford me the respect that he ought a Warlord."

"Jinzha has entrusted negotiations to me," Kitay said stiffly.

The Ram Warlord's eyes narrowed. "Ah, I understand. Injured then? Or dead?"

"Jinzha is fine." Kitay let his voice tremble just a bit at the end. "He sends his regards."

The Ram Warlord leaned forward in his chair, like a wolf examining his prey. "Really."

Kitay cleared his throat again. "Jinzha instructed me to convey that the truce can only benefit you. We *will* take the north. It's up to you to decide whether or not you want to join our forces. If you agree to our terms then we'll leave Xiashang alone, so long as your men serve in our—"

The Ram Warlord cut him off. "I have no interest in joining Vaisra's so-called republic. It's just a ploy to put himself on the throne."

"That's paranoid," Kitay said.

"Does Yin Vaisra seem like a man inclined to share power to you?"

"The Dragon Warlord intends to implement the representative democracy style of government practiced in the west. He knows the provincial system isn't working—"

"Oh, but it's working very well for us," said the Ram Warlord. "The only dissenters are those poor suckers in the south, led by Vaisra himself. The rest of us see a system that's granted us stability for two decades. There's no need to disrupt that."

"But it *will* be disrupted," Kitay insisted. "You've seen the fault lines yourself. You're weeks away from going to war with your neighbors over riverways, you have more refugees than you can deal with, and you've received no Imperial aid."

"That, you're wrong about," said the Ram Warlord. "The Empress has been exceedingly generous to my province. Meanwhile, your embargo failed, your fields are poisoned, and you're quickly running out of time."

Rin shot Kitay a glance. His face betrayed nothing, but she knew, on the inside, he must be gloating.

As they spoke, a single merchant ship drifted toward Xiashang, marked with smugglers' colors provided to them by Moag. It would claim to have run up from Monkey Province with illegal shipments of grain. Jinzha had packed soldiers into the hold and dressed the few sailors who would remain visible on deck as river traders.

If the Ram Warlord was expecting smuggler ships, then he might very well let it within the city gates.

"There's a way out here that doesn't end in your death," Kitay said.

"Negotiations are a matter of leverage, little boy," said the Ram Warlord. "And I don't see your fleet."

"Maybe your spies should look harder," Kitay said. "Maybe we've hidden it."

They *had* hidden it, deep inside a canyon crevice two miles downstream from Xiashang's gates. Jinzha had sent a smaller fleet of skimmers manned by skeleton crews out toward a different tributary to make it appear that the Dragon Fleet was avoiding Xiashang entirely by sailing east toward Tiger Province instead. They'd done this very conspicuously in broad daylight. The Ram Warlord's spies had to have seen.

The Ram Warlord shrugged. "Perhaps. Or perhaps you've taken the easy route down the Udomsap tributary instead."

Rin fought to keep her expression neutral.

"The Udomsap isn't so far from you," said Kitay. "By river or by ground, you're lying in Jinzha's warpath."

"Bold words from a little boy." The Ram Warlord snorted.

"A little boy speaking for a great army," Kitay said. "Sooner or later, we'll come for you. And then you'll regret it."

The blustering was an act, but Rin suspected the frustration in his voice was real. Kitay was playing his part so well that Rin couldn't help but feel a sudden urge to step in front of him, to protect him. Standing one-on-one before a Warlord, Kitay just looked like a boy: thin, scared, and far too young for his position.

"No. I don't think we will." The Ram Warlord reached over and ruffled Kitay's hair. "I think you're trapped. That storm hit you harder than you'll admit. And you don't have the troops to press on into the winter, and you're running out of supplies, so you want me to throw open my gates and save your skins. Tell Jinzha he can take his truce and shove it up his butt." He smiled, displaying teeth. "Run along down the river, now."

"I admit this might have been a terrible idea," said Kitay.

Rin's spyglass was trained on Xiashang's gates. She had a sick feeling in her stomach. The fleet had been waiting around the bend since dark. The sun had been up for hours. The gates were still closed.

"You don't think he bought it," Rin said.

"I was so sure he'd buy it," said Kitay. "Men like that are so incredibly arrogant that they always need to think that they've outsmarted everyone else. But maybe he *did*."

Rin didn't want to entertain that thought.

Another hour passed. No movement. Kitay started walking in circles, chewing at his thumbnail so hard that it bled. "Someone should suggest a retreat."

Rin lowered her spyglass. "You'd be sentencing my men to death."

"It's been half a day," he said curtly. "Chances are they're dead already."

Jinzha, who had been pacing the length of the deck in agitation, motioned toward them. "It's time to pursue other options. Those men are gone."

Rin's fists tightened. "Don't you dare—"

"They could have captured them." Kitay tried to calm her down. "He could be planning to use them as hostages."

"We don't have anyone important on that ship," Jinzha said, which Rin thought was a rather cruel way of describing some of his best soldiers. "And knowing Tsung Ho, he'd just set it on fire."

The sun crawled to high noon.

Rin fought the creep of despair. The later it got in the day, the worse their chances of storming the walls. They had already lost the element of surprise. The Ram Warlord surely knew they were coming by now, and he'd had half the day to prepare defenses.

But what other choice did the Republic have? The Cike were trapped behind those gates. Any later and their chances of survival dwindled to nothing. Waiting was useless. Escape would be humiliating.

Jinzha seemed to have been thinking the same. "They're out of time. We attack."

"That's what they want, though!" Kitay protested. "This is the battle they want to have."

"Then we'll give them that fight." Jinzha signaled Admiral Molkoi to give the order. For once, Rin was glad that he'd ignored Kitay.

The Republican Fleet surged forward, a symphony of war drums and churning paddle wheels.

Xiashang *had* prepared well to meet the charge. The Militia went on the offensive immediately. A wave of arrows greeted the Republican Fleet as soon as it crossed into range. For an instant it was impossible to hear anything over the sound of arrows thudding into wood, steel, and flesh. And it didn't stop. The artillery assault kept coming in wave after wave from archers who seemed to have an endless supply of arrows.

The Republican archers returned fire, but they might have been shooting aimlessly at the sky. The defenders simply ducked down and let the bolts whiz overhead while Republican rockets exploded harmlessly against the massive city walls.

The *Kingfisher* was safe ensconced within its turtleshell armor, but the other Republican ships had been effectively reduced to sitting ducks. The tower ships floated uselessly in the water. Their trebuchet crews couldn't launch any missiles—they couldn't move without fear of being turned into pincushions.

The *Lapwing*, the Seahawk closest to the walls, sent a double-headed dragon missile screeching through the air only for a Ram archer to shoot it out of the sky. Upon impact it fell sizzling back toward the boat. The *Lapwing*'s crew scattered before the shower of missiles fell upon their own munitions supply. Rin heard one round of explosions, and then another—a chain reaction that engulfed the Seahawk ship in smoke and fire.

The *Shrike*, however, had managed to steer its towers to just beside the city gate. Rin squinted at the ship, trying to gauge its distance from the wall. The towers were just tall enough to clear the parapets, but as long as the wall was manned with archers, the tower was useless. Anyone who scaled the siege engine would just be picked off at the top.

Someone had to take those archers out.

Rin glared at the wall, frustrated, cursing the Seal. If she could call the Phoenix she could have just sent a torrent of flame over the barriers, could have cleared it out in under a minute.

But she didn't have the fire. Which meant she had to get up there herself, and she needed explosives.

She cupped her hands around her mouth. "Ramsa!"

He was crouched ten meters away behind the mast. She screamed his name thrice to no avail. At last she threw a scrap of wood at his shoulder to get his attention.

He yelped. "What the hell?"

"I need a bomb!"

He opened his mouth to respond just as another set of missiles exploded against the turtle boat's side. He shook his head and gestured frantically at his empty knapsack.

"Anything?" she mouthed.

He dug deep in his pocket, pulled out something round, and rolled it across the floor toward her. She picked it up. A pungent smell hit her nose.

"Is this a *shit bomb*?" she yelled.

Ramsa waved his hands helplessly. "It's all I've got left!"

It would have to do. She shoved the bomb into her shirt. She'd worry about ignition when she got to the wall. Now she needed some way to climb up to the top. And a shield, something huge, heavy and large enough to cover her entire body . . .

Her eyes landed on the rowboats.

She turned to Kitay. "Pull a boat up."

"What?"

She pointed to the siege tower. "Get me up in a boat!"

His eyes widened in understanding. He barked a series of orders to the soldiers behind him. They ran out to the mainmast, ducking beneath shields raised over their heads.

Rin jumped into a rowboat with two other soldiers. Kitay directed the men to fasten the ropes at the ends, typically meant to lower the rowboat into the water, onto the mast pulley. The rowboat teetered wildly when they started hoisting it up the mast. It hadn't been secured well. Halfway up it threatened to flip over until they scrambled to redistribute their weight.

An arrow whistled past Rin's head. The Ram archers had seen them.

"Hold on!" She twisted the ropes. The rowboat tilted nearly

horizontal, a functional full-body shield. Rin crouched down, clinging fast to a seat so she wouldn't tumble out. A crossbow bolt slid through the bottom of the boat and cut through the arm of the soldier to her left. He screamed and let go. A second later Rin heard him crunch on the deck.

She held her breath. The boat was almost to the top of the wall.

"Get ready." She bent her knees and rocked the boat so that it would swing forward. Their first swing toward the wall fell short by a yard. Rin caught a brief, dizzying glimpse of the drop beneath her feet.

Another series of arrows studded the rowboat as they swung backward.

Their second swing got them close enough.

"*Go!*"

They jumped to the wall. Rin slipped on impact. Her knees skidded on solid rock but her feet kicked off into terrifying, empty space. She flung her arms forward and seized a groove cut in the wall. She strained to pull herself up just far enough that she could slam her elbow into the ridge and drag her torso over.

She tumbled gracelessly onto the walkway and staggered to her feet just as a Ram soldier swung a blade at her head. She blocked it with her trident, wrestled it in a circle, sent it spinning uselessly away, and then butted him in the side with the other end. He tumbled down the stairs and smashed into his comrades.

That gave her a temporary reprieve. She scanned the wall of archers. Ramsa's shit bomb wouldn't kill them, but it would distract them. She just needed a way to ignite it.

Again she cursed the Seal. She could have just lit it with a snap of her fingers; it would have been so *easy*.

She cast her eyes about for a lamp, a brazier, something . . . *there*. Five feet away sat a lump of burning coals in a brass pot. The Ram defenders must have been using it to light their own missiles.

She hefted the bomb in her hands, tossed it toward the pot, and prayed.

She heard a faint, dull pop.

She took a deep breath. Acrid, shit-flavored smoke spilled over the parapets, thick and blinding.

"We're in trouble," said the Republican soldier at her left.

She squinted through the smoke at a column of Ram reinforcements approaching fast from the lefthand walkway.

She looked frantically about the wall for a way to get down. She saw a stairwell to her left, but too many soldiers stood crowded at the base. The only other way down was across the other side of the wall, but the walkway didn't go all the way around—a ridge of wall no thicker than her heel stood between her and the other stairwell.

No time to think. She jumped onto the outer edge of the wall, dug her heels in, and began running before she could teeter to either side. Every few steps she felt her balance jerk horrifically to one side. Somehow she righted herself and kept going.

She heard the twangs of several bows. Rather than duck, she took a flying leap toward the stairwell. She landed painfully on her side and skidded to a halt. Her shoulder and hip screamed in protest, but her arms and legs still worked. She crawled frantically down the stairs, arrows whizzing over her head.

Behind the gates was a war zone.

She'd stumbled into a crush of bodies, a clamor of steel. Blue uniforms dotted the crowd. Republican soldiers. Relief washed over her. They weren't dead after all, just late.

"About time!"

Two wonderfully familiar tornadoes of destruction appeared before her. Suni picked up a Ram soldier as if he were a doll, hoisted him over his head, and flung him into the crowd. Baji slammed his rake down into someone's neck, yanked it up, and twirled it in a circle to knock an incoming arrow out of the air.

"Nice," Rin said.

He helped her to her feet. "What took you so long?"

Rin opened her mouth to respond just as someone tried to grapple her from behind. She jammed her elbow back by instinct and felt the rewarding crunch of a shattering nose. Her assailant's grip loosened. She struggled free. "We were waiting for your signal!"

"We gave a signal! Sent a flare up ten minutes ago! Where's the fucking army?"

Rin pointed to the wall. "There."

A thud shook Xiashang's gates. The *Shrike* had landed its siege tower.

Republican soldiers funneled over the wall like a swarm of ants. Bodies hurtled to the ground like tumbling bricks, while grappling hooks flew into the sky and embedded themselves at regular intervals along the wall.

She saw almost as many blue uniforms as green ones now. Slowly the press of Republican soldiers expanded through the center square.

"Get to the gates," Rin told Baji.

"Way ahead of you." Baji scattered the throng of soldiers guarding one suspension wheel with a well-aimed swing of his rake. Suni took the other wheel. Together they dug their heels into the ground and pushed. Republican soldiers formed a protective circle around them, fending off the press of defenders.

"*Push!*" someone screamed.

Rin didn't have the chance to look behind her to see what was happening. The wave of steel was too blinding. Something sliced open her left cheek. Blood splattered across her face. It was in her eyes—she wiped at them with her sleeve, but that only made them sting worse.

She lashed blindly out with her trident. Steel crunched into bone, and her attacker dropped to the ground. Lucky blow. Rin fell back behind the Republican line and blinked furiously until her vision cleared.

She heard a screeching grind from the suspension wheels. She hazarded a glance over her shoulder. With a massive groan, the gates of Xiashang swung open.

Behind them was the fleet.

The tide had turned. Republican soldiers flooded the square, a deluge of so many blue uniforms that for a moment Rin lost sight of the Ram defenders entirely. Somewhere a horn blew, followed by a series of gong strikes that rang so loudly they drowned out any other sound.

Distress signals. But signals to *whom*? Rin clambered up onto a crate, trying to see above the melee.

She spotted movement in the southwest corridor. She squinted. A new platoon of soldiers, armed and battle-fresh, ran toward the square. The local backup militia? No—they were wearing blue uniforms, not green.

But that wasn't the ocean blue of the Republican uniforms.

Rin almost dropped her trident. Those weren't Nikara soldiers.

Those were Federation troops.

For a moment she thought, panicking, that the Federation was still at large, that they had taken this chance to launch a simultaneous invasion on Xiashang. But that made no sense. The Federation had already been behind the city gates. And they weren't attacking the Xiashang city guard, they were only attacking troops clearly marked in Republican uniforms.

Realization hit like a punch to the gut.

The Ram Warlord had allied with the Federation.

The ground tilted beneath her feet. She saw smoke and fire. She saw bodies eaten by gas. She saw Altan, walking backward away from her on a pier—

"Get down!" Baji shouted.

Rin flung herself to the ground just as a spear hit the wall where her head had been.

She struggled to her feet. She couldn't see an end to the column of Federation soldiers. How many were there? Did they equal Republican numbers?

What had seemed like an easy victory was about to turn into a bloodbath.

She raced up the stairway to get a better look at the city's layout. Just past the town square she saw a three-story residence embedded in a massive, sculpture-dotted garden. That had to be the Ram Warlord's private quarters. It was the largest building in Xiashang.

She knew the best way to end this.

"Baji!" She waved her trident to get his attention. When he looked up, she pointed toward the Ram Warlord's mansion. "Cover me."

He understood immediately. Together they forced their bloody way through the throng until they broke out on the other side of the square. Then they ran for the gardens.

The mansion was guarded by two stone lions, mouths open in wide, greedy caverns. The doors were bolted shut.

Good. That meant someone was hiding inside.

Rin aimed a savage kick at the handle, but the doors didn't budge.

"Please," said Baji. She got out of his way. He took three steps back and slammed his shoulder into the doors. Wood splintered. The doors crashed open.

Baji picked himself up off the ground and pointed behind her. "We've got trouble."

Rin turned around to see a fresh wave of Federation soldiers running toward the mansion. Baji planted himself in the doorway, rake raised.

"You good?" Rin asked.

"You go. I've got this."

She ran indoors. The halls were brightly lit but appeared entirely empty—which would have been the worst of outcomes, because that would mean the Ram Warlord's family had already evacuated to somewhere safe. Rin stood still in the center of the hall, heart pounding, straining to listen for any sound of inhabitants.

Seconds later she heard a baby's shrill wail.

Yes. She concentrated, trying to track the noise. She heard it again. This time the baby's cry was stifled, like someone had clamped a sleeve over its mouth, but in the empty house it rang clear as a bell.

The sound came from the chambers to her left. Rin crept forward, shoes moving silently across the marble floor. At the end of the hall she saw a single silkscreen door. The baby's cries were getting louder. She placed a hand on the door and pulled. Locked. She took a step back and kicked it down. The flimsy bamboo frame gave way with no trouble.

A crowd of at least fifteen women stared up at her, tears of terror streaming down their fat and puffy cheeks, clumped together like flightless birds fattened for the slaughter.

They were the Warlord's wives, Rin guessed. His daughters. Their servant girls and nursemaids.

"Where is Tsung Ho?" she demanded.

They huddled closer together, mute and trembling.

Rin's eyes fell on the baby. An old woman at the back of the room had it clutched in her hands. It was swaddled in red cloth. That meant it was a baby boy. A potential heir.

The Ram Warlord would not let that child die.

"Give him to me," Rin said.

The woman frantically shook her head and pressed the child closer to her chest.

Rin leveled her trident at her. "This is not worth dying for."

One of the girls dashed forward, flailing at her with a curtain pole. Rin ducked down and kicked out. Her foot connected with the girl's midriff with a satisfying *whumph*. The girl collapsed on the ground, wailing in pain.

Rin put a foot on the girl's sternum and pressed down, hard. The girl's agonized whimpers gave her a savage, amused satisfaction. She felt a distinct lack of sympathy toward the women. They chose to be here. They were Federation allies, they knew what was happening, this was their fault, they should all be dead . . .

No. Stop. She took a deep breath. The red cleared from her eyes.

"Any of you try that again and I'll gut you," she said. "The baby. *Now.*"

Whimpering, the old woman relinquished the baby into her hands.

He immediately started to scream. Rin's hands moved automatically to cup around his rear and the back of his head. Leftover instincts from days she'd spent carrying around her infant foster brother.

She had a sudden urge to coo to the baby and rock him until his sobbing ceased. She shut it down. She needed the baby to scream, and to scream loudly.

She backed out of the women's quarters, waving her trident in front of her.

"You lot stay here," she warned the women. "If any of you move, I will kill this child."

The women nodded silently, tears streaking their powdered faces.

Rin backed out of the chamber and returned to the center of the main hall.

"Tsung Ho!" she shouted. "Where are you?"

Silence.

The baby quivered in her arms. His cries had diminished to distressed whimpers. Rin briefly considered pinching his arms to make him scream.

There was no need. The sight of her bloody trident was enough. He caught one glimpse of it, opened his mouth, and shrieked.

Rin shouted over the baby, "Tsung Ho! I'll murder your son if you don't come out."

She heard him approaching long before he attacked.

Too slow. Too fucking slow. She spun around, dodged his blade, and slammed the butt of her trident into his stomach. He doubled over. She caught his blade inside the trident's prongs and twisted it out of his hand. He dropped to all fours, scrambling for his weapon. She kicked it out of the way and jammed the hilt of her trident into the back of his head. He dropped to the floor.

"You traitor." She aimed a savage strike at his kneecaps. He howled in pain. She hit them again. Then again.

The baby wailed louder. She walked to a corner, placed him delicately on the floor, then resumed her assault on his father. The Ram Warlord's kneecaps were visibly broken. She moved on to his ribs.

"Please, mercy, *please* . . ." He curled into a pathetic bundle, arms wrapped over his head.

"When did you let the Mugenese into your gates?" she asked. "Before they burned Golyn Niis, or after?"

"We didn't have a choice," he whispered. He made a high keening noise as he drew his shattered knees to his chest. "They were lined up at our gates, we didn't have any options—"

"You could have fought."

"We would have died," he gasped.

"Then you should have died."

Rin slammed her trident butt against his head. He fell silent.

The baby continued to scream.

Jinzha was so pleased by their victory that he temporarily relaxed the army prohibition on alcohol. Jugs of fine sorghum wine, all plundered from the Ram Warlord's mansion, were passed through the ranks. The soldiers camped out on the beach that night in an unusually good mood.

Jinzha and his council met by the shore to decide what to do with their prisoners. In addition to the captured Federation soldiers there were also the men of the Eighth Division—a larger Militia force than any conquered town they had dealt with so far. They were too big of a threat to let loose. Short of a mass execution, their options were to take an unwieldy number of prisoners—far too many to feed—or to let them go.

"Execute them," Rin said immediately.

"More than a thousand men?" Jinzha shook his head. "We're not monsters."

"But they deserve it," she said. "The Mugenese, at least. You know if the tables were turned, if the Federation had taken our men prisoners, they'd be dead already."

She was so sure that it was a moot debate. But nobody nodded in agreement. She glanced around the circle, confused. Was the conclusion not clear? Why did they all look so uncomfortable?

"They'd be good at the wheels," Admiral Molkoi said. "It'd give our men a break."

"You're joking," Rin said. "You'd have to feed them, for starters—"

"So we'll give them a subsistence diet," said Molkoi.

"Our troops need that food!"

"Our troops have survived on less," Molkoi said. "And it is best they don't get used to the excess."

Rin gawked at him. "You'll put *our* troops on stricter rations so men who have committed treason can live?"

He shrugged. "They're Nikara men. We won't execute our own kind."

"They stopped being Nikara the moment they let the Federation stroll into their homes," she snapped. "They should be rounded up. And beheaded."

None of the others would meet her eye.

"Nezha?" she asked.

He wouldn't look at her. All he did was shake his head.

She flushed with anger. "These soldiers were collaborating with the Federation. Feeding them. Housing them. That's *treason*. That should be punishable by death. Forget the soldiers—you should have the whole city punished!"

"Perhaps under Daji's reign," said Jinzha. "Not under the Republic. We can't garner a reputation for brutality—"

"Because they *helped* them!" She was shouting now, and they were all staring at her, but she didn't care. "The Federation! You don't know what they did—just because you spent the war hiding in Arlong, you didn't see what—"

Jinzha turned to Nezha. "Brother, put a muzzle on your Speerly, or—"

"*I am not a dog!*" Rin shrieked.

Sheer rage took over. She launched herself at Jinzha—and didn't manage two steps before Admiral Molkoi tackled her to the ground so hard that for a moment the night stars blinked out of the sky, and it was all she could do to simply breathe.

"That's enough," Nezha said quietly. "She's calmed down. Let her go."

The pressure on her chest disappeared. Rin curled into a ball, choking miserably.

"Someone take her outside of camp," Jinzha said. "Bind her, gag her, I don't care. We'll deal with this in the morning."

"Yes, sir," said Molkoi.

"She hasn't eaten," Nezha said.

"Then have someone bring her food or water if she asks," Jinzha said. "Just get her out of my sight."

Rin screamed.

No one could hear her—they'd banished her to a stretch of forest outside the camp perimeter—so she screamed louder, again and again, bashing her fists against a tree until blood ran down her knuckles while rage built up hotter and hotter in her chest. And for a moment she thought—hoped—that the crimson fury sparking in her vision might explode into flames, real flames, *finally*—

But nothing. No sparks lit her fingers; no divine laughter rippled through her thoughts. She could feel the Seal at the back of her mind, a pulsing, sickly thing, blurring and softening her anger every time it reached a peak. And that only doubled her rage, made her shriek louder in frustration, but it was a pointless tantrum because the fire remained out of her grasp; dancing, taunting her behind the barrier in her head.

Please, she thought. *I need you, I need the fire, I need to burn* . . .

The Phoenix remained silent.

She sank to her knees.

She could hear Altan laughing. That wasn't the Seal, that was her own imagination, but she heard it as clearly as if he were standing right beside her.

"Look at you," he said.

"Pathetic," he said.

"It's not coming back," he said. "You're lost, you're done, you're not a Speerly, you're just a stupid little girl throwing a temper tantrum in the forest."

Finally her voice and strength gave out and the anger ebbed

pathetically, ineffectually, away. Then she was alone with the indifferent silence of the trees, with no company except for her own mind.

And Rin couldn't stand that, so she decided to get as drunk as she possibly could.

She'd picked up a small jug of sorghum wine back at camp. She chugged it down in under a minute.

She wasn't used to drinking. The masters at Sinegard had been strict—the smallest whiff of alcohol was grounds for expulsion. She still preferred the sickly sweetness of opium smoke to the burn of sorghum wine, but she liked how it seared her delightfully from the inside. It didn't make the anger go away, but it reduced it to a dull throb, an aching pain rather than a sharp, fresh wound.

By the time Nezha came out for her she was utterly soused, and she wouldn't have heard him approach if he hadn't shouted for her every step he took.

"Rin? Are you there?"

She heard his voice around the other side of a tree. She blinked for a few seconds before she remembered how to push words out of her mouth. "Yes. Don't come around."

"What are you doing?"

He circled the tree. She hastily yanked her trousers back up with one hand. A dripping jug dangled from the other.

"Are you pissing in a jug?"

"I'm preparing a gift for your brother," she said. "Think he'll like it?"

"You can't give the grand marshal of the Republican Army a jug of urine."

"But it's warm," she mumbled. She shook it at him. Piss sloshed out the side.

Nezha hastily stepped away. "Please put that down."

"You sure Jinzha doesn't want it?"

"*Rin.*"

She sighed dramatically and complied.

He took her clean hand and led her to a patch of grass by the river, far away from the soiled jug. "You know you can't lash out like that."

She squared her shoulders. "And I have been appropriately disciplined."

"It's not about *discipline*. They'll think you're mad."

"They already think I'm mad," she retorted. "Savage, dumb little Speerly. Right? It's in my nature."

"That's not what I . . . Come on, Rin." Nezha shook his head. "Anyhow. I've, uh, got bad news."

She yawned. "Did we lose the war? That was quick."

"No. Jinzha's demoted you."

She blinked several times, uncomprehending. "What?"

"You're unranked. You're to serve as a foot soldier now. And you're not in command of the Cike anymore."

"So who is?"

"No one. There is no Cike. They've all been reassigned to other ships."

He watched her carefully to gauge her reaction, but Rin just hiccupped.

"That's all right. They hardly listened to me anyway." She derived a kind of bitter satisfaction from saying this out loud. Her position as commander had always been a sham. To be fair, the Cike *did* listen to her when she had a plan, but she usually didn't. Really, they'd effectively been running themselves.

"You know what your problem is?" Nezha asked. "You have no impulse control. Absolutely zero. None."

"It's terrible," she agreed, and started to giggle. "Good thing I can't call the fire, huh?"

He responded to that with such a long silence that eventually it began to embarrass her. She wished now that she hadn't drunk so much. She couldn't think properly through her helplessly muddled mind. She felt terribly foolish, crude, and ashamed.

She had to practice whispering her words before she could voice them out loud. "So what's happening now?"

"Same thing as usual. They're gathering up the civilians. The men will cast their votes tonight."

She sat up. "They should not get a vote."

"They're Nikara. All Nikara get the option to join the Republic."

"They helped the Federation!"

"Because they didn't have a choice," Nezha said. "Think about it. Put yourself in their position. You really think you would have done any better?"

"Yes," she snapped. "I *did*. I *was* in their position. I was in worse—they had me strapped down to a bed, they were torturing me and torturing Altan in front of me and I was terrified, I wanted to die—"

"They were scared, too," he said softly.

"Then they should have fought back."

"Maybe they didn't have the choice. They weren't trained soldiers. They weren't shamans. How else were they going to survive?"

"It's not enough just to survive," she hissed. "You have to fight for something, you can't just—just live your life like a fucking coward."

"Some people are just cowards. Some people just aren't that strong."

"Then they shouldn't have *votes*," she snarled.

The more she thought about it, the more ludicrous Vaisra's proposed democracy seemed. How were the Nikara supposed to rule themselves? They hadn't run their own country since before the days of the Red Emperor, and even drunk, she could figure out why—the Nikara were simply far too stupid, too selfish, and too cowardly.

"Democracy's not going to work. Look at them." She was gesturing at trees, not people, but it hardly made a difference to her. "They're cows. Fools. They're voting for the Republic because they're scared—I'm sure they'd vote just as quickly to join the Federation."

"Don't be unfair," Nezha said. "They're just *people*: they've never studied warcraft."

"So then they shouldn't rule!" she shouted. "They need someone to tell them what to do, what to think—"

"And who's that going to be? Daji?"

"Not Daji. But someone educated. Someone who's passed the Keju, who's graduated from Sinegard. Someone who's been in the military. Someone who knows the value of a human life."

"You're describing yourself," said Nezha.

"I'm not saying it would be me," Rin said. "I'm just saying it shouldn't be the people. Vaisra shouldn't let them elect anyone. He should just rule."

Nezha tilted his head to the side. "You want my father to make himself Emperor?"

A wave of nausea rocked her stomach before she could respond. There was no time to get up; she lurched forward onto her knees and heaved the contents of her stomach against the tree. Her face was too close to the ground. A good deal of vomit splashed back onto her cheek. She rubbed clumsily at it with her sleeve.

"You all right?" Nezha asked when she'd stopped dry-heaving.

"Yes."

He rubbed his hand in circles on her back. "Good."

She spat a gob of regurgitated wine onto the dirt. "Fuck off."

Nezha lifted a clump of mud up from the riverbank. "Have you ever heard the story of how the goddess Nüwa created humanity?"

"No."

"I'll tell it to you." Nezha molded the mud into a ball with his palms. "Once upon a time, after the birth of the world, Nüwa was lonely."

"What about her husband, Fuxi?" Rin only knew the myths about Nüwa and Fuxi both.

"Absent spouse, I guess. Myth doesn't mention him."

"Of course."

"Of course. Anyway, Nüwa gets lonely, decides to create some humans to populate the world to keep her company." Nezha pressed his fingernails into the ball of mud. "The first few people she makes are incredibly detailed. Fine features, lovely clothes."

Rin could see where this was going. "Those are the aristocrats."

"Yes. The nobles, the emperors, the warriors, everyone who matters. Then she gets bored. It's taking too long. So she takes a rope and starts flinging mud in all directions. Those become the hundred clans of Nikan."

Rin swallowed. Her throat tasted like acid. "They don't tell that story in the south."

"And why do you think that is?" Nezha asked.

She turned that over in her mind for a moment. Then she laughed.

"My people are mud," she said. "And you're still going to let them run a country."

"I don't think they're mud," Nezha said. "I think they're still unformed. Uneducated and uncultured. They don't know better because they haven't been given the chance. But the Republic will shape and refine them. Develop them into what they were meant to be."

"That's not how it works." Rin took the clump of mud from Nezha's hand. "They're never going to become more than what they are. The north won't let them."

"That's not true."

"You think that. But I've seen how power works." Rin crushed the clump in her fingers. "It's not about who you are, it's about how they see you. And once you're mud in this country, you're always mud."

CHAPTER 18

"You're joking," Ramsa said.

Rin shook her head, and her temples throbbed at the sudden movement. Under the harsh light of dawn, she'd come to deeply regret ever touching alcohol, which made the task of informing the Cike they'd been disbanded very distasteful. "I'm unranked. Jinzha's orders."

"Then what about us?" Ramsa demanded.

She gave him a blank look. "What *about* you?"

"Where are we supposed to go?"

"Oh." She squeezed her eyes shut, trying to remember. "You're being reassigned. You're on the *Griffon*, I think, and Suni and Baji are on the tower ships—"

"We're not together?" Ramsa asked. "Fuck that. Can't we just refuse?"

"No." She pressed a palm into her aching forehead. "You're still Republic soldiers. You have to follow orders."

He stared at her in disbelief. "That's all you've got?"

"What else am I supposed to say?"

"Something!" he shouted. "Anything! We're not the Cike anymore, and you're just going to take that lying down?"

She wanted to cover her ears with her hands. She was so

exhausted. She wished Ramsa would just go away and break the news to the others for her so that she could lie down and go to sleep and stop thinking about anything.

"Who cares? The Cike's not that important. The Cike is dead."

Ramsa grabbed at her collar. But he was so scrawny, shorter even than she, that it only made him look ridiculous.

"What is wrong with you?" he demanded.

"Ramsa, stop."

"We joined this war for you," he said. "Out of loyalty to *you*."

"Don't be dramatic. You entered this war because you wanted Dragon silver, you like blowing shit up, and you're a wanted criminal everywhere else in the Empire."

"I stuck with you because we thought we'd stay *together*." Ramsa sounded like he was about to cry, which was so absurd that Rin almost laughed. "We're always supposed to be together."

"You're not even a shaman. You've got nothing to be afraid of. Why do you care?"

"Why *don't* you care? Altan named you commander. Protecting the Cike is your duty."

"I didn't ask to be commander," she snapped. Altan's invocation brought up feelings of obligation, duty, that she didn't want to think about. "All right? I don't want to be your Altan. I can't."

What had she done since she'd been put in charge? She'd hurt Unegen, driven Enki away, seen Aratsha killed, and gotten her ass kicked so badly by Daji that she couldn't even properly be called a shaman anymore. She hadn't led the Cike so much as encouraged them to make a series of awful decisions. They were better off without her. It infuriated her that they couldn't see that.

"Aren't you angry?" Ramsa asked. "Doesn't this piss you off?"

"No," she said. "I take orders."

She could have been angry. Could have resisted Jinzha, could have lashed out like she'd always done. But anger had only ever helped her when it manifested in flames, and she couldn't call on that anymore. Without the fire she wasn't a shaman, wasn't a proper Speerly, and certainly wasn't a military asset. Jinzha had no reason to listen to or respect her.

And she knew by now that the fire was never coming back.

"You could at least try," Ramsa said. "Please."

There was no fight left in his voice, either.

"Just grab your things," she said. "And tell the others. They want you to report in ten."

In a matter of weeks the last strongholds of Hare and Ram Provinces capitulated to the Republic. Their Warlords were sent back to Arlong in chains to grovel before Vaisra for their lives. Their cities, townships, and villages were all subjected to plebiscites.

When the civilians elected to join the Republic—and they invariably voted to join, for the alternative was that all men over the age of fifteen would be put to death—they became a part of Vaisra's sprawling war machine. The women were put to work sewing Republican uniforms and spinning linens for the infirmaries. The men were either recruited as infantry or sent south to work in Arlong's shipyards. A seventh of their food stores were confiscated to contribute to the northern campaign's swelling supply lines, and Republican patrols stayed behind to ensure regular shipments of grain upriver.

Nezha bragged constantly that this was perhaps the most successful military campaign in Nikara history. Kitay told him to stop getting high on his own hubris, but Rin could not deny their astonishing string of victories.

The daily demands of the campaign were so grueling, however, that she rarely got the chance to revel in their wins. The cities, townships, and villages began to blur together in her mind. Rin stopped thinking in terms of night and day, and started thinking in battle timetables. The days bled into one another, a string of extraordinarily demanding predawn combat assignments and snatched hours of deep and dreamless sleep.

The only benefit was that she managed to temporarily lose

herself in the sheer physical activity. Her demotion didn't affect her as much as she'd thought it would. Most days she was too tired to even remember it had happened.

But she was also secretly relieved that she did not have to think anymore about what to do with her men. That the burden of leadership, which she'd never adequately met, had been lifted entirely from her shoulders. All she had to do was worry about carrying out her own orders, and that she did splendidly.

Her orders were doubling, too. Jinzha might have begun to appreciate her ability, or he might have simply disliked her so much he wanted her dead without having to take the blame, but he began to put her on the front lines of every ground operation. This was typically not a coveted position, but she relished it.

After all, she was terribly good at war. She had trained for this. Maybe she couldn't call the fire anymore, but she could still *fight*, and landing her trident into the right joint of flesh felt just as good as incinerating everything around her.

She gained a reputation on the *Kingfisher* as an eminently capable soldier, and despite herself she started to bask in it. It awakened an old streak of competitiveness that she had not felt since Sinegard, when the only thing getting her through months of grueling and miserable study had been the sheer delight of having her talents recognized by someone.

Was this how Altan had felt? The Nikara had honed him as a weapon, had put him to military uses since he was a small child, but still they'd lauded him. Had that kept him happy?

Of course she wasn't happy, not quite. But she had found some sort of contentment, the satisfaction that came from being a tool that served its purpose quite well.

The campaigns were like drugs in their own right. Rin felt wonderful when she fought. In the heat of battle, human life could be reduced to the barest mechanics of existence—arms and legs, mobility and vulnerability, vital points to be identified, isolated, and destroyed. She found an odd pleasure in that. Her body knew what to do, which meant she could turn her mind off.

If the Cike were unhappy, she didn't know. She didn't speak to them anymore. She barely saw them after they were reassigned. But she found it harder and harder to care because she was losing the capacity to think about much at all.

In time, sooner than she'd expected, she even stopped longing for the fire that she'd lost. Sometimes the urge crept up on her on the eve of battle and she rubbed her fingers together, wishing that she could make them spark, fantasizing about how quickly her troops could win battles if she could call down a column of fire to scorch out the defensive line.

She still felt the Phoenix's absence like a hole carved out of her chest. The ache never quite went away. But the desperation and frustration ebbed. She stopped waking up in the morning and wanting to scream when she remembered what had been taken from her.

She'd long since stopped trying to break down the Seal. Its dark, pulsing presence no longer pained her daily like a festering wound. In the small moments when she did permit herself to linger on it, she wondered if it had begun to take her memories.

Master Jiang had seemed to know absolutely nothing about who he had been twenty years ago. Would the same happen to her?

Already some of her earlier memories were starting to feel fuzzy. She used to remember intricately the faces of every member of her foster family in Tikany. Now they seemed like blurs. But she couldn't tell if the Seal had eaten those memories away, or if they had simply corroded over time.

That didn't worry her as much as it should have. She couldn't pretend that if the Seal stole her past from her little by little—if she forgot Altan, forgot what she'd done on Speer, and let her guilt wash away into a white nothingness until, like Jiang, she was just an affable, absentminded fool—some part of her wouldn't be relieved.

When Rin wasn't sleeping or fighting, she was sitting with Kitay in his cramped office. She was no longer invited to Jinzha's councils, but she learned everything from Kitay secondhand. He, in turn, enjoyed bouncing his ideas off of her. Talking through the multitudes of possibilities out loud gave relief to the frantic activity inside his mind.

He alone didn't share the Republic's delight over their incredible series of victories.

"I'm concerned," he admitted. "And confused. Hasn't this whole campaign felt too easy to you? It's like they're not even trying."

"They *are* trying. They're just not very good at it." Rin was still buzzing from the high of battle. It felt very good to excel, even if excellence meant cutting down poorly trained local soldiers, and Kitay's moodiness irritated her.

"You know the battles you're fighting are too easy."

She made a face. "You could give us a little bit of credit."

"Do you want praise for beating up untrained, unarmed villagers? Good job, then. Very well done. The superiorly armed navy crushes a pathetic peasant resistance. What a shocking turn of events. That doesn't mean you're taking this Empire on a silver platter."

"It could just mean that our navy is superior," she said. "What, you think Daji's giving up the north on purpose? That doesn't get her anything."

"She's not giving it up. They're building a shipyard, we've known that since the beginning—"

"And if their navy were any use, we would have seen it. Maybe we're actually just *winning* this war. It wouldn't kill you to admit it."

But Kitay shook his head. "You're talking about Su Daji. This is the woman who managed to unite all twelve provinces for the first time since the death of the Red Emperor."

"She had help."

"But she's had no help since. If the Empire were going to fracture, you'd think it would have already. Don't get cocky, Rin. We're playing a game of wikki against a woman who's had decades of practice against far more fearsome opponents. I've said this to Jinzha, too. There's a counteroffensive coming soon, and the longer we wait for it, the worse it's going to be."

Kitay was obsessed with the problem of whether the fleet ought to curtail its campaign for the winter or to sail directly to Tiger Province, rendezvous with Tsolin's fleet, and take on Jun and his army. On the one hand, if they could solidify their hold on the coastline through Tiger Province, then they would have a back channel to run supplies and reinforce land columns to eventually encircle the Autumn Palace.

On the other, taking the coastline would involve a massive military commitment from troops that the Republic didn't yet have. Until the Hesperians decided to lend aid, they would have to settle for conquering the inland regions first. But that could take another couple of months—which required time that they also didn't have.

They were racing against time. Nobody wanted to be stuck in an invasion when winter hit the north. Their task was to solidify a revolutionary base and corner the Empire inside its three northernmost provinces before the Murui's tributaries froze over and the fleet was stuck in place.

"We're cutting it close, but we should be up to the Edu pass within a month," Kitay told her. "Jinzha has to make his decision by then."

Rin did the calculations in her head. "Upriver sailing should take us a month and a half."

"You're forgetting about the Four Gorges Dam," Kitay said. "Up through Rat Province the Murui's blocked up, so the current won't be as strong as it should be."

"A month, then. What do you think happens when we get there?"

"We pray to the heavens that the rivers and lakes haven't frozen yet," Kitay said. "Then we see what our options are. At this point, though, Jinzha's wagered this war on the weather."

Rin's weekly meetings with Sister Petra remained the thorn in her side that progressively stung worse. Petra's examinations had become increasingly invasive, but she had also started withholding the laudanum. She was finished with taking baseline measurements. Now she wanted to see evidence of Chaos.

When week after week Rin failed to call the fire, Petra grew impatient.

"You are hiding it from me," she accused. "You refuse to cooperate."

"Or maybe I'm cured," Rin said. "Maybe Chaos went away. Maybe your holy presence scared it off."

"You lie." Petra wrenched Rin's mouth open with more force than she needed and began tapping around her teeth with what felt like a two-pronged instrument. The cold metal tips dug painfully into Rin's enamel. "I know how Chaos works. It never disappears. It disguises itself in the face of the Maker but always it returns."

Rin wished that were the case. If she had the fire back she'd incinerate Petra where she stood, and fuck the consequences. If she had the fire, then she wouldn't be so terribly helpless, bowing down to Jinzha's commands and cooperating with the Hesperians because she was only a lowly foot soldier.

But if she gave in to her anger now, the worst she could do was make a mess in Petra's lab, wind up dead at the bottom of the Murui, and destroy any hope of a Hesperian-Nikara military alliance. Resistance meant doom for her and everyone she cared about.

So even though it tasted like the bitterest bile, she swallowed her rage.

"It's really gone," she said when Petra released her jaw. "I told you it's been Sealed off. I can't call it anymore."

"So you say." Petra looked deeply skeptical, but she dropped the subject. She placed the instrument back on her table. "Raise your right hand and hold your breath."

"Why?"

"Because I asked."

The Sister never lost her temper with Rin, no matter what Rin said. Petra had a freakishly calm composure. She never betrayed any emotion other than an icy professional curiosity. Rin almost wished that Petra would strike her, just so she knew she was human, but frustration seemed to slide off of her like rainwater from a tin roof.

However, as time passed with no results, she did start subjecting Rin to baser and baser experiments. She made Rin solve puzzles meant for children while she kept time with her little watch. She made Rin perform simple tasks of memorization that seemed designed to make her fail, watching without blinking as Rin became so frustrated that she started throwing things at the wall.

Eventually Petra asked her to stand for examinations naked.

"If you wanted to ogle me you could have asked earlier," Rin said.

Petra didn't react. "Quickly, please."

Rin yanked her uniform off and tossed it in a bundle on the floor.

"Good." Petra passed her an empty cup. "Now urinate in this for me."

Rin stared at her in disbelief. "Right now?"

"I'm doing fluids analysis tonight," Petra said. "Go on."

Rin set her jaw. "I'm not doing that."

"Would you like a sheet for privacy?"

"I don't care," Rin said. "This isn't about science. You don't have a clue what you're doing, you're just being spiteful."

Petra sat down and crossed one leg over the other. "Urinate, please."

"Fuck that." Rin tossed the cup onto the floor. "Admit it. You've no idea what you're doing. All your treatises and all your instruments, and you don't have a single clue about how shamanism works or how to measure Chaos, if that really even exists. You're shooting in the dark."

Petra stood up from her chair. Her nostrils flared white.

Rin had finally struck a nerve. She hoped that Petra might hit her then, if only to break that inhuman mask of control. But Petra only cocked her head to the side.

"Remember your situation." Her voice retained its icy calm. "I am asking you to cooperate only out of etiquette. Refuse, and I will have you strapped to that bed. Now. Will you behave?"

Rin wanted to kill her.

If she hadn't been so exhausted, if she had been an ounce more impulsive, then she would have. It would have been so easy to knock Petra to the floor and jam every sharp instrument on the table into her neck, her chest, her eyes. It would have felt so good.

But Rin couldn't act on impulse anymore.

She felt the sheer, overwhelming weight of Hesperia's military might restricting her options like an invisible cage. They held her life hostage. They held her friends and her entire nation hostage.

Against all of that, Sealed off from the fire and the Phoenix, she was helpless.

So she held her tongue and forced down her fury as Petra's requests became more and more humiliating. She complied when Petra made her lean naked against the wall while she drew intricate diagrams of her genitals. She sat still when Petra inserted a long, thick needle into her right arm and drew so much blood that she fainted when she stood up to return to her quarters and couldn't stand back up for half a day. And she bit her tongue and didn't react when Petra waved a packet of opium under her nose, trying to entice her to draw the fire out by offering her favorite vice.

"Go on," Petra said. "I've read about your kind. You can't resist the smoke. You crave it in your bones. Isn't that how the Red Emperor subdued your ancestors? Call the fire for me, and I'll let you have a little."

That last meeting left Rin so furious that the moment she left Petra's quarters, she shrieked in fury and punched the wall so hard that her knuckle split open. For a moment she stood still, stunned, while blood ran down the back of her hand and dripped off her wrist. Then she sank to her knees and started to cry.

"Are you all right?"

It was Augus, the baby-faced, blue-eyed missionary. Rin gave him a wary look. "Go away."

He reached for her bleeding hand. "You're upset."

She jerked it out of his grasp. "I don't want your pity."

He sat down next to her, fished a linen out of his pocket, and passed it to her. "Here. Why don't you wrap that up?"

Rin's knuckle was bleeding faster than she had realized. After getting her blood drawn the week before, the very sight of it made her want to faint. Reluctantly she took the cloth.

Augus watched as she looped it tightly around her hand. She realized she couldn't tie off the knot by herself.

"I can do that," he offered.

She let him.

"Are you all right?" he asked again when he was finished.

"Does it fucking look like—"

"I meant with Sister Petra," he clarified. "I know she can be difficult."

Rin shot him a sideways look. "You don't like her?"

"We all admire her," he said slowly. "But . . . ah, do you understand Hesperian? This language is hard for me."

"Yes."

He switched, speaking deliberately slowly so that she could keep up. "She's the most brilliant Gray Sister of our generation and the foremost expert of Chaos manifestations on the eastern continent. But we don't all agree with her methods."

"What does that mean?"

"Sister Petra is old-fashioned about conversion. Her school believes that the only pathway to salvation is patterning civilizations on the development of Hesperia. To obey the Maker you must become like us. You must stop being Nikara."

"Attractive," Rin muttered.

"But I think that when we wish to win barbarians over and convert them to the greater good, we should use the same strategies that Chaos uses to draw souls to evil," Augus continued.

"Chaos enters through the other's door and comes out his own. So should we."

Rin pressed her bound knuckles against the wall to stem the pain. Her dizziness subsided. "From what I know, you lot are more fond of blowing our doors up."

"Like I said. Conservative." Augus shot her an embarrassed smile. "But the Company has been changing its ways. Take the bow, for instance. I've read about the Nikara tradition of performing deep bows to superiors—"

"That's only for special occasions," she said.

"Even so. Decades ago, the Company would have argued that bowing to a Nikara would be an utter affront to the dignity of the white race. We are chosen by the Maker, after all. We are the highest evolved persons, and we shouldn't show respect to you. But I don't agree with that."

Rin fought the urge to roll her eyes. "That's nice of you."

"We are not equals," Augus said. "But that doesn't mean we can't be friends. And I don't think the path to salvation involves treating you like you're not people."

Augus, Rin realized, really thought that he was being kind.

"I think I'm good now," she said.

He helped her to her feet. "Would you like me to walk you back to your quarters?"

"No. Thank you. I can manage."

When she returned to her room, she drew the packet of opium out from her pocket. She hadn't quite stolen it. Petra had left it in her lap and hadn't commented on it when Rin stood up to leave. She meant for Rin to have it.

Rin yanked up a loose floorboard and hid the drug where no one could see. She wasn't going to use it. She didn't know what sick game Petra was playing, but she couldn't tempt her that far.

Still, it relieved her to know that if it became too much, that if she wanted it all to end and she wanted to float higher, higher, away from her body and shame and humiliation and pain until she left it permanently, then the opium was there.

If any other Hesperians shared Augus's opinions, they didn't show it. Tarcquet's men on the *Kingfisher* kept a chilly distance from the Nikara. They ate and slept by themselves, and every time Rin drifted within earshot of their conversations, they fell quiet until she'd passed. They continued to observe the Nikara without intervening—coldly amused by their incompetence, and mildly surprised by their victories.

Only once did they put their arquebuses to any use. One evening a commotion broke out on the lower deck. A group of prisoners from Ram Province broke out of their holding cell and attacked a handful of missionaries who had been proselytizing in the brig.

They might have been trying to escape. They might have thought to use the Hesperians as hostages. Or they might have simply wanted to lash out at foreigners for getting too close—Ram Province had suffered greatly under occupation and had no great love of the west. When Rin and the other soldiers on patrol reached the source of the shouting, the prisoners had the missionaries pinned to the floor, alive but incapacitated.

Rin recognized Augus, gasping desperately for breath while a prisoner wedged an arm under his throat.

His eyes locked on to hers. "Help—"

"Get back!" the prisoner shouted. "Everyone get back, or they're dead!"

More Republican soldiers crowded the hallway in seconds. The skirmish should have been resolved instantly. The prisoners were unarmed and outnumbered. But they had also been marked for their strength as pedalers. Jinzha had specifically ordered that they be treated well, and no one wanted to attack for fear of causing irreparable injury.

"Please," Augus whispered.

Rin faltered. She wanted to dart forward and pull his attacker off. But the Republican soldiers were holding back, waiting for orders. She couldn't jump alone into the fray; they'd tear her apart.

She stood, trident raised, watching as Augus's face turned a grotesque blue.

"Out of the way!" Tarcquet and his guard pushed through the commotion, arquebuses raised.

Tarcquet took one look at the prisoners and shouted an order. A round of shots rang through the air. Eight men dropped to the ground. The air curdled with the familiar smell of fire powder. The missionaries broke free, gasping for breath.

"What is this?" Jinzha forced his way through the crowd. "What's happened?"

"General Jinzha." Tarcquet signaled to his men, who lowered their weapons. "Good of you to show up."

Jinzha surveyed the bodies on the floor. "You've cost me good labor."

Tarcquet cocked his arquebus. "I would improve your brig security."

"Our brig security is fine." Jinzha looked white-faced with fury. "Your missionaries weren't supposed to be down there."

Augus rose to his feet, coughing. He reached for Jinzha's arm. "Prisoners deserve mercy, too. You can't just—"

"Fuck your mercy." Jinzha pushed Augus away. "You're on my ship. You'll obey orders, or you can take a swim in the river."

"Don't speak to my people like that." Tarcquet stepped in between them. The difference between him and Jinzha was almost laughable—Jinzha was tall by Nikara standards, but Tarcquet towered over him. "Perhaps your father didn't make it clear. We are diplomats on your ship. If you want the Consortium to even consider funding your pathetic war, you will treat every Hesperian here like royalty."

Jinzha's throat bobbed. Rin watched the anger pass through his expression; saw Jinzha shove down the impulse to react. Tarcquet held all the leverage. Tarcquet could not be reproached.

Rin derived some small satisfaction from that. It felt good to see Jinzha humiliated, treated with the same condescension with which he'd always treated her.

"Am I understood?" Tarcquet asked.

Jinzha glared up at him.

Tarcquet cocked his head. "Say 'yes, sir' or 'no, sir.'"

Jinzha had murder written across his face. "Yes, sir."

Tensions ran high for several days afterward. A pair of Hesperian soldiers began following the missionaries around wherever they went, and the Nikara kept their wary distance. But unless one of theirs was in danger, Tarcquet's soldiers did not fire their weapons.

Tarcquet continued his constant assessment of Jinzha's campaign. Rin saw him every now and then on deck, obnoxiously marking notes into a small book while he surveyed the fleet moving up the river. And Rin wondered what he thought of them—their unresponsive gods, their weapons that seemed so primitive, and their bloody, desperate war.

Two months into the campaign, they sailed at last into Rat Province. Here their string of victories came to an end.

Rat Province's Second Division was the intelligence branch of the Militia, and its espionage officers were the best in the Twelve Provinces. By now, it had also had several months of warning time to put together a better defensive strategy than Hare or Ram Provinces had been able to mount.

The Republic arrived to find villages already abandoned, granaries emptied, and fields scorched. The Rat Warlord had either recalled his civilians to metropolitan centers farther upriver or sent them fleeing to other provinces. Jinzha's soldiers found clothing, furniture, and children's toys scattered across the grassy roads. Whatever couldn't be taken was ruined. In village after village they found burned, useless seed grain and rotting piles of livestock carcasses.

The Rat Warlord wasn't trying to mount a defense of his borders. He had simply retreated to Baraya, his heavily barricaded capital city. He planned to starve the fleet out. And Baraya had a better chance of success than Xiashang had—its gates were thicker, its residents better prepared, and it was more than a mile inland, which neutralized the attack capabilities of the *Shrike* and the *Crake*.

"We should just stop here and turn back." Kitay paced his office floor, frustrated. "Ride out the winter. We'll starve otherwise."

But Jinzha had become increasingly irascible, less and less willing to listen to his advisers and more adamant that they had to storm forward.

"He wants to move on Baraya?" Rin asked.

"He wants to press north as fast as we can." Kitay tugged anxiously at his hair. "It's a terrible idea. But he won't listen to me."

"Then who's he listening to?"

"Any of the leadership who agree with him. Molkoi especially. He's in the old guard—I *told* Vaisra that was a bad idea, but who listens to me? Nezha's on my side, but of course Jinzha won't listen to his little brother, it'd mean losing face. This could throw away all of our gains so far. You know, there's a good chance we'll all just starve to death up north. That'd be hilarious, wouldn't it?"

But, as Jinzha announced to the *Kingfisher*, they absolutely would not starve. They would take Rat Province. They would blow open the gates to the capital city of Baraya, and win themselves enough supplies to last out the winter.

Easy orders to give. Harder to implement, especially when they reached a stretch of the Murui so steep that Jinzha had no choice but to order his troops to move the ships over land. The flooded riverbanks earlier had made it possible for them to sail directly over lowland roads. But now they were forced to disembark and roll the ships over logs to reach the next waterway wide enough to accommodate the warships.

It took an entire day of straining against ropes to simply pull the massive tower ships onto dry land, and much longer to cut down enough trees to roll them across the bumpy terrain. One week bled into two weeks of backbreaking, mindless, numbing labor. The only advantage of this was that Rin was so exhausted that she didn't have the time to be bored.

Patrol shifts were slightly more exciting. These were a chance to get away from the din of ships rolling over logs and explore the surrounding land. Thick forests obscured all visibility past a mile, and Jinzha sent out daily parties to root through the trees for any sightings of the Militia.

Rin found these relaxing, until word got back to the base that the noon patrol had caught sight of a Militia scouting party.

"And you just let them *go*?" Jinzha demanded. "Are you stupid?"

The men on patrol were from the *Griffon*, and Nezha hastily interceded on their behalf. "They weren't worth the fight, brother. Our men were outnumbered."

"But they had the advantage of surprise," Jinzha snapped. "Instead, the entire Militia now knows our precise location. Send your men back out. No one sleeps until I have proof every last scout is dead."

Nezha bowed his head. "Yes, brother."

"And take Salkhi's men with you. Yours clearly can't be trusted to get the job done."

The next day, Salkhi and Nezha's joint expedition returned to the *Kingfisher* with a string of severed heads and empty Militia uniforms.

That appeased Jinzha, but ultimately it made no difference. First the Militia scouts returned in larger and larger numbers. Then the attacks began en masse. The Militia soldiers hid in the mountains. They never launched a frontal assault, but maintained a constant stream of arrow fire, picking off soldiers unawares.

The Republican troops fared badly against these scattered, unpredictable attacks. Panic swept through the camp, destroying morale, and Rin understood why. The Republican Army felt out of place on land. They were used to fighting from their ships. They were most comfortable in water, where they had a quick escape route.

They had no escape routes now.

CHAPTER 19

Snow started falling the day that they finally returned to the river. At first it drifted down in fat, lazy flakes. But within hours it had transformed into a blinding blizzard, with winds so fierce that the troops could hardly see five feet in front of them. Jinzha was forced to keep his fleet grounded by the edge of the river while his soldiers holed up in their ships to wait out the storm.

"I've always been amazed by snow." Rin traced shapes into the porthole condensation as she stared out at the endless, hypnotizing flurry outside. "Every winter, it's a surprise. I can never believe it's real."

"They don't have snow down south?" Kitay asked.

"No. Tikany gets so dry that your lips bleed when you try to smile, but never cold enough for the snow to fall. Before I came north, I'd only heard about it in stories. I thought it was a beautiful idea. Little flecks of the cold."

"And how did you find the snow at Sinegard?"

A howl of wind drowned out Rin's response. She pulled down the porthole cover. "Fucking miserable."

The blizzard let up by the next morning. Outside, the forest had been transformed, like some giant had drenched the trees in white paint.

Jinzha announced that the fleet would remain grounded for one more day to pass the New Year's holiday. Everywhere else in the Empire, New Year's would be a weeklong affair involving twelve-course banquets, firecrackers, and endless parades. On campaign, a single day would have to be enough.

The troops disembarked to camp out in the winter landscape, glad for the chance to escape the close quarters of the cabins.

"See if you can get that fire going," Nezha told Kitay.

The three of them sat huddled together on the riverbank, rubbing their hands together while Kitay fumbled with a piece of flint to start a fire.

Somewhere Nezha had scrounged up a small packet of glutinous rice flour. He poured the flour out into a tin bowl, added some water from his canteen, and stirred it together with his fingers until it formed a small ball of dough.

Rin prodded at the measly fire. It fizzled and sputtered; the next gust of wind put it out entirely. She groaned and reached for the flint. They wouldn't have boiling water for at least half an hour. "You know, you could just take that to the kitchen and have them cook it."

"The kitchen isn't supposed to know I have it," said Nezha.

"I see," Kitay said. "The general is stealing rations."

"The general is rewarding his best soldiers with a New Year's treat," Nezha said.

Kitay rubbed his hands up and down his arms. "Oh, so it's nepotism."

"Shut up," Nezha mumbled. He rubbed harder at the ball of dough, but it crumbled to bits in his fingers.

"You haven't added enough water." Rin grabbed the bowl from him and kneaded the dough with one hand, adding droplets of water with the other until she had a wet, round ball the size of her fist.

"I didn't know you could cook," Nezha said curiously.

"I used to all the time. No one else was going to feed Kesegi."

"Kesegi?"

"My little brother." The memory of his face rose up in Rin's mind. She forced it back down. She hadn't seen him in four years. She didn't know if he was still alive, and she didn't want to wonder.

"I didn't know you had a little brother," Nezha said.

"Not a real brother. I was adopted."

No one asked her to elaborate, so she didn't. She rolled the dough into a snakelike strip between both palms, then broke it up piece by piece into thumb-sized lumps.

Nezha watched her hands with the wide-eyed fascination of a boy who'd clearly never been in the kitchen. "Those balls are smaller than the tangyuan I remember."

"That's because we don't have red bean paste or sesame to fill them with," she said. "Any chance you scrounged up some sugar?"

"You have to add sugar?" Nezha asked.

Kitay laughed.

"We'll eat them bland, then," she said. "It'll taste better in little pieces. More to chew."

When the water finally came to a boil, Rin dropped the rice flour balls into the tin cauldron and stirred them with a stick, creating a clockwise current so that they wouldn't stick to each other.

"Did you know that cauldrons are a military invention?" Kitay asked. "One of the Red Emperor's generals came up with the idea of tin cookware. Can you imagine? Before that, they were stuck trying to build fires large enough for giant bamboo steamers."

"A lot of innovations came from the military," Nezha mused. "Messenger pigeons, for one. And there's a good argument that most of the advances in blacksmithing and medicine were a product of the Era of Warring States."

"That's cute." Rin peered into the cauldron. "Proves that war's good for something, then."

"It's a good theory," Nezha insisted. "The country was in chaos during the Era of Warring States, sure. But look at what it brought us—Sunzi's *Principles of War*; Mengzi's theories on governance.

Everything we know now about philosophy, about warfare and statecraft, was developed during that era."

"So what's the tradeoff?" Rin asked. "Thousands of people have to die so that we can get better at killing each other in the future?"

"You know that's not my argument."

"It's what it sounds like. It sounds like you're saying that people have to die for progress."

"It's not progress they're dying for," Nezha said. "Progress is the side effect. And military innovation doesn't just mean we get better at killing each other, it means we get better equipped to kill whoever decides to invade us next."

"And who do you think is going to invade us next?" Rin asked. "The Hinterlanders?"

"Don't rule them out."

"They'd have to stop killing each other off, first."

The tribes of the northern Hinterlands had been at constant war since any of them could remember. In the days of the Red Emperor, the students of Sinegard had been trained primarily to fend off northern invaders. Now they were just an afterthought.

"Better question," Kitay said. "What do you think is the next great military innovation?"

"Arquebuses," Nezha said, at the same moment that Rin said, "Shamanic armies."

Both of them turned to stare at her.

"Shamans over *arquebuses*?" Nezha asked.

"Of course," she said. The thought had just occurred to her, but the more she considered it, the more attractive it sounded. "Tarcquet's weapon is just a glorified rocket. But imagine a whole army of people who could summon gods."

"That sounds like a disaster," Nezha said.

"Or an unstoppable military," Rin said.

"I feel like if that could be done, it would have been," said Nezha. "But there's no written history on shamanic warfare. The only shamans the Red Emperor employed were the Speerlies, and we know how that went."

"But the predynastic texts—"

"—are irrelevant." Nezha cut her off. "Fortification technology and bronze weapons didn't become military standard until well into the Red Emperor's rule, which is about the same time that shamans started disappearing from the record. We have no idea how shamans would change the nature of warfare, whether they could be worked into a military bureaucracy."

"The Cike's done pretty well," Rin challenged.

"When there are fewer than ten of you, sure. Don't you think hundreds of shamans would be a disaster?"

"You should become one," she said. "See what it's like."

Nezha flinched. "You're not serious."

"It's not the worst idea. Any of us could teach you."

"I have never met a shaman in complete control of their own mind." Nezha looked strangely bothered by her suggestion. "And I'm sorry, but knowing the Cike does not make me terribly optimistic."

Rin pulled the cauldron off of the fire. She knew she was supposed to let the tangyuan cool for a few minutes before serving, but she was too cold, and the vapors misting up from the surface were too enticing. They didn't have bowls, so they wrapped the cauldron in leaves to keep their hands from burning and passed it around in a circle.

"Happy New Year," Kitay said. "May the gods send you blessings and good fortune."

"Health, wealth, and happiness. May your enemies rot and surrender quickly before we have to kill more of them." Rin stood up.

"Where are you going?" Nezha asked.

"Gotta go take a piss."

She wandered toward the woods, looking for a large enough tree to hide behind. By now she'd spent so much time with Kitay that she wouldn't have minded squatting down right in front of him. But for some reason, she felt far less comfortable stripping in front of Nezha.

Her ankle twisted beneath her. She spun around, failed to catch her balance, and fell flat on her rear. She spread her hands to catch her fall. Her fingers landed on something soft and rubbery. Confused, she glanced down and brushed the snow away from the surface.

She saw a child's face buried in snow.

His—she thought it was a boy, though she couldn't quite tell—eyes were wide open, large and blank, with long lashes fringed with snow, embedded in dark shadows on a thin, pale face.

Rin rose unsteadily to her feet. She picked up a branch and brushed the rest of the snow off the child's body. She uncovered another face. And then another.

It finally sank in that this was not natural, that she ought to be afraid, and then she opened her mouth and screamed.

Nezha ordered a squadron to walk through the surrounding square mile with torches held low to the ground until the ice and snow had melted enough that they could see what had happened.

The snow peeled away to reveal an entire village of people, frozen perfectly where they lay. Most still had their eyes open. Rin saw no blood. The villagers didn't appear to have died from anything except for the cold, and perhaps starvation. Everywhere she found evidence of fires, hastily constructed, long fizzled out.

No one had given her a torch. She was still shaken from the experience, and every sudden movement made her jump, so it was best that she didn't hold on to anything potentially dangerous. But she refused to go back to camp alone, either, so she stood by the edge of the forest, watching blankly as the soldiers brushed snow off yet another family of corpses. Their bodies were curled in a heap together, the mother's and father's bodies wrapped protectively around their two children.

"Are you all right?" Nezha asked her. His hand wandered hesitantly toward her shoulder, as if he wasn't sure whether to touch her or not.

She brushed it away. "I'm fine. I've seen bodies before."

Yet she couldn't take her eyes off of them. They looked like a set of dolls lying in the snow, perfectly fine except for the fact that they weren't moving.

Most of the adults still had large bundles fastened to their backs. Rin saw porcelain dishes, silk dresses, and kitchen utensils spilling out of those bags. The villagers seemed to have packed their entire homes up with them.

"Where were they going?" she wondered.

"Isn't it obvious?" Kitay said. "They were running."

"From *what*?"

Kitay said it, because no one else seemed able to. "Us."

"But they didn't have anything to fear." Nezha looked deeply uncomfortable. "We would have treated them the way we've treated every other village. They would have gotten a vote."

"That's not what their leaders would have told them," said Kitay. "They would have imagined we were coming to kill them."

"That's ridiculous," Nezha said.

"Is it?" Kitay asked. "Imagine it. You hear the rebel army is coming. Your magistrates are your most reliable sources of information, and they tell you that the rebels will kill your men, rape your women, and enslave your children, because that's what you're always supposed to say about the enemy. You don't know any better, so you pack up everything you can and flee."

Rin could imagine the rest. These villagers would have run from the Republic just as they had once run from the Federation. But winter had come earlier that year than they'd predicted, and they didn't get to the lowland valleys in time. They couldn't find anything to eat. At some point it was too much work to stay alive. So they decided with the rest of the families that this was as good a place as any to end it, and together they lay down and embraced each other, and perhaps it didn't feel so terrible near the end.

Perhaps it felt just like going to sleep.

Through the entire campaign, she had never once paused to consider just how many people they had killed or displaced. The numbers added up so quickly. Several thousand from famine—

maybe several hundred thousand—and then all the soldiers they'd cut down every time, multiplied across villages.

They were fighting a very different war now, she realized. They were not the liberators but the aggressors. They were the ones to fear.

"War's different when you're not struggling for survival." Kitay must have been thinking the same thing she was. He stood still, hands clutching his torch, eyes fixed on the bodies at his feet. "Victories don't feel the same."

"Do you think it's worth it?" Rin asked him quietly so that Nezha couldn't hear.

"Frankly, I don't care."

"I'm being serious."

He considered for a moment. "I'm glad that someone's fighting Daji."

"But the stakes—"

"I wouldn't think too long about the stakes." Kitay glanced at Nezha, who was still staring at the bodies, eyes wide and disturbed. "You won't like the answers you come up with."

That evening the snowstorms started up again and did not relent for another week. It confirmed what everyone had been afraid of. Winter had arrived early that year, and with a vengeance. Soon enough the tributaries would freeze and the Republican Fleet would be stuck in the north unless they turned back. Their options were dwindling.

Rin paced the *Kingfisher* for days, growing more agitated with every passing minute. She needed to move, fight, attack. She didn't like sitting still. Too easy to fall prey to her own thoughts. Too easy to see the faces in the snow.

Once during a late-night stroll she stumbled across the leadership leaving Jinzha's office. None of them looked happy. Jinzha stormed past her without saying a word; he might not have even noticed her. Nezha lingered behind with Kitay, who wore the peeved, tight-lipped expression that Rin had learned meant that he hadn't gotten his way.

"Don't tell me," Rin said. "We're moving forward."

"We're not just moving forward. He wants us to bypass Baraya entirely and take Boyang." Kitay slammed a fist against the wall. *"Boyang!* Is he mad?"

"Military outpost on the border of Rat Province and Tiger Province," Nezha explained to Rin. "It's not a terrible idea. The Militia used Boyang as a fortress during the first and second invasions. It'll have built-in defenses, make it easier to last out the winter. We can break the siege at Baraya from there."

"But won't someone already be there?" Rin asked. If the Militia was garrisoned anywhere, it had to be in Tiger or Rat Province. Any farther north and they'd be fighting in Sinegard for the heart of Imperial territory.

"If someone's already there, then we'll fight them off," said Nezha.

"In icy waters?" Kitay challenged. "With a cold and miserable army? If we keep going north, we're going to lose every advantage we've gained by coming so far."

"Or we could cement our victory," Nezha argued. "If we win at Boyang, then we control the delta at the Elehemsa tributary, which means—"

"Yes, yes, you cut around the coast to Tiger Province, you can send reinforcements to either through riverways," Kitay said irritably. "Except you're not going to win Boyang. The Imperial Fleet is almost certainly there, but for some reason Jinzha would prefer to pretend it doesn't exist. I don't know what's wrong with your brother, but he's getting reckless and he's making decisions like a madman."

"My brother is not a madman."

"Oh, no, he might be the best wartime general I've ever seen. No one's denying he's done well so far. But he's only good because he's the first Nikara general who's been trained to think from a naval perspective first. Once the rivers freeze, it's going to turn into a ground war, and then he won't have a clue what to do."

Nezha sighed. "Look, I understand your point. I'm just trying to see the best in our situation. If it were up to me I wouldn't go to Boyang, either."

Kitay threw his hands up. "Well, then—"

"This isn't about strategy. It's about pride. It's about showing the Hesperians that we won't back down from a challenge. And for Jinzha, it's about proving himself to Father."

"These things always come back to your father," Kitay muttered. "Both of you need help."

"So say that to Jinzha," Rin said. "Tell him that he's being stupid."

"There's no possible version of that argument that goes well," Nezha said. "Jinzha decides what he wants. You think I can contradict him and get away with it?"

"Well, if *you* can't," Kitay said, "then we're fucked."

An hour later the paddle wheels creaked into motion, carrying the Republican Fleet through a minor mountain range.

"Look up." Kitay nudged Rin's arm. "Does that look normal to you?"

At first it seemed to her like the sun was gradually coming up over the mountains, the lights were so bright. Then the glowing objects rose higher, and she saw that they were lanterns, lighting up the night sky one by one like a field of blooming flowers. Long ribbons dangled from the balloons, displaying a message easily read from the ground.

Surrender means immunity.

"Did they really think that would work?" Rin asked, amused. "That's like screaming, 'Go away, please.'"

But Kitay wasn't smiling. "I don't think it's about propaganda. We should turn back."

"What, just because of some lanterns?"

"It's what the lanterns mean. Whoever set them up is waiting for us in there. And I doubt they have the firepower to match the fleet, but they're still fighting on their own territory, and they know that river. They've staked it out for who knows how long." Kitay motioned to the closest soldier. "Can you shoot?"

"As well as anyone else," said the soldier.

"Good. You see that?" Kitay pointed to a lantern drifting a little farther out from the others. "Can you hit it? I just want to see what happens."

The soldier looked confused, but obeyed. His first shot missed. His second arrow flew true. The lantern exploded into flames, sending a shower of sparks and coal tumbling toward the river.

Rin hit the ground. The explosion seemed impossibly loud for such a small, harmless-looking lantern. It just kept going, too—the lantern must have been loaded with multiple smaller bombs that went off in succession at various points in the air like intricate fireworks. She watched, holding her breath, hoping that none of the sparks would set off the other lanterns. That might spark a chain reaction that turned the entire cliffside into a column of fire.

But the other lanterns didn't go off—the first had exploded too far from the rest of the pack—and at last, the explosions started to fizzle out.

"Told you," Kitay said once they'd ceased completely. He picked himself off the ground. "We'd better go tell Jinzha we need a change in route."

The fleet crept down a secondary channel of the tributary, a narrow pass between jagged cliffs. This would add a week to their travel time, but it was better than certain incineration.

Rin scanned the gray rocks with her spyglass and found crevices, cliff ledges that could easily conceal enemies, but saw no movement. No lanterns. The pass looked abandoned.

"We're not in the clear yet," Kitay said.

"You think they booby-trapped both rivers?"

"They could have," Kitay said. "*I* would."

"But there's nothing here."

A boom shook the air. They exchanged a look and ran out to the prow.

The skimmer at the head of the fleet was in full blaze.

Another boom echoed through the pass. A second ship exploded, sending blast fragments up so high that they crashed across the *Kingfisher*'s deck. Jinzha threw himself to the ground just before a piece of the *Lapwing* could skewer his head to the mast.

"Get down!" he roared. "Everybody down!"

But he didn't have to tell them—even from a hundred yards away the burst impacts shook the *Kingfisher* like an earthquake, knocking everyone on deck off their feet.

Rin crawled as close as she could to the edge of the deck, spyglass in hand. She popped up from the railing and glanced frantically about the mountains, but all she saw were rocks. "There's no one up there."

"Those aren't missiles," Kitay said. "You'd see the heat glow in the air."

He was right—the source of the explosions wasn't from the air; they weren't detonating on the decks. The very water itself was erupting around the fleet.

Chaos took over the *Kingfisher*. Archers scrambled to the top deck to open fire on enemies who weren't there. Jinzha screamed himself hoarse ordering the ships to reverse direction. The *Kingfisher*'s paddle wheels spun frantically backward, pushing the turtle boat out of the tributary, only to bump into the *Crake*. Only after a frantic exchange of signal flags did the fleet begin backtracking sluggishly downriver.

They weren't moving fast enough. Whatever was in the water must have been laced together by some chain reaction mechanism, because a minute later another skimmer went up in flames, and then another. Rin could *see* the explosions starting below the water, each one detonating the next like a vicious streak, getting closer and closer to the *Kingfisher*.

A massive gust of water shot out of the river. At first Rin thought it was just the force of the explosions, but the water spiraled, higher and higher, like a whirlpool in reverse, expanding to surround the warships, forming a protective ring that centered around the *Griffon*.

"What the fuck," Kitay said.

Rin dashed to the prow.

Nezha stood beneath the *Griffon*'s mast, arms stretched out to the tower of water as if reaching for something.

He met Rin's gaze, and her heart skipped a beat.

His eyes were shot through with streaks of ocean blue—not the eerie cerulean gleam of Feylen's glare, but a darker cobalt, the color of old gems.

"You too?" she whispered.

Through the protective wave of water she saw explosions, splashes of orange and red and yellow. Warped by the water, they almost seemed pretty, a painting of angry bursts. Shrapnel seemed frozen in place, arrested by the wall. The water hung in the air for an impossibly long time, steady while the explosives went off one by one in a series of deafening booms that echoed around the fleet. Nezha collapsed on the deck.

The wave dropped, slammed inward, and drenched the wretched remains of the Republican Fleet.

Rin needed to get to the *Griffon*.

The great wave had knocked Nezha's ship and the *Kingfisher* together into a dismal wreck. Their decks were separated by only a narrow gap. Rin took a running start, jumped, skidded onto the *Griffon*'s deck, and ran toward Nezha's limp form.

All the color had drained from his face. He was already porcelain pale, but now his skin looked transparent, his scars cracks in shattered glass over bright blue veins.

She pulled him up into a sitting position. He was breathing, his chest heaving, but his eyes were squeezed shut, and he only shook his head when she tried to ask him questions.

"It hurts." Finally, intelligible words—he twisted in her arms, scrabbling at something on his back. "It *hurts* . . ."

"Here?" She put her hand on the small of his back.

He managed a nod. Then a sudden, wordless scream.

She tried to help him pull his shirt off, but he kept thrashing in her arms, so she had to slice it apart with a knife and yank the pieces away. Her fingers splayed over his exposed back. Her breath caught in her throat.

A massive dragon tattoo, silver and cerulean in the colors of the House of Yin, covered his skin from shoulder to shoulder. Rin couldn't remember seeing it before—but then, she couldn't remember seeing Nezha shirtless before. This tattoo had to be old. She could see a rippled scar arcing down the left side where Nezha had once been pierced by a Mugenese general's halberd. But now the scar glistened an angry red, as if freshly branded into his skin. She couldn't tell if she was imagining things in her panic, but the dragon seemed to undulate under her fingers, coiling and thrashing against his skin.

"It's in my mind." Nezha let out another strangled cry of pain. "It's telling me—*fuck*, Rin . . ."

Pity washed over her, a dark wave that sent bile rising up in her throat.

Nezha gave a low moan. "It's in my head . . ."

She had an idea of what that was like.

He grabbed her wrists with a strength that startled her. "Kill me."

"I can't do that," she whispered.

She *wanted* to kill him. All she wanted was to put him out of his pain. She couldn't bear to look at him like this, screaming like it was never going to end.

But she'd never forgive herself for that.

"What's wrong with him?" Jinzha had arrived. He was looking down at Nezha with a genuine concern that Rin had never seen on his face.

"It's a god," she told him. She was certain. She knew exactly what was going through Nezha's head, because she'd suffered it before. "He called a god and it won't go away."

She had a good idea of what had happened. Nezha, watching

the fleet exploding around him, had tried to protect the *Griffon*. He might not have been aware of what he was doing. He might only remember wishing that the waters would rise, would protect them from the fires. But some god had answered and done exactly what he'd wished, and now he couldn't get it to give him his mind back.

"What are you talking about?" Jinzha knelt down and tried to pull Nezha out of her grasp, but she wouldn't let go.

"Get back."

"Don't you touch him," he snarled.

She smacked his hand away. "I know what this is, I'm the only one who can help him, so if you want him to live, then *get back*."

She was astounded when Jinzha complied.

Nezha thrashed in her arms, moaning.

"So help him," Jinzha begged.

I'm fucking trying, Rin thought. She forced herself to calm. She could think of only one thing that might work. If this was a god—and she was almost certain that this was a god—then the only way to silence its voice was to shut off Nezha's mind, close off his connection to the world of spirit.

"Send a man to my bunk," she told Jinzha. "Cabin three. Have him pull up the second floorboard in the right corner and bring me what's hidden under there. Do you understand?"

He nodded.

"Then hurry."

He stood up and started to bark out orders.

"Get out." Nezha was curling in on himself, muttering. He scrabbled at his shoulder blades, digging his nails deep into his skin, drawing blood. "Get out—*get out!*"

Rin grabbed his wrists and forced them away from his back. He wrenched them, flailing, out of her grip. A stray hand hit her across the chin. Her head whipped to the side. For a moment she saw black.

Nezha looked horrified. "I'm sorry." He clutched at his shoulders like he was trying to shrink. "I'm so sorry."

Rin heard a groaning noise. It came from the deck—the ship was moving, ever so slowly. Something was pushing at it from below. She looked up, and her stomach twisted with dread. The waves were swelling, rising around the *Griffon* like a hand preparing to clench its fingers in a fist. They had grown higher than the mast.

Nezha might lose control entirely. He might drown them all.

"Nezha." She grasped his face between her palms. "Look at me. Please, look at me. *Nezha.*"

But he wouldn't, or couldn't, listen to her—his seconds of lucidity had passed, and it was all she could do to hold him tight so that he wouldn't shred his own skin while he moaned and screamed.

An eternity later she heard footsteps.

"Here," Jinzha said, pressing the packet into her hand. Rin crawled onto Nezha's chest, pinning down his arms with her knees, and tore the packet open with her teeth. Nuggets of opium tumbled out onto the deck.

"What are you doing?" Jinzha demanded.

"Shut up." Rin scraped up two nuggets and held them tightly in her fist.

What now? She didn't have a pipe on hand. She couldn't call the fire to just light up the opium nuggets and make him inhale, and making a fire would take an eternity—everything on deck was drenched.

She had to get the opium into him *somehow*.

She couldn't think of any other way. She balled the nuggets up in her hand and forced them into his mouth. Nezha thrashed harder, choking. She pinched his jaw shut, then wrenched it open and pushed the nuggets farther into his mouth until he swallowed.

She held his arms down and leaned over him, waiting. A minute passed. Then two. Nezha stopped moving. His eyes rolled up into the back of his head. Then he stopped breathing.

"You could have killed him," said the ship's physician.

Rin recognized Dr. Sien from the *Cormorant*. He was the

physician who had tended to Vaisra after Lusan, and appeared to be the only man permitted to treat the members of the House of Yin.

"I just assumed you'd have something for that," she said.

She stood slouched against the wall, exhausted. She was amazed she'd been allowed into Nezha's cabin, but Jinzha had only given her a tight nod on his way out.

Nezha lay still on the bed between them. He looked awful, paler than death, but he was breathing steadily. Every rise and fall of his chest gave Rin a small jolt of relief.

"Lucky we had the drug on hand," said Dr. Sien. "How did you know?"

"Know what?" Rin asked cautiously. Did Dr. Sien know that Nezha was a shaman? Did *anyone*? Jinzha had seemed utterly confused. Was Nezha's secret his alone?

"To give him opium," Dr. Sien said.

That told her nothing. She hazarded a half truth in response. "I've seen this illness before."

"Where?" he asked curiously.

"Um." Rin shrugged. "You know. Down in the south. Opium's a common remedy for it there."

Doctor Sien looked somewhat disappointed. "I have treated the sons of the Dragon Warlord since they were babies. They have never told me anything about Nezha's particular ailment, only that he often feels pain, and that opium is the only way to calm him. I don't know if Vaisra and Saikhara know the cause themselves."

Rin looked down at Nezha's sleeping face. He looked so peaceful. She had the oddest urge to brush the hair back from his forehead. "How long has he been sick?"

"He began having seizures when he was twelve. They've become less frequent as he's gotten older, but this one was the worst I've seen in years."

Has Nezha been a shaman since he was a child? Rin wondered. How had he never told her? Did he not trust her?

"He's in the clear now," said Dr. Sien. "The only thing he'll need is sleep. You don't have to stay."

"It's all right. I'll wait."

He looked uncomfortable. "I don't think General Jinzha—"

"Jinzha knows I just saved his brother's life. He'll permit it, and he's an ass if he doesn't."

Dr. Sien didn't argue. After he closed the door behind him, Rin curled up on the floor next to Nezha's bed and closed her eyes.

Hours later she heard him stirring. She sat up, rubbed the grime from her eyes, and knelt next to him. "Nezha?"

"Hmm." He blinked at the ceiling, trying to make sense of his surroundings.

She touched the back of her finger to his left cheek. His skin was much softer than she had thought it would be. His scars were not raised bumps like she'd expected, but rather smooth lines running across his skin like tattoos.

His eyes had returned to their normal, lovely brown. Rin couldn't help noticing how long his lashes were; they were so dark and heavy, thicker even than Venka's. *It's not fair*, she thought. He'd always been much prettier than anyone had the right to be.

"How are you doing?" she asked.

Nezha blinked several times and slurred something that didn't sound like words.

She tried again. "Do you know what's going on?"

His eyes darted around the room for a while, and then focused on her face with some difficulty. "Yes."

She couldn't hold back her questions any longer. "Do you understand what just happened? Why didn't you tell me?"

All Nezha did was blink.

She leaned forward, heart pounding. "I could have helped you. Or—or you could have helped me. You should have told me."

His breathing started to quicken.

"Why didn't you tell me?" she asked again.

He mumbled something unintelligible. His eyelids fluttered shut.

She nearly shook him by the collar, she was so desperate for answers.

She took a deep breath. *Stop it.* Nezha was in no state to be interrogated now.

She could force him to talk. If she pressed harder, if she yelled at him to give her the truth, then he might tell her everything.

That would be a secret revealed under opium, however, and she would have coerced him when he was in no state to refuse.

Would he hate her for it?

He was only half-conscious. He might not even remember.

She swallowed down a sudden wave of revulsion. No—no, she wouldn't do that to him. She couldn't. She'd have to get her answers another way. Now was not the time. She stood up.

His eyes opened again. "Where are you going?"

"I should let you rest," she said.

He shifted in his bed. "No . . . don't go . . ."

She paused at the door.

"Please," he said. "Stay."

"All right," she said, and returned to his side. She took his hand in hers. "I'm right here."

"What's happening to me?" he murmured.

She squeezed his fingers. "Just close your eyes, Nezha. Go back to sleep."

The remains of the fleet sat stuck in a cove for the next three days. Half the troops had to be treated for burn wounds, and the repulsive smell of rotting flesh became so pervasive that the men took to wrapping cloth around their faces, covering everything except their eyes. Eventually Jinzha had made the decision to administer morphine and medicine only to the men who had a decent chance of survival. The rest were rolled into the mud, facedown, until they stopped moving.

They didn't have time to bury their dead so they dragged them into piles interlaced with parts of irreparable ships to form funeral pyres and set them on fire.

"How strategic," Kitay said. "Don't need the Empire getting hold of good ship wood."

"Do you have to be like this?" Rin asked.

"Just complimenting Jinzha."

Sister Petra stood before the burning corpses and gave an entire funeral benediction in her fluent, toneless Nikara while soldiers stood around her in a curious circle.

"In life you suffered in a world wreaked by Chaos, but you have offered your souls to a beautiful cause," she said. "You died creating order in a land bereft of it. Now you rest. I pray your Maker will take mercy on your souls. I pray that you will come to know the depths of his love, all-encompassing and unconditional."

She then began chanting in a language that Rin didn't recognize. It seemed similar to Hesperian—she could almost recognize the roots of words before they took on an entirely different shape—but this seemed something more ancient, something weighted down with centuries of history and religious purpose.

"Where do your people think souls go when they die?" Rin murmured quietly to Augus.

He looked surprised she had even asked. "To the realm of the Maker, of course. Where do your people think they go?"

"Nowhere," she said. "We disappear back to nothing."

The Nikara spoke of the underworld sometimes, but that was more a folk story than a true belief. No one really imagined they might end up anywhere but in darkness.

"That's impossible," Augus said. "The Maker creates our souls to be permanent. Even barbarians' souls have value. When we die, he refines them and brings them to his realm."

Rin couldn't help her curiosity. "What is that realm like?"

"It's beautiful," he said. "A land utterly without Chaos; without pain, disease, or suffering. It is the kingdom of perfect order that we spend our lives trying to re-create on this earth."

Rin saw the joyful hope beaming out of Augus's face as he spoke, and she knew that he believed every word he was saying.

She was starting to see why the Hesperians clung so fervently to their religion. No wonder they had won converts over so easily during occupation. What a relief it would be to know that at the end of this life there was a better one, that perhaps upon death you might enjoy the comforts you had always been denied instead of fading away from an indifferent universe. What a relief to know that the world was supposed to make sense, and that if it didn't, you would one day be justly compensated.

A line of captains and generals stood before the burning pyre. Nezha was at the end, leaning heavily on a walking stick. It was the first time Rin had seen him in two days.

But when she approached him, he turned to walk away. She called out his name. He ignored her. She dashed forward—he couldn't outrun her, not with his walking stick—and grabbed his wrist.

"Stop running away," she said.

"I'm not running," he said stiffly.

"Then talk to me. Tell me what I saw on the river."

Nezha's eyes darted around at the soldiers standing within earshot. He lowered his voice. "I don't know what you're talking about."

"Don't lie to me. I saw what you did. You're a shaman!"

"Rin, shut up."

She didn't let go of his wrist. "You moved the water at will. I *know* it was you."

He narrowed his eyes. "You didn't see anything, and you won't tell anyone anything—"

"Your secret is safe from Petra, if that's what you're asking," she said. "But I don't understand why you're lying to *me*."

Without responding, Nezha turned and limped briskly away from the pyres. She followed him to a spot behind the charred hull of a transport skimmer. The questions poured out of her in an unstoppable torrent. "Did they teach you at Sinegard? Does Jun know? Is anyone else in your family a shaman?"

"Rin, stop—"

"Jinzha doesn't know, I figured that out. What about your mother? Vaisra? Did he teach you?"

"*I am not a shaman!*" he shouted.

She didn't flinch. "I'm not stupid. I know what I saw."

"Then draw your own conclusions and stop asking questions."

"Why are you hiding this?"

He looked pained. "Because I don't want it."

"You can control the water! You could single-handedly win us this war!"

"It's not that easy, I can't just—" He shook his head. "You saw what happened. It wants to take over."

"Of course it does. What do you think we all go through? So you control it. You get practice at reining it in, you shape it to your own will—"

"Like *you* can?" he sneered. "You're the equivalent of a spiritual eunuch."

He was trying to throw her off, but she didn't let that distract her. "And I would kill to have the fire back. It's difficult, I know, the gods aren't kind—but you *can* control them! I can help you."

"You don't know what you're talking about, shut up—"

"Unless you're just scared, which is no excuse, because men are dying while you're sitting here indulging in your own self-pity—"

"I said *shut up*!"

His hand went into the skimmer's hull, an inch from her head. She didn't flinch. She turned her head slowly, trying to pretend her heart wasn't slamming against her chest.

"You missed," she said calmly.

Nezha pulled his hand away from the hull. Blood trickled down his knuckles from four crimson dots.

She should have been afraid, but when she searched his face, she couldn't find a shred of anger. Just fear.

She had no respect for fear.

"I don't want to hurt you," he said.

"Oh, trust me." Her lip curled. "You couldn't."

CHAPTER 20

"A puzzle for you," said Kitay. "The water erupts around the ships, blows holes in the sides like cannonballs, and yet we never see a hint of an explosion above the water. How does the Militia do this?"

"I assume you're about to tell me," Rin said.

"Come on, Rin, just play along."

She fiddled with the shrapnel fragments strewn across his worktable. "Could have been archers aiming at the base. They could have fixed rockets on the front ends of their arrows?"

"But why would they do that? The deck's more vulnerable than the hull. And we would have seen them in the air if they were alight, which they'd have to be to explode on impact."

"Maybe they found out a way to hide the heat glow," she said.

"Maybe," he said. "But then why the chain reaction? Why start with the skimmers, instead of aiming directly at the *Kingfisher* or the tower ships?"

"I don't know. Scare tactics?"

"That's stupid," he said dismissively. "Here's a hint: The explosives were in the water to begin with. That's why we never saw them. They really were underwater."

She sighed. "And how would they have managed that, Kitay? Why don't you just tell me the answer?"

"Animal intestines," he said happily. He pulled out a rather disgusting translucent tube from under the table, inside of which he'd threaded a thin fuse. "They're completely waterproof. I'm guessing they used cow intestines, since they're longer, but any animal would do, really, because it just has to keep the fuse dry enough to let it burn down. Then they rig up the interior so that slow-burning coils light the fuse on impact. Cool, eh?"

"Sort of like the pig stomachs."

"Sort of. But those were designed to erode over time. Depending on how slow the coils burn, these could keep a fuse dry for days if they were sealed well enough."

"That's incredible." Rin stared at the intestines, considering the implications. The mines were ingenious. The Militia could win riverine battles without even being present, as long as they could guarantee that the Republican Fleet would travel over a given stretch of water.

When had the Militia developed this technology?

And if they had this capability, were any of the river routes safe?

The door slammed open. Jinzha strode in unannounced, holding a rolled-up scroll in one hand. Nezha followed in his wake, still limping on his walking stick. He refused to meet Rin's eye.

"Hello, sir." Kitay cheerfully waved a cow intestine at him. "I've solved your problem."

Jinzha looked repulsed. "What is that?"

"Water mines. It's how they blew up the fleet." Kitay offered the intestine up to Jinzha for inspection.

Jinzha wrinkled his nose. "I'll trust your word for it. Did you figure out how to deactivate them?"

"Yes, it's easy enough if we just puncture the waterproofing. The hard part is finding the mines." Kitay rubbed his chin. "Don't suppose you've got any expert divers on deck."

"I can figure that part out." Jinzha spread his scroll over Kitay's table. It was a closely detailed map of Rat Province, on which he'd circled in red ink a spot just inland of a nearby lake. "I need you to draw up detailed plans for an attack on Boyang. Here's all the intelligence we have."

Kitay leaned forward to examine the map. "This is for a springtime operation?"

"No. We attack as soon as we can get there."

Kitay blinked twice. "You can't be considering taking Boyang with a damaged fleet."

"A full three-fourths of the fleet is serviceable. We've mostly lost skimmers—"

"And the warships?"

"Can be repaired in time."

Kitay tapped his fingers on the table. "Do you have men to man those ships?"

Irritation flickered over Jinzha's face. "We've redistributed the troops. There will be enough."

"If you say so." Kitay chewed at his thumbnail, staring intensely down at Jinzha's scribbles. "There's still a slight problem."

"And what's that?"

"Well, Lake Boyang's an interesting natural phenomenon—"

"Get to the point," Jinzha said.

Kitay traced his finger down the map. "Usually lake water levels go down during the summer and go up during colder seasons. That should advantage deep-hulled ships like ours. But Boyang gets its water source directly from Mount Tianshan, and during the winter—"

"Tianshan freezes," Rin realized out loud.

"So what?" Jinzha asked. "That doesn't mean the lake drains immediately."

"No, but it means the water level goes down every day," Kitay said. "And the shallower the lake, the less mobility your warships have, especially the Seahawks. I'm guessing the mines were put there to stall us."

"Then how long do we have?" Jinzha pressed.

Kitay shrugged. "I'm not a prophet. I'd have to see the lake."

"I told you it's not worth it." Nezha spoke up for the first time. "We should head back south while we still can."

"And do what?" Jinzha demanded. "Hide? Grovel? Explain to Father why we've come home with our tails tucked between our legs?"

"No. Explain about the territory we've taken. The men we've added to our ranks. We regroup, and fight from a position of strength."

"We have plenty of strength."

"The entire Imperial Fleet will be waiting for us in that lake!"

"So we will take it from them," Jinzha snarled. "We're not running home to Father because we were scared of a fight."

This isn't really an argument, Rin thought. Jinzha had made up his mind, and he would shout down anyone who opposed him. Nezha—the younger brother, the inferior brother—was never going to change Jinzha's mind.

Jinzha was hungry for this fight. Rin could read it so clearly on his face. And she could understand why he wanted it so badly. A victory at Boyang might effectively end this war. It might achieve the final and devastating proof of victory that the Hesperians were demanding. It might compensate for Jinzha's latest string of failures.

She'd known a commander who made decisions like that before. His bones, if any had survived incineration, were lying at the bottom of Omonod Bay.

"Aren't your troops worth more than your ego?" she asked. "Don't sentence us to death just because you've been humiliated."

Jinzha didn't even deign to look at her. "Did I authorize you to talk?"

"She has a point," Nezha said.

"I am warning you, brother."

"She's telling the truth," Nezha said. "You're just not listening because you're terrified that someone else is right."

Jinzha strode over to Nezha and casually slapped him across the face.

The crack echoed around the little room. Rin and Kitay sat frozen in their seats. Nezha's head whipped to the side, where it stayed. Slowly he touched his fingers to his cheek, where a red mark was blooming outward over his scars. His chest rose and fell; he was breathing so heavily that Rin thought for sure he would strike back. But he did nothing.

"We could probably get to Boyang in time if we leave immediately," Kitay said neutrally, as if nothing had happened.

"Then we'll set sail within an hour." Jinzha pointed to Kitay. "You get to my office. Admiral Molkoi will give you full access to scout reports. I want attack plans by the end of the day."

"Oh, joy," Kitay said.

"What's that?"

Kitay sat up straight. "Yes, sir."

Jinzha stormed out of the room. Nezha lingered by the doorway, eyes darting between Rin and Kitay as if unsure of whether he wanted to stay.

"Your brother's losing it," Rin informed him.

"Shut up," he said.

"I've seen this before," she said. "Commanders break under pressure all the time. Then they make shitty decisions that get people killed."

Nezha sneered at her, and for an instant he looked identical to Jinzha. "My brother is not Altan."

"You sure about that?"

"Say whatever you want," he said. "At least we're not Speerly trash."

She was so shocked that she couldn't think of a good response. Nezha stalked out and slammed the door shut behind him.

Kitay whistled under his breath. "Lovers' spat, you two?"

Rin's face suddenly felt terribly hot. She sat down beside Kitay and busied herself by pretending to fiddle with the cow intestine. "Something like that."

"If it helps, I don't think you're Speerly trash," he said.

"I don't want to talk about it."

"Let me know if you do." Kitay shrugged. "Incidentally, you could try being more careful about how you talk to Jinzha."

She made a face. "Oh, I'm aware."

"Are you? Or do you *like* not having a seat at the table?"

"Kitay . . ."

"You're a Sinegard-trained shaman. You shouldn't be a foot soldier; it's below you."

She was tired of having that argument. She changed the subject. "Do we really have a chance at taking Boyang?"

"If we work the paddle wheels to death. If the Imperial Fleet is as weak as our most optimistic estimates say." Kitay sighed. "If the heaven and the stars and the sun line up for us and we're blessed by every god in that Pantheon of yours."

"So, no."

"I honestly don't know. There are too many moving pieces. We don't know how strong the fleet is. We don't know their naval tactics. We've probably got superior naval talent, but they'll have been there longer. They'll know the lake terrain. They had time to booby-trap the rivers. They'll have a plan for us."

Rin searched the map, looking for any possible way out. "Then do we retreat?"

"It's too late for that now," Kitay said. "Jinzha's right about one thing: we don't have any other options. We don't have supplies to last out the winter, and chances are if we escape back to Arlong, then we'll lose all the progress we've made—"

"What, we can't just hunker down in Ram Province for a few months? Have Arlong ship up some supplies?"

"And give Daji the entire winter to build a fleet? We've gotten this far because the Empire has never had a great navy. Daji has the men, but we have the ships. That's the only reason we're at parity. If Daji gets three months' leeway, then this is all over."

"Some Hesperian warships would be great right around now," Rin muttered.

"And that's the root of it all." Kitay gave her a wry look. "Jinzha's being an ass, but I think I understand him. He can't afford to look weak, not with Tarcquet sitting there judging his every move. He's got to be bold. Be the brilliant leader his father promised. And we'll blaze forward right with him, because we simply have no other option."

"How many of you can swim?" Jinzha asked.

Prisoners stood miserably in line on the slippery deck, heads bent as rain poured down on them in relentless sheets. Jinzha paced up and down the deck, and the prisoners flinched every time he stopped in front of them. "Show of hands. Who can swim?"

The prisoners glanced nervously at one another, no doubt wondering which response would keep them alive. No hands went up.

"Let me put it this way." Jinzha crossed his arms. "We don't have the rations to feed everyone. No matter what, some of you are going to end up at the bottom of the Murui. It's only a question of whether you want to starve to death. So raise your hand if you'll be useful."

Every hand shot up.

Jinzha turned to Admiral Molkoi. "Throw them all overboard."

The men started screaming in protest. Rin thought for a second that Molkoi might actually comply, and that they would have to watch the prisoners clawing over each other in the water in a desperate bid to survive, but then she realized that Jinzha didn't really intend to execute them.

He was watching to see who wouldn't resist.

After a few moments Jinzha pulled fifteen men out of the line and dismissed the rest to the brig. Then he held up a water mine wrapped in cow intestine and passed it through the line so the men could take a better look at the fuse.

"The Militia's been planting these in the water. You will swim through the water and disable them. You will be tethered to the ship with ropes, and you will be given sharp rocks to do the job. If you find an explosive, cut the intestine and ensure that water floods the tube. Try to escape, and my archers will shoot you in the water. Leave any mines intact, and you will die with us. It's in your interest to be thorough."

He tossed several lines of rope at the men. "Go on, then."

Nobody moved.

"Admiral Molkoi!" Jinzha shouted.

Molkoi signaled to his men. A line of guards strode forward, blades out.

"Do not test my patience," Jinzha said.

The men scrambled hastily for the ropes.

The storms only intensified in the following week, but Jinzha forced the fleet forward to Boyang at an impossible pace. The soldiers were exhausted at the paddle wheels trying to meet his demands. Several prisoners dropped dead after being forced to paddle consecutive shifts without a night's sleep, and Jinzha had their bodies tossed unceremoniously overboard.

"He's going to tire his army out before we even get there," Kitay grumbled to Rin. "Bet you wish we'd brought those Federation troops along now, don't you?"

The army was both weary and hungry. Their rations had been dwindling. They now received dried fish twice a day instead of three times, and rice only once in the evenings. Most of the extra provisions they'd obtained in Xiashang had been lost in the explosions. Morale drooped by the day.

The soldiers became even more disheartened when scouts returned with details of the lake defense. The Imperial Navy was indeed stationed at Boyang, as all of them had feared, and it was far better equipped than Jinzha had anticipated.

The navy rivaled the size of the fleet that had sailed out from Arlong. The one consolation was that it was nowhere near the technological level of Jinzha's armada. The Empress had hastily constructed it in the months since Lusan, and the lack of preparation time showed—the Imperial Fleet was a messy amalgamation of badly constructed new ships, some with unfinished decks, and conscripted old merchant boats with no uniformity of build. At least three were leisure barges without firing capacity.

But they had more ships, and they had more men.

"Ship quality would have mattered if they were out over the ocean," Kitay told Rin. "But the lake will turn this battle into a crucible. We'll all be crammed in together. They just need to get their men to board our ships, and it'll be over. Boyang's going to turn red with blood."

Rin knew one way the Republic could easily win. They wouldn't even have to fire a shot. But Nezha refused to speak to her. She only ever saw him when he came aboard the *Kingfisher* for meetings in his brother's office. Each time they crossed paths he hastily looked away; if she called his name, he only shook his head. Otherwise, they might have been complete strangers.

"Do we expect anything to come of this?" Rin asked.

"Not really," Kitay said. He held his crossbow ready against his chest. "It's just a formality. You know how aristocrats are."

Rin's teeth chattered as the Imperial flagship drifted closer to the *Kingfisher*. "We shouldn't have even come."

"It's Jinzha. Always worried about his honor."

"Yes, well, he might try worrying more about his *life*."

Against the counsel of his admirals, Jinzha had demanded a last-minute negotiation with the flagship of the Imperial Navy. Gentlemen's etiquette, he called it. He had to at least give the Wolf Meat General a chance to surrender. But the negotiation would not even be a charade; it was only a risk, and a stupid one.

Chang En had refused a private meeting. The most he would acquiesce to was a temporary cease-fire and a confrontation held over the open water, and that meant their ships were forced to draw dangerously close together in the final moments before the firing began.

"Hello, little dragon!" Chang En's voice rang over the still, cold air. For once, the waters were calm and quiet. Mist drifted from the surface of Boyang Lake, shrouding the assembled fleets in a cloudy fog.

"You've done well for yourself, Master," Jinzha called. "Admiral of the Imperial Navy, now?"

Chang En spread his arms. "I take what I want when I see it."

Jinzha lifted his chin. "You'll want to take this surrender, then. You can retain your position in my father's employ."

"Oh, fuck off." Chang En's jackal laughter rang high and cruel across the lake.

Jinzha raised his voice. "There's nothing Su Daji can do for you. Whatever she's promised you, we'll double it. My father can make you a general—"

"Your father will give me a cell in Baghra and relieve me of my limbs."

"You'll have immunity if you lay down your arms now. I give you my word."

"A Dragon's word means nothing." Chang En laughed again. "Do you think me stupid? When has Vaisra ever kept a vow he's made?"

"My father is an honorable man who only wants to see this country unified under a just regime," Jinzha said. "You'd serve well by his side."

He wasn't just posturing. Jinzha spoke like he meant it. He seemed to truly hope that he could convince his former master to switch loyalties.

Chang En spat into the water. "Your father's a Hesperian puppet dancing for donations."

"And you think Daji is any better?" Jinzha asked. "Stand by her, and you're guaranteeing years of bloody warfare."

"Ah, but I'm a soldier. Without war, I'm out of a job."

Chang En lifted a gauntleted hand. His archers lifted their bows.

"Negotiator's honor," Jinzha cautioned.

Chang En smiled widely. "Talks are over, little dragon."

His hand fell.

A single arrow whistled through the air, grazed Jinzha's cheek, and embedded itself in the bulkhead behind him.

Jinzha touched his fingers to his cheek, pulled them away, and watched his blood trickle down his pale white hand as if shocked that he could bleed.

"Let you off easy that time," Chang En said. "Wouldn't want the fun to be over too quick."

Lake Boyang lit up like a torch. Flaming arrows, fire rockets, and cannon fire turned the sky red, while below, smokescreens went off everywhere to shroud the Imperial Navy behind a murky gray veil.

The *Kingfisher* sailed straight into the mist.

"Bring me his head," Jinzha ordered, ignoring his men's frantic shouts for him to duck down.

The rest of the fleet spread out across the lake to decrease their vulnerability to incendiary attacks. The closer they clumped, the faster they would all go up in flames. The Seahawks and trebuchets started to return the fire, launching missile after missile over the *Kingfisher* and into the opaque wall of gray.

But their spread-out formation only made the Republicans weak against Imperial swarming tactics. Tiny, patched-up skimmers shot into the gaps between the Republican warships and pushed them farther apart, isolating them to fight on their own.

The Imperial Navy targeted the tower ships first. Imperial skimmers attacked the *Crake* with relentless cannon fire from all sides. Without its own skimmer support, the *Crake* began shaking in the water like a man in his death throes.

Jinzha ordered the *Kingfisher* to come to the *Crake*'s aid, but it, too, was trapped, cut off from the fleet by a phalanx of old Imperial junks. Jinzha ordered round after round of cannon fire to clear them a path. But even the bombed-out junks took up space in the water, which meant all they could do was stand and watch as the Wolf Meat General's men swarmed aboard the *Crake*.

The *Crake*'s men were exhausted and spread too thin to begin with. The Wolf Meat General's men were out for blood. The *Crake* never stood a chance.

Chang En cut a ferocious path through the upper deck. Rin saw him raise a broadsword over his head and cleave a soldier's skull in half so neatly he might have been slicing a winter melon. When another soldier took the opportunity to charge him from behind, Chang En twisted around and shoved his blade so hard into his chest that it came out clean on the other side.

The man was a monster. If Rin hadn't been so terrified for her life, she might have stood there on the deck and simply *watched*.

"Speerly!" Admiral Molkoi pointed to the empty mounted crossbow in front of her, then waved at the *Crake*. "Cover them!"

He said something else, but just then a wave of cannons exploded against the *Kingfisher*'s sides. Rin's ears rang as she made her way to the crossbow. She could hear nothing else. Hands shaking, she fitted a bolt into the slot.

Her fingers kept slipping. Fuck, *fuck*—she hadn't fired a crossbow since the Academy, she'd never served in the artillery, and in her panic she'd almost forgotten completely what to do . . .

She took a deep breath. *Wind it up. Aim.* She squinted at the end of the *Crake*.

The Wolf Meat General had cornered a captain near the edge of the prow. Rin recognized her as Captain Salkhi—she must have been reassigned to the *Crake* after the *Swallow* was lost in the burning channel. Rin's stomach twisted in dread. Salkhi still had her weapon, was still trading blows, but it wasn't even close. Rin could tell that Salkhi was struggling to hold on to her blade while Chang En hacked at her with lackadaisical ease.

Rin's first shot didn't even make it to the deck. She had the direction right but the height wrong; the bolt pinged uselessly off the *Crake*'s hull.

Salkhi brought her sword up to block a blow from above, but Chang En slammed his blade so strongly against hers that she dropped it. Salkhi was weaponless, trapped against the prow. Chang En advanced slowly, grinning.

Rin fitted a new bolt into the crossbow and, squinting, lined up the shot with Chang En's head. She pulled the trigger. The bolt sailed over the burning seas and slammed into the wood just next to Salkhi's arm. Salkhi jumped at the noise, twisted around by instinct...

She had barely turned when the Wolf Meat General slammed his blade into the side of her neck, nearly decapitating her. She dropped to her knees. Chang En reached down and dragged her upright by her collar until she was dangling a good foot above the ground. He pulled her close, kissed her on her mouth, and tossed her over the side of the ship.

Rin stood frozen, watching Salkhi's body disappear under the waves.

Slowly the tide of red took over the *Crake*. Despite a steady stream of arrow fire from the *Shrike* and the *Kingfisher*, Chang En's men dispatched its crew like a pack of wolves falling on sheep. Someone shot a fiery arrow at the masthead, and the *Crake*'s blue and silver flag went up in flames.

The tower ship now turned on its sister ships. Its catapults and incendiaries were no longer aimed at the Imperial Navy, but at the *Kingfisher* and the *Griffon*.

Meanwhile the Imperial skimmers, small as they were, ran circles around Jinzha's fleet. In shallow waters the Republic's massive warships simply didn't have maneuverability. They drifted helplessly like sick whales while a frenzy of smaller fish tore them apart.

"Put us by the *Shrike*," Jinzha ordered. "We have to keep at least one of our tower ships."

"We can't," Molkoi said.

"Why not?"

"The water level's too low on that side of the lake. The *Shrike*'s been grounded. Any farther and we'll get stuck in the mud ourselves."

"Then at least get us away from the *Crake*," Jinzha snapped. "We're about to be stuck as is."

He was right. While Chang En wrestled for control of the *Crake*, the tower ship had drifted so far into shallow waters that it could not extricate itself.

But the *Kingfisher* and the *Griffon* still had more firepower than the Imperial junks. If they just kept shooting, they might cement their hold on the deeper end of the lake. They had to. They had no other way out.

The Imperial Navy, however, had ground to a halt around the *Crake*.

"What on earth are they doing?" Kitay asked.

They didn't seem to be stuck. Rather, Chang En seemed to have ordered his fleet to sit completely still. Rin scoured the decks for any sign of activity—a lantern signal, a flag—and saw nothing.

What were they waiting for?

Something dark flitted across the upper field of her spyglass. She moved her focus up to the mast.

A man stood at the very top.

He wore neither a Militia nor a Republican uniform. He was garbed entirely in black. Rin could hardly make out his face. His hair was a straggly, matted mess that hung into his eyes and his skin was both pale and dark, mottled like ruined marble. He looked as if he'd been dragged up from the bottom of the ocean.

Rin found him oddly familiar, but she couldn't place where she'd seen him before.

"What are you looking at?" Kitay asked.

She blinked into the spyglass, and the man was gone.

"There's a man." She pointed. "I saw him, he was right there—"

Kitay frowned, squinting at the mast. "What man?"

Rin couldn't speak. Dread pooled at the bottom of her stomach. She'd remembered. She knew exactly who that was.

A sudden chill had fallen over the lake. New ice crackled over the water's surface. The *Kingfisher*'s sails suddenly dropped without warning. Its crew looked around the deck, bewildered. No one had given that order. No one had lowered the sails.

"There's no wind," Kitay murmured. "Why isn't there a wind?"

Rin heard a whooshing noise. A blur shot past her eyes, followed by a scream that grew fainter and fainter until it abruptly cut off.

She heard a crack in the air far above her head.

Admiral Molkoi appeared suddenly on the cliff wall, his body bent at grotesque angles like a broken doll on display. He hung there for a moment before skidding down the rock face and into the lake, leaving behind a crimson streak on gray.

"Oh, fuck," Rin muttered.

What seemed like a lifetime ago, she and Altan had freed someone very powerful and very mad from the Chuluu Korikh.

The Wind God Feylen had returned.

The *Kingfisher*'s deck erupted into shouts. Some soldiers ran to the mounted crossbows, aiming their bolts at nothing. Others dropped to the deck and wrapped their arms around their necks as if hiding from wild animals.

Rin finally regained her senses. She cupped her hands around her mouth. "Everybody get belowdecks!"

She grabbed Kitay's arm and pulled him toward the closest hatch, just as a piercing gust of wind slammed into them from the side. They crumpled together against the bulkhead. His bent elbow went straight into her rib cage.

"Ow!" she cried.

Kitay picked himself off the deck. "Sorry."

Somehow they managed to drag themselves toward the hatch and tumbled more than walked down the stairs to the hold, where the rest of the crew huddled in the pitch darkness. There passed a long silence, pregnant with terror. No one spoke a word.

Light filled the chamber. Gust after gust of wind ripped the wooden panels cleanly away from the ship as if peeling off layers of skin, exposing the cowering and vulnerable crew underneath.

The strange man perched before them on the jagged wood like a bird alighting on a branch. Rin could see his eyes clearly now—bright, gleaming, malicious dots of blue.

"What's this?" asked Feylen. "Little rats, hiding with nowhere to go?"

Someone shot an arrow at his head. He waved a hand, annoyed. The arrow jerked to the side and came whistling back into the soldiers' ranks. Rin heard a dull thud. Someone collapsed to the floor.

"Don't be so rude." Feylen's voice was quiet, reedy and thin, but in the eerily still air they could hear every word he said. He hovered above them, effortlessly drifting above the ground, until his bright eyes landed on Rin. "There you are."

She didn't think. If she stopped to think, then fear would catch up. Instead she launched herself at him, screaming, trident in hand.

He sent her spinning to the planks with a flick of his fingers. She got up to rush him again but didn't even get close. He hurled her away every time she approached him, but she kept trying, again and again. If she was going to die, then she'd do it on her feet.

But Feylen was just toying with her.

Finally he yanked her out of the ship and started tossing her around in the air like a rag doll. He could have flung her into the opposite cliff if he'd wanted to; he could have lifted her high into the air and sent her plummeting into the lake, and the only reason he hadn't was that he wanted to play.

"Behold the great Phoenix, trapped inside a little girl," sneered Feylen. "Where is your fire now?"

"You're Cike," Rin gasped. Altan had appealed to Feylen's humanity once. It had almost worked. She had to try the same. "You're one of us."

"A traitor like you?" Feylen chuckled as the winds hurtled her up and down. "Hardly."

"Why would you fight for her?" Rin demanded. "She had you imprisoned!"

"Imprisoned?" Feylen sent Rin tumbling so close to the cliff wall that her fingers brushed the surface before he jerked her back in front of him. "No, that was Trengsin. That was Trengsin and Tyr, the pair of them. They crept up on us in the middle of the night, and still it took them until midday to pin us down."

He let her drop. She hurtled down to the lake, crashed into the water, and was certain she was about to drown just before Feylen yanked her back up by her ankle. He emitted a high-pitched cackle. "Look at you. You're like a little cat. Drenched to the bone."

A pair of rockets shot toward Feylen's head. He swept them carelessly out of the air. They fell to the water and fizzled out.

"Is Ramsa still at it?" he asked. "How adorable. Is he well? We never liked him, we'll rip out his fingernails one by one after this."

He tossed Rin up and down by her ankle as he spoke. She clenched her teeth to keep from crying out.

"Did you really think you were going to fight us?" He sounded amused. "We can't be killed, child."

"Altan stopped you once," she snarled.

"He did," Feylen acknowledged, "but you're a far cry from Altan Trengsin."

He stopped tossing her and held her still in the air, buffeted on all sides by winds so strong she could barely keep her eyes open. He hung before her, arms outstretched, tattered clothes rippling in the wind, daring her to attack and knowing that she couldn't.

"Isn't it fun to fly?" he asked. The winds whipped harder and harder around her until it felt like a thousand steel blades jamming into every tender point of her body.

"Just kill me," she gasped. "Get it over with."

"Oh, we're not going to kill you," said Feylen. "She told us not to do that. We're just supposed to hurt you."

He waved a hand. The winds yanked her away.

She flew up, weightless and utterly out of control, and crumpled against the masthead. She hung there, splayed out like a dissected corpse, for just the briefest moment before the drop. She landed in a crumpled heap on the *Kingfisher*'s deck. She couldn't draw enough breath to scream. Every part of her body was on fire. She tried making her limbs move but they wouldn't obey her.

Her senses came back in blurs. She saw a shape above her, heard a garbled voice shouting her name.

"Kitay?" she whispered.

His arms shifted under her midriff. He was trying to lift her up, but the pain of the slightest movement was enormous. She whimpered, shaking.

"You're okay," Kitay said. "I've got you."

She clutched at his arm, unable to speak. They huddled against each other, watching the planks continue to peel off the *Kingfisher*. Feylen was stripping the fleet apart, bit by bit.

Rin could do nothing but convulse with fear. She squeezed her eyes shut. She didn't want to see. The panic had taken over, and the same thoughts echoed over and over in her mind. *We're going to drown. He's going to rip the ships apart and we will fall into the water and we will drown.*

Kitay shook her shoulder. "Rin. *Look*."

She opened her eyes and saw a shock of white hair. Chaghan had climbed out on the broken planks, was teetering wildly on the edge. He looked like a little child dancing on a roof. Somehow, despite the howling winds, he did not fall.

He lifted his arms above his head.

Instantly the air felt colder. Thicker, somehow. Just as abruptly, the wind stopped.

Feylen hung still in the air, as if some invisible force was holding him in place.

Rin couldn't tell what Chaghan was doing, but she could feel the power in the air. It seemed as if Chaghan had established some invisible connection to Feylen, some thread that only the two of them could perceive, some psychospiritual plane upon which to wage a battle of wills.

For a moment it seemed as if Chaghan was winning.

Feylen's head jerked back and forth; his legs twitched, as if he were seizing.

Rin's grip tightened on Kitay's arm. A bubble of hope rose in her chest.

Please. Please let Chaghan win.

Then she saw Qara hunched over on the deck, rocking back and forth, muttering something over and over under her breath.

"No," Qara whispered. "No, no, *no*!"

Chaghan's head jerked to the side. His limbs moved spastically, flailing without purpose or direction, as if someone who had very little knowledge of the human body was controlling him from somewhere far away.

Qara started to scream.

Chaghan went limp. Then he flew backward, like a little white flag of surrender, so frail that Rin was afraid the winds themselves might rip him apart.

"You think you can contain us, little shaman?" The winds resumed, twice as ferocious. Another gust swept both Chaghan and Qara off the ship into the churning waves below.

Rin saw Nezha watching, horrified, from the *Griffon*, just close enough to be in earshot.

"Do something!" she screamed. "You coward! *Do something!*"

Nezha stood still, his mouth open, eyes wide as if he were trapped. His expression went slack. He did nothing.

A gust of wind tore the *Kingfisher*'s deck in half, ripping the very floorboards from beneath Rin's feet. She fell through the fragments of wood, bumped and dragged along the rough surface, until she hit the water.

Kitay landed beside her. His eyes were closed. He sank instantly. She wrapped her arms around his chest, kicking furiously to keep them both afloat, and struggled to swim toward the *Kingfisher*, but the water kept sweeping them backward.

Her gut clenched.

The current.

Lake Boyang emptied into a waterfall on its southern border. It was a short, narrow drop—small enough that its current had little effect on heavy warships. It was harmless to sailors. Deadly to swimmers.

The *Kingfisher* rapidly receded from Rin's sight as the current dragged them faster and faster to the edge. She saw a rope drifting beside them and grabbed wildly for it, desperate for anything to hang on to.

Miraculously it was still tethered to the fleet. The line went taut; they stopped drifting. She forced her freezing fingers around the cord against the rushing waters, struggled to wrap it in loops around Kitay's torso, her wrists.

Her limbs had gone numb with the cold. She couldn't move her fingers; they were locked tight around the rope.

"Help us!" she screamed. "Someone *help*!"

Someone stood up from the *Kingfisher*'s prow.

Jinzha. Their eyes met across the water. His face was wild, frantic—she wanted to think he had seen her, but maybe his attention was fixed only on his own disappearing chance of survival.

Then he disappeared. She couldn't tell if Jinzha had cut the rope or if he'd simply gone down under another burst of Feylen's attack, but she felt a jerk in the line just before it went slack.

They spun away from the fleet, hurtling toward the waterfall. There was one second of weightlessness, a confusing and delicious moment of utter disorientation, and then the water claimed them.

CHAPTER 21

Rin ran across a dark field, chasing after a fiery silhouette that she was never going to catch. Her legs moved as if treading water—she was too slow, too clumsy, and the farther back she fell from the silhouette, the more her despair weighed her down, until her legs were so heavy that she couldn't run any longer.

"Please," she cried. "Wait."

The silhouette stopped.

When Altan turned around, she saw he was already burning, his handsome features charred and twisted, blackened skin peeled away to reveal pristine, gleaming bone.

And then he was looming above her. Somehow he was still magnificent, still beautiful, even when arrested in the moment of his death. He knelt in front of her, took her face in his scorching hands, and brought their foreheads close together.

"They're right, you know," he said.

"About what?" She saw oceans of fire in his eyes. His grip was hurting her; it always had. She wasn't sure if she wanted him to let her go or to kiss her.

His fingers dug into her cheeks. "It should have been you."

His face morphed into Qara's.

Rin screamed and jerked away.

"Tiger's tits. I'm not that ugly." Qara wiped her mouth with the back of her hand. "Welcome to the world of the living."

Rin sat up and spat out a mouthful of lake water. She was shivering uncontrollably; it took her a while before she could push words out from between numb, clumsy lips. "Where are we?"

"Right by the riverbank," Qara said. "Maybe a mile out of Boyang."

"What about the rest?" Rin fought a swell of panic. "Ramsa? Suni? *Nezha?*"

Qara didn't answer, which meant she didn't know, which meant that the Cike had either gotten away or drowned.

Rin took several deep breaths to keep from hyperventilating. *You don't know they're dead*, she told herself. And Nezha, if anyone, had to be alive. The water protected him like he was its child. The waves would have shielded him, whether he consciously called them or not.

And if the others are dead, there's nothing you can do.

She forced her mind to compartmentalize, to lock up her concern and shove it away. She could grieve later. First she needed to survive.

"Kitay's all right," Chaghan told her. He looked like a living corpse; his lips were the same dark shade as his fingers, which were blue up to the middle joint. "Just went out to get some firewood."

Rin pulled her knees up to her chest, still shaking. "Feylen. That was Feylen."

The twins nodded.

"But why—what was he—" She couldn't understand why they looked so calm. "What's he doing with them? What does he *want*?"

"Well, Feylen the man probably wants to die," Chaghan said.

"Then what does—"

"The Wind God? Who knows?" He rubbed his hands up and down his arms. "The gods are agents of pure chaos. Behind the veil they're balanced, each one against the other sixty-three, but if you set them loose in the material world, they're like water bursting from a broken dam. With no opposing force to check them, they'll do whatever they want. And we never know what the gods want. He'll create a light breeze one day, and then a typhoon the next. The one thing you can expect is inconsistency."

"But then why's he fighting for them?" Rin asked. Wars took consistency. Unpredictable and uncontrollable soldiers were worse than none.

"I think he's scared of someone," Chaghan said. "Someone who can frighten him into obeying orders."

"Daji?"

"Who else?"

"Good, you're awake." Kitay emerged into the clearing, carrying a bundle of sticks. He was drenched, curly hair plastered to his temples. Rin saw bloody scratches all over his face and arms where he'd hit the rocks, but otherwise he looked unharmed.

"You're all right?" she asked.

"Eh. My bad arm's feeling a bit off, but I think it's just the cold." He tossed the bundle onto the damp dirt. "Are you hurt?"

She was so cold it was hard to tell. Everything just felt numb. She flexed her arms, wiggled her fingers, and found no trouble. Then she tried to stand up. Her left leg buckled beneath her.

"*Fuck.*" She ran her fingers over her ankle. It was painfully tender to the touch, throbbing wherever she pressed it.

Kitay knelt down beside her. "Can you wiggle your toes?"

She tried, and they obeyed. That was a minor relief. This wasn't a break, then, just a sprain. She was used to sprains. They'd been common for students at Sinegard; she'd learned how to deal with them years ago. She just needed something like cloth for compression.

"Does anyone have a knife?" she asked.

"I've got one." Qara fished around in her pockets and tossed a small hunting knife in her direction.

Rin unsheathed it, held her trouser leg taut, and cut off a strip at the ankle. She ripped that longways into two pieces and wrapped them tightly around her ankle.

"At least you don't have to worry about keeping it cool," said Kitay.

She didn't have the energy to laugh. She flexed her ankle, and another tremor of pain shot up her leg. She winced. "Are we the only ones who made it out?"

"If only. We've got a bit of company." He nodded to his left.

She followed his line of sight and saw a cluster of bodies—maybe seven, eight—huddled together a little ways up the riverbank. Gray cassocks, light hair. No army uniforms. They were all from the Gray Company.

She could recognize Augus. She wouldn't have been able to pick the rest out of a line—Hesperian faces looked so similar to her, all pale and sparse. She noticed with relief that Sister Petra was not among them.

They looked miserable. They were breathing and blinking—moving just enough that Rin could tell they were alive, but otherwise they seemed frozen stiff. Their skin was pale as snow; their lips were turning blue.

Rin waved at them and pointed to the bundle of sticks. "Come over here. We'll build a fire."

She may as well try to be kind. If she could save some of the Gray Company from freezing to death, they might win her some political capital with the Hesperians when—if—they made it back to Arlong.

The missionaries made no move to get up.

She tried again in slow, deliberate Hesperian. "Come on, Augus. You're going to freeze."

Augus registered no recognition when she called his name. She might not have been speaking Hesperian at all. The others had either blank stares or vaguely frightened expressions on their faces. She shuffled toward them, and several scuttled backward as if scared she might bite them.

"Forget it," Kitay said. "I've been trying to talk to them for the last hour, and my Hesperian is better than yours. I think they're in shock."

"They'll die if they don't warm up." Rin raised her voice. "Hey! Get over here!"

More scared looks. Three of them leveled their weapons at her.

Shit. Rin stumbled back.

They had arquebuses.

"Just leave them," Chaghan muttered. "I'm in no mood to be shot."

"We can't," she said. "The Hesperians will blame us if they die."

He rolled his eyes. "They don't have to know."

"They'll find out if even one of those idiots ever finds their way back."

"They won't."

"But we don't know that. And I'm not killing them to make sure."

If it weren't for Augus, she wouldn't have cared. But blue-eyed devil or not, she couldn't let him freeze to death. He'd been kind to her on the *Kingfisher* when he hadn't needed to be. She felt obligated to return the favor.

Chaghan sighed. "Then leave them a fire. And then we'll move far enough that they'll feel safe to approach it."

That wasn't a bad idea. Kitay had a small flame going within minutes, and Rin waved toward the Hesperians. "We're going to sit over there," she called. "You can use this one."

Again, no response.

But once she'd moved farther down the bank, she saw the Hesperians inching slowly toward the fire. Augus stretched his hands out over the flame. That was a small relief. At least they wouldn't die of sheer idiocy.

Once Kitay had built a second fire, all four of them stripped their uniforms off without self-consciousness. The air was icy around them, but they were colder in their drenched clothes than without. Naked, they huddled together over the flames, holding their hands as close to the fire as they could get without burning their skin. They squatted in silence for what seemed like hours. Nobody wanted to expend the energy to talk.

"We'll get back to the Murui." Rin finally spoke as she pulled her dry uniform back on. It felt good to say the words out loud. It was something pragmatic, a step toward solid action, and it quelled the panic building in her stomach. "There's plenty of loose driftwood around here. We could make a raft and just float downstream through the minor tributaries until we hit the main river, and if we're careful and only move at night, then—"

Chaghan didn't let her finish. "That's a terrible idea."

"And why's that?"

"Because there's nothing to go back to. The Republic's finished. Your friends are dead. Their bodies are probably lining the bottom of Lake Boyang."

"You don't know that," she said.

He shrugged.

"They're *not* dead," she insisted.

"So run back to Arlong, then." He shrugged again. "Crawl into Vaisra's arms and hide as long as you can before the Empress comes for you."

"That's not what I—"

"That's exactly what you want. You can't wait to go groveling to his feet, waiting for your next command like some trained dog."

"I'm not a fucking dog."

"Aren't you?" Chaghan raised his voice. "Did you even put up a fight when they stripped you of command? Or were you glad? Can't give orders for shit, but you love taking them. Speerlies ought to know what it's like to be slaves, but I never imagined you'd enjoy it."

"I was never a slave," Rin snarled.

"Oh, you were, you just didn't know it. You bow down to anyone who will give you orders. Altan pulled on your fucking heartstrings, played you like a lute—he just had to say the right words, make you think he loved you, and you'd run after him to the Chuluu Korikh like an idiot."

"Shut up," she said in a low voice.

But then she saw what this was all about now. This wasn't about Vaisra. This wasn't about the Republic at all. This was about Altan. All these months later, after everything they'd been through, everything was *still* about Altan.

She could give Chaghan that fight. He'd fucking had it coming.

"Like you didn't worship him," she hissed. "I'm not the one who was obsessed with him. You dropped everything to do whatever he asked you to—"

"But I didn't go with him to the Chuluu Korikh," he said. "You did."

"You're blaming *me* for that?"

She knew where this was going. She understood now what Chaghan had been too cowardly to say to her face all these months—that he blamed Altan's death on her.

No wonder he hated her.

Qara put a hand on her brother's arm. "Chaghan, don't."

Chaghan shook her off. "Someone let Feylen loose. Someone got Altan captured. It wasn't me."

"And *someone* told him where the Chuluu Korikh was in the first place," Rin shouted. "Why? Why would you do that? You knew what was in there!"

"Because Altan thought he could raise an army." Chaghan spoke in a loud, flat voice. "Because Altan thought he could reset the course of history to before the Red Emperor and bring the world back to a time when Speer was free and the shamans were at the height of their power. Because for a time that vision was so beautiful that even I believed it. But *I* stopped. I realized that he'd gone crazy and that something had broken and that that path was just going to lead to his death.

"But you? You followed him right to the very end. You let them capture him on that mountain, and you let him die on that pier."

Guilt coiled tightly in Rin's gut, wrenching and horrible. She had nothing to say. Chaghan was right; she'd known he was right, she just hadn't wanted to admit it.

He cocked his head to the side. "Did you think he'd fall in love with you if you just did what he asked?"

"Shut up."

His expression turned vicious. "Is that why you're in love with Vaisra? Do you think he's Altan's replacement?"

She rammed her fist into his mouth.

Her knuckles met his jaw with a crack so satisfying she didn't even feel where his teeth punctured her skin. She'd broken something, and that felt marvelous. Chaghan toppled over like a straw target. She lunged forward, reaching for his neck, but Kitay grabbed her from behind.

She flailed in his grasp. "Let me go!"

His grip tightened. "*Calm down.*"

Chaghan pulled himself to a sitting position and spat a tooth onto the ground. "And she says she's not a dog."

Rin lunged to hit him again, but Kitay yanked her back.

"Let me go!"

"Rin, stop—"

"I'll kill him!"

"No, you won't," Kitay snapped. He forced Rin into a kneeling position and twisted her arms painfully behind her back. He pointed at Chaghan. "You—stop talking. Both of you stop this right now. We're alone in enemy territory. We split up from each other and we're dead."

Rin struggled to break free. "Just let me at him—"

"Oh, go on, let her try," Chaghan said. "A Speerly that can't call fire, I'm *terrified*."

"I can still break your skinny chicken neck," she said.

"Stop talking," Kitay hissed.

"Why?" Chaghan sneered. "Is she going to cry?"

"No." Kitay nodded toward the forest. "Because we're not alone."

Hooded riders emerged from the trees, sitting astride monstrous warhorses much larger than any steed Rin had ever seen. Rin couldn't identify their uniforms. They were garbed in furs and leathers, not Militia greens, but they didn't seem like friends, either. The riders aimed their bows toward them, bowstrings stretched so taut that at this distance the arrows wouldn't just pierce their bodies, they would fly straight through them.

Rin rose slowly, hand creeping toward her trident. But Chaghan grabbed her wrist.

"Surrender now," he hissed.

"Why?"

"Just trust me."

She jerked her hand out of his grip. "*That's* likely."

But even as her fingers closed around her weapon, she knew they were trapped. Those longbows were massive—at this distance, there would be no dodging those arrows.

She heard a rustling noise from upriver. The Hesperians had seen the riders. They were trying to run.

The riders twisted around and loosed their bowstrings into the forest. Arrows thudded into the snow. Rin saw Augus drop to the ground, his face twisted in pain as he clutched at a feathered shaft sticking out of his left shoulder.

But the riders hadn't shot to kill. Most of the arrows were aimed at the dirt around the missionaries' feet. Only a few of the Hesperians were injured. The rest had collapsed from sheer fright. They huddled together in a clump, arms raised high, arquebuses unfired.

Two riders dismounted and wrenched the weapons out of the missionaries' trembling hands. The missionaries put up no resistance.

Rin's mind raced as she watched, trying to find a way out. If she and Kitay could just get to the stream, then the current would carry them downriver, hopefully faster than the horses could run, and if she held her breath and ducked deep enough then she'd have some cover from the arrows. But how to get to the water before the riders loosed their bowstrings? Her eyes darted around the clearing—

Put your hands up.

No one spoke the order but she heard it—a deep, hoarse command that resonated loudly in her mind.

A warning shot whistled past her, inches from her temple. She ducked down, grabbed a clump of mud to fling at the riders. If she could distract them, just for a few seconds . . .

The riders turned their bows back toward her.

"Stop!" Chaghan ran out in front of the riders, waving his arms over his head.

A sound like a gong echoed through the clearing, so loud that Rin felt her temples vibrating.

A flurry of images from someone else's imagination forced their way into her mind's eye. She saw herself on her knees, arms up. She saw herself stuck through with arrows, bleeding from a dozen different wounds. She saw a vast and dizzying landscape—a sparse steppe, desert dunes, a thunderous stampede as riders set out on horseback to seek something, destroy something . . .

Then she saw Chaghan, facing the riders with his fists clenched, felt the sheer *intent* radiating out from his form—*we're here in peace we're here in peace I am one of you we're here in peace*—and she realized that this wasn't just some psychospiritual battle of wills.

This was a conversation.

Somehow, the riders could communicate without moving their lips. They conveyed images and fragments of intent without spoken language directly into their receivers' minds. Rin glanced at Kitay, checking to make sure that she hadn't gone mad. He was staring at the riders, eyes wide, hands trembling.

Stop resisting, boomed the first voice.

Frantic babbles erupted from the bound Hesperians. Augus doubled forward and yelled, clutching his head. He was hearing it, too.

Whatever Chaghan said in response, it was enough to persuade the riders that they weren't a threat. Their leader lifted a hand and barked out a command in a language Rin didn't understand. The riders lowered their bows.

The leader swung himself off his horse in one fluid motion and strode toward Chaghan.

"Hello, Bekter," Chaghan said.

"Hello, cousin," Bekter responded. He'd spoken in Nikara; his words came out harsh and twisted. He wrenched sounds out of the air like he was ripping meat from bone, as if he were unused to spoken language.

"*Cousin?*" Kitay echoed out loud.

"We're not proud of it," Qara muttered.

Bekter shot her a quick smile. Whatever passed mentally between them happened too fast for Rin to understand, but she caught the gist of it—something lewd, something violent, horrid, and dripping in contempt.

"Go fuck yourself," Qara said.

Bekter called something to his riders. Two of them jumped to the ground, wrenched Chaghan's and Qara's arms behind their backs, and forced them to their knees.

Rin snatched up her trident, but arrows dotted the ground around her before she could move.

"You won't get a third warning," Bekter said.

She dropped the trident and placed her hands behind her head. Kitay did the same. The riders tied Rin's hands together, pulled her to her feet, and dragged her, stumbling miserably, toward Bekter so that the four of them knelt before him in a single line.

"Where is he?" Bekter asked.

"You're going to have to be more specific," Kitay said.

"The Wind God. I believe the mortal's name is Feylen. We are hunting him. Where has he gone?"

"Downriver, probably," said Kitay. "If you know how to fly, you might catch up!"

Bekter ignored him. His eyes roved over Rin's body, lingering in places that made her flinch. Hazy images came unbidden to her mind, too blurry for her to see more than shattered limbs and flesh on flesh.

"Is this the Speerly?" he asked.

"You can't hurt her," Chaghan said. "You're sworn."

"Sworn not to hurt you. Not them."

"They're under my charge. This is my territory."

Bekter laughed. "You've been gone a long time, little cousin. The Naimads are weak. The treaty is shattering. The Sorqan Sira's decided to come down and clean up your mess."

"'Charge'?" Rin repeated. "'Treaty'? Who are you people?"

"They're watchers," Qara murmured.

"Of what?"

"People like you, little Speerly." Bekter pulled off his hood.

Rin flinched back, repulsed.

His face was covered in mottled burns, ropey and raised, a mountainous terrain of pain running from cheek to cheek. He smiled at her, and the way the scars crinkled around the sides of his mouth was a terrible sight.

She spat at his feet. "Had a bad encounter with a Speerly, didn't you?"

Bekter smiled again. More images invaded her mind. She saw men on fire. She saw blood staining the dirt.

Bekter leaned in so close that she could feel his breath, hot and rank on her neck. "I survived it. He did not."

Before Rin could speak, a hunting horn pierced the air.

The thunder of hooves followed. Rin craned her neck to look over her shoulder. Another group of riders approached the clearing, this one far larger than Bekter's contingent. They formed a circle with their horses, surrounding them.

Their ranks parted. A slight little woman, reaching no higher than Rin's elbow, moved through the lines.

She walked the way Chaghan and Qara did. She was delicate, birdlike, as if she were some ethereal creature for whom being anchored to the earth was a mere inconvenience. Her cloud-white hair fell just past her waist, looped in two intricate braids interwoven with what looked like shells and bone.

Her eyes were the opposite of Chaghan's—darker than the bottom of a well, and black all the way through.

"Bow," Qara muttered. "She is the Sorqan Sira."

Rin ducked her head. "Their leader?"

"Our aunt."

The Sorqan Sira clicked her tongue as she strode past Chaghan and Qara, who knelt with their eyes cast down as if in shame. Kitay she ignored completely.

She stopped in front of Rin. Her bony fingers moved over Rin's face, gripping at her chin and cheekbones.

"How curious," she said. Her Nikara was fluent but oddly syncopated in a way that made her words sound laced with poetry. "She looks like Hanelai."

The name meant nothing to Rin, but the riders tensed.

"Where did they find you?" the Sorqan Sira asked. When Rin didn't answer, she smacked her cheek lightly. "I am talking to you, girl. Speak."

"I don't know," Rin said. Her knees throbbed. She wished desperately that they would let her stop kneeling.

The Sorqan Sira dug her fingernails into Rin's cheek. "Where did they hide you? Who found you? Who protected you?"

"I don't know," Rin repeated. "Nowhere. No one."

"You are lying."

"She's not," Chaghan said. "She didn't know what she was until a year ago."

The Sorqan Sira gave Rin a long, suspicious look, but released her.

"Impossible. The Mugenese were supposed to have killed you off, but you Speerlies keep turning up like rats."

"Chaghan has always drawn Speerlies like moths to a candle," Bekter said. "You remember."

"Shut up," Chaghan said hoarsely.

Bekter smiled widely. "Remember what you wrote in your letters? *The Speerly has suffered. The Mugenese were not kind. But he survived, and he is powerful.*"

Was he talking about Altan? Rin fought the urge to vomit.

"*He has his mind for now but he is hurting.*" Bekter's voice took on a high, mocking pitch. "*But I can fix him. Give him time. Don't make me kill him. Please.*"

Chaghan jammed his elbow backward into Bekter's stomach. In an instant Bekter seized Chaghan's bound wrists and twisted them so far behind his back that Rin thought surely he'd broken them.

Chaghan's mouth opened in a silent scream.

A sound like a thunderclap ricocheted through Rin's mind. She saw the riders wince; they'd heard it, too.

"Enough of this," said the Sorqan Sira.

Bekter released Chaghan, whose head lurched forward as if he'd been shot.

The Sorqan Sira bent down before him and brushed his hair back behind his ears, petting it softly like a mother grooming a misbehaved child.

"You've failed," she said softly. "Your duty was to observe and cull when necessary. Not to join their petty wars."

"We tried to stay neutral," Chaghan said. "We didn't intervene, we never—"

"Don't lie to me. I know what you've done." The Sorqan Sira stood up. "There will be no more of the Cike. We are putting an end to your mother's little experiment."

"Experiment?" Rin echoed. "What experiment?"

The Sorqan Sira turned toward her, eyebrows raised. "Precisely what I said. The twins' mother, Kalagan, thought it would be unjust to deny the Nikara access to the gods. The Cike was Kalagan's last chance. She has failed. I have decided there will be no more shamans in the Empire."

"Oh, *you've* decided?" Rin struggled to stand up straight. She still didn't fully understand what was happening, but she didn't need to. The dynamic of this encounter had become abundantly clear. The riders thought her an animal to be put down. They thought they could determine who had access to the Pantheon.

The sheer arrogance of that made her want to spit.

The Sorqan Sira looked amused. "Did I upset you?"

"We don't need your permission to exist," she snapped.

"Yes, you do." The Sorqan Sira cast her a disdainful smile. "You're little children, grasping in a void that you don't understand for toys that don't belong to you."

Rin wanted to slap the contempt off of her face. "The gods don't belong to you, either."

"But we *know* that. And that is the simple difference. You Nikara are the only people foolish enough to call the gods into this world. We Ketreyids would never dream of the folly your shamans commit."

"Then that makes you cowards," Rin said. "And just because you won't call them down doesn't mean that we can't."

The Sorqan Sira threw her head back and began to laugh—a harsh, cackling crow's laugh. "My word. You sound just like them."

"Who?"

"Has no one ever told you?" The Sorqan Sira grasped Rin's face in her hands once more. Rin flinched away, but the Sorqan Sira's fingers tightened around her cheeks. She pressed her face against Rin's, so close that all Rin could see was those dark, obsidian eyes. "No? Then I'll show you."

Visions pierced Rin's mind like knives forced into her temples.

She stood on a desert steppe, in the shadow of dunes stretching out as far as she could see. Sand whipped around her ankles. The wind struck a low and melancholy note.

She looked down at herself and saw white braids woven with shells and bone. She realized she was in the memory of a much younger Sorqan Sira. To her left she saw a young woman who had to be the twins' mother, Kalagan—she had the same high cheekbones as Qara, the same shock of white hair as Chaghan.

Before them stood the Trifecta.

Rin stared at them in wonder.

They were so *young*. They couldn't have been much older than she was. They could have been fourth-years at Sinegard.

Su Daji as a girl was already impossibly, bewitchingly beautiful. She emanated sex even when she was standing still. Rin saw it in the way she shifted her hips back and forth, the way she swept her curtain of hair over her shoulders.

To Daji's left stood the Dragon Emperor. His face was stunningly, shockingly familiar. Sharp angles, a long straight nose, thick and somber eyebrows. Strikingly handsome, pale and perfectly sculpted in a way that didn't seem human.

He had to be from the House of Yin.

He was a younger, gentler Vaisra. He was Nezha without his scars and Jinzha without his arrogance. His face could not be called kind; it was too severe and aristocratic. But it was an open, honest, and earnest face. A face she immediately trusted, because she couldn't see a way that this man was capable of any evil.

She understood now what they meant in the old stories when they said that soldiers defected to him in droves and knelt at his feet. She would have followed him anywhere.

Then there was Jiang.

If she had ever doubted that her old master could possibly be the Gatekeeper, there was no mistaking his identity now. His hair, shorn close to his ears, was still the same unnatural white, his face as ageless as it had been when she'd met him.

But when he spoke, and his face twisted, he became a complete stranger.

"You don't want to fight us on this," he said. "You're running out of time. I'd clear out while you still can."

The Jiang that Rin had known was placid and cheerful, drifting through the world with a kind of detached curiosity. He spoke softly and whimsically, as if he were a curious bystander to his own conversations. But this younger Jiang had a harshness to his face that startled Rin, and every word he spoke dripped with a casual cruelty.

It's the fury, she realized. The Jiang she knew was utterly peaceful, immune to insult. This Jiang was consumed with some kind of poisonous wrath that radiated from within.

Kalagan's voice trembled with anger. "Our people have claimed the area north of the Baghra Desert for centuries. Your Horse Warlord has forgotten himself. This is not diplomacy, it is sheer arrogance."

"Perhaps," Jiang said. "You still didn't have to dismember his son and send the fingers back to the father."

"He dared to threaten us," said Kalagan. "He deserved what he got."

Jiang shrugged. "Maybe he did. I never liked that kid. But do you know what our dilemma is, dearest Kalagan? We need the Horse Warlord. We need his troops and his warhorses, and we can't get those if they're too busy running around the Baghra Desert fending off your arrows."

"Then he should retreat," said the Sorqan Sira.

Jiang inspected his fingernails. "Or perhaps we'll make *you* retreat. Would it be so hard for you to just go settle somewhere else? Ketreyids are all nomads, aren't you?"

Kalagan lifted her spear. "You *dare*—"

Jiang wagged a finger. "I wouldn't."

"Do you think this is wise, Ziya?"

A girl emerged from the ranks of the riders. She bore a remarkable resemblance to Chaghan, but she stood taller, stronger, and her face was flushed with more color.

"Get back, Tseveri," said the Sorqan Sira, but Tseveri walked toward Jiang until they were separated by only inches.

"Why are you doing this?" she asked softly.

"Politics, really," Jiang said. "It's nothing personal."

"We taught you everything you know. Three years ago we took

pity on you and took you in. We've sheltered you, hidden you, healed you, given you secrets no Nikara has ever obtained. Aren't we family to you?"

She spoke to Jiang intimately, like a sister. But if Jiang was bothered, he hid it well behind a mask of amused indifference.

"Would a simple thank-you suffice?" he asked. "Or did you also want a hug?"

"Be careful who you turn your back on," warned Tseveri. "You don't need the Horse Warlord, not truly. You still need us. You need our wisdom. There's so much you still don't know—"

"I doubt it." Jiang sneered. "I've had enough of playing philosopher with a people so timid they shrink from the Pantheon. I need hard power. Military might. The Horse Warlord can give us that. What can you give me? Endless conversations about the cosmos?"

"You've no idea how ignorant you still are." Tseveri gave him a pitying look. "I see you've anchored yourselves. Did it hurt?"

Rin had no idea what that meant, but she saw Daji flinch.

"Don't be surprised," Tseveri said. "You're so obviously bound. I can see it shining out of you. You think it makes you strong, but it's going to destroy you."

"You don't know what you're talking about," Jiang said.

"No?" Tseveri tilted her head. "Then here's a prophecy for you. Your bond will shatter. You will destroy one another. One will die, one will rule, and one will sleep for eternity."

"That's impossible," Daji scoffed. "None of us can die. Not while the others live."

"That's what you think," said Tseveri.

"Enough of this," Riga said. Rin was stricken by how much he even *sounded* like Nezha. "This isn't what we came for."

"You came to start a war you don't need to fight. And you ignore me at your peril." Tseveri reached for Jiang's hand. "Ziya. Please. Don't do this to me."

Jiang refused to meet her eye.

Daji yawned, making a desultory attempt to cover her mouth

with the back of a dainty pale hand. "We can do this the easy way. Nobody needs to get hurt. Or we could just start fighting."

Kalagan leveled her spear at her. "Don't *presume*, little girl."

A crackling energy charged the air. Even through the distance of memory Rin could sense how the fabric of the desert had changed. The boundaries of the material world were thinning, threatening to warp and give way to the world of spirit.

Something was happening to Jiang.

His shadow writhed madly against the bright sand. The shape was not Jiang's own, but something terrible—a myriad of beasts, so many in size and form, shifting faster and faster, with a growing desperation, as if frantic to break free.

The beasts were in Jiang, too. Rin could see them, shadows rippling under his skin, horrible patches of black straining to get out.

Tseveri cried something in her own language—a plea or an incantation, Rin didn't know, but it sounded like despair.

Daji laughed.

"*No!*" Rin shouted, but Jiang didn't hear her—*couldn't* hear her, because all of this had already come to pass. All she could do was watch helplessly as Jiang forced his hand into Tseveri's rib cage and ripped out her still-beating heart.

Kalagan screamed.

"That's enough," said the present Sorqan Sira, and the last things Rin saw were Daji whipping her needles toward the Ketreyids, Jiang and his beasts pinning down the Sorqan Sira, and Riga, standing impassively, watching the carnage with that wise and caring face, arms raised beatifically as if he blessed the slaughter with his presence.

"We gave the Nikara the keys to the heavens, and they stole our land and murdered my daughter." The Sorqan Sira's voice was flat, emotionless, as if she were merely recounting an interesting anecdote, as if her pain had already been processed so many times she could not feel it anymore.

Rin bent over on her hands and knees, gasping. She couldn't

scrub the image of Jiang from her mind. Jiang, her *master*, cackling with his hands covered with blood.

"Surprised?" asked the Sorqan Sira.

"But I *knew* him," Rin whispered. "I know what he's like, he's not like *that* . . ."

"How would you know what the Gatekeeper is like?" The Sorqan Sira sneered. "Have you ever asked him about his past? Did you have *any* idea?"

The worst part was that it all made *sense*—the truth had dawned on Rin, awful and bitter, and the mystery of Jiang was clear to her now; she knew why he'd fled, why he'd hidden in the Chuluu Korikh.

He must have been starting to remember.

The man she had met at Sinegard had been no more than a shade of a person; a pathetic, affable shade of a personality suppressed. He had not been pretending. She was certain of that. No one could pretend that well.

He had simply not *known*. The Seal had stolen his memories, just like it would one day steal hers, and hidden them behind a wall in his mind.

Was it better now that he remained in his stone prison, suspended halfway between amnesia and sanity?

"You see now. You'll understand if we'd rather put an end to you." The Sorqan Sira nodded to Bekter.

Her unspoken command rang clear in Rin's mind. *Kill them.*

"Wait!" Rin struggled to her feet. "Please—you don't have to—"

"I don't entertain begging, girl."

"I'm not begging, I'm bartering," Rin said quickly. "We have the same enemy. You want Daji dead. You want revenge. Yes? So do I. Kill us, and you've lost an ally."

The Sorqan Sira scoffed. "We can kill the Vipress easily enough ourselves."

"No, you can't. If you could, she'd be dead already. You're scared of her." Rin thought frantically as she spoke, spinning an argument together from thin air. "In twenty years you haven't even *ventured* south, haven't attempted to take back your lands. Why? Because you know the Vipress will destroy you. You've lost to her before. You don't dare to face her again."

The Sorqan Sira's eyes narrowed, but she said nothing. Rin felt a desperate stab of hope. If her words angered the Ketreyids, that meant she had touched on a fragment of the truth. It meant she still had a chance of convincing them.

"But you've seen what I can do," she continued. "You know that I could fight her, because you know what Speerlies are capable of. I've faced the Empress before. Set me free, and I'll fight your battles for you."

The Sorqan Sira shot Chaghan a question in her own language. They conversed for a moment. Chaghan's words sounded hesitant and deferential; the Sorqan Sira's harsh and angry. Their eyes darted once in a while to Kitay, who shifted uncomfortably, confused.

"She *will* do it," Chaghan said finally in Nikara. "She won't have a choice."

"I'll do what?" Rin asked.

They ignored her to keep arguing.

"This is not worth the risk," Bekter interrupted. "Mother, you know this. Speerlies go mad faster than the rest."

Chaghan shook his head. "Not this one. She's stable."

"No Speerlies are stable," said Bekter.

"She fought it," Chaghan insisted. "She's off opium. She hasn't touched it in months."

"An adult Speerly who doesn't smoke?" The Sorqan Sira cocked her head. "That'd be a first."

"It makes no difference," Bekter said. "The Phoenix will take her. It always does. Better to kill her now—"

Chaghan spoke over him, appealing directly to his aunt. "I have seen her at her worst. If the Phoenix could, then it would have already."

"He's lying," Bekter snarled. "Look at him, he's pathetic, he's protecting them even now—"

"Enough," said the Sorqan Sira. "I'll have the truth for myself."

Again, she grasped the sides of Rin's face. "Look at me."

Her eyes seemed different this time. They had become dark and hollow expanses, windows into an abyss that Rin did not want to see. Rin let out an involuntary whine, but the Sorqan Sira's fingers tightened under her jaws. "*Look.*"

Rin felt herself pitching forward into that darkness. The Sorqan Sira wasn't forcing a vision into her mind, she was forcing Rin to dredge one up herself. Memories loomed before her, haphazard and jagged fragments of visions that she'd done her best to bury. She was wrought in a sea of fire, she was pitching backward into black water, she was kneeling at Altan's feet, blood pooling in her mouth.

The Seal loomed over her.

It had grown. It was thrice as large as she had last seen it, an expanded and hypnotic array of colors, swirling and pulsing like a heartbeat, arranged like a character she still could not recognize.

Rin could *feel* Daji's presence inside it—sickening, addictive, seductive. Whispers sounded all about her, as if Daji were murmuring into her ear, promising her wonderful things.

I'll take you away from this. I'll give you everything you've ever wanted. I'll give him back to you.

You only have to give in.

"What is this?" the Sorqan Sira murmured.

Rin couldn't answer.

The Sorqan Sira let go of her face.

Rin dropped to her knees, hands splayed against solid ground. The sun spun in circles above her.

It took her a moment to realize the Sorqan Sira was laughing.

"She's afraid of you," the Sorqan Sira whispered. "Su Daji is afraid of *you*."

"I don't understand," Rin said.

"This changes everything." The Sorqan Sira barked a command. The riders standing nearest Rin seized her by the arms and hoisted her to her feet.

"What are you doing?" Rin struggled against their grip. "You can't kill me, you still need me—"

"Oh, child. We are not going to kill you." The Sorqan Sira reached out and stroked the backs of her fingers down Rin's cheek. "We are going to fix you."

CHAPTER 22

The Ketreyids tied Rin against a tree, though this time they were considerably gentler. They placed her bound wrists in her lap instead of twisting them painfully behind her back, and they left her legs untied once the extent of her ankle injury became obvious.

She couldn't have run far even without a sprained ankle. Her limbs tingled from fatigue, her head was swimming, and her vision had started going fuzzy. She slouched back against the tree, eyes closed. She couldn't remember the last time she'd eaten anything.

"What are they doing?" Kitay asked.

Rin focused with difficulty on the clearing. The Ketreyids were arranging wooden poles to create a latticed dome-like structure, just large enough to accommodate two people. When the dome was finished, they draped thick blankets over its top until it was completely covered.

The Ketreyids had also added logs to their measly campfire. It was a roaring bonfire now, flames leaping higher than the Sorqan Sira's head. Two riders carried a pile of rocks in from the shore, all at least the size of Rin's head, and placed them over the flames one by one.

"They're preparing for a sweat," Chaghan explained. "That's what the rocks are for. You'll go inside that yurt with the Sorqan Sira. They'll put the rocks inside one by one and pour water over them while they're hot. That fills the yurt with steam and drives the temperatures up to just under what will kill you."

"They're going to steam me like a fish," Rin said.

"It's risky. But that's the only way to draw something like the Seal out. What Daji's left inside you is like a venom. Over time it will keep festering in your subconscious and corrupt your mind."

She blinked in alarm. "You could have told me that!"

"I didn't think it was worth scaring you when I couldn't do anything about it."

"You weren't going to tell me I was going mad?"

"You would have noticed eventually."

"I hate you," she said.

"Calm down. The sweat will extract the venom from your mind." Chaghan paused. "Well. It'll give you a better chance than anything else. It doesn't always work."

"That's optimistic," Kitay said.

Chaghan shrugged. "If it doesn't work, the Sorqan Sira will put you out of your misery."

"That's nice of her," Rin mumbled.

"She'd do it swiftly," Qara assured her. "Quick slice to the arteries, so clean you'll barely even feel it. She's done it before."

"Can you walk?" asked the Sorqan Sira.

Rin jerked awake. She didn't remember dozing off. She was still exhausted; her body felt like it was weighted down with rocks.

She blinked the sleep from her eyes and glanced around. She was lying curled on the ground. Thankfully, someone had untied her arms. She pulled herself to a sitting position and stretched the cricks out of her back.

"Can you walk?" the Sorqan Sira repeated.

Rin flexed her ankle. Pain shot up her leg. "I don't think so."

The Sorqan Sira raised her voice. "Bekter. Lift her."

Bekter glanced down at Rin with a look of distaste.

"I hate you, too," she told him.

She was sure that he would lash out. But the Sorqan Sira's command must truly have been law, because he simply knelt down, pulled her into his arms, and carried her to the yurt. He made no effort to be gentle. She jostled uncomfortably in his arms, and her sprained ankle smashed against the yurt's entrance when he deposited her inside.

She bit back a cry of pain to deny him the pleasure of hearing it. He shut the tent flap on her without another word.

The yurt's interior was pitch-black. The Ketreyids had padded its lattice sides with so many layers of blankets that not a single ray of light could penetrate the exterior.

The air inside was cold, silent, and peaceful, like the belly of a cave. If Rin didn't know where she was, she would have thought the walls were made of stone. She exhaled slowly, listening as her breath filled the empty space.

Light flooded the yurt as the Sorqan Sira entered through the flap. She carried a bucket of water in one hand and a ladle in the other.

"Lie down," she told Rin. "Get as close as you can to the walls."

"Why?"

"So you don't fall onto the rocks when you faint."

Rin curled into the corner, back braced against the taut cloth, and pressed her cheek to the cool dirt. The tent flap closed. Rin heard the Sorqan Sira crawling across the yurt to sit right beside her.

"Are you ready?" the Sorqan Sira asked.

"Do I have a choice?"

"No. But you should prepare your mind. This will go badly if you are frightened." The Sorqan Sira called to the riders outside, "First stone."

A shovel appeared through the flap, bearing a single rock glowing a bright, angry red. The rider outside tipped the rock over into a muddy bed at the center of the yurt, withdrew the shovel, and shut the flap.

In the darkness, Rin heard the Sorqan Sira dip the ladle into the water.

"May the gods hear our prayers." Water splashed over the rock. A loud hiss filled the yurt. "May they grant our wishes to commune."

A wave of steam hit Rin's nose. She fought the urge to sneeze.

"May they clear our eyes to see," said the Sorqan Sira. "Second rock."

The rider deposited another rock into the mud bed. Another splash, another hiss. The steam grew thicker and hotter.

"May they give us the ears to hear their voices."

Rin was starting to feel light-headed. Panic clawed at her chest. She could barely breathe. Even though her lungs filled with air, she felt as if she were drowning. She couldn't lie still any longer. She pawed at the edges of the tent, desperate for a whiff of cold air, anything . . . the steam was in her face now, every part of her was burning, she was being boiled alive.

The rocks kept coming—a third, a fourth, a fifth. The steam became unbearable. She tried covering her nose with her sleeve, but that, too, was damp, and trying to breathe through it was the worst form of torture.

"Empty your mind," the Sorqan Sira ordered.

Rin's heart pumped furiously, so hard that she could feel it in her temples.

I'm going to die in here.

"Stop resisting," the Sorqan Sira said urgently. "Relax."

Relax? The only thing Rin wanted to do then was scramble out of the yurt. She didn't care if she burned her feet on the rocks, didn't care if she had to slip through the mud, she just wanted to get out into the open air where she could breathe.

Only years of meditation practice under Jiang stopped her from getting up and running out.

Breathe.

Just breathe.

She could feel her heartbeat slowing, crawling nearly to a stop.

Her vision swirled and sparked. She saw little lights in the darkness, candles that flickered in the edges of her sight, stars that winked away when she looked upon them . . .

The Sorqan Sira's breath tickled her ear. "Soon you will see many things. The Seal will tempt you. Remember that none of what you see is real. This will be a test of your resolve. Pass, and you will emerge intact, in full possession of your natural abilities. Fail, and I will cut your throat."

"I'm ready," Rin gasped. "I know pain."

"This isn't pain," said the Sorqan Sira. "The Vipress never makes you suffer. She fulfills your wishes. She promises you peace when you know you ought to be fighting a war. That's worse."

She pressed her thumb against Rin's forehead. The ground tipped away.

Rin saw a stream of bright colors, bold and gaudy, which resolved themselves into definable shapes only when she squinted. Reds and golds became streamers and firecrackers; blues and purples became fruits, berries, and cups of pouring wine.

She looked around, dazed. She was standing in a massive banquet hall. It was twice the size of the Autumn Palace's throne room, packed with long tables at which sat gorgeously dressed guests. She saw platters of dragon fruit carved like flowers, soup steaming from turtle shells, and entire roasted pigs sitting on tables of their very own, with attendants designated to carve away pieces of meat for the guests. Sorghum wine ran down gilded trenches carved into the table sides so that the diners could fill their cups themselves whenever they wished.

Faces she knew drifted in and out of her sight, faces she hadn't seen for so long that they felt like they were from a different lifetime. She saw Tutor Feyrik sitting two tables away, meticulously picking the bones from a cut of fish. She saw Masters Irjah and Jima, laughing at the high table with the rest of the Academy masters.

Kesegi waved at her from his seat. He was unchanged since

she'd last seen him—still ten years old, tawny-skinned, all knees and elbows. She stared at him. She'd forgotten what a wonderful smile he had, cheeky and irreverent.

She saw Kitay, dressed in a general's uniform. His wiry hair was grown long, pulled into a bun at the back of his head. He was deep in conversation with Master Irjah. When he caught her eye, he winked.

"Hello, you," said a familiar voice.

She turned, and her heart caught in her throat.

Of course it was Altan. It was *always* Altan, lurking behind every corner of her mind, haunting every decision she made.

But this was an Altan who was alive and whole—not the way she'd known him at Khurdalain, when he'd been burdened by a war that he would kill himself winning. This was the best possible version of him, the way she'd tried to remember him, the way he'd rarely ever been. The scars were still on his face, his hair was still messy and overgrown, tied back in a careless knot, and he still wielded that trident with the casual grace of someone who spent more time on the battlefield than off.

This was an Altan who fought because he adored it and was good at it, and not because it was the only thing he had ever been trained to do.

His eyes were brown. His pupils were not constricted. He did not smell of smoke. When he smiled, he almost looked happy.

"You're here." She couldn't manage anything but a whisper. "It's you."

"Of course I am," he said. "Not even a border skirmish could keep me from you today. Tyr wanted to have my head on a stake, but I don't think even he could stand up to Mother and Father's wrath."

A border skirmish?

Tyr?

Mother and Father?

The confusion lasted for only a moment, and then she understood. Dreams came with their own logic, and this was nothing but a beautiful dream. In this world, Speer had never been destroyed. Tearza had not died and abandoned her people to slavery, and her kin had not been slaughtered overnight on the Dead Island.

She almost laughed out loud. In this illusion, their biggest concern was a fucking *border skirmish.*

"Are you nervous?" Altan asked.

"Nervous?" she echoed.

"I'd be surprised if you weren't," he said. His voice dropped to a conspiring whisper. "Unless you're having second thoughts. And—I mean, if you are, it's fine by me. If we're being honest, I've never been too fond of him, either."

"'Him'?" Rin echoed.

"He's just jealous that you're getting married first while nobody wants him." Ramsa shouldered his way between them, chewing on a red bean bun. He dipped his head toward Altan. "Hello, Commander."

Altan rolled his eyes. "Don't you have fireworks to light?"

"That's not until later," said Ramsa. "Your parents said they'll castrate me if I go near them now. Something about safety hazards."

"That sounds about right." Altan ruffled Ramsa's hair. "Why don't you scurry along and enjoy the feast?"

"Because this conversation is much more interesting." Ramsa took a large bite of the bun and spoke with his mouth full. "So what's it going to be, Rin? Will we have a runaway bride? Because I'd like to finish eating first."

Rin's mouth hung open. Her eyes darted between Ramsa and Altan, trying to detect proof that they were illusions—some imperfection, some lack of substance.

But they were so *solid*, detailed and full of life. And they were so, *so* happy. How could they be this happy?

"Rin?" Altan nudged her shoulder. "Are you all right?"

She shook her head. "I don't— This isn't . . ."

Concern crossed his face. "Do you need to lie down for a moment?"

"No, I just . . ."

He took her arm. "I'm sorry I was making fun of you. Come on, we'll go find you a bench."

"No, that's not what I . . ." She shrugged him off and backed away. She was walking backward, she *knew* she was, but somehow every time she took a step she ended up no farther from Altan than she had been to begin with.

"Come with me," Altan repeated, and his voice resonated around the room. The colors of the banquet hall dimmed. The guests' faces blurred. He was the only defined figure in sight.

He extended his hand toward her. "Quickly now."

She knew what would happen to her if she obeyed.

Everything would be over. The illusion might last another few minutes, or an hour, or a week. Time worked differently in illusions. She might enjoy this one for a lifetime. But in reality, she would have succumbed to Daji's poison. Her life would be over. She would never wake up from this spell.

But would that be so wrong?

She wanted to go with him. She wanted to go so badly.

"No one has to die," Altan said, voicing her own thoughts out loud. "The wars never happened in the first place. You can have everything back. Everyone. No one has to go."

"But they *are* gone," she whispered, and the instant she said it, its truth became apparent. The faces in the banquet hall were lies. Her friends were dead. Tutor Feyrik was gone. Master Irjah was gone. Golyn Niis was gone. Speer was gone. Nothing could bring them back. "You can't tempt me with this."

"Then you can join them," Altan said. "Would that be so bad?"

The lights and streamers dimmed. The tables faded to nothing; the guests disappeared. She and Altan were alone, two spots of flame in a dark passage.

"Is this what you want?" His mouth closed over hers before

she could speak. Scorching hands moved on her body and trailed downward.

Everything was so terribly hot. She was burning. She'd forgotten how it felt to truly *burn*—she was immune to her own flame, and she'd never been caught in Altan's fire, but *this* . . . this was an old, familiar pain, terrible and delicious all at once.

"No." She fought to find her voice. "No, I don't want this—"

Altan's hands tightened on her waist.

"You did," he said, pressing closer. "It was written all over your face. Every time."

"Don't touch me." She pressed her hands against his chest and tried to push him away, to no avail.

"Don't pretend you don't want this," said Altan. "You need me."

She couldn't breathe. "No, I don't . . ."

"Don't you?"

He brought his hand to her cheek. She cringed back, but his burning fingers rested firm on her skin. His hands moved down to her neck. His thumbs stopped where her collarbones met, a familiar resting place. He squeezed. Fire lanced through her throat.

"Come back." The Sorqan Sira's voice cut through her mind like a knife, granting her several delicious, cool seconds of lucidity. "Remember yourself. Submit to him and you lose."

Rin convulsed on the ground.

"I don't want this," she moaned. "I don't want to see this—I want to get out—"

"It's the poison," said the Sorqan Sira. "The sweat amplifies it, brings it to a boil. You must purge yourself, or the Seal will kill you."

Rin whimpered. "Just make it stop."

"I can't. It must get worse before it gets better." The Sorqan Sira seized her hand and squeezed it. "Remember, he exists only in your mind. He only has as much power as you give him. Can you do this?"

Rin nodded and gripped the Sorqan Sira's arm. She couldn't find the breath to say the words *send me back*, but the Sorqan Sira nodded. She threw another ladleful of water onto the rocks.

The heat in the yurt redoubled. Rin choked; her back arched, the material world faded away, and the pain returned. Altan's fingers were around her neck again, squeezing, choking her.

He leaned down. His lips brushed against hers. "Do you know what I want you to do?"

She shook her head, gasping.

"Kill yourself," he ordered.

"*What?*"

"I want you to kill yourself," he repeated. "Make things right. You should have died on that pier. And I should have lived."

Was that true?

It must have been true, if it had lingered so long in her subconscious. And she couldn't lie to herself; she *knew*, had always known that if Altan had lived and if she had died then things would have gone much differently. Aratsha would still be alive, the Cike would not have disbanded, they would not have lost to Feylen, and the Republican Fleet might not be in fragments at the bottom of Lake Boyang.

Jinzha had said it first. *We should have tried to save the other one.*

"You are the reason why I died," Altan continued, relentless. "Make this right. Kill yourself."

She swallowed. "No."

"Why not?" His fingers tightened around her neck. "You're not particularly useful to anyone alive."

She reached up for his hands. "Because I'm done taking orders from you."

He was a product of her own mind. He had only as much power as she gave him.

She pried his fingers off her neck. One by one, they came away. She was nearly free. He squeezed harder but she kicked out, nailed him in the shin, and the moment he let go she scrambled backward away from him and sank into a low crouch, poised to strike.

"Really?" he scoffed. "You're going to fight me?"

"I won't surrender to you anymore."

"'Surrender'?" he repeated, like it was such a ludicrous word. "Is that how you've thought of it? Oh, Rin, it was never about that. I didn't want surrender from you. I had to *manage* you. Control you. You're so fucking *stupid*, you had to be told what to do."

"I'm not stupid," she said.

"Yes, you are." He smiled, patronizing and handsome and hateful all at once. "You're nothing. You're useless. Compared to me you're—"

"I'm nothing at all," she interrupted. "I was a terrible commander. I couldn't function without opium. I still can't call the fire. You can tell me everything I hate about myself, but I already know. You can't say anything to hurt me more."

"Oh, I doubt that." Suddenly his trident was in his hand, spinning as he advanced. "How's this, then? You *wanted* me dead."

She flinched. "No. I never."

"You *hated* me. You were afraid of me, you couldn't wait to be rid of me. Admit it, when I died you laughed."

"No, I wept," she said. "I wept for days, until I couldn't breathe anymore, and then I tried to stop breathing, but every time, Enki brought me back to life, and then I hated myself because you said that I had to keep living, and I hated living because *you're* the one who said I had to—"

"Why would you mourn me?" he asked quietly. "You barely even knew me."

"You're right," she said. "I loved an idea of you. I was infatuated with you. I wanted to *be* you. But I didn't know you then, and I'll never really know what you were. I'm finished wondering now, Altan. I'm ready to kill you."

The trident materialized in her hands.

She had a weapon now. She wasn't defenseless against him. She'd never been defenseless. She had just never thought to look.

Altan's eyes flickered to the prongs. "You wouldn't dare."

"You are not real," she said calmly. "He's dead, and I can't hurt him anymore."

"Look at me," he said. "Look at my eyes. Tell me I'm not real."

She lunged. He parried. She disentangled their prongs and advanced again.

He raised his voice. "*Look at me.*"

"I *am*," she said softly. "I see everything."

He faltered.

She stabbed him through the chest.

His eyes bulged open, but otherwise he didn't move. A slow trickle of blood spilled out the side of his mouth. A red circle blossomed on his chest.

It wasn't a fatal blow. She'd stabbed him just under the sternum. She had missed his heart. Eventually he might bleed to death, but she didn't want him gone just yet. She needed him alive and conscious.

She still needed absolution.

Altan peered down at the prongs emerging from his chest. "Would you like to kill me?"

She withdrew her trident. Blood spilled out faster onto his uniform. "I've done it before."

"But could you do it *now*?" he inquired. "Could you end me? If you kill me here, Rin, I'll go."

"I don't want that."

"Then you still need me."

"Not the way I did."

She'd realized, *finally* realized, that chasing the legacy of Altan Trengsin would give her no truth. She couldn't replicate him in her mind, no matter how many times she tortured herself going over the memories. She could only inherit his pain.

And what was there to replicate? Who *was* Altan, really?

A scared boy from Speer who just wanted to go home, a broken boy who had learned that there was no home to return to, and a soldier who stayed alive just to spite everyone who thought he should be dead. A commander with no purpose, nothing to fight for, and nothing to care about except burning down the world.

Altan was no hero. That was so clear to her now, so stunningly clear that she felt as if she'd been doused in ice water, submerged and reborn.

She didn't owe him her guilt.

She didn't owe him anything.

"I still love you," she said, because she had to be honest.

"I know. You're a fool for it," he said. He stepped forward, reached for her hand, and entwined his fingers in hers. "Kiss me. I know you've wanted to."

She touched his blood-soaked fingers against her cheek. She closed her eyes, just for a moment, and thought about what might have been.

"I loved you, too," he said. "Do you believe that?"

"No, I don't," she said, and pressed her trident into his chest once more.

It slid smoothly in with no resistance. Rin didn't know if that was because the vision of Altan was already fading, immaterial, or if Altan within this dream space was deliberately aiding her, sinking the three prongs neatly into that space in his rib cage that stood just over his heart.

When Rin breathed again it was a new and frightening sensation, at once mechanical and also terribly confusing. Was this *her* body, this mortal and clumsy vessel? One finger at a time she learned the inner workings of her body again. Learned the way air moved through her lungs. Learned to hear the sound of her heart pumping inside her.

She saw light all around her and above her, a perfect circle of blue. It took her a moment to realize that it was the roof of the yurt, pulled open to let the steam escape.

"Don't move," said the Sorqan Sira.

The Sorqan Sira placed a hand over Rin's chest, clenched her fingers, and started to chant. Sharp nails dug into Rin's skin.

Rin screamed.

It wasn't over. She felt a terrible pulling sensation, as if the

Sorqan Sira had wrapped her fingers around Rin's heart and wrenched it out of her rib cage.

She looked down. The Sorqan Sira's fingers hadn't broken skin. The tugging came from something within; something sharp and jagged inside her, something that didn't want to let go.

The Sorqan Sira's chanting grew louder. Rin felt an immense pressure, so great she was sure that her lungs were bursting. It grew and grew—and then something gave. The pressure disappeared.

For a moment all she could do was lie flat and breathe, eyes fixed on the blue circle above.

"Look." The Sorqan Sira opened her palm toward Rin. Inside was a clot of blood the size of her fist, mottled black and rotten. It smelled putrid.

Rin shrank instinctively away. "Is that . . . ?"

"Daji's venom." The Sorqan Sira made a fist over the clot and squeezed. Black blood oozed through the cracks between her fingers and dripped onto the glowing rocks. The Sorqan Sira peered curiously at her stained fingers, then shook the last few drops onto the rocks, where they hissed loudly and disappeared. "It's gone now. You're free."

Rin stared at the stained rocks, at a loss for words. "I don't . . ." She choked before she could finish. Then it happened all at once. Her entire body shook, racked with a grief she hadn't even known was there. She buried her head in her hands, whimpering incoherently, fingers thick with tears and snot.

"It's all right to cry," the Sorqan Sira said quietly. "I know what you saw."

"Then fuck you," Rin choked. "*Fuck you.*"

Her chest heaved. She lurched forward and vomited over the stones. Her knees shook, her ankle throbbed, and she collapsed onto herself, face inches from her vomit, eyes squeezed shut to stem the tide of tears.

Her heart slammed against her rib cage. She tried to focus on her pulse, counting her heartbeats with every passing second to calm down.

He's gone.

He's dead.

He can't hurt me anymore.

She reached for her anger, the anger that had always served as her shield, and couldn't find it. Her emotions had burned her out from the inside; the raging flames had died out because they had nothing left to consume. She felt drained, hollowed out and empty. The only things that remained were exhaustion and the dry ache of loss in her throat.

"You are allowed to feel," the Sorqan Sira murmured.

Rin sniffled and wiped her nose with her sleeve.

"But don't feel bad for him," said the Sorqan Sira. "That was never him. The man you know has gone somewhere he'll be at peace. Life and death, they're equal to this cosmos. We enter the material world and we go away again, reincarnated into something better. That boy was miserable. You let him go."

Yes, Rin knew; in the abstract she knew this truth, that to the cosmos they were fundamentally irrelevant, that they came from dust and returned to dust and ash.

And she should have taken comfort in that, but in that moment she didn't want to be temporary and immaterial; she wanted to be forever preserved in the material world in a moment with Altan, their foreheads pressed together, eyes meeting, arms touching and interlacing, trying to meld into the pure physicality of the other.

She wanted to be alive and mortal and eternally temporary with him, and that was why she cried.

"I don't want him to be gone," she whispered.

"Our dead don't leave us," said the Sorqan Sira. "They'll haunt you as long as you let them. That boy is a disease on your mind. Forget him."

"I *can't*." She pressed her face into her hands. "He was brilliant. He was different. You'd have never met anyone like him."

"You would be stunned." The Sorqan Sira looked very sad. "You have no idea how many men are like Altan Trengsin."

"Rin! Oh, *gods*." Kitay was at her side the instant she emerged from the yurt. She knew, could tell from the expression on his face, that he'd been waiting outside, teeth clenched in anxiety, for hours.

"Hold her up," the Sorqan Sira told him.

He slipped an arm around her waist to take the weight off her ankle. "You're all right?"

She nodded. Together they limped forward.

"Are you sure?" he pressed.

"I'm better," she murmured. "I think I'm better than I've been in a long time."

She stood for a minute, leaning against his shoulder, simply basking in the cold air. She had never known that the air itself could taste or feel so sweet. The sensation of the wind against her face was crisp and delicious, more refreshing than cool rainwater.

"Rin," Kitay said.

She opened her eyes. "What?"

He was staring pointedly at her chest.

Rin fumbled at her front, wondering if her clothes had somehow burned away in the heat. She wouldn't have noticed if they had. The sensation of having a physical body still felt so entirely new to her that she might as well have been walking around naked.

"What is it?" she asked, dazed.

The Sorqan Sira said nothing.

"Look down," Kitay said. His voice sounded oddly strangled.

She glanced down.

"Oh," she said faintly.

A black handprint was scorched into her skin like a brand just below her sternum.

Kitay whirled on the Sorqan Sira. "What did you—"

"It wasn't her," Rin said.

This mark was Altan's work and legacy.

That bastard.

Kitay was watching her carefully. "Are you all right with this?"

"No," she said.

She put her hand over her chest, placed her fingers inside the outlines of Altan's.

His hand was so much bigger than hers.

She let her hand drop. "But it doesn't matter."

"Rin..."

"He's dead," she said, voice trembling. "He's dead, he's gone, do you understand? He's *gone*, and he's never going to touch me again."

"I know," said Kitay. "He won't."

"Call the flame," the Sorqan Sira said abruptly. She had been standing quietly, observing their exchange, but now her voice carried an odd urgency. "Do it now."

"Hold on," Kitay said. "She's weak, she's exhausted—"

"She must do it now," the Sorqan Sira insisted. She looked strangely frightened, and that terrified Rin. "I have to know."

"Be reasonable—" Kitay began, but Rin shook her head.

"No. She's right. Stand back."

He let go of her arm and stepped several paces backward.

She closed her eyes, exhaled, and let her mind sink into the state of ecstasy. The place where rage met power. And for the first time in months she let herself hope that she might feel the flame again, a hope that had become as unattainable as flying.

It was infinitely easier now to generate the anger. She could plunder her own memories with abandon. There were no more parts of her mind that she didn't dare prod, that still bled like open wounds.

She traversed a familiar path through the void until she saw the Phoenix as if through a mist; heard it like an echo, felt it like the remembrance of a touch.

She felt for its rage, and she pulled.

The fire didn't come.

Something pulsed.

Flashes of light seared behind her eyelids.

The Seal remained, burned into her mind, still present. The ghost of Altan's laughter echoed in her ears.

Rin held the flame in the palm of her hand for only an instant, just enough to tantalize her and leave her gasping for more, and then it disappeared.

There was no pain this time, no immediate threat that she might be sucked into a vision and lose her mind to the fantasy, but still Rin sank to her knees and screamed.

CHAPTER 23

"There's another way," said the Sorqan Sira.

"Shut up," Rin said.

She'd come so close. She'd almost had the fire back, she'd tasted it, only to have it wrenched out of her grasp. She wanted to lash out at *something*, she just didn't know who or what, and the sheer pressure made her feel like she might explode. "You said you'd fixed it."

"The Seal is neutralized," said the Sorqan Sira. "It cannot corrupt you any longer. But the venom ran deep, and it still blocks your access to the world of spirit—"

"Fuck all you know."

"Rin, don't," Kitay warned.

She ignored him. She knew this wasn't the Sorqan Sira's fault, but still she wanted to hurt, to cut. "Your people don't know shit. No wonder the Trifecta killed you off, no wonder you lost to three fucking teenagers—"

A shrieking noise slammed into her mind. She fell to her knees, but the noise kept reverberating, growing louder and louder until it solidified into words that vibrated in her bones.

You dare reproach me? The Sorqan Sira loomed over Rin like a giant, standing tall as a mountain while everything else in the clearing shrank. *I am the Mother of the Ketreyids. I rule the north of the Baghra, where the scorpions are fat with poison and the great-mawed sandworms lie in the red sands, ready to swallow camels whole. I have tamed a land created to wither humans away until they are polished bone. Do not think to defy me.*

Rin couldn't speak for the pain. The shriek intensified for several torturous seconds before finally ebbing away. She rolled onto her back and sucked in air in great, heaving gulps.

Kitay helped her sit up. "This is why we are polite to our allies."

"I will await your apology," said the Sorqan Sira.

"I'm sorry," Rin muttered. "I just—I thought I had it back."

She'd numbed herself to her loss during the campaign. She hadn't realized how desperately she still wanted the fire back until she touched it again, just for a moment, and everything had come rushing back; the thrill, the blaze, the sheer roaring *power*.

"Do not presume that all is lost," said the Sorqan Sira. "You will never access the Phoenix on your own unless Daji removes the Seal. That she will never do."

"Then it's all over," Rin said.

"No. Not if another soul calls the Phoenix for you. A soul that is bound to your own." The Sorqan Sira looked pointedly at Kitay.

He blinked, confused.

"No," Rin said immediately. "I don't—I don't care what you can do, *no*—"

"Let her speak," Kitay said.

"No, you don't understand the risk—"

"Yes, he does," said the Sorqan Sira.

"But he doesn't know anything about the gods!" Rin cried.

"He doesn't *now*. Once you've been twinned, he will know everything."

"Twinned?" Kitay repeated.

"Do you understand the nature of Chaghan and Qara's bond?" the Sorqan Sira asked.

Kitay shook his head.

"They're spiritually linked," Rin said flatly. "Cut him, and she feels the pain. Kill him and she dies."

Horror flitted across Kitay's face. He tried to mask it, but she saw.

"The anchor bond connects your souls across the psychospiritual plane," said the Sorqan Sira. "You can still call the Phoenix if you do it through the boy. He will be your conduit. The divine power will flow straight through him and into you."

"I'm going to become a shaman?" Kitay asked.

"No. You will only lend your mind to one. She will call the god through you." The Sorqan Sira tilted her head, considering the both of them. "You are good friends, yes?"

"Yes," Kitay said.

"Good. The anchor takes best on two souls that are already familiar. It's stronger. More stable. Can you bear a little pain?"

"Yes," Kitay said again.

"Then we should perform the bonding ritual as soon as we can."

"Absolutely not," Rin said.

"I'll do it," Kitay said firmly. "Just tell me how."

"No, I'm not letting you—"

"I'm not asking your permission, Rin. We don't have another choice."

"But you could die!"

He barked out a laugh. "We're soldiers. We're always about to die."

Rin stared at him in disbelief. How could he sound so cavalier? Did he not understand the risk?

Kitay had survived Sinegard. Golyn Niis. Boyang. He'd suffered enough pain for a lifetime. She wasn't putting him through this, too. She'd never be able to forgive herself.

"You have no idea what it's like," she said. "You've never spoken to the gods, you—"

He shook his head. "No, you don't get to talk like that. You don't get to keep this world from me, like I'm too stupid or too weak for it—"

"I don't think you're weak."

"Then why—"

"Because you don't know anything about this world, and you never should." She didn't care if the Phoenix tormented her, but Kitay . . . Kitay was pure. He was the best person she had ever known. Kitay shouldn't know how it felt to call a god of vengeance. Kitay was the last thing in the world that was still fundamentally kind and good, and she'd die before she corrupted that. "You have no idea how it feels. The gods will break you."

"Do you want the fire back?" Kitay asked.

"What?"

"*Do you want the fire back?* If you can call the Phoenix again, will you use it to win us this war?"

"Yes," she said. "I want it more than anything. But I can't ask you to do this for me."

"Then you don't have to ask." He turned to the Sorqan Sira. "Anchor us. Just tell me what I have to do."

The Sorqan Sira was looking at Kitay with an expression that almost amounted to respect. A thin smile spread across her face. "As you wish."

"It's not so bad," Chaghan said. "You take the agaric. You kill the sacrifice. Then the Sorqan Sira binds you, and your souls are linked together forever after. You don't need to do much but exist, really."

"Why a living sacrifice?" Kitay asked.

"Because there's power in a soul released from the material world," Qara said. "The Sorqan Sira will use that power to forge your bond."

Chaghan and Qara had been enlisted to prepare Rin and Kitay for the ritual, which involved a tedious process of painting a line of characters down their bare arms, running from their shoulders to the tips of their middle fingers. The characters had to be written at precisely the same time, each stroke synchronous with its pair.

The twins worked with remarkable coordination, which Rin would have appreciated more if she weren't so upset.

"Stop moving," Chaghan said. "You're making the ink bleed."

"Then write faster," she snapped.

"That would be nice," Kitay said amiably. "I need to pee."

Chaghan dipped his brush into an inkwell and shook away the excess drops. "Ruin one more character and we'll have to start over."

"You'd like that, wouldn't you?" Rin grumbled. "Why don't you just take another hour? With luck the war will be over before you're done!"

Chaghan lowered his brush. "We didn't have a choice in this. You know that."

"I know you're a little bitch," she said.

"You have no other choice."

"Fuck you."

It was a petty exchange, and it didn't make Rin feel nearly as good as she thought it would. It only exhausted her. Because Chaghan was right—the twins had to comply with the Sorqan Sira or they would certainly have been killed, and if they hadn't, Rin would still have no way out.

"It'll be all right," Qara said gently. "An anchor makes you stronger. More stable."

Rin scoffed. "How? It just seems like a good way to lose two soldiers for every one."

"Because it makes you resilient to the gods. Every time you call them down, you are like a lantern, drifting away from your body. Drift too far, and the gods root themselves in your physical form instead. That's when you lose your mind."

"Is that what happened to this Feylen?" Kitay asked.

"Yes," said Qara. "He went out too far, got lost, and the god planted itself inside."

"Interesting," Kitay said. "And the anchor absolutely prevents that?"

He sounded far too excited about the procedure. He drank the twins' words in with a hungry expression, cataloging every new sliver of information into his prodigious memory. Rin could almost see the gears turning in his mind.

That scared her. She didn't want him entranced with this world. She wanted him to run far, far away.

"It's not perfect, but it makes it much harder to lose your mind," Chaghan said. "The gods can't uproot you with an anchor. You can drift as far as you want into the world of spirit, and you'll always have a way to come back."

"You're saying I'll stop Rin from going crazy," Kitay said.

"She's already crazy," Chaghan said.

"Fair enough," Kitay said.

The twins worked in silence for a long while. Rin sat up straight, eyes closed, breathing steadily as she felt the wet brush tip move against her bare skin.

What if the anchor *did* make her stronger? She couldn't help feeling a thrill of hope at the thought. What would it be like to call the Phoenix without fear of losing her mind to the rage? She might summon fire whenever she wanted, for as long as she wanted. She might control it the way Altan had.

But was it worth it? The sacrifice seemed so immense—not just for Kitay, but for *her*. To link her life to his would be such an unpredictable, terrifying liability. She would never be safe unless Kitay was, too.

Unless she could protect him. Unless she could guarantee that Kitay was *never* in danger.

At last Chaghan put his brush down. "You're finished."

Rin stretched and examined her arms. Swirling black script covered her skin, made of words that almost resembled a language that she could understand. "That's it?"

"Not yet." Chaghan passed them a fistful of red-capped toadstools. "Eat these."

Kitay prodded a toadstool with his finger. "What are these?"

"Fly agaric. You can find it near birch and fir trees."

"What's it for?"

"To open up the crack between the worlds," Qara said.

Kitay looked confused.

"Tell him what it's really for," Rin said.

Qara smiled. "To get you incredibly high. Much more elegant than poppy seeds. Faster, too."

Kitay turned the mushroom over in his hand. "Looks poisonous."

"They're psychedelics," Chaghan said. "They're all poisonous. The whole *point* is to deliver you right to the doorstep of the afterworld."

Rin popped the mushrooms in her mouth and chewed. They were tough and tasteless, and she had to work her teeth for several minutes before they were tender enough to go down. She had the unpleasant sensation that she was chewing through a lump of flesh every time her teeth cut into the fibrous chunks.

Chaghan passed Kitay a wooden cup. "If you don't want to eat the mushroom you can drink the agaric instead."

Kitay sniffed it, took a sip, and gagged. "What's in this?"

"Horse urine," Chaghan said cheerfully. "We feed the mushrooms to the horses, and you get the drug after it passes. Goes down easier."

"Your people are *disgusting*," Kitay muttered. He pinched his nose, tossed the contents of the cup back into his throat, and gagged.

Rin swallowed. Dry lumps of mushroom pushed painfully down her throat.

"What happens to you when your anchor dies?" she asked.

"You die," Chaghan said. "Your souls are bound, which means they depart this earth together. One pulls the other along."

"That's not strictly true," Qara said. "It's a choice. You can choose to depart this earth together. Or you may break the bond."

"You can?" Rin asked. "How?"

Qara exchanged a look with Chaghan. "With your last word. If both partners are willing."

Kitay frowned. "I don't understand. Why is this a liability, then?"

"Because once you have an anchor, they become a part of your soul. Your very existence. They know your thoughts. They feel what you feel. They are the *only ones* who completely and fully understand you. Most would die rather than give that up."

"And you'd both have to be in the same place when one of you died," said Chaghan. "Most people aren't."

"But you *can* break it," Rin said.

"You could," Chaghan said. "Though I doubt the Sorqan Sira will teach you how."

Of course not. Rin knew the Sorqan Sira would want Kitay as insurance—not only to ensure that her weapon against Daji kept working, but as a failsafe in case she ever decided to put Rin down.

"Did Altan have an anchor?" she asked. Altan had possessed an eerie amount of control for a Speerly.

"No. The Speerlies didn't know how to do it. Altan was . . . whatever Altan was doing, that was inhuman. Near the end, he was staying sane off of sheer willpower alone." Chaghan swallowed. "I offered many times. He always said no."

"But you already have an anchor," said Rin. "You can have more than one?"

"Not at the same time. A pairwise bond is optimal. A triangular bond is deeply unstable, because unpredictability in reciprocation means that any defection on one end affects the other two in ways that you cannot protect against."

"But?" Kitay pressed.

"But it can also amplify your abilities. Make you stronger than any shaman has the right to be."

"Like the Trifecta," Rin realized. "They're bonded to each other. That's why they're so powerful."

It made so much sense now—why Daji had not killed Jiang if they were enemies. She wouldn't. She *couldn't*, without killing herself.

She sat up with a start. "So that means . . ."

"Yes," said Chaghan. "As long as Daji is alive, the Dragon Emperor and the Gatekeeper are both still alive. It's possible their bond was dissolved, but I doubt it. Daji's power is far too stable. The other two are out there, somewhere. But my guess is that they can't be doing too well, because the rest of the country thinks they're dead."

You will destroy one another. One will die, one will rule, and one will sleep for eternity.

Kitay voiced the question on Rin's mind. "Then what happened to them? Why did they go missing?"

Chaghan shrugged. "You'd have to ask the other two. Have you finished drinking?"

Kitay drained the cup and winced. "Ugh. Yes."

"Good. Now eat the mushrooms."

Kitay blinked. "What?"

"There's no agaric in that cup," Chaghan said.

"Oh, you asshole," Rin said.

"I don't understand," Kitay said.

Chaghan gave him a thin smile. "I just wanted to see if you'd drink horse piss."

The Sorqan Sira waited outside before a roaring fire. The flames seemed alive to Rin; the tendrils jumped too high, reached too far, like little hands trying to pull her into the blaze. If she let her gaze linger, the smoke, turned purple by the Sorqan Sira's powders, started taking on the faces of the dead. Master Irjah. Aratsha. Captain Salkhi. Altan.

"Are you ready?" asked the Sorqan Sira.

Rin blinked the faces away.

She knelt across from Kitay on the frigid dirt. Despite the cold, they were permitted to wear only trousers and undershirts that exposed their bare arms. The inky characters trailing down their skin shone in the firelight.

She was terrified. He didn't look afraid at all.

"I'm ready," he said. His voice was steady.

"Ready," she echoed.

Between them lay two long, serrated knives and a sacrifice.

Rin didn't know how the Ketreyids had managed to trap an adult deer, massive and healthy, without any visible wounds, in just a matter of hours. Its legs were bound tightly together. Rin suspected that the animal had been sedated, because it lay quite still on the dirt, eyes half-open as if it were resigned to its fate.

The effect of the agaric had begun to set in. Everything seemed terribly bright. When objects moved in her field of vision, they left behind trails like streaks of paint that sparked and swirled before they faded away.

She focused with difficulty on the deer's neck.

She and Kitay were to make two cuts, one on either side of the animal, so that neither could bear full responsibility for its death. Alone, each wound would be insufficient to kill. The deer might drag itself away, cover the cut in mud and somehow survive. But wounds on both sides meant certain death.

Rin picked her knife off the ground and gripped it tightly in her hands.

"Repeat after me," said the Sorqan Sira, and uttered a slow stream of Ketreyid words. The foreign syllables sounded clunky and awkward in Rin's mouth. She knew their meaning only because the twins had explained them to her.

We will live as one. We will fight as one.

And we will kill as one.

"The sacrifice," said the Sorqan Sira.

They brought their knives down.

Rin found it harder than she'd expected. Not because she was unused to killing—cutting through flesh was as easy to her now as breathing. It was the fur that offered resistance. She clenched her teeth and pushed harder. The knife sank into the deer's side.

The deer arched its neck and screamed.

Rin's knife hadn't gone in deep enough. She had to widen the cut. Her hands shook madly; the handle was loose between her fingers.

But Kitay dragged his knife across the deer's side with one clean, steady stroke.

Blood pooled, fast and dark, around their knees. The deer stopped writhing. Its head drooped to the ground.

Through the haze of the agaric, Rin *saw* the moment the deer's life left its body—a golden, shimmering aura that lingered over the corpse like an ethereal copy of its physical form before drifting upward like smoke. She tilted her head up, watched it floating higher and higher toward the heavens.

"Follow it," said the Sorqan Sira.

She did. It seemed such a simple matter. Under the agaric's influence her soul was lighter than air itself. Her mind ascended, her material body became a distant memory, and she flew up into the vast and dark void that was the cosmos.

She found herself standing on the periphery of a great circle, its circumference etched with glowing Hexagrams—characters that together spelled the nature of the universe, the sixty-four deities that constituted all that was and would ever be.

The circle tilted and became a pool, inside which swam two massive carp, one white, one black, each with a large dot of the opposite color on its flank. They drifted lazily, chasing each other in a slow-moving, eternal circle.

She saw Kitay on the other side of the circle. He was naked. It was not a physical nakedness; he was made more of light than he was of body—but every thought, every memory, and every feeling he'd ever had shone out toward her. Nothing was hidden.

She was similarly naked before him. All of her secrets, her insecurities, her guilt, and her rage had been laid bare. He saw her cruelest, most brutal desires. He saw parts of her that she didn't even understand herself. The part that was terrified of being alone and terrified of being the last. The part that realized it loved pain, adored it, could find release only in pain.

And she could see him. She saw the way that concepts were stored in his mind, great repositories of knowledge linked together to be called up at a moment's notice. She saw the anxiety that came with being the only person he knew who was *this* smart. She saw how scared he was, trapped and isolated in his own mind, watching his world break down around him because of irrationalities that he could not fix.

And she understood his sadness. The grief; the loss of a father, but more than just that—the loss of an empire, the loss of loyalty, of *duty*, his sole meaning for existence—

She saw his fury.

How had it taken her this long to understand? She wasn't the only one fueled by anger. But where her rage was explosive, immediate and devastating, Kitay's burned with a silent determination; it festered and rotted and lingered, and the strength of his hate stunned her.

We're the same.

Kitay wanted vengeance and blood. Under that frail veneer of control was an ongoing scream of rage that originated in confusion and culminated in an overwhelming urge for destruction, if only so he could tear the world down and rebuild it in a way that made *sense*.

The circle glowed between them. The black carp and white carp began to circle faster and faster until the darkness and brightness were indistinct; not gray, not melded into each other but yet the same entity—two sides of the same coin, necessary complements balancing each other like the Pantheon was balanced.

The circle spun and they spun with it—faster and faster, until the Hexagrams blurred and melded into a glowing hoop. For a moment Rin was lost in the convergence—up became down, right became left, all distinctions were broken . . .

Then she felt the power, and it was magnificent.

She felt like she had when Shiro injected her veins with heroin. It was the same rush, the same dizzying flood of energy. But this time her spirit did not drift farther and farther from the material world. This time she knew where her body was, could return to it in seconds if she wanted. She was halfway between the spirit world and the material world. She could perceive both, affect both.

She had not gone up to meet her god; her god had been drawn down into her. She felt the Phoenix all about her, the rage and fire, so deliciously warm that it tickled as it coursed over her.

She was so delighted that she wanted to laugh.

But Kitay was moaning. He had been for some time now, but she was so entranced with the power that she'd hardly noticed.

"It's not taking." The Sorqan Sira intruded sharply on Rin's reverie. "Stop it, you're overpowering him."

Rin opened her eyes and saw Kitay curled into a ball, whimpering on the ground. He jerked his head back and uttered a long, keening scream.

Her sight blurred and shifted. One moment she was looking at Kitay and the next she couldn't see him at all. All she could see was fire, vast expanses of fire over which only she had control...

"You're erasing him," hissed the Sorqan Sira. "Pull yourself back."

But why? She'd never felt so good before. She never wanted this sensation to stop.

"You are going to kill him." The Sorqan Sira's fingers dug into her shoulder. "And then nothing will save you."

Dimly, Rin understood. She was hurting Kitay, she had to stop, but *how*? The fire was so alluring, it reduced her rational mind to just a whisper. She heard the Phoenix's laughter echoing around her mind, growing louder and stronger with every passing moment.

"Rin," Kitay gasped. "*Please.*"

That brought her back.

Her grasp of the material world was fading. Before it disappeared entirely she snatched up her knife and stabbed down into her leg.

Spots of white exploded in her vision. The pain chased the fire away, induced a stark clarity back to her mind. The Phoenix fell silent. The void was still.

She saw Kitay across the spirit plane—kneeling, but alive, present, and whole.

She opened her eyes to dirt. Slowly she pulled herself into a sitting position, wiped the soil off the side of her face. She saw Kitay looking around in a daze, blinking as if he were seeing the world for the first time.

She reached for his hand. "Are you all right?"

He took a deep, shuddering breath. "I—I'm fine, I think, I just . . . Give me a moment."

She couldn't help but laugh. "Welcome to my world."

"I feel like I'm living in a dream." He examined the back of his hand, turned it over in the fading sunlight as if he didn't trust the evidence of his own body. "I suppose—I saw the physical proof of your gods. I knew this power existed. But everything I know about the world—"

"The world you knew doesn't exist," she said softly.

"No shit." Kitay's hands clenched the dirt and grass like he was afraid the ground might disappear under his fingertips.

"Try it," said the Sorqan Sira.

Rin didn't have to ask what she meant.

She stood upon shaky legs and turned to face away from Kitay. She opened her palms. She felt the fire inside her chest, a warm presence waiting to pour out the moment she called it.

She summoned it forward. A warm flame appeared in her hands—a tame, quiet little thing.

She tensed, waiting for the pull, the urge to draw out more, *more*. But she felt nothing. The Phoenix was still there. She knew it was screaming for her. But it couldn't get through. A wall had been built in her mind, a psychic structure that repelled and muted the god to just a faint whisper.

Fuck you, said the Phoenix, but even now it sounded amused. *Fuck you, little Speerly.*

She shouted with delight. She hadn't just recovered, she had *tamed a god*. The anchor bond had set her free.

She watched, trembling, as fire accumulated on her palms. She called it higher. Made it leap through the air in arcs like fish jumping from the ocean. She could command it as completely as Altan had been able to. No. She was better than Altan had ever been, because she was sober, she was stable, and she was free.

The fear of madness was gone, but not the impossible power. The power remained, a deep well from which she could draw when she chose.

And now she *could* choose.

She saw Kitay watching her. His eyes were wide, his expression equal parts fear and awe.

"Are you all right?" she asked him. "Can you feel it?"

He didn't answer. He touched a hand to his temple, his gaze fixed so hard on the flames that she could see them reflected bright in his eyes, and he laughed.

That night the Ketreyids fed them a bone broth—scorching hot, musky, tangy, and salty all at once. Rin guzzled it as fast as she could. It scalded the back of her throat, but she didn't care. She'd been subsisting on dried fish and rice gruel for so long that she'd forgotten how good proper food could taste.

Qara passed her a mug. "Drink more water. You're getting dehydrated."

"Thanks." Rin was still sweating despite the cold onset of night. Little droplets beaded all over her skin, soaking straight through her clothing.

Across the fire, Kitay and Chaghan were engaged in an animated discussion which, as far as Rin could tell, involved the metaphysical nature of the cosmos. Chaghan drew diagrams in the dirt with a stick while Kitay watched, nodding enthusiastically.

Rin turned to Qara. "Can I ask you something?"

"Of course," Qara said.

Rin shot Kitay a glance. He wasn't paying her any attention. He'd seized the stick from Chaghan and was scrawling a very complicated mathematical equation below the diagrams.

Rin lowered her voice. "How long have you and your brother been anchored?"

"For our entire lives," Qara said. "We were ten days old when we performed the ritual. I can't remember life without him."

"And the bond has always . . . it's always been equal? One of you doesn't diminish the other?"

Qara raised an eyebrow. "Do you think I've been diminished?"

"I don't know. You always seem so . . ." Rin trailed off. She didn't know how to phrase it. Qara had always been a mystery to her. She was the moon to her brother's sun. Chaghan was such an overbearing personality. He loved the spotlight, loved to lecture everyone around him in the most condescending way possible. But Qara had always preferred the shadows and the silent company of her birds. Rin had never heard her express an opinion that wasn't her brother's.

"You think Chaghan dominates me," Qara said.

Rin blushed. "No, I just—"

"You're worried you'll overpower Kitay," Qara said. "You think your rage will become too much for him and that he'll become only a shade of you. You think that's what has happened to us."

"I'm scared," Rin said. "I almost killed him. And if that—that imbalance, or whatever, is a risk, I want to know. I don't want to strip him of his ability to challenge me."

Qara nodded slowly. She sat silently for a long while, frowning.

"My brother doesn't dominate me," she said at last. "At least, not in a way I could ever possibly know. But I've never challenged him."

"Then how—"

"Our wills have been united since we were children. We desire the same things. When he speaks, he voices both our thoughts. We are two halves of the same person. If I seem withdrawn to you, it is because Chaghan's presence in the mortal world frees me to dwell among the spirit world. I prefer animal souls to mortals, to whom I've never had much to say. That doesn't mean I'm diminished."

"But Kitay's not like you," Rin said. "Our wills *aren't* aligned. If anything, we disagree more often than not. And I don't want to . . . erase him."

Qara's expression softened. "Do you love him?"

"Yes," Rin said immediately. "More than anyone else in the world."

"Then you don't need to worry," Qara said. "If you love him, then you can trust yourself to protect him."

Rin hoped that was true.

"Hey," Kitay said. "What's so interesting over there?"

"Nothing," Rin said. "Just gossip. Have you cracked the nature of the cosmos?"

"Not yet." Kitay tossed his stick onto the dirt. "But give me a year or two. I'm getting close."

Qara stood up. "Come. We should get some sleep."

Sometime during the day the Ketreyids had built several more yurts, clustered together in a circle. The yurt designated for Rin and her companions was at the very center. The message was clear. They were still under Ketreyid watch until the Sorqan Sira chose to release them.

The yurt felt far too cramped for four people. Rin curled up on her side, knees drawn up to her chest, although all she wanted to do was sprawl out, let all of her limbs loose. She felt suffocated. She wanted open air—open sands, wide water. She took a deep breath, trying to stave off the same panic that had crept up on her during the sweat.

"What's the matter?" Qara asked.

"I think I'd rather sleep outside."

"You'll freeze outside. Don't be stupid."

Rin propped herself up on her side. "You look comfortable."

Qara smiled. "Yurts remind me of home."

"How long has it been since you've been back?" Rin asked.

Qara thought for a moment. "They sent us down south when we turned eleven. So it has been a decade, now."

"Do you ever wish you could go home?"

"Sometimes," Qara said. "But there's not much at home. Not for us, anyway. It's better to be a foreigner in the Empire than a Naimad on the steppe."

Rin supposed that was to be expected when one's tribe was responsible for training a handful of traitorous murderers.

"So—what, no one talks to you back home?" she asked.

"Back home we are slaves," Chaghan said flatly. "The Ketreyids still blame our mother for the Trifecta. They will never accept us back into the fold. We'll pay penance for that forever."

An uncomfortable silence filled the space between them. Rin had more questions, she just didn't know how to ask them.

If she were in a different mood, she would have yelled at the twins for their deception. They'd been spies for all of these years, watching the Cike to determine whether or not they would hold stable. Whether they did a good enough job culling their own, immuring the maddest among them in the Chuluu Korikh.

What if the twins had decided that the Cike had grown too dangerous? Would they have simply killed them off? Certainly the Ketreyids felt as if they had the right. They looked down on Nikara shamans with the same supercilious arrogance as the Hesperians, and Rin hated that.

But she held her tongue. Chaghan and Qara had suffered enough.

And she, if anyone, knew what it was like to be an outcast in her own country.

"These yurts." Kitay put his palms on the walls; his outspread arms reached across a third of the diameter of the hut. "They're all this small?"

"We build them even smaller on the steppe," Qara said. "You're from the south; you've never seen real winds."

"I'm from Sinegard," Kitay said.

"That's not the true north. Everything below the sand dunes counts as the south to us. On the steppe, the night gusts can rip the flesh off your face if they don't freeze you to death first. We stay in yurts because the steppe will kill you otherwise."

No one had a response to that. A peaceful quiet fell over the yurt. Kitay and the twins were asleep in moments; Rin could tell by the sound of their steady, even breathing.

She lay awake with her trident clutched close to her chest, staring at the open roof above her, that perfect circle that revealed the night sky. She felt like a little rodent burrowing down in its hole, trying to pretend that if it lay low enough, then the world outside wouldn't bother it.

Maybe the Ketreyids stayed in their yurts to hide from the winds. Or maybe, she thought, with stars this bright, if you believed that above you lay the cosmos, then you had to construct a yurt to provide some temporary feeling of materiality. Otherwise, under the weight of swirling divinity, you might feel you had no significance at all.

CHAPTER 24

A fresh blanket of snow had fallen while they slept. It made the sun shine brighter, the air bite colder. Rin limped outside and stretched her aching muscles, squinting against the harsh light.

The Ketreyids were eating in shifts. Six riders at a time sat by the fire, wolfing down their food while the others stood guard by the periphery.

"Eat your fill." The Sorqan Sira ladled out two steaming bowls of stew and handed them to Rin and Kitay. "You have a hard ride before you. We'll pack you a bag of dried meat and some yak's milk, but eat as much as you can now."

Rin took the proffered bowl. The stew smelled terribly good. She huddled on the ground and pressed next to Kitay for warmth, bony elbows touching bony hips. Little details about him seemed to stand out in stark relief. She had never noticed before just how long and thin his fingers were, or how he always smelled faintly of ink and dust, or how his wiry hair curled just so at the tips.

She'd known him for more than four years by now, but every time she looked at him, she discovered something new.

"So that's it?" Kitay asked the Sorqan Sira. "You're letting us go? No strings attached?"

"The terms are met," she replied. "We have no reason to harm you now."

"So what am I to you?" Rin asked. "A pet on a long leash?"

"You are my gamble. A trained wolf set loose."

"To kill an enemy that you can't face," Rin said.

The Sorqan Sira smiled, displaying teeth. "Be glad that we still have some use for you."

Rin didn't like her phrasing. "What happens if I succeed, and you no longer have use for me?"

"Then we'll let you keep your lives as a token of our gratitude."

"And what happens if you decide I'm a threat again?"

"Then we'll find you again." The Sorqan Sira nodded to Kitay. "And this time, *his* life will be on the line."

Rin had no doubt the Sorqan Sira would put an arrow through Kitay's heart without hesitation.

"You still don't trust me," she said. "You're playing a long game with us, and the anchor bond was your insurance."

The Sorqan Sira sighed. "I am afraid, child. And I have the right to be. The last time we taught Nikara shamans how to anchor themselves, they turned on us."

"But I'm nothing like them."

"You are far too much like them. You have the same eyes. Angry. Desperate. You've seen too much. You hate too much. Those three were younger than you when they came to us, more timid and afraid, and still they slaughtered thousands of innocents. You are older than they were, and you've done far worse."

"That's not the same," Rin said. "The Federation—"

"Deserved it?" asked the Sorqan Sira. "Every single one? Even the women? The children?"

Rin flushed. "But I'm not—I didn't do it because I liked it. I'm not like *them*."

Not like that vision of a younger Jiang, who laughed when he killed, who seemed to delight in being drenched in blood. Not like Daji.

"That's what they thought about themselves, too," said the

Sorqan Sira. "But the gods corrupted them, just as they will corrupt you. The gods manifest your worst and cruelest instincts. You think you are in control, but your mind erodes by the second. To call the gods is to gamble with madness."

"It's better than doing nothing." Rin knew that she was already walking a fine line, that she ought to keep her mouth shut, but the Ketreyids' constant high-minded pacifistic lecturing infuriated her. "I'd rather go mad than hide behind the Baghra Desert and pretend that atrocities aren't happening when I could have done something about them."

The Sorqan Sira chuckled. "You think that we did nothing? Is that what they taught you?"

"I know that millions died during the first two Poppy Wars. And I know that your people never crossed down south to stop it."

"How many people do you think Vaisra's war has killed?" the Sorqan Sira asked.

"Fewer than would have died otherwise," Rin said.

The Sorqan Sira didn't answer. She just let the silence stretch on and on until Rin's answer began to seem ridiculous.

Rin picked at her food, no longer hungry.

"What will you do with the foreigners?" Kitay asked.

Rin had forgotten about the Hesperians until Kitay asked. She peered around the camp but couldn't spot them. Then she saw a larger yurt a little off to the edge of the clearing, guarded heavily by Bekter and his riders.

"Perhaps we will kill them." The Sorqan Sira shrugged. "They are holy men, and nothing good ever comes of the Hesperian religion."

"Why do you say that?" Kitay asked.

"They believe in a singular and all-powerful deity, which means they cannot accept the truth of other gods. And when nations start to believe that other beliefs lead to damnation, violence becomes inevitable." The Sorqan Sira cocked her head. "What do you think? Shall we shoot them? It's kinder than leaving them to die of exposure."

"Don't kill them," Rin said quickly. Tarcquet made her uncomfortable and Sister Petra made her want to put her hand through a wall, but Augus had never struck her as anything other than naive and well-intentioned. "Those kids are missionaries, not soldiers. They're harmless."

"Those weapons are not harmless," said the Sorqan Sira.

"No," Kitay said. "They are faster and deadlier than crossbows, and they are most deadly in inexperienced hands. I would not return their weapons."

"Safe passage back will be difficult, then. We can spare only one steed for the two of you. They will have to walk through enemy territory."

"Would you give them supplies to make rafts?" Rin asked.

The Sorqan Sira frowned, considering. "Can they find their own way back over the rivers?"

Rin hesitated. Her altruism extended only so far. She didn't want to see Augus dead, but she wasn't about to waste time shepherding children who never should have come along in the first place.

She turned to Kitay. "If they can make it to the Western Murui, they're fine, right?"

He shrugged. "More or less. Tributaries get tricky. They could get lost. Could end up at Khurdalain."

She could accept that risk. It did enough to alleviate her conscience. If Augus and his companions weren't clever enough to make it back to Arlong, then that was their own fault. Augus had been kind to her once. She'd made sure the Ketreyids didn't put an arrow in his head. She owed him nothing more than that.

Chaghan was alone when Rin found him, sitting at the edge of the river with his knees pulled up to his chest.

"Don't they think you might run?" she asked.

He gave her a wry smile. "You know I don't run very fast."

She sat down beside him. "So what happens to you now?"

His face was unreadable. "The Sorqan Sira doesn't trust us to watch over the Cike any longer. She's taking us back north."

"And what will happen to you there?"

His throat bobbed. "That depends."

She knew he didn't want her pity, so she didn't burden him with it. She took a deep breath. "I wanted to say thank you."

"For what?"

"You vouched for me."

"I was just saving my own skin."

"Of course."

"I was also rather hoping that you wouldn't die," he admitted.

"Thanks for that."

An awkward silence passed between them. She saw Chaghan's eyes dart toward her several times, as if he was debating whether to broach the next subject.

"Say it," she finally said.

"Do you really want me to?"

"Yes, if you're going to be this awkward otherwise."

"Fine," he said. "Inside the Seal, what you saw—"

"It was Altan," she said promptly. "Altan, alive. That's what I saw. He was alive."

Chaghan exhaled. "So you killed him?"

"I gave him what he wanted," she said.

"I see."

"I also saw him happy," she said. "He was different. He wasn't suffering. He'd never suffered. He was *happy*. That's how I'll remember him."

Chaghan didn't say anything for a long time. She knew he was trying not to cry in front of her; she could see the tears welling up in his eyes.

"Is that real?" she asked. "In another world, is that real? Or was the Seal just showing me what I wanted to see?"

"I don't know," Chaghan said. "Our world is a dream of the gods. Maybe they have other dreams. But all we have is *this* story unfolding, and in the script of this world, nothing's going to bring Altan back to life."

Rin leaned back. "I thought I knew how this world worked. How the cosmos worked. But I don't know anything."

"Most Nikara don't," Chaghan said, and he didn't even try to mask his arrogance.

Rin snorted. "And you do?"

"We know what constitutes the nature of reality," said Chaghan. "We've understood it for years. But your people are fragile and desperate fools. They don't know what's real and what's false, so they'll cling to their little truths, because it's better than imagining that their world might not matter so much after all."

It was starting to become clear to her now, why the Hinterlanders might view themselves as caretakers of the universe. Who else understood the nature of the cosmos like they did? Who even came close?

Perhaps Jiang had known, a long time ago when his mind was still his. But the man she'd known had been shattered, and the secrets he'd taught her were only fragments of the truth.

"I thought it was hubris, what you did," she murmured. "But it's *kindness*. The Hinterlanders maintain the illusion so you can let everyone else live in the lie."

"Don't call us that," Chaghan said sharply. "*Hinterlander* is not a name. Only the Empire uses this word, because you assume everyone who lives on the steppe is the same. Naimads are not Ketreyids. Call us by our names."

"I'm sorry." She crossed her arms against her chest, shivering against the biting wind. "Can I ask you something else?"

"You're going to ask me regardless."

"Why do you hate me so much?"

"I don't hate you," he said automatically.

"Sure seemed like it. Seemed like it for a long time, even before Altan died."

Finally he twisted around to face her. "I can't look at you and not see him."

She knew he would say that. She knew, and still it hurt. "You thought I couldn't live up to him. And that's—that's fair, I never could. And—and if you were jealous, for some reason, I understand that, too, but you should just know that—"

"I wasn't just jealous," he said. "I was angry. At both of us. I was watching you make all the same mistakes Altan did, and I didn't know how to stop it. I saw Altan confused and angry all those years, and I saw him walk down the path he chose like a blind child, and I thought precisely the same was happening to you."

"But I know what I'm doing. I'm not blind like he was—"

"Yes, you are, you don't even realize it. Your kind has been treated as slaves for so long that you've forgotten what it is like to be free. You're easily angered, and you latch quickly onto things—opium, people, ideas—that soothe your pain, even temporarily. And that makes you terribly easy to manipulate." Chaghan paused. "I'm sorry. Do I offend?"

"Vaisra isn't manipulating me," Rin insisted. "He's . . . *we're* fighting for something good. Something worth fighting for."

He gave her a long look. "And you really believe in his Republic?"

"I believe the Republic is a better alternative to anything we've got," she said. "Daji has to die. Vaisra's our best shot at killing her. And whatever happens next can't possibly be worse than the Empire."

"You really think that?"

Rin didn't want to talk about this anymore. Didn't want her mind to drift in that direction. Not once since the disaster at Lake Boyang had she seriously considered not returning to Arlong, or the idea that there might not be anything to return *to*.

She had too much power now, too much rage, and she needed a cause for which to burn. Vaisra's Republic was her anchor. Without that, she'd be lost, drifting. That thought terrified her.

"I have to do this," she said. "Otherwise I have nothing."

"If you say so." Chaghan turned to gaze at the river. He seemed to have given up on arguing the point. She couldn't tell if he was disappointed or not. "Maybe you're right. But eventually, you'll have to ask yourself precisely what you're fighting for. And you'll have to find a reason to live past vengeance. Altan never managed that."

"You're sure you know how to ride this?" Qara handed the warhorse's reins to Rin.

"No, but Kitay does." Rin peered up at the black warhorse with trepidation. She'd never been entirely comfortable around horses—they were so much bigger up close, their hooves so poised to split her head open—but Kitay had spent enough of his childhood riding around on his family's estate that he could handle most animals with ease.

"Keep off the main roads," Chaghan said. "My birds tell me the Empire's taking back much of its territory. You'll run into Militia patrols if you're seen traveling in broad daylight. Stick to the tree line when you can."

Rin was about to ask about the horse's feed when Chaghan and Qara both looked sharply to the left, like two hunting animals alerted to their prey.

She heard the noises a second later. Shouts from the Ketreyid camp. Arrows thudding into bodies. And a moment later, the unmistakable sound of a firing arquebus.

"*Shit*," Kitay breathed.

The twins were already racing back. Rin snatched her trident off the ground and followed.

The camp was in chaos. Ketreyids ran about, grabbing at the reins of spooked horses trying to break free. The air was sharp with the acrid smoke of fire powder. Bullet holes riddled the yurts. Ketreyid bodies were strewn across the ground. And the Gray Company missionaries, half of them wielding arquebuses, fired indiscriminately around the camp.

How had they gotten their arquebuses back?

Rin heard a shot and threw herself to the ground as a bullet burrowed into the tree behind her.

Arrows whistled overhead. Each one found its mark with a thickening thud. A handful of Hesperians dropped to the ground, arrows pierced cleanly into their skulls. A few others ran, panicked, from the clearing. No one chased them.

The only one left was Augus. He wielded two arquebuses, one in each hand, their barrels drooping clumsily against the ground.

He'd never fired one. Rin could tell—he was shaking; he had absolutely no idea what to do.

The Sorqan Sira uttered a command under her breath. The riders moved at once. Instantly twelve arrowheads were pointed at Augus, bowstrings stretching taut.

"Don't shoot!" Rin cried. She ran forward, blocking their arrows' paths with her body. "Don't shoot—please, he's confused—"

Augus didn't seem to notice. His eyes locked on Rin's. He raised the arquebus in his right hand. The barrel formed a direct line to her chest.

It didn't matter if he'd never fired an arquebus before. He couldn't miss. Not from this distance.

"Demon," he said.

"Rin, get back," Kitay said tightly.

Rin stood frozen, unable to move. Augus waved his weapons erratically about, pointed them alternately between the Sorqan Sira, Rin, and Kitay. "Maker give me the courage, protect me from these heathens . . ."

"What is he saying?" the Sorqan Sira demanded.

Augus squeezed his eyes shut. "Show them the strength of heaven and smite them with your divine justice . . ."

"Augus, stop!" Rin walked forward, hands raised in what she hoped was a nonthreatening gesture, and spoke in clearly enunciated Hesperian. "You have nothing to be afraid of. These people aren't your enemies, they're not going to hurt you—"

"Savages!" Augus screamed. He waved one arquebus in an arc before him. The Ketreyids hissed and scattered backward; several sank into a low crouch. *"Get out of my head!"*

"Augus, please," Rin begged. "You're scared, you're not yourself. Look at me, you know who I am, you've met me—"

Augus leveled the arquebus again at her.

The Sorqan Sira's silent command rippled through the clearing. *Fire.*

Not a single Ketreyid rider loosed their bow.

Rin glanced around in confusion.

"Bekter!" the Sorqan Sira shouted. "What is this?"

Bekter smiled, and Rin realized with a twist of dread what was happening.

This wasn't an accident. The Hesperians had been set free on purpose.

This was a coup.

A furious flurry of flashing images ricocheted back and forth in the clearing, a silent war of minds between Bekter and the Sorqan Sira blasted to everyone present, like they were wrestlers performing for an audience.

Rin saw Bekter cutting the Hesperians' bonds and placing the arquebuses in their hands. They stared at him, brain-addled in terror. He told them they were about to play a game. He challenged them to outrun his arrows. The Hesperians scattered.

She saw the girl Jiang had murdered—Tseveri, the Sorqan Sira's daughter—riding across the steppe with a little boy seated before her. They were laughing.

She saw a band of warriors—Speerlies, she realized with a start—at least a dozen of them, flames rolling off of their shoulders as they marched through burned yurts and charred bodies.

She felt a scorching fury radiating out of Bekter, a fury that the Sorqan Sira's weakening protests only amplified, and she understood: This wasn't just some ambition-fueled power struggle. This was vengeance.

Bekter wanted to do for his sister Tseveri what the Sorqan Sira never could. He wanted retribution. The Sorqan Sira wanted Nikara shamans controlled, but Bekter wanted them dead.

Too long you've let the Cike run unchecked in the Empire, Mother. Bekter's voice rang loud and clear. *Too long you've shown mercy to the Naimad scum. No more.*

The riders agreed.

They'd long since shifted their loyalties. Now they only had to dispose of their leader.

The exchange was over in an instant.

The Sorqan Sira reeled back. She seemed to have shrunk in on herself. For the first time, Rin saw fear on her face.

"Bekter," she said. "Please."

Bekter spoke an order.

Arrows dotted the earth around Augus's feet. Augus gave a strangled yelp. Rin lunged forward, but it was too late. She heard a click, then a small explosion.

The Sorqan Sira dropped to the ground. Smoke curled from the spot where the bullet had burrowed into her chest. She looked down, then back up at Augus, face contorted in disbelief, before slumping to the side.

Chaghan rushed forward. *"Ama!"*

Augus dropped the arquebus he'd fired and raised the second one to his shoulder.

Several things happened at once.

Augus pulled the trigger. Qara threw herself in front of her brother. A bang split the night and together the twins collapsed, Qara falling back into Chaghan's arms.

The riders turned to flee.

Rin screamed. A rivulet of fire shot from her mouth and slammed into Augus's chest, knocking him over. He shouted, writhing madly to put out the flames, but the fire didn't stop; it consumed his air, poured into his lungs, seized him from inside like a hand until his torso was charcoal and he couldn't scream anymore.

Augus's death throes slowed to an insectlike twitching as Rin sank to her knees. She closed her mouth. The flames died away, and Augus lay still.

Behind her Chaghan was cradling his sister. A dark splotch of blood appeared over Qara's right breast as if painted by an invisible artist, blossoming larger and larger like a blooming poppy flower.

"Qara—Qara, *no* . . ." Chaghan's hands moved frantically over her breast, but there was no arrowhead to pull out; the metal shard had buried itself too deep for him to save her.

"Stop," Qara gasped. She lifted a shaking hand and touched it to Chaghan's chest. Blood bubbled out between her teeth. "Let go. You have to let go."

"I'm going with you," Chaghan said.

Qara's breath came in short, pained gasps. "No. Too important."

"Qara . . ."

"Do this for me," Qara whispered. "*Please.*"

Chaghan pressed his forehead against Qara's. Something passed between them, an exchange of thoughts that Rin could not hear. Qara reached a shaking hand to her chest, drew a pattern in her own blood on the pale skin of Chaghan's cheek, and then placed her palm against it.

Chaghan exhaled. Rin thought she saw something pass in the space between them—a gust of air, a shimmer of light.

Qara's head fell to the side. Chaghan pulled her limp form into his arms and dropped his head.

"Rin," Kitay said urgently.

She spun around. Ten feet away, Bekter sat astride his horse, bow raised.

She lifted her trident, but she had no chance. From this close Bekter had an easy shot. They'd be dead in seconds.

But Bekter wasn't shooting. His arrow was nocked to his bow, but the string wasn't pulled taut. He had a dazed look in his eye; his gaze flickered between the bodies of the Sorqan Sira and Qara.

He's in shock, Rin realized. Bekter couldn't believe what he'd done.

She hefted her trident over her head, poised to throw. "Murder's not so easy, is it?"

Bekter blinked, as if just coming to his senses, and then aimed his bow at her.

"Go on," she told him. "We'll see who's faster."

Bekter looked at the gleaming tips of her trident, then down at Chaghan, who was rocking back and forth over Qara's form. He lowered his bow just a fraction.

"You did this," Bekter said. "You killed Mother. That's what I'll tell them. This is your fault." His voice wavered; he seemed to be trying to convince himself. His bow shook in his hands. "All of this is your fault."

Rin hurled her trident. Bekter's horse bolted. The trident flew a foot over his head and shot through empty air. Rin aimed a burst of flame in his direction, but she was too slow—within seconds Bekter was gone from her sight, disappeared into the forest to follow his band of traitors.

For a long time, the only sound in the clearing came from Chaghan. He wasn't crying, not quite. His eyes were dry. But his chest heaved erratically, his breath came out in short, strangled bursts, and his eyes stared wide, down at his sister's corpse as if he couldn't believe what he was looking at.

Our wills have been united since we were children, Qara had said. *We are two halves of the same person.*

Rin couldn't possibly imagine how it felt to have that stripped away.

At last Kitay bent down over the Sorqan Sira's body and rolled her flat on her back. He pulled her eyelids closed.

Then he touched Chaghan gently on the shoulder. "Is there something we should—"

"There's going to be war," Chaghan said abruptly. He laid Qara out on the dirt before him, then arranged her hands on her chest, one clasped over the other. His voice was flat, emotionless. "Bekter's the chieftain now."

"*Chieftain?*" Kitay repeated. "He just killed his own mother!"

"Not by his own hand. That's why he gave the Hesperians those guns. He didn't touch her, and his riders will attest to that. They'll be able to swear it before the Pantheon, because it's true."

There was no emotion on Chaghan's face. He looked utterly, terrifyingly calm.

Rin understood. He'd shut down, replaced his feelings with a focus on calm pragmatism, because that was the only way he could block out the pain.

Chaghan took a deep, shuddering breath. For a moment the facade cracked, and Rin could see pain twisting across his face, but it disappeared just as fast as it came. "This is . . . this changes everything. The Sorqan Sira was the only one keeping the Ketreyids in check. Now Bekter will lead them to slaughter the Naimads."

"Then go," Rin said. "Take the warhorse. Ride north. Go back to your clan and warn them."

Chaghan blinked at her. "That horse is for you."

"Don't be an idiot."

"We'll find another way," Kitay said. "It'll take us a little longer, but we'll figure it out. You need to go."

Slowly, Chaghan stood up on shaky legs and followed them to the riverbank.

The horse was waiting tamely where they'd left it. It seemed completely unbothered by the commotion in the clearing. It had been trained well not to panic.

Chaghan lifted his foot into the stirrup and swung himself up into the saddle in one graceful, practiced movement. He grasped the reins in both hands and looked down at them. He swallowed. "Rin . . ."

"Yes?" she answered.

He looked very small atop the horse. For the first time, she saw him for what he was: not a fearsome shaman, not a mysterious Seer, but just a boy, really. She'd always thought Chaghan so ethereally powerful, so detached from the realm of mortals. But he was human after all, smaller and thinner than the rest of them.

And for the first time in his life, he was alone.

"What am I going to do?" he asked quietly.

His voice trembled. He looked so utterly lost.

Rin reached for his hand. Then she looked at him, really looked him in the eyes. They were so similar when she thought about it. Too young to be so powerful, not close to ready for the positions they had been thrust into.

She squeezed his fingers. "You fight."

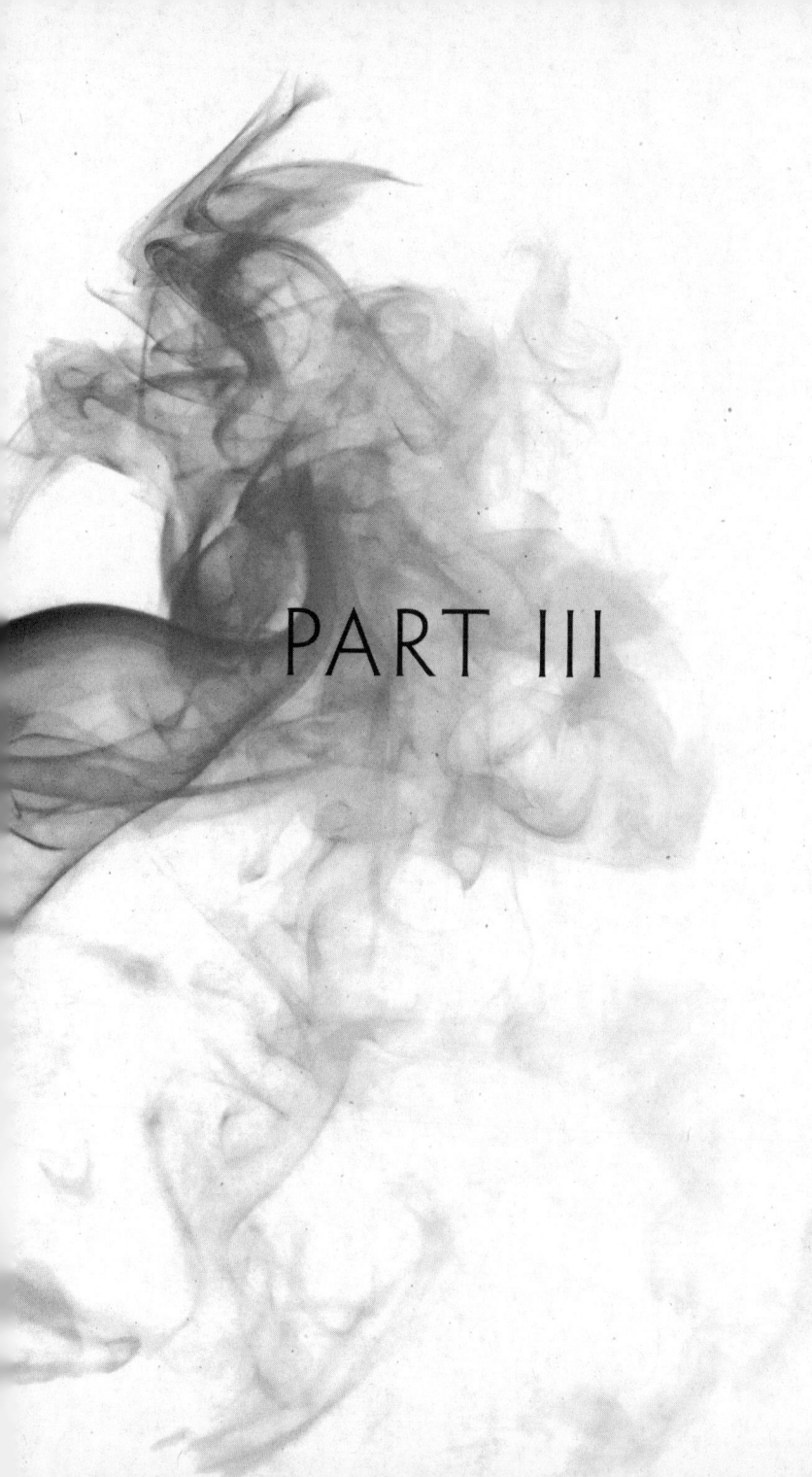

CHAPTER 25

The journey back to Arlong took twenty-nine days. Rin knew because she carved one notch each day into the side of their raft, imagining, as the time stretched on, how the war must be going. Each mark represented a question, another possible alternate outcome. Had Daji invaded Arlong yet? Was the Republic still alive? Was *Nezha*?

She took solace during the journey in the fact that she didn't see the Imperial Fleet on the Western Murui, but that meant little. The fleet might have already passed them. Daji might be marching on Arlong instead of sailing—the Militia had always been far more comfortable with ground warfare. Or the fleet could have taken a coastal route, could have destroyed Tsolin's forces before sailing south for the Red Cliffs.

Meanwhile their raft bobbed insignificantly down the Western Murui, drifting on the current because both of them were too exhausted to row.

Kitay had cobbled the raft together over two days using ropes and hunting knives the Ketreyids had left behind. It was a flimsy thing, tied together from the washed-up remains of the Republican Fleet, and just large enough for the two of them to lie down without touching.

Rafting was slow progress. They kept cautiously to the shores to avoid dangerous currents like the one that had swept them over the falls at Boyang. When they could, they drifted under tree cover to stay hidden.

They had to be careful with their food. They'd salvaged two weeks' worth of dried meat from the Ketreyids' rations, and occasionally they managed a catch of fish, but still their bones became ever more visible under their skin as the days went on. They lost both muscle mass and stamina, which made it even more important to avoid patrols. Even with Rin's reacquisition of her abilities, there was little chance they could win in any real skirmish if they couldn't even run a mile.

They spent their days sleeping to conserve energy. One of them would curl up on the raft while the other kept a lonely vigil by the spear attached to a shield which served as an oar and rudder. One afternoon Rin awoke to find Kitay etching diagrams into the raft with a knife.

She rubbed the sleep from her eyes. "What are you doing?"

Kitay rested his chin on his fist, tapping his knife against the raft. "I've been thinking about how best to weaponize you."

She sat up. "Weaponize?"

"Bad word?" He continued to scratch at the wood. "Optimize, then. You're like a lamp. I'm trying to figure out how to make you burn brighter."

Rin pointed to a wobbly carved circle. "Is that supposed to be me?"

"Yes. That represents your heat source. I'm trying to figure out exactly how your abilities work. Can you summon fire from anywhere?" Kitay pointed across the river. "For instance, could you make those reeds light up?"

"No." She knew the answer without trying it. "It has to come from me. *Within* me."

Yes, that was right. When she called the flame it felt like it was being tugged out from something inside her and through her.

"It comes out my hands and mouth," she said. "I can do it from other places too, but it feels easier that way."

"So *you're* the heat source?"

"Not so much the source. More like . . . the bridge. Or the gate, rather."

"The gate," he repeated, rubbing his chin. "Is that what the Gatekeeper's name means? Is he a conduit to every god?"

"I don't think so. Jiang . . . Jiang is an open door for certain creatures. You saw what the Sorqan Sira showed us. I think that he's only able to call those beasts. All the monsters of the Emperor's Menagerie, isn't that how the story goes? But the rest of us . . . it's hard to explain." Rin struggled to find the words. "The gods are in this world, but they're also still in their own, but while the Phoenix is in me it can *affect* the world—"

"But not in the way that it wants to," Kitay interrupted. "Or not always."

"Because I don't let it," she said. "It's a matter of control. If you've got enough presence of mind, you redirect the god's power for your purposes."

"And if not? What happens if you open the gate all the way?"

"Then you're lost. Then you become like Feylen."

"But what does that *mean*?" he pressed. "Do you have any control over your body left at all?"

"I'm not sure. There were a few times—just a few—I thought Feylen was inside, fighting for his body back. But you saw what happened."

Kitay nodded slowly. "Must be hard to win a mental battle with a god."

Rin thought of the shamans encased in stone within the Chuluu Korikh, trapped forever with their thoughts and regrets, comforted only by the knowledge that this was the least horrible alternative. She shuddered. "It's nearly impossible."

"So we'll just have to figure out how to beat the wind with fire." Kitay pushed his fingers through his overgrown bangs. "That's a pretty puzzle."

There wasn't much else to do on the raft, so they started experimenting with the fire. Day after day they pushed Rin's abilities to see how far she could go, how much control she could manage.

Up until then, Rin had been calling the fire on instinct. She'd been too busy fighting the Phoenix for control of her mind to ever bother examining the mechanics of the flame. But under Kitay's pointed questions and guided experiments, she figured out the exact parameters of her abilities.

She couldn't seize control of a fire that already existed. She also couldn't control fire that had left her body. She could give the fire a shape and make it erupt into the air, but the lingering flames would dissipate in seconds unless they found something to consume.

"What does it feel like for you?" she asked Kitay.

He paused for a moment before he answered. "It doesn't hurt. At least, not so much as the first time. It's more like—I'm aware of something. Something's moving in the back of my head, and I'm not sure what. I feel a rush, like the shot of adrenaline you get when you look over the edge of a cliff."

"And you're sure it doesn't hurt?"

"Promise."

"Bullshit," she said. "You make the same face every time I summon a flame any bigger than a campfire. It's like you're dying."

"Do I?" He blinked. "Just a reflex, I think. Don't worry about it."

He was lying to her. She loved that about him, that he'd care enough to lie to her. But she couldn't keep doing this to him. She couldn't hurt Kitay and not worry about it.

If she could, she'd be lost.

"You have to tell me when it's too much," she said.

"It's really not so bad."

"Cut the crap, Kitay—"

"It's the urges I feel more than anything," he said. "Not the pain. It makes me hungry. It makes me want more. Do you understand that feeling?"

"Of course," she said. "It's the Phoenix's most basic impulse. Fire devours."

"Devouring feels good." He pointed at an overhanging branch. "Try that shooty thing again."

Over the next few days she learned a number of different tricks. She could create balls of fire and hurl them at targets up to ten yards away. She could make shapes out of flame so intricate that she could have put on an entire puppet show with them. She could, by shoving her hands into the river, boil the water around them until steam misted the air and fish bubbled belly-up to the surface.

Most importantly, she could carve out protective spaces in the fire, up to ten feet from her own body, so that Kitay never burned even when everything around them did.

"What about mass destruction?" he asked after a few days of exploring minor tricks.

Rin stiffened. "What do you mean?"

His tone was carefully neutral. Purely academic. "What you did to the Federation, for instance—can we replicate that? How much flame can you summon?"

"That was different. I was on the island. In the temple. I'd . . . I'd just seen Altan die." She swallowed. "And I was angry. I was so angry."

In that moment, she'd been capable of an inhuman, vicious, and terrible rage. But she wasn't sure she could replicate that rage, because it had been sparked by Altan's death, and what she felt now when she thought about Altan wasn't fury, but grief.

Rage and grief were so different. Rage gave her the power to burn down countries. Grief only exhausted her.

"And if you went back to the temple?" Kitay pressed. "If you went back and summoned the Phoenix?"

"I'm not going back to that temple," Rin said immediately. She didn't know what it was, but Kitay's enthusiasm was making her uncomfortable—he was looking at her with the sort of intense curiosity that she had only ever seen in Shiro and Petra.

"But if you had to? If we only had one option, if everything would be lost if you didn't do it?"

"We're not putting that on the table."

"I'm not saying you have to. I'm saying we have to know if it's even an option. I'm saying you have to at least try."

"You want me to practice a genocidal event," she said slowly. "Just to be clear."

"Start small," he suggested. "Then get bigger. See how far you can go without the temple."

"That'll destroy everything in sight."

"We haven't seen signs of human life all day. If anyone lived here, they're long gone. This is empty land."

"What about wildlife?"

Kitay rolled his eyes. "You and I both know that wildlife is the least of your concerns. Stop hedging, Rin. Do it."

She nodded, put her palms out, and closed her eyes.

Flame wrapped her like a warm blanket. It felt good. It felt *too* good. She was burning without guilt or consequence. She was unrestrained power. She could feel herself tipping back into that state of ecstasy, could have lost herself in the dreamy oblivion of the wildfire that surged higher, faster, brighter, if she hadn't heard a high-pitched keening that wasn't coming from her.

She looked down. Kitay lay curled in a fetal position on the raft, hands clutching his mouth, trying to suppress his screams.

She reined the fire back in with difficulty.

Kitay made a choking noise and buried his head in his hands.

She dropped to her knees beside him. "Kitay—"

"I'm fine," he gasped. "Fine."

She tried to put her hands on him, but he pushed her away with a violence that shocked her.

"Just let me breathe." He shook his head. "It's all right, Rin. I'm not hurt. It's just—it's all in my head."

She could have slapped him. "You're supposed to tell me when it's too much."

"It wasn't too much." He sat up straight. "Try that again."

"*What?*"

"I couldn't get a good look at your blast radius just then," he said. "Try it again."

"Absolutely not," she snapped. "I don't care that you've got a death wish. I can't keep doing this to you."

"Then go right up to the edge," he insisted. "The point right before it hurts too much. Let's figure out what the limit is."

"That's insane."

"It's better than finding out on a battlefield. Please, Rin, we won't get a better chance to do this."

"What is wrong with you?" she demanded. "Why does this matter so much?"

"Because I need to know the full extent of what you can do," Kitay said. "Because if I'm strategizing for Arlong's defense then I need to know where to put you, and why. Because if I went through all of this for *you*, then the very least you can do is show me what maximum power looks like. If we've turned you back into a weapon, then you're going to be a damn good one. And stop panicking over me, Rin. I'm fine until I say I'm not."

So she called the flame again and again, pushing the limits every time, until the shores burned pitch-black around them. She kept going even while Kitay screamed because he'd ordered her not to stop unless he said so explicitly. She kept going until his eyes rolled back into his head and he went limp on the raft. And even then, when he revived seconds later, the first thing he said to her was: "Fifty yards."

When at last they reached the Red Cliffs, Rin saw with immense relief that the flag of the Republic still flew over Arlong.

So Vaisra was safe, and Daji was still a distant threat.

Their next challenge was to get back into the city without getting shot. Arlong, expecting a Militia assault, had hunkered down behind its defenses. The massive gates to the harbor past the Red Cliffs were locked. Crossbows were lined up against every flat surface overlooking the channel. Rin and Kitay could hardly march up to the city doors—any sudden, unexpected movement would get them stuck full of arrows. They discovered this when they saw a wild monkey wander too close to the walls and startle a line of trigger-happy archers.

They were so exhausted that they found this ridiculously funny. A month's worth of travel and their biggest concern was *friendly fire*.

Finally they decided to get some sentries' attention in the least threatening way possible. They hurled rocks at the sides of the cliff and waited while pinging noises echoed around the channel until at last a line of soldiers emerged on the cliffside, crossbows pointed down.

Rin and Kitay immediately put their hands up.

"Don't shoot, please," Kitay called.

The sentry captain leaned over the cliff wall. "What the hell do you think you're doing?"

"We're Republican soldiers back from Boyang," Kitay called, gesturing to their uniforms.

"Uniforms are cheap on corpses," said the captain.

Kitay pointed to Rin. "Not uniforms that fit her."

The captain looked unconvinced. "Back away or I'll shoot."

"I wouldn't," Rin called. "Or Vaisra will be asking why you've killed his Speerly."

The sentries hooted with laughter.

"Good one," said the captain.

Rin blinked. Did they not recognize her? Did they not know who she was?

"Maybe he's new," Kitay said.

"Can I hurt him?" she muttered.

"Just a little."

She tilted her head back and opened her mouth. Breathing fire was harder than shooting it from her hands because it gave her less directional control, but she liked the dramatic effect. A stream of fire shot into the air and unfurled itself into the shape of a dragon that hung for a moment in front of the awed soldiers, undulating grandly, before rushing the captain.

He was never in any real danger. Rin extinguished the flames as soon as they made contact. But he still screamed and fell backward as if he were being charged by a bear. When at last he resurfaced over the cliff wall, his face had turned bright pink, and smoke drifted up from his singed eyebrows.

"I should shoot you just for that," he said.

"Why don't you just tell Vaisra that the Speerly's back," Rin said. "And bring us something to eat."

Word of their return seemed to have spread instantly to the entire harbor. A massive crowd of soldiers and civilians alike surrounded them the moment they passed through the gates. Everyone had questions, and they shouted them from every direction so loudly that Rin could barely make out a word.

The questions she did understand were about soldiers still missing from Boyang. The people wanted to know if any others were still alive. If they were on their way back. Rin didn't have the heart to answer.

"Who dragged you out of hell?" Venka elbowed her way through the soldiers. She seized Rin by the arms, looked her up and down, and then wrinkled her pert nose. "You smell."

"Nice to see you, too," Rin said.

"No, really, it's *rank*. It's like you've taken a knife blade to my nose."

"Well, we haven't seen properly clean water in over a month, so—"

"So what's the story?" Venka interrupted. "Did you break out of prison? Take out an entire battalion? Swim the whole length back down the Murui?"

"We drank horse piss and got high," said Kitay.

"Come again?" Venka asked.

Rin was about to explain when she caught sight of Nezha pushing his way to the front of the crowd.

"Hello," she said.

He stopped just before her and stared, blinking rapidly as if he didn't know what he was looking at. His arms hung awkwardly at his sides, slightly uplifted, like he wasn't sure what to do with them.

"Can I?" he asked.

She stretched her arms toward him. He pulled her in against him so hard that she stiffened on instinct. Then she relaxed, because Nezha was so warm, so solid, and hugging him was such a wonderful feeling that she just wanted to bury her face into his uniform and stand there for a very long time.

"I can't believe it," Nezha murmured into her ear. "We thought for sure..."

She pressed her forehead against his chest. "Me too."

Her tears were falling thick and fast. The embrace had already stretched on much longer than it should have, and finally Nezha let her go, but he didn't take his arms off her shoulders.

Finally he spoke. "Where is Jinzha?"

"What do you mean?" Rin asked. "He didn't return with you?"

Nezha just shook his head, eyes wide, before he was pushed aside by two massive bodies.

"Rin!"

Before she could speak, Suni wrapped her in a tight hug, lifting her a good foot off the ground, and she had to pound frantically at his shoulder before he released her.

"All right." Ramsa reached up and frantically patted Suni's shoulder. "You're going to crush her."

"Sorry," Suni said, abashed. "We just thought..."

Rin couldn't help but grin even as she felt her ribs for bruises. "Yeah. Good to see you, too."

Baji grabbed her hand, pulled her in, and pounded her on the shoulder. "We knew you weren't dead. You're too spiteful to go that easy."

"How did you get back?" Rin asked.

"Feylen didn't just wreck our ships, he whipped up a storm that wrecked everything in the lake," Baji said. "He was aiming for the big ships, though; somehow a few of the skimmers held together.

About a quarter of us managed to get out of the maelstrom. I've no idea how we paddled back out to the river alive, but here we are."

Rin had an idea of how that had happened.

Ramsa's eyes flickered between her and Kitay. "Where are the twins?"

"That's a long story," Rin said.

"Not dead?" Baji asked.

"I . . . ah, it's complicated. Chaghan isn't. But Qara—" She paused, searching for the right words to say next, just as she saw a tall figure approaching from just over Baji's shoulder.

"Later," she said quietly.

Baji turned his head, saw who she was looking at, and immediately stepped aside. A hush fell over the soldiers, who parted ranks to let the Dragon Warlord through.

"You've returned," said Vaisra. He looked neither pleased nor displeased but somewhat impatient, as if he'd simply been expecting her.

Rin instinctively ducked her head. "Yes, sir."

"Good." Vaisra gestured toward the palace. "Go clean yourself up. I'll be in my office."

"Tell me everything that happened at Boyang," Vaisra said.

"Haven't they already told you?" Rin sat down opposite him. She smelled better than she had in weeks. She'd cut her oily, lice-ridden hair; scrubbed herself in cold water; and traded in her stained, pungent clothes for a fresh uniform.

A part of her had been hoping for a warmer welcome—a smile, a hand on her shoulder, at least some indication that Vaisra was glad she was back—but all he gave her was solemn expectation.

"I want your account," he said.

Rin considered pinning the blame on Jinzha's tactical decisions, but there was no point in antagonizing Vaisra by rubbing salt into an open wound. Besides, nothing Jinzha had done could have prevented what had happened once the battle began. He might as well have been fighting the ocean itself.

"The Empress has another shaman in her employ. His name is Feylen. He channels the Wind God. He used to be in the Cike, until that went sideways. He wrecked your fleet. Took him minutes."

"What do you mean, he *used* to be in the Cike?" Vaisra asked.

"He was put down," Rin said. "I mean, he went mad. A lot of shamans do. Altan let him back out of the Chuluu Korikh by accident—"

"By accident?"

"On purpose, but he was stupid to do it. And now I suppose Daji's found a way to lure him onto her side."

"How did she do that?" Vaisra demanded. "Money? Power? Can he be bought?"

"I don't think he cares about any of that. He's . . ." Rin paused, trying to figure out how to explain it to Vaisra. "He doesn't want what humans want. The god has . . . like with me, with the Phoenix—"

"He's lost his mind," Vaisra supplied.

She nodded. "I think Feylen needs to fulfill the god's fundamental nature. The Phoenix needs to consume. But the Wind God needs chaos. Daji's found some way to bend that to her will, but you won't be able to tempt him with anything humans might want."

"I see." Vaisra was silent for a moment. "And my son?"

Rin hesitated. Had they not told him about Jinzha? "Sir?"

"They didn't bring back a body," Vaisra said.

His mask cracked then. For the briefest moment, he looked like a father.

So he did know. He just wouldn't admit to himself that if Jinzha hadn't made his way back to Arlong with the rest of the fleet, then he was probably dead.

"I didn't see what happened to him," Rin said. "I'm sorry."

"There's no point speculating, then," Vaisra said coolly. His mask reassembled itself. "Let's move on. I assume you'll want to rejoin the infantry?"

"Not the infantry." Rin took a deep breath. "I want command of the Cike again. I want a seat at the strategy table. I want direct say in anything you want the Cike to do."

"And why's that?" Vaisra asked.

Because Chaghan can't be right about my being your dog. "Because I deserve it. I broke the Seal. I've gotten the fire back."

Vaisra raised an eyebrow. "Show me."

She turned an open palm toward the ceiling and summoned a fist-sized ball of fire. She made it run up and down the length of her arm, made it twist around her in the air before calling it back into her fingers. Even after a month of practice, she was still amazed at how easy it was, how delightfully natural it felt to control the flame the way she controlled her fingers. She let it take shapes—a rat, a rooster, an undulating orange dragon—and then she closed her fingers over her palm.

"Very nice," Vaisra said approvingly. The mask was gone now; he was finally smiling. She felt a warm rush of encouragement.

"So. Command?"

He waved a hand. "You're reinstated. I'll let the generals know. How did you manage this?"

"That's a long story." She paused, wondering where to start. "We, ah, ran into some Ketreyids."

He frowned. "Hinterlanders?"

"Don't call them that. They're Ketreyids." She gave him a quick account of what the Ketreyids had done, told him about the Sorqan Sira and the Trifecta.

She omitted the part about the anchor bond. Vaisra didn't need to know.

"Then what happened?" Vaisra asked. "Where are they?"

"They're gone. And the Sorqan Sira's dead."

"What?"

She told him about Augus. She knew Vaisra would be surprised, but she hadn't expected his reaction. The color drained from his face. His entire body tensed.

"Who else knows?" he demanded.

"Just Kitay. And a couple of Ketreyids, but they're not telling anyone."

"Tell no one this happened," he said quietly. "Not even my son. If the Hesperians find out, our lives are forfeit."

"It was their fault to begin with," she muttered.

"Shut up." He slammed a hand on the table. She flinched back, startled.

"How could you be so stupid?" he demanded. "You should have brought them back safe, that would have ingratiated us to General Tarcquet—"

"Tarcquet made it back?" she interrupted.

"Yes, and many of the Gray Company are with him. They escaped south in one of the skimmers. They are deeply unhappy with our naval capabilities and are *this* close to pulling out of the continent, which is a thought I assume never crossed your mind when you decided to murder one of them."

"Are you joking? They were trying to kill us—"

"So you should have incapacitated him or fled. The Gray Company is untouchable. You couldn't have picked a worse Hesperian to kill."

"This isn't my fault," Rin insisted. "He'd gone mad, he was waving an arquebus around—"

"*Listen to me*," Vaisra said. "You are walking a very fine line right now. The Hesperians are not just upset, they are terrified. They thought you a curiosity before. Then they saw what happened at Boyang. Now they are convinced that each and every one of you is a mindless agent of Chaos who could bring about the end of the world. They're going to hunt down every shaman in this empire and put them in cages if they can. The only reason why they haven't touched *you* is because you volunteered, and they know you'll cooperate. Do you understand now?"

Fear struck Rin. "Then Suni and Baji—"

"—are safe," Vaisra said. "The Hesperians don't know about them. And they'd better not find out, because then Tarcquet will know we've lied to him. Your job is to keep your head down, to cooperate, and to draw the least possible attention to yourself. You have a reprieve for now. Sister Petra has agreed to postpone your meetings until, one way or another, this war has concluded. So behave yourself. Do not give them further reason for irritation. Otherwise we are all lost."

Then Rin understood.

Vaisra wasn't angry at her. This wasn't about her at all. No, Vaisra was frustrated. He'd been frustrated for months, playing an impossible game with the Hesperians where they kept changing the rules.

She dared to ask. "They're never bringing their ships, are they?"

He sighed. "We don't know."

"They still won't give you a straight answer? All this because they're still deciding?"

"Tarcquet claims they haven't finished their evaluation," Vaisra said. "I admit I do not understand their standards. When I ask, they utter idiotic vagaries. They want signs of rational sentience. Proof of the ability to self-govern."

"But that's ridiculous. If they'd just tell us what they wanted—"

"Ah, but then that would be cheating." Vaisra's lip curled. "They need proof that we've independently attained civilized society."

"But that's a paradox. We can't achieve that unless they help."

He looked exhausted. "I know."

"Then that's fucked." She threw her hands up in the air. "This is all just a spectacle to them. They're never going to come."

"Maybe." Vaisra looked decades older then, lined and weary. Rin imagined how Petra might sketch him in her book. *Nikara man, middle-aged. Strong build. Reasonable intelligence. Inferior.* "But we are the weaker party. We have no choice but to play their game. That's how power works."

She found Nezha waiting for her outside the palace gates.

"Hi," she said tentatively. She looked him up and down, trying to get a read on his expression, but he was just as inscrutable as his father.

"Hello," he said back.

She tried a smile. He didn't return it. For a minute they just stood there staring at each other. Rin was torn between running into his arms again and simply running away. She still didn't know where she stood with him. The last time they'd spoken—really spoken—she'd been sure that he would hate her forever.

"Can we talk?" he asked finally.

"We *are* talking."

He shook his head. "Alone. In private. Not here."

"Fine," she said, and followed him along the canal to the edge of a pier, where the waves were loud enough to drown their voices out from any curious eavesdroppers.

"I owe you an explanation," he said at last.

She leaned against the railing. "Go on."

"I'm not a shaman."

She threw her hands up. "Oh, don't fuck with me—"

"I'm *not*," he insisted. "I know I can do things. I mean, I know I'm linked to a god, and I can—sort of—call it, sometimes . . ."

"That's what shamanism *is*."

"You're not listening to me. Whatever I am, it's not what *you* are. My mind's not my own—my body belongs to some—some *thing* . . ."

"That's just it, Nezha. That's how it is for all of us. And I know it hurts, and I know it's hard, but—"

"You're still not listening," he snapped. "It's no sacrifice for you. You and your god want the same damn thing. But I didn't *ask* for this—"

She raised her eyebrows. "Well, it doesn't just happen by *accident*. You had to want it first. You had to ask the god."

"But I didn't. I never asked, and I've never wanted it." The way Nezha said it made her fall quiet. He sounded like he was about to cry.

He took a deep breath, and when he spoke again, his voice was so quiet she had to step closer to hear him. "Back at Boyang, you called me a coward."

"Look, all I meant was that—"

"I'm going to tell you a story," he interrupted. He was trembling. Why was he trembling? "I want you to just listen. And I want you to believe me. *Please*."

She crossed her arms. "Fine."

Nezha blinked hard and stared out over the water. "I told you once that I had another brother. His name was Mingzha."

When he didn't continue, Rin asked, "What was he like?"

"Hilarious," Nezha said. "Chubby, loud, and incredible. He was everyone's favorite. He was so full of energy, he *glowed*. My mother had miscarried twice before she gave birth to him, but Mingzha was perfect. He was never sick. My mother adored him. She was hugging him constantly. She dressed him up in so many golden bracelets and anklets that he jangled when he walked." He shuddered. "She should have known better. Dragons like gold."

"Dragons," Rin repeated.

"You said you'd listen."

"Sorry."

Nezha was sickly pale. His skin was almost translucent; Rin could see blue veins under his jaw, crisscrossing with his scars.

"My siblings and I spent our childhood playing by the river," he said. "There's a grotto about a mile out from the entrance to this channel, this underwater crystal cave that the servants liked telling stories about, but Father had forbidden us to enter it. So of course all we ever wanted to do was explore it.

"My mother took sick one night when Mingzha was six. During that time my father had been called to Sinegard on the Empress's orders, so the servants weren't as concerned with watching us as they might have been. Jinzha was at the Academy. Muzha was abroad. So the responsibility for watching Mingzha fell to me."

Nezha's voice cracked. His eyes looked hollow, tortured. Rin didn't want to hear any more. She had a sickening suspicion of where this story was headed, and she didn't want it spoken out loud, because that would make it true.

She wanted to tell him it was all right, he didn't have to tell her, they never had to speak about this again, but Nezha was talking faster and faster, like he was afraid the words would be buried inside him if he didn't spit them out now.

"Mingzha wanted to—no, *I* wanted to explore that grotto. It was my idea to begin with. I put it in Mingzha's head. It was my fault. He didn't know any better."

Rin reached for his arm. "Nezha, you don't have to—"

He shoved her away. "Can you please shut up and just listen *for once*?"

She fell silent.

"He was the most beautiful thing I'd ever seen," he whispered. "That's what scares me. They say the House of Yin is beautiful. But that's because dragons like beautiful things, because dragons *are* beautiful and they create beauty. When he emerged from the cave, all I could think about was how bright his scales were, how lovely his form, how magnificent."

But they're not real, Rin thought desperately. *Dragons are just stories.*

Weren't they?

Even if she didn't believe in Nezha's story, she believed in his pain. It was written all over his face.

Something had happened all those years ago. She just didn't know what.

"So beautiful," Nezha murmured, even as his knuckles whitened. "I couldn't stop staring.

"Then he ate my brother. Devoured him in seconds. Have you watched a wild animal eat before? It's not clean. It's brutal. Mingzha didn't even have time to scream. One moment he was there, clutching at my leg, and the next moment he was a mess of blood and gore and shining bones, and then there was nothing.

"But the dragon spared me. He said he had something better for me." Nezha swallowed. "He said he was going to give me a gift. And then he claimed me for his own."

"I'm so sorry," Rin said, because she didn't know what else to say.

Nezha didn't seem to have even heard. "My mother wishes I'd died that day. *I* wish I'd died. I wish it had been me. But it's selfish even to wish I were dead—because if I had died, then Mingzha would have lived, and the Dragon Lord would have cursed him like he cursed me, he would have *touched* him like he touched me."

She didn't dare ask what that meant.

"I'm going to show you something," he said.

She was too stunned to say anything. She could only watch, aghast, as he undid the clasps of his tunic with trembling fingers.

He yanked it down and turned around. "Do you see this?"

It was his tattoo—an image of a dragon in blue and silver. She'd seen it before, but he wouldn't remember.

She touched her index finger to the dragon's head, wondering. Was this tattoo the reason Nezha had always healed so quickly? He seemed able to survive anything—blunt trauma, poisonous gas, drowning.

But at what price?

"You said he claimed you for his own," she said softly. "What does that mean?"

"It means it *hurts*," he said. "Every moment that I'm not with him. It feels like anchors digging into my body; hooks trying to drag me back into the water."

The mark didn't look like a scar that was almost ten years old. It looked freshly inflicted; his skin shone an angry crimson. The glint of sunlight made the dragon seem as if it was writhing over Nezha's muscles, pressing itself deeper and deeper into his raw skin.

"And if you went back to him?" she asked. "What would happen to you?"

"I'd become part of his collection," he said. "He'd do what he wanted to me, satisfy himself, and I'd never leave. I'd be trapped, because I don't think I can die. I've tried. I've cut my wrists, but I never bleed out before my wounds stitch themselves back together. I've jumped off the Red Cliffs, and sometimes the pain is enough for me to think I've managed it this time, but I always wake up. I think the Dragon is keeping me alive. At least until I return to him.

"The first time I saw that grotto, there were faces all along the cave floor. It took me a while to realize I was fated to become one of them."

Rin withdrew her finger, suppressing a shudder.

"So now you know," Nezha said. He yanked his shirt back on. His voice hardened. "You're disgusted—don't say you aren't, I can see it on your face. I don't care. But don't you tell anyone what I've just told you, and don't you *ever* fucking dare call me a coward to my face."

Rin knew what she should have done. She should have said she was sorry. She should have acknowledged his pain, should have begged his forgiveness.

But the way he *said* it—his long-suffering martyr's voice, like she had no right to question him, like he was doing her a favor by telling her . . . that infuriated her.

"I'm not disgusted by that," she said.

"No?"

"I'm disgusted by you." She fought to keep her voice level. "You're acting like it's a death sentence, but it's not. It's also a source of power. It's kept you alive."

"It's a fucking abomination," he said.

"Am *I* an abomination?"

"No, but—"

"So what, it's fine for me to call the gods, but you're too good for it? You can't sully yourself?"

"That's not what I meant—"

"Well, that's the implication."

"It's different for you, you *chose* that—"

"You think that makes it hurt any less?" She was shouting now. "I thought I was going mad. For the longest time I didn't know which thoughts were my own and which thoughts were the Phoenix's. And it fucking *hurt*, Nezha, so don't tell me I don't know anything about that. There were days I wanted to die, too, but we're not *allowed* to die, we're too powerful. Your father said it himself. When you have this much power and this much is at stake you don't fucking *run* from it."

He looked furious. "You think I'm running?"

"All I know is that hundreds of soldiers are dead at the bottom of Lake Boyang, and you might have done something to prevent it."

"Don't you dare pin that on me," he hissed. "I shouldn't have this power. Neither of us should. We shouldn't exist, we're abominations, and we'd be better off dead."

"But we *do* exist. By that logic it's a good thing the Speerlies were killed."

"Maybe the Speerlies *should* have been killed. Maybe every shaman in the Empire should die. Maybe my mother's right—maybe we should get rid of you freaks, and get rid of the Hinterlanders, too, while we're at it."

She stared at him in disbelief. This wasn't Nezha. Nezha—*her* Nezha—couldn't possibly be saying this to her. She was so sure that he would realize he'd crossed the line, would back down and apologize, that she was stunned when his expression only hardened.

"Don't tell me Altan wasn't better off dead," he said.

All shreds of pity she'd felt for him fled.

She pulled her shirt up. "Look at me."

Immediately Nezha averted his eyes, but she grabbed at his chin and forced him to look at her sternum, down at the handprint scorched into her skin.

"You're not the only one with scars," she said.

Nezha wrenched himself from her grasp. "We are not the same."

"Yes, we are." She yanked her shirt back down. Her eyes blurred with tears. "The only difference between us is that I can suffer pain, and you're still a fucking coward."

She couldn't remember how they parted, only that one moment they were glaring at each other and the next she was stumbling back to the barracks in a daze, alone.

She wanted to run after Nezha and say she was sorry, and she also wanted never to see him again.

Dimly she understood that something had broken irreparably between them. They'd fought before. They'd spent their first three years together fighting. But this wasn't like those childish schoolyard squabbles.

They weren't coming back from this.

But what was she supposed to do? Apologize? She had too much pride to grovel. She was so sure she was right. Yes, Nezha had been hurt, but hadn't they all been hurt? She'd been through Golyn Niis. She'd been tortured on a lab table. She'd watched Altan die.

Nezha's particular tragedy wasn't worse because it had happened when he was a child. It wasn't worse because he was too scared to confront it.

She'd been through hell, and she was stronger for it. It wasn't her fault that he was too pathetic to do the same.

She found the Cike sitting in a circle on the barracks floor. Baji and Ramsa were playing dice while Suni watched from a top bunk to make sure Ramsa didn't cheat, as he always did.

"Oh, dear," Baji said as she approached. "Who made you cry?"

"Nezha," she mumbled. "I don't want to talk about it."

Ramsa clicked his tongue. "Ah, boy trouble."

She sat down in between them. "Shut up."

"Want me to do something about it? Put a missile in his toilet?"

She managed a smile. "Please don't."

"Suit yourself," he said.

Baji tossed the dice on the floor. "So what happened up north? Where's Chaghan?"

"Chaghan won't be with us for a while," she said. She took a deep breath and willed herself to push Nezha to the back of her mind. *Forget him. Focus on something else.* That was easy enough—she had so much to tell the Cike.

Over the next half hour she spoke to them about the Ketreyids, about Augus, and about what had happened in the forest.

They were predictably furious.

"So Chaghan was spying on us the entire time?" Baji demanded. "That lying fuck."

"I always hated him," Ramsa said. "Always prancing around with his mysterious mutters. Figures he'd been up to something."

"Can you really be surprised, though?" Suni, to Rin's shock, seemed the least bothered. "You had to know they had some other agenda. What else would Hinterlanders be doing in the Cike?"

"Don't call them Hinterlanders," Rin said automatically.

Ramsa ignored her. "So what were the Hinterlanders going to do if Chaghan decided we were getting too dangerous?"

"Kill you, probably," Baji said. "Pity they went back north, though. Would have been nice to have someone deal with Feylen. It'll be a struggle."

"A struggle?" Ramsa repeated. He laughed weakly. "You think last time we tried to put him down was a *struggle*?"

"What happened last time?" Rin asked.

"Tyr and Trengsin lured him into a small cave and stabbed so many knives through his body that even if he could have shamanized, it wouldn't have done a lick of good," Baji said. "It was kind of funny, really. When they brought him back out he looked like a pincushion."

"And Tyr was all right with that?" Rin asked.

"What do you think?" Baji asked. "Of course not. But that was his job. You can't command the Cike if you don't have the stomach to cull."

A cascade of footsteps sounded outside the room. Rin peered around the door to see a line of soldiers marching out, fully equipped with shields and halberds. "Where are they all going? I thought the Militia hadn't moved south yet."

"It's refugee patrol," Baji said.

She blinked. "Refugee patrol?"

"You didn't see all them coming in?" Ramsa asked. "They were pretty hard to miss."

"We came in through the Red Cliffs," Rin said. "I haven't seen anything but the palace. What do you mean, refugees?"

Ramsa exchanged an uncomfortable look with Baji. "You missed a lot while you were gone, I think."

Rin didn't like what that implied. She stood up. "Take me there."

"Our patrol shift isn't until tomorrow morning," Ramsa said.

"I don't care."

"But they're fussy about that," Ramsa insisted. "Security is tight on the refugee border, they're not going to let us through."

"I'm the Speerly," Rin said. "Do you think I give a shit?"

"Fine." Baji hauled himself to his feet. "I'll take you. But you're not going to like it."

CHAPTER 26

"Makes the barracks look nice, huh?" Ramsa asked.

Rin didn't know what to say.

The refugee district was an ocean of people crammed into endless rows of tents stretching toward the valley. The crowds had been kept out of the city proper, hemmed in behind hastily constructed barriers of shipping planks and driftwood.

It looked as if a giant had drawn a line in the sand with one finger and pushed everyone to one side. Republican soldiers wielding halberds paced back and forth in front of the barrier, though Rin wasn't sure who they were guarding—the refugees or the citizens.

"The refugees aren't allowed past that barrier," Baji explained. "The, uh, citizens didn't want them crowding the streets."

"What happens if they cross?" Rin asked.

"Nothing too terrible. Guards toss them back to the other side. It happened more often at the beginning, but a few beatings taught everyone their lesson."

They walked a few more paces. A horrible stench hit Rin's nose—the smell of too many unwashed bodies packed together for far too long. "How long have they been there?"

"At least a month," Baji said. "I'm told they started flooding in as soon as we moved on Rat Province, but it only got worse once we came back."

Rin could not believe that anyone had been living in these camps for that long. She saw clouds of flies everywhere she looked. The buzzing was unbearable.

"They're still trickling in," Ramsa said. "They come in waves, usually at night. They keep trying to sneak past the borders."

"And they're all from Hare and Rat Provinces?" she asked.

"What are you talking about? These are *southern* refugees."

She blinked at him. "I thought the Militia hadn't moved south."

Ramsa exchanged a glance with Baji. "They're not fleeing the Militia. They're fleeing the Federation."

"*What?*"

Baji scratched the back of his head. "Well, yes. It's not like the Mugenese soldiers all just laid down their weapons."

"I know, but I thought . . ." Rin trailed off. She felt dizzy. She'd known Federation troops remained on the mainland, but she'd thought they were contained to isolated units. Rogue soldiers, scattered squadrons. Roving mercenaries, forming predatory coalitions with provincial cities if they were large enough, but not enough to displace the entire south.

"How many are there?" she asked.

"Enough," Baji said. "Enough that they constitute an entirely separate army. They're fighting for the Militia, Rin. We don't know how; we don't know what deal she brokered with them. But soon enough we'll be fighting a war on two fronts, not one."

"Which regions?" she demanded.

"They're everywhere." Ramsa listed the provinces off on his fingers. "Monkey. Snake. Rooster."

Rin flinched. *Rooster?*

"Are you all right?" Ramsa asked.

But she was already running.

She knew immediately these were her people. She knew them by their tawny skin that was almost as dark as hers. She knew them by the way they talked—the soft country drawl that made her feel nostalgic and uncomfortable at the same time.

That was the tongue she had grown up speaking—the flat, rustic dialect that she couldn't speak without cringing now, because she'd spent years at school beating it out of herself.

She hadn't heard anyone speak the Rooster dialect in so long.

She thought, stupidly, that they might recognize her. But the Rooster refugees shrank away when they saw her. Their faces grew closed and sullen when she met their eyes. They crawled back into their tents if she approached.

It took her a moment to realize that they weren't afraid of her, they were afraid of her uniform.

They were afraid of Republican soldiers.

"You." Rin pointed to a woman about her height. "Do you have a spare set of clothes?"

The woman blinked at her, uncomprehending.

Rin tried again, slipping clumsily into her old dialect like it was an ill-fitting pair of shoes. "Do you have another, uh, shirt? Pants?"

The woman gave a terrified nod.

"Give them to me."

The woman crawled into her tent. She reappeared with a bundle of clothing—a faded blouse that might have once been dyed with a poppy flower pattern, and wide slacks with deep pockets.

Rin felt a sharp pang in her chest as she held the blouse out in front of her. She hadn't seen clothes like this in a long time. They were made for fieldworkers. Even the poor of Sinegard would have laughed at them.

Stripping off her Republican uniform worked. The Roosters stopped avoiding her when they saw her. Instead, she became effectively invisible as she navigated through the sea of tightly packed bodies. She shouted to get attention as she moved down the rows of tents.

"Tutor Feyrik! I'm looking for a Tutor Feyrik! Has anyone seen him?"

Responses came in reluctant whispers and indifferent mutters. *No. No. Leave us alone. No.* These refugees were so used to hearing desperate cries for lost ones that they'd closed their ears to them. Someone knew a Tutor Fu, but he wasn't from Tikany. Someone else knew a Feyrik, but he was a cobbler, not a teacher. Rin found it pointless trying to describe him; there were hundreds of men who could have fit his description—with every row she passed she saw old men with gray beards who turned out not to be Tutor Feyrik after all.

She pushed down a swell of despair. It had been stupid to hope in the first place. She'd known she'd never see him again; she'd resigned herself to that fact long ago.

But she couldn't help it. She still had to try.

She tried broadening her search. "Is anyone here from Tikany?"

Blank looks. She moved faster and faster through the camp, breaking into a run. "Tikany? Please? Anyone?"

Then at last she heard one voice through the crowd—one that was laced not with casual indifference but with sheer disbelief.

"Rin?"

She stumbled to a halt. When she turned around she saw a spindly boy, no more than fourteen, with a mop of brown hair and large, downward-sloping eyes. He stood with a sodden shirt dangling from one hand and a bandage clutched in the other.

"Kesegi?"

He nodded wordlessly.

Then she was sixteen years old again herself, crying as she held him, rocking him so hard they almost fell to the dirt. He hugged her back, wrapping his long and scrawny limbs all the way around her like he used to.

When had he gotten so tall? Rin marveled at the change. Once, he'd barely come up to her waist. Now he was taller than she by about an inch. But the rest of him was far too skinny, close to starved; he looked like he'd been stretched more than he had grown.

"Where are the others?" she asked.

"Mother's here with me. Father's dead."

"The Federation . . . ?"

"No. It was the opium in the end." He gave a false laugh. "Funny, really. He heard they were coming, and he ate an entire pan of nuggets. Mother found him just as we were packing up to leave. He'd been dead for hours." He gave her an awkward smile. A *smile*. He'd lost his father, and he was trying to make her feel better about it. "We just thought he was sleeping."

"I'm sorry," she said. Her voice came out flat. She couldn't help it. Her relationship with Uncle Fang had been one between master and servant, and she couldn't conjure up anything that remotely resembled grief.

"Tutor Feyrik?" she asked.

Kesegi shook his head. "I don't know. I saw him in the crowd when we left, I think, but I haven't seen him since."

His voice cracked when he spoke. She realized that he was trying to imitate a deeper voice than he possessed. He stood up overly straight, too, to appear taller than he was. He was trying to pass himself off as an adult.

"So you've come back."

Rin's blood froze. She'd been walking blindly without a destination, assuming Kesegi had been doing the same, but of course they'd been walking back to his tent.

Kesegi stopped. "Mother. Look who I found."

Auntie Fang gave Rin a thin smile. "Well, look at that. It's the war hero. You've grown."

Rin wouldn't have recognized her if Kesegi hadn't introduced her. Auntie Fang looked twenty years older, with the complexion of a wrinkled walnut. She had always been so red-faced, perpetually furious, burdened with a foster child she didn't want and a husband addicted to opium. She used to terrify Rin. But now she seemed shriveled dry, as if the fight had been drained from her completely.

"Come to gloat?" Auntie Fang asked. "Go on, look. There's not much to see."

"*Gloat?*" Rin repeated, baffled. "No, I . . ."

"Then what is it?" Auntie Fang asked. "Well, don't just *stand* there."

How was it that even now Auntie Fang could still make her feel so stupid and worthless? Under her withering glare Rin felt like a little girl again, hiding in the shed to avoid a beating.

"I didn't know you were here," she managed. "I just—I wanted to see if—"

"If we were still alive?" Auntie Fang put bony hands on narrow hips. "Well, here we are. No thanks to you soldiers—no, you were too busy drowning up north. It's Vaisra's fault we're here at all."

"Watch your tone," Rin snapped.

It shocked her when Auntie Fang cringed backward like she was expecting to be hit.

"Oh, I didn't mean that." Auntie Fang adopted a wheedling, wide-eyed expression that looked grotesque on her leathery face. "The hunger's just getting to me. Can't you get us some food, Rin? You're a soldier, I bet they've even made you a *commander*, you're so important, surely you could call in some favors."

"They're not feeding you?" Rin asked.

Auntie Fang laughed. "Not unless you're talking about the Lady of Arlong walking around handing out tiny bowls of rice to the skinniest children she can find while the blue-eyed devils follow her around to document how wonderful she is."

"We don't get anything," Kesegi said. "Not clothes, not blankets, not medicine. Most of us forage for our own food—we were eating fish for a while, but they'd all been poisoned with something, and we got sick. They didn't warn us about that."

Rin found that impossible to believe. "They haven't opened any kitchens for you?"

"They have, but those kitchens feed perhaps a hundred mouths before they close." Kesegi shrugged his bony shoulders. "Look around. Someone starves to death every day in this camp. Can't you see?"

"But I thought—surely, Vaisra would—"

"Vaisra?" Auntie Fang snorted. "You're on a first-name basis, are you?"

"No—I mean, yes, but—"

"Then you can talk to him!" Auntie Fang's beady eyes glittered. "Tell him we're starving. If he can't feed all of us, just have them deliver food to me and Kesegi. We won't tell anyone."

"But that's not how it works," Rin stammered. "I mean—I can't just—"

"Do it, you ungrateful cunt," Auntie Fang snarled. "You owe us."

"I *owe* you?" Rin repeated in disbelief.

"I took you into our home. I raised you for sixteen years."

"You would have sold me into marriage!"

"And then you would have had a better life than any of us." Auntie Fang pointed a skinny, accusing finger at Rin's chest. "You would never have lacked for anything. All you had to do was spread your legs every once in a while, and you would have had anything you wanted to eat, anything you wanted to wear. But that wasn't enough for you—*you* wanted to be special, to be important, to run off to Sinegard and join the Militia on its merry adventures."

"You think this war has been *fun* for me?" Rin shouted. "I watched my friends die! *I* almost died!"

"We've all nearly died," Auntie Fang scoffed. "Please. You're not special."

"You can't talk to me like that," Rin said.

"Oh, I know." Auntie Fang swept into a low bow. "You're so *important*. So *respected*. Do you want us to grovel at your feet, is that it? Heard your old bitch of an aunt was in the camps, so you couldn't pass up the chance to rub it in her face?"

"Mother, stop," Kesegi said quietly.

"That's not why I came," Rin said.

Auntie Fang's mouth twisted into a sneer. "Then why *did* you come?"

Rin didn't have an answer for her.

She didn't know what she'd expected to find. Not home, not belonging, not Tutor Feyrik—and not this.

This was a mistake. She shouldn't have come at all. She'd cut her ties to Tikany a long time ago. She should have kept it that way.

She backed away quickly, shaking her head. "I'm sorry," she tried to say, but the words stuck in her throat.

She couldn't look either of them in the eyes. She didn't want to be here anymore, she didn't want to feel like this anymore. She backed out onto the main path and broke into a quick walk. She wanted to run away, but couldn't out of pride.

"Rin!" Kesegi shouted. He dashed out after her. "Wait."

She halted in her tracks. *Please say something to make me stay. Please.*

"Yes?"

"If you can't get us food, can you ask them for some blankets?" he asked. "Just one? It gets so cold at night."

She forced herself to smile. "Of course."

Over the next week a torrent of people poured into Arlong on foot, in rickety carts, or on rafts hastily constructed of anything that could float. The river became a slow-moving eddy of bodies packed against each other so tightly that the famous blue waters of the Dragon Province disappeared under the weight of human desperation.

Republican soldiers checked the new arrivals for weapons and valuables before corralling them in neat lines to whichever quarters of the refugee district still had space.

The refugees met with very little kindness. Republican soldiers, Dragons especially, were terribly condescending, shouting at the southerners when they couldn't understand the rapid Arlong dialect.

Rin spent hours each day walking the docks with Venka. She was glad to have escaped processing duty, which involved standing guard over miserable lines while clerks marked the refugees' arrivals and issued them temporary residence papers. That was probably more important than what she and Venka were doing, which was fishing out the refuse from the segments of the Murui near the refugee chokepoints, but Rin couldn't bear to be around the large crowds of brown skin and accusing eyes.

"We're going to have to cut them off at some point," Venka remarked as she lifted an empty jug from the water. "They can't possibly all fit here."

"Only because the refugee district is tiny," Rin said. "If they opened up the city barriers, or if they funneled them into the mountainside, there would be plenty of space."

"Plenty of *space*, maybe. But we haven't got enough clothes, blankets, medicine, grain, or anything else."

"Up until now the southerners were producing the grain." Rin felt obligated to point that out.

"And now they've run from home, so no one is producing food," Venka said. "Doesn't really help us. Hey, what's this?"

She reached gingerly into the water and drew a barrel out onto the dock. She set it on the ground. Out tumbled what at first looked like a soggy bundle of clothing. "Gross."

"What is it?" Rin stepped closer to get a better look and immediately regretted it.

"It's dead, look." Venka held the baby out to show Rin the infant's sickly yellow skin, the bumpy evidence of relentless mosquito attacks, and the red rashes that covered half its body. Venka slapped its cheeks. No response. She held it over the river as if to throw it back in.

The infant started to whimper.

An ugly expression twisted across Venka's face. She looked so suddenly, murderously hateful that Rin was sure she was about to hurl the infant headfirst into the harbor.

"Give it to me," Rin said quickly. She pulled the infant from Venka's arms. A sour smell hit her nose. She gagged so hard she nearly dropped the infant, but got a grip on herself.

The baby was swaddled in clothes large enough to fit an adult. That meant someone had loved it. They wouldn't have parted with the clothes otherwise—it was now the dead of winter, and even in the warm south, the nights got cold enough that refugees traveling without shelter could easily freeze to death.

Someone had wanted this baby to survive. Rin owed it a fighting chance.

She strode hastily to the end of the dock and handed the bundle off to the first soldier she saw. "Here."

The soldier stumbled under the sudden weight. "What am I supposed to do with this?"

"I don't know, just see to it that it's cared for," Rin said. "Take it to the infirmary, if they'll let you."

The soldier gripped the infant tightly in his arms and set off at a run. Rin returned to the river and resumed dragging her spear halfheartedly through the water.

She wanted very badly to smoke. She couldn't get the taste of corpses out of her mouth.

Venka broke the silence first. "What are you looking at me like that for?"

She looked defensive. Furious. But that was Venka's default reaction to everything; she'd rather die than admit vulnerability. Rin suspected Venka was thinking about the child that she'd lost, and she wasn't sure what to say, only that she felt terribly sorry for her.

"You knew it was alive," Rin said finally.

"Yes," Venka snapped. "So what?"

"And you were going to kill it."

Venka swallowed hard and jabbed her spear back into the water. "That thing doesn't have a future. I was doing it a favor."

Wartime Arlong was an ugly thing. Despair settled over the capital like a shroud as the threat of armies closing in from both the north and the south grew closer every day.

Food was strictly rationed, even for citizens of Dragon Province. Every man, woman, and child who wasn't in the Republican Army was conscripted for labor. Most were sent to work in the forges or the shipyards. Even small children were put to task cutting linen strips for the infirmary.

Sympathy was the greatest scarcity. The southern refugees, crammed behind their barrier, were uniformly despised by soldiers and civilians alike. Food and supplies were offered begrudgingly, if at all. Rin discovered that if soldiers weren't positioned to guard the supply deliveries, they would never reach the camps.

The refugees latched on to any potentially sympathetic advocates they could. Once word of Rin's connection to the Fangs spread, she became an involuntarily appointed, unofficial champion of refugee interests in Arlong. Every time she was near the district she was accosted by refugees, all pleading for a thousand different things that she couldn't obtain—more food, more medicine, more materials for cooking fires and tents.

She hated the position they'd thrown her into because it led only to frustration from both sides. The Republican leadership grew irritated because she kept making impossible requests for basic human necessities, and the refugees started resenting her because she could never deliver.

"It doesn't make sense," Rin complained bitterly to Kitay. "Vaisra's the one who always said we had to treat prisoners well. And this is how we treat our own people?"

"It's because the refugees have no strategic advantage to them whatsoever, unless you count the mild inconvenience that their stacked-up bodies might present Daji's army," Kitay said. "If I may be blunt."

"Fuck off," she said.

"I'm just reporting what they're all thinking. Don't kill the messenger."

Rin should have been angrier, but she understood, too, just how pervasive that mind-set was. To most Dragons, the southerners barely registered as Nikara. She could see through a northerner's eyes the stereotypical Rooster—a cross-eyed, buck-toothed, swarthy idiot speaking a garbled tongue.

It shamed and embarrassed her terribly, because she used to be exactly like that.

She'd tried to erase those parts of herself long ago. At fourteen she'd been lucky enough to study under a tutor who spoke near-standard Sinegardian. And she'd gone to Sinegard young enough that her bad habits were quickly and brutally knocked out of her. She'd adapted to fit in. She'd erased her identity to survive.

And it humiliated her that the southerners were now seeking her out, that they had the audacity to wander close to her, because they made her more like them by sheer proximity.

She'd long since tried to kill her association with Rooster Province, a place that had given her few happy memories. She'd almost succeeded. But the refugees wouldn't let her forget.

Every time she came close to the camps, she saw angry, accusing stares. They all knew who she was now. They made a point of letting her know.

They'd stopped shouting invectives at her. They'd long since passed the point of rage; now they lived in resentful despair. But she could read their silent faces so clearly.

You're one of us, they said. *You were supposed to protect us. You've failed.*

Three weeks after Rin's return to Arlong, the Empress sent a direct message to the Republic.

About a mile from the Red Cliffs, the Dragon Province border patrol had captured a man who claimed to have been sent from the capital. The messenger carried only an ornamented bamboo basket across his back and a small Imperial seal to verify his identity.

The messenger insisted he would not speak unless Vaisra received him in the throne room with the full audience of his generals, the Warlords, and General Tarcquet. Eriden's guards stripped him down and checked his clothes and baskets for explosives or poisonous gas, but found nothing.

"Just dumplings," the messenger said cheerfully.

Reluctantly they let him through.

"I bear a message from the Empress Su Daji," he announced to the room. His lower lip flopped grotesquely when he spoke. It seemed infected with something; the left side was thick with red, pus-filled blisters. His words were barely understandable through his thick Rat accent.

Rin's eyes narrowed as she watched him approach the throne. He wasn't a Sinegardian diplomat or a Militia representative. He didn't carry himself like a court official. He had to be a common soldier, if even that. But why would Daji leave diplomacy up to someone who could barely even speak?

Unless the messenger wasn't here for any real negotiations. Unless Daji didn't need someone who could think quickly or speak smoothly. Unless Daji only wanted someone who would take the most delight in antagonizing Vaisra. Someone who had a grudge against the Republic and wouldn't mind dying for it.

Which meant this was not a truce. This was a one-sided message.

Rin tensed. There was no way the messenger could harm Vaisra, not with the ranks of Eriden's men blocking his way to the throne. But still she gripped her trident tight, eyes tracking the man's every movement.

"Speak your piece," Vaisra ordered.

The messenger grinned broadly. "I come to deliver tidings of Yin Jinzha."

Lady Saikhara stood up. Rin could see her trembling. "What has she done with my son?"

The messenger sank to his knees, placed his basket on the marble floor, and lifted the lid. A pungent smell wafted through the hall.

Rin craned her head, expecting to see Jinzha's dismembered corpse.

But the basket was filled with dumplings, each fried to golden perfection and pressed in the pattern of a lotus flower. They had clearly gone bad after weeks of travel—Rin could see dark mold crawling around their edges—but their shape was still intact. They had been meticulously decorated, brushed with lotus seed paste and inked over with five crimson characters.

The Dragon devours his sons.

"The Empress enjoins you to enjoy a dumpling of the rarest meat," said the messenger. "She expects you might recognize the flavor."

Lady Saikhara shrieked and slumped across the floor.

Vaisra met Rin's eyes and jerked a hand across his neck.

She understood. She hefted her trident and charged toward the messenger.

He reeled backward just slightly, but otherwise made no effort to defend himself. He didn't even lift his arms. He just sat there, smiling with satisfaction.

She buried her trident into his chest.

It wasn't a clean blow. She'd been too shocked, distracted by the dumplings to aim properly. The prongs slid through his rib cage but didn't pierce his heart.

She yanked them back out.

The messenger gurgled a laugh. Blood bubbled through his crooked teeth, staining the pristine marble floor.

"You will die. You will all die," he said. "And the Empress will dance upon your graves."

Rin stabbed again and this time aimed true.

Nezha rushed to his mother and lifted her in his arms. "She's fainted," he said. "Someone, help—"

"There's something else," General Hu said while palace attendants gathered around Saikhara. He pulled a scroll out of the basket with remarkably steady hands and brushed the crumbs off the side. "It's a letter."

Vaisra hadn't moved from his throne. "Read it."

General Hu broke the seal and unrolled the scroll. "*I am coming for you.*"

Lady Saikhara sat up and gave a low moan.

"Get her out of here," Vaisra snapped to Nezha. "Hu. Read."

General Hu continued. "*My generals sail down the Murui River as you dawdle in your castle. You have nowhere to flee. You have nowhere to hide. Our fleet is larger. Our men are more numerous. You will die at the base of the Red Cliffs like your ancestors, and your corpses will feed the fish of the Murui.*"

The hall fell silent.

Vaisra seemed frozen to his chair. His expression betrayed nothing. No grief, no fear. He could have been made of ice.

General Hu rolled the scroll back up and cleared his throat. "That's all it says."

Within a fortnight Vaisra's scouts—exhausted, horses ridden half to death—returned from the border and confirmed the worst. The Imperial Fleet, repaired and augmented since Boyang, had begun its winding journey south carrying what seemed like the entire Militia.

Daji intended to end this war in Arlong.

"They've spotted the ships from the Yerin and Murin beacons," reported a scout.

"How are they already this close?" General Hu asked, alarmed. "Why weren't we told earlier?"

"They haven't reached Murin yet," the scout explained. "The fleet is simply massive. We could see it through the mountains."

"How many ships?"

"A few more than they had at Boyang."

"The good news is that the larger warships will get stuck wherever the Murui narrows," Captain Eriden said. "They'll have to roll them on logs to move over land. We have two, maybe two and a half weeks yet." He reached over to the map and tapped a point on Hare Province's northwestern border. "I'm guessing they'll be here by now. Should we send men up, try to stall them at the narrow bends?"

Vaisra shook his head. "No. This doesn't alter our grand strategy. They want us to split our defenses, but we won't take the bait. We concentrate on fortifying Arlong, or we lose the south altogether."

Rin stared down at the map, at the angry red dots representing both Imperial and Federation troops. The Republic was wedged in on both sides—the Empire from the north, the Federation from the south. It was hard not to panic as she imagined Daji's combined forces closing in around them like an iron fist.

"Deprioritize the northern coastline. Bring Tsolin's fleet back to the capital." Vaisra sounded impossibly calm, and Rin was grateful for it. "I want scouts with messenger pigeons positioned at mile intervals along the Murui. Every time that fleet moves, I want to know. Send messengers to Rooster and Monkey. Recall their local platoons."

"You can't do that," Gurubai said. "They're still dealing with the Federation remnants."

"I don't care about the Federation," Vaisra said. "I care about Arlong. If everything we've heard about this fleet is true, then this war is over unless we can hold our base. We need all of our men in one place."

"You're leaving entire villages to die," Takha said. "Entire provinces."

"Then they will die."

"Are you joking?" demanded Charouk. "You think we're just going to stand here while you renege on your promises? You said that if we defected, you would help us eradicate the Mugenese—"

"And I will," Vaisra said impatiently. "Can't you see? We beat Daji and we win back the south, too. Once their backer is gone, the Mugenese will surrender—"

"Or they will understand that the civil war has weakened us, and they'll pick off the pieces no matter what happens," Charouk countered.

"That won't happen. Once we've won Hesperian support—"

"'Hesperian support,'" Charouk scoffed. "Don't be a child. Tarcquet and his men have been loitering in the city for quite some time now, and that fleet isn't showing up on the horizon."

"They will come if we crush the Militia," Vaisra said. "And we cannot do that if we're wasting time fighting a war on two fronts."

"Forget this," said Gurubai. "We should take our troops and return home now."

"Go right ahead," Vaisra said calmly. "You wouldn't last a week. You need Dragon troops and you know that, or you'd have never come in the first place. None of you can hold your home provinces, not with the numbers you have. Otherwise you would have gone back a long time ago."

There was a short silence. Rin could tell from Gurubai's expression that Vaisra was right. He'd called their bluff.

They had no choice now but to follow his lead.

"But what happens after you win Arlong?" Nezha asked suddenly.

All heads turned in his direction.

Nezha lifted his chin. "We unite the country just to let the Mugenese tear it apart again? That's not a democracy, Father, that's a suicide pact. You're ignoring a massive threat just because it's not Dragon lives at stake—"

"Enough," Vaisra said, but Nezha spoke over him.

"Daji invited the Federation here in the first place. You don't need to finish us off."

Father and son glared at each other over the table.

"Your brother would never have defied me like this," Vaisra said quietly.

"No, Jinzha was rash and reckless and never listened to his best strategists, and now he's dead," said Nezha. "So what are you going to do, Father? Act out of some petty sense of revenge, or do something to help the people in your Republic?"

Vaisra slammed his hands on the table. "*Silence*. You will not contradict me—"

"You're just throwing your allies to the wolves! Does no one realize how horrific this is?" Nezha demanded. "General Hu? *Rin?*"

"I . . ." Rin's tongue was lead in her mouth.

All eyes were suddenly, terrifyingly on her.

Vaisra folded his arms over his chest as he watched her, eyebrows raised as if to say, *Go on*.

"They're invading your home," Nezha said.

Rin flinched. What did he expect her to say to that? Did he think that just because she was from the south, she would contradict Vaisra's orders?

"It doesn't matter," she said. "The Dragon Warlord is right—we split our forces and we're dead."

"Come on," Nezha said impatiently. "Of all people, you should—"

"Should what?" she sneered. "I should hate the Federation the most? I *do*, but I also know that dispatching troops south plays right into Daji's hands. Would you rather we simply deliver Arlong to her?"

"You're unbelievable," Nezha said.

She gave him her best imitation of Vaisra's level stare. "I'm just doing my job, Nezha. You might try doing yours."

CHAPTER 27

"I've outlined a number of tactics in this." Kitay handed Rin a small pamphlet. "Captain Dalain will have her own ideas, but based on historical record, these have worked the best, I think."

Rin flipped through the pages. "Did you rip these out of a book?"

He shrugged. "Didn't have time to copy it all down, so I just annotated."

She squinted to read his scrawling handwriting in the margins. "Logging?"

"It's a lot of time and manpower, I know, but you don't have many other good options." He tugged anxiously at his bangs. "It'll be more of an annoyance to them than anything, but it does save us a few hours."

"You've scratched out the guerrilla tactics," she observed.

"They won't do you much good. Besides, you shouldn't be trying to destroy the fleet, or even parts of it."

Rin frowned. That was exactly what she had been planning to do. "Don't tell me you think it's too dangerous."

"No, I think you simply *can't*. You don't understand just how big the fleet is. You can't burn them all before they catch on to you, not with your range of fire. Don't try anything clever."

"But—"

"When you take risks, you're gambling with my life, too," Kitay said sternly. "No stupid shit, Rin, I mean it. Keep to the directive. Just slow them down. Buy us some time."

Vaisra had ordered two platoons to sail up the Murui and obstruct the Imperial Navy's progress. They were racing against the clock, scrambling for extra time so that they could continue fortifying Arlong and wait for Tsolin's fleet on the northern shore to race back down the coastline. If they could delay the Imperial Navy for at least a few days, if Arlong could muster its defenses in time, and if Tsolin's ships could beat Daji's back to the capital, then they might have a fighting chance against the Empire.

It was a lot of *if*s.

But it was all they had.

Rin had immediately volunteered the Cike for the task of delaying the fleet. She couldn't stand being around the refugees anymore, and she wanted to get Baji and Suni well away from the Hesperians before their restlessness manifested in disaster.

She wished she could bring Kitay with her. But he was too valuable to send out on what was most likely a suicide mission for anyone who wasn't a shaman, and Vaisra wanted him behind city walls to rig up defense fortifications.

And while Rin was glad that Kitay would be out of harm's way, she hated that they were about to be separated for days without a means of communication.

If danger came, she wouldn't be able to protect him.

Kitay read the look on her face. "I'll be all right. You know that."

"But if anything happens—"

"*You're* the one going into a war zone," he pointed out.

"Everywhere is a war zone." She folded the manual shut and stuffed it into her shirt pocket. "I'm scared for you. For both of us. I can't help that."

"You haven't got time to be scared." He squeezed her arm. "Just keep us alive, won't you?"

Rin made one last stop by the forge before she left Arlong.

"What can I do for you?" The blacksmith shouted at her over the furnace. The flames had been burning nonstop for days, mass-producing swords, crossbow bolts, and armor.

She handed him her trident. "What do you make of this metal?"

He ran his fingers over the hilt and felt around the prongs to test their edges. "It's fine stuff. But I don't do many battle tridents. You don't want me to mess around with this too much, I'd ruin the balance. But I can sharpen the prongs if you need."

"I don't want to sharpen it," she said. "I want you to melt it down."

"Hmm." He tested the trident's balance over his palm. "Speerly-built?"

"Yes."

He raised an eyebrow. "And you're sure you want this reforged? I can't find anything wrong with it."

"It's ruined for me," she said. "Destroy it completely."

"This is a very unique weapon. You won't get a trident like this again."

Rin shrugged. "That's fine."

He still looked unsure. "Speerly craft is impossible to replicate. No one's alive now who knows how they made their weapons. I'll do my best, but you might just end up with a fisherman's tool."

"I don't want a trident," she said. "I want a sword."

Two skimmers departed from the Red Cliffs that morning. The *Harrier*, led by Nezha, raced upriver to hold the city of Shayang, situated on a crucial, narrow bend in the upper river delta. Shayang's inhabitants had long since evacuated down to the capital, but the city itself used to be a military base—Nezha needed only garrison the old cannon forts.

Rin's crew, headed by Captain Dalain, a lean, handsome woman, followed at a slower pace, paddling at a crawl in what was supposed to have been Jinzha's warship.

It wasn't close to finished. They hadn't even named it. Jinzha was supposed to choose a name when construction was done, and now no one could bring themselves to do it in his stead. The bulkheads of the upper deck hadn't been put in, the bottom decks were sparse and unfurnished, and cannons hadn't been fitted to the sides.

But none of that mattered, because the paddle wheels were functional. The ship had basic maneuverability. They didn't need to sail it into enemy territory, they just had to get it twenty miles up the river.

Kitay's pamphlet turned out to be brilliant. He'd sketched a series of little tricks to create maximal delays. Once they anchored Jinzha's warship, the Cike and Captain Dalain's crew spread out over a span of ten miles, and with incredible efficiency, implemented each one of them.

They erected a series of dams using a combination of logs and sandbags. Realistically these would buy them only half a day or so, but they would still tire out the soldiers forced to dive into deep water to clear them away.

Upriver from those, they planted wooden stakes in the river to tear holes in the bottom of enemy ships. Kitay, with Ramsa's enthusiastic support, had wanted to plant the same sort of water mines that the Empire had used on them, but they'd run out of time before he could figure out how to dry the intestines properly.

They stretched multiple iron cables across the river, usually right after bends. If the Wolf Meat General was smart, he would just send soldiers out to disassemble the posts instead of trying to hack through the cables. But the posts were hidden well behind reeds and the cables were invisible underwater, so they might cause a destructive backlog if the fleet rammed into them unawares.

They set up a number of garrisons at three-mile intervals of the Murui. Each would be manned by ten to fifteen soldiers armed with crossbows, cannons, and missiles.

Those soldiers were most likely going to die. But they might manage to pick off a handful of Militia troops, or at best damage a ship or two before the Wolf Meat General blew them apart. And in terms of bodies and time, the tradeoff was worth it.

Near the northern border of the Dragon Province, right before the Murui forked into the Golyn, they sank Jinzha's warship into the water.

"That's a pity," said Ramsa as they evacuated their equipment onto land. "I heard it was supposed to be the greatest warship ever built in the Empire's history."

"It was Jinzha's ship," Rin said. "Jinzha's dead."

The warship had been a conquest vessel built for a massive invasion of northern territory. There would be no such invasion now. The Republic was fighting for its last chance at survival. Jinzha's warship would serve best by sitting heavy in the Murui's deep waters and obstructing the Imperial Fleet for as long as it could.

They smashed in the paddles and hacked apart the masts before they disembarked, just to make sure the warship was destroyed beyond the point of any possibility that the Imperial Fleet might repurpose it to sail on Arlong.

Then they rowed small lifeboats to the shore and prepared for a hasty march inland.

Ramsa had laced the two bottom decks with several hundred pounds of explosives, all rigged to destroy the warship's fundamental structures. The fuses were linked together for a chain reaction. All they needed now was a light.

"Everyone good?" Rin called.

From what she could see, the soldiers had all cleared the beach. Most them had already set off at a run toward the forest as ordered.

Captain Dalain gave her a nod. "Do it."

Rin raised her arms and sent a thin ribbon of fire dancing across the river.

The flame disappeared onto the warship, where the fuse had

been laid just where Rin's range ran out. She didn't wait to check if it caught.

Ten yards past the tree line, she heard a series of muffled booms, followed by a long silence. She stumbled to a halt and looked over her shoulder. The warship wasn't sinking.

"Was that it?" she asked. "I thought it'd be louder."

Ramsa looked similarly confused. "Maybe the fuses weren't linked properly? But I was sure—"

The next round of blasts threw them off their feet. Rin hit the dirt, hands clamped over her ears, eyes squeezed shut as her very bones vibrated. Ramsa collapsed beside her, shaking madly. She couldn't tell if he was laughing or trembling.

When at last the eruptions faded, she hauled herself to her feet and dragged Ramsa up to higher ground. They turned around. Just over the tree line, they could just see the Republican flag flying high, shrouded by billowing black smoke.

"Tiger's tits," whispered Ramsa.

For a long, tense moment it seemed like the warship might stay afloat. The sails remained perfectly upright, as if suspended from the heavens by a string. Rin and Ramsa stood side by side, fingers laced together, watching the smoke expand outward to envelop the sky.

At last the sound of splintering wood echoed through the still air as the support beams collapsed one by one. The middle mast disappeared suddenly, as if the ship had folded in on itself, devouring its own insides. Then with a creaking groan, the warship turned on its side and sank into the black water.

They made camp that night to the sound of more explosions, though these were coming from at least seven miles away. The Imperial Navy had reached the border town at Shayang. The noise was impossible to escape. The bombing went on through the night. Rin heard so many rounds of cannon fire that she could not imagine anything still remained of Shayang except for smoke and rubble.

"Are you all right?" Baji asked.

The crew was supposed to be grabbing a few hours' sleep before their journey downriver, but Rin could barely even close her eyes. She sat upright, hugging her knees, unable to look away from the flashing lights in the night sky.

"Hey. Calm down." Baji put a hand on her shoulder. "You're shaking. What's wrong?"

She nodded in Shayang's direction. "Nezha's over there."

"And you're afraid for him?"

She whispered without thinking. "I'm always afraid for him."

"Ah. I get it." Baji gave her a curious look. "You're in love."

"Don't be disgusting. Just because you think the whole world is tits and—"

"No need to get defensive, kiddo. He's a good-looking fellow."

"We're done talking."

Baji snickered. "Fine. Don't engage. Just answer this. Would you be here without him?"

"What, camping out by the Murui?"

"Fighting this war," he clarified. "Serving under his father."

"I serve the Republic," she said.

"Whatever you say," he said, but she could see from the look in his eyes that he hardly believed her.

"Why are you still here, then?" she asked. "If you're so skeptical. I mean—you've got no allegiance to the Republic, and gods know the Cike barely still exists. Why haven't you just run?"

Baji looked somber for a moment. He never looked this serious; he always had such an outsize personality, an endless series of dirty jokes and lewd comments. Rin had never bothered to consider that that might be a front.

"I did think about that for a minute," he said after a pause. "Suni and I both. Before you got back we thought seriously about splitting."

"But?"

"But then we'd have nothing to do. I'm sure you can understand,

Rin. Our gods want blood. That's all we can think about. And it doesn't matter that when we're not high, we've nominally got our minds back. You know that's not how it works. To anyone else a peaceful life would be heaven right now, but for us it'd just be torture."

"I understand," she said quietly.

She knew it would never end for Baji, either; that constant urge to destroy. If he didn't kill enemy combatants then he would start taking it out on civilians and do whatever he'd done to get himself into Baghra in the first place. That was the contract the Cike had signed with their gods. It ended only in madness or death.

"I have to be on a battlefield," Baji said. He swallowed. "Wherever I can find one. There's nothing else to it."

Another explosion rocked the night so hard that even from seven miles away they could feel the ground shake beneath them. Rin drew her knees closer to her chest and trembled.

"You can't do anything about that," Baji told her after it had passed. "You'll just have to trust that Nezha knows how to do his job."

"Tiger's fucking tits," Ramsa shouted. He was standing farther uphill, squinting through his spyglass. "Are you guys seeing this?"

Rin stood up. "What is it?"

Ramsa motioned frantically for them to join him at the top of the hill. He handed Rin his spyglass and pointed. "Look there. Right between those two trees."

Rin squinted through the lens. Her gut dropped. "That's not possible."

"Well, it's not a fucking illusion," Ramsa said.

"What isn't?" Baji demanded.

Wordlessly, Rin handed him the spyglass. She didn't need it. Now that she knew what to look for, even her naked eye could see the outline of the Imperial Navy winding slowly through the trees.

She felt like she was watching a mountain range move.

"That thing's not a ship," Baji said.

"No," Ramsa said, awed. "That's a fortress."

The centerpiece of the Imperial Navy was a monstrous structure: a square, three-decked fortress that looked as if the entire siege barrier at Xiashang had come detached from the ground to slowly float down the river.

How many troops could that fortress hold? Thousands? *Tens of thousands?*

"How does that thing stay afloat?" Baji demanded. "It can't have any mobility."

"They don't need mobility," Rin said. "The rest of the fleet exists to guard it. They just need to get that fortress close enough to the city. Then they'll swarm it."

Ramsa said what they were all thinking. "We're going to die, aren't we?"

"Cheer up," said Baji. "Maybe they'll take prisoners."

We can't fight them. Rin's chest constricted with sharp and suffocating dread. Their entire mission seemed so pointless now. Logs and dams might stall the Militia for a few hours, but a fleet that powerful could eventually barrel its way through anything.

"Question," Ramsa said. He was peering through his spyglass again. "What do Tsolin's flags look like?"

"*What?*"

"Have they got green snakes on them?"

"Yes—"

A terrible suspicion hit her. She seized the spyglass from him, but she already knew what she would see. The ships trailing at the rearguard bore the unmistakable coiled insignia of the Snake Province.

"What's going on?" Baji asked.

Rin couldn't speak.

It wasn't just a handful of ships that belonged to Tsolin. She'd seen six by her count now. Which meant one of two things— either Tsolin had skirmished and lost early to the Imperial Navy, and his ships had been repurposed for Imperial use, or Tsolin had defected.

"I will take your silence to mean the worst," Baji said.

. . .

Captain Dalain ordered an immediate retreat back to Arlong. The soldiers dismantled their camp in minutes. Paddling downstream, they could be back to warn Arlong within a day, but Rin didn't know if advance warning would even make a difference. The addition of Tsolin's ships meant the Imperial Navy had nearly doubled in size. It didn't matter how good Arlong's defenses were. They couldn't possibly fight off a fleet that big.

Cannon fire from Shayang continued throughout the night, then stopped abruptly just before dawn. At sunrise they saw a series of smoke signals from Nezha's soldiers unfurling in the distant sky.

"Shayang's gone," Dalain interpreted. "The *Harrier*'s grounded, but the survivors are falling back to Arlong."

"Should we go to their aid?" someone asked.

Dalain paused. "No. Row faster."

Rin pulled her oar through the muddy water, trying not to imagine the worst. Nezha might be fine. Shayang hadn't been a suicide mission—Nezha had been instructed to hold the fort for as long as he could before escaping into the forest. And if he were seriously injured, the Murui would come to his aid. His god wouldn't desert him. She had to believe that.

Around noon, they heard a distant round of cannon fire once more.

"That'll be the warship," Ramsa said. "They're trying to blow their way through."

"Good," Rin said.

Sinking the warship had perhaps been Kitay's best idea. The Imperial Fleet couldn't simply blast it to bits—the bulk of the structure lay underwater, where cannon fire couldn't touch it. Exploding the top layers would only make it harder to extract the sunken bottom from the Murui.

Half an hour later, the cannon fire stopped. The Militia must have caught on. Now they would have to send in divers with hooks to trawl and clear the river. That might take them two days, three at the most.

But after that, they would resume their slow but relentless journey to Arlong. And without Tsolin, there was nothing left to stop them.

"We know," Kitay said upon Rin's return. He'd rushed out to greet her at the harbor. He looked utterly disheveled; his hair stood up in every direction as if he'd spent the last few hours pacing and tugging at his bangs. "Found out two hours ago."

"But *why*?" she cried. "And when?"

Kitay shrugged helplessly. "All I know is we're fucked. Come on."

She followed him at a run to the palace. Inside the main stateroom, Eriden and a handful of officers stood clustered around a map that was no longer even close to accurate, because it had simply erased Tsolin's ships from the board.

But the Republic hadn't just lost ships. This wasn't a neutral setback. It would have been better if Tsolin had simply retreated, or if he had been killed. But this defection meant that the entire fleet they had relied on now augmented Daji's forces.

Captain Eriden replaced the pieces meant to represent Tsolin's fleet with red ones and stood back from the table. "That's what we're dealing with."

No one had anything to say. The numbers differential was almost laughable. Rin imagined a glistening snake coiling its body around a small rodent, squeezing until the light dimmed from its eyes.

"That's a lot of red," she muttered.

"No shit," Kitay said.

"Where's Vaisra?" she asked.

Kitay drew her to the side and murmured into her ear so Eriden wouldn't hear. "Alone in his office, probably hurling vases at the wall. He asked not to be disturbed." He pointed to a scroll lying on the edge of the table. "Tsolin sent that letter this morning. That's when we found out."

Rin picked the scroll up and unrolled it. She already knew its contents, but she needed to read Tsolin's words herself out of some morbid curiosity, the same way she couldn't help taking a closer look at decomposing animal carcasses.

This is not the future I wished for either of us.

Tsolin wrote in a thin, lovely script. Each stroke tapered carefully to a fine point, an effortless calligraphic style that took years to master. This wasn't a letter written in haste. This was a letter written laboriously by a man who still cared about decorum.

All across the page Rin saw characters crossed out and rewritten where water had blotted the ink. Tsolin had wept as he wrote.

> *You must recognize that a ruler's first obligation is to his people. I chose the path that would lead to the least bloodshed. Perhaps this has stifled a democratic transition. I know the vision you dreamed of for this nation and I know I may have destroyed it. But my first obligation is not to the unborn people of this country's future, but the people who are suffering now, who pass their days in fear because of the war that you have brought to their doorstep.*
>
> *I defect for them. This is how I will protect them. I weep for you, my student. I weep for your Republic. I weep for my wife and children. You will die thinking I have abandoned you all. But I do not hesitate to say that I value the lives of my people far more than I have ever valued you.*

CHAPTER 28

The Imperial Navy was due to reach the Red Cliffs in forty-eight hours. Arlong became a swarm of desperate, frantic activity as the Republican Army hastened to finish its defensive preparations in the next two days. The furnaces burned at all hours, day and night, turning out mountains of swords, shields, and javelins. The Red Cliffs became a chimney for the engines of war.

The blacksmith sent for Rin the evening of the first day.

"The ore was a marvel to work with," he said as he handed her a sword. It was a lovely thing—a thin, straight blade with a crimson tassel fixed to the pommel. "You wouldn't happen to have more like it, would you?"

"You'd have to sail back to the island," she murmured, turning the blade over in her hands. "Root around the skeletons, see what you find."

"Fair enough." The blacksmith produced a second blade, identical to the first. "Fortunately, there was enough excess metal for a backup. In case you lose one."

"That's useful. Thank you." She held the first blade out, arm straight, to test its weight. The hilt felt molded perfectly to her grasp. The blade was a tad longer than anything she'd ever used, but it was lighter than it looked. She swung it in a circle over her head.

The blacksmith backed out of her range. "I thought you'd want the extra reach."

She tossed the hilt from hand to hand. She'd been afraid the length would feel awkward, but it only extended her reach, and the light weight more than made up for it. "Are you calling me short?"

He chuckled. "I'm saying your arms aren't very long. How does it feel?"

She traced the tip of her blade through the air and let it pull her through the familiar movements of Seejin's Third Form. She was surprised at how good it felt. Nezha had been right—she really was much better with a sword. She'd fought her first battles with one. She'd made her first kill with one.

Why had she been using a trident for so long? That seemed so stupid in retrospect. She'd practiced with the sword for years at Sinegard; it felt like a natural extension of her arm. Wielding one again felt like trading a ceremonial gown for a comfortable set of training clothes.

She gave a yell and hurled the sword toward the opposite wall. It stuck into the wood right where she'd aimed, perfectly angled, hilt quivering.

"How is it?" asked the blacksmith.

"It's perfect," she said, satisfied.

Fuck Altan, fuck his legacy, and fuck his trident. It was time she started using a weapon that would keep her alive.

The sun had gone down by the time she returned to the barracks. Rin moved hastily through the canals, arms sore from hours of lugging sandbags into empty houses.

"Rin?" A small figure emerged from the corner just before she reached the door.

She jumped, startled. Her new blades clattered to the floor.

"It's just me." The figure stepped into the light.

"Kesegi?" She swiped the swords off the ground. "How'd you get past the barrier?"

"I need you to come with me." He reached out to seize her hand. "Quick."

"Why? What's going on?"

"I can't tell you here." He bit his lip, eyes darting nervously around the barracks. "But I'm in trouble. Will you come?"

"I . . ." Rin glanced distractedly toward the barracks. This could go terribly badly. She'd been ordered not to interact with the refugees unless she was on duty, and given the current tensions in Arlong, she would be the last to receive the benefit of the doubt. What if someone saw?

"*Please*," Kesegi said. "It's bad."

She swallowed. What was she thinking? This was Kesegi. Kesegi was family, the very last family that she had. "Of course. Lead the way."

Kesegi set off at a run. She followed close behind.

She assumed something had happened behind the barrier. Some brawl, some accident or skirmish between guards and refugees. Auntie Fang would be at the bottom of it; she always was. But Kesegi didn't take her back to the camps. He led her behind the barracks, past the clanging shipyards to an empty warehouse at the far end of the harbor.

Behind the warehouse stood three dark silhouettes.

Rin halted. None of those figures could be Auntie Fang; they were all too tall.

"Kesegi, what's going on?"

But Kesegi pulled her straight toward the warehouse.

"I brought her," he called loudly.

Rin's eyes adjusted to the dim light, and the strangers' faces became clear. She groaned. Those weren't refugees.

She turned to Kesegi. "What the hell?"

He looked away. "I had to get you here somehow."

"You lied to me."

He set his jaw. "Well, you wouldn't have come otherwise."

"Just hear us out," said Takha. "Please don't go. We'll only get this one chance to speak."

She crossed her arms. "We're hiding from Vaisra behind warehouses now?"

"Vaisra has done enough to ruin us," said Gurubai. "That much is obvious. The Republic has abandoned the south. This alliance must be aborted."

She fought the impulse to roll her eyes. "And what's your alternative?"

"Our own revolution," he said immediately. "We revoke our support for Vaisra, defect from the Dragon Army, and return to our home provinces."

"That's suicide," Rin said. "Vaisra is the only one protecting you."

"You can't even say that with a straight face," Charouk said. "Protection? We've been duped from the beginning. It is time to stop hoping Vaisra will throw us scraps from the table. We must return home and fight the Mugenese off on our own. We should have done that from the beginning."

"You and what army?" Rin asked coolly.

This entire conversation was moot. Vaisra had called this bluff months ago. The southern Warlords couldn't go home. Alone, their provincial armies would be destroyed by the Federation.

"We'll need to build an army," Gurubai acknowledged. "It won't be easy. But we'll have the numbers. You've seen the camps. You know how many of us there are."

"I also know that they are untrained, unarmed, and starving," she said. "You think they can fight Federation troops? The Republic is your only chance at survival."

"Survival?" Charouk scoffed. "We're all going to die within the week. Vaisra's gambled our lives on the Hesperians, and they will never come."

Rin faltered. She didn't have a good answer to that. She knew, just as they did, that the Hesperians were unlikely to ever find the Nikara worthy of their aid.

But until General Tarcquet declared explicitly that the Consortium had refused, the Republic still had a fighting chance.

Defecting to the south was certain suicide—especially because if Rin abandoned Vaisra, then no one was left to protect her from the Gray Company. She might run from Arlong and hide. She might elude the Hesperians for a long time, if she was clever, but they would track her down eventually. They wouldn't relent. Rin understood now that people like Petra would never let challenges to the Maker slip away so easily. They would hunt down and kill or capture every shaman in the Empire for further study. Rin might still fight them off, might even hold her own for a while—fire against airships, the Phoenix against the Maker—but that confrontation would be terrible. She didn't know if she'd come out alive.

And if the southern Warlords defected from the Republic, then no one was left to protect them from the Militia *or* the Federation. That calculation was so obvious. Why couldn't they see it?

"Give up this fool's hope," Gurubai urged her. "Ignore Vaisra's nonsense. The Hesperians are staying away on purpose, just as they did during the Poppy Wars."

"What are you talking about?" Rin demanded.

"You really think they didn't have a single piece of information about what was happening on this continent?"

"What does that matter?"

"Vaisra sent his wife to them," Gurubai said. "Lady Saikhara spent the second and third Poppy Wars tucked safely away on a Hesperian warship. The Hesperians had full knowledge of what was happening. And they didn't send a single sack of grain or crate of swords. Not when Sinegard burned, not when Khurdalain fell, and not when the Mugenese raped Golyn Niis. These are the allies you're waiting for. And Vaisra knows that."

"Why don't you just say what you're suggesting?" Rin asked.

"Has this really never crossed your mind?" Gurubai asked. "This war has been orchestrated by Vaisra and the Hesperians to put him in a prime position to consolidate control of this country. They didn't come during the third war because they wanted to see the Empire bleed. They won't come now until Vaisra's challengers are dead. Vaisra is no true democrat, nor a champion of the people. He's an opportunist building his throne with Nikara blood."

"You're mad," Rin said. "No one is crazy enough to do that."

"You'd have to be crazy *not* to see it! The evidence is right in front of you. The Federation troops never made it as far inland as Arlong. Vaisra lost nothing in the war."

"He nearly lost his *son*—"

"And he got him back with no trouble at all. Face it, Yin Vaisra was the only victor of the Third Poppy War. You're too smart to believe otherwise."

"Don't patronize me," Rin snapped. "And even if that's all true, that doesn't change anything. I already know the Hesperians are assholes. I'd still fight for the Republic."

"You shouldn't fight for an alliance with people who think we're barely human," said Charouk.

"Well, that still gives me no reason to fight for *you*—"

"You should fight for us because you're one of us," said Gurubai.

"I am not one of you."

"Yes, you are," Takha said. "You're a Rooster. Just like me."

She stared at him in disbelief.

The sheer hypocrisy. He'd disowned her easily enough at Lusan, had treated her like an animal. Now he wanted to claim they were one and the same?

"The south would rise for you," Gurubai insisted. "Do you have any idea how much power you hold? You are the last *Speerly*. The entire continent knows your name. If you raised your sword, tens of thousands would follow. They'd fight for you. You'd be their goddess."

"I'd also be a traitor to my closest friends," she said. They were asking her to abandon Kitay. *Nezha*. "Don't try to flatter me. It won't work."

"Your friends?" Gurubai scoffed. "Who, Yin Nezha? Chen Kitay? Northerners who would spit on your very existence? Are you so desperate to be like them that you'll ignore everything else at stake?"

She bristled. "I don't want to be like them."

"Yes, you do," he sneered. "That's all you want, even if you don't realize it. But you're southern mud in the end. You can butcher the way you talk, you can turn away from the stench of the refugee camps and pretend that you don't smell, too, but they are *never* going to think you're one of them."

That did it. Rin's sympathy evaporated.

Did they really believe they could sway her with provincial ties? Rooster Province had never done anything for her. For the first sixteen years of her life, Tikany had tried to grind her into the dirt. She'd lost her ties to the south the moment she'd left for Sinegard.

She'd escaped the Fangs. She'd carved out a place for herself in Arlong. She was one of Vaisra's best soldiers. She wouldn't go back now. She *couldn't*.

For her, the south had only ever meant abuse and misery. She owed it nothing. Certainly not a suicide mission. If the Warlords wanted to throw their lives away, they could do that by themselves.

She saw the way Kesegi was looking at her—stricken, disappointed—and she willed herself not to care.

"I'm sorry," she said. "But I'm not one of you. I'm a Speerly. And I know where my loyalties lie."

"If you stay here you'll die for nothing," Gurubai said. "We all will."

"Then go back," she sneered. "Take your troops. Go home. I won't stop you."

They didn't move. Their faces—stricken, ashen—confirmed she'd called their bluff. They couldn't run. Alone in their provinces, they didn't have a chance. They might—*might*, though Rin strongly doubted they had the numbers—be able to fight off the Mugenese troops on their own. But if Arlong fell, it was only a matter of time until Daji came for them, too.

Without her support, their hands were tied. The southern Warlords were trapped.

Gurubai's hand moved to the sword at his waist. "Will you tell Vaisra?"

Her lip curled. "Don't tempt me."

"Will you tell Vaisra?" he repeated.

Rin gave him an incredulous smile. Was he really going to fight her? Was he really even going to *try*?

She couldn't help relishing this. For once she held all the power; for once, she held their fates in her hands and not the other way around.

She could have killed them right there and been done with it. Vaisra might have even praised her for the demonstration of loyalty.

But it was the eve of battle. The Militia was creeping to their doorstep. The refugees needed some sort of leadership if they were going to survive—certainly no one else was looking out for them. And if she murdered the Warlords now, the resulting chaos would hurt the Republic. The southern armies' numbers weren't great enough to win the battle, but their defection was more than enough to guarantee defeat, and that wasn't something Rin wanted on her hands.

She loved that this was her decision—that she could disguise this cruel calculation as mercy.

"Go to sleep," she said softly, as if speaking to children. "We've a battle to fight."

She escorted Kesegi back to the refugee quarters over his protests. She took him the long way around the city, trying to keep as much distance from the barracks as possible. For ten minutes they walked in stony silence. Every time Rin looked at Kesegi he stared angrily forward, pretending he hadn't seen her.

"You're angry with me," she said.

He didn't respond.

"I can't give them what they want. You know that."

"No, I don't," he said curtly.

"Kesegi—"

"And I don't know *you* anymore."

She had to admit that was true. Kesegi had said farewell to a sister and found a soldier in her place. But she didn't know him anymore, either. The Kesegi she'd left had been just a tiny child. This Kesegi was a tall, sullen, and angry boy who had seen too much suffering and didn't know who to blame for it.

They resumed walking in silence. Rin was tempted to turn around and head back, but she didn't want Kesegi caught alone on the wrong side of the barrier. The night patrol had lately taken to flogging refugees who wandered out of bounds to set an example.

Finally Kesegi said, "You could have written."

"What?"

"I kept waiting for you to write. Why didn't you?"

Rin didn't have a good response to that.

Why *hadn't* she written? The Masters had permitted it. All of her classmates had regularly written home. She remembered watching Niang send eight separate letters to each of her siblings every week, and being amazed that anyone had so much to say about their grueling coursework.

But the thought of writing the Fangs had never even crossed her mind. Once she reached Sinegard, she'd locked her memories of Tikany tightly away in the back of her mind and willed herself to forget.

"You were so young," she said after a pause. "I guess I didn't think you'd remember me."

"Bullshit," Kesegi said. "You're my sister. How could I not remember you?"

"I don't know. I just . . . I thought it'd be easier if we made a clean break with each other. I mean, it's not like I was ever coming home once I got out—"

His voice hardened. "And you didn't ever think I wanted to get out, too?"

She felt a wave of irritation. How had this suddenly become her fault? "You could have if you wanted to. You could have studied—"

"When? When you left it was just me and the shop; and after Father started getting worse, I had to do everything around the house. And Mother isn't kind, Rin. You knew that—I begged you to not leave me with her—but you left anyway. Off in Sinegard on your adventures—"

"They weren't adventures," she said coldly.

"But you were in *Sinegard*," he said plaintively, with the voice of a child who had only heard stories of the former capital, who still thought it was a land of riches and marvels. "And I was stuck in Tikany, hiding from Mother every chance I got. And then the war started and all we did every single day was huddle terrified in underground shelters and hope that the Federation hadn't come to our town yet, and if they did, then they might not kill us immediately."

She stopped walking. "Kesegi."

"They kept saying you were going to come for us." His voice cracked. "That a fire goddess from the Rooster Province had destroyed the longbow island, and that you were going to come back home to liberate us, too."

"I wanted to. I would have—"

"No, you wouldn't have. Where were you all those months? Launching a coup in the Autumn Palace. Starting another war." Venom crept into his voice. "You don't get to say you don't want any part of this. This is your fault. Without you we wouldn't be here."

She could have replied. She could have argued with him, said it wasn't her fault but the Empress's, told him there were political forces at play that were much larger than any of them.

But she simply couldn't form the sentences. None of them felt genuine.

The simple truth was that she'd abandoned her foster brother and hadn't thought about him for years. He'd barely crossed her mind until they'd met in the camp. And she would have forgotten him again if he weren't standing right here before her.

She didn't know how to fix that. She didn't know if fixing it was even possible.

They turned the corner toward a line of single-story stone buildings. They had made it to the Hesperian quarters. A few more minutes and they'd be back at the refugee district. Rin was glad of it. She wanted to get away from Kesegi. She couldn't bear the full brunt of his resentment.

From the corner of her eye, she saw a blue uniform disappear around the back of the closest building. She would have dismissed it, but then she heard the sounds—a rhythmic shuffle, a muffled moan.

She'd heard those noises before. She'd delivered parcels of opium to Tikany's whorehouses plenty of times. She just couldn't imagine how this could be the time or the place.

Kesegi heard it, too. He stopped walking.

"Run to the barrier," she hissed.

"But—"

"I'm not asking." She pushed him. "*Go.*"

He obeyed.

She broke into a run. She saw two half-naked bodies behind the building. Hesperian soldier, Nikara girl. The girl whimpered, trying to scream, but the soldier covered her mouth with one hand, grasped her hair with the other, and jerked her head back to expose her neck.

For a moment all Rin could do was stand and watch.

She'd never seen a rape before.

She'd heard about them. She'd heard too many stories from the women who had survived Golyn Niis, had imagined it vividly so many times that they invaded her nightmares and made her wake up shaking in rage and fear.

And the only thing she could think about was whether this was how Venka had suffered at Golyn Niis. Whether Venka's face had contorted like this girl's, mouth open in a silent scream. Whether the Mugenese soldiers who had pinned her down had been laughing like the Hesperian soldier was now.

Bile rose up in Rin's throat. "Get off of her."

The soldier couldn't, or refused to, understand her. He just kept going, panting like an animal.

Rin couldn't believe those were noises of *pleasure*.

She threw herself into the soldier's side. He twisted around and flung an awkward fist toward her face, but she ducked easily, grabbed his wrists, kicked in his kneecaps, and wrestled him into submission until he was lying on the ground, pinned down between her knees.

She reached down, feeling for his testicles. When she found them, she squeezed. "Is this what you wanted?"

He writhed frantically beneath her. She squeezed harder. He made a gurgling noise.

She dug her fingernails into soft flesh. "No?"

He screeched in pain.

She called the flame. His screams grew louder, but she grabbed his discarded shirt off the ground, shoved it into his mouth, and didn't let him go until his member had turned to charcoal in her hands.

When he finally stopped moving, she climbed off his chest, sat down next to the trembling girl, and put her arm around her shoulders. Neither of them spoke. They just huddled together, watching the soldier with cold satisfaction as he twitched, mewling feebly, on the dirt.

"Is he going to die?" the girl asked.

The soldier's whimpers were getting softer. Rin had burned half of his lower body. Some of the wounds were cauterized. It might take a long while for the blood loss to kill him. She hoped he was conscious for it. "Yes. If no one takes him to a physician."

The girl didn't sound scared, just idly curious. "Will you take him?"

"He's not in my platoon," Rin said. "Not my problem."

More minutes passed. Blood pooled slowly beneath the soldier's waist. Rin sat with the girl in silence, heart hammering, mind racing through the consequences.

The Hesperians would know the killer was her. The burn marks would give her away—only the Speerly killed with fire.

Tarcquet's retaliation would be terrible. He might not settle for Rin's death—if he found out what had just happened, he might abandon the Republic altogether.

Rin had to get rid of that body.

Eventually the soldier's chest stopped rising and falling. Rin shuffled forward on her knees and felt his neck for a pulse. Nothing. She stood up and extended a hand to the girl. "Let's get you cleaned up. Can you walk?"

"Don't worry about me." The girl sounded remarkably calm. She'd stopped trembling. She bent forward to wipe the blood and fluids off of her legs with the hem of her torn dress. "It's happened before."

CHAPTER 29

"Tiger's fucking tits," Kitay said.

"I know," Rin said.

"And you just dumped him in the harbor?"

"Weighed him down with rocks first. I picked a pretty deep stretch by the docks; no one's going to find him—"

"Holy shit." Kitay ran a hand through his bangs and yanked as he paced around the library. "You're going to die. We're all going to die."

"It might be all right." Rin tried to convince herself as she said it, but she still felt terribly light-headed. She'd come to Kitay because he was the one person she trusted to figure out what to do, but now both of them were panicking. "Look, no one saw me—"

"*How do you know?*" he asked shrilly. "No one caught you dragging a Hesperian corpse halfway across the city? No one was looking out their windows? You'd be willing to stake your life on the fact that *not a single person saw*?"

"I didn't drag it, I dumped it in a sampan and rowed out to shore."

"Oh, *that* solves everything—"

"Kitay. Listen." She took a deep breath, trying to get her mind to slow down enough to work properly. "It's been over an hour. If they'd seen, don't you think I'd be dead by now?"

"Tarcquet could be biding his time," Kitay said. "Waiting until morning to set an army on you."

"He wouldn't wait." Rin was certain of that. The Hesperians didn't fuck around. If Tarcquet found out that a shaman, of all people, had killed one of his men, then her body would already be riddled with bullet holes. He wouldn't have given her the chance to escape.

The more time that passed, the more she hoped—believed—that Tarcquet didn't know. Vaisra didn't know. They might never know. Rin wasn't telling anyone, and the refugee girl would certainly keep her mouth shut.

Kitay rubbed his palms against his temples. "When did this happen?"

"I told you. Just over an hour ago, when I was walking Kesegi back to the barriers from the old warehouses."

"What on earth were you doing by the warehouses?"

"Southern Warlords ambushed me. Wanted to talk. They're thinking of defecting back to their home provinces to deal with the Federation armies and they wanted me to come along, and they had this insane theory about the Hesperians, and—"

"What did you say?"

"Of course I refused. That'd be a death sentence."

"Well, at least you didn't commit treason." Kitay managed a shaky laugh. "And then, what, you just wandered back to the barracks and murdered a Hesperian on the way?"

"You didn't see what he was doing."

He threw his hands up. "Does it fucking matter?"

"He was on a girl," she said angrily. "He had her by her neck and he wouldn't stop—"

"So you decided to scorch any possible chance we have of surviving the Red Cliffs?"

"The Hesperians aren't fucking coming, Kitay."

"They're still here, aren't they? If they really didn't care they'd have packed up and gone. Did that ever cross your mind? When your back is to the wall there's a massive difference between zero and one percent but no, you'd rather *guarantee* it's zero—"

Her cheeks burned. "I didn't think—"

"Of course not," Kitay snapped. His knuckles had gone white. "You never think, do you? You always just pick whatever fights you want, whenever you want, and fuck the consequences—"

Rin raised her voice. "Would you rather I had let him rape her?"

Kitay fell silent.

"No," he said after a long pause. "I'm sorry, I didn't—I didn't mean that."

"I didn't think so."

He pressed his face into his hands. "*Gods*, I'm just scared. And you didn't have to kill him, you could have—"

"I know," she said. She felt drained. All the adrenaline had gone out of her at once, and now she only wanted to collapse. "I know, I wasn't thinking, I saw it happening and I just—"

"It's my life on the line now, too."

"I'm sorry."

"I know." He sighed. "I don't think— You didn't have— Fine. It's fine. I understand."

"I really don't think anyone saw."

"Fine." He took a deep breath. "Are you going to go back to the barracks?"

"No."

"Me neither."

They sat together on the floor for a long while in silence. He rested his head against her shoulder. She clutched at his hands. Neither of them could sleep. They were both watching the library windows, waiting to see Hesperian troops lined up at the door, to hear the fall of heavy boots in the hallway. Rin couldn't help but feel a twinge of relief at every additional moment that passed.

It meant the Hesperians weren't coming. It meant that, for now, she was safe.

But what happened when the Hesperians woke up in the morning and discovered a missing soldier? What happened when they started to search? They wouldn't find him for days at least, she'd made sure of that, but the sheer fact that a soldier was missing might derail Hesperian negotiations regardless.

If the fallout didn't land on Rin, then would they punish the entire Republic?

The southern Warlords' words rose unbidden to her mind. *You shouldn't fight for an alliance with people who think we're barely human.*

"Tell me what the southern Warlords said," Kitay said, startling her.

She sat up. "About what?"

"The Hesperians. What's this theory?"

"Just the usual. They don't trust them, they think they'll bring a second coming of the occupation, and . . . Oh." She frowned. "They also think that the Hesperians let the Mugenese invade on purpose. They think Vaisra knew the Federation was going to launch an invasion, and that the Hesperians knew, too, but neither of them acted because they wanted the empire weakened and ripe for the taking."

Kitay blinked. "Really."

"I know. That's crazy."

"No," he said. "That makes sense."

"You can't be serious. That would be awful."

"But it tracks with everything we know, doesn't it?" Kitay gave a short laugh that bordered on manic. "I'd been thinking it from the start, actually, but I thought, 'Nah, no one could be that insane. Or evil.' But think about the Republic's ships. Think about how long it took to build that entire fleet. Vaisra's been planning his civil war for years—that's obvious. But he never launched an attack until now. Why?"

"Maybe he wasn't ready," she said.

"Or maybe he needed the country weakened if he was ever going to wage a successful war against the Vipress. Needed us shattered so he could pick up the pieces."

"He needed someone else to attack first," she said slowly.

He nodded. "And the Federation was the best pawn for that task. I bet he laughed when they marched on Sinegard. I bet he'd been wanting that war for years."

Rin wanted to say no, say *of course* Vaisra wouldn't let innocent people die, but she knew that wasn't true. She knew Vaisra was more than happy to wipe entire provinces off his map as long as it meant he kept his Republic.

Gods, as long as he kept his *city*.

Which meant Hesperian passivity during the Second Poppy War had not been some political mistake, or a delay in communications, but entirely deliberate. Which meant that Vaisra had known the Federation would kill hundreds, thousands, tens of thousands, and he'd let it happen.

When she thought about it now, it should have been so easy to realize that they'd been manipulated. They had been trapped in a geopolitical chess game that had been years, perhaps decades in the making.

And she hadn't simply been fooled. She'd been deliberately blind to the clues around her, and she'd sat back and let everything happen.

She'd been stupidly, passively asleep for such a long time. She'd spent so much effort fighting in the trenches for Vaisra's Republic that she'd barely considered what might happen after.

If they won, what price would the Hesperians demand for their aid? Would Petra's experiments escalate once Vaisra no longer needed Rin on the battlefield?

It seemed so foolish now to imagine that as long as Vaisra vouched for her, she was safe from those arquebuses. Months ago she'd been lost and afraid, desperate to find an anchor, and that had primed her to trust him. But she'd also seen, over and over again by now, how easily Vaisra manipulated those around him like shadow puppets.

How quickly would he trade her away?

"Oh, Kitay." She exhaled slowly. She suddenly felt very, very afraid. "What are we going to do?"

He shook his head. "I don't know."

She thought through the possibilities out loud. "We have no good options. If we defect to the south, we're dead."

"And if you leave Arlong, then the Hesperians will hunt you down."

"But if we stay loyal to the Republic, we're just building a cage for ourselves."

"And none of that even matters if we don't survive the day after tomorrow."

They stared at each other. Rin heard a heartbeat echoing against the silence; hers or Kitay's, she didn't know.

"Tiger's tits," she said. "We're going to die. None of this even matters because Feylen is going to wreck us under the Red Cliffs and we're all going to die."

"Not necessarily." Kitay stood up abruptly. "Come with me."

She blinked up at him. "What?"

"You'll see. I've been meaning to show you something ever since you got back." He clasped her hands and pulled her to her feet. "I just haven't had the chance. Follow me."

Somehow they ended up in the armory. Rin wasn't entirely sure they were supposed to be there, because Kitay had kicked through the lock to get in, but at this point she didn't care.

He led her to a back storage room, pulled a bundle wrapped in a canvas sheet out from a corner, and dropped it on the table. "This is for you."

She peeled the sheet back. "A pile of leather. Thank you. I love it."

"Just unfold it," he said.

She held up the contraption, a confusing combination of riding straps, iron rods, and long sheets of leather. She peered at it from all angles but couldn't make sense of what she was looking at. "What is this?"

"You know how none of us have been able to defeat Feylen?" Kitay asked.

"Because he keeps flinging us into cliff walls? Yes, Kitay, I remember that."

"Listen." He had a manic glint in his eye. "What if he couldn't? What if you could fight him on his turf? Well, *turf* doesn't really apply, but you know what I mean."

She stared at him, uncomprehending. "I have no idea what you're talking about."

"You've got far more control of that fire now, yes?" he asked. "Could probably call it without thinking?"

"Sure," she said slowly. The fire felt like a natural extension of her now; she could extend it farther, burn hotter. But she was still confused. "You already know that. What does that have to do with anything?"

"How hot can you make it?" he pressed.

She frowned. "Isn't all fire the same temperature?"

"Actually, no. You get different sorts of flames on different surfaces. There's a difference between a candle flame and a blacksmith's fire, for instance. I'm not an expert, but—"

"Why does that matter?" she interrupted. "I couldn't get close enough to burn Feylen anyway, and I don't have that kind of reach."

He shook his head impatiently. "But what if you could?"

"We're not all geniuses like you," she snapped. "Just tell me what you're going on about."

He grinned. "Remember the signal lanterns before Boyang? The ones that would have exploded?"

"Of course, but—"

"Do you want to know how they work?"

She sighed and resigned herself to giving him free rein to talk as much as he wanted. "No, but I think you're about to tell me."

"Hot air rises," he said gleefully. "Cool air sinks. The balloons trap the hot air in a small space and it lifts up the entire apparatus."

She considered this for a moment. She was starting to understand where he was going, but she wasn't sure if she liked the conclusion. "I weigh a lot more than a paper balloon."

"It's about the ratio," Kitay insisted. "For instance, heavier birds need larger wings."

"But even the largest bird is *tiny* compared to—"

"So you'd need even bigger wings. And you'll need a hotter fire. But you have the strongest heat source in existence, so all we had to do was get you an apparatus to turn that into flying power. The wings, if you will."

She blinked at him, and then looked down at the pile of leather and metal. "You've got to be joking."

"Not in the slightest," he said happily. "Do you want to try it on?"

She gingerly unfolded the apparatus. It was surprisingly light, the leather smooth under her hands. She wondered where Kitay had found the material. She held it up, marveling at the neat stitching.

"You did this all in a week?"

"Yeah. I'd been thinking about it for a while, though. Ramsa came up with the idea."

"*Ramsa* did?"

He nodded. "Half of munitions is aerodynamics. He's spent a long time figuring out how to make things fly right."

Rin was somewhat wary of gambling her life on the designs of a boy whose greatest passion in life was watching things explode, but she supposed that at this point she had very few options.

With Kitay's help, she fastened the strap over her chest as tightly as she could manage. The iron rods shifted uncomfortably against her back, but otherwise the wings were surprisingly flexible, greased to rotate smoothly with every movement of her arms.

"You know, Altan used to give himself wings," she said.

"He *did*? Could he fly?"

"I doubt it. They were made of fire. I think he just did it to look pretty."

"Well, I think I can give you some functional ones." He tightened the straps around her shoulders. "Everything fit okay?"

She lifted her arms, feeling somewhat like an overgrown bat. The leather wings looked pretty, but they seemed far too thin to sustain her body weight. The interlacing rods that kept the apparatus together also looked so terribly fragile she was sure she could snap them in half over her knee. "You sure that's going to be enough to keep me up?"

"I didn't want to add too much to your weight. The rods are as slender as they'll go. Any heavier and you'll sink."

"They could also break and send me plummeting to my death," she pointed out.

"Have a little faith in me."

"It's gonna hurt *you* if I crash."

"I know." He sounded far too giddy for her comfort. "Shall we go try this out?"

They found an open clearing up on the cliffs, well out of range of anything that was remotely flammable. Kitay had wanted to test his invention by pushing Rin off a ledge, but reluctantly agreed to let her try levitating over level ground first.

The sun was just beginning to rise over the Red Cliffs, and Rin would have found it exceptionally lovely if she weren't so terrified that she could hear her heartbeat slamming in her eardrums.

She stepped out into the middle of the clearing, arms raised stiffly over her sides. She felt both exceedingly scared and stupid.

"Well, go on." Kitay backed up several paces. "Give it a try."

She gave the wings an awkward flap. "So I just . . . light up?"

"I think so. Try to keep it localized to your arms. You want the heat trapped in the air pockets under the wings, not dispersed in the air."

"All right." She willed the flame to dance up her palms and into her neck and shoulders. Her upper body felt deliciously warm, but almost immediately her wings began to smoke and sizzle.

"Kitay?" she called, alarmed.

"That's just the binding agent," said Kitay. "It'll be fine, it'll just burn off—"

Her voice rose several pitches. "It's fine if the *binding agent burns off?*"

"That's just the excess substance. The rest should hold—I think." He didn't sound convincing in the least. "I mean, we tested the solvent at the forge, so in theory . . ."

"Right," she said slowly. Her knees were shaking. Her head felt terribly light. "Why do I let you do this?"

"Because if you die, I die," he said. "Can you make those flames a little larger?"

She closed her eyes. Her leather wings lifted at her sides, expanding from the hot air.

Then she felt it—a heavy pressure yanking on her upper body, like a giant had reached down and jerked her up by the arms.

"Shit," she breathed. She looked down. Her feet had risen off the ground. "Shit. *Shit!*"

"Go higher!" Kitay called.

Great Tortoise. She *was* rising higher, without even trying—no, she was practically shooting upward. She kicked her legs, wobbling in the air. She had no lateral directional control, and she couldn't figure out how to slow her ascent, but holy gods, *she was flying.*

Kitay shouted something at her, but she couldn't hear him over the rush of the flames surrounding her.

"What?" she yelled back.

Kitay flapped his arms and ran in a zigzag motion.

Did he want her to fly sideways? She puzzled over the mechanics of it. She could decrease the heat on one side. As soon as she tried it she nearly flipped over and ended up hanging awkwardly in midair with her hip level with her head. She hastily righted herself.

She couldn't drift laterally, then. But how did birds change direction? She tried to remember. They didn't move straight to one side, they tilted their wings. They didn't drift, they swooped.

She beat her wings down several times and rose several feet into the air. Then she adjusted the curve of her arms so that the wings beat to the side, not downward, and tried again.

Immediately she careened to the left. The swift change in direction was terribly disorienting. Her stomach heaved; her flames flickered madly. For a moment she lost sight of the ground, and didn't right herself until she was mere feet away from the dirt.

She jerked herself out of the dive, gasping. This was going to take some practice.

She flapped her wings to regain altitude. She shot up faster than she'd anticipated. She flapped them again. Then again.

How far could she go? Kitay was still shouting something from the ground, but she was too far up to understand him. She rose higher and higher with each steady beat of her wings. The ground became dizzyingly far away, but she had eyes only for the great expanse of sky above her.

How far could the fire take her?

She couldn't help but laugh as she soared, a high, desperate, frantic laugh of relief. She rose so high that she could no longer make out Kitay's face, until Arlong turned into little splotches of green and blue, until she had even passed through a layer of clouds.

Then she stopped.

She hung alone in an expanse of blue.

A calm washed over her then, a calm that she couldn't ever remember feeling. There was nothing up here she could kill. Nothing she could hurt. She had her mind to herself. She had the *world* to herself.

She floated in the air, suspended at the point between heaven and earth.

The Red Cliffs looked so beautiful from up here.

Her mind wandered to the last minister of the Red Emperor, who had etched those ancient words into the cliffside. He'd written a scream to the heavens, an open plea to future generations, a message for the Hesperians who would one day sail into that harbor and bomb it.

What had he wanted to tell them?

Nothing lasts.

Nezha and Kitay had both been wrong. There was another way

to interpret those carvings. If nothing lasted and the world did not exist, all that meant was that reality was not fixed. The illusion she lived in was fluid and mutable, and could be easily altered by someone willing to rewrite the script of reality.

Nothing lasts.

This was not a world of men. It was a world of gods, a time of great powers. It was the era of divinity walking in man, of wind and water and fire. And in warfare, she who held the power asymmetry was the inevitable victor.

She, the Last Speerly, called the greatest power of all.

And the Hesperians, no matter how hard they tried, could never take this from her.

Landing was the tricky part.

Her first instinct was to simply extinguish the fire. But then she dropped like a rock, plummeting at a breakneck speed for several heart-stopping moments until she managed to get her wings spread and a fire lit beneath them. That made her come to a lurching halt so rough she was shocked the wings didn't rip right off her arms.

She drifted back up, heart hammering.

She'd have to glide down somehow. She thought through the movements in her head—she'd decrease the heat, little by little, until she was close enough to the ground.

It almost worked. She hadn't counted on how fast her velocity would increase. Suddenly she was thirty feet from the ground and hurtling far too quickly toward Kitay.

"*Move!*" she shouted, but he didn't budge. He just reached his hands out, grabbed her wrists, and swung her about until they collapsed in a tangled, laughing heap of leather and silk and limbs.

"I was right," he said. "I'm always right."

"Well, don't be so smug about it."

He groaned happily and rubbed his arms. "So how was it?"

"Incredible." She flung her arms around him and hugged him tight. "You genius. You wonderful, wonderful genius."

Kitay leaned back, arms raised. "Careful, you'll break the wings."

She twisted her head around to check them and marveled at the thin, careful craftsmanship that held the apparatus together. "I can't believe you did this in a week."

"I had some time on my hands," said Kitay. "Wasn't out there trying to stop a fleet or anything."

"I love you," she said.

Kitay gave her a tired smile. "I know."

"We still don't know what we're going to do after—" she started, but he shook his head.

"I know," he said. "I don't know what to do about the Hesperians. For once, I haven't the faintest idea, and I hate it. But we'll figure our way out of it. We've figured our way out of this, we're going to survive the Red Cliffs, we're going to survive Vaisra, and we'll keep surviving until we're safe and the world can't touch us. One enemy at a time. Agreed?"

"Agreed," she said.

Once her legs had stopped shaking, he helped her strip out of her gear. Then they climbed back down the cliff, still light-headed and giddy with victory, laughing so hard that their sides hurt.

Because yes, the fleet was still coming, and yes, they might very well die the next morning, but in that instant it didn't matter, because fuck it, she could *fly*.

"You'll need some air support," Kitay said after a while.

"Air support?"

"You'll be a very conspicuous, very obvious target. You'll want someone fending off the people shooting at you. They throw rocks, we throw them back. A line of archers would be nice."

Rin snorted. Arlong's defenses were spread thin as things were. "They're not going to give us a line of archers."

"Yeah, probably not." He shot her a sideways look, considering. "Should we try Eriden before the last council starts? See if he'll lend us at least one of his men?"

"No," she said. "I have a better idea."

Rin found Venka the first place she looked—training in the archery yard, furiously decimating straw targets. Rin stood in the corner for a moment, watching her from behind a post.

Venka hadn't fully learned yet to compensate for her stiff arms, which seemed to spasm uncontrollably and to bend only with effort. They must have hurt badly—her face tightened every time she reached for her quiver.

She hadn't taken her left arm brace off. She'd just locked her upper wrist into place instead. She was shooting while overcorrecting for a hyperextended arm, Rin realized. But for the amount of control she had left, Venka had a stunning degree of accuracy. Her speed was also absurd. By Rin's count she could shoot twenty arrows a minute, maybe more.

Venka was no Qara, but she'd do.

"Nice go," Rin called at the end of a fifteen-arrow streak.

Venka doubled over, panting. "Don't you have anything better to do?"

In response, Rin crossed the archery range and handed Venka a silk-wrapped parcel.

Venka glared at it suspiciously, then placed her bow on the ground so she could accept. "What's this?"

"A present."

Venka's lip curled. "Is it someone's head?"

Rin laughed. "Just open it."

Venka unwrapped the silk. After a moment she looked up, eyes hard, flinty and suspicious. "Where did you get this?"

"Picked it up in the north," Rin said. "It's Ketreyid-made. You like it?"

Before they'd returned to Arlong, she and Kitay had bundled all the weapons they could scavenge onto the raft. Most of them had been short knives and hunting bows that neither of them could use.

"This is a silkworm thorn bow," Venka declared. "Do you know how *rare* this is?"

Rin wouldn't have known silkworm thorn from driftwood, but

she took that as a good sign. "I thought you'd like it better than those bamboo creations."

Venka turned the bow over in her hands, then held it up to her eyes to examine the bowstring. Her arms shook. She glanced down at her trembling elbows, openly disgusted. "You don't want to waste a silkworm thorn bow on me."

"It's not a waste. I saw you shoot."

"That?" Venka snorted. "That's nowhere close to before."

"The bow will help. Silkworm thorn's lighter, I think. But we can also get you a crossbow, if it'll help with distance."

Venka squinted at her. "What exactly are you saying?"

"I need air support."

"Air . . . ?"

"Kitay's built a contraption to help me fly," Rin said bluntly.

"Oh, *gods*." Venka laughed. "Of course he has."

"He's Chen Kitay."

"Indeed he is. Does it work?"

"Shockingly, yes. But I need backup. I need someone with very good aim."

She was absolutely sure Venka would say yes. She could read longing all over Venka's face. She was looking at the bow the way some might a lover.

"They won't let me fight," she said finally. "Not even from the parapets."

"So fight for me," Rin said. "The Cike's not in the army and the Republic can't tell me who I can recruit. And we're down a few men."

"I heard." A smile cracked across Venka's face. Rin hadn't seen her look so genuinely happy in a long, long time. Venka held the bow tight to her chest, caressing the carved grip. "Well, then. I'm at your service, Commander."

CHAPTER 30

At dawn, Arlong's civilians began clearing out of the city. The evacuation proceeded with impressive efficiency. The civilians had been packed and prepared for this for weeks. All families were ready to go with two bags each of clothing, medical supplies, and several days' worth of food.

By midafternoon the city center had been hollowed out. Arlong became a shell of a city. The Republican Army quickly transformed the larger residences into defense bases with sandbags and hidden explosives.

Soldiers accompanied the civilians to the base of the cliffs, where they began a long, winding climb up to the caves inside the rock face. The pass was narrow and treacherous, and some heights could not be scaled except by using several stringy rope ladders embedded into the rock with nails.

"That's a rough climb," Rin said, looking doubtfully up the rock wall. The ladders were so narrow the evacuees would have to go up one by one, with no one to aid them. "Can everyone make it?"

"They'll get over it." Venka walked up behind her with two small, sniffling children in tow, a brother and sister who'd been separated from their parents in the crowd. "Our people have been using those hills as hideouts for years. We hid there during the Era of Warring States. We hid there when the Federation came. We'll survive this, too." She hoisted the girl up onto her hip and jerked her brother along. "Come on, hurry up."

Rin glanced backward over her shoulder at the masses of people moving below.

Maybe the caves would keep the Dragons safe. But the southern refugees had been ordered to occupy the valley lowlands, and that was just open space.

The official word was that the caves were too small to accommodate everyone, and so the refugees would have to make do. But the valley provided no shelter at all. Exposed to the elements, with no natural or military barriers to hide behind, the refugees would have no protection from the weather or the Militia—and certainly not from Feylen.

But where else were they going to go? They wouldn't have fled to Arlong if home were safe.

"I'm hungry," complained the boy.

"I don't care." Venka tugged at his skinny wrist. "Stop crying. Walk faster."

"This battle will take place primarily in three stages," said Vaisra. "One, we will fend them off at the outer channel between the Red Cliffs. Two, we win the ground battle in the city. Three, they will try to retreat along the coast, and we will pick them off. We'll get to that stage if we are miraculously lucky."

His officers nodded grimly.

Rin glanced around the council room, amazed by how many faces she'd never seen before. A good half of the officers were newly promoted. They wore the stripes of senior leadership, but they looked five years older than Rin at most.

So many young, scared faces. The military command had been killed off at the top. This was rapidly becoming a war fought by the children.

"Can that warship even get through the cliffs?" asked Captain Dalain.

"Daji's familiar with the channel," said Admiral Kulau, the young navy officer who had replaced Molkoi. He sounded as if he were deepening his voice to seem older. "She'll have designed it so it can."

"It doesn't matter," Eriden said. "If their warship even starts depositing troops outside the channel, then we're in trouble." He leaned over the map. "That's why we have archers stationed here and here—"

"Why aren't there any back-end fortifications?" Kitay interrupted.

"The invasion will come from the channel," Vaisra said. "Not the valley."

"But the channel's the obvious avenue of attack," Kitay said. "They know you're expecting them. If I'm Daji, and I have a numerical advantage *that* large, then I split my troops and send a third column round the back while everyone's distracted."

"No one's ever attacked Arlong from land routes," Kulau said. "They'd be eviscerated on the mountaintops."

"Not if they're unguarded," Kitay insisted.

Kulau cleared his throat. "They're not unguarded. They've got fifty men guarding them."

"Fifty men can't beat a column!"

"Chang En's not going to send a full column of his crack troops round the back. You have a fleet that big, you man it."

No one spoke the more obvious answer, which was that the Republican Army simply didn't have the *troops* for better fortifications. And if any part of Arlong warranted a defense, then it was the palace and military barracks. Not the valley lowlands. Not the southerners.

"Of course, Chang En will want this to turn into a land battle," Vaisra continued smoothly. "There they have the sheer advantage in numbers. But this fight remains winnable as long as we keep it amphibious."

The channel had already been blocked up with so many iron chains and underwater obstacles that it almost functioned as a dam. The Republic was banking on mobility over numbers—their armed skimmers could dart between the Imperial ships, breaking up formations while the munitions crews shot bombs down from their cliffside stations.

"What's the makeup of their fleet?" asked a young officer Rin didn't recognize. He sounded terribly nervous. "Which ships do we target?"

"Aim for the warships, not the skimmers," Kulau said. "Anything that has a trebuchet should be a target. But the bulk of their troops are on that floating fortress. If you can sink any ships, sink that first."

"You want us in a fan formation at the cliffs?" Captain Dalain asked.

"No," said Kulau. "If we spread out then they'll just obliterate us. Stay in a narrow line and plug up the channel."

"We're not worried about their shaman?" Dalain asked. "If we clump our ships together, he's just going to blast our fleet against the cliffs."

"I'll take care of Feylen," Rin said.

The generals blinked at her. She looked around the table, eyes wide open. "What?"

"Last time you ended up stranded for a month," said Captain Eriden. "We'll be fine against Feylen—we have fifteen squadrons of archers positioned across the cliff walls."

"And he'll just fling them off the cliffs," said Rin. "They won't be more than an annoyance."

"And you won't be?"

"No," she said. "This time, I can fly."

The generals looked as if they were unsure whether to laugh. Only General Tarcquet, sitting silently as usual in the back of the room, looked mildly curious.

"I built her a, uh, flying kite sort of contraption," Kitay explained. He made some gestures with his hands that clarified nothing. "It's made up of some leather wings with rods, and she can generate flames hot enough to levitate herself using the same principle that lifts a lantern—"

"Have you tried it?" Vaisra asked. "Does it work?"

Rin and Kitay nodded.

"Wonderful," Gurubai said drily. "So, assuming she's not mad, that's the Wind God taken care of. There's still the rest of the Imperial Navy to deal with, and we're still outnumbered three to one."

The officers shifted uneasily.

It was easier for Rin if she compartmentalized the battle to simply dealing with Feylen. She didn't want to think about the rest of the fleet, because the truth was there *was* no easy way to deal with the fleet. They were outnumbered, they were on the defensive, and they were trapped.

Kitay sounded far calmer than she felt. "There's a number of different tactics we can try. We can try to break them up and storm their warships. The important thing is that we don't let that fortress get to the shore, because then it turns into a land battle for the city."

"And Jun's forces won't be so formidable," Kulau added. "They'll be exhausted. The Militia isn't used to naval battles, they'll be seasick and dizzy. Meanwhile our army was designed for riverine warfare, and our soldiers are fresh. We'll just outfight them."

The room looked unconvinced.

"Here's an option we haven't considered," General Hu said after a short pause. "We could surrender."

Rin found it disheartening that this wasn't immediately met with a general outcry.

Several seconds passed in silence. Rin glanced sideways at Vaisra but couldn't read his expression.

"That wouldn't be a terrible idea," Vaisra said finally.

"It wouldn't." General Hu glanced desperately around the room. "Look, I'm not the only one thinking it. They're going to slaughter us. No one's come back from a numbers disadvantage like this in history. If we cut our losses now, we still come out of this alive."

"As always," Vaisra said slowly, "you are the voice of reason, General Hu."

General Hu looked profoundly relieved, but his smile faded as Vaisra continued to speak. "Why *not* surrender? The consequences couldn't possibly be so terrible. All that would happen is that every single person in this room would be flayed alive, Arlong destroyed, and any hope of democratic reform would be quashed in the Empire for at least the next few centuries. Is that what you want?"

General Hu had turned pale. "No."

"I have no place in my army for cowards," Vaisra said softly. He nodded to the soldier standing beside Hu. "You there. You're his aide?"

The boy nodded, eyes huge. He couldn't have been older than twenty. "Yes, sir."

"Ever been in battle?" Vaisra asked.

The boy's throat bobbed as he swallowed. "Yes, sir. I was at Boyang."

"Excellent. And what is your name?"

"Zhou Anlan, sir."

"Congratulations, General Zhou. You've been promoted." Vaisra turned to General Hu. "You can leave."

General Hu forced his way through the crowded bodies and left without another word. The door swung shut behind him.

"He's going to defect," said Vaisra. "Eriden, see that he's stopped."

"Permanently?" Eriden asked.

Vaisra considered that briefly. "Only if he struggles."

After the council had been dismissed, Vaisra motioned for Rin to stay behind. She exchanged a panicked glance with Kitay as he filtered out with the others. Once the room had emptied, Vaisra closed the door behind him.

"When this is over I want you to go pay a visit to our friend Moag," he said quietly.

She was so relieved that he hadn't mentioned the Hesperians that for a moment all she did was blink at him, uncomprehending. "The Pirate Queen?"

"Make it quick," Vaisra said. "Leave the corpse and bring back the head."

"Wait. You want me to kill her?"

"Was I not sufficiently clear?"

"But she's your biggest naval ally—"

"The *Hesperians* are our biggest naval ally," Vaisra said. "Do you see Moag's ships in the bay?"

"I don't see any Hesperian ships in the bay," Rin pointed out.

"They will come. Give them time. But Moag's going to be nothing but trouble once this war's over. She's operated extralegally for too long, and she couldn't get used to a naval authority that isn't her own. Smuggling's in her blood."

"So let her smuggle," Rin said. "Keep her happy. What's the problem with that?"

"There's no way to keep her happy. Ankhiluun exists because of the tariffs. Once we have free trade with the Hesperians, that makes the entire premise of Ankhiluun irrelevant. All she'll have left is opium smuggling, and I don't intend to be half as lenient toward opium as Daji is. There's a war coming once Moag realizes all her income streams are drying up. I'd rather nip it in the bud."

"And this request has nothing to do with the fact that she hasn't sent ships?" Rin asked.

Vaisra smiled. "An ally's only useful if they do as they're told. Moag's proven herself unreliable."

"So you want me to commit preemptive murder."

"Let's not be as dramatic as that." He waved a hand. "We'll call it insurance."

"I think the wall's ready," Kitay said, rubbing his eyes. He looked exhausted. "I wanted to triple-check the fuses, but there wasn't time."

They stood at the edge of the cliffs, watching the sun set between the two sides of the channel like a ball falling down a ravine. Dark water shimmered below, reflecting crimson rock and a burnt-orange sun. It looked like a flood of blood gushing out from a freshly sliced artery.

When Rin squinted at the opposite cliff, she could just see the lines where fuses had been strung together and tucked with nails into the rock, like a sprawling, ugly patchwork of protruding veins.

"What are they chances they don't go off?" she asked.

Kitay yawned. "They'll probably go off."

"Probably," she repeated.

"You're just going to have to trust Ramsa and I did our jobs. If they don't go off, we're all dead."

"Fair enough." Rin hugged her arms across her chest. She felt tiny standing over the massive precipice. Empires had been won and lost under these cliffs. They were on the brink of losing another one.

"Do you think we can win tomorrow?" she asked quietly. "I mean, is there even the slightest chance?"

"I've done the math seven different ways," Kitay said. "Compiled all the intelligence we have and compared the probabilities and everything."

"And?"

"And I don't know." His fists clenched and unclenched, and Rin could tell he was resisting the urge to start tugging at his hair. "That's the frustrating part. You know the one thing that all the great strategists agree upon? It actually doesn't matter what numbers you have. It doesn't matter how good your models are, or how brilliant your strategies are. The world is chaotic and war is fundamentally unpredictable and at the end of the day you don't know who will be the last man standing. You don't know anything going into a battle. You only know the stakes."

"Well, they're pretty fucking high," Rin said.

If they lost, their rebellion would be vanquished and Nikan would descend into darkness for another several decades at least, rent apart by factional warfare and a lingering Federation presence.

But if they won, the Empire would become a Republic, primed to hurtle into the new and glorious future with Vaisra at the helm and the Hesperians at his side.

And then Rin would have to worry about what happened after.

An idea struck her then—just the smallest tendril of one, but it was there; a fierce, burning spark of hope. Vaisra might have just handed her a way out.

"How do you get to the rookery?" she asked.

"I can take you," Kitay said. "Who do you want to send a letter to?"

"Moag." Rin turned to begin the climb back toward the city.

Kitay followed. "What for?"

"There's something she should know." She was already composing the message in her head. If—no, *when*—she left the Republic, she would need an ally. Someone who could get her out of the city fast. Someone who wasn't linked to the Republic.

Moag was a liar, but Moag had ships. And now, Moag had a death sentence over her head that she didn't know about. That gave Rin leverage, which gave her an ally.

"Call it insurance," she said.

Traveling at its current pace, the Imperial Navy would breach the channel at dawn. That gave Arlong six more hours to prepare. Vaisra ordered his troops to sleep in rotating two-hour shifts so they would meet the Militia with as much stamina as possible.

Rin understood the rationale, but she couldn't see how she was possibly supposed to close her eyes. She vibrated with nervous energy, and even sitting still made her uneasy—she needed to be moving, running, hitting something.

She paced around the field outside the barracks. Little rivulets of fire danced through the air around her, swirling in perfect circles. That made her feel the slightest bit better. It was proof that she still had control over *something*.

Someone cleared his throat. She turned around. Nezha stood at the door, bleary-eyed and disheveled.

"What's happened?" she asked sharply. "Did anything—"

"I had a dream," he mumbled.

She raised an eyebrow. "And?"

"You died."

She made her flames disappear. "What is going on with you?"

"You died," he repeated. He sounded dazed, only half-present, like a little schoolboy disinterestedly reciting his Classics. "You—they shot you down over the water, and I saw your body floating up in the water. You were so still. I saw you drown, and I couldn't save you."

He started to cry.

"What the fuck," she muttered.

Was he drunk? High? She didn't know what she was supposed to do, only that she didn't want to be alone with him. She glanced toward the barracks. What would happen if she just left?

"Please don't leave," Nezha said, as if reading her mind.

She folded her arms against her chest. "I didn't think you ever wanted to see me again."

"Why would you think that?"

"'It would be best if we died,'" she said. "Who said that?"

"I didn't mean that—"

"Then what? Where do you draw the line? Suni, Baji, Altan—we're all monsters in your book, aren't we?"

"I was angry that you called me a coward—"

"Because you are a coward!" she shouted. "How many men died at Boyang? How many are going to die today? But no, Yin Nezha has the power to stop the river and he won't do it, because he's fucking scared of a tattoo on his back—"

"I told you, it *hurts*—"

"It always hurts. You call the gods anyway. We're soldiers—we make the sacrifices we must, no matter what it takes. But I suppose you would put your own *comfort* over a chance to crush the Empire—"

"Comfort?" Nezha repeated. "You think it's about comfort? Do you know how it felt, when I was in his cave? Do you know what he did to me?"

"Yes," she said. "Exactly the same thing the Phoenix did to me."

Rin knew Nezha's pain. She just didn't have the sympathy for it.

"You're acting like a fucking child," she said. "You're a general, Nezha. Do your job."

Anger darkened his face. "Just because you've decided to worship *your* abuser doesn't mean we all—"

Rin stiffened. "No one abused me."

"Rin, you know that's not true."

"Fuck you."

"I'm sorry." He held up his hands in surrender. "Look—I really am. I didn't come here to talk about that. I don't want to fight."

"Then why are you here?"

"Because you could die out there," he said. "We both could." His words poured out in a torrent, as if he were afraid that if he stopped speaking they would run out of time, as if he would only ever get this one chance. "I saw it happen, I saw you bleeding out in the water, and I couldn't do anything about it. That was the worst part."

"Are you high?" she demanded.

"I just want to make things right between us. What's that going to take?" Nezha spread his arms. "Should I let you hit me? Do you want to? Go ahead, take a swing. I won't move."

Rin almost took him up on the offer. But the moment she made a fist, her anger dissipated.

Why was it that whenever she looked at Nezha, she wanted to either kill him or kiss him? He made her either furious or deliriously happy. The one thing he did not make her feel was secure.

With him there was no neutrality, no in between. She loved him or she hated him, but she didn't know how to do both.

She lowered her fist.

"I really am sorry," Nezha said. "Please, Rin. I don't want us to end like this."

He tried to say something else, but the sudden boom of the signal gongs drowned out his voice. They reverberated through the barracks with such loud urgency that Rin could feel the ground trembling beneath her feet.

The familiar taste of blood filled her mouth. Panic, fear, and adrenaline flooded her veins. But this time they didn't make her collapse; she didn't want to curl into a ball and rock back and forth until it was over. She was used to this now, and she could use it as a fuel. Turn it into bloodlust.

"We should be in position," she said. She tried to walk past him into the barracks to get her equipment, but he grabbed at her arm.

"Rin, please—you have more enemies than you think you do—"

She shrugged him off. "Let me go!"

He blocked her path. "I don't want this to be the last conversation we ever have."

"Then don't die out there," she said. "Problem solved."

"But Feylen—"

"We're not going to lose to Feylen this time," she said. "We're going to win, and we're going to live."

He sounded like a terrified child woken up from a bad dream. "But how do you know?"

She didn't know what made her do it, but she put her hand on Nezha's shoulder. It wasn't an apology or forgiveness, but it was a concession. An acknowledgment.

And for just a moment, she felt a hint of that old camaraderie, a flicker she'd felt once, a year ago at Sinegard, when he'd thrown her a sword and they'd fought back to back, enemies turned to comrades, firmly on the same side for the first time in their lives.

She saw the way he was looking at her. She knew he felt it, too.

"Between us, we have the fire and the water," she said quietly. "I'm quite sure that together, we can take on the wind."

CHAPTER 31

"I can feel my heartbeat in my temples." Venka leaned over her mounted crossbow and checked the gears for what seemed like the hundredth time. It was cranked to maximum, fitted in with twelve reloading bolts. "Don't you love this part?"

"I hate this part," Kitay said. "Feels like we're waiting for our executioner."

His hairline sported visible bald patches. He was going mad waiting for the Imperial Navy to show up, and Rin knew why. They both liked it so much better when they were on the offensive, when they could decide when to attack and where.

They'd been taught at Sinegard that fighting a defensive battle by sitting behind fixed fortifications was courting disaster because it just gave the enemy the advantage of initiative. Unless a siege was at play, sitting behind defenses was almost always a doomed strategy, because there were no locks that couldn't be broken, and no fortresses that were impregnable.

And this would not be a siege. Daji had no interest in starving them out. She didn't need to. She intended to smash right through the gates.

"Arlong hasn't been taken for centuries," Venka pointed out.

Kitay's hands twitched. "Well, its luck had to run out sometime."

The Republic was as prepared as it ever would be. The generals had set their defensive traps. They'd divided and positioned their troops—seven artillery stations all along the upper cliffs, the majority stationed on the Republican Fleet in formation inside the channel, and the rest either guarding the shore or barricading the heavily fortified palace.

Rin wished that the Cike could be up on the cliff fighting by her side, but neither Baji nor Suni could offer much air support against Feylen. They were both stationed on warships at the center of the Republican Fleet where, right in the brunt of enemy fire, their abilities might stay hidden from Hesperian observers, and also where they'd be able to cause the most damage.

"Is Nezha in position?" Kitay peered over the channel.

Nezha was assigned to the front of the fleet, leading one of the three remaining warships that could hold its own in a naval skirmish. He was to drive his ship directly into the center of the Imperial Fleet and split it apart.

"Nezha's always in position," said Venka. "He's sprung like a—"

"Don't be vulgar," Kitay said.

Venka grinned.

They could hear a faint series of booms echoing from beyond the mouth of the channel. In truth, the battle had already begun—a flimsy handful of riverside forts that constituted Arlong's first line of defense had already engaged the Militia, but they were manned with only enough soldiers to keep the cannons firing.

Kitay had estimated those would buy them all of ten minutes.

"There," Venka said sharply. "I see them."

They stood up.

The Imperial Navy sailed directly into their line of sight. Rin caught her breath, trying not to panic at the sheer size of Daji's fleet combined with Tsolin's.

"What's Chang En doing?" Kitay demanded.

The Wolf Meat General had lashed his boats together, tied them stern to stern into a single, immobile structure. The fleet had become a single, massive battering ram, with the floating fortress at the very center.

"To fight the seasickness, you think?" Venka asked.

Rin frowned. "Has to be."

That seemed like a clever move. The Imperial troops weren't used to fighting over moving water, so they might do better on a locked platform. But a static formation was also particularly dangerous where battling Rin was concerned. If one ship went up in flames, so did the rest of them.

Had Daji not discovered that Rin had figured a way around the Seal?

"It's not seasickness," Kitay said. "It's so Feylen won't blow them out of the water. And it gives them the advantage if we try to board. They get troop mobility between ships."

"We're not going to board," said Rin. "We're going to torch that thing."

"That's the spirit," Venka said with an optimism that nobody felt.

The locked fleet crawled toward the cliffs at a maddeningly slow pace. War drums echoed around the channel as the fortress moved inexorably forward.

"I wonder how many men it takes to propel that thing," Venka mused.

"They don't need much paddling force," Rin said. "They're sailing downstream."

"Okay, but what about lateral movement—"

"Please stop talking," Kitay snapped.

Rin knew their chattering was idiotic, but she couldn't help it. She and Venka had the same problem. They had to keep running their mouths, because the wait would drive them crazy otherwise.

"The gates aren't going to hold," Rin said despite Kitay's glare. "It'll be like kicking down a sandcastle."

"You're giving it five minutes, then?" Venka asked.

"More like two. Get ready to fire that thing."

Venka patted Kitay's shoulder. "Don't be so hard on yourself."

He rolled his eyes. "The gate wasn't my idea."

In a last-ditch effort, Vaisra had ordered his troops to chain the gates of the channel shut with every spare link of iron in the city. It might have deterred a pirate ship, but against this fleet, it was little more than a symbolic gesture. From the sounds of it, the Militia intended to simply knock the gates over with a battering ram.

Boom. Rin felt stone vibrating beneath her feet.

"How old are those gates?" she wondered out loud.

Boom.

"Older than this province," said Venka. "Maybe as old as the Red Emperor. Lot of architectural value."

"That's a pity."

"Isn't it?"

Boom. Rin heard the sharp crack of fracturing wood, and then a noise like fabric ripping.

Arlong's gates were down.

The Imperial Navy poured through. The channel lit up with pyrotechnics. Massive twenty-foot cannons embedded into Arlong's cliff walls went off one by one, sending scorching, boulder-sized balls shrieking into the sides of Chang En's ships. Each one of Kitay's carefully planted water mines went off in lovely, timed succession to the sound of firecrackers magnified by a thousand.

For a moment the Imperial Fleet was hidden behind a massive cloud of smoke.

"Nice," Venka marveled.

Kitay shook his head. "That's nothing. They can absorb the losses."

He was right. When the smoke cleared, Rin saw that there had been more noise than damage. The fleet pressed on through the explosions. The floating fortress remained untouched.

Rin paced toward the cliff edge, sword in hand.

"Patience," Kitay muttered. "Now's not the time."

"We should be down there," she said. She felt like a coward waiting up on the cliff, hiding out of sight while soldiers burned below.

"We're only three people," Kitay said. "We'd be cannon fodder. You dive in now, you'll just get shot full of iron."

Rin hated that he was right.

The cliffs shook continuously under their feet. The Imperial Navy was returning fire. Loaded missiles shot out of the siege towers, showering tiny rockets onto the cliffside artillery stations. Shielded Militia archers returned two crossbow bolts for every one that reached their decks.

Rin's stomach twisted with horror as she watched. The Militia was using precisely the same siege-breaking strategy that Jinzha had employed on the northern campaign—eviscerate the archers first, then barrel through land resistance.

The Republican warships took the worst damage. One had already been blown so thoroughly out of the water that its fragmented remains were blocking the paths of its sister ships.

The Imperial cannons fired low to aim at the paddle wheels. The Republican ships tried to rotate in the water to keep their back paddles out of the line of fire, but they were rapidly losing mobility. At this rate, Nezha's ships would be reduced to sitting ducks.

Rin still saw no sign of Feylen.

"Where is he?" Kitay muttered. "You'd think they would bring him out right away."

"Maybe he's bad with orders," Rin said. Feylen had seemed so terrified of Daji, she didn't want to think about the kind of torture it took to persuade him to fight.

But at this rate, the Militia didn't even need to bring Feylen out. Two artillery stations had gone down. The other five were running out of ammunition and had slowed their rate of fire. Most of Nezha's warships were dead in the water, while the core of the Imperial Navy had sustained very little fire damage.

Time to rectify that. Rin stood up. "I'm going in."

"Now's the time," Kitay agreed. He handed her a jug of oil from a tidy pile stocked next to the crossbow, and then pointed down at the channel. "I'm thinking center left of that tower ship.

You want to split that formation apart. Get the ropes going and the rest will catch fire."

"And don't look down," Venka said helpfully.

"Shut up." Rin stepped backward, dug her feet against the ground, and broke into a run. The wind whipped against her face. Her wings rippled against the drag. Then the cliff disappeared under her feet, her head pitched downward, and there was no fear, no sound, only the thrilling and sickening lurch of the drop.

She let herself dive for a moment before she opened her wings. When she spread her arms the resistance hit her like a punch. Her arms felt like they were being torn from their sockets. She gasped—not from the pain, but from the sheer exhilaration. The river was a blur, ships and armies dissolving into solid streaks of browns and blues and greens.

Arrows emerged in her line of sight. They looked like needles from a distance; gaining in size at a frightening pace. She veered to the left. They whizzed harmlessly past her.

She'd gotten within range of the tower ship. She leveled off the dive. She opened her mouth and palms; a stream of fire shot out from her extremities, setting ablaze everything she passed.

She dropped the oil just before she pulled up.

She heard the glass shatter as the jar hit the deck, the crackle as the flames caught. She smiled as she soared upward to the opposite cliff wall. When she hazarded a glance backward she saw arrows lose momentum and drop back to the ground as they struggled to reach her.

Her feet found solid earth. She dropped to her knees and doubled over on all fours, panting while she surveyed the damage below.

The ropes had caught a steady, spreading fire. She could see them blackening and fraying where she'd dropped the oil.

She looked up. Across the channel, Venka methodically shoved another round of bolts into her crossbow loading mechanism, while Kitay waved for her to return.

The muscles in her arms burned, but she couldn't afford too much time for recovery. She crawled to the edge of the cliff and hauled herself to her feet.

She squinted, mapping out her next flight pattern. She caught Venka's attention and pointed toward a cluster of ships untouched by the fire. Venka nodded and redirected her crossbow.

Rin took a deep breath, jumped off the cliff, and swooped down, basking again in the rush of adrenaline. Javelins came whistling in her direction, one after another, but all she had to do was swerve and they soared uselessly into empty air.

She felt giddy as she set sails ablaze and felt the warm heat of the fire buoying her up as it spread. Was this how Altan had always felt in the heat of battle? She understood now why he'd summoned himself wings, even though he couldn't fly with them. It was symbolic. Ecstatic. In this moment she was invincible, divine. She hadn't just summoned the Phoenix, she'd become it.

"Nice job," Kitay said once she'd landed. "The fire's spread to three ships, they haven't managed to put it out—wait, can you breathe?"

"I'm okay," she gasped. "Just—give me a moment . . ."

"Guys," Venka said sharply. "This is bad."

Rin staggered to her feet and joined her near the precipice.

Burning the ropes had worked. The Imperial formation had begun to splinter, its outward ships drifting away from the center. Nezha had seized the opening to wedge his warship straight through the main cluster, where he'd managed to blow smoking holes into the side of the floating fortress.

But now he was stuck. The Imperial Navy had lowered wide planks onto his ship's sides. Nezha was about to get swarmed.

"I'm going down there," Rin said.

"To do what?" Kitay asked. "Burn them and you burn Nezha."

"Then I'll land and fight. I can direct fire more accurately from the ground, I just have to get there."

Kitay looked reluctant. "But Feylen—"

"We don't know where Feylen is. Nezha's in trouble. *I'm going.*"

"Rin. Look at the hills." Venka pointed toward the lowland valleys. "I think they've sent ground troops."

Rin exchanged a glance with Kitay.

Before he could speak she launched herself into the sky.

The ground column was impossible to miss. Rin could see them so clearly through the forest, a thick band of troops marching on Arlong from behind. They were barely half a mile from the refugee evacuation areas. They'd reach them in minutes.

She cursed into the wind. Eriden had claimed his scouts hadn't seen anything in the valley.

But how did one miss an entire *brigade*?

Her mind raced. Venka and Kitay were both screaming at her, but she couldn't hear them.

Should she go? How much good could she do? She couldn't destroy a column of soldiers on her own. And she couldn't abandon the naval battle—if Feylen appeared while she was miles away he could sink the entirety of their fleet before she could return.

But she had to tell *someone*.

She scanned the channel. She knew Vaisra and his generals were ensconced behind fortifications near the shore where they could oversee the battle, but they would refuse to do anything even if she warned them. The naval battle had few enough soldiers to spare.

She had to warn the Warlords.

They were scattered throughout the battleground with their troops, she just didn't know *where*.

No one could hear her shout from this high up. Her only option was to write them a message in the sky. She beat her wings twice to gain altitude and flew forward until she hung right over the channel, in clear sight but high out of range.

She decided on two words.

Valley invaded.

She pointed down. Flames poured from her fingers and lingered for a few seconds where she'd placed them before they dissipated. She wrote the two characters over and over, going over strokes that had faded from the air, praying that someone below would see the message.

For a long moment, nothing happened.

Then, near the shoreline, she saw a line of soldiers peeling away from the front. Someone had noticed.

She redirected her attention to the channel.

Nezha's ship had been almost completely overrun by Imperial troops. The ship's cannons had gone silent. By now its crew had to be mostly dead or incapacitated.

She didn't stop to think. She dove.

She landed badly. Her dive was too steep and she hadn't pulled up in time. She skidded forward on her knees, yelping in pain as her skin scraped along the deck.

Militia soldiers converged on her instantly. She called down a column of flame, a protective circle that incinerated everything within a five-foot radius and pushed the approaching soldiers back.

Her eyes fell on a blue uniform in a sea of green. She barreled through the burning bodies, arms shielding her head, until she reached the single Republican soldier in sight.

"Where's Nezha?" she asked.

He stared past her with unfocused eyes. Blood trickled in a single line from his forehead across his face.

She shook him hard. *"Where's Nezha?"*

The officer opened his mouth just as an arrow embedded itself in his left eye. Rin flung the body away, ducked, and snatched a shield up from the deck just before three arrows thudded into the space where her head had been.

She advanced slowly along the deck, flames roaring out of her in a semicircle to repel Militia troops. Soldiers crumpled in her path, twitching and burning, while others hurled themselves into the water to escape the fire.

Through the blaze she heard the faint sound of clashing steel.

She dimmed the wall of flame just for a moment to see Nezha and a handful of remaining Republican soldiers dueling with General Jun's platoon on the other end of the deck.

He's still alive. Warm hope filled her chest. She ran toward Nezha, shooting targeted ribbons of flame into the melee. Tendrils of fire wrapped around Militia soldiers' necks like whips while balls of flame consumed their faces, blinding their eyes, scorching their mouths, asphyxiating them. She kept going until all soldiers in her vicinity had dropped to the ground, either dead or dying. It felt bizarrely, exhilaratingly good to know she had so much control over the flame, that she now possessed such potent and novel ways of killing.

When she pulled the fire back in, Nezha had fought Jun to submission.

"You're a good soldier," said Nezha. "My father doesn't want you dead."

"Don't bother." A sneer twisted Jun's face. He raised his sword to his chest.

Nezha moved faster. His blade flashed through the air. Rin heard a thick chop that reminded her of a butcher shop. Jun's severed hand dropped to the ground.

Jun stumbled forward on his knees, staring at his bloody stump like he couldn't believe what he was looking at.

"It won't be that easy for you," said Nezha.

"You ingrate," Jun seethed. "I *created* you."

"You taught me the meaning of fear," Nezha said. "Nothing more."

Jun made a wild grab for the dagger in Nezha's belt, but Nezha kicked out—one short, precise blow against Jun's severed stump. Jun howled in pain and fell over onto his side.

"Do it," Rin said. "Quickly."

Nezha shook his head. "He's a good prisoner—"

"He tried to kill you!" Rin shouted. She summoned a ball of flame to her right hand. "If you won't, then I will—"

Nezha grabbed her shoulder. "*Stop!*"

Jun struggled to his feet and made a mad scramble for the edge of the ship.

"No!" Nezha rushed forward, but it was too late. Rin saw Jun's feet disappear over the railing. She heard a splash several seconds later. She and Nezha hurried to the railing to look over the edge, but Jun didn't resurface.

Nezha whirled on her. "We could have taken him prisoner!"

"Look, I didn't hurl him off the side." She couldn't see how this was her fault. "And I just saved your life. You're welcome, by the way."

Rin saw Nezha open his mouth to retort just before something wet and heavy slammed into her from above and knocked her to the deck. Her wings jammed painfully into her shoulders. She was caught under a water-soaked canvas, she realized. Her fire did nothing but fill the inside of the canvas with scorching steam. She had to call it back in before she choked.

Someone was holding the canvas down, trapping her inside. She kicked frantically, trying to wriggle out to no avail. She twisted harder until her head broke through the side.

"Hello." The Wolf Meat General leered down at her.

She roared flames at his face. He slugged the back of his gauntleted hand against her head. She slammed back against the deck; her vision exploded into sparks. Dimly she saw Chang En lift his sword over her neck.

Nezha hurled himself into Chang En's side. They landed sprawled in a heap. Nezha scrambled to his feet and backed away, sword raised. Chang En picked his sword off the deck, cackling, and then attacked.

Rin lay flat on her back, blinking at the sky. All of her extremities tingled, but they wouldn't obey when she tried to move them. From the corner of her eye she caught glimpses of a fight; she heard a deafening flurry of blows, steel raining down on steel.

She had to help Nezha. But her fists wouldn't open; the fire wouldn't come.

Her vision started fading to black, but she couldn't lose consciousness. Not now. She bit down hard on her tongue, willing the pain to keep her awake.

Finally she managed to lift her head. Chang En had backed Nezha into a corner. Nezha was flagging, clearly struggling simply to stand up straight. Blood soaked the entire left side of his uniform.

"I'll saw your head off," Chang En sneered. "Then I'll feed it to my dogs, just like I did your brother's."

Nezha screamed and redoubled his assault.

Rin groaned and rolled over onto her side. Flames sparked and burst in her palms—just tiny lights, nowhere near the intensity she needed. She squeezed her eyes shut, trying to concentrate. To pray.

Please, I need you . . .

Nezha's strikes came nowhere close to landing. Chang En disarmed him with ease and kicked his sword across the deck. Nezha scrambled for the hilt. Chang En swept a leg behind his knees, kicking him to the ground, and placed a boot on his chest.

Hello, little one, said the Phoenix.

Flames burst out of every part of her. The fire was no longer localized to her control points—her hands and mouth—but blazed around her entire body like a suit of armor, glowing and untouchable.

She pointed a finger at Chang En. A thick stream of fire slammed into his face. He dropped his sword and buried his head in his hands, trying to smother the flames, but the blaze only extended across his entire body, burning brighter and brighter as he screamed.

Rin stopped just short of killing him. She didn't want to make this easy for him.

Chang En had stopped moving. He lay flat on his back, covered in grotesque burns. His face and arms had turned black, shot through with cracks that revealed blistered, bubbling skin.

Rin stood over him and opened her palms downward.

Nezha grabbed her shoulder. "Don't."

She shot him an exasperated look. "Don't tell me you want to take him prisoner, too."

"No," he said. "I want to do it."

She stepped back and gestured to Chang En's limp form. "All yours."

"I'll need a sword," he said.

Wordlessly, she handed hers over.

Nezha traced the tip of the blade over Chang En's face, jabbing it into the blistered skin between his crackled cheekbones. "Hey. Wake up."

Chang En's eyes opened.

Nezha forced the sword point straight down into Chang En's left eye.

Chang En grabbed at empty air, trying to wrench the blade from Nezha's grasp, but Nezha gave him a savage kick to the ribs, then several more to the face.

Nezha wanted to watch Chang En bleed. Rin didn't try to stop him. She wanted to watch, too.

Nezha pressed the sword point to Chang En's neck. "Stop moving."

Whimpering, Chang En lay still. His gouged eye dangled grotesquely on the side of his face, still connected by lumpy strings. The other eye blinked furiously, drenched in blood.

Nezha grasped the hilt with both hands and brought it down hard. Blood splashed across both of their faces.

Nezha let the sword drop and backed away slowly. His chest heaved. Rin put her hand on his back.

He leaned into her, shaking. "It's over."

"No, it's not," she whispered.

It had barely just begun. Because the air had suddenly gone still—so still that every flag in the channel dropped, and the sound of every shout and clash of steel was amplified in the absence of wind.

She reached out and grabbed Nezha's fingers in hers, just as the ship ripped out from beneath them.

CHAPTER 32

The force of the gale tore them apart.

For a moment Rin hung weightless in the air, watching driftwood and bodies floating absurdly beside her, and then she dropped into the water with the rest of what used to be the ship's upper deck.

She couldn't see Nezha. She couldn't see anything. She sank fast, weighted down by the wreckage. She flailed desperately around in the black water, trying to find some path to the surface.

And there it was—a glimmer of light through the mass of bodies. Her lungs burned. She had to get up there. She kicked, but something tugged at her legs. She'd gotten tangled in the flag, and wet cloth underwater was strong as iron steel. Panic fogged her mind. The flag only ensnared her more the harder she kicked, dragging her down to the riverbed.

Calm. She forced herself to empty her mind. *Calm down.* No anger, no panic, just nothingness. She found that silent place of clarity that allowed her to think.

She wasn't drowned yet. She still had the strength to kick her way to the surface. And the cloth wasn't tied in such a hopeless knot, it was simply looped twice around her leg. She reached forward. A few quick movements and she broke free. Relieved, she swam upward, forcing herself not to panic, focusing on the simple act of pushing herself through the water until her head broke the surface.

She didn't see Nezha as she dragged herself to shore. She scanned the wreckage, but she couldn't find him. Had he surfaced at all? Was he dead? Crushed, impaled, drowned—

No. She had to trust that he was fine. He could control the water itself; it couldn't possibly kill him.

Could it?

The howl of unnatural wind pierced the channel and lingered, punctuated only by the sound of splintering wood.

Oh, gods.

Rin looked up.

Feylen hung suspended in the air above her, slamming ships against the cliff wall with mere sweeps of his arm. Driftwood and debris swirled in a hazardous circle around him. With winds as fast as these, any one of those pieces might kill her.

Rin's mouth had gone dry. Her knees buckled. All she wanted was to find a hole and hide. She stood paralyzed by fear and despair. Feylen was going to batter their fleet around the channel until there was nothing left. Why fight? Death would be easier if she didn't resist . . .

She ground her fingernails into her palm until the pain brought her to her senses.

She couldn't run.

Who else was going to fight him? Who else possibly *could*?

She'd lost her sword in the water, but she spied a javelin on the ground. Fat lot of good it would do against Feylen, but it felt better to hold a weapon. She scooped it up, opened her wings, and summoned a flame around her arms and shoulders. Steam fizzled around her, a choking cloud of mist. Rin waved it away, hoping desperately her wings were waterproof.

She focused on generating a steady, concentrated stream of flame around her sides, so searingly hot that the air around her blurred, and the grass at her feet wilted and shriveled into gray ash.

Slowly she rose up toward the Wind God.

Up close, Feylen looked miserable. His skin was pallid, pockmarked, overgrown with sores. They hadn't given him new clothes—his black Cike uniform was ripped and dirty. Face-to-face he was no fearsome deity. Just a man with tattered garb and broken eyes.

Her fear faded away, replaced by pity. Feylen should have died a long time ago. Now he was a prisoner in his own body, sentenced to watch and suffer while the god he detested manipulated him as a gateway to the material world.

Without the Seal, without Kitay, Rin might have turned into something just like him.

The man is gone, she reminded herself. *Defeat the god.*

"Hey, asshole!" she shouted. "Over here!"

Feylen turned. The winds calmed.

She tensed, anticipating a sudden blast. She had only Kitay's guarantee that she could correct course with her wings if Feylen sent her spinning, but that was a better chance than anyone else had.

But Feylen only hung still in the air, head cocked to the side, watching her rise to meet him like a child curiously observing the antics of a little bug.

"Cute trick," he said.

A piece of driftwood shot past her left arm. She wobbled and righted herself.

Feylen's cerulean eyes met hers. She shuddered. She was acutely aware of how *fragile* she was. She was fighting the Wind God in his own domain, and she was a little thing held in the air by nothing more than two sheets of leather and a cage of metal. He could tear her apart and dash her against those cliffs so easily.

But she didn't just have her wings. She had a javelin. And she had the fire.

She opened her mouth and palms and shot every bit of flame she had at him—three lines of fire roaring from her body all at once. Feylen disappeared behind a wall of red and orange. The winds around him stilled. Debris began dropping out of the air, a rain of wreckage that dotted the waters below.

His retaliatory blow caught her off guard. A gust of force hit her so hard and fast that she hadn't braced herself, hadn't even tensed. She hurtled backward, tumbling through the air in circles until the cliff wall appeared perilously close before her eyes. Her nose scraped the rock before she managed to redirect her momentum and pull herself right-side up.

She drifted back toward Feylen, heart hammering.

She hadn't burned him to death, but she'd come close. Feylen's face and hair had turned black. Smoke wafted out from his scorched robes.

He looked shocked.

"Try again," she called.

His next attack was a series of unrelenting winds blasting her from different, unpredictable directions so she couldn't just ride out the current. One moment he forced her toward the ground, and the next he buoyed her upward, just to let her drop again.

She maneuvered the winds as well as she could, but it was like swimming against a waterfall. She was a little bird caught in a storm. Her wings were nothing against his overwhelming force. All she could do was keep from plummeting to the ground.

She suspected the only reason Feylen hadn't yet flung her against the rocks was because he was toying with her.

But he hadn't finished her off at Boyang, either. *We're not going to kill you,* he'd said. *She told us not to do that. We're just supposed to hurt you.*

The Empress had commanded him to bring her in alive. That gave her an advantage.

"Careful," she shouted. "Daji won't be happy with broken goods."

Feylen's entire demeanor changed when she spoke Daji's name. His shoulders hunched; he seemed to shrink into himself. His eyes darted around, as if petrified that Daji could see him even so high in the air.

Rin stared at him, amazed. What had Daji *done* to him?

How was Daji so powerful that she could terrify a god?

Rin took the chance to fly in closer. She didn't know how Daji had subdued Feylen, but she was now sure that Feylen couldn't kill her.

Daji still wanted her alive, and that gave her her only advantage.

How did one kill a god? She and Kitay had puzzled over the dilemma for hours. She'd wished they could bring him into the Chuluu Korikh. Kitay had wished they could just bring the Chuluu Korikh to him.

In the end, they'd compromised.

Rin eyed the web of fuses lining the opposite cliff wall. If she couldn't kill Feylen with fire, then she'd bury him under the mountain.

She only had to get him close enough to the rocks.

"I know you're still in there." She drifted closer to Feylen. She needed to distract him, if only for a few seconds' reprieve. "I know you can hear me."

He took the bait. The winds calmed.

"I don't care how powerful your god is. You still own this body, Feylen, and you can take it back."

Feylen stared wordlessly at her, unmoving, but she saw no dimming of the blue, no twitch of recognition in his eyes. His expression was an inscrutable wall, behind which she had no idea if the real Feylen was still alive.

She still had to try.

"I saw Altan in the afterlife," she said. A lie, but one shrouded in the truth, or at least her version of it. "He wanted me to pass something on to you. Do you want to know what he said?"

Cerulean flickered to black. Rin saw it—she hadn't imagined it, it wasn't a trick of the light, she *knew* she'd seen it. She continued to fly forward. Feylen was afraid now; she could read it all over his face. He drifted backward every time she drew closer.

They were so close to the cliff wall.

She was mere feet away from him. "He wanted me to tell you he's sorry."

The winds ceased entirely. A silence descended over the channel. In the still air Rin could hear everything—every haggard breath Feylen took, every round of cannon fire from the ships, every wretched scream from below.

Then Feylen laughed. He laughed so hard that corresponding pulses of wind shot through the air, alternating blasts so fierce that she had to flap frantically to stay afloat.

"*This* was your plan?" he screeched. "You thought he would care?"

"You *do* care." Rin kept her voice calm, level. Feylen was in there. She'd seen him. "I saw you, you remember us. You're Cike."

"You mean nothing to us." Feylen sneered. "We could destroy your world—"

"Then you would have done it. But you're still bound, aren't you? *She's* bound you. You gods have no power except what we give you. You came through that gate to take your orders. And I'm ordering you to go back."

Feylen roared. "Who are you to presume?"

"I'm your commander," she said. "I cull."

She shot her fire not at him, but the cliff wall. Feylen shrieked with laughter as the flames streamed harmlessly past him.

He hadn't seen the fuses. He didn't know.

Rin flapped frantically backward, trying to put as much distance between herself and the cliff as she could.

For a long, torturous instant, nothing happened.

And then the mountain moved.

Mountains weren't supposed to shift like that. The natural world wasn't supposed to reshape itself so completely in seconds. But this was real; this was an act of men, not gods. This was Kitay and Ramsa's handiwork come to fruition. Rin could only stare as the entire top ledge of the cliff slipped down like roofing tiles cascading to the ground.

A shrieking howl pierced through the cascade of tumbling rock.

Feylen was whipping up a tornado. But even those last, desperate gusts of wind could not stop thousands of tons of exploded rock jerked downward with the inevitable force of gravity.

When their rumbling stopped, nothing moved beneath them.

Rin sagged in the air, chest heaving. The fire still burned through her arms, but she couldn't sustain it for long, she was so exhausted. She was struggling just to breathe.

The blood-soaked channel beneath her could have been a meadow of flowers. She imagined that the crimson waves were fields of poppy blossoms, and the moving bodies were just little ants scurrying pointlessly about.

She thought it looked so beautiful.

Could they be winning? If *winning* meant killing as many people as they could, then yes. She couldn't tell which side had control over the river, only that it was awash with blood, and that broken ships were dashed against the cliff sides. Feylen had been killing indiscriminately, destroying Republican and Imperial ships alike. She wondered how high the casualty rate had climbed.

She turned toward the valley.

The destruction there was enormous. The palace was on fire, which meant the Militia troops had long ago slashed their way through the refugee camps. The troops would have cut the southerners down like reeds.

Drown in the channel, or burn in the city. Rin had the hysterical urge to laugh, but breathing hurt too much.

She realized suddenly she was losing altitude.

Her fire had gone out. She'd been falling without noticing. She forced flames back into the wings and beat frantically even as her arms screamed in protest.

Her descent halted—she was close enough to the cliffs that she could see Kitay and Venka waving at her.

"I did it!" she screamed to them.

She saw Kitay's mouth moving, but couldn't hear him. He pointed.

Too late she turned around. A javelin shot past her midriff, passed harmlessly under her wing. *Fuck.* Her stomach lurched. She wobbled but righted herself.

The next javelin struck her shoulder.

For a moment, she simply felt confused. Where was the pain? Why was she still hanging in the air? Her own blood floated around her face in great fat drops that for some reason hadn't fallen, little bulbous things that she couldn't believe had come from her.

Then her flames receded into her body. Gravity resumed its pull. Her wings creaked and folded against her back. Then she was just deadweight plummeting headfirst into the river.

Her senses shut down upon impact. She couldn't breathe, couldn't hear, and couldn't see. She tried to swim, kick herself to the surface, but her arms and legs wouldn't obey her, and besides, she didn't know which way was up. She choked involuntarily. A torrent of water flooded her mouth.

I'm going to die, she thought. *I'm really going to die.*

But was this so bad? It was wonderfully, peacefully silent under the surface. She couldn't feel any pain in her shoulder—her whole body had gone numb. She relaxed her limbs and drifted helplessly toward the river bottom. Easier to give up control, easier to stop struggling. Even her burning lungs didn't bother her so much. In a moment she would open her mouth, and water would rush in, and that would be the end.

This wasn't such a bad way to go. At least it was quiet.

Someone seized her hard. Her eyes shot open.

Nezha pulled her head toward his and kissed her hard, his lips forming a seal around hers. A bubble of air passed into her mouth. It wasn't much, but her vision cleared, her lungs stopped burning, and her limbs began to respond to her commands. Adrenaline kicked in. She needed more air. She grabbed at Nezha's face.

He pushed her away, shaking his head. She started to panic. He seized her wrists and held her until she stopped flailing madly in the water. Then he wrapped his arms around her torso and pulled them both toward the surface.

He didn't kick his legs. He didn't have to swim at all. He only held her against him while a warm current bore them gently upward.

Something shrieked in the air above them just as they broke the surface. A javelin slammed into the water several feet away. Nezha yanked them back down into the depths, but Rin kicked and struggled. All she wanted to do was get to the surface, she was so desperate to breathe . . .

Nezha grasped her face with his hands.

Too exposed, he mouthed.

She understood. They needed to come up somewhere near a broken ship, something that would give them cover. She stopped thrashing. Nezha guided them several yards farther downriver. Then the current buoyed them up and deposited them safely onto the shore.

Her first breath above the surface was the best thing she'd ever tasted. She doubled over, coughing and vomiting river water, but she didn't care because she was *breathing*.

Once her lungs were empty of water, she lay back and summoned the fire. Little flames lit up her wrists, danced across her entire body, and bathed her in delicious warmth. Steam hissed as her clothes dried.

Groaning, she rolled over onto her side. Her right shoulder was a bloody mess. She didn't want to look at it. She knew her wings were a crumpled disaster. Something sharp shoved deeper into her skin every time she moved. She struggled to rip the contraption off, but the metal harness had twisted and bent. It wouldn't give.

She felt for where it pressed into her lower back. Her fingers came away bloody.

She tried not to panic. Something was stuck, that was all. She knew she wasn't supposed to pull it out until she was with a physician, that the object piercing her back was the only thing stopping her blood spilling out. And she couldn't see well enough from this angle—she'd be stupid to try to remove it herself.

But she could barely move without digging the rod deeper into her back. She might end up severing her own spine.

Nezha was in no state to help her. He had curled into a small, trembling ball, his arms wrapped around his knees. She crawled toward him and tried to hoist him into a sitting position using her good arm. "Hey. *Hey.*"

He didn't respond.

He was twitching all over. His eyes fluttered madly while little whimpering noises escaped his mouth. He raised his hands, trying to claw at the tattoo on his back.

Rin glanced at the river. The water had started moving in eerie, erratic patterns. Odd little waves ran against the current. Blood-soaked columns rose out of the river at random. A handful splashed harmlessly near the shore, but one was growing larger and larger near the center of the river.

She had to knock Nezha out. That, or she had to get him high—but this time she had no opium . . .

"I brought it," he gasped.

"What?"

He placed a trembling hand over his pocket. "Stole it—brought it here, just in case . . ."

She shoved her hand into his pocket and drew out a fist-sized packet wrapped tightly in bamboo leaves. She tore it open with her teeth, choking at the familiar, sickly sweet taste. Her body ached with an old craving.

Nezha sucked in air through clenched teeth. "Please . . ."

She clutched two nuggets in her hand and ignited a small fire beneath them. With her other hand she hoisted Nezha upright and tilted his head over the fumes.

He inhaled for a long time. His eyes fluttered closed. The water began to calm. The little waves sank beneath the surface. The columns lowered slowly and disappeared. Rin exhaled in relief.

Then Nezha shrank away from the smoke, coughing. "No—no, I don't want that much—"

She gripped him tighter. "I'm sorry."

He'd only smoked several whiffs. That would wear off in under an hour. That wasn't enough time. She needed to make sure the god was gone.

She forced the opium under his nose and clamped a hand over his mouth to force him to inhale. He thrashed in protest, but he was already weak and his struggles grew more and more feeble as he inhaled more of the smoke. Finally he lay still.

Rin threw the half-burned nuggets into the dirt. She brushed a hand over Nezha's forehead, pushed strands of wet hair out of his eyes.

"You'll be all right," she whispered. "I'll send someone out after you."

"Stay," he murmured. "Please."

"I'm sorry." She leaned forward and lightly kissed his forehead. "We've got a battle to win."

His voice was so faint she had to lean down to hear it. "But we've won."

She choked with desperate laughter. He hadn't seen the burning city. He didn't know that Arlong barely existed anymore. "We haven't won."

"No . . ." His eyes opened. He struggled to raise his arm. He pointed at something past her shoulder. "Look. There."

She turned her head.

There on the seam of the horizon sailed a fleet, waves and waves of warships. Some glided over water; some floated through the air. There were so many that they almost seemed like a mirage, endless doubles of the same row of white sails and blue flags against a brilliant sun.

CHAPTER 33

"How lovely," spoke a voice, familiar and beautiful, that made Rin's heart sink and her mouth fill with the taste of blood.

She lowered Nezha onto the sand and forced herself to stand up. Metal shifted beneath her flesh, and she bit back a cry of pain. The agony in her back and shoulder was almost unbearable. But she was not going to die lying down.

How could the Empress still terrify her like this? Daji was just a lone woman now, without an army or a fleet. Her general's garb was ripped and drenched. She limped when she walked, and her shoes left behind imprints of blood. Yet she approached with her chin lifted high, her eyebrows arched, and her lips curved in an imperious smile as if she had just won a great victory, emanating a dark, seductive beauty that made irrelevant her sodden robes, her shattered ships.

Rin hated that beauty. She wanted to drag her nails across it until white flesh gave way under her fingers. She wanted to gouge Daji's eyes out of their sockets, crush them in her fists, and drip the gelatinous ruin over her porcelain skin.

And yet.

When she looked at Daji her entire body felt weak. Her pulse raced. Her face felt hot. She couldn't tear her eyes from Daji's face. She had to look and keep looking, otherwise she would never be satisfied.

She forced herself to focus. She needed a weapon—she snatched a sharp piece of driftwood off the ground.

"Get back," she whispered. "Come any closer and I'll burn you."

Daji only laughed. "Oh, my darling. Haven't you learned?"

Her eyes flashed.

Suddenly Rin felt the overwhelming urge to kill herself, to drag the driftwood against her own wrists until red lines opened along her veins, and twist.

Hands shaking, she pressed the sharpest edge of the driftwood to her skin. *What am I doing?* Her mind screamed for her to stop, but her body didn't care. She could only watch as her hands moved on their own, preparing to saw her veins apart.

"That's enough," Daji said lightly.

The urge disappeared. Rin dropped the driftwood, gasping.

"Will you listen now?" Daji asked. "I'd like you to stand still, please. Arms up."

Rin immediately put her arms up over her head, stifling a scream as her wounds tore anew.

Daji limped closer. Her eyes flickered over the remains of Rin's harness, and her right lip curled up in amusement. "So that's how you dealt with poor Feylen. Clever."

"Your best weapon is gone," Rin said.

"Ah, well. He was a pain to begin with. One moment he'd try to sink our own fleet, and the next all he wanted to do was float among the clouds. Do you know how absurdly difficult it was to get him to do *anything*?" Daji sighed. "I suppose I'll have to finish the job myself."

"You've lost," Rin said. "Hurt me, kill me, it's still over for you. Your generals are dead. Your ships are driftwood."

A round of cannon fire punctuated her words, a roar so loud that it drowned out every other sound along the shore. It went on for so long that Rin couldn't imagine that anything remained floating in the channel.

But Daji didn't look faintly bothered. "You think that's winning? You aren't the victors. There are no victors in this fight. Vaisra has ensured that civil war will continue for decades. He's only deepened the fractures. No man can stitch this country back together now."

She continued to limp forward until they were separated by only several feet.

Rin's eyes darted around the shore. They stood on an isolated stretch of sand, hidden behind the wreckage of great warships. The only other soldiers in sight were corpses. No one was coming to her rescue. It was just her and the Empress now, facing off in the shadows of the unforgiving cliffs.

"So how did you manage the Seal?" Daji asked. "I was rather convinced that it was unbreakable. It can't have been one of the twins; they would have done it long ago if they could." She tilted her head. "Oh, no, let me guess. Did you find the Sorqan Sira? Is that old bat still alive?"

"Fuck you, murderer," Rin said.

"I presume that means you've found yourself an anchor, too?" Daji's eyes flitted toward Nezha. He wasn't moving. "I do hope it's not him. That one's almost gone."

"Don't you dare touch him," Rin hissed.

Daji knelt over Nezha, fingers tracing over the scars on his face. "He's very pretty, isn't he? Despite everything. He reminds me of Riga."

I must get her away from him. Rin strained to move, eyes bulging, but her limbs remained fixed in place. The flame wouldn't come, either; when she reached for the Phoenix, all her rage crashed pointlessly against her own mind, like waves crashing against cliffs.

"The Ketreyids showed me what you've done," she said loudly, hoping it would distract Daji.

It worked. Daji stood up. "Really."

"The Sorqan Sira showed us everything. You can try to convince me that you're trying to save the Empire, but I know what kind of person you are—you betray those who help you and you throw lives away like they're nothing. I saw you attack them, I saw you three murder Tseveri—"

"Be quiet," Daji said. "Don't say that name."

Rin's jaw locked shut.

Rin stood frozen, heart slamming against her ribs, as Daji approached her. She had just been spinning words out of the air, hurling everything she could to get Daji away from Nezha.

But something had pissed Daji off. Two high spots of color rose in her cheeks. Her eyes narrowed. She looked furious.

"The Ketreyids should have surrendered," she said quietly. "We wouldn't have hurt them if they weren't so fucking stubborn."

Daji stretched a pale hand out and ran her knuckles over Rin's cheeks. "Always such a hypocrite. I acted from necessity, just like you. We are precisely the same, you and I. We've acquired more power than any mortal should have the right to, which means we have to make the decisions no one else can. The world is our chessboard. It's not our fault if the pieces get broken."

"You hurt everything you touch," Rin whispered.

"And you've killed in numbers exponentially greater than we ever managed. What really separates us, darling? That you committed your war crimes by accident, and mine were intentional? Would you really do things differently, if you had another chance?"

The hold on Rin's jaw loosened.

Daji had given her permission to answer.

She couldn't say yes. She could lie, of course, but it wouldn't matter; not here, where no one but Daji was listening, and Daji already knew the truth.

Because if she had another chance, if she could go back to that moment in time when she stood in the temple of the Phoenix and faced her god, she would make the same decision. She would release the volcano. She would encase Mugen in tons of molten stone and choking ash.

She would destroy the country completely and without mercy, the same way that its armies had treated her. And she'd laugh.

"Do you understand now?" Daji tucked a strand of hair behind Rin's ear. "Come with me. We've much to discuss."

"Fuck off," Rin said.

Daji's mouth pressed in a thin line. The compulsion seized Rin's legs and forced her to move, shuddering, toward Daji. One by one Rin's feet dragged through the sand. Sweat beaded on her temples. She tried to shut her eyes and couldn't.

"Kneel," Daji commanded.

No, spoke the Phoenix.

The god's voice was terribly quiet, a tiny echo across a vast plain. But it was there.

Rin struggled to remain standing. A horrible pain shot through her legs, forcing them down, growing stronger every moment that she refused. She wanted to scream but couldn't open her mouth.

Daji's eyes flashed yellow. "*Kneel*."

You will not kneel, said the Phoenix.

The pain intensified. Rin gasped, fighting the pull, her mind split between two ancient gods.

Just another battle. And, as always, anger was her greatest ally.

Rage drowned out the Vipress's hypnosis. Daji had sold out the Speerlies. Daji had killed Altan, and Daji had started this war. Daji didn't get to lie to her anymore. Didn't get to torture and manipulate her like prey.

The fire came in fits and bursts, little balls of flame that Rin hurled desperately from her palms. Daji only dodged daintily to the side and flicked a wrist out. Rin jerked aside to avoid a needle that wasn't there. The sudden movement pulled the broken contraption deeper into her back.

She yelped and doubled over.

Daji laughed. "Had enough?"

Rin screeched.

A thin stream of fire lanced over her entire body—enveloping her, protecting her, amplifying her every movement.

This was power like she'd never felt.

That's a state of ecstasy, Altan told her once. *You don't get tired. . . . You don't feel pain. All you do is destroy.*

Rin had always felt so unhinged—volleying between powerlessness and utter subjugation to the Phoenix—but now the fire was hers. Was *her*. And that made her feel so giddy that she almost screamed with laughter because for the first time ever, she had the upper hand.

Daji's resistance was nothing. Rin backed her easily up against the hull of the nearest beached ship. Her fist smashed into the wood next to Daji's face, missing it by an inch. Wood cracked, splintered, and smoked under her knuckles. The entire ship groaned. Rin drew her fist back again and slammed it into Daji's jaw.

Daji's head jerked to the side like a broken doll's. Rin had split her lip; blood trickled down her chin. Yet still she smiled.

"You're so weak," she whispered. "You have a god but you have no idea what you're doing with it."

"Right now, I know exactly what I want to do with it."

She placed her glowing-hot fingers around Daji's neck. Pale flesh crackled and burned under her touch. She started to squeeze. She thought she'd feel a thrill of satisfaction.

It didn't come.

She couldn't just kill her. Not like this. This was too quick, too easy.

She had to destroy her.

She moved her hands up. Placed her thumbs under the bases of Daji's eye sockets. Dug her nails into soft flesh.

"Look at me," Daji hissed.

Rin shook her head, eyes squeezed tight.

Something popped under her left thumb. Warm liquid streamed down her wrist.

"I'm already dying," Daji whispered. "Don't you want to know who I am? Don't you want to know the truth about us?"

Rin knew she should end things right then.

She couldn't.

Because she *did* want to know. She'd been tortured by these questions. She had to understand why the Empire's greatest heroes—Daji, Riga, and Jiang, *her* Master Jiang—had become the monsters they had. And because here, at the end of things, she doubted now more than ever that she was fighting for the right side.

Her eyes fluttered open.

Visions swarmed her mind.

She saw a city burning the way Arlong burned now; buildings charred and blackened, corpses lining the streets. She saw troops marching in uniform lines of terrifying numbers, while the city's surviving inhabitants crouched by their doorsteps, heads bent and arms raised.

This was the Nikara Empire under Mugenese occupation.

"We couldn't do anything," Daji said. "We were too weak to do anything when their ships arrived at our shores. And for the next five decades, when they raped us, beat us, spat on us and told us we were worth less than dogs, we couldn't do anything."

Rin squeezed her eyes shut, but the images wouldn't go away. She saw a beautiful little girl standing alone before a heap of bodies, soot across her face, tears streaming down her cheeks. She saw a young boy lying in a starved, broken heap in the corner of the alley, curled around jagged, shattered bottles. She saw a white-haired boy screaming profanities and waving his fists at the retreating backs of soldiers who did not care.

"Then we escaped, and we had power within our hands to change the fate of the Empire," Daji said. "So what do you think we did?"

"That doesn't excuse anything."

"It explains and justifies *everything*."

The visions shifted again. Rin saw a naked girl shrieking and crying beside a cave while snakes writhed over her body. She saw a tall boy crouching on the shore while a dragon encircled him, whipping up higher and higher waves that surrounded his body like a tornado. She saw a white-haired boy on his hands and knees, beating his fists against the ground while shadows writhed and stretched out of his back.

"Tell me you wouldn't have given up everything," Daji said. "Tell me you wouldn't sacrifice everything and everyone you knew for the power to take back your country."

Months flashed before Rin's eyes. Next she saw the Trifecta, fully grown, kneeling by the body of Tseveri, who was *just one girl*, and the choice seemed so clear and obvious. Against the suffering of a teeming mass of millions, what was one life? Twenty lives? The Ketreyids were so few; how hard could the comparison be?

What difference could it possibly make?

"We didn't want to kill Tseveri," Daji whispered. "She saved us. She convinced the Ketreyids to take us in. And Jiang loved her."

"Then why—"

"Because we had to. Because our allies wanted that land, and the Sorqan Sira said no, and we needed to win it through force and fear. We had one chance to unite the Warlords and we weren't going to throw it away."

"But then you gave it away!" Rin cried. "You didn't take it back! You sold it to the Mugenese—"

"If your arm were rotting, wouldn't you cut it off to save your body? The provinces were rebelling. Corrupt. Diseased. I would have sacrificed it all for a united core. I knew we weren't strong enough to defend the whole country, only a part of it. So I culled. You know that; you command the Cike. You know what rulers must sometimes do."

"You sold us."

"I did it for them," Daji said softly. "I did it for the empire Riga left me. And you don't understand the stakes, because you don't know the meaning of true fear. You don't know how much worse it could have been."

Daji's voice broke.

And for the second time, Rin saw the facade break, saw through the carefully crafted mirage that Daji had been presenting to the world for decades. This woman wasn't the Vipress, wasn't the scheming ruler Rin had learned to hate and fear.

This woman was afraid. But not of her.

"I'm sorry I hurt you," Daji whispered. "I'm sorry I hurt Altan. I wish I'd never had to. But I had a plan to protect my people, and you simply got in the way. You didn't know your true enemy. You wouldn't listen."

Rin was so furious with her then, because she couldn't hate her anymore. Who was she supposed to fight for now? What side was she supposed to be on? She didn't believe in Vaisra's Republic, not anymore, and she certainly didn't trust the Hesperians, but she didn't know what Daji wanted her to do.

"You can go ahead and kill me," said Daji. "You probably could. I'd fight back, of course, but you'd probably win. *I* would kill me."

"Shut up," Rin said.

She wanted to tighten her fists and choke the life out of Daji. But the rage had drained away. She didn't have the will to fight anymore. She wanted to be angry—things were so much easier when she was just blindly angry—but the anger wouldn't come.

Daji twisted out from her grip, and Rin didn't try to stop her.

Daji was as good as dead regardless. Her face was a grotesque ruin—black liquid gushed out from her gouged eye. She stumbled to the side, fingers feeling for the ship.

Her good eye locked on to Rin's. "What do you think happens to you after I'm gone? Don't imagine for a moment you can trust Vaisra. Without me, Vaisra has no use for you. Vaisra discards his allies without blinking when they are no longer convenient, and if you don't believe me when I say you're next, then you're a fool."

Rin knew Daji was right.

She just didn't know where that left her.

Daji shook her head and held her hands out, open and unthreatening. "Come with me."

Rin took a small step forward.

Wood groaned above her head. Daji skirted backward. Too late, Rin looked up just in time to see the ship's mast crashing down on her.

Rin couldn't even scream. It took everything she had just to breathe. Air came in hoarse, painful bursts; it felt like her throat had been reduced to the diameter of a pin. Her entire back burned with agony.

Daji knelt down in front of her. Stroked her cheek. "You'll need me. You don't realize it now, but you'll figure it out soon. You need me far more than you need them. I just hope you survive."

She leaned down so close that Rin could feel her hot breath on her skin. Daji grabbed Rin by the chin and forced her to look up, into her good eye. Rin stared into a black pupil inside a ring of yellow, pulsing hypnotically, an abyss daring her to fall inside.

"I'll leave you with this."

Rin saw a beautiful young girl—Daji, it had to be—in a huddled heap on the ground, naked, clothes clutched to her chest. Dark blood dripped down pale thighs. She saw the young Riga sprawled on the ground, unconscious. She saw Jiang lying on his side, screaming, as a man kicked him in the ribs, over and over and over.

She dared to look up. Their tormenter was not Mugenese.

Blue eyes. Yellow hair. The soldier brought his boot down, over and over and over, and each time Rin heard another set of cracks.

She leaped forward in time, just a few minutes. The soldier was gone, and the children were clinging to each other, crying, covered in each other's blood, crouching in the shadow of a different soldier.

"Get out of here," said the soldier, in a tongue she was far too familiar with. A tongue she would have never believed would utter a kind word. "Now."

Then Rin understood.

It had been a Hesperian soldier who raped Daji, and a Mugenese soldier who saved her. That was the frame the Empress had been locked into since childhood; that was the crux that had formed every decision afterward.

"The Mugenese weren't the real enemy," Daji murmured. "They never were. They were just poor puppets serving a mad emperor who started a war that he shouldn't have. But who gave them those ideas? Who told them they could conquer the continent?"

Blue eyes. White sails.

"I warned you about everything. I told you this from the beginning. Those devils are going to destroy our world. The Hesperians have a singular vision for the future, and we're not in it. You already know this. You must have realized it, now that you've seen what they're like. I can see it in your eyes. You know they're dangerous. You know you'll need an ally."

Questions formed on Rin's tongue, too many to count, but she couldn't summon the breath to speak them. Her vision was tunneling, turning black at the edges. All she could see was Daji's pale face, dancing above her like the moon.

"Think about it," Daji whispered, tracing her cool fingers over Rin's cheek. "Figure out who you're fighting for. And when you know, come find me."

"Rin? *Rin!*" Venka's face loomed over her. "Fucking hell. Can you hear me?"

Rin felt a great weight lifting off her back and shoulders. She lay flat, eyes open wide, sucking in great gulps of air.

"Hey." Venka snapped her fingers in front of her. "What's my name?"

Rin moaned. "Just help me up."

"Close enough." Venka wedged her arms under her stomach and helped Rin roll onto her side. Every tiny movement sent fresh spasms of pain rippling through her back. She collapsed into Venka's arms, breathless with agony.

Venka's hands moved over her skin, feeling for injuries. Rin felt her fingers pause on her back.

"Oh, that's not good," Venka murmured.

"What?"

"Uh. Can you breathe all right?"

"Ribs," Rin gasped. "My—*ow*!"

Venka pulled her hands away from Rin. They were slippery with blood. "There's a rod stuck under your skin."

"I know," Rin said through gritted teeth. "Get it out." She reached back to try again to yank it out herself, but Venka grabbed her wrist before she could.

"You'll lose too much blood if it comes out now."

Rin knew that, but the thought of the rod digging deeper inside her was making her panic spiral. "But I'm—"

"Just breathe for a minute. All right? Can you do that for me? Just breathe."

"How bad is it?" Kitay's voice. *Thank the gods.*

"Several ribs broken. Don't move, I'll get a stretcher." Venka set off at a run.

Kitay knelt down beside her. His voice dropped to a whisper. "What happened? Where's the Empress?"

Rin swallowed. "She got away."

"Obviously." Kitay's fingers tightened on her shoulder. "Did you let her go?"

"I . . . *what*?"

Kitay gave her a hard look. "Did you let her go?"

Had she?

She found that she couldn't answer.

She could have killed Daji. She'd had plenty of opportunities to burn, strangle, stab, or choke the Empress before the beam fell. If she'd wanted to, she could have ended everything then and there.

Why hadn't she?

Had the Vipress manipulated her into letting her go? Was Rin's reluctance a product of her own thoughts or Daji's hypnosis? She could not remember if she had chosen to let Daji escape, or if she had simply been outsmarted and defeated.

"I don't know," she whispered.

"You don't know," Kitay asked, "or you don't want to tell me?"

"I thought it'd be so clear," she said. Her head swam; her eyes fluttered closed. "I thought the choice was obvious. But now I really don't know."

"I think I understand," Kitay said after a long pause. "But I'd keep that to yourself."

CHAPTER 34

Rin jolted awake to the sound of gongs. She tried to spring out of bed, but the moment she lifted her head, a searing pain rippled through her back.

"Whoa." Venka's blurry face came into view. She put a hand on Rin's shoulder and forced her back down. "Not so fast."

"But the morning alarm," Rin said. "I'm going to be late."

Venka laughed. "To what? You're off duty. We're all off duty."

Rin blinked. "What?"

"It's over. We *won*. You can relax."

After months of warfare, of sleeping and eating and waking on the same strict schedule, that statement was so incredible to Rin that for a moment the words themselves sounded like they'd been spoken in a different language.

"We're finished?" she asked faintly.

"For now. But don't be too disappointed, you'll have plenty to do once you're up and moving." Venka cracked her knuckles. "Soon we'll be running cleanup."

Rin struggled to prop herself up on her elbows. The pain in her lower back pulsed along with her heartbeat. She clenched her teeth to stave it off. "What else is there? Update me."

"Well, the Empire hasn't exactly surrendered. They're decapitated, but the strongest provinces—Tiger, Horse, and Snake—are still holding out."

"But the Wolf Meat General's dead," Rin said. Venka already knew that—she'd seen it happen—but saying it out loud made her feel better.

"Yeah. We captured Tsolin alive, too. Jun made it out, though." Venka picked up an apple from Rin's bedside. She began paring it with rapid, sure movements, fingers moving so fast that Rin was amazed she didn't peel her own skin off. "Somehow he swam out of the channel and got away—he's well on his way back to Tiger Province now. Horse and Snake are loyal to him, and he's a better strategist than Chang En was. They'll put up a good fight. But the war should be over soon."

"Why?"

Venka pointed out the window with her paring knife. "We have help."

Rin shifted around in her bed to peer outside, clutching the windowsill for support. A seemingly infinite number of warships crowded the harbor. She tried to calculate how many Hesperian troops that entailed. Thousands? Tens of thousands?

She should have been relieved the civil war was as good as over. Instead, when she looked at those white sails, all she could feel was dread.

"Something wrong?" Venka asked.

Rin took a breath. "Just . . . disoriented a bit, I think."

Venka handed the peeled apple to Rin. "Eat something."

Rin wrapped her fingers around it with difficulty. It was amazing how hard the simple act of *chewing* was; how much it hurt her teeth, how it strained her jaw. Swallowing was agony. She couldn't manage more than a few bites. She put the apple down. "What happened to the Militia deserters?"

"A couple tried to flee over the mountains, but their horses got scared when the dirigibles came," Venka said. "Trampled them underfoot. Their bodies are still stuck in the mud. We'll probably send a crew to get those horses back. How's your . . . well, how's everything feeling?"

Rin reached backward to feel at her wounds. Her back and shoulder were covered in a swath of bandages. Her fingers kept brushing against raised skin that hurt to touch. She winced. She didn't want to see what lay beneath the wrappings. "Did they tell you how bad it was?"

"Can you still wiggle your toes?"

Rin froze. "*Venka.*"

"I'm kidding." Venka cracked a smile. "It looks worse than it is. It'll take you a while, but you'll get full mobility back. Your biggest concern is scarring. But you were always ugly, so it's not like that will make a difference."

Rin was too relieved to be angry. "Go fuck yourself."

"There's a mirror inside that cabinet door." Venka pointed to the back corner of the room and stood up. "I'll give you some time alone."

After Venka closed the door, Rin pulled off her shirt, climbed gingerly to her feet, and stood naked in front of the mirror.

She was stunned by how repulsive she looked.

She'd always known that nothing could make her attractive; not with her mud-colored skin, sullen face, and short, jagged hair that had never been styled with anything more sophisticated than a rusty knife.

But now she just looked like a broken and battered thing. She was an amalgamation of scars and stitches. On her arm, dotted white reminders of the hot wax she'd once used to burn herself to stay awake studying. On her back and shoulders, whatever lay behind those bandages. And just under her sternum, Altan's handprint, as dark and vivid as the day she'd first seen it.

Exhaling slowly, she pressed her left hand to the spot over her stomach. She couldn't tell if she was only imagining it, but it felt hot to the touch.

"I should apologize," said Kitay.

She jumped. She hadn't heard the door open. "Fucking hell—"

"Sorry."

She scrambled to pull her shirt back on. "You might have knocked!"

"I didn't realize you'd be up." He crossed the room and perched himself on the side of her bed. "Anyway, I wanted to apologize. That wound is my fault. Didn't put padding around the gears—I didn't have time, so I was just going for something functional. The rod went in about three inches at a slant. The physicians said you're lucky it didn't sever your spine."

"Did you feel it, too?" she asked.

"Just a little," Kitay said. He was lying, she knew that, but in that moment she was just grateful he would even try to spare her the guilt. He lifted his shirt and twisted around to show her a pale white scar running across his lower back. "Look. They're the same shape, I think."

She peered enviously at the smooth white lines. "That's prettier than mine will be."

"Don't get too jealous."

She moved her hands and arms about, gingerly testing the temporary boundaries of her mobility. She tried to raise her right arm above her head, but gave up when her shoulder threatened to tear itself apart. "I don't think I want to fly for a while."

"I gathered." Kitay picked her unfinished apple up off the windowsill and took a bite. "Good thing you won't have to."

She sat back down on the bed. It hurt to stand for too long.

"The Cike?" she asked.

"All alive and accounted for. None with serious injuries."

She nodded, relieved. "And Feylen. Is he . . . you know, properly dead?"

"Who cares?" Kitay said. "He's buried under thousands of tons of rock. If there's anything alive down there, it won't bother us for a millennium."

Rin tried to take comfort in that. She wanted to be sure Feylen was dead. She wanted to see a body. But for now, this would have to do.

"Where's Nezha?" she asked.

"He's been in here. Constantly. Wouldn't leave, but I think someone finally got him to go take a nap. Good thing, too. He was starting to smell."

"So he's all right?" she asked quickly.

"Not entirely." Kitay tilted his head at her. "Rin, what did you do to him?"

She hesitated.

Could she tell Kitay the truth? Nezha's secret was so personal, so intensely painful, that it would feel like an awful betrayal. But it also entailed immense consequences that she didn't know how to grapple with, and she couldn't stand keeping that to herself. At least not from the other half of her soul.

Kitay said out loud what she had been thinking. "We're both better off if you don't hide things from me."

"It's an odd story."

"Try me."

She told him everything, every last painful, disgusting detail.

Kitay didn't flinch. "It makes sense, doesn't it?" he asked.

"What do you mean?"

"Nezha's been a prick his whole life. I imagine it's hard to be pleasant when you're in chronic pain."

Rin managed a laugh. "I don't think that's entirely it."

Kitay was silent for a moment. "So am I to understand that's why he's been moping for days? Did he call the dragon at the Red Cliffs?"

Rin's stomach twisted with guilt. "I didn't *make* him do it."

"Then what happened?"

"We were in the channel. We were—I was drowning. But I didn't force him. That wasn't me."

What she wanted was for Kitay to tell her she hadn't done anything wrong. But as usual, all he did was tell her the truth. "You didn't have to force him. You think that Nezha would let you die? After you'd called him a coward?"

"The pain's not so bad," she insisted. "Not so bad that you want to die. You've felt it. We both survived it."

"You don't know how it feels for him."

"It can't possibly be worse."

"Maybe it is. Maybe it's worse than you could even imagine."

She drew her knees up to her chest. "I never wanted to hurt him."

Kitay's voice held no judgment, only curiosity. "Why'd you say those things to him, then?"

"Because his life is not his own," she said, echoing Vaisra's words from so long ago. "Because when you have *this* much power, it's selfish to sit on it just because you're scared."

But that wasn't entirely it.

She was also jealous. Jealous that Nezha might have access to such enormous power and never consider using it. Jealous that Nezha's entire identity and worth did not hinge on his shamanic abilities. Nezha had never been referred to solely by his race. Nezha had never been someone's weapon. They had both been claimed by gods, but Nezha got to be the princeling of the House of Yin, free from Hesperian experimentation, and she got to be the last heir of a tragic race.

Kitay knew that. Kitay knew everything that crossed her mind. He sat quietly for a long time.

"I'm going to tell you something," he finally said. "And I don't want you to take it as a judgment, I want you to take it as a warning."

She gave him a wary look. "What?"

"You've known Nezha for a few years," he said. "You met him when he'd perfected his masks and pretensions. But I've known him since we were children. You think that he's invincible, but he is more fragile than you think. Yes, I know he's a prick. But I also know that he'd throw himself off a cliff for you. Please stop trying to break him."

The trial of Ang Tsolin took place the next morning on a raised dais before the palace. Republican soldiers crowded the courtyard below, wearing uniform expressions of cold resentment. Civilians had been barred from attendance. Word of Tsolin's betrayal was common knowledge by now, but Vaisra didn't want a riot. He didn't want Tsolin to die in chaos. He wanted to give his old master a precise, cleanly executed death, every silent second drawn out as long as possible.

Captain Eriden and his guards led Tsolin to the top of the platform. They'd let him keep his dignity—he was neither blindfolded nor bound. Under different circumstances he might have been receiving the highest honors.

Vaisra met Tsolin at the center of the dais, handed him a wrapped sword, and leaned forward to murmur something into his ear.

"What's happening?" Rin murmured into Kitay's ear.

"He's giving him the option of suicide," Kitay explained. "A respectable end for a disgraceful traitor. But only if Tsolin confesses to and repents for his wrongs."

"Will he?"

"Doubt it. Even an honorable suicide can't overcome that kind of disgrace."

Tsolin and Vaisra stood still on the dais, silently regarding each other. Then Tsolin shook his head and handed the sword back.

"Your regime is a puppet democracy," he said aloud. "And all you have done is hand your country over to be ruled by the blue-eyed devils."

A murmur of unease swept through the soldiers.

Vaisra's eyes roved the crowd and fell on Rin. He beckoned to her with one finger.

"Come here," he said.

She glanced around her, hoping he was pointing to someone else.

"Go," Kitay muttered.

"What does he want with me?"

"What do you think?"

She blanched. "I'm not doing this."

He gave her a gentle nudge. "It's best if you don't think too much about it."

She shuffled forward, leaning heavily on her cane. She could still only barely walk. The worst was the pain in her lower back, because it wasn't localized. The node seemed connected to every muscle in her body—every time she took a step or moved her arms, she felt like she'd been stabbed.

The soldiers parted to clear her a path to the platform. She ascended with slow, shaking steps. Every step pulled painfully at the stitches in her lower back.

Finally she stopped before the Snake Warlord. He met her gaze with tired eyes. Even now, even when he was completely at her mercy, he still looked like he pitied her.

"A puppet to the end," Tsolin whispered, so softly that only she could hear. "When are you going to learn?"

"I'm not a puppet," she said.

He shook his head. "I thought you might be the smart one. But you let him take everything he needed from you and just rolled over like a whore."

She would have responded, but Vaisra spoke over her.

"Do it," he said coldly.

She didn't have to ask what he meant. She knew what he wanted from her. Right now, unless she wanted to arouse suspicion, she needed to be Vaisra's obedient weapon of the Republic.

She placed her right palm on Tsolin's chest, just over his heart, and pushed. Her curled fingers seared with flames so hot her nails went straight into his flesh as if she were clawing at soft tofu.

Tsolin twitched and jerked but kept his mouth shut. She paused, marveling at how long he managed not to scream.

"You're brave," she said.

"You're going to die," he gasped. "You fool."

Her fingers closed around something that she thought might be his heart. She squeezed. Tsolin's head dropped. Over his slumped shoulder, she saw Vaisra nod and smile.

Rin wanted to get out of Arlong immediately after that. But Kitay argued, and she reluctantly agreed, that they wouldn't make it a mile out of the channel. She still couldn't walk properly, much less run. Her open wounds required daily checkups in the infirmary that neither of them had the medical knowledge to conduct on their own.

They also didn't have an escape plan. They'd heard only silence from Moag. If they left now, they'd have to travel on foot unless they could steal a riverboat, and Arlong's dock security was too good for them to manage that.

They had no choice other than to wait, at least until Rin had healed up enough to hold her own in a fight.

Everything hung in a tense equilibrium. Rin received no word from Vaisra or the Hesperians. Sister Petra hadn't summoned her for an examination in months. Rin and Kitay made no overt moves to escape. Vaisra didn't have any reason to suspect her allegiances had shifted, so she was operating on a fairly loose leash. That gave her time to figure out her next move. She was a mouse inching closer to a trap. It would spring when she moved to escape, but only then.

A week after Tsolin's execution, the palace servants delivered a heavy, silk-wrapped package to her room. When she unwrapped it she found a ceremonial dress with instructions to put it on and appear on the dais in an hour.

Rin still couldn't lift her hands all the way over her head, so she enlisted Venka's assistance.

"What the fuck do I do with this?" Rin held up a loose rectangle of cloth.

"Calm down. It's a shawl, you drape it just under your shoulders." Venka took the cloth from Rin and wrapped it loosely over Rin's upper arms. "Like so. So that it flows like water, see?"

Rin was getting too hot and frustrated to care how well her clothes flowed. She snatched up another loose rectangle that looked identical to her shawl. "Then what about this?"

Venka blinked at her as if she were an idiot. "You tie that around your waist."

The biggest injustice, Rin thought, was that despite her injuries, they were still forcing her to walk in the victory parade. Vaisra had insisted it was crucial for decorum. He wanted to put on a show for the Hesperians. A display of Nikara gratitude and etiquette. Proof they were civilized.

Rin was so tired of having to prove her humanity.

The robe was quickly wearing down her patience. The damned thing was hot, stifling, and so tight it restricted her mobility in ways that made her breathing quicken. Putting it on required so many moving pieces she was tempted to throw the whole pile in the corner and set it on fire.

Venka made a noise of disgust as she watched Rin fasten the sash around her waist with a quick sailor's knot. "That looks horrendous."

"It's going to come undone otherwise."

"There's more than one way to tie a knot. And that's far too loose besides. You look like you've been caught getting frisky with a courtier."

Rin pulled at the sash until it pressed into her ribs. "Like this?"

"Tighter."

"But I can't breathe."

"That's the point. Stop only when it feels like your ribs are going to crack."

"I think my ribs *have* cracked. Twice over now."

"Then a third time can't do much more damage." Venka took the sash out of Rin's hands and began retying the knot herself. "You are incredible."

"What's that supposed to mean?"

"How did you come this far without learning any feminine wiles?"

That was such an absurd phrase that Rin snorted into her sleeve. "We're soldiers. Where did *you* learn feminine wiles?"

"I'm *aristocracy*. My whole life my parents were determined to get me married to some minister." Venka smirked. "They were a little miffed when I joined the military instead."

"They didn't want you at Sinegard?" Rin asked.

"No, they hated the idea. But I insisted on it. I wanted glory and attention. Wanted them to write stories about me. Look how that turned out." Venka yanked the knot tight. "You have a visitor, by the way."

Rin turned around.

Nezha stood in the doorway, hands dangling awkwardly by his sides. He cleared his throat. "Hello."

Venka patted Rin's shoulder. "Have fun."

"That's a pretty knot," Nezha said.

Venka winked as she flounced past him. "Even prettier on the wearer."

The creak as the door swung shut might have been the loudest noise Rin had ever heard.

Nezha crossed the room to stand beside her in front of the mirror. They looked at each other in the glass. She was struck by the imbalance between them—how much taller he was, how pale his skin looked next to hers, how elegant and natural he looked in ceremonial garb.

She looked ridiculous. He looked like he belonged.

"You look good," he said.

She snorted. "Don't lie to my face."

"I would never lie to you."

The following silence felt oppressive.

It seemed obvious what they should be talking about, but she didn't know how to raise the subject. She *never* knew how to bring things up around him. He was so unpredictable, warm one minute and cold to her the next. She never knew where she stood with him; never knew if she could trust him, and that was so damn frustrating because aside from Kitay he was the one person whom she wanted to tell *everything*.

"How do you feel?" she finally asked.

"I'll live," he said lightly.

She waited for him to continue. He didn't.

She was terrified to say anything more. She knew a chasm had opened between them, she just didn't know how to close it.

"Thank you," she tried.

He raised an eyebrow. "For what?"

"You didn't have to save me," she said. "You didn't have to . . . do what you did."

"Yes, I did." She couldn't tell if the lightness in his tone was forced or not. "How would it go over if I let our Speerly die?"

"It hurt you," she said. *And I had you smoke enough opium to kill a calf.* "I'm sorry."

"It's not your fault," he said. "We're fine."

But they weren't fine. Something had shattered between them, and she was sure that it was her own fault. She just didn't know how to make it right.

"Okay." She broke the silence. She couldn't stand this anymore; she needed to flee. "I'm going to go find—"

"Did you see her die?" Nezha asked abruptly, startling her.

"Who?"

"Daji. We never found a body."

"I gave your father my report," she said. She'd told Vaisra and Eriden that Daji was dead, drowned, sunk at the bottom of the Murui.

"I know what you told him. Now I want you to tell me the truth."

"That's the truth."

Nezha's voice hardened. "Don't lie to me."

She crossed her arms. "Why would I lie about that?"

"Because they haven't found a body."

"I was trapped under a fucking mast, Nezha. I was too busy trying not to die to *think*."

"Then why did you tell Father that she's dead?"

"Because I think she is!" Rin quickly pulled an explanation out of thin air. "I saw Feylen crash that ship. I saw her fall into the water. And if you can't find a body that just means she's buried down there with the other ten thousand corpses clogging up your channel. What I *don't* understand is why you're acting like I'm a traitor when I just killed a god for you."

"I'm sorry." Nezha sighed. "No, you're right. I just—I want us to be able to trust each other."

His eyes looked so sincere. He'd really bought it.

Rin exhaled, marveling at how narrowly she'd gotten away.

"I've never lied to you." She placed a hand on his arm. It was so easy to act. She didn't have to fake her affection for him. It felt good to tell Nezha what he wanted to hear. "And I never will. I swear."

Nezha gave her a smile. A real smile. "I like when we're on the same side."

"Me too," she said, and that, finally, wasn't a lie. How desperately she wished they could stay that way.

The parade turnout was pathetic. That didn't surprise Rin. In Tikany, people came out for festivals only because they bore the promise of free food and drink, but battle-wrecked Arlong didn't have the resources to spare either. Vaisra had ordered an extra ration of rice and fish distributed across the city, but to civilians who had just lost their homes and relatives, that was little cause to celebrate.

Rin still could only barely walk. She'd stopped using her cane, but she couldn't move more than fifty yards without getting exhausted, and both her arms and legs were riddled by a tight, sore ache that seemed to only be getting worse.

"We can have you ride on a sedan chair if you need," Kitay said when she faltered on the dais.

Rin clutched his proffered arm. "I'll walk."

"But you're hurting."

"Entire city's hurting," she said. "That's the point."

She hadn't seen the city outside the infirmary until now, and the devastation was painful to look at. The fires in the outer city had burned for nearly a day after the battle, extinguished only by rainfall. The palace remained intact, though blackened at the bottom. The lush greenery of the canal islands had been replaced by withered dead trees and ash. The infirmaries were overcrowded with the wounded. The dead lay in neat lines by the beach, awaiting a proper burial.

Vaisra's parade wasn't a testament to victory, but an acknowledgment of sacrifice. Rin appreciated that. There were no gaudy musicians, no flagrant displays of wealth and power. The army walked the streets to show that they had survived. That the Republic was alive.

Saikhara headed the procession, breathtaking in robes of cerulean and silver. Vaisra strode just behind her. His hair was streaked with far more white than it had been months ago, and he walked with just the barest hint of a limp, but even those signs of weakness seemed only to add to his dignity. He was dressed like an Emperor, and Saikhara looked like his Empress. She was their divine mother and he was their savior, father, and ruler all at once.

Behind that celestial couple stood the entire military might of the west. Hesperian soldiers lined the streets. Hesperian dirigibles drifted slowly through the air above them. Vaisra may have promised to usher in a democratic government, but if he intended to stake his claim to the entire Empire, Rin doubted that anyone could stop him.

"Where are the southern Warlords?" Kitay asked. He kept twisting around to get a look at the line of generals. "Haven't seen them all day."

Rin searched the crowd. He was right; the Warlords were absent. She couldn't see a single southern refugee, either.

"Do you think they've left?" she asked.

"I know they haven't. The valleys are still full of refugee camps. I think they chose not to come."

"What for, a show of protest?"

"I suppose it makes sense," he said. "This wasn't their victory."

Rin could understand that. The victory at the Red Cliffs had solved very few of the south's problems. Southern troops had bled for a regime that only continued to treat them as a necessary sacrifice. But the Warlords were sacrificing prudence for symbolic protest. They needed Hesperian troops to clear out the Federation enclaves in their home provinces. They should have been doing their best to win back Vaisra's favor.

Instead, they'd made clear their loyalties, just as they had to her in that alley days ago.

She wondered what that meant for the Republic. The south hadn't submitted an open declaration of war. But they'd hardly demonstrated obedient cooperation, either. Would Vaisra now send those armed dirigibles to conquer Tikany?

Rin planned to be gone long before it came to that.

The procession culminated in a funeral rite for the dead on the riverbank. The turnout for this was much larger. A mass of civilians lined up under the cliffs. Rin couldn't tell if the water was only reflecting the Red Cliffs, but it seemed as if the channel was still shot through with blood.

Vaisra's generals and admirals stood in a straight line on the beach. Ribbons on posts marked those with rank who were absent. Rin counted more ribbons than people.

"That's a hell of a lot of digging." She looked out over the stacks of drenched, rotting corpses. The soldiers had spent days trawling the water for bodies, which otherwise would have poisoned the water with the foul taste of decay for years.

"They don't bury their dead in Arlong," Kitay said. "They send them out to sea."

They watched as soldiers loaded pyramids of bodies onto rafts, then pushed them out into the water one by one. Each pyre was draped with a funeral shroud dipped in oil. At Vaisra's command, Eriden's men shot a barrage of flaming arrows onto the fleet of bodies. Each one found its target. The pyres caught fire with a sharp, satisfying crackle.

"I could have done that," Rin said.

"It means less when you do it."

"Why?"

"Because the only thing that makes it significant is the possibility that they don't aim true." Kitay nodded over her shoulder. "Look who's here."

She followed his line of sight to find Ramsa, Baji, and Suni standing by the edge of the shore a little ways away from a huddle of civilians. They were looking back at her. Ramsa gave her a little wave.

She couldn't help grinning in relief.

She hadn't gotten a chance to talk to the Cike since the eve of the battle. She'd known they were all right, but they hadn't been permitted in the infirmary, and she didn't want to make a fuss for fear of arousing Hesperian suspicion. This might be their only chance to talk privately.

She leaned close to murmur in Kitay's ear. "Is anyone looking?"

"I think you're fine," he said. "Hurry."

She shuffled, limping, as quickly as she could down the shore.

"I see they finally let you out of the death farm," Baji said in greeting.

"'Death farm'?" she repeated.

"Ramsa's nickname for the infirmary."

"It's because they'd roll out corpses every day in grain wagons," Ramsa said. "Glad you weren't in one of them."

"How bad is it?" Baji asked.

She instinctively brushed her fingers over her lower back. "Manageable. Hurts, but I can walk without assistance now. You all got through unscathed?"

"More or less." Baji showed her his bandaged shins. "Scraped those when I was jumping off a ship. Ramsa threw a fuse too late, got a bad burn on his knee. Suni's completely fine. The man can survive anything."

"Good," she said. She glanced quickly around the beach. No one was paying attention to them; the crowd's eyes were fixed on the funeral pyres. She lowered her voice regardless. "We can't stay here anymore. Get ready to run."

"When?" Baji asked. None of them looked surprised. Rather, they all seemed to have been expecting it.

"Soon. We're not safe here. Vaisra doesn't need us anymore

and we can't count on his protection. The Hesperians don't know you and Suni are shamans, so we have a bit of leeway. Kitay doesn't think they'll move in immediately. But we shouldn't drag our feet."

"Thank the gods," Ramsa said. "I couldn't stand them. They smell horrible."

Baji gave him a look. "Really? That's your biggest complaint? The smell?"

"It's rank," Ramsa insisted. "Like tofu gone sour."

Suni spoke up for the first time. "If you're worried, why don't we get out tonight?"

"That works," Rin said.

"Any particulars?" Ramsa asked.

"I don't have a plan beyond escape. We tried to get Moag on board, but she hasn't responded. We'll have to just make our way out of the city on our own."

"One problem," Baji said. "Suni and I are on night patrol. Think it'll tip them off if we go missing?"

Rin assumed that was precisely the reason why they had been put on night patrol.

"When do you get off?" she asked.

"An hour before dawn."

"So we'll go then," she said. "Make straight for the cliffs. Don't wait at the gates, that'll only attract attention. We'll figure out what to do once we're out of the city. Does that work?"

"Fine," Baji said. Ramsa and Suni nodded.

There was nothing else to discuss. They stood together in a cluster, watching the funeral in silence for a few minutes. The flames on the pyres had grown to a full blaze. Rin didn't know what was propelling the pyres farther out to sea, but the way the flames blurred the air above them was oddly hypnotizing.

"It's pretty," Baji said.

"Yeah," she said. "It is."

"You know what's going to happen to them, right?" Ramsa said. "They'll float for about three days. Then the pyres will start to break apart. Burned wood is weak and bodies are heavy as shit. They sink into the ocean, and they'll bloat and crumble unless the fish nibble everything but the bones first."

His brittle voice carried over the still morning air. Heads were turning.

"Will you stop?" Rin muttered.

"Sorry," said Ramsa. "All I'm saying is that they should have just burned them on land."

"I don't think they got all the bodies," Baji said. "I saw more corpses in the river than that. How many Imperial soldiers do you think are still down there?"

Rin shot him a look. "Baji, please—"

"You know, it's funny. The fish will feed on the corpses. Then you'll eat the fish, and you'll literally be feeding on the bodies of your enemies."

She glared at him through blurry eyes. "Do you have to do that?"

"What, you don't think it's funny?" He put his arm around her. "Hey. Don't cry—I'm sorry."

She swallowed hard. She hadn't meant to cry. She wasn't even sure why she was crying—she didn't know any of the bodies on the pyre, and she didn't have any reason to grieve.

Those bodies weren't her fault. She still felt miserable.

"I don't like feeling this way," she whispered.

"Me neither, kid." Baji rubbed her shoulder. "But that's war. You might as well be on the winning side."

CHAPTER 35

Rin couldn't sleep that night. She sat upright in her infirmary bed, staring out the window at the still harbor, counting down the minutes until dawn. She wanted to pace the hallway, but didn't want the infirmary staff to find her behavior odd. She also wished desperately she could be with Kitay, poring over every possible contingency one last time, but they'd been sleeping in separate rooms every night. She couldn't risk giving away any sign that she intended to leave until she'd made it out of the city gates.

She'd packed nothing. She owned very little that mattered—she'd bring along her backup longsword, the one that wasn't lost at the bottom of the channel, and the clothes on her back. She'd leave everything else behind in the barracks. The more she took with her, the faster Vaisra would realize that she had left for good.

Rin had no idea what she was going to do once she got out. Moag still hadn't returned her missive. She might not have even received it. Perhaps she had and elected to ignore it. Or she might have taken it straight to Vaisra.

Ankhiluun might have been a terrible gamble. But Rin simply had no other options.

All she knew was that she needed to get out of the city. For once, she needed to be a step ahead of Vaisra. No one suspected that she might leave, which meant no one was keeping her from going.

She had no advantages past that, but she'd figure out the rest once the Red Cliffs were well behind her.

"Fancy a drink?" asked a voice.

She jumped, hands scrabbling for her sword.

"Tiger's tits," Nezha said. "It's just me."

"Sorry," she breathed. Could he read the fear on her face? She hastily rearranged her features into some semblance of calm. "I'm still twitchy. Every noise I hear sounds like cannon fire."

"I know that feeling." Nezha held up a jug. "This might help."

"What is that?"

"Sorghum wine. We're off duty for the first time since any of us can remember." He grinned. "Let's go get smashed."

"Who's us?" she asked cautiously.

"Me and Venka. We'll go grab Kitay, too." He extended his hand to her. "Come on. Unless you've got something better to do?"

Rin wavered, mind racing furiously.

It was a horrible idea to get drunk on the eve of her escape. But Nezha might suspect something if both she and Kitay refused. He was right—neither she nor Kitay had a plausible excuse to be anywhere else. All of them had been off duty since the Hesperians docked in the harbor.

If she wasn't planning to turn traitor, why on earth would she say no?

"Come on," Nezha said again. "A few drinks won't hurt."

She managed a smile and took his hand. "You read my mind."

She tried to calm her racing heartbeat as she followed him out of the barracks.

This was all right. She could afford this one liberty. Once she left Arlong, she might never see Nezha again. She knew, despite their bond, that he could never leave his father's side. She didn't want him to remember her as a traitor. She wanted him to remember her as a friend.

She had at least until the hour before dawn. She might as well say a proper goodbye.

Rin didn't know where Nezha and Venka had found so much liquor in a city that prohibited its sale to soldiers. When she'd made it outside the infirmary, Venka was waiting on the street with an entire wagon of sealed jugs. Nezha retrieved Kitay from the barracks. Then they pushed the wagon together up to the highest tower of the palace, where they sat overlooking the Red Cliffs, surveying the wreckage of the fleets floating below.

For the first few minutes they didn't speak. They just drank furiously, trying to get as inebriated as possible. It didn't take very long.

Venka kicked at Nezha's foot. "You sure we're not getting jailed for this?"

"We just won the most important battle in the history of the Empire." Nezha gave her a lazy smile. "I think you're fine to imbibe."

"He's trying to frame us," Rin said.

She hadn't meant to start drinking. But Venka and Nezha had kept urging her, and she hadn't known how to say no without drawing suspicion. Once she started it was harder and harder to stop. Sorghum wine was only horrible for the first few swallows, when it felt like it was burning away at her esophagus, but very quickly a delicious, giddy numbness settled over her body and the wine began tasting like water.

It'll wear off in a few hours, she thought dimly. She'd be fine by dawn.

"Believe me," Nezha said. "I wouldn't need this to frame any of you."

Venka sniffed at her jug. "This stuff is gross."

"What do you like better?" Nezha asked.

"Bamboo rice wine."

"The lady is demanding," Kitay said.

"I'll procure it," Nezha vowed.

"'I'll procure it,'" Kitay mimicked.

"Problem?" Nezha asked.

"No, just a question. Have you ever considered being less of a pretentious fuck?"

Nezha put his jug down. "Have you ever considered how close you're standing to the roof?"

"Boys, boys." Venka twirled a strand of hair between her fingers, while Kitay flicked droplets of wine at Nezha.

"Stop it," Nezha snapped.

"Make me."

Rin drank steadily, watching with lidded eyes as Nezha scooted on his knees across the tower and tackled Kitay to the floor. She supposed she should be afraid that they might fall off the edge, but drunk as she was, it just seemed very funny.

"I learned something," Kitay announced abruptly, shoving Nezha off of him.

"You're always learning things," said Venka. "Kitay the scholar."

"I'm an intellectually curious man," Kitay said.

"Always hunkering down in the library. You know, I made a wager once at Sinegard that you spent all that time jerking off."

Kitay spat out a mouthful of wine. "*What?*"

Venka propped her chin up on her hands. "Well, were you? Because I'd like to get my money back."

Kitay ignored her. "My point being—*listen*, guys, this is actually interesting. You know why the Militia troops were fighting like they'd never held a sword before?"

"They were fighting with a bit more skill than that," Nezha said.

"I don't want to talk about troops," said Venka.

Nezha elbowed her. "Indulge him. Else he'll never shut up."

"It's *malaria*," Kitay said. He sounded at first like he was hiccupping, but then he rolled on his side, giggling so hard his entire frame shook. He was drunk, Rin realized; perhaps more drunk than she was, despite the risk.

Kitay must be feeling the way she did—happy, deliriously so, for once in the company of friends who weren't in danger, and she suspected that he, too, wanted to suspend reality and break the rules, to ignore the fact that they were about to part forever and just share these last jugs of wine.

She didn't want dawn to come. She would draw this moment out forever if she could.

"They're not used to southern diseases," Kitay continued. "The mosquitoes weakened them more than anything we did. Isn't that amazing?"

"Marvelous," Venka said drily.

Rin wasn't paying attention. She scooted closer to the edge of the tower. She wanted to fly again, to feel that precipitous drop in her stomach, the sheer thrill of the dive.

She dangled one foot over the edge and relished the feeling of the wind buffeting her limbs. She leaned forward just the slightest bit. What if she jumped right now? Would she enjoy the fall?

"Get away from there." Kitay's voice cut through the fog in her mind. "Nezha, grab her—"

"On it." Strong arms wrapped around her midriff and dragged her away from the edge. Nezha gripped her tightly, anticipating a struggle, but she just hummed a happy note and slouched back against his chest.

"Do you have any idea how much trouble you are?" he grumbled.

"Hand me another jug," she said.

Nezha hesitated, but Venka readily obliged.

Rin took a long draught, sighed, and lifted her fingertips to her temples. She felt as if a current were running through her limbs, like she had stuck her hand in a bolt of lightning. She rested her head back against the wall and squeezed her eyes shut.

The best part of being drunk was how nothing mattered.

She could dwell on thoughts that used to hurt too much to think about. She could conjure memories—Altan burning on the pier, the corpses in Golyn Niis, Qara's body in Chaghan's arms—all without cringing, without the attendant torment. She could reminisce with a quiet detachment, because nothing mattered and nothing hurt.

"Sixteen months." Kitay had started counting aloud on his fingers. "That's almost a year and a half we've been at war now, if you start from the invasion."

"That's not that long," said Venka. "The First Poppy War took three years. The Second Poppy War took five. The succession battles after the Red Emperor could take as long as seven."

"How do you fight a war for *seven years?*" Rin asked. "Wouldn't you get bored of fighting?"

"Soldiers get bored," Kitay said. "Aristocrats don't. To them, it was all a big game. I guess that's the problem."

"Here's a thought experiment." Venka waved her hands in a small arc like a rainbow. "Imagine some alternate world where this war hadn't happened. The Federation never invaded. No, scratch that, the Federation doesn't even exist. Where are you?"

"Any particular point in time?" Kitay asked.

Venka shook her head. "No, I meant, what are you doing with your life? What do you wish you were doing?"

"I know what Kitay's doing." Nezha tilted his head back, shook the last drops from his jug into his mouth, then looked disappointed when it refused to yield any more. Venka passed him another jug. Nezha attempted to pop the cork, failed, muttered a curse under his breath, and smashed the neck against the wall.

"Careful," said Rin. "That's premium stuff."

Nezha lifted the broken edges to his lips and smiled.

"Go on," Kitay said. "Where am I?"

"You're at Yuelu Academy," Nezha said. "You're conducting groundbreaking research on—on some irrelevant shit like the movement of planetary bodies, or the most effective accounting methods across the Twelve Provinces."

"Don't mock accounting," Kitay said. "It's important."

"Only to you," Venka said.

"Regimes have fallen because rulers didn't balance their accounts."

"Whatever." Venka rolled her eyes. "What about the rest of you?"

"I'm good at war," Rin said. "I'd still be doing wars."

"Against who?" Venka asked.

"Doesn't matter. Anyone."

"There might not be any wars left to fight now," Nezha said.

"There's always war," Kitay said.

"The only thing permanent about this Empire is war," Rin said. The words were so familiar she said them without thinking, and it took her a long moment to realize she was reciting an aphorism from a history textbook she'd studied for the Keju. That was incredible—even now, the vestiges of that exam were still burned into her mind.

The more she thought about it, the more she realized that the only permanent thing about *her* might be war. She couldn't imagine where she'd be if she weren't a soldier anymore. The past four years had been the first time in her life that she'd felt like she was worth something. In Tikany, she'd been an invisible shopgirl, far beneath everyone's notice. Her life and death had been utterly insignificant. If she'd been run over by a rickshaw on the street, no one would have bothered to stop.

But now? Now civilians obeyed her command, Warlords sought her audience, and soldiers feared her. Now she spoke to the greatest military minds in the country as if they were equals—or at least as if she belonged in the room. Now she was drinking sorghum wine on the highest tower of the palace of Arlong with the son of the Dragon Warlord.

No one would have paid so much attention to her if she weren't so very good at killing people.

A twinge of discomfort wormed through her gut. Once she left Vaisra's employ, what on earth was she supposed to do?

"We could all just switch to civilian posts now," Kitay said. "Let's all be ministers and magistrates."

"You have to get elected first," Nezha said. "Government by the people, and all that. People have to like you."

"Rin's out of a job, then," Venka said.

"She can be a custodian," said Nezha.

"Did you want someone to rearrange your face?" Rin asked. "Because I'll do it for free."

"Rin's never going to be out of a job," Kitay said hastily. "We'll always need armies. There'll always be another enemy to fight."

"Like who?" Rin asked.

Kitay counted them off on his fingers. "Rogue Federation units. The fractured provinces. The Hinterlanders. Don't look at me like that, Rin; you heard Bekter, too. The Ketreyids want war."

"The Ketreyids want to go to war with the other clans," Venka said.

"And what happens when that spills over? We'll be fighting another border war within the decade, I promise."

"That's just mop-up duty," Nezha said dismissively. "We'll get rid of them."

"Then we'll create another war," said Kitay. "That's what militaries *do*."

"Not a military controlled by a Republic," Nezha said.

Rin sat up. "Have any of you pictured it? A democratic Nikan? Do you really think it'll work?"

The prospect of a functioning democracy had rarely bothered her during the war itself. There was always the more pressing threat of the Empire at hand. But now they'd actually *won*, and Vaisra had the opportunity to turn his abstract dream into a political reality.

Rin doubted he would. Vaisra had too much power now. Why on earth would he give it away?

She couldn't say she blamed him. She still wasn't convinced democracy was even a good idea. The Nikara had been fighting among themselves for a millennium. Were they going to stop just because they could vote for their rulers? And who was going to vote for those rulers? People like Auntie Fang?

"Of course it'll work," Nezha said. "I mean, imagine all the senseless military disputes the Warlords get into every year. We'll end that. All arguments get settled in council, not on a battlefield. And once we've united the entire Empire, we can do anything."

Venka snorted. "You actually believe that shit?"

Nezha looked miffed. "Of course I believe it. Why do you think I fought this war?"

"Because you want to make Daddy happy?"

Nezha aimed a languid kick at her ribs.

Venka dodged and swiped another jug of wine from the wagon, cackling.

Nezha leaned back against the tower wall. "The future is going to be glorious," he said, and there wasn't a trace of sarcasm in his voice. "We live in the most beautiful country in the world. We have more manpower than the Hesperians. We have more natural resources. The whole world wants what we have, and for the first time in our history we're going to be able to use it."

Rin rolled onto her stomach and propped her chin up on her hands.

She liked listening to Nezha talk. He was so hopeful, so optimistic, and so stupid.

He could spout all the ideology he wanted, but she knew better. The Nikara were never going to rule themselves, not peacefully, because there was no such thing as a Nikara at all. There were Sinegardians, then the people who tried to act like Sinegardians, and then there were the southerners.

They weren't on the same side. They'd never been.

"We're hurtling into a bright new era," Nezha finished. "And it'll be magnificent."

Rin spread her arms. "Come here," she said.

He leaned into her embrace. She held his head against her chest and rested her chin on the top of his head, silently counting his breaths.

She was going to miss him so much.

"You poor thing," she said.

"What are you talking about?" he asked.

She just hugged him tighter. She didn't want this moment to end. She didn't want to have to go. "I just don't want the world to break you."

Eventually Venka started retching off the side of the tower.

"It's okay," Kitay said when Rin moved to stand up. "I've got her."

"You're sure?"

"We'll be fine. I'm not close to as drunk as the rest of you." He draped Venka's arm over his shoulder and guided her carefully toward the stairs.

Venka hiccupped and mumbled something incomprehensible.

"Don't you dare puke on me," Kitay told her. He looked over his shoulder at Rin. "You shouldn't be staying out with wounds like that. Go get some sleep soon."

"I will," Rin promised.

"You're sure?" Kitay pressed.

She read the concern on his face. *We're running out of time.*

"I'll be out here for an hour," she said. "Tops."

"Good." Kitay turned to leave with Venka. Their footsteps faded down the staircase, and then it was just Rin and Nezha left on the rooftop. The night air had suddenly become very cold, which at that point seemed to Rin like a good excuse to sit closer to Nezha.

"Are you all right?" he asked her.

"Splendid," she said, and repeated the word twice when the consonants didn't seem to come out right. "Splendid. *Splendid.*" Her tongue sat heavy in her mouth. She'd stopped drinking hours ago, had nearly sobered up by now, but the evening chill had numbed her extremities.

"Good." Nezha stood up and offered her his hand. "Come with me."

"But I like it here," she whined.

"We're freezing here," he said. "Just come on."

"Why?"

"Because it'll be fun," he said, which at that point sounded like a good reason to do anything.

Somehow they ended up on the harbor. Rin lurched into Nezha's side as she walked. She hadn't sobered up as quickly as she'd hoped. The ground tilted treacherously beneath her feet every time she moved. "If you're trying to drown me, then you're being a little obvious about it."

"Why do you always think someone's trying to kill you?" Nezha asked.

"Why wouldn't I?"

They stopped at the end of the pier, farther out than any of the fishing crafts were docked. Nezha jumped into a little sampan and gestured for her to follow.

"What do you see?" he asked as he rowed.

She blinked at him. "Water."

"And illuminating the water?"

"That's moonlight."

"Look closely," he said. "That's not just the moon."

Rin's breath caught in her throat. Slowly her mind made sense of what she was seeing. The light wasn't coming from the sky. It was coming from the river itself.

She leaned over the side of the sampan to get a closer look. She saw darting little sparks among a milky background. The river was not just reflecting the stars, it was adding its own phosphorescent glow—lightning flashes breaking over minuscule movements of the waves, luminous streams washing over every ripple. The sea was on fire.

Nezha pulled her back by the wrist. "Careful."

She couldn't take her eyes off the water. "What is it?"

"Fish and mollusks and crabs," he said. "When you put them in the shadow they produce light of their own, like underwater flames."

"It's beautiful," she whispered.

She wondered if he was going to kiss her now. She didn't know much about being kissed, but if the old stories were anything to judge by, now seemed like a good time. The hero always took his maiden somewhere beautiful and declared his love under the stars.

She would have liked Nezha to kiss her, too. She would have liked to share this final memory with him before she fled. But he only stared thoughtfully at her, his mind fixed on something she couldn't guess at.

"Can I ask you something?" he asked after a pause.

"Anything," she said.

"Why did you hate me so much at school?"

She laughed, surprised. "Wasn't it obvious?"

She had so many answers, it seemed a ridiculous question. Because he was obnoxious. Because he was rich and special and popular, and she wasn't. Because he was the heir to the Dragon Province, and she was a war orphan and a mud-skinned southerner.

"No," said Nezha. "I mean—I understood I wasn't the nicest to you."

"That's an understatement."

"I know. I'm sorry about that. But, Rin, we managed to hate each other so much for three years. That's not normal. That goes back to first-year jitters. Was it all because I made fun of you?"

"No, it's because you scared me."

"I scared you?"

"I thought you were going to be the reason why I'd have to leave," she said. "And I didn't have anywhere else to go. If I'd been expelled from Sinegard, then I might well have died. So I feared you, I hated you, and that never really went away."

"I didn't realize," he said quietly.

"Bullshit," she said. "Don't act like you didn't know."

"I swear that never crossed my mind."

"Really? Because it had to. We *weren't* on the same level, and you knew it, and that's how you got away with everything you did, because you knew I could never retaliate. You were rich and I was poor and you exploited it." She was surprised by how quickly the words came, how easily she could still feel her lingering resentment toward him. She'd thought she'd put it behind her a long time ago. Perhaps not. "And the fact that it's never fucking *crossed your mind* that the stakes were vastly different between us is frustrating, to be frank."

"That's fair," Nezha said. "Can I ask you another question?"

"No. I get to ask my question first."

Whatever game they were playing suddenly had rules, was suddenly open to debate. And the rules, Rin decided, meant reciprocity. She stared at him expectantly.

"Fine." Nezha shrugged. "What is it?"

She was glad she had the liquid courage of lingering alcohol to say what came next. "Are you ever going to go back to that grotto?"

He stiffened. "What?"

"The gods can't be physical things," she said. "Chaghan taught me that. They need mortal conduits to affect the world. Whatever the dragon is . . ."

"That thing is a monster," he said flatly.

"Maybe. But it's beatable," she said. Perhaps she was still flush with the victory of defeating Feylen, but it seemed so obvious to her, what Nezha had to do if he wanted to be freed. "Maybe it was a person once. I don't know how it became what it is, and maybe it's as powerful as a god should be now, but I've buried gods before. I'll do it again."

"You can't beat that thing," Nezha said. "You have no idea what you're up against."

"I think have some idea."

"Not about this." His voice hardened. "You will never ask me about this again."

"Fine."

She leaned backward and let her fingers trail through the

luminous water. She made flames trickle up her arms, delighting in how their intricate patterns were reflected in the blue-green light. Fire and water looked so lovely together. It was a pity they destroyed each other by nature.

"Can I ask another question now?" he asked.

"Go ahead."

"Did you mean it when you said we should raise an army of shamans?"

She recoiled. "When did I say that?"

"New Year's. Back on the campaign, when we were sitting in the snow."

She laughed, amused that he had even remembered. The northern campaign felt like it had been lifetimes ago. "Why not? It'd be marvelous. We'd never lose."

"You understand that's precisely what the Hesperians are terrified of."

"For good reason," she said. "It'd fuck them up, wouldn't it?"

Nezha leaned forward. "Did you know that Tarcquet is seeking a moratorium on all shamanic activity?"

She frowned. "What does that mean?"

"It means you promise never to call on your powers again, and you'll be punished if you do. We report every living shaman in the Empire. And we destroy all written knowledge of shamanism so it can't be passed down."

"Very funny," she said.

"I'm not joking. You'd have to cooperate. If you never call the fire again, you'll be safe."

"Fat chance," she said. "I've *just* gotten the fire back. I don't intend to give it up."

"And if they tried to force you?"

She let the flames dance across her shoulders. "Then good fucking luck."

Nezha stood up and moved across the sampan to sit down beside her. His hand grazed the small of her back.

She shivered at his touch. "What are you doing?"

"Where's your injury?" he asked. He pressed his fingers into the scar in her side. "Here?"

"That hurts."

"Good," he said. His hand moved behind her. She thought he was going to pull her into him, but then she felt a pressure at the small of her back. She blinked, confused. She didn't realize that she had been stabbed until Nezha drew his hand away, and she saw the blood on his fingers.

She slumped to the side. He pulled her into his arms.

His face ebbed in and out of her vision. She tried to speak, but her lips were heavy, clumsy; all she could do was push air out in incoherent whispers. "You . . . but you . . ."

"Don't try to speak," Nezha murmured, and he brushed his lips against her forehead as he drove the knife deeper into her back.

CHAPTER 36

The morning sun was a dagger to Rin's eyes. She moaned and curled onto her side. For a single, blissful moment, she couldn't remember how she had ended up there. Then awareness came slowly and painfully—her mind lapsed into flashes of images, fragments of conversations. Nezha's face. The sour aftertaste of sorghum wine. A knife. A kiss.

She rolled over into something wet, sticky, and putrid. She had vomited in her sleep. A wave of nausea racked her body, but when her stomach heaved nothing came out. Everything hurt. She reached to feel at her back, terrified. Someone had stitched her up—blood was crusted around the wound, but it wasn't bleeding.

She might be fucked, but she wasn't dying just yet.

Two bolts chained her to the wall—one around her right wrist, and one between her ankles. The chains had some slack, but not very much; she couldn't crawl farther than halfway across the room.

She tried to sit up, but a wave of dizziness forced her back onto the floor. Her thoughts moved in slow, confused strains. She tried without hope to call the fire. Nothing happened.

Of course they'd drugged her.

Slowly, her tired mind worked through what had happened.

She'd been so stupid, she wanted to kick herself. She'd been *this* close to getting out, until she'd caved to sentiment.

She'd known Vaisra was a manipulator. She'd known the Hesperians would come after her. But never had she dreamed that Nezha might hurt her. She should have incapacitated him in the barracks and snuck out of Arlong before anyone saw. Instead, she'd hoped they could have one last night together before they parted forever.

Fool, she thought. *You loved him and you trusted him, and you walked straight into his trap.*

After Altan, she should have known better.

She glanced around the room. She was alone. She didn't want to be alone—if she was a prisoner then she needed to at least know what was coming for her. Minutes passed and no one entered the room, so she screamed. Then she screamed again and kept screaming, on and on until her throat burned.

The door slammed open. Lady Yin Saikhara walked into the room. She carried a whip in her right hand.

Fuck, Rin thought sluggishly, just before the whip lashed across her left shoulder to the right side of her hip. For a moment Rin lay frozen, the crack ringing in her ears. Then the pain sank in, so fierce and white-hot that it brought her to her knees. The whip came down again. Right shoulder this time. Rin couldn't bite back her screams.

Saikhara lowered the whip. Rin could just see the barest tremble in her hands, but otherwise the Lady of Arlong stood stiff, imperious, pale with that raw hate that Rin had never understood.

"You were supposed to tell them," Saikhara said. Her hair was loose and disheveled, her voice a tremulous snarl. "You were supposed to help them fix him."

Rin crawled toward the far corner of the room, trying to get out of Saikhara's striking range. "What the fuck are you talking about?"

"You creature of Chaos," Saikhara hissed. "You snake-tongued deceiver, you pawn of the greatest evil, this is all your fault . . ."

Rin realized for the first time that the Lady of Arlong might not be entirely sane.

She raised her hands over her head and crouched against the back corner in case Saikhara decided to bring the whip down again. "What do you think is my fault?"

Saikhara's eyes looked wide and unfocused; she spoke staring at a point a yard to Rin's left. "They were going to fix him. Vaisra promised. But they came back from the campaign and they said they've come no closer to knowing the truth, and you're still *here*, you dirty little thing—"

"Wait," Rin said. Puzzle pieces fitted slowly together in her mind; she couldn't believe she hadn't seen this connection before. "Fix *who*?"

Saikhara only glared.

"Did they say they'd fix *Nezha*?" Rin demanded. "Did the Hesperians say they could cure his dragon mark?"

Saikhara blinked. A mask froze over her features, the same mask her son and husband were so adept at.

But she didn't have to say anything. Rin understood the truth now; it was lying so obviously before her.

"*You promised*," Saikhara had hissed at Vaisra. "*You swore to me. You said you'd make this right, that if I brought them back they'd find a way to fix him.*"

Sister Petra had promised Saikhara a cure for her son's affliction—this was the entire reason Saikhara had fought so hard to bring the Gray Company to the Empire. Which meant Vaisra and Saikhara had both known Nezha was a shaman all this time.

But they hadn't traded him to the Hesperians.

No, they'd only jeopardized every other shaman in the empire. They'd handed her to Petra to repeat what Shiro had put her through, just for some hope of saving their boy.

"I don't know what you think they'll learn," Rin said quietly. "But hurting me can't fix your son."

No, Nezha was likely going to suffer the dragon's curse until he died. That curse had to be beyond Hesperian knowledge. That thought gave her some small, vicious satisfaction.

"Chaos deceives masterfully." Saikhara moved her hand rapidly over her chest, forming symbols with her fingers that Rin had never seen. "It conceals its true nature and imitates order to subvert it. I know I cannot elicit the truth from you. I am only a novice initiate. But the Gray Company will have their turn."

Rin watched her warily, paying close attention to the whip. "Then what do you want?"

Saikhara pointed toward the window. "I'm here to watch."

Rin followed her gaze, confused.

"Go ahead," Saikhara said. She looked oddly, viciously triumphant. "Enjoy the show."

Rin stumbled toward the window and peered outside.

She saw that she was being held in a third-story room of the palace, facing the center courtyard. Underneath, a crowd of troops—Republican and Hesperian both—had assembled in a semicircle around a raised dais. Two blindfolded prisoners walked slowly up the stairs, arms tied behind their backs, flanked on both sides by Hesperian soldiers.

The prisoners stopped at the edge of the dais. The soldiers prodded them with their arquebuses until they stepped forward to stand at the center. The one on the left tilted his head up to the sun.

Even with the blindfold, Rin recognized that dark, handsome face.

Baji stood straight, unyielding.

Beside him, Suni hunched down between his shoulders as if he could make himself a smaller target. He looked terrified.

Rin twisted around. "What is this?"

Saikhara's gaze was fixed on the window, eyes narrowed, mouth pressed in the thinnest of lines. "*Watch.*"

Someone struck a gong. The crowd parted. Rin watched, veins icy with dread, as Vaisra ascended the dais and took a position several feet in front of Suni and Baji. He raised his arms. He shouted something that Rin couldn't make out over the crowd. All she heard was the soldiers roaring in approval.

"Once upon a time, the Red Emperor had all the monks in his realm put to death." Saikhara spoke quietly behind her. "Why do you think he did it?"

Four Hesperian soldiers lined up in front of Baji, arquebuses leveled at his torso.

"What are you doing?" Rin screamed. "*Stop!*"

But of course Vaisra couldn't hear her down there, not over the shouting. She strained helplessly against her chains, screeching, but all she could do was watch as he lifted his hand.

Four staggered shots punctuated the air. Baji's body jerked from side to side in a horrible dance with each bullet, until the last one caught him dead center in the chest. For a long, bizarre minute he remained standing, teetering back and forth, like his body couldn't decide which way to fall. Then he collapsed to his knees, head bent, before a last round of gunfire knocked him to the floor.

"So much for your gods," Saikhara said.

Below, the soldiers reloaded their arquebuses and fired a second round of bullets into Suni.

Slowly Rin turned around.

Rage filled her mind, a visceral urge not just to defeat but to *destroy*, to incinerate Saikhara so thoroughly that not even her bones would remain, and to do it *slowly*, to make the agony last as long as possible.

She reached for her god. At first there was no response, only an opium-dulled nothing. Then she heard the Phoenix's reply—a distant shriek, ever so faint.

That was enough. She felt the heat in her palms. She had the fire back.

She almost laughed. After all the opium she had smoked, her tolerance had become much, much higher than the Yins had imagined.

"Your false gods have been discovered," Saikhara said softly. "Chaos will die."

"You know nothing of the gods," Rin whispered.

"I know enough." Saikhara raised the whip again. Rin moved faster. She turned her palms toward Saikhara and fire burst out—just a small stream, not even a tenth of her full range, but it was enough to set Saikhara's robes aflame.

Saikhara skirted backward, screeching for help while the lash fell repeatedly against Rin's shoulder, slicing across open wounds. Rin raised her arms to shield her head, but the whip lacerated her wrists instead.

The doors opened. Eriden burst inside, followed by two soldiers. Rin redirected the flames at them, but they held damp, fireproof tarps in front of them. The fire sizzled and failed to catch. One kicked her to the ground and pinned her down by the arms. The other forced a wet cloth over her mouth.

Rin tried not to inhale, but her vision dimmed and she convulsed, gasping. The thick taste of laudanum invaded her mouth, cloying and potent. The effect was immediate. Her flames died away. She couldn't sense the Phoenix—could barely even hear or see at all.

The soldiers let go of her. She lay limp on the floor, dazed, drool leaking out the side of her mouth as she blinked blankly at the door.

"You shouldn't be here," Eriden said to Nezha's mother.

Saikhara spat in Rin's direction. "She should be sedated."

"She *was* sedated. You were reckless."

"And you were incompetent," Saikhara hissed. "This is on your head."

Eriden said something in response, but Rin could no longer understand him. Eriden and Saikhara were only vague, blurry streaks of colors, and their voices were distorted, meaningless babbles of nonsense.

Vaisra came for her hours later. She watched the door open through bloated eyelids, watched him cross the room to kneel down beside her.

"You," she croaked.

She felt his cool fingertips brush against her forehead and push her tangle of hair past her ears.

He sighed. "Oh, Runin."

"I did everything for you," she said.

His expression was uncharacteristically kind. "I know."

"Then why?"

He pulled his hand back. "Look out at the channel."

She glanced, exhausted, toward the window. She didn't have to look—she knew what he wanted her to see. The battered ships lying in pieces along the channel, a fourth of the fleet crushed beneath an avalanche of rocks, the bodies drowned and bloated drifting as far as the river ran.

"That's what happens when you bury a god," she said.

"No. That's what happens when men are fool enough to toy with heaven."

"But I'm not like Feylen."

"It doesn't matter," he said gently. "You could be."

She pulled herself to a sitting position. "Vaisra, please—"

"Don't beg. There's nothing I can do. They know about the man you killed. You burned him and dumped his body in the harbor." Vaisra sounded so disappointed. "Really, Rin? After everything? I told you to be careful. I wished you'd listened."

"He was raping a girl," she said. "He was *on* her, I couldn't just—"

"I thought," Vaisra said slowly, as if talking to a child, "I taught you how the balance of power fell."

She struggled to stand up. The floor tilted under her feet—she had to push herself up against the wall. She saw double every time she moved her head, but at last she managed to look Vaisra in the eye. "Do it yourself, then. No firing squads. Use a sword. Grant me that respect."

Vaisra raised an eyebrow. "Did you think we were going to kill you?"

"You're coming with us, sweetheart." General Tarcquet's voice, a slow, indifferent drawl.

Rin flinched. She hadn't heard the door open.

Sister Petra stepped inside and stood just a little behind Tarcquet. Her eyes were like flint beneath her shawl.

"What do you want?" Rin growled at her. "Here to get more urine samples?"

"I admit I thought you could still be converted," Petra said. "This saddens me, truly. I hate to see you like this."

Rin spat at her feet. "Go fuck yourself."

Petra stepped forward until they were standing face-to-face. "You did have me fooled. But Chaos is clever. It can disguise itself as rational and benevolent. It can make us merciful." She lifted her hand to stroke the side of Rin's face. "But in the end, it must always be hunted down and destroyed."

Rin snapped at her fingers. Petra jerked her hand back. Too late. Rin had drawn blood.

Petra skirted back and Rin laughed, let blood drip from her teeth. She saw sheer terror reflected in Petra's eyes, and that alone was so oddly gratifying—Petra had never shown fear before, had never shown *anything*—that she didn't care about the disgust on Tarcquet's face or the disapproval on Vaisra's.

They all already thought her a mad animal. She'd only fulfilled their expectations.

And why shouldn't she? She was done playing the Hesperians' game of hiding, pretending she wasn't lethal when she was. They wanted to see a beast. She'd give them one.

"This isn't about Chaos." She grinned at them. "You're all so terrified, aren't you? I have power that you don't, and you can't stand it."

She opened her palms out. Nothing happened—the laudanum still weighed thick on her mind—but Petra and Tarcquet jumped back nonetheless.

Rin cackled.

Petra wiped her bloody hand on her dress, leaving behind thick, red streaks on gray cloth. "I will pray for you."

"Pray for yourself." Rin lunged forward again, just to see what Petra would do.

The Sister turned on her heels and fled. The door slammed behind her. Rin slunk back, snorting with mirth.

"Hope you got your kicks in," Tarcquet said drily. "Won't be a lot of laughs where you're going. Our scholars like to keep busy."

"I'll bite my tongue out before they touch me," Rin said.

"Oh, it won't be so bad," Tarcquet said. "We'll toss you some opium every once in a while if you behave. They told me you like that."

Her pride fled her.

"Don't give me to them," she begged Vaisra. She couldn't posture anymore, couldn't conceal her fear; her entire body trembled with it, and although she wanted to be defiant, all she could think of was Shiro's laboratory, of lying helpless on a hard table while hands she couldn't see probed at her body. "Vaisra. Please. You still need me."

Vaisra sighed. "I'm afraid that's no longer true."

"You wouldn't have won this war without me. I'm your best weapon, I'm the steel behind your rule, you *said*—"

"Oh, Runin." Vaisra shook his head. "Look outside the window. That fleet is the steel behind my rule. See those warships? Imagine the size of those cargo holds. Imagine how many arquebuses those ships are carrying. You think I really need you?"

"But I'm the only one who can call a god—"

"And Augus, an idiotic boy without the least bit of military training, went up against one of the Hinterlands' most powerful shamans and killed her. Oh yes, Runin, I told them. Now imagine what scores of trained Hesperian soldiers could do. My dear, I assure you I don't need your services any longer." Vaisra turned to Tarcquet. "We're done here. Cart her off whenever you wish."

"I am not keeping that thing on my ship," Tarcquet said.

"We'll deliver her before you depart, then."

"And you can guarantee she won't sink us into the ocean?"

"She can't do anything as long as you give her regular doses of laudanum," said Vaisra. "Post a guard. Keep her doped up and covered in wet blankets, and she'll be tame as a kitten."

"Too bad," Tarcquet said. "She's entertaining."

Vaisra chuckled. "She is that."

Tarcquet gave Rin a last, lingering glance. "The Consortium's delegates will be here soon."

Vaisra dipped his head. "And I would hate to keep the Consortium waiting."

They turned their backs toward her and moved to the door.

Rin rushed forward, panicked.

"I did everything for you." Her voice came out shrill, desperate. "I killed Feylen for you."

"And history will remember you for it," Vaisra said softly over his shoulder. "Just as history will praise me for the decisions I make now.

"Look at me!" she screamed. "Look at me! *Fuck you!* Look at me!"

He didn't respond.

She still had one card left to play, and she hurled it wildly at him. "Are you going to let them take Nezha, too?"

That made him stop.

"What's this?" Tarcquet asked.

"Nothing," said Vaisra. "She's drugged, she's babbling—"

"I know everything," Rin said. Fuck Nezha, fuck his secrets—if he was going to backstab her then she would do the same. "Your son is one of us, and if you're going to kill us all then you'll have to kill him, too."

"Is this true?" Tarcquet asked sharply.

"Clearly not," said Vaisra. "You've met the boy. Come, we're wasting time—"

"Tarcquet saw," Rin breathed. "Tarcquet was on the campaign. Remember how those waters moved? That wasn't the Wind God, General. That was Nezha."

Vaisra said nothing.

She knew she had him.

"You knew, didn't you?" she demanded. "You've always known. Nezha went to that grotto because you let him."

Because how else did two little boys escape the palace guard to explore a cave they were forbidden from entering? How, without the Dragon Warlord's express permission?

"Were you hoping he'd die? Or—no." Her voice shook. "You *wanted* a shaman, didn't you? You knew what the dragon could do and you wanted a weapon of your own. But you wouldn't take the chance on Jinzha. Not your firstborn. But your second son? Your third? They were expendable. You could experiment."

"What is she talking about?" Tarcquet demanded.

"That's why your wife hates me," Rin said. "That's why she hates all shamans. And that's why your son hates you. And you can't hide it. Petra already knows. Petra said she was going to fix him—"

Tarcquet raised an eyebrow. "Vaisra . . ."

"This is nothing," Vaisra said. "She's raving. Your men will have to put up with that on the ship."

Tarcquet laughed. "They don't speak the language."

"Be glad. Her dialect is an ugly one."

"*Stop lying!*" Rin tried to rush Vaisra. But the chains jerked painfully at her ankles and flung her back onto the floor.

Tarcquet gave a last chuckle as he left. Vaisra lingered for a moment in the doorway, watching her impassively.

Finally he sighed.

"The House of Yin has always done what it has needed to," he said. "You know that."

When she woke again she decided she wanted to die.

She considered dashing her head against the wall. But every time she knelt facing the window, hands braced against stone, she started shaking too badly to finish the job.

She wasn't afraid to die; she was afraid she wouldn't bash her head in hard enough. That she'd only shatter her skull but not lose consciousness, that she'd be subject to hours of crushing pain that didn't kill her but left her to a life of unbearable agony and half of her original capacity to think.

In the end, she was too much a coward. She gave up and curled up miserably on the floor to await whatever came next.

After a few minutes she felt a sharp jabbing sensation in her left arm. She jerked her head up, eyes darting around the room to find what had bitten her. A spider? A rat? She saw nothing. She was alone.

The prickling intensified into a sharp lance of pain. She yelped out loud and scrambled to sit up.

She couldn't find the cause of the pain. She squeezed her arm tight, rubbed frantically up and down, but the pain wouldn't disappear. She felt it as acutely as if someone were carving deep gashes into her flesh, but she couldn't see blood bubbling up on her skin or lines splitting the surface.

At last she realized that this wasn't happening to her.

This was happening to Kitay.

Did they have him? Were they hurting him? Oh, *gods*. The only thing worse than being tortured was knowing that Kitay was being tortured—to *feel* it happening, to know that it was ten times worse on his end, and to be unable to stop it.

Thin, scratchy white lines that looked like scars from a long-healed wound materialized under her skin.

Rin squinted at their shape. They weren't random cuts to inflict pain—the pattern was too deliberate. They looked like words.

Hope flared up in her chest. Was Kitay doing this to himself? Was he trying to *write* to her? She closed her fists, teeth clenched against the pain, while she watched the white lines form a single word.

Where?

She crawled to the window and peered outside, counting the windows that led up to hers. Third floor. First room in the center hallway, just above the courtyard dais.

Now she just had to write back. She cast her eyes around the room for a weapon but knew she'd find nothing. The walls were too smooth, and her cell had been stripped of furniture.

She examined her fingernails. They were untrimmed, sharp

and jagged. That might do the trick. They were terribly dirty—that might cause infection—but she'd worry about that later.

She took a deep breath.

She could do this. She'd scarred herself before.

She managed just three characters before she couldn't bring herself to scratch any more. *Palace 1–3*.

She watched her arm with bated breath. There was no response.

That wasn't necessarily bad. Kitay had to have seen. Maybe he just had nothing else to say.

Quickly she smeared the blood over her arms to hide the cuts, just in case any guards ventured in to check on her. And if they saw, then she would simply pretend she had gone mad.

CHAPTER 37

Something clanged against the window.

Rin jerked her head up. She heard a second clang. She half ran, half crawled to the windowsill and saw a grappling hook lodged against the iron bars. She peeked over the edge. Kitay was scaling up the wall on a single rope. He grinned up at her, teeth gleaming in the moonlight. "Hi there."

She stared back, too relieved to speak, hoping desperately that she wasn't hallucinating.

Kitay hoisted himself through the window, dropped soundlessly to the floor, and fished a long needle out of his pocket. "How many locks?"

She jangled her chains at him. "Just two."

"Right." Kitay knelt by her ankles and set to work. A minute later the bolt sprang free. Rin kicked the shackles off her legs, relieved.

"Stop that," he whispered.

"Sorry." She was still drowsy from the laudanum. Moving felt like swimming and thinking took twice as long.

Kitay moved on to the bolt around her right wrist.

She sat quietly, trying her best not to move. Half a minute

later she heard something outside the door. She strained her ears. She heard it again—footsteps. "Kitay—"

"I know." His sweaty fingers slipped and fumbled as he worked the needle around the lock. "Stop moving."

The footsteps grew louder.

Kitay yanked at the bolt, but the chains held firm.

"Fuck!" He dropped the needle. "Fuck, *fuck*—"

Panic squeezed at Rin's chest. "They're coming."

"I know." He glared at the iron cuff for a moment, breathing heavily. Then he yanked his shirt over his head, twisted it into a thick knot, and pressed it at her face. "Open your mouth."

"What?"

"So you don't bite off your tongue."

She blinked. *Oh.*

She didn't argue. There was no time to think about it, no time to come up with a better plan. This was it. She let Kitay wedge the cloth into her mouth as far back as it would go until it was pressed down on her tongue, holding her teeth immobile.

"Should I tell you when?" he asked.

She squeezed her eyes shut and shook her head.

"Fine." Several seconds passed. Then he stomped down on her hand.

Her mind flashed white. Her body jerked. She arched her back, legs kicking uncontrollably at nothing. She heard herself screaming through the cloth, but it seemed to come from very far away. For a few seconds she was detached from herself; it was someone else's scream, someone else's hand in pieces. Then her mind reconciled with her body and she began bashing her other hand against the floor, desperate for some secondary pain to mask the intensity of the first.

"Stop that— Rin, *stop!*" Kitay grabbed her shoulder and held her still.

Tears leaked out the sides of her eyes. She couldn't speak; she could barely breathe.

"Did you hear that?" The voices from the hallway sounded terribly close. "I'm going in."

"Suit yourself, but I'm not coming with you."

"She's sedated—"

"Does she *sound* sedated? Go get the captain."

Footsteps echoed down the hallway.

"We have to do this fast," Kitay hissed. He'd turned a ghastly pale. He was feeling this, too; he had to be in agony, and Rin had no idea how he'd suppressed it.

She nodded and shut her eyes again, gasping while he yanked at her hands. Fresh stabs of pain lanced up her arm.

She made the mistake of looking and saw white bone piercing through her flesh. Her vision pulsed black.

"Try wriggling free," Kitay said.

She gave her arm a tentative pull and nearly screamed in frustration. She was still stuck.

"Put that rag back in," he said.

She obeyed. He stomped down again.

This time the hand broke clean through. She felt it, a clean crack that reverberated through the rest of her body. Kitay clenched her wrist firmly and extricated her hand with one vicious pull.

Somehow all the pieces came through still attached to her arm. He wrapped her mangled fingers in his shirt. "Tuck this into your elbow. Press down when you can, it'll stanch the bleeding."

She was so dizzy from the pain that she couldn't stand. Kitay hoisted her up by the armpits to a standing position. "Come on."

She leaned against him, unresponsive. Kitay lightly slapped the sides of her face until her eyes blinked open.

"Can you climb?" he asked. "Please, Rin, we've got to go."

She groaned. "I have one arm and I'm still high."

He dragged her toward the window. "I know. I feel it, too."

She looked at him and realized his hand was hanging limp by his side. That his face was drawn, pale, and slick with sweat. They were tied together. Her pain was his pain. But he was fighting through it.

Then she could, too. She owed him that.

"I can climb," she said.

"It'll be easy," he said. Relief shone clear on his face. "We learned this at Sinegard. Twist the rope around your foot to make a little platform. You'll be standing on about an inch of it. Slide down a little bit at a time." He ripped a square off of the shirt and pressed it into her good hand. "That's for the rope burn. Wait until I'm all the way down so I can catch you."

He patted her cheeks several times to drag her back to alertness and then hauled himself out the window.

Rin had no idea how she made it down the wall. Her limbs moved with dreamlike slowness, and the stones kept swimming before her eyes. Several times the rope threatened to come free from her leg and she spun terrifyingly in the air until Kitay yanked it taut. When she couldn't hold on any longer, she jumped the last six feet and crashed into Kitay. Pain shot up her ankles.

"*Quiet.*" Kitay clamped a hand over her mouth before she could gasp. He pointed out into the darkness. "There's a boat waiting that way, but you've got to get across the dais unnoticed."

She realized then that they were standing on the execution stage. She glanced behind her. She saw two bodies. They hadn't bothered to remove them.

"Don't look," Kitay whispered.

But she *couldn't* not look, not when they were standing so close. Suni and Baji lay bent and broken in browning piles of their own blood. The last two shamans of the Cike, victims of her stupidity.

She glanced around the courtyard. She couldn't see the night patrol, but surely they would be circling back around the palace any moment. "Won't they see us?"

"We have a distraction," Kitay said.

Before she could ask, he stuck his fingers into his mouth and whistled.

A figure appeared at the other end of the courtyard on cue. He stepped into the moonlight, and his profile came into sharp relief. Ramsa.

Rin started toward him, but Kitay yanked her back by the arm. Ramsa met her eyes, shook his head, and pointed to a line of guards emerging from the far corner.

Rin froze. They were three against twenty guards, half of whom were Hesperians armed with arquebuses, and she couldn't call the fire.

Ramsa calmly pulled two bombs out of his pocket.

"What's he doing?" Rin strained against Kitay's grip. "He's going to get himself killed."

Kitay didn't budge. "I know."

"Let me go, I have to help him—"

"You can't."

A shout rang through the night. One of the guards had seen Ramsa. The patrol group broke into a run, swords drawn.

Ramsa knelt on the ground. His fingers worked desperately at the fuse. Sparks flew all around him, but the bombs didn't light.

Rin tugged at Kitay's hands. "Kitay, *please*—"

He dragged her farther back into the shadow. "He's not the one we're trying to save."

She saw a flash of fire powder. The Hesperian guards had fired.

Ramsa stood up. Somehow the first round of shots had missed him. He'd managed to get the fuse to light. He laughed in delight, holding his bombs over his head.

The second round of fire tore him apart.

Time dilated terribly. Rin saw everything happen in slow, deliberate, and intricate detail. One bullet smashed through Ramsa's jaw and came out the other side in a spray of red. One burrowed through his neck. One embedded itself in his chest. Ramsa stumbled back. The bombs fell out of his hands and hit the ground.

Rin thought she could see the barest hint of a flame at the point of ignition. Then a ball of fire expanded out like a blooming flower, and then the blast radius consumed the courtyard.

"Ramsa . . ." She sagged against Kitay's shoulder, arms stretched toward the blast site. Her mouth worked and she pushed air through her throat, but she didn't hear her own voice until a long moment after she spoke. "Ramsa, no—"

Kitay jerked her upright. "He's bought us an escape window. Let's go."

The sampan that awaited them behind the canal bend was hidden so well in the shadows that Rin thought for a few terrifying seconds that it wasn't there at all. Then the boatman steered the craft out from under the willow leaves, stopped before them, and extended his hand. He wore a Hesperian military uniform, but his face was hidden under a Nikara archer's helmet.

"Sorry we couldn't get to you earlier." The boatman was a her. Venka lifted up her helmet for a brief moment and winked. "Get in."

Rin, too exhausted to feel bewildered, stumbled hastily into the sampan. Kitay jumped in after her and tossed the side rope overboard.

"Where'd you get that uniform?" he asked. "Nice touch."

"Went corpse-hunting." Venka kicked the boat away from shore and steered them swiftly down the canal.

Rin collapsed onto a seat, but Venka nudged her with her foot. "Down on the floor. Cover yourself with that tarp."

She crouched down in the space between seats. Kitay helped drag the tarp over her head.

"How did you know to find us?" Rin asked.

"Father tipped me off," Venka said. "I knew something weird was happening on the tower, I just wasn't able to place *what*. The moment I caught the gist of what was going on I ran and found Kitay before Vaisra's men could, but we couldn't figure out where they were keeping you until Kitay tried that thing with his skin. Neat trick, by the way."

"You realize you've just declared treason on your country," Rin said.

"Seems like the least of our concerns," Venka said.

"You can still go back," Kitay said. "I'm serious, Venka. Your whole family is here, you've got no business running away with us. I can take the sampan from here, you can hop off—"

"No," she said curtly.

"Think hard about this," he insisted. "You've still got plausible deniability. You can leave now; no one knows you're on this boat. But you come with us and you can never go back."

"Pity," Venka said dismissively. She turned to Rin. Her voice took on a hard edge. "I heard what you did to that Hesperian soldier."

"Yeah," Rin said. "So?"

"So well done. I hope it hurt."

"It looked like it did."

Venka nodded in silence. Neither of them had anything else to say about it.

"Any luck with the others?" Venka asked Kitay after a pause.

He shook his head. "Wasn't time. The only one I could reach was Gurubai. He should be with the ship now if he got past the guards—"

"Gurubai?" Rin repeated. "What are you talking about?"

"Vaisra's going after the southern Warlords," Kitay explained. "He's won his Empire. Now he's consolidating his power. He started with you, and now he's just cleaning up the others. I tried to give them some warning, but couldn't reach them in time."

"They're dead?"

"Not all of them. They've got Charouk in the cells. Don't know if they'll execute him or let him languish, but they'll certainly never set him free. The Rooster Warlord put up a fight, so they shot him when the riots started—"

"*Riots?* What the hell is going on?"

"The camps have turned into a war zone," Venka said. "They'd doubled the guard all around the refugee district—said it was for safety, but the moment the troops came in for the Warlords they all knew what was happening. The southern troops started the revolt. We've been hearing fire powder going off all night—I think Vaisra set the Hesperians loose on them."

Rin struggled to take all of this in. The world, it seemed, had turned upside down in the span of several hours. "They're just *killing* them? Civilians too?"

"That's likely."

"Then what about Kesegi?" Rin asked. "Did he get out?"

Venka frowned. "Who?"

"I—no one." Rin swallowed. "Never mind."

"Think about it this way," Venka said brightly. "At least it's bought you a distraction."

Rin retreated back under the tarp and lay still, counting her breaths to distract herself from the mess that was her hand. She wanted to look at it, survey the damage in her mangled fingers, but she couldn't bring herself to unwrap the bloody cloth. She knew there would be no salvaging that hand. She'd seen the cracked bones.

"Venka?" Kitay's voice, urgent.

"What?"

"I thought you covered your bases."

"I did."

Rin sat up. They'd moved faster than she thought—the palace was a distant sight, and they were already sailing past the shipyard. She twisted around to see what Venka and Kitay were staring at.

Nezha stood alone at the end of the pier.

Rin scrambled upright, her good hand flung outward. She was still reeling from the laudanum, but she could just elicit the smallest whispers of flame in her palm, could probably jerk out a larger torrent if she focused—

Kitay tackled her back down under the tarp. "Get down!"

"I'll kill him." Fire burst out from her palm and her lips. "*I'll kill him—*"

"No, you won't." He moved to pin her wrists down.

Without thinking she pummeled at Kitay with both fists, trying to break free. Then her injured hand whacked against the side of the boat, and the pain was so horrendous that for a moment everything went white. Kitay clamped a hand over her mouth before she could scream. She collapsed into his arms. He held her against him and rocked her back and forth while she muffled her shrieks into his shoulder.

Venka fired two arrows in rapid succession across the harbor. They both missed by a yard. Nezha jerked his head to the side when they whistled past him, but otherwise stood his ground. He didn't move the entire time the sampan crossed the shipyard toward the dark cover of cliff shadows on the other side of the channel.

"He's letting us go," said Kitay. "Hasn't even sounded the alarm."

"You think he's on our side?" Venka asked.

"He's not," Rin said flatly. "I know he's not."

She knew with certainty that she'd lost Nezha forever. With Jinzha killed and Mingzha long dead, Nezha was the last male heir to the House of Yin. He stood to inherit the most powerful nation this side of the Great Ocean and become the ruler he'd prepared his entire life to be.

Why would he throw that away for a friend? She wouldn't.

"This is my fault," she said.

"It's not your fault," Kitay said. "We all thought we could trust that bastard."

"But I think he tried to warn me."

"What are you talking about? He *stabbed* you."

"The night before the fleet came." She took a deep breath. "He came to find me. He said I had more enemies than I thought I did. I think he was trying to warn me."

Venka pursed her lips. "Then he didn't try very hard."

Two ships with deep builds and slender sides awaited them outside the channel. Both bore the flag of Dragon Province.

"Those are opium skimmers," Rin said, confused. "Why are they—"

"Those are fake flags. They're Red Junk ships." Kitay helped her to her feet as the sampan bumped up against the closest skimmer's hull. Kitay whistled up at the deck. Several seconds later, four ropes dropped into the water around them.

Venka fastened them to hooks on the four sides of the sampan. Kitay whistled again, and slowly they began to rise.

"Moag sends her regards." Sarana winked at Rin as she helped her aboard. "We got your message. Figured you'd want a ride farther south. Just didn't think things would get this bad."

Rin was both deeply relieved and frankly amazed that the Lilies had come for her at all. She couldn't remember why she'd ever hated Sarana; right now she only wanted to kiss her. "So you decided to pick a fight with a giant?"

"You know how Moag is. Always wants to snatch up trump cards, especially when they've been tossed out."

"Did Gurubai make it?" Kitay asked.

"The Monkey Warlord? Yes, he's belowdecks. Little bit bloodied up, but he'll be fine." Sarana's gaze landed on Rin's wrapped hand. "Tiger's tits. What's under there?"

"You don't want to see," Rin said.

"Do you have a physician on board?" Kitay asked. "I have triage training otherwise, but I'll need equipment—boiling water, bandages—"

"Downstairs. I'll take her." Sarana put her arm around Rin and helped her across the deck.

Rin glanced over her shoulder as they walked, peering at the receding cliffs. It seemed incredible that they had not been followed out of the channel. Vaisra certainly knew she'd escaped by now. Troops should be pouring out of the barracks. She'd be surprised if the entire city weren't put under lockdown. The Hesperians would scour the city, the cliffs, and the waters until they had her back in custody.

But the Red Junk skimmers were so clearly visible under the moonlight. They hadn't bothered to hide. Hadn't even turned their lamps off.

She stumbled over a bump in the floor panels.

"All right there?" Sarana asked.

"They're going to catch us," Rin said. Everything felt so idiotically meaningless—her escape, Ramsa's death, the river rendezvous. The Hesperians were going to board them in an hour. What was the point?

"Don't underestimate an opium skimmer," said Sarana.

"Your fastest skimmer couldn't outrun a Hesperian warship," Rin said.

"Probably not. But we have a little time. Command miscommunications always happen when you have two armies and leaders who aren't familiar with each other. The Hesperians don't know it's not a Republican ship and the Republicans won't know if the Hesperians have given permission to fire, or if they even need it. Everyone assumes that someone else is taking care of it."

Sarana's plan was to escape through command chain inefficiency. Rin didn't know whether to laugh or cry. "That doesn't buy you escape, it buys you maybe half an hour."

"Sure." Sarana pointed to the other skimmer. "Thus the second ship."

"What is that, a decoy?"

"Pretty much. We stole the idea from Vaisra," Sarana said cheerfully. "In a second we're going to cloak all of our abovedeck lights, but that ship's going to posture like it's ready for a fight. It's rigged up with twice the firepower of a usual skimmer. They won't get close enough to board, so they'll be forced to blow it out of the water."

That was clever, Rin thought. If the Hesperians didn't notice the second skimmer escaping into the night, they might conclude that she'd drowned.

"Then what about its crew?" she asked. "That thing is crewed, right? You're just going to sacrifice Lilies?"

Sarana's smile looked carved into her face. "Cheer up. With luck, they'll think it's you."

. . .

The Lilies' physician laid Rin's hand on a table, gingerly unwrapped it, and took a sharp breath when she saw the damage. "You sure you don't want any sedatives?"

"No." Rin twisted her head around to face the wall. The look on the physician's face was worse than the sight of her mangled fingers. "Just fix it."

"If you move, I'll have to sedate you," the physician warned.

"I won't." Rin clenched her teeth. "Just give me a gag. Please."

The physician barely looked older than Sarana, but she acted with practiced, efficient movements that set Rin slightly more at ease.

First she doused the wounds with some kind of clear alcohol that stung so badly that Rin nearly bit through the cloth. Then she stitched together the places where the flesh had split apart to reveal the bone. Rin's hand was already stinging so badly from the alcohol that it almost masked the pain, but the sight of the needle dipping repeatedly into her flesh made her so nauseated she had to stop in the middle to dry-heave.

At last, the physician prepared to set the bones. "You'll want to hold on to something."

Rin grasped the edge of the chair with her good hand. Without warning, the physician pressed down.

Rin's eyes bulged open. She couldn't stop her legs from kicking madly at the air. Tears streamed down her cheeks.

"You're doing well," the physician murmured as she tied a cloth splint over the set hand. "The worst part's over."

She pressed Rin's hand between two wooden planks and tied them together with several loops of twine to render the hand immobile. Rin's fingers were splayed outward, frozen in position.

"See how that feels," said the physician. "I'm sorry it looks so clumsy. I can build you something more lightweight, but it'll take a few days, and I don't have the supplies on the ship."

Rin raised the splint to her eyes. Between the planks she could see only the tips of her fingers. She tried to wiggle her fingers, but she couldn't tell if they were obeying her or not.

"Am I all right to remove the gag?" the physician asked.

Rin nodded.

The physician pulled it out of her mouth.

"Will I be able to use this hand?" she asked the moment she could speak.

"There's no telling how this might heal. Most of your fingers are actually fine, but the center of your hand is cracked straight through the middle. If—"

"Am I losing this hand?" Rin interrupted.

"That's likely. I mean, you can never quite predict how—"

"I understand." Rin sat back, trying not to panic. "All right. That's—that's okay. That . . ."

"You'll want to consider getting it amputated if it heals and you still don't have mobility." The physician attempted to sound soothing, but her quiet words only made Rin want to scream. "That might be better than walking around with . . . ah, dead flesh. It's more prone to infections, and the recurring pain might be so bad that you want it gone entirely."

Rin didn't know what to say. Didn't know how she was supposed to absorb the information that she was now effectively one-handed, that she'd have to relearn everything if she wanted to fight with a sword again.

This couldn't be happening. This couldn't be happening to *her*.

"Breathe slowly," said the physician.

Rin realized she'd been hyperventilating.

The physician put a hand on her wrist. "You'll be all right. It's not as bad as you think it is."

Rin raised her voice. "*Not as bad?*"

"Most amputees learn to adjust. In time, you'll—"

"I'm supposed to be a soldier!" Rin shouted. "What the fuck am I supposed to do now?"

"You can summon fire," said the physician. "What do you need a sword for?"

. . .

"I thought the Hesperians were only here for military support and trade negotiations. This treaty basically turns us into a colony." Venka was talking when Rin, despite the physician's protests, walked into the captain's quarters. She glanced up. "Aren't you supposed to be asleep?"

"Didn't want to," Rin said. "What are we talking about?"

"The physician said the laudanum would have you out for hours," Kitay said.

"I didn't take it." She sat down beside him. "I've had enough of opiates for a while."

"Fair enough." He glanced over at her splint, then flexed his own fingers. Rin noticed the sweat drenching his uniform, the half-moon marks where he'd dug his nails into his palm. He'd felt every second of her pain.

She cleared her throat and changed the subject. "Why are we talking about treaties?"

"Tarcquet has staked his claim to the continent," said the Monkey Warlord. Gurubai looked awful. Flecks of dried blood covered both his hands and the left side of his face, and his expression was hollow and haggard. He'd escaped the crackdown, but just barely. "The treaty terms were atrocious. The Hesperians got their trade rights—we've waived our rights to any tariffs, but they get to keep theirs. They also won the right to build military bases anywhere they want on Nikara soil."

"Bet they got permission for missionaries, too," Kitay said.

"They did. And they wanted the right to market opium in the Empire again."

"Surely Vaisra said no," Rin said.

"Vaisra signed every clause," Gurubai said. "He didn't even put up a fight. You think he had a choice? He doesn't even have full control over domestic affairs anymore. Everything he does has to be approved by a delegate from the Consortium."

"So Nikan's fucked." Kitay threw his hands up in the air. "Everything's fucked."

"Why would Vaisra want this?" Rin asked. None of this made sense to her. "Vaisra hates giving up control."

"Because he knows it's better to be a puppet Emperor than to have nothing at all. Because this arrangement plies him with so much silver he'll choke on it. And because now he has the military resources necessary to take the rest of the Empire." Gurubai leaned back in his chair. "You're all too young to remember the days of joint occupation. But things are going right back to how they were seventy years ago."

"We'll be slaves in our own country," Kitay said.

"'Slave' is a strong way of putting it," Gurubai said. "The Hesperians aren't much into forced labor, at least on this continent. They prefer relying on forces of economic coercion. The Divine Architect appreciates rational and voluntary choice, and all that nonsense."

"That's fucked," Rin said.

"It was inevitable the moment Vaisra invited them to his hall. The southern Warlords saw this coming. We tried to warn you. You wouldn't listen."

Rin shifted uncomfortably in her seat. But Gurubai's tone wasn't accusatory, simply resigned.

"We can't do anything about it now," he said. "We need to go back down to the south first. Clean out the Federation. Make it safe for our people to come home."

"What's the point?" Kitay asked. "You're the agricultural center of the Empire. Fight off the Federation and you'll just be doing Vaisra a favor. He's going to come for you sooner or later."

"Then we'll fight back," Rin said. "They want the south, they'll have to bleed for it."

Gurubai gave her a grim smile. "That sounds about right."

"We're going to take on Vaisra and the entire Consortium."

Kitay let that sink in for a moment, and then let out a mad, high-pitched giggle. "You can't be serious."

"We don't have any other options," said Rin.

"You could all run," Venka said. "Go to Ankhiluun, get the Black Lilies to hide you. Lie low."

Gurubai shook his head. "There's not a single person in the Republic who doesn't know who Rin is. Moag's on our side, but she can't keep every lowlife in Ankhiluun from talking. You'd all last at most a month."

"I'm not running," Rin said.

She wasn't going to let Vaisra hunt her down like a dog.

"You're not fighting another war, either," Kitay said. "Rin. You have one functional hand."

"You don't need both hands to command troops," she said.

"*What* troops?"

She gestured around the ship. "I'm assuming we'll have the Red Junk Fleet."

Kitay scoffed. "A fleet so powerful that Moag's never dared to move on Daji."

"Because Ankhiluun's never been at stake," Rin said. "Now it is."

"Fine," Kitay snapped. "You've got a fleet maybe a tenth of the size of what the Hesperians could bring. What else you got? Farm boys? Peasants?"

"Farm boys and peasants become soldiers all the time."

"Yes, given time to train and weapons, neither of which you have."

"What would you have us do, then?" Rin asked softly. "Die quietly and let Vaisra have his way?"

"That's better than getting more idiots killed for a war that you can't win."

"I don't think you realize how big our power base is," said Gurubai.

"Really?" Kitay asked. "Did I just miss the army you've got hidden away somewhere?"

"The refugees you saw at Arlong don't represent even a thousandth of the southern population," said Gurubai. "There are a hundred thousand men who picked up axes to fend off the Federation when it became clear we weren't getting aid. They'll fight for us."

He pointed at Rin. "They'll fight especially for *her*. She's already become myth in the south. The vermilion bird. The goddess of fire. She's the savior they've been waiting for. She's the symbol they've been waiting this whole war to follow. What do you think happens when they see her in person?"

"Rin's been through enough," Kitay said. "You're not turning her into some kind of figurehead—"

"Not a figurehead." Rin cut him off. "I'll be a general. I'll lead the entire southern army. Isn't that right?"

Gurubai nodded. "If you'll do it."

Kitay gripped her shoulder. "Is that what you want to be? Another Warlord in the south?"

Rin didn't understand that question.

Why did it matter what she *wanted* to be? She knew what she *couldn't* be. She couldn't be Vaisra's weapon anymore. She couldn't be the tool of any military; couldn't close her eyes and lend her destructive abilities to someone else who told her where and when to kill.

She had thought that being a weapon might give her peace. That it might place the blame of blood-soaked decisions on someone else so that she was not responsible for the deaths at her hands. But all that had done was make her blind, stupid, and so easily manipulated.

She was so much more powerful than anyone—Altan, Vaisra—had ever let her be. She was finished taking orders. Whatever she did next would be her sole, autonomous choice.

"The south is going to go to war regardless," she said. "They'll need a leader. Why shouldn't it be me?"

"They're untrained," Kitay said. "They're unarmed, they're probably starving—"

"Then we'll steal food and equipment. Or we'll get it shipped in. Perks of allying with Moag."

He blinked at her. "You're going to lead peasants and refugees against Hesperian dirigibles."

Rin shrugged. She was mad to be so cavalier, she knew that. But they were backed against a wall, and their lack of options was almost a relief, because it meant simply that they fought or they died. "Don't forget the pirates, too."

Kitay looked like he was on the verge of ripping out every strand of hair left on his head.

"Do not assume that because the southerners are untrained they will not make good soldiers," said Gurubai. "Our advantage lies in numbers. The fault lines of this country don't lie at the level that Vaisra was prepared to engage. The real civil war won't be fought at the provincial level."

"But Vaisra's not the Empire," Kitay said. "The split was with the Empire."

"No, the split is with people like us," Rin said suddenly. "It's the north and the south. It always was."

The pieces had been working slowly through her opium-addled mind, but when they finally clicked, the epiphany came like a shock of cold water.

How had it taken her this long to figure this out? There was a reason why she'd always felt uncomfortable championing the Republic. The vision of a democratic government was an artificial construct, teetering on the implausibility of Vaisra's promises.

But the real base of opposition came from the people who had lost the most under Imperial rule. The people who, by now, hated Vaisra the most.

Somewhere out there, hiding within the wreckage of Rooster Province, was a little girl, terrified and alone. She was choking on her hopelessness, disgusted by her weakness, and burning with rage. And she would do anything to get the chance to fight, to *really* fight, even if that meant losing control of her own mind.

And there were millions more like her.

The magnitude of this realization was dizzying.

The maps of war rearranged themselves in Rin's mind. The provincial lines disappeared. Everything was merely black and red—privileged aristocracy against stark poverty. The numbers rebalanced, and the war she'd thought she was fighting suddenly looked very, very different.

She'd seen the resentment on the faces of her people. The glare in their eyes when they dared to look up. They were not a people grasping for power. Their rebellion would not fracture over stupid personal ambitions. They were a people who refused to be killed, and that made them dangerous.

You can't fight a war on your own, Nezha had once told her.

No, but she could with thousands of bodies. And if a thousand fell, then she would throw another thousand at him, and then another thousand. No matter what the power asymmetry, war on this scale was a numbers game, and she had lives to spare. That was the single advantage that the south had against the Hesperians—that there were so, so many of them.

Kitay seemed to have realized this, too. The incredulity slid off his face, replaced by grim resignation.

"Then we're going to war against Nezha," he said.

"The Republic's already declared war on us," she said. "Nezha knows what side he chose."

She didn't have to debate this any longer. She *wanted* this war. She wanted to go up against Nezha again and again until at the end, she was the only one standing. She wanted to watch his scarred face twist in despair as she took away from him everything he cared about. She wanted him tortured, diminished, weakened, powerless, and begging on his knees.

Nezha had everything she used to want. He was aristocracy, beauty, and elegance. Nezha *was* the north. He had been born into a locus of power, and that made him feel entitled to use it, to make decisions for millions of people whom he considered inferior to himself.

She was going to wrench that power away from him. And then she'd pay him back in kind.

Finally, spoke the Phoenix. The god's voice was dimmed by the Seal, but Rin could hear clearly every ring of its laughter. *My darling little Speerly. At last we agree.*

All shreds of affection she'd once felt for Nezha had burned away. When she thought of him she felt only a cruel, delicious hatred.

Let it smolder, said the Phoenix. *Let it grow.*

Anger, pain, and hatred—that was all kindling for a great and terrible power, and it had been festering in the south for a very long time.

"Let Nezha come for us," she said. "I'm going to burn his heart out of his chest."

After a pause, Kitay sighed. "Fine. Then we'll go to war against the strongest military force in the world."

"They're not the strongest force in the world," Rin said. She felt the god's presence in the back of her mind—eager, delighted, and at last perfectly aligned with her intentions.

Together, spoke the Phoenix, *we will burn down this world.*

She slammed her fist against the table. "I am."

DRAMATIS PERSONAE

THE CIKE

Fang Runin: a war orphan from Rooster Province; commander of the Cike; and the last living Speerly
Ramsa: a former prisoner at Baghra; current munitions expert
Baji: a shaman who calls on an unknown god that gives him berserker powers
Suni: a shaman who calls on the Monkey God
Chaghan Suren: a shaman of the Naimad clan; and the twin brother of Qara
Qara Suren: a sharpshooter; speaker to birds; and twin sister of Chaghan
Unegen: a shape-shifter who calls on a minor fox spirit
Aratsha: a shaman who calls the river god
*****Altan Trengsin:** a Speerly, formerly the commander of the Cike

THE DRAGON REPUBLIC AND ITS ALLIES

The House of Yin

Yin Vaisra: the Dragon Warlord and leader of the Republic
Yin Saikhara: the Lady of Arlong; and the wife of Yin Vaisra
Yin Jinzha: the oldest son of the Dragon Warlord; and the grand marshal of the Republican Army
Yin Muzha: Jinzha's twin sister, studying abroad in Hesperia
Yin Nezha: the second son of the Dragon Warlord
*****Yin Mingzha:** the third son of the Dragon Warlord; drowned in an accident as a child

Chen Kitay: son of the defense minister; and the last heir to the House of Chen
Sring Venka: daughter of the finance minister
Liu Gurubai: the Monkey Warlord
Cao Charouk: the Boar Warlord
Gong Takha: the Rooster Warlord
Ang Tsolin: the Snake Warlord and Yin Vaisra's old mentor

THE NIKARA EMPIRE AND ITS ALLIES

Su Daji: the Empress of Nikan and the Vipress; calls on the Snail Goddess of Creation Nüwa
Tsung Ho: the Ram Warlord
Chang En: the Horse Warlord, aka the "Wolf Meat General," and later leader of the Imperial Navy
Jun Loran: formerly Combat master at Sinegard; currently the de facto Tiger Warlord
Feylen: formerly a shaman of the Cike who calls the Wind God; imprisoned at the Chuluu Korikh and set free by Altan Trengsin
Jiang Ziya: the Gatekeeper, calls on the beasts of the Emperor's Menagerie; currently self-immured in the Chuluu Korikh
***Yin Riga:** the former Dragon Emperor; presumed dead since the end of the Second Poppy War

THE HESPERIANS

General Josephus Tarcquet: the leader of the Hesperian troops in Nikan
Sister Petra Ignatius: a representative of the Gray Company (the Hesperian religious order) in Nikan; one of the most brilliant religious scholars of her generation
Brother Augus: a young member of the Gray Company

THE KETREYIDS

The Sorqan Sira: the leader of the Ketreyid clan; the older sister of Chaghan and Qara's mother
Bekter: son of the Sorqan Sira
***Tseveri:** daughter of the Sorqan Sira; murdered by Jiang Ziya

THE RED JUNK FLEET

Chiang Moag: Pirate Queen of Ankhiluun; aka the Stone Bitch and the Lying Widow
Sarana: a highly ranked Black Lily and one of Moag's favorites

* Deceased

ACKNOWLEDGMENTS

So many people helped me turn this book into something I'm proud of. Hannah Bowman saw this manuscript in its early stages and helped me in the nicest way possible to realize it was trash. It is still trash, but the fun kind. Thank you for always advocating for me, believing in me, and pushing, sometimes dragging, me forward. We burn on, boats against the current, hurtling into the future! David Pomerico and Natasha Bardon not only whipped this manuscript into a much better story than I could have come up with on my own, they helped me grow as a writer and saw me through an awful case of second-book syndrome. JungShan Ink created the cover illustrations and, as usual, somehow reached straight into my mind to depict Rin the way I've always imagined her. Thank you also to the teams at Liza Dawson Associates and Harper Voyager—Havis Dawson, Joanne Fallert, Pamela Jaffee, Caroline Perny, Jack Renninson, and Emilie Chambeyron. I'm lucky I get to work with you!

I'm blessed to be surrounded by friends, mentors, and teachers who encourage me to do more than I ever could have imagined, and who believe in me when I don't. Bennett, the Scarigon Plateau, was named after Scarigon. A great warrior. There you go. Shkibludibap! Maybe one day we will learn the fate of Gicaldo Marovi and his friend Rover . . . Farah Naz Rishi is my shining desert flower, my warm cup of stew on a cold day, the cheese to my bread, the strongest and most beautiful person I know, and the K to my J.B. May we grow old and petty together. Alyssa Wong, Andrea Tang, and Fonda Lee are incredible role models who set the standard for grace and hard work, and who inspire me to unapologetically write *me*. Professors John Glavin, Ananya Chakravarti, Carol Benedict, Katherine Benton-Cohen, John McNeill, James Millward, and Howard Spendelow turned me into the scholar that I am. I'm grateful to the Marshall Commission for its incredible generosity; the Marshall Class of 2018 are complete badasses and I want to be like all of you when I grow up. Adam Mortara reminds me through his shining example to never pull the ladder up after myself, but to reach down and pull others up. Jeanne Cavelos and Kij Johnson remain the best writing teachers I've ever encountered. Port is a very good beverage.

Huge, huge shout-out to the book bloggers, booktubers, bookstagrammers, and reviewers who talk about my work. (Incorrect Poppy War, I'm looking at you.) The fact that people get so excited about my characters is absolutely unreal. You have no idea how much encouragement and support you've given me, and I'm so glad I get to share my stories with you. #FireDick Forever. Burn on, my trash children.

And finally: if I am anything, it is because my parents gave me everything.

ABOUT THE AUTHOR

R. F. Kuang lives in New Haven, where she is pursuing a PhD in East Asian languages and literatures at Yale.

READ THE WHOLE POPPY WAR TRILOGY

The Poppy War
Book 1 of The Poppy War

A brilliantly imaginative talent makes her exciting debut with this epic historical military fantasy, inspired by the bloody history of China's twentieth century and filled with treachery and magic, in the tradition of Ken Liu's *Grace of Kings* and N.K. Jemisin's Inheritance Trilogy.

The Dragon Republic
Book 2 of The Poppy War

Rin's story continues in this acclaimed sequel to *The Poppy War*—an epic fantasy combining the history of twentieth-century China with a gripping world of gods and monsters.

The war is over.

The war has just begun.

The Burning God
Book 3 of The Poppy War

The exciting end to The Poppy War trilogy, R. F. Kuang's acclaimed, award-winning epic fantasy that combines the history of twentieth-century China with a gripping world of gods and monsters, to devastating, enthralling effect.

DISCOVER GREAT AUTHORS, EXCLUSIVE OFFERS, AND MORE AT HC.COM

AVAILABLE WHEREVER BOOKS ARE SOLD